SCOTT M. SWAINE

FORGOTTEN MASTERS IX

VEILED EMANCIPATION

Primix Publishing
East Brunswick Office Evolution
1 Tower Center Boulevard, Ste 1510
East Brunswick, NJ 08816
www.primixpublishing.com
Phone: 1-800-538-5788

Published by Primix Publishing: 02/04/2025

ISBN: 979-8-89194-174-8(sc)
ISBN: 979-8-89194-261-5(hc)
ISBN: 979-8-89194-175-5(e)

Library of Congress Control Number: 2024908033

CONTENTS

Chapter 1

BUILDING BLOCKS

It was a typical business day in Capitol Prime, the capital city of the world of Azgarén. To the south, just outside the city limits, in their main military headquarters building, known locally as Central Command, two people dressed in formal uniforms made their entrance through the lobby doors.

Ayene Ti'van and her accomplice, Petrith Girhani, two secret agents working for an underground movement disguised as a new government security agency called Azgarén Central Intelligence, were arriving for a meeting with the military chief of staff, High Commander Teranu Geilv.

The two of them passed through the lobby unhindered, as they had become familiar faces by this time working on a new high-priority security revamp project. This was due to an alleged breach being declared as the result of a similarly alleged defector who presumably stole valuable documents and security codes during a daring escape.

In actuality, Ayene and Petrith were part of a liberation force to rescue their native home from an alien supervillain calling himself Marshal Darumon. The alleged violation mentioned here was in fact a careful ruse, using the name of a former agent serving Darumon as an excuse to infiltrate the local operations right under his nose in order to disarm his control mechanisms. The two of them, along with the rest of their team, had been playing through a series of carefully scripted events intended to invoke suspicion and aversion towards the Marshal's devious propaganda and rhetoric. This would relate to his reasons for being there and presumed benevolent promises of great wisdom in exchange for their services.

On this occasion, the teammates needed to set up a new project, and for this they needed the cooperation of Central Command, and in particular the authorization of Commander Geilv, to get it off the ground. And to perpetrate this, they were disguised as military officers.

"Commander Geilv?" Ayene announces at the door.

"Yes, come in, Captain."

Ayene and her cohort both entered the room as Geilv directed them into chairs.

"How is the security overhaul coming along?" he asks.

"Quite nicely if I must say so. As you know, we have been busy retooling the old security protocols, and so far, we have managed to close what we believe to be a number of critical gaps in the old algorithms. We think we are getting close to finishing up in here, but a new concern is presenting itself as we try to look ahead at the potential for a surprise arrival of Ytani and whoever it was he joined up with."

"Wonderful. For everything else going on around here, I almost forgot about him. What do you think this new concern is about?"

"Essentially, we're thinking of public safety. If he should ever return with his newfound friends, as we're calling them, and whatever intentions he might have, especially if he should still be displaying that god complex of his…well, almost anything is possible, including some sort of attack."

"Do you think he would actually dare to attack us down here?"

"Commander, if he was behaving so poorly at that mining base with the local crews, who knows what he might be thinking the next time he comes around. I'm trying to interpret the psychology aspect here. He felt he held the authority, for whatever reason, to dominate over people's lives. It is my understanding he was responsible for a number of deaths at that base, to say nothing of all the injuries to their female crewmembers, as disgusting as that sounds."

"Yes, and we also need to consider, um…well, that weapon he stole."

"Yes, and then there is that. I cannot be sure what that weapon actually does, other than blow things up on an unimaginable scale, but if we consider he loved to control, rather than destroy, he might hold other motives for us down here and maybe simply use that weapon as a form of incentive to get what he wants."

"Oh great, Captain, that just made my day. So, do you have any ideas of how he might apply this?"

"He loved female companions, so it seems...not politely, but he certainly had an interest. And I recall someone telling me once he had this god complex where he wanted a pet world with pet people and a pet military. Does this give enough of an idea?"

"It does, and it also asks a truly fascinating question of how the Marshal might respond to it. To have his own agent using his own weapon and blackmailing him for everything else he has down here. Now there's an irony."

"I would laugh if it did not also include a target-paint on my own head. But anyway, even though we can say that weapon could probably blast away anything it comes in contact with, I must at least offer a small consolation for our people regarding any other form of conventional attack, if he should use this as a reminder."

"All right, what are you suggesting here?"

"Sir, it comes to mind that not once, during our entire history of being at war with anything, did we ever have anyone come here and attack us on our own soil. So, it stands to reason our people have no idea of what to do in case of a true emergency, like a raid."

"Should I remind you of our recent scuttlebutt about the Marshal and his insurgents?"

"You can remind me all you want, but surely in the long history we've been travelling around out there, we might have encountered something else along the way."

"Ah, good point, Captain. And so, this naturally follows with Ytani and the threat he might actually pose in this case, in relation to our history of NEVER being attacked here."

"Right, so in the case of a local attack, for instance of Ytani making random terrorist hits as a demonstration of his ability to actually hit us, I would suggest we begin installing a series of emergency systems to warn our people to take shelter in order to prevent the senseless loss of our good citizens. My officer here is actually the one to come up with the idea, so I will let him explain his vision."

She now defers to Petrith, as he leans forward to speak.

"Sir," he begins. "My first suggestion is a type of raid siren alarm network. It would need to be installed for complete coverage in every major city and town, as they would all be equally vulnerable, and controlled by some form of centralized command function, most likely leading back here for our higher command officers, like you for instance, to hold the keys. This will be part of an early-warning system to alert our people to any impending attacks once they're detected arriving here at Azgarén."

"This is a sensible suggestion, Lieutenant," he nods.

"We also need to establish a series of raid shelters, using any and all compatible underground facilities, which at this point could be custom-made, if we have the resources, or at least such as underground parking lots, basements…anything that could provide immediate shelter from an aerial attack, and with enough structural integrity to protect itself from the collateral effect of the building itself taking damage."

"Interesting."

"Not only this, but as Captain Ti'van said, our people have probably never seen anything like this before, so we'll need to conduct a number of drills, I'm sure, to teach them how to respond in an orderly manner and to learn where the nearest shelter location is, or at least to take shelter in whatever structure is available, rather than to simply stand outside and become a target."

"This is reasonable, but you are speaking of what sounds like a rather large project here."

"Yes Sir, I realize that, but in my opinion, if Ytani has friends from that other universe, we cannot know their full capabilities. He also has that weapon in his pocket, and this represents a significant terrorist potential, regardless of whether or not he should actually use it. And if he wants a toy world with toy people on it, he probably won't take no for an answer, and will use whatever coercive methods he chooses to enforce his demands on us until we eventually buckle."

"Dammit, you're a clever young man, Lieutenant. I can't argue with that, especially from what I've heard of him from our base staff. Very well, I guess we really don't have much choice but to do what we can to protect lives…as many as we can protect under these circumstances. But this also asks the question of how to ultimately defeat him, or do we simply meet his demands one day if only to stop the attacks."

"I don't know how to answer that, Sir, but we're likely to take a lot of hits before that happens."

⁘◆⁘

In the Ark'ravan Research Center, a major medical research facility and manufacturing plant located on the northwestern edge of the city, a young intern is making a visit to the office of Director Ghantil Bak'vayn, the center's chief administrator.

"Ghantil, I have a little problem I'd like you to look at for me."

"Yes, Azina, what is it?"

"As part of that new research project on the An'gamu seed, and Ayene's solution for removing it, I've been conducting a historical review of the original design concept trying to look up the coding sequence to investigate where it might be causing that synaptic feedback she described."

"Right, I recall you were going to pull out the old archives. Did you find anything?"

"Yes, I found the files relating to the original research. The seed itself is old tech, dating back almost a hundred millennia. If you recall from our history, the project started as a way to see about creating an artificial lifeform that could be used to enhance our natural biological functions, potentially to give us abilities we might not normally have."

"I recall those studies. Some of the possibilities I remember as part of the original thesis were to tolerate alien atmospheres, if for instance to colonize inhospitable worlds and the colonists would need to be modified to survive there. Also, to breathe water like a fish, or to enhance our internal fortitude to survive in heavy environments and extreme temperature ranges. But the project was discontinued after a while as the moral and ethical questions turned the public away from it, instead opting for technological solutions that kept us free from this ugly parasite."

"And it should've stayed that way," she mourns as she glances at her body and the seed entity on her back. "Anyway, then the Marshal comes in and reopens the study, but with a twist, it seems."

"Yes, so what did you find?"

"Well, of course, nowadays, to produce the seed, we simply program a production run through the factory controls and out pops the product. So, I had to go looking through the old archives on the original research which set the programming. This brought out those ancient records, plus the modern design changes, and something else."

"Something else? What is it?"

"I don't know. It's a locked file that was attached to the data record. It was stored with the modern coding schematics, so I'm assuming it has something to do with the genetic redesign work. But I have no idea how to open it for inspection to see if it holds anything of relevance."

"Do you have it with you?"

"Yes, here on this chip," she sets the item on his desk. "This is the data I pulled out, including that file. It looks like it was protected with a security code, but it doesn't carry an authoring ID, so I don't know who to ask about it."

He picks up the chip and plugs it into his terminal, then pulls up the folder listing the contents. The monitor displays a series of files involving the research and design work of the seed, along with one using a codename, but no author.

The Director tries simply opening it by clicking on the name, but the screen shows an error message. He tries using a few passwords he had become familiar with during his tenure, but none of them grants access.

"I wonder who created this file," he muses. "Was it one of the original researchers? But then why would they encrypt it. This doesn't follow normal procedure. We need these files accessible for future staff members in the event of another study."

"Right...another study," she smirks. "What study, Ghantil, because no one ever allowed any. So, whoever made this probably didn't want anyone to know about it."

The Director looks up at her sternly.

"Azina, this is a research institute. Our primary purpose is to research and design new medical technologies and procedures. If anyone had in mind to incorporate something into one of our designs with the intent of hiding it from our eyes..."

"Meaning, perhaps, the Marshal?"

"Dammit, now I REALLY want to see what's inside here."

He ponders the issue, trying a few other passwords chosen at random, but realizing it was a futile effort.

"This may be impossible without knowing precisely who made this and what they used to encrypt it."

"Can we try to reverse the process? Does anyone have any information on these encryption techniques to see about undoing it?"

"I wouldn't know...unless... What if we ask those people at the ACI? They seem to be breaking a lot of military codes anyway."

"Hey! There you go. All right, I'll call this in and see if Ayene can stop by to take a look."

"Good, you do that."

A woman is entering one of the local medical clinics in the city, along with her young son who is reluctantly tagging along. They enter the neatly appointed reception area and make their way across to the desk. As they approach, the intern greets the new arrivals.

"Yes ma'am, may I help you?"

"Yes, I have a scheduled appointment for my son here. He is due for his implantation, and I wish to register him for the procedure."

"Implantation, you mean for the Suppressor chip?"

"Yes, he is four decades now. We made this appointment a few months ago in preparation of the event."

The woman presents a tablet device on the counter and pulls up her family medical data, selecting the page with her son's medical history and appointment scheduling.

"Right here," she directs to the unit. "I will link this over to you so you can identify the record in your files."

"One moment," the intern interrupts. "We are no longer providing that particular service, and all the associated appointments have been cancelled, although it might not necessarily show on your personal ledger."

"What? But he is four decades. This procedure is mandated at that age. Where do I go now for this service?"

"There has been a change to our policies where the Suppressor chip is concerned. We are no longer producing or implanting these devices."

"Why? Has something changed with the mandate?"

"As I understand it, the Council mandate hasn't changed, but there are some new investigations currently underway. One of these relates to the reason for keeping the chip in service at all, or if it can be discontinued by now. Some new information has surfaced, although so far, the medical community is still reviewing it. But they feel confident, due at least in part to the fact that there have been no new deaths reported since the original inception of the chips, and this leads us to surmise the cause for it might have passed by now."

"Really! This is actually pleasing to me."

"I'm sure you're not the only one. And in fact, we are beginning a program to deactivate the chips for many of our clients. But one of these investigations relates to the original mandate. Can you believe it, but that old ruling actually denied the medical profession to collect any statistical feedback to see if there were any new discoveries during this time!"

"Huh? But wait, I am not a medical professional, but I think even I can see the need for this feedback as a means to learn about the progress of the condition, am I right?"

"Absolutely, you are right!" she responds enthusiastically. "But the Council denied us this service."

"Why?"

"Officially, we believe it was a preventative measure to keep the public from experiencing any new panics, as we did back in the old days when it first came out. But at the same time, it stands to reason that the medical community would NEED this in order to monitor the situation, so they could decide how to deal with it as we progressed forward with the chip solution. However, the mandate seemed to defeat its own purpose."

"Defeating its own purpose..." she muses softly.

"Yes, which is to say, to keep it for as long as it was necessary due to the threat potential. But in the absence of any feedback to monitor things, other than maybe to say we haven't seen any more deaths in that time, there is no way to actually measure the aspect of '...for as long as it was necessary...' other than to wait and see, and only indirectly."

"This sounds like bad wording in the mandate."

"Exactly, and one might also suggest it could lead us to simply keep it indefinitely, unless someone wakes up to smell the synapses frying for that awful feedback response and ask the question...is it finally finished."

"Uh oh, I sense a failure of logic here. And what does the Council have to say about this?"

"Nothing. They're not giving us any opinions for or against. They're too busy with this special deliberation to be bothered with this, it seems."

"But wait a moment. Is it not their job to be bothered with such things as this?"

"Yes, most of us would think so, but apparently whatever it is they're working on right now takes the priority...above and beyond their official duties to which they were actually hired to perform. So, in the absence of their opinions, we are pursuing a few of our own."

"I see..." the woman responds thoughtfully.

"I suppose I should also mention one other aspect of this Anomaly currently under review, just in case any new cases ARE discovered during this time."

"Oh? And what is that?"

"The investigation, which is part of this new review...you know, in the absence of the Council giving us THEIR answer, which some are beginning to question now, is going to reopen the study of what we actually saw reported during the original cases. Naturally, those death syndromes were a big cause for concern, but some of the original researchers were speculating that it might not be related, or perhaps could be regulated with better understanding, and NOT simply covering it up with a chip."

"Um, again…wait. Covering it up? I thought the chip was a remedy solution."

"No, it was a means to disable something within the neural tissues to prevent it from appearing in the first place. This is being treated as much more of an effort to cover it up, not to remedy it, as if to provide a curative solution. If it were a disease, you do not cure a disease with a control chip. If it is something else, the general opinion is to understand it better, in order to learn what it actually was, not to numb some part of our brain while claiming this will protect you from something we could never confirm even existed."

"But I… Wait. If not that, then what is this thing and what actually caused those original deaths? I recall some of my old history lessons on the matter, and those deaths were not a figment of someone's imagination…I do not think. Right?"

"This is true, those deaths were very disturbing events. But according to the journals we're being given to review, and the reports being distributed by the ARC, these people are reviewing some of the old data, and so far, they are noticing a number of inconsistencies in those early reports, and the conclusions those people were drawing."

"Really! Can you give me an example?"

"All right, for one, the first cases of children being discovered were few and far between on the timing, on the order of years, perhaps decades. This might suggest something exceedingly rare was occurring. If we are speaking of the sudden arrival of anything alien feeding off them, it must not have been very hungry in those first decades to take so few victims."

"Um, I suppose you do have a point."

"The numbers did increase, however, so maybe it was just slow to get going. Nevertheless, it was still rare, and very far between in both timing as well as geographic locations. So it could not be something arriving in some location and manifesting itself locally. These seemed random and scattered all over. This also defies the notion of one entity arriving and trying to feed off anything if it cannot even stay in one place long enough to establish a comfortable nest."

"Possibly…" she considers. "Could it be a nomadic form of life? Or more than one entity?"

"This is surely possible, and if it's alien, who knows. But you still need to be able to measure it, and no form of life we can imagine…not any we are currently aware of, or even to speculate on…should be able to come and go without leaving something behind it. Here is where we have the worst of the puzzles. On those occasions when our people arrived and tried studying it, they were in the room with both the child in bed and this ghostlike thing moving around the room."

"Right, I recall this from those old stories."

"We had biologists and med-techs in there with some of their best equipment trying to scan and register what it was, including what it was made of, any energy readings, biorhythmic waveforms… Whatever! The result? The child itself appeared perfectly normal and asleep in bed. The only abnormality, if you can call it that, was an unusually elevated level of brain activity. The people simply assumed he was asleep and perhaps having a very vivid dream. The readings were of the same wavelength as dreaming."

"Dreaming…all right."

"But as for the entity, and this is what twisted so many horns, it was essentially a hole in space."

"A what? I know it was described by some as ghostlike, but…"

"What I mean is, it did not show up as having any recognizable mass or energy readings. It simply didn't exist on the scanners. And yet, they could talk to it and carry conversations, it could interact with various objects in the room, and if you were to reach out, you could even touch it with your hand. How do you define something without mass to seemingly possess a tangible body you can feel? This is simply ridiculous, don't you think?"

"Yes! I must agree! It would seem someone did not have their scanners calibrated correctly."

"Maybe so, but the fact that it also carried interactions was puzzling, as it represented the child for its behaviors, memories, experiences, and personal knowledge. It could just as easily have been the child itself, but perhaps in some altered state. And a few were even suggesting it could be related to this elevated brain activity. As if to say, the child was dreaming itself outside its body. But this too seemed ridiculous, as it would defy any known science our society would otherwise subscribe to."

"Yes, I think I would have to agree with this, as well."

"Except for one," the intern muses casually, "which the Council never chose to recognize officially as holding any validity. And by the way, I hear a few of those people were also in the room studying this thing, and they were the only ones to come up with any viable theories on the matter, at least until those deaths occurred."

"Um, wait. Who are we speaking of here?"

"Former Council member Elder Velen Nazég and his people, a faction calling itself Metaphysics, and one to which our society would generally disagree with for all our other devotions. Unless you consider being frightened of ghost stories as being one of them."

"Him?!" the woman emits alarmingly.

This statement sent the woman reeling. The name, in this case, belonged to a highly denounced individual, and the mention of this faction having any potential to actually discover something of value seemed ludicrous, if not for the similarly ludicrous nature of the problem. She stumbled back a step as she tried to regain her balance. She glanced around the waiting room, taking notice of several other people who had turned to observe the conversation by now. She finally returned her attention to the intern behind the desk.

"Yes, him," the intern emits ironically. "When all else fails, use your imagination, which most of us forgot how to do after we hit college," she shrugs. "Here we need to bring together a few of the other clues of something OTHER than what the Council was telling us. Those children died soon after they were found, and only after the Anomaly was being studied. They were too far apart in timing, as well as location, to be anything trying to breed in our environment and establish itself in any one area. Otherwise, we would more likely see a clustering effect, not a random distribution numbering in the single digits and across decades."

"So it could not be an infestation, or else we would see a growth pattern here, am I right?"

"Exactly! It seemed to mimic the child in every practical sense. So if we say it was some kind of takeover, like a body-snatcher scenario, it was replicating those memories very accurately, as well as the behaviors. But are we speaking of an alien thing trying to take over as a hostile lifeform? You might think it would be a bit more discreet if it were, and not standing there in plain view telling us children's stories. And this thing was clearly a sentient entity, whatever it was. At least insofar as what the child represented at that time."

"Could it have been playing a role with us?"

"Maybe, I suppose many things could be possible. But it doesn't end there. For instance, how did it get in the room? The window was closed on most occasions, and all or most of the doors to the house would be closed and locked as well. It seemed to appear out of nowhere, and then disappeared back to nowhere when the body was found. And then we have the researchers themselves. Listen to this..."

The intern repositions herself in her seat as she prepares the next argument.

"Again, the child was perfectly normal as far as the medical scans were concerned, except for those brain scans. The occurrences were so rare and infrequent that initially the teams simply went out to the house where this family might live and conducted their studies right there in the child's bedroom. This is how it was for the initial occasions; I believe. They were apparently trying to understand what it was and how it got there more than anything else. Then the bodies were found shortly after. So, while they were inside the room, all was normal, but as soon as they stepped outside, maybe to take a break and review their notes, here comes a scream from what I suppose was one of the parents, and HERE is where they all rush back inside to find the body. This is where I suppose people started getting the idea of this death syndrome being more like killing the child, rather than a natural cause from an illness."

"And therefore, an alien thing, like an infestation. It didn't do anything while they were present, but when they left..."

"This would certainly be the impression. But the patterns are all wrong for it to be something attempting to manifest itself, unless like you said, it could be very nomadic. But you know, personally, if I were something that didn't otherwise show up on the scanners, and I was sentient enough to know this, I don't think I would worry about it too much. It apparently held enough impunity to conduct itself without concern of repercussions."

"This is a very interesting perspective, and it does hold a certain merit. But we also need to remember all those other deaths."

"Yes, we do. After these first deaths were discovered, and people are starting to worry, this is where the teams turned to a new course of action. We have a set of reports where they tried to relocate subsequent examples of these children to a proper medical ward under secure conditions and full observation. They say the child's body was carried in one medical van, and this thing…ghost or whatever you might call it…was influenced to follow along in another one."

"Did it obey?"

"Yes, and just like you might expect of a child, it was apparently excited to be in a real live medical ambulance whizzing along the roadways, flashing lights, sirens and all."

"Really!" she exclaims amusedly. "That certainly does sound like a child, and not something hostile trying to take over. Not unless you want to tell me the ghost thing behaves like a child naturally."

"That would indeed be a curious sight. Now, on arrival, the child was put into a medical ward and plugged into their monitors to record its full bio signs. Again, everything was normal. The ghost was taken to another room for detailed study, and this time, the researchers stayed in the room with it to monitor and oversee what it does from there, rather than leaving it alone."

"Ah, good! And what happened on this occasion?"

"According to the reports we have on file, this process was repeated only a couple of times before we saw the arrival of Sargeras and Darumon, and this also coincided with all the other troubles we started to see. But the reports go a little like this. They tried to occupy the ghost with a variety of activities you might normally ask of a child, since it resembled one to begin with. There were security cameras in the room to oversee this, so they could record anything out of the ordinary. The cameras did apparently record the people and this ghost, which again would defy the notion of an immaterial thing showing up on video."

"Yes, and another flaw in those statements."

"All seemed normal on that side. On the other side, in the Ward, the child was still sleeping, the monitors recorded its bio signs, and this too seemed normal. A few interns might come and go, but the focus at this time was on the ghost, not a sleeping child."

"Believing the ghost was the culprit, right?"

"Right. But then, something happens. This is where the data seems a little confused. This is also where a few of these new researchers are trying to review the old records to see if there was something the original people missed, maybe due to their distraction with the ghost, and perhaps also their nervousness of the situation of those deaths."

"Oh dear. And what was that?"

"The child died again. According to the video, the room seemed empty, as far as anyone could tell. There were no interns watching anything at that moment, and the bio monitors were still apparently attached and working. But then the readings went wild with some kind of surge, and then flatlined almost immediately thereafter. The alarms sounded off, and this is where the interns rushed back into the room to again find a body. It was so quick that it defied all logic of a body shriveling up like that in such a short time frame. The physics of a body partially mummifying in a matter of seconds simply do not compute!"

"And the ghost?"

"Yes, the ghost…" she nods ironically and passes her gaze across her desk as she prepares to finish up. "The ghost was in that other room, interacting with those people as if it were having a party. Then…" she waves a finger, "…according to the timestamps on the video, at the same exact moment of the death, the ghost vanishes, almost like turning off a light switch. There was no goodbye, no indication it desired to leave the room, nothing to suggest it had any intentions of anything other than interacting with the people. It simply went poof. A moment later, the med-techs are charging into the room with the news from the Ward."

"Oh dear! But how do we explain this? Do these new people have any ideas? And then, what about all the other deaths scattered around the world that caused the panic?"

"As for this incident, it looked like the ghost wasn't the cause, but as much a victim as the child itself. It seemed as though the ghost was cut off in mid-statement during those conversations."

"Cut off?!" she winces.

"Yeah, almost like turning off your vid-com in the middle of a broadcast. It was unexpected. Some of our people are now suggesting this was indeed related to the child and that unusual brain activity. If so, the child's death caused the ghost to vanish, not the other way around. And this now points us back to Elder Nazég and his ideas, which no one was ever willing to accept. If the ghost was in fact some form of manifestation of the child's mind during these unusual dreams, it's not an alien thing. This might also help to explain why it has no apparent mass or energy signature. How do you measure a spiritual presence, especially in a society that doesn't even believe in such a thing to begin with?"

"Oh wonderful… Aargh…" she grunts as she reaches up to her interface for a feedback hit.

"This death syndrome is still a mystery, but if we say it was not an alien thing, and instead something we simply do not have the proper science to measure, then we need to develop that science so we can measure it. But now, as to your other question about all those random deaths. This is also a mystery, but a few of our people are starting to associate something which has long been on the mind of some of our top experts as being a little too convenient."

"I am not sure if I want to hear this. My chip is already giving me trouble."

"Perhaps I can help. Since we already have instructions to start disabling these things, let me call someone up here to do yours."

The intern dials a number on her terminal to someone in one of the examination rooms to come forward. While they wait, she continues her explanation, which was part of the ARC's plan to slowly reveal these details and build up a picture of a hidden scandal by the Council, and ultimately involving Darumon.

"The deaths being described here were indeed as alien as anything you might imagine," the intern relates. "Therefore, it stands to reason, if someone, like the Council, told you it was an alien, you might not have any other choice but to believe it, especially as we all seem so content to believe everything they say to begin with."

"Um, am I detecting something in that statement of yours?"

"Yes, you probably are, and it relates to my earlier statement of them not doing their jobs. My chip was turned off a long time ago, so I can feel all the ire I want over how those people have been treating us during this time. That nondisclosure clause, for instance. This is a deliberate attempt to hold back critical information from us that might otherwise allow us to realize if and when it might finally be possible to discontinue these horrid little chips, among other things. But like we already said, they seem far too preoccupied with whatever it is they're deliberating in there, rather than their assigned governmental duties the people elected them to serve."

"Got it. I might actually have to agree with this perspective. I did not elect those people to sit in a room debating so much nonsense that is not apparently serving our public, when we have immediate real-world issues to resolve."

"Exactly! But this also leads a few of our top experts in a dangerous direction for the implications. These theories, if any of them are correct, could be exceedingly scandalous. So, until they can find their evidence, they need to keep this under careful control. This would also include people like you if we should choose to share any of this."

"Oops! All right, I will keep myself silent until we can find our data. But what sort of theories are we speaking of here? This does not sound at all polite."

"It is not. And the data is difficult to pinpoint so far, which might further reflect on that idea of a cover-up. The ARC is currently investigating a number of things, as we might have a series of elements involved collectively, and it all comes down to that all-too-convenient event, which is the arrival of the only alien creatures we can be sure of. Sargeras and Darumon."

The woman again reels back at the suggestion, as the traditional interpretation of those two names was that they were the benefactors of their society for their grand promises of high wisdom and an uplifting effect due to their scientific values. But to suggest something scandalous would turn this around, and given all the history they had up till now, this would probably hurt.

She paused in her reaction to glance around the room again. As before, the conversation, which was actually loud enough to be overheard, did in fact have the attention of several people by now. The intern also took notice of this, but the idea was to break the people of their dependency on the Council and its overwhelming influence of their opinions. Therefore, to mention a scandal might be enough to open the eyes of the people to finally start asking those questions no one ever bothered to ask before.

"Those deaths," the intern begins again, "at least in those children, seemed so mysterious largely due to their timing, and also the fact that people were present in the room only moments before it happened. Then boom, something happens as soon as they turn their backs. We have only two real choices here to work with. An alien thing doing something our science doesn't hold a definition for, or a hidden effort to remove something from those very same scientists who were trying to study it."

"Oh no!" the woman gasps and covers her face.

By this time, another intern had arrived and was now attempting to plug in a diagnostic probe into the woman's interface to deprogram it. The conversation paused long enough to give the other intern a chance to finish her work. Then the woman at the desk continued.

"Now, if we go back to the idea of an alien thing, this still requires us to learn how to identify it, and a nondisclosure clause that denies us even to realize if it's still out there doesn't help us to learn anything. All it does, panic or no panic, is tell us to keep using the chips...indefinitely.

That's not a solution, and this is also contradictory to the statement that they are intended to be temporary. And this is a mandate from a Council that seems not to give out any opinions on anything it doesn't otherwise care for. And here is a possible reason for a scandal. They locked themselves away in their chambers with their secrets of the universe and forgot about all of us out here."

"Yes!" the woman surges, now with more vigor, as her chip was disabled. "That would surely twist a few horns, and thank you for giving me relief from that horrid little bug, as now I can actually experience it."

"Absolutely. Just be careful where you show it, as the people who ordered us to use it are still out there and might have something to say about it. So we need to keep it calm. The next problem is more sinister, and potentially dangerous, depending on how deep it runs. If this is actually a cover-up, it means someone knows what this thing really is, but doesn't want the rest of us to know about it. This could be one reason why Elder Nazég, who apparently WAS trying to figure it out, instead got chased away and so heavily vilified by everyone. He might not have been cooperating by their rules, which may instead desire to keep it hidden."

"All right, but let me ask you this one question. When we say, not following someone's rules, could there be a legitimate reason and he was violating this?"

"This is surely a good question to ask, but it fails the logic when you consider those deaths...all of them. And this must now also include Marshal Darumon and all his efforts to...help us...find a solution to it. Most of those deaths occurred only after he arrived...or at least officially arrived."

"Officially?" she winces. "Uh oh...and HE was the one who so often vilified the former Elder. Oh great."

"He gives the Council this incredible offer of great wisdom, which no one ever hears anything about. The Council vanishes behind closed doors, and fails to serve any of their usual functions from that time forward. And WE get chips stuck in our heads with no possibility to realize when it's time to stop, or a way to monitor the progress of this Anomaly, assuming it's still out there. Also, the original study was closed, and no one was ever allowed to go back to it. This all speaks of someone telling us to shut up and stop asking questions. Further to take these chips whether we need them or not, and whether this is the correct solution or not. And the one man who could possibly help us understand what it was is chased away, and the rest of us are made not to believe in anything supernatural. But we sure do lose our horns with ghost stories!"

"Actually, you are absolutely right. I specialize in psychology studies, and I can tell you a few things where that mentality is concerned. But if you are suggesting a scandal here, I simply must permit myself to inquire on those deaths again. If no one saw anything, and the room was presumably empty, even on camera, like in that medical ward, how did it happen?"

"All I can say is what I read from one of these top experts that are mostly speculating on the idea, at least until we can find some form of data to validate any of this."

"All right, this is reasonable."

"If we are speaking of something alien, and I think this much we might have to admit to, it must involve something our science is so far unfamiliar with. How do you convert, for lack of a better word, a fully healthy, living body, to a dried-up husk? Well, some form of weapon to dehydrate it in some funny…alien…manner, might do the trick. And you might not need to be right on top of it to do it."

"Uh huh…I see your point. Even those random ones. Just fire this off from a distance, or hit them from some hidden location, and there you go. But in the case of those children, it would have to be someone who WAS present…somewhere. Those people turn their backs, someone sneaks around behind them, maybe distracting one or more simply to ensure their privacy, if only for a brief moment, and zap…fried body."

"Yes, and then, so conveniently, Sargeras and the Marshal show up after only a couple of those occasions when we had cameras on them, maybe as a way to gain control before we actually DID record enough data to make a determination. But if this is the case, it's not just the Council to be afraid of. The alien infestation is something we gave the keys to our lives, our bodies, and our world to. And the Council, for this much, might be in partnership with them."

"Oh no, and so we have our scandal. But to what ultimate end? There must be a reason…some form of motivation."

"I suppose so, but no doubt this would count as part of that cover-up, if it really is true. If these children are demonstrating a skill or something that we are unable to measure, at least with our preferred sciences, it could be that alien mind, for all HE might know, might not want us to have it. As for the Council, well, if this deliberation says anything, they got what they wanted. Everything else is moot."

"Yeah, maybe so."

"And so, this is where we are now. The Council refuses to comment on anything other than they are deliberating something so important that they can't comment on anything else. Therefore, in the absence of THEM doing their work, WE are taking the initiative to correct a few things, being so tired of waiting for them to give us any new instructions to do anything at all. And if we're right, horns will fly, you can be sure of it. Meanwhile, the ARC is looking for volunteers, anyone who might actually be exhibiting these symptoms. If we stop using the chips, we might get lucky and find another case. And this time, study it on our terms, not the Council's. Therefore, any new discoveries in our children must be reported right away for examination."

✦✦✦

"Just a few more months," Relissa ponders. "Jiggers, it feels like it's been forever, and so much hard work."

"I'm happy for you, Relissa," Marelle states jovially. "I have another year, but I'm anxious to get through it. And Haran, you have two more, right? You're going all the way to the Ninth, aren't you?"

"That's right," he affirms. "And I'm extremely excited. These next two years should be my crowning achievement in the mage studies. I was recently speaking to our former Dean, now turned priest, over at the temple. He's very proud of what I've done so far and wishes me well. Between him and the other students from our old academy, they're all cheering me on."

"That sounds great, Haran," Sulíma smiles. "I'm glad to hear you're getting so much support. I'm still in my early studies so far, but I'm excited to finally get a chance to see how it all works."

"You're also taking some courses at your new university, aren't you? That's got to be tough, dividing your time between two schools."

"It's hard, but I want to push my way through it because one day I want to be an arcanic technician. When I see all the work they're making around here, and then listen to Marelle and Petrith about what they're doing over at the BRC, I want a piece of it before it's all used up."

"Don't worry about that, Suli," Marelle soothes. "I'm sure you'll have more than enough opportunity to invent all sorts of fascinating stuff. My biggest concern is just getting far enough through this next year so I can start training up my next set of skills in my flight training."

"And for this you need the Seventh Circle. Wow, those must be some tough new technologies they're making over there."

"Yeah, they're tough, but this is also the military, so I guess it just goes with the territory."

"How is that new prototype coming along?" Petrith asks.

"They tell me most of the technologies have progressed to the point where they can create a working example of a proper combat craft. They're also working on a set of automated drones for me to play with, once I get up there."

"When you say, up there," Relissa winces. "Where is that, exactly?"

"Space, my dear little ground-based companion," she smirks. "These vessels are made to travel outside the planetary sphere."

"Jiggers; and I thought riding around on that gryphon with Thaelyn was enough to give me the willies."

"What are these drones for?" Túfula inquires.

"The new prototype will include everything this time. We have the drive system, weapons, the jump drive, full navigation and tactical readouts, scanners…the works. This is the final revision, other than maybe for a few refinements for future models. The drones are for practice fire. I'll be up there testing the scanners and tactical displays, target locks, weapons to shoot them down, and afterwards the jump drive to begin making the various waypoint markers we'll be using later for travel between worlds."

"Cu'Nar's grace, Marelle, that's not just a little gunship, it's a pocket-sized cruiser!"

"Try doing that with your traditional sciences."

"Are you going to leave anything for me to research?" Sulíma whines.

"Don't worry, Suli. Just do your studies and practice hard. Remember, most of this is proprietary for the war. We'll need to make it official one day, but that needs to be done in a more conventional manner, with real science and real invention."

"All right, so I guess that's a hint to think about for later."

Relissa and her group had been indulging in a round of camaraderie in the courtyard of the Order academy guildhall on Tae'Eladar. They were starting to look forward to the end of the school year, and the excitement was building for the commencement ceremony for the next graduating class.

Meanwhile, on the world of Therinë, the city of Rolsklinde, Thaelyn and his officers were in another meeting when the session was interrupted briefly by Ayene in projected form making ready for her latest run to check on things at the ARC.

"I'm ready, my Lord, do you have any special instructions?"

"None at this time, Lieutenant, all seems well here for the present. You are going to check on the ARC today, correct?"

"Yes, my Lord. We got a note from them about some encrypted files they found, and we suspect it might be the Marshal hiding something from us. I'm going to take a quick look, and then probably call on Petrith to see what he can do about it."

"Most excellent. As you were, Lieutenant."

She bows curtly and folds away.

Ayene arrives inside the ARC, folding directly into the Director's office. As usual, the Director jumps, although not as severely this time as he was getting used to the sudden appearances.

"Lieutenant, how are you today?" he asks after resettling himself in his chair.

"Doing well, thank you, and you?"

"We have a number of projects all occurring at once here, and as you can probably imagine, it has us all very busy. More so than usual, I might say, which is refreshing in many ways."

"Well, we can't simply have you people sitting on your tails all day. I got your note on that encrypted file, so I came to check on it. What is it you found?"

"Apparently, someone locked what appears to be a critical file on us. It was found with the rest of the genetic coding schemes for the seed, but it seems to be password protected. Normally, this would violate our standard procedures to keep these things available for later review, like reopening a project study. So, whoever did it is not likely one of our usual staff members."

"Interesting, and so this suggests the Marshal, I suppose."

"It certainly does."

"Do you have a copy here, or is it with Azina?"

"I have a copy of it, but I can't open it."

"Can you show it to me?"

He pulls up a private folder on his data terminal with a copy of the strange file inside for Ayene to examine, even though there is not much to say about it at this point.

"There is no authoring ID on it either," the Director notes, "which adds further suspicion to the idea of its potential origin."

"What about the rest of it? Do you have the full set, except for this part?"

"Everything is present except for a set of missing chromosomes, and we know these are missing by the numbers given in the other sets. Number fourteen, and then twenty-one through twenty-seven are absent, out of a total of thirty-two."

"This thing has a lot of chromosomes, I guess," she chuckles.

"Yes, but if this represents one of his little secrets, it could explain why he pushed those seeds at us so hard."

"Well, we simply can't have that now, can we..." she smirks. "Fortunately for us, the ACI doesn't stop at roadblocks like these, so if you'll allow me, I'll call on one of our top experts to see if we can help figure this out. Meanwhile, maybe you can call Azina in here to give the poor girl a break. We'll see what we can do together."

"All right."

The Director reaches for his intercom and calls Azina to his office while Ayene flashes back home, this time returning to the guildhall on Tae'Eladar, where she suspected Relissa and the gang may still be involved in their afternoon chat.

"...And then, after that," Marelle relates, "we need to test a new feature they'll be incorporating into it called linked synchronous navigation. That sounds like fun."

"What in all the nether-space is that supposed to be?" Sulíma wonders.

Ayene appears as a sudden flash in the courtyard, sending another wave of minor starts through the group. But being somewhat more accustomed to it than the Director, they made the recovery a little easier.

"Jiggers, Ayene!" Relissa yips. "Why do you keep doing that to us?"

"Sorry people, but I have a little problem, and I need to borrow Petrith for a moment."

"What is it?" he asks.

"The ARC has an encrypted file, likely by the Marshal and probably using a military grade coding. We need it unlocked so we can gain access to it."

"What kind of file is it?" he asks as he gets up.

"It's part of the design work on the seed entity, and at this point it probably relates to that bit where it links to Sargeras, or so we hope."

"That figures... Then this sounds like something from the early days after his arrival. Good. I have some backup files on my desk over at the BRC, so give me a moment to go get them and I'll meet you over there."

"Good, see you soon."

Ayene flashes away back to Azgarén while Petrith dashes out of the courtyard and down to the local gateway node, where he follows the network to a special transit station with a secured military gateway leading to the Bahlaie Research Center. This is where most of the joint research was taking place for the war effort, as well as his electronic espionage study materials.

"Petrith," calls Chief Technician Lapäli as she sees him rushing through. "You seem in something of a hurry. What's going on?"

"I'm being called to service. Lieutenant Ti'van has some sort of odd file on the computers at the ARC that's encrypted, and they need someone to try opening it."

"Really! What's this about?"

"It supposedly has to do with the seed research, but we're not too sure what's inside. But if it's locked, it's probably important, and likely the Marshal again. We'll see when I get it open. I just need to grab some of my tools."

He walks around to his desk and picks up several holo-chips, which he had been collecting during this time as he worked on his secret projects inside Central Command. He places them in a pouch to carry with him, and then moves away to a small room where he can perform his projection.

Ayene had returned to the ARC by this time and was in conversation with the Director and Azina.

"...In the meantime," the Director reflects. "I've been receiving a number of reports from our clinics around the city. These are about parents showing up since our procedural changes in regard to their appointments for their children to take the Suppressor chip."

"Are you using our new propaganda spiel?"

"Yes, we are. Our people are under instruction to inform the public that these procedures are no longer available, and offering a cleverly devised statement as to why, by describing our new research of the Anomaly, and a series of proposals and suppositions. We're also dropping hints as to the Council apparently covering something up that they didn't want us to know about using that nondisclosure clause to deny us any statistics to monitor the situation. It's being formulated as a potential scandal we still need to validate, so we don't get a lot of people crinkling up their tails, and also to keep them calm until our… data…has been collected to verify anything. It's mostly to stir things up so they stop thinking the Council is a god entity that can do no wrong. This is why we are only now doing something…because we're so tired of waiting."

"Naturally. And the response so far?"

"Shock, surprise, a bit of anger and frustration. Many of them are voters who elected a Council to do some form of work, but who are subsequently frustrated that the Council isn't doing anything at all. The reports say many of them are wondering why the Council would try covering up the statistical reporting, at the very least, which is an obvious issue if you're a medical professional who needs to maintain data on it. And then the long duration of no new research to see if the chips are still even necessary. But the most interesting is when we throw Former Elder Velen Nazég into the mix. To suggest he knew something, perhaps something revolutionary, but the rest of the Council tossed it out, along with him and his full faction, because it represented a threat to their authority to control the results, is placing them in a very bad light right now."

"A potential authoritarian body that likes playing god," she muses. "I have to take a stand with Kaliya and Thaelyn when I say I don't like placing blame on people where it's not warranted, at least not fully, as they WERE apparently drunk on their power. But they did throw him out, and they did villainize him, with or without the Marshal pushing it, and in their absence, we need a scapegoat to distract him from our other objectives."

"Yes, your other objectives…" he chuckles. "You know, Lieutenant, I took notice of that cute little public demonstration you put on recently out there with that industry. It had to be you; I've never seen anyone else do anything like that before, and you so expertly placed the blame on entities that couldn't be so easily traced."

"Oh yes!" Azina adds. "That spokesperson of yours… 'Thanks to the Marshal and our wonderful military keeping us all safe here at home, we shouldn't need this awful emergency condition of war by now. Therefore, it should be dismissed so we can all go back to normal… which also means we can finally remember we have, and always DID have, clean eco-friendly techs to convert this industry so that it stops polluting our world to the point where everything finally dies.' I need to take lessons from you people."

"I also took notice of how you placed some of the blame on the Council for not doing their normal jobs as they should, due to this long deliberation they're involved with, but you didn't necessarily make any statements that could bring down the Marshal or any of his regulators to alter the news feed."

"Yeah, it's all part of the plan," Ayene croons. "We're going to build up this nice little picture, and before long, it's going to hit a wall soon. This reminds me, I need to make a few more contacts along the way to pave things ahead of us."

Petrith had arrived downstairs in the lobby using his Suuden'kai officer's disguise. He marched in through the door, not having actually been inside the building before to go there directly, and steps up to the reception desk, where the clerk observed his elegantly formal approach.

"Welcome to the ARC, how may I assist you?"

"I believe I am expected upstairs in the research lab. Can you direct me?"

"Yes, take the elevator down the hall to Level Three. May I ask who it is you are supposed to meet with?"

"I am working in conjunction with Ayene Ti'van and Intern Nur'ten on a recent issue they just discovered."

The clerk studies him briefly, unsure what to make of him.

"Are you from Central Command, or are you…" she halts, leaving the statement open.

Petrith displays a broad grin.

"Yes…" he smirks proudly.

"I see. You're a new face. What's your name?"

"Petrith Girhani. Ignore the costume. As much as I like parading around as a military officer, I'm not quite there yet."

"Really! Well, it looks good on you. Take the lift upstairs and speak to someone at the desk. You might also want to change clothes along the way, or you might confuse them."

"Now why would I want to do such a silly thing as that? I like confusing people."

"Yes, I think I see your point. All right…Sir," she smiles. "Have it your way."

He turns down the hall to find the lift and rides it upstairs to the third floor.

"Welcome to the Research Center, Lieutenant," announces one of the interns as he approaches the desk. "Can I help you?"

"I was called here to join with Ayene Ti'van. Do you happen to know where she is at this time?"

"Ah, yes, I received a call just a moment ago to expect someone. They're currently in the Director's office on the fifth floor. Do you know where that is?"

"Not yet, but I'm sure I can find it. Thanks."

He turns and once again takes the lift. This time he arrives on the fifth floor and follows the corridor until he finds the well-appointed office of the facility director.

"Here I am, Ayene, what do we have?"

The Director and Azina both turn to see the stately form of the military officer entering the room.

"Good," she responds. "Director Bak'vayn, Azina, this is a friend of mine, Petrith Girhani. He's going to see if he can offer some help with your little problem."

"Is he another..." the Director lingers in his statement.

"Petrith, show them your true colors, will you please?"

"Aw, but the girls love a man in uniform. Just ask the one downstairs," he smiles.

"Ahem. Petrith..." she intones mockingly.

"Yes Ma'am."

"Ayene," Azina shies away. "Is he actually for real?"

"How do you mean real?"

Petrith transforms his image to his normal appearance while the room observes.

"Ooh," Azina croons. "Now that's what I call real."

"Yes, but you'll need to take a number," he affirms. "I've already got three of them back home fighting for my attention."

"In all the nether-space, how did you manage that?"

"Good breeding and a smooth approach," he grins.

"I see you have those glowing eyes," the Director muses. "Are you more of Velen's group?"

"What's left of it..."

"How many are there? I recall stories of a large number of people departing with him."

"According to our history, we started with something like three hundred thousand people on the ship."

"Three hundred thousand on a single ship?!" Azina blasts. "In all the nether-space, just how big was that thing?"

"The size of a small city... It's basically a large colony vessel design, and we were packed in tight. But with the Marshal hitting us so many times, and killing large numbers of our population, we got bumped from one world to another where we tried repopulating, only to lose more on the next one. This last time was bad though. Our numbers are only about ten thousand by now, and this doesn't count how many we lost along the way. I'm several generations away from the original group."

"Incredible," the Director wheezes. "And I am so terribly sorry for that."

Petrith approaches the desk to examine the terminal.

"So, what do we have here?"

"I'm a little unsure how you can help," the Director states. "But if you would like to take a look, I have it right here on my screen."

Petrith sets his pouch on the desk and leans in to observe as the Director pulls up the file.

"I assume you're using the standard network operating system here, right?"

"Yes, it's a common interface on most systems."

"Do you mind if I take over a moment?"

"Oh, of course..."

The Director vacates his chair to allow Petrith to sit down. He pulls out some of the chips from his bag and sets them on the desk, then sorts through them and selects one to insert into the reader. He accesses the chip and displays a folder with several applications. The Director leans over his shoulder to observe.

"May I ask what you have there?"

"I've been collecting a number of archival files from Central Command on their old security codes. And I have a few utilities to help me identify which one might be in use here so we can apply the right algorithm to unlock this thing."

"But wait a minute. You're not actually with Central Command, so what does this mean? You're a spy?"

"He's a hacker," Azina smirks. "That's what I think they were called once upon a time."

"Personally," Petrith grins. "I like the term Cyber Intelligence Acquisitions Officer. It has a certain ring to it, don't you think?"

"Yeah, right!" she huffs. "Well, I suppose if you're working for a top-secret security agency, you need to have some sort of skills."

"Skills..." Ayene muses cutely. "I heard a story about him that when he was a young boy, he hacked his way into a top-level and VERY secure Security Council mainframe, the sort of thing that was supposed to be hack proof. How is that for skill?"

"Ugh! That sounds downright dangerous. And so you put him to work for you instead?"

"Hey, you can't pass up something like that, especially in a time of war."

Petrith brings up an application and runs it on the troublesome file. The program conducts a quick analysis of the file header and pops up an identification string. He clicks on a button to have it begin decrypting the header using a master key, which serves as a type of authority override for the military to gain access to a file no matter who made it. It is applied to the string as a universal unlock to reveal the password once used on the rest of it. Then, the password is applied to the remainder of the file to decrypt the data and return the result.

Ayene, the Director, and Azina all watched as the terminal churned out the resulting file in only a few moments time. Petrith then clicked on the new file in the folder to pull up the document on the display.

The Director and Azina were both stunned at the apparent ease of Petrith's labors. The Director let out a soft chuckle while Azina simply shook her head in disbelief.

"If this guy were let loose on the street," she moans. "He would be a public hazard."

"Too late, Doll," Petrith grins. "I've already been there."

The Director stepped in closer to examine the chart.

"Look at this, Azina," he states as he inspects the data. "I've never seen a layout like this before."

The girl moves in closer while Petrith steps out of the way and repacks his bag. He and Ayene then hang back over their shoulders as the group continues to ponder the results.

"Metacytogenic Linkage?" Azina wonders. "Trans-somatopathic Induction? Asymmetric Paraneural Cohesion? In all the nether-space, who invented these terms? This isn't science!"

"Not our science, at least," the Director concludes, "which doesn't leave too many other possibilities."

"But what does it do? How do we decipher the names to understand their meanings?"

"These terms sound as if they would be right up Elder Nazég's alley for his science faction, assuming even HE could decipher them. And it makes me wonder if this was yet another reason why he, among all of them, was chosen to be contacted and removed by those strange beings."

"Maybe."

"But now we need to understand these new sequences. Azina, you have your work waiting for you. Run it through the simulator and see what happens."

"Right, I just hope I don't overload the system with it," she winces. "This pattern looks complex."

"Do the best you can. We need to understand how this works so we can find a solution to it. And then we need to retool our facility to start producing a counteragent in mass quantities. I would also like to share this with some of my colleagues, maybe to bring a few more minds into it for additional study."

"Well," Petrith accedes. "It looks like the two of you will be busy for a while. If there's nothing more, then I guess my work is done for now."

"Yes, and thank you, Petrith. You too, Ayene. We'll handle it from here, and I'll let you know of our results."

"Very good, Director," Ayene offers with a nod. "Petrith, we should report this in to bring them up-to-date."

"Yes Ma'am."

The two of them redirect their focus to the WIC building and fold themselves away, while Azina collects the data file on a new holo-chip and returns back to her workstation.

✦✦◆✦✦

At the city's primary video entertainment station and broadcast hub, known as Capitol Prime Communications, the lead anchorwoman was preparing for a nightly news broadcast. The cameramen lined up their equipment as she and her co-anchor prepared their news reports. Then the countdown begins.

"Places, everyone," the coordinator announces. "We're going online in three, two, one..."

The program begins with the classic theme music and colorful logo for the CPComm global network, followed by the announcer's voice declaring yet another episode of Capitol Prime News. First in the spotlight was the lead anchorwoman.

"This is Ileani Ur'paran for C.P. News. Our main story for today

continues to involve the protest marches occurring at industrial parks around the world. These protests have been denouncing the parks as the worst environmental disaster in recorded history, and all for the lack of due diligence by the Council to review the situation during this period in order to update the technology being used to the more ecologically friendly methods employed elsewhere. The leaders of this environmentalist movement continue to cite Article Twenty-Three of the Charter of Laws, and the failure of these industries to conform to the legal standards for environmental protection and pollution control.

Furthermore, the demonstrators are calling for the dismissal of the long-standing emergency condition of war we have been living under during this time relating to the insurgent attacks. As you know, since the time of the arrival of the Marshal and Sargeras, we have been offering our services to give aid to them against these insurgents, and after ten long millennia of successfully defending ourselves against them, the leaders of this group are demanding action to reevaluate the need to maintain this condition that forces us to apply this very same industry. They are stating there has never been a historical account of a local incursion in or around Azgarén home space; therefore, it becomes obvious these insurgents should not be regarded as a serious threat to our planetary security.

There is still no official word from the Council on this, even though a spokesperson was recently interviewed as saying they are in deep deliberation and will provide the public with their opinions once they have come to an appropriate conclusion.

Meanwhile, the protests seem to be attracting the public's attention during this time, and several of the demonstrations have been seen to be growing in numbers, as local residents join the march in their support of this clear and obvious concern for public health and the harm being conducted to our world's ecology…"

Chapter 2

HIDDEN REPRISALS

Ayene was making another covert visit to Azgarén, this time at the main courthouse located near the government center. Her plan today was to visit the office of a well-known magistrate to make a quiet deal with him and to pull him into her circle for a later play on the airwaves. As with so many other offices, she first arrives at the secretary's desk.

"Welcome, Ma'am," the middle-aged woman states politely. "May I help you?"

"Yes, I have an appointment to meet with Magistrate Par'lakur."

The woman checks her terminal for the scheduling.

"You are…Special Agent Ayene Ti'van?"

"Yes I am."

"A special agent? What branch of service are you from?"

"Azgarén Central Intelligence, we're a new planetary security agency specializing in internal security, for instance relating to corruption by government officials, also such things as espionage, and foreign and domestic threats like terrorism."

"Terrorism! My goodness, do we actually have that occurring now?"

"Our department has been involved in a number of recent investigations, and we hold a solid opinion that we might be in danger of exactly this, although the details of it need to be maintained as confidential so far in order to protect the public interest. We certainly do not want any new panics occurring in the streets."

"I see. Well, I believe the Magistrate is currently available, so you can go right in."

"Thank you."

Ayene nods politely and turns to enter the private office of the Magistrate. As she steps inside, she closes the door behind her.

"Magistrate Par'lakur? I'm Special Agent Ti'van. A pleasant greeting to you..."

The mature man behind the desk looked up at her and offered his return greeting.

"Yes indeed, Special Agent Ti'van," he responds formally. "Come and sit down here. What is it you desire on this occasion? I am curious as to this title of yours...a special agent. It is not a very common title to see."

"No, I suppose it isn't, but you should get used to it, as you'll likely be seeing more of it soon."

"Really. Then what seems to be the concern that it would call on someone like you?"

"Magistrate, I need to tell you a story, and then I need you to agree to offer your professional aid. We have an issue of planetary security at stake here. Right now, my department is working on a series of highly sensitive projects in cooperation with a foreign body, and in relation to the Marshal, who as it turns out lied to us about who he is, where he came from, and why he's here."

The Magistrate instantly turned a sour face at the blatant suggestion. He leaned in to listen more intently.

"What sort of allegations are we speaking of here?"

"First, the Marshal and Sargeras are better described as fugitives and refugees of an ancient war between their society and a rival faction over a legal issue they were discovered violating. When these others tried to apply their own form of justice, most of Sargeras's people were punished and removed, but it seems Sargeras and Darumon escaped and went into hiding. Unfortunately, they came out looking for this so-called aid to their great cause, which is actually a revenge attack on their former rivals, and here is where we come in."

"A revenge attack," he muses. "What manner of conduct is this you say they were found performing?"

"We are speaking of societies that exist on a scale that could easily be described as gods in comparison to us. Their level of development would truly dwarf ours by any measurable evaluation. Sargeras and his kind were discovered to be committing a series of atrocities on lesser lifeforms, more like on our scale, and using them as a form of entertainment sport. These others simply took offence to it."

"Indeed! So, what was this elaborate story of his insurgents?"

"Elaborate story," she smirks. "Yes, elaborate indeed."

The Magistrate took quick notice of the emotional display, as it tended to stand out.

"Did I just see you reacting to something?"

"Yes, Magistrate, we are disabling our interfaces. We believe them to be a part of his elaborate story."

"What?" he jerks back.

"The Tav'ageen Anomaly, for instance, is being regarded as a hoax. The demand for these seed entities he pushed at us is also being regarded as a ruse of some kind, and likely with ulterior motives. As for his insurgents, it was simply a cover to push everything else at us. He has no interest in giving us any gifts of wisdom. He's just using us for our military and perhaps our technology, and all for ulterior motives relating to this revenge attack."

"Against these others? But one moment, using US for OUR technology? If he is so much higher, why use us?"

"Very simply, he is in exile from his natural element, so we are the next best thing."

"Oh, how unfortunate."

"Yes," she smiles tenderly. "He recently made an advance on a world owned by them. It was a secret maneuver. They regard Sargeras and his kind as a dead society by now, so this would've accounted as a terrorist attack by unknown forces. Fortunately, the Marshal, and I use the term loosely, was discovered along the way. Meanwhile, our organization made secret contact once we learned of these events. We were curious about these people, because of all the stories HE was giving out. He retreated from this encounter rather hastily, and also with an excuse for why, which has nothing to do with the actual cause, and naturally this stood out."

"Naturally. Because he was discovered, I suppose, and he is essentially in hiding."

"Yes. And for all his stories of insurgents, you might think we were on the offensive, not making a sneak attack."

"Indeed, that might stand out to anyone who is paying attention."

"Here is where we found out who he really is. And as you can probably imagine, we're not happy about it."

"I suppose I can understand that. What sort of plans do you…or these others…have to correct this?"

"This is where I need your help. Sargeras and Darumon are regarded as a flight risk, and being godlike entities, they don't need spaceships to do this. They presumably hold the power within their minds to fold space directly. This is dangerous, for a number of reasons, not the least of which is to escape to places unknown and try again elsewhere. So, our first concern is we need to play a careful game on them to distract their attention while these others make their own secret advance."

"All right, so far this sounds reasonable, but this also sounds more like a military maneuver. How would someone like me play into it?"

"Where we are concerned, our role is part of the distraction, and also to release ourselves from what the Marshal did here on our world. He played a lot of tricks on us during this time for all his stories, and virtually all of it behind our collective backs. We need to unravel some of this. Think of it this way. He built a house of brick and stone, and layered it with thick weatherproofing on the outside. But he is armed and dangerous inside that house to anyone he might see through the windows. We need to peel away that weatherproofing, and then erode the brick and stone, while at the same time not openly revealing ourselves to him through those windows. Do you see my point in this curious little picture?" she smiles.

"That is a very interesting depiction, but I think so."

"My department is currently working on unraveling some portion of this already. For instance, we found out he installed regulators in our media stream who were censoring and fabricating news reports for the public."

"What?! That is a clear violation of Article Nine, Section Fourteen!"

"Yes, and this might represent those windows. He was managing us with his stories, maybe also monitoring us for whatever reactions we might have, all through them."

"Interesting. And I see here a demonstration of your point with that depiction."

"Naturally, we arrested them, but quietly, as we don't want him to know we're on to him yet. Then we replaced them with our own people to simulate his management schemes, but working it our way, so we can send our countermeasure actions out to the people. But it has to be done in such a way that it might not stand out as open defiance."

"Is he really that dangerous?"

"We believe so. Just look at the Tav'ageen Scare. We believe HE is responsible as the alien infestation."

"Oh no…" he moans.

"But from here, it gets nasty, as it has to involve the Council. Those regulators were said to be mandated by them, which would mean THEY ordered this, perhaps on behalf of the Marshal."

"Uh oh, and now this suggests a cooperative effort."

"I suppose you could claim a valid reason, meaning that Scare, in order to keep the people calm. But regulating frightening detail and fabricating false information are two very different things."

"Yes! I would agree."

"Now, if we are speaking of the Council, this would run deep and very sensitive to our world population. But this next part is under a high security rating to keep it quiet until we can make a few other movements first. You need to understand the severity of the situation before I can reveal it to you. Agreed?"

"All right, I will abide by your terms, but I will tell you ahead of time, this is starting to wear on me."

"I know, so hold on a bit more. So far, only a handful of people actually know of this. We are playing this as a series of steps with critical thresholds where something breaks and part of that brick wall of his falls away. This is the eroding aspect of the game."

"Got it."

"To put it simply, the Council is missing."

The Magistrate frowned sternly, and quickly clutched at his interface for a minor feedback hit. He pulled back in his chair and glared at her.

"They are missing! How do you mean? Do we know why, and what happened to them?"

"My people do, and it's not pretty. Let's first build another picture. It would seem there is some critical detail gathering up, but a lot of people slipped the tip for putting it together during this long period of time. For instance, that deliberation. I did some research on the DataNet recently and found the last time anyone saw one of them physically was during the release of the Tav'ageen Suppressor chip back in 9765.31. Then they vanish from view as part of this alleged deliberation. That was nearly ten millennia ago, Magistrate. You do recall our average lifespans, do you not? And some of them were old-timers back then," she grins shyly.

"That would be a problem, right there. They might not even still be alive at this time. But it also represents another immediate problem, and that would be the elections we had since then."

"Yes, it would. So, this carries us to the next part. My research also indicated those elections simply reelected the same people during this entire period of time. So we are speaking of what seems to be the original people from way back then."

"Incredible! Even though the time offset would leave some of them deceased by now…possibly?"

"Possibly. And not seen physically during this entire period of time. This led me to another item on the list. Why didn't anyone, like close family members, say anything during this time."

"Uh oh…I am getting a tingling in my horns now."

"I'm not surprised. They are also missing. Here is what I found. It would seem, in the early days of the Tav'ageen Scare, the military quarantined them as a means of protecting them from potential harm. But no one was told about this, as it was classified behind a high-level security clearance, which itself doesn't make sense. Who are they hiding from if the Scare was some alien thing harming our people, rather than any part of our native population that should know what their elected government is doing out there."

"Yes, I would agree."

"This includes both the Council proper and their immediate family members. The Council would then be returned only for press releases, but taken away again as a continuation of this quarantine procedure. At the end of the Scare, they were supposedly brought back and went into this long deliberation. However, they were never actually brought back, or at least, this is to say, not to the Grand Hall. The Grand Hall is empty, and not simply empty, but nearly in a state of collapse, as the doors were kept locked and not even a building inspector allowed inside. I managed to push my way past the receptionist guarding the door and saw it. Then I arrested the Internal Secretary for a number of fraudulent acts he admitted to, including, get this, election fraud to keep this one Council in power during this full period."

"You must be joking!" he shouts and clutches at his interface harder.

"No, I'm not. This is not simply an oversight for building maintenance, and not even a Council gone AWOL. This is a deliberate attempt to hide something. Especially if you consider the condition of that room, where they could not even bother themselves to check the light bulbs on occasion. Somebody ordered it closed, and maintained an order to keep it that way, and further hid it behind all these so-called spokespeople giving out their tail-crazy excuses that the Council is deliberating something. And still, none of us were told anything, other than they WERE in there, and they WERE deliberating something."

"This does indeed go well beyond simply covering up an oversight or a Council with PR issues. Even if we say they cheated the elections and went into hiding, they should be dead of natural causes by now… at least some of them. And to be quarantined for any reason is one thing, but not to tell the rest of us is unreasonable censorship. These are our public officials who should be serving the public interest. I will also admit, this touches on a private ire I have been holding for some time relating to this deliberation, and the complete lack of any other form of service."

"I think you would not be alone in that, and here is where we need to peel away that weatherproofing layer I mentioned earlier."

"Interesting. All right, how do we imagine this part of your most curious metaphoric depiction?" he attempts a soft smile.

Ayene returned the smile, realizing she was making a good impression on the esteemed legal counselor.

"The first thing you need to know is the military carried them away to a place identified as Site One-Alpha, according to military records. This is the quarantine site. Unfortunately, even though the statements claim the Council is in deliberation, their families are still locked behind that same security roadblock. You cannot determine where they are or if they are alive or dead. Not unless you can tap into the secure government files for such things as tax returns and other personal information," she smirks.

"Why do I get the impression you already did that?"

"Why, Magistrate," she emits innocently. "Do I look like the sort of person who would peek under the tail of something like that?"

"I think I will reserve judgment on that for now. What about this quarantine site, are we saying they never left? The families should not be a security issue, not like the Council, so what else could be the cause?"

"I don't think any of them left. According to my research, not even Central Command knows any of this, which is disturbing if they are the ones doing the work. But Site One-Alpha was destroyed in the early moments of these insurgent attacks. Which means the Marshal, for all his stories, and very likely one or more of his cover-ups telling the military to hit something, hit THEM as well. But the military, like the rest of us, never knew the Council was actually out there."

"How, in all the nether-space, can those people not know what they themselves did with our Council?"

"This is a fine question to ask, Magistrate. The answer is very unfortunate, however. The Marshal applies these security restrictions to literally everything he does, and independently to each person he gives instructions to. To Person A, he might say, 'Take the Council and quarantine them…'. Then, to Person B, he says, 'Hey, look! Insurgents! Go kill!" she flourishes theatrically with her hands. "Finally, to Person A again, he simply thanks him for helping, but not to worry, as some Person C finished it by bringing them home. And to each and all of them…this never happened."

"Unbelievable! This would require a work effort to fabricate and manage this level of intrigue."

"Therefore, the brick house and its weatherproofing. And worse, you should also know, he expects his pet military to follow every command he gives out. One of his famous mandates, which is what he really wanted out of the Council to gain control of the rest of us, was a top-secret military grade neural implant to literally take control of their minds. All those so-called insurgents were probably innocent worlds he blasted simply for his personal pleasure, as would fit the psychology of their kind, and thus the reason for these ancient crimes. With the push of a button, our military becomes his private killing machine."

"Oh please!" he moans.

"Yeah, here is where we need to be so careful and peel away his control mechanism. We have control of our military again, thanks to Commander Geilv turning over to our side, but the Marshal doesn't know it yet, and could still be a danger by himself. He lied to us about virtually everything, and used fear tactics to gain control. The Tav'ageen Scare is his doing. He took advantage of a situation and exploited it against us. The trouble is, the real cause behind the original Anomaly is still an issue, and the public needs to be made aware of it, so he doesn't hold the power to do it again."

"Oops! Would this represent more of that weatherproofing, or the brick itself by now?"

"It has to go in layers. And here we come down to someone like you. We are a pet society to him. A society that is expected to behave a certain way, as per his instruction. This would account for his regulators, the perception of the Council doing anything, and the rest of us stuck in a holding pattern waiting till the end of time for that great wisdom of his."

"Thank you so much for the encouragement," he shakes his head ironically.

"But things are about to change," Ayene asserts. "His pet society is starting to wake up to those long-duration clues that have been building up under our noses, regardless of his efforts to hide them. It's very innocent, you see. All you need to do is ask one little question, and here comes a tide of controversy. You can't stop a full planetary population from realizing someone slipped the tip on something so clearly obvious."

"Uh huh. It sounds like you people were taking lessons from someone out there."

"Yes, I suppose so," she chuckles softly.

The Magistrate once again pondered her clear freedom of emotional expression. It was starting to wear on him that she could experience this while so many others, including himself, were so restricted.

"By the way," he asks. "If you people are turning these things off, can this be done for anyone else?"

"Yes. We are working alongside the ARC on a number of side concerns, like these chips and the seeds. They are organizing a very quiet program to disable the chips. I would recommend it, but keep it under control for now when you're out in the open."

"Thank you, I would love to be able to laugh again without having half my brain fried for the favor of it."

"Absolutely. Now, on to this next part. Have you been paying attention to the recent news by Ileani Ur'paran? That specialized military industry out there that's been polluting the place to all the nether-space."

"Actually, yes. I have noticed recently there have been a number of demonstrations out there protesting that industry."

"This is our work. The protests started out as staged events, but we are calling attention to this discrepancy, and it seems to be working. We're playing it up like the Marshal and our military, for all their wonderful efforts, have protected our world from harm. Therefore, we can no longer justify this enduring emergency condition that permits the industry in the first place."

"All right, this is a good start. But what if he tries something to reestablish himself?"

"We think he cannot do that by now. Ten millennia, and we are undefeated in battle against his superior alien forces. To start something now, right when someone is asking questions about it, would stand out as VERY coincidental."

"Ouch!" he blasts satirically, and then lets out a minor chuckle, but is quickly stifled with a feedback hit. "That one was worth it. Yes, he seems to have backed himself into a corner. So this, I think, would be some of that weatherproofing, to tear away at his reasoning to have it in the first place."

"Very good," she nods. "Another aspect has to reflect on another clear element that the people seem to have forgotten, but we are holding this in reserve for now to pop it out later. Elder Nazég and that ship. The Marshal claimed THEY were his insurgents. This means, we are chasing all across the galaxy hunting someone who clearly knows where we live, and have jump drives to reach us. And their primary target should be Sargeras, not anything else. This discrepancy should stand out to ask why we were out THERE to begin with. So, if the Marshal should argue, we'll simply hit him with this and see how he likes it."

"Yes, and that should twist a few horns along the way…ten millennia of them."

"And all this will eventually cascade into other things when the Council, for all their deliberation, fails to respond to this most important real-world issue. Here we will start to see a bit of that brickwork come off."

✦✦✦

"Your grace, do you have a moment?"

"Lady Sehnisavain, such a pleasure. It has been a while since the last time we spoke. Please come in."

Priestess Sehnisavain was making a visit to the WIC building from her home in Kynesoth, where she and the other High Elves, who were once slaves to Darumon and Sargeras as the Flame Elves, had made a successful rehabilitation in the years after the war. Accompanying her was another familiar face, also from that period. The two women approached the table for their consultation with Thaelyn.

"And young Mynae," he observes. "Are you also making a visit on this fine day?"

"Yes, my Lord," she responds pleasantly. "It's been a while, and I've been keeping myself quite busy, as you may know. But on this occasion, I asked the Lady here if she could bring me forward to you with something that has been returning to my mind of late."

"Indeed. And what might that be?"

Mynae looked up at Sehnisavain for her blessing to present herself. The Priestess nods politely, and the girl continues with her address.

"Well, if you recall those first days after you liberated us from… our most unfortunate affair, we spoke about possibly one day when we might have a chance to redeem our honor for his treatment of us. I have been in deep thought many times these past several years, as the memories are difficult to overcome, and I still feel as though I would wish to afford some small role in this matter. I have been in discussion with others, as well, and there are many of us who feel this way. I have also tried to keep myself abreast of our progress, as best I can, to see if there might be any opportunities for us."

"I see, and I do recall this conversation once before. But we must keep in mind, however, you are rated as a civilian, not a member of our military, and I generally do not bring civilians out onto the battlefield."

"Yes, I can surely understand this. You are a very wise and compassionate ruler, and the people do love you so. I once considered military service, but that thought quickly subsided as I fell into the calmer setting of civilian life, and I think I am quite content there. However, this does not necessarily quell all of my feelings. And so I decided to investigate a little more to see if there might be at least some small element of service I could perform, if only to bring that tiniest amount of satisfaction to my mind that I made a stand, and he knew about it."

"He, meaning Darumon? All things considered, making a stand in front of such a creature as that is not always a safe course of action, dear Child."

"I suppose not," she grins. "But even so, it would surely bring a curious turn of affairs before his eyes to see his long-lost servants turned against him. I cannot be sure if he would take any sort of action, but if I understand this correctly, he might be there merely for the entertainment value, and I had a thought."

"A thought… Oh dear, now what?"

"To help me understand better what was occurring out there, I had to find consultation with someone who seems to hold very close ties with you and the people who are actually performing most of this. And so, I found two young women who seemed very knowledgeable."

"Please, not them," Thaelyn mutters softly. "Do not tell me you spoke with those two…"

"They were a human named Marelle and a Night Elf named Relissa."

"Dear Powers, not another one!" he lays his head in his hand. "General, prepare my private list again, we have another name."

"Yes, my Lord," he responds. "Gracious, we may need to start a new page soon."

"Very well, Mynae, what sort of errant mischief did they set you upon?"

"Oh, they did not necessarily set me upon anything; this has yet to come into full fruition. Here is my situation. Since that day when we were liberated, some of us went into service for our trades, and others decided to take advantage of the wonderful academies you have available. As a mage, I was particularly excited to find I could enter into your arcane studies, although granted I was in the civilian course. But still, it was a luxury for me. With such a rich diversity of possibilities, I was having a hard time deciding my final school of study, but I found I was moving mostly into elemental magic, since that was what I was studying before."

"Yes, I believe I recall some small mention once, although you were still under the effect of his control at the time you threw that one out," he grins.

"Yes, burning everything to the ground. My deepest apologies, but I think you probably understand the situation well enough."

"Indeed, but if you are thinking of using elemental forces on our enemies, I hope you were made aware during your consultation that our only true enemies here are Darumon and Sargeras. If we go into any sort of action against the Suuden-Aryku, I am hoping not to cause any serious harm, as they are also victims in this affair."

"Yes, they told me that, but I would hardly stand much of a chance to throw fireballs at Sargeras and live to tell the tale."

"Absolutely! Therefore, I am at something of a loss to suggest how you could play a role, unless those terrible twins suggested something," he raises an eyebrow suspiciously.

"Well, no, not directly, and recall that I said we are more likely to be involved in the entertainment aspect of it. So, whatever display I put on should be reasonably harmless, but yet to show my stand against him. This is something of a game, after all. The Suuden-Aryku are his playing pieces, and we are yours. Therefore, why not add a little wildcard into it."

"A wildcard, yes, this sounds just like them. Very well, Mynae; let us hear what this wildcard is about."

"As I said, there are a fair number of us who have come together and expressed an interest in making this statement on behalf of our people. To the best of my understanding, you are building a type of arena battlefield. Somewhere, you will have your front line of soldiers, and your support troops will be in the rearward positions. As a mage, this would normally be my place anyway. The game you will be playing with Sargeras is mostly to hold his attention until you can make whatever final move you have in mind to bring him down."

"Yes, but also keep in mind, this scene has a large number of variables we cannot yet fully realize. So, many things are subject to change."

"Of course, I suppose that is the nature of it. But if I cannot throw something like a fireball, I must throw something else. And if it is not intended to harm, it must at least represent something like a slap in the face for what he did to us."

"But slapping him, or the Suuden-Aryku?"

"Again, if I tried assaulting him directly, I might not live long enough to see the end result. Also, if to use an unfortunate term, we're all just pawns anyway."

"I suppose you may be right, in some respect," he nods solemnly. "The gods sometimes play these games, and the small ones are made the pawns. Although, I will admit, in the case of the Estelar, they typically play this in order to solve a larger issue. Very well, but how do you envision this slap in the face?"

"I toyed with many thoughts, but my studies in elemental magic were not appropriate for most of it. And I doubted much of this would be a part of the civilian course anyway. I thought about a conjuring of some sort, but it cannot be a vicious animal that could bite and cause harm. I then considered illusionary magic, but this is a very different school from where I am. Then another thought came to mind that actually fit my selected school. I could summon forth a conjured elemental."

"An elemental… We must be careful here, Mynae," he cautions. "One must not trifle with such things. How would you use this?"

"A single strike hit. A row of us, thusly trained, could bring up a line of elementals, in this case water elementals. We would keep it simple, using lesser forms of the conjuring. We would then send them off as a wave to splash across the faces of the enemy line, perhaps simply to knock them off their feet and give a thorough soaking before the creatures drain off into that river I hear is on the other side. But, of course, we would need a local water source on our side to call them forth."

Thaelyn leans back in his chair to consider the notion. The image might actually be rather amusing to see for anyone, if only for the exception that it was on a battleground during a skirmish. And yet, for Sargeras, he might find it entrancing enough to capture his attention, while not actually causing any real harm to the opponent.

"Curious," he muses, then producing a grin and followed by a boisterous laugh. "Incredible! General! Why am I surrounded by so many mischief-makers on this world with such innovative ideas?"

"I cannot know, my Lord," he returns with a grin. "It is a wild world, and so are those who live here."

Mynae smiled brightly that she made such an impression, but she still waited for his final response.

"Mynae," Thaelyn continues. "This idea of yours is a most interesting formulation. But the conjuring spell you speak of is a rather high-level spell and, well, so far at least, reserved mostly for military use, with only limited civilian potential."

"I am aware of that. It's a Circle Seven spell. I already learned about that from Relissa, who is currently in that class. I'm at Circle Six right now, but again the civilian course. This is my problem. If I were to be allowed to make this play at all, I would need to take a Circle Seven course to study this spell. But this is the advanced school. If I am not part of the military, or otherwise involved in a profession that would demand this class, I am unsure how I might be allowed to do this. And so, I come before you to ask if you could offer your advice."

Thaelyn leans to one side in his chair and taps a finger to his cheek.

"You say there are others involved in this desire. Are they all mages, and how many?"

"To the best of my understanding, we have heard from a few

thousand who have an interest in this pursuit, but not all of them are mages. They come from many walks, and therefore some might simply stand in the background as we perform our play. But in practice, we could limit this study to just enough to make a single line across the field."

He continues to ponder the idea, trying to visualize it in his mind. It would indeed make a good play, and perhaps even serve to draw Sargeras deeper into the action. But this was a military action, not normally given into civilian hands. If he were to grant this request, he would need to make a special exception to the rule for it.

"Very well, here is what we will do. Mynae, I will place you and the Priestess here in charge of this. Select your combatants. General, I will have you draw up a document granting special privileges to this girl and her team to study Seventh Circle elemental conjuring, specifically the water elemental. And we will bypass the testing procedure on this occasion to grant them this privilege."

"Very good, my Lord," he nods.

"Mynae, it is certainly possible, if you have such a desire, to enter the full class as a technical skill, assuming you can meet the entrance requirements, as it does involve this under certain applications. But for now we will grant this to you for this one occasion."

Mynae perks up with a brilliant smile, glancing at Sehnisavain for her response before replying.

"Oh, thank you, my Lord! I thank the gods above for sending you to us. If it were not for that, I shudder to think what may have become of us."

+ ﹢ ﹢ ◆ ﹢ ﹢ +

A new week was passing and Ileani was in the process of giving out another follow-up news bulletin.

> *"…In the news today, continued protesting has been reported to be causing disruptions of some local workforces at the specialized industrial parks ordered and maintained by the Council emergency war protocols. Although no violence has been reported, security forces have been called on at least a few occasions to oversee the crowds that continue to grow in response to the rising concerns over the pollution levels being generated by these industries.*

Sources inside the Council Grand Hall continue to maintain that the Council is in deep deliberation of these and other matters, but a growing outcry is mounting of protesters who are becoming impatient with the Council issuing the same statements every time. Because of this, claims are being made that the Council is showing signs of negligence to review the policy in question, as well as these facilities at any time during this period we have described ourselves to be at war with these insurgent forces. Some leaders are even threatening lawsuits, not only against the industries for the damage they have caused, but also the Council for its apparent lack of concern of the underlying issues..."

Ayene was making a return visit to the Grand Hall as a continuation of her plans to develop an image of the Council's lack of real work at serving the people. A young woman sat at the reception desk in an intersection of corridors leading off to the various offices, as well as the large ornate doors leading inside the Grand Hall central chamber where the Council was said to be conducting their work. When she saw Ayene's face, she felt a cold snap rush through her. She watched Ayene carefully as the officer approached the desk.

"Hello again, Lena," Ayene announces pleasantly. "Keeping yourself busy?"

"Yes Ma'am," she replies tepidly. "And you?"

"Doing well enough..."

Ayene passes a quick glance around the area before moving in closer and leaning on the desk to converse more discreetly.

"I need a private word with you," she whispers.

Lena cautiously scans the lobby to see if anyone might be in proximity, but the coast was clear for now. She then returns to Ayene.

"What do you need this time, Lieutenant?" she mutters softly. "I'm still trembling from your last visit, and this time I can actually feel it, after having my chip disabled."

"We're not finished here, Lena, and it's likely to get worse before it gets better. But I need everyone in line to get the job done, and that means you too."

"All right, so what is it you have this time?"

"I recall you said you work this shift for only six hours, and then you trade off with others, right?"

"Yes Ma'am."

"I want you to start passing word to all the other girls who work this desk. Have them meet with one of our people over at the ACI office. You still have the address, right?"

"Yes Ma'am," she nods.

"Good. As for you, I'm going to give you some instructions directly, as we're already familiar with each other, and like it or not, this now places you in a special role."

"Uh oh…"

"Relax, but you will probably need to improvise a little on your acting skills."

"Acting skills… Now I wish I took that course we had back in my junior school," she grins softly.

"Yes, and I'm sure you're not the only one," she smiles.

Ayene makes another pass around the area and waves for the girl to follow her behind the desk towards the double doors leading to the inner chamber. There, they retreat into a corner for a close chat.

"All right, listen carefully," Ayene begins quietly. "As for the other girls, tell them they'll get their briefings in our office. But you, young lady, are about to make history…at least in a small and perhaps indirect way."

"Um, I never really wanted to make history. I'm just trying to make my way with a job that pays the bills."

"Yes, well, this job is about to get noticed. I'm going to send some people in here, including a reporter, to interview you and our temporary Internal Secretary for some important details relating to how things work in here. She'll have her instructions, and you'll just follow along with your usual story…the same one you gave me once upon a time."

"All right, that sounds easy enough…so far."

"The other group will come later, and they'll be dressed as maintenance workers, so that no one takes any special notice of them. They'll want access inside the room here, but we need to make sure no one actually sees them go in or come out again."

"Um, all right, I suppose I can do that. But what are they actually going to do in there?"

"Fix the roof…" she grins and chuckles wickedly.

Lena's eyes began to bulge, and she almost felt like running away.

She glanced at the door, trying to recall the clutter of debris that littered the floor, and the extreme decay they found in there after Ayene forced her way inside to discover the truth of the Council.

"And then," Ayene continues, "you're probably going to hear a few odd noises. So, like a good little girl, you'll call C.P. Security, as well as the emergency rescue services. Got it?"

"In all the nether-space, I thought you said you were trying to avoid a big sensation."

"THIS sensation is likely to be inevitable. You saw what it looked like in there. But we're engineering it according to our schedule, not some random event, so that it falls in line with a sequence of other events we're putting together, like those protests you've probably seen on the news lately."

"Oh! Is that your work? Yes, I've been paying attention to that. It's the most exciting news I've seen for…well, ever, actually."

"Yes, that's the whole point. We need to turn a few heads on things around here, but do so in an indirect manner. Once word of this sensation gets out, horns will fly, but we're predicting someone, like the Marshal, may try offering some kind of story to cover it up."

"And what will you do after that?"

"So far, this is subjective, depending on the reactions we see, as we have a few directions we can travel. But the picture we're going to build will hopefully drive him into a corner."

"Hopefully… All right, I'm in, I suppose…like it or not. Just give me a little warning beforehand."

<hr>

Another week was closing, and Kaliya and Ayene were making a return to the WIC building for a late meeting to fill in Thaelyn and the others on their work, as well as to review several new ideas they had, and adjustments to a few old ones.

"My Lord," Kaliya announces as she approaches the table.

"Ah, there she is," Thaelyn muses. "I had almost thought the two of you had gone AWOL on us for all your work on Azgarén."

"Not in this lifetime," she smiles. "But I'll admit we have been very busy coordinating those protest marches, as well as drumming up that civilian support. But now we need to move forward with a few of our other plans, and I wanted to update you on our ideas."

"Indeed. And will this require my private list again?" he eyes them suspiciously.

"Um…we're trying to keep a modest profile on this one so far," she grins sheepishly.

"I see, very well, what do we have today?"

"First, we're ready to start taking these protests into the courtrooms. Ayene made contact with a prominent magistrate who isn't very happy with how things are being portrayed through our campaign. The Council, as you might expect, is completely silent in any appropriate form of response to these charges, so it's going to fall to the courts to overturn their emergency protocol."

"How clever, and this generally resolves the problem without pointing any fingers directly at any one individual the Marshal can make disappear."

"Not only that, but to do so would cause an even bigger sensation, and this could turn ugly after a while, so he's going to find himself limited in what he can do about it. The people are simply tired of this continued situation that never gets resolved. He can't possibly expect us, even as trained animals, to sit on it for this long without saying something about it."

"I suppose so."

"Along the way, we need to pave ahead for a few things. One of these is Geilv. He's the HC, the guy who's supposed to be in charge of Central Command…chip or no chip. We have what is essentially a planetary emergency occurring where Ytani is concerned, even though he hasn't officially shown up yet. But the fact that Geilv is receiving advice from his officers that Ytani could make a return at any moment means he needs to keep his horns sharp so he can make decisions on it, and that damnable chip just doesn't give a person the possibility."

"Uh huh…and so, what is he going to do about it? And then, what will the Marshal do about it afterwards?"

"We're thinking of some nondescript young recruit signing up inside Central, fresh out of training and already complaining about the treatment he gets. He's going to start a little behind-the-scenes gossip about his chip, and how he was forced to take it even though he felt he could surely perform without it, at least up until the med-tech informed him it was a standard piece of equipment used as a training aid."

"Uh oh…and so we have these words leaking out now, I presume."

"Oh yes! This is going to cause a minor sensation inside Central, and probably spread to the rest of the military. Those chips are designed to be training aids...that's all they're supposed to be. So, why do all the veteran soldiers in there still have them? And then we return back to Geilv, who will take unilateral action to turn his off, saying he was military since even before the Marshal showed up, and surely didn't need additional training to fight insurgents that never won a single battle."

"Good gracious, Kaliya," the General moans. "While this would certainly resound with a justifiable cause, how do you think the Marshal will take it?"

"Our prediction, if it is worded correctly, is the Marshal might be offended, but Geilv isn't rebelling against the Marshal, only the chip, and the fact that he's a VERY well-seasoned military man, therefore the justification to keep that blasted chip is entirely moot. We feel Geilv is too valuable for the Marshal to take action, not when you factor in Ytani and so many other things. To train up a replacement just isn't practical."

"Well, that's certainly one way of putting it," he chuckles. "He's too valuable to throw away, rebellion or no rebellion."

"Our thoughts on this are highly variable for the timing," Ayene adds. "We don't want to raise any unnecessary issues between them, so we might just keep this in reserve in case it's ever needed to justify his manners. But we need the story to give a viable alibi."

"Absolutely," Thaelyn notes.

"This could possibly allow us to make other movements with reasonable liberty, but ultimately, he should still try to stay in good sorts with the Marshal so as not to raise suspicion. Although, one of these occasions might relate to something we expect to occur after the Council Grand Hall roof collapses."

Thaelyn gazes at her, and then passes to Kailen and the General before returning to Ayene.

"Are we expecting something unfortunate to occur in there, young miss secret agent?"

"Well, I think it goes without saying, that place was a wreck, so it's quite reasonable to suggest it COULD collapse...if given enough time...or a helping hand," she grins.

Thaelyn glares at her a moment longer until he raises a finger at the General.

"Prepare my list if you please. Keep it handy a moment. Just what sort of helping hand are we suggesting here, Ayene?"

"A group of maintenance workers is going to visit the place for that long-overdue inspection. They'll of course be carrying their…inspection…equipment in a set of large cases. Unfortunately, the requisition forms delivered a set of cutting lasers rather than welding torches. Oops!" she rolls her eyes away innocently.

"Oh! Oops, is it? General?"

"Yes, I see it already," he moans and shakes his head.

Ayene passes a cute smirk at Kaliya for her achievement.

"Are you trying to play catch-up on me now?" Kaliya huffs playfully.

"Anyway," Ayene continues. "Lena, that young girl outside at the reception desk, will give them access, out of sight of anyone else, and they'll go to work to weaken some of the steel reinforcement bars, which at this point is the only thing holding what's left of the roof up there. We'll perforate a few of them and leave, and let gravity do the rest."

"Dear Powers, I feel for that young receptionist when it finally caves in. You should at least give her instructions to take cover at the first sound of it. The shock wave from the air burst might be enough to blast those doors open, and spray a considerable volume of debris through the room."

"All right, good point. But as I said to her, we need this according to our schedule, not something random, so we can combine it with our other efforts."

"Yes, I understand, and this would certainly provide a hefty wake-up call to the general public out there."

"Right. This will open up the sensation of the missing Council, and likely force the Marshal to invent one of his famous excuses, and we're expecting he'll probably hang it on Geilv's horns to deliver the message. But the message will be modified our way, which will turn it around at the Marshal again, in case he should get any funny NEW ideas about anything," she smiles.

"Indeed, and I am already very anxious to see how this turns out. So, I will give you each one mark for the story, and likely another one at the conclusion of it. General?"

"Oops!" Kaliya mutters.

"Oh well," Ayene relents. "At least we both got one."

"Yeah, but I'm still ahead of you," she grins.

✦ ✦ ✦ ◆ ✦ ✦ ✦

In the city of Capitol Prime, near a large courthouse complex, a gathering of local citizens is forming in the plaza outside the building. So far, word on the street is that a high-level case is being proposed and reviewed by a resident magistrate relating to the recent protesting by environmentalists around the world on the dirty industry and the Council's apparent irresponsiveness in taking any corrective action. Ileani was on the scene in an interview with Magistrate Par'lakur to report on some of the details.

"Magistrate," she begins. "Can you explain how the courts might hope to overturn a mandate once issued by the Council, which is regarded as the highest position of law in our society?"

"Miss Ur'paran," he responds courteously. "We are a society of laws, first and foremost. Even the Council needs to recognize this and abide by those same laws they once placed into action over the rest of us. To do otherwise is a clear and obvious violation of their elected roles as lawgivers. They are still citizens of our society, no different from any other, regardless of how so many people seem to treat them as holding such high esteem that they cannot possibly do wrong in the eyes of the people. Therefore, they must be expected to hold due diligence to the needs of the people and our world. And while some may argue this deliberation was a gift that could potentially uplift us as a society, their FIRST duty should be the one we elected them to perform to begin with. As such, in the absence of them apparently doing this in relation to that industry, we are simply taking the appropriate action to ensure those laws are upheld in the spirit they were intended."

"And what sort of response do you expect the Council to give, assuming they actually give one at all, as so many people are claiming negligence on their part for their complete lack of response."

"At this point, if they make any sort of response, I should imagine the first thing they will need to do is give an explanation of why they didn't give any other explanations before now. Their silence is inexcusable, Miss Ur'paran, as a government authority whose responsibility it is to serve the people. The stories we've been told are nothing more than stall tactics. Therefore, we must now decide for ourselves if the condition of war we were placed into is still justifiable for the obvious results we have seen during this time, with or without the Council giving an opinion about it. Once we have this, we can move forward with our decisions on these mandates that were once placed on us for this industry and other things."

"I see, and thank you, Magistrate, for your perspective."

In Commander Geilv's office, he was receiving a familiar visitor. Navina Lar'akan was making a return with additional instructions from Ayene and Kaliya. As she peeks through the door, he calls out to welcome her.

"Come in, Agent Lar'akan. What can I do for you today?"

He directs her into a chair, where she pulls out a data tablet for review.

"Commander, we have some instructions for you. We need to press forward with some of our objectives, but in order for us…meaning you… to perform our duties as we must, we need to ensure our full capacity to meet up to the challenge that will soon be facing us."

"Why do I suddenly get the idea you have some kind of hidden agenda here?"

"Oh, Commander, one person's hidden agenda is another person's revelation! And this revelation is surely long overdue. Follow along with me a moment. Do you have a tablet? I have a file I wish to link over to you."

"Um…"

Geilv reaches behind him to a side table and a tablet he has laying there. The unit was seldom used, but he maintained it just in case. He sets it on the desk and brings up an app to receive a document file.

Navina links hers via a wireless connection and transfers a page of wording over to him. As Geilv studies the file, she continues with her depiction.

"In a nutshell, Commander, we will say you have a new recruit that recently signed up fresh out of training. He is an ambitious young man with hope in his eyes to serve a great and noble cause within our illustrious military. Unfortunately, he is also a bit disgruntled, largely due to the fact that even though he graduated with top honors out of his academy studies, someone told him they needed to stick a chip in his brain before he could go into active service. Naturally, this deflated his ambitions somewhat."

"You know, something tells me you people spend a lot of time inventing stories over there. All right, and what happens to this unfortunate young man?"

"He argues with his med-tech about this chip, as it seemed entirely unnecessary. But when the med-tech explained to him that this was a standard piece of equipment applied to all military personnel as a type of training aid…" she raises her brow conspicuously. "He instantly argued that this should be a violation of his rights as an individual who desired to serve a valuable cause, but NOT as a trained animal with a restraining collar."

"Really! That does indeed sound unfortunate. What ultimately happened to him?"

"His case is still pending, but in the meantime, he has been campaigning to drum up support, as well as awareness, for what he believes to be a vital cause relating to the original stated purpose of these chips, which as it turns out is known by the medical community in some obscure reference dating all the way back to the beginning when the thing was first pushed through the Council. However, due in part to the Council being currently under review for other forms of negligence, as seen in the recent news broadcasts… Do you watch the news broadcasts, Commander?"

"Actually, I fell out of that habit a long time ago, but several of my officers have been bringing reports to me on a protest going on over that industry out there, and the Council's apparent lack of response or action to correct it. Now we have some sort of legal action taking place. This should be interesting to see."

"Right, so this is now prompting a few other things, it would seem. These training aids were one thing they mandated, and apparently, after so long a period of successful campaigns against the Marshal's insurgents, it would seem, according to the argument, that the need for these training aids is no longer justifiable, especially in our most senior officers at Central Command."

As Navina closes, she sports a broad smile at the Commander and leans back in her chair.

Geilv studies her smug expression, and then reads more of the document on his tablet.

"And how am I going to use this as my…revelation? Because I'm getting an impression here that you're telling me to use this for myself."

"Clearly, Commander, you have a long history that dates back even before the Marshal. How can you, he, or anyone else around here, truly justify your need for a training aid to serve in any military. Now, I am aware of the conversation you shared over at the ARC. But we are in a situation where surely, we have a few critical concerns that we feel are necessary for a man like you to require his full faculties to contend with. And let's face it, that chip is very restrictive. Therefore, at some moment, you will simply have had enough of it. You are not currently on active duty on the front lines, and there are events occurring around us right now that might require your attention. The Marshal doesn't seem to concern himself with domestic issues, and as the HC, it naturally falls on you to serve and protect. It's that simple."

"Yes, it is, I must admit. And you, for all your storytelling, are a very clever young lady. All right, I'll look this over and think of a good way to present this. But the next question is when do I actually need to present this?"

"This is difficult to predict. We might keep it as a secret weapon to justify why you suddenly behave as a man who now controls his own affairs. For instance, the events occurring right now of the protests and the lack of Council response might lead us in certain directions. I believe you already know what those directions are. But the Marshal, for all his benevolence to our own cause, might choose to offer alternative explanations as to the reasoning. As we move forward, we might see him being pushed farther and farther into a corner until ultimately it may become necessary for you to demonstrate yourself as a man with a mind of his own to take charge. But generally speaking, play it softly as long as you can, and only pull this one out when the situation grants you enough ground to stand on."

"I swear," he shakes his head. "I wish I knew where you people learn this stuff. All right, I think I get it, though this one seems tricky. So, I'll study this, think of my approach, and if I see a moment for it, I'll play it, but I think only as a last resort if I want to keep him under control."

"Very good, Commander, then I should be on my way again. Good day to you."

Navina gets up and strolls out of the office, leaving the Commander with his tablet and a new set of questions circling through his mind.

◆◆◆◆◆◆◆

Ayene was visiting her office in the city. This was the building they were occupying as part of their operations for the ACI. She was riding the lift upstairs, even though she could simply fold her way up there, but chose not to on this occasion, as she and the other officers were trying to live and work as if they were all corporeal and using traditional methods. This was at least in part due to the fact that some of their resident secretaries were local employees, and didn't otherwise know about the projection skill.

She arrived at the office of the organization's Director, passing through the reception area, and waving at his secretary, then entering into his private office. The Director, in this case, was her former Commander from the mining base they once managed, and also in projected form.

"Lajivi, we're gearing up for our operation inside the Grand Hall. We just received our shipment of cutting lasers, and according to our testing, they should work while in projected mode."

"This projection skill is turning out to be more and more dangerous with each new discovery we make. Very good, Ayene. Once we have our latest set of interviews, we should give ourselves a little bit of time in-between, so it doesn't seem too coincidental, and then we are Go for the Big Hit."

"And big will be the word for it. This will shake the history books."

"Yes, but then I think a lot of things we're doing right now will shake the history books. I just hope there's still someone around later to read them."

"Keep the faith, Commander; we're working a very intricate plan here."

In another part of the city, Ileani was making another foray to conduct an interview. It has been a couple of days since her meeting with the Magistrate, and the court reviews were well underway. On this occasion, she was following up on a little investigative reporting to fill in some background detail.

She was arriving in the plaza with the Council Grand Hall, pausing briefly outside to take in the beauty of the majestic building with its ornate architecture. She glanced around the plaza at the benches and planters, the sculpture and artwork, all of which depicted the grandeur of their world government body, and then reflected on Ayene's instructions concerning the reason for her visit. She pulled out her data tablet for a quick review before proceeding through the front doors. As she enters inside, the first thing she sees is young Lena at the reception desk.

Lena took notice of Ileani almost immediately, as her nerves had become rather tense after Ayene's last visit. Ileani, being a famous vid-com personality, was easily recognizable. And as she and her cameraman approached the desk, Lena struggled to contain herself as she perked up to offer her usual greeting.

"Welcome to the Council Grand Hall. How can I help you?"

Ileani knew they were both working as agents in cooperation with the ACI, so she smiled gently and introduced herself.

"I'm Ileani Ur'paran, and I represent C.P. News."

"Yes Ma'am, I recognized you as you first walked in. You're a little hard to miss. Um, you're smiling, so does that mean…" she raised her brow cautiously.

"Yes, they had me disable my interface. It seems they're doing that for a lot of people lately."

"So it seems. All right, so what do we do now? You're here for an interview, right?"

"Yes, and since we both have our scripts, we'll just put on a little show together. First, we'll have you call up the Internal Secretary, as I understand he's also a part of it, and I need to include him as well. Then, we'll take up a position just over there with those doors in the background," she directs at the Council chamber entrance.

"All right, one moment…"

Lena makes a quick call on her vid-com to the Internal Secretary's office, which at this time was occupied by one of Kaliya's people in projected form, although neither Lena nor Ileani knew about the projections. In several moments, the man comes around the building into the lobby.

By this time, Ileani had positioned Lena just offside of the doors, and she further directed the Secretary to line up next to her, while she oriented herself in front of the doors for the cameraman. She begins the interview with a brief introduction.

"This is Ileani Ur'paran for C.P. News. I am inside the Council Grand Hall, hoping to fill in for the obvious discrepancies we have been experiencing lately due to the recent protests over that polluting industry and the Council's lack of response to the allegations currently underway in the court system. Behind me…" she directs over her shoulder, "…are the doors leading to the inner chamber where the Council is said to be conducting this long and supposedly arduous deliberation that seems to be occupying so much of its time away from other matters of State."

She now steps over to Lena and the Secretary, both of whom stood professionally at attention.

"This young lady here," she glances at Lena, "is one of the

receptionists who works at the front desk here in the lobby area. Miss, can you give us your name, please?”

“Yes, my name is Lena Nybaan.”

“Thank you. Now, Miss Nybaan, how long have you worked here?”

“I believe it’s going on four decades by now.”

“And during that time, have you ever seen any of the Council members pass through these doors?”

“Not personally, but then my work shift is only six hours long.”

“I see. Then what about any other people who work in your position. Do you know if any of them ever saw anything?”

“I can’t be entirely sure, as I only know of two others, the one who comes before me and the one who comes after. I meet with them briefly when we change shifts, but we don’t really have much opportunity for idle talk. I usually just go home and take care of other things in my life.”

“All right, but then what about the public. Don’t we have the occasional tourist crowd passing through here who might want to see the inner chamber? I was always under the impression it was such a marvelous sight to behold, for all the glamor of the architecture, and the artistic beauty of the mosaic tiling. I recall hearing stories of it when I was a girl growing up and going to school.”

“Yes, and I probably heard those same stories, and had those same dreams. But the Council has been in this really delicate deliberation, and they tend to keep the doors locked, for security reasons, so that they aren’t disturbed during this time.”

Ileani now turns partially to the camera as she continues.

“But does this also mean they don’t come out even for press releases or statements of any kind? For this, we need to ask the Internal Secretary for his perspective,” she turns in his direction. “Sir, for as long as I’ve been alive, at the very least, I’ve always heard of the Council being inside their chambers conducting this very intense deliberation. I’ve often wondered what sort of deliberation they might be conducting, and I can attest that as a journalist, I have conducted research on a number of occasions on the DataNet hoping to learn of something new. But unfortunately, it’s always the same story. Can you explain to us why the Council can’t seem to offer us even a hint of what they’re doing in there?”

“Miss Ur’paran,” he begins. “I can only say that I inherited my position from my predecessor, just as he inherited it from his, along with our associated instructions. And those instructions tell us that for as long as the Council is inside this room, those doors need to remain locked as part of this high security restriction. This is due largely, as I understand it, to the suggestion that the Council may have, at one time, received something special from the Marshal as part of his promise to grant us some of his great wisdom in exchange for our services to him and Sargeras."

"But Mister Secretary, how long does it actually take to deliberate this tidbit of knowledge, and what about the rest of their legislative duties? My understanding is that none of the science factions have seen any new research objectives during this entire period of time when they first went in there. This has left many of our top research specialists longing for something to do. And then we have this new crisis developing with that polluting industry and this legal action, and a public outcry that the Council simply isn't doing its job. How do we respond to that?"

"The only statement I'm allowed to give out on these matters is that same one we have given out so many times before. And although I realize there may be those who have grown impatient with the same response repeated time and again, until we see one of the Council members actually step through these doors to give us a review of what they've been deliberating during this time, there simply isn't anything else to say about it."

"But what does this actually say about the Council then? How long have they been locked away in there with no one seeing them come outside? These are the questions I think the public are beginning to ask."

"Yes, I'm sure they are, and likely for as long as this one Council has been inside there."

Ileani halted her interview and suddenly felt an eerie chill at that strange statement. She knew they were each following a kind of script as part of this show, although she wasn't personally familiar with his. But that statement hinted at something new. She glared at him briefly, realizing she needed to respond somehow, but her words were failing her as this represented going off her own script.

"What do you mean, this ONE Council? You mean the one most recently elected, right?"

"Oh, well, uh, yes! Naturally, they are the elected body. I mean, who else would be inside there."

Ileani was starting to catch a hint at something. It was a potential leak he was letting out. His apparent faltering had to be part of his script, but he wasn't letting it go easily, probably as part of his cover. So she decided to play into it.

"Of course, naturally, but these people have been in there for such a long time. Like I said, during my full lifetime, I never heard of anything different. What about the Council membership that came before?"

"Before? Oh! As I understand it, this one particular Council has been reelected quite a number of times so far. I guess somebody really likes them."

"Reelected, yes, but…um…wait. One particular… Just a moment!" she urges as she starts to pick up the tune. "When did this…one particular Council…first take office, reelection or otherwise?"

"First take office? Oh, wow, that would be a while ago now. Probably when they first received this special gift of wisdom. After all, they had to go into this private deliberation, you know."

"When they first received…" she flusters. "In all the nether-space… When they first received… You mean when they FIRST received it?" she shouts.

"I suppose so. After all, someone had to be first. I heard this gift of wisdom was a great privilege. I can only imagine what they might be deliberating in there that they were reelected so many times to keep it up."

Ileani's eyes bulge as the message starts to sink in. The man's innocent gaze and puerile manners played out as someone who apparently didn't fully realize the implications of the offence. It was as if he inherited something that was intended to be this way.

"Reelected to keep it up!!" she shrieks. "Are you saying they were actually reelected just to keep it up?"

"Well, if the doors are locked and no one ever sees them for anything else, I guess this must be the reason," he shrugs with a cocky undertone.

Now Ileani loses control. She backs away and screams, grabbing her horns and twisting in the direction of the doors, as if hoping she could use x-ray vision to see inside.

"Shut it down!" she shouts at the cameraman. "You people tricked me!" she issues sternly at the Secretary. "And by the way, that was very well played, but aargh!" she screams again. "I thank whatever power governs the universe that you people turned my chip off. Now I can justifiably pull my horns out."

"You are most welcome, Miss Ur'paran. As for tricking, we needed a genuine reaction, and simply acting doesn't do it. Also, my act had to be that of someone who apparently inherited a position so commonplace by now, that you might think the Council and their god complex doesn't need to abide by such things as election rules. Not when they have the Marshal passing out the secrets of the universe on a golden platter."

"But just a moment, help me to understand the full meaning here. Who is inside there right now?"

"As far as the public is concerned, this is the same Council that held office back in the days of the Arrival. And for reference, in case you forgot what century it is, it's been almost a hundred of them passing by now. This…great privilege…overrode the elections, as the Marshal and his superior wisdom doesn't seem to adhere to such mundane issues. You can do a bit of research on the DataNet for some of your answers. Just look for the last time ANY Council member was seen in public. Also, when any NEW Council member was elected…or any other change in the seating. You will see the same people have held these seats during this full time. What this says is those elections were all likely faked, even after some of these people should have died of old age by now."

"Unbelievable! But how could it be possible that no one noticed this before?"

"Was anyone actually looking, or were you all too busy listening to their rhetoric of '…any day now, blah blah…' and then went back to your own business."

"You know, you may hold a point, and for all that mind-numbing rhetoric, this could very well be true. But I swear to you, this will blow a few horns into orbit."

"I'm sure it will."

He then smiles, nods, and proceeds to walk away back to his office.

Ileani simply shook her head at the apparent scene in front of her. She followed him with her eyes as he casually sauntered off. She then turned to glare at Lena, who simply smiled and shrugged, as she felt there was nothing more to say, so she returned to her desk. This left Ileani alone and smoldering as she gazed at her cameraman, who didn't seem any better for it.

"I swear," she grumbles. "The next time I see that special agent…"

She directed the cameraman to pack up and they left the building to return to her office.

Chapter 3

A POLITICAL BOMBSHELL

At CPComm, the news wires were steaming hot as one sensational revelation after another was being broadcast in recent times. Over the course of the week since her last interview, Ileani found herself with more excitement than she had ever experienced in her career.

Ayene made another visit during this time to give out continued instructions, now informing the news team to keep the ages of the last set of Council members hidden until later. Ileani conducted her research on the DataNet to learn the full extent of the duration for this one Council party and was beginning to make her own association for their ages, where many of them should no longer be alive simply due to old age.

"But Ayene," she wonders. "Why shouldn't we tell them about this?"

"I want to see what the Marshal does first. He probably isn't paying as much attention to their ages, like we are. I feel this would represent a level of micromanagement that he doesn't personally care for. Instead, if he makes any kind of excuse for it, he'll be shooting himself in his own hoof once we go public with this."

"You're simply nasty! All right, I can go with that. But what's the next bombshell you're going to drop on me…and everyone else, for that matter?"

"You'll know it when you see it. We're going to put a little bit of time between this and the next one, so we don't push them too closely together. Just be sure you're first on the scene. Do you ever monitor such things like C.P. Security or any of the emergency channels for accidents and such?"

"We have people who do that occasionally, though there's never really that much to report on. Most vehicle accidents are minor, due to the anti-collision controls they use. If anything does actually hit anything else, it's barely worth running out there to look at, much less to report on."

"What about disasters, like fires, or other emergencies?"

"Yes, but again, for all the safety protocols out there, this doesn't usually have much opportunity to erupt into anything big. Not unless you're talking about an earthquake or something. But this region is very stable. And we don't get any serious storm activity around here, either."

"I see. No wonder my life was so boring while I was growing up," she giggles. "Well, on this occasion, you might want to put a few extra people on watch and keep your camera teams on alert. You won't want to miss this one."

"Uh huh…and will you be paying for my new set of horns this time, or do we leave it to the company medical policy?" she smiles timidly.

Meanwhile, in Central Command, Geilv was receiving a call from the Marshal.

"Commander," the raspy voice ushers through the com-link. "We seem to have a bit of malcontent growing out there."

"Malcontent?" he responds innocuously. "What do you mean?"

"Have you been paying attention to the local news media lately? I should think a few things would stand out by now."

"Yes, actually… A few of my officers have been reporting to me on a number of recent events. Personally, I fell out of the habit half an eternity ago. What part of it do you refer to as malcontent?"

"All of it, to be honest. We have those protests occurring against our lovely industry that has been serving our needs so well. Then, eh… well, we have some claims of the Council not living up to expectations. But the most disturbing is a recent broadcast about the elections. This brings me to wonder about a few things, actually."

"And what are those?"

"Well, first of all, who is it that's allowing all this on the airwaves in the first place. I mean we had, eh…well, our regulators should be trying harder to keep things calm for us. You know, because we surely don't want any more panics, like we did that one time."

"Naturally, Marshal, and I do recall that period of our history."

"Absolutely, Commander! And then there was that one relating to the elections. In all Creation, how could that blundering idiot let that one slip?"

"Let it slip, Marshal?"

"Yes…I mean, no…I mean, eh, it was clearly a sensational statement that could only cause a public disturbance. And it seems to be doing exactly that! I think it's only a matter of time before they, eh…that is to say before they start, um…well, never mind. But Commander, we may need to think of a few good excuses to solve this problem and bring things back under control. I'm already getting a few ideas, but I'm going to wait to see how this turns out first."

"Yes, Marshal, as you say."

They end the link and the Commander gazes at the vid-com with a tiny smile curling up from his lips.

"I'm starting to enjoy this," he mumbles softly.

✦ ✦ ✦ ✦ ✦

Later in the day, as vid-coms around the world were blazing with news reports portraying controversy and intrigue, Ileani was preparing for another update as the station coordinator signals the cameras.

> *"This is Ileani Ur'paran for C.P. News. The outpouring of public response to the recent review of the election results has not only turned the political parties upside-down, but it's also invoking numerous new lawsuits against the Council for possible election fraud. As stated before, the last recorded change in a Council seat was the expulsion of Former Elder Velen Nazég back in the year 9764.53. Since that time, research conducted on the DataNet shows the election results to be consistently reelecting the same people to the same seats.*

> *A group of analysts has joined together to review the voter opinion polls for each election held during this long period of time in the hopes of either validating or invalidating the results. Although the volume of data is expected to be immense, they have vowed to conduct a thorough review to discover the truth of this world-shattering controversy.*

Meanwhile, sources inside C.P. Security have informed our station that they have arrested the Internal Secretary, as well as several of his predecessors, who were all implicated in covering up these fraudulent acts. An additional investigation is underway to discover the duration of this obvious cover-up, and when it might have first begun.

In a related story, leaders of each of the science factions are outraged at these reports, and many are coming forward with their own complaints and discontent over the Council and its blatant lack of service to provide any new research grants, investigative review, or the release of new discoveries. Several of the factions are even taking the initiative to pick their own research topics and pursue them independently. This is in opposition, as we have learned, to their usual practice of simply waiting for an official grant or other directive to do any work, as given out explicitly by the Council.

One long-standing topic being considered by the medical community is the continued need for the An'gamu seed. According to sources, the seed was originally created as part of that same emergency war protocol that demanded the dirty industry. The reason behind this was the urgent need to evacuate from our native home due to the old Tav'ageen Anomaly…that alien infestation once described to be affecting our population, and therefore our need to escape from it.

But some top experts are coming forward with their arguments that since the development of the Tav'ageen Suppressor chips, which were created for us by the Marshal as his solution to this terrible plague, their application has been so effective at relieving our population of the concern, that technically there can be no further justification to abandon our natural home. These officials have claimed that after nearly ten millennia of no reported cases, it would appear as if the Marshal's solution has found its own answer.

As a corollary result, this has led some medical officials to another enduring complaint against the Council. The An'gamu seed was originally interpreted to serve as a temporary solution relating to our imperative need to evacuate, but the medical community has argued that the Council never once allowed any further research on the topic to find a curative solution to remove them. This leads one to surmise these otherwise temporary parasitic implants would

*become permanent, with or without the need to evacuate. Needless
to say, the medical community is now considering potential methods
in which to remove the seeds."*

◆ ◆ ◆ ◆ ◆ ◆ ◆

"This is outrageous, Commander!" the Marshal blasts on the com-link.
"Just who do these people think they are?"

"Which ones, the Council?"

"NO! I mean those impudent fools who are questioning all of our
precious little mandates. We had those in there for a reason!"

"As I understand it, from the statements being made, those reasons
may be moot by now."

"What do you mean moot! They're just as important as ever! Gah!"
he screeches. "This is getting completely out of hand now. The next
thing you know, they'll be questioning the chips! Aargh!"

He ends the link.

The Commander studies the vid-com after the conversation ended.

"I think I can see where this is leading now. Very clever, people…"

◆ ◆ ◆ ◆ ◆ ◆ ◆

Ayene chose to allow a few weeks to pass before starting any new
sensations. The courts were still processing the complaints, the public
outrage over the Council was simmering, and several investigations were
underway relating to their corruption and past activities. But so far, no
one tried entering the Grand Hall to drag them out for questioning.

Outside the building, Ayene was now assembling a group of people
appearing as a maintenance crew. They all wore the uniforms of a local
utility company, and each of them carried a large hard-shell tool case.
Ayene was again in her ACI suit.

Once the team was assembled, they held back to one side of the
building while Ayene peeked inside the lobby. When she saw the area
was clear, she marched inside and up to the desk.

Lena had just arrived on her work shift for the day, and barely
had time to settle into her seat when Ayene's abrupt appearance sent a
sudden tremor through her. She studied Ayene's approach carefully,
scanning for anything else in the area. When Ayene arrived at the
desk, she leaned in privately.

"Do you have the key?" she asks softly.

"Yes Ma'am."

Lena opens a drawer and pulls out a large old-fashioned brass key used on the architecturally antique door lock. She conceals it in her hand as she glances over her shoulder at the door.

"Are we ready?" she asks.

Ayene surveys the lobby and the adjacent corridors leading off in both directions. It was a slow time of day, so no one was present at this time. She nods silently and returns briskly to the front doors to wave her team in, while Lena rushes to the chamber doors to unlock them.

The crew hurriedly paces across the lobby floor and ducks inside the chamber, with Lena closing the door behind them. She turns again to Ayene.

"What are they actually going to do in there, as if I couldn't guess?"

"They're carrying a set of cutting lasers to perforate some of those steel reinforcement bars, which are just barely holding things up. Our people estimate that we only need to cut through a portion of them, and then the roof will slowly begin to buckle and finally collapse. You'll probably hear a few noises as fragments begin to crumble off, so my suggestion is to take cover behind your desk, away from the doors, which may blast off their hinges at the sudden air burst. Got it?"

"Yes Ma'am. And then I need to call in the emergency people to check for whatever casualties might be inside. This should be fun, but it'll also create a lot of trouble."

"And I'll have more work for you afterwards, so stay handy and don't run off immediately."

The two of them return to the girl's desk for additional instructions and a bit of idle banter while the crew works, making it seem like a normal day with some official conversation of the recent political events.

After nearly an hour of work, the door creaks open slightly, and a worker waves his hand for attention. Ayene motions for them to come out and Lena rushes up to attend to the door, closing and locking it behind them. Ayene now directs her crew to leave the building as casually as possible, while she offers a parting wave to Lena on her way out. The team is sent back to the ACI office to return their bags while she returns to the WIC building to report in.

"My Lord, Operation Party Crasher is engaged."

"Party Crasher..." Kailen chuckles ironically. "I especially love the crashing part of it."

"Yes, well..." she smiles. "Now I need Kaliya and her people to offer their assistance to manage things."

"Absolutely, Lieutenant..." Thaelyn responds. "Kaliya, kindly prepare your people."

"Yes, my Lord," she replies pertly.

Kaliya rises from her chair where she and the others were in one of their usual meetings. She offers a salute, and then leaves to return back to Tae'Eladar, where she would once again assemble members of her team.

"Meanwhile," Ayene continues. "I think it would be prudent of me to return and observe, just to make sure we keep it in our favor."

"Very good," Thaelyn affirms. "As you were, Lieutenant."

Ayene now offers her own salute and flashes back to Azgarén.

She arrives back in the plaza outside the Council building, where she takes up seating on one of the benches and pulls out her tablet to peruse the local news articles and shopping ads. This was simply to occupy time until the main event.

Kaliya had assembled her people on the training field outside the guildhall in Bya'an Tamoranth, where she was giving them a final briefing for their latest game play. On this occasion, they would dress up as C.P. Security officers and merge with the locals in the general area, only to respond when the emergency occurred. When she felt they were ready, she gave orders for everyone to return to their rooms to project.

She entered her own room and sat down, then relaxed into her meditation to project herself out-of-body. Once she had fully emerged, she folded her image to Azgarén to join with Ayene.

"All right, Ayene," she announces as she sits down. "Everyone should be converging locally by now, so it's just a matter of time."

"Good. I just now made a call to Captain Bein'talan to inform him of our plan. I want him on the scene to assist me in my presentation. I'll ask you to play the role of one of his officers rushing up to him with an urgent report of what you saw inside, as if you were looking for survivors, and I'll position myself behind Ileani's cameraman to direct the play."

"Cu'Nar's grace, Ayene, we should put you to work in a studio!" she chuckles.

"Maybe!" she grins. "I also left instructions with Lajivi to have our other agents project themselves inside the inner chamber a few times just to check on things and make any…adjustments…to our work to make sure we don't have to wait too long. I want this over before Lena's work shift ends today. I need her in this picture as well."

"And then we have Ileani enter the scene. I wonder how she might react to this."

"Fortunately for her, her interface is turned off, so she won't need to suffer that horrid feedback hit from it."

"No, but she will probably need psychiatric help before you're finished with her."

The two of them usher up a bold laugh while they wait and watch the people passing by.

Several hours had passed and Lena's nerves were on edge. She found herself starting and jerking for every little sound that echoed into the room. It could be someone's hoof steps walking by, or a door closing. One time, a female officer was passing through when she fumbled with her handbag and dropped a personal article on the floor.

She studied the clock, counting each passing moment, wondering if the event would actually occur at all, or if the roof in there was actually sturdier than previously expected. Then she heard something. It sounded hard, like a rock falling from a great height and hitting a solid surface. She turned an ear to it, wondering if she was simply hallucinating or if there might be another one. She waited several long moments, and she thought she could hear a few smaller sounds, like additional pieces falling down. It sounded like a rain of hard particles, where the clicking and clattering rose and fell in amplitude…and then came a loud crash.

She jerked around at the boisterous commotion as additional clanks and bangs continued to echo through the doors. She tenuously rose from her seat, feeling a sudden urge to run away. She slid her body around the desk to the other side where she hoped to find shelter and ducked down.

Another crash resounded through the lobby, and now additional people were rushing out of their offices to see about the disturbance, only to find Lena crouching behind her desk and staring at the chamber doors. And then it happened.

A heavy creaking, followed by a thunderous roar boomed through the building, smashing its way through the doors, and sending a large cloud of dust and debris into the lobby. The shockwave continued until it hit the glass entry doors, shattering them onto the ground outside.

Lena instinctively hit the floor, and while the desk generally sheltered her from the brunt of the force, she could feel the pressure wave as it rushed over the counter, carrying with it a spray of particles. She covered her face and screamed, but her voice was drowned out by the loud rumbling of the collapse. The other people who had gathered in the room ran in any direction they could find. Some were hit by the spray of debris while others were choking on the dust.

When the initial commotion had settled, Lena sprang to her hooves and dashed outside to clear herself from the dust cloud. She pulled out her trans-com and quickly dialed in to the local emergency hotline.

"Emergency Services," the voice calmly announces. "Please state your name and the nature of the emergency."

"My name is Lena Nybaan," she urges. "I'm a receptionist inside the Council Grand Hall. We've had an accident, or something. In all the nether-space, I think the roof just caved in! We need people out here now!"

"Calm down, Miss Nybaan. You say the roof caved in? Are you injured?"

"I'm alright, I think. Dusty, but I'm still here."

"What about any other injuries?"

"I can't be sure. I saw some people running, but not much else through all the dust."

"What part of the building collapsed, Miss Nybaan?"

"I think it was the inner chamber. A huge cloud of dust came through the doors at me."

"All right, I am sending our crews out there right now. I will ask you to stay in the area, but do not try going back inside there in case the remainder of the building is unstable."

"Right, I'm in the plaza right now."

"Very good, and try to stay calm."

They end the link and she put the trans-com away. She then turns to scan the area. A large crowd of people were gathering to observe the scene. They were coming out of local cafés and nearby offices, and some were rushing into view from the sidewalks along the streets. Then she sees Ayene standing near one of the benches, so she rushes over to meet her.

"What now, Ma'am?" she ushers nervously.

"Now we wait a few moments for the people to assemble."

In the offices of CPComm, a worker who was monitoring the emergency channels perks up at the announcement of a crisis occurring at the Council Grand Hall. He turns to his local supervisor.

"Sir, we have something here."

The man steps over to examine the report being broadcast for rescue crews and security forces.

"This looks serious," he muses. "All right, I have special instructions for Ileani to go out there. Call her up and get her ready."

Ileani was at her desk editing a recent report when the call came in. She instantly jumped out of her chair and grabbed her bag before rushing out the door. She shouted out orders for her camera team to pull itself together, and they all convened in the parking lot with one of the news vans.

Outside the Grand Hall, Kaliya was directing her teammates to search the building and bring out anyone who might still be inside. She also directed several of them to assist in crowd control of the growing mass of people assembling in the plaza.

By this time, Ayene's former boss at C.P. Security was arriving to meet with her.

"Captain Bein'talan," she calls to him. "Good. Now, quickly, I want to introduce you to my immediate CO, Captain Kaliya Nazég," she directs at Kaliya standing next to her.

The security captain studied Kaliya for her uniform, which resembled a C.P. Security styling, but it didn't carry a captain's rank insignia. Instead, Kaliya was dressed as a lieutenant.

"A Captain?" he wonders.

"Yes Sir, she's military, so this is a disguise. Also, many of these people you see out here belong to her," she further directs at the other security officers in the area.

"I see, all right."

"Now, once Ileani shows up, I need you to be a part of our little play. We're going to reveal what we see in there to the public, but it has to be in such a way as to represent a type of revelation."

"Are you sure about this, Ayene? I remember what you said once about sensations."

"I know, but at this moment, we're ready for it."

"If you say so…"

Lena stood by watching and listening, and also studying Kaliya's presentation as she directed her team around the area. It seemed so professional and well-coordinated.

A series of emergency teams were now arriving, including medical teams from the nearby clinics. Kaliya began directing her people to move the victims from the building into a group on one side of the plaza where the medical teams could set up a triage center, in case there were any serious injuries.

Captain Bein'talan watched the quick and efficient work Kaliya made with her team, which seemed even more coordinated than his own. He examined her closely, taking note that she appeared rather young to be a Captain.

"Excuse me, eh, Captain Nazég…such an interesting name, by the way. Just how old are you?"

"I'm four centuries, Captain. And yes, I can already hear it coming. But I had to push hard and travel far to arrive here."

"Well, you do seem to know your stuff…for such a young velvet horn," he grins mildly.

"Oh, Captain, I think I could even teach an old bull like you a few things."

"Really!" he chuckles. "That I'd like to see…"

Ileani and her news team sped along the roadways on their way across town, soon to arrive in the clutter of emergency vehicles and crowds of people.

"In all the nether-space," she winces. "What happened here?"

They pull over and unload the van, and she leads them into the plaza, politely pushing her way through the crowds of people. Once in view, she struggles to interpret what her eyes were seeing as she spies the masses of security officers, rows of people sitting on the ground with medical personnel attending to them, and a large cloud of dust billowing up from the remains of the Council building's dome roof. In the center of the plaza, she spots Ayene and the other officers in charge.

"Ayene!" she shouts and tries pushing her way over to them. "What in all the nether-space happened here?"

"Ileani, you're just in time. Get your cameraman over here. Orient on the building. I'm going to direct you for this part."

"Oh no! Are you going to pull another of your little tricks on me?"

"Just play along with it, Ileani. You know how these things need to go by now."

"I swear, when this is over..."

Ileani positions her camera team, where one man was handling the camera, and another was carrying a portable transmission booster that linked with their van to channel the signal back to the office. Ayene stood behind the camera, and Kaliya moved away from the scene. Finally, Lena was positioned in view for a quick interview. Ileani took a deep breath as she made herself ready.

"CPComm, I'm ready. Give me a count."

"We hear you, Ileani," the voice ushers through her headset. "Stand by... We're going live in three, two, one..."

Once again, on vid-coms around the world, an urgent bulletin was being announced on the air, preempting the existing entertainment programming with an important news broadcast.

"This is Ileani Ur'paran for C.P. News. I'm currently live in front of the Council Grand Hall building here in the government district of Capitol Prime. The scene is chaotic as people are gathering from all over the area to witness what appears to be a disaster with the Grand Hall building. What I'm looking at right now is the remains of the famous dome roof that covered the inner chamber of the Grand Hall, but now it is gone, having apparently collapsed inside the building. We have emergency workers assisting the injured, and a virtual army of security forces cordoning off the area and searching for survivors. The details of how this happened are uncertain so far, but with me now is Lena Nybaan, that same young lady I interviewed not long ago when we found ourselves reporting on the election fraud. Lena, can you tell us what you know of the events inside this building?"

"Yes, I can," she asserts. "I was at my desk when it happened. At first, I could hear a bunch of noises echoing through the doors leading to the inner chambers. Normally, I might not pay too much attention to this, thinking it's just someone inside moving around and doing their work. But then I heard this horribly loud crash, and just after that, this terrible blast that broke through the doors with this huge

cloud of dust spraying all over everything. I just barely had enough time to hide behind my desk before it hit!"

"Lena, from what I'm seeing up there, it would appear as if the roof caved in. Are you aware of any issues relating to the building maintenance procedures that should normally discover and correct this before it might become so critical?"

"Ileani, I have to say it again that during my little six-hour work shifts, I never once saw anyone come or go through those doors. But I will offer you this much. Since our last meeting, I started asking around with those other girls who work in that same position. We started exchanging stories together to see if anyone might have something to say, and believe it or not, for as long as any of us have been working that desk, which at this point amounts to several decades on average, none of us saw anyone open those doors for any reason. Not a Council member, and not even a simple custodial worker."

Ileani glared at the girl for the outlandish statement. She then turned partway to the camera and further to Ayene on the other side of it, before returning to the young receptionist.

"Let me see if I understand this correctly," she states flatly. "For what could be perhaps several decades that we can be sure of, no one sitting in front of those doors ever saw someone actually passing THROUGH those doors?"

"That's right..." she shrugs.

"And this is our exceptionally studious Council that's presumably deliberating something in there?!" her voice surges. "In all the nether-space, are they so iron-horned that they can't even take a break for dinner?" she screeches.

As Ileani tries to catch her breath from this latest shock, Kaliya sees her cue. She runs up from a crowd in the background towards Captain Bein'talan. Ayene waves at Ileani, and further taps the cameraman on the shoulder to follow her motions. Kaliya rushes up to the Captain with her sensational report, which was now being broadcast live as if it were an incidental attraction.

"Captain!" she ushers conspicuously. "We just now managed to get inside there. I can't believe what we saw!"

"What is it, Lieutenant?" he roleplays. "Is there anyone still alive in there?"

"Sir! The place is a wreck! And when I say it's a wreck, I mean it looks like it was a wreck even before the collapse! We don't see any bodies in there at all. The place looks like it was abandoned several millennia ago, for all the decay and crumbling furniture."

Ileani listened to the report, realizing this had to be part of Ayene's sensational play. But rather than glare at Ayene for another of her tricks, her eyes simply bulged, and she gasped sharply. She then grabbed her horns and let out a raucous scream.

She abruptly turns and starts running towards the building to see for herself, waving for her cameraman to follow her. She arrives at the broken remains of the front door, which by now had been covered by a heavy tarp to allow passage over the sharp debris. Taking care to step gently across the threshold, she passed inside the lobby. Both she and the cameraman surveyed the scene, including the broken chamber doors and the clutter within.

They worked their way through the lobby to peek inside. There they beheld the remains of the once-great inner chamber of the Council of Elders, the seat of their planetary government, now reduced not simply to ruin for the collapsed roof, but also showing the clear signs of decay and neglect of some untold amount of time. The furniture had rotted away, the mosaic tiling and plaster of the walls had crumbled to the floor, and the remaining structural components showed obvious signs of corrosion and deterioration due to extreme age without any form of maintenance.

She stood there, staring into the room while the camera continued playing the live broadcast, until a voice came on her headset.

"Ileani, this is CPComm, can you hear us? Can you tell us what you see in there?"

"CPComm, do you actually want me to respond to that?" she snaps. "In all the nether-space, this place is unbelievable! I'm looking at the major portion of the roof after it collapsed inside the room. There is a lot of dust," she pauses to cough softly, "but that's minor compared to the furnishings. I'm looking at rows of chairs here, which I believe were for political overseers when they might attend the proceedings in here. But they look like something out of a horror movie involving a lost civilization after a holocaust. And the walls look like they've been crumbling for…I don't know how long. CPComm, I don't know how to say this, but this gives me the impression that no one has been inside here since the Council was said to be engaged in that long deliberation. And this simply leads me to ask where they actually were if they were supposed to be deliberating something. It's no wonder they never responded to anything. It also makes me wonder again about those elections. Who were we electing if there's no one present in here?"

"All right, Ileani, we're going to recommend you go back outside before anything else falls down and causes injury. Clearly, this will require someone to come forward and answer for this, but at this moment, I can't be sure who that someone might be."

"Yeah, you got that much right."

She slowly works her way back outside into the plaza and returns to her former position near the Captain.

"CPComm, I don't think there's anything else for me to do out here, so I'm going to wrap this up for now."

"Understood, Ileani."

"Right, so this is Ileani Ur'paran…or what's left of her…as well as everything else out here…live on the scene."

She motions for the cameraman to shut down, and she turns to glare sternly at Ayene and Kaliya.

"All right you two, before you pull out the remains of my horns with any more of your pranks, I'm going to want a few answers."

Ileani had returned to her office, along with Ayene and Kaliya, after finishing their report outside the Council building and giving it over to Captain Bein'talan to clean up. Now they were convening in a conference room for a private chat.

"All right, Ileani," Kaliya begins. "Listen up carefully. First, we never wanted to hurt you, but your reactions were necessary as someone who needed to see it with their own eyes and respond accordingly. And with respect, I can't be sure how much acting experience you had while attending journalism school."

"Fine, I can understand that part. Acting isn't something they normally teach over there. But this goes a little above and beyond what a person can take, acting or otherwise. What's really happening? I know the Marshal is our enemy in these matters, but what happened to the Council?"

"He happened to them, most likely. Some of this information is still being kept classified, and some of it will be slowly released through you. For now, most of the big hits are done. Over the course of this next week, we'll have people come in with individual stories. These people will claim to be family relations. If we can arrange it, we'll use actual relatives, if we can find any. Otherwise, actors. But not immediate family, like husbands, wives, or children. Rather, more distant relations, like cousins. The reason being this... If you search on the DataNet and look for any immediate family members for the Council, there is no information of their proper existence. Ask if they're alive and well, and you get nothing. Ask if they're dead, and you'll hit a military security roadblock."

"Why?"

"According to military records," Ayene offers. "During the time of the Tav'ageen Scare, the Council was taken away to a quarantine site without any of us knowing about it. The whole thing was hidden behind this security wall, and probably due to the Marshal covering up so many of his actions, even to most of our own military. They would be brought back only for press releases, but they weren't actually inside the Grand Hall during this time. Then the Scare ends and presumably they go into this deliberation. But here is where it gets ugly. The quarantine site they were stationed at got hit by these insurgents the Marshal kept talking about."

"Oh no..."

"Now, we cannot be sure where the site was, as it used a codename, but one thing we do know is his insurgents are fake. The only thing that was blasting anything out there was our own military under his orders using a classified military-grade mind-control chip. Therefore, our only conclusion is he pointed a finger and told them to pull the trigger."

"You must be kidding me!" she gasps.

"We're expecting him to respond to this somehow," Kaliya resumes. "This simply cannot go unanswered without it leading to some kind of uprising, and surely, he wouldn't want that. We're like a pet society to him, so he's going to want us to behave ourselves as good little animals where he can simply throw us a treat to pacify us."

"Oh, pacify, is it?" Ileani snaps. "I'll show him a little pacification."

"But not quite like that, Ileani," Ayene cautions. "He's a very powerful creature that doesn't take no for an answer. People die on such occasions. So, we need to play this little game on him to slowly inform the people and make them aware of each piece in turn that he's played on us. Right now, we're working our way through the Council's situation, but only up to a point, as we're expecting him to make an excuse for where they REALLY are while in this deliberation, and you'll publish it as if it were our answer. This is to pacify HIM."

"Unbelievable, so as he's trying to pacify us, we also have to pacify him. All right, what comes after that?"

"We're going to run on this for a bit," Kaliya continues. "Since we already have so many other scandals where the Council is concerned, we're expecting a few of these court reviews to declare them illegal, along with any and all mandates they made relating to that emergency war protocol. This is going to pave the way for us to make a few more movements, one of which being another…discovery…the medical community is going to realize. But for this, I think I'll leave it open. After all, we can't let those horns of yours grow too big," she grins.

"Thank you, Captain…" she smirks sarcastically. "But in the end, how are we going to solve any of this? Can you at least give me a little hint, so I don't lose what's left of my sanity?"

"All right, but this is entirely confidential, just between us. I'm building a military force with the help of a foreign authority, the REAL ones the Marshal is hiding from, and we plan to launch against him once we have our stage set for a little show we plan to put on. And you, Miss I-Want-To-Be-A-Sensational-World-Reporter, will see your dream come true."

◆

"Commander!" the voice of the Marshal screams through the com-link. "If we don't gain control of this situation, we might lose complete containment of everything we worked so hard to build!"

"I cannot be sure what it is you were trying to build. I am just a military officer trying to fight a war against your insurgents."

"Yes! But of course, Commander! What I meant to say is, eh…we were working so hard to, eh…provide for, eh…the future of all these lovely little people as they offered so many of their services to our great cause. Yes! But this scandal of the Council could ruin everything. Have you seen it?"

"I did not see the actual broadcast, but one of my officers brought it to my attention afterwards. I was quite surprised by it."

"Naturally! In all Creation, that Internal Secretary and all his blundering couldn't even check the roof on occasion."

"Yes, I found this rather disturbing, but not quite as disturbing as the Council being absent from the one place we all believed them to be…including myself."

The link went silent for an extended moment as the Commander listened and waited for a reply.

"Oh, um, you weren't briefed on this? I thought you were. I mean, it was quite a long time ago, and we were all under a lot of stress during those terribly hectic times. You know, with the arrival of those incorrigible insurgents, and then that Tav'ageen, um, thing. I'm sure it must've simply slipped by. Eh, yes, Commander, actually this is something that was being kept a very highly classified secret… for security reasons, you know, and due to, eh…well, actually, that Internal Secretary was right about one thing. They were deliberating some very delicate matters, and had to be sequestered away in a highly secure facility to ensure not only their privacy, but also their security for the nature of this information. Yes…"

"Very well, Marshal, as you say, but as the High Commander of the Azgarén military, it falls to me that I must know the precise location and condition of our world government at all times as part of my duty assignment."

"Oh, but of course, Commander, this is surely understood. So, don't you worry about it, as they are neatly tucked away in this secure facility while they conduct these very important deliberations. In fact, since we find ourselves somewhat exposed, it may become necessary to finally reveal this to the world, at least as a way to explain how and why the Council has been so completely out of communication, as these deliberations are indeed so very delicate that they cannot be interrupted."

"And how do you plan to do this, Marshal? Will you offer a press release from your office?"

"Actually, Commander, since you mentioned your role as the High Commander, I think this may fall better within your own context. So, here is what we'll say. The Council was once sequestered away due to that old Tav'ageen condition, as you know…eh, you do recall that, right?" he asks tactfully.

"Yes, Marshal, this much I remember."

"Good! So, this is actually where they still are, since it seemed like such a fine location to begin with, being isolated and secure from any manner of tampering."

"This is reasonable, but what about that mention of the elections? This will cause a sensation in and of itself."

"Yes, well, at this point, we might not be able to escape that. But when you have such a thing as this highly delicate and extremely valuable wisdom I once granted them, you simply cannot afford to pass it around too much. You know, corruption, intrigue, misuse of things…"

"Ah, but of course, that does make sense."

"Right! Therefore, this one Council body had to focus itself entirely on the purpose of decoding this information, which by the way was rather elaborate, and therefore the reason it's taking so long."

"Excellent, Marshal, and I think this will help to satisfy some of those complaints."

"Good, Commander, I'm so happy you agree. So, get out there and deliver this for us, will you?"

He ends the link, leaving the Commander to once again glare at the vid-com.

"I wonder who the better storyteller is around here, you or those people at the ACI."

He reaches again for the com-link, this time calling the control booth.

"Captain Ta'yeen here…"

"Captain, please report to my office immediately."

"Yes Sir."

They end the link, and the Commander waits for the Captain to arrive.

"Yes, Commander," he announces as he enters the room.

"The Marshal is ordering me, as the HC, to give an excuse for the missing Council. Can you believe it?"

"What sort of excuse?"

"He's trying to explain how they never actually returned from Site One-Alpha after that quarantine. Now, according to our own files, that place was hit by his insurgents. So, how do you think he can justify using it if we already have this recorded in our files?"

"An oversight, maybe? He classifies everything so tightly, maybe he simply thinks it's secure. Do we know the true condition of that place?"

"My personal suspicion is he sent one of his classified active-mode surgical strikes in there. But maybe it would be prudent to send a ship out there just to make sure. Look up the old records of Site One-Alpha and find out the coordinates. Then send a scout to investigate. Report back to me on what you find. In the meantime, I need to make an appointment with that Miss Ur'paran. We'll give her this much for now, and then I think I need to consult with the people at the ACI for the rest. They might also find it interesting to have this information, assuming they don't have it already."

"So…" Ayene relates. "The Commander was told to release the secret of Site One-Alpha, at least in principle, which is essentially what we were hoping for out of the Marshal. Although, just like the Commander, we're wondering how he might justify using that if Central's records show it was blasted once upon a time."

"Indeed," Thaelyn muses. "And how do you think you might respond to this?"

"As for the Marshal, Geilv thinks he might assume it to be secure behind his wall of secrecy. But Geilv himself is ordering up a scout to check on the condition of that place, for his own information, as well as the ACI. We'll see what that report says first and go from there. But we expect it to be gone."

"Meanwhile," Kaliya submits. "We're going to bring up the little issue of the relatives. We need to remind the people of the Council's average ages, and again of this long duration of time. We'll let them come to their own conclusions after that. I don't think it should take too much to incite this curious revelation. This will leave at least some of them out there asking who's still alive in that high security enclave of theirs."

"This could also lead to one or more additional scandals," Ayene adds. "First, it could incite claims of a conspiracy relating to why they didn't replace the lost members, which brings us full-circle with the elections."

"When you say to incite these claims," Thaelyn wonders. "How do you mean?"

"As you know, the Council is made up of representative members of each of the science factions, rather than a political body like in your parliament where they're all legal experts and politicians. But they're supposed to represent ALL of our active science factions equally. If to lose one, say due to old age or some other cause, you MUST replace him with someone new, or else risk alienating that science faction. And this could lead to scandals of conspiracy and discrimination."

"Ah, I see it now. Powers behold, that could invoke a bit of discord."

"And a bit of civil unrest, I should think," Kailen adds. "It could also cascade into other actions if not corrected."

"Right," Ayene continues. "When you consider they who might have died of old age by now, and with no valid elections to bring in fresh blood, we could be disrupting our whole political system over there!"

"Gracious," the General moans. "This insurgency of yours could escalate into a true revolution."

"At this point, it's a little out of our hands, as they need to be made aware of these facts, one way or another. To do otherwise is to keep them under the Marshal's thumb."

"Of course, do go on."

"Another issue relates to why their families are involved and the security restrictions over their absence. It's the COUNCIL who should be so secretly secluded. Why hide the families if they're not supposed to be involved in politics?"

"Interesting…" Thaelyn notes. "But will you try to pursue any of this?"

"For the moment," Kaliya responds. "We're going to let this simmer. To push it any further might push the Marshal too far. Instead, the medical community is going to remember that nondisclosure clause in the Suppressor chip mandate. And since it doesn't actually serve anyone when trying to study the current situation, they're going to start analyzing it."

Chapter 4

CHANGING PERSPECTIVES

"Commander?"

"Yes, Captain, come in."

In Central Command, Captain Ta'yeen was visiting Geilv with a summary report on the scout vessel sent to investigate the quarantine base.

"Sir, the science team we sent has finally completed the investigation of that location once used for Site One-Alpha."

"Good, but now, what did they find? They've been out there for a week by now, right?"

"Yes Sir, and they found what you might expect of a former research base. They conducted a careful examination of the remains, even to take specimens for their forensic studies to determine if they could identify how and when it occurred."

"I see, but this already sounds bad for our Council."

"Yes Sir, it does. They found the remains of a base. It was on a barren moon, so without anything like an oxygen atmosphere or moisture to corrupt the results, they were able to identify scoring on the base materials consistent with plasma fire, such as what we might have been using in those early days, and the age calculations date it right back during that same time period."

"Any bodies?"

"They were able to identify a number of bodies, including body parts, scattered across the region from the explosions. Some samples were taken, along with a number of personal effects, which they were able to identify as the Council and their families."

"So, this is what happened," he sighs morbidly. "Those people at the ACI were right with their assumptions. But now, what are we going to do with it."

"Did they give you any instructions?"

"Technically yes. The Council is hidden away at this classified site due to these high security protocols and the extremely delicate nature of the donation of the Marshal's great gift of wisdom. In other words, we're going to leave it be for now so as not to push him over the edge with some new death toy, or whatever he might try next."

"Wonderful."

"I think it needs to be this way to keep a status quo until they can make their next move. They expressed an interest in our findings, so I'll need to pass this along to them, and then I suppose they'll play another of their little games at some moment."

"This should be interesting to see."

◆◆◆◆◆

A news broadcast was underway giving a recent update of the families of the Council members voicing their concerns.

> *"In the news today, more family members are coming forward to express their concerns for their missing relatives. Ever since the revelation given out by High Commander Geilv of Central Command explaining how the Marshal gave this special authorization to the Council, there have been numerous cries of foul play. According to the High Commander's statement, this decision was largely due to the highly sensitive nature of this gift of wisdom the Marshal granted, where the Council should be allowed to conduct these deliberations exclusively within this one group, citing the potential for misuse if it was spread too far and without any controls. But now, these family members have been coming forward inquiring about the health and welfare of their loved ones due mostly to the long duration of time the Council has apparently been absent from view."*

The report changes scenes to a previously recorded interview with one such family member, which in this case was one of Kaliya's teammates impersonating a local resident.

> *"I am simply without any way to comprehend how he might still be alive after all this time. He was already an elder member for his age, so by this moment he should have passed on long ago. But if those elections were all falsified to reelect the same people, who is it that would have replaced him?"*

The scene now returns to the reporter.

> *"Due to this and other similar statements, the leaders of many of the science factions have been in heavy debate over who should still be alive and who might have passed on due to their last-known ages. This naturally leaves many to ask about these elections again, and the nature of the political system we use for our society that demands full representation among all the factions equally within our Council body. A few factional leaders are even going so far as to suggest this could be part of a larger conspiracy to usurp our traditional system of government and replace it with a more conservative form that excludes those factions not otherwise desirable. One leader even had this to say..."*

Again, the scene changes to an interview clip using another of Kaliya's people, this time as a well-dressed woman in a suit.

> *"Ileani, I am reminded of one occasion in our history where the Council did, in fact, take sides to oust a legitimate factional component purely out of prejudice for what that factional component represented. This was the faction once represented by Former Elder Velen Nazég. Now, I realize we all regard him as one who presumably joined this insurgent group, or at least this is the story given to us by the Marshal, but for those of us who might actually recall the occasion, the Council held a form of aversion to his faction from the beginning. So, a few of us are now wondering what part of his action to leave our world was due to joining anything at all, versus how much was simply the prejudice of the Council chasing him away."*

━━━━◆━━━━

"Aargh!" the Marshal screeches into the com-link. "Now they're bringing HIM up again! Can't we find any peace around here?!"

"Marshal," Geilv attempts to maintain his composure. "I can hardly imagine this would result in anything more than another moment of their desire for something to talk about. It occurs to me the news media tends to be lacking on many occasions. Now that they have some new subject matter to follow, they are simply exploiting it."

"Do you think so, Commander? Personally, I feel this could blow up in our faces as another sensation."

"Maybe you are simply taking this too personally, especially after that unfortunate occasion of the quarantine site being exposed."

"Yes! Of course! You may be right. Thank you, Commander. I just need to take a deep breath and tell myself it'll be over soon enough."

The link ends, this time leaving Geilv almost ready to burst out laughing. He allows himself a few hearty chuckles until his thoughts begin to settle into the curious meaning of this new reference. This naturally leads him to recall his time in pursuit of Velen and his people, and further to reflect on the Marshal describing them to be a part of this insurgent faction.

"Interesting," he muses privately. "I wonder where that came from. Is it simply a coincidence where someone mentioned something that came to mind, or is the ACI playing another of their games? The Marshal declared them to be part of these insurgents, but if there really are no insurgents, what actually happened to cause Elder Nazég to run away. And also, where did that huge ship come from?"

✦✦✦✦✦

Ayene was filing her most recent report at the WIC building with Thaelyn and his officers. On this occasion, Kaliya was occupied elsewhere.

"So far," she relates. "My parents have helped us in establishing some new contacts in the commercial advertising field. They brought in the administrators of their local manufacturing center, and with a little help from me in my ACI costume, we've managed to assemble a number of associated industries to participate in this new ad campaign. In fact, to make it seem even more legit, I had some of our people at the ACI check around for more office space so we can go fully commercial on this."

"Commercial?" Thaelyn raises his brow. "Are you now trying to enterprise off this war, young miss?"

"No..." she smiles and shakes her head. "I may be coordinating this, but there's a direction to it. As a law degree holder, I feel the need to at least try to uphold some kind of legally viable operation where this goes. We are creating a piece of intellectual property which we hope to license for advertising and entertainment venues. This requires legal representation and copyright protection to keep it under our control. For this, we will need to establish a business entity to carry our service, likely in the form of a new corporate body."

"Very interesting, and this is indeed very clever of you. So, how do you see this unfolding?"

"First, we need an office, and people working the problem to keep the books straight. So far, I'm running off the mention specified in Adalon's prophecies about the Eracyodines, which seems solid enough. The Director at the ARC tells me some of his associates are close to releasing a result to us. He says he should be hearing something soon, but a few early reports are suggesting a lot of new, previously unknown results are coming in, and this sounds like the Marshal was indeed hiding something. In the absence of anything else he COULD be hiding; we have to assume it's the truth of our evolution. And if this is the case, it'll shake the research community to the core once it's out."

"This is likely to be unavoidable."

"A lot of things are that way around here. But for now, we put together a few concept drawings and a computer graphics modeling of our cute little Eracyodine cartoon character."

Ayene pulls out her tablet and calls up a series of images she had collected from the artists she was working with. She shows it to the group. The images represented a bipedal animal figure, representative of the Suuden-Aryku, but in a more primitive animalistic form, in some ways resembling a dinosaur-like ancestor, but in this case with a much thicker tail and broader horns that stretched behind the head more so than the modern-day example. It was hunched slightly at the pelvis, and with a noticeably smaller cranium.

"How cute..." Thaelyn smiles. "And this will be animated in some fashion, I suppose?"

"Yes, we'll be using CG animation for this point, which is popular in most forms of children's entertainment. In fact, I'm actually hoping to develop this image into a type of children's cartoon series."

"Indeed! That sounds rather inventive."

"But so far, we're going to plant a few of our images simply as product advertising..."

<hr />

Kaliya was taking the afternoon away from her usual duties to conduct a little personal experimentation and practice. Over the course of time when she had been studying and practicing in the academies, then to learn of her projection skill, and again when she was helping Ayene in the initial steps to learn her own, she had been reminded of a very curious talent she apparently exhibited once, if completely by accident.

Her thoughts drifted on a number of occasions to her first time inside the chamber used for the Ritual of Redemption, which she had to take after that initial fail for the Spirit Test. Although at the time she had no idea of what she was doing, she would later realize, with the help of Aelwyn during her official Prodigy Gift training, that she apparently held the power to alter the fabric of Reality around her. She learned to perfect this, within reason, inside the chamber, which held an unusual form of spatial continuum relative to the outside world. She also used this when she was helping Ayene. Now she wanted to see if she could learn a little more about it.

She was on her way through the guildhall courtyard towards the administration office, where she would find the testing rooms. As she passes the desk, she waves at the resident officers.

"Kaliya, how are you this fine day?" calls a middle-aged man behind the desk.

"Quite well, Master Sagrid. Do you mind if I borrow the use of the ritual chamber for a little practice?"

"Practice? What could you possibly find of interest to practice in there?"

"Oh, a little of this and a little of that," she grins.

"Right. You know, young lady, I've heard a few things about you in recent times. Just try not to tear any holes in our local plane."

"No, tearing holes isn't quite my thing," she muses naughtily. "I'm going all out on this one. I'm going to...create!" she flutters her fingers theatrically.

The Master eyes her cautiously as she continues on down the hall.

She arrives at the door leading into the antechamber for the ritual rooms. As she passes inside, her thoughts reflected on that first day when she came in here in an almost dreamlike state for the hallucinogenic incense she was given as a preparatory procedure. She paused to study the curved back wall with an arrangement of doors on it.

She recalled how she once chose a door out of this long array that led into one of the chambers, although in reality, it's all one big room, and the array of doors are simply for the psychological effect. She picks one, as it was all the same for this point, and strolls forward to it. She opens the door and steps inside.

The inside of the chamber itself was pitch-black. The room was empty, with no other objects inside, nor any lighting. It was entirely up to the visitor, and typically while under that hallucinogenic effect, to imagine what might be inside as part of a process to reveal their inner demons and bring them out in order to contend with them somehow. But on this occasion, it was not her inner demons she wanted. Those were already taken care of.

"In the beginning, there was darkness," she muses humorously. "At least until I came along," she snickers. "Let there be light!"

In her mind, she forced her will to imagine a point source of light appearing directly above and aiming down at her. This part was easy, as she had done it before. And according to her will, an illuminating beam appeared out of nowhere and spotlighted her.

"And I saw the light, and I felt this was a good start…but I'm not finished yet. Let's make that chair I used once before."

She turns to one side and recalls a favorite chair she once enjoyed during her downtime at the Naarg uy'Sodrad. It was a soft, comfortable lounge chair found in a recreation area.

She places this image in her mind and projects it as an overlay onto the space in front of her. Again, she had done this before, multiple times by now, during her early projection training. As she enforced her will upon the fabric of Reality, an outline begins to form, filling in with a shape and slowly taking on substance. She continues to apply herself until the object fully materializes into Reality.

"And here we have a chair," she affirms proudly. "But can I make anything else? Aelwyn seemed to think this could be another hidden talent. But cu'Nar's pity, this is the riddle of metaphysics brought to life! So, let's see how far I can go with it. One day, I might find this important to know. And having a little practice can't hurt."

She now applies her skills in a new direction, creating a table to go along with the chair. She kept her designs simple for now, if only to gain a better understanding of the practice.

"And to think," she considers privately. "Thaelyn once told me there are societies in the Outer Planar regions that can sculpt entire cities this way."

She next imagines a broad wooden floor, followed by a set of walls circling around it, therefore creating a simple room. She stepped inside to examine her work, then to modify one of the walls to include a hole for a window. She sticks her head through to peek outside.

"I'm going to need more light."

She calls up additional spotlights to further spread across the local area. She steps outside her little house and imagines a roof covering it, building it up in pieces as she mentally assembled the beams and supports, and finally a layer of shingles on top.

"Girl, what have you done here..." she whispers distantly to herself. "If Father thought I was a Prodigy Child before, he'd lose what's left of his horns if he saw this."

She continued playing with her ideas, creating and removing objects as she slowly began to grasp this extraordinary new talent.

"I think I'll need to keep this one quiet for now," she admits. "This is simply too much to let go this soon in the game. But I'll be back for more. I need to know what else I can do with it. That Darumon created a true monster in us. Someone needs to understand the parameters of it."

✦

As a new week begins, the news reports were now showing additional concern, as well as complaints and accusations of corruption over the Council's membership being well beyond their natural lifespans by now, therefore asking who was actually conducting any deliberation at all. Each of the science factions were demanding the Council be declared invalid, due in part to this as well as the election fraud that failed to appropriately declare any new form of membership.

In Commander Geilv's office, the Marshal was in conversation over this discrepancy.

"This is getting out of hand, Commander," the Marshal groans. "Now they're saying the Council was too old to begin this long deliberation as they were, and this could backfire on us with that, eh... unfortunate situation of those elections. But, eh...well, I think at this moment, I need to confess a small detail that went along with this gift I gave them and the subsequent deliberation they've been indulging in."

"Oh? And what is that?"

"Well, first, Commander, you need to understand that this knowledge is well above where your society is in the present day, so it has to be treated very delicately as, um, people have a tendency to behave strangely when confronted with such things…"

As Geilv listened to the Marshal, he felt a curious sense of intrigue at what sort of inane excuse the Marshal would come up with this time.

"…And so," the Marshal continues. "Even though the Council was filled with a group of rather mature individuals, I didn't want this to spread around too much by seeing so many members come and go, thereby potentially allowing for leaks of information…you know, to contain it due to our need for security."

"Of course, Marshal. This is a very sensitive matter."

"Right, Commander, very sensitive indeed! So, one of the things I donated, just to be sure all remained well during this time, as I suspected it might take a while, was a, eh…special medical supplement. You see, Commander, where I come from, time is an obstacle we managed to overcome long ago, and the aging process was one of the first things we would solve as we once sought our own form of enlightenment. Therefore, one of these gifts was to teach them these same principles so that they could, eh…find some relief from the burdens of this long duration they would need to invest in as they deliberated on everything else."

"A medical supplement to…extend their lifespans?"

"Yes! Now wouldn't that be a miraculous achievement to bring home. But before they can do this, they need to finish their other work. And then, Commander, you will see these discoveries elevate your society to new levels of prestige. I think this alone is worth that trifling bit of disruption we are seeing now. But now we need to convince the people out there of this matter."

"Ah, I understand, Marshal. Although I am not entirely sure if I might hold enough influence to do this myself. This would fall a bit outside my level of expertise."

"Oh, um…well, perhaps…yes! I suppose this might require a special touch. After all, I was the one to grant this extraordinary gift of wisdom. So, what I will do is simply issue a statement through my secretary here to be sent to the news media, as I sometimes do, and this should cover things for us."

The Marshal ends the link, leaving the Commander shaking his head.

"Unbelievable…" he moans.

It was morning on Therinë, and Thaelyn was joining with his officers for their daily review. Kailen was examining the latest spy-cam videos, including the most recent conversation between Geilv and the Marshal, and Ayene was reporting a series of notes left at her desk at the ACI office.

"So…" she explains. "The Marshal will be issuing a special announcement to the news media of this crazy excuse of a longevity drug he used on our Council in this hidden research base to grant them the time they need for this ridiculously long deliberation."

"This one is almost laughable," Thaelyn muses. "He must be growing desperate to settle this controversy. Very well, and do you have a response to this, or are we following through with our other plans instead?"

"I think we'll let this slide for now. I'll pass the word to the Director, to pass to his associates, to relax a bit on these complaints. We might still see a bit of grumbling, but we need to allow him some time to recover his sense of containment. We're not ready yet for our next phase, which at this point still requires Marelle and her combat pilot training."

"Agreed, and she needs to spend at least a fair amount of time this next year in her Seventh Circle mage training to qualify for those weapons and the jump drive."

"Yeah, and that's still a couple of months away from us. And this still doesn't consider where it will eventually lead us, which has to be into our final stage. And that requires our base to be complete…"

On Azgarén, the Director was in his own meeting on the vid-com with one of his associates, where they were discussing the results of their hasty review of their evolutionary history.

"Director, our investigation, which I will admit up front was conducted rather quickly as compared to our usual procedures, is turning up some very surprising results."

"Oh? And what sort of results are those, Professor?"

"These are hitting us on multiple levels right now, and I had my people go back to recheck their findings several times, and using different techniques, just to make sure our tests were giving us what we thought they were. Director, I am shocked! We all are! Nothing…and I mean NOTHING about our previous studies on the Eracyodines appears to be accurate to what we're seeing now, except that they existed and were our early forebearers."

"Well now, just a moment, Professor," he leans forward on his desk. "Just how do you mean that? Can you give me an example?"

"Examples?!" she blasts. "Yes! I'll give you some examples. First, let's review what we thought we knew, and we'll go from there. We're measuring our civilization to be approximately two million years old by now, based on chronological records and early forms of archeological remains, which so far appear normal. From there, the first signs of these Eracyodines evolving to use tools, organizing themselves, and ultimately to become this young civilization, began about half a million years before this."

"Bringing us to the familiar number of two and a half million years from that evolutionary shift, correct?"

"Yes. This is when that extraordinary environmental event took place that forced our early ancestors to make this wonderful do-or-die leap of evolutionary faith."

The Director glared at the vid-com with a quizzical smirk at her boisterous outburst.

"We also have the transitional period," the Professor adds, "which presumably ran for something like fifty millennia for this evolutionary transformation to actually occur, giving our early ancestors time to make this change from what we most often refer to as the Classic Eracyodine to the later Modernized Eracyodine."

"Right, I recall this from my own history lessons."

"But the fossil evidence has always raised questions for the dating methods and the expected results as compared to any other form of life on our world. The numbers just don't add up politely."

"And therefore, all the controversy for the findings."

"Right. So, I had my people investigating every fossil we could find, whether in storage in our archives, or on display in museums. I decided to take the position of trying to refute your statements of this artificial process, and instead to approach it in an objective manner where we would try to justify our original findings. After all, how many times, and how many people have tried to understand this in the past?"

"Of course."

"Director, like so many others in our world, I was raised on the belief that our early ancestors made this beautiful, and in some ways romantic struggle to survive in a changing world. It makes for a great bedtime story, how they were said to be tenacious and clever, even inventive, to the point where they demonstrated the ability to rise above all odds and overcome these new obstacles."

"Yes, I think we all had that, actually."

"To be honest, it tends to fill you with a sense of pride that you come from an ancestral line filled with such ingenuity."

"I know what you mean. And as for your new results?"

"The results..." she sighs wearily. "What we're uncovering right now is leading some of my people into further study trying to understand why we're getting these results. I even recruited some people at a particle physics lab with a high-resolution electron microscope, along with more precise testing for the age of our samples as we try to refine our figures. One group even got the idea to compare the studies of bone growth in other species to the Classic form, hoping to test the longevity of the individuals to see how many generations may have passed during that transitional period. But now, the trouble we're running into is that transitional period doesn't seem to exist anymore!"

"What? How do you mean?"

"Our species, as it is in the modern day, has this exceptionally long lifespan as compared to all other forms of life in our world. This is one of the biggest controversies in our history, as we have no idea where it came from, except to suggest that wild idea someone once had of this environmental...thing. But this environmental thing apparently did more than give us this crazy long lifespan. It changed our bone structure, too. As a medical professional, I'm sure you know what I'm talking about, with the unusual ring structure we have within our bone fibers."

"Right, of course..."

"And this ring structure, which in some ways resembles the rings of trees, as new bone material is generated in the core and radiates outward, can be measured to give us a fairly reasonable idea of the age of an individual, even in fossils. But this is where that microscope comes into play. In order for us to count those rings and gain any idea of the ages of the individuals in this case, we needed some very precise measurements."

"Naturally."

"Now, we sampled a lot of random specimens from our archives, but eventually it came down to that one most controversial of all discoveries…The Nest."

"Yes, I was actually thinking of that during this time. That one tends to stand out, as if to say the origin of our species began in that one location, as crazy as it might sound."

"Not so crazy by now! The Nest, as it's called, has always been the most extraordinary find in archeological history. Here we have what appears to be multiple generations of Eracyodines, both Classic and Modernized, inhabiting the same location during what many have suggested to be the same general period of history. But this is ridiculous if we have a transitional period of fifty millennia. So, the conclusion was that the site was probably sheltered from the elements during this period, therefore the older remains were exposed as newer generations may have abandoned and reoccupied that same space."

"And this would allow their newer remains to mingle with the older ones in the same layer of stratum. Although, if you were to ask me, I'm not so sure I would want to live in a cave littered with so many ancient bones. It doesn't sound very healthy, or comfortable."

"Yes, well, that point aside," she chuckles. "And therefore our dating methods, if based on the rocks, would be skewed due to this anomaly. We would see both sets being laid down at roughly the same time."

"All right, I got it. But now, what about these new findings?"

"Director, my people are pulling their horns out trying to understand what they're looking at here! When we went back to retest these samples, our testing showed up consistent dates throughout. First of all, that transitional period has vanished. In that Nest grouping, those fossils that seem to be mingling actually do seem to be mingling. And worse, some of my people went back out there to the original dig site to make another study of how they were laid out. Director, we're seeing evidence of ritual burial of those Classic remains!"

"The Classic ones?" he shouts.

"Yes! Complete with remnants of stone tools and such, for whatever reason, as if to say they were the direct parents of the Modernized ones, and being honored with gifts from their descendants to carry into the afterlife."

"In all the nether-space, if that doesn't put a burr under the tail."

"Furthermore, those Modernized fossils show this ring pattern, whereas the Classic ones do not. But it's much smaller than in our modern day, and yet we see later specimens showing it to be growing at an alarming rate. The Classic form might have lived maybe half a century, by our best estimates. But the Modernized form was several times that number and grew almost exponentially."

"Exponentially!" he winces.

"And now, for the big one... The half-million year offset from that wonderful environmental whatsits that caused the whole thing to begin with, was only about five thousand years before our earliest recorded civilization."

The Director gaped at the vid-com, wheezing and nearly speechless.

"Five...five..." he croaks.

"Yeah, there's a couple of zeros missing in that number, which makes me wonder who did those early calculations and how they could've fouled it up so badly."

"But that's... Professor! That's..."

"Tampering is the word I think you're looking for...pure and simple tampering with our natural evolution, and further tampering with our ability to study it accurately."

"In all the nether-space, Professor, a little piece of me was holding out hope that this was just a story, but now I'm feeling very weak."

"You're not the only one, Director. Right now, my people are working to study and reclassify the other specimens we have here, and it's all coming out about the same. The Modernized form started using tools very abruptly and only a touch before they started doing such things as inventing writing, agriculture, and early tribal living."

"Incredible. Five thousand years..." he muses. "Given the lifespans, maybe also the ground they needed to cover, this could be enough time, I suppose, to grow a local population and start taking over the place. All right, I'm sure our friends will need to see this data to include as part of their own records, and then they tell me they're working on some clever method to release it without the Marshal taking any immediate notice."

"How do you release something like this without someone, especially HIM, taking notice of any kind?"

"I don't know right now, but it'll probably be a method to hide it as actual fact so far, at least until they're ready to expose it fully."

◆◆◆◆◆

Over the course of the following weeks, the news media saw a lessening of the scandalous intrigue being generated in relation to the missing Council, but the trials were still ongoing, and there was still a level of outrage simmering. Once again, Ileani found herself releasing a follow-up news broadcast with the latest report.

"Many of the science factions are still fuming over the controversy of the Council taking so long with these alleged deliberations, and further in relation to the Marshal's press release a month ago concerning his gift of some sort of longevity drug which he gave to the Council as a means of preserving them so that they could see this deliberation through to the end.

Among these factions is the medical community, saying that if the Council did in fact make use of this extraordinary new medical treatment, why couldn't they at least reveal this much to our public, as this would surely represent a functioning product that could be studied openly. In the absence of this, here is what one spokesperson had to say..."

The view now changes to a clip of a press meeting and a female speaker.

"The Council is clearly negligent, regardless of any other statement. We are a society of scientists. Even if this wonder drug was a private allowance for the duration of this deliberation, in the ten millennia they have been hiding themselves away, they should've at least had some sort of report to publish, if for no other reason than to keep us posted that they are IN FACT doing some kind of work and didn't forget any of their other obligations.

Therefore, it becomes clear to many of us that in the absence of a functioning government body here at home, performing their duties as they must, we must consider declaring the Council invalid if they cannot respond to any of these allegations with even a simple progress report. We will therefore grant them a grace period from the moment of this news release to get their tails in motion and prove to us that they are still a government body capable of performing government functions. If not, we may find ourselves forced to replace them with one that does."

The report now returns to the newsroom.

"In other news, the trials relating to the emergency war protocols are proceeding to a decision phase, in which arguments will be presented on whether or not to dissolve the condition and return our world to a peacetime setting again."

Another press meeting clip comes on the screen of a male legal consultant.

"We have been examining many aspects of these complaints, not the least of which are the legal violations, but also the lack of supportive evidence to suggest we are, or ever have been, under direct threat of these insurgents here at home. Therefore, even though the fear of a potential attack may have presented itself at one time, it never materialized. According to our historical records, our military has travelled across the galaxy and back again, dispatching these insurgents with great success. Not once did they ever manage to penetrate our native space with a hostile assault force, even though we are fairly sure they ought to know where we live and have the jump drives to reach us."

And again, the report returns to the newsroom to finish up.

"When later questioned on his statement of these insurgents knowing where Azgarén is found, and having jump drives to reach it, he said this was based on the Marshal's avid claim of that huge alien ship that once arrived in our skies and carried away the Former Elder Velen Nazég. He said, 'If they know where to find us to carry him off, they know where to attack us if they actually wanted to.'

Meanwhile, several of the factions that have been most vocal during this time are now promising to investigate some of the Council's other actions during that period as a review to verify the integrity of their decisions in relation to the events that may have prompted them."

◆ ◆ ◆ ◆ ◆

"This is simply intolerable, Commander," the Marshal groans on the com-link. "We give one explanation, and they come up with a new complaint. We give an explanation for that one, and they hit us with yet another."

"It would seem that way," he states calmly. "But at the same time, it would also seem they have a viable perspective to work from."

"Viable?!" he blasts abruptly, and then forces his temper down. "Eh, yes, I suppose you have a point, so what we need is a way to explain what is truly occurring out there while at the same time trying to maintain some semblance of control over the situation. I'm going to put together another statement to release to our agents in the news media. I'm still wondering how and why they're allowing all these sensational reports to pass through. This is clearly stirring up a lot of public controversy, and the whole point of those agents was to keep things within some level of, eh...well, containment. You do recall that moment we had once upon a time with the Tav'ageen panic, right? Such an unfortunate moment that was."

"Yes, that was a tragic moment in our history."

"Indeed, Commander! And we surely don't want any more of that!"

He ends the link, which left the Commander staring at the vid-com once again wondering what the Marshal had in mind this time.

"I hope you're not thinking what I think you're thinking..."

99

Chapter 5

STRANGE ARRIVALS

"Ghantil, I believe we have a solution to the seed entity," Azina declares as she enters his office.

"Great! What did you find, Azina?"

"After carefully decoding and simulating that strange alien genetic data, we had to make a few assumptions based partly on our results, and also that demonstration we ran on a cloned replicant in the lab. By observing the clone and applying the Belvik Spore solution the Captain gave us, we saw a systemic bioelectrical feedback emission erupting out of the seed entity…a bit like a last gasp before it dies. Then, when analyzing the remains, we found ourselves left with little more than a process of elimination to find the source. Nothing in the original seed coding would generate that feedback, so it had to be this alien set. That stuff is just weird, and it seems to involve something that demands the host to behave like a slave platform to something higher. When it failed, we think it probably sent this feedback into the host as a means of taking it down with it."

"So sinister," he huffs. "So, we really are little more than food for that creature. But now, how do we disable this effect?"

"I spoke to Captain Nazég about this as we were performing the study, and she informed me that the rifle-propelled version didn't hit as hard. In that case, it was only a strong stun, and the victim could recover with only minimal medical aid. So, I pulled up the records on that one to compare a few notes. The coding was altered in such a way that it seemed to debilitate some aspects of this alien set. For lack of a better term, the control mechanism was broken, and it wasn't as strongly enforcing itself in that case."

"Interesting, but this is a completely different formulation. How can we apply it here?"

"We tried another series of tests using clones, this time creating an array of them, and applying a number of different drug agents to see if we could simulate this same effect when the seeds died. The objective here was to daze or zonk the capacity of the seed entity so that it couldn't function at its best. A bit like giving it a narcotic. Along the way, I suddenly had this crazy idea. Would you believe it? I decided to try that fungal narcotic they pushed at us once, and it worked!"

"It did?" he perks up. "But what about the host in this case?"

"We still had the old research docs in the archives, and if you recall, they told us to try researching it for any potential pharmaceutical purposes. What an irony!" she giggles. "We had already discovered and eliminated those heavy metals and the narcotic effect as it relates to our native neural tissues. So, what I did was to compare ours to the seed entity and recalibrate a few molecule chains to hit the seed instead."

"Incredible, that's a fine piece of work, Azina. And the result?"

"The result essentially incapacitates the seed entity so that it no longer has such refined control. A bit like dumbing it down, and wiping its sense of what's going on."

"A little like the story of those miners," he reflects. "And so, we're using another of his death toys to fight on our side. This is a sweet bit of revenge. Now, where does this put us? Are we ready for a field test?"

"I believe so. According to the parameters provided to us by the Captain, their medical team was taking a slow cautious approach, so we decided to bump it up for better efficiency. After all, we made the thing, and we hold a lot more detail on its tolerance levels."

"Good, and this might allow us to process the treatments a little faster."

"Our testing allowed us to halve the time the Captain and her people spent. I've already given instructions to produce more of this drug. The Captain was kind enough to inform us they still had one of those farms on Morndindor, and another one on Therinë, neither of which were actively being managed, but both still seemed viable. Initially, they were going to destroy them, but decided against it for now, instead to leave it for later study."

"Ours or theirs?"

"At this point, probably theirs, as it represents a curious biological specimen. But I'm sure they'll share the results if we ask for it."

"Very good, and now this could benefit all of us. Amazing. This is a good turn for us, Azina. So, I'm assuming they'll provide us with some sort of deliveries?"

"Yes, she said she would speak to that Lord Thaelyn of hers about this. The farms in question are rather small, and again not actively in use. So, first they need to restart their production, then probably add more facilities, since we would need to ramp up the production considerably to provide for our world population. It's a case where either we need to start producing our own, but on a large agricultural scale, or else they would, and then make trade with us."

"A trade agreement…with a foreign society. In all the nether-space, that's a new one."

"Either way, to get us started, we'll need to produce more of that fertilizer Central was asking for once. They'll agree to trade what they have for more of this, at least until we can settle on a better arrangement."

"Excellent! Then I should get down to writing up some sort of contract. Let's show them we can be responsible businessmen here."

"Sounds good to me," she smiles. "Next is to ask for volunteers. We need actual bodies this time to observe the full results. But the Captain cautions me to keep them in the lab during that final let-go moment in case we see another of those shock-induced comas."

"All right, then we'll put out the word for a closed study and ask for volunteers to participate. We already know it worked for Ayene, so we can feel at least some confidence to find a positive result."

✦ ✦ ✦ ✦ ✦

"Your Lordship," Chief Tech Lapäli calls as she enters the room. "We have our first production-line model of the Harvester ready. Ayene and Petrith have informed me that they hope to install one of these in their office basement, so we've managed to put together a small unit to fit the space, and custom-designed a bank of fuel cells to power it. Trying to get it up and running will be an exercise in itself, but it should make a good example to learn from."

"Everything needs a beginning," he nods. "And this one allows us to keep it under our control. Good. Package it up and we will have some of Kaliya's people deliver it for us."

"All right, but we're fairly certain you'll need actual people to install it, not projections, and they'll need to know what they're doing. This means we might need to import a group locally so they can conduct their work."

"Very well, we know we can use our portals to bring them in, and we can use spell scrolls to bring them home again, if we must. It will not be efficient, but it will work, at least until the Harvester is fully charged. What about a conjuring pad? Do we have a functional design for that yet?"

"Yes, the Professor and his people were able to assemble something to concentrate these energies for a person to stand on and cast spells. It should work well enough once the capacitors are charged. But this unit won't win any awards for the charging rates."

"Fair enough, Chief Tech, this is our first time, and it is still a learning experience. We can work on optimizing things at a later moment, maybe to have a better design ready for our base."

"Good, then I'll have our people prepare it for delivery right away. In the meantime, our production lines are churning away at more component modules, but I need to tell you, we're running through our supply of adamantium rather quickly, and I know how valuable this stuff is."

"Indeed, but the need is similarly great. I have given word to our mining teams to continue their production as best they can, and we have a few additional survey groups out there investigating new supplies. We will see to it, Chief Tech, one way or another."

"Our next goal is to make this compatible with our ships, and maybe some kind of personal unit. For now, I think we can scale it down, using nanotech alternatives to some of the components, and we already have a scaled-down version of a reactor we can use, derived partly from our studies of those cute little units we found on Ruuki uy'Daan. We've actually been using something like that in some of our ships."

"Speaking of which, I have heard of your progress with our new combat craft. Marelle should be finishing her year very soon and beginning the new one after. Then she will be available to assist in your testing. But once we finalize the design, we will need a small fleet of them constructed."

"Right, I'm already thinking ahead for that day. We have some new industry we've been working on lately to help us fabricate the parts. Once we get it running, the rest should come much easier."

"Excellent, this seems to be coming together nicely. Continue your good work, Chief. I will see about procuring the resources and forward them to you."

Morning was rising on Morndindor, and a messenger had arrived with a letter to the home of Tol and Eiki Bronzeheart in the city of Glimmerheim. The cycles of day and night were almost opposite between here and Therinë, and so the letter was the last business of the previous day on Therinë, sent to be delivered to their home first thing in the morning, local time.

"Tol, we've received word from our good King that he has a need t' see ye on Therinë."

"Does he now, ay? I wonder what he be a-workin' up with the war they be a-fightin'?"

"The last bit of tellin' was they found their way t' that place they call Azgarén, an' were a-sneakin' 'round real careful like under the nose of that nasty titan. I'll tell ye true, I nay be a-wantin' t' be a-sniffin' up his backside, ye can be sure of that!"

Tol shares a rowdy laugh with his wife at the thought.

"Did he say what this be about, lass?"

"The note here says he has a need t' talk about some diggin', an' makin' up somethin' with the Daanen-Aryku t' carry their magic t' that new world, since it be right poor on it. An' it seems he'll be a-needin' a plump mountain or two of Adamant for it."

"Oi! This will need t' be brought t' the lads in the mines. Right then, I'll go t' see him this eve, when it turns t' be their morn."

"D' ye want me t' stay up till ye return?"

"Nay, me love. I don'na know how long it might take, an' ye need yer sleep as much as any. Mayhap it nay will take too long, an' I can join ye back for a few winks."

"Aye then… Be quick, an' don'na forget t' tell me what he has t' say."

Tol and Eiki had finished their morning ritual and were making ready to attend to their daily chores. Tol was the Chief Forge Smith in the city, a service he was proud of, especially since Thaelyn and his people liberated them from the oppression of the Marshal and his servant Ytani, an unmodified Suuden'kai Prodigy Child installed as the local Thane.

Tol made his way down to the forges, which processed ore into metal almost on a continual basis. Some of this was used locally, but a large amount was being exported outside their mountain home to the outer portion of the city, and other outlying regions, to provide for a large reconstruction effort of their wrecked world.

He directed his work crews during the day to load the smelters and cast ingots for the outside industries, while another team of forges worked their molds and castings into tools and parts for the local trades.

By the end of the day, he felt weary, as did most of the laborers. But his spirit was still strong, as he knew he made good work with his team, and now he had another duty waiting for him. The evening was closing. He made a quick visit to a local tavern for a bite to eat, and then headed off to the local gateway node which would take him across to Therinë and Rolsklinde.

It was morning in that city when he arrived. He shielded his eyes briefly as the sudden change in lighting was shocking to him. He made his way outside and across the plaza to the WIC building, a place he had not visited for quite some time since the liberation of his home.

"Milord! How be ye today?" he shouts in a sturdy voice as he enters through the door.

"Chief Bronzeheart, so good to see you. We are well, though we have been keeping ourselves very busy of late with all our little projects. And what of you and your lovely wife, Eiki?"

"Aye, she be workin' as hard as ye can imagine, what with all the fine goods that be comin' into town. The tradin' with the other cities and worlds has brought many a fine ware to our humble home. So, what be the need ye have of me this fine day? I got yer note, and it told a tale of diggin' and a mighty pile of Adamant."

"Indeed, make yourself comfortable here and we shall begin."

Tol takes up a chair at the table as Thaelyn prepares himself.

"We have two goals to meet, and they are connected in a few minor ways. First is Azgarén. As you may already know, we have been engaged in a number of missions to disrupt Darumon's activities there. Along the way, we also discovered some fascinating details of how the people are largely oblivious to the truth of Darumon and Sargeras, living their lives thinking all is well right in their own home."

"That nay be a good thing, if they be anythin' like our people under the Thane."

"This is true, and largely you are right. Apparently, they have been lied to about virtually everything, if only to keep them complacent to Darumon's whims."

"Oi, that be a sad tale to me ears. How do ye think ye'll be goin' about helpin' them?"

"We have already found several people who have converted to our side, much like you and your wife, and Belrum and the others once did."

"Aye, that be grand. So, ye yay have a few good words for it after all."

"Indeed, we do. And furthermore, some of them have agreed to help us make our initial incursion, but we must do so in a very cautious manner, for that very same reason I explained to you once about Sargeras, keeping beneath his sights until the last moment."

"Aye, I recall the tale. How do ye think ye'll be doin' this?"

"We have a group of local people conducting some work for us, clearing a large area, and building some facilities for us to use as our staging post for an assault. But this is being done under the guise of a local project, in order to defray questioning by anyone who might become curious."

Tol lets out a boisterous laugh at the thought.

"So, Darumon was makin' tales to put the people under his way, and ye'll be makin' tales to put them under another. It'll be a fine sight when it all comes 'round. But now, how do ye think I can help here?"

"Part of this facility is inside a mountain."

"Oh!" he resounds enthusiastically. "I see it now. And ye need some good strong dwarven arms to help ye carve it out, do ye?"

"You are a wise man, Tol," he smiles. "We will need some special work done to open up space for the equipment and people we will need to house inside there. We will provide you the details later, but for now, if you think you have the men for it, we would like to begin organizing them and the tools they need to do their work. I think this might also offer you and yours some modest opportunity to earn back a little of your esteem from what he did to you."

"Aye to that! Ye can be sure of it! I'll spread the word back home and tell them the tale. Ye'll have yer work team, a good hearty crew of me best."

"Excellent. We shall coordinate our efforts as we move forward, but we also have a minor issue to be tolerated thus far. We do not as yet have a functioning method of travelling to and from this location efficiently. We can send people in, but until we have the space to establish our equipment, we will not have an easy way to bring them out."

"Hmm, this equipment ye speak of, mayhap it be includin' yer gateway node?"

"Anything that uses our magical energies," he nods. "The equipment I speak of will begin to provide for that, and once it goes into operation, the rest will arrive soon after to establish a reliable service for us. But your team will need to essentially camp inside that mountain until that time and keep themselves carefully hidden from any unwanted eyes."

"Aye then, but to do that, we'll be needin' supplies, like food and such."

"Of course, we will provide a steady supply to keep you in good form. We will use some of our agents, such as Kaliya and her people, to ferry the supplies to and from, as well as any other items, like care packages and letters from home."

"'Tis a grand deed ye make. Aye, I think this will do us well enough. Now, on to this bit about the Adamant. I hear ye'll be needin' a great heap of it, ay?"

"Yes, one of our most important projects involves a new form of technology we are developing to allow us to bring our magical capabilities into that world."

"This be a part of that tale of the equipment ye need to set up before ye can do anything else, ay?"

"Yes, and once this is working for us, many other things become possible. But to do this, the design calls for a large quantity of adamantium."

"About how much?"

"We have several applications occurring simultaneously, but in total…" he coughs gently, "…a few tons, maybe more depending on the productivity ratios."

"Great All-Father!" he extols with a loud whistle. "Right then, this may take a wee bit, even with the supply ye gave us back from that mine to the south, which our people still haven' found a use for."

"To put it to this purpose would be a valuable cause. We also have the mine to the north, with some of our people working there, and you have that same mine to your south. In addition, we have found more deposits on Ruuki uy'Daan and elsewhere we could tap into, and

I think we may need to tap into everything we possibly can to see this done on time."

"Right then, so how much time do we have?"

"That depends on a great many variables, not the least of which is the time for your people to carve out that mountain. We also need to prepare our friends and all these little stories we are spreading amongst the public, and of course the time to actually build this equipment, which is the most important. We want it ready by the time the mountain has space for it. Therefore, let us simply say, time is of the essence."

"Aye to that. So, I'll have our people start makin' up tools and such for it, and workin' the Adamant mines again hard and heavy. Do ye want bricks, or forged in some way?"

"Our people are currently using some custom industry to forge custom components, so whatever is convenient for transport. Ingots are a generic form, and easy to use, so if you can do this for us, that would be very helpful."

"Right, especially if this be some fancy bit of work ye're makin'. Good then, be there anythin' else ye need?"

"That is all for now, Chief. We will have our people work closely with yours to see this through."

"Fine and good… Then I should be returnin' home to give the word, and mayhap find a few winks of sleep before settin' off on this."

He gets up from his chair and offers a bow, then turns and briskly makes his departure.

✦✦◆✦✦

The streets of Capitol Prime were a constant flow of activity, just as it was in most large cities. Vehicles passed by on the hover lanes as office workers were either commuting to work or returning home. Pedestrians, including business professionals and shoppers, casually walked along the sidewalks as they visited the local shops and malls.

Throughout the city, there had been a flurry of utility workers installing the public raid sirens Ayene and Petrith once ordered during their visit to Commander Geilv's office. A large number of emergency signals and public address announcers were being erected on utility poles all across the city and linked to a wireless communication network. The scene was being repeated in every major city and town around the globe.

In addition, city engineers had been sent out to evaluate many of the buildings, sorting through their design specifications to identify those with underground facilities to be designated as raid shelters, and posting new signs for public direction in case of emergency.

Very few people paid any attention to this in the beginning, as most were only interested in attending to their personal affairs. But as the work became more apparent, some began to take notice. The sights were unusual, and the public had no idea of their intended purpose. Some of them paused to ask questions, only to be told there would be a public announcement in the near future giving an explanation.

In the downtown section of the city, where the commercial district boasted tall skyscrapers and robust plazas and malls, there were several large-format video boards displaying global news and product advertisements. A new product campaign was underway, and advertisements were popping up everywhere, including shopping malls and home vid-com entertainment channels.

The campaign featured an adorable new spokesperson, representing a prehistoric Eracyodine cartoon character. On this occasion, the cute little critter was seen digging in the dirt, as if searching for grubs, when it stumbled into a shopping cart. Realizing the futility of its former task, it takes this and proceeds into a local supermarket, where it begins browsing the aisles. The ad was accompanied with a whimsical caption.

> *"Every boy and girl should start the day with a hearty bowl of Fruit Crunchies, the meal for the growing Eracyodine in you."*

In the offices of the ACI, Ayene and the agency director, meaning to say Commander Kriv'tik, were calling in one of their veteran office workers for a meeting.

"Director," she announces as she formally enters the office. "Do you have something for me?"

"Miss Kaetaal," he begins. "I've been reviewing a few of our personnel records to see about offering a promotion or two, and your name came up. According to your file, you once served with C.P. Security for some period of time, correct?"

"Yes Sir! I actually served with them for six centuries, starting out as a city patrol officer and working my way up to a Class 8 security rating in their forensics research division."

"Just out of curiosity, Miss Kaetaal, why would you choose to leave them and come to work with us? C.P. Security is a fine institution to serve."

"Yes, it is, but when I heard of this new service, I was hoping to find myself with an opportunity to apply my skills on a broader spectrum. The pamphlets that were circulating through our old office were calling for people with strong interests in top level security investigation and data collection. I hold a minor degree in law, another one in forensic statistics, and a major in criminal justice. Therefore, I felt this position might afford me an opportunity to apply myself more fully."

"Indeed, and for all the work we have lining up ahead of us, this is quite possible. But now, Miss Kaetaal, if we are to see you apply yourself more fully, we will need to bring you up a notch or two and begin introducing you to a few of our innermost secrets which only a select few are aware of. For this, we would need to modify that security rating of yours."

"Of course, Sir, and you can be sure I will strive to meet up to your expectations."

"This is good to hear, so on this occasion, I am bumping you to a Class 5 rating. This is a big move, Miss Kaetaal, but we need you up there."

Her eyes bulged momentarily, and she gasped sharply.

"Five! But...in all the nether-space, that's three levels above my last position."

"We have a number of critically pressing needs, and with six centuries of experience, I think you know the demands by now. Most of our agents work in the field, but we need someone here in the office too. So far, you're at the top of the list, so it's time to see what you're made of. And to start you off, Agent Ti'van here is going to give you a special tour to educate you on a few very important details."

"Yes Sir!" she asserts boldly. "I promise I won't let you down."

Ayene and the younger woman leave the office and begin making their way to the lift.

"Your name is Kita, right?" Ayene asks.

"Yes Ma'am."

"And how old are you?"

"I'm soon to reach my first millennium."

"Nice, that's a special moment. All right, from now on, you're going to be privileged to some very delicate information that only a handful of others in the world actually know about, and aside from those of us here with this understanding, most of them are over at the ARC."

"The ARC?"

"Yes, because we're working very closely with them on a number of discreet projects."

"I see, and will I be informed of these projects, or are they part of another classification?"

"I'm going to bring you in on a number of things, so hold on to those horns of yours, or you might lose them."

"Oh dear…all right, I'm ready."

They enter the lift and Ayene hits the button for the basement. The doors close and the lift begins moving.

"First and foremost, unknown to anyone in our world, at least outside our little circle, we here at the ACI have made contact with an outside authority."

"An outside authority…" she whispers. "Someone from another world?"

"We can say, technically, yes. But a part of it also relates to something Central recently discovered, and who normally lives there."

"Uh oh…what did they discover?"

"Nether-space, the real thing, meaning to say, a four-dimensional spatial continuum. It does actually exist, despite our science trying to deny it for so long."

"Wow! That would sure send a few horns flying."

"I'm sure it would. But the beings that live there are quite different from our example. And yet, again technically speaking, THESE are the Marshal's true enemies, not anything you might find in our galaxy, or even our universe."

"Oops!" she yips softly. "There go all his stories!"

"Absolutely. And we're currently working with them on a number of very sensitive projects where our planetary security and the Marshal are concerned."

"Uh oh… Um, may I speak a moment?"

Ayene nods.

"I've been paying attention to some of the news recently, and I've had a number of questions going around in my mind. I know we've been investigating the Council, and recently I heard the Marshal give this excuse, and this is all I can say about it…an excuse…for how and why the Council, who should probably be dead by now, could still be alive and in some odd outpost deliberating something. Are my suspicions correct, or am I simply imagining things?"

"Kita, you're a very intuitive young lady, so I'll answer yes, you are right. It was an excuse, and a bad one at that, but so far, we're instructing Ileani Ur'paran to release it as a viable explanation of why they're absent from their posts."

"Wait! A viable explanation… So, Ileani is working for us?"

"She is, at least as an outside agent we can leak information to."

"Wow, so we're intentionally leaking information to her. Then all those recent news sensations she's been putting on are your work?"

"Most of it. A few pieces are collateral with other factions getting involved. But now…"

As the lift arrives in the basement, the doors open, allowing Ayene to lead the younger woman into a corridor. The basement was finished with hallways, supply rooms, and utility centers. One segment had been recently remodeled in preparation for the Harvester unit to be installed. Ayene leads them along the corridor to a door. She halts just before entering.

"Kita, the Marshal lied to us about everything he said. He's not some beneficent alien bearing great gifts. He's a fugitive from another authority body, and he's currently in hiding, along with Sargeras. The people we made contact with belong to a faction serving that other body. Inside this room, they are currently installing some custom technology to allow us better interaction here within this building. Using this, we'll be able to pass information, among other things, about our operations on both sides so we can grab the creep that killed our Council, took us as his pets, infested us with his parasites and fake medical chips, and generally wants to use us for a revenge attack on his old rivals, those ones in that extradimensional space. Now, with all that being said, how do your horns feel?" she smirks.

Kita stared blankly at Ayene and wheezed.

"Rather soft, actually… Wow, is this what it feels like to earn Class 5 security?"

"Yours is probably a special case, but we need the extra hands to help us with these intimate details. Also, we'll need to hit our full population with it one of these days. The trouble is, the Marshal is a being of very high potential, some might say nearly godlike as compared to us. The old Tav'ageen Anomaly was a fake. Let me show you what it really is…"

Ayene now steps away to allow herself some room. She then begins transforming her image into several of her favorite practice shapes, much to the fear and hesitation of the younger agent. She finally returned back to her normal Suuden'kai image, but this time without her seed or cranial implant.

"This is how I actually appear in real life," she asserts. "My interface and seed are both removed, thanks to our friends. But the Tav'ageen thing is a fabulous quality born into our species, and Darumon hates it. This is the reason he went to so much trouble trying to hide it."

"A quality? But can you actually explain to me what I just saw?"

"What you're looking at right now is a type of mental projection of my spirit outside my body. To better understand this, you need to think of Former Elder Velen Nazég and the science faction he once represented."

"Ah hah!" she blurts boldly and jabs a finger at Ayene. "I thought there was something suspicious to the sudden mention of his name recently…and not just once! Never in my life did I hear his name mentioned so prominently in the news media."

"You're quick! I like that. Just remember, this is all very sensitive. The Marshal, above all others, cannot know what we're doing."

"Got it!"

"Anyway, Elder Nazég once had an idea of what this was, but of course the rest of the Council didn't care much for him. And the Marshal simply made things worse."

"Right, I recall some of the stories now."

"The projection skill is what he once described as a Prodigy Gift, and it is everything that word might suggest, perhaps even more. The image doesn't need to be your own body, and we can move around to any place we can recall in our minds, simply by thought. Right now, my body is on a completely different world, and in a completely different universe, Kita. I'm not even supposed to be alive, thanks to the Marshal and his secret games."

"Uh oh. And a new universe? You mean, aside from that extradimensional space?"

"Yes, both of which Central discovered, and to which he forgot to tell our science factions about, even after ten millennia of promising us great wisdom."

"Oh, yes!" she tosses her hands up. "I'm sure that will go over wonderfully once it gets out. But what did he do to you?"

"I was stationed at a top-secret mining base in this other universe. He had us mining an unknown mineral to produce an unknown explosive material he then hoped to use against his true enemies. Fortunately for us, but unfortunately for him, he was found out and chased away, and the weapon confiscated."

"Good, I think. But he's still here."

"So he is…"

Ayene now opens the door to allow them to enter. Inside the room, Kita's eyes began to focus on a small army of gnomes hauling the oversized pieces of the Harvester into place and connecting them to power couplings on the fuel cells.

"Wow!" she croons. "Are these the people you met? How did they get in here?"

"They use a form of conveyor which we call a portal, and it works on a personal level. There are actually several races involved. This one does a lot of their research."

They enter more fully inside the room to find a few others supervising, one of them a human in an elaborate robe.

"See this man here?" Ayene directs. "He's known as a mage. You might find this hard to believe, Kita, but in this other universe, they have actual real magic. It's all powered by a special energy layer they have over there. And this device they're installing here will begin making some for us in this room."

"Magic?" she frowns. "Like…as in…um…"

"Yeah, fireballs and lightning strikes from the fingertips magic," Ayene nods.

Now her eyes bulge even bigger.

"You're kidding me!"

"No, I'm not. I've seen it, and I'm also taking a few of my own lessons in it. I'm attending one of their academies right now."

"In all the nether-space…" she whispers.

Kaliya was also standing in the room in her Order military uniform. She was in physical form on this occasion to assist with the spell scrolls to help move people around. When Ayene began introducing the younger agent to the activity, she turned around to make an official greeting.

Kita noticed Kaliya standing there, but her back was turned at the time. When she saw her turn around, her first reaction was shock at seeing the glowing eyes. She fell back a step as Kaliya approached.

"What happened to you?" Kita wheezes.

"Nothing special, outside of being born," she grins. "But if you mean the eyes, this is what my father brought to us when that ship came to take him away."

"Your father? A SHIP!!" she screeches. "In all the nether-space, are you trying to say...um..."

"Velen is my father."

Kita now felt faint, and she reached out for a wall to lean against.

"And so, we have his name in the news...and not just once. Does this mean, well, wait a minute...actually, wait another minute...um... is he dead, or was this the Marshal making up another story?"

"It's a story. We're still alive...barely."

"Barely. All right, so does this mean he actually was chasing you all over the galaxy?"

"And into another universe..."

"Wow, that part didn't make it on the headline news, apparently. And the eyes?"

"We met another race who helped in delivering that ship. We call them the cu'Nar, a race of what are known as elementals, pure light and energy. They shared a little of this with us as a way of guarding us against Sargeras and his influence...maybe also as a way to cleanse us of his essence."

"His essence? How do you mean?"

"We believe Darumon artificially engineered us using his own seed. So technically, he's our father."

Kita grimaced with an audible whine, and her body trembled reflexively as she pressed herself harder against the wall and shook her head morosely.

"Oh please, are you serious? I suppose you are if your eyes glow from something to purify you from it."

"Yeah, we're not any happier about it than you are, but we need to press forward."

"By the way," she examines the uniform. "Who are you and who do you work for?"

"My name is Captain Kaliya Nazég, and I serve Lord Thaelyn, King of a world we call Tae'Eladar," she offers a polite salute.

"A King," she muses. "That's interesting. But a Captain? You look even younger than I am."

"Yes, well, things move much faster on that world," she shrugs. "And I was something of a rush job to bring us to where we are now."

"Yeah, and something tells me my horns are going to take a long time to grow back from all this. But now, what are we going to do about the Marshal, if he's such a bad person?"

"We're playing a series of little games on him to slowly tear down everything he played on us, while at the same time preparing a hidden advance on him. This here," she thumbs at the installation work behind her, "will allow us to coordinate things a little easier, at least until we can better establish ourselves."

"And Kita," Ayene adds. "Now that you're aware of this, we're going to have you help coordinate things, like communication and any people that need to use it."

✦

"How is that chamber coming along?" the construction foreman shouts. "We need to be sure it's stable before we move to the next phase."

"Yes Sir, we seem to be ready. The final mold forms have been removed and it looks like the room is ready for use. We just need to report back to the Director with the news so he can forward it to the supplemental work crews."

"Good. Next, we should finish up the aqueduct from the river. They're going to need water inside there. I also have instructions to create a channel of some kind running roughly midsection across the field."

"What's that for? Irrigation?"

"I don't actually know. It was a recent revision, so they must've made a few changes on their side. Then we have the access tunnels."

"That part I think I can understand if they're going to build anything up here to serve as buildings or structures, but shouldn't we be excavating something more like a basement rather than long tunnels?"

"These plans show there will be some sort of wall on either side of us, and the tunnels are for utility service. Apparently, there will be another one running down the center connecting to something that will come up to the surface. This seems to be part of their custom technology."

"All right then, we'll get to work."

The foreman and one of his lead jobsite managers were reviewing the plans for the work being done in the valley outside of Capitol Prime.

The project was more than four months along by now, and a lot of progress had been made outside. A large region had been cleared of debris and leveled out. A substantial portion of the lower mountainside had been blasted away down to the bedrock and shored up with concrete reinforcement, establishing the foundation for the future base facility to be built. An underground aqueduct was being dug from the river further upstream to provide water to the project site. A junction midway would divert some of it into a connecting branch leading across the future battlefield as an open channel covered by a grate. The rest would be carried by a pipeline into the main facility on the mountainside.

Deep ditches were being cut into the ground to be made into underground tunnels running the length of the field in multiple areas. Some of these branched off to side chambers where a surface access would be built. The outer edges of the project also had the beginnings of tunnel corridors running three quarters the length up to the river.

Inside the mountain, one large chamber had been carved out and reinforced, representing an arrival zone and storage yard. Other tunnels had been started, but the work was on hold until a supplemental work crew could be brought in to finish it, since they were designated as specialists. They would attend to the inner workings while the Suuden-Aryku maintained the appearance of activity on the outside.

Back in the city, Ayene was escorting Kita as her latest apprentice, and together they were visiting the ARC for an introduction.

"I want her scheduled as soon as you have an opening for the procedure," Ayene asserts. "I would like to see our people free from this horrible little bug with all due haste."

"Absolutely, Lieutenant," the Director affirms. "Azina is currently taking volunteers for a closed study of our solution. Once we have our final results from that, we'll open it up for everyone else."

"A way to remove the seed..." Kita muses distantly. "I always thought that was impossible. I firmly believed I would have this awful thing stuck to my back for the rest of my life. Oh, Ayene, I will be loyal to you until the end of time for this."

"Meanwhile," she smiles. "Director, I got your note on the project out there in the valley."

"Yes," he responds. "The foreman just recently called in about the arrival zone, saying it's ready for you to start bringing in your people."

"Good, then we shouldn't delay ourselves. We have our people assembling on the other side, so let's schedule a meeting out there once we're all together."

"Sounds good to me…"

It took several days for the Marshal to compose his thoughts well enough to write up his latest press release. He went through many drafts by this time, scratching out most of them as he tried crafting his words such that they would be acceptable to the need, but without the potential to generate more conflict with all the naysayers. Many thoughts passed through his mind along the way, reflecting on numerous concepts and ideas, as well as several past desires and ambitions. He found himself finally settling on a general direction, albeit reluctantly, as it represented the one and only possible way to resolve this, while at the same time, not revealing those details he had been trying to withhold due to his other private concerns.

Those concerns, which he had argued with himself on many occasions, were starting to plague him by now. On one hand, he had a delicate desire to teach the Suuden-Aryku such knowledge as what he reflected on during the events at Morndindor and Madzurki. But on the other hand, to do so might push the limits with his master, as the Suuden-Aryku were already a very mature race, and to advance them further might be too much.

When the document was ready, he submitted the result through his usual channels, and they were now arriving on Ileani's desk via one of Ayene's agents.

"And here we have his latest excuse?" she asks.

"Yeah, and this one is a work of art," Navina remarks. "Kaliya took a look at it earlier and she's already getting ideas about it."

"And what am I supposed to do with it?"

"He'll expect it to be broadcast verbatim. After all, it's supposed to be going through his regulators. This is actually one of Kaliya's thoughts, as well. This could open up a few things for later."

"How so?"

"It reflects on something we learned about him once. We have some spy video on him in private thought. It was interesting, as he was speaking of something very similar to this. To be honest, I'm surprised because it looks like he actually did it, at least partially."

"Uh huh, whatever that means," she smirks. "And what are you going to do to tear this one up?"

"In the near term, I think Ayene has a few ideas floating around her horns, so I'll leave it to her," she grins brightly.

"I thought so," she sighs. "Just so long as she allows me to catch mine before she causes them to go flying off again."

As the meeting breaks up, Ileani submits the statement to her news crew for a report scheduled later in the day. When the time finally comes to make her report, she situates herself in her anchorman's chair as the set coordinator gears up for another presentation.

"This is Ileani Ur'paran for C.P. News. Our top report for tonight is a press release just received today from the Marshal as he generously offers his aid to help the people of the world find solace in the many controversies surrounding the extended absence of the Council. This statement seems to be in response to the recent press releases coming out of the science community about the Council's lack of proper demonstration of their capacity to perform the more traditional government functions that are necessary in our society.

According to the Marshal, the Council has been out of communication during this time largely due to the matter of secluding themselves from outside distractions so they could more purposely focus on this deliberation. But he says this deliberation is not your traditional discussion over common inventions or scientific principles. No, a gift of wisdom of this sort could seriously impact every aspect of our way of life, and to such measures that everything we thought we knew about our traditional sciences would be turned upside-down.

'There are forces out there,' he states, 'that we cannot understand with what we have in our hands today. Such forces as these are not a part of the physical sciences as we know them. Instead, if one were to study these in earnest, one might think them to belong to the realm of magic and mysticism. And indeed, the physical sciences, as we know them, may in fact one day simply fall into the background. Such concepts as these would naturally demand a supreme level of discipline, not simply for the potential they hold to invoke progress, but also their potential to cause harm. Simply to know of them is to bring a new level of interpretation to the reality of existence around us.

Out there, amongst the great seas of what some might call Creation, are societies that understand these philosophies; societies that are much older and better travelled than ours, and they might hold the power to build vast empires using these principles. And his, admittedly, is one of those.

Therefore, to simply hand out such knowledge as this to a young society like ours could result in such great turbulence that, if it is not handled properly, could potentially lead us into disaster. It is because of this, where not only does the Council need to take so much time in this deliberation to decode these principles, but they must also understand ways to apply them, and then to merge this with what our society represents in the modern day. This is no simple task, as our society is a complex one, but also a young one. To understand the magnitude of what this represents, we must evolve into it. But as we all know, evolution takes time, and we simply cannot rush that. Our youth might inspire ambition, but this must also be tempered with patience. And as such, the Council must take it's time without any outside interference to see it through successfully.'"

"Powers behold," Thaelyn croons. "If I did not know better, I would almost say he is taking a lesson from the Estelar for this point. Such inspirational words."

"He must be at his wit's end if he's going this far out," Kaliya notes. "This reminds me of Morndindor, and the processor at Madzurki. Do you recall the video we have of him in that factory? He suggested teaching them this stuff, but then turned away from it due to Sargeras and his opinion."

Thaelyn and his officers, along with Kaliya and Ayene, were in a meeting the following day after Ileani's latest report.

"Indeed! Kaliya, this is a truly fascinating association. Could it be we have backed him into such a corner by now that he might actually be reconsidering these principles?"

"This almost makes it seem as if he holds special care for them," the General muses.

"Well," Ayene offers. "He did apparently spend a lot of time on us, and we are serving as a life support machine for his master, so I guess we do hold some value, after all."

"Value…" Kailen huffs. "But now, do you have any plans for unraveling this one?"

"I had a few things come to mind…" she grins. "Not so much to unravel. This is simply too good. Our people could actually learn from this one. And I, for one, would like to keep this example as a reference for something higher. Naturally, as I said before, we want to relax a bit to offer some time from this last batch of sensations before we hit him with the next one. But we're going to drop one final little piece… indirectly, just to rub him in the nose a bit."

"Oh dear…" Thaelyn moans. "And what sort of rub are we considering on this occasion?"

"Velen… This runs right up his alley for his old science faction. Therefore, it could finally offer some credence to his beliefs."

"Oh, Powers help us," he chuckles.

"Another thing, it opens a few avenues for those topics our sciences seem averted to admit to, like other universes and nether-space. If we say these lessons may provide the viability for such things, the sciences will have something new to chew on for later. And this naturally opens a new channel for us. Ooh, I like where this is going."

"General… The List…"

"There you go, Ayene," Kaliya smiles. "You're getting closer."

"I wonder," she muses. "Do you earn any kind of reward for how many you collect in a certain time frame?"

The group lets out a hearty laugh for the remark.

"And what is this new channel you speak of, Ayene?" Thaelyn asks.

"It would relate to the Tav'ageen Anomaly, but we'll wait a bit first. We'll reflect back on this when we make ready for our next hit."

"Very good…"

Ayene and her recent charge, Kita, along with the Director and Azina, were convening at the construction project in the valley adjacent to the city. They were arriving at the temporary office located onsite where the foreman and his team were coordinating the effort.

Kita surveyed the area curiously, as this would represent her first time out here. Ayene had briefed her on the project back at the office, and she would work closely to assist in coordinating between this and the other activities occurring within the ACI building.

Neither the Director nor Azina had actually visited the area during this time, so as they pulled into the makeshift parking lot, they took a moment to stroll around.

The large-scale project was easily seen from the main road. It covered a broad expanse of land from the mountain on the far side and across to the riverfront. Large vehicles were loading up debris to be carried away for disposal, while earthmovers continued to work the land. A number of smaller hover-shuttles were scattered around the area, some as personal transport for the work crew and others for their supervisors.

As the group assembled, the foreman came outside to greet them.

"Director Bak'vayn, so good to see you," he calls. "Everything is ready here for our specialists to arrive, although I'm still asking myself how we expect to bring them in if they need to be so discreet."

"Our friends have something special in mind. We just need the space for them to arrive in, and from there we'll move forward."

"If you say so… Would you like to make an inspection?"

"I would, but I'm waiting for a representative to arrive first. Ayene, do we have a time frame for that?"

"We do…" she affirms.

Ayene looks up into the sky, where she spies a pair of birds circling overhead. She raises a hand high above to make a fist, and as she gives the signal, the strange creatures make a determined dive to the ground.

Kita, the Director, and Azina all watched in amusement as the flying curiosities landed on the ground just in front of them. The foreman and his immediate officers all stepped back when they saw the strange animals arrive in view.

"These are your representatives?" he mutters softly.

As they landed, the two hawks, which were technically a nonnative species to this world, began to transform into their normal shapes. Kaliya and Navina stepped out of their disguises to meet the rest of the group.

Kita studied the transformation in awe, having been made somewhat familiar with it by now after Ayene's demonstration in the ACI basement. But as she saw Navina come into view, she felt compelled to speak.

"Agent Lar'akan? You're one of them?"

"Yes, most of us who don't actually work inside the building are like this. The Director is another one, by the way."

"In all the nether-space, so I'm working in an office filled with ghosts?" she chuckles.

The foreman and his officers were stunned by the display, and further with Kita's remark. He studied them, as well as the Director and his group for their obvious lack of surprise.

"Um, Director," he ushers tenderly. "What did I just see? Where did these people come from, and what did she mean by ghosts?" he glances at Kita for her comment.

"This is the Tav'ageen Anomaly," he asserts confidently. "Assuming we might ever have the opportunity to explore it fully, which it seems we do not."

"Do not?"

"Yes, in part due to the chips and the interference they cause. And this naturally brings us to the Marshal, as these are HIS invention... meaning to say he knows what it is, but doesn't want US to know."

"Great, so this begs me to ask the question of why."

"The why is a complex scenario, but to put it simply, he is a godlike figure that doesn't like little things like us pretending to be godly in any way."

"Oh! So THAT is the reason for the Anomaly. I suppose this can also explain those original death syndromes and the panic we had once."

"It would indeed. But the Captain here, along with her people, have been exploring it outside his view, and they have learned some fascinating details about it."

"I would love to hear about this someday. How might this reflect on our own project to discover something?"

"Our best theory for NOT discovering anything might entail a lingering effect from the chip, and maybe also our schooltime brainwashing not to believe in ghosts, or anything else Former Elder Nazég was trying to teach us about."

"Oh! Is that so! Thank you, Director. That made my day," he shrugs ironically. "But now, what about our work out here?"

"I would first like to take a quick peek inside," Kaliya states. "Then we'll arrange for our delivery."

They moved off as a group towards the entrance of the mountain, stepping around the fencing and screens that were erected to keep away the occasional unwanted visitor, and into the tunnel that would eventually become the entrance to the hidden facility. They travelled deep inside to a neatly carved out room, reinforced and supported by columns, affording a central lane for traffic and side compartments for storage and temporary accommodations for the workforce, at least until something better could be arranged.

Kaliya examined the setting and approved the design. She then led them back outside again.

"You've made some good work here," she admits. "This will be our starting point. From here, you should put on a nice little display outside to keep up the appearance of your labors, while our people work on the inside."

"Will any of your people require assistance or materials?" the Director asks.

"From time to time, maybe, but we can arrange that as the need arises. Many of the materials will likely be imported from home, since we're accustomed to certain design concepts, and then of course is our custom technology and equipment."

"I'd really be interested in seeing some of that," Azina interjects.

"I already saw some of it in our basement back at the office," Kita muses.

"Really! And how does it look?"

"Weird," she smirks. "You know that statement the Marshal made recently? Well, this could qualify as an example."

"As we move forward," Kaliya continues. "We will have our people at the ACI, Kita here being one of those, assist in coordinating things for us. As she said, we're installing some custom tech in their basement, one of these being a communications device to link back home with our own leadership."

"Just a moment," the Director interjects. "You're installing some kind of communication device from your basement to a world which, if I'm not mistaken, is in another universe from us?"

"That's right. It's a remarkable little invention that one of His Lordship's people came up with a while back. It's truly amazing, actually, and it blew the horns right off our topmost engineering technicians. But it requires the flows to function properly. We'll eventually install one of those here, as well."

"Incredible," the Director mumbles as he surveys the local area for any additional visitors. "So, when do we begin this process of importing your people?"

Kaliya turns towards the mountainside and waves her arm in a wide arc over her head. From further up the peak, a large flock of birds rises up and begins descending down to the ground around her.

The Director and Azina gazed in awe at the number of bodies coming in. The foreman steps back impulsively as the wave settles on the ground and reshapes themselves into people. Every one of them was in uniform, a full platoon of them.

"Navina," Kaliya instructs. "Return back and fetch my bag, please."

Navina salutes and flashes out of sight.

"A bag?" Azina muses. "Are you going shopping now?" she grins.

"Not this time, although I did notice a sale going on at one of your downtown malls. Who would've thought that a bunch of emotionally restricted people would carry such inspiring fashions?"

"Hey! We might be emotionally restricted, but we do still have a sense of taste."

"Yeah," Kita smiles affectionately. "Some might even suggest that sense of taste is to compensate for the emotional restrictions. My boyfriend certainly seems to like it!"

The young ladies shared a laugh as they waited for Navina to return.

Navina had travelled to the WIC building and retrieved Kaliya's bag, which was actually a hard-shell suitcase, rather than a cloth bag, and it was sitting on the floor next to the table in the strategy room. She then flashes back to Azgarén.

"Here we are, Captain," she declares.

"That looks rather professional," the Director muses as he studies the case.

"Yeah, the term bag is mostly affectionate," Kaliya affirms. "Now, everyone back inside. What comes next will be…magic!" she announces with a bright grin and a fluttering of the hands.

The assembly now returns back into the large chamber. Kaliya and Navina take up positions at the far end, while Ayene, Kita, the Director and the others move off to the side to observe.

Navina sets the case down and opens it, revealing a collection of parts neatly cushioned within their custom foam packing inserts. Kaliya then starts picking out pieces and assembling her effigy apparatus.

"That's very strange," Azina mutters as she studies the odd pieces. "What is that?"

"Normally," Kaliya explains. "I would do this with my natural body, but in projected form, I need an effigy device to act as a replacement. This serves as a surrogate to conduct the energies."

"This is interesting," Kita notes. "When you were in our basement, you used these scrolls of yours directly. So, were you actually corporeal at that time?"

"Yes, I was, in order to assist in moving our people around. But this time, I'm projected."

"And so, here the process must be applied differently due to the fact that you are not corporeal. I am becoming even more fascinated by this. I wonder; would it be possible at some moment for me to learn something?"

"Absolutely, but it might need to wait a bit until after we can bring our immediate situation under better control."

"All right, this is reasonable."

"You would also need to travel to Tae'Eladar at that moment to find the study materials."

"Wow, that sounds a little scary, but also exciting."

Kaliya assembles a tripod as the base before hauling out the other pieces. As she begins assembling the rest of it, the Director and Azina study the peculiar apparatus carefully.

"Um, and what are those things?" Azina asks.

"Normally, like Kita said, I would use a spell scroll if I were physical and channeling the energies directly. The scroll is a specially formulated paper, which uses specially formulated and also enchanted ink, and this would be applied by a mage to inscribe arcanic glyphs representing the conceptual form of the commands to invoke whatever spell you are trying to use."

"You know," the Director ponders. "As you explain this, I am once again reminded of Elder Nazég and his Metaphysics faction, and here describing something that could be a practical application of some of those ideas he was inventing."

"Exactly. However, in projected form, I need to use this instead. This is a fairly new invention by those people during their more modern Industrial Age, and it almost replaces the mage entirely. I nicknamed it a semiautomatic conjuring device, as it does a lot of the work for me."

"Can you explain the theory of operation?"

"I could, but you'll need new horns afterwards."

"Uh huh, like always. Well, I'm willing to give it a try."

Kaliya first pulls out a round base unit and sets it on the tripod.

"This is like a battery pack for an arcanic charge. It has a limited use before you need to recharge it, so you need to make it count."

"Of course."

"Inside here are some special storage crystals that are designed to contain the arcanic energy. The formulation of these crystals is most often synthetic, although as I understand it, some native forms do exist on Tae'Eladar. However, it became more practical for them, due to their technological demands, to synthesize them in a laboratory environment, rather than trying to harvest anything natural."

"Very innovative."

She now pulls out another round container and sets it on top of the first, aligning a set of mounting pins and connecting fibers for the power relay. The Director and the others try to peer over to see inside.

Nestled inside this short cylindrical housing were a series of interlocking gears and wheels. These gears are further attached to a wire framework hovering above the unit holding a series of six mithril disks in a vertical orientation. The disks each had softly glowing glyphs inscribed onto them, and were arranged in a ring formation around a central mounting bracket for a rune stone. The bizarre contraption looked like some sort of mechanical museum gizmo from an old sci-fi movie.

The Director further peeked inside to see more components, including two counterrotating sets of crystals, some wiring, and finally a rodlike object mounted in a set of clips.

"Is that some sort of power cell there?" he points at the item.

"Yes, good old-fashioned chemical energy," Kaliya smiles.

"Uh huh, I suppose it fits. And the rest of it?"

"These disks you see here are made of a metal called mithril, which is another form of that special enchanted metal like adamantium. They are enriched with these glyphs to attune them to certain arcanic harmonics. We use this as part of the channeling process to contain the energies. You might say it creates a mini containment field, but these energies don't follow your classic laws of physics. Do you see these crystals here?" she points at the two rings inside the unit. "These are more of the same as I mentioned before, but these are designed to direct the flow of arcanic energy from below into the center here, which we might call a reaction chamber, for lack of a better term. From there, the containment field is derived from what we call the 'perspective' of these glyphs building the field."

"That simply doesn't make sense to me."

"I had to go through a lot of classes back on Tae'Eladar before I could understand half of this."

The unit also included an inclined shelf rising up from the rear, and what appeared to be a small microphone positioned along the bottom edge. The edge itself appeared as a slot, and the top edge sported a retainer clip.

The Director now found himself studying the shelf assembly.

"This looks almost like a docking port for something like a tablet device."

"Very close," Kaliya nods. "It is a docking port, but not for a tablet device as we would understand it. This is part of that new tech they invented. Are your horns ready for this?"

"I'm not sure, but go ahead."

She now reaches into the case to pull out a thick envelope with something rigid inside. She opens it up to pull out a plastic prototype board with a prearranged series of iconic plates mounted on it. The plates were made of molded glass with a thin mithril framework surrounding them. They each held a set of small, embedded crystals of various configurations and compositions. Along the lower edge of each plate was a word inscribed into an enamel glaze.

As Kaliya set the board into its docking port, the Director and Azina both stepped in to inspect the curious arrangement. Kita peered over Kaliya's shoulder, and the foreman and some of his officers took turns to study the apparatus.

"I'm going to need a careful interpretation of what I'm looking at here," the Director shakes his head. "This one looks like a work of art, but to think it could be a part of a functioning machine of any kind..."

"Yes, Director, I have to agree with you, at least in theory. This is like a program board. These plates each represent that conceptual algorithm I spoke of earlier that you might find on a spell scroll. Once again, I need to speak the name of the glyphs, which are inscribed on the bottom of each one, and collectively they spell out the incantation I'm trying to invoke. The arcanic energies have to be channeled through here first, to empower the wording, and the result funnels to this cradle you see in the middle here."

"And what goes in that cradle?"

"This..."

Kaliya now pulls out a rune stone from a side compartment in the case. She holds it up for review.

"Is that a rock?" the Director winces.

"Well, yes, essentially it is," Kaliya offers. "This stone is what we call a rune stone. It acts as a storage vessel to the dimensional index of our exit point."

"A rock?!" Azina screeches incredulously.

"Yeah, Azina, a rock, although I'll admit it's a special kind of mineral you might find on worlds like Tae'Eladar. How it works is like this…"

Kaliya clears her throat, even though she wasn't physical with a throat to clear, but as a habit to separate statements.

"Do you see this microphone here?" she points at the unit. "Once Again, if I were physical with a spell scroll, I would use my body for this. Here, my voice, at the very least, can manifest into the local space such that a device can detect me."

"Ah!" the Director erupts. "This now reminds me of those early children. We couldn't detect them on the scanners, but we COULD record them on video and audio."

"Yes! This much you can do. And we're using it here. You might not need this with a physical person, as a physical body can produce sound with physical force in space. Mine has to be simulated mechanically. Then we have these plates. They're each embedded with crystals of certain harmonics. The arrangement is keyed to these words. The whole thing is programmable, so you have a library of these plates to choose from. But I will caution how you arrange them to make sure you have a valid configuration."

"Just for the sake of discussion, what happens if you don't?"

"Well, we were joking on this back home about blowing up labs."

"Uh huh…joking," he chuckles softly.

"Much like with the scroll, the glyphs react to my voice commands as each one is read off. Together they form a kind of sentence with a conceptual meaning. This interacts with the arcanic energies to create an effect. And that effect focuses on this stone to imbue it with our result."

She places the rune stone into the cradle and checks the configuration to make sure all is well. She then turns the unit on with a small switch on one side, and the wheels begin to spin up to full power. A soft whirring sound emanates from the device as everyone watches the spinning disks and crystals. They also take notice of the glyphs on the plate lighting up with a soft glow, as if backlit by some form of gentle illumination.

With the device now ready for use, Kaliya positions herself to begin the chant. Azina closes in to study the action, along with the Director.

Kita stood in the background behind Kaliya, keeping a safe distance so as not to interfere. And the foreman and his people circled around the other side for a better view.

She begins calling out the glyphs in sequence. As each one is engaged, the lighting effect alters to a bright radiance. This is accompanied by a soft whispering echo of her voice repeating the name back to her.

Azina watched with bated breath, and on seeing and hearing the reactions of the plates, she was tempted to gasp audibly. She had to cover her mouth to stifle herself so as not to interfere with the process.

Kaliya proceeded through the full set, until all the glyphs were glowing brightly. Then, a soft hissing issued up as the arcanic energies were funneled through the apparatus and focused into the center. The crystals flashed with energy, causing most of the people in the room to jerk back. This was quickly followed by a lateral spiraling of energy around the tripod in a broad sweep, quickly expanding, and then immediately collapsing back into the stone, causing it to glow briefly.

Azina instinctively ducked behind the Director as she saw the swirling energies fill the local space. Many of the others simply cringed as they watched the otherworldly device behaving in ways that would otherwise defy their understanding of science.

Kita, who had some previous experience with Kaliya and her spell scrolls, managed to hold firm better than most, but the spectacle was still surprising. She studied the results on the tripod.

"It didn't spend the program this time," she notes. "So this one is reusable?"

"Yeah, that's the best part, no more spell scrolls," Kaliya smiles. "But it might also put a few people out of business along the way."

"Yeah, remind me not to apply for a job in that area," she giggles.

Kaliya pulls out the rune stone and holds it up for display. The surface of the stone seemed to alter its hue slightly.

"This one is now marked for this location," she asserts. "Meaning to say this precise three-dimensional vector where the stone was physically located during this time. You can tell it's marked by looking at it, as the surface tends to carry a faint image of the place, almost like a snapshot of our location. It's what we call a perception image…a little bit like a memory."

"Unbelievable!" the Director muses. "A form of recording process that doesn't use any manner of electromagnetic encoding. Not digital, and not even analog, as far as I can tell."

"That's right. Although, we're developing a new form of tech for these jump drives of ours that would fit better with your expectations. It resembles a data block that can be transmitted between ships and other devices, but it still needs the proper interpretation hardware."

She sets the rune down on her equipment case and pulls out another one. She then picks up the apparatus and relocates it a couple steps off to the side, where she would repeat the process to create a small line of these markings. She did this twice, for a total of three in a row.

During this process, Azina felt an urge to ask about the reasoning behind it.

"We typically process this in what we call way-lines," Kaliya explains. "It increases the flow capacity for more people to arrive."

With all three runes now marked, Kaliya packed up her equipment.

"All right, return these back to base. I'll wait here to direct the traffic."

Navina picks up the case, along with the runes, and flashes back to Therinë.

Azina was breathing heavily by this time. The mysterious activity defied her understanding of science, and everything else she thought she ever knew about. She could feel her nerves tensing up in expectancy.

"Let's move away to allow a bit of room," Kaliya suggests to the group. "Meanwhile, we need to start bringing in our supplies. Let's line it up against that wall there," she points to one side.

The squad members all flashed away to attend to their duties, returning back to Rolsklinde and the WIC building, where a large number of bags, crates, and other containers were waiting for transport, along with equipment, bedrolls, cooking appliances, and other essentials. Also, in Rolsklinde, a small army of dwarves, each carrying a bag of tools and personal items, waited for their turn.

Navina arrived in the WIC building to return Kaliya's gear and the marked runes. Thaelyn examined each stone and passed it along to a group of mages, who then went outside to the dwarven workforce and began opening portals.

In the mountain chamber, three circular apertures formed in midair in a line near the back wall. The Director and his group stared at the extraordinary anomaly.

"Ghantil," Azina murmurs hesitantly. "What are we looking at right now?"

"Although I've never seen it myself, that looks like the exit point of a conveyor rift."

"Amazing! You don't see this anywhere except maybe a vid-com adventure video."

"And especially not on this scale, OR inside a mountain!"

"Yeah, especially that," she giggles.

"This one is small compared to some of the configurations we use," Kaliya explains, "if only because we're inside this close space."

"Who is doing this part?" the Director asks. "And how are they doing it?"

"Mages. People who specialize in the Art, as we call it, of spellcasting. It's a professional occupation over there."

"I met one of those in our basement," Kita accedes. "He was a very nice fellow. He dresses a bit strange, though," she smiles.

"They hold the rune stone in their hand and cast an enchantment on it directly to open the rift from their side."

The three rift apparitions gleamed, and in their virtual windows, Azina and the others could see a modest city square and a group of people lining up on the other side. Azina leaned in to study the image.

"Is that... And are those people? Captain, what are we looking at in this window?"

"In this image, you can see a small piece of a city we call Rolsklinde, along with a few of its residents passing by. Those standing in front are our labor force from that world we spoke of once, called Morndindor. They're called dwarves and are very good at working stone and metal."

"But they're so small."

"Yes, but don't let that fool you," Kaliya laughs. "First, they're tough little guys, and this set comes from that world where Ayene had her mining base. It's a heavy gravity world, so they're a lot stronger than they appear."

"Fascinating," she croons. "I wait all my life to hear something about the universe, and not until I learn I was never intended to hear anything at all, that's when I start to see wonders."

The dwarven troupe begins marching forward. One by one, in each of the three columns, they seem to disappear momentarily, only to flash into view again on the near side of the window. Azina and the others stared down at the undersized fellows as they marched past.

"Chief Bronzeheart, welcome to Azgarén," Kaliya calls to the lead member.

"Aye lass, 'tis a fine day, although me nostrils are already tellin' me the air here is just a wee bit thin and smoky."

"Yes, it is, so try to contain any of your outbursts to a modest level. We don't have any priests handy as yet."

"Right to that! Where do ye want us?"

"So far, this room here is the only one we have available for occupation. We have a set of plans for you to follow to dig out the rest of it. This mountain seems to be a mix of sediment on the outer layers and bedrock consisting of metamorphic layers deeper inside."

"Aye, that should nay be a problem for us. We'll work our way through it, ye can be sure of that. We've got some of our finest strong-arms with us, and many a bag of our best diggin' picks."

"Excellent. We will bring in fresh supplies as needed, and my people will make routine visits to check on you."

"Sounds grand enough. I'll be settin' up me worktables and sortin' through the drawin's in just a bit, once I get me kin settled."

"Great. Now, let me introduce you to some of our contacts here. This is Agent Kita Kaetaal, and she is part of our local operations. You may be seeing her from time to time, although we have a language difference to deal with along the way. Next is Director Bak'vayn, who is one of our most instrumental contacts here in this world, and this one is Azina Nur'ten, both of whom work at a local medical facility. So, if you need anything, we might call on them for medical support. Finally, we have the local foreman in charge of our efforts on the outside. You'll need to work with him, at least somewhat, to coordinate some of your work and conceal yourselves until we can make our move."

"Aye, good to know," he nods.

Now Kaliya turns to the Director to make the return introduction.

"Director, this is Chief Forge Smith Tol Bronzeheart. He's the one who will be overseeing the operations. As you can probably already tell, we have a language issue, but we'll try to overcome that later."

"Is there a way for us to possibly learn this language?" Kita asks.

"Yes, but again you would be best served to go to Tae'Eladar for that. They have a language course that runs about three months to teach you the local tongue."

"Only three months? Is their language so primitive?"

"It's not that the language is primitive, it's that the course is highly compressed, therefore the normal time is reduced down to that much."

"In all the nether-space! How can a person remember anything if it rushes past you so fast?"

"I took that course once," Ayene affirms. "For me, it was actually a bit longer, due to that horrible bug on my back, but I was astonished by the result."

"The bug?" she raises her brow. "The seed did something to interfere with your lessons?"

"They use a special agent you need to drink, and this has the effect of accelerating your brain function, but the seed didn't like it."

"Wow, but still, three months... Maybe, once I get mine removed, do you think I could make visits?"

"We can certainly see about it."

"This is such a fascinating process you have here, Captain," the Director admits. "How does it look on the other side when you use that stone of yours?"

"Normally, I would hold it in my hand, like this..." Kaliya demonstrates by holding out her open hand. "I would summon up the local energies with my thoughts, channel them through my body and into my hand, and modulating them with a few carefully chosen words of power, which in my mind hold special meaning and invoke my thoughts to alter the energies into whatever form is called for. The result, in this case, creates another rift like what you see here, but from the source perspective."

"Incredible, and this again reminds me of your initial visit and what you said about these other beings you met once."

"And curiously," Ayene notes playfully. "This is generally what the Marshal was hinting at with his most recent crazy excuse. This opens a very interesting door for us."

They continued to watch the parade of dwarves entering through until the last of them arrived and the portals closed. Meanwhile, Kaliya's team was bringing in the supply of goods and lining them up on one side of the room. The dwarves then began sorting through their equipment and making their plans to go to work.

◆◆◆

A news broadcast was currently airing with the latest report.

> *"In recent news, a coalition of scientists representing each of the major factions has come together to respond to the Marshal's most recent statement..."*

The report turns to a press conference with a female speaker.

"Although not everyone can be said to be completely satisfied with his announcement, in light of the Marshal's recent account relating to his extraordinary depiction of this special allowance of his great wisdom, we have come to the conclusion that this could indeed justify their extended absence. Still, we are a society in need of more than just wisdom. We have our domestic needs as well, such as legislation, social services, and budget allowances.

We are therefore willing to come to a compromise arrangement. We would still desire the Council to provide us with some manner of progress report on occasion, but for now, the needs of the people must also be met. And so, with the Council apparently so heavily involved in this intense deliberation, we have decided to organize a special emergency committee as a temporary solution to see to the rest of it."

The scene returns to the newsroom.

"The summit meeting went on to say that they will assemble this emergency committee after a special vote is taken to select the members. Once elected, they will begin examining the requirements of our government operations and delegating assignments as needed to bring our services back into conformance with the needs of the people.

Meanwhile, the courts have made a decision, based on the evidence presented, that the emergency war protocols should be dissolved. According to the arguments, there can be no true justification in the modern day that these insurgents can be regarded as a threat to Azgarén security, as there were never any direct attacks in our native space.

The arguments also compared the imperative needs of our world population, and how those needs were interrupted by the long-standing conditions bypassing our native demands. These demands should now be a primary motivational concern for the health and welfare of the people. As such, this now paves the way for action to be taken on these other issues, thus allowing us to return to the way things once were."

Chapter 6

QUIET LIBERATION

Another school year has come to an end, and the graduation ceremony was underway at the guildhall. The graduating class was gathering in the main hall, along with Thaelyn to oversee the event, while the Master of Ceremonies prepared himself to conduct the affair.

Relissa was among the crowd, while Marelle, Haran, Sulíma and the others stood on one of the balconies overlooking the assembly. Also present on the balcony were Relissa's parents, Lord Throdeth and Lady Amariyn, former members of the Elven Council in Solinaia. Amariyn was now a member of Thaelyn's High Council, and Throdeth was a distinguished scholar and a member of the Therinë parliament. They each watched as the presentation moved forward, where one after another of the students was called up. Eventually, it became Relissa's turn, and the MC called her to the front.

"Scout Ranger Relissa Moonshimmer…"

She steps out of her row and marches forward along the runway carpet that lines the aisle in the middle of the hall. Her nerves were jittery, but she was just as excited to get this over with. She approaches the stairs and salutes, then kneels to listen to his traditional declaration.

"On this day, you who have come before us do hereby honor us with your devotion. Now, the time has come for you to choose, with final determination, your course to become a member of our brotherhood, the Order of Tyr, fully and completely, and for the duration of your lifetime. How do you plea?"

Relissa perks up to meet his eyes with her usual quirky grin.

"I plead…you bloody better believe I do!" she announces proudly.

The room erupts with cheery laughter as the MC turns with a smirk to meet Thaelyn.

"My Lord, are you sure about her?"

"I would expect no less from this one," he responds with a prominent shrug and a broad smile. "And surely, as she represents the first of the Morier to join our ranks, we should anticipate more to come."

"Well then, we should not delay in giving her a diploma so she can get straight to work."

"Aye!" Relissa agrees with a soft chuckle.

"Then in the eyes of our gods, rise Sister of the Order, Relissa Moonshimmer…and may those same gods help us forever after."

He hands over a scroll with her completion record on it and the room offers up a majestic applause, while an attendant steps up to pin the guild heraldry symbol just below the neckline on an overlapping fold of her vest. She rises up and takes a step back for another salute, then makes an about-face and returns to her former position.

As always, after the ceremony, those who were watching on the balcony came down to meet with their friends and family. Kaliya and the others joined up with Relissa to share her success.

"Throdeth," Amariyn croons. "Can you believe it? Our little girl, finally grown up and ready for the world."

"Mum," Relissa corrects. "I was grown up a while ago, and already out there running the fields and making trouble."

"Yes, well, that seems like a different age by now. I consider this as a renewal for you. You are not the same person as you once were."

"Aye, in a lot of ways… But don't think that other part is dead and buried just yet," she winks.

"I still recall you as a young tot in the classroom," Throdeth reflects. "Disobedient, disrespectful, short-tempered, and so often lost in her dreams. But now look at you," he pauses with a wide grin. "Audacious, impetuous, roguish, and still lost in her dreams. Don't ever change, my dear. You are a delight just as you are."

Relissa leans in to give each of them a firm hug, while the others come up to offer their congratulations.

"Well, kid, you made it," Kaliya announces. "So, are you ready to start chasing around with me, or do you think you'll take a desk job?"

"In all the bleedin' hells, if you think I'm going to let you run off again without someone supervising…" she teases. "Do you remember how many times you got into trouble without me at your back?"

"I think I even got into trouble once or twice WITH you at my back."

"Aye, but at least I was there to unravel your horns from it. The trouble now is you're using this projection bit and going off to Azgarén, so I'm a wee bit restricted by that."

"Yes, and so far, we need to keep it that way until we can stabilize our foothold. Right now, you would stand out a bit too much if you tried going there."

"More like I'd be standing under you, you're all so bloody tall," she chuckles. "But aye, I guess I'll need to find something else to do for now. I'm hoping Thaelyn can offer something keen for me. I want to be a part of it, but I'm not quite sure how I'll fit in."

"Yeah, as a ranger, there might not be too many possibilities for scouting since it's so urbanized, and you're more of a woodsman for this point."

"And the woods over there are a wee bit sickly. Hey, what about that. You know, Priestess Rumoren is stationed over on Ruuki uy'Daan with her latest project in that big conservation center they built as a research facility. She was working on that problem to help save the ecology on Morndindor. I wonder if I could help somehow with Azgarén."

"There's an idea, although I hear they have a lot of conservation centers already, but maybe you could coordinate something with the Priestess to offer some new insight."

"That's a good one. Maybe I could pair up with a few druids and we can go take a peek at it, but quietly, and then see what the Priestess has to say about it. Hmm, I wonder if a Tree of Life would work over there," she muses privately.

"It's going to be lonely here without you, Relissa," Marelle pouts. "I have another year, and then I'm off to war after that."

"Just be sure to watch your back," Relissa states. "Because you can be sure I won't be covering you in those dinky little flying toboggans."

"And that just leaves me," Haran notes, "and these three," he thumbs at their Daanen-Aryku friends. "A man can only take just so many flirtatious suggestions. Poor Petrith, I don't know how he can hold himself still for it."

"Aye, it makes you wonder what they're doing after class in that shower for so long," she snickers.

"Now just a minute…" Sulíma protests. "I happen to be a very hygienic young lady. It's not my fault if that shower is so luxurious, I could fall asleep under it."

"Sleeping isn't what I'm worried about."

"Yeah, but that's my story," she grins.

"Trust me," Túfula offers. "I'll watch her. After all, I want a piece of him, too."

"Girls," Petrith begs. "Didn't I say I need to take this in sequence?"

"Yeah…one, then the other, and maybe the third if she can get time off work for it."

"Dear cu'Nar, have mercy."

The group continued their conversation well into the evening, moving to a local tavern for a meal and some musical entertainment until it was time to split up and go to bed.

In the days that followed, Marelle signed up for her new classes, including her Seventh Circle mage study, which she had worked so hard for. Now she needed to build herself up and get ready for her grand performance. Haran signed up for his Eighth Circle class, anxious to make his way up the ladder, while Sulíma and the others continued with their own selections.

◆◆◆◆◆

It had been about a month since the Marshal's last statement, and Ileani was conducting a new interview in preparation for her latest report. On this occasion, she was meeting with Ayene and another of Kaliya's teammates dressed up as a professional businessman.

"All right, Ileani," Ayene begins. "We're not trying to start any new scandals on this occasion, but instead to touch upon a forbidden subject that seems to have been so conveniently opened up for us due to the Marshal's last release."

"A forbidden subject?" she muses as she examines her notes, which at this moment also included a new script. "This is interesting. I'm becoming very curious about your direction for some of this."

"Trust me, Ileani, you'll learn when the time is right, but we can't afford to let too much out at one time."

"Yeah, and I still remember that incident at the Grand Hall. I hope you're not going to pull another of those on me."

"Whether or not I do is irrelevant, at this point. I need your support as we slowly build up our imagery."

"All right, so let's get this going."

Ayene steps out of the picture as the other two arrange themselves in their seating, and then the cameraman takes aim and gives the signal.

"This is Ileani Ur'paran, here with Lenik Lan'traval, who describes himself as a theoretical sciences analyst. He has come forward with a fascinating new interpretation that he claims has presented itself only just recently after studying a variety of elements from the different science factions, both past and present, and then combining these perspectives with the Marshal's most recent press release, which he says ties it all together so remarkably. Mister Lan'traval, how would you explain this new revelation of yours?"

"Ileani, as a theoretical sciences analyst, I make it my purpose to interrogate the direction and future potential of many of our scientific studies, then to publish my perspectives in the hopes that we may find new ways to evolve ourselves as we move forward in these studies, rather than to simply stagnate in the mire of our ancestors. Now, granted, the science factions out there do strive to push the boundaries of our understanding, but the sciences we study now may not be the only sciences that CAN be studied."

"And do you think there may be something else out there we missed?"

"Oh, most certainly, but not necessarily that we missed, as it could be something new that we haven't even encountered yet. If we take ourselves back in time to the early days of our civilization, we can easily see where our ancient ancestors had to push themselves into new frontiers to discover something they never knew existed before. The discovery of chemistry, the discovery of electricity, the discovery of the atomic sciences... These are all clear and obvious steps we took as a society that was growing and evolving to higher positions of intellectual prestige. But here we find ourselves perhaps on the edge of something new, and our Council might be the first to make this discovery, all thanks to the Marshal."

"Ah, so this relates to what he had to say about them last month. Does this hold any special meaning to you?"

"Indeed, it does, and not simply for what we have now. It also rings with something we might have previously discredited as so much nonsense. And perhaps not just one principle, but others as well."

"Others? Can you give us an example perhaps?"

"I suppose I could. I am aware of theories that have gone unproven, if only due to the inability to actually validate them. These might include the possibility of alternate universes, and even the true existence of nether-space itself, which so many think to be only a myth, and not a viable destination to actually travel to."

"Yes, I have heard this on many occasions, especially as we like to use that term in our language relating to some fantasy void space, and probably the last place you might want to find yourself."

"Yes, such is the way of our culture," he offers a tiny smile. "But one might want to seriously consider this, if four-dimensional space, which would be the better term to use here, might truly exist in some form or another. And if so, one might ask oneself what we would need to do to explore it."

"Do you have any suggestions?"

"Well, as the Marshal said so aptly, we would surely need to evolve, if only to meet the needs of travelling through it. But if to consider any part of this, to say nothing of what else he might have shared with them, it's actually no wonder the Council would take so long in their deliberation, as I would imagine it would require them to rethink virtually everything they thought they knew about the sciences they represent, especially those certain few sciences, coincidentally governed by the direction of the Council, who seem particularly avoidant to even consider these concepts."

"Oops! What do you mean by that?"

"For instance, how long have we denied the existence of nether-space, even though one might think the simple use of a jump drive through a hyperdimensional conduit might prove otherwise. All you would need to do is look out a window."

"Wow, that ought to say something to someone."

"And yet, our sciences, who are so often dependent on the Council to advise what, if anything, they are permitted to research, should have taken notice of this on countless occasions. I mean, after all, for as long as we have had jump drives and used them to travel across our galaxy, even a simple passenger should ask the question relating to the view."

"That sounds like someone slipped the tip on this topic."

"At the very least! And perhaps it is a simple matter of denial to recognize the thing CAN exist. But that statement by the Marshal was a true work of art. He is effectively saying there may be things out there our sciences do not know about, and perhaps CANNOT know about in our present form. And his gifts might reflect on this to some degree. Therefore, whatever it was he gave them would most likely NOT represent any science they would be familiar with."

"That would surely create a dilemma for them, and also prove difficult to interpret into anything practical."

"And this now brings me to my most important topic, as his statements reflect on a few principles I once examined in a rather obscure branch of study. And most curiously, this is one the Council simply threw out as so much rubbish."

Ileani studied him, as it was part of her script, before responding to this seemingly irrational statement.

"Mister Lan'traval, can you please clarify your meaning here?"

"Absolutely, Ileani. When the Marshal declared in his most recent statement, which I must regard as a historic piece of documentation, how there are…things…out there that we are simply too young to know about, but that SOME societies might be so privileged, meaning to say his, as one example, then we are speaking of a concept we may call the nature of Knowing. But Knowing, as a concept in itself, may be a bit obscure to some. You either know something, or you don't know it. This is the general perception of most people. But this principle, as a philosophical construct, is known as epistemology, although I doubt too many people would have heard this word uttered very often in common speech."

"As a matter of fact, I might agree on this."

"There is another philosophy we could associate with here, and which I feel can come into play if we theorize more on the principles of what COULD be out there, and what we CAN know about, but it might be outside our immediate reach, or perhaps our present evolutionary station. Consider a simple insect if you will. What can that insect Know about such a thing as mathematics? What can it Know about the nature of matter and energy? Even if you take a higher animal species, it would not be able to perceive of these concepts. It is not until you arrive with our example when you might see this level of comprehension, as our higher minds can now ask these questions."

"I hate to say it, but this is starting to rise a little above my own level of Knowing as well, at least in theory for the direction you're taking."

"Maybe so, but stay with me, Ileani, and maybe you'll learn something. Consider how you hold the power to ask questions, as we all do. But the questions we ask may be limited to our capacity to perceive what might be around us to ask these questions about. Therefore, we must now look beyond this, beyond our common perceptions, and ask something new."

"And what is this you would ask about now?"

"Ileani, the principle I am describing now is sometimes known as the study of ontology. Ontology, as a philosophical construct, can lead you to ask such fascinating questions as, 'what is a thing,' or 'what can be said to exist,' and coincidentally, this would tend to oppose our traditional manners of scientific deduction and empirical thought. The Marshal's statement is exactly that, although perhaps not in such precise wording. But the principles are the same and lead us to wonder what he might be alluding to."

"And therefore, what the Council could be deliberating right now."

"Exactly. Especially if this level of wisdom could eventually cause all our other sciences to fall into the background, as he said. This now forces us to consider a higher form of meaning, and by association, that higher form of Knowing, where a higher intellect might come into its awareness by means that is NOT empirical. To understand a thing, to know how to define it that does not require a measuring device. This is almost literally trying to answer the Age-Old question relating to the meaning of existence. But existence is much more than a question. It is not simply a body you can hold a set of calipers to. It is all around us. We are a part of it. We are composed of mind and body, of substance and energy, of form and function. We exist, but how do we measure ourselves? As a series of mathematical equations? Or can we measure ourselves by the presence of our perceptions alone. Does the mind define existence? And for this, you need a very different form of science, which could possibly make all the others obsolete, and to which the Council once refused to accept."

"And just for clarification, why did they choose not to accept it?"

"Likely, it was not one of those they could hold authority over. If the others require empirical evidence to define, and you choose to regulate this by either allowing or disallowing any form of research, you control the direction of it…a little like saying there are no other universes out there, and nether-space is a myth…just pull down the window shades and ignore that view outside."

"Uh oh… And so, which science are we speaking of here?"

"Metaphysics, the domain of Former Elder Velen Nazég. How ironic it is that the Council might now have to force itself to reconcile this notion after they so fervently condemned him, along with his... fanciful...science faction once upon a time."

Ileani gaped at the man, in part as her role in the script, but in larger part due to the clearly suggestive statement. She held her gaze for a pensive moment until she remembered to redirect herself back into the script.

"But Mister Lan'traval, as I recall it, Former Elder Nazég, um, well, although he was often downplayed by the Council for his factional beliefs, he was more severely downplayed due to his departure on that massive ship that arrived in those early days. In fact, I recall it was actually the Marshal himself who claimed that ship belonged to these insurgents he spoke of so often. This event seemed to mark him as an enemy to the people."

"While this may be true, it does also ask us about a motivation. He was trying to present our people with a new direction in our studies. Now, I suppose, on one side of the argument, you might say his rejection by our Council would cause him to simply want to look elsewhere."

"Look elsewhere...hmm..." she muses conspicuously.

"Such as with those people, as the Marshal referenced in his statement, who DO know what this is, and who might actually listen to him, whereas our Council would not."

"Oops! Yes, that might represent a motivation."

"However, in fairness, I suppose a skeptic might argue he simply rebelled against the Council. But again, why? What motivation might cause a man, who was otherwise unappreciated by the governing authority of our scientifically minded society, to rebel against that same society, if only because they refused to accept his form of science?"

"Uh, I think I am detecting a paradox in that statement, am I not?"

"Maybe so, Miss Ur'paran. If I were a man who was so badly rejected for my beliefs by a society so dedicated to seeking out new beliefs, I might be offended by it."

"But...seeking out new beliefs..."

"Miss Ur'paran, surely you are familiar with the preamble of our Charter of Laws. There is a clause in there that very clearly states that ALL forms of knowledge shall be our domain. But it would seem someone forgot about that little mention on this occasion. And yet, that statement by the Marshal, and this long deliberation, clearly suggests there is in fact more out there to learn, at least some of which is outside our current capacity, and which might even DEFY that capacity. And now our Council has to contend with that which they apparently did not wish to contend with before. Oh…" he croons prominently. "If only Former Elder Nazég could see it now. I think he might be silently laughing at the irony of it."

✦✦✦✦✦

In Central Command, in Commander Geilv's office, and indeed throughout the rest of the building, a sudden shock blasted through the structure. It was as if a tremendous wail resounded across the local area, echoing through the buildings, and thundering across the field.

Geilv was at his desk when the burst rumbled through. He jerked up and jumped out of his chair, then hurried out of his office towards the control room. On his arrival, he sees most of the officers peering out the window and observing many more on the ground all turned to one side and staring at something.

"What happened here?" he asks urgently.

"Sir, I have no idea," the Captain relents. "It sounded like some kind of scream, and by what I'm seeing down there on the tarmac, it might be coming from the Marshal's office."

"Interesting…" he smirks. "I wonder what just happened to cause him to scream like that. Call up the lounge and see if there's a news broadcast going on."

The Captain obliges and makes a call on a local intercom to the officer's lounge, where a refreshment bar attendant answered.

"Officer's Lounge… Can I help you?"

"This is Captain Ta'yeen in the control booth. Are you watching the news channel?"

"Yes Sir, we are. That Ileani Ur'paran is on again with another of her sensational reports."

"Really! What did she do this time?"

"Well, she was interviewing some kind of analyst, and they just let go that Former Elder Velen Nazég might not have defected away after all. At least not the way it was always told."

"No? What are they saying about it?"

"This apparently relates to the Marshal's recent press release. It seems to reflect on that exact science faction the former Elder was trying to give us, but no one took him seriously, especially the Council. So, either he ran away to find someone else who would listen to him, or he rebelled against a hostile entity that was trying to suppress him in our…scientifically minded free and open society. It goes on to say the Council, who never once took it seriously, might be choking on their own words by now. All ten millennia of it."

The Captain glared at the intercom and gasped at the virtual bombshell hit. He then turned to the Commander, who gazed blankly into space.

"In all the nether-space," he mutters. "That'll certainly do it! Commander? What do you think?"

"He chased them all across the galaxy, and then sent our people in, like Lajivi, to hit anything he could find. But Captain, if we held so much military power to blast away whole worlds, why couldn't we hit one colony ship and a single group of refugees? This wasn't his plan. He just played with them and used them to lead us on his grand crusade."

"And Elder Nazég? I recall the Marshal came home once with a final hoorah that he finished him."

"No, this was on Therinë. He apparently sabotaged their ship somehow to crash there intentionally, and then took three and a half centuries to toy with them, until that new invasion arrived."

"Commander!" he shouts. "In all the nether-space, the more I hear about that creature over there, the more I want to take a plasma mortar and finish him myself."

"This also causes me to ask how we were able to follow him during this time. I recall something now. A couple of things, actually."

"What was that?"

"First, a conversation I had on Therinë. It was that man who arrived. He related to me how the Nazég vessel made a wild jump to arrive in that other universe. But Captain, how do you track a ship through a jump…ANY jump, especially a wild one."

"Sir, I don't think you can, and a wild one is just…well, wild!"

"Yes, and arriving on a world the Marshal apparently had control of."

"That doesn't sound so wild to me. That sounds planned."

"Planned, yes," Geilv nods. "Our side was told of some odd beacon probe that miraculously attached itself just as they departed. I wonder who had the horns to do THAT, especially on this occasion!"

"Oh yes! And after so many millennia of hunting him."

"This reminds me of that second point. The Director at the ARC said he can apparently fold space independent of anything else."

"Fold space?"

"Personal point-to-point transport. This means, he can go anywhere he has in mind to travel…literally in mind to travel, as this is what he uses."

"In all the nether-space, THAT would be a potent ability."

"And a dangerous one, especially if he was riding on that vessel as a passenger. Then, he returns here with his famous scouting reports of insurgents."

"Oh! Wonderful!" he blasts. "And so, this could account for all our sightings. Oh, hey everyone…" he mocks. "We found the Nazég vessel. Let's go make a big scene in their skies and give them a chance to escape from us…again. Then blast the rest of the area to clean up."

"Precisely, Captain. Toys, like everything else his kind were said to be playing with. So, the story of the insurgents was fake, and so was his claim. But Captain, there WAS a ship, and it WAS huge and very alien. So, who did it belong to? Because it apparently came for HIM."

"That might suggest someone else knew the situation and was trying to evacuate him in front of that hostile body posing as our free and open scientifically minded government."

"That's an interesting suggestion, Captain…posing as one, at least on this occasion. After all, they certainly did give themselves over to the Marshal and all his ideas."

"Do we know if Elder Nazég is still alive out there?"

"I can't be sure who's still alive in that thing, but our estimates weren't good for the possibilities."

"Wonderful. So we have the Council, who is presumably in this deliberation to study something they probably haven't a clue over, and this assumes they're actually alive, which we already know they are not. And then the one man who might hold the answers was chased away by the Marshal."

"Yes…" he muses distantly. "Chased away, this is actually a good way of putting it. What if he did hold an answer of some kind? He was never very highly regarded by the Council, from what I recall, therefore he would be expendable…unless someone knew he held value."

"Like the Marshal? But in his case, as a potential threat?"

"And whoever was on that ship to rescue him."

On the northern edge of the city was a large and well-renowned university complex, known honorably as Capitol Prime University, or

CPU. This was one of the more prestigious institutions, for its age and history, as well as due to being located in the capital city of Azgarén. Within its aged halls, thousands of students moved between their classes attending their studies.

Among these was one young lady anxiously rushing through the corridors to a study hall where she and several others belonging to a local discussion group would sometimes gather for debates and to compare notes from their class schedules.

"Look! Look here!" she shouts to the group at one of the tables. "I told you! I swear! And finally, someone out there figured it out!"

The commotion attracts the attention of the group as she makes her hasty approach.

"Latena!" calls one member. "What do you mean?"

She arrives and clumsily plops down into one of the chairs, displaying her tablet for the group to see. On the screen was a recording of the recent news report by Ileani with the analyst and his perspectives of the Marshal's last press release, including the statements relating to Velen and his faction.

"What did I say, people? It is a conspiracy! Just like I told you. And this counts as my proof!"

"Hold on, Latena," ushers the leading member. "Not that I would wish to argue with you, but we all know how excitable you can be where this theory of yours goes, and we need to take this with a level of rational evaluation."

"Oh, you! You always were a party pooper. All right, did you see the news report that just came out? It was that Ileani Ur'paran again, doing another of her sensationalist broadcasts."

"Another one? I have not had time to watch anything so far today. What did she do?"

"All right, first, you surely recall the Marshal and that press release he made a while back, which I personally think is just another of his excuses, like with that longevity drug."

"Are you still thinking the Council ran away with this secret wisdom?" asks another member. "They should be dead by now, regardless of anything else."

"Yes, well, they certainly are not doing anything else useful around here. Dead or alive, they are not serving as our government body. Not that I ever expected they were to begin with."

"Latena, carefully," the lead member cautions. "You may not approve of them, but we do have a long history of their service. Just look at everything we did since we first converted to this form of government."

"Halin, I will admit to this much, but let me ask you this. Was it for US or for THEM, and we simply took benefit along the way? Remember what I said about the Charter of Laws. It could just as easily be they took what they wanted, and it coincidentally benefited us."

"Coincidentally is a very subjective term, but I will not argue this for how you describe those statements. Let us first analyze what you have this time."

"All right, here..." she presents her tablet. "Watch this video I recorded from today's broadcast. We will begin there."

She plays the recording for the group, setting her tablet on the table for everyone to see and allowing it to run. At the end, many of them are picking up their jaws at the clear, and very controversial implications.

"In all the nether-space..." gasps one member.

"Really?" states yet another one. "Is that before or after the clearly suggestive notion that it could be real, and our overly controlling Council might be denying anyone to actually research it."

"Or even to look out a window to see it!" a third one considers.

"And Halin, your idea of coincidental?" he wonders.

"Is a bit softer now," he admits. "This does indeed suggest a subversive act, and not just one, but potentially a string of them... much like Latena was suggesting. And so, Elder Nazég did not defect, but either ran away to find people who would actually listen to his unorthodox science faction, or else he ran away from those who were actively hostile to him, and this being within a society that is not supposed to be actively hostile to new ideas."

"And therefore," Latena urges. "What I said about the Charter of Laws. It is a dictatorship. They pick and choose what they want for themselves, and he was not one of them. If even the Marshal would say to us, this is a valid science, according to this guy, that means the Council was wrong. It also says, whoever came to carry him away was removing him for a reason, and probably NOT as a defector. My research on the guy says he probably could not hurt a marsh wisp. What sort of military analyst would he make to a bunch of militants who come from this supposedly higher tech society than ours. Furthermore, who is he informing on? Our people? They want Sargeras, not us, or at least it should be."

"She does have a point there," offers the third member. "I also heard it said in one of those reports that these people should know where we live and have jump drives to reach us. This might therefore cause a person to ask why they did not come here to finish Sargeras, but instead took away someone no one cared for to begin with. And for all this time, making us chase them when THEY should come HERE for it."

"And if the Marshal is saying this is a valid form of science," Halin notes. "These insurgents of his, who would come from that same society where they might understand this, WOULD find value in his unorthodox ideas."

"But just a moment," the second one interjects. "Find value for what reason. If they are more advanced than we are, which has always been the suggestion, they probably know all this already. And Elder Nazég might therefore represent a neophyte by comparison."

"Maybe so, but a neophyte with correct ideas in a society that wants him silenced. This now points a new finger at the Marshal, by the way. If HE knew this, why would HE want him silenced. I think Latena just found herself some new ground to stand on, and the Council is taking sides here."

"Wait a moment!" shouts a fourth member who had been silent up until now. "In all the nether-space, am I glad our sect turned against him in those early days! This sounds exactly like what they were claiming after a while…he is a false prophet."

"Auryn, what do you mean?" Halin asks.

"Well, um…" she glances around discreetly. "You know about our sect, right?"

"Of course, you told us, although this sounds almost as, um…well, never mind."

"Laughable? Yeah, I know what you are thinking. I will just ignore it, since I know virtually everyone around here would laugh if they knew we were trying to hold on to a religion."

"Yeah. Sorry, Auryn. But what do you mean with that false prophet thing?"

"When the Marshal and Sargeras first arrived, our sect, along with many others, were all looking at them as possibly harbingers of a higher form of wisdom. We have long believed, or at least hoped for, the existence of a higher mind of some sort that could guide us on the path of true enlightenment. Our ancestors once believed in a religious icon they called the Creator, as you know. But this was thrown out long ago by our society as mysticism, ever since we converted to the scientific pursuits."

"Right."

"Anyway, after a while of waiting, and with no real results of this promise of anything, we gave up and declared him a false prophet, as he never delivered on his promise. Surely not as a higher mind that ought to be able to deliver more efficiently than this."

"I think I see your point. Ten millennia is a long time for a higher mind to actually deliver anything…high."

"Exactly. But now, if we are saying he DOES know something 'high', and this might also relate to Elder Nazég and his faction, and he was chased away AND so badly vilified, this suggests that not only did these insurgents carry away someone valuable for his beliefs, but the Marshal should also know this, and between him and the Council, they are removing this from us to learn about. This does not simply make him a false prophet, but also a collaborator with the idea of a dictatorial Council. Now I am asking myself about these insurgents. Who are they, and why did they REALLY take Elder Nazég away, or send the Marshal and Sargeras out from their side?"

"For that matter," the third member adds. "Why has the Marshal been leading us on this long crusade of his to fight them. Also claiming the Elder is a public enemy if his only real crime is knowing something someone wants silenced. What if the Marshal is wrong and those insurgents were right?"

"Hmm…" Halin muses distantly. "False promises, dictatorial methods, and possible slandering of an innocent victim. That would be reason enough to kick someone out. But it also represents a tail-yanker of a problem for the rest of us."

✦ ✦ ✦◆✦ ✦ ✦

"Ghantil, we have some results from our studies."

"Good, Azina, how do they look so far?"

"We've processed two full groups by now, and our data is looking very consistent. The first group experienced a slight problem, due to our application of the drug being a little on the conservative side. But they still recovered with only minimal trauma. The second group received a heavier dose, about thirty percent more, and the results were much more favorable. They did take a hit, but it was mostly a stunning effect, leaving them delirious for several moments until we could apply a few stimulants to bring them back around."

"Excellent, then it sounds as if we have a workable solution at last. I want to put this into production as quickly as possible. Our only limiting factor right now is that drug. We're working with Lord Thaelyn and his people to produce more of that fungus, and I recently received word that they're investigating how to extend that farming of theirs to increase their productivity. But in the meantime, we'll need to pace ourselves."

"Where do you think we should begin? As I recall, the plan was to process as many emergency personnel as we could, including all the medical staff."

"Right, so we'll start with this, and the ACI is asking us to take a few of their people as well. The shipments we've been getting so far are enough to get things started, but we still need to refine the removal process. So, we'll begin with our native staff and expand outwards from there. Also, we should call in some medical personnel from the other clinics and surgery rooms to observe and study the techniques, and in this way spread it around."

"All right, but now, who goes first?" she raises her brow inquisitively.

"Naturally, we need to process everyone, but Azina, I would like you to be part of the first official group. I'm going to need you operational on the other side of this."

Azina smiles brightly at the suggestion and claps her hands enthusiastically.

"In the meantime," the Director continues. "I'm receiving reports from the clinics concerning our efforts to disable the chips. Not only have they been sending out notices to the families to return their children for the disabling process, but now they're scheduling them for the full removal of the interface."

"Good!" she asserts firmly. "And let this be the end of that!"

"Not only that, Azina, but we're also informing them, quietly so far, that if any of these children should suddenly show any symptoms of the Tav'ageen, um…" he sighs. "No, we'll start calling it the Prodigy Gift, because that's what it is. Anyway, our hope is by disabling those chips in the children, we might finally have a chance to discover one of these examples again. So, we're explaining to the parents what to look for and how to handle it. After all, we don't want to start any new panics. This time, we want to keep it under control, so it doesn't go out to the world before we're ready."

"And so, after all this time, the Project we once tried so hard to keep secret is about to be revealed to the world...sort of."

"Yes, in an indirect manner of speaking. But we need our results first, and in such a way that the Marshal, even if he does somehow hear about it, can't do anything to stop it."

"Or make any new trouble...at least not this time without us knowing where it's actually coming from."

◆◆◆

A new ad campaign was starting up within another industry and borrowing the same cute Eracyodine cartoon figure. This one was showcasing a new model of hover shuttle.

> *"The new DynoDart 600 will turn your daily commute into a dreamy experience. You might not even take notice of the smooth flight characteristics while you enjoy the luxurious interior of soft synthetic leather seats, a rich sound system, and the advanced environmental comfort controls. Standard equipment includes a broad-spectrum network uplink, advanced anti-collision safety features, and a satellite-guided autopilot. You will spend more time enjoying the drive rather than actually driving it. It is so easy, even an Eracyodine can do it!"*

Ayene was visiting the ARC for a follow-up to Azina's success in finding a workable solution to the seed removal. The next objective was to provide for those people who would soon be shedding this awful parasite.

"Azina just entered the program last week," the Director admits, "along with a selection of other interns and a few of our resident med-techs."

"Good luck with it," she offers. "Removing that horrid little bug is probably the worst of it. But now, I would recommend you begin distributing some kind of filter masks. This will help cover for the one obvious benefit it does seem to give, that being to filter out the pollution."

"Right, but as I understand it, you have your people going around trying to shut down that industry now, correct?"

"Yes, and for a while now, but the air isn't going to clear up anytime soon. Some of us are considering trying to find counteragents to this, maybe some form of detergent that can be spread around to decontaminate the place. But in the meantime, the people will need some form of protection."

"All right, we can certainly put together some designs and distribute them to a few supplemental industries for production. The next question is this drug we've developed as a counteragent to this death feedback. When the time finally comes for your people to launch against Sargeras, we need a way to provide this to the general public. How do you propose we do this AND achieve universal coverage with any measure of guarantee? I certainly don't want to see our world population suffering from these feedback coma conditions."

"The logistics of this are certainly a tough nut to crack, I'll admit. But we're working with Central right now to install a raid siren network… just in case we actually do start seeing hostile forces in our local space," she grins. "If you can provide enough supply, we'll try to combine these as a form of incentive for the world population to open their eyes and demand this as part of a new emergency safety procedure."

"Ugh…" he lays his hand on his brow and shakes his head. "Are you trying to incite another world panic?"

"Not trying, but there is really no other way to push people into doing something they might not otherwise do on their own."

"Yes, you have a point. The Marshal did this with his seeds and chips, so we may need to do this again with our countermeasures."

"And lives are at stake here, so panic or no panic, we do need to push them."

"Right, so this means we need to ramp up our production considerably. This also means you with your fungus farms."

"For this point, it may be necessary to expand with some specialized farming here. Maybe we could also locate the original world they came from and use that as well."

"Are you able to do that?"

"I can check around Central and see what they know about it. We also have that ship we acquired once…a science vessel, as it turns out… so this could give us access for a little field study."

"Good, and finally, we have the most obvious problem of how to excuse ourselves once these people start going out on the streets without their seeds."

"Yes, this is a good one," she considers. "We already had a news release of the medical community taking the initiative, due in part to the questions surrounding that Council war protocol. And with the dismissal of that protocol, the medical community feels itself free to research a countermeasure to it. We're simply going to have to admit that they found one. I don't see any other practical way around it. After all, we're a society of scientists…this is what we do. He made us, so he can't possibly argue that we're doing something other than what he made us to do."

"Except that he didn't make us to do THIS," he chuckles. "And the end result of the people taking it?"

"It was never intended to be permanent…never advertised this way… and certainly NOT a desirable thing to have regardless. He's going to learn that we're not his pets to be used as food."

"And what if he tries reasserting this urgent need to evacuate due to the Tav'ageen Scare that started the whole thing?"

"First, we're going to remind the world that we don't need the seeds to colonize anything. We have all sorts of wonderful technology to serve the same purpose."

"Right, I recall this flashed across the newswires once."

"Second, the chips, which are perhaps his most fabulous invention to solve that Scare, are working so many wonders for us that we don't have any urgent need to do anything. We can take our time with it."

"Uh oh… And this might back him into a corner. If he tries anything, like more of these random attacks, this could place those chips into question."

"Yes, and so very suddenly and inconveniently for the timing of the message," she smirks. "After all, with ten millennia of unqualified success, and then to see something as unfortunate as a new attack… right after we remind everyone of HIS fabulous invention…"

"Ouch! Got it. This might then bring HIM into question for his integrity."

"Exactly, as the coincidence would speak for itself, especially after everything else has been said."

"Lieutenant, I think you actually do have a mean streak in you."

"And I'm not done yet," she smiles. "Director, I think it's time to reveal to the world the medical community's…discovery…of that hidden genetic code you found under a security lock. After all, if you're supposed to be researching something, you need something to research, right?"

◆◆◆◆◆

These last few days seemed to pass slowly for Azina since she received her treatment for the seed entity. The procedure at the ARC was calibrated to run approximately ten days, as opposed to the Daanen-Aryku version which was more conservative. Azina was anxious to see it through, but she was also nervous since this was the first official application of the treatment. She limited her travels, restricting herself to only the necessary excursions for food and personal items while shopping, and during the final days she admitted herself to the ARC's medical ward in anticipation of her final stage.

"How do you feel today, Azina?" asks a resident med-tech.

"Sluggish... Hard to focus..." she murmurs softly.

"Give me one moment to run a scan on you. Just relax, you know the drill."

"Yeah... This thing feels like it's close to the end."

The med-tech runs a program default scan over the girl as she lies on the bed. The monitor showed numerous systemic fluctuations throughout the entity, and further within her body for the organs it was attached to.

"You were given your medication this morning, right?"

"Yes. Do I need more? It feels so..." her voice trails off.

The medical technician had been studying the monitors when Azina stopped talking. She noticed a sudden alteration of the girl's vital signs, first a spike, and then a distortion of the rhythms. She quickly turned to see Azina's face had gone blank and her eyes were drooping. The girl's voice began to gurgle, and she appeared to be incoherent. The bio-monitors on the bed were sounding off a flurry of alerts as the med-tech quickly scanned the panel again and scrambled for the intercom.

"Medical alert in Examination Room Fourteen," she shouts into the unit.

She reaches for a hypo-spray and pulls out several vials from a nearby cabinet, inserting one and applying it quickly to the girl's neck.

Several additional people rushed into the room and began taking readings from the monitors. They brought out a respirator and attached it to Azina's face, checking her eyes and taking her pulse, while further monitoring the biorhythms on the display as they slowly settled into a natural pattern.

"Azina, can you hear me?" the med-tech inquires.

The girl was still gurgling, as if trying to respond but unable to control her motor functions yet.

"Can you blink your eyes for me?"

She was only barely able to comply, nudging her eyelids only partway and back again.

The med-tech grabbed the hypo-spray again and applied another drug to help stimulate the girl's neural function.

Azina tried speaking again, and this time her voice became more pronounced.

"Diz-zy… Spin-ning…"

"Just relax, Azina, your rhythms are returning to normal."

The med-tech runs another full scan on the girl for an updated image. The monitor showed the entity with no activity now, and Azina's body was slowly recovering.

"Such a horrible little thing," she remarks to herself. "If this is the standard behavior, we're going to have our work cut out for us."

"And we still need to remove it," adds one of the interns.

"Yeah, and that's the worst part of it. So many people, how could we have allowed ourselves to get this way."

"Med…tech," Azina stammers slowly.

"Yes, I'm here. How do you feel? Your rhythms are looking much better now."

"Slightly…better… Still…fuzzy… Horrible…little…bug…"

"Easy does it, Azina. You're in good hands here. We'll watch you for a while longer and wait until you fully stabilize before going to the next step."

"All right. Does the…Director know?"

"Not yet. So far, we only called a local alert when you went down. Thankfully, you were already on the table."

"Good timing… I guess."

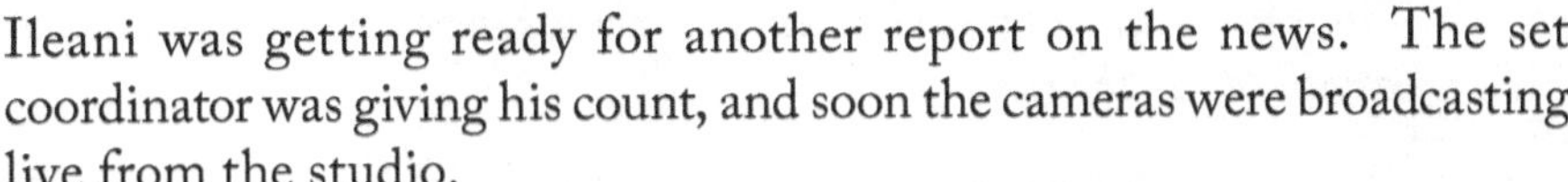

Ileani was getting ready for another report on the news. The set coordinator was giving his count, and soon the cameras were broadcasting live from the studio.

"This is Ileani Ur'paran for C.P. News. Today's news is about the medical community and their efforts to research the An'gamu Seed in order to find a solution to remove it from the host body. As we reported a few months ago, due to the complaints of the Council's emergency war protocols and the court's efforts to overturn this condition, the

medical community has taken it upon themselves to finally investigate this long-overdue concern of the mandates relating to the seeds as a means to evacuate our home world due to the old Tav'ageen Scare.

According to a spokesperson for the medical community, it seems the Council neglected to authorize a curative solution to remove the seed from the body. Even though the seed was never advertised as a permanent feature, this oversight lent to the consequence that it would stay with us for the foreseeable future, with or without any actual emergency. The spokesperson further went on to say that this technology, which was once the product of a much earlier research project to investigate the means of modifying the body, thereby allowing for our survivability in an otherwise uninhabitable environment, was later shelved due to its inherent disfiguring qualities and the general public's disfavor for the result.

However, as part of the medical community's new research into the removal process, sources say they came upon a stumbling block in the form of an unknown encrypted data file found in their old archives from the days of the revised design work. An official from a leading research institute was quoted as saying this would tend to violate the protocols of virtually any laboratory practice to maintain open files for review and revision by later generations of technicians. He said, 'Whoever locked this file under a security password should be locked away behind bars.'

Naturally, this is raising a new outrage within certain circles, especially when combined with the original Council mandate and their apparent lack of foresight to authorize a countermeasure to this alleged temporary emergency protocol. Some are even going so far as to describe it as a conspiracy to infect us with these seeds for some ulterior motive not relating to the emergency, especially when combined with the preexistence of all the other colonizing technologies available at the time.

But on the bright side to this story, C.P. News recently came into knowledge that the security lock on this file was successfully cracked. Sources say a private firm with access to some very talented professionals, was able to reverse-engineer the security encryption protocol, which they describe to resemble a military-grade hashing algorithm once used in the early days at approximately that same time period of those war protocols. This now clears the way for the medical community to finish their studies in the hopes of soon finding their answers."

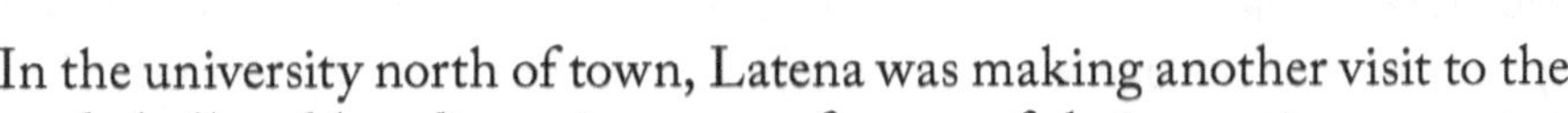

"They're doing it again!" the Marshal screams into the com-link. "In all Creation, what has gotten into these people?!"

"Marshal," the Commander responds calmly. "I am sure this is not a serious concern. After all, I seem to recall the seeds were only intended for our evacuation procedure, and the statements I have heard do lend some credence to their desires to see this corrected, as it is clear we never did evacuate."

"That's not the point! We still need them, because… Um, because… eh, well, you never know when we might actually need them…eh… in case of… Argh! But they're getting inside that file, and it was classified!" he roars. "Doesn't anyone around here have any respect for private matters anymore? Gah!"

The link ends abruptly, and the Commander glares at the vid-com.

"Private matters, is it now?" he muses.

In the university north of town, Latena was making another visit to the study hall and her discussion group for one of their meetings.

"This sounds typical of them," moans one member. "Given the last conversation we had about them, I am not actually surprised to hear this one now."

"You mean their 'accidental' failure to tell anyone how to remove the seeds?" grumbles another member.

"Yes, and then that locked file the news report mentioned. Locked under a military grade code from that same time period. That should tell you who REALLY owns this world."

"Unfortunately," Latena issues. "This is how a dictatorship tends to operate. A hostile military body and a corrupt government, often owned by one or more power hungry people with a lot of authority."

"But Latena," Auryn interjects. "Hold on. If the Council is missing, or lost in some far away research outpost, and if that power hungry military actually owned everything, would this not include the media telling us about it?"

"Um, well, all right, Auryn, I suppose you have a point. But it could have just as easily slipped out, too. If the military thought it could own everything simply by putting a security padlock on it, they might not have anticipated that company breaking it open. So the next thing I would expect to hear is how someone shut it down. Then probably arresting those people, and 'suddenly' the research has been cancelled for some lame reason. And the news, with that Ileani Ur'paran, might also get turned around. You do not just see something like this vanish. They do not go away that easily. Not when you own the military, and any other authority that keeps the place operational."

"Well, if that is the case, I am really sorry, as I was hoping to hear more about that research. We will be graduating soon, and hitting our second centennial, as you know. And you know where that leads."

"Yes, Auryn, and I have been dreading that for the past century."

In the ARC, the seed removal process proceeded ahead like clockwork. Ayene was in another meeting with the Director about their enhanced effort at procuring more of the fungus for processing into the drug.

"We found the location of that fungus," she reports. "It's a Class L warm moon circling a gas giant in a star system identified as Lyeenka, and apparently in that same alternate universe where we have Morndindor, Therinë and the others."

"Sounds to me like Central did a bit of exploring out there," the Director concedes. "And still, no one around here knows anything about it."

"Well, maybe one day, but it might have to wait. Anyway, we sent the Ghan'aju out there to investigate. Captain Va'tyn reports that they did a few surveys, and so far, it seems there is a large abundance of this covering the surface. The moon has a heavy methane atmosphere with only traces of oxygen, but not enough to actually cause ignition… thankfully," she chuckles.

"Indeed! I would hate to see the fireball that would create."

"The temperature is just above freezing, so there are pools of liquid water, and it has a variety of strange lifeforms on it, all naturally adapted to live under these conditions."

"From the perspective of a biology study, I know a few people who would pull their horns out for an opportunity to see that."

"I'm sure you do," she smiles. "And then we have this fungus, which seems to play a major role in the local ecosystem. In fact, our last word from the Captain is that he could easily load up his cargo hold with stockpiles of the stuff without any significant impact on the local environment. And I recall from our observations in those farming cells that this stuff tends to grow rather quickly in the right conditions."

"Good, so how do we do this? Are we still working a trade agreement here since this Captain of yours is technically working for this Lord Thaelyn during this time?"

"Essentially yes. Although we realize there is a pressing need, and lives are at stake here, we also see this as a labor effort, with expense on the other side of it. Therefore, we feel it is worthy of someone getting paid for their work as compensation. Besides, this is largely going to the economy of the old Daanen'kai city, which we're calling Daazh uy'Sodrad, and is populated mostly by our people as refugees we, um… Acquired as part of our, uh… Liberation efforts," she grins innocently.

The Director glared at her for the discreetly impish statement.

"Uh huh… Hmm, Daazh uy'Sodrad…Spring of Freedom. That doesn't sound too bad. And further that he named it using our language. Doesn't he own that world now?"

"He does, but since the city once belonged to the Daanen-Aryku, he's giving honor to them and what they suffered along the way. I also heard once that they might rename that world one day to something a little more appropriate as a colony world, rather than a place of exile, which doesn't sound too pleasant."

"Wow, now that says something. All right, so we're making trade with our own people, I guess, rather than his kingdom at this point. Interesting. Do we call this a type of colony now?"

"Maybe so. The money His Lordship's kingdom uses is very different from what we use here. So, to use our own people makes things a little less complicated for now."

"Ah, yes, good point."

"They'll also see about building some additional local farming inside these specialized enclosures to optimize things for us as time goes forward."

"Good, because I suspect we'll be using this up rather quickly once we standardize the treatment process."

✦✦✦✦✦✦

In the months that followed, the staff of the ARC was processed for their seed removal, and slowly the other clinics were called to send staff members to take their turns. The procedure was shared in other cities around the world, as more and more centers began the laborious chore of first processing their local staff, and then the regional clinics.

In addition to this, the ARC opened up slots for the local staff of the ACI to be processed, meaning Kita and others who were native residents were taking their turns.

It has been nearly three months by now, and Kaliya had her team in rehearsal for their next mission, which would need to be handled very delicately…as if any of their missions could afford it any other way. This would represent the last month before the ARC would presumably finish production on the Marshal's latest invention.

She and her selected crew were at the Cormyr Training Grounds, where Kaliya and her original team first practiced some of their projection skills while in training.

"So, Captain," calls one of the members. "What's the game plan for today?"

"We have some new tricks we need to study in order to make this work. By this time, some of you are in the Seventh Circle and well enough practiced in marking portal runes that I don't have to do it all myself," she snickers. "This is important for us to improve our efficiency. I will select three of you, along with a partner, as part of our initial phase."

"Three?"

"We are expecting Commander Geilv to send those same three ships out there. We need to mark runes on them to import mages for our later exercise. You will mark a rune in each of their shuttle bays, but your partner may need to cover for you in the event of any crewmembers lurking about. Not that I actually expect anyone to just be standing around in a shuttle bay, since they shouldn't be planning on going anywhere, but for safety reasons…you know."

"Right, so the partner distracts them while the conjuror marks the rune."

"Our first objective will be to make our way to the surface of Sigil. We'll be using that same access point they made originally as our arrival zone. We will convene there and hope the ships arrive in the same general area where they were before. We may need to fold over to them again manually, since our previous memory perspectives may be altered due to their absence and subsequent return."

"So, we may not be able to simply fold inside like the last time. Got it. And do we try to gain entrance the same way as the first time?"

"If it seems convenient enough, but do take care, as always, of any observers."

"Acknowledged."

"Each of the three teams will choose a ship. Once inside, you'll make your way to the shuttle bay. You'll need to memorize where you are, since you'll need to make a brief return to the WIC building to pick up your bags. Then go back, mark your rune, and return for delivery. And this completes the first stage."

"When do we use these runes?" asks another member.

"The runes will be handed over to a group of mages who will use them to get inside. They'll be wearing disguises to look like, um…well, something you might find in a place like Sigil. They'll come equipped with runes leading to Ruuki uy'Daan, where Commander Kriv'tik and his people will wait for the new arrivals, along with some Order troops to help contain the situation until a full explanation of our little game has been made."

"That's a lot of people to contain, but hopefully, if they follow orders, we can keep it under control."

"At this moment, they know the Marshal is at fault here, and the Captain of the Tul'ryk is aware Kriv'tik is alive and working on a top-secret investigative project. This is a plus on our side, so we're expecting this to move along fairly smoothly. Furthermore, those same teammates will also train my new ethereal apparition image and voice simulation. I'm also recruiting Ayene to assist me on the bridge of the Tul'ryk. The teammates will act as guides to direct the crews through the portals. Having you present in this form will surely convince them to leave."

"You're not kidding! I think having someone like that present would convince anyone to leave, no matter the cause," he chuckles, inciting the rest of the group to join in.

"We also have the Commander and Captain Va'tyn of the Ghan'aju, and his people, who have been helping us train a few of our own on how to pilot a star cruiser, and again using the Ghan'aju as their example. Those teammates will remain corporeal and arrive after the ships have been evacuated. As for those of us here, we will be in projected mode, and this is why we are here now."

"Captain, are we going to try impersonating mini dust storms and dead leaves again?" asks a member with a modest grin.

"Not quite. We're going Wrath of God style on this occasion," she responds with a laugh.

"Dear cu'Nar, I'm sorry I asked. All right, what do you have in mind?"

"We can't use flash-bangs or fireballs inside the ships for our special effects, like we did at the base on Morndindor, at least not without possibly causing damage, and I don't want to do that. So, we need to simulate the sounds of angry gods attacking from outside."

"Cu'Nar's pity," moans one of the female members. "What kinds of sounds do we make for that?"

"In projected mode, when we speak, we're not actually talking in the traditional manner. Just like with our image projection, where it's a matter of the perspective of our mind manifesting our image in physical space, the same goes with the sounds we make. I believe in my mind I am talking, therefore my mind manifests sounds that resemble speech. Some of us have also mimicked animal sounds during our practice with various shapes. Now we'll be playing thunder and lightning, explosions, like that of ship equipment blowing up, and such like. Thaelyn has also been coaching me on a special role I need to play at a specific moment as a message to the Marshal."

"What's that?"

"He needs to be told, in a roundabout way, that the Estelar are aware of him and will not permit any future incursions. I have a series of lines I've been practicing for this, but for right now, let's just get the sound effects ready. Remember, think big. This is why we're out here in the middle of nowhere, so we don't disturb anyone with our ruckus."

Kaliya now leads her team into the production of thunderous roars, sounds of lightning strikes, booming and crashing, and other horrific clamors. Each member conjured up memories from their lifetime experience of nature sounds and imitated those echoing out from their projected images. The scene resembled a titanic barrage of apocalyptic destruction, if only by the sounds emitted from the teammates. If it were not for the fact that it was only an act by a group of projected images, one might suggest the world was coming to an end.

✦✦✦

It was the end of the month, and the Director of the ARC was reminded of an important schedule that was coming due. On this occasion, he had to make a fated call to Commander Geilv.

"This is Commander Geilv speaking…"

"Commander, this is Director Bak'vayn at the ARC. How are you today?"

"Just barely holding together. I've been expecting your call, but not very anxiously."

"I don't blame you, Commander. But I need to inform you that our contacts within the ACI tell us they are ready to move forward with their plans for that city structure you found. Therefore, we are releasing our hold on that new project the Marshal ordered."

"I see. And here is where we need to send our ships back out there, and the Marshal essentially gets his tail spanked."

"Yes, to put it mildly. But overall, this will lead us to another sequence of some kind. I don't envy you for your position, Commander, but if it helps any, we're all in this together, so we need to stand by each other as best we can."

"Thank you, Director. I'll let you know how it goes once we have a result."

They end the link, and the Commander calls up the local Captain.

"Sir?" he announces as he enters the room.

"Captain, sit with me a moment. I just got a call from the ARC. The schedule for the Marshal's latest pet project is complete and it's time for us to put the plan into action. I need you to call up Captain Kan'vrij and tell him we are redeploying the Tul'ryk and its escort into that, um…Abnormal Space…or whatever those people normally call it."

"All right, and as I recall the plan, they're supposed to deploy this new death toy device, and then get into trouble for it, leaving the owners to retaliate and, well…"

"Right, and we have to make it look good on our side, no matter what happens on the com-link. This means, like it or not, we're playing actors."

"Wonderful. So where do we begin?"

"Send them out there. Make sure the Captain knows the plan. I'll make a call to the Marshal to inform him we have his latest special order ready, and it is being deployed. I will suggest to him, for all his recent woes for these news sensations, perhaps he would like to oversee this operation as a means of redirecting his thoughts to this very important work. I think he might like that," he smirks.

"Oh, Commander, how generous of you," he chuckles.

"Once we have his participation, we'll coordinate with the ships, but at this point, my understanding is the ACI and their contacts will be taking over the operations and offloading the crew to some waystation."

"Commander, with respect, I would personally like to verify the safety of our people somehow. Do you think it might be possible to pass a message of some kind, if only for a simple status report?"

"I suppose I can ask. This shouldn't be too much to ask for. But I think I would not want to ask too many questions about it, for that same security risk I have under the Marshal."

"That's not a nice place to sit, Commander. All right, I'll get on this immediately."

The Captain gets up and leaves the office while the Commander contemplates his call to the Marshal. He leans back in his chair staring at the vid-com and tapping a finger on his desk, then leans forward again to dial up a number.

"This is Darumon," issues the course voice. "What is it, Commander? I hope we do not have yet another disaster waiting for us on the news broadcast."

"Actually, no, Marshal. I wish to inform you that your special order has arrived from the ARC and is currently on its way."

"Ah! Yes! Good!" he chuckles wickedly. "Finally, we can see some real work done around here."

"Perhaps you would wish to oversee the operation during its initial phase? It could provide you with some amount of distraction from your other concerns."

"Why, Commander, this is actually a very considerate suggestion. Yes! I would most certainly wish to oversee those first moments. I have very little else to do around here lately. My terminal continues to drive me crazy for this new security demand. Now it is asking me for such nonsense as my mother's unmarried name, my favorite color, and which was my most popular childhood sport, among other things."

"Yes…" he furrows his brow modestly and glances at his terminal. "I see some of the same over here, but as I said before, this is deemed necessary due to the issue of Ytani."

"And relating to that issue, have you heard anything from him lately? I'm expecting him to make some sort of appearance one of these days."

"Nothing as yet. None of our sensor buoys have alerted us to any incursions in our local space."

"This worries me, but I suppose there is very little we can do about it until he makes a showing. But Commander, I want you to be extremely cautious if and when he does arrive. I've been trying to think of ways in which to bring that situation under control, but first I need a target."

"Understood, Marshal. In the meantime, I will inform you when the Tul'ryk is in position and ready to deploy."

"Good, I'll be waiting."

They end the link, and the Commander continues to stare at his terminal.

"He is STILL having trouble? But..."

He pauses to consider the situation, as his terminal had been behaving normally during this time. He reaches over to engage the monitor and pull up his default screen. All appears normal, with no random login boxes.

"I'm not getting that over here. Why only him? Oh, wait..."

He leans back again and glances at the door, trying to visualize the security revamp that was going on elsewhere in the building.

"You little sneaks!" he mutters under his breath. "No wonder you were able to break so many of our codes. You're right under our noses!" he chuckles. "All right, I won't complain. Just so long as you give it back to us when all this is done."

✦✦✦✦✦

In orbit over the planet, in the Saakerav Military Space Dock, Captain Kan'vrij and his senior officers received their instructions and made their way through the docking port into the ship. The crew was already onboard and waiting. As the Captain arrived on the bridge, he signaled back to base.

"This is Captain Kan'vrij on the Tul'ryk. We are ready for departure and awaiting confirmation."

"This is Captain Ta'yeen in Central Command. Do you understand your orders for this mission?"

"Affirmative, and although it disturbs me for the potential outcome, we must think of Azgarén and everyone down there. We will comply with our instructions and hope for the best. And if it becomes possible, with the aid of our friends, we will try to pass a message of our status to settle your feelings back home. Central…" he sighs deeply. "We all wish you success in ridding our home of that monster. I hope one day to return and see that I still have a home."

"I understand, Sanuri, we all feel the same for this point. You are cleared to depart. You will notify us of your arrival and whatever time delay is required for your team to…theoretically…deploy themselves."

"Understood."

Captain Kan'vrij gave the order, and the ship's docking controls were released from the station, allowing it to drift away. The Captain ordered the helm to bring the ship around and proceed ahead slowly, soon to be accompanied by its escort as they also launched from the station. They continued for several moments until they reached a safe distance to engage their jump drives.

"Helm," the Captain announces. "Set our coordinates to our previous exit point in Abnormal Space. And one of these days, we should probably assign a better name to it."

"Sir, yes Sir!" shouts the ensign.

The other two ships received their coordinating navigation protocols and made ready to follow the larger cruiser in formation. Their jump drives began charging up while the helmsmen called off the numbers, eventually to peak and flash away as the ships phased out of the local space.

✦✦✦✦✦✦✦

"My Lord, they're away!" calls a scout just arriving in projected form.

"Good," Thaelyn nods. "Kaliya, your time has come. Make it a good one."

Kaliya and her team were standing by in the WIC building and waiting for word of the launch. Some of her team was in projected form while others were corporeal.

A group of nine mages, each with a rune to Ruuki uy'Daan, waited on the side. They were wearing special costumes on this occasion to conceal their features. The garment was a flowing white robe with a narrow blue band leading from the neckline down the full length in front. It had a blue sash around the waist, and blue cuffs for the wrists and lower hemline. The head was covered in a hood, with a heavy veil over the face, and they wore white gloves, leaving no part of the body visible to the outside. The design was very clean, with no outward signs of identity.

As for the incursion team, six projected forms would make their way into the shuttle bays where they would mark the arrival runes. Three equipment cases, much like Kaliya's bag with her effigy device, sat near the table. They each held a similar set for the operations crew. The team would return for these once they found their way in.

Kaliya directed her projected team members to begin folding themselves to the outside of Sigil, arriving near the airlock she first used as her focus point on previous missions. They arrived on the outer surface as a group and began surveying the skies around them for the appearance of the ships.

Several moments later, they spied the flashing of the hyperspace rift in the distance, and three dots appeared out of it. Kaliya waved to her team, and they directed their attention to fold across the extended distance to their marks. They arrived on the hull of the larger vessel, where two pairs of agents broke away from the group to travel onward to the two escorts.

Kaliya's group included Ayene and Navina, plus the one remaining pair to mark the rune in the shuttle bay. They found their way inside through a nearby window, where they each took up their Suuden'kai disguises. Kaliya and Ayene took military costumes, while Navina took her ACI dress code. Then the agents split off to find the shuttle bay while Kaliya, Ayene, and Navina sauntered up to the bridge.

"Navina," Kaliya whispers as they ride the lift. "You'll represent yourself as the Azgarén contact. Ayene and I will scope the place as tiny bugs so no one will notice. But before we can make our move, we need to allow time for the crew to…presumably…enter the city and set themselves up."

"Presumably…" she smirks. "And this should give our people more than enough time to set up on the other side."

"Right, so we'll allow maybe an hour to work their way through those sewers."

"Sounds good to me. Then I'll just engage in a little chatter along the way."

As they arrive on the bridge, Kaliya and Ayene alter their shapes to small flying insects. Navina steps out of the lift as the others buzz their way up to the ceiling for concealment.

The Captain takes quick notice of the oddly dressed agent arriving on the scene. He turns to glare at her.

"May I ask who you are, young lady?"

"Special Agent Navina Lar'akan," she pulls out her trans-com with her ID. "Azgarén Central Intelligence…"

"Azgarén… The ACI, here? Young lady, I've been hearing a few things about you people. So far, it sounds like you're insidious. And by your presence here, I think that might be an understatement. All right, so what are we supposed to do now?"

"My information tells me that the Commander only now informed the Marshal of our departure. So, to make it seem more realistic, we should allow ourselves a little time for your crews to enter the city."

"I see. All right, as you wish. But then what? Do you have contact with these other people?"

"Yes, I do. They are watching us as we speak, but keeping themselves concealed until the appointed time. We will simply relax a moment for now."

"Easy for you to say…" he sighs tensely.

"Captain, I realize you are under a lot of stress right now, but I assure you, we are working hard to save our world and everyone on it."

"Yes, but it doesn't help when you know you're going to be locked away in some strange place with strange people watching over you."

"It may not be as strange as all that. And besides, along the way, you and your crew might also learn a few things. So, you should consider it an opportunity to indulge in a little of that great wisdom the Marshal kept promising, but never delivered on, as you'll be among people who might actually be able to teach you something."

"Really! Well, maybe that's not so bad after all."

+ + + ◆ ◆ ◆ + +

About an hour passes and a call comes in from the control room.

"Commander, this is Captain Ta'yeen. The Tul'ryk is in position, and by this time, the Captain tells us his team would've made full penetration inside the structure, enough to make a deployment. So, I guess we are Go for our operation."

"Acknowledged, Captain, I'm on my way."

They end the link and Geilv gets up to leave his office. He makes his way through the hallways to another segment of the building, where he arrives inside the control center. All the resident officers offer a salute as the stoic elder Commander makes his presentation.

"What is the status of the Tul'ryk, Captain?"

"They are in a standby condition and awaiting confirmation to proceed."

The Commander casually glances around the room at each of the other officers at their stations, then back to the Captain with an inquisitive gaze.

"Yes Sir," the Captain affirms. "They're all in on it. They'll try to keep silent during this time, leaving most of the acting to us."

He nods and makes another cursory pass at the assembly before continuing.

"Very good, but this is not something they normally teach us in military school. Open a channel for us."

The Captain directs the comms officer to call up the Tul'ryk.

"This is Central Command to the Tul'ryk. Are you receiving?"

"Central Command, this is the Tul'ryk, we are receiving you."

The Commander steps forward.

"This is Commander Geilv. I understand you are in position and currently in a standby mode, correct?"

"Yes Sir. Would you like to speak to the Captain?"

"Affirmative."

The Captain of the ship now comes on the line.

"This is Captain Kan'vrij. Commander, we are ready to proceed here. We have an agent from the ACI with us and she will make contact with these others to get us going. We're just waiting on your confirmation."

"An agent of the ACI is on your ship? Interesting. I really wish I knew how they did this. May I speak to her?"

"Yes Sir."

Now Navina approaches the station.

"Commander, good day to you, this is Special Agent Navina Lar'akan again."

"You? Young lady, how did you manage to infiltrate our military base, and then to infiltrate one of our ships?"

"I'm very talented, Commander, this much I can assure you."

"Yes, like those people I suspect you have in our offices down here working that new security revamp. The Marshal seems to be having a lot of troubles with his terminal lately."

"Oh, but I'm so very sorry to hear that. Maybe it'll keep him from developing any new death toys for a while."

"Right, so where do we go from here?"

"Our first step is to make contact, then to offload the local crew. We have a number of other agents on hand, although located elsewhere for now, who will play our actors, along with a number of sound effects we brought along. For as long as we are audio-only on the com-link, this should make for a scary demonstration. Then we finish up with a type of message the Marshal should be familiar with, if his old rivals were ever to discover him. This should turn him away from making any future attempts at this place. After that, we hope things will quiet down a little until our next move."

"Understood. Then I suppose we will wait for your signal when you are ready with your demonstration."

"Absolutely, Commander."

They end the link and Navina moves away from the com-station.

"Now, Captain," she asserts. "These people are a rather strange race with strange appearances and manners. We are working cooperatively on this, but our efforts must dissuade the Marshal from making so much mischief out there."

"Mischief? Is that how you describe destroying worlds?"

"In an unfortunate manner of speaking, yes. Their terminology redefines certain baseline standards. This is a condescending term we adopted along the way to describe such manners as what he has been exhibiting lately. None of us is pleased about his actions, but at the same time, there is not much we can do about it except to prevent any more."

"Yes, I would most certainly agree on that. Now, as to calling these people, how do we do this?"

Navina smiles gently and moves to the center of the room, where she lifts a hand to her temple, as if using a telepathic form of summoning.

The Captain and his officers studied her intensely, glancing at each other and the rest of the bridge crew trying to interpret what she might be doing. But before he has an opportunity to question her, a pair of mysterious shapes begins to appear out of a misty haze in front of the room. The Captain and the other officers freeze in their steps.

Kaliya and Ayene had been waiting during this time for the moment to appear. As Navina made her false play at telepathy, the two of them emerged from their hiding places as tiny bugs in the crevices of the ceiling tiles, then to take shape in their special ethereal bodies.

The Captain leans in gently to speak to Navina.

"How did you do that?" he whispers.

"Captain, it would seem our species is capable of a few rather extraordinary talents no one knew about until recently. One of those is telepathy. This was actually the domain of Former Elder Nazég and his science faction. But unfortunately, the rest of the Council, and likely the Marshal as well, all took great pleasure in discrediting him."

"Discrediting?" he surges. "So, what was that long chase the Marshal claimed during this time?"

"An excuse for him to blast away all his famous insurgents the Former Elder was presumably stirring up. The Marshal is a fiend, and the Council behaves as a god entity, Captain. They like to control things. But this is one thing they wouldn't be able to control, because it's in our full species."

"Oh, how lovely."

Navina steps forward and offers a polite bow to her two Celestial guests. The Captain and the others watched and felt compelled to offer the same. Then he steps forward to make an introduction.

"A, uh, pleasant greeting to you," he offers uncertainly. "My name is Captain Sanuri Kan'vrij, and I welcome you to our ship which we call the Tul'ryk."

"Thine offer is well received…" Kaliya emits in her ghostly voice.

The strange vocalizations sent shudders through the bridge crew.

Kaliya continues, "We are here as part of our agreement to conduct a demonstration in the eyes of the Ancient One, that he may know we are aware of his intrusion into this fold. He must be deterred from his future endeavors, as we will not allow his encroachment of the ancient Door leading to the prison fold that once and forever more cages the others of his kind."

"I understand, and I think I should also offer my deepest apologies for disturbing your fine city here. I'm told the Commander once offered some form of reparation, but you declined as you have your own preferred methods. Is this correct?"

"This is correct. She who governs the construct will attend to its ways with her own devices."

"All right, so now, you need to remove my crew from these ships as you prepare for this demonstration. How do you propose we arrange this?"

"We will open the Doors from this fold into another, where thee and thine will pass into that domain where thou wilt seek thy refuge."

"I, uh…" he flusters.

"Captain," Navina interjects. "Allow me to translate a bit. My interaction with them has allowed me to interpret their wording somewhat by now. Their native language has surely evolved beyond what we might use back home, and some portion of it is fully telepathic, meaning more conceptual than verbal."

"That would be a fascinating thing to study, assuming my horns could handle it."

"Yes, and for each of us, I'm sure. But a 'door' to them is like a conveyor to us…a dimensional rift aperture. They apparently have the ability to create these rather easily, and also on a personal level."

"Really! That would be interesting to see."

"Also, the term 'fold' represents a dimensional plane, or a universe to people like us."

"Incredible. I can only imagine what level of sophistication a society would need to achieve in order to hold such perceptions as these."

"Indeed, my experience suggests that when you reach a certain level, such complex terms as we might use are no longer necessary. The new standard for them becomes much like the older standard for people like us."

"And where will these…doors…of yours be applied?" he asks the apparitions.

Kaliya responds, "The Doors will be opened in those locations where the smaller vessels take refuge within the larger."

"Smaller vessels…" the Captain struggles with the cryptic message.

"Captain," another officer submits. "Maybe they're speaking of the shuttle bays."

"Ah, yes, thank you, Lieutenant. That makes good sense, actually. Plenty of open space to work with."

Kaliya turns to Ayene and nods. Ayene folds herself away, returning to the WIC building to give instructions for the mages to be sent. A local group opens a series of three portals, one for each of the ships.

The Captain instructs the comms officer to open a secure link to the escort ships, giving instructions that contact has been made and all crewmembers are to be evacuated through some manner of exit to be provided inside their shuttle bays. The ships are placed on standby mode and the crews begin filing through the corridors.

In the shuttle bay on the Tul'ryk, the crewmen were accumulating as a gathering of confused stares. They were presented with a row of three strangely clad individuals in white robes holding up something that looked like a small stone, and a vertical manifestation of what vaguely resembled a conveyor rift hovering in the air.

"Well, so much for that definition of those inside the city being of a technologically inferior designation," mutters one crewman to another.

"I agree. These look similar in size and physical description, but the clothing is different from the observations in the scouting reports."

"Probably another grade, as with those who were seen levitating."

"Yes, and this thing they are using," he directs at the rune stones. "I recall mention of devices that could be based on this Abnormal Energy, and this would certainly be abnormal by our standards."

"It also suggests a form of technology alien to ours, but comparable to some of our own designs."

"If so, then our interpretation of technology might not even apply in this space."

Among the alien visitors were two more apparitions on either side of the mages directing the crew into the portals, forming them up in columns and timing their departure for a comfortable spacing in-between.

On the other side, on Ruuki uy'Daan, Order troops assisted the Suuden-Aryku crewmen as they stepped out. The crew, being unaccustomed to such mode of transport, at least outside of a ship travelling through hyperspace, were having difficulty gaining their proper footing on arrival, so the troops would catch them and assist in steadying them while moving them out of the way for the next one.

Commander Kriv'tik and his next-in-line, Lieutenant Az'krun, stood by as the crewmen arrived. They watched the growing assembly of disoriented and clearly disturbed faces as the crew moved to one side and waited.

On the Tul'ryk, the Captain and his first officer were the last to leave. He took one final look around inside the shuttle bay, wondering if he'll ever see his ship again. He sighed despondently before jumping through the aperture, and then the mages closed the portals.

On his arrival on Ruuki uy'Daan, one of his first sights was Commander Kriv'tik. He suddenly felt much more relieved at the familiar face, and he stepped up to greet him.

"Commander, you don't know how glad I am to see you."

"I think I have a fairly good idea, Captain. But now, hold that thought a while, as we need to talk."

<hr>

"Ayene," Kaliya announces as they reconvene on the bridge. "Based on our conversation, how do you feel on imitating the Captain's voice?"

"I feel good. I was paying close attention to it, so I think I can play that role."

"All right, first we need our people. The mages are going home, and the others will be sent to us using those same runes into the shuttle bays. Once we take up our positions on each of the bridges, we need to coordinate our efforts through our shard-coms."

"Understood."

"And Navina, once we're arranged, we'll have you call in to Geilv and let him know the game is on."

"Got it."

Kaliya waited patiently for her team to follow through on their orders. The corporeal crew arrived on each of the ships and took up their places on the bridges, including the Tul'ryk. They were equipped with shard-coms to communicate locally, and also to their base in Rolsklinde. At the same time, the projected members assembled on the bridge of the Tul'ryk to make ready for their latest performance. Kaliya took up a position in front of the helm station, ready to conduct the affair.

"Ayene, you're the voice of Captain Kan'vrij. The rest will be background, including the other officers and crew, and the occasional scream or shout. We have our projected sound effects crew in position, and we all have our scripts. Along the way, we'll start to lose ships, first one frigate, and then the other. Finally, we have this ship, where the gods are generally having their way with it. I need our spy to go to Central and hide out. I want eyes on the other side to watch Darumon's reaction."

The crew takes their places and one projected member flashes away to the ventilation duct in the control center at Central Command. Kaliya waits a few moments before beginning.

"Navina, call us in, please."

The young lady steps over to the comms station where one of Kaliya's officers was manning the controls. She then calls in to announce their status.

"Central Command, this is Special Agent Lar'akan. We are ready on this side."

"This is Central Command. We are receiving you. What is your status?"

"Everything is ready for our little play. The crew is secure, and our Special Ops team is in place."

"Acknowledged. The Commander wishes to share a word before we begin."

"Understood."

"Agent Lar'akan, this is Commander Geilv. I'll need a moment to call in the Marshal."

"All right, Commander, we'll wait for you. But from that moment forward, our actors will need to play the roles of the former bridge crew, including Captain Kan'vrij. So, you will be addressing him on your return."

"Acknowledged."

Ayene grinned widely in expectation of her upcoming performance. She was almost feeling giddy at the idea.

"You need to hold it together, girl," Kaliya jibes.

"Yes, Kaliya, I've just never done anything like this before. I can't even recall any decent vid-com shows with something like this."

"In a society without emotion, what kind of vid-com shows do you have?"

"Boring ones, you can be sure of that. You don't dare involve anything to invoke an emotional response, or else…you know."

"Yeah. Ouch!"

Several long moments pass, and the comm station buzzes with an inbound signal. Kaliya points at an agent holding a shard-com to alert the other ships of the game, then to Ayene to respond.

"This is Captain Kan'vrij speaking," she announces formally.

"Captain," ushers a harsh rasping voice. "This is Marshal Darumon. Such a glorious moment. Finally, we might be able to accomplish our objective. What is your current condition?"

"Our people are ready to make our first launch. We have positioned them at strategic locations for greater efficiency. We are now waiting for your word to begin."

"Excellent, then the word is given, begin your operation, and do be sure to provide me with frequent updates as to your immediate progress."

"Acknowledged, we will keep the com-link open for you to listen in on our progress. Team leaders, this is the Captain, you will begin your application of the devices."

Kaliya points to another member for a reply. The voice echoes as if funneling through a com-link.

"Affirmative, Captain, initiating the procedure now."

Kaliya pauses a few moments before giving her next cue, pointing to the same agent.

"Captain, the devices seem to be functioning within parameters. The results appear to be effective."

She now points to another agent, following a sequence like a director on a movie set.

"Lieutenant, look there. I see one of those levitating entities. It appears to be moving away quickly."

"Captain," the Marshal urges. "You must be sure to enforce your position if that being should appear."

"Acknowledged. Lieutenant, gather the troops at your location. Prepare to hold that position."

"Understood."

Kaliya holds the action for another few moments before continuing.

"Captain, we have a sighting on the authority being. It is approaching from above."

"Engage when ready."

"Engaging..."

Kaliya now points to a group of sound effects members. They start letting off muted sounds of gunfire, then a wailing scream that seemed to echo through simulated urban streets, followed by sounds of crashing, and a roar like a fiery shockwave.

"Captain! It is retaliating against our assault. This is strange, where is that coming from? Sir! It appears to be sending out something like a firestorm, but...I do not see a weapon of any kind! Look out, men!" he shrieks. "It is coming this way..."

The channel is now filled with the screams of the military troops.

"Captain!" he shouts. "We cannot defend against this! We need to...aaaagghh!"

"Lieutenant!" Ayene shouts in her imitated voice. "Dammit! This is the Captain to any available squad member, report!"

Kaliya now points to another member in the room.

"Captain, our scanners are detecting something outside the ship."

"Outside? Here? Put it on screen."

"It appears to be some manner of storm developing outside. Scans are classifying it as a high-intensity plasma storm, developing rapidly."

Kaliya points at the next sound effects crew. Distant thunder echoes out.

"Where did THAT come from?" Ayene issues in her roleplay. "Tactical, this looks serious. We need our shields at maximum power."

"Acknowledged."

"Captain," shouts the Marshal on the com-link. "What's happening out there?"

"There is a sudden surge of turbulence developing outside the ship. It appears as a plasma storm, but there was nothing on the scans a moment ago, so I have no idea where it came from."

"Never mind that, you need to pull back, now!"

Kaliya jabs a finger at the crew again. Now the thunder crashes loudly with sounds of impacts, and a groaning of metal as the hull begins to buckle.

"In all the nether-space!" the tactical officer exclaims. "That thing hits hard! Captain! We just took a direct hit to the aft section! We sustained heavy damage! I'm showing a breach on several decks midship."

"Seal off those sections and redirect more power to the shields!"

"Sir," issues another officer. "That last hit seemed to damage some of the conduits. I'm showing a loss of power to the starboard nacelle."

"We need more power to the shields! And engage the stabilizers!"

Another crash of thunder roars through, along with the sounds of an electrical explosion, followed by a scream.

"Captain!" the Marshal screeches. "You must retreat!"

"Marshal, we are taking a series of direct hits! This storm seems to be launching against us with a directed purpose! Engineering, what is our status?"

"Our engines have just gone offline, one nacelle is destroyed," responds another agent.

Kaliya points again.

"Captain!" shouts another one. "We just lost one of our escorts. I'm showing a direct hit that cracked it in two! And I'm reading collateral explosions ripping it apart further."

Now more thunder, plus sounds of additional hull impacts, and more screams as equipment explodes.

"Captain, I'm showing a breach in the engineering section! Main power is failing. We're switching to backups."

"Sir," shouts another officer. "We've lost contact with the second escort. Scans are showing explosions and a debris cloud at their last position."

"Dammit!" Ayene curses. "Helm, do we have ANY maneuvering power? We need to pull away from this!"

"The helm is not responding! All maneuvering control is dead! The main drive is offline, and even the thrusters are down."

"This is bad, people!"

Kaliya suddenly waves her hands for a pause. The sounds die out, and she gently points again.

"Captain!" shouts one of the background voices. "Look there, on the monitor!"

"What is THAT?" Ayene shouts in her Captain's persona. "It looks like some kind of entity!"

"Captain!" the Marshal demands. "What is it? What do you see out there?"

"I see something on the monitor. It looks like...faces, reflecting off the clouds, or something."

"Sir!" the background agent adds. "It appears as multiple entities of an unknown specification. They do not register as material bodies. More like, well, something abnormal. And they are converging on us!"

"Could they be the cause of that storm?"

"For the lack of anything else out here, um... And I am showing high concentrations of that Abnormal Energy surrounding them."

"In all the nether-space, is that where it comes from?"

Now it was Kaliya's turn. She makes herself ready for her special performance, recalling her practice session with Thaelyn on recreating a divine announcement, and shouts out her lines using three different simulated voices.

"Intrusion...!" her voice booms in a feminine tone.

"Transgression...!" she echoes in a different feminine manner.

"Contamination...!" she sounds off in a deeper masculine voice.

"Recognition...!" she reverberates using the first voice again.

"Impossibility...! Extinction...!" she responds in the male tone, as if carrying a conversation with her alter egos.

"Correction...! Observation...! Prime Manifestation...!"

"Perseverance...?"

"Affirmation...! Secondary Encroachment...!"

"Secondary...?!"

"Recollection…" she reflects in the second female. "Notification…! Preparation…!"

"Prosecution…?"

"Negation… Solitary iteration… Recommendation… Observation… Anticipation… Recursion…? Eradication…!"

"Concurrence…" she finishes in the first voice.

She again points assertively at her group. They now give a grand finale of thundering crashes, explosions, screams, and finally, as she points to the comms officer, he cuts the link, along with all the other signaling, just as the escort ships did on their cue.

The team rests, and all faces glare at Kaliya for her exemplary role.

"Dear cu'Nar, Kaliya," Navina whimpers. "I don't know about Darumon, but that would frighten the wits out of me, you can be sure of it."

"Yes, but it's Darumon we need to impress on this occasion. Now, let's see if we were successful. We'll wait for our spy to return with a report. Meanwhile, tell the other ships to make ready for departure. We'll park everything in orbit around Ruuki uy'Daan for now, just like the Ghan'aju."

"That place is going to become a bit cluttered if we keep this up."

✦

In Central Command, in the control center, a shocked and very disturbed crew of officers had just finished listening to the sounds of what seemed like a cataclysmic attack on their ships. Commander Geilv and Captain Ta'yeen stared at the com-link, speechless over the presentation. They tentatively glanced at each other, and then over at the Marshal.

Darumon was also gazing at the com-link, in his case with a blank stare, which soon turned to trepidation. He rolled his eyes around the room, and gradually leaned over to the window, looking outside and up into the sky, then quickly withdrawing away from it several short paces. He was clearly affected, and unable to respond at first.

The Commander decided he needed to make the first effort, if only to gain some perspective of the situation.

"Marshal, it would seem we have lost our ships. What are your instructions?"

"It would seem?!" he retorts acerbically, and then tries to recompose himself. "Yes… It would seem. Instructions? Instructions, yes… I think, eh… Yes, I think our activities there have been averted…for now."

"Should we make another attempt?"

"NO!" he shouts urgently. "No, no… This will require some, eh… reconsideration. Yes! Clearly, we should delay any future activities in that region. At least until, eh… Actually, we may need to cancel that operation altogether. After all, I am sure we can proceed without that element of our plan. And…and…" his mind seems to wander off momentarily. "I wonder if I should report this to him…" he muses privately as he glances hesitantly out the window again. "No, maybe not… Not at this time. After all, he's sleeping…he needs his rest, you know."

The Commander and the Captain glanced at each other as if trying to interpret the Marshal's curious meanderings.

"That is, not unless, eh…" he continues mumbling to himself. "Well, yes, this is what we must do. They, eh…they seem, ehm…not as interested in pursuing. Maybe. Solitary iteration, they said. Yes. This is the answer. I'm simply not worth it," he issues solemnly.

The officers looked on as Darumon seemed to descend into a moment of melancholy, lowering his head as he reflected on those final words.

"This is where we stand. As if it should be any surprise by now," he shakes his head despondently. "Commander…" he perks up briefly and turns to the elder officer. "We should perhaps relax our posture for a while. You will keep a strong security force in operation around us. I want to know the absolute instant anything shows up on those screens! Though, at this moment…" his voice trails off.

He then dashes out of the room.

The Commander and the Captain follow him with their eyes, uncertain which of the two events, the activity on the com-link or the Marshal's reaction, was the more distressing.

"Commander," the Captain wonders. "Two thoughts occur to me on this occasion. The first being his reference to reporting this to… someone. And there is only one person he might have in mind to report anything to."

"Agreed. And it sounded as though he intended to keep this away from him."

"Sargeras, that is."

"Yes."

"But that other part. He's not worth it? This is where we stand, as if it were any surprise? I'm unsure how to interpret that."

"I think I can offer a suggestion, but given his past manners, I would be surprised to hear those words, regardless. He appeared disappointed, or maybe depressed."

"That they aren't interested in pursuing him? After all that he did?"

"I am going to suggest this is a tactic to defray any, um, determined interest. We both know they are already pursuing him, but secretly."

"But of course!" the Captain nods. "So, they simply put on this show that he can keep on hiding. That's clever, if also a bit nasty. But then, no more so than anything he did elsewhere. And yet, he seemed upset over it."

"He's the last of his kind, and not worth them travelling all this way simply to finish it…or at least this is the impression they are trying to give."

"To break him, I suppose. And he did appear broken on this occasion."

"Yes, he did."

"And Sargeras? He would not want to share this with him? This would represent something of a noteworthy result, win or lose."

"Agreed, and that runs against what I might otherwise expect of him, unless there is something we're missing about those two."

+‧+‧+◆+‧+‧+

"Captain, I have your result from Central," the spy states as she returns from her run.

"Good," Kaliya nods. "I've been waiting for you. What did Darumon do?"

"Well, I have some good news, some bad news, and some very strange news."

"Already it sounds like trouble."

"Not really, it's actually working in our favor. The good news is we have three shiny new military ships to play with."

"All right, I suppose I can agree with that. Next?"

"The bad news is the Marshal is a sad little puppy for losing them," she affirms woefully.

"Well now, if he feels so badly about it, maybe we should just go up and apologize, and give him back the keys."

The room erupts in a hearty round of laughter.

"But overall, what did he do?" Kaliya inquires.

"Here is where we have the strange news. It's a positive result for our efforts, but it is also noteworthy for the implications, just as the Commander and his Captain were taking notice of on the other side."

"Those two make a good team together. What happened?"

"He behaved mostly as we had hoped. We definitely put the fear of god into him, or maybe several gods, the way he reacted. You'll probably want to review the video when we get back. He's cancelling all future forays into this space. He seemed frightened, skittish, and he even looked out the window briefly as if he were expecting to see fire and brimstone to rain down on top of him."

"Wow, that's not bad."

"Yeah, and then he went on to order up increased sector security, as if they needed any more, and demanded to be informed if anything should show up at all, and suggesting they should essentially lay low for a while."

"Very nice. This should keep him in his place, at least for now."

"But now, we have the strange part, and both the Commander and his Captain took notice of it. He started talking to himself, asking if he wanted to tell Sargeras about this, but then decided against it, since the poor guy was sleeping and he didn't want to disturb him with anything really, really bad."

"Huh?" Kaliya blurts impulsively. "He's keeping this to himself, as if to keep it a secret? Dear cu'Nar, Darumon is Sargeras's right hand man, loyal to the end of time, and he's keeping a secret from him?"

"Curious," Ayene muses. "I wonder what other secrets he's been keeping."

"But that's not all," the spy continues. "He was also speaking about that message of yours. Solitary iteration. This must've hit something deep inside, and it hurt. Everyone took notice of it. He was sad, despondent, even disappointed. They're not interested in chasing him because, as he said to himself in there, he's simply not worth it...as if it could be any surprise by now."

"These are his words?"

"Yeah. Geilv and his Captain both suggested this broke something inside."

Chapter 7

A HIDDEN CONSPIRACY

"Broke something?" Thaelyn muses inquisitively.

"This is not something I would've expected out of him," Kailen suggests.

"My spy overheard Commander Geilv and Captain Ta'yeen also mentioning this." Kaliya recalls. "And in fact, we're retrieving that spy-cam footage even now for a better review."

"Then that message must have hit a tender spot," Thaelyn considers. "And by your observations, I suppose this should be expected. After all, they are the last of their kind, and this ought to leave a mark."

"But could he actually be keeping secrets from his own master?" the General wonders. "Incredible!"

"At this moment," Thaelyn considers. "I am forced to reflect upon Adalon's prophecies. That one towards the beginning, where the master sleeps and his servant, meaning Darumon, is the one who is most active. Darumon is working a plan, and likely as his own form of revenge attack in his master's honor."

"Like a good little servant would," Kaliya notes.

"Yes, I feel this may be the case. If we interpret this line in such a manner, then everything he did was his own work. Surely, Sargeras would not have commissioned him to artificially evolve the old Eracyodines into this new breed. Sargeras would probably foresee the possible outcome and forbid it. But in his absence, Darumon was left to make his own decisions, and hope he could contain the outcome using whatever control mechanisms he could muster."

"Like his seeds and the chips."

"Indeed, where in the absence of the dynamistic flows, he would need a more conventional means of taking personal management of his creation once those early children began to appear. Furthermore, I find it unlikely Sargeras, in his present condition, would sanction any form of attack on the Estelar for the simple reason of the imbalance of power, with or without the use of that weapon. Even the Estelar would shy away from the production of that material for any reason."

"But if he's desperate..." she proposes.

"Yes, desperation can certainly drive many irrational acts, and especially if you are in such a position as the last of your kind. What else do you have to lose at that point?"

"Darumon has been associated as a terrorist on many occasions during this time, and he's making a lot of risky decisions along the way, like the attack on Sigil."

"I cannot pretend to know the mind of a Primordial, but I think even one such as he would know better than that, and surely Sargeras. Even with that weapon, and even with a terrorist tactic, desperate or not, it is still highly prone to discovery and the associated repercussions."

"Then how do we explain his actions here," Kailen wonders. "Desperation... Last of a kind... This would be nearly suicidal under those conditions. And then to keep it a secret that not only did he fail, but that he might have exposed himself to his old enemies, and not just once, but twice."

"Could it simply be to avoid getting in trouble with his master?" the General offers.

"Oh yes!" Ayene snickers. "This wouldn't go over well if he were ever to find out. I don't know if we could use the term, 'horns will fly', but something would certainly go into the stratosphere."

"Indeed, it would," Thaelyn affirms. "For instance, in the Outer Planes, the servants of the Estelar can sometimes make an error...even the Estelar themselves, though it is extremely rare. After all, they are still people, and people can make mistakes on occasion, regardless of their station in life. But the Estelar tend to be rather forgiving of their servants, especially if you factor in the Measure of Balance, which is largely about a learning experience."

"Ah, but of course."

"And this might hold a clue for us. If we consider how the Primordials treat lesser lifeforms, where Darumon may also be included as a servant, and yet he is likely held in much higher esteem than most, he may still wish to appear infallible, if only to prevent any punitive action for his mistakes. And I would expect this to be a grand one."

"What about this," Kaliya wonders. "Desperation…maybe, but what if there is another factor involved here? They're alone, the last of their kind, and spending the remainder of eternity hiding under a rock. I would think that simple desperation might also be compounded with a last gasp at trying something…anything."

"Yes, good, this can certainly be another driving factor, and therefore taking so many risks. He SHOULD know better, but this is overridden with the obvious alternative, which is essentially oblivion, one way or another, even if to remain hiding under that rock."

"Ouch!" Ayene winces. "That leaves a lot of possibilities for what he might try. But it might also give an explanation for his behavior with that message. Last of their kind, and simply not worthy of consideration by those who own the place. Hiding under a rock or otherwise, it's already an oblivion."

"Yes," Thaelyn nods tenderly. "And a small part of me must feel for the sensation."

"If this is the case," Kaliya submits. "Then, what about any other mistakes he may be covering up?"

"Like the Prodigy Gift?" Ayene wonders. "That would be a huge one, if you ask me."

"Yes, it would," Thaelyn affirms.

"All right, but then what are we saying here?" Kaliya ponders. "He creates us and hopes to use us as part of his revenge attack. But is he doing it as a service to his master? Did Sargeras at one time suggest this course of action? Or did Darumon choose this for himself, and when he makes a mistake, he wants to cover it up along the way."

"This is a curious statement. Did, perhaps, the two of them plan this from the beginning, or is Darumon taking a unilateral approach to serve his master in some way?"

"To serve his master…" Kailen reflects. "To attack and destroy some part of the Estelar, particularly those who started the whole thing with that last battle…and also to free the others in that prison… Oh, that would be a service, all right! It would also solve that 'last of a kind' business, at least partially."

"Ah, yes," the General adds. "And this might ultimately lead to restoring Sargeras and the other Primordials to power. Recall what he said once in that spy recording from young Leesa at the Governor's office. They were in decline, and he apparently feels pain for their loss. Such as this would represent a fine service to restore their former prestige."

"And all with Darumon to thank for it," Kaliya concludes. "A great gift to his most beloved master..."

"Yes, a gift," Kailen asserts. "To earn favor as his loyal and faithful servant who can do no wrong. Furthermore, to present him with such a gift as restoring the old ways of the Primordials. Dear cu'Nar, can you imagine what sort of favor he might earn for this?"

"A considerable amount, to be sure," Thaelyn agrees. "It might even elevate him to a new level of prestige. And so, when we see him making a mistake, he would surely not wish to reveal it openly. Perhaps he will simply cover it up and wait for another day to try again."

"So..." Kaliya grins. "What would happen if we made a little more trouble for him?"

"More trouble?" Thaelyn raises his brow. "As if you are not doing enough already?"

"Well, what I mean is, we still have this issue of the Prodigy Gift. And for this, we have Ytani out there with the potential to make a little noise."

"And this little noise will carry some big repercussions," Ayene finishes.

✦✦◆✦✦

"I am astonished at this story of yours, Captain," the Director relents. "Thunder and lightning, sounds of explosions...is there anything you can NOT do with this talent?"

"So far," Kaliya offers. "I don't know how to answer that. We do have a few limitations, but most of these are mechanical when interacting with certain items, or each other. Everything else is simply a manifestation of the mind."

"And to think of what that mind might be capable of."

"Yeah," Azina sighs. "And then to think I was once laughing at the whole idea. I'm really sorry about that now. So, where does this leave us?"

"We have new instructions for you," Kaliya notes, "which will carry us for now, and then we're waiting on a few things back home before we can take this to the next step. One of these is a test flight of a new combat fighter."

"A combat fighter? But, um…are you actually going to war with someone, or…"

"We need to make a showing in your skies, and it has to appear real in the eyes of any interested parties, meaning to say Darumon, your military, and all those people out there who never saw anything during their lifetimes. You can't do that with a projection."

"Oh great! And does this relate in any way to Ayene telling us about this raid siren network she has underway?"

"Actually, yes…" Ayene replies. "Even though we're building up the image of the Marshal's insurgents being so impotent that they can't even find us a second time to launch a proper attack, we still have Ytani out there with his god complex. It will be during this general moment in time when we're going to expose another of the Marshal's little secrets and major foul-ups."

"Wow, you people seem to be having a lot of fun with this."

"By the way, Captain," the Director recalls. "I think we should be aware of our timing for your final play versus when we can achieve full coverage of our population for this drug. According to Ayene, she thinks you can use this raid siren network to, um, encourage them to take it on demand. But we need to be sure everyone has something to take."

"Right, and I know Commander Kriv'tik is putting the crew of the Tul'ryk to work on a new project building a series of large, specialized farming enclosures to bump up the production of that fungus. But it might not be in full operation until later this year. However, once it goes online, we should have a much more reliable flow coming in. This will help a lot. Then it's just a matter of having it ready. But if I understand the timing of this thing, you need to apply it just before it hits, so how much time do we have with a single application?"

"When we apply it for the seed removal," Azina mentions. "We're using a treatment plan to cover the final few days. But if we're talking about a preventative before Sargeras goes down, I could make the usage simple enough, if to package it like a pill, or maybe an oversized chewable tablet. But for this, we need to consider potency and maybe also a time-release quality to calibrate the duration. Nevertheless, I think they would still need to take it very soon before he goes down, just to be sure."

"Then, what I'm hearing in all this," Ayene accedes, "is the biggest problem being the delivery and distribution of the drug for universal coverage. If we can accomplish that, the next issue is telling them when to use it, so we'll need to include that in the raid siren broadcast. That should be easy enough, if we somehow advertise an imperative need for it to be kept on hand for a special emergency. That'll get their tails in motion. The Marshal did this for everything else he pushed at us, so we'll take a lesson from him and turn it around."

"All right," Kaliya nods. "So, we have our final attack, like a raid of Ytani's unknown friends, and this invokes a worldwide scramble alert. Ooh, yes, I like where this is going now. The alert tells them it's time to take their medicine just before they go into the shelters. This also gets them off the streets to prevent any collateral damage from either Darumon or Sargeras taking out their anger on anyone."

"You know," Azina winces. "I'm not sure who is worse; Darumon, or the two of you."

✦✦✦

It has been several months by now since medical staff members everywhere were being processed for their seed entities, and many of them were now moving around the streets in this altered condition. At first, they were few and far between amongst the public masses, and did not cause as much concern amongst the other citizens, where many of them didn't pay close enough attention to each other to begin with. Initially, for those who did take that passing notice, these people were presumed to belong to the younger generation, not yet come of age for implantation.

However, the application of the new filter masks did cause a few heads to turn. Some questions began to arise, but initially, so as not to draw too much immediate attention, the explanations were kept casual, relating to the pollution for those without the seeds. But soon after was the discovery that, in addition to this, the cranial interfaces were showing up absent. This began to invoke a considerable amount of interest. Those were another mandate entirely, and ever since childhood. Eventually, as these occurrences began to increase in frequency, it was starting to get out that the seeds were coming off, and the chips were being removed.

Ayene was visiting the ACI building to speak with Kita after she finished her procedure.

"Kita? How do you feel today?"

"Much better, thanks. That was scary. Those last few days, I felt like something bad was about to happen…and it did."

"Fortunately, you have the ARC watching over you. I was actually the first one to take this procedure, and that was with the Daanen-

Aryku. We weren't expecting such a severe feedback hit, and it put me into a coma. Fortunately, they pulled me out, and I'm much better now."

"Wow, I didn't get hit that hard, but it was still frightening when it happened. And when I got home again, I took a good look at myself, expecting to see all sorts of scars and blemishes on me. They said they had to use a lot of tissue restoration to patch up the holes, but overall, it doesn't seem so bad."

"Same here," Ayene affirms. "Let's hope we're the last ones ever to see that horrid thing used again. And if that monster should even try it, I'll give him a little piece of my own."

"I haven't told my boyfriend yet, or my family. I'm wondering what they'll say the next time we meet," she giggles softly.

"As for your boyfriend…hmm. Do you ever wear anything sexy for him?" she grins playfully.

"I do, sometimes," she smiles.

"Well then, have him make a visit and then casually saunter around your apartment as if everything is normal and see how he reacts. I think you shouldn't have any trouble after that."

"Oh! You! But that's a really great idea," she snickers.

"As for the rest, we'll be releasing an official notice in the news once we achieve a critical threshold with the emergency services. That should help cover for you. Beyond that, just go easy on them. I had to do the same with my parents. But in my case, I had a complication with the chip. They were a bit skittish on that part since I was known to be displaying those Tav'ageen symptoms as a child."

"Uh oh… How did you handle that?"

"I had to tell them what it actually is, so they wouldn't lose their next year's supply of horns," she smiles.

"That wouldn't be much fun," Kita chuckles. "But now that I'm free of it, I was thinking of that language class you mentioned. Do you think it might be possible to get into one?"

"Actually, now would be a good time for it. We have those people from the Tul'ryk, some of whom are soon to enroll in a course, so you could join up with them."

"Good. Then, I'd like to have some time off so I can do this. I'll also need transportation."

"Of course, I'll see about getting someone assigned to assist you, and maybe we can involve a few others around here as well."

Inside CPU, the end of the school year was approaching soon, and the graduating class was gearing up for its final exams. Many of the students were anxious to find careers for themselves, while others were deep in contemplation of other matters. Among these were two young ladies meeting in the local cafeteria during a break.

Latena and Auryn were both taking time for a quick snack. Each had arrived separately, and Auryn was just returning from the food bar when she saw her friend sitting at a table. So she strolls over to say hello.

"Latena? I did not see you at the meeting earlier. Is something wrong? You hardly ever miss an occasion."

The girl circles around the table to sit down. She studies her friend's glum expression, or at least as much of an expression as might be possible for the debilitating effect of the Suppressor chip.

"You look depressed today. What is wrong?"

"I am, and you should be too, Auryn. We graduate in just three months, and this next month I need to go in for my preparatory appointment."

"Oh, that…" she grimaces. "Yes. Ugh…" she gestures a gag. "I hate that one most of all. It has not left my mind, not since that talk we had a while back with the news reports, and that 'alleged' research someone is promising. But I really do not see any point in reminding myself, as there is really no alternative."

"No alternative!" Latena blasts mutedly. "Someone finally starts questioning that godlike Council with their oversized horns, and they even go so far as revealing some super-secret genetic code no one was probably ever supposed to know about. Then you have this report about a private firm breaking it open and this research that is supposed to do something. Right. Have you heard anything new since then? It seems the news is quieting down more than anything else."

"Just like you said. Yeah, I know, Latena, and so I do not see a point in fighting it. They clearly hold all the authority, and I think little people like us do not stand much of a chance."

"Is this your religion talking? Simply sit back and allow your horns to droop while those people continue to destroy what is left of our world?"

"Well, now, just a moment, Latena. We should remind ourselves of that industry out there and those court cases. That actually did succeed in something. The old war protocols were cancelled, and I hear there are actions being taken on the industry. Some of it is being shut down, others are being retooled."

"Yeah, you are right. I saw that too. All right, maybe I should take back a few of my words. But it does not change the fact that once my appointment comes due, that will be the end of it. The industry I can understand. That stuff is simply nasty, and I think even the power-hungry military, or whoever is behind all this, would probably want that cleaned up after a while. I mean, who would want to breathe this stuff all their life?"

"Yeah, I would agree on this much. But a little piece of me is holding out hope that whoever discovered that secret file is also watching their tail enough to know who made it in the first place, and whether they might want to keep it where it is."

"Oh, Auryn, that really DOES sound like your religion talking. Take it on faith that someone is out there trying to bring down the Big Horns."

Latena attempts a soft smile through her distress while hoping not to invoke a feedback hit from her chip. She glances around the room at the other students passing by before returning to the conversation.

"It still puzzles me why they would want us to have those seeds in the first place. It was supposed to be for that big evacuation, which no one ever did. I swear to you, Auryn, that much had to be a hoax. If the Marshal was able to give us this chip as a solution to the Tav'ageen thing, why did he encourage the Council to apply this big emergency drive for an evacuation?"

"And therefore the seeds?" she wonders.

"Yes! We have the Saakerav station up there in the vacuum of space, and I know from all my other studies that we were capable of colonizing something from long before HE ever showed his horns."

"Do we want to involve the Scare in this equation, or leave it out?"

"I say leave it out. How long does it take to load up a cargo vessel with a colony pack, and compare that to how long it takes to find a place to deliver it? Now ask yourself about infecting a world population with these horrid seeds no one ever wanted OR used according to specs. And by the way, even after all this time, WITH the chip solving our problems, just like those reports were hinting at."

"Yeah, hinting at!" Auryn nods. "You know, Latena, if I did not know better, I would say you are not the only conspiracy theorist around here."

"I…well…but will it ever actually amount to anything? Auryn, how long has it been overall? Even if there were others out there, they must not have been very successful in drawing attention."

"I would say the same unless we are speaking of something recent. Those news sensations were all recent, and for all this duration, they came fast and furious, like something new happened out there."

"Yeah, and then…pbbt," she animates. "It all goes quiet, nearly as suddenly as it started."

"And you think those power-hungry people finally clamped down on it?"

"It had to be. For instance, that scene at the Grand Hall, I think it was too coincidental. Someone starts arguing about the Council being in this long deliberation, as if no one took notice of this earlier…"

"Actually, I was listening to some people talking not long ago when I was with my family at a local restaurant, and they apparently did NOT notice it."

"Auryn, how can you NOT notice the Council absent from any of their assigned duties?"

"When your horns are so badly turned down from all this boring news filling you with the same stories every day. Also, I think a lot of people simply do not care anymore. During most of their lives, nothing ever happens, so they stop paying attention since it is always the same story."

"Oh wonderful, that makes my day. And it simply exasperates the situation. This is perfect, Auryn. If you want to turn people's horns down, fill them with so much boring, repetitive detail that they stop asking questions."

"That is for sure!"

"Anyway, then you have that guy, the Internal Secretary. He was a work of art! I am truly wondering how anything gets done around here with people like HIM in office!" she shakes her head. "But you know, I think he was a plant."

"You mentioned this once before. But the Internal Secretary?"

"Yeah, and would you like to know why? You will love this one, Auryn."

"All right, sure. What new scandal do you want to throw at me this time?"

"I did a bit of research on him since that time. The real one, and I will use this term for now, as opposed to that one we saw on the news."

"All right."

"He had been in office for a long time, more than a century. This is surely long enough that if you have a secret, you know how to keep it. But this guy, I swear to you, Auryn… He intentionally led Ileani on a road to an information leak. I see words, Auryn, you know this. And I saw a series of words he dropped in front of her that she picked up on to ask about. In fact, I am almost wondering if she was in on it from the start."

"Ileani? Are you thinking she could be part of a conspiracy to intentionally leak these sensations?"

"It is always HER releasing these stories, so unless you want to tell me she got lucky on the news bulletins, then I might say she is on the inside of something, maybe because she is a big name in the business."

"Oh wow, but that would make sense."

"As for that guy, first he pointed out this ONE Council was in this deliberation for so long, and then he hummed and hawed, until she poked him for more, like when they first got elected. This led to that RE-election bit, and ultimately to the point dating back to the beginning. That is a sequence of leaks, Auryn, but built up in such a way that it might look accidental, as if from a guy who might be totally raw in his position and does not know how to keep a critical secret."

"Oh, Latena, you should bring this to the group. They would love to hear this one."

"Right, and then, not long after that, boom, there goes the Grand Hall roof. And then another leak. It had to be, Auryn. Here we have Ileani, AGAIN, live on the scene. Live, Auryn, I think this is a clue. If it were recorded, it could be altered, maybe even covered up. But you cannot stop a live broadcast."

"Ooh! Yes, you have a good point. And this is where she is making so many of the really big sensations."

"And then we have that one C.P. Security officer, which I am wondering about. Who was she, and was she REALLY C.P. Security? But she comes running up, right in front of the camera, which so conveniently turns to listen in, and there you go with the missing Council, the leak of the millennium!"

"I think I would have to agree. This played out almost like it was staged. And this then leads us to the other stuff, like those elections again, the Marshal's excuse of this deliberation, and the longevity drug, in case no one was paying attention to how old they were in there. You know, Latena, this does actually build up a picture of someone working out there to expose a series of conspiracies."

"Yeah, it does…but who," she muses thoughtfully. "They must know something, and they are leaking it to the rest of us. But it seems to have gone quiet for a while. What does THAT mean. Were they caught? Or are they simply out of ammunition now that the Council is exposed? But Auryn, that roof. That was WAY to coincidental to be an accident."

"Yeah. When you add up the other pieces, it could have been staged."

"How long does it take for a building to collapse, Auryn, if you do not maintain it properly? Now, maybe we can say the construction was exceptional, and I heard one report relating to the doors being closed and locked during this full time, so I think we can say it was very nearly hermetically sealed…nearly, but not perfect."

"Right, I think we can say this much. Therefore, it might take a very long time before any significant amount of decay builds up, like from moisture and such, before it reaches a point where it actually does collapse."

"Yeah, and this was not long after that leak of the elections. In all this long history, no one says anything, and then boom, and boom again. I think someone knew the Council was gone, then maybe sabotaged whatever was left of that roof, and let it go. And that C.P. Security officer, I am willing to bet she was working for them, maybe someone in disguise. That Captain…hmm. I need to review that clip again, but he behaved almost as if he was acting a role with her."

"Acting!" Auryn blasts. "But hold on, Latena. This is C.P. Security, or at least it appeared that way. If we say they were REAL C.P. Security, that means we have a law enforcement element out there doing something. But doing it secretly with a lot of 'accidental' leaks. So, who are they hiding from?"

"The power-hungry element, no doubt. Auryn, maybe you were right, they do know how to watch their tails, but went silent maybe as a cover to let things soften a bit. Too much at one time can expose you."

"Yes, I would agree."

✦✦✦✦✦

"Sir, I'm ready," Marelle shouts as she enters the training center at the BRC.

"Ah, Marelle," the flight instructor responds. "How are your skills at using rune stones coming along?"

"Progressing well. I'm five months into my class and I've been putting in extra time on the weekends to practice marking and conjuring portals. My instructor tells me I should be ready for this by now."

"Very good. The ship is ready for you out on the pad. This is our full prototype, except for the software upgrades for the nav linking function and the arcanic Harvester unit. They're still working at miniaturizing that to fit."

"That new software feature sounds interesting. I'm trying to imagine it, linking multiple ships into a flight formation, all synchronized to follow the leader."

"It's necessary for the way we're handling the jump drive, and it can also be useful for attack runs and other functions."

"I can't wait to try it out, except that I need a team."

"Don't worry, Marelle, we have other pilots training up alongside you. The biggest challenge right now is testing our equipment and building a fleet of them, but we're moving forward nicely enough on that already."

"So, what's the plan for today?"

"Right, now listen up. We've already sent out several other pilots to conduct cartography runs. We've mapped the full Tae'Eladaran star system by now, including all the planets in their orbits, their moons, and anything else of interest out there...which isn't much, as it turns out."

"Isn't much? What do you mean?"

"Usually when we investigate a new star system, we see a lot of general debris, like asteroids, comets, and such. But not this one, it's virtually barren. According to our information of how it was formed, since this universe once belonged to the Primordials, they probably created everything with only those pieces they wanted."

"Maybe so, and then we have the Shell out there."

"Yeah, and then there's the Shell. In the cu'Nar's Name, I've never seen anything like that before, and not just for what it's made of, but the sheer size of it!"

"Did you run a scan on it trying to figure it out?"

"We sent someone out there during one of our mapping runs to take a closer look at it, but the scans still need analyzing. It appears to be some form of synthetic material, similar in nature to a crystalline latticework, but the composition almost seems...well, unnatural...abnormal."

"Oh! Abnormal, is it? A little like those people on Azgarén with all their Abnormal this and that?"

"Yeah," he chuckles ironically. "And likely the same kind of Abnormal, creating something that appears as a solid barrier. And what's even more bizarre, our scans are picking up some sort of nanotech droids moving through it. We think they probably maintain it over time, which would make sense for the apparent age of the structure."

"Wow, so now we know a little bit more about ourselves and our home."

"That's right! We're all taking small steps towards a new future. But now, you need to take a few steps of your own, and they won't be so small, Lieutenant. This is the one we've been waiting for. Today, you'll be testing the final few important systems on your craft, and along the way, begin marking our jump points to the other home worlds."

Marelle forms a wide grin as she anticipates the fantastic new journeys she'll be pioneering.

"Yes Sir, I'm ready."

They step outside and stroll over to her ship, which had undergone a few renovations since the last time to accommodate the new technology. It had a larger reactor than previously, and an arcanic inductor to gather up from the local environment. It had winglike projections on the sides, but sweeping forward with a crescent curve, befitting an elven architectural design. But these were not for any aerodynamic purpose, as they did not function using those principles. They were largely for appearance, and to serve as mounting points for the engine nacelles, which were an upgrade from the previous versions, and a set of weapons mounted at the points. It looked like a real combat craft this time, ready for action, graceful but deadly to anything that got in its way.

"These weapons you see here," the instructor gestures at the devices, "are linked to your conjuring orbs inside. We've already briefed you on the activation sequence, but you'll need some practice to get a good feel for it. The power discharge is relative to your perception, so the bigger the target, the bigger you need to think for the output levels, at least up to a certain cap."

"That sounds tricky. It'll definitely need some practice, and on a variety of targets of different sizes."

"Correct, but so far, we only have a series of drones ready for you to try. Unfortunately, we don't have any of that really big, and subsequently very dirty industry Darumon was using to build anything larger," he chuckles. "So you may just have to play with it if you ever go into actual battle. My suggestion, from what I understand of it, is to take it in steps until you find a happy medium."

"Good point."

"Next is the jump drive. It works very similarly to what you should already be familiar with from your mage studies. There is a conjuring orb on the front console next to the nav computer. The nav computer is like what you trained with on the simulator. Normally, you would select your destination from a list or enter a series of coordinates calculated from your current position. But so far, it's just the list. The coordinate system isn't functional yet until we can improve the tech some more. And, in fact, some of our people are still scratching their tails over how we might apply that."

"You think your traditional methods wouldn't work?"

"Not as likely here. But cu'Nar's grace, Marelle..." he shakes his head. "I was listening to some talk earlier between several of those gnomish technicians. They were speaking of something called a Seer's Pool and how it can peer into remote locations, and then some of the old mages who might use this to conceptualize a destination in order to assign a portal outlet. Ugh. That simply hurts."

"I know, but I've also heard of this from some of my history classes. That would probably rip those horns of yours right off," she giggles.

"Yeah. Then, the rest is magic, as they say. You conjure up your energies into the orb and it channels into the rift generator."

"Is there any possibility of me getting lost out there?"

"All things considered, I can't really see how you can get lost, at least not permanently. So long as you have at least one valid jump point recorded, you should be able to return back to it."

"All right, is there anything else?"

"At this time, I think that's all."

Marelle offers a salute, and then climbs into her new ship, settling herself into her seat and strapping in. She dons her helmet and secures it, making sure the environment seal is tight, then closes the hatch and powers up.

The instructor returns back to the control booth and takes up a seat by the monitors. He calls her up on the com-link.

"You will notice, if you examine your nav computer, there are several destination endpoints already recorded. These are actually temporary, for safety reasons. Like I said, for as long as you have at least one in there, you have a way home."

"Where do they go?"

"They were recorded previously using drones marking points on each of our home worlds. Here on Tae'Eladar, on Therinë, on Ruuki uy'Daan, and on Morndindor. But the drones were only airborne, not in space. Your objective is to jump to those locations and reposition yourself outside the planetary sphere for an official marking. This will become our waypoint for later travel."

"Acknowledged, Sir, and the combat drones? Where are they right now?"

"Over our heads... There are six, some in stationary orbit, and others moving at random. Your objective there is simply to shoot them down. We want you to use both firing modes, the blaster and the EMP. I'll be watching from here. We'll have you perform this first, then proceed to the jump drive."

"Got it, ready on deck..."

"You have permission to depart. Good luck, Lieutenant."

Marelle positions herself with the controls, orienting her hands over the holographic sensors, with her palms resting on the conjuring orbs. She gradually runs a finger up the strafing cross, bringing herself off the ground to a comfortable height, then applying thrust and direction to glide away from the field.

She had become much more confident in her skills by this time, and the ship responded promptly to her control. She took it up swiftly through the layers of atmosphere and finally into low orbit, where she activated her targeting scanners to locate her prey.

In the distance, the scanners detected several objects marked by identifier signals. Some seemed stationary while others were in motion.

"Sir, I have targets on my scope. Requesting permission to engage."

"Permission granted, Lieutenant. Engage at will."

She moderates her cruising speed, pacing her approach as she closes in while selecting her first target. In this case, she chose one of the stationary units, judging it carefully for its general size, and considering the EMP firing mode first. She tracked her target with her eyes while focusing her mind into the conjuring orbs, treating them as a part of her body, and spoke her first sequence of invocation words.

Outside the ship, the guns fired their first official shot at a live target, even though it was only a test drone. The twin orbs of electrical discharge rocketed out along a directed path to their mark, and Marelle veered off to find her next victim. The shot made impact in a spray of static bolts.

The instructor was monitoring the drones from the ground, when one of his displays suddenly spiked and went dead.

"Nice shot, Lieutenant. Which one was that?"

"That was EMP, Sir. How does it look on your side?"

"From this side, it all looks basically the same…dead. The only real difference is the target simply being disabled or splattered halfway across the sector."

"Well, this one is just sitting there for now, wondering which way it wants to go next. I hope it doesn't fall on someone's house."

"These are too small for that. They'll burn up long before they reach the ground."

"Right, coming up on the next one…"

She sights her next target, another stationary unit, choosing this one for the convenience of proximity. She charges up again, this time using just one conjuring orb, to test their functioning independent from each other.

A single shot flies out and strikes the target using the blaster mode. The drone explodes in a bright display of fire and small debris.

She turns to find her next target, locating one that's making a sweep across in front of her, then turning and sweeping back again.

"Clever little guy, he thinks he can outwit me," she mutters devilishly.

She takes up pursuit of her latest opponent as it makes another pass, sighting it in her scope and directing her thoughts at the virtual object the blip represents.

"You think you can escape? We'll just see about that."

She loaded up an EMP charge on one orb and let it go. The projectile launches out, tracking her quarry as it moved along, then making impact and knocking it off course into a wild trajectory back into the atmosphere.

"Bye-bye little fella, see you on the other side."

Marelle was enjoying herself. She felt the power to dominate the skies. She decided to try another trick, considering multiple targets at once. Each gun could fire independently, based on her ability to focus on the different targets and conjure from either orb. She located another two, both of them in motion making zigzags.

She made her approach, diving between them and sweeping first to one side and launching a shot, then making a quick return to fire at the second one. The two shots zipped away in different directions, each making a solid hit and blasting their targets to dust.

"Lieutenant," ushers the voice on the com-link. "Did you just make two at once, or are my screens showing a malfunction?"

"Sir, these little guys don't stand a chance up here. I can use these orbs independently on different targets and in close succession."

"Dear cu'Nar, Lieutenant, I'm very happy you're on our side."

Lastly, she spies the final mark, one more stationary drone.

"This makes six, I believe. I'm almost sad to see him go…or maybe not."

She fires off one more EMP and watches as the pulse makes a solid strike.

"Sir, I believe that's all of them."

"Very good, Lieutenant, I'm showing all targets are dead…some more than others I would imagine," he chuckles. "Now, for your next objective, we are going to assign your jump markers. For this, since we want to establish safe zones for our future transit, we do not want them to be in line with any other bodies that might be moving around out there…like a planet, for instance."

"Yes Sir, that wouldn't make for a very lovely return home. Where do you suggest?"

"Traditionally, we would make these outside the orbital plane, either above or below, and often at the edge of a star system. But for our purpose, since we're using these small vessels, we'll mark it just outside the normal orbital ring of the local planet. I would advise moving above the plane and away from the planet and its moon to keep outside of anything that could get in the way."

"Affirmative, I'm on my way."

She turns away from the planet and hits the throttle again, switching her nav computer to show a 3D tactical chart of the Tae'Eladaran star system, which diagrams the planetary orbits and their associated moons. She marks a destination waypoint on the screen and orients outward and above the orbital plane of Tae'Eladar, continuing along until she reaches a point beyond the normal orbital path of its moon. When she arrives, she reorients to look back at the planet.

"Sir, I am in position. This looks like a good spot. Any special instructions before I begin?"

"According to my sources, meaning those people who designed this thing, you must select a reference point for your marking perspective. Ordinarily, when we calculate our indexing schemes using our old technology, we base it on the star itself, rather than any one particular planet. Our nav computers will then make further calculations for the planets, assuming we have any special desire to arrive there, but this is secondary to the star. Therefore, we are suggesting you select the star as your focal point. We'll worry about where the planet is in its orbit at another time."

"Got it. Using the star as my perception target."

Marelle sights her gaze on the local star. Her visor automatically polarizes to shield her eyes from the glare. She visualizes her perspective relative to the star and other bodies, including distance and orientation. She reaches up to the nav console and punches up the configuration for marking a jump point, then lays her hand on the conjuring orb and makes ready to begin her chant.

The ship's arcanic induction coils charge up and the energies gather in the storage capacitors. The status indicator rises to show the charge progression until it peaks, and an alert beep sounds off. Now it was time, and she began her chant.

She directs her energies into the orb while keeping her eyes on her focus and her mind subtly aware of her relative location in space. She recalled the planets, their moons, the star, and the planar Shell surrounding them, all as part of her perspective, and as her chanting came to its climax, the ship began to glow.

The vessel wrapped itself in a bright aura which erupted into a spiraling vortex, rapidly stretching outward on the horizontal plane of the ship, and then collapsing back again with one final flash before settling. An acknowledgement beep sounds off on the console and the nav screen shows the new marker highlighted.

Marelle held fast as her eyes tried to recover from the brilliant display which seemed to permeate the full ship. The vessel's small size allowed the energies to completely overcome her. She shakes her head, trying to bring her senses back in order.

"Wow, that was a new one."

"Are you alright, Lieutenant? I show a successful operation."

"Yes Sir. It's just that the flash was a little unexpected, but it would seem I have what I came for."

"You're the first person to perform this operation, so we really didn't know what to expect with an actual pilot inside."

"Gee, thanks for the heads-up on that," she chuckles. "Now what, do we go to the next mark? Perhaps we should test this to make sure it works."

"Good idea. Move away to another point in space and try jumping to your recent mark."

"I'm on it."

She takes off once again, this time setting a waypoint marker on her nav screen and allowing the autopilot to carry the distance. She zips across to the opposite side of the planet, which placed her at a respectable distance from her previous location, then turns again and looks back.

"I am at my new location, now initiating my jump sequence."

She enters her nav computer and displays her latest mark, which so far has only been identified by a default ID and time stamp. She selects the line entry and engages the sequence. Once again, a status indicator displays the charging process. She studied the numbers.

"Ten…twenty…thirty…" she reads softly to herself.

She held her hand on the orb, ready to invoke the arcanic energy dump into the drive system.

"Forty…fifty…sixty…"

Her tensions built with the rising numbers. She had to force herself to remain calm.

"Seventy…eighty…ninety…"

Now was her time, she had to begin the chant to start cycling the flows into the jump nacelles. As before, her conjuration invoked the ship to begin glowing, and as she finished, the ship was consumed by a bright flash of light, sucking it away from the local space and into a portal rift.

The travel time, in this case, was negligible since the physical distance was so short. It was not even long enough for the initial flash to subside before she found herself reemerging back into real space, precisely where she was when she marked her jump point, including her physical orientation towards the star.

"Woohoo!" she squeals. "We are there!"

"Congratulations, Lieutenant. I must admit, I envy you a little. You are the first of your people to make this effort. This is truly a momentous occasion. You just made history."

"Thank you, Sir! It feels good. Now to get on to our other objectives. I still have a few other worlds to mark."

+ + ◆ + +

"Priestess Rumoren, I've got your new samples."

"Relissa, I've been waiting for you. What do we have today?"

"I've been running through that wood in the northwestern

mountains. Jiggers, it's hard work running that bit. I need to keep a strength chant on me just to stay on my feet."

"Yes, I know. I recall this from the time we were stationed there. That heavy gravity makes it hard on us. Tana has also made the run, but in her case, she seems to have a little more strength to manage it."

"I still wish she'd learn to wear a little more covering. That girl doesn't leave much for the boys to guess over."

"She is what she is, and she seems very comfortable with herself, so I will not argue…just as long as she maintains a dress code within reasonable measure."

Relissa was returning from a research expedition on Morndindor, where the Priestess and her team, which included druids, rangers, and several Daanen-Aryku, were conducting their ecological restoration research. The druids were slowly trying to evolve themselves from priests of nature to biologists and conservationists. And the elaborate facility they built on Ruuki uy'Daan, located west of the city, provided a comfortable environment in which to collect and process specimens.

The facility was huge, and still growing, as new wings were constructed in a continuing effort to collect and study the endangered species from Morndindor, as well as various species on Ruuki uy'Daan that also appeared to be in danger after so many years of overhunting by the orcs who once resided there.

It was an architectural curiosity due to the combined design concepts between the people of Tae'Eladar and the Daanen-Aryku. It was largely a brick and wood beam building with multiple floors and high ceilings, many windows and skylights, several large greenhouses and enclosed animal pens, plus office space and a number of research labs.

The animal habitats were designed to match their native environment, along with research stations to study their habits, and nurseries for the new offspring. In the greenhouses, they were collecting seeds and young plant shoots to nurture and develop for later transplantation, as well as to assist in furnishing the animal pens with bedding and food. Everything being collected was carefully sorted and cataloged, using technology donated by the Daanen-Aryku.

Relissa had been in training as an assistant to the Priestess, along with one of the young Daanen'kai girls named Tana Lar'akan, Navina's daughter, who was an aspiring druid. So far, they were assigned to make runs on Morndindor, and occasionally on Ruuki uy'Daan, collecting plant and animal specimens for new research. Relissa also had hopes of conducting work on Azgarén, once an opening was found, and combining that with her desire to join her friends in the final stages of the war.

"Relissa, I received a note for you from Rolsklinde. I put it in your box."

"Oh? I wonder what they want over there now."

She strolls over to an array of mailboxes, which were essentially a matrix of enclosed compartments mounted on a wall. The mail service functioned like any other, where the postal delivery was sorted and filed into the appropriate boxes. She opened her box and pulled out a letter, then found a chair for herself to relax in and read it.

"Looks like I'm invited to lunch with Kaliya and the gang," she mentions.

"That sounds nice. It's been a while since you've had time with your friends."

"Aye, but I have to wonder, is this just a nice little getaway, or does that oversized door-banger have something up her tail again?" she snickers.

✦✦✦✦✦

"Now wait, Latena," Halin asserts. "Are you saying this could be the work of an actual body out there conducting all these sensations?"

"Halin," she responds firmly. "Look at the pieces again. You have that Interior Secretary, who had to be a plant. The original guy would probably know better than to let something like this out. If the Council has been falsifying the elections since the beginning, and the Internal Secretary knew about it, which I think had to be the case if he was essentially covering it up all this time..."

"The current one, or all of them? It would have to be a continual thing, for all the changes of staff."

"Yes, that as well. Then, each new one had to be brought into it and given the same instructions. But this guy..." she shakes her head. "You know my rep for seeing words, right? He let it go piece by piece to Ileani, so she had to dig to finish it. It was intended to look accidental. What this tells me is she might be on the inside, and HE was a plant. So, whoever is on the outside is the enemy they are hiding from, and secretly trying to expose."

"But is it the Council itself, or something else? What about the secret code on that research file?"

"They say it was military, but you know, this could also lead to the Marshal. He built that military, and he also invented all this stuff."

"Uh oh…" moans another group member. "This brings us back to that one talk we had. Could he actually be wrong, and those insurgents out there are right?"

"And then, all his excuses," offers a third member.

"Yeah," Latena waves a finger. "This is where I am beginning to suspect these latest scandals. Someone started asking questions, and it had to follow a progression to where the REST of us would start asking them as well. Auryn told me a little while ago about something she overheard while out with her family; right, Auryn?"

"Yeah," she replies. "We were on a family outing, and I overheard some conversation. People stopped asking questions about these things a long time ago, in part because life is too boring around here for all the repetitive news broadcasts, and no real progress. So, they simply lost interest."

"Great!" Halin tosses his hands up. "And so…what? It falls to us who are still young enough to show a little enthusiasm?"

"Probably so, Halin," Latena nods. "That polluting industry was an obvious issue. But it was supported by those war protocols, which was ANOTHER obvious issue. But to get rid of one, you had to get rid of the other. So, it goes to the courts. This must mean whoever is in control, is NOT in control of our court system if they actually did the job."

"Yes, I think you have a point."

"Then, once you got rid of those protocols, it cleared the way for a cascade of other things, including this research. This might also suggest the researchers are not a part of it, and outside the control circle. We have that leak about the elections, meaning that guy, whoever he really was, had to be a plant to leak that critical detail. And not long after that, we have what I might call the leak of the millennium, the Grand Hall roof collapsing! And probably right on cue with Ileani covering it live, and with a C.P. Security officer, maybe a fake one in costume, running up almost into the camera telling us they're missing."

"And it had to look incidental," Auryn adds. "Because most likely, whoever is in this control circle is probably watching us. These people are likely trying to expose something he has been hiding from us during this time."

"And what this says," Latena surmises, "is the Council, for all of its deliberations, did not simply…forget…something. Assuming they are still alive after all this time, they probably ignored it completely and ran off with those secrets."

"You do not think that one about the longevity drug holds any merit?" Halin asks.

"I might have to agree with the medical faction. Real or not, this would be a functional product. Why not give it to us as a holdover to show they are actually doing something. Whatever ELSE they are deliberating; THIS one was an end product."

"I have to agree," the second member nods. "This much they could surely release openly if they had any such interest. They probably ran off with that, as well."

"Latena, a question," the third one wonders. "A fake security officer in a costume?"

"At the Grand Hall? My guess is yes. I reviewed that video again, and that CPS Captain out there, his posture and wording, looked like an act. He was real CPS, by the way. Captain Bein'talan of the East City Center Precinct. I looked him up. So, this tells me at least THEY, and likely the rest, are also in on it. This is starting to narrow our focus, and it is not our native government authority…at least not for whoever it is they are hiding from. If the Council is gone, dictatorship or otherwise, the active authority is something else."

"Active authority?!" Halin blasts. "Are you actually saying…"

"Halin, at the very least, I think we can say the Council is NOT actively doing any real government business. Not when you have all the science factions out there with their tails all crinkled up forming an emergency committee to fill in."

"She has a solid point there," the second member admits.

"Yes, she does," Halin nods. "And if these people know something, and they are actively hiding from it, it has to be whatever is actively controlling things. But Latena, this does make me ask one thing. If this active authority was so active and authoritative, it should also be in control of such things as the courts, CPS, and probably a lot more."

"Unless all these sensations are designed to break that," she offers. "Halin, if we ARE speaking of the Marshal, he is just one guy."

"And that military? We were thinking once they might be involved."

"Yes, we were. After all, he built it. But do you actually see them roaming the streets to set things back to normal?"

"Um, no, not yet…" he attempts a simulated chuckle. "With emphasis on the not YET aspect."

"All right, granted. But what if we have a secret movement occurring, and they are pulling together a variety of pieces that used to be under the authoritative control of this, um, we will call it a body, and revealing a series of these control mechanisms to the public as a means of exposing the truth?"

"Latena, the first thing to come to mind is why go through this very elaborate effort if they actually know who is on top and they want him, her, or it, out."

Latena paused to consider this opinion. It was certainly a valid perspective, but it needed reconciliation. And for this, she would need to gather up some of the myriad of elements they had seen pass across the vid-com screens in recent times.

"Him…" she muses softly. "His name. Yes. There must be a connection."

"Latena?"

"Halin, we were speaking that one time about the Marshal's insurgents, whoever they actually are, and in relation to Elder Nazég. That name has not been mentioned in the news, other than a reminder of who our military is supposed to be chasing halfway across the galaxy, and certainly not with any mention that he might hold a viable perspective on anything."

"Yes! So, what do you think about it?"

"There has to be a connection, and it is likely that we made a big mistake in not listening to him once. This is an effort to raise awareness in our population. Now, if you want to turn someone's opinion about anything, what do you do, but raise awareness over something no one previously considered before. But here we have the Marshal and the Council, both of whom were vilifying him during this time… badly. If the Council is crooked, the people need to be made aware of THIS. If the Marshal is in collaboration with them, we need to know about THAT too. But everyone believes the Council is our perfect government, and HE is our society's benefactor."

"Ouch, there go my horns," the third member complains.

"Yeah," Halin nods. "This does hold merit. If you simply go out there and start berating any of these people, you will likely get your tail chewed a few times for it. Everyone was hoping for that great wisdom that never arrived."

"Now," Latena continues. "If those insurgents want Sargeras and the Marshal so badly, they should have sent a massive military ship into our atmosphere, not whatever that thing was that took Elder Nazég away. And they probably would have had a much better chance at succeeding before the Marshal did whatever he did to our military that we are winning each time."

"Yes, that was a bad move and with no true logic to it."

"Next, if we reflect on that idea we had once, Elder Nazég knew something, and the rest wanted him out. What could he have known? Well, I think we need to reflect on what the Marshal did to us during this time, along with the Council. And coincidentally, what this movement seems to be UN-doing to us after those war protocols were cancelled."

"In all the nether-space, Latena!" Halin gasps. "But yes! He locked us up on our own world with a heavily polluted environment, empty promises of his wisdom, and this story of these insurgents. Have we become prisoners here?"

"Do not forget the seeds and the chips, and this comes back down to the Tav'ageen Anomaly. HE gave us the answers to that, and this is one of those statements on the news. NOW they are researching a way out of it, but they had to break that security thing first…with a military grade code attached to it. This must be HIS work. He did something to those things. The science community is up-in-arms at this 'violation of protocol' that should be reprimanded. This means, that lock should NOT have been there. Furthermore, we have all sorts of colonization tech no one ever bothered to think of, and instead that panic forced us to become infested with these parasites. What if that secret code was something he did to keep us bottled up using those seeds?"

"Oh please!" the second member groans. "I did not need to hear that. And I have an appointment coming up soon."

"So do I. In fact, I need to go in tomorrow for my preparatory exam…to which I think I am going to argue, if they are indeed trying to break the thing. But what if he took advantage of a situation, possibly made it worse, collaborated with the Council, maybe with the 'payment' of this wisdom they ran off with, and leaving the rest of us stuck in this perpetual war with insurgents that never stop? Now I am asking about those insurgents. Such a convenient excuse to keep us locked down…

as if we EVER had the opportunity to actually leave. You DO know the Council never let us colonize anything, right?"

"Yeah," Halin asserts. "But now, we will be graduating soon, so what do we do about any of this? Do we play like everyone else, turn our horns down and pretend the world is business as usual? If Latena is actually right, and we have someone else out there making noise, furthermore that they are hoping to drum up some form of awareness, I wonder if they need any help."

"Halin," the second member issues. "Help from a bunch of velvet horn university grads?"

"Well, we do have the enthusiasm to actually DO something, unlike what Auryn said of everyone else out there."

"All right, I suppose you have a point, but we are more likely speaking of some form of authority body. I doubt C.P. Security would recruit people like us to go out and tear down a corrupt government and chase off an alien being with his own designs."

"At the very least," Latena muses. "I would like to know who is doing all this. I wonder if we could contact someone, like C.P. Security, and ask. Surely, if they ARE trying to find support, a few extra bodies out there on the protest lines would not hurt."

"Maybe."

"It is such a shame, though," Auryn mourns. "Our sect, and so many others, were hoping this could lead us to find that higher mind that could actually grant us some form of enlightenment. It is such a shame how this one turned out to be such a tail-yanker."

"Auryn," Halin soothes. "I cannot pretend to understand your religion, but I think if one exists out there, we might find others one day. So, if it means anything, keep the faith."

"Thank you, Halin, that was very sweet. But you know, Latena might have something. What if our people could add a few numbers to that protest march? Many of them are seasoned adults, rather than velvet horn university grads, and a lot of them are ranking tech specialists, so they should carry a bit of weight."

"This would help. How many do you actually have?"

"We have hidden sects in all the major cities. I do not know the numbers, but I am sure it counts as a respectable quantity."

"Um, Auryn," Latena proposes tenderly. "Are we speaking of a protest against the Council, or are we also speaking of opening up your religion to public scrutiny? If we are hoping to bring down a corrupt government, might this also pave the way for a rebirth of your old religion?”

“Oh wow, that would be a sight to see. I do not think I could hope for something like that, but if we did have the chance, it would be nice to let the people know about it. Our people do believe that there must be a higher form of life out there to represent a divine image. The Marshal does actually resemble one such example, at least to some degree, but his failure to bring forth his promises in a timely manner made us declare him a false prophet after a while. But regardless of this, we believe there must be room for both a scientific study as well as the veneration of a holy figure, as we feel a need to serve both the mind as well as the spirit.”

Latena attempts a modest smile, as she humorously shakes her head.

“Auryn, your faction is a little weird even for all my conspiracy theories to cope with. To think that in all this time, there might still be some people out there who want to worship a god.”

“So, Kaliya,” Relissa muses playfully. “What’s the real reason you called us, because if I know you right, you must have something wacky bouncing around upstairs.”

“Oh, Relissa,” she smirks. “Can’t I simply have a desire to join up for a little talk amongst my friends?”

“Aye, you can, but I don’t see Haran here this time. And we all know the rep we have as a group with Thaelyn.”

“Some of us more than others,” Marelle adds.

“Well, that’s simply coincidental,” Kaliya smiles. “But I can see you catch on too quick, so all right. I do have a little problem, and I need some of my best brainstormers to help me out.”

“Brainstormers, is it now?” Relissa winces. “And you’re asking US for it? Jiggers, and how many marks do you have on Thaelyn’s list by now?”

“Enough to fill a few pages, probably,” she chuckles. “The General even threatened to write a biography on me. But I need your help because I know you two have some great ideas in you, and I wouldn’t want to leave you out of any opportunities for your own contribution… to the list,” she grins brightly.

“Buggers to you, girl!” Relissa laughs. “Aye then, so where do we start?”

"Ytani… We know he needs to make a new arrival, and we recently found out Darumon is keeping secrets from his master, like that fail at Sigil."

"Jiggers! He's actually keeping a secret from his own bloody master? And here I thought the rest of it was enough to rattle your brains."

"I know, it hit all of us the same, but it also opens a very interesting door for us…the Prodigy Gift. Initially, I was simply going to have him pop in to say hello, preferably on a live news feed, and like so many others, completely by accident with Ileani giving some innocent report of some kind."

"But I suppose this just isn't good enough for you, ay?" Relissa wonders.

"I don't think it was ever really good enough, because I also want to demonstrate his bad manners as well as his Prodigy Gift. He's got that god complex, after all, and I want to see about incorporating that with an attitude of making trouble for the Marshal."

"Aye, I get it. So, we're saying he wants to take his pet world, this time being Azgarén."

"The first thing I can think of," Marelle considers, "is you need to build the image. The people of Azgarén probably have no idea who he is, and with everyone locked up behind those Suppressor chips, to see someone actually behaving with an attitude of ANY kind will be unusual."

"Good, so this is our first point," Kaliya nods. "He'll need to make an appearance, and thoroughly demonstrate his LACK of the chip and seed. I can do this if I reflect on when I saw him that one time in his room. He was without his shirt, so if I can replicate that image, it would surely demonstrate his unmodified form."

"Didn't he also go without his pants during that time?" Marelle smiles impishly.

"Um, well, yes, but I was turned the other way by then," Kaliya grins shyly.

"Oh! Relissa, do you hear that? She must take after her boyfriend."

"Jiggers," she moans. "There goes any possibility for kids."

The group shared a brisk laugh.

"Anyway," Kaliya continues. "Then I think I need to consult with someone, like Petrith, for a little tutoring on how men like to show off to the world."

"Is that with or without Suli participating in the mix," Marelle muses. "Because she'll probably get very upset if you have him perform for you without her supervising."

The group erupted in another quick laugh.

"Then I need my lines, and I want to ultimately disclose a few things about the Prodigy Gift, but in pieces. This is where I think I should have Ayene involved in an interview with Ileani where I make my appearance and she...accidentally...films it."

"Buggers, that poor girl..." Relissa moans.

"We need this as another of our sensations, but here is where I need to decide how to present it. One thing we know is we don't want Darumon trying to refute it, and so it has to go out live."

"Aye, that's a good one."

"I might also suggest building up something before this," Marelle offers. "Ytani is making a return, and he wants the world to know it. This reminds me of our plans for the incursions into their space. We're making a demonstration to build up a picture of something happening that needs people to take notice of it."

"All right," Kaliya muses. "So, what does Ytani do to get people to take notice?"

"My first suggestion is this... To get noticed big time, he needs public coverage...large-scale public coverage, which means to take it out on the streets. If we reflect on your time with those orcs, you used a giant-sized image. But here, I don't think it'll work as well with all those tall buildings. In such a heavily urbanized city like Capitol Prime, if it's anything like the images on my flight simulator, you're not going to get decent visibility unless you're in the air. This can also allow you better mobility to cover more ground."

"Good, I like this. A large flying...thing...works nicely, but it also has to be noticeably alien."

"Aye," Relissa submits. "A big flying beasty would get their attention...hmm..."

She pulls out a pad of paper and a pen from her bag and sets it on the table. She then ponders a few ideas and starts drawing several lines and shapes on the paper.

"What sorts of animals do you have over there, anything with feathers or scales?"

"Um, keeping in mind that I'm not a native, so I don't have the native education like I should. But I don't recall anything from my early school. I think anything with scales would be ground-based, not flying, and I don't recall anything with feathers."

"So, we might be speaking of bare skin, like webbed across the wing?"

"Maybe, although I suppose anything works if you want it to look alien."

"All right, but then, how big are they?"

"I doubt there is anything large, certainly not big enough to represent something noticeable from the ground that would turn heads."

"Legs?"

"Best I can recall is a species with two rear legs, and then a pair of wings."

"And where do they usually live?"

"Wow, um, I believe we're speaking mostly of tree-dwellers here, like in a jungle environment, or forested areas."

"Sounds ducky enough…"

Relissa draws a few rough concept images, but scratches them out.

"Are we speaking of things like mammals, reptiles, amphibians?"

"Cu'Nar's grace, Relissa," she giggles. "You're really going into detail on this. As I recall, this is a mammal, I think."

"Aye, so we don't want one of those if we're going alien."

She finally tries another idea, this time combining a few others. She begins refining it with sucker-like amphibious feet, and a broad amphibious head and toothless mouth, then eyes with vertical slits. She then pulls out another pouch from her bag with a number of colored pens.

"Wow, Relissa," Kaliya leans forward. "What all do you have in there?"

"I use these as part of my conservation work over on Ruuki uy'Daan, drawing up pictures of the things I see out on my runs."

"Sounds like you're doing well with that job."

"Aye, except for the bleedin' heavy gravity," she chuckles.

"And the artistry? I didn't know you could do that."

"You're right! I didn't realize I had it in me till I got into some of those scouting classes."

She fills in some coloration, giving it a mottled green-brown patching and leathery skin. She eventually turns it around to show the others.

"Think of something the size of a cow, but with wings. This'll turn a few heads I think, especially if you go around squawking all over the place to announce yourself."

Kaliya studies the image with a broad grin forming across her face.

"All right, so now the plan… I first make a few appearances in the city, just to draw attention…maybe over the course of a few or several days, to spread it out. So, if Darumon wants to make any of his excuses, he'll be quickly overruled by the massive display I'm making. Then we have our show. Let's see. Do we have it in a city plaza?"

"Coming down to ground level would certainly make a scene," Marelle chuckles. "That'll send the crowds screaming off in all directions! You can't very well hide that."

"But I need Ayene with Ileani, so this much needs to stay put. We'll probably have to clue her in at least a little bit, so she won't lose her horns too badly."

"Lose them? Are you sure she grew any new ones since the last time?"

"And when do you think you'll be doing this?" Relissa asks.

"That's another problem," Kaliya relents. "Because I suspect this will eventually lead to our final sequence. He makes his appearance, probably makes some number of demands of the people, or rather Darumon, just to make noise and get him angry. But after a while, when he's not getting what he wants, he needs to send people in to reinforce his idea of being the new god-king of Azgarén."

"And this is where my team comes in," Marelle muses.

"But here we have a problem, and that is we need our base up and running too."

"And that's still a long way off."

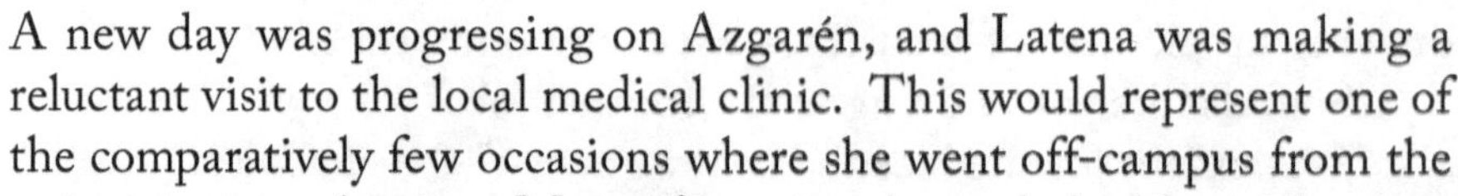

A new day was progressing on Azgarén, and Latena was making a reluctant visit to the local medical clinic. This would represent one of the comparatively few occasions where she went off-campus from the university into the city. Most of her time in study had her either in a study hall or in her dorm room.

She entered the clinic, which was a local office near where her family lived and where she grew up as a child, so it was very familiar to her. A number of other people waited in the lobby for their turn to see one of the resident professionals. Latena would first need to check in at the desk before taking a seat.

She approaches the desk to speak with the intern, fumbling with her bag to pull out her tablet device which held her medical information. She was expecting to have an argument about the seed, as she certainly did not want one, and also in regard to her recent debates at the university. But as she arrives at the counter and looks up at the receptionist, her voice catches in her throat and her jaw drops.

The first thing she took notice of was the obvious absence of the seed entity on the woman's body. The intern was clearly mature enough that she should have one, and as far as Latena could recall from her previous visits, the woman did at one time, as did everyone else in the office.

Latena stands there, speechless and with her eyes bulging. The sight would not be so unusual if it were anyone in her university environment, as they were all too young for it still. And as she gawks at the abnormal image, she begins teetering, catching herself as she steps back a pace.

The woman looks up at her most recent client and smiles. This sends Latena stumbling back yet another step. But before any words can be spoken, a soft giggling can be heard echoing from across the room. This surreal utterance caught her attention, and her eyes grew even larger as she stiffly swivels around to find the source. Sitting in one of the waiting room chairs was a mother and her young daughter. The girl, who might be around her first centennial, which equated to middle childhood, was glaring at Latena and grinning, while letting out soft laughter at the poor university grad's reactions.

"That's funny," the girl mutters humorously.

Latena gapes at the girl for her obvious emotional display, even though she was clearly old enough to have the chip. She cocks her head at the young attendee, and the girl turns sideways and points to show the absence of her interface unit. It had apparently been removed at some recent point in time, and there was a small medical patch covering the area.

"What in all the nether-space…" Latena wheezes.

"It's gone," the girl admits. "I'm in here for a follow-up. It feels great. I hated that thing."

"Gone? As in…what? They removed it?"

"Yeah."

"Why?"

"It's a new thing they're doing. Ask her…" she points at the receptionist behind the desk.

Latena jerks back around to the intern behind the desk again. The woman was still smiling, more now than previously, and raising her brow in anticipation.

"Welcome, Miss. Can I help you today?"

"Help? Me?" Latena flusters and glances back at the girl. "I think the first thing would be to help me understand if I just stepped into a fantasy world, or if this is still the real one."

"It's the real one, although with a few of our long-term problems finally being corrected. Yours would not be the first reaction we're seeing lately, but it certainly is a bold one. Is there something I can do for you?"

Latena glares at the woman and her figure, which she was again studying for the lack of a seed entity covering it.

"I, uh…well, I, uh…was, um…uh… In all the nether-space, I thought I knew what I came in here for, but now I am not sure."

The intern followed her gaze and knew what was going through the young woman's mind.

"Yeah, it's gone, much like that young lady's chip over there. And my chip is disabled, although it's still present so far."

"Still present?"

"I'm waiting my turn until we can process a few others first. I think I can hold out a little longer."

"And the seed? Gone? How?"

"It's a new procedure being released, although quietly so far, by the ARC."

"Quietly? Why quietly?"

"Well, there are a couple of reasons, not the least of which is we would expect a mad rush of new applicants, and we are trying to maintain some level of control to pace ourselves."

"Yeah, I am sure of that much!"

"Another reason is to process the more critical elements, such as medical and emergency personnel, as they tend to hold a high priority to see about the rest of the public needs."

"All right, I suppose I can accept that."

"Then, once we can reach a certain threshold, we will open it up, but a little piece of me is dreading that moment for all the applications likely to come in. I would expect a huge waiting list to form up almost instantly."

"Probably so. Ouch, I would not want to be in your hooves at that time."

"Absolutely! But now, are you here for an appointment?"

"Oh, yeah, but, um..." she again studies the woman's body. "It was for a, uh..."

"Let me see if I can guess before you lose your horns completely. Judging by your approximate age, and the fact that you do not...yet... have your seed, are you here for your second centennial preparatory?"

"Yes."

"All right, this gives us a starting point. And what is your name, please?"

"Latena Ta'yeen. But if the ARC is removing them..."

"Yes, yours will be cancelled."

"Cancelled!" she shouts. "Ergh..." she flinches as she grabs her interface for a feedback hit.

"Ouch!" the girl in the waiting room emits sympathetically.

Latena turns her attention to the girl again.

"You should get that turned off," the girl suggests.

"Turned off?" Latena whimpers.

"Yeah, at least get it turned off before you go asking any more questions."

"You think?"

Latena turns back around to the receptionist with inquiring eyes.

"Yeah," the woman nods. "We're providing a service for all of our patients lately."

The intern now turns to her terminal. She had been entering Latena's information, but now she pulls up an app to make a call to one of the examination rooms.

"I need someone up here at the front desk with a D-probe," she announces into the link. "Make it quick, this one is having a meltdown."

"A meltdown! Ergh..." Latena grunts from another hit. "Just what happened here that I must have missed."

"First and foremost, the ARC has discontinued the seeds and the chips, and instigated a program to disable the chips already out there."

"Disable?! Argh!" she whines. "Dammit..."

"I told you!" the girl behind her issues.

Latena turns to look over her shoulder at the child, who simply shrugs.

"And what about her?" Latena points at the girl.

"Yes," the intern admits. "We are also scheduling some of them to be removed, starting with the younger children and slowly working our way up."

"And who ordered all this? The Council?"

"Pah! Them! No, the Council is too busy with whatever it is they think they're doing in their top-secret hideout no one ever told us about."

"Really! Argh…" she clenches the interface harder.

"Wow," the girl giggles. "You don't know when to stop, do you!"

Latena glares at the girl and playfully raises her finger. She then returns to the receptionist.

"So, you people are essentially disobeying the Council mandates by now, I guess," she states.

"Yes, technically speaking, they did not give us the opportunity to do our job the way it was supposed to be done, so we are taking our own action now."

"Would this relate to any of that talk about those court cases and that emergency board being established right now?"

"Partially. It goes a little deeper than that. Have you been paying attention to the news broadcasts recently, beginning with that industry out there?"

"Yes! I am part of a debate group over at the U that gathers on occasion. We talk about all sorts of ideas, mostly political, and lately it has been centered around these recent sensations. Things like who is doing what, where, how, and why. But so far, it is all just a lot of hot conspiracy theories. One thing we have generally come to a conclusion about is the Council is crooked, and the Marshal probably collaborated with them on one thing or another, and this resulted in them running off with that great wisdom he promised. We think he might also be lying about a lot of stuff, and this might also include his insurgents."

"Really! And all this as conspiracy theories?"

"Yes, but it is unlikely you will find a lot of people out there who would listen to a bunch of, um, well, as one of our members said recently, a bunch of velvet horn university grads."

The intern chuckles vigorously at the suggestion as she takes notice of another woman coming through a door behind her with the probe to deprogram the interface.

The new intern arrives next to Latena and begins attaching the probe to the diagnostics port on her unit.

"Hold still, this will only take a moment," she notes. "You will feel a soft twinge as it goes offline. You might want to steady yourself on the counter here."

Latena complies by leaning on the counter as the woman runs a reconfiguration process on the interface unit. She soon feels a soft twinge within her neural tissues. She closes her eyes as she tries to hold her composure. When the process is complete, the intern disconnects the unit and pats the girl on the shoulder, then smiles and returns back to her station.

Latena holds her position as she tries to recover her senses. The release of the control effect would take a few moments.

"How do you feel now?" the girl behind her asks.

Latena turns slowly and opens her eyes to view the girl, who was smiling at her.

"Give me a moment, I had that thing in there for a long time."

"You'll feel better soon. Just like my mom," she glances at the woman next to her. "She had hers a long time too. Oh, you might also notice you can say things like I'm, you're, can't, won't, and so on now."

"I can? Why?"

"The chip blocks some of that. It's one of the side effects."

"Oh, really! So THAT is the reason. So nice of them to tell us about that little detail."

"Now..." the receptionist continues. "As far as the seeds go, the Council never permitted us to research any countermeasures during this time, so the otherwise temporary application of the seeds became permanent by default, if for no other reason than because no one told us to stop."

"This is one of the things we were talking about in our group. They did not simply forget to say something, they explicitly ignored it."

"Right. And recently, the ARC came into a possible solution to safely remove them. They conducted a number of closed tests to validate the procedure and refine the techniques, and now they're releasing it on a limited scale to the public, beginning with the medical community itself to give us the first step at relief so we can help everyone else."

"But wait, this suggests a process that has been underway for a while now. How long ago did this all get started, because I recall that security lock on some critical file."

"It was actually before that. The report on that security lock was delayed to the press."

"Delayed? Why delayed?"

"To give us time to find our solution before anyone could otherwise stop us...again."

"Oh! Wonderful!" she blasts. "So, whoever it is in control of our fake government is STILL in control, and you people are all working behind their back? Incredible, wait till I tell Auryn about this. She'll… she'll…she will…" Latena pauses in confusion.

"There you go!" the girl ushers up from her seat. "That didn't take long!"

Latena turns once again to gaze at the frisky young female behind her.

"You know, you…you are…you're…right. You're going to cause your mom's horns to sag prematurely."

"She's already doing that," the mother smiles tenderly.

"Anyway, this friend of mine, Auryn, will likely be so happy, she'll get down on her knees and start praying to something."

"A fake government?" the receptionist wonders. "Is this part of your conspiracy theory?"

"Yes, the Council is a front. I knew this from a long time ago. I've long debated with my group how I believe them to be a hidden dictatorship, picking and choosing what they want, and all under a false guise of our alleged free and open society."

"This is interesting, and a bit controversial. Not that I would actually argue with you, based on what I know, but can you give me an example?"

"Yeah, Former Elder Nazég. His name was mentioned several times recently as if he might hold a clue to something the rest of them wanted silenced. Then they basically vilified him with the Marshal claiming these insurgents of his getting involved. But our group has decided it's the Marshal who should be discredited, and all these news sensations are proving my point. And this would be the evidence…" she points at her interface, then the girl and hers, and the woman with her seed. "He invented this, and now you are UN-inventing it."

"All right, I suppose I can't argue with that obvious example. But in fairness, the seeds were originally said to be the result of the old Tav'ageen Scare and the push to evacuate from our native home."

"Yes, a panic causing us to forget we have loads of other preexisting colonization tech. And probably made worse by HIM frightening us to take these seeds as his superior solution."

"Yes, this is how it seemed to work out. But then, as the chips came out, we had no further official reason to vacate. But again, no one told us to stop."

"No one told you to stop likely due to that secret file holding something we were never told about, and maybe the REAL reason for the seeds."

This statement stifled the receptionist, who had a fairly complete understanding of the truth, as what had been released privately through the ARC to the medical community. It reflected upon the true nature of the seeds and the hidden link to Sargeras. She frowned at Latena and leaned forward.

"Interesting. Is this also part of your conspiracy theory?"

"Yeah, and I think I just hit on something. Your reaction. I see words, and I know how to read people for their postures. You know something, and it's the real reason behind all this, isn't it!"

"You are a very clever young lady. And you must be causing YOUR mother's horns to sag prematurely," she smiles softly.

"I was doing that from a long time ago, chip or no chip," she smirks and glances at the girl again. "I'm a student at CPU, and majoring in political science, political history, and with a minor in social history. I'm also something of a conspiracy theorist and activist."

"Uh huh, I should've guessed by your manners. The exuberance of youth. You glow with it."

"Hey, I'm not the only one! We have a whole group, and we're all very determined to understand all these recent sensations. It's all WAY too sudden and coincidental. So, who is behind it? Because if you people are involved, and maybe also the ARC for this point, and probably C.P. Security, that fake Internal Secretary at the Grand Hall, and what I suspect to be a fake CPS officer telling us the Council was missing... this tells me there is someone behind all this, and they're pulling strings the active authority out there isn't supposed to know about."

"Active authority?" the receptionist frowns.

"Yeah, and it's not our native government. This doesn't leave too many choices, but one of them is alien."

"Uh huh... All right, listen," she asserts cautiously. "Before you go out and start protesting anything, you need to know something. Yes, I do know a few things, as what has been released to us through the ARC. Among other things, the Council is currently under investigation by a new planetary security agency trying to answer some of these same questions. So far, they are keeping it very quiet, because the implications could send shockwaves through our entire world population, and we don't want this so far."

"Shockwaves…" Latena muses. "Anything like they're crooked, the Marshal lied to us, and there's no great wisdom coming to us after all?"

"Something like that, yes, although this might also be considered minor if you count the seeds, the security file, and so on. I think a lot of people would lose their horns over that."

"Yes, likely so. And those insurgents? Why would they take away an undesirable member of our Council unless they knew something about him?"

"I don't know if I could give you a precise answer to that one, but I do know Elder Nazég knew something that someone else wanted silenced, and further to discredit him for his beliefs so the rest of us would stop asking about it."

"Oh great!" she scorns. "Yes, that's a dictatorship in action. This is what a dictatorship does, you know?"

"I'm not a political specialist, but I suppose it might seem that way. And the Marshal has ulterior motives to his designs. Beyond that, what I can tell you is this. First, you need to know there is an issue of planetary security here. If you and your group try any of your activism, you might find yourself splashing in a very bad puddle. The Marshal is the enemy here, and he is not a nice guy. But even though he might currently be alone, which is to say without his custom military machine serving him, he is still a powerful being, with abilities our science doesn't understand, and that Scare was an example of it."

"Uh oh. But wait, a custom military machine?"

"Yeah, one of his top-secret mandates from the Council was a type of mind-control chip none of us were ever supposed to know about. He presumably used this as a training aid, so it is said, against his so-called insurgents. This is how he treats people who might not otherwise cooperate voluntarily."

"Oops!" Latena backs off. "All right, you got my attention. But if we can't go out and do anything, who is? Because I still have my studies on the Council and their history, with or without the Marshal. Whatever they are, we can't trust them anyway."

"Perhaps what you need to do is speak with a representative and share your thoughts. You and your group must have spent some time on these theories of yours, and they might find them interesting to hear. Meanwhile, as to the rest. This agency was not established by the Council, but a secondary body trying to investigate them AND the Marshal."

"A collaboration, just like I said."

"At least in part. But this is all I can say about it for now. I don't carry the authority to say anything more, due to that planetary security business, which is scary."

"All right, I won't push. But if I want to learn anything more, I need to know who to talk to."

"Our resource is over at the ARC. What we have learned on this side is the Tav'ageen Anomaly, compounded by that old Scare, was actually a hoax. The Marshal took advantage of something in us and made it worse."

"A hoax!" she shouts. "In all the nether-space…but, um…but… um…" she flusters with a sudden nervous overtone.

"Is there something wrong?" the receptionist asks.

"Um…sort of…I think. First, why do you think it was a hoax?"

"Well, for one thing, we were told to use the chips as a solution. But like the seeds, it was supposed to be temporary until that famous evacuation. Then, once we had this 'solution'…" she flutters her fingers for emphasis, "…the Council effectively closed the book on it. They refused any future research on the Anomaly, and incorporated a nondisclosure clause in the mandate that disallowed the return of any statistical detail on its progress, or lack thereof, which might inform the medical community if it was still a threat of any kind."

"More dictatorship mentality. They took an easy way out and did it for a reason. And this can still reflect back on the Marshal, as he was advising them."

"One explanation for this clause was to prevent another public panic. But you might think we would need to know if the thing could still be out there that would continue to require the chips. Combine this with the obvious success, and the fact that we are still here, not evacuating, and a lot of things are brought into question, including the Anomaly. We believe the seeds hold this ulterior motive, and if so, the chip was a secondary solution only after something else was applied, and THIS is what brought us back under control. But no one told us to stop any of it. This is also where the mention of Elder Nazég comes in, as his faction was one of those trying to study it."

"Ah hah! But did he learn anything?"

"My information is a bit vague, but I don't think he had time. And certainly not before the Council turned against him."

"Figures! But this now suggests a correlation with those insurgents, that ship, the Marshal getting so upset, and a few other things."

"Including this dictatorship you mention? Tell me, how do you figure this one?"

"Well, like I said, I am a student at CPU, with my majors in politics. One topic that fascinates me is the study of alternate forms of government, either those we actually had…you know, way back in ancient times, or at least what we might theorize about. Along the way, I wrote a number of essays comparing these to each other, including their pros and cons, and then comparing this to the modern day when we describe ourselves to be in this Enlightened Era. But I have an issue with the Charter of Laws, starting right up front with the preamble, where I feel there is a flaw in the wording. If you interpret it a certain way, it could carry a hidden meaning."

"Really! How do you mean?"

"Read it for yourself sometime and try to compare with what you actually see the Council doing right now. All this you just now told me, how they are NOT doing this, NOT doing that, restricting something else. But the Charter is all about fairness, equality, and the pursuit of ALL forms of knowledge…or so it makes you think. The thing is we are not doing it."

"Interesting. And why do you say it only makes you think this?"

"Because if you look more closely at the wording, it hints that the Council is actually in control of WHAT you think, WHAT you research, or NOT research. The science communities do NOT have the freedom to choose their own. The Council is directing it from behind this hidden clause. But we are all trained to think in terms of this spirit of the wording, which I think is a prefab excuse to stop us from asking questions. We're not allowed to have a religion, but we treat the Council as a god entity, and never question its integrity. That election fraud, for instance. Did anyone ever bother to check up on them to see if they were following their own laws, or did we simply assume they were doing as we always expected of them."

"You know, I've had similar discussions as this with a few others. We took too much for granted with them. And this also reflects on that new security group. I wonder if these people would like to hear about this. It could provide some interesting background information."

"Well, if they do, I hope they are a little more open-minded than my teachers. They do not see things the same, but most of my group does by now, and we all think it is a hidden conspiracy. And these recent news sensations are simply compounding it. A Council that is supposedly deliberating the mysteries of the universe and using a super longevity drug to stay alive long enough to actually do it, while at the same time defying our legal process of elections and everything else. This is a load of nether-bilge, if you ask me, and all this while no one around here has any real work to do, like you people and these seeds, or the Tav'ageen thing. Then to see that bit with the Grand Hall, and finally the Marshal's lame excuse of where the Council is REALLY supposed to be..." she shakes her head.

"Yes, there are some curious discrepancies here, I'll admit."

"But now, back to the Tav'ageen Anomaly," she asserts. "You said you learned something, and I am also very concerned about this after you just turned my chip off."

"Did I actually say I learned something?" she raises her brow.

"Oh, don't try pulling Little Miss Innocence on me. Remember, I see words. And I'm not some dull-horn who tucks her tail whenever someone orders it. First, you said the thing was a hoax, and then you said the Marshal used something in us...IN US...and made it worse. That tells me there IS something in us, and you know it. Further, you must KNOW what is in us, otherwise you wouldn't be turning off the chips, if there was still any concern for a Scare."

"Dammit, you're good!" she chuckles boldly. "In fact, you could be dangerous if you ever DID get out on the street protesting something!"

Latena smiled at her achievement, and this time she made it real, as there was no more threat of a feedback hit from it. And it also felt good, as on this occasion, it counted as a victory for all her arguments.

"All right," the receptionist continues. "First, as you might know, the science community could never fully identify what caused it. Then the Marshal shows up and helps us find an answer, but he never really demonstrated his evidence. And yet, the Council took his word for it. In our society, to simply take someone's word is preposterous without evidence to back it up. Then you have the chips, and the nondisclosure clause, and the case is closed indefinitely."

"Right."

"Next, we have some people wondering if it was ever real to begin with. We have those early deaths, and of course the panic, but none of it made any sense to the medical community, or that it showed any relationship."

"No relationship? One seemed to follow the other, isn't that a relationship?"

"Indirectly, yes. But much of the original detail from that time period was apparently hidden as part of that old Scare and a cover-up to allow people to calm down again."

"A cover-up?!" Latena screeches.

"Yes, this is basically what it was. You have a world panic, so how do you settle it down, except to cover up some portion of it. Unfortunately, the deaths became worse, as we now have the Scare occurring in the streets. But the original deaths are what is being questioned here, and whatever came after might be part of a scandal instead."

"Oh no…"

"Here is what I'm telling other people who ask about this. The original few children were examined in their bedrooms, not a medical facility. The occurrences were so few and far between, that it didn't play out like anything arriving and attacking someone. If you have an arrival, it should be clustered in one place and showing a growth pattern in that area, not scattered to all sides, and over such an extended period of time that one cannot follow to another as the same entity."

"All right, so far it sounds good. Instead, it's completely random and seemingly unrelated."

"The medical scans showed no signs of abnormalities or illness, and the deaths were virtually instantaneous…just when the people's backs were turned."

"Uh oh! That doesn't sound good."

"And the timing was quick. What I mean is, one moment the child is fine, then they leave the room, and bam, the child is dead and appears partially mummified. The physical laws we understand relating to a process like this do not add up nicely…not by any natural causes."

"So, it has to be unnatural."

"Finally, as they grew so concerned about this, they decided to bring these children into a lab for the study. The body was brought in one vehicle, and that ghost thing rode along in another one."

"I don't recall hearing this story before."

"This is probably one of those that was buried. The ghost behaved just like the child might behave, riding along in a medical van with the sirens blaring. It enjoyed every moment of it."

"Just like a child would."

"Once at the lab, the body was plugged into monitors while the ghost went into another room with a small army of researchers. The body was mostly ignored, except for an occasional intern checking the readings. Instead, the focus was on the ghost, not a sleeping child."

"Oh, blast you people."

"Yes, well, it was assumed the ghost was at fault here. What possible harm can a sleeping child perform?" she shrugs.

"Yes, I suppose."

"This ghost was in the same room as the child in the earlier studies before the child was found dead. Therefore, we have the idea of something alien arriving. But HERE we find some data, if only to hint at something."

"All right, good. What kind?"

"The ghost was under constant surveillance, including security cameras. The child's body was also being watched by cameras. The ghost spent all its time chatting with the people, and then boom. Gone. The timing was exactly when the monitors shot up erratically on the child, and then flatlined. There was no one in the room on the monitors, and the interns responding to the alarms found the body again, same as before. Meanwhile, that ghost got cut off in midsentence as it was carrying its conversation, just like pulling a plug."

"Pulling a plug? But that sounds more like murder than anything else."

"But in the absence of anything visible on camera, it was not on top of the body doing so, so it had to be at range, or at least enough range to avoid the cameras. This could possibly mean a doorway, and then possibly using an alien form of weapon to partially dehydrate the body."

"In all the nether-space! And alien, you say?"

"These security people believe it was the Marshal. An unofficial arrival we were not aware of. We had only two of these instances before he and Sargeras showed up, this time officially, and here is where he insists on helping us solve this problem. But then we have the Scare and his 'solution' to run away at all costs."

"Wonderful!" Latena shrieks. "So, a dictatorial Council isn't the only thing to worry about around here. Then how do we actually explain this if it wasn't what they said? Because I have, um, a personal reason for asking."

"A personal reason?"

Latena takes a deep breath and sighs tensely as she glances around the room.

"I don't usually talk about this… In fact, I don't talk about it at all. I received my chip at four decades, the same as the rest, but my mother secretly revealed to me that I was suffering this Anomaly. She was given instructions to apply the chip immediately as a corrective procedure. So, what is this chip supposed to do, and if it's actually a hoax of some kind, what is this Anomaly in reality, especially if you're calling the Marshal's name into it, as well as Elder Nazég who might know something. Because all this now points to this being a center of attention for everything else."

The intern gazed at the girl with her mouth agape. For a moment, she was speechless, until she forced herself back into perspective.

"You're really dangerous. I need to refer you to the ARC, and not just for this. You experienced the symptoms? They'll want to know about this. They're asking for volunteers who may have experienced those early signs to participate in a secret study project. But as for the rest, you need to speak with Director Bak'vayn. Tell him what you told me and see what he has to say about it. He may even refer you to this security agency for this other issue of yours."

The intern turns to her terminal and starts punching in the details to make a new appointment for the girl at the ARC.

"Latena Ta'yeen, right? All right, Miss Political Activist who doesn't like tucking her tail on command, I'm at the limit of what I can say here, so if you want more, you need to go to the ARC. They're working directly with this new security agency on these and other matters. So maybe, if you play your game right, you might get lucky. But let me give you one very valuable piece of advice. The people in question who might be covering this up killed children to do so. Don't be another example of this, please."

"Oops…suddenly I'm sorry for mentioning the part about tucking my tail."

"I don't necessarily care about that…we're all doing it to some degree or another, but we're doing it quietly."

"Got it."

"A political activist, is it?" the Director muses. "That's a new one."

"Does it actually show that in there now?" Latena blushes.

"Yeah, she put a note in here saying you're a very strongly outspoken young lady with some controversial perspectives that the ACI might be interested in."

"The ACI? Is that this new security agency she mentioned?"

"Yes. Azgarén Central Intelligence, a planetary security agency with the will and the authority to push their way into any locked room they want, all because someone locked that room away from the rest of us for their secret games."

"And this would include the Council, I suppose, and maybe the Marshal?"

"It would. But before we go into that, let's talk about your experiences. It says you had these symptoms as a young girl?"

Latena was visiting the ARC as part of her follow-up from the local clinic and her earlier visitation. It was quickly becoming aware that she was a hidden Prodigy Child.

"Yes Sir, my mother once told me about it. She said our family med-tech diagnosed it as the Tav'ageen Anomaly, and that he required an immediate scheduling for the chip."

"Yes," he concedes. "That was the procedure in those days. And I am truly sorry for all those people out there that had to suffer for this. But until recently, we simply didn't know any better."

"The woman at the clinic said something about how Elder Nazég was in there trying to study this, but the result was indeterminate. What was all that about? This scares me a bit if I'm one of those who had this, even though you seem confident enough to turn off the chips."

"First, I want you to know that you are not in any danger of anything. Not for as long as we keep this under wraps. We know what it is, but we can't let it out to the public yet. If you think it caused a panic before, what we have now would cause a massive scandal, probably a lot of confusion, perhaps some hysteria, maybe also some paranoia, and likely a huge outrage, and we can't let that happen so far. So, from this moment, you need to keep it quiet. Understood?"

"All right," she whispers cautiously. "But wow, that's quite a laundry list you have there. That sounds at least as bad as the old panic, if not worse. Is it actually as bad as to cause all that?"

"This largely depends on who you talk to and what they have to say about it. But ultimately, this could be THE biggest sensation in the history of our species…well, one of them."

"Only one of them?" she winces. "What's the other one?"

"Where it came from, but that's another story so far."

"Uh huh...and when do I actually learn all this so I can answer my own questions?"

"Let me begin with those of us here at the ARC. Our study hopes to find people, maybe like you, from a younger age group, as we believe those of us who had the chip for a certain length of time may have become so desensitized by now for the emotional dampening effect that we might not be able to rediscover it as easily. Therefore, a younger example, like yours, might be our best hope to find it again, at least to get the study off the ground."

"Fine, but this still leaves the question of why and what this thing actually is."

"It's thought to be a latent ability we believe is in our species. This was the original theory of Elder Nazég. But it's only recently showing itself, and the Marshal hates it. That's the reason for his chips, to cover it up."

"So, it's the chips that do the cover-up...at least in part, and with these nondisclosure statements to prevent any of you from following up on anything. This sounds very neat."

"Yes, it is, and he covered for himself quite nicely."

"He...so we can't be speaking of the Council here, as you would use the word THEY instead."

"You're a clever young lady, and very observant."

"I have to be, if I'm going to be a political activist," she smiles gently. "But THEY are the ones who passed the mandate, so how do they fit into it?"

"I can't be sure, other than to suggest they simply took his word as a being that carried superior knowledge that couldn't be wrong. And they wanted that superior knowledge, seemingly at all costs."

"Wonderful, and so we have another example of my conspiracy theory," she sighs. "I swear to you, Director, one thing I want to do is share these thoughts, or at least some of them, with my group at the U. They'll go tail-crazy over it."

"I won't try to stop you if it fits with these theories of yours, but do take care of the more sensitive details relating to the Marshal. We do not want him hearing about this, as he probably won't be at all happy."

"All right, I'll step around it carefully. But now, what is this latent ability? What does it actually do?"

"Let me first ask if you recall anything from that moment in time."

"Um, it's hard to say now. I don't know what part of it was real or a dream. I do remember something about seeing myself in my own bed, but it just didn't seem real to me. And it bothers me to think that something happened, and no one knows what it was. I remember how my mother worried about a relapse, and I often had these little fears in the back of my mind that something might be coming for me one day."

"Hmm, yes… We had one other report so far, and she gave something similar, saying she thought she had an imaginary friend she would talk to. So, in her case, she apparently managed to contend with it on more familiar terms, but I suppose each of us is different. Do you recall anything of the original descriptions?"

"Yeah, how it was originally described as ghostlike images that closely resembled the child in bed, and people saying it could be something like an alien infestation trying to mimic the child in a body-snatcher scenario. This was scary in itself."

"Yes, and probably part of that cover-up to invoke panic. In reality, it was the child projecting an image outside their own body, a type of spirit manifestation that could take a tangible form, and able to interact with people and objects in much the same way as the original body would…at least within reason."

"A spirit projection?" she muses. "Do we know how it happened?"

"In those cases, most likely by accident. We find it highly unlikely the child knew what it was doing. This is the purpose of our new project, to find people like you who might hold a closer association to that inner child that we could possibly tap into, and therefore learn ways to control it better."

"When you say to control it, how do you mean this?"

"There are a number of ways in which to answer that question, not the least of which is to understand what one can do with it, for better or for worse, as this could lead to some very serious security issues, as well as a potential for crime and other offences. On the other hand, it could hold extraordinary utility value, and we can only begin to imagine where this could take us. But again, we need to learn how to control it so that it can be called on demand, and then contained by the one doing it. Maybe also monitored to prevent abuse."

"Interesting. But then, how do we find it? Put me to sleep and hope I wake up outside my body again?"

"I was conducting a secret project for just this purpose over the course of a long period of time, but no one was ever able to come forward with any results. Then, I had some people come into my office with a rather fantastic story, as well as a demonstration of what this thing can actually do. These are the people at the ACI."

"Them?" she shouts. "I thought you said they were a planetary security agency. What are they doing studying something no one is supposed to know anything about?"

"Because Miss Ta'yeen, they were working outside the Marshal's influence. They also had help."

"Help? From whom?"

"Beings of godlike proportions who recognized what this was, and had the knowledge to teach them how to use it."

"Gods?" she wheezes. "But…but…but…um… Gods?"

"Yes, gods…actual real gods, it would seem, and the Marshal and Sargeras are both in hiding from them."

"Why?" she squeaks timidly.

"They're fugitives from an ancient battle that took place where the rest of their kind was destroyed for some very high crimes. But these two managed to escape their justices, and now they're taking up refuge here…unfortunately for us."

"Oh! Yes! So unfortunate!" she blasts. "And these others, do they know they're here?"

"They do…now, at least."

"Only now? What…these gods aren't some all-seeing, all-knowing thing?"

"They're people, not much different from us in many ways, but of such a supremely high evolutionary station as to put the rest of us to shame. Such a definition as what you might find in a textbook for a godlike figure is technically unrealistic, as it tries to squeeze an infinite capacity into an otherwise finite body. You just can't do that. But on a more practical scale, you CAN have a being of such godlike proportions as to fulfill many of those same qualities, but still fit within the boundaries of our empirical measurements. Well, sort of, as this would now go beyond our form of science. Do you recall that famous statement by the Marshal of his gift of wisdom to the Council?"

"You mean, all that gibberish of our science falling into the background of something for higher minds to chew on?"

"Yes. So try not to mock it too severely," he smiles, "as such beings like these tend to live by that principle, and not in a three-dimensional universe like ours. This is where the REAL concept of nether-space comes into play."

"Oops. And therefore, that analyst and all his statements…more leaks, but this time to open up something we previously took for granted. Wow."

"The Marshal apparently had little or no choice by that time to reveal something, which could easily relate to his great wisdom, but done so reluctantly in order to justify the Council's long deliberation."

"Incredible!" she gasps. "But I don't believe what I'm hearing, Director! Are you saying we actually do have something like gods out there that someone can offer worship to?"

"We do, though the worship part is largely voluntary, if you would wish to engage in any form of interaction. And I learned of some people who are doing exactly this."

"Of OUR people?"

"Yes, our people. And they say this one deity they offer their worship to is actually ideal for our otherwise empirical-minded society, as he holds authority over a certain domain, as they call it, of knowledge and wisdom, much like a scholar in profession. It's said that he will bestow upon them the occasional bit of guidance on those occasions when they are ready for it, but never to such an extent as to promise the secrets of the universe just for the taking. These beings believe we must grow into it first."

Latena was stunned by the suggestion. Like with most people, she never really believed in such things. But now, she found herself suddenly very curious about this notion, and not simply on behalf of her friend from school.

"But anyway," the Director continues. "Both the Marshal and Sargeras are considered a flight risk, so these people need to make a cautious approach to prevent them from another escape."

"Uh huh," she mumbles vacantly. "And meanwhile he covers up this otherwise potentially amazing Gift that takes a god to teach us how to use it. In all the nether-space, Auryn, you'll flip when you hear this one."

"Is that a friend of yours from school?"

"Yeah, and she's, um…special, you might say."

"Oh, how so?"

"I'm not so sure I want to say it, but um…I, uh…well, you didn't hear this from me, but she belongs to a local sect that wants to worship a religion."

"A what?" he blurts as he lurches forward in his chair. "A religious sect? In all the nether-space, we still have people in our world who try to worship a deity?"

"Yeah, and they have sects in all the major cities, it would seem, so this isn't an isolated thing. But they have to keep it hidden since, um, you know, it's generally forbidden."

"This I need to see! We haven't seen anything like this in…um…"

"Since before King Saakerav, the old, OLD days…"

"Yes! What sort of religion is it?"

"They're apparently trying to borrow from something ancient, although it almost seems pointless as what they really want…" her voice drifts off momentarily as she shakes her head feebly. "What they want is something real that they can look up to for spiritual guidance and maybe support as we grow. They say the Marshal might resemble something like this, but for all his empty promises, they're describing him as a false prophet, and unworthy of any sort of worship."

"Well, you got that much right. But this is unbelievable! Then you definitely need to speak to these people. But now, what was this about your conspiracy theory?"

"Oh, Director, you probably don't want to get me started on that now."

◆◆◆

Latena had returned to her dorm at the university. It was later in the day after her meeting with the Director, and her head was swimming in controversy. The Director had encouraged her to meet with the ACI about her conspiracy theories, as well as this idea of these gods, but she was suddenly very uncertain if she actually wanted to get involved on something of this scale. So, she decided to call up her good friend.

"Hello?" the delicate feminine voice answers.

"Auryn, this is Latena," she announces excitedly. "Are you busy right now?"

"Not really. I was just reading a book for my history class…"

"Good…right…it was actually rhetorical. Put it down and come over to my dorm room. We need to talk."

"Oh? What about? You seem really anxious about something."

"Me? Anxious?" she flusters. "Don't ask! Just get your tail over here now. I'm pulling my horns out, and I need someone to catch them for me."

"Wow. All right, give me a moment."

They hang up and Latena tries to relax on her bed. She props up her pillows to offer comfort and leans against the headboard, nervously twiddling her thumbs. Several moments later, the door buzzer rings. She jumps up to answer it and lets her friend in.

"All right, Latena," Auryn soothes. "What happened? You sound upset."

"Upset? Me?" she mutters tensely. "Auryn, you have NO idea what just happened today. But trust me, you'll be pulling your horns out right next to me by the time I'm finished!"

She directs her friend into a chair as they sit down together.

"Auryn, do you recall all that talk our group has been chewing on lately? Well, um, let's just say I got a little confirmation out of some, eh..." she coughs emphatically, "...people."

"People? Confirmation? Latena, are you feeling alright? You seem to be...um..."

"What... Excited? Nervous? On the edge of my mind? Oh Auryn, if only I could tell you what I learned today...which is exactly what I plan on doing," she titters. "And it not only answered all those questions, but a few older ones for me, as well."

"Latena, are you actually showing emotion right now?"

"Oh! THAT..." she begins cackling hysterically. "Yeah, you might say so."

Auryn glared at her friend as she was clearly demonstrating something she should not be demonstrating, and also, she wasn't suffering any feedback hits from it. She watches as Latena releases some of her tensions until she can pull herself together again.

"We had a little, um...thing...that happened today," she chortles.

"Latena! What happened to you?"

"My chip has been turned off."

"Turned off?!" she shouts uneasily, and quickly reaches for her interface unit.

"Yeah, and we should do yours too while we're at it. They're turning them off."

"Who is turning them off?"

"Auryn, I had my appointment today...you remember, that preparatory thing, right? Well, they told me the seeds have been discontinued...FINALLY discontinued!"

"You are kidding me! So, we are not going to get poisoned by those things anymore?"

"Better! The ARC apparently found a way to remove them safely, and so far, the medical community is applying them to their own staff as part of a prelude to a global announcement. But Auryn, it goes deeper, and I need your support to figure out what I'm going to do about it."

"What do you mean, what YOU are going to do about it? This is a medical thing, and you are a politics student."

"Auryn, there's a big, BIG conspiracy here, and I've just been vindicated. I was RIGHT!" she shouts. "The Council IS corrupt, but it goes even deeper than that, as the Marshal is also in on it!"

"Like what our group was talking about? But...wait!" she raises her hand in pause. "Latena, you are going too fast. Try to slow down and tell me what happened at that appointment of yours."

Latena halts to take a deep breath before she explains.

"All right, I went in, and the lady at the desk was absent her seed. She also had emotion...she was smiling at me as I approached. Then, as I'm having my shock reaction to that, I hear giggling from a young centennial girl in one of the chairs. I'm glaring at her for the obvious emotion, and she turns to show me a medical patch where she recently had surgery to remove her interface. They're taking them out in some cases, starting with the younger children."

"Taking out the interfaces? Not just turning off the chips?"

"Everything that alien monster did to us is being undone, Auryn. HE is the conspiracy. The Council may be whatever it is, but at the moment, HE is that active authority I spoke of. I think he took over the place."

"Uh oh..."

"So we're talking, me and that lady at the desk. Here's where I start asking my questions. In a nutshell, it goes like this. There is this secret planetary security agency out there, brand new, I never heard of them before, which doesn't surprise me if they're keeping a low profile in front of a very obvious planetary threat."

"How much of a planetary threat?"

"Tav'ageen Scare sized. The Marshal is likely the reason for it. He and Sargeras are both criminals, not running from insurgents, but rather a government authority for crimes their whole society did to others. These two are likely the last of their kind by now."

"Oh wow! And here goes that false prophet thing again. My mom will lose her horns big time for this one."

"Yeah. The Tav'ageen Anomaly is something completely different. He just came along and exploited it to panic us into his seeds and whatever. And everything else was a lie to keep it that way. And Elder Nazég knew about it, but was chased away."

"Him?!" she shouts. "No wonder he became a scapegoat. But what about that ship?"

"I was sent to the ARC by this intern for some of this. And according to Director Bak'vayn, he was evacuated by someone trying to save him. He told me the ARC is working with this security body, called Azgarén Central Intelligence, or ACI, to undo all the Marshal's tricks. THEY are the ones who cracked that security file, THEY are the ones responsible for those protests with the industry, the court cases, the Grand Hall incident, and whatever else. I wouldn't be surprised if that fake Internal Secretary was actually one of them, and maybe also that CPS officer with the news on the Council. They ARE leaking information to us, but with the Marshal likely watching the same show, they can't let on they know who he is. The REAL authorities are planning on taking him down, and we don't want him running off into another hole."

"In all the nether-space, what did we get ourselves into here?"

"Yeah. So the medical community, among others, are breaking from the Council authority that keeps them locked up like animals, and choosing their own research topics. For instance, that bit with the seed research and that locked file. The news report we saw was real, but it was also delayed, to allow time for them to make some progress before the Marshal got any funny ideas of trying to stop it. They already have a solution to remove the seeds, and the procedure is spreading to all the labs out there, so he can't interfere. But HE is the one to worry about, more than any missing dictatorial Council. He kills people who get in his way."

"Oops!"

"Case in point, the Tav'ageen Anomaly. Those deaths were his action to hide the truth from us."

"But Latena," she gasps. "These were children…at least some of them."

"Yes, Auryn, children who accidentally found something he wanted to hide from us. It's a latent ability we are developing only recently, and they were forerunners who discovered it by accident. Then he comes along, and as soon as the researchers turn their backs…boom, dead kid."

Auryn's eyes bulged as she listened to the horrific depiction.

"This intern said some of the investigation those people made included moving those kids to a medical lab for study. I don't recall hearing of this, and she says it was apparently buried to hide it from us…supposedly to prevent a panic. They had cameras on the child in one room. He was plugged into an array of monitors, and that ghost thing was in another room with more cameras and a team of researchers. They were all so focused on the ghost, they didn't pay much attention to the child itself, leaving it generally open to…whatever."

"Great! Thanks for the thought, but you missed the target, right?"

"They were of the opinion the ghost was the thing to watch, not a sleeping and otherwise uninteresting child in bed. But yeah, they technically missed it. Then, the monitors go haywire with a spike of some kind, and then flatline. At the same time, that ghost, who was happily carrying on conversations with people, simply went poof, almost like pulling the plug on something."

"Wow, but do they at least know what it is? It sounds like these people you spoke to must have learned something, right?"

"Yes, and this is where Elder Nazég comes in. HE was getting ideas about what it could be, but the rest of them refused to accept his controversial opinions. It's a kind of projection of one's spirit into physical space, a sort of out-of-body experience that can become tangible."

"Unbelievable!" she whispers. "An actual spirit projection?"

"Yeah, the ACI knows what it is because they're using it. And the ARC is setting up a special project to study it, for real this time. Auryn, I never told anyone this, but I once had those early symptoms as a girl. My mother told me about this once, and that our family med-tech ordered the chip as a way of 'correcting' it. But the intern said I needed to visit the ARC to see about this project. I just now got out of a meeting with that Director over there, and this is where I learned a few things about the other side of the Marshal and Sargeras. But Auryn, you're going to lose a year's supply of horns when you hear this next part."

"Oh please, I am almost overloading with my chip as it is."

"Hold on a bit longer and we'll take care of that for you. You said the Marshal is a false prophet, right? But he might resemble a higher form of life for your religion?"

"Yeah."

"Well, Auryn, you and your entire movement have just found yourselves a god. The authority he's running from IS a higher form of life…god-sized. Real ones. And the Director says he knows some of our people who are already offering worship to them for guidance and support."

Auryn now went speechless, and she stared blankly into Latena's eyes. She could barely wheeze as she tried to interpret the meaning of that statement. Even with her religious devotion, this was a big chunk to swallow.

"Actual gods?" she gasps. "But Latena, not that I would try to debate this, I must still try to understand what it is."

"All right, recall the Marshal and that crazy statement he made about science, higher minds, and so on, like what that analyst was talking about."

"Uh huh."

"The Marshal might have found himself pushed into making that statement due to all these sensations. Beings of this sort live by those principles, and also in that place we might otherwise call nether-space. Four-dimensional space, Auryn. It's apparently real after all, which makes me think of yet another conspiracy if the Council, or whatever, was denying us to ever realize it."

"Oh great! Yeah, just look out a window and bam, you can see it. But does anyone ever pay attention? I guess not."

"And likely due to the Council denying THAT piece of research. Recall what we said earlier…overly controlling. This is who they are. Anyway, these would count as beings of such supremely high evolutionary standing that we are insects by compare. But they apparently take a parental role with beings like us. They don't give out the secrets of the universe, but they DO offer guidance to help us grow up and earn it ourselves."

"Well, this is acceptable, but I would still like to see it for myself so I can make my own judgment. I am not as high as some of our people, but if you are suggesting I bring this home, I think I should have something I can demonstrate."

"Right. The Director is telling me I need to speak to these people at the ACI, and this is where I'm pulling my horns out. I want to, but I'm really nervous. Maybe you could join me, and we can both find something to bring home."

"Maybe."

"But Auryn, what this says is the ACI learned FROM these gods what the Tav'ageen Anomaly actually is. Now think, if we're in possession of something that requires gods to teach us how to use it, what does that say about us now? And you call the Marshal a false prophet? He's much worse than that. He's a bigot that doesn't like little people like us pretending to have nice things. And I'll bet this is part of the reason he got in trouble with those others."

"But Latena, what does this mean for us as a people?"

"Well, one thing is we have something we don't know how to use, and wouldn't even accept from the scientific standpoint, especially if it takes someone like Elder Nazég to identify it for us," she chuckles ironically. "That guy on the news, that analyst. Oh yeah, now I know what he was saying about Elder Nazég laughing at us. I would too if I were in his hooves."

"Yeah, that would yank a tail or two. So we are showing a godlike ability, and the Marshal, who might also be a godlike entity, if he rivals these others, does not like it. But by teaming up with this OTHER godlike body, we could learn more about how to be our own example... or something?"

"This all goes a little above me, but maybe something like that. Auryn, didn't you tell me your sect was looking to find a higher mind to associate with? Well, the Director says one of these gods is supposed to be perfect for our society of scientists to find their spiritual support. They each have domains of teachings, and this one is a bit like a scholar teaching other scholars. How can you argue with that? It's the best of both worlds!"

Auryn stared at her friend, almost thinking the girl had lost her mind. But the suggestion, in and of itself, couldn't go unanswered. And her sect was indeed dissatisfied with their existing direction. Maybe this could prove interesting after all.

"So, what do you suggest we do first?" she wonders. "We should probably bring this to our group sometime. But do we go to this ACI place first to see what they have to say?"

"Yeah, that would be my first suggestion. He gave me an address. They have an office over in the government district. But let's also take care of your chip, because if you're anything like me, you'll be pulling your horns out before this is done."

✦✦✦✦✦

The two girls were just arriving outside the ACI office, after having made a quick stop at a local medical clinic to have Auryn's chip disabled. Now they were walking up to the front entrance of the building. They paused briefly before going inside.

"Latena," Auryn begins. "Are you absolutely sure about this? I mean, this is a government security operation, and by the sound of it, they are involved in something big. I...I am...I'm..." she frowns at the unusual sensation as she was still recovering from her procedure.

"It's part of that horrible chip, Auryn. Just go with it."

"Right. I'm, uh...not so sure how I feel about getting involved in something like this. I mean, I know we were talking about maybe joining a protest, or something, but I could never have believed it would escalate to anything like this!"

"Neither did I, but here we are. So, we should at least share what we have and see if anyone will listen. The Director at the ARC seemed eager to think I had a good point to offer."

"Well, all right, if he thinks so, but my side is a little different."

"Yeah, and he was fascinated to think we might have people out there like you."

"You told him?" she asks nervously.

"It's alright, Auryn. I think he might actually support you, under these conditions."

"Well..."

They proceeded inside the lobby to find a small sitting area, along with a desk and a neatly dressed officer.

Kita was working at her desk when the two young ladies came forward. As they approached, she brought her attention to them.

"Good greetings, citizens. Is there something I can help you with?"

"Yes, um..." Latena steps up to introduce herself. "My name is Latena Ta'yeen, and this is a friend of mine, Auryn Táwgari. We're both students at CPU, and recently I had a visit with Director Bak'vayn at the ARC about his special project concerning the Tav'ageen Anomaly. We got to talking about a few things, and he suggested I might want to come over here and speak to an officer about some ideas I have, along with a discussion group we have at the U."

"What sort of ideas are these?" she asks as she starts referencing her terminal.

"Well, um…I'm something of a conspiracy theorist, although my teachers always tell me I'm too young and full of ambition to know what I'm talking about. But I'm a student of political science and political history, and along the way, I've been noticing a number of things which I felt were wrong about the Charter of Laws, and the Council's management of things. And apparently, all these recent sensations we've been seeing in the news lately…which I think is probably your work, are simply adding into it that I may be right with my suspicions. He thought you might be interested in hearing what I have to say."

Kita pulls up a journal where she finds a memo sent by the Director relating to the girl's potential visit.

"Latena Ta'yeen…yes, he sent a note over here about you. A conspiracy theorist…and a very outspoken young lady," she raises her brow.

"Great, so am I starting to develop a reputation now?" she chuckles lightly.

Kita took quick notice of the girl's emotional display.

"Is your chip disabled?"

"Yes, both of us, actually."

"Interesting. Well, if the Director thinks you hold something of interest, perhaps we should listen to it. Can you give me a brief synopsis?"

"All right, first, we have a discussion group at the U, and we like to talk about these things on occasion. We've long held an opinion of something wrong with the Charter of Laws, and I found in my studies a number of sections where I feel the wording could be hiding something. I've studied all sorts of government styles, both real and theoretical, and written a number of essays about them, and I think ours is behaving like a type of authoritarian dictatorship, even though no one outside our group chooses to see it this way. But this stuff on the news lately only seems to be confirming my suspicions."

"Then let us first try to identify what it is you think you're seeing and go from there."

"Sure… Case in point, the Council seems to hold absolute power over what, if anything, each of the science factions is allowed to research.

The factions themselves don't hold the authority to choose their own studies, as it all comes down from the Council. So, IF the Council wants them to study something, THEN they have the opportunity to do so. And right now, as far as I know, no one is studying anything, and the Council is presumably in this deliberation, which I have serious doubts over, and hoarding it all to themselves…and this is another of my arguments."

"All right. On this, you do hold a valid point, at least until recently when many of those same factions began to break from that control mechanism and choose their own topics for independent study, with or without the Council offering any direction."

"So I've heard."

"But you think the Council is actually keeping things to itself?"

"Look at it this way. If they didn't want it, they didn't authorize it. And the Charter says ALL forms of knowledge should be available to us, but they're not pursuing ALL forms of knowledge, only those portions THEY want. And if you factor in Elder Nazég, he was one they didn't want. Therefore, the Tav'ageen thing, which as I recently learned is false. The Charter gives them the power to pick and choose what they want, and discard anything else or simply cover it up, so we're not as free and liberated as we thought."

"This is interesting, but then let me ask you this. I have a minor in law at the U, with a major in criminal justice, so I know a few things about what you mean from that perspective. But if you are suggesting the Charter, which has been with us for so long, has a fatal flaw, can you explain how and why no one took notice of it before now?"

"First, we're all taught to think it's the spirit of the wording that counts. I think this is an excuse for a dictatorship hiding behind our collective backs. Then, the preamble says this body of statesmen, meaning our Council, will DRIVE our motivations, and to me this sounds like they intend to control it. It's a very clever manner of wording to fool us into thinking we have something, when in fact we don't. And when you consider the truth behind the Tav'ageen Anomaly, among other things, and the fact that all our other science factions are running on empty while the Council hides itself in this secret base, taking this secret longevity drug the Marshal claims he gave them, there is something wrong with the whole scenario. And it all comes out of King Saakerav, who started the whole thing."

"Why him? I mean, why do you suspect him of something?"

"What King would go to such trouble as uniting the world, and then simply walk away from his work? For instance, what would be the cost of all that? And you simply walk away after it's done? No. I think he was a figurehead for a hidden movement."

Kita gazed at the girl for the suggestive mention, as it was starting to sink in that this could be a missing piece of a larger puzzle. She briefly glanced at her terminal to review her memo.

"All right, wait a moment. Let me call someone to assist with this. We have a special agent here who might hold some insight. Have a seat here..." she directs them into a set of chairs at the desk.

Kita now reaches for her trans-com and tries making a call, but the line doesn't answer immediately.

"Hmm, I wonder if she's over there..." she mumbles to herself.

She now reaches out to her vid-com and links into a router to channel the signal through the special shard-com interface in the basement. She dials a number and waits. In a moment, the line answers.

"Ti'van here..."

"Ayene, this is Kita at the office. We have a pair of young ladies in here with some interesting ideas about the Charter of Laws and the Council behaving as a form of hidden dictatorship. This causes me to wonder if there may be a secret element we're discovering that needs closer inspection. Do you have a moment to join us?"

"Sure, give me a few moments to project and I'll be right over."

"Good, see you then."

They end the link and Kita smiles at her guests.

"We should wait for her to arrive. I think it will not be too long."

The group relaxes in their seats while Ayene makes her way across.

Ayene had been in a conference with Thaelyn in the WIC building at the time. She excused herself to find a seat in the adjacent conference room, where she would sometimes make her projection. After several moments, she was ready to travel. She folded her way to Azgarén, there to arrive in a local office space for privacy, and from there, she made her way downstairs to the lobby. On her arrival, Kita rose to introduce her two guests.

"Ayene, we have two people sent to us by the Director at the ARC. This one is Latena Ta'yeen, and her friend Auryn Táwgari."

Ayene presents herself for an introduction.

"Good greetings to you, I'm Lieutenant Ayene Ti'van. So, you have some sort of a story to tell? Maybe you'd like to come up to my office?"

"Sure," Latena smiles cautiously.

Ayene leads them back up the lift to her office, where they sit down together for a pleasant chat.

"Um, Lieutenant," Latena begins nervously. "I'm what you might call a political activist, which may or may not give much credence to my purpose here. I'm also a conspiracy theorist, and part of a group at the U where we sometimes talk about current events, and especially all these recent sensations on the news."

"How old are you?"

"Almost two…both of us…"

"And did you say your name was Ta'yeen? Do you know of anyone over in Central?"

"Yeah, my uncle is a Captain and works in the control center. Is that a problem?"

"Not specifically, but we have a series of security issues, so we need to walk a careful line, along with Central, on a number of sensitive topics. So, whatever we talk about here needs to be kept secret. If Central needs to know anything, we'll be the ones telling them."

"I see. All right…"

"So, where should we begin?"

"Um, all this here started as I had to go in for my preparatory for the seed recently, only to learn it was cancelled, which was surprising. Although not quite as surprising as seeing the intern without her seed, and a young centennial girl with a surgical patch on her head who was laughing at my reactions," she chuckles.

"Yes, that might tend to stand out," Ayene smiles.

"Here is where I learned we have the chips being turned off, even removed in some cases, and a few other things relating to the Council, the Marshal, and all these news sensations. You are researching stuff they forbade us to research, like removing the seeds. You're pointing fingers at the Marshal for subversive acts where the Tav'ageen Anomaly goes, calling it a hoax. Also, I believe you might know something about those seeds where that secret file is concerned. And you're apparently investigating the Council for corruption, and undoing a lot of things they did to us during this time. It sounds like you people discovered something…finally…and are taking action to reverse it, but all without exposing yourself in front of the Marshal and Sargeras, who are actually godlike criminal entities, according to the Director over at the ARC."

"All right, so far, so good."

"And finally, the Council hasn't been doing its work, at least not the real work, and let's not forget that election scandal. This points at them being corrupt and breaking their own laws."

"It would certainly appear that way."

"But where the Council goes, whatever they might be doing, assuming they're still alive and doing it, it also sounds like they are NOT our currently active authority. The Marshal is, and behind our backs with the Council acting as a front to distract us."

"Wow, you're a clever one."

"Yeah, I see words and I know how to interpret things. Like what I believe to be your fake Internal Secretary and his 'accidental' leak of the elections, and then your fake CPS officer with the Grand Hall fiasco. Am I right?" she smiles cautiously.

Ayene frowns at the girl for her bold assertion.

"I think I am going to need to keep a close eye on you. If the Marshal was paying even half as much attention as you, he might already know about us."

Latena giggles gently as Ayene continues.

"Yes, we are responsible for most of these sensations, although some of it is collateral as other people get involved."

"All right, this makes sense. After all, there have to be a few people with the horns to ask questions."

"Yes, more than you might think, if only you look in the right places. But admittedly, most of the general population fell into a bad habit for all the Marshal's fake and censored news media feeding us his rubbish, rather than the REAL news," she grins.

"What?" Latena shouts. "Fake and censored?"

"He had secret regulators in the news media, directed by a man inside the Grand Hall, and receiving bulletins from the Marshal's office. And this was also stated to be mandated by that missing Council due to those same war protocols and the Tav'ageen Scare."

"Wow, now there you go for a dictatorship. This sounds like it rides right up the tail. Could this be where Ileani Ur'paran is coming from lately? She works for you now?"

"Yeah, we recruited her to help us leak the real stuff, but indirectly so the Marshal still thinks his people are in there, just not living up quite to his full expectations."

"This sounds complex," Auryn muses. "And according to that

Director, apparently there is some sort of authority body out there hoping to come in and grab him, or something, right?"

"Yes, but that plan isn't as easy as simply walking into the room and throwing a set of binders on him. First, I doubt binders would work on something like him, and the two of them might see these others coming and try running instead. So we need to play a careful game to undo his work and distract his attention while they sneak in behind him. But now, what is this curious little story of yours about something secret?"

"It was originally about the Council and the Charter of Laws," Latena offers. "But it seems to be getting lost in all this new stuff."

"All right, let's focus on what you have, and we'll go from there."

"Sure. First, I believe they represent a hidden dictatorship, a form of authoritarian government body. For instance, anytime they actually did authorize any form of real research, it was never intended to serve us, unless it became incidental. They might authorize something that could serve the people, but it first had to serve them to have it. They seem to pick and choose what research they want, as well as their membership, especially if you involve Elder Nazég's name in the news recently. They didn't want him or his faction. If you look at the Tav'ageen Anomaly, and if we say Elder Nazég was getting ideas about it, they wanted it buried. Of course, now I hear the Marshal was involved, and clearly, HE didn't want it either. So, between the two of them, they chased Elder Nazég away and thoroughly berated him and his faction."

"They most certainly did. And we all listened to it for so long."

"Then, we have the science factions without any real work to do… UNLESS the Council tells them to do it. And if the Council doesn't care for it, they don't do anything. In other words, we do NOT have the freedom to choose ALL forms of knowledge we are promised in the preamble of the Charter. You do know how it reads, right?"

"Yes, I do. I hold a degree in law, and so I'm very familiar with the Charter. But let me ask this, although maybe you've heard this before. How would you define this as a dictatorship? Because the Council holds the authority to govern our direction as a society. This is their job, regardless of this recent business of the deliberation and the complications we are seeing from it."

"Look at this, and I'll show you my meaning…"

Latena pulls out her data tablet and loads a document showing the Charter of Laws. She zooms to the first page where she finds the preamble.

"If you read this for the spirit of the wording, as they always teach us, it sounds great. But I think it's a clever play of words intended to turn our horns down. Listen to this."

She clears her throat and prepares to read.

"We the People, who hereby declare ourselves to enter into this agreement, to dissolve and dismiss our ancestral rivalries and materialistic pursuits, to unite our population into one collected body, and from this moment to seek the challenges of higher intellectual ascension, do now this day create for ourselves a new Enlightened Era, where all people are created equal, where all forms of knowledge and wisdom shall become our domain, and where the direction of our society shall be governed by an attendance of statesmen who will drive our motivations on behalf of the many."

"All right," Ayene offers. "Now, explain to me what YOU see in it."

"It's fine up until these last couple of lines. We're supposed to be pursuing ALL forms of knowledge. But where is Elder Nazég in that statement if he was so often downplayed? He was chased off due to what might otherwise be a hostile body denying HIM the freedom for HIS pursuit of knowledge."

Ayene halts as the connection quickly rings a bell.

"Worse," Latena continues. "If you throw in the Marshal and that famous explanation of 'something out there', which that analyst said was so much like Elder Nazég's faction, this now says HE should know what it is, and if Elder Nazég was on the mark, he chased him away for it."

"In all the nether-space, young lady, you're dangerous to have around."

"Yeah, that's what the lady at my medical clinic said. This then leads us to suspect he is hiding something, perhaps in collaboration with the Council. And it likely involves the truth of the Tav'ageen Anomaly, which according to the Director is actually a latent ability in us. The Council behaves as if it wants to own everything, but I doubt they could own this."

"Absolutely not! Once you start turning off those chips, it'll be out on the street like wildfire. But this is where we and the ARC need to conduct research on ways to contain it, so it doesn't actually go wild."

"Yeah, he mentioned this to me. Wow, I'm not sure if I want to see that. But the Council never liked Elder Nazég. Every time a new form of science came into our society that the Council wanted, the Charter was updated to involve a new Elder to represent it, but HIS never was.

Best case scenario, he was probational, and highly skepticized. And then this last line: They will DRIVE us for our motivations. That's a control word. It doesn't say they will guide us; it says they are the ones in absolute control here. Compare this to how they clearly behave with the science factions. No one does any work unless they tell them to do so. And so, this is where I feel we have an authoritarian dictatorship. And it all got started with King Saakerav, as he's the one who wrote this. He spent untold riches to unite the world, only to walk away and leave it in the hands of this Council."

"Saakerav!" Ayene shouts. "Dammit! That creature did it to us again!"

Ayene's sudden outburst startled both Latena and Auryn. Now she was darting around her desk to her vid-com.

"Kita! Get Kaliya over here. We have a new problem."

"Yes Ma'am!"

Latena and Auryn both glared at each other at the heightened level of tension.

"Um…" Latena wonders timidly. "So, does this mean something to you?"

"Yes, it does! And you, young lady, for all your youthful ambition and controversial statements, may have just opened up another little secret. I'm going to ask you to wait a moment as another of our officers makes her way over here. She needs to hear this one."

"All right, but now I'm getting a little nervous."

"You weren't nervous before this?" Auryn asks.

"Well, yes I was, but it's getting worse."

"Yeah, but at least we don't have those horrible chips bugging us this time."

Kaliya was also in that meeting with Thaelyn at the WIC building when she got the call on her shard-com.

"It would seem I'm needed," she muses. "Will you excuse me?"

"Of course, Kaliya," Thaelyn nods. "I hope whatever is occurring over there is nothing too serious."

"It's probably just Ayene twisting up someone's horns again," she chuckles.

She moves away to the same conference room and sits next to Ayene's body to project her own image. A few moments later, she is arriving in the basement of the ACI building, as she didn't have an actual office of her own. She works her way up to Ayene's office to join the meeting.

But as soon as she enters, the two young visitors gasp at her glowing eyes. Kaliya was using her natural image, not her Suuden'kai disguise.

"In all the nether-space," Auryn wheezes. "Look at her eyes."

And yet, even with this, Latena almost immediately recognized the face.

"You!" she points. "I know you. You're that fake CPS officer."

"Oh dear," Auryn whimpers. "But Latena, those eyes?"

"Yeah, the Director said something about these people taking lessons from gods. Maybe she got blessed or something."

"In all the nether-space, Latena, are you actually developing a belief in something?"

"Well, I suppose I have to. We have people here worshiping actual gods."

Kaliya halts as soon as she steps through the door. She passes her gaze between the two excitable young ladies, not sure which one to focus on first.

"Oops... You have guests?"

"It's alright," Ayene waves at her. "Come on in, they know about the Prodigy Gift already...well, I presume they do. This one said she knew it was a hoax, and that it's an innate Gift."

"Yeah, but..." Latena gushes frantically. "He didn't actually say what it looks like on the outside."

"Well, now is as good a time as any to introduce you. This is Captain Kaliya Nazég, Elder Nazég's daughter. And she's a projection right now."

"You're kidding me!" she shouts. "How did you do that? And is it normal for your eyes to glow like this?"

"Not actually..." Kaliya admits. "You mentioned a blessing. Well, you're partly right. My eyes glow naturally, so I simply create the image to match. The image can be anything we choose, with the only true limitation being the capacity of our imagination to create something. And before you ask, since I know you will, all our eyes glow like this due to a gift we received from a race of beings we encountered on that ship that took us away. They say it was to cleanse us of something in our bodies."

"Cleanse? Cleanse what? I'm almost afraid to ask now."

"Let's come to that a bit later. You look like you're close to losing your horns as it is, and we just cleaned up recently," she smiles. "But they are strange energy beings, so this energy tends to reflect in our eyes now."

"I see, and thank you. And clearly you have emotions."

"We weren't here at the time Darumon gave you all his little toys. So, Ayene, what are we talking about here?"

"These two are students at CPU," she directs at the girls. "This one's name is Latena Ta'yeen, the Captain's niece, no less," she chuckles.

"Oh no! You're kidding me!"

"Just crazy luck, I guess. She also describes herself as a political activist and a conspiracy theorist."

"Now wait just a moment!" she bellows and sets her hands on her hips. "Captain Iron-Horn has a niece who's a rabble-rousing activist?"

"Yeah, go figure," she laughs.

"To my Uncle," Latena grins playfully. "I've always been his sweet innocent young niece. He knows I like to come up with these crazy ideas, but like the rest of my family, they all hope it'll settle down once I graduate and get into a normal life."

"Uh huh…normal. Kaliya, be aware, she could probably put Thaelyn to the test for her deliberating skills. She's already decoded half of our indirect clues and deduced their actual meaning."

"Uh oh…" she retracts mockingly. "That sounds bad, in and of itself. So, do we lock her away, or put her to work?"

"I don't know. She probably doesn't know how to use the skill yet, so I don't know how she might behave while peeking at people in the shower," she grins.

The two of them break out laughing at the thought.

"That must be one of those…inappropriate…uses of the thing… hmm…" Latena muses mischievously. "I wonder if I can check on Halin sometime."

"Not without me, you're not!" Auryn protests naughtily. "That guy's cute, and such a body on him!" she coos.

"Oh no, not another one," Kaliya smiles. "Ayene, we're giving them bad ideas. But you," she directs at Latena, "with that cute little smirk on your face. Sweet and innocent… Yeah, we probably do need to put her to work for us."

"My thoughts as well," Ayene nods. "I think we might have a special gem here. She was sent over by the Director at the ARC."

"Him? Why was she in there?"

"I was in there originally as a reference from my local clinic," Latena offers. "It would seem I'm one of you people for this Gift thing. I had the symptoms as a girl."

"Really! Ooh, I like that already."

"Also," Ayene adds, "because she has this theory about the Charter of Laws and the Council being a hidden dictatorship. Although you and I both know where it comes from, I think it was made that way from the beginning, and I don't like this."

"All right, one thing at a time, how do we define this?"

"Are you familiar with the preamble?"

"I recall this from my junior school. We had to memorize it as part of our studies."

"Good, so the Charter tells us we should have full freedom to choose our way through the path of knowledge. But even though the preamble tells us we should be pursuing the FULL range of knowledge, your father was cut out of it. Meaning to say, they didn't want him OR his faction as part of that term ALL knowledge."

"Wow...that cuts a little close. All right, next?"

"She also points out, the Council behaved as a hostile entity where our blessed idea of 'free and open' are concerned."

"Ouch, that hurts."

"Yeah, more of that spirit of the thing clouding the issue, like I said with Article Nine, Section Fourteen and those regulators. 'They must publish true and accurate information to the best of their ability...' so long as no one is curtailing that ability."

"In all the nether-space," Latena gushes. "So you already know some of it?"

"We figured this one out as we learned of those people in the news feed. There is something similar in Article Twenty-Three for that industry. Cute little bumps for who actually controls things. But Kaliya, you need to hear this one. That final line in the preamble. They will DRIVE us on our motivations, and according to her, this is a control term, not a guidance term. They are taking absolute power and disguising it as a form of freedom to fool us. Look at the science factions. We already know they don't get any real work unless the Council tells them to do it."

"All right," Kaliya nods. "So we have the Council taking a level of authority above and beyond what the Charter otherwise suggests they should have."

"And Saakerav wrote it."

Kaliya's face goes blank at that mention. She gapes at Ayene, and then briefly glances at the two girls.

"Grace of the cu'Nar!" she shouts. "He did it to us again!"

"That's exactly what I said! He set us up so we could be driven like hill cows to the slaughter. If we look at our history, we moved along a rather precise course to be where we are now. And of course, once he got what he wanted out of us, he came in and took possession of it."

"What are you two talking about?" Latena wonders openly.

"And what did she mean with that word cu'Nar?" Auryn adds. "They that follow?"

Both Kaliya and Ayene glance at each other wondering who will take this one.

"What does she know about any of this so far?" Kaliya asks.

"I don't know. Latena, how much did the Director actually tell you?"

"He said that the Tav'ageen thing was a hoax," she admits. "A big cover-up for a latent ability, and the Marshal and Sargeras are hiding from a god society. And you people are investigating a lot of stuff, and apparently making a lot of noise on the news lately. All those people leaking details to us, but indirectly so the Marshal, who is probably listening, doesn't get any funny ideas for another public Scare."

"Yeah, that sounds fairly boilerplate to me. Kaliya?"

"All right, the easy one first... The cu'Nar is that race of beings we found on our ship. They apparently assisted in delivering it to us, and we think they are a form of servant to one of these gods who is currently watching Sargeras...thus the name, as they are apparently following him and acting as spies for someone. Along the way, my people took up a kind of reverent mention of them in our language, that's all."

"So..." Auryn responds. "This isn't some kind of god you actually worship?"

"Not in this case. Not for the cu'Nar. We offer thanks for their help, and we honor them by showing our respect with certain terms we developed along the way."

"And this other god you mentioned? Who is that?"

"This is curious. Why are you so interested in learning of these gods?"

"Well, um, it's fascinating to learn of something that might be described as a god. I mean, after all, if we use the word god..."

"What was your name again?"

"Auryn Táwgari."

"Is this part of some kind of university study program, like to study early culture and their associated religions or something?"

"Um, well, partially, yes, we do have something like that. And it's true that I majored in our old-world cultural studies. But this is, um, different. Latena and I both belong to this discussion group with conspiracy theories and such, but I also belong to another group...which is technically forbidden."

"Technically forbidden... What can be technically forbidden in a society like ours?"

"Religion."

Now both Ayene and Kaliya go blank-faced. They gape at each other and the two girls in succession.

"A religion? Here?" Kaliya gushes. "Incredible! What is it you worship?"

"It's one of the older religions of our world. It gets passed down through our families, mostly. When King Saakerav brought the world together and turned us all to the study of science exclusively, religion essentially became outlawed, a forbidden topic of a past era, relegated to the history books and nothing more. But those of us who felt it was too important to simply throw away, kept it alive, if only in secret. We realize it's mostly just a bunch of mysticism, but there are those of us who feel there should be a higher form of existence out there, a higher mind that we could look up to for guidance and spiritual support, that we are not alone and there is someone we can follow to a true form of enlightenment."

"But do you actually have a god image of some kind right now?"

"Sort of, but it's an ancient idol. It's not something we can empathize with, as it doesn't truly represent anything physical. We call it the Creator, and we believe it stems from some really ancient society...very Early Age stuff, you know."

"Is there a history to it?"

"Yeah, and this is actually part of my university course. As best we can figure, from the old archeology studies, it dates back to some early moment in our history when our ancient ancestors believed there was this one they called the Creator who lifted us up from the dirt and gave us minds to think. He was the Father of our people who then guided us on our path of growth. This is also where we believe we take our name as a society...Suuden-Aryku. The Lifted Ones."

By this time, Kaliya was grabbing her horns and gasping. Ayene stood there with bulging eyes and her mouth agape, astonished by the story being given.

"In all the nether-space!" she howls. "Could it actually be?"

"If it is," Kaliya retorts. "This would be one of the most important elements of our history yet. No wonder he forbade it after a while, to put some distance away from it."

"Just like the Eracyodines!"

"What are you two talking about now?" Auryn wonders anxiously.

"Wait, please," Kaliya begs. "First, explain how you see this in the modern day. How can you find solace in worshiping some ancient idol?"

"Um, well, we feel there should be something like a higher mind out there. When the Marshal first arrived, some of us thought HE might represent something. But his false promises and distant behavior turned us away from him, calling him a false prophet."

"Thank the cu'Nar for that!" she praises boldly.

"Yeah, I suppose so. And yet, if he can exist, we started asking if there could be something else out there that could actually fulfill our desires to meet a truly enlightened mind. Then Latena met the Director, and heard his story, so she came and dragged me by the horns to see if I could find what we're looking for with these new gods you people found."

"I don't believe what I'm hearing…and from our own people. All right, Auryn, you want it, you got it. How about one called Lord Oghma, otherwise known as Sage of Wisdom, and Adherent of Inspiration. He's one of these gods we found. They're a society called the Estelar. Sargeras and his kind are known as Primordials, at least where the Estelar are concerned. It's more of an interpretation than an actual name. And the two of them got into a fight once, where the Primordials lost."

"Why did they get into this fight?" Latena asks. "The Director mentioned something about a crime of some kind."

"Yes, the Estelar found them creating young forms of life and using them as playing pieces in a kind of gladiatorial entertainment sport. This, in addition to just not allowing young species to ever actually grow up, cutting them off when they got too high for the bigoted attitudes they held."

"Oh! How nice! Well, Auryn, how is that for your false prophet idea?"

"Yeah, that'll certainly do it."

"Naturally," Kaliya continues. "The Estelar took offence at this, as they believe life is precious and should be allowed to grow, so they put an end to it. But Sargeras and Darumon apparently escaped and went into hiding. Now, here they are, trying to get a little revenge."

"Revenge!" Latena snaps. "Is that what he's doing? It figures!"

"Yeah, but it goes a little deeper than that now. Here's the part where most people start losing their horns. Darumon created us. So Auryn, your Creator figure might actually be him."

"Oh wonderful…" she moans and hangs her head. "But I would actually expect if HE was the one, he would WANT us to worship him, wouldn't he?"

"Maybe, maybe not… It sort of depends on how he wants to use us, and worship might not be a part of it. Those seeds, however… They WERE a part of it."

"How so?"

"Are you paying attention to the news about that secret data file we found? It's a bunch of alien coding to provide a type of life support machine to bring Sargeras back to full health after being in hiding for so long."

"Ew!" she shudders. "I'm so glad you got them to stop those things now."

"You and a lot of others, I'm sure. But now, we need to figure out how best to use you for this new information. That Charter has to go, I think. And the Council…well…"

"It has to go as well," Latena asserts. "Who ever heard of a government body composed of scientists whose sole purpose is to assign research projects?"

"Well," Kaliya considers. "Technically, I would agree with this one example. But ours is also called a technocracy, which is a valid form of government by some estimates, if also an unusual one."

"Well, all right, unusual. But if you ask me, governments are for politicians and lawmakers. I should know. This was my specialty at the U. I wrote a number of essays on the different kinds of governments and how they relate to each other, and there was no precedent for King Saakerav to create what he did, and certainly not to simply walk away from it after he spent so much time building it."

"She has a point…" Ayene relents. "Darumon wanted us all in one basket. So here comes Saakerav to save the day."

"Yeah," Kaliya nods. "And with his non-violent form of government to build up this fantastic technology machine."

"Wait! Him?" Latena blurts.

"He can change his shape, Latena," Ayene asserts. "So he can impersonate anyone or anything he wants. Saakerav was probably one of those occasions."

"And that would be the missing piece!" she blasts. "He WAS a figurehead, at least of a sort. So he comes in, spends whatever it takes to unite the world, sets up this outlandish new form of government, and then walks away, leaving us to develop according to whatever ulterior motive he has for us until we find ourselves here and now."

"And probably dropping in on occasion just to make sure things stay that way."

"So," Ayene muses naughtily. "Do we bring both of them up to him, or just the one?"

"Latena is the activist," Kaliya considers. "And I'm getting some good ideas for her already. Auryn is the religious kook, so she should go see Aerlie."

"Hey!" Auryn protests. "I'm not a kook. I can't help it if I'm doing something no one else in our world would think of doing…and therefore might say I lost my mind…which sometimes I think I have…but I'm not a kook!"

"Trust me," Latena smiles. "She's only a minor kook, but I'll watch over her."

"Where we're going," Kaliya notes. "She'll fit in wonderfully. Most of our people are taking some level of devotion, if only due to Darumon. If he were to try peeking in on us at any moment, he wouldn't like what he sees. But this also brings up another mention. We can't let this out publicly here. If he should even smell the Estelar, or hear any mention of the name, he might take off and we'll lose him."

"What about you, Kaliya?" Auryn wonders. "Is it alright for me to call you Kaliya, or do you prefer I use a formal address?"

"It's fine, go ahead. I'm only two centuries ahead of you, so we're not that far off. And a lot of us are on a first name basis. In fact, let's be friends and take a more relaxed approach, shall we? I'm always open to make new friends."

"Sure!" she smiles pleasantly. "But what about you, do you actually worship this god you mentioned?"

"I'm a paladin of Oghma. It's a type of holy warrior that's also part priest. I'm creating an army of them, and this also includes Ayene here."

"Wow, holy warriors. This actually reminds me of some of our old stories."

"Darumon romanticized some of those stories. I'm reinventing a few. But what I'm going to recommend is we drop you off with Aerlie. She's a priestess, so she can start teaching you about our gods. Ask any question you like and see how it matches up to your expectations. We'll meet up again later to see what you think of it. Meanwhile, I want to bring Latena to Thaelyn, and share some of this new detail."

"All right. So, um, why are we standing here in your basement?"

The group had finished their meeting in Ayene's office, and now they were reconvening in the basement of the building. Kaliya and Ayene were still both in projected form, and they were standing near the conjuring pad and Harvester unit. In a corner was a human male sitting at a desk. He was a mage who was assigned to this post as part of the duty to provide passage out of the building to Tae'Eladar.

Latena and Auryn both took notice of him as they arrived in the room, but were trying to keep quiet about the clearly alien being sitting in the room with them.

"Yeah, about that," Kaliya responds. "The people we're working with have a very unusual form of technology, which will probably blow your horns off a few more times. To us, it looks like magic. This guy over here," she points at the man. "He's a mage, someone who uses this like a profession. This device you see here," she now points at the Harvester, "is a piece of custom technology we have on loan to provide a form of energy we don't normally have in our universe."

"Um, wait..." Latena interjects. "Not in OUR universe?"

"Darumon led our military...or rather I should say YOUR military, into a completely new universe, as well as a location in four-dimensional space, as part of his plan to chase his old rivals, but none of you are supposed to know about this."

"You mean, we already found something?" she shouts. "So, that analyst on the news wasn't just hinting at something, he was trying to open up an idea for later!"

"That's right. My father was chased to this other universe as part of Darumon's games to play with us along the way. In that other universe, we found these people, and now we're all coming back here to put things right. But that other universe, and indeed MANY other universes, has this special form of energy. Ours does not, which means people like us don't know what it is or how to use it. This is again part of Darumon's statement about something 'out there'..." she waves a hand figuratively. "But trust me, this blows the top off of any traditional kind of technological evolution."

She now turns to the mage and waves him over. The man grabs a rune stone from his desk and strolls over to the conjuring pad.

"He will call up something we call a portal, which is a variation of a conveyor. This will send you to a world we call Tae'Eladar, where we'll reconvene and go from there. Ayene and I need to take our own path by folding our images back to that location directly."

"You can do that?"

"Yes, our bodies are currently on a world we call Therinë, so this is truly a powerful Gift."

"Wow, can you teach me how to do this?"

"I can, but let's see about that later on."

Kaliya directs the mage to begin. He positions himself on the pad and begins conjuring up the energies into the rune. Latena and Auryn both gaze in wonder as the odd-looking stone begins to glow with a ring of light circling around it.

"All right, Ayene, why don't you go ahead and catch them on the way out. I have my doubts either of them has ever travelled this way before," she grins.

Ayene smiles and nods, then flashes away. Her sudden disappearance startled the two girls.

"Now, who wants to go first?" Kaliya smirks.

"How do we do this?" Latena asks.

"Just touch the glowing stone with your fingers, and poof, you're gone."

"When you say, poof you're gone, I hope it's not a permanent issue."

"I will mention one thing, the journey is rather long from here, so keep your wits about you as you pass through the conduit."

Latena nods as she cautiously lifts a hand over the strange glowing artifact and gingerly brings her fingers in a group down onto its surface. In an instant, she is enveloped in a bathing glow which carries her away.

Auryn jumped back at the sight of seeing her longtime friend vanishing in a ball of light. Suddenly, she was both frightened as well as fascinated by this form of travel.

"You're next, Auryn," Kaliya urges. "We usually give a small delay

in the timing to allow the people to move out of the way. Go ahead.
I'll meet you there in a moment."

"Uh huh…"

Now Auryn brings up a hand, and just like her friend, touches the
glowing stone.

Kaliya nods to the mage, and then she follows behind, folding away
to Tae'Eladar.

Ayene was waiting in the guildhall courtyard, where the exit point of
the portal would arrive on a special pad most often reserved for official
use. Latena's awkward transit through the dimensional conduit left her
screeching as she made her fumbling exit, forcing Ayene to catch the
poor girl on the way out.

Latena was panting from her fright, but as she found herself in
familiar arms, she slowly pulled herself together to realize she had
arrived in a completely different world.

As she stepped away from the pad, she glanced around in awe at
the variety of people passing through the courtyard, along with the
nostalgically romantic, if also alien architecture, and most importantly,
the fresh air and clear skies. This, more than anything, caused her to
stop and stare. A moment later, Auryn arrived, and soon after that
was Kaliya to join them.

"Is that real up there?" Latena wheezes. "I can see actual clouds,
just like on the old vid-com historical programs. And the air!"

"Look there!" Auryn points at a nearby planter box.

The two of them rushed up to the planter to breathe in the aromatic
fragrances of the local foliage and numerous flowering shrubs. They
gazed at the surrounding ornamentation and the people wandering
around, some of whom stopped to stare back at their curious visitors.

"All right, Kaliya," Auryn whines. "I think I want to live here. How
much are apartments? And what kind of jobs do these people have?"

"Well, I'm sure there are people you can talk to about that, but let's
try to stay focused for a moment. We still have lots of time for that."

"Right, and I need to bring the rest of our sect over here, assuming
these gods of yours can, um, you know…help us."

"I think they probably can. Let's go, follow me."

Kaliya leads the group out of the courtyard and onto the avenue
leading down the hill to the main cross street. Latena and Auryn both
study the quaint city setting, which reminisced of their ancient culture
back home. On the street ahead, they observed people walking by on

the sidewalks and horses pulling wagons. The two of them halted to stare at the abnormal sight.

"In all the nether-space," Latena balks. "You have personal conveyor devices, and yet you still use wheeled vehicles pulled by animals?"

"Yeah, it's like I said, these people evolved by different means. This aspect of magic changed a lot of things for them, so we can't measure them by our own example."

"But wheeled vehicles pulled by animals? Couldn't they invent a hover shuttle by this time?"

"Well, they're only in their Industrial Age so far, so give it time. Maybe a century or two…"

"A what or two?" she shrieks. "It took us a few hundred millennia to do that!"

"Yes," Ayene issues. "But then we also have ridiculously long lifespans, so we probably took our leisurely time with it."

"Oh, leisurely time, is it now?"

They continued along to the cross street and turned, then strolled down to a large temple complex.

Auryn stared at the ornate building coming up ahead. It was clearly a very important structure for the architectural styling, but she couldn't very easily associate it as a temple of any kind, as her society didn't have any more by this time, and certainly nothing this elaborate even from the perspective of their history.

They arrived at the door and entered inside. She could almost feel the reverence of the building in the grandeur of the interior adornments, the statuaries, and other furnishings. And up on the dais, she could see a wide array of icons lining the platform, each depicting a different deity. She started feeling weak in the knees, and she began hunching over penitently.

As they approached the platform, Kaliya waves to one of the priests.

"Ah, Kaliya," he announces politely. "Do we have some special guests on this occasion?" he asks as he takes notice of the two new additions.

"Yes, we do," she smiles. "This young lady," she directs at Auryn, "if you can believe it, is an aspiring worshiper from Azgarén. She simply needs something to worship. Do you think we can accommodate her?"

"Oh! Well, but of course!" he chuckles. "But from Azgarén? I thought they were all too heavily devoted to their science, not any kind of religion."

"That's what we thought, until this girl walked in the door. They're part of a hidden sect trying to hold on to something from our ancient past. The trouble is they're not happy with what they have and are looking for something better…like our gods. Is the Lady around? I'll need her help since she speaks the language."

"Of course, one moment…"

The man directs one of his younger clergymen to rush off towards Aerlie's office in the rear. The group waits, with Auryn taking special notice of the priests in their robes, and the chanting in the background as a group was in rehearsal of a daily prayer. Then Aerlie emerged from her office, and Auryn felt her knees buckle completely. She gazed at the graceful, winged figure arriving in view as she nearly fell to the ground.

Kaliya, Ayene, and Latena all turned to find their friend kneeling on the ground and hunched over as Aerlie arrived in front of them. Kaliya and Ayene both offer polite bows, which causes Latena to follow suit to mimic their actions.

"Uh, Kaliya?" Aerlie muses curiously. "Do we have guests today?"

"Yes, this timid little girl down here is looking for salvation. Think you can help? They don't speak Tae'Eladaran, so we need to use our native form."

"Of course," she smiles.

Aerlie bends down to take the girl's hand and speaks softly to her.

"What is your name, Child?"

"Auryn Táwgari," she replies shyly.

"And Kaliya says you seek to learn the ways of our gods?"

"Yes, Holy One. But I feel very weak right now. This place is so beautiful, and a little overpowering."

"Perhaps it is, at that," she smiles. "What is it that brings you here? Your people are not known to hold such a desire as a religion."

"No, not in our modern day, but I belong to a secret sect. We have chapters in most of our major cities back home, as far as I know. We always felt there was a need to find support for the spirit, but we have to keep it hidden because it's generally not tolerated in our society to worship a religion. It's technically forbidden to us."

"This is a most curious statement, to think of a society of intellectuals, in your case of scientific devotion, forbidding such a thing as a religion. Could it not be that a god might desire you to seek knowledge every bit as much as a scientist would?"

"I don't really know how to answer that, but I think the traditional belief is that the two sides tend to exclude each other."

"Yes, in some societies they do. So, do you have anything specific in mind?"

"We've been trying to hold on to an ancient form of idol that once belonged to our ancestors, but it's just a hunk of rock, not something we can feel anything for. What we really want is a higher mind that can help us find a form of true enlightenment, and Kaliya suggested I look at what you have here, especially one she calls, um...Oghma?"

"Ah yes, her people have found a special interest in him. Perhaps what I can do is simply give you a little introduction to all of them, as a nice well-rounded tour. Are you thinking of taking up studies of some kind?"

"I don't know. I'm still a little afraid."

"Well, there is nothing to be afraid of here. Come, stand up and I'll show you around. My name is Lady Aerlie, by the way."

"Lady Aerlie?" Latena wonders. "Is that a noble title?"

"Indeed, it is, although I'm actually the royal Queen of this world."

Now Latena felt a chill rush through her. She wasn't informed of this little detail before they embarked on their rambunctious excursion. She instantly felt her legs give out, and she collapsed to the ground next to her friend.

"My deepest apologies, but I didn't actually know you were a Queen."

"Oh, silly!" Aerlie giggles. "I'll bet Kaliya did this just to see your reaction. She has something of a reputation around here."

"Yeah," Kaliya grins. "Watching people's horns go flying off is fun."

"Oh!" Latena blasts. "Is THAT how you like to play it?"

"Are you also looking to learn from us?" Aerlie asks. "What is your name?"

"Latena Ta'yeen, but I'm actually here to meet...um..." she glares at Kaliya a moment. "Maybe I should ask you about this if she's playing these sorts of games. Thaelyn?"

"Yes, my husband...and our King," she smiles.

"Uh huh...that's what I was thinking. All right, so how do I address him, so I don't make a fool of myself twice?"

"Just relax, Latena. Thaelyn and I are both very easy to get along with. He goes by the title of Lord most often. We like these as they hold a nostalgic feel for our earlier beginnings."

"Really! All right, but do you use anything like 'Your Majesty' or some other traditional form here?"

"Anything that would normally apply to such stations as ours is fine," she nods. "But most of all is to relax. What is it you wish to talk to him about? This should be interesting, if Kaliya brought you all the way over here for it."

"I'm, uh…a political activist?" she smiles bashfully.

Aerlie stands back up as she cocks her head and raises her brow. She sets her hands on her hips and makes a brisk flutter of her wings, and then glances at Kaliya.

"Are we trying for another mark on his list today?"

"It's been a slow month, so…you know," Kaliya shrugs and smiles.

"Of course…" she chuckles.

She draws Auryn with her, and the two of them move away to give the young girl her first lessons in the local gods. Kaliya then leads the rest of her troupe back outside to the local gateway node.

✦✦✦✦✦

"Incredible!" Latena shouts. "So, even without a proper space industry, you can travel between worlds just by using these things?"

"We still need that initial index to find our destination, but essentially, yeah."

"And again using wheeled vehicles, although in this case a motorized one."

"Yes, that's a recent improvement as we found ourselves crossing these new worlds we discovered along the way."

Kaliya's group was just arriving on Therinë through the gateway hub station. As before, Latena had to travel separately through the portal, while Kaliya and Ayene, who were still projected, followed independently.

"And you use this as a form of public transportation…so common, so easy!"

"That's right. Now, we'll go across the way here, where Ayene and I need to pick up our bodies."

"That just doesn't sound right…to pick up your bodies. Can I watch?" she grins impishly.

"Sure, but it looks a little weird if you're not used to it."

"I'll keep that in mind. After all, this might finally help me understand what happened to me that one time."

They stroll outside and across the plaza, with Latena taking in the new sights, sounds, and smells. They make their way back to the WIC building where Kaliya leads them to the conference room to find both her and Ayene's bodies sitting in the chairs. Latena halts at the surreal sight.

"Yeah, maybe you're right," she mutters uncertainly. "This is a little too weird."

"Just wait till you see us merge," Kaliya smirks.

Latena hovers in the room as the other two women return to their bodies. She partially covers her face as she observes their spirit projections seem to turn translucent while they sit back down and merge their images back into their bodies. A few moments later, both of them wake up.

"Yeah, um," she hesitates. "I think I might have changed my mind about learning how to do that."

"It's actually not as bad as it seems," Kaliya responds. "It just takes a little getting used to."

"A little?"

Kaliya now leads them back into the main strategy room where Thaelyn and his officers were still in their meeting. As they arrived at the door, Thaelyn took quick notice of the returning officers, along with their guest.

"Eh, General," he mumbles cautiously. "We seem to have a stray lamb arriving in the wolf den."

"Oh dear gods, now what," he chuckles.

"Kaliya and Ayene, so good to see you return. But now, who is this you have here?"

"My Lord," Kaliya begins. "We'll need to speak in our native language, since she doesn't speak Tae'Eladaran. But I wish to present to you Latena Ta'yeen, Captain Ta'yeen's niece."

He raises his brow at the mention of the name.

"Are we abducting family relations now?"

"Well, I figure, better us than Darumon," she smiles sweetly.

"Oh, naturally," he throws his hands up. "Why did I not think of this sooner? And should I ask why this occasion is so special?"

"Why, of course, my Lord! After all, she's a special young lady."

"Uh huh..." he covers his eyes. "General, I am developing a strong suspicion that we will need the list again…and also my medicine. As I will likely have another headache before this day is out."

The General smiles and laughs silently.

"Very well," he continues. "Come join us here at the table. And just how did you come upon this sweet innocent young lady?"

"Oh, well…" Ayene interjects. "You see, she's just a lost little girl who wandered in off the street and found her way into the basement of the ACI building, and then, uh…kind of bumped into one of our portal runes just as the mage was conjuring up the energies."

"Oh! How tragic! General, we need to improve on our safety protocols where those are concerned."

They all erupted in a quick laugh as Kaliya and her gathering approached the table, with Latena feeling a little self-conscious for the special occasion. She cautiously steps forward to make her introduction. As she does, she feels nervous, but attempts a polite curtsy.

"Your Majesty, I hope you can pardon my lack of proper form, but we are not as well-practiced where I come from."

"Most interesting," he rises partially and bows. "And yet you do seem to have a fair amount of culturing in you. Where did you even learn this much? Or did one of these mischief-makers impart a few lessons?"

"Oh no, not of this sort, at least," she flashes an impish smile at Kaliya. "I'm a student at the university in Capitol Prime, and I study such things as political science, political history, and also social history. And I suppose, like a lot of people, I tend to romanticize our ancient history a bit, so you might say I just picked up a few ideas along the way…although I never once imagined I might ever use them."

"Indeed, but your demonstration might suggest you would make a good politician, or even a diplomat or an ambassador if you keep this up," he smiles.

"Wow, Latena," Kaliya grins. "That's already a very good impression you made, if he's offering this sort of advice."

Kaliya directs her people into a row of chairs at the table as she begins to explain.

"Latena is a curiosity for us," she admits. "This is what called both of us away a short while ago. She came in to the ACI building as a referral from the Director at the ARC."

"She was… And for what reason?"

"Originally, she was apparently sent there as the result of a recent visit to her local medical clinic, where they found out she's a hidden Prodigy Child."

"Ah, I see, and so she was referred to him for further study."

"Right, but then he began talking to her, and this is where she started bringing up some of her own ideas about things."

"Ideas…and do any of these ideas require a mark on our list?"

"Probably…" she rolls her eyes. "Ayene was interviewing her when I arrived, and says we need to watch out for her. She apparently has a few skills in deliberation, to say nothing of deductive reasoning."

"Indeed! I may wish to examine this."

"We also learned something which I think none of us realized before now, at least not directly, but it certainly caught our attention."

"Very well, how do you wish to proceed on this?"

"Latena, since this is your discovery, I'll let you handle this part."

"Oh, thank you," she retorts playfully. "You push me through a hole in space that takes me to a completely different universe where they have public transportation conveyors to carry you from one world to another, but from there you need an animal hauling a wheeled vehicle to go across town," she giggles. "And now I need to explain my case to nothing less than a King."

Thaelyn smiled as he watched the young girl, and he could feel the youthful energy emanating out of her. She clearly carried an attitude, and her interactions told him she was quick to learn.

"You say you are a student, Miss Ta'yeen? Do you have a direction for yourself yet?"

"Well, I'll be graduating in a couple of months, and my family has been trying to get me to settle down and find a job. Since I'm into politics, I was hoping for something along those lines, but so far, I'm still a little undecided. You see, I don't like our existing political system."

"Indeed, and just for the sake of discussion, what is it about your current system that disturbs you so, although I can probably guess at a few issues just from our own experience."

"Yes, those would be a good place to start. I'm what you might call a political activist."

"Oh! Now I get it! And is this where we begin dispensing the marks, Kaliya?"

"Just wait till she gives you her sales pitch."

"Of course…" he nods. "General, keep yourself handy."

"Your Majesty," Latena continues. "First of all, I'm majoring in political science, also political history, and a minor in social history, so I have a range of studies that I brought together, and along the way, I began to take notice of something. My teachers often said I have too much youthful zeal, but I also belong to a debate group at our university, and once I shared my perspectives, many of them also began to see it. This was further compounded by all these recent sensations in our news media, which I now understand is largely your work, along with the ACI."

"So, it would seem our efforts are paying off a bit. Very good..."

"Not simply that," Ayene asserts. "But she's deciphering them and coming up with the actual meaning."

"Oh dear. Does she make any visits to Central Command and Darumon's office? If so, we may need to detour her through one of our public transportation conveyors, and then send her off for a leisurely ride through the country in one of our horse-drawn carriages."

"That actually sounds lovely," Latena smiles. "The air here is so fresh; I could fall in love with the place."

"Indeed, as compared to your own, I can understand that."

"Anyway, I've also written a number of essays comparing one form of political system to another, along with the benefits and drawbacks. Studying the different forms of government was always a fascinating subject for me, and ours just isn't right."

"When you say it is not right, how do you mean this precisely?"

"Well, for instance, have you ever heard of a government body that is composed entirely of scientists who do little more than dole out research grants?"

"Specifically of this sort, I have not. When Kaliya and her people first came forward, and I learned of your ways, it did in fact seem as a rather unusual form of government body, one we might call a technocracy, where instead of the more traditional political agents, you might have people of a business or perhaps technical background guiding your society. In fairness, I have seen a few such examples during my lifetime, albeit not very often."

"All right, maybe so, but are we speaking of a world where the concept was unheard of before that time, and so atypical of the norm that one might wonder where the idea could have come from in the first place."

"This might carry a curious paradox."

"And therefore, my biggest issue of why we have it. It came into existence during a time of feudalism and monarchial authorities. Such a concept as democracy, like to elect a body of statesmen, was virtually unknown. We are speaking of people who like to take absolute power unto themselves and hold it. And yet, here we are. A government body, such as an elected body, should be composed of politicians, not scientists…or, if to take your example, at least of people who are dedicated to the general spectrum of government policies, and not so specialized to one thing. A government entity is too complex to be managed by anyone with such a singular purpose of mind."

She pulls out her tablet and steps around to show him. He directs her into the chair next to him so she can make her presentation.

"In here," she displays her tablet. "I have the Charter of Laws, the main legal document that governs our people. During the course of my studies, I began to see what I believe to be a hidden message within the wording of this document. Small captions and phrases embedded here and there that could be interpreted in a certain way, such that if someone wanted to, they could take control, and no one could say or do anything about it. And apparently, you also found some of these relating to this recent work of yours."

"Indeed, so you, at the very least, among any others who might otherwise study this, did take notice of something. This is at least promising."

"And I believe it points to a deception for how our government is intended to be ruled, as opposed to how we are made to believe in it. My teachers call it the spirit of the words."

"Interesting, and I recall Ayene here using that statement once. Very well, let us take this apart for a moment. We will begin with the suggested meaning."

"Sure. The suggested meaning is to say we have a free and open society that is motivated to study all forms of knowledge as some grand goal to carry us forward into what we call an Enlightened Era. Here, allow me to read it to you. This is the preamble of the Charter of Laws."

She pauses to clear her throat and begins referencing her tablet.

"We the People, who hereby declare ourselves to enter into this agreement, to dissolve and dismiss our ancestral rivalries and materialistic pursuits, to unite our population into one collected body, and from this moment to seek the challenges of higher intellectual ascension, do now this day create for ourselves a new Enlightened Era, where all people are created equal, where all forms of knowledge and wisdom shall become our domain, and where the direction of our society shall be governed by an attendance of statesmen who will drive our motivations on behalf of the many."

"That sounds so very familiar to me," Kailen reminisces softly.

"Did you learn this in your own schools, Commander?" Thaelyn asks.

"I did, as we all did, and we still carry this with us. In fact, if you were to ask my father, or even Elder Vankkar, they could probably recite many parts of it by heart. But now, if she's right, and there's something wrong with it, I'll be very upset."

"Kailen," Kaliya reaches a hand over to his shoulder. "Hold on to your horns, my dear brother. This will be a wild one."

"Very well," Thaelyn muses. "On the surface, if we take it at face value for what we might suggest as the spirit of intent, we have a declaration of a world body coming together, discarding all their old rivalries, and aligning themselves on the pursuit of intellectual esteem. Then we have a body of statesmen, meaning to say your Council, which is chosen to direct this course on behalf of the masses. This would certainly give the impression of a strong spirit of intent to create a representative governing body like what you have now to guide your society along this new path."

"Yes," Latena affirms. "And apparently, during all this time, the people believed this to be the case. But your recent propaganda campaign has alerted our group, who always liked to discuss these topics anyway, and me with my youthful zeal and conspiracy theories, to believe something hidden has just been revealed."

"And how do we explain this hidden item?"

"To start with, this line that says ALL forms of knowledge shall become our domain. So, how do we factor in the expulsion of Elder Nazég's faction?"

"Uh oh..." Kailen moans. "She's right, now I smell something."

"Perhaps so," Thaelyn offers. "But let us approach this objectively for a moment. We also know Darumon was involved, and if Velen was coming to a conclusion regarding the Prodigy Gift, surely, he would want him removed from the equation."

"Probably."

"Maybe so," Latena submits. "But there's more to it. My history studies tell me it was never popular to begin with. The other factions often downplayed his form as too fanciful and intangible. Here is where I see the beginning of our problem. If you read the rest of the Charter, you'll find amendments where we add some new science faction, along with an Elder to represent it. And these occur whenever our history shows a new discovery, which is to say a discovery I believe the Council WANTED to have, but Metaphysics was never included. Elder Nazég had to push to gain any form of recognition, and even after he had a hoof in the door, the Charter was never updated to formally include his faction. His was regarded as probational, never firmly accepted, often ridiculed, and…" she waves a finger. "The Council essentially turned hostile towards him during that expulsion. And we call ourselves a free and open society in the pursuit of ALL knowledge. His was excluded in that…with hostility."

"Great Powers," Thaelyn whispers. "Kaliya, I think you were right; this young lady does carry some potential for debate."

"She's good with her facts too," Ayene adds.

"Very well," Thaelyn nods. "But can we explain this by some conventional means? Prejudice aside for the moment, could it be a simple oversight? Or, if we ARE suggesting a form of prejudice, could his have been an unusual example of it?"

"You're starting to sound like my teachers now," she smiles gently.

"He does that," Kaliya grins. "You need to watch him for it."

"Really! Thanks, I'll keep it in mind. But anyway, while these are certainly valid arguments, I don't think so. The Council holds an obligation, at the very least, to support those factions it actually does represent. If we consider this eternally long deliberation, and our science labs being virtually empty, they're not even doing this much. Then, we're seeing all your new sensations on the news, and this is pointing us at even more discrepancies."

"Such as?" Thaelyn wonders.

"Well, clearly, you don't need perfectly sharp horns to look up in the sky and see all that pollution, and then realize how long it's been since they built that industry. The Council, regardless of their deliberation, should see this much at least. As should most of the people, if it were not for that fake news you brought down. This looks like a deliberate effort to keep it, and further a deliberate effort to distract us from that other effort."

Thaelyn studied the girl, and took note of how she was formulating her statements so neatly. Even though she was quite young, it was clear she did have some skills at presentation.

"In our group at the U," she continues. "We've generally come to the conclusion that the Council may not even exist among us. We think they probably took that great wisdom and ran off with it, or something. Assuming they are still alive. That longevity drug is nonsense. And even if it were real, it would represent something they could offer, if only to keep us interested in what they are doing out there. In the absence of that, they abandoned their posts. Here is where I might say we are reduced to what I call an active authority, and it is not our native one."

"An active authority?"

"Someone or something else taking over. We WERE looking at the military at one time, due potentially to that secret lock on the research file. But this began to dissolve as we considered the courts overturning the war protocol, and then that fake Internal Secretary and his leak of the elections, along with C.P. Security and the Grand Hall incident. If the military was behind it, they might work harder to cover it up."

"Interesting..." he ponders. "A fake Internal Secretary, do you think?"

"It had to be. If he were real, he would know better. The guy who was supposed to be in there held that position for more than a century. I looked it up," she smirks.

"Of course..." he raises his brow. "General, put down a small mention to pay close attention to this young lady. If she performs this level of background checks, she could pose a danger to someone... although I am unsure who at this time."

The General smiles and chuckles, as Latena continues.

"Anyway, like I said, I see words, and he led Ileani on a clear path to unravel something."

"Yes, I suppose if you are clever enough, maybe also youthful and ambitious enough, and certainly one who actively looks for conspiracies, it might stand out."

Latena felt a warm comforting sensation at the positive appraisal.

"And then," she continues, "we have C.P. Security and Kaliya over at the Grand Hall. In all our long history, these events are occurring rather quickly, and very conveniently. Maybe it's just me and my conspiracy theorist mind, or maybe it's my youth and ambition that I like to see things happen on a scale that doesn't extend over centuries and millennia, but this would also stand out."

"Quite possibly. But do you think anyone else would see it this way?"

"My group agrees with me, but then we're all young, ambitious, and looking for trouble."

"Uh huh… Commander, we have another example here. Your society is proving itself to be rather challenging."

"Yeah," Kailen nods. "And here I thought Kaliya was bad."

Latena continues, "But that Grand Hall incident was right in front of the camera, almost like an act. That CPS Captain looked like he was playing a role, and she was intended to…accidentally…reveal something to the public. You people are worse than the Marshal for all his pranks," she giggles.

"Point your finger not at me, but those two at the end of the table there," he directs at Kaliya and Ayene.

"Well, whoever it is, they sure stirred up a pot of trouble."

"I have no doubt, and further that they are not finished."

"But I figure, if the military held this authority position, we would likely see them marching through the streets to put things back the way they want them."

"Very clever, and this does hold merit. Although, admittedly, it might also reveal the true nature of who your authority is and spoil some of that spirit of the wording."

"Yes, but if the people are growing wise to it by now, they might not have a choice. And yet, whoever is in control SHOULD control all these independent elements, but they do not…or at least not anymore. This now suggests to us there could be a body out there of some sort revealing these things independently. And if THIS is the case, the Council, at the very least, was NOT providing the service it was supposed to be providing, and someone knew this, especially if you look at that emergency committee they're forming right now. And this body, whoever it is that's revealing these secrets, is clearly hiding from someone, and it is not the Council, maybe not even the military, but instead that active authority…the one actively controlling things."

"Good gracious!" the General murmurs. "This girl should go to work as a secret intelligence analyst."

"Perhaps even her full group," Thaelyn infers. "Maybe the ACI should consider a junior training program."

The assembly ushers up a vigorous laugh.

"The Council was entirely focused on one thing," Latena admits. "Which was technically nonessential to any of us. And this again brings us to this picking and choosing aspect. I'm sure the other science factions out there would love to have some actual work pass their way, but no one did anything UNLESS the Council gave the word. And the Council knew this, which follows behind the clause in that document. 'Do as we say and only as we say, but only those we care to say it to.' And so we have a dictatorship. It's all in this final line. They will DRIVE us, not guide us as a role model, but drive us as a control authority. And we are told to believe, as if on faith, in the spirit of the thing."

"Fascinating…" Thaelyn muses distantly.

"I swear!" Kailen moans. "That one is simply sinister. And we still teach those lines to our children."

"My Lord," the General submits. "I think I must agree. As I look at this, I must ask about that statement of ALL knowledge being OUR domain. That last line suggests this body of statesmen is lifting themselves above that initial part saying, 'We the People.' This would mean their Council is a false body of public representatives, and instead an authoritarian body above them. If they only research those items they desire, or if we suggest Darumon and his interests, this could lead us to this path they took along the way."

"Much like we were seeing with the ARC in recent times." Kaliya nods.

"And with the rest of us only receiving anything at all as incidental returns," Ayene adds.

"Quite possibly," the General offers. "While I am sure they did need to research a fair amount to the greater benefit of the people… after all, you still need to evolve as a society. Nevertheless, there would be a general direction to it."

"Right," Latena issues. "And this would surely reflect on their picking and choosing aspect. We might benefit from some of it, but again, what about Elder Nazég? If we say he was a potential new form of science we might need to study, and if even the Marshal might admit to this study as real, when we consider that statement he published, followed by that analyst who associated it with Elder Nazég's faction, it might be controversial, but it seems like it was justified as rational."

"Even though no one might realize this UNTIL the Marshal made that statement," Kaliya shrugs.

"Yes," Ayene notes. "How ironic."

"One thing I would like to point out is that analyst again," Latena asserts. "If we say the Marshal understands this same principle, and he gave it to the Council to study, they would now be forced to accept that which they did not want to accept before. But since BOTH of them were vilifying Elder Nazég, and further to suggest these insurgents and their massive ship carrying him away for some reason, this might suggest someone else knew the situation. My group agrees with those people of yours. If those insurgents could drop a ship of any kind in our space, they should've dropped a military ship instead, if Sargeras was the real target. Why take away an undesirable member of our government unless there is another reason. And I happen to know from my research that Elder Nazég was a very gentle man, not a militant."

Kaliya smiled affectionately at the suggestion.

"Yes, Latena, he is, although he is also a wreck from all the hits we took."

"I am sorry about that. But this also leads our group to point a finger, as you say, at the Marshal. Is he wrong and these insurgents are right?"

"Powers behold," Thaelyn muses. "That would be a dangerous question to ask openly in this situation."

"Probably so. Regardless of the story behind the Marshal, we still have the opinion of the people over our perfect government body and this highly regarded benefactor to our society. They all wanted this great wisdom, and they believed he would actually give it to us."

"This is unfortunate, to say the least."

"Therefore, this might represent an intentional effort to hide something. And naturally, once again, this is picking and choosing, not the full pursuit of all knowledge. But in this case, it now involves the Marshal collaborating with them, even WITH his promises of great wisdom…which never materialized."

"It does indeed."

"But here we come into a problem."

"Oh, and how do you define this one?"

"The Marshal, that secret code, and the seeds."

Thaelyn raised his brow and glanced at both Kailen and the General.

"Very well, and how does this one appear?"

"He invented everything. He also built that military. That lock was dated from about the same time period, and it related to this seed research. It's clearly an effort to hide something, and likely the real reason why he frightened us into taking THAT rather than all our other colonization tech. The messages you have been playing to remind the people that we actually DO have that tech is a clear indication we were NOT supposed to be running away from home using anything OTHER than that. But he started a panic with the old Tav'ageen Scare. This suggests he took advantage of something, made it worse, and forced his solutions at us for a reason, but not the one stated."

"This is a clever bit of deduction."

"Right, especially when you consider that hidden code. So, the question is, what is really inside those seeds he pushed at us that you are now overturning his war protocols to clear the roadblocks that prevented us from removing them? This points at a conspiracy to infect us with something we might not otherwise want."

"Do you actually know what is in those seeds?"

"I do now, after these two informed me. It's awful, but it simply confirms the suspicion. Combine that and this projection skill, which is the real Tav'ageen Anomaly, and this validates most of what I am saying here that the whole thing was fake from the beginning, and Elder Nazég was right. But the rest of the Council, maybe also in collaboration with the Marshal, was trying to hide it. THEY didn't want it, and likely because they wouldn't be able to own it, like everything else."

"Yes, young Miss Ta'yeen, you are a dangerous one. Fortunately, we found you first. If the Marshal were to see you, I fear for what he might do. Very well then, let us see where we stand on your more recent teachings. Kaliya, you and Ayene were both called away for this. What have you told her thus far?"

"I think, at this point," Kaliya considers. "She has most of it. The Primordials, the Estelar, the Prodigy Gift, um…like she said, the real reason for the seeds, also those chips, and then we have, oh…Saakerav and his role, and a lot of storytelling."

"Let me see…" he pauses to think. "The Eracyodines?"

"Um, partially. Not the full story."

"And the Council?"

"Ah, not yet."

"All right, let us attend to this first."

"Right. Um, Latena, do you recall our discussion of Darumon making us?"

"Yes," she nods. "And I dread to hear what he did. Are we his actual children?"

"Yes, half him, half Eracyodine. Part of our efforts involve giving those hungry researchers something new to chew on. We are working mostly through the ARC and the Director. He and all his science associates are helping us with a bit of background research. Darumon arrived a little more than two million years ago, it would seem, not long before our 'official' entry into a civilized form, and he essentially mated with some of those Eracyodines to uplift them to a sentient form. He then began to grow them into what we are today."

"Mated?" she grimaces. "You mean him...and an animal? Ugh..." she shudders. "To think of the imagery alone. So that ancient religion of ours actually holds some merit. The Creator is actually Darumon, in a literal sense of the word."

"The Creator?" Thaelyn wonders.

"Yes, I have a friend who majors in early cultural studies. The Creator is an ancient Early Era religion, probably dating WAY back to the beginning, where we have this mythology bit. According to the story, he is the father of our race, lifting us out of the dirt and giving us minds in which to think."

"Interesting...hmm... Lifting. Could this be where your society gets its name, the Lifted Ones?"

"Yes. According to her studies, this is where our name comes from. We probably took this as a result, or maybe this old religion gave it to us. But then we have Saakerav, and you say it was HIM again, posing as one of us and uniting our world. But Kaliya, you didn't actually say why he would want us to STOP worshiping him as the Creator."

"I could possibly offer a suggestion here," Thaelyn considers. "If his true intention is to direct you on this path of an otherwise unorthodox technocratic pursuit, religion might need to be discouraged, as it could potentially conflict with the idea. Science has a tendency to refute the presence of a divine Creator image. Also, this is Darumon we are speaking of. Not Sargeras. HE is the divine image, and Darumon is simply a servant under that. I think it unlikely he would want to steal the limelight away from his Master. There may be repercussions from that."

"Ouch!" Kaliya winces. "But yeah, and Sargeras may not even know what Darumon did to them...or rather us, that is."

"Indeed, and therefore to turn them away from it completely."

"All right, next is this. Latena, the Council isn't deliberating anything. They're dead...blasted away on some lonely moon somewhere as the result of Darumon's fake insurgents destroying our outposts during his so-called war."

Latena grimaces at the thought as she tries to visualize it.

"Well, there goes the missing Council and their grand efforts at uplifting our society with his false promises. So, the active authority is what... Him?"

"Yeah. He basically took control once he got his famous mandates to lock up the people with his seeds and chips."

"So our group was right to start pointing fingers. Although we at least held out hope that the Council was still alive somewhere, just running away with their precious secrets of the universe. But then, is this to say our glorious civilization of free and open scientific pursuit was really just him driving us for his personal needs?"

"I think so, mostly. And Kailen, for all the spirit of the words and everything else, you might want to know something. Latena, who wrote the Charter of Laws?"

"Uh oh…" she glances between the two of them. "And this guy is big. I'll bet he works out a lot," she grins softly.

"Once upon a time in my early Sentinels' days," he smiles. "But not as much now."

"All right. It was originally written by Saakerav himself during that time to set things up. And after what I have to assume to be a rather hefty expenditure to unite the world, he simply walks away from it."

Kailen moaned and covered his eyes. The General sighed and leaned back. Thaelyn glared at the girl, raising his brow, and gazing at the other faces in attendance. He then closed his eyes and shook his head.

"How typical," he sighs. "And I suppose this provides the final confirmation. It fits so neatly with all his other manners we have seen elsewhere. He invents that image, spends what could be untold amounts of wealth to unite the world, and finally, he leaves it in the hands of a previously unconceived form of government."

"Then, it's like we said in our group," Latena concludes. "He and the Council were, in fact, figureheads, and in this case with the Marshal serving as a shadow body behind it. And as the result, we never had a real free and open society," she mourns.

"Not the way it was advertised," Ayene affirms. "And then we have that 'spirit of the words' they keep pounding into our brains. Surely, Latena, you're not the first to question it, but they hammer it right out of you."

"And here we have my earlier argument. A king spending all his wealth to unite the world. But only to walk away from it? Kings don't do that. They're, um…" she glances timidly at Thaelyn. "Well, they're quite often powermongers."

"I will not argue this," he admits. "As you are right in many cases."

"She has a point," Kailen considers. "I would hardly believe anyone spending so much effort as to unite a full world would simply hand over the keys and walk away."

"Absolutely not," Thaelyn affirms. "We could take my example, for this point. Albeit I cannot be described as someone who simply woke up one day with the fantastic idea to bring a world under my control, I did spend a considerable amount of time and resources on it, and I am still here to oversee the result."

"Wow," Latena croons. "A real live example of it? Can I ask how it makes you feel to achieve all of this? This would make for a fascinating interview with someone who actually did it."

"I am sure it would. Perhaps, if you are so inclined, we could sit together for a nice chat on some of my experiences."

"Oh, that would be wonderful!" she smiles brightly.

"And so, we have Saakerav," Kailen reflects. "Or rather I should say Darumon, bringing our misbehaving little world population into order to serve his ultimate needs. He installs a false government body, romanticizes his actions, denies us a religion, but plants this idea of the spirit of a belief, and hides virtually everything else to conceal himself until he is ready to take personal control."

"One question, if I may," Latena asserts. "I know you told me he is hiding from this other god society, but what can he possibly do about it? He might be hiding, but why go to all this JUST to hide? He could do that anywhere, couldn't he?"

"He wants revenge. He had a secret mining base where we found Ayene and her people. He was then using this to build a kind of doomsday weapon to attack the Estelar. Then, he was hoping to release whatever few remaining Primordials might still be out there, but perhaps in prisons, and restore them to power."

"Ouch! I don't think I like the sound of that. Where are you at this time fighting back?"

"The weapon is gone, his military has been alerted as to who he really is, although very quietly and with instructions that he is very dangerous, and to play like everything is business as usual until we can make our move. And of course, we need to unravel his games and your public opinion poll over your favorite benefactor."

"Sounds like fun. Can I help?" she grins impishly.

"Eh..." Thaelyn hesitates. "Are we speaking of with or without this conspiracy group of yours? And then, what about your uncle in Central Command?"

"Yeah, my uncle. I love him dearly, but he really doesn't know who I am on the inside. Much like my mom. She thinks I'm her precious little girl, and like I said to these two," she directs at Kaliya and Ayene, "they think I'm just a sweet innocent young lady who will eventually grow out of this and get a normal life."

"Oh!" he roars. "Is THIS the game you play on them. Commander, I said it before, the females of your society are trouble. And it would seem, the younger they are, the more trouble they cause."

"Yes," he nods. "And this one has a group behind her encouraging the issue."

They all rise up with another brief round of laughter.

"If my mother argued about my activist side before..." Latena reflects. "Oh wow, I'd never hear the end of this one," she chuckles. "Travelling to another world, speaking to a King. Oh, this would unravel her horns in a big way. And oh! In a completely different universe! That alone would blow a few horns away for the mere sensation. You know, it reminds me of that time our star navy made a visit to our neighboring galaxy."

"Oh?" Thaelyn muses. "Did they find anything interesting?"

"I don't know if they did or not, but my history lessons described it as a great technological achievement. But then it was shut down for some lame excuse as to take advantage of what we have at home... which we never did."

"Sounds like more of that chokehold from the Council," Kaliya offers.

"I suppose you may have a point," Thaelyn nods. "He would surely not want his creation to go running off to some other galaxy, especially if he never let you colonize anything locally. You were clearly showing your ambition to explore, but now he wants to restrain you. How long ago was this?"

"As I recall..." Latena ponders. "I think this was about, um... thirty-five millennia ago."

"Thirty-five... Well, at least it is not that ten we keep hearing so often. Thirty-five would place him...eh..."

Thaelyn suddenly perks up in his chair as he makes a connection.

"Thirty-five! That is the age of Tae'Eladar since the Sarrukh came to visit."

"Sarrukh?" she emits tenderly.

"Cu'Nar's grace!" Kaliya snaps. "A turning point!"

"Indeed!" Thaelyn affirms. "The Maker must have seen this and took it for the same meaning. He was now curtailing them so he could more assertively direct them on the course HE wanted. If they held the capacity to jump to another galaxy, surely by this time they could take him home."

"And so, now SHE brings in the Sarrukh to refurbish Tae'Eladar, and of course here YOU come into it."

Latena watches the discussion, and glances around the table at all the heightened emotions.

"You people are scaring me now. Who are we talking about?"

"Maker Kuroku," Kaliya notes. "She's a member of the Estelar. Just as Darumon made us, the Maker is responsible for Tae'Eladar. We believe she has something personal against him and Sargeras. So, she created a kind of contender society to challenge Darumon's side."

"Do these gods do this sort of thing often?"

"I doubt anything quite like this, but she's playing a very delicate game here to catch him off-guard. Remember what I said of him being a flight risk. If she came at him directly, he might take notice and run. But if WE came at him, he's likely only to laugh at it."

"Oh! How nice! And how should I interpret that if you really ARE coming after him?"

"You should interpret it as we hold a number of secrets he wouldn't be expecting out of such little things like us, and we have HIM guiding us," she points assertively at Thaelyn.

Latena turned hesitantly to look at Thaelyn, who only smiled playfully.

"All right, I suppose I need to ask this now, if only to finish what's left of my horns. What's so special about you that he wouldn't be expecting it?"

"I am what we call a Celestial, half born of the Estelar."

Latena wheezed as she gaped at him. She was not expecting to hear this one. She studied him carefully, but as far as she could tell, he looked very similar to any other example she had seen so far in this world, with the only curious difference being his eyes and hair.

"Uh huh…" she mutters apprehensively. "And what does that mean? You're half-god or something?"

"Many might use such a term. We are a hybrid form to cross the gap between such as the Estelar and the Child Races, meaning people like you."

"Child Races?" she squeaks. "We're children to you? All of us?"

"This is how we tend to see you, yes."

"Oh dear, well that certainly puts things into perspective. So, um, how do you expect to fight him? With your animals pulling the wheeled vehicles, or the public transportation conveyors?" she grins cautiously.

Thaelyn leads the group in a pleasant laugh and pats her comfortingly on the shoulder.

"Since my arrival, I have been leading the people of Tae'Eladar, and more recently those outside, on a slow and careful path of development, as we believe in the growth experience more than anything else."

"Wait, Kaliya said something about this with these other gods. They don't give out the secrets of the universe for the taking, but only guidance to help us grow, right?"

"Precisely! It is a policy we maintain for ourselves that we call the Measure of Balance. If you look outside, as well as on Tae'Eladar, our local society is not as technologically adept as yours in the modern day, but in time it will be. Meanwhile, we had to make a number of compromises within our military to rise to our current challenges. But once these two Primordials have been dealt with, we must shelve most of this until such a time as the people are worthy of their secrets. However, given how quickly these races tend to evolve, I would not expect this to be an overly long period."

"About how long, do you think?"

"They move much more quickly than yours, Miss Ta'yeen. Under normal conditions, if given how we WERE progressing before all this occurred, I would suggest perhaps two centuries at most before they make their first forays into space."

"Two centuries at MOST?!" she shrieks. "From animals to spaceships? I won't even be ready for a family before that time! In fact, I doubt I'll even be ready for a steady boyfriend by then."

"Indeed," he smiles. "Kaliya and her friends have said the same. And this is further influenced, even without my teachings, by their involvement with her people and the things we had to share along the way. So, that number is likely to be much less by now."

"That's enough to cause my horns to fall off and stay that way," she sighs.

"Welcome to the club," Kailen smirks.

"But now," Thaelyn continues. "As to this offer of help, maybe along with your group. I would not encourage anything that could draw such attention as to bring down Darumon's wrath."

"To be honest, our group WAS actually thinking of joining our voices to some of those protests out there. But what I have here will likely prompt us to rethink a few things."

"Yes, I would highly recommend it. Our people are mostly in projected form, which denies Darumon any potential for retaliation. I would not recommend placing a physical body out there that he could somehow track, and then do away with as he once did with those early Prodigy Children."

"Oh, I would agree, but if you people could allow us some kind of a role, even if to conduct some sort of publicity effort to raise awareness."

"Possibly. You do have some fine skills, and I am not one to throw away talent. Kaliya, did you have any special plans for this young lady, or is this simply a social visit to reveal these issues of your local government?"

"I actually do have a few ideas for her," she considers. "She's an activist, and we have a clear issue with the Council, assuming we actually had one, and the Charter which needs revising, or maybe all-out replacement. Even without Darumon, this represents a loophole that could be exploited, if only due to the potential for future abuse by anyone who might actually try doing this to us."

"Very well, but if you are thinking of inciting any sort of rebellion against this government authority, regardless of the fact they no longer exist, I think I should point out that they represent a foreign body as compared to ours, and therefore it does not necessarily fall within our authority to invoke an alteration of their political system. We have you, the Commander here, and others, but you also regard yourselves as external, with many of you also joining my kingdom by now. We would need an authority figure to take this responsibility that does not otherwise hold fealty to me or mine."

"We have Kriv'tik, and he's basically already representing an insurgent force."

"Who is that?" Latena asks.

"He's a former Fleet Commander in the Azgarén navy, now the Director of the ACI."

"Oh, well that would certainly do the trick."

"And what about Kailen?" Kaliya resumes. "He's an HC, and although he's joined as an ally force with the kingdom, he's not...yet... declared himself a part of it."

"Are you trying to pull a technicality on me, young lady?" Thaelyn intones suspiciously.

"Only if it works, and I believe this one holds merit, as he IS working on behalf of the rest of our people."

"Powers pay pity… General…" he hangs his head.

Now the General reaches over to pat Thaelyn on the shoulder to comfort him.

"Your Majesty," Latena begins. "She's absolutely right. I would welcome your help with this, regardless of any political fireworks it may cause, and for good reason. Listen… Technically, you don't NEED a military or a political leader to lead a revolt. Anyone who can rally the people can lead a march, and I already have people behind me… my debate group at the U. And I feel confident I can bring more into it. For all that you've already done, if I was able to use this to convince anyone at all, I should be able to do more. And the fuel I've received here only adds more potency to it."

"But you should be careful how you apply that fuel."

"Of course… But you're also out there making noise against the Council, as well as the Marshal. This, in itself, is a form of insurgency. Then, you're out to dispose of the Marshal and Sargeras, but HE is basically the leader of our world, that hidden shadow body, regardless of any Council, and regardless of anyone actually knowing about it. Take him out, and we have no more government, so you're already interfering with it."

"Powers behold!" Thaelyn moans. "General, are you listening to this young lady?"

"My Lord, technically speaking, she does seem to hold a valid point here."

"Now," Latena continues. "To have one sovereign body influencing the politics of another sovereign body can be regarded as offensive, maybe even an act of war. But you're already at war with him, with the intention of taking him out of power. Along the way, you're a liberation force against a dictator. In the eyes of our people, you would be celebrated for your efforts, whether you think it is your authority to do so or otherwise. The seeds, the chips, this is already your work, and I for one thank you greatly."

"General," Thaelyn covers his eyes. "Do we have space on our list for someone of this caliber?"

"Good gracious," he winces. "I can't be sure. I may need to start a whole new chapter for this one."

"As for me," Latena resumes. "I would do this anyway, but I'll need backing. A young girl like me doesn't turn a lot of heads without someone backing her up. The Charter has to go, along with whatever form of government it calls for, and I still say we need a more traditional form of political body, leaving the scientists to do their own thing. For this point, I think even THEY would thank you. So, no matter how you look at it, it's a revolution, and you're already involved. So, you might as well finish it."

"Uh huh…" Thaelyn mutters. "And you are Captain Ta'yeen's niece, no less. I would never have guessed he might have one like you in his family. Powers help us… Commander, are all your females like this? How do you manage over there?"

"I'll admit," he relents. "It's hard. I can recall a few moments with Ankhia, and then Kaliya and her friends when they were children, and even now. But HER example is enough to twist a few horns."

"And I'm only on my second centennial," Latena grins. "Besides, I'm not as sweet and innocent as the rest of my family thinks I am."

"Oh, indeed!" Thaelyn accedes firmly. "What a surprise. Then how do you suppose we should proceed with this moment of political intrigue?"

"I can start with some rallies in town, but I'll need to take it global to get any real coverage. If you can feed me the resources I need, I'll do the leg work. You can simply be a hidden supporter if you like."

"This will require time and a great amount of effort. You said you are still a student? I would not wish to interfere with that. A solid education is an important investment."

"Yes, but graduation is only two months away. Maybe we could start after that, and then I could put all my time into it."

"Good, this is acceptable. In the meantime, we should coordinate our efforts and make a few plans. Ayene, you should pass this along to Kriv'tik to assist in providing some support through your office, since this is essentially an extension of our operations there. She will need funding, probably transportation, perhaps also printing services, or whatever you use to distribute literature, as well as…well, maybe an office to handle calls for inquiries, and let me see…presentation lectures at some sort of meeting halls."

"Wow!" Latena smiles. "That's already a lot of effort. Thank you."

"As you said," he sighs deeply. "If we are to do this, we should not make such trivial pursuit of it. I can call on some of our own people to provide assistance with ideas, maybe even scripts for your lectures. I might also suggest, if you are to interact with any of our people, as I suspect you will, you should take a course in our language. Kaliya can assist with that. This could serve us greatly in the future."

Chapter 8

SUBVERSIVE ACTS

A new day was breaking on Azgarén, although the measurements of day and night were very different for them as they were elsewhere. Latena and Auryn had returned to their dorms at the university in Capitol Prime after their visit to Tae'Eladar. Each had found their new calling, with Latena's mind swirling around her new thoughts of a political activist movement, and Auryn with her newfound religion.

At the end of the classes for the day, they split up. Auryn was preparing to return home to share her discovery, while Latena was making a visit to the study hall where her group was meeting.

As she arrives, she finds the usual members gathered around their favorite table. She struts up and sits down with a clearly confident smile on her face. This, in itself, stood out as unusual, because it related to emotion, and therefore the chip.

"Um, Latena," Halin wonders. "Why do you appear that way?"

"Appear what way, Halin?" she responds jovially.

The tone of her voice also rang out with something abnormal. He glances around at the rest of the group as they all studied her.

"Did something happen to your chip, Latena?" asks another member.

"You might say that. It's turned off."

"Turned off? How? And also why?"

"Guys, we have a problem, and I need your help, all of you, and anyone else you can call into it. But we need to keep it reasonably quiet, just between us. I met with those people we suspected to be the cause of all these sensations. We were right about several things, and wrong about a few others, but the reasons are actually worse than we thought."

"Whoa, slow down, Latena," Halin ushers. "You know how I like to rationalize things. What do you mean? What people and what problems? And how is it you met with someone?"

"The meeting was unexpected, but it followed as a sequence of events where one led to another, and so on. But Halin, while you may like to rationalize everything, you'll be losing your horns soon, trust me. I'll try to summarize this for you, but we have a job to do, and we have outside help offering itself to make it work."

"Outside help? Those people you mentioned, maybe?"

"Yes. These are the REAL people the Marshal is hiding from. And they're not insurgents. We were right, he is NOT who he said he was."

"All right, one thing at a time. From the beginning, Latena. And also, what is this with your chip?"

"The ARC has discontinued the seeds and the chips. They did this some time ago, but the news we're seeing is being intentionally delayed in order to allow them time to make some progress before releasing the fact that they are actually doing it."

"And why is this?"

"The Marshal is watching. He's our enemy. And he won't like what he sees. That secret file DID hide something in those seeds, and THAT is the reason for the Tav'ageen Scare. You might say HE is the alien thing plaguing our society."

"Uh oh..."

"I went in for my preparatory, and they told me the seeds were cancelled, and the ARC already has a way to remove them. The lady was missing hers, and she said the medical community, as well as emergency services and other critical elements, are going through this now as a prelude to a general release."

"Well, that certainly would be a relief," emits a third member. "I had my appointment coming up soon, so now I can forget it?"

"Yeah, it's gone now. They're also turning off the chips and removing them in some people, probably as they can find time and opportunity. There was a young centennial girl in that office just recently out from her surgery."

"Oh, I would certainly like to take a look at that!"

"But Latena," Halin wonders. "How does this relate to the Anomaly itself, and everything they said about it?"

"The Anomaly was a hoax for the stated causes, and the Scare was Darumon exploiting it. Darumon is the cause of those deaths…murder to hide the truth from us. Then he and the Council chased Elder Nazég away as he was beginning to figure it out. That ship belonged to an outside body that was following Sargeras. They evacuated him to find help from this other body who is now coming in to take those two criminals out."

"Criminals!" he urges. "Who are they and what did they do?"

"First, you need to understand the seriousness of the situation. Darumon kills people who get in his way. So don't get in his way. Let these other people do that. They're better trained and equipped."

"All right, got it."

"The Marshal, and I use that term loosely here, as he's probably not even military, but he and Sargeras are the last survivors of a dead society of supremely advanced beings that were killed off by another society of supremely advanced beings for crimes relating to abusing lesser beings like us."

"That sounds bad," the second member winces. "The whole society?"

"Yeah, it seems they all took pleasure in the form of entertainment over watching little things like us, but only to a certain point. After that, boom, I guess we're no longer entertaining, but instead a bother."

"Ouch!"

"So, they're in hiding, and the Marshal, for all his stories, is actually on a revenge attack, hoping to stab these people in the back with some kind of super weapon he was building in a secret outpost he had once. Everything else was a lie."

"But wait," Halin asserts. "How do we figure the seeds and the chip, which he made all of us take?"

"The seeds, with that secret code, serve as a kind of life support thing for his master, Sargeras. His form of life, in our environment, wouldn't be able to survive very well, so the seeds create a kind of field effect energy layer for him to tap into. This is how they live."

"I do not like the sound of THAT!" the third member exclaims. "And to think, I almost got one."

"As I understand it, this energy layer is normally an ambient thing in some places, but not here, so the seeds create an artificial one."

"And therefore," Halin surmises. "The full coverage of our world population."

"Right, and therefore the panic to push us into it. This was a critical step for him. And then we have the chips. These are a solution to the Tav'ageen Anomaly all right, but not the one we were told about. The Anomaly is a latent ability our species is just starting to realize, but it's the sort of skill NONE of us is prepared for. Therefore, the big mystery of what it is that ONLY a science like Metaphysics would understand. This might give you an idea for why Elder Nazég's name has been mentioned so much recently. They're trying to rub it in the faces of everyone out there who laughed at him, and basically tell them not to laugh at our free and open society that was supposed to embrace it instead."

"Great!" the second member tosses his hands up. "Yeah, that will certainly yank a few tails."

"But it runs even deeper, as our Council WAS a figurehead…for the Marshal. Our species was originally engineered by him; therefore, we have this crazy Tav'ageen thing showing up now. He holds a special interest in us as his 'children', or perhaps I should say as a pet society intended to do his work for him with this revenge thing. He is a nearly godlike being that has been driving our society during our full history, like with Saakerav uniting the nations, and our technological evolution to serve HIS needs. He's like a shadow body behind our Council."

"Oh wow…" mutters the third member. "That will hurt when it finally gets out."

"Now, as for these others. He apparently made a secret advance recently on his old rivals, but was discovered and chased away. Elder Nazég is still alive and now in THEIR custody. That ship was a delivery to evacuate him, and the Marshal chased him like a hunted animal just for fun. The military found a new universe out there, as well as real nether-space, so that analyst and his 'hints' are suggesting something to blow a few more horns away later on. And this is where the Marshal brought us to fight his enemies."

"Nether-space!" Halin intones emphatically. "That would break a few important theories. No wonder he described them as overly controlling, and denying us even to recognize what we might see out a window."

"Yeah, part of his promises of great wisdom he never delivered on," she chuckles. "But now that they know he's still alive, they are mounting a counterforce. The trouble is, he has us locked up here with his seeds and his stories, and our people bought the whole basket."

"We sure did," Halin nods.

"They're making their plans right now, but he and Sargeras could run if they see trouble coming. So they're taking this by stealth. Meanwhile, they're helping us realize what he did to us by feeding leaked information through the news, which by the way was originally controlled by him through regulators censoring everything."

"What? He was managing our media feeds?"

"Yeah. This is why we never learned anything. HE didn't want to share it. So much for our benefactor."

"Unbelievable!"

"And here we come to all of us. I'm going to lead a revolution. And you're all going to help," she smiles cutely.

Halin and the others all glanced uncertainly at each other before Halin leaned in cautiously.

"A revolution, Latena? I know you sometimes call yourself an activist, but..."

"Halin, the Council is dead, not just missing. He killed them after he got all his mandates. HE is our government now, and probably always was. He would be that active authority I mentioned once. So, to lead a revolution against him isn't such a bad idea. And you already know about the Charter of Laws. It has to go. And besides, these people intend to destroy both of them anyway. If they are the ones running the show, this is already a revolution. So we may as well make it official. A technocracy, as this is called, where the sole purpose of our government seems to be giving out research grants, which they never do anyway, and especially if you consider it was mostly for the benefit of an outside body with ulterior motives, is ridiculous. We should go back to something normal that works."

+ + + ◆ + + +

Auryn was making a return to her family home for a visit. She hopped into her hover shuttle and sped along the roadways to the eastern suburbs where her parents lived. As she arrived, she parked in the driveway and took a moment of pause to consider what she had to deliver to her family, and indeed to their full religious sect. Then she got out of the vehicle and anxiously strode up to the door, where she briskly knocked before entering inside.

"Mom? It's me. Where are you?"

"Auryn?" echoes a mature voice from another room. "I am in the kitchen. Are you finished with your classes for today?"

"Yes, and I wanted to make a quick visit. I need to tell you something. Where's Dad?"

"He is out in the garden. He is still fighting with that awful little vine that keeps creeping under the fence."

"Again? In all the nether-space, why doesn't he just jump over the fence, find the root, and pull it out?"

"Well, my dear, he is not as young as some of us."

A young woman comes out of the kitchen area, and they shared a quick hug. But she did not immediately take notice of Auryn's exuberant state.

"Not as young," Auryn huffs. "As if fourteen isn't young," she smirks playfully. "I think he's just lazy."

Her mother gazed at Auryn curiously for her vivacious statement, as well as her obvious manners.

"You seem quite energetic today. Did something happen?"

"Oh Mother! You'll never guess what happened," she grins brightly and begins bouncing. "It's what we've been waiting for all this time. I finally found it! But I need Dad to hear it too. And then we need to share it with the group."

Now her mother was glaring at Auryn for a clearly emotional display, and not a simple one at that.

"Auryn, what happened to you? You look like you are actually showing emotion."

"Oh, right, my chip was turned off. But now, listen..."

"Huh? Your chip has been turned off? Why?"

"Oh, that...yeah... They're turning off the chips now. But anyway..."

"What?" she urges tensely. "What do you mean, turning the chips off? Who is turning them off?"

"Oh! Right! The medical community is turning them off now. But now, like I was saying..."

"Auryn!" she blasts, now reaching for her interface. "Why are they turning off the chips?"

"OH! Yes! The Tav'ageen thing was a hoax. But anyway..."

"A WHAT??" she screams and clutches hard at her interface.

"Mom, will you stop with the nether-wild chip and listen to me. I found a real god!"

"A…god…?" she wheezes and reaches for a chair to lean on.

Auryn sighs frustratingly and turns to find the back door. She rushes up to it and peeks outside.

"Dad?" she calls.

"Auryn, is that you?" he shouts back. "What are you doing home today?"

"Trying to kill Mom with her nether-wild feedback, now it's your turn. I need you in here so I can tell you something."

"Feedback? Auryn, what sort of game are you playing today?"

"Dad, please. Stop fiddling with the neighbor's plants and get your crinkled old tail in the house. It's important!"

The man was on his knees working in the garden when the girl's clearly excited demand echoed across the yard. He turned to peer over his shoulder and saw her waving anxiously at the door. He sighed softly, put down his tools, and pulled out a cloth to wipe his face and hands as he rose up to stroll back inside.

"All right, my little sugar-horn, what is it?"

As soon as he comes within reach, she takes his hand and pulls him inside.

"Now, both of you listen," she instructs firmly. "I learned a lot of very sensitive details yesterday that we can't let out in public. There's a new government-level security agency out there investigating the Council and the Marshal. So, whatever THEY have been telling us these past ten millennia is probably wrong. For instance, the Tav'ageen thing was a lie, a hoax, and the chips are nothing more than an elaborate cover-up for the real reason behind it. It's a scandal that could blow the lid off the entire planet, but this security agency needs to keep it under wraps for now because the real villain is the Marshal, and he's bad. Got it?"

She glares at both of them, as now even her father was reaching for his interface.

"The Council is also being implicated in wrongdoing," she continues. "Partly for concealing the facts and behaving as a corrupt body."

"A corrupt body?" her father issues disbelievingly.

"Yeah, and this is not the first time. You know my friend Latena at the U, the conspiracy theorist? Well, she's been vindicated. Meanwhile, the medical community is turning off people's chips, like mine, and also removing them, as part of a secret operation to relieve us of these horrible little torture devices. Also, the ARC found a way to remove the seed. You recall the news on the new research? Well, it's actually old news now, delayed as a stall tactic to give them time to actually do it before the Marshal can put a stop to it. He WANTS us to have the seeds, and it relates to that secret code they found once."

"Why?" her father asks. "What does it do?"

"It feeds Sargeras as a kind of life support engine. They're using us to support him."

"In all the nether-space... But Auryn, wait. Where did all this come from so suddenly?"

"Latena had to go in for an appointment at the clinic recently...her preparatory thing. They told her both the seeds and the chips have been discontinued, and when she started asking why, they gave her... well, part of the story, the part they're allowed to share at the clinics. But so far, most of it is being carefully classified by this new agency called the ACI, Azgarén Central intelligence. She was told to meet with the Director at the ARC for more detail, and then she came back to the U and grabbed me. She said this ACI made contact with a foreign authority, the REAL reason the Marshal and Sargeras are in hiding. They're criminals, not benefactors. There's no such thing as insurgents, and his promises were all false."

"Criminals! No wonder he never followed through with any of his promises."

"More than that, Hani," Auryn's mother relents. "Our group declared him a false prophet, remember? A good thing, too..."

"Yes, but Marna, this goes a little beyond simply failing to live up to his promises, when you consider what she said about those seeds. THAT would be criminal!"

"The whole thing runs really deep," Auryn affirms. "But now, Latena came to me and asked me to join her as the Director referred her to speak with an agent at the ACI about some of her conspiracy theories. This is actually where she got vindicated, as the Council is just a front for a shadow body controlling things. Our free and open society isn't as free and open as we thought. It's actually a dictatorship controlling us like animals. And further, it fills our heads with stuff like 'the spirit of the words' to keep us from realizing it."

"So THAT is where it comes from," Hani muses. "But if it is not the spirit of the wording, how are we supposed to interpret it?"

"As you know, Latena is a major in political studies. The Charter of Laws has a lot of subversive little clauses that could be exploited as control mechanisms. They allow someone to come in and take over the functioning of something, and excuse themselves by saying the 'spirit of the wording' allows them to basically have it their way. The preamble is a good place to start, as it says the body of statesmen will DRIVE us for our motivations. The word 'drive' is a control word, not a guidance word."

"Yes, I think I can see that perspective. And so this is what they are doing behind our backs while teaching us to think in terms of the spirit of the wording…meaning guidance, not control."

"Exactly. We're supposed to have the freedom to seek ALL forms of knowledge. But if you've been listening to the sensations on the news lately, which is part of the ACI's work, Elder Nazég was right, and the rest of the Council was prejudiced against him. They kicked him and his faction out, denying us that element of ALL knowledge and discrediting his whole faction. Now compare this to the recent statement by the Marshal and that analyst that basically validated Elder Nazég's faction as being technically rational. This represents a contradiction if the Marshal was part of the discrediting action. He wanted Elder Nazég out of the picture, and the Council joined with him. They are a dictatorship that couldn't otherwise OWN the faction and what it had to offer. And this was relating to the real Tav'ageen Anomaly."

"The real one?"

"It's a latent ability our species is just now developing. But we, as a society, probably aren't ready for it. The Council refused to accept the principle of Metaphysics, which is THE science you need to interpret the thing, and naturally, this turned them against Elder Nazég and his theories. Then the Marshal…a being who actually IS very godlike in a lot of ways, but also prejudiced against others playing god with fancy skills."

"Oh! Really!" Hani blasts. "Yes, and no doubt this goes along with that criminal aspect again, I suppose."

"Right. So the Council tends to pick and choose what THEY want, not what the science factions or the people might find interest in. Here is where that line in the preamble comes in. None of the science factions have any work to do right now…well, outside of this new practice of breaking from the Council controls…and they never got any unless the Council decided what they want out of it."

"Well, that might explain a few things, but what about this deliberation?"

"The deliberation is a visible example of the Council doing what it wants and ignoring everything else, like that pollution and the obvious need to clean it up, but never actually doing it, even after all this time. This is to justify the continued need for the seeds. But there's another secret here, and you need to promise to keep it. Let the ACI deal with the problem. The Council isn't just missing. They're dead. The Marshal actually owns us and our world, and the Council was a front for HIM. He engineered us as a species, and set us up for everything else. He has enemies out there he wants revenge on, and we're just tools along the way. Worse, the Creator is actually him. So don't go praying to it anymore. He's not worth it."

"Oh no," Marna moans. "So our religion is actually worshiping him?"

"Well," Hani shrugs. "That spoils whatever remained of it for me."

"But not all of it is bad," Auryn soothes. "Listen to this. The ACI is working with this other side, those enemies I mentioned. They're like a governing authority. Latena and I learned a lot of details, but at least half of it has to be kept secret until the ACI can slowly leak it out as part of a careful education effort. The Marshal is watching, and we don't want him going tail-crazy over losing too much control too quickly."

"I can certainly understand that much. But who does this ACI work for if they are calling him and the Council illegal? You said this is a government security service, right?"

"Yes, but not owned by the Council. They're a hidden movement to bring down the corruption in our government, which means the Council."

"Oh wonderful. But if they are actually dead…"

"Yeah, this technically makes them a revolutionary force. We have to rebel away from what the Marshal made of us…actual insurgents, if you can believe it," she giggles.

"Oh dear…" Marna winces.

"When the Marshal arrived in front of us, it was to 'officially' take over the place, and he apparently succeeded, which I suppose wasn't too difficult since he owned so much anyway. But so far, he can't know we're catching on to him, because he's a very powerful creature as compared to us."

"What about the military," Hani asks. "Are they doing anything?"

"He thinks he owns them. After all, he made them, and apparently with a secret Council mandate to push special devices to control their minds. None of us was supposed to know about this. The ACI got those turned off now, so even though they COULD turn against him, they need to keep a low profile and play the game like he STILL owns them, at least until the ACI and these others can make a move. If things turn against him and Sargeras too badly, they could try running away, and we don't want them doing anything to anyone else. So we have to keep them here until this authority body can deal with it."

"Great. And how long for that?"

"We still have a few things to work out, but they're currently planning a covert action to take both of them down. Meanwhile, our population needs an education to break us out of our ignorance habit."

"All right, I understand."

"Auryn," Marna asserts. "What is this you said about a god of some kind?"

"A god?" Hani muses. "Are we speaking of the Marshal again?"

"No, not him. She was very excited when she first came in, and she said something about finding a god."

"Yeah, this is the good part," Auryn smiles. "Well, good with a bit of bad, if you consider the Marshal and Sargeras. These beings are all part of true god societies, false prophet or otherwise. Sargeras and his kind are simply a bad example of one, but they're all dead now, thanks to this other one. He and his were ALL criminals of one kind or another, mostly for abusing lesser lifeforms like ours. The Marshal is simply a servant being under him, so don't expect anything out of him except trouble. But this other society took over, pushing the previous one out."

"One society of gods pushing another one out…how interesting."

"When Latena and I went to see the ACI, they explained a few things about these people, although I use the term people a little loosely. So naturally, I wanted to see it for myself. But to do this, um…well, we had to make a little excursion…to another world…in another universe," she titters.

"You went to another world AND another universe?" Hani shouts. "Such a thing actually exists? And how? I mean, YOU did this?"

"I had help, Dad. It's not like my little shuttle is capable of interdimensional travel. And yes, other universes AND nether-space both exist. That analyst was hinting at something we were previously made to disbelieve in, and likely as a tactic to keep us boxed up."

"Wonderful. Well, all right, but why go all the way over there?"

"Well, that's where they live, or at least this one group. So we got an escort using a type of conveyor device in the basement of the ACI building, and it delivered us to this other world."

"A conveyor device!" her mother screeches. "In a basement? What, a simple star cruiser is not good enough?"

"Mom, they use these almost like a public transportation system. This world we visited is owned by a civilization that isn't even capable of normal space travel yet. Instead, they're only about Industrial Age. I saw animals pulling wheeled vehicles on the roads over there, and Latena told me she had to visit another world they own, and using a motorized vehicle through a conveyor as their form of transit."

"Unbelievable!"

"But they also have this field effect energy layer that allows them access to a completely different form of technology. This allows them to build conveyors using tech that looks like magic to us. In fact, this is where Elder Nazég's faction would find its heyday. So, go figure…" she shrugs. "And this is where that analyst comes in. This may one day be the future of our society."

Both of her parents glared at each other trying to visualize this seemingly contradictory scenario.

Auryn continues, "When we arrived, Latena made a meeting with the leader of that world, who is a royal King, and I met with his wife, a Queen, who is also a priestess in this HUGE temple," she waves her hands to emphasize. "I could feel the reverence of the place, and they had rows of icons depicting the images of their local gods. And Mom, Dad, when she brought me up to them, I laid my hands on their nameplates, and I could hear their voices speaking to me in my mind. They're telepathic. This is how they speak."

"Telepathic… That would certainly be a high example."

"We apparently have some of our people over there already, Elder Nazég's people. He's still alive, so the Marshal lied about that also. And some of them are taking up worship of one they call Lord Oghma, who holds a special dominion over things like knowledge and wisdom, and scholarly pursuits. So he's perfect for people like us."

"But wait… Who or what is this society of gods? You mentioned people, if only loosely. Can we define them in some way that fits what we have been looking for to fulfill our parameters of a higher mind?"

"Yes, we can. They're people, but so high on the evolutionary ladder that they made godhood. It's a huge society of what I suppose are MANY individual races who all came together like this to rule over everything else. They don't live in a common three-dimensional universe like ours, but in higher dimensional spaces above us. And not as corporeal lifeforms, but something evolved into those other spaces using whatever occurs naturally out there. I learned that there is a progression of life, beginning with beings like us, corporeal lifeforms, then transitioning into the next dimensional layer as a kind of intermediate form. They use the word Celestial for this one. Then, after some amount of additional evolution, you ascend again to this final form, which they call the divine form, no longer corporeal at all, but pure mind and energy. But it takes maybe billions of years to do all this."

"Billions! Yeah, that might do something."

"By this time, they see people like us as child societies, and from time to time they take an interest in one or another to offer guidance. But they have rules on how they do this, all based on a principle they call the Measure of Balance, which is mostly derived on evolutionary growth, not simply dumping the secrets of the universe in your lap."

"And here we have the Marshal offering this," Hani muses. "Even if it was a false promise, it could qualify as part of that criminal thing, if he was violating a kind of rule."

"Yeah. This woman, her name is Lady Aerlie, and she gave me some special instruction. These beings are called Estelar. But be really careful where you speak that name. If the Marshal should hear it..." she whistles emphatically. "They're absolutely ancient, like many eons by now...I don't know the exact number. They cover the greater majority of what she calls Creation, which means all the universes out there."

"All the universes..." Marna winces. "So there are other universes out there besides ours. And people who might travel among them."

"Yeah, and our wonderful benefactor brought our military to one as he was attempting a sneak attack on his old enemies. But he forgot to tell the rest of us for all his promises of great wisdom."

"Yes, how considerate of him," she huffs. "And as for these gods, you actually spoke to one of them?"

"Several, in fact. Lady Aerlie gave me a little instruction. There's a special process to it, where you call their names and offer up your thoughts in a certain way to communicate with them. And you really do feel their minds as they link up. They shared images with me, which is their form of language, and I finally felt like we're not alone. There ARE higher minds out there, and we can reach out to them, but we have to do it quietly, behind the Marshal's back, and probably do it on that other world."

Auryn's parents both gazed at their enthusiastic daughter, and then at each other.

"Well, Marna," Hani considers. "I think, before I would feel comfortable bringing this to our group, I would like to see it for myself. Auryn, is there any possibility for this?"

"The ACI can help us," she nods. "I made some friends over there, so I can call on them to offer transport. Then you'll see, and then we can bring it to the rest."

⁘⁘◆⁘⁘

"Have you seen how far those dwarves have gone already?" asks one worker.

"Yes, I peeked in on them a few times," responds another one. "Those tools of theirs are cutting through this rock like butter."

"What are they made of? I've never seen a hand tool like that before."

"They look innocent enough, by their design, but from what I hear, they're made from some new kind of metal."

"New to us, you mean. But they look like they've been using it all their lives, by the way they're clearing out those tunnels and opening up new rooms."

"Well, the story is they tend to live underground anyway, so this is probably an old habit for them."

"Probably, and we're just barely keeping up by hauling away the debris to a dump site."

"The way it looks, by the plan I was reviewing with that foreman of theirs, we should have several new rooms ready by the end of the year. Most important, I think, is that one in the rear they apparently hope to use for this special technology of theirs."

"I'm anxious to see that. I wonder if they'll let us in to take a look."

"I hope so. But ultimately, we'll just have to wait and see."

A pair of Suuden'kai workers engage in a conversation during a rest period between work shifts at the construction site. The dwarven laborers had been industriously digging out the mountain using their adamantium picks and chisels, which were making short work of the native rock. The precision craftsmanship of the stonemasons and miners revealed they knew exactly how to carve out a cavernous room so that it required only minimal auxiliary support.

New tunnels had been dug and flags posted for further development to open up space for the Harvester and a reactor assembly, which were priority areas. The plans also called for accommodations for the work crews and staff members stationed onsite, along with a kitchen facility and cafeteria, and an employee washroom. The design was intended to offer some measure of future potential beyond the initial function as a battlefield arena, in the hopes that one day all this hard work might find a new life for itself.

As the construction moved forward, they had plans for a control booth protruding from the mountainside overlooking the field. This is where the initial planning stages and execution of the invasion would take place. On a lower level, they would dig out a large assembly room, to be used as a staging area, with a ramp leading up to a wide exit located under the booth and onto the field.

Finally, the plans called for an observation deck above the control room. The facility would be designed with what was essentially a broad lounge area. Again, it was hoped this might find future use after the war, perhaps as a visitor center and recreation lounge. These designs were as much to provide for Thaelyn and his people, as it might for the investors financing the project.

Meanwhile, on Tae'Eladar, work at the Bahlaie Research Center was progressing smoothly.

"Chief Tech Lapäli, I have the most recent progress report on our production lines for the Harvester modules."

"Good," she responds as she takes the data-pad. "The combat ships shouldn't be too much longer, I think. They can get by with smaller units. But that one for the base, that'll take some time for the sheer size of it."

"Yeah, and those materials are going quick. As soon as we get a shipment in, it's sent through the processor to fabricate the parts, and then fuse them into the superstructure."

"Well, so long as we keep getting the shipments, we'll keep up the work. We know we need it. It's not an option."

"Yes Ma'am."

"We also need to finish the capacitors. We have that new design we're using now, smaller and more efficient. But we need to update our ships again so they can be ready for use. I hear they're anxious to move forward over there."

"Cu'Nar help us, these people move so fast. I hope we can get a chance to catch our breath once this is done."

"Don't get your hopes up too high," she smiles. "We might get a little time, but once the rest of their population catches up to us, we'll be on the run again."

Chief Technician Lapäli and one of her engineers were reviewing a report of their progress of building the new Harvester units. The innovative designs were as much a work of art as it was technology, but it used a lot of adamantium along the way. The general design represented a toroidal shape with multiple channels leading to a spherical collector at the center, and this would funnel the energies into a bank of capacitors circling the perimeter.

The research and industrial park had grown during this time as new buildings were added to house the specialized industry to produce the components for a small fleet of combat craft. The production line moved along slowly but methodically, with an initial order to produce three flights of ships. Then, depending on the sequencing of events relating to the war, more could be produced as needed.

The Chief dismissed her assistant back to his duties while she paused in reflection over the many projects in the works, and the great volumes of new knowledge they had accumulated in this short time. She surveyed the large tarmac outside her window. It didn't look anything like a traditional airfield or spaceport, but considering where the general technology of this world was right now, the view was very futuristic. There were industrial facilities, aircraft hangers, landing pads, and then the large construction hanger on the far side.

This remarkably large hanger was for yet another project. It was the big carry-all Thaelyn ordered. This ship was approximately the size of a midrange cruiser class vessel, where their traditional spacecraft categories go, as these designs tended to be larger than the classic oceanic varieties. As their research progressed, work on this one crept along slowly.

It had been two months since Marelle's jump drive test. Now, part of this new technology for the drive system had been installed, along with the reactor and many of the internal systems, like power conduits and life-support, but the bridge section was still under development.

It also called for a much larger Harvester unit, as this was the largest ship they were yet building onsite.

One feature had yet to be finalized, and it was the cargo suspension field generator. This would attach inside the framework of the ribcage-like armatures on either side. The ribs were hinged to be pulled up while landing or extended down when grappling an object. The cargo would be captured in a suspension bubble and retracted inside the cage. The cage would then be lowered to encapsulate the item in a secure containment field. The technology was still in development, but expected to be finalized soon, based on a similar mage spell for enveloping an object in a secure container environment.

The Chief then noticed some activity on the field. It was Marelle and a small team making their way to a set of training craft for a group run. She was now leading her own squad. The training craft would be used on this occasion for simple air travel, but once a flight of combat craft was ready, they would be promoted to space travel.

Thaelyn was sitting in a lounge towards the front of the WIC building. It was a pleasant retreat from his work in the strategy room where he spent so much of his time. The large picture window looking out on the plaza afforded a view of people passing by, with horse-drawn wagons rumbling across the cobblestone pavement, occasional street vendors hawking their wares, and town criers shouting out the most recent daily news.

The General and Kailen both pulled up a chair next to him, and they all sat staring out the window.

"My Lord?" the General inquires softly. "You seem rather pensive at the moment."

"Seven and a half centuries," Thaelyn muses reflectively. "When I first arrived on Tae'Eladar, it was in chaos. It was only through much effort and hard work that I brought the people together, and this is what we made from it. A world at peace, a world that prospers with new science and wisdom. Slowly, step by step, this process takes time, and for good reason."

He sighs and glances at his two companions before returning to the window.

"But those first few centuries were just to arrange the elements.

The real progress did not truly begin until we had a firm grip on the world around us and could afford ourselves to delve into the greater mysteries of discovery. And yet, when I look out this window, although I see people who are precisely where they need to be at this moment, this is not Tae'Eladar. It is another world far from our native home. And more, it is not the only one. The kingdom is now home to four complete worlds, all due to this war and the meanderings of a creature that should no longer exist."

"This is true, my Lord. But in my mind, although we might not see this for some untold number of years, perhaps centuries, here we are, and your wisdom still runs pure through the core of it."

"It's actually very curious," Kailen offers. "The conversation we had with Latena and our early explorations, and yet not once did we ever colonize anything, even though we apparently wanted to."

"Indeed," Thaelyn suggests. "He wanted to keep you in one place so he could more effectively manage you. One might even suggest your lethargic development was another trick he used. You have these exceedingly long lifespans of yours, which affords you more than enough time to take things slow. And if he has no special hurry to push forward, he might find this desirable to ensure you take the path he lays out."

"I don't think I like the idea, but I may have to agree. But not in your company!" he chuckles. "Cu'Nar's Grace, you push hard. I hear poor little Suli and Túfu over there comparing notes to our old school, or even the new university we have, and how they can barely keep their tails in pace with the other students."

"I think with the right kind of conditioning, we can find a happy medium together. The pressures we are under right now may not necessarily be ideal, or even stay this way as we settle into our eventual rhythms."

"So far, I'll keep myself to my more immediate work, if I can manage it, and leave the extended education for a later time. At least until well after things settle on Azgarén."

"This is reasonable," Thaelyn nods. "And yet, when speaking of Azgarén, as I look outside here, I see our people in such a state that would leave anyone but to imagine we could reach other worlds. Even with the use of our rune portals, one still needs to find a way to that place before they can use it the first time. We were lucky in at least a few ways, none of which could be described as normal. Kaliya and her Gift, Darumon and his conveyors on Ruuki uy'Daan, and then

Ayene with her Gift. How does one describe this except to say it is miraculous? And in the few or several generations yet to come, we will see the slow release of all we have learned during this time, and then to see our society take to the stars in earnest. And this too is a miracle, for we are not even in our home universe."

"And not only that, but you have TWO new universes to play with at this point."

"Indeed! And how long did it take you even to explore the one galaxy back home?"

"Good gracious," the General chuckles. "Yes, and here we might say we have two of them to get us started."

"Possibly three," Thaelyn considers, "if you consider the Sarrukhan Gate. Wherever it leads, if we were to send a new mission over there, and bring some of our new technology with us, we could mark a waypoint, then send in one of our scouting vessels, and use it to mark a local index for a later return. If it points to yet another galaxy, there is one more for you. How do you define a society like ours under those circumstances?"

"You don't," Kailen relents. "You can't even compare it with ours and all we have."

"I must agree," the General accedes. "And not simply for his people with what they can or cannot accomplish, as we have yet to include Tae'Eladar being trapped inside the Shell. You need a portal or a jump drive simply to find an exit of any kind, and this again requires somewhere to exit to."

"You know," Kailen admits. "I think, even with that limitation, you might still move so much faster than we did. First, you have your association with the Estelar, and I suspect they would probably help you for this much. After all, they built that thing, so they should offer a little support."

"Perhaps," Thaelyn affirms. "Maybe this is another positive use for the Sarrukhan Gate. If nothing else, it could lead us outside."

"Yes, a nice little backup plan. The next problem is you'll be there so much faster than it took us simply for the way you people move. My newborn son might not even be an adult before you evolve all this outside to their Space Age."

"Maybe, Commander," he chuckles. "If only for the shorter life cycles we have here and their inherent drive to see faster development. But now we come back to my original reason for sitting here. We have, between those of us here in this room, more science pending to be delivered than an army of wise men could attest to. Normally, one might see this as a natural evolution over the course of centuries for such people. But here we are, and the people are already aware of at least some portion of it, and well before they can understand the mechanics of what it is or how it works. Therefore, we must decide very carefully how to dole it out such that we can bring these people into some semblance of equilibrium. And this speaks only of what we have in our hands now, not that which we might yet come into possession of before we are finished."

"Cu'Nar's pity, I don't envy you on this, but then I suppose I have my share of it, for all I've contributed. You can be sure I'll stand by you if you need me."

"My deepest thanks, Commander, this is no small matter. We will need to bolster the education levels, carefully calculating a progression to bring them through a series of new eras, then to release these inventions slowly as each new era comes into play. But to go from a horse-drawn carriage to a star cruiser?" he chuckles ludicrously.

"It would seem we have our work cut out for us," he grins and nods.

"Personally," the General admits. "I am very pleased to have had this opportunity to glimpse the future, my Lord. I may not live long enough to see it come into common play for our people, but to have this cautious peek is a pure delight. A man does not often have such pleasures, if ever at all. Even if he were to spend a lifetime with an oracle, or stare into a magic pool that foretells the future, such as this might never appear."

"And yet, General," Thaelyn asserts. "I still look out this window, even though I have seen such magic pools in the achievements of other races and the history books of those who have reached much higher stations, and I see a society that simply is not ready for it, but still, here we are."

"Perhaps, unless you consider the Elixir of Visions and what potential it offers. That has surely played a role to increase our rate of movement."

"Yes, and I will admit, our society has seen some remarkable results from it in the past. And so, here we are, having it pressed upon us for all these new demands. We have four worlds within our grasp, and more space to cover than we could hope to achieve in a dozen lifetimes. And then there is Azgarén. Whatever our final outcome may be with the people there, I suspect we will maintain contact in some way. What influence might that have on our society that is so far behind?"

<hr>

Latena was in another conference at the university. This time with a larger body of friends and other students. She was developing a following, but she still needed to reel them in so they would actually follow.

"Latena, are you sure about this?" asks one student. "I have heard of your political group. But what you are suggesting now sounds illegal."

"No more illegal than those who illegally control us," she asserts. "Plus, I have support behind me. There is already a movement in progress doing exactly this. You remember all those sensations on the news recently, right? That was them. They already oppose the Council, and now they see the flaw in the Charter as well. They hired me to be a part of it…the voice of the people. Just as soon as I graduate, I'm going to work for them."

"In all the nether-space, then are we speaking of an actual rebellion?"

"And what will your parents think of this?" another one offers. "They still do not know how much of a troublemaker you actually are."

"Yes, well…" she shrugs. "This goes a little beyond that. But I need additional support, people like you, as many as we can get. Spread the word to the other universities. Bring in more students…people with the horns to take action. Maybe we can call in support from some of the science factions out there. They sure have enough reason to protest, for all they suffered. Like he said, this is a revolution we're speaking of here. The Council has to go, as well as the Charter. We need to bring a new Era to our people, complete with a new government that works in a more predictable manner."

"And what about the law enforcement, do you think they will simply stand around as we try to overthrow our own government?"

"Believe it or not, the ACI has them on their side already, as well as the military. For instance, that bit at the Grand Hall… C.P. Security knew about it ahead of time. The fiasco on the news was simply to show the rest of us."

"You are kidding me!" he gushes.

"These people shared a lot of critical details with me, but I'm only allowed to reveal some parts of it so far. They know the Council is corrupt, picking and choosing their favorite research topics and throwing the rest out. They also know the Marshal holds illegal influence, partially directing this. This is enough to demand a change, as it all points to a secret takeover of our world with a dictatorship hiding behind the mask of our supposedly free government."

"Latena, I do not believe this!" interjects one more student. "So, what we have is an illegal government, possibly controlled by an alien being, and we are simply taking it back for ourselves?"

"Yeah, as ironic as it might seem, WE are now the insurgents."

"But Latena," the first one urges. "If the military is already against them, why do THEY not do something about it?"

"Because the Marshal is trouble on a scale that's bigger than us down here. He made the military, and he thinks he owns them, and he expects THEM to behave this way as well."

"I do not understand. If they are our military..."

"They're not OUR military, they're his, and always were. I learned he pushed a secret mandate through the Council once to stick control chips in their heads to make them work exclusively for him. With the push of a button, they become indiscriminate killing machines. And he used them on anything he didn't like out there."

"Uh oh..."

"Now, the ACI got it turned off, so they have control of themselves again. But the problem is the Marshal is a known murderer. And who do you think might be his first target if they turn against him? Just pick a direction, and there you go."

"In all the nether-space, so are you saying they are powerless against him?"

"It gets a little complicated, so we're taking a cautious approach. The ACI is planning a series of moves to take him down. But until they're ready, we all need to play like it's business as usual. Well, other than for this rebellion," she giggles.

"Right, business as usual as we try to take over the world."

"The sensations on the news are going to lead in this direction regardless. It's part of the plan to disassemble everything he built up with his lies and deception."

"Yes, but Latena," the third student offers. "If this is the sort of guy who likes to make people disappear, are you sure you want to protest against him?"

"I'll be the primary figurehead in this, and the ACI will protect me. They have some special methods they can use, so we feel confident in this. But he can't stop a world revolution. And so far, we're not pointing a finger directly at him…not yet. Not until we have a threshold of control on our side. So, we have to keep a certain image until his REAL enemies are ready. He's running from them, and they don't want him to run any further. This is why we need to play like business as usual on the outside. From one sensation to another, they are building up a visible representation of the Council's corruption. But only the Council so far. The Marshal will be called into it slowly as we associate his interactions. But by then, we hope to have the bulk of our world population in an uproar for the injustices played on us."

"And therefore denying him an easy target for retaliation. By then, he will have lost most of his control element, right?"

"Right. It all has to fall into a pattern of our people growing tired of how things are and demanding something new."

"So…" the first one surmises. "What you are really saying is we are inciting a form of civil unrest on a global scale, based initially on the Council's errant deeds over time, and calling either for reforms, or a new government entirely, as well as revisions or a rewriting of the Charter. This would exclude the Marshal from direct mention, at least until you pull the plug with his involvement on some of these other things."

"Correct. And we need people out there in support of this to demonstrate our message. And since we already have the backing of this other 'insurgent' body…" she chuckles, "as well as such like C.P. Security and other offices, plus the military, even though they probably can't get directly involved, it's a sure thing we can get this across, if only we work on it."

"All right, I think I see where this is going. Ultimately, it will bring a revolution, in one form or another, and as it turns out, we are simply doing our part to offer support to it."

"Yes, we need to make an official plea for these changes and reforms, and it has to go out to the public to gain their attention and support."

"You know," the second one considers. "As I see it, if the only real finger-pointing is at the Council, even though he might actually be behind it, in the absence of his name being mentioned, all he can do is complain about us not following our local government policies. But he should not hold any right to argue this in the first place. This is not supposed to be HIS world, not unless he actually wants to come out of hiding and tell us he illegally took control, which will simply invoke an even bigger outrage. And I think, at that time, it WILL involve our military going on the offensive for an alien being taking over our local government."

"It sounds like we are pushing him into a corner with all this," the third one suggests.

"Yes, I suppose we are. We are overwhelming him with numbers, as well as exposing his games indirectly, slowly tearing down all the toy inventions he was using to cage us like animals. Those seeds, for instance… Like Latena said with that secret code. If they hold a special purpose, and not the one he originally told us about, this will amount to a criminal offence just by itself."

"That's right!" Latena nods. "And the Suppressor chips also hold a special purpose, but not the one advertised. I got mine turned off, and I'm going to ask all of you to do the same. Go to your nearest medical clinic and ask them to turn it off as part of the ARC's secret program to disable these horrid little devices."

"And the Tav'ageen Anomaly?" asks the second student. "As I recall, this was the original reason for it."

"Yes, but it was also a lie, a hoax. The Tav'ageen Scare was the Marshal turning a potential medical sensation into a world panic. This is where Elder Nazég's faction would normally come into it. One of these agents told me she's planning a kind of public demonstration using a special association to expose it to the world, and this will put the eye on the Council for kicking out Elder Nazég, who knew the truth, as well as the Marshal for conspiring to hide something."

"Hide something!" he gasps. "Such as what?"

"For now, I'm not allowed to say. The repercussions are delicate, and need to be carefully defined. But you'll know it when you see it. Meanwhile, do as I say and get yours turned off."

She pauses as she glances around the room. They had collected in the school cafeteria. Most of the students were sitting in clusters around tables listening to the debate, while others sat quietly eating their meal.

"Now listen," she picks up again. "We graduate next month. These people are currently gathering up resources, like campaign funding, literature, transportation, and so on. I'm going to be taking time to study this foreign language…it'll help me interact with them better."

"A foreign language? For this foreign society? Where do you need to go for that?"

"To their world… I've already been there once. It's a beautiful place, so I'm anxious to go back there. They say this language course is only three months long, highly compressed and accelerated. For this, I'll be spending some time away, but in my free time, I'll work on these demonstrations here in the city. Then we go global, and we make history."

<hr>

Graduation day has arrived for the students at the university in Capitol Prime, and among the student body receiving their diplomas were Latena and Auryn. Their families watched and waited as the ceremony proceeded along until each student was processed with the traditional congratulations and well-wishes. At the end of the ceremony, Latena and Auryn moved away from the crowd to find their loved ones within the masses of family members.

"Have you told them yet?" Auryn whispers.

"No," Latena admits softly. "How do you tell your parents, who think you're such a sweet and gentle young lady looking to make her way in life, that she's about to become a revolutionary fighting to change the world around her."

"They're going to find out eventually. Just one shot of you on the newswires and boom, there goes the image."

"I know. But in the meantime, I don't want to listen to the nagging. Let them see it on the newswires, AFTER I've made some progress on it, so they'll realize I'm not crazy."

The two of them giggled quietly as they made their way to find their families.

At the end of the day, the crowds at the graduation hall filtered out. Latena and Auryn were cleaning out their dorm rooms and preparing to go home again. They both had plans to attend the language class on Tae'Eladar, but they still needed to sign up. By this time, Kaliya and Ayene had assembled a number of campaign scripts, and they were reserving space in several prominent lecture halls, both locally as well as in other major cities. Meanwhile, Latena would need to make a little noise on the streets, just to get noticed.

Auryn, on the other hand, had decided to go deeper with her religious devotion. She carried several more conversations with Aerlie during this time, along with some of the other priests in the temple in Bya'an Tamoranth, and she was now leaning towards the idea of becoming one herself. And so, as the week rolled by, the two girls enrolled in the language class at the academy, and Auryn also investigated the priesthood course.

"Now, Latena," Ayene begins. "We're going to have you start your demonstrations out on the streets here in C.P. This will draw the initial attention, but we're not going to bring any serious news coverage into it just yet. We're going to allow it to build some steam first, and put on only a few bulletins about the activity, but without the specific mention of who is behind it or what your ultimate motives are. This is to give the appearance of something starting out small, and then growing in momentum."

"All right, got it."

"Kaliya will throw in a few of her people to serve as crowd warmers, and this will pull additional people into it. Then, as we achieve a critical mass, we'll go public."

"Good, and thanks. This sounds like a lot of work, but I'm excited to be a part of it."

Over the next few days, Latena began to assemble her people, who at this time were mostly her friends from the university discussion group, and a random gathering of other students, along with a number of people from Kaliya's team to add visibility to it. She studied her lecture scripts and by the end of the week she felt she was ready for her first public demonstration.

Ayene's people had made arrangements to assemble a small podium with a microphone and a set of loudspeakers in a busy downtown plaza. Latena took up her place on the podium, surrounded by many of her fellow protesters with signs claiming the errant nature of the Charter of Laws and the Council itself. They began marching along the sidewalks, chanting their slogans, and calling out to the public to bring them into attendance to listen to her speech.

"My fellow citizens!" she announces boldly. "I come to you to announce a great injustice. One that has gone unnoticed since the beginning of this so-called Enlightened Era we hold so proud. For as long as we have lived, we held the Council and the Charter of Laws to represent our highest achievement of social esteem. It changed the world, from a rampant assemblage of warring nations to a harmonious world body directed at a singular purpose. But there is a curse that hangs over us, and to our dismay, no one has ever taken notice of it."

She glances around the gathering, which was starting to draw people from around the local area.

"This curse has gone unnoticed if for no other reason than to say we gave our trust to the Charter of Laws and the Council, that they held their beneficent design for the purpose of lifting us up to a new purpose. But in reality, this is not the case. Recently, we have seen in the news a number of sensational press releases describing one thing or another, and this in itself turned many heads to ask what they were looking at. But I saw something new, and when I demonstrated this to my fellows, they saw it as well. And when I took it to others in even higher positions, they also saw it. Finally, I brought it to the attention of people in the position of law and government, and even THEY began to see the truth of it, much to our combined despair. These are not the simple ramblings of a young girl with too much energy to spend. They have been validated by those in the positions of authority to make decisions."

She pauses to catch her breath and study the crowd's response. Many more faces were gathering and paying close attention by now, if only due to their curiosity.

"The Council, as we have all heard it, is in this strange deliberation, but I say it is a lie. It is a lie that they hold any deliberation to give US anything. It is a lie to say they are in deliberation to give any of the existing science factions anything. Instead, if they are doing anything at all, they are doing it for themselves alone. Listen to these words, which come from the preamble of the Charter of Laws. Many of you probably know this already, but have you ever heard it spoken this way before..."

She now holds up her tablet device and prepares to read.

"We the People, who hereby declare ourselves to enter into this agreement, to dissolve and dismiss our ancestral rivalries and materialistic pursuits, to unite our population into one collected body, and from this moment to seek the challenges of higher intellectual ascension, do now this day create for ourselves a new Enlightened Era, where all people are created equal, where all forms of knowledge and wisdom shall become our domain, and where the direction of our society shall be governed by an attendance of statesmen who will drive our motivations on behalf of the many."

She holds a moment to let that sink in before continuing.

"These words are very inspirational, but I say there is a hidden message here. I recently graduated from the local university, where I earned a degree in political science and political history. When I once showed this to my teachers, they simply told me it is the SPIRIT of the statement that holds us so high. But there is no spirit here. How can you tell a society that chooses not to follow a religion to believe in the spirit of a thing, which is essentially to take it on faith? But there are words here that tell of something much darker, and when I reflect on those recent news releases, I can see it in action. Listen as I repeat some of these words."

She pauses to redirect herself to the tablet for reference.

"One thing it tells us is we will become a united society, and this much I can attest to. And I would say this is a benefit, as we are no longer making war with ourselves. It also says we are all equal, which is also good, as we do not hold any rivalries or prejudices against each other based on so many trivial differences. We are bonded together as a whole society working towards a common cause."

She glances around the gathering to gauge their responses.

"But then," she continues. "It says that ALL knowledge shall become our domain. To me, the word 'all' means just that...all. It does not selectively pick and choose what it wants. It does not cast out that which it does not hold personal value in. All is all. And yet, all does not seem to involve Elder Velen Nazég and his science faction, which he felt was a valid form of knowledge we should investigate, but the Council felt differently. That analyst we saw recently on the newswires, when the Marshal made that so-called famous press release, made a very important point. If the Marshal's statement might suggest this form of study to be valid, how laughable it is for the Council to have their noses rubbed in their own mistake. And for all that Elder Nazég tried to teach us, to see the rest of our population laughing at him was inexcusable in this allegedly free and open society where ALL knowledge shall be our domain."

Latena studied the gathering crowds. Many of the people were whispering about the obvious shortsightedness of the situation where the Charter was supposed to permit this level of openness.

"Yes, this is where we are supposed to be a united, and also an equal society. One that does not hold prejudice or hostile opinions of anything proposed by another. We should actually be ashamed of ourselves for this point. And this really has nothing to do with what some CLAIM Elder Nazég did by running away. If you were so heavily ridiculed by your peers in such an allegedly free and open society of unbiased people, would you not also run away and join something else? And perhaps to those very same people who chased off that one individual who was especially vocal in ridiculing you."

This invoked a subtle rise of voices as the association suddenly turned a number of opinions around for the potential reason. And at this point, it was not to violate anything, but to escape from that prejudice…a clear and obvious, justifiable cause.

"Therefore, I say they CHOSE not to include this, and they pushed him out. And worse, they did this with a form of hostility to that word 'all', where we are supposed to support anything that should come our way, even if it might hold a new perspective of wisdom, one that might even defy some of our older ones. How many times have we seen old theories disproven, and so we needed to update our perspectives to match? Could his have been one of those, but on this occasion undesirable? This is a violation of that line in our preamble, and it is not up to the interpretation of any one individual or body."

She again pauses to catch her breath and see if the audience showed any reaction.

"Throughout our history, whenever the Council found a science it took preference to, it amended the Charter to involve a new Council member to represent that faction. But Elder Nazég was an exception to this, even after he pushed so hard to get in the door and show his work to us, they still refused to write him into the Charter as an official member. Instead, they often ridiculed him and his faction, and it would seem they spread this poison to many others in our society."

The crowd was stirring with several murmurs as they reflected on the recent news reports relating to his name, and further the history of the Council's position.

"And if this is not enough, I have recently spoken with a number of people who represent the leadership of several prominent science factions, asking them if they have had ANY valuable research grants or assignments given to them in recent times. And they all tell me the same story. None of the science factions have received anything since the Council went into this deliberation. And even before this, they were ONLY allowed to research those subjects the Council DICTATED to them. This is the word we need to understand here. This final line… We will have a body of statesmen who will DRIVE our motivations. This means they will CONTROL it…a dictatorship in disguise, and an authoritarian one at that….one that picks and chooses what it wants, not for us, but for themselves. And Elder Nazég was an example of one they did not want for themselves. Even now, no one in any science faction has any true work to do, as the Council does not give it out unless THEY want it! And then they hide themselves behind this statement of the spirit of the words. It is an illusion to deceive us, and our education system seems programmed to maintain it."

This caused the crowd to begin grumbling.

"Case in point, just look at yourselves…these horrible seeds. How many of you can honestly say you should be wiser than this to know we have more than enough technology to colonize anything we want in space, but we took these seeds because the Council told us to. And worse, they made a legal mandate for it, and we followed along, as the dull-horns we are, thinking they know what's best for our society… this idea of the all-powerful beneficent government body carrying us to higher intellectual esteem. They forgot to tell us we DO have this higher esteem. And when that panic hit us, we ran as frightened animals into their loving arms, only to be infected by this horrid parasite no one truly wanted, and all because they said it was good for us."

This accusation caused another rise in the voices of the assembling crowd, as they felt it necessary to agree with this obvious error.

"Well now," Latena continues. "Do you feel so much more enlightened, having been blessed by our most beneficent Council and their most cherished spirit of the word, with that thing sucking away at you? And they further denied…yes, denied…as I cannot accept this as any simple oversight. Not ten millennia of it. They denied the science community to devise a way to remove them, even when it became painfully obvious that we weren't going anywhere. This is dictatorship in action!"

Now the crowds were shouting even more vigorously, albeit with many of them taking feedback hits along the way.

"It is not until NOW, when we have these controversies, and people actually taking action to disband those old war protocols, and for good reason, that NOW someone has the capacity to actually do something about it. This tells me, and it should say to you, it was never intended to be remedied. Not by that dictatorial Council. They mandated it, and kept it that way, and I say this for a reason, when you consider the recent report of a secret file associated with it. That file probably holds the reason."

This revelation caused the full assembly to reel back and moan, also to grunt and whine with new feedback hits. The association of something secret and hidden with the demand to take the seed, regardless of any alternatives, now resounded with ulterior motives.

Latena continues, "I'm also a student of history, political as well as social. This document, the Charter of Laws, was written by King Saakerav, perhaps the most celebrated figure in our history. This man was a powerful ruler, with a powerful military, that crusaded out to essentially conquer the world and unite the people together for the benefit of all future generations. Like many of you, I romanticized this for the obvious prestige of what he created. A man...a king...a ruler, who must have spent a LOT of time, and a LOT of resources, to accomplish a LOT of work...and for what, to simply hand it over to a dictatorship? This makes me wonder who and what he truly was, if not some great ruler that intended to actually hold on to what he created for himself. For HIMSELF!" she shouts.

The crowds continued to gather as newcomers tried to catch up on the conversation topic with others standing nearby. As more of them assembled, more words were being exchanged on her direction of intent here.

"He did not stay for the duration of his lifetime. He did not pass it on to an heir. No King in our history ever did anything to simply give it over to someone else and walk away. Therefore, it is irrational to spend everything you have to achieve something no one else has ever achieved, and simply walk away from it the day after you have your result. It is further arguable why we so often romanticize this man, which is VERY highly encouraged in us, as if he did a wonderous thing for our people. Yes, this sounds a little like that spirit of the words again. Now, maybe he did actually do a good deed for us. After all, uniting the world such that there are no more wars and internal strife IS a good thing. But why do they constantly bombard us with this romance, unless they want to delude us into thinking this Council he made was actually good for us?"

The crowds all roared and raised their fists in agreement.

"There was no precedent in our history to create something like a Council dedicated only to science, like some might dedicate themselves to a god. This was regarded as a phenomenal change in philosophical direction in a time of feudalism, and certainly NOT such altruistic pursuits as this. Where did THAT come from? Who could even imagine such a thing? Unless there was an ulterior motive behind it. Materialistic values may be fleeting, but SCIENCE...oh yes!

Knowledge is power, as they say. And who is it that holds this power? The Council! And who is it that gave them this authority? King Saakerav! Now, the question is, why did he do this? Was it to benefit himself? No, he vanished almost as soon as he finished conquering the world. My studies do not even show a proper death record for him."

The crowd suddenly gasped and groaned at this sudden flaw in the records.

"This, in itself, might suggest he was NOT the one to romance, but rather his work and the end result, the Council, whom we DO seem to worship as a god. We certainly never question their alleged beneficence. We simply follow whatever they say is good for us."

The crowds again shout and grumble for this clear inconsistency.

"For instance, we hold the power to travel across this galaxy and back again, and we had this for hundreds of millennia…long before the Marshal and his insurgents found us. We even found a way to launch out to our nearest galactic neighbor. It was an astonishing achievement in its day. This says, we should be well capable of colonizing anything and everything we come across that looks halfway decent. Why then are we still sitting on this ONE ROCK? The answer is actually quite simple, and it is not because we do not have the technology for it. Just look at the Saakerav space station up there…so aptly named for our romance. That is an example of building something in an environment not so pleasant for our lifeforms. Building on a moon or a planet would actually be easier."

Once again, the crowd shouts in agreement with the statement.

"The reason is simply that the Council never permitted it. But why THAT, I ask. Surely, more territorial domain would mean more to control, do you think? There must be another reason. Maybe a control reason."

She again lifts her tablet to reference the document.

"The Council serves its own needs, not ours. The preamble hides a secret in the wording, camouflaged by that spirit of the thing. And this secret lifts them above the statement 'We the People.' The domain of all knowledge belongs to THEM, not us. And though we might say our society did receive many benefits, as surely knowledge is power, and a knowledgeable society that can produce even MORE knowledge for them would give them even more power! But ultimately, there were many things we did not receive. And this keeps us locked up on this one world, caged inside these seeds and chips, neither of which they allowed the science factions to research proper solutions for. And this can be further exemplified by that voyage to our neighboring galaxy, which represents one of those achievements they actually took away from us!"

She pauses for emphasis and observes their reactions so far. Then she references her tablet again to wrap up.

"Thirty-five millennia ago, we made that historic venture to our neighbor. But did we do anything about it? No! Why? Because someone…and I mean someone who dictates to our science community… told us to stop. A simple, flat order to stop. They said it wasn't important enough to bother with, and that we should spend our efforts to use what we have locally. All right, fine, but have we done this? No! We're still sitting on this one rock, and no closer to colonizing anything now than we were then. And this was long before the Marshal's insurgents came into it to hold us back. Therefore, the control issue. We are a neat little society that is nicely limited to our one little world, where we are easily managed. Not chasing all across the galaxy where the Council might actually lose control of us. And all this, while they run off with what might seem like the secrets of the universe, and all of US still quoting such fashionable sayings as the Council is serving our public needs with so much unquestioned responsibility."

Now the crowd was shouting in anger, alternating with grunts from their feedbacks. Latena then directed her friends and colleagues to begin their protest march again, chanting in the streets for a new system of laws and a new government body, this time directed at more traditional political values.

◆◆◆

Another month passes by, and the protests are spreading to other cities, with a little help from Kaliya's people who were providing additional speakers to share Latena's message. The subject matter was becoming a trending news topic, but so far Ileani was being told to keep it down to a few passing bulletins, saving a full interview until much later.

While Latena conducted her crusade, Auryn was leading another one, but quietly. She and her family were pulling in other members of their local group and beginning to share the news with other sects in other cities. At the ACI building, a large assembly of people was arriving in the lobby. Kita was working at her desk when the commotion caught her attention. She glanced up at the congregation entering through the doors and sighed heavily.

"More pilgrims, Madam Táwgari?" she utters faintly.

"If you please," she submits politely. "I know this may not be convenient for you, but it is all we have for now."

"Let's hope they get the base working soon. Then you'll have a much simpler means of travel."

She leads the group downstairs and instructs the resident mage to open a portal for them.

Meanwhile, in the ARC, Azina was making a quick visit to the Director's office with an update.

"Ghantil, I have a report from our affiliate labs and clinics. It's been nearly nine months now since we began the removal procedure. Our primary medical staff here is done, and many of the clinics have been processed. We're making good progress through the labs, and we're starting to call in some of the security forces for theirs. But Ghantil, this is going to show up in a big way soon. We're already receiving a lot of calls asking about the staff at the clinics, and now about some of the security forces. We're going to need to go public on this soon."

"Yes, I know. I spoke with Ayene on this not long ago, and she's preparing a statement for the news telling them about our apparent success at finding a solution to the seed. The trouble is we're going to have to put our name on it, even though we've been trying to keep a low profile in the eyes of the Marshal. After all, we made the thing, so it simply stands to reason that we will be on the front line to unmake it."

"Wow, and what if he gets angry?"

"They're watching things very closely. My understanding is they have an army of people in projected form surveying the city right now. But at this point, there isn't much he can do about it. The word is out, the procedure is now becoming commonplace in multiple locations, and so we have the benefit of numbers on our side."

"Well, that's a good thing. So, even if he does get angry, he can't be in all places at once, and trying to stop it now would make a really big scene."

"I think it could become worse than simply a big scene. The Council refused to allow research on a countermeasure, even though it's clear by now it was never intended to be permanent. So, making a scene to stop it would simply open up a bigger scandal that someone is intentionally trying to force it on us beyond that initial idea of the temporary thing for an emergency evacuation of the planet, to say nothing of the pollution, which is easily covered with a simple filter mask. This could erupt in a planetwide rebellion."

"Ouch."

The following week, Ayene begins briefing Ileani for their latest sensation. In the studio of CPComm, the veteran reporter prepares to go on the air again. As always, the set coordinator positions his cameras and calls out the count.

"Places everyone, and…here we go," he points assertively at Ileani.

"This is Ileani Ur'paran for C.P. News. In today's report, and in response to a number of public inquiries, the ARC has finally come forward with the revelation that they have indeed found a solution to the removal of the An'gamu seed entity from the host body. Here is what one spokesperson had to say."

The scene changes to a press release with a male medical speaker.

"It is to our great joy that we have successfully found a viable method of removing this horrid relic of ancient technology, which was once discarded as holding no desirable value to the general public. The Seed was originally the product of an old research project that sought ways to modify the body to survive in otherwise uninhabitable environments, such as underwater or in atmospheres that might otherwise be toxic. And while we might admit, the study was fascinating, from the academic perspective, the procedure itself was dismissed for a number of ethical reasons, as well as the simple preference to use other forms of technology that were available to provide the same function, but without modifying the body in any way.

After all, as it has been said before, we did then, and still do now, have sufficient technologies to build habitats in virtually any environment we choose, including barren space. Although the civilian population didn't do this as much, there were certainly enough military and government level projects to explore and discover our galaxy.

Our project, which we took on for ourselves, despite the Council's lack of presence to grant this research, brought together some of our best minds and a number of innovative ideas, including the suggestion to borrow a few concepts from a number of projects we were once involved in, thanks to the military. These were part of some classified work they once ordered, and the only research opportunities we had during these past several centuries. But with those projects now cancelled, we felt it was time to move forward.

One of these called for a special formulation of the Belvik Spores, originally customized with a cytoplasmic decomposition agent keyed to an alien tissue sample they once provided, but here reprogrammed to match the Seed's unique genetic coding we found inside that strange data file that was once hidden behind a security blockage. As we all know, the Seeds tend to be very reactive to any form of physical injury. But this process allows us to bypass this reaction, therefore permitting us to effectively destroy the entity and thus allowing us to remove it without any further incident."

The report now returns to the studio.

"Needless to say, there is a new public outcry developing as people are visiting their local clinics to see about this revolutionary new procedure. This outcry is being further compounded by a new series of protest rallies occurring on the streets of Capitol Prime and spreading to other major cities around the world. These rallies are claiming foul play on the part of the Council, as well as the Charter of Laws that provides for their authority, suggesting a hidden form of control that has gone largely overlooked by the public under the guise of a government body doing its job, as some say, in the spirit of the wording of our most honored Charter. But these new allegations are now telling a different story, one of deception, and how this has been demonstrated in several key statements and reports recently portrayed in the news media."

A video clip of a female speaker now comes online.

"It has been made clear in recent times, as well as many moments in the past, that the Council is not in fact guiding our progress, but instead directing it with hidden intent. The most obvious of these began to emerge into clarity with the recent sensations of the denial to reverse the An'gamu seeds or to review the war protocols and their associated demands on our people. And where are they even now, after we have called upon them so many times to answer for these oversights? They are in some alleged deliberation that apparently

excludes the people, and even those science factions they are supposed to be supporting with new research."

The report again returns to the studio.

"As these protests continue, it is quickly becoming clear that a solution will need to be found. But until the Council comes forward with any sort of official response, it seems as if these demonstrators will continue to grow, and from this, they will find reinforcement in their own statements."

"Commander," issues the course voice of the Marshal on the com-link. "We seem to have a new problem developing out there."

"Oh, Marshal? I haven't been paying as much attention to the news recently since things seemed to settle from the last one."

"Yes, well, now it would seem there are a new series of protests occurring against the Council, so it would appear they are making a comeback. And then, they apparently found a way to remove the seed, eh…which I suppose was inevitable, but, eh…well, this is most unfortunate because we, eh…we…we NEED those seeds due to all this awful pollution! Yes! And STILL…for as long as it takes…eh, until we can find a way to solve those other issues that prompted all this in the first place! Commander, I am becoming very displeased at this situation. We need to remind those people how unhealthy it is out there, and those seeds are so very important to have."

"Marshal, I'm just a soldier, not a medical professional or a scientist who can quantify that sort of demand. My only suggestion is that since you are the one to originally designate this need, you should provide the demonstration of proof that it is still necessary. They might listen to that more than anything I have to say."

"Me?!" he shouts, but quickly recoils. "Eh, but of course, I suppose that makes sense. But I think it should be obvious. I mean, just look out your window! Do you actually need so much quantitative proof of that smog out there?" he pauses to grumble something unintelligible. "Very well, Commander, I will think of an appropriate response and release it to our agents."

He ends the link.

The Commander gazed once again at his vid-com, this time

wondering what sort of ludicrous excuse the Marshal might bring up this time.

"You can release anything you want, Marshal, but at this point, it probably won't matter. They'll just argue the point with something else. Especially if the industry that created that smog is being shut down."

The following week, Ileani was preparing another report. Ayene had delivered a new script for her during this time, and arranged for a set of new spokesperson clips to be broadcast as the latest effort to thwart the Marshal's stubbornness.

"How many more of these do you think he can take?" Ileani wonders.

"He'll take as many as we throw at him until he begins to realize his pets have minds of their own to solve their own problems. His excuses aren't going to be accepted any longer."

"If you say so…"

Ileani positions herself in her anchor's chair and waits for the coordinator to give his signal.

> *"This is Ileani Ur'paran for C.P. News. In today's report, we have an official response from a spokesperson representing the medical community coming forward to comment on the Marshal's statement last week. As you may recall, the Marshal hoped to encourage the public to reconsider the utilitarian value of the An'gamu seeds in relation to the terrible pollution that still hangs over our heads. But the medical community made this statement in rebuttal to his claims."*

The scene changes now to one of the prerecorded spokesperson clips.

> *"The medical community, and in fact, I am sure all of Azgarén, wishes to thank the Marshal for his generous concern over our health and welfare, but we would also like to remind him that he is not the only one here with a valued reservoir of wisdom that can be applied to solve our problems. We are a society that has a considerable amount of our own wisdom, and solving such a problem as this unfortunate pollution is certainly within our capacity.*
>
> *At present, the cause of this pollution is being corrected, and though it is true this pollution may be with us for some time to come, it is our responsibility to care for our native home, since it is all we have to live on. Therefore, the sooner we apply ourselves to cleaning up our environment, the sooner we can be done with it. In the meantime, I am aware the*

medical industries have been releasing a new line of filter masks for those people who are removing the seed, and this will serve us in the interim until the other concerns have been fully dealt with. And I am sure having a filter mask is a far more desirable alternative than the seed."

The report returns to the studio.

"The Marshal's statement, while well-received in some circles, only incited further outrage in others as protesters once again came forward with their oppositional perspectives."

Now another clip comes online with a male medical professional.

"We wouldn't have this problem in the first place if the Council didn't rush that dirty industry into production. Therefore, this suggests a clear and evident intent to pollute our bodies no less than they intended to pollute our environment.

I am further aware that much of the dirty industry which caused it has been examined by independent authorities to find it was not apparently making anything recognizably useful. This causes me to wonder who designed it and why it was put into operation at all. Fortunately, most of it is now being dismantled or refurbished to serve other, more productive purposes."

The report again returns to the newsroom.

"Of course, as you might expect, this is renewing a number of arguments with the Council, and it further seems to be reinforcing the more recent protests and anti-government rallies occurring around the world. Meanwhile, many labs and clinics are reporting a waiting list is developing for the procedure to remove the seed. At the same time, a growing number of people have been asking about that strange genetic coding the ARC found in its files that was locked behind a security password. One spokesperson had this to say..."

And now, yet another clip is loaded, this one with a female professional.

"After a careful review of that coding sequence, we have come to the conclusion that it does not represent anything originally found in the

design specifications of the old research, therefore it had to be from the revised work done during the proclamation of the war protocols. To the best of our ability, we are so far describing it with the term 'asynchronous trans-somatogenic linkage.'

Now, we realize this language may seem a bit ambiguous to some, so in more generic terms, our interpretation is that it seems to be designed to create some sort of organic network, generating a type of harmonized biorhythmic energy release, and keyed in some way to make it sympathetic with others of the same. And what is especially strange is it seems to draw from our natural bioenergy emissions, such as what our cellular mass normally creates as part of our life functions, and converts this into what we think might resemble an aura effect. This is to say, it behaves in a mild symbiotic manner to create a field effect of this energy. But the energy itself does not fit any of our existing scientific profiles. In fact, a few of us have simply described it as…abnormal.

Needless to say, why this was included, and what purpose it was intended to serve is still a mystery. Because on the surface, it does not seem to represent anything to allow us to survive on inhospitable worlds…or to serve any other functional purpose for US, as WE cannot apparently use this energy."

The scene returns once more to the newsroom to finish up.

"When asked about the remainder of the seed entity, the medical community explained that the design, as we see it today, seems to include very little of the original specification for colonizing hostile worlds. Although it clearly seems to interact with most of the body's internal organs, the only one that seems to be benefitting in any way would be the lungs, where it appears to be reinforcing them against harsh atmospheres. One researcher went on to say this would certainly show value in light of our local pollution, but this alone is not reason enough to enforce its application, war protocols or otherwise."

Shortly after the broadcast finished, Commander Geilv was again at his desk when another resounding wail echoed through the building. He pulled away from his terminal and warily glanced around the room and out the window. Then he called up the Captain on his com-link. "Captain Ta'yeen here… Let me guess, you heard it too."

"I suppose it goes without saying, Captain. Was that him again?"

"Yeah, it sure looks like it. The people on the ground are again staring in the direction of his office. And the comms officer here is telling me a few are reporting crashing sounds echoing out of his window. I was just about to call in to the Officer's Lounge to see if they had something special on the newswires."

"Good, let me know what you find out. This should make my day."

On Tae'Eladar, the year proceeded forward smoothly. It was now eleven months into the school year and Marelle was getting anxious for her graduation. But even though she had progressed far in her training, her team still had more combat lessons to complete before they would be battle-ready.

On the tarmac outside the Bahlaie Research Center, she was leading her new team into another series of practice drills. By this time, they had enough operational combat ships to make up a single flight of six vessels. The pilots settled themselves in their seats and donned their helmets. Marelle then issues her directives as they begin to power up.

"All right, today we're going to try out the new group synchronous navigation feature. Once we get up there, we'll make a few test circles, and then we're going to jump to Therinë for a little target practice."

They each lift off their pads and Marelle leads them on a quick ascent into low orbit. Once they reach their objective, she gives her new instructions.

"Alpha Flight, this is Specter Prime, I am enabling group navigation," she sets a new control on her console. "I am now broadcasting my carrier. Link up and authorize your helm command to my control."

The other team members comply by linking their navigation consoles to Marelle's carrier signal, thus allowing her to control their helm functions as a mirror to her own. As each ship links up, Marelle's navigation computer pulls them into a tight formation to move as one body. Once the group was brought together, she gives her next command.

"Now, pay close attention and be ready in case we need to make any abort maneuvers. I'm going to take us for a little ride. We'll start out slow and build it up as we move along."

She powers up her engines and begins leading them on a series of gentle turns and rolls. As she feels more confident, she brings their speed up and tries a number of dips, dives, banks, and attack runs. The other ships keep in alignment with their tight formation.

"So far, it looks good," she reports. "Now we'll have some fun. I am configuring a group jump procedure. All pilots; engage your arcanic jump fields."

She calls up her jump index menu on her navigation console, where she selects today's coordinates.

"Selecting Therinë as our destination… Now powering up…"

The other pilots begin charging up their arcanic capacitors as Marelle coordinates the affair. She calls out the count as the ships hold a tight configuration.

"Ten…twenty…thirty…forty…"

The group huddles close together as the energies build.

"Fifty…sixty…seventy…eighty…"

A soft aura forms around the group as the energies begin to peak.

"Ninety… Approaching critical dump load… Mark! Dumping now, the rift is folding."

The full group now gets sucked into a dimensional rift and flashes away from the local space.

Marelle's ship leads them in their tight grouping as they shoot along the hyperspace slipstream. The navigation console goes into autopilot during this time to smoothly govern the passage as it gently twists and turns. Strange shapes pass by outside the conduit as they travel from one dimensional plane to another. Soon, a wall appears ahead of them as their destination universe comes into alignment.

"Such a fabulous sight," she murmurs softly. "And to think, we're the first to actually do this."

"Yes Ma'am," responds one of her officers. "Even though the Naarg uy'Sodrad made that one wild jump, we didn't ever do anything like THIS before."

"This one is ours, not some wild thing pushed at us by a creature who likes to play mini-god over us. We made this one ourselves."

They plunge into the new dimensional membrane and travel along to their final endpoint, flashing back into normal space in the Therinë star system. Marelle then plots her new destination on her navigation computer.

"All right, today's objective is a little target practice. For this, and with nothing else to play with, we're going to the outer band where we have a bunch of rocks. So, let's go make some gravel, boys and girls!"

She now leads them on a hot pursuit to a remote ring of debris in the outer solar system.

✦✦✦✦✦

"Be that the last of it in there?" calls one dwarven miner.

"Aye, this part of it be done by now," replies another one. "A right tidy job, if I d' say so me'self," he laughs heartily. "What be next for us, Chief?"

"Lads," Tol declares. "These plans here still show a wee bit t' the lower side, an' a shelf above us. We be a-makin' good time, but we should'na take t' restin' just yet."

"Aye t' that. Mayhap we can clean off the shelf a bit so the crew outside can start t' buildin' the tavern, or whatever they be a-callin' it."

"Methinks they be a-callin' it somethin' like an observin' deck, or some such," responds another dwarven laborer. "A fine one, that! Observin' a battle from a bar!"

The rest of the dwarven work crew joins in with some rowdy laughter.

"Just so long as they serve up a fine brew when we be done."

"Aye lads," Tol offers. "But t' d' that, they need t' be a-bringin' in their special fixin's. So, get out there an' show them how badly ye be a-wantin' yer ale!"

The dwarven mining crew had just put the finishing touches on the main portion of the facility they were excavating from the mountainside for Thaelyn's incursion point. This also included the space for the Harvester unit. The space for the reactor was completed several months prior, and a specialist Suuden'kai team was called in to assist in assembling the reactor components. The technology and components were imported separately from Tae'Eladar, along with schematics and assembly instructions.

Along with these utility spaces, they also cleared away space for the establishment of kitchen facilities, crew quarters, and other amenities with the aid of the Suuden'kai labor force outside.

The outer structure was also under development, now including the control booth, and beginning the upper deck for the lounge, which included a recreational bar, and an observation platform. Once again, these features were included in the hopes the facility might find usefulness after the initial issue of Sargeras had been dealt with.

Back home on Tae'Eladar, Kaliya was visiting the Bahlaie Research Center to report in.

"Chief, they're ready on Azgarén. We need to start moving our equipment into place, as well as some of our people to install and operate it."

"Good, we have everything ready here. Most of it is broken down into components that should be fairly easy to move around, except for that Harvester primary enclosure. The Professor says he'll need to use what he calls precision portal positioning, which is apparently a fairly new procedure they've been perfecting recently as they've been going into their Industrial Age. It would seem this isn't the first piece of heavy machinery they've had to move around. So, they use portals in a carefully measured alignment to zap it into place with minimal physical labor to manhandle things."

"It just goes to show you how people can find exceptional ways of achieving their goals using methods we might not otherwise think of."

"Yes, it does!" she giggles. "And then, the Professor is gathering up a group of his people to assist in installing and engaging the equipment."

"What about the, um, breeding stock?" she grins.

"It's preloaded. Since the whole thing needs to be delivered in one heap, it might as well be functional from the get-go."

"Perfect, so we can start installing the other stuff almost immediately."

"As far as I understand it, the reactor is already online, and we've been sending out fuel tanks to keep it alive, at least until the Harvester goes into operation to produce our own onsite. But we need to be sure to plug it in as soon as it pops. The power cells we're using won't last long."

"Got it. All right, get the team ready and send them in using the existing rune transport. We have Ayene and Kita on location to act as guides and interpreters, and the Director and Azina are both present, as they wanted to oversee the operation."

"Good, but be sure to tell them to keep at a safe distance. Some of these pieces are big."

Kaliya nods and rushes off to the WIC building in Rolsklinde to report in. She then flashes across to Azgarén to join the others just as the gnomish crew begins arriving.

Ayene, Kita, Azina, and the Director were all watching as a crew of exceptionally small men in overalls and hardhats began arriving on the scene.

"Who are these little guys?" Azina croons. "They're so cute!"

"Unbelievable," the Director mutters. "They look like a completely different variety from the others."

"These are gnomes, Director," Kaliya advises. "And unlike the other hired help, which hasn't had time yet to make the study, these people understand and speak our language. So, if you have questions, or require explanations of anything, at least within reason for what we're allowed to divulge, you can ask them. Just be careful, as they're a fidgety group. They'll talk your horns off if you let them."

"I can vouch for that..." Kita smirks and raises her hand.

"All right," he grins. "I'll try to keep that in mind. But at least we have the possibility of communication now, which is exciting enough. Now, about this equipment of yours..."

As they continue to watch, several gnomes begin marking off lines on the floor for the arrival zones of their equipment, and then pull out a collection of spell scrolls and rune stones to begin their marking enchantments.

The Director and Azina both watched in amazement as the little fellows each position themselves at different intervals and orientations and called out the glyphs on their scrolls, which then invoked the classic swirling energies to mark their runes.

"And that's how it's done from a physical perspective?" the Director muses.

The gnomes then scribbled a series of notes on several scraps of paper and tied each one to a rune to identify its numeric positioning within the grouping. They then packed them into a box, and used another spell scroll and a return rune to send it home.

"Fascinating!" he relents. "So, you can send both people and objects through, much like a postal service."

"Oh, Director," Kaliya grins. "These people are clever. When you've been using a method like this for so long, it becomes like an old habit after a while."

A few moments later, several flashes erupt as bundles of equipment arrive. The work crew now begins moving and unpacking them, soon to be assembling cranes on wheeled platforms, several hydraulic mounts, a number of fuel cells and hydrogen cylinders to provide power, and a couple of large upright cylindrical storage units that seemed to glow through their window slots.

Azina stepped in closer to examine the fuel cells and strange cylinders.

"What are these?" she asks.

"Those boxes are hydrogen fuel cells, which is a tech we should be familiar with. Now, even though you might think this to be a little above your average Industrial Age society, they cheated a little and borrowed from a time capsule they found belonging to those Sarrukh I told you about once."

"Sarrukh…oh! They're the ones that restored that world out of an ice age, right?"

"Right. Along the way, they left behind clues about who they were, and a bit of technology. Even though Thaelyn has rules on what, where, how, and why to use stuff like this, he made a small allowance once to borrow a little from this. Now they have fuel cells, which is essentially a jump start into their current Age."

"Oh, how nice of him!" she smiles. "And these things?" she points at the larger cylinders.

"Those are a recent invention as part of our push to reach where we are now. Those are arcanic power cells. They store arcanic energy for some of our local devices to use, like our communications."

Kaliya steps over to a table they had established on the side of the room where one of the gnomes unpacked several shard-coms. She picks one up.

"Do you recall from our original meeting, I mentioned they made a recent invention for communications? Well, this is it," she displays the unit. "This is what we call a shard-com. It's a bit like our own trans-coms, and in fact we're borrowing from our naming conventions, but the principle of operation differs in the antenna. Whereas ours use EM transmissions, this one uses a principle I might not be able to define accurately, assuming I could define it at all under these circumstances. But suffice it to say, this gives them the capacity to communicate with any other compatible device. Anywhere. And I do mean ANYWHERE."

Azina felt pale at the implications for the small handheld device which on the surface seemed so innocuous. It bore many similarities to her previous experience with trans-coms, but if to use such a fantastically different form of transmission as to allow it virtually unlimited reach, it clearly surpassed anything her society might possess.

"I remember what you said in that meeting, but this little thing?" she winces. "That would break at least a few laws of physics, wouldn't it?"

"At least… You should've seen our resident Chief Technician when it first came out," she rolls her eyes. "I suppose I could say the theory of operation might associate to what we think of as quantum entanglement, but the way in which they apply it is enough to cause your horns to fall off."

The gnomes vigorously labored to assemble their work platforms, as well as measuring out the space for the Harvester unit. A group began making lines on the floor for the dimensions, and then a series of geometric shapes to help with the alignment.

"Um," the Director wonders cautiously. "What is he doing now?"

"The Harvester unit is huge, and it has to be delivered in one piece. So, to do this, they use a process of precise measuring and alignment, and then mark a rune according to a careful plot coordinate and orientation. Once they have that, they send it home and use it to transport the machine part directly into its final resting place, with minimal need to move it afterwards."

"Incredible. That will be a sight to see."

"Just be sure to stand back. I would imagine the arrival will send out a bit of a shockwave."

"All right, thanks for the warning."

The gnomes continue their plotting on the floor, then use a set of calibrated triangulation frames with a rune mount on top. One of the gnomes takes out a fresh rune and another scroll, and climbs up a small ladder to reach the mounting bracket, where he arranges the rune and once again begins calling out the enchantment. As before, the swirling energies rise up and funnel back into the stone. He then takes it out and orders the framework to be removed from the area while he forwards the stone home.

"And here we go..." Kaliya announces expectantly.

The group stands back against the far wall as the gnomes all clear the area. A series of jacks had been set up around the perimeter of the marked area to act as a landing site for the large device to arrive on, and from there they would make whatever finishing touches were necessary for the final positioning.

In several moments, the room is filled with a sudden bright flash, and a pressure wave strikes the people, causing most of them to duck and cringe as a gigantic tri-helical toroidal apparatus enters the local space. The loops circled around a central spherical enclosure as a gathering pod, and beneath it was a large junction box for the power connection. The metal shell glimmered with its own internal glow, as the adamantium radiated its inherent arcanic energies.

Strapped to the sides at intervals around the structure were several large temporary utility boxes holding the power cells to keep it functional in low power mode until the utility service could be attached. The gnomes quickly went to work, with some of them checking the alignment while others brought a thick high-voltage power cable around from a nearby power relay box to the junction at the base of the unit.

They opened the box to find the primary input connectors, along with the temporary ones from the power cells. Several gnomes began laboring with levering rods to wrestle the heavy gauge cable into position while another one took a wrench to bolt it into place. Then they began pulling a set of power switches on the relay box to take over the operation of the unit so they could relieve the temporary boxes of their duty. From there, they would remove the boxes and send them home again.

The Director and his group watched in amazement at the quickness and apparent efficiency of the gnomes in their duties.

"They sure seem to know what they're doing," he notes.

"No doubt they rehearsed it a few times," Kita suggests.

"That would make good sense, actually. This looks like a time-critical operation if you need to transfer the power so quickly.

"What is this material?" Azina asks as she studies the unit. "And is it just my eyes, or is it glowing?"

"That's adamantium," Kaliya responds. "And yes, it glows. This is what the Marshal had Ayene and her people mining on Morndindor, but our application is far more constructive than what he had in mind."

"This is that super metal you were talking about?"

"Yeah, and it took a lot to build these. That stuff doesn't grow on trees. It's a rare material, although we're fortunate to have several worlds now supplying it."

"Meaning," the Director concludes. "These units might be regarded as very expensive to build."

"Yes, you might say that," she smirks ironically. "I don't know the numbers, but I think this could be worth as much as all the rest of it combined."

"And you're spending it on a single battle just to destroy one opponent?"

"Well, two if you count both the Marshal and Sargeras. But considering their threat potential, it's actually a small price to pay.

Besides, even though we have four worlds right now, there's always more out there."

"Indeed, then the potential for more discovery is always available."

"And when it's over, we can always recycle it elsewhere, so it's not like a one-time use-it-and-it's-gone situation. Although, a piece of me is thinking this might eventually go into a historical museum."

"Oh? And why is that?"

"First, this is on loan to us, so it's unofficial. Once we're done here, it gets mothballed. The people need to officially 'invent' the tech before they can earn it. But I doubt we will simply scrap it, because it does represent this moment in history, therefore..." she shrugs.

"Got it. Keep it for future generations to learn from. But now, what does this unit do? You said this is the Harvester, right?"

"This is the one that holds the farm-like environment inside with a colony of arcanids to make our arcanic energy."

"A farm-like environment, but how does this environment appear?"

"The native environment is another dimensional layer outside our own, so this creates a superconductive containment shell to simulate a pocket dimensional aspect of that same environment."

The Director grimaces at Kaliya as he tries to comprehend the depiction.

"And these people are only Industrial Age? In all the nether-space, what will they be like when they hit our level?"

"I hesitate to guess," she chuckles. "But we should also remind ourselves this tech was donated by someone, so it's not our own invention."

"Donated by someone...do we know who, and what level they are?"

"When we received it, the statement was simply, someone who has been there already. In other words, they're not revealing themselves to us. But my personal guess might be the Sarrukh again. Maker Kuroku seems to hold a connection with them, and we suspect she has used them on multiple occasions by now, including our ship."

"That might explain a few things. But simply to see it here, and among these people, who themselves should not have a clue to its operation, and yet working it like it was yesterday's news."

As the Director made his statement, several of the gnomes, who were busy with their work but also listening in on the conversation, began giggling hilariously.

"Yes," Kaliya nods. "And these people actually do understand a few things that reach outside of your classic Industrial Age specs."

Once the gnomes were happy with the placement of the Harvester, they let it down on a set of permanent mounting anchors and bolted it in. From there, they began calling in additional deliveries, in this case more of those arcanic capacitors, but larger in scale to attach to the Harvester as external storage. After positioning those, the gnomes began connecting a series of cabling from the gathering sphere on the Harvester to the capacitor array.

"Can you explain these units to me, Captain?" the Director asks. "They look like more of these storage units of yours, but how do they work?"

"Just like this smaller one I showed you before, these are capacitors. They use superconductive magnetic fields passed through more adamantium plating, which converts it into a retainer field to hold these unusual energies. They don't normally follow your classic laws of physics, so simple EM fields generally don't affect them. The plates create a vortex of compressed space, which will then hold our arcanic charge. You can see in the crown at the top what looks like a connection port. This will attach to cabling from the Harvester to draw off energy for storage."

"Excuse me," Azina yips. "Did you say compressed space?"

"Yes, I did. Don't ask how it's done, that would take too long to explain right now. Just trust me. I have a handbag back home with the same enchantment on it. It's wonderful."

"A handbag!" she screeches.

"I wouldn't mind one of those," Kita smirks.

The gnomes continued their work assembling the pieces and attaching the cabling for the arcanic storage, finally to connect the conduits to the reactor fuel generator. The Director and his group followed along to examine this new element of the assembly.

"And now that thing," he points at the new piece of equipment.

"That, Director, is one of the wonders of magic," Kaliya announces merrily. "This one will blow your horns clear off the planet. It converts the flows into fuel for the reactor, and it does this more efficiently than what the reactor would spend on maintaining the Harvester itself, leaving us with surplus energy AND surplus flows for other things."

He glared at her with his eyes bulging. Azina gaped at the wild declaration. Kita simply shook her head gently.

"But wait…" the Director gasps. "That defies everything we know about the laws of physics! I'm not a physicist, but even I know about the law of Conservation of Energy."

"This is true, but you're only working with half of the coin. This is the other half."

"Then, what you're saying here is that by using this other half, we could effectively provide ourselves with free and unlimited energy! This, by itself, would be yet another discovery of the millennium!"

"It would. In their natural form, the flows are a renewable source, so we technically have a fuel input, but it's virtually unlimited in supply and freely available. Here, we need to provide for our own, but the flows are potent enough to give us our surplus. However, once again, keep in mind, this particular unit is on loan to us. So, if we want it on an official level, we need to invent it on an official level."

"Very well, I don't think I would argue that. But where do we even begin to study this?"

"I have a friend back home who is already on her way to doing just that. So, let's give her a little time to finish her classes. After all, she wants to get a hand on a few of these ideas."

"All right, but then, let me ask you this. This arcanic energy, I know you said it covers most of everything out there…except our universe, as it turns out. But just for the sake of discussion, what would happen if this energy were released here locally?"

"The energy itself would probably dissipate after a while. Just think of those seeds and Sargeras for a moment. That recent news release, where we opened up the idea of this…abnormal…energy. That's a hint for later. Although that example is probably the wrong harmonic for our purposes, as it seems very specific to serve him, the flows are created by these arcanids as a form of symbiosis with other forms of life, like ours. They tend to cluster around dimensional bodies where they can find their source and emit this wherever they make their homes. Eventually, it builds up in a layer that spreads out to cover more space."

"This is interesting. And assuming we might be encapsulated within that space, we can learn how to use it?"

"It would take time to develop, and in that time, you might not notice it until maybe you hit a threshold, where you also develop a form of sensitivity to it. In the much longer term, and we're talking centuries or millennia, you might also see plants and animals develop some capacity to absorb and reflect its energies within their bodies or tissues. And this would represent an evolutionary adaptation."

"An evolutionary change," he muses. "Wow, from a biology perspective, this might be fascinating to watch."

"Even in our own people, as much as I hate to say this, we'll also see a change."

"As much as you hate to say it? Why?"

"According to my history studies, the human population on Tae'Eladar started out with lifespans ranging up to something like five decades on average, depending on their lifestyle, which often involved a lot of manual labor. This was before the average person knew anything about how to use this stuff, as it was often a privileged study in those days. But after Thaelyn began teaching them how to use this on a global scale, and they started developing so many industrial uses for it, their lifespans grew to an average of eight decades. Some of this can be attributed to improvements in lifestyle, like medicine and mechanization. But if we're just barely in the early Industrial Age, that's not a big step from their previous beginnings, and we're only counting a few centuries, which is fast, even for them. So, this is a significant increase in longevity just by cycling the flows through their bodies."

"Oops," Azina mutters. "And I think I can see where your 'hate to say it' part comes in."

"Right, the elven population has been using this for much longer, and they can measure their lifespans in terms of many centuries. Now, consider the numbers involved here, and then adjust for our lifespans. I dread to see how long any of us would live after even a few millennia of this."

"How does it work?"

"It seems to purify the body of the effects of time, basically slowing down the aging process by a certain amount, dependent on how much and how often you use it. It apparently also invokes a type of adaptation effect from generation to generation to exaggerate this process."

"So, if we have such ridiculously long lifespans now, after using this stuff, we'll have supremely ridiculously long lifespans," she grins.

"That's right!" she chuckles. "And some more than others. This is where we might start seeing our real evolutionary transitions occur. The Celestial Races were once people like us, already evolved with some very high capacity, and in their case using the flows habitually.

As compared to such like the humans, we might not be very far from that point, with the only exception being the use of the flows."

"I'm not so sure I'm ready for that."

"Neither am I, so we need to pace ourselves and bring the rest of our population up to meet the need."

Over the course of the following week, the gnomish workers continued installing the remainder of the essential components of their arcanic technology in the base on Azgarén. The reactor had been switched over to use the arcanic fuel converter, the Harvester was running at full capacity, and now they were putting the finishing touches on the local gateway node, linking it to the same power conduits as everything else.

The Director and Azina were once again in attendance to oversee this aspect of the operation. Ayene and Kita were supervising from this side while Kaliya was on Therinë to coordinate from that side.

"And this is what you call a gateway node?" the Director wonders.

"Looks a little like a conveyor to me," Azina muses. "But a lot smaller."

"They've been using these for a few centuries on Tae'Eladar," Ayene affirms, "which is already a lot when you consider they're only NOW entering their Industrial Age. This technology is another example of what they borrowed from that Sarrukhan time capsule. And according to my lessons, they had portal rune stones even earlier than that."

"That time capsule sounds like it was a nice little treasure cache," the Director nods.

They had assembled back in the original room where Kaliya first imported the dwarven workforce. This room was now serving as a type of port of entry from Therinë. They watched as the gnomes made their final calibrations of the gateway, in this case a custom designed model to interface with the Harvester power links.

"As you can see," Ayene directs. "It again uses those rune stones, although I'm hearing lately back home the teams are drawing up ideas for a redesign using some of this new technology they're inventing. But that's another thing. The gnomes first need to mark a local index, and they often do three stones, to keep a couple of backups."

"A clever strategy," he admits.

"This is part of the philosophy behind the redesign. The new technology using these jump drives creates a data element that can be programmed into any compatible device. And since it all comes down to a fairly familiar practice to begin with, they figure they can extend it to other devices, such as new gateways and portable units."

"Incredible, and to think it requires us to fit this into no less than a frigate-sized ship or a large industrial-scale conveyor just to get anything at all."

"Yeah, this would blow a few minds around here once it gets out. But on the other side, common transportation might go right out the window. Imagine using THIS instead of a traditional form of long-distance transport to move between cities and around the world. The tourism industry, as well as commercial and industrial cargo transport would be pumped on steroids for the ease of travel and rapidity of delivery times."

"That would change a few things."

A group of gnomes were standing around while one was working behind a control box on one side of the unit. A round stone was inserted into a U-shaped slot on top of the box, and he pulls a lever. The ring flashes briefly, causing the Director and Azina to flinch.

"Is that normal?" he asks timidly.

"Yes, that's the action of marking a stone."

The gnomes repeat the process two more times, and a mage then collected the set and moved back into the Harvester chamber. Azina followed along curiously, drawing the Director and Ayene behind.

In the next chamber, the mage stood on a round pad that had been recently installed.

"And this thing?" Azina asks.

"That's a conjuring pad," Kita remarks. "We have one of those in our basement. The mages use it as a localized source of their energy."

As they watch, the mage puts the stones in his pocket, pulls out another rune, enchants it in his hand and clamps down on it, flashing away from sight.

"And that's how it works under normal conditions, I suppose," the Director relents. "So simple, so straightforward..."

"Ayene," Azina wonders. "Do you know how to do any of this yet?"

"I'm still enrolled in the early course," she accedes. "I only just recently signed up at the academy. The course runs several years, depending on how high you want to go with it. I'm going to work my way up to join Kaliya in her military unit, and for that I need the Eighth Circle, which is a rather high-level grade of accomplishment."

"How high do they go?"

"Nine in all, so this is nearly top level. I could take it higher if I want, but her military demands need at least eight."

"That sounds potent," Azina winces. "I don't really know what that involves, but if it maxes out at nine…"

"Yeah, this is a well-respected level to achieve. And you could say I'm the first citizen of Azgarén, other than the Daanen-Aryku, to take up studies."

"I wish you well, Ayene," the Director offers. "Now what happens?"

"Let's go back out to the other room. He'll return home and give one of those to the operators configuring the other side. Then we have the fun part."

They returned to the room with the gateway node. By now, the gnomes had placed a new stone in the slot and were awaiting Ayene's return to receive her signal. She nods, and they engage the device.

The Director, Azina, and Kita all watched, along with the Suuden'kai project foreman and several of his crew who joined for the occasion. The ring came to life with a flash and a subtle rush at the appearance of a swirling vortex.

Azina gazed at it in awe. She recognized the sight from her science class studies as a child, but could never actually imagine seeing something like this personally. A moment later, she witnessed a small opening in the center, which rapidly expanded outwards to fill the window aperture.

In the window, they could see an elegant city plaza. The setting seemed almost medieval by their standards, like something out of a history book, brought to life with cobblestone pavement, wood and stone buildings, sidewalk market stands and people walking by. And then she saw wagons being drawn by sturdy animals.

"In all the nether-space," she gasps. "Animals pulling wheeled vehicles, combined with conveyors that link all your cities? That doesn't even make sense!"

"I know. But they didn't evolve the same way. When you have magic, it's a matter of the mind imagining how to use it, not your level of science limiting your capacity. I guess someone got tired of walking, so they invented portals."

"Oh!" she snaps. "So, they got tired of walking? How unfortunate!"

"The trouble is," Ayene explains. "Most of the technologies being developed as part of this operation must be carefully maintained as military secrets, at least for now. The Estelar have some very strict rules on how and when to evolve younger societies. I encountered this on several occasions when I first arrived in their world, and it surprised me how strict they are. But after spending some time with them, I began to realize how right they are to do this. Darumon made a big mistake offering us his promises, not that he would actually care…he didn't plan on delivering anything, anyway. And neither that our Council would care about it either, as all they wanted was power."

"You may have a point there," the Director concedes.

"But for these people, and due to their shorter life cycles, they tend to demand much faster progress. So, while it might take us on the order of millennia to achieve something, Thaelyn has estimated they might grow enough to earn this much in only a couple of centuries, maybe less."

"Centuries?!" Azina yips. "Only centuries…to go from wagons pulled by animals to spacecraft jumping across the universe?"

"Yeah," she sighs. "Which means, before we may be ready for our first child, they could be entering an entirely different age."

"And even with that," Kita adds. "They'll be there before that child is even grown up."

"And worse," Azina muses. "Even if I live a full life, I probably won't see as much progress as they will in a fraction of that time."

"You and me both, Azina," Ayene admits. "Although I'm technically a citizen there now, so I'll just follow along as best I can, assuming I can keep my horns from getting tangled up along the way."

In the window, they now see a pert young officer step into view, apparently speaking to one of the gnomes on the other side. She turns and steps towards the window, disappearing briefly from sight, and then reappearing on the near side.

"Ghantil," Azina whispers. "Did you see that, how she just vanished and came back into view?"

"It's just like they teach us in school about passing through a conduit," he responds quietly. "You exit from real space on one side and reemerge back on the other."

Kaliya had arrived in the room, dressed neatly in uniform, and making a professional appearance for her friends and colleagues. She steps up to the Director's group and offers a formal salute.

"Greetings Director, and Azina, and our other friends. This might count as our first formal visitation to Azgarén, at least in the flesh."

"Captain Nazég, welcome," he replies. "Such a fascinating process, you just step through on one side and pop out the other, is that it?"

"Yeah, it's simpler than flying a ship through nether-space, although that first step is a bit tricky."

"And Ayene says these connect all your cities?"

"That, as well as the four worlds we own now, although Ruuki uy'Daan and Morndindor don't have much to show for themselves yet, but I'm sure that'll change in time."

"So, you're actually physical this time?" Azina wonders. "This is the real you?"

"Yes, it is, and as you can see, in case you were wondering, my eyes really do glow."

"Amazing, I wish I could study this. Unfortunately, I might have to dissect you. Nothing personal, you understand," she grins shyly.

"You'll have to catch me first," Kaliya responds with a broad smile.

"Is it possible now for us to go visit your world?" the Director inquires gently. "I mean, you wouldn't mind if we drop in on occasion?"

"Absolutely! If you should wish to make a visit, all you need to do is walk through the gate. Initially, I might suggest you have an escort handy, or else you might get lost. In fact, now that we have this, His Lordship would like to make a formal greeting, and to offer his thanks for all your help. Would you like to make a visit now? I could bring you to meet with him, and we could become a little more familiar."

"But..." Azina flusters. "You said he's a King, right? I'm not really anyone special to go up to a King and..."

"Azina, just hold onto your horns and follow me. We'll make a quick visit and say Hi."

Kaliya leads them back to the gate and passes through. She assists Azina and the Director as they arrive, helping them to stabilize their footing since they were unaccustomed to this mode of transport. Kita followed closely behind, having more experience while she was in training for her language class.

As Azina looked around the scene, the first thing she noticed was the clean air and a variety of pleasant aromas. She begins sniffing the air vigorously.

"Do you smell that?" she angles around trying to find the source.

She spies a nearby planter with fresh flowers in bloom and runs up to it, burying her nose in the fragrant shrub.

"Ghantil, get over here and smell this. It's wonderful!"

She soon picks up another scent, which leads her into a local bakery. She nearly toppled over when she saw the arrangement of fresh baked breads and rolls. Tears started welling up as she reflected on her home and the absolute lack of these pleasures. They exited the shop and found a market with fresh fruit on display. The smell of citrus and other ripened produce tantalized her.

"Suddenly, I don't want to go home," she pines. "Ghantil, would you mind if I moved over here to live?"

"Just so long as you find a small apartment or something for me as well."

She looked up into the clear blue sky with a few sparse clouds of billowy white and could only shake her head morosely.

"Will we ever have anything like that in my lifetime?"

"Easy now, Azina," he comforts the girl. "Once we take care of our immediate problems, I'm sure we'll get to work on the rest."

"Are you ready yet?" Kaliya grins. "All this will be here for probably a long time to come, and you're welcome to return and spend your money anytime."

"I doubt these people would know what to do with the type of money we use," Azina relents.

"Yes, well, minor detail."

Kaliya leads them over to a large building on the other side of the plaza and through the double doors into the lobby.

Ayene had returned to her body by this time, having been in projected mode during her visitation to oversee the activation of the gate on Azgarén. She met with them inside the building and accompanied them the rest of the way.

✦✦✦✦✦✦✦

Thaelyn was in conference with several of his top officers, including Chief Tech Lapäli and the Professor from the BRC, along with Marelle and Relissa.

"Chief Tech," Thaelyn advises. "One of our most immediate priorities will be to finish the control center in order to facilitate the operation of the shield walls, and further to regulate the flow of the energies through the emitters on the field. We also need to establish our communications links with our people locally as well as back here at home."

"Yes, Your Lordship. We already have several component systems ready to plug in. Our people are putting the finishing touches on the console stations, and Petrith has been good enough to provide us with samples of the technologies they use on Azgarén that will allow us to interface with their local network. As such, we'll be able to send and receive through their native com-links."

"Excellent, but let us not forget that raid siren network. We need access to it in case we need to assert a little of our own influence to ensure the course of events. I am still trying to imagine how we might successfully draw Sargeras out of hiding in case Darumon should not submit to our challenge."

"Accessing the network shouldn't be a problem, and again Petrith has supplied us with the network protocols and access codes. As I understand it, it includes a PA system, so if you need to make any special announcements, you can do this from the control room."

"The most interesting, in my mind," the Professor adds, "will be this new shield wall. While in theory it follows the same design as our original model, like what we used around Firstfall during your initial arrival here, this one is scaled much larger. The concept is certainly familiar, but I'm anxious to test it to make sure it works before committing ourselves."

"Of course, Professor," Thaelyn accedes. "And I would further suggest, before we commit to any movements, we must also make sure we have a full charge available in storage. We cannot know how things will turn out."

"Are we doing anything special with that lounge area upstairs?" Marelle wonders. "That's what I'm waiting for. A nice little place to sit and enjoy a drink or two while the game is on outside," she giggles.

"Indeed, Marelle," Thaelyn smiles. "This is where we will be stationing Master Velen and his people, along with a few others I would imagine will be visiting to oversee the events outside. But we need them to be easily visible in case Darumon and Sargeras should have in mind to try tapping their knowledge."

"I don't necessarily like the idea of putting my father on the front line like that," Kailen relents. "But I suppose this is the unfortunate position of being who he is."

"Yes, and I sympathize with you, Commander. But where Sargeras and Darumon are concerned, we need their focus to be on those events we have planned. At least up until that moment we are ready to spring our trap.”

“But will we at least have a place to order drinks?” Marelle wonders.

“Absolutely!” he responds cheerily. “What good is a lounge without a refreshment bar?”

The room shares a brief laugh before he continues.

“Now Relissa, we will have you make a few visits to examine the situation with their environment. Perhaps the Director can meet with you, maybe even to introduce you to a few of his more trusted colleagues to offer some new ideas and perspectives on how we can help at a later time.”

“Aye, I’ll be there,” she nods readily. “I’ve been working with the Priestess here on a few ideas,” she thumbs at the wood elf druid sitting next to her. “We’ve made some good work collecting specimens on Morndindor, but where most of that’s dying out from heat and dry air, from what I’ve heard of this one, it’s being poisoned by all their bleedin’ pollution. That’ll be a tough one to fix if we can’t clean the air quick enough.”

“Indeed, this may require special attention, but at least the industry that was causing it is being corrected by now.”

“Aye, and there’s a good one for you. How in all the bloody hells did he manage to tangle that one up on them.”

“No doubt he put a fair amount of thought into it,” he grins gently.

“What about my thought of using a Tree of Life over there?”

“While the idea is certainly unique, I am unsure how it might perform in the absence of the arcanic energies, as this is one form of life originally born in that environment. This may require some additional study.”

As the conversation came to a pause, Thaelyn noticed some people standing near the door, so he waved to call them in.

Kaliya was waiting patiently with the others just inside the room. The Director and Azina were staring slack-jawed at the wide variety of races represented at the table. This was further compounded by the glowing eyes of the resident Daanen’kai officers. When Thaelyn saw Kaliya’s entourage, he stood up and worked his way around to meet them.

“My Lord,” Kaliya steps forward, speaking the Suuden’kai tongue for the benefit of her guests. “I would wish to introduce our most recent visitors. This is Director Ghantil Bak’vayn and Intern Azina

Nur'ten from the ARC on Azgarén. And I believe you already know Kita over here."

"Indeed, I do, and welcome to our humble home. I am Lord Thaelyn, at your service."

"At my service?" the Director blurts breathlessly. "Your Lordship, it seems you have done more service for our entire race, and apparently much more beyond that, than any man could account for. I should be the one at service here, if only to pay back for all you have done."

Thaelyn smiles pleasantly at the Director, and next turns to see Azina timidly trying to hide her face in the Director's shoulder.

"And this must be the young intern our fine Lieutenant once met, and almost as if by accident to discover she has emotions. Young Miss Nur'ten, if it were not for your, shall we say, episode, we might not have been able to accomplish nearly as much work as we have."

Azina smiles bashfully and nods.

"Thank you, um, Your Lordship," she responds softly, glancing at the Director to follow his address.

"Come now, Child," he reaches to gently take her hand. "You do not need to hide here. We are friends, and I prefer a casual manner with my guests. Allow me to introduce you to some of our officers and others who have been most instrumental in our work."

He brings them back to the table and the other officers rise up to meet them.

"This is General Gabarleine, my senior officer in command of our military. Then we have High Commander Kailen Nazég of the Daanen-Aryku Sentinels."

"Another HC?" the Director wonders. "So, do we have a little competition with Geilv?" he smiles cautiously.

"He works the problem from his side," Kailen offers. "I work it from mine."

"But you're only a Sentinels service, not a full military?"

"Yes, we follow in the path of our forebearers from the days of my father on Azgarén."

"Your father… We're speaking of Velen again?" he glances at Kaliya. "Does this mean you two are brother and sister?"

"Yes, we are, and it's been a hard road for us."

"Brother and sister, working together to bring your people back, in honor of your father. That would be a fine story for the history books. It even carries a little romance to it."

"We still need to write a few pages, however."

"How is he, by the way? He would be rather old by now, wouldn't he?"

"Yes, and the years, as well as that same hard road, were not easy on him."

"I'm sorry to hear that, but maybe we can pave a new one together for him."

"I certainly hope so."

"And then, over here," Thaelyn continues around the table. "We have Chief Technician Tanjhira Lapäli, the one who has done most of our work from the Daanen-Aryku side, and then Professor Cogswoggle, our native scientist, working together to create this hybrid technology."

"Chief Tech Lapäli, a pleasant greeting," the Director nods. "And Professor, you appear as another member like those currently working in that base...a gnome, is it?"

"Right-a-diddly-do, Director!" he affirms energetically.

"Yeah, he's definitely one of those," Azina smirks. "I caught one of them trying to peek up my lab coat once."

The Professor giggles bashfully at the mention.

"He does that to me quite often," Tanjhira nods.

"Next, we have Lieutenant Marelle Carronel," Thaelyn continues. "She is the first of our citizens to learn how to fly anything other than a gryphon, and more so to fly it in space. She is currently training up our modest taskforce of combat ships."

"Wait a moment," the Director hesitates. "I'm not sure what a gryphon is, but if I'm interpreting this correctly, you people are new to powered flight, and yet not only are you flying in space, but training others in combat vessels? Didn't you miss a step in there somewhere?"

"A small one," she admits cheerily. "You see, it all started with a Suuden'kai heavy transport. I had no idea what I was doing, but I had to move it somehow. So, I asked Padriyl over here," she directs to the younger officer behind her, "if he could offer some help in translating things."

"Ah, and is he a pilot?"

"No, he's more of a security officer working a desk job."

"Oh, really...how nice... So, he offered translation services."

"And between the two of us, and with Relissa here in the copilot's seat..." she turns to point at the dark elf. "We managed to get it off the ground."

"Um, does SHE know anything about flying?"

"She rode a gryphon once."

"Uh huh…and just so I know what we're talking about, what is a gryphon?"

"A winged animal they use as a flying mount."

"Really!" he frowns worriedly. "A winged animal…used as a flying mount…"

"You're not getting ME on one of those," Azina winces.

"Right, but now, how does this relate to flying a transport?"

"Technically, it doesn't," Marelle affirms. "With a gryphon, the driver uses a special lance-like rod to direct it through the air. They're really clever little critters, too."

"I see."

"Other than that, she's a ranger, which is a completely different trade. They mostly work with animals."

"Oh, of course, I should've guessed. And she was your copilot."

"Yeah. So, we powered up, lifted off, flew around a bit, just to get a nice feel for it, and landed neatly by our outpost, which is in a valley to our south."

"And during this time, you said you had no idea what you were doing?"

"Well, I knew I was flying, but as for the mechanics of it, um…no."

"And you flew a heavy transport without killing yourself and at least a dozen others on the ground?"

"Yeah. It wasn't really that difficult. Push this, go this way, pull back, go the other way. Turn here, press that button…"

"Oh, well, not having ever been in one of those before, I was always under the impression you needed special training for it. And now you're flying combat craft and training others to do the same. Ayene was right, you people will run circles around us."

"And these are sweet little babies as compared to that transport," she asserts eagerly. "Virtual holographic controls, tactical HUD, arcanic induction for at least half of the components…"

"In all the nether-space, I think I'll take up a religion, because I'm going to need divine strength to help me through this."

"We can teach you," she offers with a smile.

Thaelyn grins and shakes his head, then moves to the next set.

"Finally, we have Priestess Rumoren and Relissa Moonshimmer."

"I don't believe I've had the chance to meet any like you before," the Director remarks. "May I know what you call your people?"

"Generally, our mother race is called Tel'Quessir," Relissa answers. "More commonly we call ourselves elves. My clan goes by the name Mori, meaning dark, to match our skin. And my people call themselves Night Elves."

"Most interesting, so you segregate yourselves into clans based on physical features?"

"Not in all cases. Sometimes we have a few other differences, for instance where we prefer to live, like the Priestess here."

Relissa passes off to the druid.

"My people," the Priestess asserts, "use the clan name Taur, and we might use the conjugation Taurerea, which translates as the woodland ones, or Wood Elves. As you can see, our appearance is different, but we have another quality, and that is we prefer to live only in wooded areas, surrounding ourselves by the living caress of nature. We cannot abide living in stone buildings and false furnishings."

"Fascinating. So, is this to say you build your homes entirely out of organic materials?"

"We may often build our homes among the boughs of our wooded glades, for instance in the tops of the trees, and only from living materials, nothing deceased, unless we speak of the smaller items we might use for our furnishings. But in a normal city, like back home where I live, which is the capital city on Tae'Eladar, we have a district that is very organic in nature with lush vegetation everywhere. And our architecture is often comprised of the natural elements blended in as part of our structural designs."

"That would be an interesting sight to see. And you're a priestess? Our society isn't religious in any way, but I recall a few moments from our early history where religion was once practiced. And, I might also say," he smiles tenderly. "Your manner of dress is quite different from anything I might have seen before."

"Manner of dress?" Azina murmurs scandalously. "She's wearing feathers and pieces of wood."

The Priestess smiles and continues.

"Yes, we also dress ourselves in accordance to our bond with nature… nothing artificial. We give ourselves to our goddess Mielikki, the Forest Queen, and she governs how we must live in harmony with the natural world. I am a druid, a priestess of nature. I commune with the essence of nature, of plants and animals, and I attempt to bring harmony to our existence with the world around us."

The Director was uncertain how to respond to this ridiculous notion, but he didn't want to offend, so he simply smiled and nodded apprehensively.

"Um, and so, just to be sure we catch every last part of my horns falling off, are you in any way associated with these operations?"

"Partially," she submits supportively. "My current assignment is mostly relating to Morndindor, where we are engaged in a large-scale biological study and conservation effort. I'm managing a new conservatory on Ruuki uy'Daan, where Relissa and others, including one young Daanen'kai girl who is currently in training as a druid, are assisting in collecting specimens for study and cultivation for an eventual reseeding effort on Morndindor."

"Yeah, that finished it," he mumbles feebly. "So, you're some kind of biologist that worships trees or something. Furthermore, you're Industrial Age, not even space-capable, and yet you're hoping to restore and reseed a planet in an environmental collapse. Just wait until I bring this home to our own biology departments. They were pulling their horns out for nothing to do, but this might actually kill a few of them."

"Granted, this is an unusual situation," she smiles. "But we are all natural creatures, Director, including you and your dedication to technology. This does not change anything."

"I will admit, you are right, and we do hold a tradition of caring for our world…or at least we were until the Marshal came along. Um, is this to say you might offer some sort of assistance one day?"

"We have a few interesting things to offer, but first we must attend to the larger issues."

"Naturally. I know a few people who might be interested in this. Maybe I can give them a call when I get back and let them know you're coming…so they can run the other direction."

The priestess chuckles and smiles pleasantly, hoping to calm his awkward stance.

Azina decided she would give the Director a break, although she was extremely hesitant by now to hear what the next one might bring. She looked at Relissa, who was neatly dressed in a leather jacket and a cloth shirt, and sturdy woven cloth pants. It wasn't quite the same as the fashion style back home, but it was better than feathers, and it gave the appearance of someone who might spend a lot of time outdoors. Relissa's jacket seemed to bulge in front, but Azina didn't want to stare, thinking it might be impolite manners.

"And Relissa, was it?" she begins. "You are…a ranger? What is it you do?"

"A ranger is a scout profession here," she replies with her typical quirky smile. "And like she said, we tend to work with animals a lot."

"Oh, well that sounds reasonable enough. Do you train them in some way?"

"Aye, we do! But it requires a special kind of temperament to do it right. Some of them can be a little fidgety."

"Yes, I suppose so," she admits, feeling a slight relief for the soothing topic. "I don't have a lot of experience with animals. I had a few pets in my day, but that was a long time ago. So, what kind of work are you involved in?"

"Most recently, I've been helping collect samples from around Morndindor for study, and hopefully to culture and grow so we can reseed the place. I also go out to make drawings of things, like landscapes to document what I see, along with whatever I find living out there."

"That actually sounds like a very professional job. So, you basically go out on expeditions to study and catalog whatever might still be out there?"

"Aye, but that place is a mess."

"Oh yes, from what Ayene told me, I can only guess what it might be like."

"Right. Try hot, dry, and barren. Ugh! And it's also a heavy gravity world, so it's a mite hard to get around out there."

"Heavy gravity… Wow, I can understand that…well, at least in theory. I've never been off-planet before, but I can imagine it might be hard on a person."

"Figure roughly twice what we have here, maybe a bit less."

"Twice?" she winces. "Ouch, yeah, that puts it into perspective a little."

"Aye, and not just for me, but also my little friends."

"Little friends?" she asks tentatively, now feeling uncertain about this situation. "Are we talking about these animals you train?"

"That's right. A ranger uses animal companions in their trade, small critters to help scout, and bigger ones for support."

Now Relissa opens up her jacket to reveal an oversized pocket inside one flap.

"In all the nether-space," Azina mutters to herself. "I thought that was her body."

From just under the lip of the pocket, a pair of little noses pop up to test the air, and then further to reveal two furry little heads. Relissa coaxes them out onto her shoulders.

Azina steps back and ducks behind the Director.

"This is Scratch and Snickers," Relissa announces. "Two of my little friends."

"You keep those inside your clothing?" she whimpers.

"Aye, I made a little home for them inside there. I also have a pet hawk I can take with me, and a wolf."

"What's a wolf?"

"It's a bigger critter I use for support."

"Uh huh… And what do you do with these?"

"I can have them run out ahead of me and take up roosts for spying, then report back. I can also ask them to do other tricks for me."

"To ask…to report…" she winces. "Wait a minute! This suggests a form of mutual communication. Are we saying that you talk to them… as if to tell them something, and they do it?"

"That's right. Come over here a minute and I'll show you."

"I…uh…"

"Come on, they won't hurt you."

Azina cautiously steps closer as Relissa brings her to the table, setting the girl's hands on the surface. The others hang back and watch. Kita moves to the side to give the girl space and wearing her own little smirk in anticipation of the playful game.

The young elf then steps back and puzzles out a cute trick. She walks over to one of the supply shelves and looks for a couple of ribbons which she fashions into loops. The rest of the room waits to see what the mischievous dark elf has in mind.

She sets the ribbon loops on the table and calls her squirrel companions down next to them. She then begins a series of chitters and clicks, intermixed with a few special keywords.

"Ghantil," Azina whispers. "I'm not so sure about this. Maybe having Sargeras around isn't so bad after all. He's quiet, keeps to himself, and we live happy little lives, completely ignorant of anything else out there."

Relissa finishes with her instruction, and the two little animals each give bouncy chirps in acceptance of their mission. They each then pick up one of the loops and dash across the table in the direction of the jittery young intern. As she sees them coming, her instincts tell her to jump away, but her legs were frozen. All she could do was watch with her eyes bulging as they scampered up her arms and onto her shoulders.

Her voice was stuck in her throat, and she couldn't move her head, only to roll her eyes to either side, trying to see what they were doing. She could feel them gripping her shoulder as they steadied themselves, and finally she felt something occurring on her head. The squirrels were hooking the loops over the tips of her horns.

The little creatures then sat back and waited for her reaction, holding perfectly still, as little statues staring at her.

"I think she looks cute," Ayene remarks. "What do you think, Director?"

The Director was glaring rigidly at the girl, stiffly turning to glance at Ayene, and then back again, trying to make a judgement.

"Well, yes, it does go nicely with her complexion. That is, it would, if she had one."

Azina cautiously rotated her view to each of the animals and tried desperately to form a smile.

"Uh…thank you."

"I think she needs to unwind her horns a little," Kita remarks cutely.

"Oh, and you think you can do better?"

Kita smiles and reaches a hand across to Azina's shoulder. She holds it in place as she scratches her upper arm to draw attention while emitting a series of soft purrs and coos to call the animals over to her. The two little squirrels then turn and scamper across onto her arm, where Kita rubs her finger against their necks.

"Hey!" Azina snaps. "How did you do that!"

"I have a little experience by now. I met Relissa during my time studying for the language course. Kaliya introduced me to a few of her friends, and Relissa showed me a trick or two. So, I've already made my adjustment to these people. I guess I'm a little more adventurous than some…maybe it goes with my job."

"Probably your age, as well," the Director relents. "The younger crowd always did tend to be more ambitious."

"Hey, I'm not that much older," Azina protests. "But maybe I spent too much time behind a desk."

"Aye," Relissa admits as she comes back around the table. "Stuffy rooms tend to do that to you. But then, the outdoor life for you isn't all that grand, either."

"No, it's not. Most of our wildlife is in shelters by now."

Kita passes the two little critters back to Relissa as they continue.

"We have a lot of different ways about us," Relissa explains. "Not everything works the same as how you invented it. We can get the same job done, but in ways you might not normally follow yourselves."

"I suppose I have to agree with that," the Director relents. "And most certainly with the little demonstration you just gave. I've never seen someone interact with animals like that before."

"Some of us have special ways of seeing the world around us. We have different races, each with their native cultural skills and manners, some of us good with one thing while others are good with something else."

"And you're able to interact with each other like this? I would rather think this might conflict more than anything else."

"Not at all! Well, in the old days, maybe, but this was before Thaelyn came into it. Since then, we learned to accept each other, and even to learn how to cover for those areas we're not as good at. This is his gift to us," she thumbs at Thaelyn. "And then, with our magic, we can do a lot of things you might do with your science, but it comes around a different way."

"Incredible," he accedes, now relaxing a bit from the polite candor. "I've noticed this already with some of your devices, and it certainly defies anything we might hold any experience with back home. Furthermore, you people must be very tolerant of those like us and how we tend to behave. But to think this could be the result of someone piecing it together like this," he glances at Thaelyn. "Your Lordship, this surely could not have been an easy challenge for you."

"It was not," he relents. "You can be sure of it. Tae'Eladar, in those early days, was a rather untamed example. But over the course of time, we brought it into harmony."

"Aye!" Relissa chirps. "You should've seen us here, like Kaliya in those early days. The Daanen-Aryku didn't understand any of this either, just like you. Not until Thaelyn came in and showed them how it's done. They were isolationists, and she always described magic as some kind of mysticism. We have a friend named Haran, he's a mage. He tried a few times to show her, but she just couldn't get it inside her head."

"But now she's doing it on her own."

"Aye, and she's good at it, same as a lot of others who took up the study. But this didn't start until after Thaelyn showed up and made it easy for them."

"And to think," Azina considers. "I went to a university and studied hard to become proficient in my trade. And yet, there is so much we're not even aware of."

"Try taking a few classes here with us and see how you feel about it. You'll see things in a whole new way."

✦✦✦✦✦

"Ileani?" calls the receptionist at CPComm. "What happened to you?"

Ileani was returning after a medical leave during the last days of her seed removal. She was laid up for a brief time after her surgery, but was now ready to go back to work, and people were taking notice of her. As she entered the building, she was wearing her new filter mask, but took it off once inside. She strolled up to the reception desk to check in.

"Oh, hello, Teela," she responds innocently. "What do you mean?"

"Ileani, I'm not blind. Your seed is gone."

"Oh, that…" she grins softly. "I signed up for it a while ago to be processed once the majority of their critical people were done. You should do it too. My camera team is also in line to be processed."

"So, it really does work? I'm a little afraid to try it, even though I'm hearing a lot about it lately."

"It works, but the waiting lists are growing fast, so you should get in line quick before you get lost in all that."

"All right, but now what happens. We have it removed, and I see people using this new filter mask. How long do we need to keep this up?"

"Until we finish cleaning up the mess out there, and it's a big mess."

"And the Council, and the Marshal?"

"Let the ACI deal with them. Our business is to report the news… whatever news it is they give us to report," she sighs. "But it's better than what those regulators were giving out."

"Yeah, but I'm wondering how much longer we have to keep this up."

"They tell me they're waiting on a few critical projects to finish, one of these being that construction project out in the Bintavyan Valley. They also have one or two additional sensations to hit us with, although I'm not so sure I want to see the aftermath of it."

"Well, just look at it this way; at least you have something interesting to report on."

Chapter 9

EXPOSURE

Another year had come to a close at the guildhall, and graduation day was commencing. On this occasion, Marelle had finally completed her studies through the Seventh Circle, along with all the other training she required from the academy. The only thing left for her now was to continue working her skills at piloting and commanding a flight of wingmen for her future role in the coming engagements around Azgarén.

In the ceremonial hall, the Master of Ceremonies once again gave his oratory to each graduate to come forward for their diploma, until it came time for Marelle's turn.

"Lieutenant Marelle Carronel."

She steps forward from her row and up to the dais, offering the traditional salute, and then kneeling. She held herself confidently as the MC made the familiar speech.

"On this day, you who have come before us do hereby honor us with your devotion…"

It was the same for each student. She listened attentively and prepared herself for her response as he came to a close.

"…How do you plea?"

She speaks up boldly for the audience to hear. She was the first student to graduate at the academy from her hometown of Rolsklinde, and she wanted to make it special.

"In the memory of my father and mother, in the memory of all those of my home, the city of Rolsklinde, who suffered needlessly at the hands of our former governor, and to all those of our world who lost their lives only for his gain, I do hereby plead yay with all my heart to serve and protect that which we hold so dear."

The crowd offers up a resounding cheer as the MC finishes his presentation and hands her the scroll. She stands up and meets with Thaelyn's eyes wearing a bright smile.

"Very well pronounced, Marelle," he offers. "We are privileged to have you with us."

The new school year was beginning and Thaelyn was spending the morning in his office at the guildhall reviewing the academy's financial affairs and student registration. This would be his normal routine if it were not for the demands of the war. He would also spend time offering occasional lessons in some of the classes, such as the combat hall and mage academy. He took great pleasure in sharing his wisdom and personal experiences with the younger generation, but this was a rare delight in recent times as so much of his time was spent elsewhere.

A knock sounds at the door, and an attendant peeks inside with a message.

"My Lord, you have a most honored visitor."

The attendant steps aside to allow the guest to enter. The form of a stately tall female emerges into view, entirely in silver hues from head to toe, and with cat-like eyes. She sauntered casually into the room.

Thaelyn jumped out of his chair at first sight of her, circling around his desk and approaching her reverently. He took her hand and touched his brow to it in a moment of respectful deference.

"Sister Adalon," he offers kindly. "It is so good to see you out and about. To what pleasure do I owe this special occasion?"

"Thaelyn, we mussst talk..." she responds with her elongated hissing. "There are mattersss... Of concern... Within my mind. Our fated encounter... On Azgarén... Mussst proceed... With great care. He mussst not... Essscape from usss... Again."

"Again? Do you mean in relation to what apparently occurred during the Celestial War?"

"Yesss. His kind... Once made their mark... Upon the realmsss. But that time... Is at an end. He mussst not... Be allowed... A return... Nor to continue... Elsssewhere."

"It is our intention to end his reign, this much you can be sure of."

"I know thisss. I have watched… And waited… And I am pleased… With our progressss. But thisss is not… The focusss… Of my concern. He cannot… Be allowed… An essscape. He mussst be… Prevented thisss."

"Do you have any visions occurring to you about this?"

"I do. His kind… Can fold ssspace. You should know thisss. We mussst… Hinder him… Until he is… Defeated."

"Naturally, this is a concern of mine. I had been hoping to use distractions to keep his mind on us while we make that final approach. But such a power as that is difficult to prevent outright."

"Difficult, perhapsss… But it mussst be. And I happen to know… Of one individual… Who could be of ssservice. If perhapsss you should call… Upon a ssspecial friend… You may find… Your ansssswer."

"Adalon, do you recall how I feel about such ambiguous statements?" he grins.

"Yesss…" she smiles. "And I recall… How you enjoy… The challenge… To decipher them. But thisss one… Should be easy… As the one in quessstion… Is already here."

Adalon turns back towards the door and another figure steps into view, having apparently been waiting outside for her cue.

Aelwyn enters the room in her usual priestly manner with her hands clasped in front of her and her head sheltered beneath her hood.

"Adalon," Thaelyn ruminates curiously. "What is on your mind at this moment?"

"The circle mussst close. I have waited long… For thisss day. Ssso much has passssed. Ssso many livesss. Ssso much sssuffering. Finally… The wait… Is nearly over. We will sssee thisss… To itsss end… Each of usss…. In our own way."

She turns and leisurely makes her way out of the room, leaving Thaelyn and Aelwyn staring at each other, wondering what she meant by her last statement.

"Aelwyn, do you have any idea what she has in mind?"

"Only as much as you, spirit-brother," she relents tenderly. "She came out of that well of hers and called upon me, but as I stood there listening to her, I had an idea occur."

"Very well, let us hear it. But if this has to do with folding space…" he pauses unexpectedly. "Wait a moment. Aelwyn, you hold such a power, correct? Your power over the fabric of Reality allows you to fold space even outside the Outer Planar sphere."

"Yes, although I will admit I do not engage this talent often, if at all. Only in the Outer Planes, and never inside Sigil, as the Lady would not appreciate this conduct. But my Father did endow me with this Gift, as well as others that affect the reality of space around me. And I have practiced this well enough to conduct it on a Prime world. But Thaelyn, this is to fold space, not to rend it such that another cannot do the same. This actually goes against my morals."

"You may need to make an exception to that rule, in this case. This is a matter of justice, not simply playing games to foil something out of mischief."

"Perhaps, but also recall that I am not a soldier, and we are speaking of a Primordial here. His power should dwarf mine. And to perform this would be to announce myself to him. Thaelyn, this carries a great risk, if he should turn on me."

"I know, Aelwyn, but the risk travels in many directions here. If he should escape from us by folding his local space and eluding our advance, we might not ever find him again. We must take these risks, if only to preserve the Seas of Creation from the threat he represents."

"Indeed," she sighs. "I know the danger, and I know what may come of it, but I am afraid."

Thaelyn ponders the situation for a moment, trying to find reconciliation for her fear.

"Let us consider…"

"Oh, spirit-brother, are you now playing this trick on me?" she smiles gently.

"Aelwyn," he grins softly. "In many ways, you are like a sister to me, virtually a part of my family, if I could ever believe myself to have one. But tricks or otherwise, I would not hesitate to approach this any different, not even with you."

She rolls her eyes and chuckles at the audacity of his manners.

"Very well, my younger brother who believes himself so bold, let us consider what?"

"First, he cannot and should not be expecting anything like us on the field of play. If he, like Darumon, has become so complacent with the diminutive stature of those around him, we hold the element of surprise."

"Granted…"

"Therefore, we must use this to our advantage," he paces across the room and back again.

"And here he goes with his classic pacing," she mumbles privately.

Thaelyn pauses to glance at her, then at the ground where he was standing, but he can only shrug and continue his train of thought.

"Our play must follow a certain course in order to keep his mind on our little game. But in that final moment, when we are ready for our most important strike, he may choose to run rather than fight. This is where you come in."

He continues pacing around the room in deep contemplation as Aelwyn watches him curiously, folding her arms as she waits for him to resolve his thoughts.

"He keeps to himself inside that so-called sanctuary of his in the city," Thaelyn considers. "According to our sources, he never comes out, and is presumably sleeping during this time. I suspect this is largely to conserve his strength. And at this point, I doubt he would hold as much as he might in his native element."

"So, you think my test against his would not be as one-sided?"

"Keeping in mind we are also disabling portions of his life support machine in those seeds. Granted, there is still a sizable population to be considered, but we are making dents here and there."

"Very good, but this leads us to ask how many dents it will take to weaken him sufficiently for one such as I to overtake him. But then, I suppose we should also ask how potent he is to begin with under these conditions."

"That, and maybe also if we can surprise him with our own play. The element of surprise here might be just enough to throw him off-balance. If we suggest he has been largely sleeping, or otherwise out of contact with the development of the Planes during his absence, he might not expect to see such beings as we to begin with. Recall how they were not known to allow the younger races to develop this far."

"Yes, as opposed to the Estelar. And so, to see a Celestial would indeed be surprising, as we might be interpreted the same as the mortal societies, based on our outward appearance. He might then underestimate our capacity. But the question remains if we can keep him in his place long enough for that final blow."

"Indeed, these are questions we may not be able to answer from where we stand, but at the same time, I am brought back to Adalon. If she sees this occurring, we should hold faith in her judgement."

"Ah yes," she smirks. "And then we have dear Adalon, with her reputation of keeping so many curious secrets to herself. Very well, I suppose I must concede that portion of it. Then it comes down to mustering all that I have at my disposal to see this through, but for this I will need practice. And yet, we still come back to the risk that he will surely discover me once I expose myself to him. Even if he is weak enough that I can overcome his power to fold space, I doubt he would be so weak as not to retaliate."

"Then you will need a protector. And for this, I might suggest Haran. I had hoped to bring him in at some moment…he certainly deserves a role of some kind…and this would be a good one. As an Elder Mage, he would be ideal to raise a shield to hold back whatever Sargeras might throw at you. And at this moment, I think the Infinity Shield should be sufficient against whatever power he might have over there."

"You seem to place a great deal of faith in that conjuration."

"It has certainly proven itself on many occasions."

"Very well, and then what? I am still rather curious as to how this final play will proceed. Who is it that will ultimately take him down?"

"Adalon's prophecies suggest a heretofore unknown or unexpected player will arrive. I am already aware Adalon herself will be present, and her strength will certainly tip the scales to our favor along the way. Therefore, I feel confident that we will have sufficient help to contain things."

"I see, and I certainly hope you are right. But if I am to perform this way, I must conduct some research on a viable method if I should have any hope of succeeding. I will need to return home to Bitopia for this."

"I understand, dear spirit-sister. Study well and practice hard. This may be a crucial aspect of our advance."

"Ghantil," Azina calls as she enters the office. "We're getting a LOT of calls recently to schedule the seeds. We're developing a waiting list that's starting to run on for months now."

"I don't doubt it, and further that it'll get worse before it gets better."

"We should probably think about trying to distribute that remedy, but I'm also concerned about the shelf life and how long before we're ready to take this to the final stage."

"And here we run into that logistical problem again. But you're right, we should try to stockpile those pills of yours and distribute them. Shelf life or no, something is better than nothing."

"All right, I'll see about refining the packaging to maximize the result. Meanwhile, I wanted to ask you about that new girl they're talking about, Latena Ta'yeen. She's really getting into that activist business lately. How do you feel about what it all means?"

"She carries a number of valid points, and I suppose I have to agree on a few issues, not the least of which is the science community, to which we actually belong to one faction, and how we may or may not get any activity, all at the whim of the Council."

"Assuming the Council has any whim to begin with."

"Right," he nods. "Our society has used this form of government for longer than most of us can even recall from a historical perspective. If we should one day find ourselves converting to anything else, it'll be a massive culture shock. But if to reflect upon it from her perspective, a government body composed of the more traditional political values and procedures, where the science community is not restricted to someone telling us what we can or cannot research, and then how and why we should do it at all, would likely allow us to finally overcome those stranglehold restrictions we've been suffering for so long."

"And all those arguments I kept complaining about. I can't believe it, but this is what it actually comes down to."

"Just imagine, Azina, if not for this, we might not be in this predicament in the first place. It was apparently the Marshal who created this in the days of King Saakerav to constrict our manners to fit within his own designs. I now have to ask myself how much more advanced we might actually be today if it were not for this holding us back."

✦✦✦

Another demonstration was in progress in a popular downtown plaza, where a large crowd of people had been assembling to listen to Latena making her speech. But on this occasion, Ileani had her news crew out there giving a survey report.

> *"I'm here in downtown Capitol Prime standing in front of the most recent in a series of anti-government rallies being held, where people are gathering from all around the local area to listen to the speaker arguing the hidden agendas of not simply the Council, but also the Charter of Laws.*

This is not the same group of people who were once protesting the Council's emergency war protocols, but a group that has been steadily growing in number as more and more people come to realize the issues being debated here may represent a viable concern for our public way of life. Not only are they protesting in the streets, but I have heard of organized forums in lecture halls throughout many of the major cities. This is a formal movement we are seeing here.

As I stand here and listen to these statements, I cannot help but to ask myself where it may ultimately lead us. But one thing is for sure, it is certainly drawing a lot of attention, and for this I feel a confrontation may soon be approaching."

In the officer's lounge in Central Command, Commander Geilv and Captain Ta'yeen were taking a break to watch the news. The two of them were making it a renewed habit to pay closer attention to these broadcasts, as it was becoming clear to them that at least some of it might be part of a hidden campaign by the ACI to reveal certain critical details to the public about the Marshal.

"I certainly hope my little Latena doesn't get involved in any of that," the Captain relents. "This is exactly the sort of thing she was going on about so often during those university discussion groups she would attend."

"I'm actually becoming very curious about the topic here," Geilv mentions. "If it's drawing so much attention, what is it they're actually trying to say?"

"From what I heard one time, there's talk about some kind of hidden agenda in the Council, which we might dismiss anyway as we both know what happened to them..."

"But the rest of the world does not, so is this the ACI building up to something?"

"Do you think? I suppose it could be, but to what end? They're also talking about the Charter of Laws here, and how there's something wrong with it. Personally, I'm just thinking it's yet another conspiracy theory looking to get attention."

"You don't like those, do you," he chuckles.

"I'm a firm believer in the spirit of the Charter, that it was written to serve a purpose, and that purpose has led us through a lot of innovations."

"Maybe so, Captain, but when I look at what we have around us right now, I have to ask where we'll find ourselves when all this is over."

Thaelyn and his officers, along with Kaliya and Ayene, were gathering for an important meeting in the WIC building.

"We need to start planning a timeline here for Ytani," Kaliya states. "I've been spending some time with Relissa and Marelle to generate ideas on how we might do this, but as I understand it, we can't bring this to its full fruition until the base is ready, and all our players are fully prepared."

"This will need to include Haran and Aelwyn, by the way," Thaelyn asserts. "She will need to accompany us and apply herself in the event Sargeras should try folding space to escape our reach."

"Can she actually do something to stop that?" Kailen wonders.

"She holds the ability to fold space as well, but to prevent another from doing the same requires a special effort. Therefore, she has returned home to Bitopia for a bit of research and some practice. Adalon seems to think she is qualified, so we should give her some time for this. As for Haran, he will need to serve as a bodyguard in case Sargeras should take exception to the fact."

"Wow," Ayene relents. "Taking exception to someone trying to prevent him from folding space. That should be a fun one to watch."

"So, our timeline will need to carry us through this next graduation to be sure we have our best potential."

"All right," Kaliya concedes. "Then we will need to stretch things out a bit. First, Ytani needs to make his grand arrival, and I want this on a live news feed, so Darumon doesn't have any opportunity to refute it as fake. I'm going to portray a strange flying creature in the skies of C.P. for a few days, just to draw the attention of the general public. This gives us visibility for something new and exciting happening."

"When you say exciting, how does a strange flying creature become exciting?" he raises his brow.

"When it eventually makes a landing and turns into Ytani."

"Uh huh... And should we mark you down on the list before or after you make this showing?"

"I, uh... Well, maybe we should wait until after, so you can get a really good impression of just how exciting it actually was."

"Oh, but of course!" he chuckles.

The rest of the room joins with a hearty laugh.

"Now," Kaliya continues. "Among other things, we're going to have him clearly demonstrating the Prodigy Gift. This is going to finally expose the Marshal's biggest secret. We won't give away ALL the details, not immediately, but Ayene will be in an interview with Ileani about our new raid siren network when he arrives, and she'll go into her secret agent mode once he finishes. This will give off a clue we can hook into later."

"You like those hooks, don't you," Kailen remarks.

"They're certainly useful. He'll also have to demonstrate his bad manners and make a few statements to the Marshal, one of which relates to the mining base and his weapon. But we're going to downplay the issue of the weapon for now. We don't want to start a new panic."

"This is good," Thaelyn nods.

"I'll also probably have him make some sort of demand for a playmate. After all, he's a god-king, so he needs a little tribute delivered to him now and then."

"Tribute...right..."

"Here is where we have to play for time, but we also have a lot of variables to think of. Our plan is to involve multiple presentations, and likely to be played by ear, depending on the Marshal's response."

"And what sort of response are you aiming for, in this case?"

"At first, I'm going to assume he'll refuse to cooperate. He's not the sort of mentality to give in to something like this without a serious amount of convincing."

"Indeed, I might agree."

"And so, we have Ytani making multiple additional visits, again demanding tribute. In the absence of this weapon, Ytani is presenting himself as little more than a show-off with bad manners. Therefore, most of Azgarén might shrug him off as a megalomaniac, which certainly holds merit."

"Indeed!" he chuckles.

"Now, the Marshal might know the limits of this skill, but I doubt anyone else would at this point. And so, no one else on Azgarén would suspect Ytani to be off-planet making these projections, instead thinking he's local and simply misbehaving. This would add to the illusion of a false play, and only to draw attention."

"Much to their chagrin when they learn the truth," Kailen muses softly. "And worse, that SHE is the one misbehaving," he chuckles.

The group erupts in a quick laugh as Kaliya continues.

"Ytani's demands for a girlfriend will likely fall on deaf ears in the beginning. I'll make another one to reinforce the idea, but to stretch things out, we might say he forgot to tell them where to send it, so we will begin releasing some instructions…piecemeal of course…relating to his hiding place."

"Piecemeal?" Thaelyn wonders. "How do you mean this?"

"This appearance will tell them she needs to be delivered to such-and-such planetary location, since Ytani, being new to this role, forgot to give an address."

"Oh no…" Kailen moans and covers his eyes.

"Well, he wasn't really trained for this sort of thing, you know."

"Oh, indeed!" Thaelyn blasts. "Going from a dwarven Thane to a god-king is a rather steep learning curve."

They all shared another hearty round of laughter.

"Now, getting back to reality," Kaliya asserts. "It doesn't help matters that we're demonstrating the absolute worst side of this Gift. On one hand, it could be useful as a learning tool, as if to say this is what NOT to do. On the other hand, it'll hurt us when we try to say this is a truly fabulous item, if used the RIGHT way. In other words, we'll have our hands full trying to educate the people."

"I do not envy you, Kaliya," the General offers. "This is surely a monumental task you have set before you, and it is made worse by the fact that it is simply not an option for you to do it. I certainly wish you well."

"Thank you, General. In the meantime, he'll make a few additional appearances with his demands, the next one releasing the unfortunate fact that the Marshal, in his haste to chase his insurgents halfway across Creation, neglected to tell the science communities back home that he…discovered…a new universe out there."

"Good gracious! That will send a few shockwaves through the public."

"I'm sure it will, and one more thing Darumon kept hidden without justifiable cause for the discovery alone, especially if you factor in all his promises. And being Ytani on this occasion, who do you complain to about revealing all your intimate secrets?"

"Yes, very convenient, and completely outside his ability to govern."

"And this will tie in with that analyst and his statements hinting at such things the Council denied anyone to research, like nether-space, and it can also provide another hook or two we can use later for his presumed insurgents, saying if he spent so much time hunting them in THIS universe, what is he doing over there in THAT one."

"Will you be announcing the part relating to their Abnormal Space on this occasion?"

"I think not, so far. Let's take it in smaller steps. We need to give those people time to grow new horns before we blast them off again."

"This will build a rather substantial controversy against him," Thaelyn surmises.

"Especially when you would need a jump drive to reach it," Ayene asserts. "This takes us back to Elder Nazég again, and that ship. It only reinforces the idea of them using this against us. Therefore, why bother with outposts in our galaxy when they might not even live here?"

"Naturally. Yet another suggestive controversy."

"As I look at this," Kaliya continues. "We are moving closer to Adalon's prophecy of this Child breed turning against its Creator."

"Indeed, we are."

"By now, Ytani will be growing increasingly impatient with what we're going to assume to be the Marshal's noncompliance. Now, if we suggest he does NOT give in by offering up 'sacrifices' to the god Ytani, then Ytani's musclemen will have to make one or more appearances to enforce the idea that he has a military behind him. This is where Marelle comes into it."

"Oh dear," Thaelyn moans. "And made worse with Marelle's inclusion..."

"Then, depending on a few factors, not the least of which could be a visit of Ayene with Commander Geilv to help him resolve a few of his own variables, we may see a form of escalation develop between our two sides. Marelle's first run may only invoke a curious little scout to examine what just showed up on the scope, meaning to say the Ghan'aju bringing her team in for the first time to mark their index. She'll take that one out and depart the area."

"A quick hit-and-run tactic..."

"This will put Central on alert," Ayene begins. "It will serve as our first time ever incursion of hostiles in Azgarén local space. But such a small showing as this won't suggest anything more than a surprise ambush that got lucky."

"Oh, got lucky, is it?" Thaelyn smiles.

"Here we wait for the Marshal to respond, but I doubt it will result in anything, and so we come to Round Two, where Central will likely beef up security, now that they have a REAL threat arriving in their local space. My best guess is the next run will probably involve something bigger, on the order of a cruiser on this occasion, like what we had with the Tul'ryk, along with an escort, and all of them on alert."

"And how does Marelle tackle this with only a simple flight of one-man ships?"

"I would imagine, given the capabilities I'm hearing of those ships, she shouldn't have any real trouble with it other than taking a little time to make the extra hits. Her shields will also act as cloaking devices, and this will block any target locks, so the Azgarén navy may not be able to track their opponents at all. This may cause them to attempt a manual override, but this is problematic, as small craft like hers are difficult to target manually."

"I am starting to feel for those poor crewmen by now," he muses. "And so, we have our second run. Are we going for a third, and if so, what do you suggest they might use on that occasion?"

"By now, we might need to be working with Geilv, as I'm sure he'll be losing his horns over it…same as most of them. I might even suggest this, at least in a small way, from the get-go, but again this depends on variables relating to the Marshal. Meanwhile, the Marshal may still be adamant, thinking bigger is better. Central will have reports by this time of a cluster of small combat ships, and even with the obvious benefit of spatial inversion drives and a cloak, surely a heavier ship can blanket-fire the area and hit something. Therefore, our next run will likely involve something big, like a heavy cruiser with a flotilla escort."

"Good gracious!" the General relents. "I'm not entirely sure what that cruiser might look like, but I would hesitate to approach it, even if I was Marelle in her cloaked ships."

"And for this," Thaelyn considers. "I think we should be sure to give her a little extra firepower with additional vessels. She will surely need the added capacity. But do you actually believe we should travel this far?"

"My suggestion is yes," Ayene affirms. "We must demonstrate our capacity to rule the skies. This is to suggest there ARE indeed powers out there that our illustrious navy cannot counter, and this can open up Geilv's position a little, such that the Marshal essentially lied about his insurgents, especially if you factor in his encounters at Therinë and Sigil."

"This is a curious point, and I can see where it could benefit him somewhat for his own position, as this would now need to involve all this…Abnormal Energy."

"But here is where Kaliya and I have a twist…and probably cause for another mark," she grins.

"Ah, good, I was beginning to wonder about that. General?" he waves a finger.

"So far," Kaliya reflects. "We have a full flight of combat ships in operation, plus Marelle in hers, for a total of six, and with more on the way. Chief Tech Lapäli tells us the industry is pumping out as fast as it can, but there's a limit on getting everything assembled, checked, verified, and even tested before we can ensure it's ready. This is just another reason to stall for time, but our estimates suggest we might have three flights ready by the end of the year. However, for Round Three, I have an alternate idea…" she snickers.

"Young lady," he eyes her suspiciously. "Before we begin, did either Relissa or Marelle contribute to this idea? I think I should know so I can distribute the marks fairly."

"Although we did confer with them, especially Marelle for the dogfighting aspect of it, this one is mostly between the two of us this time. Since we're speaking of attack runs on star cruisers, Relissa is a little outside her field, and Marelle is more of a pilot, rather than covert ops."

"Right; and thank you. All right, and what is this new and most ingenious element of mischief you have in mind?"

"To capture the cruiser…"

Thaelyn glares at her and makes an emphatic blink before continuing.

"Um…this is curious. Yes, I think I will most surely need to ask about this, and then consider how to mark this down on the list."

"Once again, we need time to plan this, as well as some training."

"And this will involve both of us on different aspects of it," Ayene adds.

"Interesting," Thaelyn considers. "But how do you plan on doing this in the first place? First, you would need access. And what sort of crew complement are we speaking of here?"

"If they throw in a heavy, we might be looking at a thousand to fifteen hundred crewmembers."

"That is a fair number, to be sure. But next is how you might approach it. This should be good," he chuckles.

"We're going to, um…steal it?" Kaliya smiles sweetly.

"Uh huh, and this is coming from a paladin."

"We are simply arranging the combat conditions to work more to our favor, that's all."

"Oh, is this your justification? General, make a note of this, will you?"

"The bridge is the most critical element here," Ayene asserts. "Since I hold a command rank, I would wish to lead an assault on that in projected form, while she lands a full company in their shuttle bay."

"A single company versus as many as fifteen hundred?" Kailen winces. "Cu'Nar's pity, Kaliya, this reminds me of that time when you were an Ensign and tried taking on that camp full of orcs."

"Yes," she reflects. "But I didn't have the Stormhooves with me on that occasion. This is where some of our special training comes in. First, we need to practice a few things. For one, can a projected image follow a ship, like Marelle's fighter, through a hyperspace jump?"

"Indeed, this would be a curious one," Thaelyn muses.

"This could be a deciding factor in itself. Otherwise, we'll need to travel on the Ghan'aju and just memorize the area, as best we can, to arrive separately. But this will be tricky, as there really isn't anything like a landmark to focus on."

"No, there is not."

"Next, we need to be able to target the enemy vessel in space and fold over to it, then to enter it. I'll need a bunch of people capable of marking runes, so we'll need lots more of our effigies, a good way-line of at least twenty opening up inside their shuttle bay, which I'm hoping to be clear at the time."

"That's a full-scale assault!" the General winces. "And to do so on a ship of any kind, just popping out of portals!"

"It most certainly holds the merit of never having been tried before," Thaelyn considers. "And if she can do it at all, this would represent a very unique form of strategic advance."

"We need a fast way to move a lot of bodies," Kaliya states. "And the shuttle bay is our best choice. But for combat, our best advantage is to bring them into OUR space where we have the flows, and for this, Ayene will have her mission."

"No love and kisses this time?" Kailen smiles.

"Not this time," she accedes. "They'll be expecting hostiles. So, we'll go in with a stun-and-capture technique, like we did with the mining base, and use runes to transport them away. Also, I want to demonstrate our new combat skills. And I'll need Kriv'tik, and a healthy number of troops to help contain things on arrival."

"Very well," Thaelyn nods.

"But we need our magic for this, and all of us in full battle armor, first to offer protection, as well as a disguise, and also for our shields, in case anyone is armed."

"Good gracious, Kaliya," the General mutters. "That sounds like a very vigorous effort you have planned."

"As for Ayene, well, this is another practice session."

"My team will be projected," Ayene submits. "So, while Kaliya's people assemble in the shuttle bay, hopefully undetected, I will lead an infiltration of the bridge. But the bridge configuration of that ship is likely to be different from anything we have experience with, so we'll need to practice with the Tul'ryk, and then just try to interpolate from there. But for this we need time."

"Yes, time," the General interjects. "And how do you deal with the existing crew during this time?"

"This is part of our new practice. We figure there are two scenarios here. First is simply to wrestle the crew to the ground while someone pilots the ship into our space. But this is problematic to keep it that way while Kaliya makes her way up there with physical forces to take over properly."

"And during that time, almost anything could happen. I would not recommend this one."

"It also places us in view a little too readily, and we want this to appear...alien!" she flutters her fingers pretentiously.

"Oh dear..."

"So, here we come to the next one, which will probably do very nicely for us. This one is to block access to their control systems, and for this, I'll need to create something so icky, they'll just want to back away from it...something like a slime monster covering all their consoles... which, as it turns out, can interact with them to commandeer the ship."

"Great gods, I'm sorry I asked."

"Cu'Nar help us all, Ayene," Kailen moans. "And here I thought Kaliya was bad."

⟡ ✦ ✦ ✦ ✦ ⟡

Latena was taking a little time for herself, rather than inciting any new rallies. On this occasion, she decided to visit the ACI office for a bit of gossip. She was mostly curious about Tae'Eladar and what else it had to offer besides clear skies and sweet smells. And being a political science graduate, she was also interested in learning more about their system of politics, regarding it as a living example of something that apparently provided many opportunities for its people.

She entered the lobby of the ACI office and stepped up to the front desk where Kita worked. The young agent took quick notice of Latena and offered her greeting.

"Hello, Latena, how are you today?"

"I'm just taking a little break, trying to gear myself up for my first official interview, so I'm hoping to find someone to talk to, and maybe to help me relax a little. Is Ayene or Kaliya around?"

"I think they're both working on something these days. I got a memo here saying they're both training teams for a new series of projects."

"Wow, they must be really busy over there. I wonder what they have in mind this time."

"I don't know. Even though I'm in the loop, some of this stuff is still secret until they can get it ready. Is there anything I can help you with?"

"Oh..." she sighs. "Have you ever been over there?"

"On Tae'Eladar? Yeah, I took that language course and spent a little time getting to know a few people."

"That portal ride was scary, but also amazing in a lot of ways. I was riding on something that looked like a river of light, and it felt like I could be flying. I've never been on a ship jumping through nether-space, but the sights were just like what you might see in a vid-com space adventure. The part about landing on the other side is a little tricky, at least in the beginning, but the real treat was Tae'Eladar itself. Oh, it was beautiful."

"Yes, it is..." she reflects dreamily.

"Clear skies, clean air...and I mean it's so clean, you almost fall over from the pure delight of it. They have plants and trees and flowers everywhere, so every step you take is scented by something natural, not this artificial deodorizer spray we use here. The city and the people, other than the fact they're all aliens compared to us, seem so modest and uncomplicated, and yet they strike me as having such vivid personalities and colorful attitudes."

"I came to know a few like that, actually," Kita chuckles.

"And then we have their technology, which is strange to say the least. Some of it is clearly below us for what I could recognize, but they also have this other aspect involving their magic, and some of the devices I saw could easily rival our own equivalents. I'm tempted to take a few courses in their schools to see if I could learn how they do it."

"You and me both."

"But the whole thing reminded me so much of that old romance of ours, and here it is right in front of us. A society with a form of political rule that not only works, and the people experience freedom and liberty, but also progress and even a sense of family, because I saw a lot of different people of different races all living and working together. Now THAT is worthy of a good history book."

"Sounds like we might lose you over there," she grins.

"I don't know," Latena wonders as her mind drifts away. "What would it be like if we had something like that here? Kita, if we're successful at throwing out our old Council and its system of laws, we're going to need help to put it back together again. How do we do this? Do we choose from the myriad of alternate government designs? And if so, which one, because my studies tell me there are quite a few possibilities…in theory at least."

"In theory…but it sounds like you might have something in mind already."

"Kita, in theory we could go in virtually any direction, but it's really all the same at this point, as we need to teach the people what it is and how it works, and not all of them are political history students. We have become so dependent on this one idea of a government that we don't even know how the others work. I have little doubt in my mind that it's going to cause havoc in our culture and the management of our world until things settle again, whatever method we choose. We're going to need help, and for this, I can't think of anything else but to ask Lord Thaelyn for it."

"Maybe. And he is certainly the type to offer that help."

"From the things I've learned, he's like a father to his people, extremely wise and compassionate, and even though I felt so small in his presence…well, figuratively, as I stand head and shoulders above him," she giggles.

"Yeah, we all do, which is strange."

"But he's a King! And, well, who am I? I'm just a young girl with too much energy and a lot of wild ideas. But he listened to me, and even found value in what I had to say. We even shared a few laughs together. Where do you find something like that around here?"

"I wouldn't know. Our world doesn't behave like that."

"Exactly, Kita! If only we had something like that here in our world. But we don't have anyone we can follow who can inspire us like he did for his people. This reminds me of King Saakerav again, at least as far as the history books tell the story. But here is a living example of it. Even those Daanen-Aryku, as they call themselves, are turning to his side."

"Yeah, I met a few of them at the guildhall, some of Kaliya's friends from her old school."

"And then we have Auryn and her people taking up that new religion," she chuckles. "This Lord Oghma who presides over knowledge and wisdom, something we're supposed to be doing anyway."

"Now there's an irony!" Kita grins. "We turn away from religion in our world to follow science, but to follow that science, we need to turn back to religion again."

The two of them share a laugh as they consider this curious twist.

"And to compare that with our…god…and I use the term loosely."

"Kaliya once told me her father and his group took this blessing thing from those cu'Nar, and this was a way to cleanse them of whatever Darumon did to us, although I don't know exactly how that works. And by the way, this is the reason for their eyes now."

"Yeah, I don't like the idea of him being the father of our race, Kita. If these Estelar want all of us to take this, I wouldn't be against it. Even if it only gives me a psychological release, it may be worth it."

"What about the glowing eyes?"

"Well, they do offer a curious attraction," she giggles. "But then, I wonder what else these gods of theirs can teach us. I'll bet it's more than what Darumon ever gave us."

"This much I'm certain of, since he didn't give us much anyway."

"Hmm…" she ponders distantly. "You say you met some of her friends from school?"

"Yeah, they're currently enrolled in that academy of theirs. In fact, she introduced me to this group she has. They're something of a wild bunch, so you'd probably fit in nicely. And they're smart too, with some fascinating insights."

"Really! I wonder if they could teach me something."

"One is what they call a Night Elf named Relissa, the other is a human named Marelle. She's involved in their piloting program while Relissa is a conservationist."

"Sounds like a nice little diversity. But how do I meet them?"

"You should go out to the new base in the valley. They have a gateway unit working now. Are you familiar with those Daanen'kai students at the guildhall? Their names are Suli, Túfu, and Petrith. Ask them and see if they can help you."

✦✦✦✦

"So…" Relissa recalls. "What we've got right now is she'll play this big flying beastie that goes sailing around the city a few times, just to draw attention."

"A big flying beastie, is it?" Latena wonders. "What does it look like?"

"Here, I drew up a picture of what we're aiming for."

Relissa, Marelle, and Latena were sitting in a sidewalk café in Bya'an Tamoranth for a relaxing little chat and discussing Kaliya's plans for her Ytani play. Relissa pulled out her notepad and turned to the page where she once drew the large flying frog-like creature Kaliya would use for her Ytani demonstration.

"Here we go. What do you think of this? Does it look alien enough for you?"

Latena leans in for a close look and quickly grimaces at the depiction.

"Yeah, that's alien, all right. How big will it be?"

"We're thinking the size of a cow or thereabouts."

"I'm not sure how big that is, but I think if I saw one of these flying around, I'd sure take notice of it…and then I'd take off the other direction."

"Good, that's what we're hoping for. We want to get noticed with something Darumon can't hide from."

"All right, so you're flying around, and then what?"

"We were thinking she might settle down in a town square or a plaza of some kind, scare a few peeps, and then we have Ayene in an interview with that news reporter dame, probably giving off some information about that raid siren network, so they'll be out there to catch it."

"It needs to be a live broadcast," Marelle interjects. "And again, so that Darumon can't slither his way out of it saying it was fake or something. And for this, Ytani will transform into his normal shape as part of our demonstration of the Prodigy Gift."

"I see," Latena ponders. "So, ultimately, you're trying to show off this Gift, and this is where we have the latest and greatest news sensation. Oh, this will be fun to watch."

"By the way, Relissa, we did invite those two to this party, didn't we? Where are they?"

"Aye, they're a wee bit late. They must've been out in the fields practicing again."

In another area of the city, Kaliya and Ayene were both arriving through the gateway hub station. They diverted to the local transit node and took it to the Palace District, which is where they expected to meet the others. As they arrived, they crossed the street and turned onto the main avenue, where they strolled along to the pleasant café setting.

"Oh great!" Kaliya moans sarcastically. "Are you two trying to corrupt this sweet innocent young lady now?"

"Ay!" Relissa yips. "There's not much left of her to corrupt after the two of you got your meat hooks into her. We're just tidying up the leftovers."

The gang all erupts in a bold laugh as Kaliya and Ayene sit down to join them.

"And how many new marks are we aiming for today?"

"Oh, a few here and there… We're just going over your ideas for the Ytani play."

"Uh huh… Are we trying to clean it up, or rework it altogether?"

"If your goal is to set down in a plaza," Latena offers. "That'll certainly make a scene, but I wonder… Ooh! Wait a minute. If you're flying around anyway, and you want to show off this skill of yours, can you pass through a window, like to an office building?"

"I'm sure I could figure that one out easily enough," she grins.

"And you want to make a scene, right?" she also begins to grin. "Are you familiar with those tall financial towers downtown…the ones with the skywalks?"

"Ooh, yes!" Kaliya affirms.

"One of them is called the Vaanil Esluna, and it's a high-class financial tower. It has a sister building on the other side with a connecting bridge between the two observation decks. If you fly around and land on the side of the window, like maybe to cling to it, and then pass through it, I think you'll enter into an office area on one side. This will certainly cause a scene when you scare the curl out of everyone's horns, and they run away. Then chase a few across the bridge and put your news team on the other side to catch it arriving."

"Oh, Latena, you're a doll. I like it. And I can bring in some of my people to add to the flow, just to exaggerate the effect. Then we can have Ayene up there, and this would make a nice little scenic background for an interview, at least until the stampede comes rushing through."

"But now, how do you plan on using this for the demonstration of the Gift?"

"We need to make a few statements, one of which being Darumon's secret mining base where Ytani came from, and this will eventually lead to the extraordinary discovery of a new universe no one knew about... nor was ever intended to know about."

"Yeah, that'll shock a few scientists, especially those who don't have any real work to do...which is most of them," she giggles.

"But I want to leave a few hooks in there relating to Ytani and his Gift. So, he'll make a statement about it, and this will lead Ayene, in her secret agent persona, calling out an alert that he's returned and using his Gift. This will draw attention to it, and that it IS a Gift rather than some crazy ghost thing or a fake video edit."

"And that someone knows about it," she nods. "Clever move, but how do you bring this into better perspective with your hook?"

"We'll need to have some scientists trying to figure it out, once again calling my father's name into it, um..." she pauses to consider her thoughts.

"If you were to ask me, I think you need something to stretch that hook a little. If all you have is a video and a few people speculating on what they saw based on one or two words spoken..." she shakes her head. "No, you need someone up close and personal to give a report. An eyewitness account that was close enough to smell his breath...or the lack of it."

"She's got a point, Kaliya," Marelle notes. "This would be a nice little hook to sink into. And we still need to demonstrate his bad manners for his later demands of tribute."

"Tribute?" Latena wonders. "What do you mean by bad manners?"

"Ytani was a madman. He let his Gift go straight to his head, as well as his favoritism to the Marshal. In that base, he was using the female staff as his personal brothel. He was abusive, vulgar, and even killed a few women along the way for his wild sexual fetishes."

"Killed?" she winces. "In all the nether-space, don't we have laws anymore?"

"Not apparently with the Marshal running things. He wanted his metal, and Ytani believed himself to be a favorite child who could have anything he wanted. He developed a god complex after a while, and even began boasting over how he wanted a pet world with pet people in it."

"Oh wonderful! But all right, this gives me the perfect idea. He needs a victim in that crowd. So, he comes in, plays a little tail-tag with the office workers, and chases them across the skywalk. But we have ONE cute young girl who gets caught up in the confusion, maybe also knocked to the floor just as he arrives and looms over her," she grins playfully.

"Uh oh, and who is this cute young girl?" Marelle raises her brow warily.

"Me!" she asserts eagerly. "And this could play into my own campaign, as here we find our hooks and tie them together. This is one of his and the Council's biggest secrets, so if you're going to expose it, we need to expose it fully that the Council hid this from us due to THEIR god complex."

"Cu'Nar's pity," Kaliya whispers. "Relissa, you were right, she was already bad before either of you came into it."

"Yeah…" Ayene notes. "And I'm still trying to imagine how Captain Ta'yeen has a niece like this."

"If you play this right on top of me," Latena continues. "This gives me access to see him up close. If you're just a projection, I think if I'm paying close enough attention to it, I might detect something strange, right?"

"Yes, you could," Kaliya admits. "But you also need a little forewarning about it to make that connection."

"Forewarning, or maybe a little hindsight. And for someone who's a conspiracy theorist to begin with…" she chuckles wickedly. "Ayene was going to make some sort of secret agent announcement for the camera. So, if she hauls me away, like to bring me into protective custody for my experience, this could give me an excuse to learn a few things as I'm being…interviewed…by her office. I can then bring this into a news interview later, since as we all know I'll need to do something with the news media one of these days anyway."

"Wow," Ayene croons. "That's not a bad play, and it follows with some useful corollary effects."

"And we all get new marks on Thaelyn's list!" Kaliya chuckles ironically.

◆◆◆◆◆

"Now let me see if I understand this correctly," Thaelyn asserts worriedly.

"Relissa is responsible for this, um, remarkable drawing…" he pauses to examine her notepad. "And then Marelle suggested it had to be airborne for best visibility, as well as mobility. Ayene has her role with the reporter, where she ultimately drops a potentially vital clue where the Prodigy Gift is concerned. Kaliya plays the role of Ytani. And then we have YOU, young Miss Ta'yeen," he eyes her warily. "I still cannot believe you are the Captain's sweet innocent niece. Speaking of which, if this is going out live, how do you think he will react to seeing you in this role…and for that matter, the remainder of your family?"

"They'll probably lose their horns in a big way," she admits. "So, I'm not really looking forward to the aftermath, but on the other hand, like I said, I'm not so sweet and innocent. I'm scheduling an official interview with Ileani soon. Up until now, I've been keeping myself to lectures and public rallies. But I need to go on record with my motives so I can officially tell the world what we're doing and why we're doing it. Once I do that, well, the sweet and innocent image will be blown regardless."

"Indeed, it will, but this is an introductory interview so far. And then your explanation of carrying this role to get up close and personal with Kaliya's projected image is a rather unique perspective to apply here. This will indeed provide some curious new material to throw into the mix for a follow-up. And of course, combining this with your existing statements relating to the Council…" he sighs heavily. "General, we may need to throw out some of our books on how to play these games, as this group seems to be rewriting most of them."

"I think it largely revolves around this projection skill," he admits. "Without that, I am quite sure we would be falling back to the more traditional methods."

"To be honest," he throws up his hands. "I am at a loss to imagine how most of this might be played even at that. First is simply to gain access to the place. Then, if you consider the ACI, the infiltration of so many sensitive locations impersonating local employees, bypassing so many roadblocks and other barriers, and whatever else these people have to their credit so far, I think we would be far behind our present location."

"So, my Lord," Kaliya smiles pleasantly. "What do you think? Shall we go with it, or do you think you might want to change something?"

"At this moment, I cannot be sure what I would want to change. This carries many ingenious elements already. Therefore, I will simply give it my sanction and my best well-wishes."

"Thank you. Then it just comes down to the timing. If our final move revolves around this next graduation period, we need to pace ourselves accordingly."

<hr>

Ileani was wrapping up her most recent report of the rallies and the growing malcontent over the Charter of Laws and the Council. The end of the month was approaching, and she was preparing for her upcoming interview with Latena.

> *"…And as we look back on the sequence of events that brought us to this point, we may be looking at a world event that could reshape our society and our history. But to understand this movement, we'll be hosting a special live interview later today with the leader of this hot new political controversy. Be sure to join us as we listen to what she has to say and test her radical ideas with some of our own analysts. This concludes our report at this time. I'm Ileani Ur'paran for C.P. News, signing off."*

Later that day, Commander Geilv and Captain Ta'yeen were convening in the officer's lounge to catch the news broadcast that was preparing to air with the live interview. They were both curious as to what this political activist might have to say, and how it might fit in with everything else going on in the world lately.

Inside CPComm, Latena was getting set with Ileani in the newsroom, along with a couple of analysts to offer a debate. The analysts, in this case, were Navina and Petrith, and all using scripts to bring out certain details. They had arranged themselves in a comfortable setting using a semicircle of leisure chairs.

"Here we go everyone," the set coordinator issues. "We are going live in three, two, one…"

The set coordinator waves his hand and points his finger assertively at Ileani on the set, where the camera zooms in for a close-up as she begins with her traditional introduction.

"This is Ileani Ur'paran for C.P. News. Good evening, everyone, and thank you for joining us as we present this special live interview of what some people are describing as the most controversial political activist rally in memorable history. With me today is the leader of this movement, Miss Latena Ta'yeen, a local university graduate who holds majors in political science and political history."

In the officer's lounge of Central Command, Captain Ta'yeen gaped at the monitor as it panned out to include his niece on the set. He rigidly rose from his chair and stood there speechless as he pointed at the monitor. Commander Geilv, on the other hand, started grinning as he erupted in a hearty laugh.

"Well, there goes that image of the sweet innocent young niece," he chortles. "And look at who she's interviewing with," he directs at the monitor. "That woman there, she was that ACI agent in my office that one time."

The Captain glared at Geilv briefly, and then turned back to the monitor, leaning in to identify the other members.

"Him…" he points. "That young man, I know him. He was involved in that security revamp."

"And another of their agents," Geilv nods. "No doubt, along with Ti'van. All right, so it would seem they're involved with this new movement. In all the nether-space, Captain, I think this speaks for us. This is a revolution they're invoking. And at this moment, I suppose I can't blame them. The Council is dead, the Charter is apparently flawed to create a dictatorship, and we both know who is ultimately behind it. So, sit down and let's see what they have to say for themselves."

"I swear to you, Commander, those people are insidious!"

Ileani went on to introduce the other guests on her set.

"Also with us today are two political analysts who have joined with us to debate these issues: Mister Petrith Girhani and Miss Navina Lar'akan."

"I'll bet they're setting up to leak something to us," Geilv muses. "And it would seem they're using Miss Ur'paran for it."

"That would explain a lot, right there," the Captain responds. "All those sensations, one after another… They're turning the public against those enemies we're supposed to know about, rather than what the Marshal kept pointing at."

"And doing so in a very backhanded way."

Now Ileani prepared herself for the interview as she turned to her guests.

"Miss Ta'yeen," she begins. "First of all, it's been said that you're something of a conspiracy theorist. Can you explain what this means?"

"Yes, I can, Ileani," Latena submits. "During my time at the university, I belonged to a debate group, and we might often come together to discuss current events and other topics, many of them political. Naturally, we are unsettled with many aspects of the world we live in, and for a number of valid reasons. The pollution is one, but as we saw, there are lots of other people out there who are also tired of that. The Council's persistent absence is another, and again, as we saw, it seems we're not alone. And then we had that incident at the Grand Hall, which simply made things worse."

"It most certainly did, and I for one was especially shocked by it."

"I'm sure you weren't the only one. I nearly lost my horns when I saw that report, but at the same time, it got me to thinking, and this brought me back to my so-called conspiracy theories. I would like to think not all of us are so complacent that we sit on our tails century after century listening to the same old rhetoric. We're a society that's supposed to be moving somewhere. But we're not, and we haven't been for a long time."

"And therefore, you came to some of these controversial ideas of yours?"

"That's right. It's simply natural for people to ask questions. But when all you hear is the same old story, you get tired of trying after a while, as you're simply waiting for someone else to do something. Well, Miss Ur'paran, who is that someone else, if not that authority body that is supposed to be doing their work, but apparently isn't?"

"I suppose you have a point."

"Therefore, some of us in our group would try to look at the world with a different set of eyes as a way of testing alternative scenarios. And along the way, we've seen a number of what we call discrepancies in how things seem to work. Then, when we compare this with what we might perceive to be the most predictable outcome, the reality doesn't meet with our expectations."

"Can you give us an example? For instance, we've been hearing a lot lately about your rallies, and this movement of yours seems to be spreading worldwide by now."

"Yes, it would seem our message is hitting home with a lot of people who are similarly confounded by the same old monotony of life. But my movement isn't JUST about listening to the same news repeated every day, or the same report from the military about this insurgent or that insurgent, or whatever else it is they're trying to feed us that means virtually nothing as far as real progress is concerned. It's about WHO is delivering this news, and WHY it sounds so familiar all the time."

In the officer's lounge, Geilv and the Captain glanced at each other briefly.

"I think that was a message," Geilv notes softly. "She's setting something up."

The Captain nods as they continue to listen.

"And for this," Latena continues, "one of my key points must refer to the Council itself, while another one refers to the Charter of Laws. These are the most immediate culprits to focus on in our modern time."

She now pulls out her tablet device and holds it up as her reference.

"In here, I have a copy of the Charter of Laws, which was an important part of my school study material. When I first began my studies, I took notice of a curious form of wording being used in the preamble of the Charter. Then, as I progressed through my classes, I saw similar phrases and references that began to take on a certain perspective in my mind. You might say, this drew my attention, and perhaps when combined with my natural inclination as a conspiracy theorist, it started to highlight itself."

"And this is what brings you to us with these rallies now?"

"Yes. I have a tendency to see words, and not for the spirit of their meaning, as our teachers always proclaim, but for their literal meaning, which is how I feel they SHOULD be interpreted. But when I brought this up to my teachers, they simply referred back to that spirit of the wording that we must place our faith into, which to me sounds a lot like trying to worship something, as with a religious devotion. But I, like so many others in our world, am not religious. Therefore, I turned to how this wording actually laid itself out. And what I found was surprising."

"I see. And what was that, Miss Ta'yeen?"

"A deception, which I feel is made worse by this perpetual encouragement that we're supposed to place our faithful focus on the spirit of the wording, rather than our intellectual focus on how the thing actually reads. This is one of the most curious aspects of this theory, Ileani, as we're not supposed to be a religious society. That part of us presumably died out in the days preceding King Saakerav. I have a friend who studies cultural history, and she once told me about a really ancient form of religious worship our early ancestors had relating to a figure called the Creator. This is very Early Age stuff, presumably stemming out of our earliest origins as a civilization. In fact, I am aware of a cute new cartoon series called Era the Wise that's becoming popular with kids these days that uses this as part of the cultural background."

As the Commander and the Captain listened to the interview, they both began to lean forward, and each for their own private reasons.

"That was a plug, I think," Geilv mumbles. "Do you know of that cartoon, Captain?"

"Not personally. Why? Are you suggesting we now start watching cartoons?"

"We should at least look into it. It may be trying to tell us something."

"Now that's a new twist…teaching us something about a revolution through cartoon entertainment."

"Yes, but it's the last place the Marshal might look."

"Granted…albeit a strange one."

Latena continues, "But surely, if we're to describe ourselves as intellectuals in the modern day, why are we told, generation after generation, to believe in a spirit of any kind?"

"I might agree, Miss Ta'yeen," Ileani continues. "As a journalist, I certainly would not be one to believe in spirits, ghosts, divine entities, or any other form of supernatural phenomena. So, this statement would tend to run contrary to how our society should otherwise behave."

In the officer's lounge, Geilv reacted to this statement.

"Ooh! That sounds like a ticking time bomb to me."

"Interesting," the Captain nods.

Back in the newsroom, Ileani continues.

"So, when you say there is a problem in the wording, can you point out what you mean by this?"

"Yes, allow me to recite the preamble for you, and then I'll point out my meaning."

She clears her throat and pulls up the document on her tablet.

"We the People, who hereby declare ourselves to enter into this agreement, to dissolve and dismiss our ancestral rivalries and materialistic pursuits, to unite our population into one collected body, and from this moment to seek the challenges of higher intellectual ascension, do now this day create for ourselves a new Enlightened Era, where all people are created equal, where all forms of knowledge and wisdom shall become our domain, and where the direction of our society shall be governed by an attendance of statesmen who will drive our motivations on behalf of the many."

"Very good, Miss Ta'yeen," Ileani nods. "I know this so well from my own university studies, and I'm sure a lot of others would agree. But now, what do you think is wrong with this?"

"It starts out great. We're a society that wants to move forward, away from all the rivalries of our past, which means all the different nations we once had that so often competed with one another, and sometimes even fought wars. We want to enter into a future direction for the pursuit of knowledge, as a peace-loving society, united under one power, and where that one power carries us towards this Enlightened Era. But here is where I think that spirit of the wording comes into play. We enter into this agreement by choice, and apparently, we don't ask questions about it afterwards because we have this sense of faith that all is well…at least until we come to these final lines."

"The final lines," Ileani muses. "All right, then tell us about those final lines."

She momentarily redirects to her tablet again.

"We enter into this agreement…to dissolve and dismiss so many old rivalries…to come together in this great Enlightened Era…where everyone is equal, and where all forms of knowledge become OUR domain. So far, the spirit tells us that 'We the People' are the ones desiring all this knowledge, and therefore nothing should stand in our way of acquiring it. But when you look at the science factions out there right now, most of which are empty without the Council offering any new research grants or other forms of direction to search for this knowledge, it makes you wonder who slipped the tip here."

"I suppose it does."

"This would naturally point us at this body of statesmen who are the ones supposedly motivating us. But the wording is wrong for any form of governing authority that is supposed to be motivating 'We the People' on this pursuit of knowledge. The words say to DRIVE us, not GUIDE us, as a true governing authority might do for the general public. And to me, the word 'drive' is a control word. It has nothing to do with 'We the People', but everything to do with this body of statesmen, who appear to be lifting themselves above the rest, and claiming that knowledge to be THEIR domain, not ours."

"All right, for this point, let's hear from one of our analysts to see if they have anything to say. Mister Girhani, maybe you would like to go first."

"Thank you, Miss Ur'paran," Petrith responds politely. "The first thing I might wish to point out is the term 'to drive' can also be defined as an assertive statement to push our progress forward, to inspire as opposed to simply allowing nature to take its course. And when combined with such an association as our motivations for pursuing knowledge, this might further involve inspiring the science factions to pursue one or another path explicitly, if it should present itself to hold any special interest."

"While this may be true," Latena rebuts. "It doesn't say where 'this' or 'that' specific form of knowledge shall be our domain. It distinctly says ALL, and this would include even those items that might prove interesting to know, or perhaps might hold some incidental value, rather than a mainstream path we're intended to take. It might also say that we found something of value, and this might lead to a consequential path of research, but unless we actually take that path, we are failing to pursue that term 'ALL knowledge.' And this then brings me back to where the science factions are presently. If there was any form of inspirational force occurring, they should be working on something, and you can't tell me there's nothing more out there to learn. Furthermore, the Council seems to control what, if anything, they actually study. The science factions apparently don't have the freedom to choose their own. They need to be TOLD to do it."

"Then, Miss Ta'yeen," Ileani resumes. "What is it you actually see in these words that you say is hidden behind this control term and that mention of a spirit of the wording?"

"What I see is a hidden form of domination, and I also see this in practice throughout our history, including the modern day. The Council is supposed to be the one motivating us, but at the same time, they also hold us back for those elements they don't otherwise wish to motivate us on. Case in point, if you look at the recent history where these war protocols are concerned, this is one aspect of them controlling the show regardless of the best interests of either the public OR the science factions. For ten millennia, we have those war protocols demanding that dirty industry. And in those same ten millennia, the Council never once authorized, whether by inspiring or letting nature take its course, any of our science factions, or even the general public that ought to know better, to make corrections to it with cleaner technology. It is as if to say, they took the cheapest road intentionally and denied us anything better."

"But couldn't there be a rational explanation for it, rather than simply accusing them of wrongdoing? I mean, they're also in this deep deliberation, as you recall, and apparently out of communication."

"Out of communication with a society where they hold Responsibility Number One?" she balks. "With respect, Ileani, that deliberation cannot be more important than the health and welfare of our public, who elected them to serve our world needs, not some fantasy in some unknown research lab. And neither can it be more important than the environment we're destroying along the way. And this brings up yet another issue currently being corrected by that same science community that is tired of waiting for them to realize it…the seeds. Just look at yourself, you're one example of it, having removed it by now. Those seeds aren't necessary…they never were. But the Council pushed them at us, or if I use Mister Girhani's words, inspired us to take them rather than any of the existing, and very useful technologies we had then, and still do now, to do the same work. The explanation was we had to evacuate from our homes due to this Tav'ageen Scare that was creating so much havoc. But for this, I have a side argument to offer."

"A side argument. All right, what kind?"

"I was once with my debate group when we spoke of this. How long does it take to load up a cargo vessel with a colony pack? Then, how long does it take to actually find a viable location to set it down? We don't need a perfectly habitable world if we have loads of technology to build artificial habitats just about anywhere. Therefore, why the rush to use something no one would want to use in their right mind? Am I expected to run around out there tail-naked with only the seed providing for me? I don't think so. But THIS is the demand our Council made, and nothing else."

"All right, I can certainly see this perspective. Even if the Tav'ageen Scare was causing a panic, you still need to find a place to go, and in that time, you might have a fleet of ships with conventional technology ready to launch at a moment's notice."

"And so far, this has nothing to do with the fact that we never did actually evacuate. But if we say the reason was these insurgents, and this went on for so long that we had to invent this alternative solution to the Tav'ageen Anomaly, meaning the Suppressor chip, suddenly there is no more rush. This chip solved the problem, and we technically don't even NEED to evacuate now. And yet, the Council continued to…inspire us…to take these seeds, even after we had enough time to realize the alternatives, and long before any of that dirty industry had actually contaminated our home to the point where it became toxic."

"But Miss Ta'yeen," Ileani begs. "We can say this now in hindsight, but at the time, it might not have been as apparent, as we were always told this condition with the insurgents would be corrected and the evacuation would proceed as stated."

"Yes, in hindsight, which is unfortunate. And yet, even in hindsight, we were perpetually told to ignore the mess we were making, even after centuries, and then millennia of making it. Hindsight? I think after one decade of hindsight, someone had to grow the horns to realize a corrective procedure. But during this time, the Council neglected to remind us we had better techs available, both for that industry and for a colonization effort. And furthermore, doing so across the full length of time necessary to infect our world population. Hindsight or no, this time period was more than enough for someone to realize that dirty industry was in fact dirty, and we surely could have revamped some part of it to clean things up before it became critical. But the Council continued to 'inspire' us with this imperative evacuation procedure, to the exclusion of everything else, including our natural sensibility to realize we actually DO have time to correct for the earlier rush job they pushed at us."

"Yes, I suppose this does make sense."

"What this now says is they wanted us to have the seeds as a priority, despite anything else. So, the question is why, especially if you consider the recent discovery of that alien genetic coding no one knew about. This represents a hidden agenda to intentionally infect us with something we might not normally want. And it is made worse by that one statement of it creating this area effect of some kind of energy no one knows anything about, and probably couldn't use it if we did. One medical representative even went so far as to describe it as some kind of Abnormal Energy, whatever that means."

In the officer's lounge, the Commander and the Captain both perked up at the mention.

"That, Captain..." Geilv asserts as he points at the monitor, "... must be a plug for something. It points right back at what we found in that other universe, and also that Abnormal Space. WE cannot use it, but THEY most certainly can."

"Great..." the Captain moans.

Latena continues, "This is indeed inspiring us, Ileani, because how else do you force-feed something like that hideous bug. And here we are with our beneficent Council everyone thinks can do no wrong for the spirit of these words they can twist to their personal needs whenever their tail itches."

Back in Central, Geilv and his Captain both shook their heads morosely.

"Yes, I see her point now," the Captain relents. "And I'm sorry I missed it before. It's quite shameful to think we did this to ourselves."

In the studio, Latena concludes, "And this isn't the only example I can bring forward, either."

"Not the only one," Ileani muses. "But is this actually enough reason to essentially go to war with them?"

"Like I said, this is not the only one, and collectively, I must answer yes. This is what you do when you are faced with an enemy that is offending your people. These seeds are undesirable AND unnecessary. They seem to carry an ulterior motive we were NOT told about. They are also dangerous for their injury reaction. I cannot and will not accept this deliberation, or even the gift of wisdom by itself, could override their concern for our health and welfare. I similarly cannot and will not accept it would take ten millennia to figure it out, and STILL they have not made any corrective action. They pushed this at us and kept it that way, Ileani. That's a hostile act, made worse by incorporating something hidden and subversive. Is THAT not worth going to war over?"

Ileani retracted from the argument, as part of her script, and as it was intended to demonstrate a clear and evident cause for a potential rebellion.

Latena continues, "And this is not the only time they have taken the lead in inspiring, or perhaps I should instead say driving our motivations. Throughout our history, we have seen many remarkable innovations and discoveries, so we can say at least some of them were a benefit to us. After all, even the Council might want advanced medicines to care for their illnesses. Hover-enabled vehicles are certainly a step above old, wheeled vehicles. Industrial tech, materials sciences, energy production... All of this can serve both the Council AND the people because these represent tangible goods that will naturally filter down to the rest of us. But what about space exploration, Ileani? When, where, and how do we declare we've had enough? We must've crossed from one side of this galaxy to the other by now, but apparently this is all we need. They haven't asked us to do anything more than that, with or without the Marshal's insurgents getting in our way. In fact, as I understand it, those insurgents don't seem to be doing much at all to actually cage us up on this one planet, so why are we still here? And yet, if it requires the Council to actually TELL us to do this or that, why is it they once told us to STOP?"

"Huh? To stop what?"

"We've been a space-faring society for hundreds of millennia, but in that time we've never actually…officially…colonized anything, even though we have the technology to do so. We may have set down a few outposts here and there, but our population has always been restricted to our home planet. And then, one day, we made a historic achievement. We sent an expedition to our neighboring galaxy. It was fantastic to see how we could break our barriers and travel to places well beyond our previous reach. And just after that, someone says, no more. We stop here and should now focus on using what we have locally. This was thirty-five millennia ago, Ileani. So, why haven't we done it?"

Ileani glared at the girl for the curiously provocative statement.

"Um, although this does carry a certain undertone, surely there must be a logical explanation for it."

"Oh, there is!" she asserts strongly. "This line, 'where the direction of our society shall be governed by an attendance of statesmen who will DRIVE our motivations on behalf of the many.' This says, they tell you what to do, and you simply have to do it. To say inspiring isn't even accurate anymore. This is a dictatorship. And even worse, it's an authoritarian form of rule, where they demand you to obey. And what better way to control the public than to restrict their movements."

"Oh dear…"

In the officer's lounge, the feelings were similar.

"That niece of yours has a point," Geilv nods. "If we were to spread out, they, or maybe I should say the Marshal, would quickly lose control of us. We'd be everywhere."

Latena continues, "I've spoken to many leaders of the science factions, and they all tell the same story. They don't do anything UNLESS the Council authorizes it. This is an example of a dictatorship. The science factions don't have the freedom to choose their own way. They have to wait for the Council to actually give them permission to do something, and ONLY what the Council gives permission on. Suddenly, that statement of freedom for all forms of knowledge falls into the hands of those who just placed themselves above the rest."

"But if we're not speaking of a true form of freedom here," Ileani wonders. "What could be the motive of the Council, or any body of statesmen, to take this form of control over such a thing as knowledge?"

"They say knowledge is power, but power can be defined in many forms and be used for many purposes. The more active forms of power, such as military authority to storm the streets and manhandle people to do your bidding, is one clear example. But this one is more subversive, as it hides behind words. It can fabricate falsehoods and make us think we have something, when in fact we do not. It can motivate us to a purpose, when in fact it might not necessarily be to our best interests. When you brainwash people to think in terms of the spirit of something, even though we are not permitted to worship a religion, and therefore to take something on faith, this is distracting us with a hidden intent. And this leads me to one final point of contention, as it can keep us from learning something they might not otherwise want us to know."

"All right, this is interesting. This suggests you have a direction to demonstrate. What do you think they might be trying to hide with that statement?"

"I'll give you a name...Former Elder Velen Nazég."

Ileani drew back at the blatant mention, as it was actually part of her script at this point.

In the officer's lounge at Central Command, Geilv nodded subtly.

"And there he is again."

Ileani leaned back into the conversation.

"I know that name has been mentioned a few times lately, but what relevance does it have here?"

"He once presided over a science faction he felt strongly about called Metaphysics. But the rest of the Council often ridiculed him for the fanciful nature of those beliefs. Here is where we have another aspect of the Council's dictatorial nature. They kicked him out because they didn't want him involved."

"But wait a moment. For this, I think we should give another of our analysts a chance to speak. Miss Lar'akan, can you offer any perspectives?"

"Yes, and thank you," Navina offers. "Miss Ta'yeen, I recall that moment of our history quite well, not the least of which is how Elder Nazég and so many of his faction members apparently ran away from us on that ship that came along. The Council, and for that matter the Marshal as well, all declared him a traitor who was joining up with his insurgent enemies. This, in itself, would be justifiable cause to expel him."

"Justifiable, Miss Lar'akan?" Latena rebukes. "To run away from so much abuse and harassment? Is this now permitted in our Charter along with that statement of driving us towards that fabled pursuit of ALL knowledge?"

"Ouch, girl," the Captain winces as he listens. "That would hurt."

"No..." she continues. "For this, I have not one, but two counterarguments for you on this matter."

"Oh?" Navina wonders openly. "All right, this should be interesting. Where do you want to begin?"

"Let's take the easier one first, that ship. I recall the history of it saying it was huge, possibly the size of a small city, and it simply went poof...here it is in our upper atmosphere in a powered orbit. This means it had to have a jump drive and some really powerful tech to keep it up there. But Ileani, if that ship belonged to these insurgents, why is the Marshal, and for that matter Sargeras, still here among us? That ship arrived well before we had a military to fight back. And anyone capable of building something like that must be pretty high on the ladder. But if these were insurgents, they sent the wrong ship. They should have NO interest in us. Not unless you want to say they would wish to punish us for harboring a fugitive from their form of law, whatever they might call law in this case. And they had a perfect opportunity to do exactly that. But they didn't. Instead, they took away someone we didn't otherwise care about, and for what reason. To ransom him? Ha! I doubt the Council or anyone else around here, for all their prejudice, would bother to pay it. What a waste that would be, don't you think?"

"Ransom?" Navina frowns prominently.

"My research on Elder Nazég says he was a pacifist, not a militant. You do not make a militant out of someone who is hardcore against warfare. Therefore, he would hold NO military value to those people. An example of this could be made if you look at our military and their undefeated record at holding back those insurgents. If Elder Nazég is leading them, he is doing a VERY poor job at it. Therefore, it is irrational to say he could be leading something amongst a society said to be much higher than we, and who were apparently so successful in ousting Sargeras in the first place. In my opinion, they don't need anyone else, and certainly not any of us pacifists down here telling them how to conduct warfare. This is contrary to reason. But then, I suppose, if you are so often brainwashed to believe in the spirit of something, you might also allow yourself to think you know something about warfare in a society that hasn't practiced it in a thousand millennia. What do you think, Miss Lar'akan?"

"Um, yes, this WOULD represent a very clear contradiction."

In the officer's lounge, both Geilv and Captain Ta'yeen grimaced at the depiction.

"And another ouch!" the Captain winces. "That would certainly bite you in the tail."

"Yes, it would," Geilv admits. "And not just the general public, but also those of us who actually DO think we know something about warfare."

Back in the studio, Latena continues her argument.

"This leaves very few alternatives, with ransom being one of those, if these insurgents really are such bad people. But I don't recall hearing anything about them ransoming him, so it must be another, and at this point, completely unrelated reason."

"I see."

"But this statement also returns us to our primary argument, because if that ship really did belong to those insurgents, not only did they send the wrong ship, but they also took away the wrong target."

"Um, well, I suppose that would stand out, under these circumstances. But the Marshal DID claim them to be his insurgents."

"I have no doubt he would know his insurgents if he should see them. But Ileani, it also strikes me that he and Sargeras were freshly arriving after running away from them. Sargeras was said to be in very poor health when he arrived. This tells me they were running and desperate to find refuge. It also tells me they were probably under a lot of stress. So this ship, which clearly did NOT behave as a hostile force sent here to finish the job, must have been someone else, and the Marshal simply misinterpreted the nature of it. Furthermore, it had to be coincidental to our other problems."

"Wait, Latena," Ileani ushers. "First, misinterpreted? What about this long pursuit he claimed he was on? And then, coincidental? To what?"

"The pursuit..." she muses. "I can't say who might have actually owned that thing, but his insurgents must be another body entirely. If THIS was those same people, it is clear they DO know where we live. And if they're so capable of building something like that, I would expect no less than half our planetary surface to be incinerated from it, if it were actually them in a proper military ship."

"Ouch."

"As for the pursuit, I am forced to reflect on a few other people in recent times and their statements. Ten millennia, Ileani. If WE have to chase THEM halfway across the galaxy just to fight them, THEY clearly do NOT know where we live, nor have the means, or perhaps a desire to actually come to us, as that ship did. That, in itself, should represent a clear and obvious contradiction to anyone with the horns to actually realize it. This also again reflects on the spirit of the thing, for a bunch of pacifists who don't know a single tail-yanking thing about warfare."

"Boom!" Geilv muses in the officer's lounge. "That should rub it in our faces that we couldn't associate these elements any earlier, as we probably should have."

"Absolutely," the Captain nods. "Good work, Latena."

"Furthermore," Latena continues. "Even during all those ten millennia, if these insurgents can't win a single fight in that time, they must be the universe's most iron-horned AND dull-horned people ever. And I doubt you can be insurgents, who were so successful in ousting their former leader, and be all THAT at the same time."

"You know," Ileani relents. "This might also reflect on a few statements we heard in recent times by others coming forward. Maybe not using these same words, but our military was indeed very successful in our defense, so it might make you wonder why they keep trying."

"Exactly. In this time, you might think they would either change tactics, improve their methods, or give up entirely. But now, let's look at that long-time accusation against Elder Nazég again. He was vilified as a traitor in the eyes of the people during this time. If we say Elder Nazég really did turn against the Council, what he did was to turn against a hostile body that ridiculed his beliefs in a society that claims itself to be free and open for all forms of wisdom. Traitor? Yes, we have a traitor here, Ileani, but it was not Elder Nazég. It was all of us who chased him away while we claim ourselves to be pursuing all forms of knowledge. We're a society of hypocrites, and he was a victim."

Ileani closes her eyes and hangs her head, at least in part for her own blame as for all the rest.

In Central Command, many of the viewers did the same, as did many home viewers and others.

"Next," Latena asserts. "We move on to the coincidence aspect, which would fit nicely with my second argument for Miss Lar'akan here. Relating to Elder Nazég again, the Council has a history of prejudice against him predating the arrival of the Marshal AND his insurgents. For each new science faction they wanted to include, the Charter would be amended to include an Elder to represent it. But his faction never was. Ever."

"No? But if he had a title…"

"For a time, he was regarded as probationary, which I suppose is reasonable for a new faction to demonstrate its viability. But some have even suggested he was given this much if only to keep his faction from protesting against these same prejudices."

"Oh no!"

"Yes, this is our history now. His faction was never taken seriously, and ultimately, never made official. None of the other science factions gave him enough credit to know which way his tail was swinging. And the Council behaved, on at least a few occasions, with outright hostility to his faction, in contradiction to our idea of a free and open society in the pursuit of all knowledge. I can even give you an example of one other occasion that stands out in history, where they cut off the research belonging to those factions they actually DO support, even though there was a significant amount of controversy over the results of an all-important study that still needed to be resolved."

"All right, which one is that?"

"The evolution of our species, and those factions that were studying it. As we all know, the study of our early ancestors, the Eracyodines, was always held in contention for the crazy results those early researchers were finding, in relation to every other form of life in our world, and how the numbers didn't add up nicely for our example. And yet, generation after generation of researchers, using more and more advanced techniques trying to refine and interpret those otherwise crazy results, all led to the same conclusion, which simply perpetuated the controversy. Eventually, the Council simply pulled the plug, saying, effectively, we don't want to hear all you people crying over your calculation errors, so we're taking this and filing it away permanently."

"But wouldn't this mean they were actually satisfied over the results? Wouldn't this be the same as saying those results are THE results?"

"No, and I'll give you two reasons for it. First, they got tired of listening to those people, and took an answer that our empirically minded society in the pursuit of all knowledge now has to take on faith, in the spirit of the words, even though the data didn't justify it. Maybe a later generation, perhaps with better research methods, or simply more freedom to do the actual research…which would lead to my next argument on this matter…but having this, they might find the truth. And yet, the study was cancelled and remains that way to this day."

"All right, I suppose this could stand out after a while, especially if you're one who likes to point out potential conspiracies. But now, that comment you made about having the freedom to actually do the research. This is puzzling to me."

Commander Geilv watched and listened, along with Captain Ta'yeen.

"That hints at something…I think," Geilv comments.

"Maybe," the Captain muses. "Or are we just becoming paranoid for anything that might be a clue?"

"I don't know, but I would imagine this interview is here for a reason, so all of this might be part of a message."

Latena continues, "Yes, that comment. First, if you're a dictatorship, you tell people if and when you want them to do something. So, the idea of freedom is therefore rendered null and void. Next, we have all those…alleged…calculation errors that brought those consistently crazy results. Among other things, one of the science factions I spoke with was the archeology faction, and this same topic came up in conversation. With so many of the factions now going off the Council authority, they are reviewing a few old notes. They said, during many of those early studies, evidence seemed to go missing, and papers seemed to be rewritten."

"What?" Ileani shouts. "But that would represent tampering, wouldn't it?"

"Tampering, falsifying data, hiding things…the sort of thing you might find in a dictatorship that was trying to own the results and feed us something different, and precisely what I was saying before about hiding behind words."

Again, in the officer's lounge, the viewers moaned.

"Dammit!" Geilv scorns. "This has to be related to HIM again."

"And what was it they were feeding us?" Latena continues. "This becomes my second reason to your question of this being THE answer. Because we love the romance of it so much. It's part of our cultural delight. After all, how many of us as children loved to hear that epic story of our early ancestors beating impossible odds simply to survive and rise above everything else. This sounds a little like that spirit of things again, taking something on faith for a society once denied worshipping a god. Because I think you would need divine intervention to win that level of success."

Again, in Central Command, Geilv perks up at the mention.

"That, Captain…" he shouts anxiously and points at the monitor.

"That's your answer to my paranoia. The faulty research results and questionable evolutionary history. These beings are described as godlike as compared to us. Maybe he did this, and then interfered with our research to prove otherwise."

"Oh please, Commander," the Captain groans. "I didn't need to hear that one."

Again, Latena continues, "And this brings us back to Elder Nazég and his faction, where we had one OTHER occasion of something being studied, in this case leading to controversial and potentially conspiratorial results we had to accept on faith. But on THIS occasion, the faith involved ghost stories to frighten our empirically minded society, and again treating us like children. The Council then force-fed us their so-called solution to it, and with a clearly hidden motivation."

"Uh oh…" Ileani emits uncertainly. "And what was this one about?"

"The Tav'ageen Anomaly."

In the officer's lounge, the audience ushered up another series of moans at the suggestion.

"Dammit again…" Geilv spurns under his breath. "They know something. And they're associating it to this hidden motive and those damnable seeds."

"Especially with that hidden code involved," the Captain nods.

Ileani pauses in apparent contemplation of Latena's latest statement.

"All right," she relents. "Let's try to examine this. I'm assuming you are speaking of the seeds here as the force-fed solution. But how would this relate to the Tav'ageen Anomaly, other than for the Scare we had once and the motivation to evacuate? If we had preexisting colonization tech to use instead of this, these seeds were a moot choice. If we could just as easily load up a colony pack on a star cruiser, and likely in easy timing after finding a place to actually travel to, this makes the imperative rush a moot choice. So it really comes down to why the seeds at all?"

"Yes, and it likely involves that secret code hidden behind a security wall. It does something NOT relating to the design specs of why the seeds were invented in the first place. And something our people apparently don't know how to use. But, if memory serves, the Marshal assisted in designing them, and the Council, for this gift of great wisdom, approved it. So, while WE might not know how to use it, someone else does."

"Uh oh…"

In homes, offices, lunchrooms, and other locations where people had gathered to watch the news, a collective groaning ushered out as they made this subtle association.

"It has to be," Latena asserts. "Consider this if you will. Elder Nazég and his faction were part of the research teams studying that thing. Unfortunately, due to the persecution his faction was receiving, no one cared to listen to his results. They were too fanciful for our empirically minded society that is otherwise told to accept the Council's word, above any other, on faith for the spirit of its meaning. Some might even go so far as to say Elder Nazég's faction was too mystical, too supernatural. Yeah, too supernatural to take on faith, like whatever the Council was trying to feed us."

"That would certainly represent a contradiction in terms, based on everything you've said so far."

"Once again, it would represent an authoritarian body that wants to own things. And so, here we are. I could easily argue that Elder Nazég, for all the persecution and hostility he was receiving, would WANT to run away if his faction was so often being dismissed, maybe even threatened for its excessively supernatural theories. It was said he was coming into a possible explanation for the Tav'ageen Anomaly. But the Council essentially turned it into a world panic, forcing us to take something no one wanted as THE solution, and further poisoned with a hidden element they didn't want us to know about. This is surely a justifiable reason to go to war with them. I would even describe this as a form of attack, especially when I consider the Tav'ageen Scare."

"Oh, really! And how would you suggest this?"

"This would have to be considered as a perspective of hindsight. We have the Scare, and it seems like people are dying all over the place, seemingly at random. Then we have this pressing message by the Council, and I suppose we must also consider the Marshal and his influence, since we all know he offered to help us during this time. But Ileani, he's an alien being, and therefore should not be such an influencing factor in OUR planetary government authority making such critical decisions for our people, superior wisdom or otherwise."

"Yes, I suppose this does follow naturally. It should be our native authority making these decisions, especially if it involves the health and welfare of the people. He can advise us, but this is probably the limit."

In Central Command, in the officer's lounge, Geilv claps his hands together in a congratulatory announcement.

"Boom! That's definitely a plug to point out an important issue. Place the blame on the Council, BUT the Marshal was actually the one doing it. I'll bet this is a plug for later."

"Therefore," Latena issues, "we can only say that the Council is the one invoking this situation of the panic and the solution to it. But here we have to look at it in hindsight for how it played out. Their solution was the seeds and this hidden code, which means there is a hidden agenda to have those seeds above all else. If we were simply intended to evacuate, we had all sorts of viable methods available to us, but none of these were considered. Instead, this other method was force-fed to us, as I seriously doubt anyone would willingly take one of those unless you literally put a gun to their head. And therefore, the Tav'ageen Scare."

Ileani gasped, this time for real, as it represented a serious violation of rights, to say nothing of the criminal action for all the deaths.

"And Ileani," Latena concludes. "According to my history lessons, although the Scare came after the Arrival, the Anomaly, as a discovery, predates the Marshal and his insurgents. So we cannot place any blame on Elder Nazég for turning against anyone. He was out there trying to HELP us!"

In the officer's lounge at Central Command, the viewers shook their heads at the predicament. And in homes around the world, and again in lunchrooms and other public venues, where a video monitor might be displaying the interview, people were reacting to this revelation with similar revulsion. Moans and urgent whispers were echoing amongst them as they reflected on this revealing announcement.

"Therefore," Latena resumes. "If we say Elder Nazég was coming up with a potential answer, and if it seemed supernatural, like it or not for our society that doesn't care to worship a religion, you may have to simply accept it, spirit of the words or otherwise. After all, those researchers called these things ghosts, and a ghost is a supernatural entity. Unfortunately, whatever the REAL answer, we lost it, partly due to the Council's prejudice, maybe also for the Marshal's unfortunate misinterpretation of that ship, and the rest of us who don't worship a religion. Elder Nazég was wrongly vilified by the people, and then chased away…along with our answers."

Again, inside the officer's lounge, Geilv and the Captain were watching.

"Blast that monster," Geilv scorns. "This must be suggesting Elder Nazég found something, and the rest wanted him silenced."

"Maybe better to say the Marshal wanted him silenced," the Captain considers.

"Yes! Good point."

"And why is she referencing a religion so many times here?" the Captain muses curiously.

"Do you think it could hold a clue?"

"A religion? I, uh…well, I uh…should probably hold my opinion for now."

In the newsroom, Petrith leaned forward for another statement.

"So, your argument against the Council seems largely based on these occasions of prejudiced control, and in particular this one with the An'gamu seeds, where the Council seems to be behaving with personal, perhaps also malicious intent against the people?"

"It's not simply the Council," Latena replies. "We also need to consider the Charter of Laws."

"All right, let's touch on that. You are apparently demanding a revision, or perhaps a full replacement to the Charter of Laws. You said once before that it carries these clauses, but do you have anything that might lend credence to the fact that it was designed this way intentionally? Maybe it was just a flaw in the wording that slipped past those people who first wrote it."

"This is certainly a viable argument, so let's go into the history of the document. Those…people…was one man in the beginning, and whoever followed him for the rest of it. And once again, we find ourselves with one of our favorite cultural romances, King Saakerav."

"Um, all right, are you suggesting something wrong here? Why him?"

"Recall what I said about our 'theory' of evolution relating to the Eracyodines. It's a romance over how we succeeded when it may actually seem irrational by empirical standards. Any upheaval of the natural environment would more likely cause a mass extinction when the food chain fails. This is one of those points of contention in that old controversy, and so the need for resolution, but the Council closed the book on it. And our ancestors are believed to have been herbivores, the first on the list."

"That would represent a problem, but as for Saakerav?"

"Going back to the Early Age, where the world was dominated by feudal kingdoms and city-states, along comes Saakerav. He has this wonderful idea to bring it all together. Surely, uniting the world from all those warring nations and the waste of life and property WAS a good thing, and therefore we romance him and what he did for us. But then he walks away from it. He doesn't RULE that nation he likely spent untold riches on to build. Instead, he hands it over to this Council, and the Charter of Laws, which HE invented. After that, he vanishes without a trace…and I mean without any real indication of where he came FROM, or went TO. Now, if you want a controversy, how do you explain a person who goes through that much trouble to solve a problem, and doing so without any perceived interest to KEEP it? And worse, apparently without a personal life of any kind?"

"No personal life?" Petrith balks conspicuously. "But surely, there must be a history of some kind."

"As part of my…major…in political history, I studied him thoroughly. But I didn't just stop at the romance of his Great Gift to Society," she flutters her fingers theatrically. "Unlike so many others, including my teachers, who simply said to accept the spirit of the words that he was a great guy with a fantastic idea, I wanted to know WHY he did it. After all, there must be a reason why someone would go to that much trouble for something."

"Yes, I suppose you may be right."

"But what I found was a bit odd for a man as celebrated as he was. There is no written record of a past, no family tree, and no heirs to follow him. He arrives virtually out of nowhere, raises up a mighty army, which must have been very expensive, then crusades across the land, and all the while, his scribes and scholars seem to praise every step he makes, until he essentially conquers the world away from everyone else. Then he writes the early beginnings of the Charter, and he establishes a fantastic new form of government no one ever heard of before…a technocracy."

"A technocracy…meaning a form of government body entirely devoted to a scientific or perhaps a professional pursuit, and similarly governed by these same professionals, as opposed to a more traditional political body."

"Right. So, in a time of feudalism, when you have royalty owning everything…and to emphasize for those who don't fully understand my meaning, these are often pompous and egotistical aristocrats who like OWNING things. To suddenly convert from that to a democratic form of government, but one entirely devoted to selectively issuing out research grants to promote certain avenues of intellectual growth. It makes you wonder who he was in reality, and where, in all the nether-space, he got that wild idea. And at this point in time, I might actually need to emphasize the nether-space aspect of it, for the fanciful nature of that term!"

"And another boom!" Geilv claps his hands. "That's surely a plug for something later, especially if you consider our discovery of Abnormal Space."

"I swear…" the Captain moans. "These people…"

Latena continues the debate, "And maybe also if he worked for someone behind the scenes with ulterior motives. No king, no matter how altruistic he might be, is going to spend his entire national budget to conquer the world and simply walk away from it. At the very least, the people who were so often praising him would wonder where he just disappeared to that HE is no longer leading them."

"I suppose I might have to agree," Petrith nods. "This would lead at least a few people to wonder where their historic leader vanished to, and probably long before his time."

"It therefore follows that if HE didn't take the ruling position, someone else did, and he was only a figurehead for the campaign. And again, we're made to romance it, much like that same spirit of the words he wrote about. We are denied a religion, but we were given a body of statesmen who will drive us for whatever tickles their tails. And we listen to their spirit of the words, as if to say we worship THEM as our new god. We follow whatever they tell us to do, as followers of a faith, believing they are always right. This is now called totalitarianism, where the governing body holds so much control of our minds, we actually believe them to be as gods."

In the officer's lounge, Geilv leans back in his chair.

"Well, Captain, there you have it. That mention of religion is us worshipping the Council as a god entity that can do no wrong, and we follow every little thing they tell us. And I can tell you from personal experience during my lifetime, this is exactly how it works."

"Yes Sir!" he nods vigorously.

Latena continues, "The only thing we can say with certainty about Saakerav is he brought the world to peace. But this is actually to say uniting all those misbehaving little nations that were so often squandering all their national resources on warfare. In the absence of that, and with everyone now in one basket, they were much more easily managed as a group. NOW, all those national resources are being directed into someone's pet project...research for all those fascinating little sciences that might make someone powerful, if only they could apply them just right. Some of this could possibly make one rich, and some of it could enforce a control aspect."

"And, as you said earlier," Navina proposes. "The rest of us only receive something as an incidental benefit if it crosses paths with us."

"Right. He who owns the show usually controls the show. The Council can't travel very far if the world around it is still living in the Stone Age. But how much did they give us and how much did they keep for themselves. What sorts of technologies were they aiming for, and which ones did they ignore? Why are we still on this one planet and not spread all across the galaxy by now? And why did they stop certain research projects and force us to accept the results on faith, saying there is no more to learn from it. On the surface, it would seem someone had some very long-term plans here, and at least part of it seems to revolve around making us romanticize things that are otherwise irrational."

"Romanticizing things...which might cause us to stop asking about them, if only due to our...faith...that this is how it should be? Interesting. But long-term plans? Are you suggesting some portion of this was planned from so long ago?"

"One might suggest, if only speculatively, and we might need to do this by now, if there could be an ultimate direction to it. After all, Saakerav had to come from somewhere, and for a reason. The idea of a technocracy, which likely didn't even have a definition at that time, also had to come from somewhere and for a reason. And like we said before, there must be a final motivation why someone would want to accumulate knowledge as a form of power. Therefore, we have the Council, which behaves as a god entity over us, forcing us to swallow their spirit of the words, almost like a religion, and filling us with so many fanciful romances to misdirect us from the research that might otherwise disprove them."

"Oops."

"But this began nearly a thousand millennia ago, so it's a little hard to say those people would want to run off with the Marshal's great wisdom so long before we even knew who he was. But to grow a civilization like ours, maybe to see what sorts of new technologies might come out of it, maybe also to modify their interests along the way as new ideas came forward, and so on, might provide some fascinating possibilities. Then we come to the modern day, where they found the ultimate prize and apparently ran off with it."

"That sounds a bit opportunistic," Petrith muses. "But nevertheless, it does actually paint a rather interesting picture of a body with ulterior motives, and a solid image of how they might do it. And like you, I am forced to consider why any man, king or otherwise, would go to THAT much trouble for anything at all, and then leave it to someone else. At the very least, he might want to hold onto it for the duration of his lifetime, and THEN bequeath it to this other body, if he did not otherwise have an heir or something."

"But we might still have a puzzling aspect to resolve here. The Council is known, on at least a few recognizable occasions, to have pursued one form of knowledge but not another. Further to outright reject still others. Then it runs off with the biggest prize in the universe, leaving us with their trash. But this, in itself, might not necessarily carry justification, unless you can qualify the reasoning for running off, even with the universe's biggest prize. After all, we're still a society of scientists, and potentially we could still be useful."

"Yes, I agree."

"Especially as WE are the scientists, and WITH all the laboratories to actually study something. The Council shouldn't be the ones studying things. They gave up that role to take on their political duties. The science factions should be the ones studying things, and in all their dedicated labs. One might say the Council could be taking forever to deliberate something because they don't have any proper researchers or lab equipment in that hideout of theirs...not unless you can tell me they have the universe's best technicians and the universe's finest laboratory to do it with."

"Indeed, this does make sense, and one thing I think people might tend to overlook, especially if they thought the Council was still in their chambers, which is NOT a laboratory environment."

Viewers around the world all let out a collective cry at this obvious rub, which should have stood out from the beginning, especially with those science factions who did not otherwise have any work assigned, and were waiting so long for the Council to finish something.

Latena concludes her argument, "Unless we say this puzzle in front of us relates to the Tav'ageen Anomaly...the REAL reason behind that Scare."

"This is interesting," Ileani offers. "How do you think this plays a role?"

"Let me tell you a story, and maybe you can find your own answer.

Word right now is the medical community is researching not only the seeds, but also the continued need for these chips. Which means they're reopening a few things the Council ordered closed. Those mandates, so I hear, had a number of nondisclosure clauses in them to prevent any further research, even for a follow-up or statistical review, to check the status of things. This means, the Council set things up as a permanent feature, even though the word on our side, in that famous spirit of the thing, was they were all temporary. But it was never temporary. Not when you are denied a way to reverse it."

"I suppose I must agree, when I look at our recent history."

"This means, someone wanted it. They did not care for any true empirical results, and is using this as a type of control mechanism over us, much like that industry to justify keeping the seeds, and especially if you factor in the perpetual inspiration that, any day now, we will all find our answers. But that day never comes."

"Uh huh…" she nods.

"But now, a good researcher does not simply stop researching because there is nothing more to research. Much like a good conspiracy theorist doesn't give up proposing conspiracy theories. Let's pull together a few things to get started. The early studies, Elder Nazég's faction and his possible theories, and also the Marshal for his original involvement in the study, plus his recent, and also famous, as some have said, statement relating to that deliberation. Going back in time to the beginning of the Anomaly, we have those early children exhibiting something…ghostlike. They were very few and far between, and apparently distributed at random around the world. This could not be an infestation in the sense of how it was described, as I think you would see a pattern to it. At first, a clustering effect where these things came down, and then a growth pattern as it spread out from there. But this was completely at random."

"I suppose, unless you suggest a broader distribution of these entities."

"But even at that, you would still see a pattern, as they would need to grow in those areas. Even if we say they are mobile, you should still see a pattern of development, beginning at a source point and moving along."

"All right, this is reasonable."

"I had a conversation with a representative of the medical faction recently, and it seems they still had a few old files in their archives from that time period. They're currently reviewing some of this trying to find out what those people did, and how they did it, that it got fouled up so badly. Here is something I learned. Initially, those first few children were at home when this thing was discovered. At that time, with the Anomaly being unknown to us, the researchers simply went out to the house to study it, since this is where it was found, and they didn't otherwise know what to do with it."

"At the house?" Navina leans forward. "Not a lab where they could put it under a microscope for better study?"

"That's right. They probably didn't know how, or even if it could be moved, so this is how it went. The children were asleep, and there was nothing medically wrong with them. The only thing standing out was some elevated brain activity, which they figured was simply the child having a vivid dream. People do that, you know, and the brain patterns are well documented."

"Yes, I am actually aware of this."

"But we also have this ghostlike thing in the room. This is where our science goes haywire, as it defies anything…rational. We might actually say this would be better described by Elder Nazég's faction and their crazy supernatural stuff. And, in fact, after some time, he was apparently getting a few ideas."

"But the rest of them rejected these ideas."

"Yeah. Unfortunately, as we all know, those children died, and of some really nether-wild causes, which also defied all of our sciences. BUT…the part that may not have been so commonly advertised is this. It was only in a time frame of moments when those researchers turned their backs and left the room for a bit. Then, boom! A parent, who probably went back in there to check on their child, discovers the body instead. It was that fast. And the bodies were described to be partially mummified, which is both medically and scientifically impossible to occur in mere moments."

"Moments! As if to say, you see the child one moment, step outside, turn around, go back in, and boom, there you have a dead body?"

"Yes."

"And the ghost thing?"

"Gone. Therefore, people are suspecting the ghost to be the culprit."

"Yes, this would be my first guess, as well. And therefore the concern for what it is."

"Exactly. Now, after a few of these were found, and this end result occurred, the researchers are getting anxious for an answer. People are becoming afraid for all the publicity going out."

"Wait a moment. Publicity? I recall there was some mention here and there, but..."

"It would seem there was more than just a mention. It became a sensation after a while. This extraordinary...thing...and followed by this extraordinary...death. That sounds like someone wasn't being very discreet for the health and privacy issue of the child or the family."

"Really!"

"You know," Ileani interjects. "As a journalist, I would have to agree. There has to be a line drawn to protect a person's privacy, especially in a private home."

"But this does sound like someone intentionally leaking something," Petrith mentions. "If you don't actually know what you're dealing with, and you don't want to cause a public disturbance along the way, perhaps with a lot of fear and speculation, you should not advertise it so boldly. It's not professional, and it's not wise without reasonable cause."

"This is true," she nods. "Normally, we might say the public has a right to know, but at the same time, we might not want to broadcast such unrealized discoveries until some form of confirmation can justify raising awareness for public safety. And this here, at least at that time, might not have represented itself as a public hazard to be broadcast as if it were. A few isolated incidents here and there is NOT a global issue to start a panic, even if we are speaking of ghosts."

"So we have these ghost things in the room," Latena continues. "Which is as much a spectacle as it might be a concern for what they are, where they came from, and how they got inside a closed room, inside a private house. Furthermore, why they resemble the child in every interpretable manner. The researchers used everything they had to scan and measure these things, but according to the documentation under review right now, these things didn't represent a body of any kind. There was no measurable mass, no energy signature, nothing. Even though, if you were to reach out with your hand, you could touch it, and it might even feel tangible. But the machines couldn't see anything, except maybe for the cameras."

"This would certainly confuse a lot of people. You can see something, but you can't measure it."

"Right. But then you have these deaths that occur as soon as their backs are turned. Now you have worry."

"I'm sure you do."

"I suppose, this might also represent where the Council begins to cover things up, maybe due to that issue of public concern, assuming you want to credit them with this much."

"Why do you say that? I mean, given everything else, sure, but is there some specific reason here?"

"I could suggest a few things, like where that leak originated, and who's idea it was, and for what reason. But for now, keep listening and you tell me. Here we see those researchers getting the idea to move this to a lab. I don't personally recall any news bulletins about these children being moved from their homes to a medical lab, but I suppose it would follow eventually."

"Yes, I would agree."

"This is where it gets a little interesting...if you can call it that. The child was still sleeping, so its body was loaded into one medical van while the ghost was asked to follow along in another one."

"Asked?" she winces. "Is this to say they were actually talking to it, and it was following their instruction?"

"Yes! Like I said, it behaved just like you would expect of the original child. It even seemed excited to be riding in a real live medical van, with sirens blaring and lights flashing," she shrugs. "And so, we now arrive at the lab. The child's body is moved to an analysis room and plugged into a series of monitors to study his life signs. All appeared normal. The ghost, on the other hand, is another thing. They took it to another room with a small army of researchers to study it. It was under constant observation, and not just by people, but also cameras. But just like before, they were pulling their horns out trying to figure out what it was made of or how it could exist at all. And by the way, they were still talking to it, and like before, it resembled the actual child for its memories, experiences, and whatever."

"Interesting, like as if it somehow absorbed those memories into itself somehow."

"That body-snatcher scenario everyone spoke of? Yeah, maybe. But this is reality, not a science fiction horror show. Remember, monsters aren't supposed to be real, and we're a society of empirically minded people who outright reject anything supernatural," she flutters her fingers.

"Yes, this is true, but this one certainly did bring up some ideas with it."

"The belief, at this time, was the death syndrome might be related to the ghost, and nothing else. Therefore, everyone is in the room watching it, leaving the child's body in the lab plugged into the monitors, with only an occasional intern making visits to check on things. Otherwise, it wasn't doing anything interesting. It's asleep, you know."

"Yes, of course."

"Now, somewhere along the way, something strange happens. And this is where my conspiracy theorist mind goes into action. The monitors attached to the child go crazy with spiked readings, and suddenly flatline. The child is now dead. Interns respond to the alarms, and once again find the body in that awful condition."

"Oh dear, so even in a medical lab, they still lost it?"

"Yeah, and this seems to be where that leaked sensationalism trips on itself. THIS part didn't go out on the news, except to say, 'Oops, there goes another one,' and the people go into an even bigger panic as one more statistic adds up."

"All right, I can see the problem with the additional statistic, and the part about the leak is becoming a concern. They leak the news of the death, but not the fact it was inside a medical lab plugged into monitors and with people everywhere watching things. But now, what about that ghost?"

"Yeah, the ghost, and another important aspect that did NOT get publicized. In fact, it would seem this whole incident, other than for the statistic, got buried."

"Buried!" she shouts. "Oh, NOW they decide to bury the frightening details."

"And who do you think might hold enough authority to bury something in our news media, but the Council. No one else would hold such overriding authority to hide something like this."

"Yes, I suppose only THEY would hold this level of authority. None of the factions would hold the authority to tell US what to do."

"As for the ghost, it went poof, gone, and at the same exact time of death."

"Was there any indication of how or why? When you say poof, is this to say it simply vanished?"

"Yeah. The reports by those who were present say they were interacting with it, like to carry conversations and such. The poof thing happened unexpectedly and right in midsentence, almost like pulling the plug on a device and it simply goes dead on you."

Ileani reels back in her chair, feeling a sudden chill creeping along her back.

"But how do we interpret this? It was said the ghost was responsible for all those deaths."

"And no doubt the reason THIS one was buried. It was NOT responsible. The death of the child also resulted in the death, if you can call it that, of the ghost. The ghost wasn't even in the same room, and neither did it show any indication of wrongdoing. It was talking one moment, then bam, it's gone, and a moment later, shouts arrive from the lab about the child in the other room. And the time stamps on the video show it was simultaneous. So now, we need to interpret the data, as this time we have something to show for it. We might not be able to measure the ghost, but that child is another thing. Its life signs showed an instantaneous spike, and then flatline. And the body was discovered shriveled up like a mummy."

"Did the cameras in the lab show anything?" Petrith asks.

"That's the problem, they did NOT show anything…IN the room. The interns were absent at the time, and the room was empty…as far as the cameras could actually see, as they were pointing into the room. But a conspiracy theorist might ask, what about a corner or a doorway?"

"Ah! Yes, all right, so we might be speaking of something at range, not right on top of it, and not in direct view of the camera, correct?"

"I think we have to if we didn't see it on the video. And the doorway, as far as I'm told, was NOT in view of the camera in question. So, if we suggest someone or something passing by in the hallway did the deed, it would not be recorded, and this leaves us with a mystery. But this is NOT a ghost story mystery. This is now a murder mystery. Something killed that child…in a very alien manner of speaking. And this new death, like all the others, went out to incite a public panic, or maybe to FURTHER incite that panic."

"Are we suggesting it was intentional to incite that panic?"

"Well, if you look at where it led us, we might have to. They pushed unnecessary solutions at us to solve a problem that seems to involve a false suspect."

"Is this occasion before or after the Marshal got involved?" Navina asks.

"This is still before, and there were apparently two of these occasions before he arrived and offered his help. But here is where it gets sinister, because that 'help' apparently resulted in the Scare, which frightened the horns off people so badly, it was like holding a gun to your head to take those seeds."

In the officer's lounge in Central Command, Geilv and the others were still watching.

"So, it was a big cover-up for something," he muses. "Made worse with ghost stories, and likely Elder Nazég knew something, but was shunned and discredited."

"Worse, if you consider the Marshal," the Captain notes. "That long pursuit, the perpetual claims of his villainy…"

"He was made a scapegoat for something. This is obvious now."

Back in the newsroom, Navina was still responding.

"Um, but are we suggesting the Council, or the Marshal, as he did offer to help."

"Yes, he did," Latena responds. "Surely, it might appear as more of that opportunity. Someone comes along with his…superior knowledge. The Council sees treasure in this, so they take his 'advice' and give us the seeds. Then they run off with their prize and leave us with their trash. That deliberation, for instance, which is stretching on forever. The Council behaves as if it can control information at a whim. Not for our benefit, but for theirs. That spirit of the words is an excuse to distract us. They tell us they are in deliberation when they are not even at home. They forget to tell us they have this super longevity drug keeping them alive, and they violate our election rules to stay in power. This extended for ten millennia with no correction to it. It was not intended to be corrected, much like that industry was never intended to be cleaned up. Neither were we ever intended to evacuate, and these seeds and chips were never intended to be temporary, because no one ever gave instructions to the contrary. What they DID do is perpetuate their stories to the point where we stop asking questions."

"I hate to say it," Ileani moans. "But I might have to agree, after all has been said here. I had hoped one day to report on some of those revelations. But in my lifetime, all I got was more of these same stories, and the public knows it because they were watching. And you can't just keep turning people's horns down for so long before someone begins to notice."

"This is true. And then the claim that they're hiding in some secret outpost conducting this research. These people clearly had no intention of doing any real work to solve our more immediate problems, things we NEED to have solved, that would otherwise put these nether-wild secrets of the universe as secondary to our health and welfare. And you expect me to believe these people, with their super longevity drug, will unravel the secrets of the universe and give US anything out of it? They did not even go so far as to tell their families not to bother with funeral arrangements. No. If the Marshal wants to give the people of Azgarén the secrets of the universe, I'll gladly accept it. But all our best research labs are HERE, along with armies of researchers with no other work to do. I think we can handle it."

"Well, yes, I suppose. And there are some clear legality issues relating to this."

"Legality issues?" Latena balks. "Miss Ur'paran, let me reinforce one of those. How many deaths were there during the Tav'ageen Scare? And WHO was responsible for it that they pushed these seeds at us as their Great and Wise answer to the panic?"

"Uh oh..."

"Yes, this is called mass murder, and likely intentional to hide something they ran away with, or else chased Elder Nazég away if he held the answer. This was then followed by that gun to our heads for the REAL infestation...those seeds, which do, by the way, have something alien inside."

This revelation caused masses of people around the world to gasp in shock as the final message was nailed down for the purpose of the Scare. Many of them reflected on the seeds attached to their bodies and instantly felt a pain of revulsion, not simply to have the seed, but to think of who did it and why it was there.

"Miss Ta'yeen," Petrith issues. "This does, by the way, cause me to recall the Suppressor chips. I believe the Marshal is the one to actually invent those, with the help of our people. This was supposed to be the solution to stop those deaths, claiming again this alien infestation."

"Mister Girhani, regrettably, I am forced to conclude he is in collaboration with the Council and their designs. He is also said to be instrumental in the design, or RE-design, of those seeds. Whatever the Council had in mind, they must've made a backroom deal with him, and this is the result. In case you forgot, it was at least partially HE who recommended to all of us that we need to evacuate, and the Council accepted this. Then we have the seeds, which according to a recent statement, serve no functional value to survive in hostile environments, other than our polluted one. This redesign seems rather limited to a single purpose. This is followed by those insurgents getting in the way and keeping us pinned down. This was then followed by the dirty industry, which seems NOT to be producing anything other than a closed loop of recycled parts. But it IS polluting our otherwise clean environment, thereby forcing us to keep those seeds even here at home. So far, this is not a nice picture."

"No, it is not."

"And then, FINALLY, we have those chips, which arrived as a secondary solution to the original problem. But note I said secondary! If this alien super mind knew how to solve the problem, this should have been the first thing to come out. But it wasn't. But who can we place the blame on here? Him? He came to us asking for help in exchange for knowledge. Note that word…knowledge…which in this case might represent a considerable amount of power. So the Council grants their aid, takes that knowledge, and perhaps uses him to stab each of us literally in the back with those seeds. The chips, as far as I can tell, do nothing more than act as restraining collars for that zapping effect. But they sure did make a fine excuse to solve that final element of panic."

"Yes, I must agree on this, as I'm sure a lot of people have experienced that zapping at one time or another, but they seem to tolerate it, if only due to the panic that started it."

"I might also reinforce my statement that if he knew what the Council was doing to us, and carried any moral values, he might object to our world government offending its people with all these so-called solutions. After all, by his stories, he was running from something else…criminal."

In the officer's lounge, Geilv and the Captain almost felt like laughing.

"Ooh," the Captain muses. "That'll hurt when they expose the rest of it."

"This is where we might say, horns will fly," Geilv smiles.

In the newsroom, Petrith responds to Latena's last statement.

"I don't know if I could speak for that, but as for the Council, this is surely cause enough to go to war with them for these offences. This represents multiple charges against them, and over a long period of time. And in the absence of them responding to ANY of these allegations, it would seem to validate itself by default. So, I suppose, unless the Council actually comes forward with a response of any kind, you will continue your rallies to see them brought down?"

"I think I have to, Mister Girhani. Someone should be held responsible for all those deaths. Many of those people were found in alleyways and even behind closed doors, and NOT in the company of ghosts. We're not speaking of children who went to sleep here. We're speaking of adults walking from the office to a local café and back again. Those original children died of something in those labs, plugged into monitors to watch them, and with cameras surveying the room. And then ZAP!" she animates with a finger pistol. "According to those medical officials, the suspicion is those children were killed by some new kind of weapon, and likely out of view of the camera. And if THIS is the case, it's a cover-up to hide the truth of the Tav'ageen Anomaly, which the Council, maybe in collaboration with the Marshal, figured out, either with or without the aid of Elder Nazég and his unappreciated faction. This represents not only those multiple charges, but a premeditated effort combined with placing false blame on an innocent man, who was then hunted like an animal for our viewing entertainment. And if we should ever find those people, I would imagine they'll find a happy little home in an outpost, all right. A prison outpost, where we lock them up with their super longevity drug, and keep them there for the rest of their unnatural lives!"

Once again, in the officer's lounge, Geilv was chuckling to himself. "She's a feisty little one."

"Yes," the Captain admits humorously. "She is that much, at least."

"Does she get it from your side of the family?"

"I don't know. Her mother is also a feisty one. My brother tends to be a bit more like me, in some ways. Very procedural."

"This simply leads me to one final point," Latena continues. "Which would also make a viable cause to expel Elder Nazég, as he might have been a burr under their tail to reveal the truth. We have the seeds, the chips, all these statements about him, the long pursuit, and this clearly implicates the collaboration aspect. The Marshal is just as much responsible for vilifying him as the rest."

"Uh oh..." the Captain mumbles. "Go gently here, Latena."

"Miss Ta'yeen," Navina asserts. "Not that I would wish to argue this point, given what was said, but is this to say we should break our agreement with him, if he is being implicated here in this collaboration effort? And we still have those insurgents out there, as poor as they might be in actually posing any kind of a threat."

"Miss Lar'akan, unless HE would like to come out and explain all these discrepancies, rather than simply giving excuses why the Council is not doing this, or anything else we hired them to do, then I think the people might want to know what he and the Council are doing together. For instance, he is an alien being. HE should not be the one calling the shots around here. HE should not be the one excusing our government body from its government duties, and especially not outside our citizenry knowing about it OR approving it. WE elected those people. They should be serving US, the people of Azgarén. And yet, not counting the Scare in this statement, they violated a number of legal points, some of them severe, and did so on the orders of someone who should not hold any true authority around here to grant this. After all, with respect to the Marshal, what actual authority does he have to violate OUR laws?"

In the officer's lounge, both Geilv and the Captain reeled back.

"Ouch, Latena," the Captain whispers.

"Yes," Geilv submits. "But that was a direct hit on his perceived authority, and clearly a follow-up to everything else. He shouldn't be making ANY decisions, and the Council shouldn't be taking authority to violate its own laws on the advice of an alien creature."

"Yes, I would have to agree. This alone ought to invalidate their authority to serve their positions."

In the studio, both Petrith and Navina paused to consider Latena's words.

"This would indeed represent a valid argument," Petrith states. "The Council is a body elected by and serving the people of our world, spirit of the words or otherwise. Regardless of anything else, they should NOT be violating our native laws, and this should also include researching even the most precious secrets of the universe. If we reflect on the preamble again, it should be 'We the People' who hold the authority in this democratic society, especially if we are taught to respect the spirit of those words. In fact, we should enforce that teaching, deception or not. Like she said, not counting the Scare and what it represented, their selfish behavior alone should be enough to see them expelled."

"Also, I hate to say it," Navina adds. "But that same statement might similarly force 'We the People' to reprimand the Marshal for exerting an influence that violates our laws without first presenting it to that same 'We the People' for approval."

In the officer's lounge, the audience watches.

"Ooh!" the Captain winces. "That'll hurt."

"Yes, but it'll hurt on both sides, I think," Geilv muses. "Because that same 'We the People' allowed it to happen when we opened the door for him."

"Do you think we honestly had a choice, given who he is?"

"Maybe not."

In the newsroom, Latena continues, "And this should also involve our military. After all, the Council seems to have given him control of it, and again illegally."

"Wait," Navina urges. "Illegally? How do you mean?"

"We are all told, for nearly ten millennia, that our military is chasing around the galaxy fighting those insurgents who don't seem to know how to use their superior technology to finish what they started. Neither do they know when to stop trying. Now, if you belong to a society that hasn't a clue how to fight wars, you might simply shrug it off that we got lucky… again, and again, and again…" she shakes her head. "I cannot say I know anything about wars any more than the next pacifist, but I think this would stand out as a bit odd, perhaps even a bit convenient. This, compounded by the idea that…any day now…we'll evacuate, and all this trash…meaning the seeds and the chips…will be gone. It's all part of the same story. But let me ask you this. Who is leading our military during this time?"

"Well, the highest-ranking officer in our military is the High Commander, naturally."

"Yes, naturally…"

Geilv leans forward in his chair as he listens closely to this part.

"Hmm, this hints at something, and I wonder…"

"Wonder what?" the Captain asks.

"That special message to me from the ACI."

Latena continues, "…But, who MADE our military, and is actually leading this crusade against those nasty insurgents? I'll give you a hint, it's NOT the HC."

"Well, all right," Navina nods. "I am aware the Marshal is mostly instrumental in leading this crusade. After all, this is part of the agreement the Council made once for this aid. He actually built the military we have now."

"Absolutely, and no doubt he might hold a bit more military knowledge than the rest of us. But if HE is the one leading OUR military, what role does the HC have, but to follow HIS direction. This is to say, our military is actually his military. Because WE never had a full military before this. We're pacifists, remember? We stopped fighting wars a thousand millennia ago, thank you King Saakerav."

Geilv and the Captain both reacted to this statement.

"Boom," Geilv mutters. "That tells a story."

"Once again, he's an alien," Latena continues. "What actual authority does HE have to do ANYTHING in our world outside our native government OR our native society to govern? We might offer aid, but it should be 'We the People' offering this aid, not an alien body taking control of something that should otherwise belong to us. In the absence of the Council doing anything at all, this is to say they gave HIM full administrative control of our native military body to fight his wars. THAT should be one of the highest crimes yet. The Council should not hold the power to grant this level of authority to a foreign entity, and that foreign entity should not be accepting it without the rest of us realizing what was happening, or to approve it."

"Oh dear..." Ileani moans.

In the officer's lounge, Geilv perked up at the mention.

"Ka-boom!" he claps his hands again. "And that might be a clue, not only for the people, but maybe also for me to realize an illegal takeover action."

"Yes," the Captain nods. "But even though I realize it might need to be said, it also comes very close to a line we might not want to cross."

"Maybe so, but now that it's out, the people will gather up on the other side of that line, which shifts the balance a bit."

"Best case scenario," Latena continues. "We might work as a co-op effort. He points a finger, and we go in to analyze the situation, then to take whatever action is necessary. Instead, the Council essentially gave him the keys and ran away. And worse, he also seems to be managing the rest of it if he is giving excuses for why the Council is not doing its work...ANY of its work. Who is actually in control of our government at this time, Ileani? Because it's not those people we thought we were electing."

"She has a point," Petrith muses. "Aside from the fact those people abandoned their post and violated the election rules, and aside from the fact of the Tav'ageen Scare and who might be responsible for it, our government body should NOT be delegating authority over any of our native functions to an outside entity... Ever."

Again, in the officer's lounge, Geilv nodded.

"She's good," Geilv muses.

"She always was a smart girl," the Captain admits. "But how much is hers and how much is the ACI?"

"I don't know, but she's holding her own very nicely."

"Yes, and they seem to be pulling together a lot of pieces here. Now I see where all those other sensations came from."

"It must be part of a much larger plan," Geilv nods, "and very well-conceived."

"Therefore," Latena concludes. "The Council has violated the trust of the people, and again on multiple counts. Opportunity? Yes, this represents a nice one. I would describe this as making transgressive subjugating maneuvers behind our backs. They sold us off to someone else."

The Captain was getting tense by now listening to her statements.

"Latena…" he stresses. "Not only will you get yourself in trouble with him, but you're liable to start a riot!"

"That's probably the whole point," Geilv accedes. "She's instigating a rebellion here."

"Granted, but do we want pitchforks and torches parading through the streets?"

"Well, he probably couldn't oppose that very easily."

"But Miss Ta'yeen," Ileani wonders. "Are you saying they might have used him for this?"

"An opportunity presented itself," she alludes. "And they took advantage of it. And this would represent one more facet of their corruption. That Scare, those seeds, his involvement in all this, and that secret code with the alien stuff inside. I recall the medical community trying to give it a name, which sure sounded alien enough, and saying it looked like it functioned as some kind of organic network link, with a sympathetic feedback effect…this Abnormal Energy stuff. I don't think I like that…being linked to a network of any kind, and which gives off this aura effect for some unknown purpose. We can't use it, so who is? And given how that Scare went along, this could be the Council's ultimate objective for a control device, especially if that secret code was locked behind a security block, which would normally violate protocol for the research labs. For all we know, this aura effect could link everyone into some kind of self-destruct mechanism if someone amongst that authoritarian dictatorship doesn't like how we're behaving. And since they pushed it so hard at us in the first place, they must expect us to behave a certain way."

Around the world, viewers were drawing another collective gasp at this blatant accusation. It didn't matter now if it was true or false, the mere suggestion was bad enough. In the officer's lounge, Geilv and the Captain also reacted to the statement.

"Blast it!" Geilv growls. "That has to be a clue."

"If it is," the Captain relents. "He's got a full planet by the tail. But now, what are we expected to do about it?"

"This may be a lead to something for later."

"But one moment please," Ileani begs. "Miss Ta'yeen, what do you think he might have to say about all this?"

"The Marshal?" she wonders. "The first thing I would like to hear out of him is an explanation for how all this got started, and why we have it in the first place. Why do we have these seeds? What actually happened with that Scare that pushed this on us in the first place? Where, exactly, is the Council, and what, exactly, are they doing outside our view? And if he wants to give us the secrets of the universe, he should give it to those people who are professional researchers, in their professional research labs, who otherwise don't have anything else to do but professional research. Furthermore, I think it would be prudent to ask why it's taking so long for these insurgents of his to back off and stop wasting themselves against our military, thereby forcing us to keep these war protocols for so long that it nearly destroys our native home and pollutes our bodies with someone's trash. Beyond that, if he wants to stay with us, taking refuge from…whatever, I say he will need to renegotiate his terms once we have a new and proper government authority that actually behaves as a proper government authority."

"And so, this is your argument for these rallies, and it is certainly a detailed and complex argument."

"Yes. We are demanding not only a new government, but also the remake of the Charter of Laws, which brought us here in the first place. And I personally would prefer to see something a bit more traditional, with a proper form of political rule. Even if we exclude the Scare, saying perhaps it was a criminal gang taking advantage of something outside anyone's view, we still have all the rest of it. This was clearly the Council's work, maybe with the Marshal's input to provide some functionality."

"All right," Ileani concedes. "But Miss Ta'yeen, this movement of yours. It would seem you've managed to stir up a lot of contention amongst the people out there. Clearly, it appears as though you intend to rally the people to overthrow the Council. But what do you have in mind afterwards?"

"First and foremost, I think we need to know who our friends and who our enemies are. The Council is not a friend. I will reserve mention on the Marshal since he IS an alien entity, and he DID presumably come here for help, despite the fact that it might appear, at least on the surface, that he collaborated at least once or twice with the Council for these…opportunities…we spoke of. So, whatever relationship he has with the Council notwithstanding, it is the people he should be working with if he wants OUR help. And if he wants to give us any special gifts of wisdom, my first suggestion is a reversal process to all the havoc our world is suffering."

The Captain felt a moment of relief as he listened.

"Nicely said, girl," he whispers.

"Next is the Charter of Laws, and this clearly gives the Council their questionable authority. It also has to go. We can call on legal experts, and I happen to know a few with full credentials, who can assist in writing up something new and with proper language giving us true freedoms and realistic laws without the loopholes."

"All right," Ileani nods. "I suppose this is reasonable, given what you've said so far."

"Finally, as for our people, we have become so accustomed to tucking our tails on command that we don't know how to run our affairs without explicit instruction. A proper government uses politicians, not scientists pretending to know politics. This is not their specialty. We've had a Council ever since Saakerav, and we basically forgot how to do anything else. In those early days, you might see something like a monarchy or some other form of imperial rule, where the leadership represents someone, or maybe a body of some kind, who dedicated themselves to their political roles."

"Which means, we need more of the same now?"

"Surely something along this category, yes. Not all of these were bad, mind you," she waves a finger for emphasis. "There is such a thing as a good king, who can inspire his people to great moments. But I am not trying to say we need a new king over us. It DOES, however, need to be someone who spends all his time doing this line of work. Not pretending to hold the power or authority to unravel the secrets of the universe outside anyone else's ability to share in the discovery."

"Do you have anyone, or anything in mind who might serve this role? Do YOU feel like you want to take this role?"

"Me? While I may be ambitious enough to lead this revolt, I'm only two centuries old, so I doubt I could gain that level of support to lead an entire world into a new Era. And I doubt we have any single individual who currently carries this level of esteem, or wisdom, as to take that position through any other means. But as a student of politics, one thing I CAN say about it, regardless of what form of government we ultimately take, the people are going to need an education on how it works. They spent too much time allowing someone else to do the job, and then simply assuming they were doing the job right. We can't afford another of those."

In the city of Rolsklinde, Thaelyn and his officers were reviewing a terminal with a replay of the interview, which had been delivered by Kaliya's teammates from Azgarén.

"And she's so young," Kailen muses. "In some ways, she reminds me of Kaliya during those early years, but here a little more responsible for herself."

"I'm truly fascinated by her presentation," the General adds. "She seems so well-organized with her details, and so precise with her statements."

"Indeed," Thaelyn asserts. "This young lady is likely to go far in her life. I think my suggestion of a diplomat, or an ambassador may not even be sufficient. This sort of character is what I might choose for my High Council if she were available to us. If only for her age, but that will always change."

"Slowly, but yes," Kailen nods. "And if to choose her like this, you'll be guaranteed a very LONG duration of service."

They all join in a hearty laugh at the idea.

"So," he continues with a grin. "Are you thinking of annexing yet another world?"

"Oh, Commander, please..." he chuckles. "Yours would be a fine one, but I would not dare to presume we might find ourselves in that position. And yet, this young lady does hold a number of valid points, one of which is to educate those people with a proper form of political rule, whatever form they might choose."

"I wouldn't be against that, I suppose. But the culture shock would take time to settle."

"Yes, it would, but just as you once offered to stay at my side for our woes, I would stand by yours the same, Commander."

"My deepest thanks, Your Lordship," he smiles. "Your society is the finest example of a friend my people could ever hope for."

Back in Capitol Prime, in the ARC, Azina was visiting the Director's office.

"Ghantil!" she calls as she rushes inside. "Did you see that interview last night? Wow, that girl is fierce! I think she's my new hero."

"Yeah, but being a hero is one thing. Living long enough to enjoy it is another. But at least this part is out now, and I'm already getting reports from our clinics of people calling in about the seeds and what we think of that unknown component versus her statements. I think we just found our logistical breakthrough. Her fear tactic, if we can call it that, is going to start our own panic syndrome where the seeds are concerned, and this will provide us an outlet to ensure we spread that inhibitor drug around."

"Well, this is good, but it doesn't help us for telling them when to use it."

"I'm sure that'll come out at a later moment. I was paying attention to her wording, and I think I heard one or more keywords mentioned which our friends might have a use for later. That mention of Abnormal Energy, for one thing. She seemed to be placing emphasis on it for some reason, and I recall where Captain Nazég said the military was using this term for that stuff they found in that other universe. And if they hope to use this image of Ytani and his newfound friends, well, it's building a picture where this might be a trigger. So we need to be sure we have a good supply ready."

"All right, but the next obvious thing to ask is about the Marshal. Do we have any ideas on his reaction, or what it could be?"

"For what was said during this occasion, he can complain that we aren't taking his seeds as he so desires, but a world population now fearing that unknown component is enough to thwart anything he could throw at us to counter it. Even if he told us the end of the world was coming, if only to keep the seeds to survive it, I think the people would likely demand to see the evidence to prove it by now."

In Central Command, Captain Ta'yeen was in conversation with Latena on the trans-com.

"Uncle, please," she begs. "I don't need you to preach to me about what I'm doing."

"I know, Latena," he relents. "But I just finished speaking with your parents, and you can probably imagine the horn-twisting they gave me."

"Yeah, I got the same once that interview was over. It's really sad that they were apparently more offended that I was on center stage and NOT what I had to say about it. Even though a complete dull-horn could figure it out by now. But at this moment, and with love and respect to all of you, I'm in this for a legitimate cause that needs to be done. We can't just keep living under these rules, and you apparently know what I mean."

"Yes, I do, but your parents are another matter. I tried to impress on them, during my own conversation, that they should be paying more attention to the message, and that the majority of the public is realizing these issues, including legal experts, magistrates, law enforcement, and who knows what else out there."

"And what did they say to that?"

"Well, other than to say the world is going crazy around them, and most of it sounds too outlandish to believe, I think I settled them down enough to try listening to it for once. Even though we have our own security restrictions, I felt it necessary, if only for their own health and safety, to shut their mouths and pay attention, because this is a war, but not the one the Marshal kept telling us about. He lied to us, and WE, here in that famous military he built, know about it. Unfortunately, his insurgents, in their true form, are advising us to keep quiet until they can make that official move to actually finish it."

"Oops! And what did they say to THAT?"

"They didn't have much else to say by that time," he chuckles. "I'm going to assume the ACI has a plan of some kind relating to those seeds and that threat potential, and I don't want to see any unnecessary victims, including my own brother and his wife. I wouldn't be able to live with myself if I let that happen."

"Thank you, Uncle."

"I'm actually more concerned right now for your safety. If he should get angry over what you said, or that you're making so many waves..."

"Yes, I know, and these people also know. First, I'm moving around a lot, so trying to find me at any given moment would be problematic. Only a handful of people know where I am, and they're all ACI. Next, I have a set of bodyguards on me, and they're also providing me with, um, private transport, so it'll be a little hard to track my movements, if even you were to try it," she giggles.

"Really! All right, if you say so. Then, I suppose I don't have much choice but to trust these people to take care of you. But be careful anyway."

"Yes, Uncle, I will."

In another part of Central Command, Geilv was involved in one of his own conversations.

"I am growing very impatient with these rabble-rousers, Commander!" the Marshal growls into the com-link. "This is getting completely out of hand! And I'm STILL wondering where in all Creation those regulators are during this time!" he shrieks. "I've sent numerous statements to them, but it seems they're not reporting our news the way we want it!"

"Did we perhaps see a change in staffing recently?"

"Not that I'm aware of…although I suppose I might want to check on that. Maybe if I send an inquiry to our agent in the Council building. He usually keeps good track of these things."

He pauses in silence as he mulls this thought.

"But then we have that new conspiracy…activist…noisemaker!" he howls. "With all her statements and accusations, her rampant squabbles about this and that. Aargh!" he shouts. "She should be arrested, along with all the rest! We need to remind those peasants who they are. The Council is the one who makes the decisions around here, and it makes them because this is what they do. And it's not the place for these little people to argue about it!"

Geilv waits silently as the Marshal again takes a moment to catch his breath. He held his comments to himself on this occasion in order to hear what comes next, although he was already growing very impatient with what was said already.

"Just who does she think she is," the Marshal snarls, "going out there pretending to be the savior of the world?! Don't we have laws against such people making so many disobedient statements? Commander, I want you to find that young…" he grumbles something unintelligible, "…well, just find her and put her somewhere so she can't possibly make any more noise!"

"This is not precisely my department, but I could always inquire about it."

"Good! Do so! And while you're at it, see about the rest of them who are parading around out there! We need to bring this situation back into order!" he screeches.

He ends the link, leaving the Commander glaring angrily at the vid-com.

"Back…into…order…is it?" he scorns through his teeth.

He reaches for the vid-com again to make another call.

"Control, Captain Ta'yeen here."

"Captain, to my office, if you please…" he barks.

"Yes Sir, right away!"

They end the link and Geilv waits, although not very patiently at this point. Soon, the door buzzer rings, and the Captain marches in promptly.

"Sir, you look like you just got off the line with HIM again. What happened?"

Geilv points assertively into the chair opposite the desk.

"My apologies, Captain, but he is wearing on my nerves now, so I need a buffer, and unfortunately it has to be you."

"I understand, Commander. I'm here for you."

"As you can probably expect, he's not at all happy with your niece. Neither is he happy with MOST of what is happening out there. He's commanding them to learn their place, as 'peasants' should, and leave the business of making decisions to the Council, as little people who have no right to argue with it. He's also ordering me to find your niece, arrest her, and bury her somewhere, so he can find the peace and servitude he so desires."

"How nice of him," he huffs. "Does he know it's my niece, or just some girl who happens to be making a public disturbance?"

"He didn't say, and at this point, he probably doesn't care. We're all little creatures who should jump whenever he calls for it."

"Figures… Then, Commander, I need to ask what you have in mind to do about this?"

"My only solution right now is to consult the ACI. They surely must have a contingency plan for this."

He again reaches for his vid-com and makes another call.

"ACI, Agent Kaetaal speaking."

"Miss Kaetaal, this is High Commander Geilv over at Central Command."

"Ah, Commander," she responds pleasantly. "I was actually expecting your call today. Do we have something special with the Marshal?"

"Yes, we do, and I would like some advice on how to contend with it."

"Of course, Commander, what is the situation this time?"

"He's angry, to say the least. He wants to bring things back into order, as he calls it, and he wants that Miss Ta'yeen arrested and made to disappear. Now, how would you suggest we respond to this, because I suspect you might be anticipating something."

"Absolutely, Commander," she chirps. "And I have a very appealing little statement for you today. Are you ready?"

"Yes Ma'am…and you seem rather cheerful about it."

"Commander, I can imagine you are in a hard position over there. But just remember, WE are the ones in control here. There is little he can do at this time to return back to the way things were. And besides, you, being the HC, have a rather powerful military at your disposal. If he once ordered you to turn your weapons on a member of the Estelar, I think those same weapons could be turned on him and Sargeras with similar results."

Geilv raised his brow at the mention, and glanced at the Captain.

"Perhaps you're right, although Sargeras is inside that building in the middle of town."

"I know, but in relation to what he is capable of, we might need to use it. It is the unfortunate nature of being in the military that we might find ourselves forced to make such dire decisions."

"Acceptable losses…" he closes his eyes and sighs. "Yes, I understand. Thank you, Miss Kaetaal."

"Now, as for the response, I'll vid-mail this document to you in just a moment. But here it is. Due to Miss Ta'yeen's many statements and accusations, as well as her clear examples in practice, and the large support base she has accumulated thus far, there are now multiple legal investigations taking place by various security offices and law firms that are intensely reviewing the Charter of Laws for these deceptive statements. In the meantime, she is being exonerated of any wrongdoing, such as for making public disturbances or other rebellious movements, until such time as one or more of these can be verified by independent sources. If, in fact, she should be found guilty of anything, the law enforcement services will take their actions according to the appropriate legal mandates. However, if she is correct in her claims, she will be vindicated, and those same security forces and law firms will more likely take to her side for the next rally. The Council and its Charter of Laws will be declared invalid, their authority dismissed, and the world will essentially demand a replacement."

"Wow," the Captain croons. "Now there's a statement. I wonder how many windows he'll break on this occasion," he grins.

"Didn't he just get the last one repaired recently?" Geilv smirks.

✦✦✦

On home vid-coms everywhere, a new cartoon show was becoming popular with children and adults alike. It featured that same lovable Eracyodine figure that had been making its arrival on the scene in advertising, but now granted its own time slot for an entertainment series.

Era the Wise was an educational entertainment show featuring a mother Eracyodine and her family solving the problems of a changing world. The family was part of a Stone Age tribe just starting out, and having to conquer such issues as providing food, building homes, making tools, and later to discover such things as fire, the wheel, and constructing simple machines to aid in their work.

> *"Era!" shouts a young child. "Look what I found. These two rocks, if I hit them together, I see little flashes of fire!"*

> *"Let me see that," the mother replies. "Ooh! What if we bring them close to this dry grass over here..." they trot over to a fire pit filled with twigs and brush. "Now let's try it. Hit them close to the grass."*

The two of them strike the flint rocks together to create a series of sparks, catching the dry grass on fire.

> *"It worked!" he shouts. "Oh Era, the Creator will be so pleased with us. He gave us the power to understand fire, and now we can make it on our own!"*

> *"And I think this will allow us to make many more things. But for now, it's time to eat!"*

In the WIC building, Kaliya and Ayene were giving their most recent report, along with a sample video on the terminal situated at the far end of the table.

"I love this idea, Ayene," Kaliya grins. "This has to be one of our better achievements, if only for the positive contribution it offers."

"Yes, it is," Ayene smiles. "Initially, the hard part was to find sponsors, so I established that new company and put a few of our people to work for us. Then, once we got our sponsors and collected a bit of funding, we began assembling the pieces for the actual show, including the airtime."

"And for this," Thaelyn submits. "You made a deal with that CPComm to grant you some privilege, correct?"

"Yeah, they're a major entertainment company, and our work with them in recent times has opened a few doors."

"It must be nice to have friends like that," Kailen notes.

"Indeed," Thaelyn accedes contentedly. "It is good to have people on the inside who can offer such assistance. Especially if they have contacts that can offer further assistance in those areas we are not as specialized in. It is actually moments like these that bring me the greatest pleasure."

"We had to recruit quite a few people for this," Ayene admits, "including the idea machines for the episode storylines. You're not going to find too many of those on Azgarén, not with those chips installed. Our vid-com programs are exceptionally dull, so we hired a few local people here, including the Daanen-Aryku for the technical detail and voice acting, and from Tae'Eladar for the artistic and cultural aspects."

"And this further demonstrates my point for an example of cooperation between people of different cultures working to solve a common problem. There is great strength to be found here, and this is precisely how I brought the kingdom together in those early days. You do me a great service by once again exemplifying these same qualities."

Ayene and the others felt a warm sense of accomplishment at the suggestion.

"We're also borrowing from Latena's friend for this idea of the Creator image, that old religion they once had."

"A little cultural review, perhaps?"

"Yes, this is a little rub in the face," she smiles brightly. "Not that I would expect him to watch cartoons, though."

"Indeed!" he chuckles. "But this is certainly a good play, and I suppose you are opening up another hook of some kind when you release the true details of your history."

"Yeah, and then we'll see horns fly."

✦✦✦✦✦

Another month passes by, and Latena's rallies are stirring up the science factions for the implications of deposing the old government body they've been using for so long. The Director found himself offering a little of his own support where his fellow colleagues were concerned.

"Director," the Professor argues. "How am I supposed to interpret that young lady and her protests? We've been using this form of government, and doing quite well with it…um, well, at least until the Marshal came in and…"

"Professor," he interjects. "Regardless of the Marshal, our system of government is atypical of anything normal. If you listen to Miss Ta'yeen, you'll notice that if it were not for this dictatorial control mechanism, we might have far more flexibility to find our own studies outside of someone telling us what to do and when to do it. I am actually aware, from a visit I made with our friends out there, that their form of government, as one example, leads them to great discoveries and rapid advance, and with few or no restrictions outside what might be reasonable for the population to grow into what they have before moving on to the next step."

"And what sort of government is that?"

"Theirs is actually a modified form of monarchy, with an elected civilian parliament, and all of it…well, except for the royal family, being composed of politicians doing the actual political work. Their leaders are truly inspirational, and the examples I saw in those people I met told me they have found ways to overcome their limits using some rather ingenious methods. They also have a form of religion that associates with this other god society, which sometimes offers guidance and a sense of purpose that rises above our own values. So, if we compare this to ours, they'll run circles around us before we can even pull our horns into place. And that's in the best of conditions for our side."

"Wow! Then what are you actually suggesting with this movement? Are we supposed to take up sides with it and demand a new government?"

"If the Council is already dead, we are missing that much even now. And if the Marshal is actually the one in control, it is for his own reasons, not ours. This much needs to be corrected, at the very least, and preferably away from his own design work, as it seems engineered to serve his needs. So, this would be my best advice, and I am technically siding with them already. I am aware that the ACI is currently directing a number of independent services, like legal experts and security officials, to conduct a review of the Charter. And so far, they're discovering what could easily be interpreted as hidden agendas in the wording. They're now cross-referencing this with historic examples of when this might have come into actual play, and building a list of offences along the way. It's not looking good for the Council OR the Charter at this point, so you might want to get on the bandwagon for a change. I think we are heading for a historic occasion in our world."

"A historic occasion, but it sounds a little frightening too. We might not know how to manage things until it settles again. This could create turmoil in our society if we lose all control of law and security."

"I think our friends out there will offer their help along the way, so while I might feel as you do for the implications, whatever Darumon did to us, it was only for his plans of revenge against his enemies, none of whom we were ever intended to know about. Therefore, I would be in favor of throwing everything out and starting over from scratch."

"That's a big step, Director, but I suppose I can't argue with it. We became his puppets right after we became his children. How horrible..." she sighs. "Then I'll spread the word on this side, and we'll add our support to it. And let's hope we can eventually find our true salvation."

"Very good, Professor, and try to share this with as many others as you can who may also contribute into it. We want as many people involved as possible. He can't possibly stop a full planetary revolution. And if he should try it, he'll find himself massively outnumbered. I doubt even HE could fight something like that. And even if he did, we would all know where it's coming from by that time."

They end the link and the Director glances around the room, and then out the window. From his office, he could just barely catch a glimpse of the tall black tower that was Sargeras's sanctuary building.

"And as for you," he mumbles under his breath. "You should be feeling a pinch coming up soon."

He turns to find his vid-com again and calls up Azina.

"Intern Nur'ten here," she answers pleasantly.

"Azina, how is our progress coming along for the inhibitor drug?"

"We're dividing it between the removal treatments and stockpiling it for our general distribution. They tell me they have a partial production on Ruuki uy'Daan with that new farming enclosure. It's ramping up slow but steady, and with new sections being added to extend it further."

"That's good to hear, but we still have a lot of people out there. According to my numbers, we're processing thousands each day throughout the world, and it seems the numbers are growing slowly, which is good. But I just had a recent visit from the Captain. She's settling on a final objective with a timeline attached. Here is where things start getting tricky for us. We have just under a year before they hit."

"Wow, so that means we need to push this drug to the people and have them fully supplied soon. All right, I'll put a priority on the packaging side for general distribution. All they need is one dose, but the timing issue is what worries me.”

Kaliya was in another meeting with Thaelyn in the WIC building.

“…And so, here we are. Last month, when the Marshal went wild over that revelation that his lovely law enforcement wasn’t working as he desired, he was also griping over his regulators again. Well, it’s time to relieve him of that worry as well,” she smiles innocently.

“To relieve…” Thaelyn muses. “I like how she uses that term. Is it not such a quaint suggestion, General?”

“Indeed, my Lord,” he grins. “It almost makes you think she cares for him.”

“This one is coming up real soon,” Kaliya offers. “The science factions are getting involved with the rallies now, and this is an important step for us. This will allow us to finally throw in the revelation of the Eracyodines. But first, we’ll let it build a little. After all, from the time they went off Council direction to the time they got the idea to do this work, then to get a result…well…” she shrugs. “Meanwhile, the Council is losing authority…at least in theory, and so will be the last pieces of their machinations, including those regulators. And here is where we start opening ourselves up a bit,” she snickers.

“Uh oh…” Kailen moans. “I feel another news scandal coming.”

“We won’t give our name just yet, but enough of a hint to say there is…someone…out there doing some background work that does NOT serve the Council or the Marshal. And that someone is tearing things apart.”

“If the term, to pull one’s horns out, could apply to the Marshal, he’ll be making a really big mess soon.”

“You should see his office lately,” she winces. “To say nothing of the roadway down below…”

Over the coming weeks, the world was turning upside-down for all the protests as more people joined in, now involving many top officials relating to the science factions. Ileani was preparing for her latest broadcast to report on this.

"This is Ileani Ur'paran for C.P. News. A world in turmoil, this is how people are describing the situation outside and around the globe. Laboratories are going on strike, scientists are turning to dissidents, and researchers are joining the rally lines that have taken on a life of their own. It all comes down to the message being portrayed by the speakers of these protests claiming the Charter of Laws restricts the freedom of the public to progress forward, and the Council withholds research it otherwise desires for its own use."

The report now turns to a recorded press clip with an agitated female speaker.

"The science factions of the world are no longer going to serve the Council's whims! We have minds of our own and we are surely capable of making our own decisions on what to research and when to research it! If the Council wants to regulate anything, they can regulate their own tail-wagging."

The scene returns to Ileani in the newsroom.

"As always, the Council has no statements to offer to justify its actions, and neither to excuse its long absence. The traditional spokesperson that used to represent the Council has apparently been arrested as part of the election fraud scandal, and we at CPComm have recently been released from a long-standing security restriction imposed by a highly secretive planetary security agency. The restriction relates to a group of regulators that had been stationed in our offices since the time of the old war protocols and the Tav'ageen Scare.

These regulators, which were originally mandated by the Council to control the flow of sensational news that once caused the world to go into a panic over the Tav'ageen Anomaly, were recently arrested and removed, not only in our station, but globally throughout each major news media outlet. We are further aware that a contact that linked this chain, the public relations officer inside the Council Grand Hall building, was similarly arrested as part of a sting operation where they were found to be delivering false media releases and other alleged violations of Article Nine, Section Fourteen of the Charter of Laws.

However, this Article, which relates to the Truth in Reporting Act of 3752, has been carefully reviewed and found to contain clauses that provide for the Council to impose a form of override authority on our media services. Security officials are now suggesting this is yet another example of a hidden motive to prevent the free flow of information to the public, regardless of its sensational nature, and therefore preventing that which may hold critical importance to inform the public of the true nature of events in the world around us.

Needless to say, once this began to leak out, there was a renewed fervor amongst protesters over yet another scandal caused by the Council, and this seems to be adding new fuel to the already heated opposition. Rally attendants are demanding an immediate response from the Council to answer for these violations, despite whatever deliberation they are conducting or how sensitive it might be. As one protester was heard to say, 'There is simply no excuse for the Council to treat our population this way as to feed us false information while they take all the good stuff.'"

Once again, in Central Command, the officers heard, and in some cases felt, the monstrous wails echoing through the building. Commander Geilv stopped his work to listen, feeling a tender sense of mischief as he pondered what could be the cause on this occasion. But rather than hearing just one long wail, this one seemed broken up into several shorter ones, and further it was interspaced with what sounded like muted thumping noises. And so, he called up the Captain on his com-link to inquire what he had to say.

"Control, Captain Ta'yeen."

"Captain, what am I hearing out there? It sounds like something hitting something."

"Yes, Commander, I'm currently in contact with some of our ground crew out there, and I have another officer calling in to the Lounge again. It would seem the Marshal is going berserk this time. We have people outside reporting him screaming, and apparently tossing pieces of furniture out the window. One moment..."

The Captain held the conversation as he listened to another officer reporting from the Lounge attendant.

"Sir, I just got word from the Lounge. It would seem the ACI is opening the door a little. They just revealed their presence, but only enough to say they're out there, and that they arrested those regulators for broadcasting false news in the media stream."

"So, one of the Marshal's toys has just been broken," he smiles.

"And that, combined with the fact that the whole world is turning against his pet Council. None of the science factions are listening to them by now."

"Yes, that'll do it. But if they're letting this out, they must be planning something big soon."

"I don't know, Sir, but these are becoming interesting times."

✦

Ayene was visiting CPComm again to meet with Ileani in her office. It has been roughly two and a half months since Latena's now-famous interview, and it was time to release a new sensation.

"You know, Ayene," Ileani begins. "If I should ever survive this moment of our history, I think I should earn an award for my acting performance. So, what do you have this time?"

"Another horn-puller, so be ready for it."

"A horn-puller, all right," she takes a deep breath. "Go…"

"A couple of years ago or so, we had the Director of the ARC call a very quiet symposium of his fellow scientists."

"Wait a moment, a symposium… Would this relate in any way to that construction work out in the Bintavyan Valley?"

"Indirectly, yes. The real reason was in part to share some of these stories privately. Another was to begin a secret research project we had them perform for us to find evidence of something we believe had been hidden from us since the beginning of…well, however long it's been that we were trying to research this particular item."

"Um, all right, and is this where I start pulling my horns out?"

"Yes, it is, so make sure you have your spares ready," she grins.

"Yes, thank you, I believe I have a set in the drawer here. So, what was it you were trying to research that has been hidden away all this time, and should I ask who it was hiding it, as well?"

"We suspect it was Darumon hiding it, and for good reason. Let me first ask, have you checked on that new cartoon, Era the Wise?"

"Yes, I did, actually. It's really cute. But I'm wondering where a planetary security agency comes off producing a children's cartoon."

"Oh, we're a comprehensive service, Ileani," she smiles. "It carries a couple of messages inside, so it's not only for entertainment; it's also for education, a little like a hidden history lesson of our early beginnings."

"Oh dear, I'm starting to feel tingles in my horns now."

"Once upon a time, our early ancestors apparently worshipped a deity they called the Creator. Like Latena said, this entity, sometimes called the father of our race, presumably lifted us out of the dirt... well, figuratively, and gave us minds in which to think, to grow, and to develop into a sophisticated society...eventually. This is a history lesson to play on our ancestral origins, meaning the Eracyodines as they evolved into something higher."

"And those tingles just got stronger."

"Yeah, and we're not done yet. Coincidentally, this is where our race name comes from, in case you ever wondered...Suuden-Aryku."

"Really! Now that is something I didn't know. I sometimes wondered about that, and simply figured someone labeled us that way for our pursuit of knowledge."

"No, this goes way back. Now, recall what Latena said about missing evidence and falsified reports. This symposium was to confirm a suspicion that was brought forward by a statement we received from this one individual who has apparently been watching Sargeras and Darumon ever since they went into hiding. She says Darumon came here once and apparently modified our ancient ancestors to create us. So, the Creator is Darumon."

"And there they go..." she mourns and hangs her head.

"And I'm sorry to say, there is one more piece I need to lay on you. We're related to him. He actually is our father."

Ileani turns away and visibly shudders, as she leans on her desk and begins whimpering. Ayene gently lays a hand on her shoulder to comfort her, patting her reassuringly.

"Ileani, none of us like the idea, but we also inherited something from him."

"Inherited?" she whines. "What?"

"Well, one thing that becomes immediately obvious is our life spans. That most unusual thing that differentiates us from everything else in our world."

"All right, that's not too bad...I suppose."

"You can also see it in our bone structure, from what I understand of the medical or biological side of it."

"Yes, although this isn't my specialty, but I am aware of this."

"There's more, but this now becomes the domain of Elder Nazég and his faction. Darumon is nearly a god figure, and we're half of that, but I don't think I want to burden you with too much all at once. So, we should probably leave the rest for later," she smiles softly.

"In other words, you want to leave something for my next set of horns. I really think I hate you," she attempts a partial smile. "So, how did he do it? Or do I even want to know."

"He was outside his natural element, meaning to say his native home where he might have all his usual tools to work with. So, he had to resort to the most primal method he had available. From that, we became a hybrid of Eracyodine and Darumon."

"Right, that's what I was afraid of, and it doesn't help my horns any. It also paints a rather unorthodox, if also obscene picture of him doing it with an animal."

"I know. And once the initial shock passes, we'll be letting out a few more secrets he didn't want anyone to know about, and also relating to Elder Nazég. So, make sure you have a few extra sets of horns available."

"All right, point taken. I swear, for all he did to us, I think I'll retire when this is done. So, how are you suggesting we do this, the usual way with a few careful scripts and a couple of speakers?"

"Yeah, but we can't point our fingers directly at him. We just want him to know we finally figured it out, so all his attempts to hide it from us in the past are now out, and there's nothing else he can do about it."

"I'm wondering, this mean streak of yours, is it contagious?"

"Only if you spend a lot of time with me in close proximity," she grins.

✦✦✦✦✦

Ileani was preparing her latest and greatest world-shattering sensation. As always, the set coordinator called out the count, and the cameras began rolling.

> *"This is Ileani Ur'paran for C.P. News. In today's groundbreaking headline, the long-standing controversy within the archeological faction has finally been resolved! This debate, which has confounded scientists for hundreds of millennia, and raised one salvo of volatile questions after another, but never once demonstrating a satisfactory level of empirical data to qualify any of these results, has finally been broken.*

At the same time, this also seems to validate Miss Latena Ta'yeen's statements of missing evidence and falsified reports from all those earlier attempts to resolve this issue. And this has further prompted the science community to once again protest the Council's authoritarian practices and their attempts to feed us their fabricated romances.

In a recent press release, a representative for a leading research institute came forward with this astonishing new finding."

The video now changes to a prerecorded press conference with a female professional, who also happened to be the Director's personal friend.

"My name is Professor Tireen Nad' livan, Senior Coordinator of the Brym Yitan Research Institute of Archaeological Studies. For as long as we have asked the question of the origin of our species, we have searched for clues in the fossil record to identify where we came from and how our species climbed the long ladder from the earliest ancestors to where we are today. But to so much of our frustration, our past efforts always resulted in inconsistencies of data and a timeline that simply did not compare favorably with any other species of life in our world. There have always been missing elements and unsatisfactory comparisons between ours and others over how we came to be who we are, and how our biology differs from anything else around us. And every time we tried to revise our findings; it seemed that something was getting in our way of a rational result. At least, that is, until finally the Council simply forbade any future research on the subject. Yes, people, I said they forbade it, as if to say, 'No more, we have all that we want out of it.'

But since the time of these revelations with the Council, the Charter of Laws, and the controversies relating to this deceptive conspiracy, and further to include those statements by that young Miss Ta'yeen, during that one interview of hers, we began to seek our own direction of study, regardless of what the Council may, or more often, may not allow us to have. The recent mention of that cartoon, Era the Wise, brought some of us back to this Age-Old question, and now that we have liberated ourselves from the grip of the Council's prohibiting manners, we decided to revisit the study to see if perhaps THIS time we could find our answers. And we did. But the answers we found are very troubling, and they suggest this deception may run very deep as to what someone…somewhere…was trying to hide from us.

As many of you probably know from the history lessons given in our schools, the Eracyodines can be divided into two groups, what we refer to as the Classic form, meaning the pre-transitional species, and the Modernized form, which is the post-transitional one. All our previous attempts to define our origin as a species led us to the same conclusion, where the transition occurred approximately half a million years before our earliest records of civilization. And as you all know, our civilization is measured at about two million years. Also, during this period, which we sometimes refer to as the transitional phase, we have a time offset of roughly fifty thousand years between these two species. This was suggested to be the period of our extraordinary evolutionary leap from one to the other, thus bringing us into the age where we could move forward as a dawning form of sentient life now on the path of enlightenment. Well, it is no more.

The recent study, which began at our institute, but quickly spread to other facilities, not only to find additional opinions, but also additional technologies to interpret our findings, led us to a truly shocking, as well as an extremely disparaging result. Not only has that transitional period vanished completely, but the original calculations for the timeline were off by a couple orders of magnitude. I cannot be sure who made this error, or if it was indeed an error or rather a secret attempt to hide something, but our findings have turned our origin as a species completely inside-out.

What we have found, and this time verified with reasonable confidence, as we compared to other species in our world, is that the Classic Eracyodine and the Modernized form were virtually side-by-side in our evolutionary past. We even sent expeditions into the field to verify our fossil evidence with fresh examples, and found the Classic form laid to rest in ritual burials with Stone Age tools resembling those from the Modernized form. There can be no viable explanation why a member of a species fifty millennia offset would bury an ancient ancestor with its personal treasures, UNLESS that ancestor came just before the individual as a direct parental figure. And when we counted our dating methods again, we found this did NOT occur five hundred millennia before our earliest recorded civilization, but rather only...FIVE millennia...before we first invented writing."

An ushering of voices from the press conference began welling up vigorously in the background as she continued.

"We further examined the fossils to discover the Classic form may have had an average lifespan of perhaps half a century at best, but the Modernized form displayed the telltale ring structure we see in our modern-day bones, and those rings counted a lifespan several times that number, and then growing at an alarming rate, almost approaching an exponential factor over the following generations, until we eventually arrived at our current figures, where it seems to have leveled off. And we have remained this way for most of our history."

A voice from one of the press agents rises up.

"Professor, just what sort of results are we speaking of here that can give these kinds of figures?"

"The figures we are speaking of here suggest there was a sudden, virtually instantaneous transition from the Classic form to the Modernized one, meaning to say, the last Classic example was the parent of the first Modernized example. Now, according to what we understand of evolution, and judging from every other example of life we have in our world, this pattern follows a slow and predictable path. But ours made a very serious turn, and it could not have been natural. Something external entered into the equation to deliberately alter our ancestors. It changed our bone structure, and also our potential longevity, as we refined ourselves over those following generations. I can only guess what else it did to us that we are not even aware of yet.

My friends and fellow citizens, I am sorry to inform you, but it would seem someone or something from outside our world likely interfered with our natural evolution and altered our species. This may also reflect on that old religion of the Creator, as it would seem someone held a memory of this. But it cannot be a benevolent one if they further interfered with our ability to realize this at an earlier moment as we tried asking our questions. Which means, whoever it was has been with us for a very, very long time. And with the

Council ultimately denying us this continued research, I might also suggest they knew."

Once again, in Central Command, in the officer's lounge, Commander Geilv and Captain Ta'yeen were taking a break to watch this latest clip.

"In all the nether-space," the Captain wheezes. "Commander! Are we actually saying...?"

Geilv was turning pale as he watched the monitor. He rotated slowly to face the Captain, and simply gazed at him in a moment of silence.

"That monster..." he whispers. "No wonder he likes to control us. He made us!"

"And by the sound of it, he wants to keep us as his pets."

At this moment, another tumultuous shrieking echoed through the building, along with more sounds of thumping and crashing. The two of them sprang up and launched out of the room towards the control booth. On their arrival, they found the resident crew on the com-links with the ground personnel as the scene outside was turning chaotic. People were running in all directions, but mostly away from the Marshal's office next door.

"What's happening?" Geilv asks hurriedly.

"Sir, I have someone on the line. He's telling me the Marshal is going wild out there. He's seeing pieces of material flying out of the Marshal's window, including wall fragments...um, a door...a cabinet... no, two cabinets now...um, and now a sink..."

"So, he got everything, including the sink," he chuckles. "Sounds like he ran out of furniture, and now he's tearing up the building. All right, have our people keep clear of the area until things settle...if they ever do at this point. I don't know if I want to go back to my office, but I suppose he might be making one of his famous calls soon to rant about something."

Chapter 10

YTANI RETURNS

It had been a month since the last sensation, and the revelation of their evolutionary tampering was still reverberating in some circles. Several science factions had taken up speculation of what else might be evident in their artificial evolution, and a series of new examinations were underway to compare their genomes with any known exobiology studies, hoping to identify the source of their hybridization effect.

Back on Therinë, Kaliya was in a final prelaunch meeting with Thaelyn and his officers in the WIC building.

"This is it!" she announces. "The beginning of the end…"

"I'm not so sure if I like the way you say that…" Kailen winces.

"Well, it is, in a very real sense of it. This is what we've been building up to, and now it's ready."

"I'm aware that Marelle has been training her team rather vigorously lately," Ayene offers. "She's up to two flights now, and we're expecting the third to be ready in several more months, which puts us on schedule."

"We should be sure of this," Thaelyn asserts. "I do not want to push our people, only to see them make mistakes at a critical moment."

"Absolutely! We're checking and double-checking everything. We'll be ready for it. We also have that carry-all coming close to completion. But we're going to need someone to Captain it. Do we have any suggestions?"

"At this moment, I am actually thinking of Marelle again. I recall that mention once by Adalon of the two of them sharing some sort of moment together, and I suspect this is the one. Furthermore, she has most certainly earned it, for all she has done for us. She has almost single-handedly pioneered space travel for our society. I would like to see her moved to a position to carry us even beyond this point, once everything else is complete. This would make for a fine career for her after the war."

"Industrial Age…with space flight," Kailen shakes his head. "I think I'll need to retire after this."

"Well…" Ayene shrugs. "She is certainly a good choice for it. All right, so once it's ready, we'll need to give her a few crash lessons," she grins.

"You know," Kailen grimaces even more. "You make it sound even worse than this girl," he thumbs at Kaliya.

The group erupts in a quick laugh together.

"This next week," Kaliya submits. "I'll start my initial flights around C.P. as that creature. I'll make a few circles, just to see the sights, and then disappear somewhere. I'll need to make a few of these over the course of the week, to ensure we get the coverage. Then we put on our show with Ileani. I just hope her horns can take it."

"By this time," Thaelyn moans. "I would imagine her to be in a much-weakened state after all your other antics. Just remember, we would like her to join with us on that final day, so we need to leave something standing until then."

"She's handling it so far. But all these revelations don't leave you a lot of room to breathe. Darumon really fouled things up for those people. But except for the final play, this should amount to the last of the major hits, and Ayene did lay a small hint on her the last time they met."

"Good, but a small hint as opposed to what you and that mischievous young Miss Ta'yeen conjured up, are two entirely different prospects."

"Well, all right, so the term is subjective," she smirks.

Over the course of the following week, the extended circadian cycles of Azgarén saw the beginnings of daytime arising. This would be the time for Kaliya to make her first presentation, as she wanted broad daylight in order to be seen prominently in the skies over the city.

In the skies above Capitol Prime, soaring gracefully above the rooftops, a strange creature makes its appearance. No one notices it at first, being so high above the ground. Not even the elevated lanes of hover traffic took notice, as their eyes were directed on their travels. It makes several circles, eyeing the movement of people and vehicles below, before deciding to descend lower, passing between some of the taller buildings.

Inside one of the tall office towers, the workers sit at their desks attending to their daily accounting and management work. A row of secretaries was lined up in their cubicles along the window and focused intently on their assignments. Then they thought they saw the flash of something big pass by outside. They impulsively turned to see what it was, but it had already moved out of view. So, they simply returned to their work, shrugging it off and assuming it was a hover shuttle, probably a security vehicle making a patrol.

The creature circles between several buildings, until finally it gains the attention of those inside, this time with someone catching a clear glimpse of it as it moved away.

"What is that?" calls one office worker. "Look there!"

Several other workers quickly turned to see the tail end of the creature as it sailed off further along the avenue.

Moving above the street level was a lane of hover shuttles, common traffic in a flow moving through the city at altitude. The creature turns and dives through the lane, forcing some of the vehicles to take sudden evasive action to avoid a collision. It then twists and circles a corkscrew around several other vehicles before descending further, then ducking around another building.

It makes a circle around a city block and back towards the main avenue running through the heart of the city, diving low this time, and letting out a loud shriek.

The vehicles on the ground swerved, and pedestrians on the sidewalks turned to find the source of the sound. It was large, almost the size of a small passenger vehicle, with leathery skin decorated in mottled green and brown spots. It had two legs in the rear with amphibian-like sucker feet, broad wings, and an elongated head with a wide frog-like snout, seemingly toothless and with large eyes.

It glided over the scene placidly, not making any aggressive moves, simply passing through, flapping its wings as it made its way over a substantial segment of the road, then picking up altitude and veering off, eventually to disappear from the city.

✦✦◆✦✦

"Ghantil!" Azina shouts as she enters his office in a flurry of giggles. "Did you see the news earlier? Mysterious creature is sighted over the city…scientists are baffled. Is it a new species, or some research project that got loose into the wild?"

"Yes, that was good for a few laughs. I've already been in contact with a few of my colleagues informing them to remain calm. We'll see how this plays out, but it should make life a little more interesting for us around here."

"A little MORE interesting? In all the nether-space, how much more can people take?"

Over the next several days, Kaliya made more appearances similar to the first, where she was simply flying around the city. More people were paying attention to the skies now, and she was sighted on numerous occasions. On some of her appearances, she found herself being followed by the city security patrols. They did not make any aggressive moves, instead just keeping a cautious distance and appearing to be watching her, and probably recording her on video.

In the news, Ileani was preparing another of her reports.

> *"This is Ileani Ur'paran for C.P. News. In today's report, we have another sighting of that strange lifeform that has been spotted flying over the city recently…"*

The news feed changes to a prerecorded video clip of Kaliya's animal image in flight.

> *"C.P. Security provided us with this video as they observed the creature from a safe distance. So far, scientists and zoologists are still baffled as to the origin of this entity, as there is no recorded example of species known to us in our world to match this description. This leaves some to suggest it to be a genetically altered specimen that somehow escaped from the laboratory. But no lab has officially come forward to claim responsibility for this mishap, and this leaves a few to speculate whether it might hold extraplanetary origins."*

The video now returns to the studio.

> *"In other news, an official spokesperson is finally coming forward to offer a long-overdue explanation of the curious activity occurring on our streets of what appears to be a series of siren horns and alert signals being erected throughout each of our major cities, and with more of them being installed in smaller cities and towns around the*

world. Join with us tomorrow as we host a live interview with a security specialist who will explain this new technology network and how it will affect our world population."

The next day, now inside the Vaanil Esluna tower in downtown Capitol Prime, Kaliya, Ayene, and Navina, along with Latena, and Ileani and her news team, were convening for a pre-broadcast meeting.

"Ileani," Kaliya smiles gently. "How do your horns feel today?"

"When I woke up," she mutters. "They were fine, but that's quickly changing by now. What do you have in mind for me this time…horn-pulling or tail-yanking…or maybe a little of both?"

"A little of both, so bear with us and we'll explain what we have in mind. But Ileani, this one will hit hard."

"Hard…all right," she sighs. "At least you're giving me fair warning this time. What is it?"

"First, Ayene is going to play a military Captain who's been working with Central Command on a new security revamp. As part of this, she's been working with High Commander Geilv on installing that siren network out there everybody's been talking about recently."

"Is this for real or just a story?

"Real. The HC does know her as a military Captain, but at the same time, he's recently come to realize, through a little of his own deduction, that she's probably with the ACI. He's a clever man."

"All right, good. So, she'll play this role, and through this role reveal to us what this new network is about."

"Right. Central has a legitimate worry, and therefore the network is a precautionary step."

"A legitimate worry? Uh oh. Does this relate to the Marshal's fake insurgents?"

"Actually, no, it relates to someone who was working for him once, but presumably defected."

"Defected! Oops!"

"Now, this next part is for you, and you alone. Remember, this is an important element we need to paint a picture of, but it needs to come in steps."

"Yeah…and I'm getting flashbacks of the Grand Hall now."

"Oh, Ileani, this is what makes life so interesting around here."

"And you think I like this level of interesting?" she grins.

"Yes, you love it, and you know it."

The group exchanges a soft round of laughter, trying to keep it down in the setting of the busy observation deck.

"Now, we have Latena again..."

"Yeah, and I'm wondering what she's going to do this time. She almost started a riot after our last broadcast."

"Yes, well, she's playing a sweet young girl who's just trying to get along this time."

"Sweet young girl? Her?" she snaps. "Getting along? I doubt it! This little tyke must be a serious burr for her mother. All right, what's she supposed to be doing?"

"She's simply visiting this nice luxurious observation deck, with all these high-level businessmen that would make very good campaign targets for her rally. So, she'll be passing out fliers."

"Uh huh. So simple and innocent..."

"Well, up to a point."

"Yeah...up to a point."

"Navina," Kaliya directs. "You're the cue to send her off. You'll be watching me on the other side, and when I make my move, you'll fold over here and give her the word."

"Yes, Captain," she affirms.

"Fold?" Ileani wonders.

"Yeah...fold," Kaliya admits. "This is the part that's going to hurt. Latena already knows. But, um, Ileani, I might just want you to remain as you are for that first impression effect...you know, the horns flying off," she smiles innocently.

"Right. You know, between you and Ayene, I'm not sure which of you I hate more."

"What if I treat you to something sweet afterwards? Do we have any nice little cafés nearby?"

"Actually, yes. I'm familiar with a really expensive one," she grins gently.

"Great! As a reward for your service, and a little payback for all the times we sent your horns flying, I'll treat you to something nice to smooth over all these feelings."

"All right, I'll accept that."

"But now, what's most important is to keep that camera rolling and catch all of it. This is why we're doing it live, to make sure the people take notice. We're going to make a new sensation of the millennium here, and this is going to inflate to something that'll blow the rest of it to nether-space."

"Wow, you sure like to talk big. As if we needed any more of those, after the last one."

"They tend to tie together after a while. All these little pieces will fall into place as we follow up later."

"Uh huh, sure..." she sighs. "All right, I'll do my best to act like I have no idea what you're talking about...because I don't," she chuckles.

"Good. So, I'm going to move over here, out of the way. Just pretend like I don't exist. You and Ayene will orient with that bridge in the background..." she points at a channel leading out across the skywalk. "Latena, you have your fliers, so you'll move to that corridor across the way, like you're coming through it, and when Navina flashes you the signal, you come out to introduce yourself and pass around a few here and there."

"Yes Ma'am!" she nods eagerly.

"And everyone...action!" she grins and waves her hands theatrically while backing away.

Ileani smiles and shakes her head humorously as she prepares to call in to her office.

"CPComm, this is Ileani. We're ready on this side. We need to make this one count. I don't know what sort of tricks these people are playing this time, but this shot needs to be historic, got it?"

"Yes, Ileani, we are with you. We are setting ourselves up now. Going live in three, two, one..."

Inside Central Command, Captain Ta'yeen and Commander Geilv were once again taking a break in the officer's lounge. Ayene had contacted Geilv earlier to ensure he was present on this occasion, as he needed to be as much a witness as anyone for this event. As for the Captain, well, he would result as collateral damage when he saw the acting crew. They both turned their attention to the local vid-com as the broadcast began.

> *"This is Ileani Ur'paran for C.P. News, currently live on the observation deck of the Vaanil Esluna building in beautiful downtown Capitol Prime. With me today is Captain Ayene Ti'van of the*

Azgarén military Security Protocols Division. A pleasant greeting to you, Captain."

"And a pleasant greeting to you too, Miss Ur'paran."

In the officer's lounge, Geilv and the Captain glared at the scene. "Her again!" Geilv mumbles. "All right, they're active again. Watch out, Captain, there's not much left of that building next door."

"Captain, I am aware that there have been a number of inquiries in recent months relating to this new network of towers being installed throughout the city, and in fact this same scene is being observed in every other major city around the world, plus their associated suburban areas and many towns. This is a massive undertaking, but what does it all mean?"

"Miss Ur'paran," Ayene replies. "The Azgarén military is dedicated to safeguarding the health and welfare of the people of the world from all forms of potential harm, and this includes anything that might offend us from foreign sources. When we reflect on our long battle against these insurgents the Marshal brought to us, even though I recall it being said that they never arrived on our own shores to threaten us personally, we realize that there is still the potential that they, or perhaps some as yet unknown body, may actually attempt this. And what surprises us is that at no time during this period has any effort been made to ensure the local safety of the people from a possible attack."

"So, is this purely a precautionary step to ensure the safety of the people in the, hopefully, unlikely event that there may ever be such an occasion?"

"Naturally, we feel this is important, and further that it may be overdue. Therefore, we are taking the initiative to see to this while we have this opportunity of calmness. The clear and evident long duration of these insurgents, and the seeming lack of their progress, has caused a few of us to wonder if there may be a hidden purpose, perhaps in the form of a covert effort to distract us with these losses while they plan something else."

"This sounds like it could be a serious issue. And it's also giving me this strange feeling that maybe you know of something, if only due to the reason that NOW you choose to make these changes, rather than

*at any moment in the past. Did something change in recent times
to provoke this?"*

As Ayene engaged in her interview, Kaliya moved away quietly
to a nearby restroom, where she flashed away from the scene. She
reappeared on a rooftop several buildings away and transformed into
her new alien creature image. From there, she leapt off the edge of the
building and began flying gracefully along the avenues, making sure
she could be seen vividly by people on the ground, in office buildings,
and the hover traffic in the elevated lanes.

She dove between buildings, letting out a series of loud squawks,
twisting and zooming in front of windows, as if simply to show off
her flamboyant acrobatics. Then, as she circled around one more tall
skyscraper, she saw a convenient landing spot. She arcs upward, flapping
to gain altitude, and slams against the sturdy glass windowpane, much
to the surprise and horror of a secretary inside her office cubicle.

The young woman screeched and jumped out of her seat, instantly
clutching at her interface for the heavy feedback she was receiving,
then anxiously backing away from the window as she observed the
huge alien creature peering in at her, like a tourist at a zoo studying
the caged specimens.

The creature gave the appearance of a huge amphibious lifeform
with sucker-like toes on the rear feet and cups on the inner wing joints,
a broad toothless mouth, and bulging eyes with vertical slits. It clung to
the outer surface of the glass, while the secretary, now joined by several
others in the room, glared at it from across the way.

Navina was also present in the room, having taken up an
inconspicuous disguise as part of a piece of wall art. She watched the
scene and made ready for her move once Kaliya made hers.

Time seemed to stand still for a moment as the office workers
exchanged glares with the creature, until it began to move again. It
angled its head into the glass window and began to press against it. The
office workers all gasped as they saw it attempting to break through.

"It will break the glass!" shouts one of them.

"How is it even holding on out there?" queries another.

But before they could make any assessments, the creature began to
seemingly pass through the glass without disturbing it, slowly emerging
inside the room as it hooked its claws on furniture and cubicle partitions
to pull itself along.

"That is impossible!" shrieks one of the workers, and they all began screaming as they ran out of the room.

Once Kaliya had fully penetrated through the window and onto the floor, Navina flashed away from her tiny perch and back to the other tower to give her cue. She arrived near to Latena, where the immediate area was clear of observers, and reimagined her image back to its normal shape.

"All right, Latena, it's time," she whispers to the girl.

Latena nods and casually saunters out onto the deck with her stack of fliers in hand, giving a few greetings to people as she hands them out. Ileani discreetly glanced around as she was listening to Ayene and took notice of the girl making her approach. She felt a cold shiver wriggling its way up her back as she tried to hold herself together for whatever new horrific surprise lay in wait. But while on this side of the bridge, things were quiet, with the only interesting activity being the interview; the other side was in chaos.

"RUN!" shrieks one of the office workers as she dashes through the other observation deck. "It came inside! It is behind us!"

A small army of Kaliya's people were present on that side, simply milling about in casual conversation. But when a flurry of frantic bodies came out of one of the offices, they all perked up. They turned to study the commotion, only to see a rush of people darting through the area, followed by Kaliya's alien image lumbering along. One lead man began running across the skywalk, gaining a head start while the rest began to file in behind him, and everyone screaming at the top of their lungs.

In the officer's lounge in Central Command, the Commander and the Captain sat quietly listening to the interview on the vid-com.

> *"Miss Ur'paran," Ayene responds calmly. "While I'm sure the sequence of recent events may have caused a number of sensations around us, what with protests, court trials, this new rally occurring out there, that recent news release…my goodness, that was a shocker…and so much of it seeming to lead us in some rather curious directions, I want to assure you that while it may appear as though something may have changed in recent times, we of the Azgarén military are quite confident in our position…"*

As she makes her statement, the first of the runners arrives on the scene, shrieking in terror as he emerges from the skywalk and rushing past Latena in the background, causing the poor girl to freeze her motions and jump back. The ruckus causes Ayene to halt her statement and turn reflexively to the noise as the man disappeared through the corridor at the far end.

"Now, that was curious indeed!" she notes conspicuously.

But before they could react further, the minor disturbance was soon followed by a much larger one, as an army of people began to pour into the room, all of them screaming and running in different directions. Ileani and her cameraman both turned to follow the unexpected surge with a growing sense of dread.

Latena found herself suddenly trapped in a rush of bodies flooding through the skywalk. She ducked and pulled her arms around her head, then seemed to stumble and fall to the ground.

In Central Command, the alarming scene drew the officers in the lounge closer to the monitor, when the Captain began to take notice of the girl's apparent identity.

"Latena?" he whispers.

"What is she doing there?" Geilv mutters. "And with Ti'van in the scene..."

The flow of panicked citizens eventually ran out, leaving Latena crouching on the floor, where she briefly pulled her head up, as if trying to gauge what just happened. But before she had enough time to assess her situation, a heavy galloping charged up behind her. Kaliya's alien creature had arrived.

The Captain gaped at the scene on the monitor, and Ileani gasped and fell back a step at the alien lifeform that had somehow found its way inside the building, and was now standing directly over Latena, who seemed frozen with fear.

The girl stiffly turned to look over her shoulder to see the oversized head peering straight down at her. She screamed and fell back, trying to scoot away on her haunches, but Kaliya's alien simply lunged at her to pin her in place.

"No!" the Captain screams at the monitor, but it seemed futile.

The young girl laid there motionless as Kaliya's alien seemed entranced by its immaculate catch.

"CPComm! This is Ileani!" she sputters. "I don't know what I'm looking at, but this looks like that...thing...we were getting reports of flying around the city lately. In all the nether-space, how did it get inside here! And that girl..."

At this moment, Kaliya's alien began surveying the surrounding sights, which had largely cleared out by now, except for Ileani and Ayene. When it spies the cameraman, it returns back to the girl and begins to deform its shape, reducing down to the size of a well-toned muscular young man wearing only a set of shorts.

"What in all the…" Ileani wheezes breathlessly.

Kaliya's Ytani image now hovered over the young girl as he gloated over her fine youthful body.

"Hey there sweet-hooves!" he announces lasciviously and with a slight reverberation to his voice for an enhanced effect. "I haven't seen you before. That's a fine-looking tail you've got there. Need any help carrying it around? I've got the touch that drives the girls wild!"

"Huh?" she shudders nervously. "Who are you? What are you! And how did you do that!"

"Oh, this little thing?" he laughs boldly. "It's just a little trick I once learned. It comes in handy on occasion. You'd be amazed at what I can do."

Now he turns back up to the camera.

"Ooh! Are we on video? I always wanted to be a star! Wait a minute, do I know you?" he directs at Ileani, and then stands up. "Yeah, you're that lady that does all the news stuff. Oh, this is great!" he boasts.

He now begins flaunting himself for the camera, taking in the glamor of his celebrity. He preens himself, and then flexes his muscular arms for a little showmanship. He then raises his hand and flutters his fingers in a childish wave.

"Hi Mom, hi Dad…" he offers in a juvenile voice, "…well, in theory, at least." Then he turns serious and grins malevolently. "Hello Marshal…" he announces wickedly. "Remember me? Of course you do. Ytani is the name."

He then bellows out a roar of maniacal laughter, displaying himself to the room in all directions.

In Central Command, both the Captain and the Commander perked up at the mention.

"It's him!" Geilv shouts and points assertively at the monitor.

Ytani regains himself briefly and glares at the camera again.

"Lose any secret mining bases lately?" he taunts with even more laughter. "And my goodness, Marshal, what WERE you doing on Madzurki? When I peeked inside that storeroom of yours on Ooduan, I found so many lovely, um… Well, I'm not sure what you call them, but WOW! Do they go boom in a big way! It's a good thing my friends suggested using a remote timer on that one we were testing. There wasn't anything left of the entire star system when it finished!"

He follows with another uproarious bellow of laughter which filled the room with an unnatural rumble.

"Oh, and by the way," he feigns with mocked tenderness. "It was so nice of you to provide that star cruiser. Such a lovely one, too!" he again grins maliciously. "It made such a wonderful going away present."

Once again, he emits another outburst of maniacal laughter.

In the officer's lounge of Central Command, the Captain glared at the scene.

"He's completely mad! Commander Kriv'tik wasn't joking about that!"

Ytani seemed to be enjoying his moment of fame in the spotlight. He panned his view across the full observation deck, even though it was mostly empty by now except for a few people peeking around corners.

"You know, Marshal," he reflects. "I had a lot of free time in that house you set up for me. And the job was so remarkably dull," he swipes his hand nonchalantly. "But this skill you taught me...oh, now THAT was interesting. But shame on you, that you didn't tell me just how much it can actually do. Were you holding out on me? Well, not to worry, because I'm trying all sorts of things now. I met some fascinating people, too. They have all this weird...stuff, and they have this thing that, um, well they go like this..." he tries fumbling a curious gesture with his hands. "I don't know how it works, but strange things happen. Maybe, one of these days, I'll have them teach me something. They say it goes along with some kind of weird energy stuff they have over there."

He pauses again to glance salaciously at the girl under his feet.

"Meanwhile, I'm back home, and oh it feels so good...well, except for this awful air you have here. But I suppose that's just how it goes. Maybe, once I get my palace built, I can order all my new minions to clean it up for me. After all, even a god-king needs to place to live!"

He begins another boisterous round of hearty laughter.

"Can you imagine it?" he roars. "Me, little Ytani, left all alone in that house, so far away from home...all grown up and now a GOD-KING!!" he thunders.

He now descends into an uproariously maniacal cackling which seemed to echo unnaturally throughout the building.

Back in the officer's lounge, the Commander shook his head at the scene.

"He's worse than mad, Captain. He's psychotic."

"Sir, I doubt even THAT would be enough to explain it."

When Ytani finally brings himself back under control, he returns to the camera.

"Now, let's see, I'm going to need a few things to fill my new palace…"

He begins glancing around, then back down to take notice of the girl under his feet again.

"Yes, we'll start with this one," he casually waggles a finger at her. "Package her up in a cute little black lace thingy and we'll see how far she can go. Meanwhile, I need to attend to my new subjects. A god-king's work is never done, you know! But don't worry, as we'll be seeing each other again one day. Just make sure you have my tribute ready. We wouldn't want any…accidents!"

He finishes with another round of wild laughter, and then vanishes in a puff.

As the Captain watched the monitor, his blood began to boil.

"Over my dead body, you little…" he spurns.

Ileani could barely find her breath after that display. When the image of Ytani vanished from the room, she stood there, wondering what she was supposed to do next. But it was Ayene who went into action now. She hastily pulled out her trans-com and pretended to dial in an important number, then slapped it to her ear. Ileani found herself drawn to this overt display.

"Control!" Ayene urges strongly. "We have a Code Amber-One. He's back! Yes, Ytani! No, not corporeal, he was using his Gift."

Ileani jerked around to gape at Ayene at the strange reference.

"I need a full sector security scan," Ayene orders. "See if there's anything out there in proximity! I'm coming in!"

She ends the link and stuffs the item back in her pocket, then rushes over to help Latena. She pulls the girl back to her feet and they rush off together down the corridor, leaving Ileani sweating from the ordeal and wondering what part of it was a play and what part was real.

✦✧✦✦✧✦

"Commander!" the Marshal screeches into the com-link.

"Yes, Marshal, I saw it. Ytani is back."

The Marshal then let out a horrendous scream into the com-link, which was followed by several crashing sounds, and finally the sound of breaking glass just before the signal cut out.

The Commander gazed at his vid-com, wondering if the Marshal had just tossed his terminal out the window.

"Well, you made him…" he mutters. "As well as that weapon."

He then tries calling the Captain, who had returned to his office by now hoping to make a few of his own calls.

"Captain Ta'yeen here," he responds with a weary voice.

"Captain, have you been able to reach anyone?"

"Latena's trans-com must be turned off or something. All I'm getting is her message box. I got her mother, who apparently missed the broadcast. I wasn't sure if I wanted to tell her, but I figured she'll probably see it as a replay later, so I cautioned her to take it slow. Commander, if that errant young man so much as touches that sweet little girl in any way…"

"At ease, Captain, there isn't much we can do about it from where we are now. I'm still trying to figure out how he did all that…the shape-changing, and then that enhanced voice of his. No part of it makes any sense to me."

"Didn't Commander Kriv'tik once say something about him using some special trick to fool the local population of that mining world they were on? The Marshal apparently taught him something, but what was it?"

"I don't know, but Ti'van seemed to know something. I heard her call it a Gift, and that he wasn't apparently corporeal."

"But, Commander, that makes even less sense than anything else I can imagine."

"Yes, it does. I'll need to think on this, maybe see if the ACI can shed some light on it. They seem to know things they shouldn't otherwise know about."

"Well, they do share that relationship with those others, so maybe they received some sort of education."

"Maybe. Anyway, try to relax. Ti'van apparently helped Latena out of the scene, so maybe she's in protective custody of some kind."

"All right, and if this is the case, I'll give them my kindest thanks for the favor."

✦✦✦✦✦

Kaliya was making a follow-up visit to the offices of CPComm, where she hoped to put Ileani at ease for the most recent excitement and fill in a few critical details. They met in a local conference room and closed the door for privacy.

"I'm not so sure I want to talk to you, Captain." Ileani mumbles nervously. "Sweet treat or otherwise, that one was bad."

"Ileani, please, settle yourself and let's sit a moment. Your performance was exquisite. We got just what we wanted out of it. And I clearly owe you not only that sweet treat, maybe even a double dose to smooth things over, but also an explanation, and at this point, to fill you in on the rest of it. You've earned it by now."

"All right, I'll accept that offer. But when you say you got what you wanted, what do you mean?"

"What I mean is Darumon went haywire. This is perhaps his biggest secret, and one he would literally kill for to keep quiet."

"Literally kill for?" she winces. "Captain, I don't think I like the way you say that, especially after everything else."

"Right, so let me explain, and you must understand, until our picture is complete, this is entirely confidential, got it?"

"Yes, all right," she sighs. "I'll try…but I hope there's not much more ahead of us."

"This relates to the ever-popular…da-da-da-dum…" she intones musically, "…Tav'ageen Anomaly."

Ileani glared at her for the obvious demonstration, and further raised her brow at the infamous term.

"All right, so what are we talking about in reality? Because if you're using this little theatrical play of yours, there must be another sensational mystery he's hiding from us. This also reminds me of Latena's interview. She seemed to be centering a lot of her statements on those old war protocols and the Scare."

"Good, you're catching on. The focus in her statements was aimed at the Council, as they are supposed to be our primary concern for our world authority. She had to build that image to point a finger at an obvious target, which would be the one we might expect to be the culprit doing questionable, and even illegal acts, when in fact, as you already know, the real one is the Marshal."

"Right. So we are raising awareness, but trying not to point our fingers directly at him, and therefore paint ourselves as a target for retaliation, I suppose."

"Good. But now, here we go with the real story. We had to build up this complex image for our society of people who don't otherwise believe in a religion, magic, mysticism, or anything that might seem supernatural. This is where my father comes in...or tried to."

"Your father?" she gasps. "You mean..."

"Velen Nazég is my father," she nods confidently.

"In all the nether-space, no wonder his name has been coming up so much lately. Are you trying to get revenge in his honor for what the Council did?"

"Maybe a little, and also the Marshal, who hunted us like animals for his personal pleasures. My father is still alive, so forget what he apparently said once about killing him. He chased us all across the galaxy, and then some, but never to kill. We were just a game to him. This is how his kind likes to treat others."

"Wonderful. Now I see why you might be playing these games on HIM. Talk about payback."

"And now, we're building a correction to the old imagery. Darumon lied to us about a lot of things to cover for himself. HE is the Creator we had in our old religion, as HE is the one who made us. So, we might say someone got the idea for that religion, perhaps due to some old memories or something. But as part of his methods, we inherited a little more than just ridiculously long lifespans, and the Tav'ageen Anomaly is one of these just now coming out. It's a latent ability those first children probably found by accident. But naturally, in a society like ours, we wouldn't have a clue how to interpret it. Not unless you want to consider something supernatural, because if your father is a god, YOU now become a part of that. And the things you might inherit would actually seem godlike."

"Oh wow," she shakes her head nervously. "I don't think I would know how to handle something like that."

"None of us would. But in the case of someone like Ytani, it could easily go right to your head and cause all sorts of trouble. This becomes a serious issue of concern for those of us who might realize the potential, and that we, as a society, must learn ways to contain and control this skill. We must educate the people in methods of discipline and respect for what it has to offer. But unfortunately, for our society that, again, doesn't choose to believe in gods or supernatural...whatever...we will need to come to terms with the fact that we ARE half god, and all those other teachings are what THEY learn as their form of 'science'…" she flutters her fingers for emphasis.

"Their form of science…what we might call magic and mysticism?"

"Yes, as OUR form of science falls into the background by that time."

"Wow, this will send a few horns into orbit. But if you are hoping to teach discipline and respect, I think you missed the target. That little demonstration out there would be a bad example."

"Yes, this would be a very bad example, but Ytani is a known entity in the eyes of the Marshal, so we need to use him for now. We'll worry about the rest later. And so, here we are with our story."

Kaliya pauses to consider her direction.

"That ship that came for us belonged to someone who was watching Sargeras and Darumon, probably since the early days when there was this long series of battles between two god societies, with Sargeras and his kind being on one side of this. During what we suspect to be the last of these battles, we think these two ran away and went into hiding, while the rest of their kind were exterminated for crimes that were very similar to what we're seeing now. They like to treat younger societies as entertainment devices, and often expendable."

"How nice of them. And this is what we might call a god?"

"This is clearly a very bad example of one. But this other society arrived on the scene sometime later, and challenged the older one in the name of their form of justice, which is a principle they call the Measure of Balance. This younger society is a collection of races who managed to evolve up to that level where they could join together and take control away from this other one, and from there begin to govern everything else. They are called the Estelar."

"All right, I'm with you so far, although it sounds a bit fantastic."

"Yeah, and I'm just getting started," she smiles. "The Estelar finished off these others, which they refer to as Primordials, meaning to say that which preceded them, or an earlier form of godlike existence."

"They don't have an actual name?"

"We don't know for sure, and the hatred between the two sides might occlude anything like a name."

"Ouch, it was that bad? Wow."

"Here we come to this one member who apparently saw him go into hiding, but since he probably wasn't expected to be of any concern at the time, he and Darumon were both forgotten and ignored."

"Forgotten AND ignored?"

"We have a couple of historical references used in this case. Forgotten, as if to say by all the rest, who think the Primordials are all dead by now. We might also describe Darumon this way, if he is a lesser being under Sargeras, and not worthy to remember to begin with."

"Interesting."

"Sargeras, for his part, might also be ignored, as he would be regarded as impotent in our local space, which as it turns out, is absent his natural support layer…what some of our people have recently been describing as Abnormal Energy."

"Oops! That name has been circling around lately."

"Yes, it has. As a result, he probably went dormant for a long period of time to conserve his strength."

"All right, I think I can see it."

"But then Darumon, who seems to be the one most active here, came out of hiding, and boom, we have our history of weird evolution. We became the instruments of his revenge on the Estelar. He wanted a minion species to do his work for him."

"Uh huh. Now give me a moment. Let me guess. From all that Latena gave us, he directed us along our history, the Council and their selective research to serve HIS needs, maybe also Saakerav building that united world so HE can control us better as a group, and then where we are now with his crusade against his so-called insurgents, right?"

"Generally so," Kaliya nods. "Darumon can alter his shape, so he can impersonate other beings. Therefore, he probably came and went on many occasions to direct our history."

"Great, that makes me feel so much better."

"You're not the only one. So, here we are. Until recently, the Estelar didn't know he existed. His movements were designed as a surprise hit, using a super weapon he was building on a secret mining outpost. This one individual who was watching him apparently had something personal in it, so she was waiting for him to make a move in her direction, as that was apparently where it all started. Then we have that ship, along with some beings on it who brought it to us. My father received a warning from them, which he tried to pass to the Council, not to listen to Sargeras and Darumon, and turn them away. But as we all saw, it didn't work…not that it might have ever had the chance to begin with."

"Yes, this much becomes obvious."

"I suppose, all things considered, it might not have mattered. One way or another, Darumon would likely have his way of things. But then we have the pursuit, where we were mostly just pushed along in front of him as he made this long chase back home. But it was not so much a chase, as it was a game. He also had to build up your fancy military, with all your fancy, and dirty industry, and then test it on anything he could find out there with life on it. Those were your insurgents, Ileani; whatever OTHER forms of life this galaxy once had in it."

Ileani shuddered and closed her eyes, then turned away, still trembling.

"Oh please, don't tell me we could be responsible for all that."

"I'm sorry, but according to Central Command, they apparently blasted a lot of worlds out there that never saw it coming."

"But how could our people be so dull-horned as to do all that without at least trying to analyze what they're shooting at?"

"This one is bad. It also relates to Latena's statement of that co-op effort, where he points a finger, and we go out to actually analyze something, and THEN see what we can do about it. But analysis isn't his concern. One of the famous mandates the Council passed, but classified behind your backs, was a military authority override chip to literally take control of their minds. So, with the push of a button, you have a custom killing machine that doesn't ask questions."

"Oh great! That really makes my day."

"Eventually, we arrived on a world where we met with the other side of this. Darumon was getting ready for a final push, but he was discovered by agents belonging to the one who was watching him. She is keeping a very low profile here, probably again for personal reasons. We think she wants a piece of him, but wants to make it a surprise as much as he was trying to do on his side."

"This all sounds very sneaky. Do these gods actually play war games like this?"

"I don't know the answer for your average example, but if Darumon or Sargeras should see them coming, they might try running, and we don't want that."

"All right, got it."

"And so, right now, we're coming back, and I'm leading part of this."

"Uh huh, and making a lot of noise along the way."

"We need to unravel all his games here, and do so in a way that doesn't point a finger at us. The people need to have their eyes opened to these games of his, but they also need to realize we are a society of thinkers, and so to remind them how to actually think."

"I see. Fine, I won't argue."

"We're an old society, Ileani. Maybe not as old as some of them out there, but certainly old enough to know better. Unfortunately, due to Darumon turning our horns down so many times, we aren't nearly as mature as we probably should be for what we do have."

"I suppose, if you say we are in possession of something we should actually know more about, but we refuse to accept even the concept of it."

"Exactly. But now, about our latest sensation. First, you need to know the Anomaly, as it was advertised, was a hoax. Or at least, whatever HE said about it was a hoax, just to frighten people into taking his solutions to 'correct' it."

"I think I recall some part of this from the Director over at the ARC once upon a time. And so, we have the Scare, with Latena placing so much emphasis on it as the Council's doing, but it's actually him?"

"Right. As I said, it's a latent ability just now developing in our species, with these children as early examples. That ghost thing is actually the person's mind, or spirit, projecting outwards in a kind of out-of-body experience where it can move around independently and interact with things, much like the actual body would. But it's a projection, not a material body. Therefore, machines would not normally see it, other than for a camera."

"And those deaths?"

"Darumon, trying to hide his 'evidence' of his artificial influence in our species."

"He would kill children for this?" she shouts. "In all the netherspace, he must be the worst out of all of them."

Kaliya could only shrug as she prepared to continue.

"Look at me. Look at Navina, Petrith, and many others right now working for the ACI. These are mostly our people, what's left of us following my father. Ayene is one of yours, but she was found in that mining base, and now she is working for us. We're all projected when we make our runs here. My body is currently on another world, and my mind is projecting all the way over here. It's a VERY powerful, and VERY godlike ability. Even those societies that serve the Estelar would say so, and they ARE half-god."

"Unbelievable," Ileani whispers.

"But my father was coming to these ideas back then, even though no one else cared to listen to him. I suppose it's excusable, in a small way. After all, who would ever expect US to have something like THIS?" she chuckles.

"Yes! I would have to agree."

"He called it the Prodigy Gift, and since that time, as we found these others who could actually teach us what it is and how to use it, we have come to learn we have even more beyond this, like telepathy. This places us on a very high pedestal, and our people will NEED to learn how to manage it. It's not a choice by now. It's in us, so we will need to go through a special education program, maybe with the help of these other societies, until we can mature into it."

"Will they actually help us?"

"Yes, I'm sure they will. They behave like a parental body over younger societies like ours."

"All right, that's good to hear."

"Anyway, now we come back to your side of it and Darumon's games. That Scare was him forcing his solution for you to swallow. Those seeds serve an ulterior motive to provide for his master in this space… that Abnormal Energy, or at least an artificial layer of it. You recall how Sargeras appeared in poor health when he first arrived? Well, his form of life would not normally take up residence in a universe like this. They are extradimensional beings. And as such, they require certain environmental conditions, like this energy layer. Unfortunately, our universe doesn't seem to have it as a natural resource."

"Why would they choose to hide here if we don't have what he needs to survive comfortably?"

"Likely due to the fact that it would be the LAST place to find a being like him, if he is hiding from others of the same kind, like the Estelar."

"Ouch! Yes, I think I can see that one."

"Therefore, Darumon serving his master as a priority, meaning the seeds, and a full world population using them. We think they produce a kind of aura effect to feed into him."

"Ugh! I swear, I am REALLY happy I got that thing removed from my body."

"Yes, and we're trying to help as many others as we can, but we have a long way to go."

"Yes, you do."

"The chips are his secondary solution to disable the discovery of this Gift. So, I guess they're not called Suppressors for nothing," she smirks.

"Oh, thank you, Captain. But now, how does this relate to what I saw earlier, because you frightened the wits out of me, and probably a lot of other people."

"A lot of those people you saw run by were mine, simply to add to the background confusion. As for Ytani, that was me in an alternate shape. The projection doesn't have to be my own body. I can make virtually anything my mind can imagine, and it comes out looking real."

"So, that weird creature, and then him, was actually you?"

"I needed to make a scene, and it had to be public…very public, so Darumon can't hide from it. And I had to leave clues, statements, to suggest what it was. These are hooks for later news sensations, one of which will involve Latena again. Now that it's out, people are going to ask about it, and horns will fly when these all begin to reflect back on my father and his original ideas, and further the Council, and even the Marshal, rejecting and vilifying him. And once again, with Latena pointing fingers."

"In all the nether-space, Captain, you have a bigger mean streak than Ayene."

"Well, she's still in training." she grins.

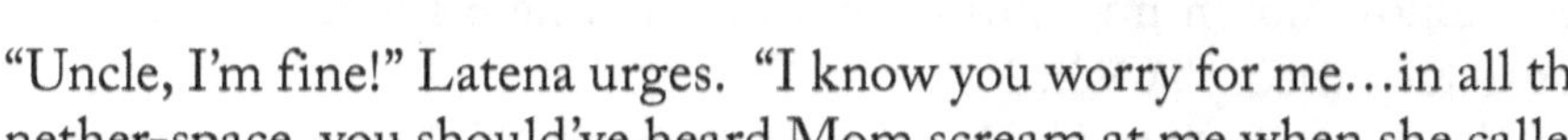

"Uncle, I'm fine!" Latena urges. "I know you worry for me…in all the nether-space, you should've heard Mom scream at me when she called a little while ago."

"Latena, it's just that…well, that man, above all others, is a lunatic, and he's considered to be extremely dangerous."

"Yes, Uncle, I was told this by that woman who was in that interview. She works for the ACI, and apparently you already know this. And since you also know I'm working for them as well, um, you know. So I'm in very safe hands. Anyway, the chances of him finding me among all these people are zero-to-none."

"Yes, well…" he sighs.

The Captain had finally managed to reach Latena on his trans-com, and of course he was the typical example of a worried uncle.

"What were you doing up there, anyway?"

"Passing out some fliers…" she responds innocently. "It was part of my rally work, looking to pull in more people, especially those in the high finance and executive levels. They could be really useful in the longer term."

"Trying to make a few contacts, are we?"

"Hey, I'm receiving a lot of coaching right now, so I'm still building myself."

"Yes, you are. But you're also turning out to be a little rascal," he grins. "You know that?"

"Oh, Uncle, you know me…" she giggles playfully. "Aren't I your favorite niece?"

"Yes, although you're also my only niece, but you would still be my favorite even if I had another."

"Thank you, Uncle, you're also my favorite. So, just keep sticking people with your regulations and protocols, and don't let anyone tell you different."

"Are you now trying to give me orders?" he grins.

"Hey, I'm your niece! I hold a special privilege."

They share a final laugh and end the link.

Latena put her trans-com away and returned to her discussion with Ayene in the ACI office.

"All right," she reflects. "So, my next interview will come up once I supposedly get debriefed by the ACI and pull my horns around again for a follow-up on my movement. This is where I give off my latest conspiracy theory. Ooh, I like this."

"I pity your poor Uncle," Ayene mourns. "That man will need therapy before we are done, right alongside Ileani. But now, while we're moving ahead and making progress, we're still concerned about any wildcards the Marshal might throw at us. He already had one breakdown where you are concerned, demanding you to be thrown into a hole somewhere. So far, he was counting on his…minions…doing his work for him. But in the absence of his minions actually doing any work, he might just get desperate and see to it himself. This is where we need to make a few careful statements to let him know HE is on the spot if anything 'bad' should happen again, like another Scare or otherwise."

"Right, and for this, we need to rehearse another script. You know, I should probably go into acting after this."

"It wouldn't hurt. Our future studies where this Gift is concerned will likely involve theatrical training to help us boost our skillset."

"You're kidding! So, you actually have a training course for this thing now?"

"And it's growing with each new discovery we make."

✦✦✦

The news desks at CPComm were buzzing again as calls rang in from science factions offering theories and proposing potential solutions to the mystery of Ytani's outlandish performance on the live feed a week before. Ileani found herself busy once more as she made one after another follow-up report.

"This is Ileani Ur'paran for C.P. News. In the news today is the figure we have come to know of simply as Ytani. As you recall, last week, Ytani made a public appearance during our interview with the military officer who was filling us in on the raid siren alert network. We have since come to understand that the REAL reason for this new emergency broadcast network is due to Ytani being a former operative working for the Marshal on what was described as a top-secret project, but now he is a defector who joined forces with an unknown foreign body.

Furthermore, according to military sources, his reference to a ship being handed over to him, which was obviously an allusion to a theft of military property, refers to a science exploration vessel called the Ghan'aju. There is no word as to the true whereabouts of this ship, as a spokesperson from Central Command told CPComm that the ship simply vanished off the scopes and is most likely running silent.

But when questioned about this explosive material Ytani described, and the references to the names Madzurki and Ooduan, Central had only this to say..."

The report changes to a press release clip with a male military officer.

"These names reference a classified operation that was underway at one time relating to a mining expedition to explore a new mineral resource. Unfortunately, the substance was highly volatile and quite unstable, so it had to be kept at a secure facility while we investigated its potential industrial value. But Ytani, who was temporarily in charge of the operation, clearly developed a form of mania, as was evidenced on the live broadcast, and it is believed he stole the ship and possibly some portion of this substance as well."

The report now returns to the newsroom.

"In other news, there is a vigorous debate ongoing between several prominent science factions on the issue of how Ytani was able to perform the amazing feats as observed not only on the live broadcast, but also apparently as he was seen in the skies of Capitol Prime in the form of that alien creature. An interview with several office workers from downtown, who were present at the time Ytani made his arrival on the sister building to the Vaanil Esluna tower, tell how he apparently clung to the outside of the window and simply passed through without affecting the glass.

This statement stunned many scientists, who are now scrambling to find answers to this incredible achievement, which Ytani himself describes as a kind of talent, and apparently taught to him by the Marshal himself. One spokesman had this to say, as he was trying to associate this to any other recorded events or theorized qualities that might describe this apparent phenomenon."

Another recorded news clip comes on the scene with a male speaker sporting a rather condescending attitude.

"Some people might say this could represent a supernatural ability, but those of us who belong to the more fundamental practices would simply brush aside such fantasies. There's really only one faction I could ever possibly recall that might claim this to hold any definition, but that one hasn't been supported for…well, a long time. No, we're not talking about ghosts here, as this young man was clearly very real. And we cannot be speaking of shape-shifting aliens, as there haven't been any reported cases of the Tav'ageen symptoms since the introduction of the Suppressor chip back in, I believe 9765.31 or so. This chip, which has served our people so effectively, has completely removed any and all threat of that unfortunate blight, so clearly, we cannot be speaking of that now, can we."

The scene returns again to the newsroom.

"However, another spokesperson came forward not long after reviewing this clip, and had this to say…"

Now another news clip comes online, this time with a more deferential female speaker.

"As a psychologist, I can already tell you this young man suffers from an extremely disturbed mind. Even the average layman can tell you that. I also took notice, as most others did, that he was missing his seed entity, and from how he was flaunting himself at the camera, he was clearly enjoying his perfect unaltered form. In addition, as it was so blatantly obvious, he expressed emotion. This naturally prompted me to examine the imagery to see he was missing his cranial interface, and as we all know, the Suppressor chip is a Council mandate for everyone at four decades. What this suggests to me is either he never received one, or he had it removed at some moment, likely an early moment in order to allow time for this behavior to manifest. This could easily account for his manic behavior and further his developmental abnormalities.

But I do not wish to advocate the idea that having the chip can prevent such behavioral abnormalities, as we all know a normally developed individual would not display such behavior. Instead, I might suggest how this, combined with the absence of the seed, created a type of megalomania complex, perhaps also an aversion to any and all forms of modification, therefore causing him to elevate himself above the rest for his perceived level of perfection.

One other attribute, which I believe we should mention here, was he had a very clearly developed physical prowess. As many of us might be aware, when a young man, perhaps of his age, engages in extensive physical exercise, such as weightlifting, he can develop a condition we often refer to as the Alpha Male Syndrome. And his disrespectful attitude where that young lady was concerned clearly demonstrated this. This is just one more aspect of his behavior we can describe as abnormal, and cannot be associated with anything else.

However, when we involve his statements of being trained by the Marshal in some strange ability, this now causes me to reflect on the Council again, and the long deliberation they are supposed to be conducting. Did the Marshal also bestow upon this young man some special gift of wisdom? And if so, for what purpose, especially if you consider this was apparently related to something as simple as a mining expedition. Needless to say, if he now places himself on the level of a god, he is clearly in need of psychiatric aid."

And finally, the video returns to the newsroom again.

"The science community vows to continue these debates as they work their way through the possibilities, but one thing is certain. If Ytani did somehow manage to escape the Council mandates for both the seed and the chip, one must then ask how and why this occurred, and along the way, ask again about this top-secret project he was serving on behalf of the Marshal. Could there be a relation?"

"Commander," the raspy voice of the Marshal mumbles over the com-link. "I'm not sure how much more of this nonsense I can take. Protests on one side, rallies on another, the Council being overthrown, and our own security forces taking up arms!" he pants. "And then, people removing their seeds, which we spent so much time on to ensure full coverage. And now THIS! That insolent little speck revealing so many of our delicate secrets, and THEN, the rest of them now asking a new volley of questions over it! This is intolerable!"

The Commander stared at the com-link as the Marshal made his rant, and carefully studied the wording along the way. But he still had a role to play, despite anything else.

"Marshal, I understand," he pretends to comfort. "Unfortunately, Ytani made an appearance not simply on a live news feed, but on multiple occasions in open view of the public. And I am quite certain he did this intentionally. He further demonstrated a very curious ability which no one can explain, and naturally this will generate questions, and for a number of reasons, not all of which relate to our delicate secrets."

"Granted, Commander, and this simply complicates things for us. I was hoping he might make a phys…phys…" he coughs subtly, "…a, eh, common showing…where I could possibly take some sort of action against him and therefore remove his threat potential. But if he's learned how to better control this…eh, well…yes, curious practice I once showed him, this could represent not only another threat to us, but it could, eh…complicate, yes, a number of issues we have been trying so hard to keep under our control."

"As you say, Marshal, but I am unable to target something I cannot see. So, I may have no choice but to wait for his next appearance and hope for a better opportunity."

"Of course, Commander, but under the circumstances, I have my doubts he'll actually grant us such a luxury."

"Marshal, one thing that bothers me is that demand he made. It causes me to reflect on Morndindor and the statements given to us from the base crew of his behavioral abnormalities, especially with the female staff. He demonstrated another of the same here, and he mentioned demanding tribute of some kind. How do you suggest we should respond to this?"

"This is a good question, Commander. I, eh… Well, yes. Despite so many of my outbursts, where I may hold many opinions of things, there are a few lines I would not choose to cross, if only to uphold at least some semblance of dignity for my own creed. And the wanton abuse of females by males is one of those. When we heard of that incident at Morndindor, I was offended, though I tend not to show these feelings often. My kind are conditioned that way."

"But you do seem to have a temper, as is clearly evidenced by your office and that space below your window."

"Oh. That. Yes, with apologies. But this is special. And I would never willingly permit such a thing as to give in to that young, eh…" he grumbles something, and then coughs it away. "That young man, and I will use this term loosely, as I would surely expect a male to uphold higher standards than that with a member of the opposite gender."

"Of course, Marshal, as I am sure many of us would."

"Exactly, Commander! I may not have had the pleasure of my own experience in my lifetime, but this much I feel is important. Therefore, naturally, I would never give in to such an insolent little pest like this, and I find it inconceivable that he would dare speak to me in such a manner as he did on that feed. I don't know who he thinks he is, but if he's going to call himself any kind of god, he'll need to show himself worthy of that title, and do so right in my face!"

He ends the link.

The Commander glares at the vid-com once again. As was most often the case, it was in audio-only mode for these conversations. He contemplates the Marshal's words deeply for several moments, and then reaches over to call up the Captain.

"Control, Captain Ta'yeen here."

"Come to my office, please, Captain, we need to talk."

"Yes Sir, I'm on my way."

The link ends, and the Commander waits several moments for the Captain to arrive. Soon after, the door announcer buzzes, and the younger officer enters inside.

"Sit with me," Geilv states.

"What is it, Commander? You look like you just spoke with the Marshal again."

"Does it actually show that much?" he smirks.

"That, combined with the habit you're developing lately of calling me in here for private chats whenever he calls in."

"Yes, I suppose I need an outlet, and you are a very kind conversation partner."

"Thank you, Sir. So, what do we have this time?"

"Right off the top, do you recall that day we lost Morndindor?"

"How could I forget it. Why?"

"Think of the Marshal for a moment, his reaction to Ytani and the claims of his mistreatment of the female staff members. Can you recall his expression, or any of his manners?"

"The Marshal?"

"Yes, I think by this time you had me drugged up on sedatives..." he chuckles.

"Indeed!" he smiles. "I had a few of my own by that time. And even at that, your horns were smoking by the time we finished. Let's see. I don't recall he showed up much reaction to that report. Why?"

"He tells me he was offended, but apparently, his kind is somehow conditioned NOT to show much of a reaction to some things...and this is despite his obvious tantrums in his office."

"Oh! So this is how he does NOT show emotions? In all the nether-space, I'd hate to see a true response."

"I'm going to make a guess here and suggest these other occasions are hitting a different nerve, but this one relates to what he calls his dignity relating to a creed...males who are wantonly abusive of females. It's a line he says he would not wish to cross."

"Well, all right, I suppose it may be possible that even he has limits."

"Maybe so. I heard once how he is a type of servant to Sargeras, and he might sometimes use the word master for him. Maybe his station is so dedicated, he doesn't have time or opportunity for it. But anyway, we were speaking of Ytani's appearance. Of course, he's upset...still... and I suppose, for this point, I can't blame him. But I think there is something missing here, and I need to figure it out."

"And you would like my help? All right, sure… Where do we begin?"

"I've been pondering that interview these last several days, trying to interpret what we saw, as well as the players, and it seems a little too coincidental."

"Coincidental?"

"First, the Marshal's conversation made a circuit around all his… delicate little secrets…as he calls them, meaning his seeds, and who-knows-what-else, and the world crashing down around him, which as you and I both know is due to the ACI."

"Uh huh…" he nods.

"Now he's talking about Ytani and this talent he taught him," Geilv considers. "He didn't seem to care as much for the weapon in this conversation, mostly about Ytani misbehaving on a live feed. But the only thing Ytani misbehaved over, at least overtly, was to direct a few words here and there, including at him, and behaving as a god figure by demonstrating that talent of his."

"Um, Commander, what about Latena?"

"If we're going to ask about her, we might also want to ask about Ti'van, whom I suspect to be part of the ACI, and we already know they're working together. And then, why did they choose that time and place for an interview relating to the siren network? My thoughts are, it was public, in a closed space, easily containable, and it would make a fabulous sensation if you wanted to show something off."

"What?" he gushes. "Are you saying it could've been staged?"

"This is one of the questions going around my horns right now. Listen to this…" he leans forward onto the desk. "The Marshal is angry that people are now asking about this latest and greatest little secret. So, this tells me he was hiding something."

"Uh oh…"

"Ytani popped into view by altering his shape from that animal creature, and we can be fairly certain he made those other demonstrations in our skies intentionally as a public showing. It was a prelude, he wanted to be seen. And since he's demonstrating himself with a message aimed at the Marshal, he wants HIM to know about it, at least as much as the rest of us."

"Fascinating, but are we suggesting he is simply flaunting it for the Marshal, or trying to demonstrate it in the eyes of the public? My interpretation was he was showing off for the Marshal, at least as much as anything else."

"Probably so, but was it simply showing off, or giving out a message? The Marshal gave him something, and it was supposed to be a secret, but here he is showing it off not only to him, but everyone else, AND on a live feed that can't be covered-up."

"So, he was showing off to all of us the same, but with a message for him."

"To spoil his secret…" Geilv nods.

"Wow, that's a good rub in the face," he chuckles.

"But now we need to ask why, if we suggest there could be a motive other than to satisfy his god complex. This also brings me to his behavior and his demand for tribute…females, just like we learned of him on Morndindor."

"Yes, and my poor little niece being his first victim."

"Yes, your poor sweet innocent niece," he smirks.

The Captain glares at him a moment, and soon begins to feel an upwelling of laughter ready to break out.

"All right!" he chortles. "So, it was staged, and using Ytani, or maybe someone claiming to be him, as a demonstration of this talent. Thank goodness if this is the case. But then, what did we actually see?"

"Captain Ti'van came in here once to request my authorization to install the siren network. So, if she's actually working for the ACI, why would they ask for this? We've heard many of their sensational reports already claiming the Marshal's insurgents aren't a bother, so it can't be them. Her original suggestion seemed to hint at Ytani and his unknown friends, and now here he is, or so we think. But did he arrive with a military fleet to assault us? No, at least not on this occasion."

"Meaning they're building up to something."

"Most likely, but there are secrets along the way they want to reveal, like the mining base, which brings me back to the Tul'ryk and that agent who was leaking information. They had an informant of some kind, probably from Morndindor, so they must know who Ytani is."

"All right, and so they're simulating him here. But this still doesn't answer the question of what we saw."

"No, but Ti'van made a very overt call on her trans-com, and it was seen on that feed. She called in to someplace she described as Control, where she used some obscure command reference, and said he was not corporeal, but using a Gift. Was it real, or a part of her play? Either way, I think she just leaked something to us. They know what this thing is."

"Interesting, but I'd like to know where they're learning all this stuff."

"Now, this conversation I just had with the Marshal. He's angry that Ytani made this showing, and especially using this Gift. He started to say, or at least I think this was the word he was going to use, that if Ytani had shown up 'physically', he could've taken some sort of action to correct it. But he changed his wording to say a common showing. This is our clue. The Marshal taught him something about creating an incorporeal image."

"Fascinating…" he croons.

"Now let's go back to Morndindor again. He was supposedly using some sort of talent or skill the Marshal taught him in order to interact with the natives. If he can create an image, maybe like a projection, and use that to arrive on the scene, he could portray an authority figure and drive them to do his bidding. This could be where he got his god complex after a while."

"All right, I'm with you so far. Although I'd really like to know how he does it, because if he can create any kind of image, he could potentially impersonate anyone or anything."

"Yes, this can be a problem. But that last news broadcast is tying my horns in a knot. One of those speakers mentioned his mania, and without the chip, he might develop abnormalities due to the modifications everyone else had, especially if you involve the Alpha Male Syndrome, which could certainly raise a person's attitude. But the story wrapped up with a final note of a potential connection between having, or NOT having, the mandates installed. Maybe this is another clue…that chip!"

"The chip…" the Captain wheezes. "Another of the Council's mandates, another of the Marshal's inventions," he pauses to consider. "It was also mentioned by Latena, at least indirectly, with her reference to continue the Tav'ageen studies. Blast it, Commander!" he shouts. "THAT must be his secret. And he buried it under those chips."

The two of them sighed deeply and leaned back in their chairs.

"Such a sweet innocent young lady," Geilv grins. "My crinkled old tail, she is!" he chuckles. "Let's see, this would've represented Elder Nazég's domain too. And from what I recall, he was developing some ideas about it back in the day, at least until those children died. And this now brings those deaths into question. If the Marshal was trying to cover it up…"

"…Then he's the one who did it," the Captain nods. "That murderer killed our children to hide his secret."

"And he made it worse with the old Tav'ageen Scare to force everything else on us."

"So then, we need to understand what this is and how it works."

"And if Ti'van used this reference of a Gift..." he frowns. "But if the Marshal buried it by demanding ALL of us to take these chips... hmm..." he halts to consider his thoughts. "All of us... Captain, this might represent a rather extreme talent, wouldn't you say?"

"Yes, I suppose it would."

"And if someone, like the Marshal, who apparently made us, made a mistake along the way..."

"In all the nether-space, are you saying he actually gave it to us?"

"And now he is trying to hide it. It was an accident. And we might ALL have it. It could be a racial feature in us."

"Oh, how delightful, Commander. So, we receive some sort of godlike Gift, and he doesn't like it. Now he wants to remove the evidence and bury the rest under these chips," he sighs again and glances around the room. "Fine! But now, Commander, what do we say about Ytani...this play of theirs? What is the ultimate purpose here, especially if you say Ti'van ordered that siren network? And along the way, what about the real Ytani?"

"Yes indeed. As for this image, I'm starting to wonder if this is building up to the ACI's mention of these other beings making ready to launch against us. The siren network might be to tell the people to go into hiding, maybe for protection."

"Well, if that's the case, whatever they have in mind doesn't sound good for us down here."

"Maybe not, but it does get them out of the line of fire...theirs, ours, and the Marshal's."

"Oh great!" he howls. "More collateral damage... If he was so anxious to cover up everything else, he might not let go of us once they arrive."

"Yes, but this is a clever way to avoid a disaster. They're clearly trying to save lives here. We probably need to pay special attention to the sequence of events coming up."

"All right, you certainly got my attention. I just wish I knew what events I'm supposed to be paying attention to. Commander, not that I wish to complain over the ACI and their methods, but I don't like this feeling of helplessness that I'm not the one in control here."

"You and me both, but we're dealing with gods here, so this rises a little above us, I think."

"Would it help if I were to start praying to something?" he smirks faintly.

They shared a brief chuckle at the notion.

"As for the real Ytani," Geilv continues. "If they're using his image, I have to wonder what happened to the real one. I think we need to ask ourselves how long ago the ACI came into authority, and maybe also where and how they learned these things. It sounds to me like they must've had help from an early moment to learn about this Gift, maybe also to train a few of their people with it. That agent used telepathy in here to call that alien into attendance, so this must be another part of it, which means they had to have some form of training."

"Granted, but then who...these aliens, maybe? If this was Elder Nazég's faction, but he's gone, it couldn't be him."

"True, but I do recall the Director of the ARC confiding in me he was part of an underground movement to maintain the old faction. So, they're not completely gone, just in hiding."

"Well, isn't that convenient!" he blasts. "All right, this is a possibility. Then, back to Ytani. We have Morndindor, the Ghan'aju, and also that weapon, none of which we can say was fake...or can we?" he raises his brow curiously.

"The weapon... He mentioned it on the feed, so they knew about it, and if they're mentioning it here..." he lurches forward. "In all the nether-space, Captain, if the ACI is the one playing the message, THEY are the ones to take that weapon. The Marshal once said it had to be a message. One unit, Captain, just one...the rest had to have been removed elsewhere. It was a message, and this was the other side of it, but for the Marshal, not us. Someone took his weapon, left a message behind, and put Ytani's name on it. And it has to be related to the ACI."

"Then what about Ytani, and then the Ghan'aju. And the base! We heard it destroyed on the com-link... Uh oh..." he trails off.

"Yeah, Captain, uh oh. A show on the com-link, just like with the Tul'ryk."

Geilv relaxes a moment and allows his mind to drift back to those early memories.

"Remember my words, my old friend..." he reflects gently. "Lajivi, what did you do over there, you old bull!" he shouts.

He abruptly turns to his terminal and starts punching up the military personnel records. As he does, he types in a few search terms.

"Let's see," he muses privately. "Let's start with her. Ayene Ti'van."

"Sir, what are you doing?"

"I think we should try verifying some of this. For instance, who was that informant? Captain Ti'van came in here with her security revamp and requests for the siren network, but she also claimed to be military. Is she actually military, or could it be someone else?"

"Well, between her and that young man, Lieutenant Girhani, they made a good show for themselves."

Geilv punches in Ayene's name on his terminal and it pulls up an old service record. He frowns deeply as he studies the information.

"This can't be..." he retorts. "First of all, this says she's a Lieutenant, not a Captain, and secondly, it says she's dead, but I know different!"

The Captain leans forward to examine the monitor.

"C.P. Security..." he mutters. "Admin and patrol service... That's not us, Commander, that's the civilian side."

"But...dead? How do you describe someone as dead...?" he halts as another flashback hits him. "Kriv'tik... The Captain of the Tul'ryk said he was listed as dead with a false record."

Geilv now punches up Kriv'tik's record. Both he and the Captain begin to read it.

"An exploding asteroid?" the Captain rebukes. "And planted by these insurgents? Oh yes, that smells of the Marshal's hand right there. Him and his cover-ups..."

"All right, let's say Ti'van is the same story. The operation was classified, so if he's covering up, he might not even show her assigned to the base at all. Kriv'tik's record here shows the same...the base never existed."

"Then how do we prove she was ever there? Personally, before I go making accusations, I'd like a little proof."

"Right, Captain, so we need to figure out how we can prove something here. The base never officially existed in our military files, so everyone who ever worked there might show the same story."

"Then we need something else to show we were working at that site. Wait, what about supply deliveries? We had constant supplies coming and going."

"Ah, good!" he nods. "And then, what about the invoices from all that."

Geilv now calls up the accounting files and begins browsing through them, entering a few search filters in the hopes of pulling up something of relevance.

"Let's try it on her name," he mumbles. "To see if she ever signed-off on anything."

He enters her name as a signee for the receipt of supply deliveries, and this creates an extended list of invoices for a base listed under a codename.

"Here we go! Codename Agent-U…whatever that means. She looks like the primary one signing-off for all their supplies."

"Then she must've worked as part of their command staff. How long ago was this?"

Geilv examines the topmost entry for the date.

"According to this," he muses. "She must've started at the opening of the base, roughly four centuries ago."

"And for how long?"

Geilv now scrolls through the list all the way to the end. When he hits the bottom, he gazes emptily at the final date, almost as if he were seeing a ghost.

"Commander?" the Captain prods gently. "What is it?"

"She was present at the time the base was lost."

"At the time it was lost…but she's obviously alive, so she didn't die with it. And if she didn't die with it…"

"No one else did…or at least we can suggest that if we involve the ACI making another show for the Marshal. And he WAS present at the time, Captain. He heard it just like the rest of us."

"Yes, he was," he nods.

"Let's try to recall the scene. They were calling the Ghan'aju for a survey mission, right?"

"Yes, I remember this now. The existing mining was apparently running out, so they requested the ship to find new deposits."

"And then Ytani goes up, rather than any qualified base staff member, and the next thing you know, the ship vanishes without a trace. Yes, that sounds like it could be a cover-up to take a ship and give an excuse for Ytani to leave the area after he blew up Ooduan."

"But this is now suggesting Ytani is completely out of the equation."

"If the ACI got involved, maybe they did something. But now, we should try to understand the timing. Ooduan was gone by the time the Marshal got there, and presumably around the time of the ship arriving. We have him make his inspection, he sees Ooduan is gone, and he orders a pullback. But then we have the attack. So, the ACI had to be right under our noses at the time, watching us and him, and further to ensure he was present in the control booth when the show was on."

"But this sounds as if we have spies in our own offices!" the Captain winces.

"Let's not concern ourselves with that for now. They're working on our side. But the real question is where that weapon went, and for that matter the base crew. Because if the base was gone by that time, at least in theory, no one would be returning through the conveyor, and to my knowledge, we didn't have any other traffic except our routine sector patrols."

"Then it must be a hidden base…" he ponders. "What about this… the Tul'ryk. They had to be offloaded somewhere, right? Maybe we're speaking of a site where they're pulling all these people together into a kind of refugee camp."

"That's an interesting idea, and it does offer an outlet. So, we have the Tul'ryk, the Ghan'aju, and maybe the base. But this means the ACI had to be arranged for quite some time to organize all this. If we suggest they got involved a while ago, I'll bet Ytani is dead. Let's consider for a moment. It probably began somewhere along the way, maybe between one and another of those murders he committed."

"My guess would be around the time of that last one. I think the murder was not long before the base going down. The med-tech recalled it when we were in there talking about it. So maybe shortly before, and they witnessed it, or shortly after, and they followed up on the evidence. Then they sprang into action to seek justice, since no one else was doing anything."

"Good, but now for the timing. How long ago was this? Captain, I'll have you gather a few people and do a little research for me. Find out when we had the last victim, and then the one that came before her, assuming we can actually trace these things by now for all his cover-ups."

"All right, I can see about this. Maybe the medical records will help us."

"Let's also send a ship out there to scan the location of that base. I want to know if it's still there, or if there's a big blast crater from the reactor going critical."

"We can do that easily enough, but do we interact in any way?"

"No, I just want a simple recon. If there's anything out there, I don't want to splash in any puddles I don't belong in. We still have the Marshal hovering over us here, and that warning to keep low."

◆◆◆◆◆

A new week was beginning and Ileani was conducting her latest news report.

"…In response to the statement of Ytani defecting to the other side, some have asked whether or not these unknown forces he sided with are more of the same insurgent forces the Marshal has been fighting during this time. But military sources say they are keeping a very close watch on our local space, and no sightings of any kind have been detected, not even during Ytani's presentation. This leads some to wonder where he actually is, if no ships have been seen arriving to deliver him in order to make any form of appearance at all.

In a related article, the medical community has been investigating if the presence, or in Ytani's case, the absence of the Suppressor chip could have played any role in his extraordinary display, as seen during that live broadcast. Some faction leaders are speculating about a connection between this talent of his, which was apparently the result of special instruction by the Marshal, and how it coincides with the absence of the chip.

But the suggestion, by itself, is inconclusive, as it turns out. The medical community is once again complaining about that nondisclosure clause in the Council mandate. This clause was originally stated to prevent any form of feedback of reported cases during this time, presumably to prevent another public panic as we once had in the days of the old Tav'ageen Scare. But at the same time, it also prevents the medical community from collecting vital data and other statistical results to track the Anomaly, or lack thereof, as a means to see if it is still out there and therefore a continued danger.

Several medical professionals have come forward to express a recurring vexation during this period where a general opinion felt as if this lack of feedback was stifling their ability to determine if the alleged alien infestation, as it was always interpreted to be, might even still be a valid concern. The reason being, in this proposition, that if it was using our population as a food resource, then during this entire time of the great success of the Suppressor chip preventing any new cases, it should have simply starved out of existence…in this proposition. But these same professionals are now questioning the original claims entirely, based on the recent scandals over the Council and their intentions."

A prerecorded video clip now comes on the air with a female medical professional.

"During the time of the original study of the Tav'ageen Anomaly, our archival records show the researchers involved were never able to qualify the presence of anything representing a physical entity, or even an energy signature of a body present in the room. In fact, the entity, and I use the term loosely, appeared and behaved exactly as the young child itself, almost as if it were awake and interacting with its surroundings. With the recent scandalous claims against the Council, and the highly questionable nature of the Tav'ageen Scare, including the potential causes, and the unprofessional nature of the selective news releases, some of which were very provocative, it is being assumed, with reasonable confidence, that the studies were being manipulated for someone else's benefit, and not ours.

As a result, we are now instigating several new programs. One of these is to review and conduct surveys of anyone who did actually experience the symptoms during their lifetime, but who got buried under that nondisclosure clause preventing anyone, including our medical analysts, from realizing it. Another is to begin disabling the chip, first to relieve our public of their effect, since it should no longer be an issue if this situation was being fabricated for the sensationalism of creating a public disturbance, and second to search for any new cases to be brought into a proper study program, this time without the Council and their machinations interfering with things.

However, we would also like to make note that these new studies, assuming we can find any fresh examples, are NOT going to be advertised so blatantly that whatever element was interfering with things once before can do so again. If, according to the statements of Miss Ta'yeen and her conspiracy theories, which do actually hold relevance to us, are in fact true, we are going to employ security measures to oversee these new studies. If that same element would like to try it again, they'll need to contend with armed guards along the way. But if this condition represents anything of such importance that it might cause the expulsion of such a fine example of a man as Elder Nazég, followed by the tragedy of the Tav'ageen Scare and whoever was responsible for it, we are going to do our part to understand the truth, and bring it out to the people."

The scene returns to Ileani in the newsroom.

"In addition to this report, a spokesperson for a previously unregistered science faction came forward to C.P. News recently with a remarkable statement."

The report now turns to another recorded clip of a male professional in a business suit.

"Since the time of Elder Nazég and his faction being excommunicated within the Council, the faction once known as the study of Metaphysics was effectively abolished, at least in part to the questionable practices of the Council and their preferential fetishes, and unfortunately, due to a lesser degree of the other factions out there who held so little regard for it. However, due to the recent scandals relating to the Council, and these same fetishes being exposed to the world, we feel it may be time to come out of hiding.

Our faction, which was never truly disbanded, had to go underground due to the negative support of the Council. We will excuse our fellow scientists, as we understand the controversial nature of our faction, but the Council is another matter. During this time, our hidden membership has attempted to continue their work, in the tradition of our founder, the Former Elder Velen Nazég, who opened our eyes to the possibility of a larger universe out there, one which might not fit the tradition of the more conventional sciences, but which might represent a new form of study for a dawning new Age. And if we reflect on the remarkable statement once made by the Marshal, that there are things out there we might not be ready for, we must make ourselves ready for them, especially if we, as a society, are still evolving, and that evolution might lead us in that direction anyway.

We will offer our thanks to the Marshal for whatever contribution he once offered to give aid to the Tav'ageen Anomaly, in the hopes of relieving us of a potential crisis. But if the crisis was actually the

Council promoting an intentional scare, and if that aid was simply a part of a collaboration effort to hide the truth, we intend to apply ourselves to discover that truth, to vindicate our founding members and their theories, and THIS time, demonstrate to the world that we ARE a viable form of study they need to pay attention to."

The scene changes again to the newsroom.

"This extraordinary revelation of the continuation of the old Metaphysics faction has led some to the speculation that the recent mention, multiple times, of the former Elder's name, might be alluding to a possible contribution to our knowledge base of what they have discovered during this time. Although, others are cautioning, that if it represents anything on the scale of what the Marshal himself once suggested in his famous statement on the Council's deliberation, it could truly carry us to a new dimension of understanding, but not one so easily digested with our traditional values."

✦

"Commander!" the Marshal shrieks. "This is escalating out of control now! Not only do we have Ytani on one side flaunting himself, but now the rest of them are starting to realize, eh…that is, to question what it is he was flaunting! And WORSE! We still have those…those…people out there. Aargh!"

"People? Which ones?"

"Didn't you see it? That old Metaphysics faction still has supporters. In all Creation! If they actually have anything to say about anything… I mean, we had that closed up once upon a time. And now they're back! That insolent young man has opened up something he truly has no idea of. Commander, this is serious! I… I…"

The Commander listens as the Marshal seems to descend into a muted whimpering.

"I tried so hard…" the Marshal moans softly. "If any of this should get out… Commander, we need to gain some control of it again. This one piece, above all others."

"Marshal?" Geilv emits cautiously. "What do you mean?"

"Commander, I fought with myself on many occasions over several factors of our progress together, but the outcome was always the same.

There are…well, let's just say certain things that cannot be made known. I have my reasons, Commander, but this situation is falling apart. There is a danger here, and I have been…um, well… I have found myself having to make certain, um…decisions. You know, what I can and cannot disclose. Some things are simply better to keep under tight control."

Geilv gazed at the com-link as he pondered this statement.

"Marshal, could any of this perhaps be due to those regulators being removed? Clearly, if they were part of the mechanism to keep the calm, now the people have free access to everything to realize all these little secrets we were trying so hard to maintain."

"Absolutely, Commander!" he shouts. "And then we have that! Who do these people think they are, coming in here and tearing things up?! We had those people in there for a reason. And as for this other thing, there is nothing more for them to concern themselves with as far as that old Tav'ageen business goes. It was closed once…and it should have stayed that way…" his voice seems to become sullen. "But now, they might actually…"

The Marshal pauses again from his heated outburst, and again seems to sink into his personal thoughts. But his manners seemed to darken. The Commander could hear him groaning in the background.

"In all Creation," the Marshal mutters privately. "If any of this should find its way up to him, I don't think I'll hear the end of it…not in this lifetime or the next. First, we have that, and now this…and then, well… And if he should begin to realize… No, we can't allow that. Not this one. I worked too hard on it."

He half-mindedly ends the link, leaving Geilv staring into his vid-com.

"Interesting…" he wonders openly. "Are we keeping another secret of some kind? But on this occasion, you sound genuinely concerned."

✦✦✦✦✦

Auryn's mother, Marna, had been trying to share their newfound religious worship with the rest of their cultist movement around the world. Her local sect had been making routine visits to Tae'Eladar during this time, originally by borrowing a ride through the mage portal in the basement of the ACI building, but more recently using the gateway at the new base. Now, regular tours of pilgrims were making their way into the region to jump across the gateway network, often with Auryn acting as an escort, and now with a few others signing up for language courses on Tae'Eladar to offer further aid. Today, Marna was in conversation on her trans-com with one of the head clerics in a new sect she was reaching out to.

"We have been hearing a few words about this whispered through our private channels," the woman responds. "But we feel the Creator would be angry if we should turn from him to find another god. Even though he may not speak to us, we feel he must be out there still."

"Listen to me," Marna asserts. "King Saakerav is the one responsible for banning all forms of the old worship, right? Whatever his motives, if he was part of this hidden agenda, we can't be sure what he had in mind or why he did it, unless you consider a few things said recently in the news. Just stop and think a moment. You want to continue following the Creator? Then you need to ask yourself who the Creator actually was, idol or otherwise. That recent revelation about our natural evolution, or maybe I should say the UN-natural evolution. Something came and lifted us out of the dirt all right, and then went to a lot of trouble to hide his efforts by interfering with our ability to learn where we actually came from. If the Creator really wanted us to know of his existence, he wouldn't be fighting our researchers by writing a false history."

"I, well…"

"And then we have Saakerav. Why did he put it down? Was he simply trying to create a new Era of science? These conspiracies, which are picking up more than just momentum, are also picking up credence as more people begin to realize Miss Ta'yeen was right. This means, if there was a hidden agenda, it could be related, and the Creator, still being with us, is still fighting us to understand who he is and why he's here. Then we have the oppression created by the Council. So, if THIS is part of his design, we weren't lifted out of the dirt for our own benefit. We were lifted out for HIS benefit, and it can't be good if it demands us to be infested with these seeds, and more recently they're suggesting this Tav'ageen thing might also be related."

"It is? How?"

"The Council pushed these chips at us, but what do they actually do, other than cause us so much suffering for the feedback. It's being said they could be hiding something if you look at the example of Ytani. Granted, he's not a very polite example, but he didn't have his chip, and he also exhibited something extraordinary. I'm aware that Miss Ta'yeen, who's a close friend of my daughter by the way, has a new theory about this, and she'll be going on the air with it soon. This could be the most sensational moment in our history. And if the Creator is responsible for it, and THEN went to so much effort to cover it up with those chips as part of his grander plan, I think we do NOT want to offer any worship to him."

"But he's just an idol, Marna."

"Just an idol?' she balks. "And you complain about him listening to something? Is that 'just an idol' anything like our Eracyodine ancestors accidentally uplifting themselves to sentient beings overnight? And the archaeology faction so unfortunately misplacing all the critical data to prove it?"

"Uh, yeah, all right. I see it. But the Marshal, he is…um… He…"

"He invented the chips," she affirms. "As well as all of these stories. And the Council took his advice over anyone else. More cover-ups. If Latena says they're all a front for someone, and that same someone created us, then interfered with us knowing about it, then to unite us into one body…for easier management…further to direct us, even to interfere with what it didn't want us to know about…then Lana, who do YOU think manipulated our Eracyodine ancestors, because you don't go from animals to intelligent people overnight! And if you were to do this for any reason at all, it had to be important. And here we must ask the reason why. And those two were clearly running away from someone."

There was silence on the line for several moments as Marna waited for the woman to respond.

"In all the nether-space," she whispers. "And these others you say you found?"

"His sworn enemies, Lana," she informs. "A rival society who owns the place. So, it makes sense to make friends with them as protection from him."

"Where do we go for this?" she asks urgently.

"Commander, do you have a moment?"

Captain Ta'yeen was peeking into Geilv's office for a meeting to follow-up on his research project where the mining base was concerned.

"Come in, Captain," Geilv waves at him. "I seem to have a lot of those lately."

The Captain enters and takes up a seat. He was carrying a data tablet with him.

"Sir, I have a couple of reports to hand in relating to Morndindor, but some of it is a bit confusing."

"All right, where do you want to begin?"

"First, I have a scouting report from the Niv'zatan, which we sent out there to scan the location of the base and report on what they see. I also have a summary of medical reports, and I was able to track down one individual who was apparently a victim out there."

"Really, although I hesitate to hear what she has to say."

"She was not easy to find, and reluctant to cooperate, but I managed to talk her into coming to my office for an interview. I told her I was trying to conduct an investigation of what happened out there for a criminal report."

"Sounds like her experience must've been bad."

"It was, by the things she told me, and not just with her, but for the rest of the staff. But first, let me tell you about the base. The Niv'zatan found the area apparently empty."

"Empty?" he frowns. "As if to say what…no structures?"

"Yes. There was no blast crater, and no scarring or signs of anything bad happening. They made a detail scan of the area, and they say it looks like the result of simply packing up and leaving."

"I see…and I suppose this is the part that confuses you, right?"

"One of them… So, I gave further instructions to scan the surrounding region, thinking it was simply relocated…just in case anyone came looking for it…but still nothing. We conducted a scan for the materials used in the base construction, for instance in case the locals tore it down and recycled them elsewhere, but still nothing. I have no idea where it went, but it's nowhere to be found on that planet."

"Interesting…and this would suggest it was disassembled and removed completely. But it also seems to confirm it was NOT destroyed by a local uprising, as we heard on the com-link. And this would then tell us the base staff is probably elsewhere as well."

"Yes, it would, with at least that Lieutenant Ti'van being here and conducting herself as part of this ACI."

"All right, so something happened, and it likely involved an external element. Whether this was the ACI proper, or otherwise, is so far uncertain, and then they thoroughly cleaned up after themselves. What else?"

"The Niv'zatan also mentioned something very curious. The planet was clearly in a state of environmental collapse, probably due to the heavy bombardment we gave it in the beginning. But just in front of that one surviving city of theirs, they saw what they described as an oasis of grasslands and wooded glens, along with new settlement."

"That's interesting…so we can say the locals are coming out of hiding, and trying to reclaim the area, but grasslands and woods on a deteriorating world?"

"Sir, this stood out as something remarkable, as if a very potent force was trying to reclaim that world."

"A potent force…" he muses and leans back in his chair. "And this sounds like it would have to be very potent, indeed. All right, if we include those godlike aliens, maybe we can say they're trying to undo the damage we caused. And if the place was wrecked down to just one surviving city, they're starting small and working their way outwards."

"This is reasonable, and those aliens may have removed our structures to clean up after themselves for the loss of the base."

"Good, and the base crew is most likely working for them and the ACI now. Interesting…" he ponders distantly. "So where would Lajivi be right now?"

"Sir, this also brings me back to the Ghan'aju. What happened to it?"

"Yes, and if we reflect on our earlier conversation, it was probably no different from the base, at this point, maybe also the Tul'ryk. Captain, we seem to have a lot of people around here turning mutinous," he chuckles. "It was called in as a decoy to use as an excuse. Ytani needed an escape. They called it in for a survey, right? Then Ytani took control and vanished. So, either the ACI intervened, or maybe Kriv'tik himself did, pulling rank and simply sending it away into hiding."

"All right. So far, so good…" the Captain smiles. "This gives us our answer for Morndindor, but now, what about Madzurki and Ooduan?"

"Madzurki was hit by an atomic device, and I'll bet it was another clean-up effort. The Marshal made a visit to see it was shut down, and also to see Ooduan was absent from the conveyor linkage. This was part of that message. Then Madzurki was removed later to finish the process."

"Using a common atomic? Wouldn't a godlike society have something bigger than that by now?"

"Maybe, but perhaps their objective was to leave something behind as another statement, or to cover up for a godlike weapon doing the job."

"Ah! As if to say, Ytani and whoever he found."

"That makes better sense to me."

"Then the only thing remaining is that weapon."

"Right. If we say the ACI is involved, especially with Ytani's mention on that live feed, then they must know what it was, removed it, and I hope destroyed it, or whatever is necessary to diffuse the issue."

"We hope…" he sighs. "Perhaps we could ask about this? If we're putting some part of this together, do you think we could get a little confirmation out of them by now?"

"I suppose I could ask. But I swear to you, Captain, if a single unit can blow a five-lightyear hole in space, I hope they realize what they're dealing with."

"I might suggest if they're associated with this alien society, they might have access to some private detail."

"Maybe so. But you know, this brings me back to a conversation I had with the Marshal on this. I was asking him what the full amount might do, and his response was strange."

"How strange?" the Captain asks warily.

"He said, '…if it was detonated in THIS universe…' And when I asked what he meant by that, he simply tried covering for himself by saying it gets technical."

"Oh! Technical, is it? I recall the Captain of the Tul'ryk and his idea of a fuse igniting the whole space out there."

"Yes. That. All that Abnormal Energy we're hearing mentioned so often lately, and what we were seeing so much of out there. And I recall that alien representative saying the stuff we call abnormal is actually far more common than we can imagine, and it's actually abnormal for us NOT to have it. Yes, that would certainly do a nice job on his old rivals. No matter where they might be, just drop one of those in the local space and boom, no more universe."

"But Commander! That sounds like some kind of doomsday weapon. This certainly WOULD be a godlike device."

"And he had lots of it," Geilv considers. "If these others own everything, he might have been planning to blow ALL of it up."

"Unbelievable!" he sighs. "Yes, let's hope that weapon is long gone by now. But now this leaves us with the Marshal and this false Ytani. What are we supposed to do about that?"

"For lack of any new instructions, I think we need to play it like we don't know anything. Now, what about the base and that survivor?"

"Right," he pulls up his tablet for reference. "She gave me a rather detailed story about him and the history of the base. I think I should also mention her dismay that it took this long to review anything, so I had to explain a few things to her."

"I understand, and I'm sorry for that."

"She prefers to leave her name out of it for the shame she feels, so if you don't mind…"

"Of course, Captain, we'll let the poor girl have her privacy."

"It starts out as she, along with the initial group, all arriving to establish the base. She tells me she was once part of C.P. Security, same as Ti'van, and several others that she can recall. So, it would seem he was pulling people out of there for this operation."

"That figures, and probably part of his cover-up, to bring them out of some other service that can't be tracked as easily."

"At the time, Ytani was established in his own house, mostly alone except for some entertainment devices he had, like a vid-com, music, games, and such."

"And how old was he again?"

"She says at this time he was only seven decades."

"That's still a child, and a prepubescent one as well."

"He was supposedly in possession of some unique skill the Marshal helped him learn to do his job, which was to interact with the native population in some way to cause them to deliver this metal to a storage room. From there, the base crew would pick it up and forward it to the processor. He would also call for these mining crews and feed them this stew using an alien fungus material with this drug component."

"Where did they find this fungus?"

"It was provided separately. She recalled a mine they were managing south of their location which had a custom environmentally sealed compartment to farm the stuff locally."

"Environmentally sealed? This suggests it came from elsewhere and likely needed some unique conditions to grow."

"Yes, it does, and she generally confirmed this. Furthermore, at approximately one-year intervals, they had to call for replacements due to this stuff being fatally toxic after a while."

"How nice… So, he feeds them poison, tells them to work literally to death, then calls for more."

"Now, as for Ytani, he started out well enough for a young boy, but with one exception. He did not have his Suppressor chip. She recalled how he once said it was taken away as a special gift to play his role with those people."

"Ah hah!" Geilv snaps his fingers. "There you have it, Captain. That chip must be related to that skill. Having it disables the skill, therefore the name, Suppressor."

"And this now points a clear finger at the Marshal. He DOES know what the Tav'ageen thing is, and he seems to be intentionally hiding it from us."

"This reminds me of a recent conversation we had together. He seemed worried about…him…finding out. I'm going to assume Sargeras again, and I'm starting to think that Sargeras may hold a special aversion to the idea. The Marshal said there was a danger, and on this occasion, I think we may need to pay attention. If Sargeras should learn we have something…well, how do we describe it? If he's godlike, and if the Marshal made us, did he make such a blunder that he gave US something godlike?"

"And so, Sargeras, being godlike, might not like the competition? Wonderful. Commander, we may need to tread lightly here. He spends all his time in that sanctuary building of his, so if he should ever come out, we should try to play it very low."

"All right. I can speak to the ACI on this to see if they have any ideas, but this would be a good suggestion."

"Anyway, back to Ytani. He was living alone, and no one ever saw any family visit him during this time. I asked her if she had any ideas of why, and she vaguely recalled him give an explanation once, and I don't like the sound of it."

"I'm already getting visions, so let's hear it."

"He said something about them being in an accident."

"Oh, an accident?" Geilv blasts. "How unfortunate! Well, yes, it is unfortunate, but also very convenient. And so, he has no other surviving family to take him in, I suppose. Or maybe he's listed as dead as part of that same accident. Hmm, I wonder if we can trace this," he muses distantly. "Do you think you could call in a few favors with some of the civilian security departments, like C.P. Security, to check on it? It was four centuries ago, so look for any family accidents, probably with fatalities of all members involved, and with a seven-decade old child named Ytani."

"Yes Sir, I think I can do that."

"And so, here we are," Geilv concludes. "As the result, the Marshal, out of the kindness of his heart, assigns him to a top-secret mining outpost that officially doesn't exist, and teaches him his deepest secret that no one else is supposed to know about, so he can pull out this material to build a super doomsday weapon. Yes, this would go nicely with all those sensations out there."

"Are you thinking of actually releasing this information?"

"Me? Oh, hardly that. I'm supposed to stay low. But the ACI, they might find it interesting," he chuckles mischievously. "What sort of structural integrity is still remaining of that building next door?"

"Not much, by now," the Captain grins. "Now, the base crew tried serving as surrogates while he was growing up, but he became rather reclusive after a while. However, as he was maturing, she says he started developing a curiosity about boys and girls."

"And so, it begins," he chuckles faintly.

"He was asking for playmates…girls, in this case. She said he was apparently starting to develop his urges, but he was still a bit young, so they asked for one of the younger non-coms to go in as a simple playmate…you know, like a Big Sister image to occupy him with games or some other form of social interaction."

"Sounds innocent enough, so far…"

"It wasn't long after this, however, when she returned appearing blushed, saying he was placing his hands all over her trying to explore what a girl is actually about."

"Oops, and this would clearly relate to the lack of proper upbringing and social manners."

"It sure would, and precisely the sort of young man I would never allow my daughter, as well as my niece, to come in contact with."

"I don't blame you."

"But he didn't stop there, he kept asking for more, and the crew had to decide on how to resolve this. If his only desire was a female companion to interact with, and due to their isolation and the classified nature of their operation, then it came down to choosing one of their staff members. He was roughly one and a half by now, still underage, but she said he was actually growing up into a fairly attractive young man, especially if you consider the lack of the seed or the chip."

"All right, I suppose I can see that."

"They did not want to become an escort service, but without the Marshal offering any control methods, and with no family or anything else, they found themselves pressed into asking one of the staff members to volunteer herself to the cause."

"To essentially be his playmate," he shrugs. "Which would include benefits by now."

"Right. Now, here we get to the dirty part. Again, one of the younger non-coms gave herself to him, and allowed him to have his fun. But at this point, he was still young and inexperienced, so she apparently had to explain a lot of things. Then, of course, as a young boy might, he apparently wanted her again, and again, and again…" he sighs.

"And here it goes…free sex, anytime, anywhere."

"And in any form, as it seems, because now he's starting to learn something and wants to experiment."

"Oops."

"She says he was still within reason for his behavior at this time, and the girl apparently started to like the interaction, probably because she was also lonely, as most of them were out there."

"I suppose this is reasonable. They weren't working under the best of conditions to begin with."

"But now, as we're moving into the second centennial, he starts getting bored with this one girl and stops asking for her. This apparently hurt her feelings as she felt they were developing something together."

"I'm sorry to hear that, but this also sounds like the beginning of his fetishes."

"Yes, it does, because now he's starting to call for them at random. Also, it's no longer a simple form of interaction. Now he's taking them in different ways, and not all of it politely. Now he's playing rough."

"How often was this?"

"Apparently, it slowed a bit as he matured into an adult, and he had a lot of other entertainment devices in there, like his vid-com, games, and such."

"I'll bet he was watching some kind of adult theater in there to get some of these wild ideas of his."

"Maybe, and when he couldn't hold onto himself any longer, he would call for someone to relieve his tensions. Then, towards the late second, going on the third, he ordered a set of weightlifting equipment. The staff was hoping this would turn into a new hobby to distract him somewhat."

"Weight training equipment," Geilv muses. "I don't like the sound of that, actually. We've heard a few people speak on this in those interviews. The Alpha Male Syndrome. I've heard it said that young male body builders tend to develop higher hormone levels, and this can result in stronger sexual urges."

"Yes Sir, and this is what she said. And he did. And without the usual conditioning and discipline counseling those weightlifters normally receive as part of their training, he starts losing control. Now he gets wild. His cravings turn into hardcore encounters using strange positions and rough handling. This is also where he begins casting insults for their seeds and the use of vulgar terms."

The Commander simply hung his head and sighed.

"At this point," the Captain continues. "We're starting to see some minor injuries, like bruising and scrapes, and stories of him abusing them with slapping and pinching. Then we come to his fourth centennial, and he apparently purchases a prisoner restraining mount."

"A what?" Geilv blasts and leans forward. "What in all the nether-space does he hope to use that for…as if I couldn't guess!"

"That's right, Commander, we're talking about acts of bondage. Now he's tying them up, and using his new pleasure toys on them. And I use that term very loosely, because the way she described it to me, it sounded as though he had been searching around every adult fetish store on Azgarén for the worst implements he could find. And if he couldn't find it, he apparently made something custom."

"Like what?" he frowns.

"He had a number of female pleasure sticks, some of them modified to inflict pain. He had a set of electrocution clips, which he would apply to the sensitive parts, and again which he claimed would stimulate, but all they really did was inflict more pain, and sometimes burns. And then he had some sharpened and pointed implements he might use to cut or pierce."

"That's simply dangerous, and not only for the seed. A person could draw a serious infection from something like that."

"Yes, and according to our medical reports, many of his victims were returned for exactly that, and even more. This young lady explained to me she was one of the more recent examples, and by the dates I referenced, I'm guessing she was the second to the last. She suffered a number of vaginal injuries, burns, and a few minor lacerations, but fortunately not the seed in her case."

"All right, so let's make an estimate here. We were asking when the ACI may have originally found that base. If we suggest Ytani is dead as justice for his murder of the most recent victim, then I think we might be looking at a time between these two, as I doubt they would allow this other one to simply slide by. If the victim had already been returned to us, maybe also reassigned elsewhere and out of sight, it may be down to witnessing only that final one."

"Right, either that, or perhaps catching it very soon after. But Commander, here is where I have another of my confusing mysteries. If we measure from the moment when we lost the base, which was easily a couple of years ago, the last victim was a good year or more before that."

The Commander glared at him for the clearly inconsistent timing.

"When you say the last victim, are we speaking of a murder, an injury, or what?"

"This reflects on our episode in the control room. According to our med-tech in the lab, he recalled that last victim that came in with the ridiculous excuse of an animal attack. Do you remember that? You were present at the time, and this was when Kriv'tik called in to us."

"Right, I recall this now. And I also recall I was ready to blow a fuse or two."

"Yes, even with your chips AND a sedative," he chuckles. "Anyway, that was a year prior. There were no new cases since that time. But BEFORE that time, and this girl confirmed this for me, he was calling for them at roughly one-month intervals to coincide with his result of the mining production, and which was described as a reward for his services."

"Incredible..." he shakes his head. "But now this doesn't make sense. What happened to him during that final year...unless..."

Geilv's eyes drift away as he ponders this idea.

"Unless we're saying he suddenly learned to behave himself, especially after committing murder. Captain, he must've been taken out a year earlier. It had to be between these two, but if this occurred a year prior, what was Kriv'tik doing in the meantime over there?"

"And for that matter, who took him out...the ACI, or Kriv'tik himself? I can't imagine he would let something like this pass."

"No, he wouldn't, but he also said this wasn't the first time, either."

"It's got to be those chips!" he scorns. "Especially the authority chip. He may have let the others pass due to the threat of the chips, but this last one probably tipped the scales."

"Maybe. But are we saying he mutinied, or did the ACI intervene?"

"Maybe both, especially if we consider the Ghan'aju. It had to go somewhere, and Ti'van had to find a way back home, which means there must be a transport link somewhere. This could offer us a possible explanation. Maybe they snuck back inside somehow."

"It further tells me Ti'van switched sides along the way. This might then correlate with others doing the same."

"All right, but now, what about the missing year?"

"If I were to guess," Geilv muses. "I'd say he was making some sort of plan. At this point, he was probably mutinying to some degree, ACI or otherwise."

"Right, I think I might have to agree."

"And that plan eventually led up to the Marshal's inspection. The Ghan'aju was sent out to conduct a survey..." he halts and snaps his fingers. "Yes, the mining was running out, and they needed the ship. This has to be the link. They were building up a need to call for that ship."

"Ah! Of course! And a clever plan, too. I recall now how those mining reports were thinning out over time. Then, I would expect by now the ACI is likely involved to some degree. They probably shut down their production and stopped imposing themselves on the locals. They file a number of false mining reports to build up this image of failing production, and then they call the ship for this new survey, and boom, trouble happens as Ytani goes berserk."

"Very good, Captain. And then the Marshal makes his visit, and then we have the clean-up effort."

"Yes, the clean-up... But one moment, Commander, this seems to be opening up a new hole for me. This is now placing us farther back in time than I previously expected. If we say the ACI has a hidden base, and we're not seeing any unusual traffic through our local sector, they must have their own private fleet of ships to pull some of this off."

"Well, Captain," he chuckles. "We don't know precisely how long they've been in operation, and by the sound of it, for their interaction with these aliens, and time to train such things as telepathy, maybe also to train a few of their people to use this projection skill, it could be a while now. But I'll admit one thing; whoever is behind it is playing a very quiet game on us. This is starting to look like a secret operation to detach themselves from all the control methods the Marshal has been playing on us. Maybe also setting up some kind of secret liberation force, and now they're coming back to set things right."

◆ ◆ ◆ ◆ ◆

It was morning on Therinë, and Thaelyn was in his usual meeting in the WIC building reviewing the activities occurring on Azgarén. Kaliya and Kailen were just finishing up with the previous day's spy-cam video when she decided to report in at the conference table.

"My Lord, we have something you might want to hear."

"Ah, do we have anything new and interesting on our cameras?"

"Yes, a continuation of Geilv and Captain Ta'yeen in conversation trying to interpret all our clues to piece together the puzzle. They're actually a very clever team, and Geilv is showing himself to be a smart man."

"I am pleased to hear that, but I do hope he recalls our warning about his position where the Marshal is concerned."

"Yeah, I think he does, and he's stepping around things very carefully."

"Good. Then what do we have today?"

"First and foremost, he's been trying to collect all these reports and sensations we're dropping into a kind of plotline, a bit like reading a book and skipping ahead to the last chapter, which might represent my visitation with him as that ghostly image, then trying to fill in the missing pages to see how it arrived there."

"How interesting… And where is he now?

"His most recent discussion is suggesting the ACI to be very active in some areas. He's interpreting my Ytani image as just that, an image, like a performance for the camera. He has suspected Ayene to be part of the ACI for a while now, and recently he got curious enough to look up her record. Of course, she's listed as dead, but with a false cause, like everyone else at the Morndindor base, and this is enough to say the Marshal is covering up that operation. But the simple fact that she's clearly alive now suggests the whole base could actually be alive, and the show we put on for the Marshal was fake. This actually helps us finally correct for our little oversight where his long-lost friend is concerned."

"This is good to hear, as I recall that moment, and it was unfortunate but necessary as we had to play this role in Darumon's eyes. Commander Geilv was simply collateral damage."

"This essentially tidies up those clues we've been dropping in other places, like the Tul'ryk. Then, he couldn't find any official record of Morndindor in his computer, so he looked up the invoices for the supply deliveries and found Ayene signing off on most of them."

"This is curious…and rather ingenious. So, Darumon apparently missed a step."

"Yeah, some of the complexity is biting him in the tail now. This would go along nicely with his recent statement of how Sargeras might somehow hear of this new sensation."

"With the Prodigy Gift, yes… So, he is keeping yet another secret.

This is just as we had hoped, and good for us to know, in case we might find an opportunity to use it."

"But Geilv also made a mention of this here in this video, and I think we should pay attention to it. During one of those recent calls, the Marshal showed what might be a sign of genuine worry, and Kailen and I would have to agree. If Sargeras should ever hear of it, this might be the tipping point for his tolerance level. This now reminds me of Madzurki and Darumon's private thoughts there."

"I may have to agree. Those people may be borderline for this point, even without these Gifts. So surely, he, above all others, needs to be monitored. I would recommend we keep a careful watch, and if he should show any signs of activity, we might need to make a countermove, if only to preserve lives."

"All right, we'll watch for it. Anyway, Geilv had the Captain do a little research on Morndindor, and now we have his results. He sent a ship out there to find the base physically removed, and since it wasn't anywhere else locally, it had to be off world. They saw that green spot in front of Glimmerheim and interpreted this to be a hard effort to reclaim that world from the ecological collapse. This would require someone big to do the job, like maybe my godly alien image. He also researched the history of Ytani's victims and found one survivor who came just before that one we saw. She apparently came in for an interview and gave a rather interesting, if also disturbing story of Ytani and the base staff. Further, that he was calling for them at roughly one-month intervals with the last victim being approximately one year before the loss of the base, and this represented a surprising discrepancy in the timing for the attack."

"I am sure it would."

"So, in summary, between all of his recent conversations, he is suggesting either the ACI or Kriv'tik himself did Ytani in after that final straw of the last murder. Then a year to plan the mines running out, resulting in the call for the ship, and Kriv'tik probably went up there to take charge and send it away. By this time, the ACI is likely involved, where they put on a show for the Marshal, and then removed all their evidence, including Madzurki and Ooduan."

"Fascinating..." he croons.

"He's also suggesting the ACI must have a base off-world, in part as a refugee camp for all these people we're abducting, and also perhaps as some kind of super-secret liberation force that must've separated from Azgarén at some moment. Then they went into hiding, maybe in association with these aliens, and began privately training such things as telepathy and the projection skill, as he calls it, and now they're making a return to set things right back home."

"This is a most curious turn," he grins. "Quite ingenious, indeed, and so close to accurate for what he has to work with. This is a very clean path of deductive reasoning. I would not mind, one of these days, to have an opportunity to sit down with him and share a few thoughts."

"Yes, and so would I," she smiles. "Along the way, that last victim also recalled Ytani being an orphan with the special privilege of his chip being removed for his job specs. This clearly tied in their speculation for the Tav'ageen Anomaly, and further to point a finger at the Marshal for hiding it. But it also opened up something else, which I'm already getting ideas on," she grins impishly.

"Oh no, and will this be deserving of another mark? Recall, you are in competition with Ayene now, so let us not be rude."

"All right, after all, the ACI will have to be the one to release it… indirectly that is. Geilv gave an instruction to see if they could trace Ytani's origins, searching the local law enforcement files from four centuries ago for any accidents involving whole families with a seven-decade old child named Ytani. It's likely he is also listed as dead. Therefore, he can be assigned to the base with no questions asked. If they can find anything, Geilv is suggesting passing it along for another sensation."

"And your thoughts on the matter, dear young Miss?" Thaelyn eyes her cautiously.

"Well, it's actually very reasonable to think someone, like a law enforcement or investigative agency, will want to research who this errant young man is. So, if you simply look up a few things, based on his…leaked…details, I think you might discover something."

"Quite possibly. And considering the disturbances you have in mind; it is very reasonable to think someone would investigate this. All right, be sure to save me a copy of that one, and whatever Darumon does afterwards. I would imagine that office of his will require major refurbishing before this is over."

"Finally," Kaliya continues. "The two of them were able to come to a few conclusions about the Prodigy Gift, but only up to a certain point."

"Meaning to involve the Suppressor chip," Kailen adds.

"Right, and this allows them to speculate on how a person can project an image of some kind, but so far that person is still local."

"And this is already bad enough, from a certain perspective. But then to include his recent revelation that it could instead be the ACI playing these games, he's going to want a few answers after a while, if for no other reason than to understand the permutations."

"Yes," Kaliya nods. "And this might then involve Ayene making a visit, especially after this next interview with Latena," she grins.

It was late in the week, and Ileani was preparing for her latest interview with Latena. They were setting up in the studio again, this time just the two of them.

In the officer's lounge at Central Command, Geilv and the Captain were both taking time to relax and listen to this latest report.

"That niece of yours is taking on a serious role in all this," Geilv muses. "She'll go down in history if she keeps this up."

"Yes, but what kind of history are we speaking of here?"

"I don't know, but if she's working with the ACI to bring in a new Era, and also leaking so many of the Marshal's little secrets of the past one, she may end up as a kind of national hero when all this is over."

"My little Latena...a national hero," he ponders. "If only I could share any of this with her parents. I was only able to clue them in on a very few pieces. But overall, they're pulling their horns out for all the trouble she's raising."

"One of these days, Captain, we'll get there."

In the studio, they were making the final arrangements. The set coordinator checked his cameras one last time and prepared to give his count. He called out the numbers and pointed at Ileani for her cue.

"This is Ileani Ur'paran for C.P. News. Welcome everybody, to another meeting with today's hottest celebrity and revolutionary, Miss Latena Ta'yeen. Today, we're going to hear about a new theory she recently came upon during the course of her recent activities, and that unfortunate encounter with that figure we have come to know of only as Ytani. Miss Ta'yeen, how do you feel today after your ordeal?"

"I feel much better, thanks," she admits. "Although that experience was certainly shocking, and not simply for this horrible creature rampaging in places you wouldn't expect to see it."

"Yes, I can certainly appreciate that. I was standing only a few paces away when it came across that skywalk. But when it transformed into that impertinent young man, I just couldn't believe my eyes. And yet, here you were, right under him. How did that make you feel at first?"

"Very vulnerable, and on multiple levels…"

In the officer's lounge, Geilv and the Captain watched expectantly.

"Ha!" Geilv blurts. "I would hardly expect that, you little faker."

"She's playing a role here," the Captain accedes. "So, she needs to say it."

"Of course…"

"But now, Miss Ta'yeen," Ileani continues. "You claim you came up with this new theory, and I'm going to assume this follows with your manners of devising conspiracy theories, right?"

"Yes, I must admit, it does," she affirms eagerly. "This one resulted from my experience up there on that observation deck, and then a debriefing I got from that woman in your interview."

As Geilv watched and listened, he nodded impulsively.

"Here it comes."

"Can you explain to us what she might have told you?" she asks.

"I got a lot of the same information about who this guy was, as what I think they let out to the public by other means. He was apparently running this mining base somewhere, but he went a bit tail-crazy with things, and next thing you know, boom, he takes off in the first star cruiser he can hijack from Central. It would make a great vid-com action movie, I suppose, but he's apparently still out there, so we still need an ending."

"Yes, I suppose we do. But now, as for this theory of yours, what is it you think you can draw out of this experience?"

"The first thing I needed was some time to myself to recover from my shock. I reflected on that surprising, and also frightening encounter, where that…thing…rampaged across the skywalk and into the room. Then to see it, or maybe to see HIM, transform like that, well…" she shrugs. "But as I found time to relax and go over my experience, my mind started ticking again. And I began to assemble a few pieces that stood out about him. The most obvious was his vulgar attitude. I swear; if my boyfriend ever tried treating me like that, he's going to lose a few parts," she chuckles satirically.

"I would agree! I've known a few men in my lifetime, but never one like that."

"Yes, but I'll bet all of yours had their chips installed. This guy clearly did not. And he apparently was completely out of control. He was clearly very obsessed with his physique. He also seemed to believe himself to be some sort of god figure, probably for this strange ability to change his shape. His statement of losing a mining base tells me something bad happened over there, and their operation went down to the nether-realms. Could he be responsible? It sure sounded like it. The statement by the military sounded like a classic example of '... there is nothing to see here, move along now...' So, they're not spilling anything they don't want to spill. This means, there's another cover-up of some kind, and I'm fairly sure it revolves around that thing he said goes boom. And this one simply must point at the Marshal, if Ytani was working for him."

"And the military?"

"We already established they work for him, especially if we say the Council illegally gave him authoritative control over them."

"Yes, I recall this now."

"This now suggests some sort of covert operation. Now, I can certainly see how a military body would conduct a covert operation. This is the military, after all, and historically speaking, a military body might often perform such things to sneak up on their enemies. So this falls nicely into place. Although why they need something that goes boom in such a big way, I don't know, since they are doing so well against these insurgents even without that."

In the officer's lounge, Geilv smiled tenderly.

"Yes," he nods. "Why would he want something like that if there's no real threat potential to warrant it."

In the newsroom, Latena continues, "Of course, this also makes me ask why the military, rather than an industrial firm, would be mining something. This seems a little outside their specialty. So, one thing we might want to ask is what were they mining and why does it go boom in such a big way as to take out an entire star system. They mentioned something about the industrial potential, but in all the nether-space, something so volatile that it goes boom and takes out a full star system? What sort of industry needs to clear the galaxy of its surplus stars?"

This statement causes Geilv and the Captain, along with many of the other viewers in the room, to erupt in a bold laugh.

"Therefore," Latena asserts. "This simply makes me think their 'industrial' use might be more military than industrial, especially if it was covert. After all, why do you need to run a covert military operation to investigate a potential industrial material? And why would the Marshal be the one to order it, unless maybe it involved something relating to his crusade. He shouldn't be out there mining up mysterious minerals for their industrial value. He is supposed to be out there fighting his insurgents. As such, this simply has to be related to that. And with a boom quotient on a stellar scale, that sounds like a bomb to me."

"I suppose it might seem that way on the surface."

"And this simply defies reason if our military has proven itself so proficient at keeping his feeble insurgents at bay so well that they can't even find us again in this big, huge galaxy. And so, my guess is he had something special in mind. What was it? Well, it certainly couldn't involve anything like sector defense. It would be a little self-defeating to use one of those to blast any new alien ships that might come along to carry away our unappreciated Council members, assuming you could find any by now."

"Maybe so," Ileani muses humorously.

"And if our military is already doing such a fine job with everything else, then he must have a plan for it elsewhere. But this also causes us to ask where he originally came from, and why he hasn't apparently made any attempts to return there by now to reclaim what those insurgents took from him so long ago…so VERY long ago. Could THIS be related? And if so…WOW! He must really want to kick them hard in the tail! As if our military, that's so proficiently kicking their tails everywhere else across the galaxy, can't do the same in his native backyard."

In the officer's lounge, Geilv leaned in to listen to this statement.

"Fascinating…" he croons softly.

"Commander?" the Captain ushers quietly. "Do you hear something in that?"

"I think I do…maybe. Maybe I'm just getting a little paranoid, wondering what is and is not a message, but that one carries something."

"Like what, something for the Marshal?"

"Maybe, but it also opens a door for me. On the outside, it suggests we should be able to lead his crusade right up to his backdoor without the need for any super weapons. Further, in all this time, why haven't we done it. Then, the Marshal keeps saying we need to keep his insurgents oppressed, but when it came to a REAL enemy force, like what we saw on Therinë, or even that city structure, he ran with his tail between his legs, like a frightened child from a nightmare monster. You saw it in the control booth with the Tul'ryk, right? THAT is his enemy force, and he's afraid of it. So, who is it he had us fighting that we were so successful at keeping oppressed? It couldn't be the same as over there where it actually mattered. And where were we at that moment? Not in our native universe, but in nether-space, of all places. And I doubt WE could fight anything out there. This opens a door for me to challenge him on his own terms."

"Congratulations, Commander, I think they just gave you a gift. But could this be in preparation for something?"

"Probably so, and it's called Ytani. Captain, I think our military just realized those training chips are no longer necessary."

In the studio, Latena continues.

"But anyway, I'm sure the military can handle this. What was really interesting was Ytani himself. We had that mad dash coming across the skywalk, and then him in this animal shape, and poor little me on the floor, trying to figure out what just happened. But before I could do anything, he pounces on me!"

"And I can only imagine what might be going through your mind at that time."

"Initially, yes. But my mind is that of a conspiracy theorist, and I suppose I conditioned myself over the course of time to see through what's on the surface. I tend to notice things. My mind kicked into overdrive at that moment and noticed his hands, which were pinning mine to the floor, but they didn't seem to carry the sort of weight I would expect of a big man like him. It just didn't feel right."

"Oh?" Ileani leans forward to show an increased interest in the topic. "How did it feel to you?"

"There was something tangible to it, like a physical body applying itself, but without the expected mass of that body. He was a big guy, muscular, like he works out a lot. And as a fully mature male, where their bodies are bigger than ours anyway, this must involve mass, lots of it, maybe twice that of a girl like me. But he didn't feel heavy at all."

"Not heavy?" she wonders.

"It felt fake, like something that looked real, maybe even felt solid, but it wasn't. Maybe like a shell, where on the outside it looks real, but without anything on the inside filling up the space."

"That is a very strange depiction."

"Now, I hate to use the word here, but I'm reminded of one of your reports where we had spokespeople talking, and one of them was some guy who apparently doesn't believe in supernatural stuff. He mentioned the word ghost. Well, other than the fact that he did seem to hold a solid form, the word ghost is probably the most accurate term I can think of to describe what his hands felt like. And then I had a brainstorm: Ghostlike images."

"Uh oh…"

"But this now leads me to several disturbing thoughts. It was like a cascade hitting me. When I look back on our previous interview, and several recent news reports, especially that one where we had that hidden Metaphysics faction come out of secrecy, I had a revelation. But the implications of that revelation nearly turned my horns inside-out."

"How so?"

"It effectively turns our finger-pointing in a new direction, and I started building a new picture out of it. There is even logic to it now."

"Logic! This is interesting."

In the officer's lounge, they continued to watch.

"If she's preparing for what I think she's preparing…" the Captain intones warily.

"Maybe so," Geilv nods. "And this is going to start something big, maybe also to finish it off."

"I wish you didn't just now use those words."

Latena continues, "And unfortunately for our world population, I think we've been misled by a lot of people during this time."

"All right, one thing at a time," Ileani issues. "First, this revelation."

"In order for me to paint this picture accurately, I think I should first rehash what was said before in our earlier interview. The Council is responsible for numerous occasions of either withholding their duties from the people and our science factions, or exerting irrational control measures on us. This has also been verified by independent sources, so we know this to be true by now. Also, on at least a few recognizable occasions, they falsified our research data in the name of their spirit of the words, and they behave as a type of figurehead for some hidden body or purpose. We have Saakerav who came out of nowhere, did something extraordinary and without precedent, and then disappears back to nowhere, leaving us with something no one ever heard of before, and romanticizing it so heavily that we all fall in love with the idea… regardless of the logic of how or why it actually happened."

"All right, and although this is a very serious summary of statements, if we look at the world out there right now, we can't help but to agree with it."

"This naturally follows with where we are now, with the war protocols, the associated industry and its pollution, and then the seeds and their hidden code. We have the Tav'ageen Scare, and what that did to us, and our direction to place the blame on the Council for so many NEW hidden agendas."

"And this generally brings us up to where we left off with the last interview, I believe."

"Right. But now we have a few new reports, like that astonishing revelation of our evolution. Ileani, I'm sure you, as a young girl, and me, and probably everyone else, loved to hear the story of our Eracyodine ancestors. But like I said before; that old research was apparently interfered with, and the science factions who were involved know this. Then they go back and try again, this time apparently outside the knowing of whatever body was interfering with it in the first place, as it had to be an ongoing thing, and for each time they made the attempt. I could potentially qualify this statement by saying the Council ordered it closed, and they expected them to behave themselves, as good little followers of our god entity Council should."

"Oops, but yes, I suppose I can see your point."

"We could also qualify this by saying each and every other attempt was WITH the Council's knowledge of it, so they COULD interfere if they wanted to. In other words, it was no secret."

"Yes, this is reasonable."

"But this time, they got an answer, because the god entity Council, or whatever body it is controlling the show, had ITS back turned. And wow! What an answer! It's no wonder someone was interfering with it. They were probably the ones who caused it."

"But one moment. Are we actually saying whatever it was that seems to have artificially engineered us as a species might actually still be among us?"

"The archeology faction sure seems to think so, especially if you consider the missing evidence and falsified reports. Unless you KNOW the reason, why would you otherwise try to hide it?"

"Well, I suppose this does hold merit. But it was so long ago..."

"Long ago... Yes, long enough that you might need a super longevity drug, or something similar to survive that long. Maybe your species has evolved so far by now that time no longer matters."

In the officer's lounge, Geilv and the others wince at the statement.

"Ouch! Yes, that will hit a tender spot. And he did use this same excuse."

Latena continues, "But then, we might need to ask for what purpose. Is there something out there that likes going around and engineering any odd lifeform into sentience simply for the fun of it? I can't pretend to know if a godlike entity with this level of potential would do so for the fun of it, but maybe there could be. But then to see…something… going to so much effort to hide it from us? This hints at an assertive effort to interfere with our ability to discover the truth of it. So, are we now saying there is a godlike entity out there that likes going around engineering new sentient lifeforms, and then perpetually covering up for itself over the long duration of their history? That seems like an excessive effort if all you want is a little fun for doing the deed."

"I think that statement would not be rational," Ileani considers. "I might have to agree there must be a motive in doing so."

"Yes, because this would surely represent a work effort, and you don't go through a work effort like this unless you have a good reason for it. Our biology doesn't match anything else in our world, and neither do our…" she smirks softly, "…ridiculously long lifespans. This clearly stands out, and would naturally invoke any number of questions and controversies. Then we have this early image of a Creator, which our ancestors once worshipped. This would likely represent some kind of early memory of what happened that developed into a religion. Later we have Saakerav, and I am still quite sure he has to be a figurehead for a hidden body. He comes along, does his part, and along the way, abolishes that religion."

"But wait," Ileani interjects. "Not that I would wish to add fuel into this argument, but if I'm interpreting you correctly, this sounds like whoever or whatever it was that evolved us, may have also portrayed or directed Saakerav and his efforts. If he is the one to create the Council, which would later interfere with our research, and further to say they might be a front for something hidden, as you are saying for Saakerav himself, this is now suggesting whatever this body might have been may not WANT us to worship it. But wouldn't this be a contradiction in terms for a god entity that created us?"

"Normally, I might say it could be, but I think it might also be subjective to the original intent. If your original intent is to create a society that would worship you, you might portray yourself openly to that society so they would know who you are in order to conduct that worship, maybe even to enforce it. But this one never did. In fact, it did just the opposite. It hid itself from us. It interfered with our ability to identify it, interfered with our ability to realize where WE came from, and how we came to be who we are now. This means, worship is not the purpose here. It has other motives."

"All right, I suppose this is reasonable."

"The trouble is, we must now ask about those other motives. Because to do anything at all on this scale, and to go to this much trouble to hide it, means the motives are more likely subversive. Hiding stuff, falsifying other stuff, and then if to include Saakerav and the Council as a false image with its own god presence, reinforced with this romance and their spirit of the words as a cultural fetish, this means THAT is the purpose. But still, there must be an ultimate direction. This is still a work effort, even if you have a figurehead body doing the work for you. So, what is the ultimate goal here? Well, the first thing to come to mind is if you are some sort of god entity, and likely with such capacity as to do all this, one thing I might suggest is time is on your side."

"Such as with this super longevity drug, or whatever?"

Latena nods, "The Marshal, for instance, once told us his kind overcame the aging process long ago. So, if he can do it, it stands to reason any other sufficiently advanced society could do the same. It might simply go with the territory of such exceptionally advanced beings. After all, look at us. We have a lot of science, and we already have ridiculously long lifespans. If we could push this a little more, wow, I don't know how it might appear, but it would be fun to watch."

"I suppose. And so, if we suggest this entity already has this, he could likely survive all this time to keep up his efforts to monitor things."

"I would say, if you want to play god, you probably need to be at or near true immortality. Evolution isn't a fast process, Ileani, even if you do give it that jump start in the beginning."

"This is true."

"But if we are now to say this entity is still here with us, it must have a final direction. We see our history with all these complications along the way, so we can say some or all of it may be part of this plan. If our purpose is to evolve along certain lines, directed by the Council and their motives, then we can perhaps suggest our purpose is to evolve with certain useful forms of knowledge. But can THIS be useful to a god entity? He probably has a lot already, so why would he need us?"

"Yes, this does actually make some good sense."

"Unless we suggest he does NOT have everything he started out with."

"Um… All right, how do you mean?"

"We may need to make a few assumptions here to get a possible idea. This entity, he goes out, finds a world with a viable form of life that is easily manipulated. And so he does. He has no true interest in a society of beings who bow down to worship him, but he DOES need them for some other reason, and not one where he openly presents himself. So he hides and directs that society from behind their collective backs. He leads them up the evolutionary ladder, developing as a potent society with some rather fancy tech along the way, until one day they're capable of travelling through space. Now, are you with me so far?"

"Yes, I am, and so far, this is a curious picture."

"Curious up to the point where they now have the capacity to jump from our galaxy to the next one, but then they're told to stop. They don't need to go any further than that. And by the way, they're never allowed to go off-planet to colonize anything. After all, he wants them to stay right at home, where he can monitor them."

"Uh oh…"

"And so we come back to the ultimate purpose. He wants servants. But not just any servants. He wants servants with certain key technologies he can use, maybe because HE lost something and needs someone else to do his work."

"This is a very interesting picture. Very subjective, of course, but also interesting."

In the officer's lounge, Geilv and the Captain continued to watch.

"Oh, Latena," the Captain muses. "You're a sly one here. But do be careful if you hope to point a finger at someone."

"Unfortunately," Latena continues. "Now we come to our recent history and something funny happens. Maybe due to the way in which he engineered us, he made a critical error along the way, or else he used a method that might be…well, let's just say, unorthodox."

"Oh?" Ileani wonders.

"Yeah, because if we are now suggesting he wants these servants as a replacement to something he lost, whatever method he might normally use to evolve a species might not be available by now. So he might need to resort to something else, maybe a bit crude, but one that would ultimately serve his purpose. Unfortunately, it also creates a side effect."

"A side effect. This is a new one. How do you mean?"

"Well, one clear example is our alien biology as compared to everything else here, and this reflects in our bone structure as well as our ridiculously long lifespan. This might be one side effect. If he is a godlike thing with perhaps a form of extreme longevity, or maybe true immortality, we must've inherited some of that…from him."

"Oh dear…and so your idea of something unorthodox?"

"Yeah, in the absence of whatever he might normally use to create new life, he was reduced to the most primal of tools. That one between his legs."

Ileani turned and grimaced, forcing herself to act out a shudder of revulsion for the camera, which really wasn't that hard to do under the circumstances.

"And so, here we are…" Latena continues, now glancing at herself. "You know; that old religion of the Creator being the father of our race may hold some actual truth to it. Although it probably wasn't a benevolent god. Not if he only wants us as servants to replace something he lost."

"All right, but this is a lot of conjecture so far. It's a fascinating story, but how do you finish it with something that might tie it together with this revelation of yours?"

"I'll give you two words, Ileani, and what I suspect to be another form of inheritance from him. The Tav'ageen Anomaly."

"Oh dear!" she retracts with an aura of surprise.

In the officer's lounge, Geilv nods assertively.

"Here it goes. This is where those horns will fly, I'll bet."

"Once again," Latena continues. "The Council interferes with our research to understand something, probably at the demand of this shadow entity behind them. We have Elder Nazég, who was trying to understand it, but his faction isn't welcome to begin with. And at this moment, I am going to point a finger at this shadow body again, because the Elder might be the only one to know how to interpret the data successfully. We have those first children who are discovered, and publicized with such sensationalism as to cause a public stir. But those nether-wild alien deaths stumped everyone. We have the medical community taking further action by moving them to those labs, and under much more careful scrutiny, including cameras. But this now places too much attention on it, and with too much potential to actually learn something. So, after only two of these occasions, that god entity finally shows itself. The Anomaly is SO serious, he has to come out of hiding to take personal action."

"Wait!" Ileani gasps. "You don't mean…"

"Well, let me tie this up for you. Who is it that told us to use the chips? But at the same time, who is it that apparently taught Ytani how to use this otherwise alien infestation for a practical purpose? This means, it's NOT an alien infestation, it's a Gift we have inside of us, and likely inherited by accident. And HE knows it."

Ileani playacted a role of shock as she sat there gaping at the girl.

"So now we have the Scare," Latena continues. "It's so mysterious and frightening that we forget we're a society of high technological esteem, and also that we aren't supposed to believe in ghost stories, that as a result, we take our god entity Council at its word that we need to run away, naked and screaming if need be, to the nearest planet with a halfway viable atmosphere, using nothing more than the seeds, which were coincidentally engineered by that same shadow entity as a survival device. Unfortunately, as the story goes, those insurgents get in our way before we can actually escape. Now, if we compare to the idea that we were never intended to leave home for any reason, because this shadow entity wants to keep us nice and neat in one place, this makes perfect sense."

"Um, maybe...but, um..."

"Yeah, the ultimate reason. It still needs to be rationalized. If the Tav'ageen Anomaly is so bad that this god entity had to come out of hiding for it, then why the seeds? For that matter, why the story of insurgents, and why all the rest of it? The chips should've been the first and only solution presented if this was the only real problem. But I think there is another problem here. One we probably missed, or maybe just didn't know about, or realize fully, because it's so...alien. Sargeras."

"Him? Why him?"

"The old reports say he was in a very poor state of health when he first arrived. The Marshal said our medical technology would be inadequate to help, and so he would do it himself. He just didn't say HOW he would do it, especially if he is missing his native tools to do anything with. He's essentially in exile, remember?"

"Um, well...yeah, I suppose."

"Much like he didn't say WHAT the Tav'ageen Anomaly actually was, or WHY we need to run away from it, and then WHY we can suddenly stay at home with these chips, which were a much better solution than those seeds they pushed at us. For someone who was promising so many secrets of the universe, he seems to have forgotten a few important details to explain real world issues right here at home," she shrugs. "But I'll tell you something. For someone who seems to serve Sargeras so devotedly, I might suggest Sargeras to be his first priority to support by any kind of solution. And those seeds have something very alien inside that no one told us about. It creates a kind of organic network link, with such nomenclature terms that sound almost supernatural. I wonder where THAT came from, especially if Elder Nazég's faction was banished, as this almost sounds like something he would invent. And what does it actually do, because the medical community has no idea from their side of it."

"Uh oh…"

"It creates this energy aura, which WE don't know anything about. But if HE helped invent them, and the original survival code for colonizing alien environments was largely omitted, THIS was their primary purpose, and his FIRST solution to solve a problem. And his first problem to solve wasn't ours. It was his."

"Then that aura effect…" she begins tentatively.

"…Is likely a life support machine for his sick master," Latena concludes. "We don't know what sort of alien beings these two actually are. And if our science once called the Tav'ageen thing 'ghostlike', that our people couldn't otherwise detect by conventional means, these two might also represent something our science couldn't define by conventional means. This would then coincide nicely with the statement that WE wouldn't be able to help him. He's probably right. After all, this energy can't be native to our local space. In fact, I had a brief conversation with a member of the astrophysics faction about this, to see if they ever detected, or even theorized about this energy as a natural resource anywhere within our local space. And he said, based on the specs he had a chance to study one time from the medical community sharing a few scans, it didn't resemble anything recognizable. It seemed organic in nature, which itself defies meaning. Rather than using EM scanners to detect something, you might be better off using a medical biorhythm scanner on it instead."

"Really!"

"But it is otherwise unknown to exist in our local space, and further not within our local galaxy, and maybe not even within our universe. Now, where do you think they actually came from, if this is something they use for any reason?"

"Wow! That would twist a few horns."

In the officer's lounge, Geilv and the Captain both nodded at the statement.

"That has to be something for later," Geilv asserts.

"Yes, and it will likely result in the 'discovery' of that other universe, maybe even, like on the Tul'ryk, nether-space itself."

"Yeah, and that'll send a few horns flying, for sure."

Latena continues, "And so, now we have those insurgents that never know when to quit, and this is combined with the war protocols that never let up, providing for that industry that pollutes the place, and therefore the continued and perpetual need for those seeds, which should've been cut out after a while, but no, this was not the plan. They serve a purpose, Ileani, but not ours. Therefore, those chips were secondary, AFTER the first priority was achieved."

In the officer's lounge, both Geilv and the Captain gasped at this revelation.

"And there's your link for those seeds!" Geilv asserts. "And if the ACI has people coming for him, this could be a message for the rest of us."

"Dammit!" the Captain scorns. "An organic network link…a power feed, maybe also with a feedback loop."

"That would be simply nasty if that ticks off at the wrong moment. We have a whole world full of them. The only ones who might survive, if this goes critical on us, would be the younger generation."

"And Sir, I can already see this would hit hard for the loss of knowledge, expertise, technical skills…" he shakes his head. "This could send our civilization of high technological esteem back to the Stone Age, simply for the loss of people to keep it alive."

Back in the studio, Ileani was trying to recover from her roleplaying reaction.

"But Latena," she issues. "While this MAY represent a purpose if you say this developed in recent times, you began all this from two million years ago with the Eracyodines."

"Yes, I did," Latena responds. "But then, how long has the Marshal and Sargeras actually been running away from those insurgents. And what do you need a star-destroying super bomb for that our glorious military can't handle after ten millennia of success? This might suggest another target, one we don't know about, and probably one that isn't local, if you consider this energy and wherever it comes from. It might also represent the reason why that god entity who created us is now out in the cold without his usual toolkit. His original story was being chased out of something, his holdings seized, and his loyalists imprisoned. That doesn't sound good, but a super bomb might save the day. So we need to ask a very important question here. What was the Marshal chasing halfway across the galaxy claiming to be his insurgents? Especially if his kind is in need of some crazy Abnormal Energy that isn't even believed to exist in our home universe?"

"Oh dear!" Ileani winces.

"And why hasn't he found his way back home yet? If he's so high on the ladder with his great wisdom, he should be able to simply program a jump drive, now that we are clearly able to jump to such exotic locations as our neighboring galaxy, and take us to any location he desires. And surely, the ONE location he should desire most is to go home, like he said in the beginning."

"Yes, I suppose it ought to be."

"But, if that home is currently the home of some other god entity, a super bomb might be necessary to take it back, if it doesn't destroy it outright. Therefore, he needed us to evolve up to the point where we might actually be able to make one for him. AND have that jump drive to take it there. But this now suggests he lost that home a LONG time ago. Now, that's patience for you to find a solution!"

"It most certainly is!"

"But using us as what might be a life support machine isn't nice. I might ask if there could have been a more polite solution, if not for the emergency of the Anomaly getting in the way. And using us for this ultimate goal without actually telling us what that ultimate goal might be, also isn't nice. I would imagine that other god entity might be a bit tougher to fight than his feeble insurgents. I might further suggest they also use this Abnormal Energy as their native environment. And if it's not found anywhere remotely near to us, I simply have to ask where they really are found, especially if their bodies are so bizarrely different from ours that our science can't interpret them. And then we have that military woman during your interview in the building downtown, and her use of the word…corporeal."

"Oops!" Ileani blurts.

"I know! How do you measure, using devices we are most often familiar with, something that is incorporeal…meaning to say ghostlike. We don't even believe in such nonsense; much less would we know how to measure it. This might even be one of those sciences that hidden shadow body explicitly denied us to study, as it would help us to identify HIM."

"I suppose…"

"Which causes me to wonder what other sciences were explicitly denied, or otherwise interfered with, that might help us to realize who he is and where he actually came from. Especially if this energy is such an important aspect of his existence, but doesn't otherwise exist in our universe. We don't believe in such things as other universes…do we?" she raises her brow inquisitively. "Where would you otherwise find incorporeal bodies as native inhabitants? Three-dimensional space is full of three-dimensional matter and energy. But if this stuff is so abnormal, where does it come from, as it doesn't seem to fit those same three-dimensional parameters."

In the officer's lounge, the audience reeled back at the assertion.

"Oh, Latena," the Captain croons. "If you're hoping to pry open something on that scale…"

"It's likely a plug for something later," Geilv nods. "After all, we did find it."

Latena continues, "And here we are, chasing away someone like Elder Nazég, as he certainly WAS trying to study something…and likely against the Council's better interests."

"Oh no," Ileani gushes. "And so, you are suggesting this whole affair might not be what it seems?"

"It certainly smells of a lot of cover-ups, and most of it with ulterior motives. And with Ytani out there going tail-crazy with his god syndrome, it simply fills in a few things we didn't know about before now. Maybe those pieces are the pieces our 'god' was hiding from us. But it also means we have something that needs careful consideration, and is not subject to the whims of whatever it was out there trying so hard to hide it from us. If we actually did inherit something…godlike… In all the nether-space, Ileani, this could be a very serious situation for us as a civilization! It might even mean we need to evolve up to that level where we can not only understand it, but know how to contain and use it responsibly. Because that example of Ytani is a really bad one."

"I would most certainly agree. But this also hints at something, and this might be that we have problems on both sides of us now."

"It sure does. Whatever that ulterior motive, it may have backfired on him."

In the officer's lounge, both Geilv and the Captain frowned at the statement.

"And there is your connection, Captain," Geilv suggests. "Ytani is the newest enemy to fear."

"That's right, Latena…" the Captain moans. "Start a new panic."

"She may need to, if our people only respond to such things to enact any kind of countermeasure on a global scale."

"True, unfortunately. That motivational factor, much like with the original Scare. Now we need to undo it. But these are also some bold statements she's making."

"My interpretation here," Geilv considers, "is they might be over an important hump, with the world on the edge of a revolt, so she's simply putting the final few nails in it. The Council is out, the Charter is out, his control mechanisms are out, and he's basically losing control. So, the scales must be tipping in our favor by now. Her arguments are turning it around so the people know who the culprit really is in case he should try anything new."

Back in the studio, Ileani winces at the last accusation.

"Backfired! That would be a dangerous situation, if this Ytani actually does have any friends out there in the possession of a super bomb. And even if not, if he is hoping to play god over us, and making demands of our people, what if he should actually try following through with some manner of enforcement?"

"Enforcement..." she muses conspicuously. "I can't be sure what this Gift may be fully capable of, but if his only demonstration was to pin me to the ground, and then gloat over my body, I might not tend to worry about that too much. If he's only a ghostlike image, I must wonder how much harm he can actually cause by himself."

"And if he actually does have friends?"

"Yes. On the one hand, I think our military has enough firepower to handle it. After all, feeble insurgents or otherwise, I've heard good things about it. And I also recall some reports suggesting Ytani might not even be...out there..." she waves a hand figuratively above her. "Instead thinking he's just a local thick-horn with a bad attitude. So, unless we actually DO see something...out there...we might be looking the wrong way. However, this does bring to mind a curious little note that stuck in my mind about him."

"And what was that?"

"Well, he might have simply been bragging, maybe also picking up a few of his own ideas from our other interviews, but he said they have this...stuff...if you recall, based on what he called weird energy. His wording seemed a little amateurish, like he didn't receive a full education."

"Yes, I noticed that in his behavior, like he was stuck in his adolescent years."

"But it also seemed a little too coincidental to use this term...weird energy."

"Like we are using the term Abnormal Energy?"

"Yes, if he was simply imitating us, he should use the same words, right? But his example seemed detached, and then how he said they used this in some way. If his friends do indeed understand this same energy, and know how to use it in a form of technology, I hesitate to think what it might be capable of, especially if this is the same energy used to power a god figure."

"Oh no!"

"But surely, these friends of his couldn't be anything like THAT!" she chuckles demurely. "I mean, after all, HE thinks he's a god, and I doubt any other god society would bow down to a dull-horn like him!" she shrugs.

"Absolutely!"

In the officer's lounge, Geilv pulled back in consideration of this thought.

"That must be hinting at something, especially if they're using his image."

"Yes," the Captain nods. "That new hostile force they're promising. And the sudden arrival of something our military can NOT handle might be that trigger for the countermeasure."

"With the raid sirens. Yes, of course."

"And especially if it uses this Abnormal Energy. I recall your story of Therinë and those new people who arrived. That sounds dangerous for the implications."

Back in the studio, Ileani prepares to wrap up.

"Well, Latena, this is certainly a fascinating bit of work on your part. I suppose the people will simply need to draw a few of their own conclusions for now, but with your revolution in full force, and with so many new supporters joining up, it certainly does appear that whoever, or whatever may have begun this process, is going to find itself with the product of its efforts developing minds of their own to lead their own lives. Perhaps we can say, we've grown up now, and are ready to take charge of ourselves."

"Absolutely, Ileani," she smiles softly. "And I'm sure we are more than capable of doing exactly that."

"I don't know how much more of this I can take!" the Marshal screeches painfully into the com-link. "That young lady will ruin everything!

And not just that, but she could possibly bring down all my hard work here! Somehow, we have to silence her impetuous ranting!"

It was later in the day when Geilv found himself in yet another heated discussion with the Marshal. But this time, he had a little ammo of his own to throw at it. And yet, he knew he still had to measure himself carefully.

"Marshal," he responds calmly. "At this point, given what we see out there by now, I think we may have crossed a threshold. If you recall, it actually began before she came into it with those protests over that industry. And even without her giving out these lectures and interviews, the rest of the world would likely keep on going as it is. From the appearance of things out there, we are on the edge of a planetary revolt. The Council has lost its authority, the Charter has been declared invalid, and all or most of the legal and security forces are taking sides with her. In fact, I think if any efforts were made to silence her now, it might add further credence to her statements about that control authority she was speaking about, and the world would descend into rebellion even farther and faster."

"Argh! It's not just about that! Her statements could turn against us. The civil unrest, all the noise she's making... In all Creation, Commander, all you need to do is look outside your window. You can almost see the fireworks from the protesting and marches she's inciting. We need containment, it's that simple! We have a powerful military here, Commander. Surely, THEY can take some action to enforce control again!"

"Yes, I suppose if that military were to take action, they could possibly make a work effort. Although, at the same time, I think it would be rather messy along the way. We may have the full planetary population to wade through at this point, and that's a lot of people to quell. I would think, in very short order, this would incite a rather furious revolt against us, and they would take up arms, making our effort even worse by comparison. And so far, this doesn't even take into consideration that many of them are the friends and family members of those military persons doing the quelling."

This suddenly silenced the Marshal, and Geilv could only hear the rasping of his breath.

"And what are you suggesting by this statement, Commander?" he issues nervously.

"Marshal, our military personnel are citizens of this world, and subject to those same issues that are offending everyone else due to the old war protocols you and the Council pushed at us. And they are further offended by many of those same statements echoing through the streets by those protesters. And even worse, they are also reminded, at least indirectly, of those military chips you so cleverly passed underneath the awareness of the public. And under the guise of being training aids. Well, for all my years of service, I think I have had enough of mine, and so have all the rest."

"Oh no, not you too," he mourns.

"Yes, Marshal, me too, and for some time, as well. That last incident you drove us into with the Tul'ryk and that odd city structure was a kind of turning point for me. Whoever THOSE people are, they cannot be the same insurgents we were hitting all across OUR galaxy. Especially if they are found in an environment so alien to us that you, for all your promises of great wisdom, neglected to inform us of where we were sending our people. To my knowledge, nether-space is simply a fanciful term our younger generation grows up with. It's not a physical location you can actually travel to. And yet, the crew of the Tul'ryk could see it right outside their windows, and this naturally caused a few of them to ask what they were looking at. People do that, you know."

"Yes, Commander, they do," he relents feebly.

"So, this simply causes me to ask who they are in relation to anything else, including the example of Therinë. And then to question everything else you claimed we were doing out there. Many of those fleet commanders you sent out on the active mode of their chips were friends of mine, and they shared a few private thoughts with me of what they saw along the way. And it was not a godlike society to match those others we found. Maybe you would like to explain what they were in reality, or should I simply guess."

"Commander, I think you would not want to hear my response. And I actually suspect by now you might already have an answer."

"Fascinating... Your tone is much different now. Is this to say that young lady with all her rabble-rousing is actually correct? I somehow think it is. It certainly makes good sense from where I stand and the things I've learned along the way."

"All right, Commander, let's not rub it in."

"Rub it in?" Geilv surges. "Let me first rub in Site One-Alpha and our Council, for whatever good it actually did."

"Yes, I might expect this one. I found myself being forced to excuse the discrepancy, but it was a vain effort. The Grand Hall roof collapsing was a fatal element here."

"Next would be this crusade of yours. How many worlds did you order us to destroy? I don't know what sorts of laws you have where you come from, but around here we take special pride in ours. And if YOU actually wrote the Charter, you must also hold at least a few principles, as some of those same laws involve the aspect of murder."

"Yes, Commander, I realize this, but…"

"Although I might also admit," Geilv interrupts, "that our laws may not even be adequate for the sheer scale of what you caused. Full planetary genocide. I am now thinking of that world Therinë and what we did there, plus what apparently happened at Morndindor with that mining outpost, and you sending someone out there to clear out the competition."

"Commander, please…"

"And then, making that unwise incursion of that new world which drew that undesirable attention. And finally, to make yet another attempt, this time with that city! That was simply reckless! And then we have Ytani and your star-destroying bomb!"

"Commander! Please! Yes! You are correct. Now, please allow me a chance to speak. First, that new world was an unexpected event. I did not expect to see a Celestial over there. I learned only too late how that world was someone's garden project. This was towards the end when we had that final confrontation, and he apparently began to let it out who he was. And even if I did know about this, to find a Celestial on a world like that would be abnormal, as they tend not to inhabit such places."

"All right, perhaps I can give you this one."

"As for Ytani, this is not my doing, this much I assure you. I weighed the options very carefully when I shared those teachings with him, and I felt it was an acceptable course of action at the time. I left it in the hands of the base crew to watch over him, and from the reports I received here…most of them at least…I felt it was still an acceptable solution, given our needs in that area."

"Most of them?"

"Yes, a few complaints came in, but I was hoping it was simply a phase he was going through as a young man in a lonely house. And my needs to achieve our quota were rather important. I did NOT, however, realize he was losing himself to this complex, nor that he committed murder amongst the base crew. I do actually hold an opinion on that, in this case. You mentioned laws? Well, yes. The society I came from did have laws, and murder was among them. Do you recall my mention about those females?"

"I do. So you might have a limit in this area. But only in this case? Nothing else out there? I am thinking of your frequent use of the terms peasant and peon in this case."

"Eh…well, all right, you do have a point. I suppose I would need to admit to this. But before you scream at me for yet another atrocity, try to see it from my perspective for a moment. What might seem offensive to you held perfect rationality to us…once. And there is a rather specific context to understand here."

"All right, I am listening."

"We may need to admit to several contexts, and these come at different moments in our history, as we grew and evolved over the course of time. Commander, I am a younger member of what we once had. Most of this is ancient history to me by now, handed down by elder members who once told such beautiful tales of brighter days, and the glory of our once great empire. It filled me with visions and dreams of grander moments. I would sometimes sit and reflect on how it might have been in our earliest times as we were still growing…the challenges we faced, the triumphs…" he sighs. "You may have your romances, but we had ours as well. It was a bygone era, now lost to us. By the time I came into it, our once great empire was in decline, and all I saw was a slow decay."

"A slow decay. Yes, this would certainly be depressing."

"Commander, my entire existence is to serve my master. I am not an evolved being, like you. Mine is a custom grown race, where each of us is uniquely crafted for our specific masters."

"Really! That's certainly interesting. So, is this to say, you are created for the sole purpose of serving that one and only individual?"

"Yes, and for the duration of my lifetime, which can be just as eternal as his, as we tend to be linked. But now, let us go back a bit into our history. Much like so many others, ours was once a young society fighting our way up the evolutionary ladder, and very often in fierce rivalry with countless others. We did not share common accord with anyone. Our people believed the only way to the top was to dominate. We were not alone in this, by the way. I recall there were many others, so it came down to a contest of who would win."

"This might surely pose a problem…for someone at least."

"It would, and the prize was to ascend to a higher station of existence, whether physical or technological. And as we slowly defeated our rivals, we found ourselves with the privilege of moving up. The rush of victory drove us to push even higher, passing through the different levels of ascension as we evolved into new forms. But the rivalry with others did not truly find an end until we arrived within sight of the highest goal we could perceive of."

"Would this be something like godhood now?"

"Yes, Commander. But a true god society, as your kind might describe it, must now measure itself on the scale of eons. And ours was quite old by the time I came into it."

"Eons!"

"Here is where I must caution you to understand what this can do to a society. For all our hard work simply to arrive there, we regarded ourselves as an overseer society, and we felt no other should hold the authority to challenge us. After all, when you struggle for so long to win such a prize as this, you would surely not wish to see another come along and take it away from you. It is simply too precious a thing to let go."

"Yes, I suppose I can see that, and especially for all the time you put into it. But this is also to say, you hold a philosophy that there can be only one at the top, unlike what we might have in our Council, an elected body."

"Yes, Commander, we were not such as a democratic authority to politely choose our leaders, who then politely step down as we choose another. Therefore, sharing our prestige with any other society was out of the question. Ours was an empire, an oligarchy of a privileged upper nobility ruling over the rest. It suited us, as our culture was oriented in this way. But this permitted only OUR culture, no others."

"I see. And on the order of eons…"

"Yes, but those same eons, Commander, can take their toll on a society. An eternity of perpetuation, where we now hold the power to oversee everything else out there. And for a society that covers the greater Seas of Creation, which involves MANY universes, Commander, this is a lot to behold."

"I am trying to think of a society simply overseeing ONE universe, let alone MANY."

"It is not a thing to take lightly," he chuckles softly. "However, when we first arrived in that place, we found one last obstacle…a forebearer society. They were already in their late stages of decline, and ours, being who they were, simply felt it was time for retirement."

"Uh huh, one more to push out of the way."

"Keeping in mind, Commander, we felt the only way to win was through strength of will and the tenacity of perseverance. So, we took that position and ruled the rest for a long while. Initially, we tried to hold ourselves to certain virtues. You mentioned laws. Oh yes, we were a very lawful society in those days, at least within our own. But here is where one of those contexts must come into play. Within our own, Commander, as we did not care for rivals who might take away our most coveted prize. Therefore, we would not allow any others to reach high enough to challenge us. To do so was as much a sin to us as outright murder might be, as this would be tantamount to committing suicide for all our own efforts."

"Very well, I suppose this makes sense. In such a harsh rivalrous scenario, it's an either-or situation. And if you simply allow them to rise up, no doubt, you are going down at the same time…much like your predecessors."

"Yes, much like them. I do not know of their history. I guess we did not ask them about it, but I would imagine they might have had something similar once. Nevertheless, once we arrived in that place, we were so proud of our achievement. We were gods, in the truest sense of the word," he croons dreamily. "The very mention of it carried a level of esteem that lifted our spirits and empowered our culture to reflect the grandeur and aristocratic appeal of that station. But Commander, this became a trap for us."

"A trap?" he frowns.

"I can look at this in hindsight now, and see it as a progression of attitude. Albeit, at the same time, I was in denial of it. I had hoped, during this time, that we might find another chance for ourselves, maybe this time to realize our failure and correct for it, to rejuvenate ourselves to that earlier prestige."

"An earlier prestige? What kind?"

"In the beginning, we once had a philosophy that life can hold a form of…fascination, to see how it evolves. It allowed us to observe, even to study other forms, maybe for that bit of lost nostalgia of our own. We called it the Challenge of Creation. It was an ancient pleasure for us. And while we might ultimately find ourselves having to put them down, it was at least as much to keep ourselves alive, rather than to fight yet another rival, quite likely destroying them anyway, or to be destroyed by them. So, do you see the context, Commander? It's a case of do it now, or do it later, but if you want to survive, you must eventually do it."

"Yes, I can see that perspective, and it is unfortunate, but if this is how it works for you, I might have to agree, it may be an unavoidable eventuality."

"And here is where that trap begins to show itself. Life, Commander, is plentiful out there. And if you belong to a god society that covers so much of Creation… So many universes, with countless galaxies, and countless stars and planets in each, the numbers are simply boggling."

"Absolutely!"

"Therefore, you become numb to it after a while. You lose the sense of fascination. It becomes at least as much a chore just to keep things under control…all those potential rivals you do not want to see creeping up on you."

"Now it's a work effort…and a rather arduous one at that."

"Indeed! And the longer you go at it, the more tedious it becomes, such that, when you have seen as much as we have, it tends to lose its independent value, as there is always more to be found. Also, you might see it coming and going on its own, even without you. Evolution, natural disasters, calamities. One moment, you find something of interest, but the next moment, it gets hit by a stray asteroid or a supernova burst."

"Oh no."

"Therefore, to hold special value in it becomes futile after a while."

"And is this where you take on those attitudes when you play it down so much?"

"It can turn that way. The aristocracy of the position causes you to feel yourself above all other things. You lose any and all respect for life as an essence, regardless of the rivalry aspect. They are all simply…" he coughs gently, "…little things," he intones with a soft tremor. "Such that your position rises above the rest, and nothing else matters. Worse, you might tend to berate them after a while, especially if they offend you somehow. After all, little things are unworthy to think themselves to be anything comparable to our own."

"And this is your trap, a form of animosity that creeps up on you, much like those rivals you so often feared. Therefore, your statements, using such words as peasants and peons."

"It also becomes the reasoning for such as Morndindor. A rivalry to compete with my own purpose, which is to serve my master, as HE must rise above all other things…at least to me. I fell into this condition on many occasions, if only because we lived by these principles so often. I did not like having my position challenged by others. It was offensive, as I felt MY cause was paramount to any other. But in the end, here we are."

"Yes. Here we are," Geilv muses.

"Commander, I know this may sound offensive to some, but the society I came from held certain opinions, and over time, this is how it became for us. We did not live to be judged by others. We did the judging. At least until THEY arrived. Those Estelar. They began to judge us for THEIR principles, and this was perhaps the biggest insult of all. Not only did one of those younger societies succeed in rivaling us, but they began to best us. It was the one thing we dreaded most of all. Many couldn't believe it was happening. They tried to shy away from the reports we would hear, believing it was…over there… somewhere, not here with us. Then, slowly, our society, which was already in decline, began to vanish. We were not simply being replaced by a rival; we were being deliberately hunted into extinction. Not even simple survival was possible anymore."

"Yes, that might certainly motivate a person."

"We are the last of our kind, my Master and I, and I was ready to do whatever it took to bring us back to our former glory. Call it desperation, call it hopelessness, but to hide under a rock for the remainder of eternity is not a life. What else can you expect a person to do but to go to the extremes to fight back. And yet, I think, even if we were successful in any part of this, it would only truly amount to little more than another moment of borrowed time."

"All right, I will take this into consideration, as it does carry its undertones. But as the High Commander of the Azgarén military, I also have my duty to my people. Regardless of the fact that you may have created us at one time, and perhaps for similar reasons of survival, I must now apply myself to my people. You have demonstrated yourself to be unpredictable, as well as determined beyond rational principle, although admittedly, it may carry a justifiable cause, but one I can no longer permit. I suspect, if you were able to teach Ytani how to alter his form, you must also have a similar capacity, and this might further reflect on such occasions as Saakerav and perhaps others in our history. Am I right?"

"Yes, Commander, I was Saakerav at one time, and I have also impersonated numerous others to help direct your society. I admit to this. That young lady out there, for all her rabble-rousing, is actually a very clever one."

"Very well, but this is a dangerous skill, and I will not tolerate you attempting any more of your games. As of this moment, I am placing you under house arrest. I will be posting guards around you, who will call in routinely with status updates, just in case you get any ideas of vanishing in a puff of smoke. I will also be giving instructions for frequent and random genetic scans of all my officers, including myself, in case you get any ideas of impersonating anyone new. And furthermore, just to make sure we have full coverage, I am giving orders to our flagship, the Ralg Hitan, to position itself over our heads with explicit instructions to turn their guns at that towering eyesore in the middle of town."

"What?" the Marshal shouts nervously. "No! Commander, what are your intentions there?"

"I want you to comply with MY instructions…I served for so long under yours. You say you are very servile under him, and for this I can understand if this is your sole purpose. So I'm guessing he means a lot to you. You once said we should be able to turn our guns on that one authority figure with some measure of success. Well, I'm doing it to him now."

"But, but…he's not a threat to you. Well, not…not as he is. He's sleeping…and not at his best," he whimpers. "My poor beloved Master. All right, Commander, I yield. Please do not go any further. I realize by now it's over. And I am actually very tired. But I must still assert the trouble that young rabble-rouser out there is causing, as there IS a very real threat, and you should know of it."

"All right, what is that threat?"

"You may think what you will of me for all of my…games. But you should know, at least some of it held a dire purpose that needed to be contained. That Tav'ageen business, for example. Yes, I am responsible, but it was actually to preserve…well, myself as well as my work here."

"Preserve? How do you mean?"

"Your society carries personal value to me, not that I would expect you to appreciate it. I worked long and hard for it. I may be, um, your father, but it runs a little deeper than that. I knew from the beginning there would be complications for my methods, but like that young lady said, I was without my usual means to do it any other way. And this now reflects back on what I just said about our society. My Master and his kind…that trap, and the attitudes that can develop. They would normally forbid such a thing as the hybridization of species, especially involving ours. It is regarded as vulgar, and the results would be seen as abominations. They would never be permitted to exist."

"Uh oh…all right, I'm getting the picture now. So, if HE should discover this…"

"It runs in both directions, Commander, as I would surely be punished for this act. But you…your full society…if he should realize this, he would erase it from existence. And this is simply for the hybridization aspect. It does not even consider these new Gifts you are discovering. This would only exasperate the idea."

"When you say to erase from existence…"

"Yes, Commander, Elder Nazég and his faction were closer to this than anyone could realize. As fanciful as it might sound, the mind CAN define the existence of Reality if it is potent enough. Recall that statement I made once…and that so many have been flaunting lately," he sighs again. "The simple force of one's will, if carefully focused, can alter the reality of existence around us. But you need to have reached at least a certain threshold of development to do this. And such beings as my Master are one example. Although, in his current state, he is weak after arriving here. His form of life cannot survive comfortably in this space. Therefore, those seeds. Commander, I must serve him, it is my purpose in life, as we are made this way. My first priority had to be to rescue him, therefore the seeds. But that Tav'ageen ability also had to be squelched, before he took notice of it, as it would surely stand out. Fortunately, his condition has him resting most of the time, and I have been walking a very fine line here trying to keep him calm while still growing your society."

"All right, I understand. I will pass the word on my side to see if we can settle a few things where that skill goes. But Ytani is outside my control, I think."

"If we can find him, I will ask you to allow me to deal with it. My skills might be enough to contend with it neatly and quietly. Beyond that, I will not make trouble for you. But I would like to know what your ultimate intentions are for us."

"The first thing on my mind is to wait until our planetary population finds stability again and we establish a new government. I may need to apply some of our military authority, but in this case to security and law enforcement along the way."

"Yes, this might become necessary if things become messy, as you said."

"Aside from that, I find myself currently torn between permitting you continued sanctuary from those Estelar you described, or if I should simply turn you in so they can finish the job. But I think I will leave that to our new government body to decide. For all the criminal acts you committed here, I'm sure they might have something to say about it."

"I see. I suppose this may be as much as I can expect. But I would not necessarily suggest returning to that city, not after our last visit. I do not guarantee their reaction on seeing you again."

"Perhaps, but last time, you had us attacking them with that thing you ordered. If we tried it again, this time I would hope for conversation, not devastation. But I will keep this on hold for now. By the way, speaking of them, what about that weapon of yours. What was it in reality, and what purpose did you have in mind for it? To attack these others?"

"Yes, it is all I have now. That weapon is a form of technology your kind is simply not ready for. And pray, Commander, that you never have the occasion for it, because it is truly frightening, even for us. We call it the Agent of Unmaking. It is a terrible product of our level of invention. But as I said, I am reduced to desperate measures. My enemies are far more powerful than I am, and yet I am pressed to serve a cause in the name of my Master. There is no other purpose for my existence now."

"Of course. But if we should ever get our hands on the rest of it..." he pauses in contemplation. "Well, I'm certainly not giving it to you. How do you disarm that stuff?"

"There is a process, but also on our level of invention. It is not easy, however, and very delicate. If we should have the occasion, I could perhaps share it with you. But I would advise extreme caution simply to approach it."

"Yes, this much I can understand. Based on what we found at Ooduan, you once told me it only blows a gigantic hole in space in THIS universe. What does it do in that place where we found your opponents? Would you like to tell me? Because if not, I can guess..."

"This is an interesting statement. Just out of curiosity, Commander, what might be your guess on this occasion?"

"We saw a lot of Abnormal Energy out there...or whatever name you might use for it. My guess is, since we don't see that here, it might be related, perhaps to ignite the whole cloud along the way. How does this sound to you?"

"Not bad, Commander, you are right. My kind describes it as the dynamistic flows, and it's a form of energy you might find in many places, actually. The weapon would normally be derived from the flows themselves, but in the absence of anyone capable of doing the work, we had to resort to other means, which meant Morndindor. And if detonated in that space, it would indeed create a reaction to erupt the full envelope. If you were to examine Ooduan a moment, then try to imagine that same effect, but on the scale of that entire environment."

"That sounds a little like overkill. You once said you wanted to recover something from them."

"To recover..." he chuckles faintly. "They have spread out rather far by now, taking control of everything we once owned. And with respect to your people, we couldn't hope to account for all of it, not without a form of firepower that is very literally godlike to meet the need. Therefore, the Agent, to open up some space that we might make a return. But this will not happen now, even if I did still have this possibility. They know about us now, and no doubt they'll be watching. Maybe they already are."

"Indeed, then we should just keep a low profile for now."

✦✦✦✦✦

It was a new morning on Therinë when Thaelyn and his officers were in their ritual meeting at the WIC building. Ayene was waiting with her report when Kaliya and Kailen were arriving at the table after a careful review of the spy-cam footage from the previous period.

"Um, my Lord?" Kaliya announces cautiously. "We, uh, have a kind of result."

"A kind of result," he raises his brow. "What kind of, in this case?"

"Geilv and Darumon, and I sent a spook out there a moment ago to verify things."

"You did, and the current result?"

"The same kind of...sort of..." she smirks timidly.

He glares at her uncertainly, and then passes to Kailen and the General.

"You know, General," he muses. "Having females in our employ is a problematic scenario."

"Indeed!" he smiles. "Especially the younger ones. Right around four centuries or so!"

"Uh huh… But now, Kaliya. What is this kind of we are speaking about?"

"A face-off on the com-link, and I believe generated by our recent interview with Latena. He actually did quite well, and the city is still standing…so far."

"So far?"

"Well, except for the Azgarén military flagship hovering over the place ready to blast that, um…" she coughs softly, "…towering eyesore, as he calls it."

"Oh dear Powers. Do we know anything about that vessel?"

"I can answer that," Ayene issues. "And yes, this is something to be concerned over. Just a few shots out of that beast could level the city. Although, I might also say it's a precautionary thing to keep Darumon in his place. Apparently, he has a soft spot with his…Master. Point a gun at HIS head and Darumon buckles."

"Indeed!"

"The ACI got a call from Geilv's office shortly after that meeting to pass a few words. Apparently, all of Latena's rabble-rousing, as he calls it, with the Tav'ageen Anomaly can potentially backfire on us if Sargeras catches wind of it. This represents a threshold level of intolerance that seems to be racial on their part, describing the hybridization of species, especially involving their own kind, as vulgar, with the results being abominations. So, this might give you an idea of where this is going."

"Yes, it does. He would find it especially offensive."

"To the point of wiping us out of existence. So we should be careful with our future Ytani plays, and have Latena and the rest soften up a bit with the Tav'ageen Anomaly statements, at least until the situation is finally resolved."

"All right, agreed. We do not need to see HIM rampaging through the streets."

"As for the ship, it's called the Ralg Hitan, which is a Han'amaku class battle cruiser, the pride and joy of the Azgarén Space Navy," she smiles.

"A battle cruiser?" the General raises his brow.

"Yes, and it's huge. I recall reading some specs on it once, and reviewing some promotional video. It's an impressive vessel, from the technological side, with something close to seven thousand crewmembers, and capable of devastating whole continents."

"Powers help us!" Thaelyn jerks back. "And he hopes to use it on a single building?"

"Yes, well, it has a large battery of weapons of different sizes, and the surgical strike ability is supposed to be very precise. And that building is actually a rather large target. Remember, it covers an area of four city blocks."

"Incredible," he shakes his head. "But this is precautionary. Let us hope we can attend to our side of it before that one turns against us. What about this confrontation? Where does this lead us now?"

Kaliya displays a holo-chip and sets it on the table.

"This is the video; in case you'd like to see it. That last interview by Latena essentially exposed the remaining pieces. This allowed Geilv to make his move based on what he had on his side. The evolution, the long-time direction of our society, Saakerav, the Council, the Tav'ageen Anomaly and the Scare, the seeds, and so on. Also, that attempt on Sigil and the discovery of something truly…godlike…" she flutters her fingers, "…which was enough to actually frighten Darumon, meaning to say that which is most likely his actual opponents, instead of all his stories of insurgents, and furthermore, to be found in nether-space, which he forgot to tell anyone about. So, the association of all these pieces is enough to alert Geilv, and the rest of the military, and even the world around them, that Darumon isn't who he claimed he was."

"And Darumon himself? Where is he now?"

"Under house arrest with guards on him, and a gun pointed at his Master's head if he should try any more games. And Darumon even surrendered after he realized he was finally beaten. His tone of voice changed on the com-link, and he started to explain himself. It's a fascinating story if you're interested."

"Great gods," the General winces. "Now, there's a twist."

"Yes," Thaelyn muses as he picks up the chip to examine it. "This would be a curious end result."

"I would like to point out a couple of highlights briefly," Kaliya offers. "We've all been saying the Primordials are horrors from beyond, but it didn't apparently start out that way."

"No? How was it?"

"Let me first ask you what you know, or perhaps what the Estelar know of them from their earliest history."

"Hmm…" he leans back in contemplation. "I am unsure if I could give you an answer from their earliest history. All I am aware of would involve that portion the Estelar were personally present to witness, and therefore to record."

"As I thought. But it would seem there is a history lost to us by now. And Darumon's story recalled a few pieces of that."

"Yes, this does seem reasonable."

"For instance, they were always a very rivalrous society, always in competition with someone to win the top prize. And their native culture seems to follow a sole survivor mentality. This equates to simple survival...the determination to win. Essentially to say, there can be only one at the top. Nothing else."

"Most interesting, and quite contrary to the Estelar. It is no wonder they did not get along."

"They were apparently an empire ruled by an oligarchy, and very aristocratic. This can give you a direction."

"Yes, an authoritarian form of rule. This much does stand out."

"In the beginning, they were a society of laws, much like any other, at least within their own. They found it interesting to study younger forms of life, maybe for the nostalgia of their past. But the eternity of time numbed their senses, and the tedium drove them into a bigoted attitude. Life, being everywhere, and constantly rivaling them if it should ever go that far, became arduous to keep under control. This rivalry aspect meant they had to defend against anyone who would take away their prize. And this meant, 'kill them now, or kill them later,' with the only difference being to face a rival that could destroy them instead. And to them, allowing this is the same as committing suicide. Therefore..." she shrugs.

"Yes. I see it. Survival. As this rival, at this point, would likely try taking them down, much like the Estelar ultimately did. And you know, this mentality also reflects on the Measure of Balance in some ways. The Estelar are also quite absolutist with their own. Conform, or else. As they will not tolerate anything with such capacity as to disturb the harmony of balance across the rest of Creation. Very well..."

"This attitude later blew up on them. Darumon described it as a kind of trap. Once you've seen so much of it, you lose that fascination. Further, they were very proud to be gods, but this manifested as a pompous attitude. Here is where Darumon recalled some of those statements he made. Words like peasant, peon, and so many other... little things. This attitude believes nothing else should hold such high esteem as their godhood, for all they suffered simply to achieve it. Furthermore, as a custom-grown entity specifically for Sargeras, HE is the primary motivation for Darumon to do his work. Nothing else matters. It's all about him."

"Therefore, he holds such a need to serve, but he is willing to go to the extremes, and some rather reckless ones at that."

"That idea of hiding under a rock. It's not a life."

"Indeed, it is not. So, our earlier hypotheses might be correct."

"Meanwhile," Kaliya continues. "Geilv issued instructions for a press release to give a response to Latena's recent interview and expose a few select details which they feel they can let out now, but keeping a few other things closed for security reasons. They still have Ytani out there, you know."

"Yes, they do."

"This will certainly aid us in containing him," the General considers. "But for how long?"

"Until the rebellion settles," Kaliya responds, "and Azgarén gets a new government to make decisions. Geilv mentioned they'll likely have a few things to say about all these games. But Geilv also stated, probably for his own personal containment, that he was undecided to grant a continuation of the sanctuary condition, or to simply turn him in to his enemies for all he's done."

"Oh dear. And this might be enough to keep Darumon in an unsteady condition, maybe to enforce him to stay low and not to invoke any reactions. I hope it works."

"Personally, I found Darumon's story to be a little bit sad. He begged for Geilv to see it from his side, the last of his kind, a dying race, being hunted into extinction, and without any hope even for simple survival. This might lead him to do things not otherwise wise or even typical of his kind, simply to have a life of some sort."

"I suppose I can certainly see this much," Thaelyn nods. "I would not wish to be in that same position. We cannot completely deny him this desire, but his acts still stand for the loss of life, and they who now govern do hold their rules. And it is these rules we must now follow, even if he never did care for them."

"And so, here we are with Geilv pointing his guns at Sargeras's head. Darumon practically begged for mercy at that one. It makes me wonder, if it was this easy to bring him down, why couldn't we do this from the beginning."

"Indeed, this surely would have made things easier for us."

"Now, moving on, I think we'll be making our move before anything new has time to occur. Ytani will serve as our distraction, and Latena and her people are under instruction to stall for time until we arrive."

"For your Stormhooves introduction, perhaps?"

"Yeah, I suppose at least that much. And this probably finishes Adalon's prophecy for this line. We turned against him."

Ayene now begins with her report.

"Among other things, Geilv, in his conversation with Darumon, also mentioned he is going to order random genetic scans of himself and his officers to make sure everyone is who they appear to be."

"This is a wise course of action," Thaelyn nods. "Just in case."

"This actually brings up another issue. Kaliya and I have each spoken with Director Bak'vayn at the ARC about this, and we all generally agree that this Prodigy Gift will force us to modify, at the very least, many aspects of identification and law enforcement practices for our people. The most important is a full revamp of our government ID cards. What we use now is often just a simple photo ID, typically with an embedded chip to scan for personal details. We might use biometrics in some cases, like secure access to sensitive areas, but for the general population, the security levels are comparatively low. However, the Prodigy Gift will change all that to the max."

"How do you see this now, Lieutenant?" the General asks.

"Nothing less than a full genetic fingerprint hash code imprinted on a holo-chip to be used for virtually everyone, everywhere, for everything. No exceptions. It's the only way to tell if a person is physical and who they appear to be. It's perhaps the highest form of security that money can buy."

"That sounds like a lot of work, and I must admit, although I can generally understand your meaning, our science has not yet reached that point to give us as broad an education on this matter."

"Maybe so, but this isn't a choice now. The Director has passed this along to some of his associates; people in different areas of science and mathematics to invent the technology and hashing algorithms, and a few designs have been presented in prototype form."

"And how would you use this, for example?"

"It would be a chip, probably larger on average than our existing holo-chips," she points at the one Thaelyn was using. "And you would insert this into a reader device to access your information. BUT you need to maintain physical contact with it, with your finger pressing on a special sensor pad to read your genetic coding in order to unlock the chip's function. Then, the reader, depending on who it is you're working with, like a shop merchant or a medical clinic, would be granted access through a secure link to a government database where we'll basically lump your entire life into one file, including finances, medical records, government security clearances, and so on. It's one-stop shopping for all your life's needs. There's no point in breaking things up into multiple cards anymore."

"That sounds like a very complex system, although very convenient for the simplicity of use. But what if a person loses their chip?"

"Another person wouldn't be able to use it. If their finger registers a different code, a red flag goes up and that person will probably find themselves in a lot of trouble. Also, the best designs use sensors to tell if the finger pressing on the pad is still attached to a living body, so no fakes by cutting someone's finger off. And if you lose it, you'll need to visit a registered government security office for a replacement. We need this to be tight...real tight."

"No doubt!" he chuckles.

"Meanwhile, I need to make a visit to Geilv's office and help him out on a few issues. I want to post bodyguards on him, just in case. He might have his own people, but I would feel better if we added a few of ours, as well. He generally already knows we're an off-world militant body, so there's no point in hiding that aspect of it now. And I want him to be our first customer for this new security ID chip."

"That sounds like a fine suggestion, Ayene," Thaelyn affirms. "Then I will wish you to be on your way when your people are assembled."

◆◆◆◆◆

Later in the day, an announcement buzzer rings at Geilv's door. His nerves were on edge, ever since his last communication with the Marshal, even though he felt he might have the situation under control. But the uncertainty factor of dealing with such an advanced being with unpredictable manners had him anxiously jumping with each noise he heard.

"Enter..." he calls.

Ayene casually steps inside the room with a pleasant smile on her face.

"Hello, Commander."

He looks up at her, feeling a subtle sense of relief for the friendly face. "Captain, or should I say, Lieutenant Ti'van?"

"Yes Sir, it's Lieutenant. I'm still waiting my turn for a promotion, but perhaps not much longer...I hope," she grins.

"But do you actually serve us for this point, or someone else?"

"Someone else, but I'm not allowed to give out the details, if you please."

"Of course... So, what does the ACI have to say for itself today?"

"First of all, congratulations for your work with the Marshal. So far, he appears to be sulking over there in his office, but a few of us are uncertain how long this might last. We think, for as long as you keep your guns pointed at Sargeras's head, he might actually behave himself. He does seem to have given up the game."

"Yeah, but that was a hard battle we fought together...all of us."

"Yes Sir, this much is true, and not just you in this office."

"It also makes me wonder how you know of it, although at this moment, I'm going to guess you have spy cameras on me, right?"

"Yes Sir. No offence to you, but we need to know what interactions you have with him. It's important for us to plan our own moves."

"All right, but can I at least trust that once this is done, you can give us back our own security?" he raises his brow.

"Yes, I think once things return to a normal routine, we can all relax a bit. But not completely, as we still have the Prodigy Gift, and that alone demands a new form of governing authority."

"Yeah, and then there's that. I can't believe we might be his creation, but with some side effect that made us half-god."

"It's not an easy life, and I doubt it'll get any easier as more people begin to realize it. Therefore, I would like to offer you a few things to begin a new process for us."

"What's that?"

"First, can you call Captain Ta'yeen and your chief med-tech in here? I would like to share this with them."

"All right..."

He makes a set of calls on his vid-com as he directs Ayene into a chair. They wait several moments as the others join them in the room. The Captain takes one look at Ayene and nearly falls back a step.

"Aren't you supposed to be dead, young lady?" he muses humorously.

"The stories of my death were only slightly exaggerated," she smiles. "Now that we're here, I wish to inform you of a few details we need to begin working on to ensure our future security as a race. Regardless of the Marshal and what he represents, either by himself, or in relation to our world society, we are born with a number of abilities that are nearly godlike in capacity, and we are not ready for them."

"Not ready for them?" the med-tech wonders.

"We're not mature enough to be worthy of them by any natural means. For instance, if used correctly, these could be revolutionary for the things we can accomplish. But if used incorrectly, as with the depiction of Ytani, they could be devastating on multiple levels, not the least of which is crime and security violations."

"Yeah," the Captain offers. "This has been crossing my mind a lot lately."

"And so, when I say we are not ready for them, this is to say, a society naturally evolved to earn this as a consequence would also be naturally evolved to understand the responsibilities that go along with it. And a lot of those more primitive tendencies might also be evolved away by that time, as well."

"But we're not there yet, even for all we have now."

"Correct. There are societies out there who are MUCH more advanced than we are, and they might have earned these Gifts as the result of their development. Some might say we could parallel them for what we have, but not the wisdom that goes along with it."

"Ouch. But how do we correct this?"

"Probably with outside help, because we'll need to evolve the rest of the way manually, and do so rather quickly to compensate. So far, we have a few ideas, and a few solutions, but this will also require a considerable amount of redevelopment of our social values, discipline, ethics, morals, and other things, just to make sure we minimize the potential for abuse. We don't have a choice in this, it has to be done. We are still a young society, and these abilities are well above where we might otherwise be, if only for our hybridization with a being well above us."

"I can only barely imagine what this might entail. What sorts of ideas are you putting together for this?"

"First, we are assembling a body of authority to propose a new set of rules we will need to learn as a society. We cannot go halfway on this; there's no room for it. But so far, this is for later. Right now, we need to secure ourselves from our more immediate factors. For this, Commander, I want to offer you a few bodyguards from our people. They will watch over you full-time and trade off with replacements periodically, at least until Darumon and Sargeras are finally dealt with. Will you accept them?"

"I suppose it couldn't hurt," he shrugs. "It might also help settle a few of my personal tensions. But what's so special about them that might be different from our own?"

Ayene now turns and reaches her hand up to snap her fingers. From out of nowhere, four men in full livery, slate blue uniforms with silver and white trim on the collars and cuffs, flash into view, and this causes everyone in the room to jump.

"These are projections using the Gift," she informs. "Combat in this form, so far at least, tends to be problematic, as it comes down to a battle of wits, as much as anything. The mind is the governing factor here, so if you can apply your mind to override your opponent and what his mind can generate, you might hold an advantage. We have examples where we can cause injury, and even death, if we can apply ourselves with sufficient effort, and yet in this form, we are generally immune to the same."

"That's bad!" moans the med-tech. "You can attack someone else, but they can't hit you?"

"Yeah, I know, so this is one thing we may need to keep under our control, so no one gets any funny ideas. Nevertheless, they can act as barriers, delay tactics, and they can call for additional help. They will trade off with others on occasion, and we use our own form of protocol for identification in this case."

She motions for one to come forward. He raises his right hand to reveal his palm, and within his palm he creates Thaelyn's Order heraldry symbol, which would be unknown locally. The others study it in awe.

"How is he able to do that?" the med-tech asks.

"It's all controlled by the mind. The image is simply a reflection of his perspective and the imagination he creates it with. And we've become quite fluent with it by now."

"Amazing."

"I will station two of these outside and two inside. Commander, if you don't mind sharing your space, I feel this is necessary to ensure your protection. You're basically the only remaining governing official we have in this world. We don't want to lose you."

"I thank you, Lieutenant," he affirms. "It's good to have people supporting me. All right, I'll accept them, and let's hope they don't become necessary. Now, what else do you suggest for our security?"

"We've been in contact with Director Bak'vayn at the ARC. He knows a lot of people in other fields, and we've been organizing a kind of consortium of experts to devise a new form of government ID. So far, we're calling it the Universal ID chip. It's a holo-chip, a bit larger than the usual ones, but it'll combine all other forms of ID, security cards, personal finance and medical information, and so on, into one chip, accessing a high security government database, and secured behind a genetic fingerprint. There's no point in having multiple chips or cards by this time, as we need THE maximum level of security for each and every citizen amongst us. The Prodigy Gift can be used to impersonate any individual, plant, animal, piece of furniture, or spot on the wall. It's that powerful."

"In all the nether-space," the Captain wheezes. "I never would've imagined it could go THAT far."

"Oh, trust me, Captain; it can even fool such a near-godlike being as the Marshal, like we did on Morndindor. He wasn't talking to our actual base staff, he was talking to a bunch of projections, and he had no idea of it."

"Incredible! So, the show we heard on the com-link wasn't even actual people?"

"That's right, the same as with the Tul'ryk. Just as we can simulate virtually any image, we can also simulate any sound. It just takes a little practice and a lot of imagination."

"Um, by the way," Geilv hesitates. "What about Kriv'tik?"

"Yes," she nods gently. "Commander, from all of us, we want to apologize for hurting you during that show. We had no idea the two of you were friends. He's fine and working on our side. You are right about one thing though. That last episode with Ytani and our female staff had him on the verge of mutiny, if not for being intercepted by this other group first. But I can't say anything more than that for now. We'll see to your reunion at a later time."

"All right, fine, and thanks," he sighs and leans back. "He always was a clever one, and very determined."

"Indeed!" she affirms. "Now, Ytani is going to make a few additional visitations where he basically makes a nuisance of himself with more demands. Despite the Marshal's warning about Sargeras and his tolerance levels, we need to make a showing to further release a few details, and also to prompt a kind of confrontation. We need this to lead us into our final play."

"And what sort of final play is this?"

"Those beings who are planning their offensive want him exposed, preferably away from anything that could represent collateral damage. So, Ytani will make his demands, to which we doubt anyone here will accede to, and the Marshal, whom we would like to be a participant in this charade, will likely grow increasingly impatient with him. But all things must have a breaking point, and Commander, we need your cooperation on this. You're going to lose a few ships along the way... theoretically."

"Theoretically..." he muses.

"This is classified to just us in this room. We need to build an image using actual examples. And the Marshal needs to hear these reports...or at least that portion where you lose the ships."

"And in actuality?"

"In actuality, your peaceful sector security is going to become less peaceful with a real insurgent force the illustrious Azgarén Space Navy will NOT be able to counter. We will use non-lethal methods, but your ships will become toast along the way. This will serve two purposes. We need something physical to justify a world panic, thereby to send the people into those shelters out there, and also to use a new drug the ARC is putting together to counter the feedback effect of the seeds when Sargeras goes down."

"A feedback effect?" the med-tech winces. "So, that's what it does?"

"There is some amount of speculation here, but we have information on our side where the people are linked into something that could cause a harmful response. That alien coding the ARC found is a feed into him as a form of life support. It creates an environmental layering effect of bioenergy as a substitute to the normal environment his kind would otherwise need as a support layer. He taps into it as a feed, but we think if he goes down, we could see a reflex where it could feed back into the people. And it could be bad, possibly putting them into a coma, or worse. Now imagine a full world population going into this. It would be a disaster we don't even want to think about."

"Absolutely!"

"Our second point is simply to demonstrate what happens when you anger a society with technologies you might not otherwise be familiar with, meaning to say, based on this Abnormal Energy. The Marshal needs to see this, or at least to hear it over the com-links, and like all things, it has to sound real. But on this occasion, the logistics don't favor us for a stage play, so we're going military on you, with respect."

"Is this to say," the Captain wonders. "You have ships that will arrive here to attack us?"

"Yes, but not anything you would expect to see in this universe, Captain."

"And do you expect us to fight back?"

"Oh, please, knock yourselves out, if you think you can," she grins. "This is the whole point, Captain. Darumon and Sargeras come from a society that takes pleasure from military combat as a type of entertainment sport. We need to put on a show, and it needs to draw them out of hiding. But to do this, we have to appear as a force to be reckoned with. So, as far as the Azgarén Space Navy is concerned, you have hostiles to fight in order to defend your home, and you will do so with all due diligence."

"But what about your people?" he grimaces. "We don't use non-lethal weapons on our ships."

"So be it," she smirks. "But first you need to catch us."

Ayene now gets up from her chair and directs her officers to their positions. Then she steps back a pace, offers a gentle wave goodbye, and flashes out of sight, which causes another round of starts in the group.

"That little scamp!" Geilv mumbles. "She's one of them!"

"I swear, Commander," the Captain shakes his head. "If I said we are entering some interesting times, I clearly didn't know what I was talking about."

Chapter 11

DISTURBING IMAGES

Ileani was preparing one of her reports at CPComm, this one as a follow-up to the appearance of Ytani during her interview with Ayene, and combining a recent delivery from Central Command, by way of the ACI, of the research Geilv ordered from Captain Ta'yeen on Ytani's family history. As usual, the set coordinator gave his count and the camera turned to the news desk.

"This is Ileani Ur'paran for C.P. News. In today's news, we have a press release received from our correspondent at Central Command, which is the result of an investigation of the figure we came to know of as Ytani. According to our correspondent, Ytani was an agent once assigned to this classified mining project by the Marshal. But due to the lack of a family name, and the clear violation of public safety protocols during his appearance, as well as his portrayal of that strange flying creature, local security officials felt it necessary to conduct an investigation to identify him and his possible point of origin as a prelude to filing charges for the theft of military property, causing a public disturbance, possibly also assault charges, and perhaps more if you consider his threats relating to that weapon he claimed he stole.

The investigation began by questioning the officials at Central Command to gain some perspective of who he is and where he came from, and further to see if they could pinpoint his current whereabouts, assuming he is actually on Azgarén at this time, as some officials are still skeptical, based on his statements. The result, however, led to a series of further investigations, as Ytani's surname was apparently unknown to those same officials.

This led the investigation to locate any other personnel who might have once served alongside him in that mining base. The investigators were able to locate a few leads, but the new results they found were even more surprising. It would seem Ytani's surname was not even known by his coworkers, as he was assigned independently by the Marshal, and likely due to this unusual skill he exhibited.

Finally, the investigation found itself forced to follow up on statements made by those individuals, hoping to find other elements that could lead them to identify Ytani, if only indirectly. Here is where things go from strange to stranger.

According to these officers, Ytani was first assigned to his role in that outpost approximately four centuries ago, when it first opened, and as a young boy of seven decades. This now refutes the earlier statement by the military that he was only temporarily assigned to the base. When questioned about this, the spokesperson had this to say."

The news feed now turns to a prerecorded press clip of a male military officer.

"The Azgarén military command wishes to apologize to the public interest for this oversight, but we have a series of delicate security issues where Ytani is concerned, as well as the nature of that mining operation he was assigned to. The Marshal had a special interest in the operation, as part of his claim to pursue his insurgent forces, and Ytani was given a special role due to his unusual talents. But the nature of the operation was so highly classified that most of us didn't even know the full extent of what was happening out there."

The video feed returns to the newsroom.

"This statement has led several of the investigators to speculate on the true origins of Ytani and how he, as a boy of only seven decades, could be assigned to such an operation as that. At the very least, his family might have something to say about it, and question why he

wasn't in school, instead. But in the absence of a surname, trying to locate his family was proving to be problematic. At least until one individual had an idea, based on so many other cover-ups and false pretenses surrounding many of the Marshal's activities.

A careful review was made in order to confirm a suspicion by this one team member, and the result was shocking as well as disturbing. The theory was that Ytani may have been assigned to the base outside the knowledge of his closest family members. But in the absence of anyone claiming a missing child, the theory also suggested the family itself might be missing. Therefore, a search was made of the death records from approximately four centuries ago where all close family relations might be lost, including a young seven-decade old child named Ytani. And a result was eventually found.

Ytani Ankadin, a former resident of Capitol Prime, along with his mother and father, were reported as deceased due to a boating accident four centuries ago, off the shore from the local town of Tul Braka, just west of C.P. The report speaks of a fire and explosion, killing all onboard, and leaving wreckage in the waters away from the shoreline. However, even though an investigation at the time found the bodies of both parents, Ytani's body was never found and believed to be swept out to sea.

A computer imaging service was then appointed to conduct an age progression of the last known photograph of Ytani from his youth, to see if they could match it with the image most recently captured of his appearance in downtown Capitol Prime, and the results appear positive.

This now leads investigators to wonder how Ytani managed to escape from the accident and find his way into the Marshal's employ, especially if to consider the highly classified nature of the operation and this unusual skill he exhibited, which itself seems to be the result of a cover-up. Needless to say, this is just one more point of contention adding up to a long series of charges the Marshal will likely face once the current revolutionary action finds stability and we appoint a new government body."

✦

During the following week, Kaliya was assembling a new team on the grounds of the Cormyr Training Fields, where some of the Order's trainees go for combat exercises. On this occasion, she had in mind to test a few ideas for another play.

"All right, listen up," she directs. "We need to experiment on a few things to see what works best. I have in mind a new play for Ytani's second showing, and it's going to be huge…godlike to be exact. But to do this, we might need to assemble it in pieces, where each of us takes a component of a larger artwork."

"An artwork?" ask one member. "Are we now going on display in a museum?"

The group ushers up a quick laugh.

"Not quite a museum, but I suppose this will be one for a few awards. In my mind, I see him sitting on a throne-like chair that spans that major boulevard running through the middle of town. The chair legs will reach from one side to the other on the sidewalks, and he'll be in the middle."

"And the local traffic…?"

"…Will likely find it hard to get by with him in the way," she chuckles. "But that's beside the point. He's displaying himself as their new god-king, and he wants to look the part. He'll also be a little upset that he didn't get his last period of tribute. But we'll say he's just starting out and needs to condition these people, so he'll give them a little bit of leniency this time."

"How much leniency?" asks one female member.

"Initially, and since we need to stall for time to get Marelle's team up, and also to finish the base, we'll just say he forgot to provide a mailing address to deliver her to."

"Oh, well, how thoughtless of him!" she smirks.

"Yeah, these things happen. After all, he's still young and trying to settle into his new role. Later, however, and we might need to play this a few times, he'll become increasingly frustrated at their clear lack of cooperation. For this, he might increase his demands somewhat."

"Increasing it… Uh oh… Increasing to what?"

"He can't very well bring fire and brimstone down on their heads, so he'll simply demand a few extra girls as we move forward."

"Oh, is he now building up a private harem?"

"Well, yeah! He's a god-king! Don't they ALL have harems?"

They share another laugh before she continues.

"But eventually, as time goes by, he'll become irritated by their lack of compliance. This might also depend somewhat on the Marshal's response, which I doubt will be favorable. But again, we need to see about stalling for time to get Marelle into play for when he gets REALLY angry and sends his bouncers in to rough them up a bit."

"Kaliya, are you sure this is part of being a paladin?"

"Well, Oghma does preside over the domain of inspiration, and we do need to inspire them."

"Oh! Now wait a moment. I don't think THAT form of inspiration is part of his domain."

"Maybe not, but we still need to play the game if we're going to draw the Marshal out like we want him."

<hr>

A new month was beginning, and Kaliya and her team were preparing for another Ytani showing. They had been rehearsing their latest procedure during this time to play out in the city, and by now they felt they were ready. In the field outside the guildhall, the team assembled in projected form and made a final check.

"All right, people, this is it. Let's give them a good scare in downtown C.P. After all, Ytani is hungry, and he's not any closer to having fun now than he was a month ago."

The team lets out a bold whoop and flashes out of sight.

In downtown Capitol Prime, people casually walked along the avenues, and vehicles drove along the roads as the population attended to its usual duties. When suddenly, an eerie sight began to emerge in the skies just over the rooftops. It formed a swirling vortex in the smoggy clouds, but tinted an orange-red, as if lit by fire, and it emitted a low rumbling sound that echoed along the streets.

The hover shuttles on the roadway, at ground level and also the elevated lanes, all slowed to observe the sight, not knowing for sure what it was, but clearly it wasn't natural, and neither was it pleasant to see. Several vehicles began turning around to speed off the other way, while still more simply halted, causing traffic to jam up.

Pedestrians stopped in their tracks, and many more came outside the shops and offices to observe the abnormal disturbance. Whispers and shouts began to erupt as fear washed over the assembling crowds. And then, from out of the sky, as if emerging from the vortex, came a series of frighteningly large objects hurtling towards the ground.

It began as a set of elongated geometric posts, like legs of a gigantic chair being cast down and landing upright on either side of the roadway on the sidewalks. They impacted with a mighty crashing that resounded in all directions. Once the four chair legs had landed, a throne seat descended down to settle on top of them, again with a powerful booming effect. This was followed by the back of the chair, and finally a giant-sized Ytani, levitating out of the cloud and landing neatly onto his new seat.

Ytani sat erect on his colossal throne, with a proud grin broadcasting abnormally wide across his face as he rotated his prominent gaze around the city.

"My dear subjects!" he thunders. "Oh, what a grand day this is! Long have I dreamed of my own private world with people who will bow to my every desire! But naughty, naughty you…you did not give me my playmate as I requested. But not to worry, for I shall be kind on this occasion, as it would seem in my previous presentation, I was so overjoyed at my return that I forgot one little detail. Oh, woe is me, for I forgot to tell you where to send her!"

He begins laughing hilariously, which bellowed around the city and drew even more attention from office workers inside their buildings.

"Well now," he regains himself. "It's really quite simple. You see, all you need to do is place her in a smallish transport…nothing fancy, mind you…and send her to my new home on a world we call Tufar Awayish. It's such a happy place, and everyone loves to kiss my hooves. But just remember, I want her wrapped up cute and cuddly, so I can enjoy every moment of her. And when I'm done, I'll be back for more. I'm accustomed to taking these at…oh, maybe one-month intervals, so I'll let you decide how to pick and choose the next sacrifice and have her ready. Now, tootle along, my yummy little minions!"

He again bellows out his maniacal laughter as he slowly rises back into the sky, along with his throne, as the full assembly reverses direction the way it came. Finally, the fiery vortex settles and vanishes.

The people on the ground, as well as the remaining vehicles, all glanced around at each other as they tried to interpret what they just saw.

✦✦✦✦✦

"Ghantil!" Azina shouts as she rushes into his office. "In all the nether-space, did you see the news a little while ago? Monster-sized Ytani blocks traffic in downtown C.P., people run in fear of his terrifying presentation. They had video taken by several onlookers, and a few C.P. Security patrols with their cameras."

"Yes, and I could hear some of it from the window here. It's unbelievable! The Captain gave me a bit of fair warning a short while before this, but if to imagine, you can create truly godlike visions with this thing!"

"I wonder what the Marshal will do about it."

"Last I heard, Commander Geilv put his own restraining collar on him, but we're still playing like Ytani is a threat. So, he'll probably balk at the idea unless…Ytani…decides to get physical. And apparently the Captain has a few plans in the making for that too."

"Is she able to get physical in this form?"

"Not in such way as that. This is where her people on the other side start making real incursions into our space, and poof; there goes our happy little sense of sector security."

"Uh oh…then we need to think of Central Command and what THEY might do."

"I received a briefing that Ayene made contact and laid down a few ground rules for this part of the game, although I'm at a loss on how they hope to pull it off."

"What did she say?"

"They're launching a non-lethal strike force on our otherwise very lethal Azgarén Space Navy, and apparently they expect to win."

"Oh really!" she smirks sarcastically. "Wow, they must be confident! What are they using?"

"According to my information, those small one-man fighters they spoke of once."

"In all the nether-space!" she shouts. "And they hope to knock down our cruisers with that? They must be insane."

◆◆◆

Inside Central Command, Geilv was once again in conversation with the Marshal.

"That insolent little speck!" the Marshal groans on the com-link. "Does he actually expect us to offer him sacrifices now? This is intolerable! Commander, clearly, we would never give in to such a thing, I don't care how capable he is with this talent!"

"Marshal, do you think he can cause any actual harm in this form?"

"I, eh…would not expect so, Commander. I will admit, I may not know what he has learned in this time, but my expectations are not especially high. He can take up any image he desires, but I think physical harm is another thing. Worst case scenario, I would imagine he can maybe knock over a few refuse bins, but as for his impertinent demands…" he grumbles something unintelligible. "Commander, we need to find a way to remove him. I had an idea come to me briefly, but that ridiculous mention of the world he's hiding on leaves us with very little to go on. However, if he should afford us any clue as to where we can actually find him, perhaps we could launch a special little surprise on him in place of his so-called sacrifice," he chuckles acerbically.

"What sort of surprise?"

"Of course, first we need a positive target, but if we were to send some kind of infiltration team, we could sneak in and eliminate him before he causes any more trouble. Maybe we can find the rest of that weapon along the way and have an opportunity to…" he sighs deeply, "…confiscate it. Right, Commander?"

"Yes, Marshal, this much I think we can both agree on, but just remember my statement."

"Yes, Commander, I've been sitting here contemplating a number of things relating to that, and further reflecting on a long history of other moments. It's all I have for now. I will not make trouble for you. In fact, I find myself becoming a little curious right now."

"Curious? Over what?"

"At present, over what sort of direction this society might take as it finds its new stability. But so far, it looks like they're still pulling together supporters, maybe also resources. It's a very big movement, Commander, to choose a new form of planetary government over what you had for so long, especially for a society as complex as yours," he muses distantly. "That young lady was right about one thing; you will need to reeducate many of your people."

Geilv stares at the com-link trying to interpret the Marshal's wording.

"Marshal, are you feeling well?" he asks.

"Why, yes, Commander, and thank you for asking. Call it… sentiment. Recall what I said before about that ancient pleasure we once had, the Challenge of Creation. I did not really have such an opportunity in my lifetime…not before coming here. Much of that had already passed, and our society, whatever remained of it, had transitioned into something else. But I find myself sitting here reflecting on our history together. I even took an opportunity to examine that cartoon series that young lady mentioned. Era the Wise. It is actually rather cute, and it's causing me to recall a few things from my own experiences."

"Really! That's interesting. To think of someone who might be godlike watching cartoons."

"Yes!" he chuckles faintly. "Who would ever think? But we do like entertainment on occasion. However, this one was special to me...this effort. It was mine, and mine alone. My Master and his kind might be the ones to create life, if they had such a desire, but those like me were just servants to manage things. This one, however..." he sighs wistfully. "This one was special."

"Not being someone in your position, I would not know that particular sensation."

"Perhaps not, but it does offer the occasional bit of wonder. You find yourself asking what will fall into place next, where next will you travel, what next will you invent..." he pauses with a slight tremor in his voice. "But this is a game for the immensely patient," he concludes. "Anyway, I suppose there will be no more of that now. Like that woman said, you've grown up now. What more do you need from me?" he clears his throat as he tries to compose himself. "Keep me informed, Commander, in case you should see anything else out there. We need to be ready for a quick movement if the opportunity should arise."

"I will."

"And maybe, if he doesn't get his delivery as planned, he might remember we don't actually know where that world is, and he might offer us another clue. Be on the alert, Commander. Our day is coming!"

The Marshal ends the link, leaving Geilv still staring at the vid-com.

"Strange..." he muses softly.

He reaches for the terminal again to make another call.

"Control, Captain Ta'yeen here."

"Captain, it's me. I need to speak to you again."

"Right away, Sir..."

They end the link and Geilv waits several moments for the Captain to arrive.

"Sir?" he announces as he enters the office.

"Captain, the Marshal is now suggesting we wait for...Ytani...to provide a final clue as to the location of his hideout so we can launch a covert strike to take him out. Now, my question is, what does the ACI have in mind to carry this to the next step."

"Did the Lieutenant give any new instructions since her last visit?"

"No, so I'm guessing we'll just have to play it by ear for now. Maybe the clues will present themselves."

"This is reasonable. But I'll say one thing: How in all the nether-space did they actually pull this one off! The reports on the news say the thing was huge and clearly resembled something of godlike proportions. So, whoever is doing this must be enlisting help of some kind, that's all I can say about it."

"The ACI must be training a lot of people with a lot of high-level skills. This makes me wonder who started it now. If everyone had these chips stuck in their heads at four decades, who was the first to unstick it and experiment with this thing?"

"Do you think maybe someone hid themselves from the mandates, or simply went undercover to experiment? We had that release of the Metaphysics faction still out there. Maybe they found something, and this is their comeuppance," he chuckles.

"Wouldn't that be ironic!" Geilv smiles. "But it must've been quite some time ago if they can afford to donate bodyguards," he glances at the two men by the door. "And they don't talk much, so clearly they're highly disciplined."

The Captain also glanced at the two men, who held their perfectly stoic stance by the door, not flinching or reacting to the conversation.

"Well, all I can say is, once this is over, I'll be looking forward to a nice return of our operations."

He rises from his chair and offers a salute, then leaves the office.

✦ ✦ ✦ ✦ ✦

The month passed by rather uneventfully, as Latena continued her campaign. But as time progressed, and she developed her foundation, even though she was told to keep things static until Thaelyn's launch, it was becoming clear that at least a show of progress was necessary to build an interim form of government until a more official body could be assembled. Ileani was preparing her most recent report to discuss this action.

> *"This is Ileani Ur'paran for C.P. News. In our report for tonight, Activist Latena Ta'yeen has been assembling a coalition of legal advisors to review once again the Charter of Laws, but this time to extract those Articles and Sections that can serve as a foundation of principle in developing a new document. In a recent speech, she had this to say..."*

The video changes to a recorded moment of Latena standing behind a podium at a press interview.

"My fellow citizens. I know we have a long way to go if we are ever to reform our government body, and likely to reinvent many aspects of what we once held so high, if only for all these scandals and controversies we have recently uncovered. I do not expect this to be easy, and I would implore our public to be patient, and give us the time and opportunity to see it through without any new disasters.

Of the many concerns on my mind, we have security and law enforcement. This much should be maintained above all others. I would strongly advise our existing services, which do serve quite well as they are, and always have, should be maintained, at the very least until we find stability in other areas. There may be adjustments along the way, as we revise the Charter of Laws, and we will surely update our procedures and practices as we refine our efforts.

We next have that temporary body once assembled by the science factions as an interim to the Council in their long deliberation. We should build on this, since it seems quite apparent by now the Council, wherever they are and whatever they are doing, might not have a job waiting for them should they ever return home again. This can surely serve us as a temporary replacement, but my longer-term visions see us converting to something else, where we will find a body of proper statesmen, in this case politicians, performing the duty of government as their primary function, and our scientists are just that...scientists."

The news broadcast now returns to the studio.

"It is expected by many that this new government will represent a democratically elected republic, although most historic examples tended to follow a top-level leadership position, such as a monarch or prominent military leader. But according to Miss Ta'yeen, there are alternative examples that may instead employ an elected chief executive, alongside a parliamentary body who would provide the legislative action.

In other news, the figure known as Ytani is raising a new controversy as his recent demonstration in downtown Capitol Prime stirred a public outcry for law enforcement to locate and detain the one responsible for what they're describing as his outrageous public disturbance, and further for the science community to explain how he does it.

In response to this, a spokesperson from the recently announced return of the old Metaphysics faction came forward expressing an interest in examining any new discoveries of the Tav'ageen Anomaly, and also to call for volunteers, especially of young adults or children who may have, at one time, ever been diagnosed with the symptoms. When asked why this selective age range, the spokesperson explained that the Suppressor chip, over the course of time, may carry a lingering effect on the ability to first discover the Gift. Therefore, younger persons would possibly hold a greater potential to rediscover it, and therefore allow researchers something to study.

And finally, in a related article, the medical community is offering a free service, in part due to these renewed studies, to disable and remove the Suppressor chips."

Another video clip now loads up of a female medical professional.

"Our faction, the medical community, feels it should serve as our responsibility, when you consider we should have conducted this study so long ago, with or without any official sanction from the Council, as part of our commitment to the public. It was once said we had to follow behind this nondisclosure clause to keep things quiet, but at the same time, our internal policies must still hold us responsible to serve a greater public interest, and that public interest must be to find a final solution to that old Anomaly condition…whatever it might be. And the chip, which on one side was always said to be temporary, and on the other side was not a very desirable solution to begin with, had to be revisited.

Therefore, in light of these new revelations, we feel it is only fair that we should provide this new service to remove that which we put there on the orders of the Council. If the Tav'ageen Anomaly is in fact something else entirely, the truth needs to be understood, and this means these chips need to come out."

The news feed returns once again to the studio.

"Naturally, this has several of the science factions offering up opinions as to the repercussions, suggesting if, for instance, the chips did indeed

serve as a cover for something that could get out of control, it will need careful monitoring, study, and some form of regulation. Medical professionals are cautioning that if any new symptoms do in fact make themselves present, the individuals should not panic, and instead report the occurrence to their local medical ward for investigation."

✦ ✦ ✦ ✦

Back on Tae'Eladar, Kaliya was preparing another of her Ytani portrayals.

"Here we go, people," she asserts. "This is Number Two of his god image, and this time we're going to make a little noise for where he's coming from."

She signals her troupe, and they all vanish from the area.

Once again, in downtown Capitol Prime, the same large disturbance appears in the sky. And as before, the people and traffic all came to a standstill. Above them was the swirling fiery vortex, and then came the immense objects tumbling out of it.

Many vehicles quickly turned and began moving off. Voices cried out as the populace screamed and ran the other way, while the gigantic throne began to assemble itself on the ground, and finally to receive the godlike Ytani levitating down onto his seat. And as before, his oversized grin spread across his face as he gazed down at his questionably loyal subjects.

"Praise be! For Ytani the Magnificent has returned!" he bellows. "Ah, my precious little minions, but I am sad, for I STILL have not received my delightful tribute. But just as I was about to bring forth my wrath upon my disloyal subjects, one of my favorite advisors reminded me of a most unfortunate oversight. Oh, how silly of me!" he boasts.

He began roaring with riotous laughter at the realization of this most recent slip-up.

"My poor, poor little minions, but of course, you might not know exactly where to find me to deliver my precious tribute. After all, I was originally stationed on that...ooh," he croons and waves his hands, "...top secret mining base our dearest Marshal was operating behind your backs. Yes! It is true! He had our illustrious military mining up some kind of weird metal no one knew anything about, and sending it off to some kind of processor to make something that goes BOOM!" he gestures an explosion with his hands.

He pauses to gaze down at the street as many of the people were now staring up at him.

"But I'm sure this isn't of any real importance to you down there," he waves it off. "After all, this all occurred in a completely different universe!" he laughs again. "Yes, our operation was so highly classified, it would seem none of you ever knew we found a new universe out there!" he cackles some more and shrugs.

On the ground, many of the people were starting to mumble amongst themselves about the implications of this statement, as it was becoming clear Ytani was giving out sensitive information that was otherwise being hidden away.

"But anyway, I digress. Needless to say, this is where I can be found. Now, I'm quite sure Central Command spent enough time out there to explore a few things, so it stands to reason that somewhere in their navigation logs they should have a reference to a world called Tufar Awayish…yes!" he beams at the crowd. "That's the name…well, that's MY name for it…whatever THEY call it is another thing."

He lets out another thundering laugh at his own joke.

"But you know, I think if they tried hard enough, they could probably find it. After all, it's a planet, and it goes around a sun…how many of those could we possibly have?"

He bursts forth with yet another maniacal outpour of laughter before departing the area the way he came, leaving some of the people on the ground now asking themselves who he actually is and what he's doing.

"Marshal," Geilv addresses on the com-link. "I presume you took notice of that last message?"

"Yes, Commander, and I'm sitting here contemplating a few things relating to it."

"You usually call me on these matters, rather than me calling you."

"Yes! So I do…did…" he muses silently.

"And then you tend to scream about it," he adds.

Geilv was making a call to the Marshal, rather than the other way, and becoming increasingly concerned for the Marshal's distant manners in recent times.

"Yes, you are correct, but on this occasion, I don't see the point. After all, he was in that other universe when he vanished, therefore it simply follows that he might still be over there."

"Can his projection actually travel that far?"

"If he is claiming still to be over there, then I suppose so. But I will admit, I am rather impressed by this much. That Gift is a rather potent one."

"And his obvious manners to leak this sensitive information?"

"Commander, if you're trying to incite a reaction out of me for his behavior, I hate to disappoint you, but on this occasion, I am neither going to complain nor argue with it. It simply stands to reason, if we were asking ourselves about him giving out more information, this is the information he will give. It was simply a matter of time…" he falls silent a moment. "Time… Time for them to realize another of my failures…another of my hidden secrets…my promises…" he trails off.

"Marshal, I am uncertain of your direction, and growing more concerned about your own behavior."

"Commander, you have people outside my door. Have I left my office? Have I made any attempts to defy your instructions? Have I tried assaulting anyone new? No. Therefore, my manners are exactly as you want them, and for as long as you keep your guns pointed at my beloved Master's head. And I suppose for as long as you and your people allow us sanctuary here. There is nowhere else for us to go."

"Yes, Marshal, but this is not precisely my point. You do not sound yourself lately."

"Oh, that…yes. Forgive me, but I find myself lost in thought a lot lately, and most of it depressing."

"I suppose I can understand, given all you have said before. Very well, but now, what about Ytani, do you have any suggestions?"

"My best is that he must've found someone over there, or maybe someone visited Morndindor, and he made contact in some way. Now, if we apply a little logic, we might suggest it could be nearby. Do we have any survey logs of other populated worlds in the near vicinity of Morndindor?"

"I am not personally familiar with any, but I could certainly have our people conduct a search."

"Yes! Do so, Commander. Send a small fleet of scouts out there and have them scan everything within, oh…let's start with the local cluster and work our way outward. If we're lucky, we can find him on OUR terms, not his, and then we can play our little trick on him and be done with it."

The link ends.

The Commander glares at the com-link, trying to determine his course of action. He pans his gaze around the room as he contemplates this new instruction. Then he reaches for the com-link again.

"Control, Captain Ta'yeen here."

"Captain, I'm worried about the Marshal. He's not behaving quite like himself lately."

"Oh dear... How is he behaving?"

"Like someone who lost the most important battle of his life, and now he's waiting for the executioner to arrive."

"Huh? Commander, how do we interpret this?"

"That's the problem, I don't know. He seems depressed, and he even admitted to this just now, as he reflects on a lot of old memories. He didn't even call in to scream about Ytani's last appearance, OR what he said."

"All right, depression might be expected by now. Based on what you told me before, he's essentially lost his purpose in life. Depression would be a natural result of that. Maybe he has nothing at all left to live for, just to sit on a rock for the rest of eternity."

"Yes, maybe so. I almost feel for him, but then again, he did a lot of ill deeds out there. Somewhere, justice must prevail. But anyway, aside from that, he offered a suggestion for a response."

"What kind?"

"He is suggesting we search the local stellar vicinity of Morndindor to see if there are any other populated worlds out there where...Ytani... might be hiding."

"Is that so. And your instructions?"

"I'm asking myself if Ytani's last message was a hint, or simply a distraction."

"Well, if nothing else, it was giving away some critical detail."

"Yes, this much I took notice of. Another leak to expose the Marshal's hidden operations. But he..." he hesitates. "The Marshal... He didn't even say anything about it, other than to say it was inevitable to come out."

"He probably realizes the futility of it by now. It's out of his hands and he lost control...of him...of us...of everything."

"Yes, most assuredly. All right, let's go ahead and give our people something to do. He's ordering up a small fleet of scout vessels to survey the local star cluster and radiating outward from there. But tell them only to search for potential forms of life, not interact in any way. We'll see where we can go from there."

"Understood, Commander."

In the WIC building, Kaliya was sitting down at the table with her latest holo-chip in hand. She appeared disturbed.

"My Lord?" she utters softly.

"Yes, Kaliya, what do we have this time?"

"I think we broke the bastard."

He frowns grimly at her as she hands over the chip.

"How do you mean? What is he doing?"

"Moping would be one word for it. He's not even arguing against the news anymore. Not that one where we revealed Ytani's origins, and not this one, either. Ytani let out one of his most sensational secrets relating to that other universe, and all he had to say was, 'oh well, so it happens.' Even Geilv took notice of it."

"Did he give instructions relating to looking for him?"

"He did, saying to search the local star clusters to see if anything is out there, maybe to find him and launch a covert-ops move on him to take him down."

"Curious…"

"And then Geilv called Captain Ta'yeen, and they've generally agreed he's given up."

"Can we call this a victory?" Kailen wonders. "Against the one who has done so much of his own?"

"And where do we go from here?" the General adds.

Thaelyn examines the chip in his hand and sticks it in the vid-com reader.

"All I can say," he offers, "is we have a process that must complete somehow, and we are not there yet."

Ileani was preparing another primetime news sensation in the newsroom. As the set coordinator gave his countdown, she turned to the camera for her latest report.

> *"…Our headline for tonight revolves around the most recent visitation by Ytani presenting himself in his god-sized image over the streets of*

downtown Capitol Prime. Once again, citizens were sent running as he came down out of his strange atmospheric disturbance to sit on his enormous throne overlooking the public below.

On this occasion, he announced yet another oversight in his instructions for his proposed tribute to be delivered to him, this time referencing his home being located in, of all things, another universe! Some experts are speculating he was simply exaggerating, as part of his obvious portrayal of bravado. But several science factions are now asking if he held a note of truth to his statement, as he once again referenced that mining operation, which was actually confirmed by military officials as a highly classified operation being conducted by the Marshal.

One spokesperson came forward with the statement that if our military did, at the instruction of the Marshal, discover a completely new universe out there, it would be the discovery of the millennium. He went on to say, 'If this was indeed the case, it now brings into question the Marshal's statement of giving such a profound gift of wisdom to the Council to deliberate, when in fact this discovery could be of immediate value to the science community at large, regardless of his classified project or anything else.'

Rally protesters are outraged that such a claim could lead to any number of extraordinary new findings to fill our otherwise empty science labs, and that this further professes the Council's lack of support to keep their represented factions busy with new research, to say nothing of the Marshal holding back on his promises of sharing any part of his own knowledge with us. A spokesperson for the astrophysics faction had this to say..."

A clip with a female professional comes online.

"There was a time when the Marshal came to us promising to share the secrets of the universe if we were to help him with his troubles. Well, if he knew there was ANOTHER universe out there, I would certainly like to know why he didn't tell us about it, especially after we've done so much for him already.

This also forces me to recall, if only in passing, that statement by Miss Ta'yeen, even if hers was in jest. And this may further demand an interpretation of her suggestions relating to this thing being described as Abnormal Energy, with the need for it as a support environment, and what relation, if there can actually be one by now, of anything in OUR universe representing an opposing force described as insurgents to the Marshal and Sargeras, if they may not even be native to this one."

The video now returns to Ileani.

"So far, there is no comment from either Central Command or the Marshal on these matters. But one thing is for certain… Ytani has let a rather significant ball drop if he was once part of this operation and let go one of its most important aspects. This now brings many to wonder what it was the Marshal was actually doing over there, and how it relates to any of his other…known…operations."

"Commander," the Marshal announces. "I would ask you to do something for me…one of these days."

"What is that, Marshal?"

"I once came here offering something. I may have lifted up your race from those early moments, and it may have carried its hidden intent, but there were other times when I argued with myself about those teachings that could bring you even higher. Therefore, let it not be said that I didn't at least give out one small piece of it. That other universe… Once the issue of Ytani is out of our way, I will have you share whatever information we have of stellar cartography, planetary studies, jump indexes for future expeditions, and so on. Give it out freely to those people who can make the best use of it."

"Huh?" he blurts.

"What, didn't you understand the request?"

"I understood it perfectly. I'm simply surprised to hear you say it."

"Why? It's already out that I held back, and the people are angry. Commander, you know full well the world has discovered virtually everything I've done…or not done. What more is there? You have the information in your records, so let's make it official. And since I'm the one who directed it in the first place, it makes sense I should be the one to release it. There is nothing more to keep secret about it. Morndindor is lost. Madzurki is lost. Ooduan is…well, I wouldn't even suggest going back there. My only suggestion is to take care around those places where we made our enemies.”

“Yes, Marshal, I’ll keep this in mind. And when Ytani has been found and removed, I’ll let our people know…and I’ll put your name on it.”

“Thank you, Commander.”

He ends the link, leaving Geilv gaping at the com-link.

“In all the nether-space…” he glances up at his bodyguards, both of whom had their eyes turned at him. “Can you believe that?” he wonders.

The two men standing by the door glanced at each other and returned back to him, but they could only shrug and shake their heads faintly.

✦✦✦

“Father, are you busy?”

“Túfu! How have you been lately? You seem to be quite occupied with your studies. Are you doing well?”

Túfula was making a visit to the Naarg uy’Sodrad and her father’s quarters. Elder Vankkar was relaxing in his study and reading a book he borrowed from the library in Bya’an Tamoranth on Tae’Eladaran history. He set it down when the girl arrived.

“I’m doing fine,” she responds. “But it’s very intense. We’re learning more in a few years than what we might get in a century back home.”

“Well, keep in mind our schools were also adjusted to pace themselves with your growth rate. I suppose you might be pushing so hard right now in order to fill in for what you need just to get to work.”

“I think the answer is both yes and no. They go fast under most conditions, largely due to the short life cycles of the local races, as well as to simply compress it so they get more study in less time anyway.”

“Creating a society of super geniuses, it would seem. And all made possible due to that strange elixir they use over there. I recall when I was taking their language class. I couldn’t believe how fast they cram this stuff down a person’s throat, and yet you still catch every word of it. If it were not for our slow rate of development, I certainly would not debate applying it to our own children.”

“So, what are you reading?” she asks as she notices the book in his lap.

“Oh, you know me, Túfu,” he sighs nostalgically. “Always the history teacher… This one is fascinating, however. It has tales of epic adventure, with people overcoming extraordinary odds, as well as moments of fantastic discovery, momentous world-shaking events, and finally how a lot of little kingdoms were brought together as one global society. Cu'Nar's grace, it reminds me of the old tales of the Stormhooves. Do you remember when you were little, and I would tell you the story?"

"Those were sweet times, Father," she reminisces, though she had not told him of the revival Kaliya was making. "You and Mother would sit with me and tell me stories of Azgarén, and all the wonderful things we had."

"Yes, and now I sit here alone," he reflects solemnly. "The only thing I have left is melancholy for what we once had in those days."

"Oh please, Father, let's not go into that again."

"It's hard, Túfu. I've seen too much. My time began…what was it? Several jumps into it, I believe. We had already been pushed across a number of worlds by the time I was born. For a while, I was a teacher, trying desperately to hold on to our history through all we had suffered. It was fascinating to me, and I wanted to keep it alive, although in the end it was a vain hope."

"No, Father, it wasn't. It was never vain. We needed it. How would I ever know about the Stormhooves if it wasn't for you?"

He pauses with a muted chuckle.

"Velen had his original Council," he continues. "But then one of them was killed during a raid we suffered where they launched a ground assault. Velen chose me, for some reason, to be the replacement, not that this was any way I had hoped to receive a promotion."

"You're not the only one. I hear Kailen also got bumped when you arrived here."

"Yes, he was, and it was very hard for him, but Velen made the choice since we were reduced to whatever we had left at the time. I think it was a good one, though. He has performed very well for us."

"He comes from a good family, so I'm not surprised."

"A lot of us came from good families. And a lot of those families no longer exist, due to the way we've been hunted like animals."

"Yeah, like animals," she muses. "So, instead, you read up on Tae'Eladaran history and dream of how the world used to be."

He smirks and glances down at the book in his hand.

"If only we could've had such remarkable people as this along the way during our journey, it might have made the voyage a little more interesting. Maybe even a bit more tolerable, if such a thing as our misfortune could ever be tolerable."

"Yeah," she sighs. "It's a part of our history now, a form of suffering that'll mark us for the rest of our lives, and perhaps many more after that. We have a lineage that makes us unique in all Creation. We can never escape from that."

"Túfu, if you're trying to hint at something here, you need to remember those security rules we have to live under. If it involves what His Lordship is doing out there, I'm not allowed to know, and neither is Opadna. Neither is Velen, for that matter. Especially him, in case Darumon or Sargeras decides to use us as an information tap."

"Yes, Father, I remember, except for one small difference. Well, maybe two, if you consider Sargeras, who is most likely sleeping, and maybe not as much a bother to begin with."

"No? But I thought..."

"Yeah, we all thought that, but the evidence is pointing the other way by now...mostly. As for Darumon, Kali told me today they broke him. He's given up. So, we don't think the threat is as great by now."

"Huh?" he gasps. "What... How... What do you mean? How could... What have you people been doing over there? Are you removing the security barrier now?"

"Partially, just enough to say we have a partial victory."

"But Túfu, how do you get a partial victory on something like this? Have we actually arrived on Azgarén?"

"Yes, and they've been conducting a number of covert operations over there. Suffice it to say, that place was a wreck for all he did to them."

"How long have they been there?"

"Several years, not long after you found us on Ruuki uy'Daan."

"But..." he wheezes. "Túfu! How do you go from Ruuki uy'Daan to Azgarén? It's in a completely different universe!"

"Yeah, that's the fun part," she smiles. "But you'll need to wait for the official release. Meanwhile, here..." she holds up her trans-com. "Got yours? I have a photo album I'd like to share with you."

He fumbles with his book and reaches into a pocket to pull out his trans-com. Túfula links over an album, which includes a collage of photos and a few videos.

"Majestic cities of lights and glamor..." she muses. "Illuminated hover lanes and elevated channels of traffic flowing through the city virtually day and night."

He begins browsing the album on his unit as she reflects on their scouting expeditions into the city.

"Túfu, you little rascal, you probably shouldn't be doing this."

"It's alright, Father. Having pictures doesn't really hurt. Everybody has those. Although some things aren't as pretty as you might remember. They created a lot of pollution along the way."

"Great, so how does the natural landscape look these days?"

"Bad. We're going to have our work cut out for us to restore things."

"And the people? Are they all like those…monsters…that kept chasing us?"

"They all have the seeds," she responds informally. "It became a Council mandate at two centuries as part of the Marshal's secret program to create a type of life support engine to care for Sargeras."

"Huh? A life support engine?"

"Yeah, he was probably starving over there for lack of these arcanic energies their form of life needs to survive. And then we have those awful chips that turn them into emotionless creeps. Do you know what they were for?"

"Um, is that a rhetorical question?" he grins softly.

"You catch on quick…" she smirks. "They're called Suppressor chips. One thing they seem to interfere with is emotion, but that's not their primary purpose. It's to…suppress…a thing they call the Tav'ageen Anomaly. It's a medical implant."

"Oh wonderful! And how do you justify a medical implant that cripples your emotional output?"

"It could be incidental. Who knows at this point? But it was mandated for their full population. Go figure."

"And why is that? Did they suffer some sort of pandemic?"

"Almost. It was causing a world panic at one time."

"Wow, that might do it. Now I'm unsure if I even want to go back."

"Well, hold that thought a bit longer. We still have a little way to go before we open it up. So, this is fair warning. The final play is coming soon, and we'll need you and the others to participate in it."

She gets up and offers a delicate wave, before strolling out of the room.

✦

In the city of Bya'an Tamoranth, one of the resident priests was approaching Aerlie's office in the rear of the temple. He knocks politely before peeking in.

"My Lady, do you have a moment?"

Aerlie was attending to some accounting work when the man came inside.

"Priest Malorn! How are your duties coming along?"

"Oh, glorious, my Lady! I'm pleased to say I've helped a fair few people this month to overcome their woes."

"Excellent. What can I do for you?"

"Well, I've been paying attention to the local gossip, trying to keep up with our progress over there on Azgarén. Recently, word seems to have trickled down that we will be making our arrival soon and, well…" he shrugs. "I was wondering if perhaps I might ask for a tiny moment to make my own little presentation…just for old time's sake. I was hoping to say hello to our former Governor. I do miss him, you know," he grins broadly.

"Uh huh…I'm sure you do," she smiles. "Well, I don't see anything wrong with it. We're already involving Sehnisavain and a group of her people, so we should be able to fit you in amongst that easily enough. It could be like a reunion of old fellows."

"Oh yes! That would be just grand. And I do thank you."

He offers a polite bow as he backs out of the room, leaving Aerlie grinning as she tries to envision this final play.

"Thaelyn will probably bring out that special list he has just for me before this is done, especially with those pilgrims we keep getting from over there. I still haven't told him about that," she giggles and shrugs as she places herself back into her work.

✦✦✦

In Capitol Prime, Azina and the Director were in conversation about her recent visit to the construction site.

"…And that's not all," she reports eagerly. "They're building something like a curved row of tall spires on the outer sides of the field, stretching out from the mountainside."

"Did they mention what they were?"

"Some kind of wall… Apparently, the field is supposed to channel the battle through a corridor, to keep it contained."

"I see, so they're trying to keep the enemy away from their flanks. I suppose that makes sense. But spires, you say? A wall is a solid structure. Maybe these are just the foundations of something to be added later."

"They don't look like it. They're tall and arced almost like a ribcage, with a buttress holding it up. It looks like an independent structure, not something you would attach something to later."

"I see. All right, we'll go take a look together once it's done and see if they can demonstrate it to us. Meanwhile, that Ytani figure is drawing a lot of attention lately. We're almost due for another one, too. I wonder what he'll demand this time," he chuckles.

"I don't know, but I hope they don't start up some kind of lottery to select his sacrifices," she giggles.

As the two of them wrap up their meeting, a sound gushes up outside. It was the wailing of the raid siren making a practice run in the city. They have heard this broadcast several times in the last couple of months, and although the sound was disturbing to the ears, the people were becoming accustomed to it by now. The practice drill involved a polite but firm female voice issuing over the broadcast network.

> *"This is a drill. All citizens must comply with the Emergency Alert Network. Please stop all non-critical activities and seek out your nearest shelter immediately. All vehicles must pull to the side of the road to allow for emergency traffic only. All passengers must exit to find their nearest shelter. The medical community also declares that all citizens currently in possession of the An'gamu Seed must procure a special medical supplement to keep on hand in case of an emergency relating to a feedback reflex condition. These can be found at any local medical clinic or laboratory."*

As the announcement bulletin resounded from the loudspeakers, vehicles came to a halt on the roadways, and the elevated lanes descended to the ground. People were then scurrying off to the nearest shelter, or any other indoor safety zone. Even though they knew by the warning broadcast it was only a drill, it was still unsettling, especially after witnessing the live news feeds of Ytani being repeated on the air.

* * *

In the Bahlaie Research Center, Chief Tech Lapäli was reviewing the final completion report of the big carry-all with one of her supervisors. The large vessel that had been under development for so long was finally ready for its initial trial.

It bore the general appearance of a long slender cargo vessel with an oversized cage resembling a giant ribbed grappling claw. The armatures retracted upwards, serving in part as a landing array to allow for the body to settle on its central landing gear, a bit like a huge insect at rest. It wasn't pretty, but it would certainly get the job done if you needed to pick up something especially large from the ground.

"Chief," he asserts. "We're ready for a flight test. The last of the internal systems are installed, the Harvester is working at full capacity, the bridge is configured, and all the diagnostics check out. We just need a crew."

"Excellent, we've been waiting for this for a long time, but now we need to make a few test runs. The most important is to check to make sure the grappling arms work, and then see if the suspension sphere functions like it's supposed to."

"That's the trickiest part. We have a test body out on the field with sensors and measuring equipment on it, but our primary concern at this moment is that the bubble is based on a rather high-level mage spell which has never been applied in this manner before. We need to be sure it meets up to our specs for a full environmental containment."

"Right, so we'll use our test body, first to pick it up, and next to move it around. We also need to take it into space and back again, and finally to drop it. This should be fun. I'll send word to His Lordship so he can make the arrangements."

⬧

"My Lord!" Marelle announces cheerily as she enters the WIC building.

She was just arriving from one of her recent training flights, and taking a break to review her log results, when an urgent summons came in from Rolsklinde. She enters the room briskly, but hesitates as she sees the large assembly of people, including Kaliya, Relissa and Haran, and her husband, Roderick.

"Wow, are we having a party or something?"

"Ah, Marelle, yes," Thaelyn announces jovially. "A little revelry can be a healthy thing from time to time. Even I enjoy it, although it seems to come so rarely of late. Perhaps once this war is finally done, we can return to the business of building empires rather than dismantling them."

"Not that I would call what Darumon created to be much of an empire."

"This is true in many ways, but he most certainly did put a fair amount of work into tying this one in knots."

"So, what's the special occasion?" she asks as she steps over to give her husband a brief hug.

"We have a special task that requires attention, but at the same time we also have a minor complication which needs to be addressed."

"Oh great, are we doing those complications again? I thought we got over those."

"Dear Child, life is filled with them, even for the finest of us. However, we do have a solution to this one, which I believe should be fairly simple. But it requires your participation."

"Me? Sounds fair enough, what do you need?"

"I need you to present yourself to this gentleman over here," he directs at the General.

"Uh oh…" she mumbles.

Marelle quickly pulls herself to attention and makes a formal approach in front of the General, who had been standing silently next to Thaelyn while the rest of the group stood waiting on the side. She offers a quick salute and waits.

"Lieutenant Marelle Carronel," he announces. "During the comparatively brief term of service you have held in our company, you have given us a series of pioneering firsts which have set the records for countless new generations to come. You were the first native member of our society to take us into powered flight. You were the first native member of our society to take us into space flight. You were the first native member of our society to test the arcanic technologies to enable aerial and space combat, as well as the arcanic jump drive to enable us to travel outside our native sphere to other worlds. And although we must give credit to our friends and allies for their role in aiding us to develop these technologies, as their society already held this privilege, ours is still young and needed to make those first forays. Therefore, it goes to you that you will carry this forevermore as your legacy."

"Thank you, Sir," she beams.

"This marks you most indelibly in our history books. But as we march forward, we have even greater needs presenting themselves before us, and for this, you must now rise to a new level of privilege to carry us that additional step."

He pulls out a small case that was concealed in his hands behind his back and presents it to her.

"In the tradition of our Order, and to the admirable service you have provided to our cause in the course of your duty, it is my great pleasure this day to grant you this token of our favor."

He opens up the case and displays it to her. She looks down at it and gasps, then quickly, but nervously, tries to recompose herself as he removes it from the box.

"From this moment forward," the General continues. "You shall lead others in the service of our cause, and no doubt continue to be the first to perform that which no one else has brought to pass before in our world. Wear this with pride, Captain Marelle Carronel."

The General pins her new rank insignia on her lapel and steps back. The assembly then offers a salute to the new officer.

"Thank you, everyone," she mutters through her anxiety.

"Marelle," Thaelyn asserts. "Now that this little complication is resolved, we can get on to that new task I spoke of. The Commander here is going to assign you a tutor, and dare I use the word, give you a crash course in a new form of flying."

"Um, a crash course?"

"Yes, and let us hope it is not a literal example," he chuckles. "We have word that the large carry-all vessel is complete, and we need someone to captain it. This means you, as we already know Adalon offered her suggestion that you and she will apparently go in together."

"Wow! And that thing is big. I've been watching the construction effort ever since it got started. All right, but I'll need a bridge crew. Do we have something selected already? It would actually make sense to borrow from those people on the Tul'ryk or something at this point, right?"

"It would, and between them and Kaliya's team, we are assembling a crew to serve our needs on this occasion. Commander Kriv'tik will be your tutor, as he has the best experience to pass on to a young greenhorn like yourself," he smiles.

"Absolutely, I'm sure it'll be a pleasure to study under him. But aren't we cutting this a little close if our due date is coming up just after this next graduation?"

"It is, so we need you to spend as much time as you can on it. The final operation should be fairly straightforward, but we need it to run as smoothly as possible. We will have your combat team continue independently for now, but ultimately you will need to train together, as the Commander here tells us they have a military protocol where anything carrying what is designated as precious cargo must be accompanied by a combat escort."

"Sounds like fun, so we get a little bit of both."

◆◆◆

"My Lord," Kaliya begins in their latest meeting. "We're gearing up for Round Three of the God Ytani image. This time he'll be upset that the scouts Geilv sent apparently zipped right past him without saying hello, to say nothing of dropping his tribute package at his doorstep."

"How unfortunate," he grins. "Did he not put out the welcome mat beforehand?"

"I guess not!" she chuckles. "So, to make up for lost time, this is where he starts upping is demands."

"I see, and how many does he want on this occasion?"

"We'll just say two for now."

"Uh huh… General, what do you think about this young lady? She calls herself a paladin, but have you ever heard of a paladin taking multiple young ladies as pleasure victims?"

"Not in the history of OUR world, to be sure," he admits. "But maybe her race has some unusual social manners."

"Ah, but of course, how could we miss that point. Very well, Kaliya, but let us now ask about Darumon's proposed response."

"I'll hint that he passed by us, or maybe an outpost with long range scanners. This might cause Geilv to send more ships, and maybe a few science vessels with cartography labs to plot their destinations more predictably."

"This is an interesting thought."

"But ultimately, this is going to make it seem that his friends aren't local, so we'll be moving into the realm of using jump drives to travel within their local space."

"Naturally, and this opens up a much larger arena of possibilities."

✦✦✦✦✦

A new month rolls in, and Kaliya and her team prepare themselves for yet another public disturbance in the form of Ytani. As before, the sky erupts with the swirling fiery vortex, and this again causes people and traffic to recoil and turn away. The local vicinity of his landing area quickly evacuates as the huge pieces of his throne tumble out of the cloud and impact on the ground, assembling into another gigantic visual display. Ytani follows shortly thereafter as he settles neatly onto his seat.

"All hail!" he bellows. "For it is I, the Great and Powerful… Ytani!" he finishes with a bold laugh.

On the ground, many people are simply fleeing the area, while others take shelter around buildings and inside doorways peeking out at him.

"Indeed, my little minions, for I am rather displeased by this time. Did I not give you sufficient time AND instruction to deliver my luscious tribute? One of my advisors recently informed me that a remote watch outpost apparently detected some of your ships passing by, but you did not even stop to say hello! For shame! Now, perhaps I simply misjudged the people at Central Command. Maybe they did NOT catalog every planet and star over there. After all, they were over there for one specific reason. So, I will be gentle on this occasion, and simply demand ONE additional young lady to be added into my tribute. But be sure you deliver them on time! Because if you should fail again… well, let's just say I won't be happy."

He finishes with another thundering laugh as he lifts back up to the sky, along with his throne.

✦✦✦

In Central Command, Geilv was in conversation with the Marshal.

"That Ytani is seriously grinding my nerves, Commander," the Marshal grumbles. "But we may be moving in the right direction. He mentioned something about passing by, so we need to recheck our results. What have your people found so far?"

"We found a number of worlds with lesser forms of life, but nothing of such level as to account for an advanced civilization. And then I had the thought to call in a couple of science vessels with stellar cartography labs to see if we could plot our courses more efficiently. But if he mentioned an outpost, I'm starting to wonder just how far away they actually are from Morndindor."

"Yes, I had this thought as well. If they are so far that they might need jump drives to explore these regions, maybe also to establish frontier outposts as waystations, this is bad for us to find anything. There are a lot of stars out there, Commander, and we don't have enough ships to cover them fast enough before he becomes so irate, he takes some sort of action. And now I worry over what that action might actually be."

"Do you think it might involve that weapon? Personally, if his primary demand is female company, I doubt he would wish to destroy his one and only source."

"True, so he might simply send in something to make trouble for us.

Hmm, Commander, I wonder if this might afford us an opportunity in itself. If we could track them somehow, or else capture something and interrogate the crew..."

"This is a feasible idea. I'll look into it. We can requisition a number of magnetic beacon pods, and if we get a chance, see if we can stick one or more to their ships as they pass through. Otherwise, it looks like it might be coming down to a skirmish out there."

"But try to leave something to capture, if you can."

"Acknowledged."

+ ✦ ✦ ✦ +

Chief Bronzeheart was making a visit to the WIC building for an update on a special order he was assembling. He had returned home once the gateway was ready at the construction site, and now was involved in his next project.

"Milord, we look to be on schedule, just so ye know."

"This is good to hear, Chief Bronzeheart," Thaelyn asserts. "We will stockpile them here until the time is ready to make the delivery."

"Aye to that. I've been workin' with yer Forgemaster from the guildhall to fill this order. This will make for a grand show. Methinks even the All-Father himself might care to sit a spell and watch. I've been tryin' to picture it in me mind, how they'll be out there swingin' and dancin' around, and nary a one will actually know what to do with a good cold piece of steel in his hand. Har!"

"We will be recording this event for others to see, and we will try to secure a copy for ourselves, just so we can have a record for future generations to learn from and enjoy."

"Aye, and I'd yay be glad to take a wee peek at it someday."

"Absolutely, Chief, you and so many others."

The Chief bows and leaves the room while Thaelyn returns to his meeting with the other officers.

Kailen was softly chuckling to himself, and Kaliya displayed a generous grin, while Ayene shook her head in disbelief.

"My Lord," she admits. "How are our people supposed to fight using swords and shields? We haven't used such items as these for a thousand millennia."

"Precisely, Lieutenant, but it levels the playing field with our own. But do not fear, as we will be gentle on them. Many of our people have learned your language for this occasion, and as for the rest, they will give visual cues to aid the Suuden-Aryku in their presentation. It should not be too difficult. We just need to make a good showing."

"A showing? This would make a better comedy. I might also want to point out the inherent risk with the seeds."

"Yes, this is also true. But the swords, in this case, will not be sharp. These are the sort we more often use in combat practice at the academy. Then, after this first tournament round is complete, we have what we might call an intermission, where we apply Sehnisavain and her people, and Aerlie also informed me that Priest Malorn wants to participate briefly. You speak of comedy, although we might not take as much pleasure out of it at this time, the point here is to rivet Sargeras and Darumon to the scene, and then desire to know what comes next."

"And thus, keeping their focus on the game," Kaliya suggests. "This will likely do the job. And then I get my turn; if I'm not mistaken."

"We will need to set up the right conditions and be sure our supplemental assets are arranged. Yours will be the one to hold their attention while we make our final play."

"What about Aelwyn? We still need her."

"Yes, and I am aware she has made some good progress in her studies. I believe she has also recruited some of her old friends, both from Sigil as well as Bitopia, to assist in her practice."

"Um, we're talking about preventing someone like Sargeras from folding space, right? Who do you practice with that might be as powerful as a Primordial and keep them from folding space?" she winces.

"Fortunately, dear Child," Thaelyn smiles. "She and I, and others of our kind, know a few people. I cannot judge how they might compare to a Primordial, or even to Sargeras, if he is in a weakened state, but they are certainly potent. We have such as the seraphim, for example. They would certainly make a formidable opponent to try oneself against."

"Yes, I suppose they would."

"And I am aware she did, in fact, call a few of these to her aid in this matter. They have been in training on the barrens of Cynosure since that represents the closest analogy to a Prime world in a universe devoid of the flows."

"I just hope she can perform as well on Azgarén. This is a critical step for us."

"She knows well enough the importance of this, so we will give her the time she needs."

"Meanwhile," Ayene continues. "It seems the majority of our construction is complete on Azgarén. We're still working on a few of the spires for the wall, but other than for a little internal decorating, and a few last-minute touches on our control room equipment, we're almost ready."

"Very good. I wish I could go see it for myself, but I think I should refrain from entering that space personally just in case my presence can be detected by either Darumon or Sargeras. Therefore, I shall wait until that final moment. And speaking of which, Aerlie tells me some of our own work back home is coming along nicely. We have been arranging some of our new broadcast technologies with microphones and speakers positioned outside many of our larger temples and plazas to link into a type of global network signal we can bring in."

"A broadcast signal from Tae'Eladar? Are you planning on making some kind of public address?"

"In a manner of speaking, I suppose we could describe it that way. We will have our people engage in a special song of praise. And while I can already feel your questions rising up over why we would want this, let us simply say, well…it is a kind of announcement, as if to give praise that we are finishing something that once began so long ago."

"But you're not giving out the details of it," she muses curiously. "General, does HE have any marks on that list of his?"

"I think he holds a special form of immunity, actually," he grins. "Too bad about that…"

Kaliya was taking time to conduct a brief inspection of the base where several Daanen-Aryku technicians were making continued adjustments of the equipment to install new monitors and communication relays. The shield wall was nearly complete, and the power cables were being connected through the underground utility tunnels to the spire channeling conduits. A narrow aqueduct crossed the field at midsection, covered by a grate and filled with a supply of river water directed from a source coming in from the side of the field.

At several intervals along both sides of the field were bulwarks, offset in staggered rows adjacent to a central avenue where the main flow of troops would funnel through. Although the bulwarks were technically functional, they were mostly for show, concealing an array of emitters popping up from the underground utility tunnels to release the flow of arcanic energy onto the field for the troops to use.

"Professor," Kaliya calls to the gnomish scientist. "How are we looking with the final pieces?"

"It's moving along nicely, Captain. My only true concern is the amount of time we might have once we release the flows onto the field. The walls will drain a fair amount, but simply filling up the field, with or without our mages using it, will empty the capacitors rather quickly."

"Right, as I thought. We'll need a full charge before we begin, but maybe once we have that, we could prime the field a little with the excess before letting go."

"That's a good idea. Also, we should be getting ready to test our walls very soon now. I remember the Director and that lovely little dear, Azina, wanted to watch the show."

"Professor, don't tell me you found another female to romanticize over."

"Oh, Captain, you know us gnomes. Whether tall or short, with tails or no, a pretty face will always show."

"That's very sweet. All right, I'll go let them know and meet you back here."

"Abso-diddle-lutely fantabulous!"

Kaliya grins and shakes her head, then moves forward to the control room, which by this time had been interfaced with the local communications network. She steps up to the vid-com, pulls up a directory listing, selects the appropriate line entry for the ARC, and waits.

"Ark'ravan Research Center, reception area," announces the clerk on the link. "How may I help you?"

"This is Captain Nazég, how are you today?"

"Captain? In all the nether-space, you're on the com-link now?"

"Well, someone needs to put all this expensive hardware to good use, now that it's working. Is the Director available?"

"One moment and I'll connect you."

Kaliya waited while the line transferred, quietly reflecting on her childhood back on Ruuki uy'Daan, where they once had a similar network. Although they didn't have the population count like what was here in Capitol Prime, it was still filled with nostalgia. But then her thoughts drifted back to Tae'Eladar, and filled with anticipation over what wonders they were now developing on that side.

"This is Director Bak'vayn."

"Director, this is Captain Nazég."

"Captain, it's a pleasure to speak with you. As you can probably appreciate, this form of contact is much more familiar than having a ghostlike apparition popping in and out all the time," he chuckles.

"Yes, well, times change, I guess. I wanted to inform you that we are just about ready to test our walls. You mentioned an interest in observing this, correct?"

"Ah, yes. Azina and I have both been very curious as to what new tricks you plan on pulling. She's made a few inspection tours, and all she can figure is that they look like tall spires that vaguely resemble a warped ribcage."

"I suppose that's to be expected, coming from a medical professional. Anyway, if you want to see it, come on out. The Professor is anxious to see how it goes in case he needs to make any adjustments."

"Right, I'll gather her up and we'll be out shortly."

Kaliya ended the link and went outside, where Relissa was inspecting some of the local soil near the wall along the base of the mountain. The young elf and her wolf companion were just returning with a specimen, one of many she had been collecting from the local area to take back to the conservation center on Ruuki uy'Daan, when Kaliya caught her attention.

"Hey there, Relissa," she shouts. "It looks like they have you doing the dirty work."

"Aye, but it's a start. I don't mind, so long as it helps set things right around here. So far, the dirt looks about as bad as everything else. Smells funny, too..."

"I'm sure a lot of things smell funny to us these days, we're all so used to the sweet smells on Tae'Eladar. One of these days, though... So, who's this little fella?" she kneels down to the wolf and scratches his ear.

"This is Rocky. He's one of my pals from my ranger training. I brought him along with me to give him a little exercise. So, are we testing the walls today, or not? I've been waiting ever since I got here to see these go up."

"Yeah, I'm just waiting on the Director and Azina to arrive before we begin."

"I remember back in the beginning with Firstfall. Jiggers, that first day when Thaelyn showed up and he hit those orcs with that Mystra's Fury bit. And the shield bubble we had over our heads."

"That was scary. I understood the science of it, if just barely, but to see it done with magic," she whistles emphatically. "You were paralyzed with fear, Haran was trembling, and I was simply in shock, at least as much for seeing that cloud as I was to realize I was still alive afterwards."

"And here we are getting set to tackle a god head on. I thought Thaelyn was whacked back then, but now here I am standing in the middle of it."

"We all are," Kaliya laughs. "But the craziest part is I never thought I'd be standing on our ancestral soil preparing for a battle to liberate our most hated foes."

"Aye, and I have to admit I was befuddled just for the quick end of the war back home. Then to think we'd be frog-hopping across two other worlds just to come here."

"And not just us, but everybody is getting a little piece of it. Sehnisavain and Mynae, Priest Malorn, Marelle, you, me...Haran, once he gets out of school..." she sighs.

"It sounds like quite a show. What whacks me is that bugger hurt so many along the way, and then with what you told us recently... Jiggers, I can't believe he's falling apart now. You did a real number on him."

"That was not easy, though. This took teamwork and a lot of planning."

"And some of it just ad hoc when something nasty comes around."

"That too... I'm asking myself what he's doing in there right now. Does he even know what's coming for him yet?"

"Ay, don't say that too loud, he might hear you," she chuckles.

"The circle closes, the last will fall," Kaliya muses. "From time to time, I still think of Adalon's last prophecy. I'm waiting to see it start to unfold, but she makes them so difficult to decipher."

"That's just the way she is, I think. She doesn't like giving it up too easy."

"Maybe, but I wonder what else she's hiding. She seems so very mysterious."

"I think she's just eccentric. Dragons are like that, so I hear."

"Yeah, maybe so..."

They continue waiting until a vehicle pulls into the parking lot just outside the field. The Director and Azina both step out and stroll over to join the others, hesitating precariously as they see Relissa's pet wolf.

"Is that..." Azina stalls in her statement.

"This is a wolf, Azina," Relissa states. "Come on over and say hello.

He's actually very gentle. Just don't be too frisky when wagging your tail, or he might get the wrong idea," she giggles.

"Thanks, I'll keep that in mind. So, is the show ready?"

"Just about," Kaliya submits. "Let me go tell the Professor we're ready out here. You might want to step off to the side just in case we fry the upper half of the valley."

"Um...sure..."

Kaliya dashes away back inside the control room to inform the Professor and supervise from there, while Relissa and the others move away from the wall for a better view.

The two walls wrapped around the game field in a gentle arc, with an open end facing the river on the other side of the valley. Beyond that was a range of low hills, then the outskirts of the city.

The Director and Azina stared at the tall spires, now fairly certain this was not your typical wall, as there was nothing connecting between them.

"Azina," he advises. "When this goes active, you should watch your distancing. This looks more like a force field arrangement here."

"Ghantil, a force field made by people who use animals to haul wagons?"

"Yes, well, those same people also have a public transportation network of conveyors, and apparently, they're gutsy enough to try taking on our cruisers with only small combat fighters. Let's not take too much for granted here."

The Professor inside the control room engages the power flow to the spires. It was difficult to make out in the daylight, but the attendees began to notice the surging energies forming a glow along the pylons. It became more pronounced as the glow pulsed and formed a columnar cloud of energy enveloping the length of each spire.

Azina instinctively stepped behind the Director as she watched the energy columns begin to crackle, suddenly to erupt in sprays resembling lightning shooting across the length of each wall, expanding and coalescing into a continuous surface. She yelped as she felt the abrupt shockwave echo across the field.

"Aye, that's a good one, if I might say so," Relissa remarks quietly.

The Professor and his assistants hurried out onto the field to make an inspection, checking each spire along the full length.

Azina felt a little calmer now, and stepped forward for a closer look. It didn't look like any force field she had ever learned about from her school science class.

"Carefully, Azina," the Director warns. "These things are usually composed of extremely high energy fields."

"Right, I just want to try something. I was always curious about these, but in my field of study, you never get a chance to actually see one."

She looks for a small rock on the ground, picks it up and tenuously casts it at the wall, expecting to see it get vaporized on contact. She flinches as it coasts across, but then sees it abruptly halt, and uneventfully fall to the ground.

"Huh? That's not right."

She looks for another one, bigger this time, and tries again. Relissa stands back and watches with a crafty smirk on her face.

Again, Azina throws the rock, a little harder this time. The rock sails across until it seemingly strikes a surface, but halts without any recoil and falls away.

"What is happening here?" she argues.

She carefully steps over and grabs her rock again, taking great care to lean away from the shield. She withdraws and examines the stone in her hand. It appeared as a normal rock, like so many others. She looks at Relissa, who only raises her brow without speaking.

"You know something, don't you!" she charges.

"Me? I'm just a ranger, what do I know about these things."

"Yeah, right, like I believe that coming from someone who talks to animals."

Azina puzzles for a moment the validity of her own statement before throwing the rock again, this time overhand with all her strength. Once again, it seems to strike a firm surface, but without any bounce, instead simply to slip downward.

"Dammit! It's supposed to vaporize!"

She rushes over and grabs the rock again, now holding it in her hand like a weapon and prepares to attack the wall.

"Azina..." the Director issues and moves to intercept her.

"Uh-uh," Relissa grins broadly and grabs his arm. "Let her have her fun."

They both watch the frustrated young woman as she pounds her rock into the wall. Azina finally lays a hand on it to test its firmness. She then drops the rock and places both hands on it, feeling around the shape.

"Ghantil, this thing is solid!" she screeches. "It's a solid form, hard as anything."

She tries pounding on it, grabbing her rock again and attempting to smash it, but the shield resists the impact with no marks or reactive forces.

"This breaks the laws of physics! I'm pounding on it, but it's just absorbing my energy."

The Director steps over to take a closer look, at first touching it warily, but then to start striking it. He takes her rock and tries hitting the wall, expecting at the very least to see damage occur to the rock as it crumbles from the impact, but nothing.

"It's absorbing our inertia. Relissa, what is this thing?"

"It's based on a mage spell we call an Infinity Shield. And aye, it's tough. It can absorb probably anything you can throw at it, including atomic blasts and worse."

"Incredible! If you were to put one of these on a battle cruiser, you could make it completely invulnerable."

"Aye, likely so! Now, what do you think our chances are against your fleet out there, ay?"

The Director and Azina both turn in awe at the suggestion.

"Are you saying…" he begins.

"This is what we'll be using against you, if you get any wacky ideas about shooting us. We already know it works against your plasma guns, and it also holds up nicely against a negative matter bomb."

"Negative matter? An antimatter device? In all the nether-space, I don't think I want to meet you in battle."

"Maybe so, but I'll bet you wouldn't mind being on the other side of it."

They step away from the wall and take another look as the gnomes finish their inspection and return inside to power it down. The shield erupts in another spray which retracts and fades from sight.

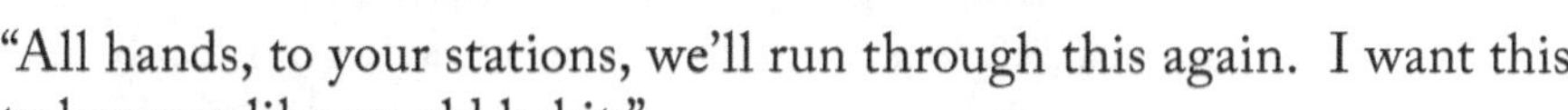

"All hands, to your stations, we'll run through this again. I want this to become like an old habit."

Marelle was settling into her new position as a Captain. Kriv'tik had spent the last two weeks giving her a crash course in captaining a cruiser. Now, he was simply standing by supervising her first few independent runs before letting her go on her own. They were still training the crew, but many of them had already gained some experience from previous operations involving the Tul'ryk.

She stood on the bridge overlooking the crew assembling at their stations. She appeared stoic and professional, surveying the operations like a true leader. But even though she put on the façade of a seasoned officer, deep down she still felt like a young greenhorn learning to sow her oats for the first time.

She recalled her previous experience in the Allegiance Guard back home in Rolsklinde, which seemed like an eternity ago. So much has changed during this time. She went from an officer in the city's Civil Watch, whose only function was to keep the local peace, to flying spaceships and now a star cruiser, even if it was only a utility vessel.

The bridge crew took up its stations, which involved a helm and navigation console in the center front, a comms station to the right, an engineering station to the rear, and the suspension field control on the left. Her seat, according to the traditions of the Daanen-Aryku, and therefore the Suuden-Aryku, was in the middle, along with her first officer.

"All stations check in," she orders. "Helm…"

"Helm is on standby, ready for your orders."

"Navigation…"

"All systems ready for your orders."

"Comms…"

"Comms station is ready. Telemetry is good."

"Engineering…"

"Engineering section reports all systems are nominal. Reactor power is good, arcanic induction is optimal, charge is good."

"Bubble control…"

"The suspension field is powered and ready. Diagnostics are good, and the grappling arms show ready."

Marelle casts her eyes over her shoulder at Kriv'tik, who was standing to the rear behind the scene. He simply smiles and nods his approval as she turns back to her command.

"All right, we have multiple targets to play with this time. We'll take them in sequence. One is a bundle of equipment going to Ruuki uy'Daan, another is a large stack of packaged cloth and leather to be delivered to Morndindor. We also have a load on Morndindor going to Therinë. Let's put this baby to some good use, now that we have her. Helm, power up and lift us away gently."

The helmsman plays over his console to power up the engines, forming an inversion field around the ship and lifting up gently. He pulls in the landing gear and begins moving away from the base.

"Our first load," Marelle continues, "was conveniently delivered to us near the utility hanger. Bring us around slowly. Bubble control, check your targeting scanners and make ready to lock on."

"Acknowledged."

The large vessel hovers above the ground, lethargically swinging across the tarmac along a marked taxiing avenue. Ground workers observed in suspense and delight as the ship makes its way across to another section of the base where a delivery had been assembled in the form of a well-bound package designed for shipment to a new location.

"Easy now," she orders. "Bubble control, how do we look?"

"Coming into position, just a little more."

The ship moved gradually over the package as the suspension field station monitored its tracking reticle on the screen.

"Captain, we are in position."

"Good. Helm, hold us steady. Bubble control, acquire the target."

The officer complied and engaged the suspension field controls. A laser positioning matrix was projected over the target and the grappling arms splayed out, revealing the field emitters inside. The target was small in comparison to the huge ship. Nevertheless, the beams engaged and projected an aura around it which expanded into a bubble just large enough to fully encapsulate the object.

"Captain, we have acquisition. The field is stable."

"Pull it in."

The officer now works the controls to retract the suspension field off the ground and into the confinement space within the grappling claws, which then closed around it like a massive set of jaws swallowing its food.

"Captain, our cargo is locked and ready."

"Excellent. Helm, take us up. Bring us out to our jump point. Nav, plot a course to Ruuki uy'Daan."

The navigation officer pulls up the jump indexing menu and selects his destination while the helmsman pilots the ship out of the atmosphere to a predetermined position suitable for jumping.

"Ready, Captain."

"Engage..." she issues confidently.

The helm charges up the jump drive with the traditional count, and the ship slowly begins to glow until that final tick on the meter sees them flash out of sight. They arrive in the Ruuki uy'Daan star system, and then make their way to the planet, setting their coordinates to a delivery pad arranged outside the conservatory where Priestess Rumoren was working on her environmental research.

As they arrive, they simply reverse the process, lining up with the delivery pad and opening up the grappling claw, then lowering the package to the ground and releasing it. She then orders a return trip to Tae'Eladar for the second package meant for Morndindor, and the process repeats like clockwork.

On Morndindor, they set their latest delivery down on another pad, much to the awe and excitement of the local population who were watching. They picked up the next shipment, which was another bundled arrangement of large crates, and took off again, this time going to Therinë, where they set it down on a pad just outside the city of Rolsklinde, before returning to base.

+⬦◆⬦+

Another month begins with another visitation by Kaliya in her Ytani god image. As before, the sky erupts, the throne comes down, and here comes Ytani in his godly seat. Although, on this occasion, he appears a bit sour.

On the street level, people once again need to scurry out of the way, but by this time, the repeated appearances are clearly becoming obnoxious and offensive for his manners and demands, to say nothing of the disturbances he creates to the local venues and traffic.

"My DEAREST minions!" he blasts with his godly voice. "What does it take to make you realize I want my tribute?! All I asked for was two little ladies to play with…THIS time. But are you capable of that? Apparently not! So, it would appear you need a little disciplining. After all, I am the GOD-KING of this world, and you will obey my every wish. And this time, I am not going to be so nice. I want no less than ten, count them…TEN…" he fumbles incompetently with his fingers as he counts the number, "…fresh young girls sent to me immediately. And if I do not get them delivered at my doorstep soon, I might just get angry enough to send my OTHER minions to remind you how this game is played."

He pauses to glare at all the little people cringing on the street below. Then he flashes a mockingly delighted grin across his face.

"And have a nice day!" he croons.

He follows with his usual hilarious laughter as he abruptly rises back into the clouds, along with his throne.

A few hours later, Ileani prepares her latest report.

> *"This is Ileani Ur'paran for C.P. News. Today's top news is another visitation of that individual calling himself Ytani. Once again, he made his appearance on the streets of Capitol Prime, this time showing his apparent frustration and disapproval over the lack of cooperation of what he describes to be his minion species at providing his alleged tribute. But rather than simply giving another extension to his demands, or further instructions on where we are supposed to be delivering it, he instead levied a new, higher demand, this time asking for no less than ten young ladies to be delivered to his service, or else, as he calls it, he will send his other minion species into our space. A spokesperson for Central Command had this to say…"*

The video changes to a male military speaker.

> *"We seriously doubt Ytani has any sort of military power that could threaten the legendary Azgarén Space Navy. But if he is so eager to lose his ships, he is freely welcome to try. Meanwhile, we clearly have no intention of giving in to his, or any other terrorist demands. This young man is simply a delusional pervert who allowed this strange ability of his to literally go to his head."*

The image now returns to the studio.

> *"Citizens are outraged at Ytani's immoral statements and salacious demands, saying they want him found and incarcerated, not only for his obvious manners, but also for his total disregard for public safety, and disruption of everyday life. But when speaking of the use of his strange ability, one spokesperson for the medical community had this to say…"*

Another clip comes on the screen, this time a female speaker.

> *"I think it might be important to point out that, from what we believe we understand of this Gift, this demonstration would clearly represent the absolute worst example of how to use it. Clearly, Ytani is deranged, but while this Gift could be a most remarkable quality in our species, I would not wish the people to interpret that it can ONLY be used in this way.*

The studies we are carrying out right now have demonstrated many positive advantages to its application. So, it becomes clear there will need to be a considerable amount of education, conditioning, and discipline in order to ensure those who might learn how to use it, do so properly. This might also demand an entirely new social climate and fundamental way of life, rooted right down to the foundation of our cultural and moral values. When presented with such a capacity as this, if it is indeed a property to be found in all of us, we can no longer afford to describe ourselves in the same terms as we once did. Perhaps Ytani is simply a very visible example of this, and therefore we should all learn from him how NOT to use it."

❖

"Marshal?" Geilv prods on the com-link. "Are you there?"

"Yes, Commander, sorry for my lapse. I was a little lost in thought just now."

"Is there a problem?"

"Well, I suppose that would depend on your perspective. With Ytani, oh yes! There is indeed a very serious problem. Now he seems to be threatening us with some manner of military force. Commander, remember my words from last time. If he should send anything into our local space, we must be ready with either that tracking technology, or else attempt to capture and interrogate."

"Yes, Marshal, I have given instructions to all our ships to be on the lookout for anything out of the ordinary."

"Good, and maybe we'll get lucky and find out where he is. Then we can send that covert team in there and finish with it!" he pauses briskly. "And bring a little peace back into our lives," he mumbles softly.

"Yes, I think I would appreciate that, as well. But what about that problem, is there another perspective you wish to comment on?"

"Oh, that…eh, well, Commander… Simply put, it relates to some of the recent news out there. You know, people making statements, analyzing things, coming to conclusions…" he sighs wistfully. "But I think, ultimately, it doesn't really matter, and I doubt you would want to hear it from me anyway. I think that will be all for now. Let me know if you see anything out there."

He ends the link.

Geilv gazes at the vid-com, wondering what could be on the Marshal's mind this time.

"Something is bothering you…but you don't think I want to hear it… from you?" he muses. "Statements, analyses, and conclusions. No doubt, all those people who are trying to interpret things. Are you suggesting I don't want to hear it due to all your other games…or because…"

He leans back in his chair to ponder the notion.

"Are you holding back on something, or…afraid I simply wouldn't accept it from you."

+ + ◆ + +

"Commander?"

Ayene was making a quick visit to Geilv's office for an update. He looks up to see her arriving at the door.

"Lieutenant, come in. What is happening today?"

"An impending attack… I just wanted to give you fair warning. From here, we alternate the intervals of Ytani's outrageous demands with his attacks."

"I see, and this is where we start losing ships, I suppose. Is this really necessary?"

"We need the evidence on the com-links in case he's either present or wishes to review it later. We will also combine this with Ytani's future statements of conquest versus your PR guys trying to downplay the severity of it. So, I may be passing a few scripts to you on occasion."

"Scripts? Are we actors now?"

"You'll need to play a few roles here and there. Also, we are gathering up some supplies to deliver here soon for our final play. And we'll need you, your officers, and a few thousand troops involved in a game to draw Sargeras out of hiding."

"Thousands of troops," he winces. "Just what do you hope to do with all that?"

"Are you aware of the construction project in the Bintavyan Valley?"

"I believe I heard something about that once. But wasn't that a conservation effort?"

"It is…for our entire world population," she smiles.

"Wow, that's quite a project. And how do we use it?"

"You'll know when you get there. But you'll need to practice a little with your new toys…those supplies we'll be delivering."

"Should I ask what those are?"

"Again, Commander," she grins. "You'll know when you see it. And with a little deductive reasoning, you might even catch our meaning. Good day, Commander."

She waves and flashes out of sight, leaving Geilv staring into the empty space she left behind.

"You young people must not appreciate walking anymore," he chuckles.

✦✦✦

Ayene was in a new training session with her own command involving a platoon of soldiers. This represented her first official command role, and she wanted to get it right. They were all in projected form for this occasion to test a new trick, and visiting the Bahlaie airfield, along with Marelle and her combat assault team. Marelle's team, on this occasion, only involved a single flight of combat craft, and was preparing to depart on their first official mission.

"All right, here's the drill," Ayene issues. "For one of our future plays, we might be challenging a heavy cruiser, assuming it actually does play out like this. We have a plan, but in order for this plan to work, we need to test ourselves for a new capacity. This one might be hard, or it might not, but we don't know until we try. Our purpose on this run is to see if we can follow a ship through a hyperspace conduit."

She pauses to judge their reactions. They all glance at each other before she continues.

"We are going to take up small forms, hide inside Marelle's combat ship, and travel along with her as she jumps to Ruuki uy'Daan. If we can do this, we should be able to do anything relating to travelling inside a ship jumping through nether-space."

She pauses again briefly.

"Now, as a safeguard, we're projecting ourselves from the Ghan'aju. If anyone gets lost, simply return home. Again, if we can do this at all, we'll practice a few more times to be sure of ourselves. But if this does not work, our fallback is to travel on the Ghan'aju to Azgarén local space and somehow see if we can memorize the area to fold there directly... which may be difficult to impossible unless we're near a moon or a planet to act as a landmark...or maybe from the Saakerav station, assuming the cruisers launch from there and we can follow them. So, everyone needs to focus carefully on your perspectives to travel with the environment."

They all let out a whoop as Ayene turns to find Marelle waiting in her pilot's seat.

"Are you people just about ready out there?" she mocks.

Ayene grins as she directs her troupe to take up small bug images and fly up to the ship, then tuck themselves neatly into the crevices to make it easy to locate their relative environment.

Marelle closes her hatch and powers up.

"Specter Flight, this is Specter Prime. Signal your condition."

"This is Specter One Leader, ready on deck."

"Base, this is Specter Prime. We are ready to proceed, and we have bugs onboard. Does anyone have a flyswatter?" she chuckles.

"Specter Prime, you might want to look in your emergency pack. Other than that, you are cleared to launch. Good luck, Captain."

The flight lifts off and takes up a standard chevron formation as it rises through the atmosphere. When they reach their low orbit objective, she directs them into a new configuration.

"Specter Flight, prepare to link up. I'm sending my carrier...now."

Marelle activates a special navigation carrier signal for her team to link into, creating a synchronized group helm and flight control, which represented a unique feature engineered for their ships. She programs a new formation that clusters them tightly together.

"Specter Flight, prepare for a group jump on my mark. Charging up...now..."

She engages the arcanic charging sequence in each ship, creating a field aura around the entire group. Marelle watches the numbers on her status display.

"Ayene and company," she instructs. "Get ready, here we go. Setting destination for Ruuki uy'Daan... All hands, stand by. Initiating now..."

The full group is enveloped in a bright flash and vanishes from the local space, travelling through the hyperspace conduit together and functioning as a single unit. The tunnel stretched out in the distance, and Marelle allowed her autopilot to guide her along the slipstream. She glanced around her cockpit to see if the tiny visitors were still with her and took notice of a variety of little bodies appearing to be desperately clinging on. Soon, the tunnel opens up as they reemerge in the Ruuki uy'Daan star system.

"Are you people still here?" she mutters into the compact space. "Come up to my console if you are, so I can see you."

A small swarm of insects begins to converge on Marelle's forward console.

"Gods above, I hope this isn't contagious," she chuckles. "All right, we seem to have success. Go home and we'll meet you on the other side."

The bug swarm vanishes.

Marelle now engages her tactical scanner and releases the group to each pilot's independent control. The flight resumes a normal formation again while she targets Ruuki uy'Daan on her scope and leads them away.

"This is Specter Prime to the Ghan'aju. We are inbound."

"This is Captain Va'tyn. We have you on our scans. Proceed ahead."

Marelle and her team made a steady line from their jump point to the planet, then around to meet with the ship. As they saw it come into view, she directed them to align themselves to land inside the shuttle bay. One by one, they glided along the marked landing strip and settled neatly into position.

"Ghan'aju, this is Specter Prime. We're all set on this side, Captain. We'll just wait until we have word on our arrival."

"Understood, stand by..."

The Captain and his bridge crew prepared the ship for its first return home since being captured around Morndindor. They break orbit and move away to find a comfortable jump point.

"Set our destination for the Azgarén outer band."

"Destination set and ready, Sir," the helmsman replies.

"Engage."

The young officer powers up the jump drive, calling out the numbers as the engines come to life.

Ayene and her team had returned to their bodies by this time, not wanting to get lost from their anchors. They joined the Captain on the bridge to oversee the rest of it. A few moments later, the ship passes through the dimensional rift. The scenery, in this case, was more elaborate, as they were passing between two different universes, ultimately to arrive among the outer band of planetary rings in the Azgarén star system.

"Helm, power down to station-keeping," he orders. "Specter Prime, we have arrived at our destination. You are cleared to launch."

"Understood," Marelle responds. "Specter Flight, launch and go dark as soon as you're clear."

She leads her group out of the flight deck. Each craft then activates its cloak and takes up a standard formation again, and Marelle leads them away at distance from the mother ship. She watches her tactical screen carefully, not only to monitor her distance from the Ghan'aju, but also looking for anything else out there.

In the Saakerav Military Space Dock, in orbit around Azgarén, a signal alert flashes on a local security scan monitor.

"Sir, we have a blip on the screen," calls the operator.

"What is it?"

"Scanners have detected a jump signature in the outer band, Sector Sixteen."

"Do we have a beacon signal on it?"

"Negative."

"Comms, are we receiving any activity?"

"No Sir," another officer replies. "The only traffic I'm hearing is local security chatter."

"There is something wrong here. Check the scanners again. Maybe it was a glitch. Is there an actual body out there?"

The operator runs another scan, this time a narrow-beam high-resolution scan to pinpoint the target of the previous disturbance.

"Sir, I'm detecting an object. It appears to be stationary."

"Stationary? Are we expecting a return from any of our patrols? Maybe one of them experienced trouble and is disabled."

"I'm not aware of anything," the comms officer admits. "Nothing came through on the distress channel."

"I wonder if this could be that Ytani character."

"If it's him, I think the blip would be in motion."

"Yes, you're probably right. Maybe we have an emergency condition. Send a security patrol out there to check on it, but have them make a cautious approach. If they see anything, I want to know immediately."

"Yes Sir."

The station sends out a message to the nearest available patrol ship, which was a frigate passing through an adjacent sector. The frigate diverts from its route and makes its way towards the mysterious visitor.

Marelle studied her tactical scanner. She could see the approach of the new ship. Her com-link was open, to listen in on the local channels, though her mic was off so she would not reveal herself.

"Specter Prime to base," she announces through her shard-com link. "I have an inbound blip. The computer identifies it as a frigate class vessel."

"Acknowledged, Specter Prime. Stand by until the designated moment of engagement."

She continued to watch as the frigate made a slow approach.

"Saakerav base, this is Sector Patrol Four," calls the ship to the space dock. "We have an object on the screen. It appears to be a ship. We are moving to investigate."

"Sector Patrol Four, are there any other targets in your local area?"

"Negative, the screens are clear, only this one vessel. It appears stationary with minimal power readings."

"Life signs?"

"Also minimal… Stand by, we'll see if we can identify it."

Marelle studied the screen, pausing occasionally to glance out the window where she could just barely see a dot in the distance where the glow from the ship reflected in the starlight and the internal lighting shined through the windows.

"That's it, come a little closer," she grins. "After all, it's your own ship, what do you have to fear from it?" she snickers.

"Saakerav base, we're making a close approach. All seems quiet. We have it onscreen now. Sir! It appears to be the Ghan'aju!"

"Sector Patrol Four, confirm. Did you say it was the Ghan'aju?"

"Affirmative, we can see it on the screen. The upper hull shows the ship name and naval registry code. What are your instructions?"

"Sector Patrol, what is the condition of the ship? Does it appear damaged?"

"Negative, scans are showing no damage."

"Make another full scan of the area. The Ghan'aju is believed to have been pirated. It is irrational that it would simply appear like this. Not unless maybe some part of the crew escaped. In any case, we have orders to try to capture it."

"Understood."

"That's our cue, boys," Marelle notes. "Specter Flight, we're going in. Use EMP only. Confirm."

"Specter One Leader, setting for EMP to disable, confirmed."

Marelle's team now comes to life, powering up their transport spheres and accelerating to attack speed.

"Lock on target. We'll make a series of strafing runs to knock it dead, then move off to mark a jump point and exit."

The sector patrol ship was making another full scanner sweep of the area when the tactical officer noticed something on his screen, but it didn't register as a proper blip.

"Captain, I have something…I think," calls the officer.

"What do you mean, you think? Either you have it, or you don't."

"Yes Sir. Scanners are detecting something approaching on an intercept vector from our starboard flank."

"Dammit. It's a trap," the Captain snarls. "Saakerav base, we are detecting inbounds, closing fast."

"Sector Patrol Four, can you specify. What do you have?"

"Sir, I can't lock onto it," the tactical officer complains. "All I'm seeing is a spatial inversion field with no body underneath."

"What? What are you talking about?"

"I have six spatial bubbles, but no ships."

"They must be using some form of stealth technology. What size bubbles?"

"Sir, this doesn't make sense," he pauses to redirect the main viewing screen to his target. "The bubbles are small. I'm estimating a small corvette size."

"A corvette? That's impossible! That sort of technology can't fit into a vessel that size!"

"Sector Patrol Four," sounds the base on the com-link. "Can you identify the inbound vessels?"

"Negative, they're using some sort of cloak. We can't lock onto them. They don't even register on our scans."

On the screen, the Captain and his officers squint at the tiny dots making their approach.

"Saakerav base, we have them on visual. This is unbelievable! Our scans show they're using spatial inversion drives, but they're tiny, maybe between a heavy fighter and small corvette category."

"Captain, you must engage and destroy. Try to recapture the Ghan'aju and bring it in."

"Acknowledged, but our targeting computers can't get a lock. Tactical, try firing in the direction of the bubble images."

"Yes Sir, but I have to aim manually, and they're moving too fast."

"All right boys," Marelle announces to her team. "Let's light 'em up."

Marelle's flight had come within firing range of the Suuden'kai frigate. She charges up her weapons through her conjuring orbs and fires her first salvo, taking aim at the ship's engine nacelles to cripple its drive system. The other members of her team followed suit, striking the rearward engineering segment, and strafing along the side.

"Saakerav base!" the Captain shouts. "We are under attack. Our shields are blown, and our engines have taken a direct hit."

"Sector Patrol Four, are you able to engage your attackers?"

"Negative, we were unable to get a target lock. They made a run along one side that knocked everything out, and they look like they're coming around for another pass. We need help out here!"

"You must make all efforts to return fire. We'll send additional forces out there to assist."

"I just hope there will be something left of us to give assistance to."

Marelle and her team made another pass, now along the port side, strafing from stem to stern, further disabling the ship's capacity to operate its weapons and scanners. Even the view screen was going dead, and now the reactor was going into failsafe.

"Saakerav base, we're going down!" the Captain shouts through the static, and then the link goes dead.

"This is Specter Prime to Ghan'aju," Marelle issues. "The target is down. You must now depart. We'll mark our location and return to base."

"Acknowledged, Specter Prime, see you back home."

The Captain issues his orders to his bridge crew and they bring the ship back up to full operation, quickly charging the jump drive and leaving the area.

Marelle and her team divert away from the immediate area at high speed to find a clear space. She brings the ship to a stop and engages her arcanic marking procedure. The energies light up as the ship records its current location, reflecting her new index on her nav screen. She then types in an identifying codename for it and gathers up her team once more in a tight formation to jump away.

✦✦✦✦✦

"Commander!" Captain Ta'yeen issues urgently. "We have a problem. Someone has entered our local space and attacked one of our patrol ships."

Commander Geilv and the Captain were both aware of Ayene's attack plan, but the rest of them were not, so they had to act it out as if it were real.

"Do we know who?" he asks.

"No idea. Saakerav station reported the appearance of a lone jump signature in Sector Sixteen. They sent a patrol ship to investigate. It was the Ghan'aju. They reported it to be operating at minimal energy and life signs. Then, as the patrol ship was reporting in, a group of cloaked ships apparently attacked out of nowhere."

"Cloaked? That sounds bad already."

"Yes Sir. The reports said they were small, something like a small corvette class combat craft. But Sir, they were said to be using some kind of spatial inversion drive!"

"A what?" he shouts. "Just a moment, Captain, cloaking devices AND inversion drives in a corvette class vessel? Inversion drives require at least a frigate class or better. As for the cloaks…"

"I know, this doesn't look good for us. Saakerav said this could be Ytani making good on his threat."

"If it is, they have some rather advanced technology on their side."

"Yes Sir. The report said they were unable to lock on their target. All they could see was the bubble. As best we can understand, they made only two passes, and the patrol ship was completely disabled in the process…everything, right down to emergency power and life support."

"Incredible…just two passes? What kind of weapon can make this sort of work in just two passes?"

"I don't know. Saakerav says they sent additional vessels into the area to assist and track the attackers, but they were gone by this time, as was the Ghan'aju."

"This tells me they were using the Ghan'aju as a carrier, if we're speaking of such small vessels. Maybe this is a weakness we can exploit next time."

"Maybe. Anyway, the scout ship was drifting, but didn't show any physical damage, so they landed a boarding party and found it was without power. Commander, I'm going to assume we're speaking of some kind of energy disruption weapon here, what do you think?"

"It sounds reasonable, but strange. This would represent only a disabling weapon, so are we saying they went easy on us this time? Or is this their best?"

"If they're going easy, I don't want to see them going hard," he chuckles uneasily. "They report there were no serious injuries, only a few minor burns on those who were standing too close to a panel as it blew out, and fortunately, the reactor went into scram mode."

"Well, this is one good thing. But now, how many ships are we speaking of here?"

"According to a quick debriefing of the bridge crew, they saw six bubbles circling around."

"Six? Only six? Ha!" he feigns bravado. "Surely, Captain, we can take out six little ships. If that Ytani should dare come back here, we need to be better prepared."

"What do you recommend, Sir?"

"I would say a midrange cruiser and a pair of frigates. I doubt a measly six tiny ships could hold up against that."

"Yes Sir. We'll make sure they don't report back home."

"And next time, be sure you catch that science vessel. If they're using it as a carrier, we need to take it away from them!"

"Absolutely, Sir!"

✦✦✦

"So, it was a quick hit-and-run, was it?" the Marshal muses. "How typical… But I will agree we need to take away that ship if they're using it as a carrier. If they're only hitting us with small combat vessels, we cannot allow them such convenience to deliver them into our space. At the very least, if you see the Ghan'aju again, tag it with your beacon pods. Perhaps we can track it to their hideout. At best, try to capture it. At worst, well, we may need to destroy it. But while this can deny them to use it again to deliver their impetuous little attack waves, it also closes a door on us to find that insolent nit."

"Understood, Marshal," Geilv affirms. "I'm giving orders that the next time we see a blip, we'll send out a much sturdier combat force. Saakerav base reported they believe the incursion only involved six of these small ships. But the problem is they were using cloaks and inversion drives. Marshal, you know as well as I those technologies require a much greater volume to install and operate, and yet these were reported to be perhaps the size of heavy fighters or small corvettes. This would represent a form of technology we might not be familiar with."

"Granted, Commander, so perhaps I should offer a small piece of my wisdom on this occasion. Ytani apparently found these people in that other universe, and we already covered the topic once of the dynamistic flows. For a society that may be native to that environment, or simply to spend enough time in it, they can learn ways of using these flows, and even to create a form of technology out of it. The methods used here do not follow in the same footsteps as your classic laws of physics, so what you might be familiar with from your earlier studies would no longer apply, at least not fully. Here, it becomes possible to create some rather elaborate technologies, but using methods you might literally describe to be magical. How is that for a piece of my wisdom, Commander? Would this make up for my long lapse?"

"Indeed, it would, Marshal, and I thank you greatly for it. This actually sounds a bit like that statement you made once about the Council's deliberations."

"Yes, it would," he sighs despondently. "Perhaps I should have given this to you much earlier, but I was once again concerned about my Master. This could possibly push you over that limit, and I was trying to play it safe. But just imagine, Commander, what miracles you might discover if you were to apply yourselves in this area. Your society..." he hesitates a long moment, "...holds a lot of potential."

And with this statement, he ends the link.

Geilv studies the vid-com after the conversation closes, and as he pondered the Marshal's words, he felt a strange sensation come over him, as if he were coming to a curious realization.

"Did you actually complement us?" he mumbles distantly.

"Ghantil, here is the latest report on our production line," Azina announces.

"Let me see that...hmm. This will take a lot of work, Azina, to produce enough of this drug to cover the full population of the world."

"Yeah, I know. We're placing the greater part of our production into packaging it up for general delivery, and we're seeing a lot of people coming in and ordering it. They say those raid drills are causing people to worry about that alien coding versus Latena's statement associating it with some sort of self-destruct device. Even that other one, about being a life support machine, is causing a lot of revulsion over being used like this. But they're starting to panic a little, the more we run those drills."

"At least it covers the logistics issue."

"It does, but I'm also hearing a few people wondering what relation this has to Ytani, if those sirens are actually relating to him."

"Yes, this might confuse people, as it may seem unrelated. But our story has to be the repeated reference to this Abnormal Energy, then to associate between him and Latena out there for that other universe, and whatever strange environment they might have locally, and if this becomes a weapon of some sort, as it might have uses beyond simple life support."

"Yeah, but try to explain that to a bunch of people who don't believe in anything supernatural," she giggles.

"I know. And next is we need to set aside something for the military. At the very least, I want to be sure they survive this episode so they can get to work assisting the rest, along with the medical teams."

"Right. I have packages going out to numerous bases around the world, along with instructions on when and how to use it. We also have every medical lab and clinic stockpiling pharmaceuticals for a worldwide disaster, in case we have a lot of people who don't get a chance for the inhibitor drug before our time runs out. This is starting to worry me, Ghantil. We're looking at a potential catastrophe here."

"Yes, and it's at least partially our own fault. Our Council took the advice of a creature with ulterior motives rather than the wisdom of one of our own. Although, if we say the Marshal was controlling the show from behind the scenes, who knows how much of it we could've actually avoided."

"It sounds like we were simply driven, like Latena said about the Charter preamble…to 'drive' us. That's all we ever were to him."

◆

Kaliya was visiting the Bahlaie Center as part of a process to export a supply delivery to Central Command. They had in mind to use Marelle and the large transport under the guise of the ACI making the delivery, but they couldn't use the existing assault jump point for her arrival, as it would stand out as too coincidental.

"All right, Kaliya," Chief Tech Lapäli begins. "This is only a prototype, but it's based on the designs we used on that initial drone we had once to test the jump drive technology. This one is simply an index marker, and in this case attached to a large arcanic power cell. You orient the device and push this button," she points at the unit. "Then it goes through an automated marking process, just like what we used on that drone. From there, the data object should be compatible with our ship nav systems."

"Tanjhira, between you and the Professor, we're creating some fantastic new technologies that I'm sure will be useful in a wide variety of applications. But on the other side of it, you just put people like me out of business!" she laughs.

"Well, it's still unofficial," she chuckles. "But yes, I suppose we are. Just think, Kaliya. Drop one of these in any location, and with or without the flows, you can mark an index for a later return. The whole universe just opened up to us."

"More than that, I'm sure! But you still need to be there to use the unit. By the way, how durable is this thing for application in space? That's where I'll be, you know."

"Yes, do you recall our usual protocols for marking a jump arrival point relative to a star system?"

"Yes."

"Good. Now, this unit was designed to withstand the vacuum of space, so we're advising you to find your way to Azgarén, and either fold your way to a convenient marking location first, then return back here to retrieve the unit, or if you have the opportunity, maybe you can find a secluded spot where you can import the device first, and then fly it up to a nice location."

"If I try flying it up, I need to be away from anything that could observe me, so I don't show up on the scanners. They might still be able to see the unit, even if they can't see me."

"Azgarén has a local moon. Can you try for that?"

"Ah! There you go. All right, give me a few moments to arrange myself."

Kaliya was already projected, so she flashes out of sight on a quick trip to Azgarén.

On her arrival, she begins searching the sky for their local moon, which was a smaller example in their case. It was daytime, so trying to see it in the bright daylight was difficult, especially for the pollution. She decides to make like a bird and fly to a high altitude, above the smog for a better view.

As she ascends above the landscape below, she passes through the clouds, and then pushes even higher into the stratosphere for a better vantage point to see around the curve of the planet. But as she looks back down at the planet below, she can begin to see the local continents and oceans assembled as a planetary body. She gazes at it for a pensive moment.

"Our home..." she muses silently in her thoughts. "As dirty as it is, but still..."

She turns to search again for the moon, and spies it just above the horizon, so she attempts to fold her image across the vast distance towards the lunar surface.

"I'll bet no one ever did THIS before," she thinks to herself. "The first one to set a projected hoof on the moon...and no one even knows about it."

She arrives on the surface and pauses to study the local landforms so she can memorize her location.

"Walking on the moon, no space suits necessary. It's a whole new concept in space exploration. I could probably travel to any moon or planet I can set my sights on, habitable or not, and explore at my leisure."

When she was satisfied, she folded herself back to Tae'Eladar.

"All right, I'm on the moon over there," she states.

"Wow, Kaliya," the Chief Tech grins. "You're boldly going where no projection has ever gone before!"

They share a hearty laugh as Kaliya picks up the new marking unit. She again flashes out of sight with her aim returning back to the lunar surface. As she arrives, she now places her mind on a suitable marking location, and furthermore how to carry this thing up to it.

"Flying is no longer an option," she thinks privately. "Not out here in space. So, it's down to drawing my perception across the emptiness and trying to judge my general location relative to the planet and the moon. Their alignment with each other will reflect on the solar orbital plane as a whole."

She holds onto the device tightly and imagines her image lifting off the surface, then to soar through the blackness of space at a tangent to Azgarén, trying to judge the alignment of the moon's orbit as a relative perspective for the solar system in general.

She pushes her projected image at high speed to distance herself from both the planet and the moon, and also to lift up above the orbital plane to find an appropriate jump point. Soon, both objects become small spheres in her view, and as she arrives at what she hopes to be a satisfactory location, she gazes back down at them.

"You know, if I wasn't projected right now, I'd be feeling a little vulnerable out here."

She tries to steady herself as she releases the marking device from her grip, thereby allowing it to re-phase with the native surroundings. She gives it a moment, and then pushes the activation button.

The unit appears to spend a brief moment charging up and is quickly consumed in a bright flash of light spiraling around it, then to reabsorb it and displaying a series of flashing lights and a data display showing a result.

"And here we have a mark. Our first official arrival mark for our new arcanic jump-drive technology…that isn't otherwise part of our game play out here."

She takes the unit into her arms again and now flashes out of sight to return home.

◆◆◆◆◆

The rest of the month followed without any new incidents. It was coming close to the end when Ayene made another visit to Geilv's office.

"Commander?"

"Yes, Lieutenant, come in. Are we getting ready for another test of yours versus ours?" he smiles delicately.

"Not quite yet, Ytani needs to play his next demand. He's not a happy guy, you know."

"I'm sure of it. A young guy like him has a lot of hormones to satisfy. Then what do we have today?"

"I have a special delivery for you, but I need to be present to ensure we don't have anyone getting anxious out there."

"A delivery…out there? Are we speaking of an arrival of some kind?"

"Yes Sir, we have a transport ship that will be carrying a package for us. It will arrive in near vicinity and make its way down here for the delivery."

"Interesting, so we're speaking of something like a space-capable ship, like a cruiser, but with landing capability? This I'd like to see. Most of ours are space-only, and then we use smaller shuttles for transfer to the ground."

"Well then, Commander, maybe we can finally teach an old bull a new trick!" she smiles.

They get up and proceed out of the office to the command booth. On their arrival, the Captain and the other resident officers give their salutes as Geilv prepares his instructions.

"Captain, it would seem the ACI has a special delivery to offer us in our upcoming challenges to our local issues. Send word to the Saakerav base to expect an arrival."

"Yes Sir."

They wait as the Captain relays the order to the space dock in orbit. When they receive confirmation, he turns back to Geilv.

"We're ready, Sir."

Ayene now pulls out her trans-com and makes a call.

"ACI, Agent Kaetaal speaking."

"Kita, it's Ayene. Pass the word through our special channel to have our delivery sent forward."

"Yes Ma'am."

They end the link and wait.

Marelle's crew was already assembled on the large carry-all ship at the Bahlaie flight center.

"Captain Carronel," a voice issues on the com-link. "This is control, we have just received word that the mission is Go. You are clear to depart."

"Thank you, Control. Helm, bring us up," she orders. "Take us out to our jump point. Nav, set for Therinë and the city of Rolsklinde."

The ship darts off through the sky and into space, to a low orbital position where they make their jump. On arrival to Therinë, they make a standard approach down through the atmosphere on a glide path towards Rolsklinde, where they arrive near the cargo delivery pad.

"Bubble control, target our load. Helm, easy does it."

By this time, she felt much more confident, and the crew was performing expertly in their tasks. The large bundle was enough to fill a couple of heavy cargo transports, and secured to a broad steel pallet frame, but it was still dwarfed by the size of this ship. The suspension field operator acquired and lifted it into place, then closed up the containment claws.

"Good. Helm, bring us up to our jump point. Nav, set our jump index to Azgarén local space."

"Yes Captain! Setting our jump index, all systems are ready."

They travel once again outside the local planetary sphere and prepare for their jump.

"Charging, ten percent...twenty...thirty..."

They wait for the energy to build up. Marelle felt a bit nervous on this occasion. Even though they were working under the guise of a friendly force, this carried a different feel for the visitation.

"Sixty...seventy...eighty..." the helmsman continues. "Reaching critical energy dump… Ninety… Dumping now… We have an arcanic rift, the envelope is folding."

They glide along the slipstream through a seemingly endless tunnel. The sights outside had become somewhat familiar by now, as seen through the windows and on the main viewer. It was a scene of light and energy, of impossible shapes and wispy plasma streams. The ship coasted on autopilot, tracing the meandering contours of the pipeline until they could see the filmy shell of a new dimensional membrane approaching ahead.

They plummeted into it, soon to be surrounded by streaks and ghostlike trails of stars and galaxies, oriented at a single dot which grew larger as they closed in. Then, with a flash, they made their exit back into real space.

In the Saakerav base, an alert signal comes in.

"Sir, we have a jump signature," announces the tactical officer. "Local space, downspin and above…"

"Let's make a quick scan of it, just in case."

"Yes Sir."

The officer targets the ship on his scanners for a careful analysis.

"This is a strange one," he muses.

"What do we have out there?"

"Sir, I don't know how to answer that, other than to say I've never seen a configuration like this one before. It carries an energy signature of a midrange cruiser, but the hull configuration is long and narrow, and it has something like a huge grappling claw underneath. And wait, I'm detecting an object in there! In all the nether-space, if I'm interpreting this correctly, this thing must be capable of lifting objects directly off the ground and carrying them as cargo."

"Amazing," he croons as he studies the screen. "Try hailing them."

The officer engages his com-station.

"This is Saakerav Station to unknown vessel. We request you identify yourself and your intentions."

Marelle was expecting this, but her mission had to carry a note of secrecy to it, so she ordered her com-station to respond.

"Saakerav Station," she answers. "We identify ourselves with the codename of Mouse-catcher. We are working in accordance with the ACI and are carrying special cargo to be delivered to Central Command."

"Acknowledged. Your vessel configuration is very strange. Are you saying this delivery goes directly to Central, or can you offload it here?"

"It is intended to go straight down to the ground. We will offload onsite, and then depart the area."

"Understood, stand by as we relay this detail."

Marelle and her crew held their position for several moments while the station relayed the instructions to Central Command on the ground. In another moment, they come back on the air.

"Mouse-catcher, we have received authority to pass you through."

"Thank you, Saakerav."

They close the link, and she gives the order to descend to the ground. They pass through the hazy layers over a broad ocean, approaching the coastline and a range of mountains.

"That would be our new base down there," she observes as they cross over the top of the range.

They keep low and move slowly around to the south, crossing the valley, and then a river, and swinging around the low end of the hills separating them from the city as they came into view of the military base.

Along the way, they crossed over a local highway passing through the area. The huge vessel, certainly in comparison to anything that might otherwise be seen travelling through the area, caught the attention of the drivers on the ground, several of which pulled out their trans-coms to take photos of it.

From inside the control booth, Ayene and Geilv waited, along with the other staff members. They watched the local monitors as their scanners tracked the arrival of the vessel.

"They're making a very cautious approach, Commander," the Captain suggests. "Slow and low to the ground..."

"I suppose they need to if they're trying to avoid any unwanted attention by the Marshal. But what is that thing?"

"So far," Ayene notes. "It's a one-of-a-kind ship, but it's proving itself to be very useful. Who knows, maybe we'll make more of them one day."

They could see it much more clearly now as it emerged from behind the hills and proceeded across the outer base perimeter.

"That's bigger than any cargo transport I ever saw!" the Captain shouts. "And what is that hanging down from it? It looks like a giant claw."

Marelle orders her ship to swing around gently and precisely to the far side of the base. She was opposite where the Marshal's office building was located, coming in just out of view from any of his windows and descending to the ground within reach of the bubble control release.

"Look at that thing!" the Captain croons. "It's the size of a midrange cruiser, at least. How does something like that land? Or does it?"

"That claw splays out," Ayene submits, "and acts as an assist to lower it to the ground."

"Unbelievable! Where did you find something like that?"

"We had a little help to build it, but we have some truly fascinating minds working on our side."

"No doubt!"

The ship had finally maneuvered into a satisfactory position for its delivery.

"Bubble control," Marelle directs. "Lower it down gently."

The Commander and his staff watched as the huge claw-like projections began to open up. Inside they could see the form of a large bundle being gently lowered to the ground.

"In all the nether-space," the Captain marvels. "Those things work like grapplers, and what's that inside? It looks big enough to fill a warehouse, and it's held in some sort of suspensor field! Commander, that thing could pick up a small building and carry it away."

"Amazing, Captain," he nods. "And it doesn't even need to land. Just leave the cargo outside and it can pick it up, carry it away, and deliver it, then go back for more. I wonder if we could copy this design. It could save a lot of work for our people moving things in hover-trucks."

"Assuming we actually had something that big to move over distance."

"Maybe one day, Captain," he muses thoughtfully. "Just imagine building a pre-fab outpost, then to pick it up and just drop it in place somewhere."

"That would save a lot of work on the job site. Our people could move in the first day."

"And best of all, we could remove it back home or elsewhere as needed."

Marelle's crew had finished, and they were closing up the claws. They could see outside the windows a number of ground personnel moving in to inspect the delivery.

"Comms; open the channel again," she issues.

"Ready Captain…"

"This is Mouse-catcher to Central Command."

"This is Central, High Commander Geilv here."

"Ah, High Commander, it's a pleasure to speak to you. How do you like this little lady?"

"That's a fine piece of hardware you have there. Perhaps one day you could show us how it works."

"I would look forward to that, but be advised, some of the technology is proprietary. Now, a few words before we go. You should store these in your armory for now, and use them when the time comes, rather than your own equipment."

"What is it?"

"I'll leave that as a little surprise. I see people down there now trying to figure it out. You will likely need a bit of time to play with it, but do be careful. We don't want any injuries."

"I'll take it under advisement."

"Excellent. Good day to you, Commander."

They close the link and Marelle orders her crew to pull back the way they came. They circle back around the hills and angle up, there to dash away quickly back into space and jump home again.

The Commander and his staff peered out the window at the delivery, which was being examined and unpacked by the ground workers. He then glares at Ayene, who was simply smiling.

"Lieutenant, I don't know who it is you're working with out there, but they must be some fascinating people."

"More than you know, Commander. When all this is over, maybe we can all sit down for a nice little chat."

She waves and leaves the room, while Geilv and the others ponder the implications.

"Captain, I would like to know what we have down there. See if you can bring up some samples to my office."

"Yes Sir."

Geilv then returns to his office and sits down, again trying to involve himself in his work to keep his mind occupied for all the confusing circumstances and statements circling around lately. About an hour passes and there is an announcement at the door.

"Enter."

The Captain comes in carrying two very unusual objects, both of which looked like they belonged in an ancient history museum.

"Commander, this is what was in those crates, or at least part of it. Am I going insane here, or is this something out of a medieval history lecture?"

The Commander gets up from his chair and steps around for a better look. He takes one of the items and examines it.

"In all the nether-space, a sword and a shield? You say only part of it? What else was there?"

"When the call came in, I went out there to see it for myself. I had a few of our workers pull together a full set so we could see it in its entirety. I don't know what I'm looking at or why, but we have these numbering in what could be the thousands, along with what one of them called a suit of medieval plate armor. It's incredible! They look like they were fashioned out of thin steel sheets, big enough to cover the critical areas, and with a chain mesh for the joints. We have chest pieces, arms and legs, helmets, gloves… It looks like we have both male and female choices here, so we'll need to select who gets it. But Sir, what are we expected to do with this?"

Geilv examines the sword closely, gently running his finger along one edge.

"This isn't sharp. Is it supposed to be? Or wait, I think I know. Of course! This is the sort of thing you would use in a stage play. The ACI is setting us up for a physical battle scene, another play for the Marshal…and Sargeras. She once said they needed him out and away from the city, and we're looking at that construction project out there in the valley. Now, let's think. I recall that one agent, and she said these beings were once found conducting something the others didn't like. It must be something like a game, a kind of…yes! A gladiatorial sport! And we're the gladiators."

"But Sir, that means we're supposed to go up against someone, and we have no idea how to fight using this."

"Well, then it's time for a little refresher course."

◆◆◆

Haran and his friends, those who were still attending classes, such as Petrith, Sulíma, and Túfula, were meeting in the guild courtyard again. The end of the school year was coming in just two more months, and Haran was both excited as well as tense to make the grade by year's end. He had been studying hard, and putting in extra time on practice, because he knew he would have a special role coming soon, and he needed to get it right the first time.

As he and the Daanen'kai trio enjoyed their chat on matters of academics and other amusing topics, Haran noticed an odd apparition developing in the open space of the courtyard near the front.

A two-dimensional vertical plane was forming, rippling outward in concentric circles. The sight was familiar to him, as he had seen it once before when the dabus came to visit from Sigil. He directed the others to observe.

"Uh oh," Sulíma moans. "Another one?"

"I shouldn't think they would have the need," Haran notes. "We solved that one."

From within the image, a shape emerges, stepping through the nearly transparent window as if coming out of an upright pool of water. It was female and dressed in a priestly robe of dark blue. From under her hood, they could see her eyes glowing brightly.

"Cardinal Aelwyn!" they shout together.

The youthful lady stepped forward as the rippling planar door closed behind her. She looked around briefly at the surroundings, and then strolled over to meet the group.

"Cardinal," Haran announces. "We missed you. Are you finished with your studies?"

"I am, Haran," she replies serenely. "And I am prepared for my duty. I took special counsel with my Father to aid me in my purpose. He instructed me in the Ways, even to gift me with greater strength to see it through successfully."

"It must be nice to be the daughter of a god," Petrith offers.

"It certainly has its benefits, but at the same time it is not easy for me, as I sometimes find it difficult to associate with mortals. But I must also admit my time here has been rather interesting, and my interactions certainly more enlightening than my experiences in Sigil."

"So, does this mean you might actually stay on with us?" Túfula wonders.

"If I do, I must also consider my beau, who still makes his home in Bitopia. He is a very jovial fellow, with a rather spirited persona. I have conversed with him on several occasions, and his interest is certainly peaking. I hope to convince him to join with us here as well."

"Is he another Celestial?"

"He is Aasimar, like me. He is also the child of Oghma, so you should get along very nicely with him. His name is Aristan. But do be aware, as he can be very flashy at times," she grins as she reflects on her relationship. "Of all the people I know, he is the one who so often made me feel so at ease with my own anxiety. Other than Thaelyn, of course."

As she recalls her memories, she also experiences an inward expression of delight, which soon leaks away, leaving the others in the near area to feel a similar level of warmth wash over them from her strong empathic emission.

"And then we have Nemelle. She is also, and perhaps finally, finding enough motivation to make a visit to investigate a few of her own interests."

"What sort of interests does she have?" Sulíma asks.

"Her mother was a former member of the Drow society here on Tae'Eladar. She has long held a desire to liberate them from their current predicament. They are, in a manner of speaking, cursed into exile from their parent society, the Tel'Quessir, and their native pantheon of deities, the Seldarine. She wishes to correct this and bring them back into the light. And with Tae'Eladar as it is, this would represent a natural conclusion to finally, and completely, unite everyone."

"Yes, it would."

"And with the recent discovery of the Night Elves on Therinë, she is eager to seek ways in which to use this opportunity. She is currently making a few studies and collecting some detail on how she might proceed, but no doubt this will require a substantial effort."

"Yes, I'm sure it would," Haran nods. "Relissa might be able to help. And I recall Adalon mentioning something about this once."

"Indeed, and all the more reason to investigate this matter. Speaking of which, has anything exceptional occurred in my absence?" she asks.

"We get occasional notes from Kaliya and the others. At last word, Commander Geilv placed the Marshal under house arrest after a confrontation over all our sensational news releases."

"What?" she gasps and sends out a pulse of emotional shock at the group.

"Yeah," Sulíma flinches. "That's Aelwyn, all right!" she smirks.

"How do you place such a creature as Darumon under house arrest in any way?"

Haran chuckles briefly as he responds.

"By turning your glorious military, and all their bristling guns, at his master's head."

"Powers behold! And it worked?"

"Apparently so," Petrith offers. "And not only that, but Darumon seems pretty broken up about it. His behavior has changed rather dramatically since then. Some of us are wondering what it all means."

"I would never have guessed something like this. Very well, I should probably present myself to Thaelyn, so he will know I have returned. Perhaps I can review some of your recordings from this time period, as well."

She turns around to another open spot and brings her mind into clarity, focusing her thoughts on the WIC building, specifically the strategy room, and begins a subliminal chant to fold the reality of space. The others watch as she speaks in her traditional detached mannerism, as if giving instruction to restructure the laws of physics to serve her needs.

"Space will flex and fold, pinching itself, narrowing the gap between these two points to create passage…"

Her voice reverberated and her eyes again glowed brightly as a new planar door opens, precisely in accordance with her will.

"Gracious," Haran mutters. "She makes it seem so easy."

The Daanen-Aryku friends just shake their heads as she steps through and vanishes from the local scene.

"And there you have the riddle of metaphysics," Túfula concedes.

Inside the WIC building, Kaliya was in a quick briefing before her next show as Ytani, when the group took notice of a disturbance within the room. A planar door opened up, drawing the attention of the meeting as a figure began to emerge.

"Grace of the cu'Nar," Kaliya mumbles. "That looks almost like what Darumon did that day on Morndindor."

"Perhaps so," Thaelyn accedes as he steps around the table. "But thankfully, this is not him."

Aelwyn had now emerged fully into view and her eyes were just beginning to return to normal. Thaelyn walks up to her and gently takes her by the shoulders, then leans his forehead into hers as a sign of welcome greeting.

"Aelwyn, it is good to see you return, and with fair timing. We are close to the end of the year, and graduation will soon be upon us. I would not wish to delay much longer after that."

"Indeed, and as such, I am yours from this moment. As unbelievable as it may sound, from what I once mentioned of the concept, here I am ready to serve at your side. To think of it, me, a Cardinal Sensate from Sigil, joining an army of mortals on a Prime world to combat a Primordial, of all things," she smiles.

As Aelwyn envisions the thought, a wave of paradoxical incredulity strikes the other people in the room, causing each of them to reel back and launch into uncontrollable giggling.

"Cardinal," Kaliya sputters through her laughter. "I thought you always tried so hard to hold this back."

"I did, and in Sigil I was very introverted. But from my experiences here, and with all of your support, and further with some new counseling by my Father, I hope to have finally broken that. While I will still monitor myself, I hope no longer to be as timid."

Kaliya felt another wave hit her, now a sensation of determined confidence.

"Welcome to the family, Aelwyn," she offers.

◆◆◆

"We seem to have a lack of understanding here," Ytani booms at the people of the city. "I ordered a certain tribute to be given to my Greatness, and you simply ignore it."

Kaliya was in her most recent Ytani guise, and again disrupting the affairs of Capitol Prime. She had already descended to the street level as her godly image and was giving out her latest oratory.

"Now, I'm quite sure you took notice of my grand display out there when I took on your imperious military," Ytani asserts brashly. "So, THIS time, I will expect you to pay closer attention. However, due to the long duration of my suffering without a pretty little lady to play with, and also due to your apparent lack of understanding of my GODLY needs, I'm upping the number again. Let me see, what was it last time? Oh! I remember now. But this time, I want MORE!" he thunders. "I want you to bring together twenty! Yes! Twenty! This is a good number to work with. I could start building up my own breeding stock with that number!"

He bellows out another tumultuous roar of laughter at the people down below, many of whom were now simply glaring at his audacity and growing increasingly impatient with his boisterous yowling.

"And this time, I want you to actually deliver them to me! Because if you do not..." he bends down in his throne and grins wickedly at them. "Well, I might just need to make a return visit with my...enforcers!"

He finishes with another riotous laugh as he withdraws from view.

Later in the day, Ileani goes on the air with a special report.

"Once again, the image of Ytani appeared on the streets of Capitol Prime, which seems to be proceeding like clockwork these days, and

once again he made his most recent demands on the people of the city, or perhaps the world in general. His most recent figure has increased the tribute to twenty young ladies to be given over to him.

In response to this, word on the street suggests the people are growing just as impatient with him as he apparently is with them. Many are demanding the cessation of his antics, whoever and wherever he might be, if for no other reason than to halt his outrageous behavior and crude social conduct.

In a related article, when asked about his statement concerning some sort of presentation in our local space, a spokesperson had this to say…"

A news clip with a male military official comes online.

"While it is true that we did have an incursion in our local space of an unknown force, the details of it need to be maintained in confidence due to the inherent security risk where we believe these broadcasts could possibly be intercepted by Ytani and his so-called minion servants. But our reports say a small group of combat craft entered, and then quickly evaded us. They did NOT, however, make any direct approach to our home world, which suggests our military was able to deter them effectively."

The video now returns to the studio.

"Only time will tell if Ytani will ever realize his unwelcome presence and discontinue his antics. But some citizens are concerned that his next appearance in Azgarén space might involve more than just a simple demonstration."

<hr>

"Commander, we need to be ready for his next showing," the Marshal decrees. "Make sure your forces are on full alert. Remember the plan. When the Ghan'aju appears, we'll try to capture it, but at least tag it if nothing else. Then we can track it back to his base and this should be enough to put an end to that horrible little pest."

"Yes, Marshal, our people will watch and wait. We have everything ready for his next appearance, and we've increased our sector security to respond faster to his incursions. We'll be ready for him."

"Good, and be sure to report in when you have something."

He ends the link, leaving Geilv mildly curious as to how this next encounter will appear, but also subtly dreading what sort of outcome it might have.

It was the middle of the month, and Marelle was preparing her combat flight for another run. She was still using just one flight, although by this time she had three available to her.

"This is Specter Prime, on deck."

"Specter Prime, you are clear to launch."

The team lifted off their pads and formed up. Then Marelle led them away from their base and out of the atmosphere to their jump point.

"Specter Flight, link up," she announces on the com-link.

She sends out her navigation carrier signal to link the group in synchronous control mode, forming up a tight cluster and engaging the group jump capability. The flight flashes out of view, arriving back in Azgarén space.

In orbit around the planet, the Saakerav base immediately detects the disturbance.

"Sir, we have another one!" shouts the tactical officer.

"Dammit, they're back. All right, we have orders to hit them hard this time. Send out our defense force. Tell them to make all efforts at tagging the Ghan'aju so we can track it home. As for their fighters, let's see how well they can hold out in a crossfire, and maybe this time we'll take a few of them down."

The comms officer calls up a patrol fleet involving three ships, the lead being a cruiser class with two frigate escorts. The ships launched from the space dock and began on their way to the location of the jump signature.

"Specter Flight," Marelle calls to her team. "Expect inbounds of multiple ships. We will relocate to another vector before making our assault."

She leads them off from their arrival zone in the direction of the suspected path of their prey, hoping to surprise them from another angle. When they arrive, they go silent again, shutting down their drive systems.

In the Saakerav station, the Commander monitors his screens.

"Do we have anything showing out there?"

"No Sir. The precision scan isn't showing up any bodies at all this time."

"Not even the Ghan'aju?"

"No Sir, so unless they departed already, I don't know what it was we detected."

"All right, tell the patrol to take it slow and easy. It could be another ambush attack."

The sector patrol fleet made its way hastily into the outer band, then slowing its approach as it drew near. They were watching much more carefully on this occasion, based on the previous occurrence, but the scans were clear, indicating the enemy was likely laying low for an ambush.

"Captain, I'm still not showing anything," the tactical officer submits.

"They're out there, I can feel it. Get Saakerav on the line."

The comms officer calls in to their base.

"Saakerav, this is the Sul'tav. We are in position, but the scans are clear. The Ghan'aju appears to be absent this time."

"Acknowledged, Sul'tav, be on alert. It might have simply moved off."

"Understood."

"They hit by surprise the first time," the Captain recalls. "All ships; stay on alert. On the first sighting, we coordinate together. Even if we can't track them, we'll blanket the area with fire."

Marelle listened to the com-link as she observed the fleet coming into range of her scope.

"Well now, isn't that nice," she remarks to herself. "Base, this is Specter Prime. I have inbounds, three of them. They appear as a cruiser and two frigates. They're getting smarter out there."

"Acknowledged Specter Prime, advance with caution, you are clear to engage."

"Understood. Specter Flight, on my mark, we go in and hit the cruiser from behind. We'll take out its engine's, then break and redirect to the frigates."

They wait a few moments longer as the patrol passes by overhead, still oblivious to her flight sitting there under their cloaks.

"They don't even know we're here. All right, here we go, power up and follow me in."

The team powers up and takes off, angling from behind the group and zeroing in on the cruiser.

"Sir! Inbounds!" shouts the tactical officer. "They're coming up from behind."

"Dammit…" he growls. "All ships; turn and engage."

Marelle's team came in quick on the cruiser. They charged up their weapons together and fired off a combined salvo at the hindquarters of the large vessel. The strike spread out over the full width of the ship. It began listing. The team then broke off, diving below the taskforce and splitting up to tackle the frigates, hitting the aft undersides.

"Captain, we've been hit! Main engines are offline."

"Impossible. How can they take those down so fast? What's the status of our shields?"

"Aft shields are blown. The hits were just too powerful. The scanners showed them approaching and seemingly firing as a unit."

"A neat little coordinated strike. Where are they now?"

"Captain," the comms officer interjects. "I'm getting distress calls from our escort. One ship is losing power along its starboard aft section, the other along its port side."

"How can they move so fast? These little things must have remarkable maneuverability. Tactical, can you get a lock?"

"No Sir, they're running under stealth again. All I'm seeing is a spatial inversion field."

"Well, try firing a few shots, at least get something out there!"

Marelle's team had circled under the frigates, hitting along the sides, and partially knocking out their engines. They quickly came back around for another strafing run.

The Suuden-Aryku ships were now firing out at random, hoping to catch something in their line of sight. But without a proper target lock, the shots simply scattered into space.

Her flight team made another pass along the frigates, strafing across the other side and taking down the weapons and scanners. The ships were now failing and beginning to drift.

"Sir, we're losing our escort," the comms officer urges.

"Keep laying down fire, see if you can concentrate it in the general direction of those blips. Maybe a clustering effect will actually hit something."

"Yes Sir!"

"How many do we see out there?"

"I'm picking up six bubbles, Sir," the tactical officer replies.

"Six…only six…" he shakes his head. "In all the nether-space, who built those things? Contact Saakerav with an update, these things are too swift and agile."

The team had just finished another run at the frigates and was now regrouping on Marelle's lead, coming around in a leisurely circle.

"Saakerav base, this is Sector Patrol Seven" the comms officer calls into his link. "We've lost our escort, and our engines are down. Scans show they're coming around for another pass. We have six bodies out there, but we're unable to make a target, so we're firing at random in their direction hoping to land a hit."

"Sector Patrol Seven, can you evade? If not, we'll send assistance to reinforce you."

"Saakerav," the Captain asserts. "Reinforcements would be nice, but unless you have something big with flak guns, I don't think anything else will serve us. We need heavy firepower to take these things down."

"Understood, we'll get someone out there ASAP."

Marelle listened to the chatter on her com-link, once again with her mic turned off for that channel.

"I feel sorry for these people, but we have a job to do. Let's finish it before we get more company. We'll make another couple of quick runs. Let's swing a circle, hit them on the sides, and take out those guns."

They make another strafing run, first along one side, then circling around for a pass on the other one.

"Captain," the tactical officer exclaims. "We are taking hits on our flanks. Our weapons are going down sequentially. The precision of their hits is unbelievable."

"Saakerav base!" he shouts. "They're running our flanks and shutting us down. We're losing power...going down..."

The signal cuts out with static as Marelle's team finishes up.

"All right, listen up," she issues. "I want to mark two additional jump points out here while we have a moment. Mark them as tactical jumps. I want them spaced fifty clicks to either side of our present location. Let's get to it quick, then go home."

The ships split up with two of them travelling off in opposite directions at distance, where they quickly engage their index marking procedures. Each of them begins to glow brightly with a swirling vortex of energy, and then fades as the energies coalesce. They regroup, and Marelle signals the group jump feature again, where they flash out of sight.

"Commander!" the Captain hurries into his office. "You're not going to believe this! We just lost our second battle to those same six combat ships…a cruiser and two frigates!"

"So much for our perfect ten millennia record," he chuckles ironically. "Do we have the same result?"

"Yes Sir, major system malfunctions all around. The frigates appear to be mostly fried, and the cruiser will need major replacements of the engines, weapons, scanners, comms, and a lot of supplemental components."

"No wonder that Lieutenant seemed so cocky to let us have our fun. Whatever those things are made of must be very durable as well as powerful. At this rate, we could lose our entire space navy to those things."

The Captain hands over a data-pad with a brief summary report. Geilv takes a moment to read through it.

"Spatial inversion drives, cloaks, fast and maneuverable… But wait, no Ghan'aju?"

"No Sir, and Saakerav said it ran a precision beam scan to verify, but it didn't show up. So, now I'm asking myself something."

"Do I dare ask what?"

"Not if you want to keep your horns," he smirks. "But if they can pack inversion drives in those things, do you think they can include a jump drive?"

"In all the nether-space, Captain, if they can do that… Let me think…yes, maybe the Ghan'aju was only needed one time, to deliver them into our space and these little things made their own index. Dammit! Captain, if these people come from that other universe…" he sighs and leans back in his chair. "Sit with me a moment."

The Captain takes up a seat opposite of Geilv at the desk.

"I was speaking to the Marshal recently," Geilv reflects. "It was just after that last attack. He's not going to like this one, I'll tell you that right away."

"I'm sure of it."

"But he started talking. He actually gave me a piece of his advanced wisdom; can you believe it?"

"Really! What was it?"

"It relates to that Abnormal Energy, what he calls the dynamistic flows. This also apparently relates to that famous statement he gave once. You know, about the Council's deliberation."

"Oh? Is he elaborating on it now?"

"Somewhat. He says this stuff can be applied to create a form of technology that doesn't follow our current understanding of physics. A society native to that place can learn how to use it and do things we might describe as magical. Now, this reminds me of Therinë again. He had possession of a society of locals that he somehow converted to his side…probably using coercion, like all the rest. He would sometimes refer to them as using magic in their trade. If this is an example of the application, and then to reflect on those people we encountered over there, that new arrival, they were more advanced with it, I think, and had some devices that apparently used this."

"Really! This is interesting. So, we could be looking at a completely new form of science, and some examples of the technology associated with it."

"Yes, and he said it can create some elaborate achievements, but not in the same way as we would do it. So, if these people can squeeze spatial inversion drives into combat fighters, I wouldn't be surprised to see a jump drive as well, and who knows what else after that."

"Well, if this is the case, maybe the Lieutenant holds a valid point to feel so confident. But now what? Are we going for another round?"

"I can't be sure, but if we do, it will have to involve something much bigger, and here I'm not so sure I want to lose any more ships."

"Saakerav tells us the Captain of the Sul'tav recommends something big with flak guns on it. That means a heavy cruiser. And if we involve one of those, it will also include a support flotilla."

"The flotilla probably wouldn't last long if these things are so quick to take them out. But flak guns? That would certainly do some damage to those fighters, cloaks or no cloaks. I think, before I commit to this, I might want some confirmation. Still, if they're thinking they can take down a heavy… Captain, those things typically run with as many as fifteen hundred crewmembers onboard. Knock one of those out of power and the rescue operation becomes problematic."

"I'm tempted to say the ACI should know this, especially if they have any of our military persons on hand as advisors. So, if they're expecting anything at all for a third round, it would certainly be interesting to see the result. But like you, I'm not so sure I want to see the losses."

"All right, I need to give this to the Marshal anyway, and I think I'll also call the ACI to see if they have anything to say about it. These things are going on a monthly basis, but I wonder how many more we need to endure."

✦

Thaelyn was again reclining in the lounge area of the WIC building, overlooking the plaza outside. But rather than simply enjoying the sight, his mind was deep in thought. The General and Kailen joined by his side and the three of them gazed out the picture window at the people moving through the plaza.

"What do you have on your mind this time, my Lord?" the General asks. "You seem very pensive, so I doubt it is the sale at the market across the way," he smiles gently.

"No, it is not…" he responds distantly. "Although, I might admit, that fruit they have on display out there is very tempting," he chuckles faintly. "No, I am pondering which might be the best way to draw Sargeras out of hiding with our game. Do we announce it as an open address on the streets? Do we somehow try to get Darumon to call his attention to it, which might be problematic in itself. Or do we try sending a messenger in there."

"Gracious, my Lord, each of those sounds problematic, in one way or another. If we try to challenge Darumon directly, he may not wish to accept it simply because it would ring with intrigue in his mind, especially coming from you. A public address, as if to use a crier or that siren network, may fall on deaf ears if Sargeras does not otherwise come outside for any reason, or if he may not care to participate in that society and its native events. This might leave us to the messenger idea."

"Either that, or if we try disturbing Darumon to such extreme that his temper takes over, and perhaps this might call his master to investigate. But this is not the same as a call to a game."

"No, it isn't."

"If we try using the messenger idea," Kailen offers. "The first thing on my mind is how do you approach someone like him? And then, how do you present these things. Did they have some sort of protocol? And who was it to actually arrange these games?"

"Indeed!" Thaelyn admits. "Unfortunately, this detail seems to be lost to us by now. We do not know how his kind might interact with the Child Races, if at all. If their only interest is to watch the game as a spectator sport, it may actually fall to such like Darumon to organize it, and this again leaves us to him calling the attention."

"And therefore, our original problem of getting him to cooperate," he nods.

"And if we refer back to the idea of a messenger, I suspect they would need to approach him very reverently. But here I have another issue.

Throughout this time, we have had the trouble of language standing in our way. What language, and for that matter, what form of ANY communication does one carry with a Primordial? The Estelar have their own unique form, which they use amongst themselves, and it is entirely telepathic, representing thoughts and images of concepts and memories. When interacting with their servants, meaning the Celestial Races, we have another common form which is the Celestial language. But the Primordials are a precursor race, and generally unrelated to the others, as far as I understand. Therefore, surely, they would have their own form."

"This doesn't leave us too many options. If we're reduced to trying our own approach, but have no idea how to make that approach, how are we expected to arrange this game?"

"This is a most curious one," he sighs deeply. "But at the same time, Adalon's prophecy, if we are interpreting it correctly, seems to imply we have an option available to us. And in the absence of Adalon correcting us, as I am sure she would if we were making a mistake, I am now asking myself if this is one of those cases where we will discover a clue along the way."

"Cu'Nar's pity!" Kailen moans. "She would be cutting it awfully close to the mark if we're waiting for this at the very last minute."

✦✦✦✦✦

Ayene was making yet another visit to Commander Geilv's office as a response to his most recent inquiry relating to a heavy cruiser and flak guns.

"Lieutenant," he asserts as she enters. "This is starting to wear on me, you know?"

"I understand, Commander, but at the same time, we have an ultimate plan that'll lead us to a final conclusion."

"I suppose, but this ultimate plan leads ME to an ultimate question. Why can't you just rush in there and deal with it without playing all these games on us?"

"I wish I could answer that, but I'm not the one making the plan. Most of us are running on scripts made by someone else, and she's the one directing this ultimate plan. So, all we can do is follow and see how it unfolds."

"That sounds tricky just by itself. So, not even you know what's happening until it actually happens?"

"Mostly. We're making up a lot of things along the way, but it all tends to fall under the guise of Fate. Basically, something will happen, it will happen in a certain way, and everything we do during this time is simply the path we are Fated to follow."

"That's…simply…weird…" he mumbles hesitantly. "And who is the one directing this…Fate?"

"We're not allowed to say, other than maybe to suggest she is one of those on the other side. But suffice it to say she's a very powerful, if also very elusive being. We suspect she has something personal in this, so she must want it a certain way. I recall once hearing how she is likely involved in a form of law enforcement and secret intelligence, so this might be setting up like a sting operation."

"Interesting. All right, then I suppose we're all in for a rough ride… and losing a lot of ships along the way."

"Ships can be replaced. And technically speaking, you don't need them anyway, not if there's nothing out there to fight."

"Yeah…technically. So, what's next? Do you know of the latest suggestion for our counterforce to your little incursions?"

"A heavy with flak guns, yes. This should be fun to watch. Now, Commander, those smaller ones will likely fall quickly, and I believe you already understand this. Our fighters are quick and dangerous, but remember we're using EMP, so keep your rescue ships on standby. That big one, however," she whistles emphatically.

"Yeah, how do you think you'll handle one of those? These are flak guns we're talking about here. Cloaks or no cloaks, they WILL hit, if only for the explosive shockwaves and shrapnel blanketing the area."

"Just try not to hit your own ships. That's a little self-defeating," she grins.

"Yes, well…"

"This is just between you and me, Commander. Our ships, for all they're capable of, have limited energy charges in this space. We use that special energy for many of our subsystems, and in this universe, we have to bring our own storage packs. Even though we can recharge them from a special device to create the stuff, it's a slow process. This leaves us with a small disadvantage, at least for the tech level we're using so far. If to go up against a heavy, it would be a hard fight to bring it down fully, given what we might have to throw at it initially."

"Ah, so you do have a weak point."

"But we're not dumb enough to allow ourselves to hit that threshold. We'll do what we can to thin things out, but as for that heavy, and not simply for the reason of this weak point, we have something special in mind."

"Something special," he muses. "I'm not so sure I like the sound of that."

"First of all, we want to take it out more efficiently than what a group of little fighters can accomplish. Second, like you, we don't enjoy fragging things any more than the rest. So, while you might hope to engage us with your flak guns, we are going to engage you using other means, and this leads me to my third point. That's an expensive piece of hardware, and it seems like such a waste to simply knock it out of commission."

"Yes, this much I can certainly agree on. So, what do you have in mind?"

"Commander, if I were to tell you that, it might spoil the surprise," she grins. "So, let's just say we'll keep it intact and hand it back to you later. This can serve as a cute little exercise in combat tactics."

As Ayene finishes up, she rises out of her chair and offers a friendly wave before departing the room in a flash.

Geilv simply glares into the open space left behind, and then glances at the two guards at the door, who continued their watch without flinching.

"I swear, you people are going to force me into an early retirement."

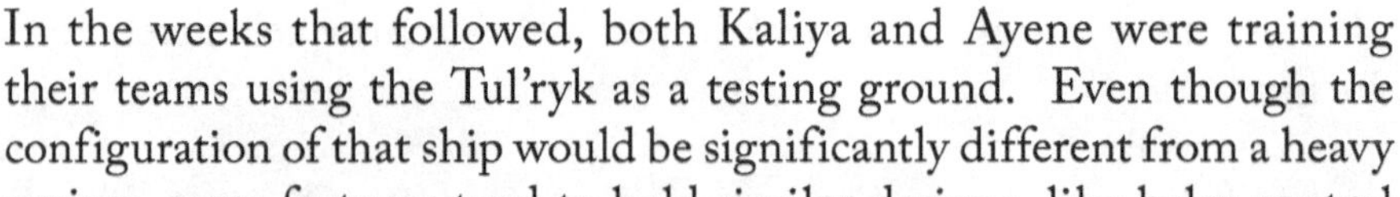

In the weeks that followed, both Kaliya and Ayene were training their teams using the Tul'ryk as a testing ground. Even though the configuration of that ship would be significantly different from a heavy cruiser, some features tend to hold similar designs, like helm control and com-stations.

Ayene was leading a platoon of projected teammates while Kaliya commanded a company of Stormhooves in full battle armor. They ran the routine multiple times, with Kaliya's people on the ground while Marelle assisted by carrying Ayene's team in a shuttle into orbit where they could spy on the Tul'ryk as their intended target. From there, Ayene led her team by folding across to the warship and infiltrating their shuttle bay. Once inside, they studied the area for a quick memory image of the location and folded back to the ground to retrieve their portal indexing devices. With these in hand, they folded back inside the shuttle hanger and formed up a long way-line, where they began marking their rune stones. When they were finished, they returned to the ground again.

On the ground, Kaliya had a line of mages waiting to receive the runes. They opened up the way-line and she led her troupe through to the ship, stacking them up on the inner wall of the shuttle hanger. Ayene, for her part, waited for confirmation of Kaliya's team to be fully assembled before proceeding to the next phase of her role, and that was to discreetly infiltrate the bridge and take up hiding until Marelle's official assault on the enemy fleet.

The Tul'ryk, in this case, had its original crew onboard and participating as the opposing team, presumably unaware at first of a hostile boarding party arriving within its shuttle bay. Once the scene was set, Marelle gave the order on her shard-com to commence.

"This is Specter Prime to all units," she begins. "The stage is set. Begin the scenario. Tul'ryk, you have hostile inbounds, go to attack mode."

"Acknowledged, Specter Prime... All hands go to simulated battle alert."

The klaxons began sounding off and the bridge crew went into their simulated attack mode. This was generally Ayene's cue to go into action. Her team folded themselves into position to cover the bridge consoles and control stations, and then reimagined their forms to a sickly green slime that seemed to be emerging out of the equipment and smothering the controls. The bridge crew quickly withdrew from their consoles in disgust and apprehension.

"Sir!" issues one officer. "We're unable to access our controls! This stuff appears to be alive and growing right out of the consoles!"

The slimy growth continued to expand, forcing the crew to back away from it.

"Everyone," the Captain exclaims. "Fall back! Don't let it come into contact with you, it could be dangerous. We'll move back to the lift and get down to auxiliary control."

As the bridge crew slowly files into the lift, Ayene's team seemed to pulse and quiver on the consoles as they secretly turned their attention to the controls just underneath their slimy bodies. Since their perceptions didn't technically need eyes to see with, they were able to study the arrangement of the controls to begin manipulating the switches and buttons, presumably to turn off all comms and gain control of the helm.

Kaliya's team waited for Ayene to gain control of the bridge. Once the crew was out, Ayene restored herself to her natural form and called for her team to follow suit. She had a shard-com with her which she had been concealing within her slimy shell. She brought it out to call in.

"This is Spook Prime to base; we have the bridge, stand by for jump simulation."

She counts a set period of time to allow for a jump sequence as she directs her people to commandeer the bridge controls. As the count reaches an appropriate amount of time, she calls in again.

"Spook Prime to Phantom Prime; jump sequence complete. You may begin your operations."

"Acknowledged," Kaliya asserts.

Now Kaliya's team goes into action. They infiltrate the ship through the hatchway from the shuttle hanger and begin systematically marching their way through the corridors of the ship. She used a combination of cloaked units to move ahead and hit some elements sight-unseen, while others isolated the crewmembers inside their rooms and hit them either with simulated weapons fire or physical attack.

The Tul'ryk was small as compared to a heavy cruiser, so the simulation didn't last long, but it was enough for a good exercise, and it left a fearful impression on the crew as they watched the expertly trained Special Forces unit taking charge of the ship. After the operation was complete, they reunited on the ground for a review.

"Captain Nazég," the Tul'ryk's Captain reflects. "You're simply scary. If this is how you're able to operate, given this magic stuff of yours, in all the nether-space, may whatever god you people worship help the rest of us."

"That's the whole point, Captain," she smiles.

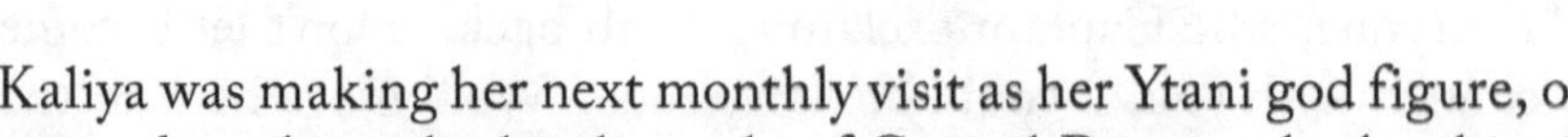

Kaliya was making her next monthly visit as her Ytani god figure, once again disturbing the local people of Capitol Prime, who by this time were not simply annoyed, but now shouting back at him.

"You people aren't being nice to me!" he roars at the protesters on the ground. "I'm supposed to be your god-king, and you don't even give me my tribute! This time I'm very, VERY upset, so I want fifty girls.

Yes, that's right, I said FIFTY! And don't you give me that look down there!" he directs at one woman who was flipping her tail at him. "I'm going to build my own harem, and then you'll see just how great and powerful I am. Oh yes!" he boasts immaturely. "Just make sure they're all packaged up nice and neat. And tell the Marshal he owes me this after losing that nice little operation at that base. I had a great little arrangement out there, my own private little party where I could call on any of those girls I wanted, and they couldn't do anything about it."

He makes one final glare around the public below before departing through his usual swirling vortex.

On the ground, the people were making a series of calls to the local security forces, once again to complain about his obnoxious presentation. Eventually, the news released their most recent report, and this eventually filtered back to Central Command.

"This is unbelievable, Commander," the Marshal groans. "That… that…" he sighs. "I had to pay closer attention to it, that's all I can say. I thought he was doing so well in that place, but clearly, I was wrong."

"Marshal, I suppose you could not have predicted his alteration of manners."

"Could not? Maybe, but I should've paid more visits to at least monitor him. I became distracted on Therinë…more of my poor judgment while indulging myself in my larger plans. Things seemed to be moving forward so nicely, I thought we might actually be successful. It was exhilarating! But in the end, here we are," he pauses in contemplation. "So, our latest plan is to send out a heavy cruiser. Good, if nothing else, we'll blanket the area with flak fire. I have serious doubts those pesky little fighters can survive that!" he chuckles. "But as always, Commander, stay on alert."

"Marshal, just for the sake of argument, what if this does not work? I do not want to lose any more ships to him, so we need to find an alternate solution to this."

"Yes, I suppose a contingency plan would be a wise course, but a contingency to losing ships only results in giving in to his demands, and I certainly wouldn't want that. Let me think about this for a while. If we're lucky, we can solve this with the next wave. We'll see where we stand after that."

"Very good, Marshal."

Chapter 12

LAYING THE FIELD

Two weeks had passed, and Marelle's team was once again preparing for their attack run in Azgarén space. But this time, she was going with her full team, which included three flights of five ships each.

Ayene had her team ready and in projected form inside the WIC building, along with Kaliya in her battle suit. The rest of her team was on the field at the Bahlaie Center, using it as a staging post, and waiting for their insertion once the rune stones were delivered.

"Kaliya, Ayene," Thaelyn begins. "This is a most curious and complicated operation, and one without precedent in our history. If you succeed, you will not only make history, but you will also be establishing a solid foundation for yourselves within it. But for now, we must focus ourselves on the duties at hand. The training you have undergone during this time is unique for any military body. Our people may train for many situations, but the precise combination of skills your Stormhooves have at their disposal will allow them to perform in ways most common military troops would require supplemental support to achieve. Yours is truly a Special Forces unit worthy of that mention."

He pauses to study each of the officers in the room before continuing.

"I would imagine, at some moment, the crew will eventually get wise to your infiltration and sound an alarm, and this will likely make things harder for you. But if you pace yourselves, and use your resources to their best advantage, I feel you will triumph well in the face of these overwhelming odds. And quite likely make it that much more difficult for the rest of us to catch up with you," he chuckles.

"Absolutely, my Lord," Kaliya affirms. "This is where the Stormhooves will set a new standard for themselves. I doubt even our own history could meet this challenge."

"Kaliya," Kailen muses. "Our history didn't involve magic, adamantium battle armor, arcanic pulse rifles, or portal runes to infiltrate star cruisers."

"Well, minor detail," she grins.

"Young lady," the General offers. "Even by OUR standards, you are setting a new standard. Good luck to you and make us proud."

Kaliya and Ayene both offer their salutes and leave the room. Ayene and her team flash back to Tae'Eladar, while Kaliya uses a custom portal rune for her transit. And as they reconvene at the research center, they make their final preparations.

"All right," Kaliya instructs. "Ayene and her troupe will hide inside Marelle's ship as bugs while she makes her way to Azgarén space. Be sure you concentrate your efforts at following her through the hyperspace conduit. This is important. Once she arrives, and our targets are in place, we'll work on marking our runes and importing our infiltration team. Then we wait. This ship will be big, so we need to be sure of our movements. Leave no crawlspace unchecked. We'll take them down and portal them away quickly, then move forward. Also, we need to be sure to capture both the bridge and engineering as primary targets."

"Meanwhile," Marelle adds. "I want Specter Squadron to take special care around that ship. Our targets are the flotilla, not the heavy. We will make long strafing runs with sharp evasive maneuvers. We will strike at their blind spots and leave the area. We have two tactical jump points we can use for an advantage. But we go active only after the infiltration team is in place. We will make use of our tactical jumps twice before Spook team goes active. I'm expecting the local chatter inside the bridge to count the numbers for us. This should give us enough time to take down a few of their flotilla ships to remove any witnesses."

The assembly breaks up with Marelle's pilots climbing into their ships and Kaliya's troopers moving off to the side where a row of mages was waiting. Ayene and her projected team changed into bugs and followed Marelle to her ship.

Marelle climbed into her pilot's seat and strapped in, then donned her helmet and ensured a tight seal. She powered up her flight controls and called out to her team.

"Specter Prime to Specter Squadron, all flights check in."

"Flight One, check."

"Flight Two, check."

"Flight Three, check."

Now she calls in to the control station.

"Base, this is Specter Prime, we are ready on deck."

"Specter Prime, we are Go for launch. You are clear to depart."

She engages her controls and lifts off the pad, followed by the rest of her team. Ayene and her people huddled in the nooks of the ship, trying to keep their focus on their immediate perspectives to maintain their positioning. They had been practicing this several times so far, and were becoming more familiar with the process, as it tended to distort their perceptions travelling through the slipstream.

"Here we go, people," Marelle submits expectantly.

She takes off from the field and leads her group at a steep incline out of the atmosphere and into space, where they make their way to the local jump point.

"Form up on my signal."

She engages her group formation carrier signal, and the mass of combat ships links up to form a tight cluster. She then begins her jump drive count.

"Once we arrive, I want everyone to preload their jump charges, so we can minimize our tactical jump delay time. We're not going to get too many of these."

They finish charging up and flash away from the local space.

In the Saakerav station, the tactical officer was monitoring his scanners. They were expecting an arrival anytime now, as the scheduling seemed to be following a predictable pattern.

"Stay sharp, people," the station Commander instructs. "I don't know why, but I can almost feel something coming."

A few moments later, a signal lights up on the tactical station.

"Sir! We have a blip in Sector Sixteen!"

"Well, what do you know," he muses. "I must be developing a knack for this. Either that, or I'm becoming paranoid. Give me a quick precision scan. Do we have any bodies out there?"

The officer orders a precision beam to scan the area.

"I'm not seeing any bodies, Sir. It appears as empty space."

"So, no Ghan'aju this time, I suppose. This just means we have those pesky little fighters again. Dammit, Central was right. They must have jump drives installed. I swear, if I could get my hands on one of those, I'd love to take a peek inside. Well, we have instructions this time to send them to the nether-realms. Send the Naal Balai out there. Let's see how well they hold up against that baby."

"Yes Sir!"

Marelle and her team had just arrived, and she released her group control feature.

"Now listen up," she announces. "Flight One will move to Tactical One. Flight Two to Tactical Two. Flight Three is with me. We're advancing forward a bit. On your arrival, everyone goes dark. We'll wait for our targets and proceed once they're within visual."

One flight moves off to the first tactical jump point while another moves in the opposite direction to the other one. As they arrive in place, they turn around and shut down their inversion fields, leaving them completely silent in space, with only their shields acting as stealth cloaks. Marelle leads the third one forward some distance and again turns to wait for her prey, shutting down her engines to become invisible.

"Ayene and company, front and center," she orders.

A swarm of bugs begins to flitter up to her forward console.

"I really don't understand why I have to travel with so many bugs in the works," she smirks. "All right, make yourselves ready."

✦✦✦✦✦

"Commander!" the Captain calls on the vid-com. "Saakerav reports another incursion. Your presence is requested in the control booth."

"Understood," he replies briskly.

Geilv wanted to be present on this occasion to oversee this operation, since he was curious, as much as anything, to see what they had in mind up there. Also, with this sort of heavy deployment, he felt he should make a personal appearance for support. But as he got up from his desk, he pondered if he should invite the Marshal for the occasion. He glanced at the two guards at his door briefly.

"What do you think, should I call him over, or is this a private occasion?"

One of the guards turned to respond.

"As far as I understand it, Sir, they're playing it like it's for real. It shouldn't matter if he's present, but it might be interesting to see his reaction."

"All right..." he considers as he calls up the Marshal on the com-link.

"Darumon here; what is it, Commander?"

"Marshal, Saakerav just reported we have a new incursion. I wanted to see if you would like to join with us as we oversee the operation."

"Oh? Yes, I would, actually. This should be good. I'll be right over."

The large cruiser and its convoy raced along through the solar system from Azgarén outward to the edge of the system, where it expected to meet with the enemy force. They were on full alert, with their scanners intensely surveying the area, but so far nothing had shown up. As they arrived, they slowed to a crawl and studied their surroundings.

"We know they like to attack by ambush," the ship's Commander issues. "And they use cloaks to deter our target locks. So, we're going to blanket the area with flak fire until we hit something. Just be mindful of our fleet."

"Yes Sir!" the tactical officer replies.

The mighty ship slows to a halt, along with its escort, as they continue their observations.

Marelle and her team watched and waited as the cruiser arrived on the scene and came to rest.

"That's a nice one," she muses quietly. "Base, this is Specter Prime. I have my target on visual. We have a heavy cruiser and a cluster of smaller ones. I'm showing two light cruisers and four frigates."

"Understood, Specter Prime, you are clear to engage. Take care out there. They're not playing for fun this time."

"Neither are we. All right, Ayene, set your sights on that big boy and fold over to it. Make your marks, import our people, and call in when ready."

Ayene and her assembly of bugs turn to face out the window at the distant objects, where the cruiser and its fleet had moved away some distance to the approximate location of Marelle's initial arrival point. They altered their forms to provide a simulation of bioluminescence, as a means of aiding them in tracking their movements out in space, then zipped along at high speed across the long distance to the ship. They circled around, searching for the shuttle bay entrance, but found it was closed at this point in time. So, they next turned to look for the nearest window to fold inside the ship and take up their military disguises. Once inside, Ayene turns to her team.

"We need to get to the shuttle bay through the lift network," Ayene states to her assembly. "I'll go in as a Lieutenant, the rest follow as small shapes creeping along the walls and ceiling. Try to keep up with me as I find a lift."

The others nod and change to tiny bugs again. They exit the room and Ayene begins determinedly strutting along the corridor as she looks for a lift. She passed several other crewmen along the way, but her stern demeanor didn't raise any questions as to who she was or where she was going. After all, who would expect an imposter onboard a ship like this? She eventually found a lift and called a car to her service. She stepped inside and waited a moment for her bug team to follow. She made a quick head count as she examined their arrival.

"Good, we're all here. Let's go."

She selects the destination on the control pad for the shuttle hanger and the lift begins to move.

On the bridge, the Commander waits pensively for something to occur outside.

"Tactical, do you see anything yet?"

"No Sir. I'm almost thinking they might be having second thoughts about it."

"Ha! So, they're tucking their tails on us? Good, this means we hold an advantage out here. Keep on those scanners. They could come out of hiding at any moment."

Inside the control booth at Central Command, Geilv and the Marshal had assembled for a review.

"And so far…" Captain Ta'yeen reports. "The Naal Balai tells us they don't see anything on their screens, which could mean the enemy is afraid of showing itself."

"How nice!" the Marshal grins. "So, we seem to have found their limit, have we? Good, but do not become lax, Captain. This delay could be nothing more than a stall tactic, waiting for us to relax our posture."

"Absolutely, Marshal."

Ayene and her team had arrived at the door to the shuttle hanger. It was a large double-wide reinforced door with small windows peeking inside. She casually glanced in both directions along the corridor, but no one was in the immediate area. She also checked for security cameras. The upper corners of the corridor had one in each direction.

"All right team," she whispers. "This door has windows. Get in there and secure our position. I saw a restroom back there. I'm going inside to change, and I'll join you in a moment."

Ayene now turns and saunters back down the corridor towards the restroom, where she ducks inside and alters her image to another small bug. She then returns outside to the hanger door and follows the rest.

The rest of her team had moved over the window by now and sighted the interior of the shuttle bay, where they folded themselves onto the floor, maintaining their diminutive images until they could be sure of their security.

There were no people in the room, so their first objective was to scout the area for more security cameras, sighting a couple in the upper corners along the rear wall. One of the team leaders signals for a couple of teammates to fly up there and cover the camera lenses to conceal their movements. It was unlikely anyone might be watching the shuttle bay security at this moment, but they had to cover themselves.

The teammates flew up and positioned themselves next to the cameras. But before they actually covered the lenses, they made a careful survey of the scenery, including walls, floors, any and all markings, any ships in view, and so on. This would represent a complex image, but they had to simulate this for the lens. When they felt they had a satisfactory result, they quickly covered the lens and portrayed a false image of an empty hanger bay. They then extended an appendage to flash a signal of their success.

Once the cameras were dealt with, Ayene and the rest of her team reimagined their shapes to their natural form.

"Good!" she asserts. "Now, quickly… I would imagine the bridge crew is getting antsy to see something outside. Record this location and go pick up your gear."

The team members make a hasty survey of the local surroundings, trying to quickly record a memory image of their positioning. Then, one by one, they start flashing out of sight.

On the bridge, the Commander was feeling tense by now.

"Where are you," he grumbles. "I know you're out there!"

"Sir," the First Officer wonders. "Do you think we should lay down a little blanket fire just to see if we can stir something up?"

"Maybe. Fire off a few salvos at random. Let's see what happens."

Kaliya and her team were waiting anxiously at the Bahlaie Center when they were greeted with the sudden arrival of a group of projections. Ayene's team proceeded to grab their equipment cases, which were all neatly lined up along a wall outside the main research building.

"How do things look in there?" she asks.

"We have a secure base," reports one of the teammates. "We covered the cameras, and as far as we can tell, no one knows we're in there."

"Good, try to keep it that way until we're in position. Worst case scenario, if someone comes in the door, try to grapple them until one of us can take them down proper."

"Yes Ma'am!"

In Central Command, the officers were also feeling the pressure.

"I don't like this extended silence, Commander," the Marshal concedes. "It means they're up to something. They must be studying us. Either that, or...hmm... I wonder if they could've moved off somewhere else."

"If that is the case," Geilv reflects. "They could be almost anywhere by now."

"Have them conduct a few long-range scans for those inversion signatures."

Marelle was still waiting for her cue. She sat silently in her ship, watching the large cruiser as it began firing a series of random shots.

"Base, this is Specter Prime. They're getting nervous. I see them firing off potshots to wake us up."

"Understood, Specter Prime. Are you in any immediate danger?"

"Negative, they're too far away and aiming the wrong direction."

"Acknowledged, stay on alert. We have word on this side of the infiltration setting up marks now."

"Got it."

Ayene's troupe had returned with their conjuring devices, and she was now setting up a long way-line to begin the marking process.

"Make it count, people," she commands. "This is an important step. Keep the calm and knock it out!"

The assembly had lined up twenty-wide and arranged their equipment, quickly assembling the devices with their control boards, then the runes in their cradles.

"I can't wait for the day when we begin using that new indexing tech," she muses privately. "That'll make this process a dream."

The row of devices began lighting up, and erupted in a series of swirling vortices of energy spiraling into the rune stones. With this step complete, the team quickly pulls the equipment back a few paces to allow room. One member then collects the rune stones into a bag for immediate return, while the rest repack their gear and return independently.

At the research center, Kaliya and her people continued to wait, until the first of the projected team members arrived and set their marked runes down on a nearby table.

"Very good!" she applauds. "Now for the fun part. Mages; open us up a way-line! Company, form up!"

The company of troops begins to form up in columns with the mages as they enchant the runes to open a line of virtual rift apertures. Row by row, the soldiers filed through at close invasion timing intervals of only a few seconds apart.

On the other side, Ayene's people were reassembling in the shuttle bay after returning their equipment. They were now preparing for the next maneuver as Kaliya's troops began to emerge out of their portals and move to one side. When the final row had arrived, the portals closed again.

"Captain," Ayene salutes. "We're ready to begin our conquest of the target."

"Excellent, Lieutenant," she affirms. "Now, I need you to station someone at the entrance to their auxiliary control, and then bring the rest of your people up to the bridge. You will wait for our scenario to begin before proceeding."

"Yes Ma'am!" she salutes proudly.

Ayene now collects her assembly and changes back into bugs, then folds back outside the door to the corridor again where they travel off to their next objective.

Kaliya calls in on her helmet com-link to her base.

"This is Phantom Prime to base; we are in position. Begin the scenario when ready."

"Phantom Prime, this is Base, acknowledged. Specter Prime, do you copy?"

"This is Specter Prime, we copy here," Marelle issues. "Beginning scenario now... Flight Three, power up, we're going in for a quick strike. Follow my target; we're taking down one of those light cruisers first."

The Flight powers up their engines and forms up on Marelle's lead as she takes them in fast.

On the bridge, the tactical officer picks up the inversion bubbles almost immediately.

"Sir! Incoming! I'm picking up five bubbles on an intercept vector from behind us."

"It figures! But five? Last I heard it was supposed to be six. They must've lost one somewhere. Whatever. All ships, engage! I want that vector flooded with plasma fire."

The fleet suddenly comes alive as each ship attempts to spin around for an optimal firing solution. Marelle leads her team forward quickly, making a series of dodging movements as they target the drive system of one of the smaller cruisers. They let off a couple of salvos, which blasted their way through the ship's shields, landing a direct hit on the engines. The ship begins listing as Marelle continues leading a long drive away from the scene.

"Where are they going!" the Commander growls. "Saakerav, one of our escorts took a hard hit and is without maneuverability. The attackers are now moving away from us at high speed."

"Understood. You will pursue and engage."

Ayene and her team of bugs flew through the corridors back to the lift, where she attempted to push the call button. In her bug form, this was difficult, but she managed to engage the service. In a moment, a car arrived, and they all filed inside. Once the door closed, she returned to her natural form.

"Computer, where is Auxiliary Control?" she orders.

"Auxiliary Control is on Deck Twelve, Section Five," the voice responds.

"Don't you just love technology," she giggles. "All right, I need our supplemental asset to go there and wait. If the bridge crew should try to reach it, you need to block their access. If it appears as we expect, you'll have a door leading inside a room. Simply blocking that should limit their access."

She now returns to the lift control.

"Computer, take me to the Bridge."

"Destination: Bridge. Stand by."

They wait as the lift begins to move. Ayene felt the pressure by now. She needed to secure her positioning on the bridge, but timing was critical to coincide with Marelle's movements.

"Once we arrive, I need our special assault team to memorize the place and prepare for our little surprise. This is going to be tricky, so keep to your focus."

As they arrived, she reimagined her shape back to a bug, and led all but one of her people onto the bridge to discreetly take up hiding among the cracks between ceiling tiles and other nooks around the room. The one who stayed behind waited for the door to close before returning to his normal shape.

"Computer, take me to Auxiliary Control," he orders.

"Destination: Auxiliary Control. Stand by."

As the lift began to move again, he took his bug shape once more and waited.

Outside, Marelle led her quarry on a little chase, but the heavy cruiser was nowhere near as agile as she was. She gained some distance and quickly shut down her engines.

On the bridge, the tactical officer reported in.

"Sir, they just turned to silent running! What are they doing out there?"

"If they shut down their engines, that means they're just sitting out there. Let's hit them while we have the chance. Bring us around to fire."

Marelle watched as the cruiser closed in.

"Specter One, go active and engage. Hit the other light cruiser and veer off sharp to the first one. Make a run at it to knock it out. Then leave them behind and go silent."

"Understood, engaging…"

The next Flight powers up and immediately takes off.

"Huh?" the tactical officer blurts unexpectedly. "What in all the… Sir! I don't understand this. I've got a new set of blips on the far side of us, advancing fast."

"What do you mean? How did they get over there?"

"I have no idea, but they're making a hard push at us…starboard side!"

"All ships, turn and engage!"

The next set of combat ships streaks in and swings around to make another hit, this time taking out the second light cruiser's engines.

"Dammit, they're thinning out our support ships. Saakerav, are you getting this? We lost the second LC, and they're now advancing on the first one to finish it."

"Acknowledged, Naal Balai. You must continue to pursue and engage."

"These things are buzzing circles around us out here! Tactical, lay down some more flak fire!"

Kaliya and her people continued to wait in the shuttle bay as they listened in on their shard-coms to Marelle's orders.

"Flight Two, prepare to go active and engage. I want you to finish that other light cruiser before breaking off. You will retreat to Tactical One and wait for them to align with you. Then jump to Tactical Two and go to standby. And prime your jump charge again. I would imagine these people are getting tired of chasing us by now."

"Flight Two, understood."

The large ship lethargically struggled to follow the small fighters as it turned and pursued them around the first light cruiser, which was now completely dead in space. The frigate escort was a bit nimbler, but even they had difficulty turning and engaging efficiently enough for this. And then, before they could bring themselves into a new firing position, the previous Flight had vanished from the screen.

"Dammit, Sir, they're gone again," the tactical officer scorns. "They're using quick hit-and-run tactics with some really weird maneuvers."

"Keep on those scanners. They must be using some kind of strange translocation technology."

In another moment, the screen shows a new blip.

"Sir, I got them again! In all the nether-space, they've moved to the other side of the field!"

"I swear to you… All right, helm, bring us around again. If we keep this up, we'll lose everything out here. I want a full blanket effect in that direction!"

Once again, the ship sluggishly turns around, but it quickly realizes the target is well behind them.

"It looks like they're aiming for the other crippled LC," the tactical officer comments.

"They're picking us off slowly. Next will be the frigates, I'll bet."

"And after that, probably us…"

"They'll need to cut through our weapons fire before they do that. I can't see how those little things can bring down one of these so easily. That's why they're taking out the smaller ones. It's more to their liking."

"Yes Sir. I see them hitting the LC in a swarm attack…now moving off again."

"They'll probably go silent and use that translocation thing again. And these waypoints they're using are just wide enough to make us run for it."

In Central Command, Geilv, the Marshal, and the others, all listened in on the chatter.

"I have to admit," the Marshal muses. "It's a clever tactic, if also very annoying. But in the end, once the heavy is isolated, these things may make a series of strafing runs at it. My suggestion is to have them hold their position. Clearly, chasing these little mongrels around isn't working. And then just use their flak fire to blanket everything within range. If you create a large enough hazard zone, these little pests might not be able to approach as easily."

"Good idea, Marshal," Geilv nods. "Saakerav Station, we have new instructions for the Naal Balai…"

By this time, the heavy cruiser was attempting to track the last Flight of combat ships towards its tactical waypoint. It was angling off to one side, along with its escort.

"Sir," the tactical officer emits. "I'm picking up something strange in that group. It's come to a standstill, but not silent this time, and I'm detecting a buildup of…Abnormal Energy? Sir! They're forming a rift distortion wave! They're jumping!"

On the screen, they observe the classic flash as the body dives into a rift vortex, but almost as soon as it does, the tactical officer notices a new blip.

"I don't believe it!" he screeches. "Sir, it looks like they just made a tactical jump across the field from us!"

At this point, the Commander was almost ready to pull his horns out, not only for the aggravating tactics being played, but also the taunting nature of the game. He sighed heavily as he gazed at the view screen.

"Well, I'll admit one thing, they're applying some clever tactics. What are they doing out there now?"

"They appear to be hovering in space."

"You can still see their bubbles?"

"Yes Sir, and it looks like they're waiting for us."

"Oh, of course they're waiting for us!" he balks. "And I'll bet they're laughing at us along the way. All right, bring us around to face them. Let's see if they make any moves."

The ship circles around slowly as Marelle watches. It was off to the right of their playing field, while Flight Two was on the left. Marelle and Flight Three were north of it, while Flight One was south. They were in a good position for a crossfire assault, should the enemy try moving through the field.

The Commander and his bridge crew wait. It appears as a standoff.

"All right, listen," he announces. "My guess is these two extremes are their target zones for these maneuvers, like waypoints. When they first engaged us, they hit us from the lower end of the field, and took off to the upper, then reappeared at one of these waypoints, and diverted to finish the first LC. The next time was to reappear at the other waypoint and go straight across, hit the second LC, and then jump back to the beginning. Are you with me so far?"

"Yes Sir. So, how do you suggest we counter this?"

"Like Central said, chasing between these two points isn't working for us. So, my suggestion is to position ourselves in the middle and orient our guns to either side. That way, no matter which way they come at us, we'll hit them."

"Good choice, Sir!"

The helmsman now begins advancing ahead slowly. They maneuver the ship gently into position roughly between the two tactical points and turns broadside to them, now orienting generally north on the field with the frigates hovering above and behind them.

Marelle monitors her scanners as they reposition themselves.

"This is Specter Prime to all units. These people look like they're getting smarter out there. They're taking up a station in the middle, waiting for us to come to them. Well, boys and girls, we don't want to disappoint them. Flight One, you have a clear run at those frigates. Go active and hit them fast. But try to stay in the blind spot of that heavy. Flight Three, get ready. If we can turn them around, we'll hit from the other side."

The tactical officer continued to study his scanners.

"They're still not moving, Sir..."

"Something's wrong with that. Could they be disabled?"

"That would be a fine bit of luck for us," the First Officer admits. "Maybe we should press our advantage while we can."

"That might not be such a bad idea."

"Sir!" the tactical officer shouts. "Dammit, I have a second blip. It's behind us! I'm now showing two groups on the screen!"

"Two of them! That explains it. They're not translocating, just toying with us. Turn and engage!"

"They're moving in fast. I think they're taking aim at the frigates this time!"

The Flight zipped in quickly and took aim at the frigates as they tried coming around. Two of them took hard hits to their engines before the Flight veered off.

"Flight Three," Marelle charges. "Now! Go active and hit those frigates."

Now her Flight powers up and takes off.

"Sir!" the tactical officer shrieks. "Another one! In all the nether-space, who is piloting these things? They're coming in from our rearward port quarter."

"Sir," the comms officer asserts. "I'm getting distress messages from our frigates. Two of them have lost power to their engines and their weapons are failing."

"Commander," the First Officer asserts. "They've got us in a crossfire! I don't know what's holding those things together, but our flak guns don't seem to be fazing them!"

"What about that stationary unit?" he orders. "Where is it?"

"Still stationary," the tactical officer responds. "They haven't moved since they arrived there."

"All right, we're losing our escort anyway, so let's at least try to take SOME of them out with us. Helm, aim for that stationary unit. I want full guns at the ready."

The ship now makes a hurried turn on its axis towards the one Flight still sitting at the jump point. It powers up its thrusters and makes a determined line at it.

"Specter Prime, this is Flight Two. They appear to be coming at us."

"Got it, Flight Two. Wait until they get within firing range and jump to Tactical One. Phantom Prime, do you copy this order?"

"This is Phantom Prime," Kaliya notes. "Copied and understood. We are standing by in a Go condition."

In Rolsklinde, in the WIC building, Thaelyn and his officers listened in on the chatter coming through the shard-com links as the scenario unfolded. He glanced around at the General and Kailen to see their reactions.

"I have never been involved in a naval action," he muses. "And certainly not a space battle, but this is quite a show of coordination. I think this will give many generations to come something new to think about."

Back on the cruiser, they were approaching their target.

"Sir," the tactical officer announces. "We're coming into firing range of that stationary unit."

"Good, at least we'll bring one of them down. Make ready to fire."

As the large ship moves into range, the Flight leader gives his order.

"Flight Two, link up..."

He sends out his carrier and the Flight begins to change their configuration into a tight huddle.

"Sir," the tactical officer notes. "They're moving into a new formation, very tight together."

"Tight? That doesn't sound right at all. One shot and we can take the whole group like that."

"Yes Sir, but…wait a minute. Oh dammit! Sir, they're jumping again! I just got a quick flash of that energy and…of course…" he shrugs. "They're on the other side of the field again."

"I don't believe it! They were toying with us! It was some kind of trap to separate us from the rest of our fleet! Where are the rest of them?"

Ayene and her team were sitting in the crevices of the room when the report came in of the second jump. Now she had to wait for her special group to perform its function.

A small team of five individuals folded their way back outside, recalling their initial arrival through the window, and working their way around. They travelled away from the hulking ship as it once again turned to find Marelle's other combat flights.

They had to maneuver carefully, so as not to lose track of their mission target. When they managed to sight one of Marelle's ships, they quickly folded over to it and transformed into large glowing orbs, zipping out from the fighter as if it were a strange form of attack aimed at the cruiser.

"Sir!" the First Officer shouts as he observes the view screen. "What in all the nether-space is that?!"

"Prepare for impact!" he orders. "Tactical, what are those things?"

"Sir, I have absolutely no idea. They're not showing up on the scans."

"What do you mean, not showing up? They're in plain sight of us!"

The five orbs streaked in and appeared to impact on the upper hull of the ship, spreading out across its surface before dissipating.

"Damage report!" the Commander demands.

The tactical officer checks his screens.

"No reports of physical damage, no electrical disruption…nothing showing up here."

"Then what were those things?"

Marelle also happened to take notice of the orbs, as she was waiting for this by now.

"Phantom Prime; jump two complete, wisps are away, and now awaiting takeover and removal procedure. All Flights, let's clean up and take a holding pattern."

Ayene was also waiting for this moment, as was the rest of her team on the bridge. When the impacts were reported, this was their cue to move.

On the Saakerav station, they listened in on the conversation.

"Naal Balai, what do you have out there?"

"Saakerav, we just observed what appeared to be a cluster of brightly glowing objects coming at us. They impacted on the upper hull, but we have no idea what they did…if anything."

"Acknowledged. Are you able to take down any of your attackers?"

"Negative, Saakerav. They're either evading us, or else they have something around them, like shields or something, that must be protecting them. Even with the blanket fire, and I'm sure we must've come close enough by now, they're still out there."

"Understood. We are ordering you to pull back. We'll call in additional ships to reinforce you. Maybe with some extra firepower, we can actually take them out."

"Acknowledged, pulling back."

But as the Commander gives his orders, the helmsman starts to notice something occurring on his console.

"Ugh! Sir! What in all the…"

The officer jumps out of his seat as a sickly green ooze begins gushing out of the control panel. The navigator sees more of it on his side and similarly lurches back.

"What?" the Commander wheezes.

All around the bridge, the consoles began swelling up with the same green slime.

"What is that stuff! Saakerav, are you still there! We have a problem here. Something is invading the bridge. It's some kind of slime coming out of the control panels. Ensign, get away from that stuff, it could be dangerous. Saakerav, are you receiving this?"

"Naal Balai, affirmative, but in all the nether-space, where is it coming from? Can you tell?"

"It just appeared out of nowhere, like it came out of the equipment. It's everywhere! And it's growing!"

The slime monsters were beginning to cover all the consoles throughout the bridge. The officers were pushed out of their seats and were now gathering in the middle of the room.

"Saakerav, we are unable to reach the controls. This…thing…is taking over the bridge, preventing us access to control the ship."

At this moment, the monitors began showing an alteration of their statistics. The comms station was the first to go.

"Sir!" the comms officer announces. "I think it's interfering with the communications. I see a shutdown procedure occurring."

"A shutdown? Like what, a malfunction?"

"I don't know, but comms just went dead."

"Sir!" the helmsman issues next. "I think we're coming to a full stop. The helm is going dead."

"And so is tactical!" the other officer reports. "This stuff is shutting us down."

"All right, whatever it is," he winces. "I don't want to come in contact with it. Abandon the bridge! We'll go down to Auxiliary and try to retake control from there. These people are insidious. This must be that little surprise they launched at us…some kind of organic weapon."

The crew now files through the lift as they begin to leave their stations. When the last of them were gone, Ayene folds into the room and takes her natural form.

"All right, lock us down in here," she orders. "Secure that lift! Make sure all comms are silent, including telemetry and ping response. Helm, check our coordinates. Do we have Ruuki uy'Daan in there? Anything at all in our home universe…"

The rest of her team all came out of their slime disguises and returned to their proper images. They started taking up positions at all the critical stations. One sat down at the helm while another took the navigation console. A third was at the comms station, while one more arrived at the tactical station, and each of them shutting down the unnecessary systems, like the weapons and comms, while the new helmsman checked the jump point indexes.

"Lieutenant, I show Ruuki uy'Daan here. It must be a generic shared log of indexes with all their ships."

"Good, this makes it easy. Set course and take us out, fast. I'm flashing to the shuttle bay to clue them in. You will hold this position until our team arrives."

"Yes Ma'am!"

Ayene now takes a moment to quickly recall the shuttle hanger, and she flashes out of sight. She arrives in the compartment to find Kaliya and her crew still on standby.

"We're launching to Ruuki uy'Daan. Give us a moment to charge up."

"Good! Marelle made some good work out there, by the sound of it."

"You should've seen it from my perspective. The Commander up there was ready to pull his horns out for all the games she was playing on him. He'll be a tough nut to settle down on the other side of it."

"Well, we have plenty of support troops in the area, so if nothing else, we'll just bundle them up as prisoners of war until we can talk them down."

Marelle had finished her work on the last of the frigates and she was observing the large cruiser by now. A moment later, she began to see it glow, then flash away in a large rift event.

"Base, this is Specter Prime, the target is away. Specter Squadron, form up, we're going home now."

Kaliya could feel the motion of the ship as it penetrated through hyperspace, and she was starting to feel some of the arcanic energies welling up as they arrived at their destination. When the word came over her com-link that they were moving, she started pushing ahead. She opened the hanger access door and ordered her people into the ship.

Ayene glanced up at the cameras again to see they were still covered.

"Camera team, front and center… We'll take up as bugs again and follow them in."

She once again took up a bug shape and was quickly joined by her cohorts who were covering the cameras. They followed Kaliya into the corridor and began spreading out through the ship.

The cruiser had arrived in Ruuki uy'Daan local space, and the helmsman began piloting it towards the planet to place it into an automatic station-keeping orbit.

"We need a scout to report that we have arrived," orders one member.

One of the members steps forward and flashes away to report in. The rest stayed where they were to continue securing the area.

Kaliya could feel the arcanic energies strongly by now, and she knew she was at full capacity to push forward.

"I need people to go dark and scout ahead. I need a front line with shields in case we get any surprises. Guns at the ready, stun only."

They began working their way through the corridors, shooting anyone that came in the line of sight. The crewmembers were not expecting hostiles to be lurking around onboard the ship, so they went down fast. And almost as soon as they were knocked down, someone took a portal rune and sent them away.

The Commander and his people had made their way down to the Auxiliary Control area. But as soon as they arrived at the door, they took notice it was covered by the same green slime, almost as if it were oozing out of the door itself.

"This is bad, people," he groans.

He searches for a nearby intercom and switches it to ship-wide mode.

"This is Fleet Commander Kansi Sak'taran to all hands. The ship has been invaded by some kind of alien slime entity. All hands are advised to be aware and do not make physical contact. The Bridge is overrun. Auxiliary is also overrun. I need a science team to Auxiliary Control to see if we can figure out what this thing is."

Kaliya listened to the announcement, and she knew she needed to take that bridge crew out as one of her priorities. But her objectives were keeping her busy for now just working her way through the rest of it.

Her spies scouted ahead and reported back what they saw, and she sent teams in to take down her prey as quietly as possible. Side compartments were investigated and cleaned out. She had multiple deployments by this time, moving along different decks, and as they cleared one area, they locked down the lift system in that section to prevent people from moving around as easily, leaving it to the stairways instead. On the stairs, they placed guards, some under a cloak, to hit anyone sight unseen if they should try coming through. Eventually, she came up to the engineering section.

"All right, people, this is Engineering. Be careful of what you shoot in here. I want people under cloak to go in and position themselves. We'll have another team rush in to draw their attention while the cloaked units take them down."

One squad calls up a cloak on themselves and makes ready while Kaliya ducks around the door frame. As she hits the button to open it, the cloaked units move in and make a quick survey to position themselves near the crew. Then Kaliya sends her second squad in to surprise the people.

The resident crewmen all turn at the sudden rush of invaders, but before any of them are able to take any kind of action, the cloaked members pop into view and attack with a stunning strike to the forehead.

"Sorry about this, people," Kaliya soothes. "But that's what war is about. Base, this is Phantom Prime, we have Engineering."

The Commander was waiting for his science team to make a judgement on what they were looking at with the slime monster covering the Auxiliary Control door.

"Sir, I'm not getting a reading on this thing. It doesn't show up at all on my scanner."

"Technician, it has to show something, just look at it!"

"I know, Sir. But according to the scanner, it doesn't even exist."

"Doesn't exist? What kind of scanner are you using here?"

"It's a medical scanner, but this thing doesn't show any kind of organic life signs."

"Nothing organic? Try something else. Maybe it's a form of life we haven't encountered before, and doesn't fall within our usual parameters. Like maybe an inorganic variety."

Kaliya's team pushed forward briskly. She needed to find the Auxiliary Control center to take down the bridge crew before they could find a way of retaking the ship.

"Ayene, where are you?"

Ayene pops into view out of her bug shape to respond.

"I'm here."

"Where is Auxiliary?"

"On Deck Twelve, Section Five. That's one more deck above us."

"All right, we need to get up there and secure that place, and also the Bridge. Everything else will fall into place after that. I want you to flash up there quickly and scout the area. Be discreet and report back."

"Yes Ma'am."

"And Ayene, you don't technically have to address me as Ma'am. We're friends, remember?"

"Well, yes, but this is official."

"Cu'Nar help us, if this becomes a habit," she chuckles.

Ayene flashes out of sight as she works her way to the nearest lift, leaving Kaliya to continue forward in search of more people.

"Sir," the technician muses. "This stuff doesn't register on any scan mode I try. I'm picking up the door, the wall, the wiring inside, but not this green stuff."

"All right, let's try a plasma torch and see if we can burn it away."

He moves again to the intercom to make an announcement.

"This is the Commander again; I need an engineering team with a plasma torch to Auxiliary Control."

He waits a moment for a reply, but after an extended period, nothing comes through. So, he tries again.

"Engineering, I need a plasma torch to Auxiliary... Respond."

Kaliya knew this was the beginning of trouble because she had only recently taken the engineering section, and she wasn't interested in faking any responses at this time.

"This is Phantom Prime. All units; expect trouble. They're trying to call Engineering, but they're going to realize any moment now that Engineering isn't there. This will probably put them on alert."

Ayene had arrived in the corridor with the Commander and his bridge crew. She hid in the corner of the wall and ceiling as a bug while she observed them.

The Commander was becoming concerned by now over the lack of response.

"Could it be overrun as well?" the First Officer wonders. "Maybe they had to evacuate the section."

The Commander frowns at the implications and turns to the intercom again.

"This is Commander Sak'taran to anyone in the area of Engineering. Respond."

They waited several moments, but again there was no response.

"Is there anyone on Deck Thirteen? Reply!"

Again, there was no response. Now he felt a chill running through him. He glared at his First Officer and the other officers around him.

"This is the Commander; I want any crewman on any deck below Deck Twelve to respond immediately!"

Ayene knew what was coming as she watched the affair. Kaliya could also feel it as she listened to the intercom.

"He's figuring it out, people. Get ready for an alarm soon."

Kaliya and her team hurried to finish the current deck and find the stairs to the next one, cutting off the lifts in the process to prevent any access. She sent a team of cloaked scouts up the first stairwell she could find to survey the area, but it was generally clear. She held her position to wait for the rest of her immediate squad to catch up and they cautiously moved up the stairs.

The Commander glanced around at his officers.

"I think this slime creature isn't the only thing that came onboard with that weird attack. The shuttle bay is also down there."

"But Sir," the First Officer submits. "It should've been closed to the outside."

"I don't think that stops these people. If they can fit jump drives into combat fighters, who knows what they need to infiltrate a battleship. This is why they didn't attack us directly. And that long delay tactic of theirs," he waves a finger. "They were landing a boarding party."

"In all the nether-space!" he shouts. "Then they must be right under us by now!"

The Commander turns once again to the intercom. He locates an alarm bell and hits the button.

"This is Commander Sak'taran to all crewmen. We may have a

hostile boarding party onboard. They likely came in through the shuttle bay and are working their way up. All hands, battle stations! Take up whatever defensive positions you have available!"

He quickly studies the surrounding corridor and waves his group to follow behind.

"Phantom Prime here," Kaliya asserts. "They're on to us. All squads, shields in front, take a defensive advance. I want scouts to survey the area and report to your team leaders. I'm going to Deck Twelve where Auxiliary is found. All units, move forward with all due haste."

✦✦✦✦✦

"Central Command," the Commander at the Saakerav Station reports. "We're still unable to locate the Naal Balai. The ping responder appears dead, and there is no telemetry or comms. Their last signal said something about a slime creature invading their Bridge control systems, but shortly after that, the signals cut out on us. And our support fleet arrived to find the rest of them, but no Naal Balai."

"Not even any wreckage?" the Captain asks.

"No, Captain. Our thoughts are on the last orders we gave to have them pull back. If they were underway at the time, they could be flying off somewhere out of control. We are now trying to scan for any inversion bubbles of that size category, but they might be moving out of range."

"What about the invaders?"

"No sign of them, so they must've finished whatever it was they had in mind. We found an energy trace for a jump signature, but the signs were dissipating by the time we arrived, so it's hard to say how many were involved in this attack."

"Understood, Saakerav," he sighs. "Keep looking and send a few scouts out there on a search pattern. Maybe, if their systems were starting to fail, they dropped out of nether-space and they're drifting. Let us know what you find."

"Affirmative."

They close the link and turn back into the room.

Geilv studied the faces of the other officers in the control booth. He also glanced at the Marshal, who appeared visibly stricken.

"I'm truly sorry for this, Commander," he states morbidly. "I should've been paying closer attention to that young man. He seemed to be performing so well for us at first, but clearly..." he sighs.

"Marshal," Geilv attempts to soothe. "This cannot be directly him. It would need to apply to those friends of his."

"Granted, but he must be the motivating factor behind it, otherwise I doubt they would be here. Commander, his mania can be easily attributed to this skill of his, but whoever he took up sides with is simply dangerous. And with a jump index to our local space, that makes them even more so. We may need to address this issue some other way."

"What way, Marshal? Do we actually give in to his demands?"

"I would hardly desire us to do that, and we still don't know where that little pest is hiding. So, giving in or otherwise, where are we supposed to send it? We are left with only a few options. One is to give him his foolish little tribute, but if he wants it, he'll have to come here to get it. If we can draw him here, or even one of his followers, we could again try to tag whatever it is he uses with a beacon and follow them home. But we're not going to spend any more ships on him."

"What if they're cloaked again?"

"Once again, if he wants it, he'll have to come down here for it. I may need to confront him myself out there. He makes these appearances on a regular schedule it seems. So, if I could be ready for him the next time he shows himself, maybe I could have a little...chat... with him," he scowls. "He's going to have to prove himself worthy of that title if he wants his tribute, and he'll have to come before me with it. And then, well, I'll try to deal with it personally, rather than have any more of your people go out there. At the very least, if we do give him anything, I want it to be carrying a beacon with it, or weapons, or something! He's not simply going to take any of these people as his playthings!"

He turns abruptly and charges out of the room.

Geilv and the Captain look on as he stomps his way down the hall. They then turn to each other.

"Captain..." Geilv muses distantly. "All things considered, and although we can attribute many potential factors into this equation, that seemed to demonstrate a protective attitude towards us."

"Maybe," he nods delicately. "Didn't you once say he mentioned our people holding some kind of potential...as if to say he complemented us?"

"He did, as well as that opinion of Ytani and those female victims. So maybe, between this and that creed of his, he holds a personal interest in all his work. It might make sense, after a while. It would surely be a work effort."

"All right, fine. But Commander, how in all the nether-space did they do that?"

"This has to be the ACI, but that slime stuff, what was that?"

"It sounded like it came out of nowhere."

"Came out of nowhere…hmm… Captain, what if it wasn't actually slime? Ti'van said this projection gift can create virtually anything if you just put your mind to it…in a literal sense of the word. How do we know if it wasn't a team of operatives pretending to be slime, just to commandeer the Bridge? She said she didn't want to harm the ship, so maybe they abducted it instead."

"Abducted a heavy cruiser?" he grimaces. "Unbelievable! But Sir, this one had fourteen hundred crewmen onboard! First of all, how do you land a boarding party on a ship that should be boxed up tight and on battle alert? You couldn't even get close enough without being blown to bits. And these fighters of theirs were running circles around them, not making any kind of approach."

"Maybe something else got in there. There was that mention of something hitting the ship just before it went down. Maybe it was some kind of invasion force using a form of technology we don't know about."

"Well, if that's the case, I dread to see what they have in mind for the next one. I sure hope these people are telling us the truth about trying to save our world, because they could just as easily conquer it."

✦ ✦ ✦ ✦ ✦

Kaliya's troupe was advancing on the last few sections of the ship by now. But she found herself in a situation where the bridge crew was concerned.

"Phantom Prime to all units," she orders on her com-link. "Status report…"

"Platoon One here, up on Deck Two forward, still working, but not much to see here."

"Platoon Two, Deck One, just arrived and now advancing forward. Platoon Four is right behind us moving aft."

"This is Platoon Three; we're just mopping up the leftovers on Deck Two aft. It looks like mostly crew quarters up here. Not much left by now, but several of them were occupied with people hiding in corners."

"Acknowledged," Kaliya responds. "We found the Commander

and his bridge crew held up in the mess hall, along with about fifty crewmen all barricaded behind a wall of tables and other furniture. They look like they're ready for a final showdown. But I'm getting a few ideas. Keep clearing the rest of it and report to my position when you're done. I have two platoons with me, but I think one more would be in order for an effective takedown."

"Understood."

Kaliya and a portion of her troupe were stationed not far from a large mess hall further along the corridor. A cloaked scout had reported a large number of people inside, seemingly armed and ready. Most of the ship had been conquered by now, and it was just down to a few stragglers.

"Ayene, you have two Spooks from the cameras down below, right?"

"Yes Ma'am."

"Good, I suspect we must have a restroom inside there. Check on it quickly and report back. See if it's empty and how visible it is from the room."

"Right away," she nods and flashes away.

She takes up a bug form and arrives at the entrance to the mess hall, which represents an open frame, rather than an actual door. She carefully enters inside, crawling along the wall and camouflaging herself to match the wall colors. She glances around to see a mass of tables and other items forming a makeshift barricade across the room, and with many people huddling behind it, most of them clearly distressed. She felt sorry for them in their situation, but she had to comfort herself that this was mostly regarded as an exercise, not a real battle. She spied a sign on the wall at the far end of the room, so she flashed across to it.

There were two doors in a recessed alcove leading to the restrooms, representing both male and female facilities. She began by altering her form to fit between the crevice of the door and the wall to slip inside. Once inside, she quickly scouted the area to see it was apparently clear of anyone currently using it. She exited the room to investigate the other one and found the same result. She then returned outside to report.

"Captain," she asserts. "There are two rooms at the far end, the doors are located in recesses, and both areas are clear."

"Good, take these two spooks with you, one to each room. We're going to use rune transport to import a couple of platoons into the area and advance from that direction, but only on my orders, got it?"

"Yes Ma'am!" she smiles.

"And Ayene, didn't I say you don't need to be so formal with me?"

"Yes Ma'am, but like I said, this is official, and I also want to annoy you," she giggles.

"Grace of the cu'Nar…" she shakes her head. "You must be taking lessons from Marelle."

Ayene now calls the two projected members standing by and they all take off together as bugs. She leads them inside, again concealing themselves for the coloring, and flash to the rear of the room to the restroom doors, where she calls them into a close huddle.

"All right, one to each room," she whispers in bug-like tones. "Study the area, flash to Bahlaie, pick up some conjuring devices, and return. Mark a rune in each room and deliver them to the Captain."

The other two chirp a response and move off to their duties. They each infiltrate one of the restrooms and reshape to their natural form. They take a quick look around to record their location and flash away to the Bahlaie Center to again pick up the equipment cases for marking runes.

On their return, they take up positions to the rear of the room, giving space for the troops to accumulate in the area. They assemble their devices, install fresh rune stones, and engage the enchantment. The process was quick and efficient, with the swirling energies cycling down into the stones. When they had finished, they packed up again and flashed out to where Kaliya held her station. Ayene had already returned there and was waiting for her next order.

"Good job," Kaliya notes. "Now, once we get another platoon freed up, we're going in. We'll open portals to each of those rooms, one platoon to a room. There you will wait until my signal. I want those two Spooks to follow and handle the doors for us. The teams will go dark and sneak up on our prey. I'll toss in a stink cloud to confuse the issue, and that's when you hit. But try to take the Commander and his First Officer upright so I can talk to them. I'll try a little of my love and kisses approach, as I'm sure they're both going to be fuming by the time this is over."

They all nod in acceptance of their tasks and two of them take the runes. They wait a short while until another platoon is available, and then they begin.

"Captain, Platoon Three is here," ushers a returning team leader. "We're all set."

"All right, here we go. Spooks, recheck the area quickly to verify it's clear."

The two projected members flash away to quickly inspect the restrooms again. They only take a moment and return back.

"It's clear, Captain."

"Good, open the portals. Platoon Three is with me, we'll go in the front to clear the debris. Five and Six will move into position. Once you assemble, you'll go dark. Spooks, you'll open the doors to let them out. You won't be able to see them in this condition, so just hold them open until we're done here."

Again, they all nod and the projected members flash away. Two teammates begin casting the enchantments on the runes to engage the energies, and the two platoons begin flashing out of sight to arrive inside the restrooms, where they accumulate to one side. Once they were all assembled, they reported in and cast cloaks on themselves. The Spooks then carefully opened the doors to allow the hidden members to sneak outside.

Ayene relocated herself into the room to observe the activity, although she couldn't see the cloaked members. But she could see the doors opening and guess what was coming.

Kaliya waited several moments for the process to complete before making her move.

"This is Phantom Prime to assigned units, stand by, I'm moving into position."

She now moves forward, drawing her remaining platoon with her, ready to spring into action. When she arrives at the door she signals again.

"This is Phantom Prime in position. On my mark, I'll cast the stink cloud, and all cloaked units will take down their targets. Three, two, one..."

She now calls up a new spell, conjuring up a sickly green ball within her hands. She quickly pops out from hiding to sight a target in the room and hurls the ball at them, then briskly ducks back again.

"Incoming!" the First Officer shouts.

In an instant, the ball explodes to create a thick cloud of green choking gas. The crewmen began coughing, and they were unable to see anything immediately around them. But the greater effects of the gas didn't cause them to lose consciousness, as it would for some. Much like with the effect Thaelyn once used as a demonstration on Therinë during the last moments of the war, the seeds again filtered out some portion of the gas. Nevertheless, before any of them could react to the attack, dozens of hidden troopers popped into view and instantly began taking down the crewmen. The attack was swift and decisive, and virtually without warning.

Once the majority of them were down, a small group of soldiers lunged forward to grab both the Commander and his First Officer, disarming and restraining them. Kaliya then rushed in with her final troupe and began clearing away the furniture. She called up a divine chant to clear the air, and the cloud rapidly dissipated away from her.

"Who in all the nether-space are you people!" the Commander growls. "How dare you attack us!" he shouts.

"Easy does it, Commander," Kaliya attempts to soothe. "This is better regarded as an exercise, not an official attack. And personally, I think it went rather well, with respect to you."

"Oh! An exercise?! You took out our entire fleet, and I'm going to guess captured this vessel and its full crew, and you call it an exercise?"

"Yes, we're an elite combat unit and working as part of the ACI. This was a simulation, Commander. We couldn't inform you of it beforehand because we needed it to appear real. It was also a demonstration of our technique."

"The ACI?!" he roars. "Blast you people!" he pants. "And what do you mean, a demonstration?"

"Please, calm down and allow me to explain. It is my understanding that Darumon was present on this occasion to oversee things inside Central, and from the report I got a short while ago from one of our operatives, it most certainly left an impression on him. We needed this, but at the same time, we didn't actually want to damage this ship, as we did the others. We used EMP to disable that fleet of yours, but small ships are more easily replaced than larger ones."

"Not for the quantity you people have taken out so far."

"Maybe so, but I think this is the last one. Next time has to be on the ground. We need Darumon and Sargeras outside so we can target them."

"Unbelievable! But then, what's this about that errant young man, Ytani?"

"Ytani WAS an agent working for Darumon. But no more. We took care of him a while back. Ours is an image we're using to fool Darumon, that's all. He's used similar distractions on just about everyone else out there, and now we're doing it to him. We're using the image of Ytani as a figurehead to distract him from our own advance. And Geilv knows this, but he's under orders to keep it quiet."

"Him? In all the nether-space, if the ACI is now giving HIM orders, I think I'm retiring from this business. But how did you actually get inside here?"

"It's all a series of cute little tricks we played to conceal our actions. First, you took notice of a strange form of attack hitting your ship, right?"

"Yes! And shortly after that, this horrid slime starts spreading all over our controls."

"Right, well, allow me to introduce you to some of the people who were playing that role. Spooks, front and center," she orders.

Ayene and her two available Spooks flash into view and come to attention.

"These people," Kaliya directs, "are projections, not corporeal bodies. This is your famous Tav'ageen Anomaly, or as we call it, the Prodigy Gift. They can create any image the mind can imagine, and as you can probably tell, we have a bit of practice by now. They simply frightened you away so we could take the bridge."

"You must be joking! A simple fear tactic?"

"Hey, it worked!" she shrugs. "And we have an army of them by now."

"Sir," the First Officer muses. "This would probably explain that thing we saw on the Auxiliary door."

"Right, it didn't show up on any scans," he notes. "How do you explain this?"

"The image is a projection of the mind and spirit," Kaliya informs. "So, it won't show up on any type of scan because it's not technically a physical object. In fact, I'm quite sure we'll need to invent a whole new form of science to be able to help us on these occasions in the future. Those things you saw hitting you were more projections to act as a potential source to bring the slime creature inside the ship. Cause and effect, get it?"

"Uh huh… So, you hit us with what LOOKS like an attack, but it's not, just something visual to draw our attention while you apparently had people inside all along, is that right?"

"Yes, but it still required a little work. First, we had to make the actual arrival inside here. For this, one of our combat groups out there had an infiltration team in projected form sitting and waiting for you to show up. They folded over to your ship, found a way inside, probably using a window to sight an interior area, folded inside, and worked their way to the shuttle bay."

"Folded? Is this how you describe transportation in this form?"

"Yeah, we're borrowing a few terms from a society with a much higher understanding of these things."

"And using this, you did actually come in through the shuttle area."

"That first team made a foothold. After that, we had to use portals, which work like conveyors, and imported a full company of troops inside."

"A company!" he shrieks. "A mere company?! Young lady, we had fourteen hundred crewmen onboard this ship, and you say you took them out with a single company?"

"Commander, we're an elite Special Forces unit, not a simple military body. Your people never saw us coming, and as you can see around us, they couldn't do anything about it even if they did. We're using methods you simply don't have any countermeasures for."

"And you can use conveyors to import troops into places you simply pop in and out of with his Gift? That makes you extremely dangerous."

"Yes, it does, but it's not just the Gift, we're also trained in magic. This is where that Abnormal Energy comes in. It allows you to perform actual magic. That cloud was one example. I conjured it up, tossed it in, and while you were choking on it, we had another group who were imported into those restrooms right behind you and came out under an invisibility cloak. They were standing right next to you as I launched my attack. So, unless you can fight that, there's no way you can resist."

"In all the nether-space," he wheezes. "An invisibility cloak? So, even though we barricaded ourselves in here nice and tight, it didn't stop you. You just found a backdoor and hit us from behind in such a way that we didn't even know you were there. Who do you people actually work for? Because you couldn't have learned this from any of us."

"This is true..."

Kaliya now takes a moment to lift her visor and show her face. The Commander and his First Officer gaze apprehensively at her features, including her glowing eyes.

"I'm Captain Kaliya Nazég, daughter of Velen Nazég. I'm reinventing the old Stormhooves and leading a liberation force back home. Some might say this is payback for your Council not listening to my father's advice way back in the beginning. Some might also say we were brought away on a kind of pilgrimage to discover the truth out there, and now we are returning home with it. But regardless, the ACI is ours, not yours, and we're very literally trained by gods, and serving THEIR rules. Now, how do you feel about us offending your military protocols?" she smiles sweetly.

"I'm not so sure if I know how to answer that."

"Uh, Captain," the First Officer relents. "Where are we right now? Because I somehow doubt you could do all this and still be in Azgarén space. You spoke of this Abnormal Energy, but this isn't native to our space, and I think someone would've come to support us by now out there."

"Yes," she affirms. "Our Bridge infiltration team jumped the ship to an area of controlled territory we own. We're currently in orbit around one of our own worlds."

"Uh, wait...one of OUR own worlds?"

"No, not yours, ours. I'm not technically a citizen of Azgarén, and certainly not after that long chase you put us through. Our military is essentially a foreign body serving a foreign government that's aiding us to retake our home."

"I...um...right... So, where does that leave us? And Azgarén, for that matter?"

"Well, technically speaking, you might call yourselves prisoners of war, but we're not technically at war with you, or Azgarén, just Darumon and Sargeras. Even though Azgarén isn't my native home, as I was born elsewhere...all of us...we are still loyal to our people, even after you hunted us like animals for so many millennia."

"Oh, so gracious of you," he chuckles ironically.

"Yeah, I know. You should've seen me as I was growing up. I had some serious issues with your people for all that. At least until we found our saviors who helped us realize who those two really are and what needed to be done about it. Then we created this special unit to fight back. But unfortunately, it also makes you, like so many others, unwitting pawns along the way."

"Oh, pawns, is it?" the Commander huffs.

"Commander, this game is being played on the scale of gods, so we're all pawns. They don't usually involve themselves directly in affairs like this. But they do give guidance, and along the way, we are expected to learn a few things. Therefore, it is to be a pawn with the purpose of solving a problem and learning a lesson, and all part of a growth exercise, so we do NOT see this again."

"Oh... All right, given where we are, that does sound rather important."

It was a new day, and Ayene was making another visit to Commander Geilv's office, although she expected this one to be a bit rough after the recent skirmish. She was carrying a holo-chip with her in the hopes it might smooth things over a bit. She buzzed the door and entered cautiously.

Geilv eyed her warily as she arrived in the room, and studied her intently for her actions.

"I'm not entirely sure what to think of you at this moment, Lieutenant. That show you put on was scary, to say the least, and this one wasn't a simple stage play. So, what actually happened out there, and are our people still alive from it?"

She approaches the desk and presents the chip, setting it on the table for him.

"Bear with me, Commander, please. This is for you, and I'll ask you to give me a moment to explain what happened. Maybe you would also like to call Captain Ta'yeen in here, since we need his participation as well."

Geilv takes the chip and examines it, then turns and calls the Captain on his vid-com. While they wait, he inserts the chip in his terminal to see what was on it. He pulls up a browser app and finds a single file that appears as a vid-mail message.

"What's this? Who is it from?"

"Fleet Commander Sak'taran. It's a summary report of his condition for you, since I doubt you're in a very good mood right now."

"You got that much right."

They wait a few moments longer until Captain Ta'yeen arrives. As he enters, he spies Ayene in the room.

"You again," he emits hesitantly. "All right, what do you want this time?"

"Captain," Geilv instructs. "Sit with us. We have a report to listen to."

The Captain joins Ayene at the desk as Geilv opens the file.

"High Commander Geilv, this is Fleet Commander Kansi Sak'taran of the Naal Balai. Good greetings to you, as much as we can call it under the circumstances.

First and foremost, we are alright. Our ship and its full complement were captured as part of a battle simulation where we were declared technical prisoners of war. Although, this is largely due to the involvement of the ACI and their battle against the Marshal and Sargeras, where we became, as they call it, unfortunate pawns.

I was recently in conference with Fleet Commander Kriv'tik, much to my surprise, as I thought he was dead. I am currently under orders as part of a security blackout not to provide any information as to our whereabouts, as the location is highly classified for now. However, it is apparently part of a controlled region of territory where the ACI is maintaining a type of refugee camp. We have people from the Ghan'aju here, the Tul'ryk, and that secret base the Marshal was operating at Morndindor.

But Commander, I swear to you, if these people ever DID have any designs to take control, I have no doubt in my mind they could do it. I shared a conversation with the young lady...and I do mean young...who was the military Captain of the company of soldiers... and yes, I did say only a company...who infiltrated our ship and took us down so efficiently, it made my horns fly off. They describe themselves as a kind of elite Special Forces unit, and I think they very effectively demonstrated their capacity on this occasion. I had the last of my people held up in our mess hall, fully barricaded and ready for anything. But before we even knew what hit us, we were ambushed by two platoons of invisible operatives hitting from behind and literally out of thin air!" he chuckles satirically.

"Needless to say, they must've received some very advanced training from somewhere, and it apparently comes from this other side. Sir, if this is what we would be up against when the Marshal speaks of insurgents of any kind, I really doubt we would've had ten millennia of so many victories. These people don't even need to walk to their target. They just use conveyors and jump in right behind you.

Anyway, they tell me we need to hold out here until the final battle, whatever that final battle looks like, where they will eventually bring the Marshal and Sargeras down. Then we'll all go home. Until then, all I can say is to keep following their instructions. These people apparently have actual gods calling the shots, so none of us is truly in charge here. Sak'taran out..."

Both Geilv and the Captain retracted at the conclusion of the video and leaned back in their chairs. Neither of them appeared especially happy, but they were at least somewhat settled for the message.

"Where do we go from here?" Geilv asks.

"We've been asking ourselves a few of these same questions back home," Ayene offers. "The variable is now the Marshal. According to our most recent report, his reaction to this tells us he wants to make a direct showing in front of Ytani. But here we have what we call a paradox on how to call Sargeras outside to play. We need them exposed and away from anything else, like the city. We know his kind likes entertainment in the form of a game of sport, and we hope to attract him with one. But the question is, how do you approach someone like him with an offer like this? Who is it that normally does this? Is it the Marshal? And how do you entice HIM to do your work for you? Or perhaps there could be another way."

"It's a little late in the game to be asking that one," the Captain winces. "Isn't it?"

"Yes and no, because like I said before, we are following this path of Fate, and the sequence of events seems to be governed by someone who knows what's going to happen before it actually occurs. If she saw an error in our path, we think she would've said something by now, and she hasn't. So, we are left to conclude that we are following this path correctly, and it will unfold according to what comes naturally, and this will give us our answer even without us knowing what it is or how to reach it."

"I don't even understand what you just said, let alone think I would trust it," he chuckles.

"Yes, well, you need to be a part of it to know the meaning. I once believed as so many others do in this world, but my time with these people has taught me a few things. These gods are exceptionally powerful, so space, time, the fabric of Reality; this is their playground as much as we have our own."

"Then, I suppose we just have to wait and see what he does next, and follow this path accordingly, and something will open up for us to lead us to the next step. In all the nether-space, is this how you've been playing it all along?"

"Parts of it, to be sure," she nods. "Some of it was apparent, while other parts had to be discovered only at the appropriate time when it was revealed to us. We're working on a series of prophecies here, and they tell the story of what it is, where it comes from, and how it ends. But the messages are often very cryptic, leaving us to guess what's coming until it finally hits."

"What good is a prophecy if it doesn't give you a solid idea of what's coming?"

"Ordinarily, I would ask the same. But these are unique. The way we interpret them is she doesn't like giving out the answers directly, instead turning it into a kind of learning experience to see how we solve the problems along the way. This is how these gods work, as they regard us as their Children, and as children, we must grow and evolve."

+·+◆+·+

Ileani was preparing another of her news reports based on the recent encounter in Azgarén space. Even though Central was not giving an official account, Ayene made a visit to leak a few details which needed to be sent out in order to set up the situation for later. As she gets ready in the news studio, the set coordinator gives his direction to begin.

> *"This is Ileani Ur'paran for C.P. News. A spokesperson for Central Command came forward today with a surprising announcement. This is to follow up on the proposed threats that have been laid down on multiple occasions by the figure we call Ytani. According to this military informant, who wishes to remain anonymous, he revealed that on three separate occasions, unknown forces entered Azgarén local space and launched surprise attacks on our sector security forces. Until now, Central had been attempting to downplay this in order to prevent any public anxiety, but the most recent assault has forced the issue that public safety is now becoming a serious concern.*
>
> *According to this anonymous source, the first hit involved only a single frigate-class vessel which was very quickly lost due to the fierceness of the attack. The second hit involved a much sturdier mid-class cruiser and dual frigate escort. But this was also lost, and with no apparent damage done to the enemy. Finally, according to this informant, a new attack was launched just recently, this one apparently of a larger assault force, and on this occasion, facing off against the Naal Balai, a heavy-class cruiser which was accompanied by a flotilla of lighter cruisers and frigates. The result of this battle was a total loss of the flotilla, and the Naal Balai gone missing, presumably damaged as it made a retreat, and now lost in space.*
>
> *Central Command has come to the conclusion that the level of technology used in these ships, as well as their apparent effectiveness in battle, leaves our space navy vulnerable to any future attacks.*

Talks are underway between top officials on what course of action to take next, but along the way is a high level of concern over whether Ytani and his followers should launch another attack that might come all the way down here, as well as what sort of measures they might use, as it would seem their effectiveness in these battles made extensive use of this strange Abnormal Energy. What this tells us is these people know what it is, know how to use it, and apparently have a military application available.

This naturally brings us back to the emergency broadcast network and raid siren alert system. According to military sources, this network was originally installed as part of a precautionary procedure in the event Ytani should make any appearances in our native skies. While, at the time, they did not anticipate the severity of his follower forces, it becomes clear now that if they do make another appearance, public safety should be our primary concern. We here at CPComm are committed to keep you informed in case of any emergency to ensure our citizens are made aware of this, and any other requirements to find safety.

In a related article, that new planetary security agency, which so far wishes to remain unnamed, but that once revealed itself as arresting the media regulators, among other things, as part of their investigation of the Council's corruption, has come forward with a new statement.

A spokesperson for the agency, after reviewing these recent reports of the military action in our local space, is concerned for these alien forces and their application of this Abnormal Energy, as it might also reflect on the An'gamu Seeds and the aura effect they give off. She says that if this Energy holds such potential as a military application, and since our world seems to be enveloped in this cloud, as she calls it, generated directly by the Seeds, it may be possible to launch a strike that could trace its way along this cloud, resulting in a feedback effect through that organic network we once heard about linking all these Seeds together. This could then result in an unknown, and potentially harmful response in the Seed, which could therefore translate into the bodies of those who still possess them.

While we do not want to alarm our citizens unnecessarily, this represents a clear and evident danger, one that cannot be ignored, even if it does seem fanciful. Therefore, they strongly urge all citizens still in possession of the Seed to seek out their nearest medical clinic for a special inhibitor drug the ARC has been producing recently as a counteragent in the hopes of preserving the lives of our people. They also tell us at C.P. News that the raid siren network will give instructions, if and when there should be an actual emergency, on when to use this drug as the people are advised to seek shelter from any impending attacks."

"Mom," Auryn asserts. "Latena tells me those other people are getting ready for their final launch. But once all is said and done, the people of this world are going to have their horns spun backwards as we bring all these pieces together into the final story. And for this, I think it's important for our group to be present to offer aid."

"What kind of aid, Auryn?" Marna wonders. "We're not med-techs...well, most of us, that is. And although we've spoken of this in the past, I'm still a little unsure how you expect us to teach a world of nonbelievers about any sort of god or religion."

"Yes, well, regardless of that, Lady Aerlie told me once how we should gather our people together to make an open presentation. The people need to at least see this much to realize there IS a god AND a religion out there, and it's real. Not this nether-wild tail-slapping we got from the Council or whoever was telling us to stop. We'll probably end up going public with it, one way or another, so now is the time for us to come out of hiding."

"All right, if you say so. But we'll need to organize ourselves, and maybe to call in people from the other sects."

"We also need to be sure of that medicine for the seed, in case anyone still has it and gets a hit from it."

"Yes, and then we have that. Our family was lucky to get in early and have it removed, but I know of a lot of others who are on a long waiting list."

"And we should be sure to bring all our new worship items. We want to make this look good."

"Auryn, you are becoming more of a follower than I am. Are you sure of yourself here?"

"Yes, Mom," she smiles sweetly. "I'm signing up for classes on Tae'Eladar soon. I'll be the first new official cleric our people have known since the old days, and I hope one day to teach others."

In the WIC building, Thaelyn and his officers were discussing the most recent series of events.

"So, he is hoping to challenge Ytani himself," he muses. "This might prove interesting, but how would it play out. Kaliya, you will need to improvise rather heavily on this occasion. You cannot be too aggressive, but at the same time you cannot seem too soft as to allow him to push you off your pedestal. Our objective is to see if we can draw Sargeras out of hiding, although how we might accomplish this during your meeting, I cannot say. It might even be inappropriate to demand such a thing for this occasion. Maybe this would need to wait until I have my fated encounter."

"If Ytani is only demanding girls," she responds pensively. "Or maybe I should say tribute, claiming he has a godly right to it, and Darumon is suggesting he needs to demonstrate this right, and do so right in front of him, this is to say he hopes to challenge Ytani to a face-off. One common theme here is to find him and bring him into the open so Darumon can...deal...with him."

"And in this case," Ayene adds. "To deal with is to say to put an end to," she chuckles. "But the trick here is to invoke a final conclusion. Based on what we're seeing in the Marshal, he wants this brought to a close, and I think you're right, it might not be appropriate to involve Sargeras in this discussion, at least not as a direct reference. The Marshal wouldn't want to bring HIM into it if it involves the projection skill."

"This is very true," Thaelyn nods.

"What we have here is Ytani pretending to be a god, and the Marshal, whom we can say is probably as close to a god as we might want to come, is offended. This makes sense to a certain degree, regardless of who the Marshal might be. I think anyone in that position might feel this way."

"This much may also be true."

"Next, Ytani is demanding stuff without a proper destination to deliver it to, which is typical for someone who hasn't a clue over what he's doing. Therefore, godly right or otherwise, if he wants his girls, either he needs to be more specific on where to send them, or else come get them personally. And if the Marshal can get at least this much out of him, he can send a beacon probe to track his location, or maybe a Special Ops team to finish it for him."

"A Special Ops team..." Kailen wonders. "This would assume Ytani's friends don't take notice of the weapons they're carrying. I think that might stand out a bit."

"Yes, it might, but he sounds like he's getting desperate. He's even behaving as if he's genuinely sorry this happened in the first place. Even Geilv took notice of what seemed like a protective attitude in him this last time."

"This almost sounds as if he has feelings, and this is not something I would expect of him. Not after everything else he's done."

"Maybe so, but we do have that one occasion of him speaking about his former society, and then of the male versus female behavior policy. And I feel as though this might actually be genuine. Geilv and the Captain also think this, for Darumon's portrayal in recent times. Then we have our recent observations of him telling us he's not only sulking in that office of his, but he seems to be reminiscing about his old memories, which I suppose makes sense if this is all he has by now. He even went so far once as to say our species has a lot of potential. He seems to hold something personal in us, which may hold merit if he made us for a reason, but he seems reluctant to say any more. And then there was that time when he told the HC how he might not even want to hear these words…from him."

"This would certainly make sense for all the offences he's made. I'm sure a lot of people probably wouldn't want to hear what sort of personal feelings he might have by now."

"And so," Kaliya notes. "This leaves us with the final presentation. Darumon wants to be present at the time, so we need to be sure we get the timing right. So far, I've been trying to maintain a schedule so the people will know when and where Ytani will show up. This means, we can only hope Darumon will be on time."

"I would also like to see about monitoring the situation," Thaelyn asserts, "if and when we do get Sargeras to come outside. I think it would be prudent for us to station a series of surveillance cameras at those locations where he might best be seen. For instance, just outside that sanctuary building of his, and perhaps along the way he might take to exit the city. Ayene, perhaps you could arrange something with CPComm to assist."

"I can certainly do that," she states. "And then what? Should we wire it into our base control room? That place will look like a newsroom before long."

"Quite likely, but we cannot hold back at this time. Information is vital to see these last moments unfold according to a predictable plan."

<hr>

Tae'Eladar was enjoying a weekend break, and while this might normally involve relaxation and entertainment for most people, it was an especially celebratory moment for Kaliya, Ayene, and their military unit. Today would be the official day of inauguration for the Stormhooves.

The ceremony was arranging itself inside the Great Hall of the Order in the guildhall in Bya'an Tamoranth. The room was packed solid with people, mostly Kaliya's troops who needed to be present at the official service. Both the floor and balconies were filled to capacity.

Tucked away in the recesses were Relissa, Marelle, and Haran to watch the show, and just behind them, squeezed into the tight space, were Sulíma and Túfula, and others who held relation, but were not technically part of this military body. Petrith was among those in the gathering, as was Navina, both of whom were enlisted.

Kaliya and Ayene were both in full dress uniform and on the carpet running up to the platform, where Thaelyn and Aerlie stood waiting, along with Kailen on one side and the General on the other. Padriyl Lapäli, who so often loved to film everything for historical purposes, also stood up there with a professional video camera donated by his mother, the Chief Technician at Bahlaie. She was also among the observers on one of the balconies.

Thaelyn raises his hands to draw the attention of the room as he prepares to speak to the assembly.

"We who are gathered here on this occasion are making history in a way never before seen. We have amongst us a people, the likes of which may have never before existed, with such skills and training that were likely never before combined in this way, and who are already developing a reputation that quite possibly has never before been witnessed. We are therefore blessed to have them here among us. We are similarly blessed to be the ones to honor them with these gifts. We are blessed to be the ones to begin them on this long journey. And we are blessed that they honor us with their uniquely inspirational service. It is indeed a proud day for us all, that on this occasion, we give official announcement to their name and their creed, that they will travel far and share this with many more for countless generations to come."

The room rises up in bold applause.

"But while it is one thing to give rise to a new military Order, it is another thing entirely to see it brought literally to life by the efforts of so few, who took it upon themselves to begin on this journey…a journey that required such a profound alteration of their own beliefs as to virtually remake them. And then to see this spread among so many others who came together in this same belief, then to grow, as more were added, until we have the foundation not of a simple military unit, but an army! And what an army this is, for they could easily challenge the gods themselves if they should feel such purpose!" he laughs.

The room joins him as they rise up in a hearty round of laughter.

"For this occasion, we called in a few people to do a little research for us to find the appropriate insignia to serve our needs."

He now turns to a pair of flagbearers standing nearby who were carrying poles with banners rolled up and tied with a ribbon. He waves for them to step forward.

The two men were standing on opposite sides of the platform. They presented themselves forward in military prose and officially set the poles in their mounting bases on the floor.

"Let it be known that on this day, and forevermore, this symbol shall represent the covenant of this new military service, the Order of the Stormhooves!"

A row of trumpeters announces a short tribute, as the two men now untie and remove the ribbons, allowing the banners to unfurl. The banners revealed the official heraldry for the ancient fellowship of the Stormhooves, but now fully restored and with a new purpose in life. The image depicted a sunrise on the bottom, with a symbol like a caduceus staff hovering above it, along with a pair of inverted swords bracketing the sides, with lightning bolts for blades, and at the top was a set of angelic wings floating over the scene.

The room rose up in another rowdy applause, along with whistles and cheers as they all praised the official announcement of the new Order. As the trumpeters finished their revue, Thaelyn brought the room back into order.

"But what is a new military without its commanders?" he begins again. "The Stormhooves bears another unique quality, as this intrepid incarnation was conceived and devised by one young lady who previously held only a faint hope in her heart that one day, she might serve a valued role. Unbeknownst to her, and anyone else for that matter, that role would carry her across worlds and to the far reaches of the realms before she could realize her true purpose. And though it can easily be said she was not alone, she very nearly singlehandedly created this body in principle and philosophy, and from there, she guided so many others to follow her. And along the way, she made her own history…multiple times, I might add," he chuckles.

The room offers up another mild round of laughter and whoops.

"Then came another young lady who challenged the impossible right alongside of her. She too held her desires, and realized her own worth, in the ingenuity and the creativity of her own design. And together they carried this even farther, creating new rules, new practices, and new forms of mischief for our foes. May the Powers help us all," he grins as he glances around at those on the platform.

The room again rises up in a hilarious surge of cackling.

"Captain Kaliya Nazég and Lieutenant Ayene Ti'van, present yourselves forward and be recognized."

Now Kaliya and Ayene begin marching in rhythm to a horn and drum beat in the background. They proceeded along the carpet up to the platform where they halted just in front of the steps. Here they saluted and kneeled.

"I was never personally involved in naval combat," Thaelyn admits. "But this recent demonstration of yours was extraordinary. It was both expertly performed and frightening for the result. To be able to infiltrate AND capture a large naval vessel while in battle-ready condition, with the crew on full alert, and do so without any damage to the ship or harm to the people, is an exquisite piece of tactical maneuvering, and in itself worthy of another commendation award. And we will see to this just as soon as the guild artisans can devise something appropriate. Of course, we should also give proper credit to your cohort, Marelle, for her role in it," he flashes to the side where the visitors were watching. "Her tactics on the outside are also worthy of a special mention, if for no other reason than to match a simple squadron of combat fighters against a fleet of large warships."

Marelle smiled at the mention and waved.

"Meanwhile, the two of you have surely earned a new merit for yourselves, not only for this, but the accumulation of so many other deeds leading us up to where we are with Azgarén and all your work there. And in fact, it would seem your Stormhooves is developing into a hybrid service as both ground forces and naval, which may require us to revise a few of the ranking protocols at some moment."

He turns to a set of attendants and waves at them to come forward. They each held small cases in their hands as they approached the two women. Each man opened his case to reveal a new rank insignia for the officers, and they pulled these out to apply to their lapels.

"From this moment," Thaelyn concludes. "I suspect you will invoke even more mischief for us, as well as others. But the sort of mischief will surely be one for the history books to come, and will likely set new standards to make life even harder for those who would dare try to follow in your footsteps…or perhaps I should say, hoof steps," he grins.

The crowd ushers up a loud chuckle.

"Rise and be recognized, Colonel Kaliya Nazég and Captain Ayene Ti'van."

The two of them stand up with proud smiles and offer another salute, and then they make an about-face to present themselves to the crowd.

+ +✦+ +

The final week was upon Kaliya and her team. This was the one to make or break the Ytani image. She and Ayene were in the WIC building for a final review.

"I want to see his reaction as you make your meeting," Thaelyn asserts. "Therefore, we need Ayene out there with a camera to record the occasion. This can hopefully provide a way to judge how I might approach the later encounter as we call in to Central Command. And we must be sure to have him present in their control booth, which means the Commander needs to issue a general alert, and we will use this to summon up a global alert, which will eventually filter down to our raid sirens."

"And this will trigger our new world panic," Kaliya muses humorously, "where everybody is tripping over each other to first, take their pills, and second, scramble into the nearest shelter."

"Yes, well, this is unfortunate, but essentially outside our control as those pills, above all else, are vitally important."

"But how is this actually going to appear?" Ayene wonders. "We still don't know how you're going to get Sargeras outside."

"I know," he nods. "This is beginning to look like one of those occasions of private knowledge, and there are very few people left to acquire it from by now."

"Wonderful, so we're waiting for some unknown tidbit to come from some unknown source and right at the last second. Wow, talk about nerve-racking."

"Indeed, but we must proceed forward, nevertheless. The prophecies have not led us awry thus far, so we must hold our faith that Adalon, at the very least, is watching and knows what she is talking about."

"Then that just leaves me with the final Ytani showdown," Kaliya considers. "I wonder how I'm going to handle this."

"Just keep an open mind and follow whatever clues you might have available. If nothing else, try to arrange a confrontation with Darumon, and maybe we can go from there."

"Right, well, here I go."

Kaliya and Ayene both get up from the table and offer salutes before retiring to the next room, where they sit down to project their images. After several long moments, they're each on their way to Azgarén where they arrive on the streets in downtown Capitol Prime.

"I'm not going to do my fancy image this time," Kaliya notes. "Ytani is angry by now, so he's just going to flash into view, maybe with only a little special effect."

"Are we going with an angry god image now?" Ayene grins.

"Yeah," she smiles. "Let's see, the swirling firestorm is cute, but maybe if he simply funnels down to the street level. We'll skip the chair, and just have him stand there. It might be more appropriate for when Darumon arrives. Just keep the camera rolling and try to stay clear of any fire and brimstone."

"Oh, thank you!" she smirks.

Ayene moves off to the side where she takes up a casual stand near the corner of a building, mostly out of view of anyone passing by. She takes out her trans-com and begins filming.

Kaliya moves to a secluded alcove where she can't be seen and flashes out of sight. A moment later, the telltale vortex lights up the sky above the street.

Once again, the people and vehicles come to a stop and moan over yet another of Ytani's appearances. Several of them begin shouting at the disturbance, and already a few are calling in to the local law enforcement.

The fiery disc swirls with a thunderous roar, but instead of the typical chair pieces falling out of it, the storm itself begins to funnel down to the ground, striking the street and coalescing into the body of Ytani, who towered above the rest by gigantic proportions. But despite the intimidating size of his image, many people in their hover shuttles began blowing their horns in annoyance of his image blocking traffic and generally causing a local disruption.

"You people down there," he bellows, "are just not behaving like good little minions giving me what I deserve as your god-king! My OTHER minions…well, they are MUCH more obedient. Oh yes! But playing with them just isn't the same as having a cute young lady to toy with. I remember all the fun I had at that base. I'm beginning to wish we still had it now. At least there, I had a captive audience to play with…"

In Central Command, Geilv was on the line with the Marshal.

"Marshal, I just got word from C.P. Security that Ytani has arrived and he's out there making another scene."

"Good! Then I need to get out there right away before he leaves."

"Do you need a vehicle for this?"

"No, Commander, I have my own means…that vanishing in a puff of smoke you once mentioned," he chuckles. "But I shouldn't delay this with idle chatter, so if you will excuse me, I'll be on my way."

"Understood."

They end the link and Geilv makes another call to the Captain to share the word while the Marshal prepares himself.

In his office, Darumon moves away from his desk and draws in his focus of mind. A rippling pattern quickly surrounds his body, and he is soon enveloped in a folding of space from the local environment.

Ayene was on the street with her camera focused on Kaliya's public disturbance, and a resulting backlash of protesters who were accumulating in the vicinity. She was attempting to survey the area, hoping to find evidence of the Marshal arriving, when she began to notice a strange effect appearing just down the way on the street. She turned her camera to focus on it.

Several other people also took notice of the pronounced visual distortion appearing and growing in size in the area. Much of the protesting quickly faded as more people were called to the attention. Even Kaliya's Ytani image, which had gotten into an arguing match with several protesters, also settled as she took notice of the spatial distortion wave forming on the ground.

The wave represented a concentric rippling pattern, like waves on a pond after tossing a stone into it. But it was upright and developing in size to match the proportions of Ytani himself. As it intensified, a body began to emerge to form the giant-sized shape of Darumon.

Many of the people shrieked and rushed away from the scene, pulling back towards the buildings, and ducking around corners and into local shops and lobbies. The Marshal towered above the street much like Ytani did, with his eyes blazing and his voice rumbling.

"Ytani, you little worm!" he roars. "How dare you even suggest yourself to be a god of any kind. You have no idea what it means to carry that title. And I should know, for I serve one!"

Darumon briskly turns and points assertively at the tall black tower in the middle of the city that represented Sargeras's sanctuary building.

"You are nothing more than an insolent little child," he continues, "with delusions brought forth by this skill of yours. In this form, you are merely an apparition, and apparitions do not count as gods, neither are gods counted as apparitions. They are as physical as I am, and as these are down here," he waves his hand at the people below. "And true gods do not demand tribute of any kind. This is a fantasy created by lesser beings with their primitive religions."

"Oh?" he balks. "And what about you, Marshal? Didn't YOU ask for something once upon a time?"

"Indeed I did, but my reasons were different, and they were personal, and I am regretting those actions now, as it has become clear to me that it was a futile effort resulting in a great amount of waste."

Kaliya sensed a sudden dramatic shift in the context of attitude with that statement. She felt a shudder rush through her, but she knew she had to remain stoic in her presentation.

Ayene also felt this alteration as she continued to watch and record the video. She glanced up at Darumon, but his obvious rage at Ytani's errant behavior didn't reveal much more.

"Ytani," he continues. "No true god would demand such as tribute or material wants from their followers, and they certainly would not display such infantile fetishes for female service. In fact, there is absolutely nothing these little creatures have in their possession that a true god would find of value. Any being that might describe itself as a true god can simply alter the fabric of Reality and bring forth what he desires by the will of his mind alone. But as for you, not only have you failed to demonstrate any of the qualities of a true god, you also have not even demonstrated the qualities of someone who would dare pretend as much!"

"Pretend? But didn't you once tell me I was special, and this is why you taught me how to do this?"

"The only thing special about you is that I chose to teach you something I dared not teach anyone else. And being able to perform this does not make you a god. At best, it might grant you certain advantages over the more common forms of life, but gods are a far different breed, Ytani. They have eons of evolution to their advantage. You and your kind are far from that point, despite this newfound power of yours. In my estimation, your civilization would need to travel a good half an epoch before you could even begin to touch the domain of gods, skill or no skill."

"Civilization! Ha! I am UNIQUE! The One, the Only..."

"Ytani!" he resounds harshly. "The only thing you are 'The One' of is an insolent pest. Your entire species has this skill! And I know this to be true because I'm the one responsible for it!"

This silenced Kaliya for a moment. To hear him actually admitting to this fact was unexpected. In her Ytani guise, she pulled back in surprise.

On the ground was a sudden emergence of murmuring and whispers, which collectively began to rise above the street as more people had gathered by now to witness this standoff.

Ayene was similarly shocked at Darumon's apparent change in demeanor on this occasion as she continued to record the scene.

Darumon realized what he did, but since it was already out, it didn't matter as much by now. If Commander Geilv could put it together, so could the rest. And so, he paused briefly to catch his breath and glance around at the streets below. He also cautiously looked over his shoulder in the direction of the large sanctuary building to see if there might be any reaction by Sargeras.

"This ability is present within your entire race," he resumes a little more calmly. "So, you are better described as a mere common individual amongst a society with an accidental feature, and this feature is only now beginning to show itself," he sighs. "The Suppressor chips were simply an attempt to conceal it, as my Master would never permit such a thing as a species like yours developing such a talent as this. I was trying to hide it, for my protection...as well as yours," he glances again briefly at the people below.

"Protection?" Ytani mumbles softly. "And the feedback effect?"

"The chip isn't a perfect solution, so the feedback was necessary to contain the individual's potential to a minimum level in order to keep it hidden."

"Interesting."

"So, Ytani, you are treading on very thin ground here with the REAL gods out there who might take actual offence over you claiming this for yourself. And further, they would not spend the time arguing about it. You have failed to reveal to us where you are hiding to receive this… tribute…of yours, but true gods aren't limited to star cruisers and jump drives. They have the ability to find you no matter what world you are on, in what galaxy, or in what universe. If it represents a valid location within the Seas of Creation, they can find you. And this also includes that famous nether-space your kind finds so fascinating to jest over."

"Nether-space…" Ytani wheezes.

This statement caused an instant rise of oohs and ahs on the street below, as it was still believed by many to be a fantasy used only in their language.

Darumon continues, "And I should know THIS also, because I once tried to hide from them, but this too turned out to be a futile effort."

Kaliya paused in contemplation of his meaning, but this was not the time to react. She still had to maintain her image of bravado.

Darumon takes another moment to glance around at the people below who were gathering on the sidewalks. The area was becoming cluttered with onlookers by this time as people came out of their offices and shops to observe the scene.

"Therefore," he concludes. "If you want anything at all, you will have to come here and take it yourself. This pitiful display you are making is not only annoying, but it also carries no significant value to accomplish your goals. You want tribute? Come and get it, and take it directly out of my hand, if you dare, because for as long as I stand on this world, I will defend it as my territory against such like you. If you want to play god, Ytani, you'll need to push me out first."

"Is that so, Marshal?" he sneers. "All right, you're on. But you'd better tell all these little people to go hide somewhere, because if I'm going to bring my Greatness down here, I'm going to make a little noise along the way, and we'll see what it takes to push you off your pedestal. And while we're on the subject, maybe we should also ask about…your Master!" he jeers. "Does he ever come out to play?"

"I would not even trouble him with such nonsense as you. And I would further caution you, Ytani. If HE should ever discover you with this talent, he WILL be displeased for it. Tribute will no longer be an issue, as I doubt you OR your friends will last long enough to collect it. His kind is known to hold the power to wipe whole civilizations from existence, and simply with a wave of his hand, as any true god can!"

This statement caused an instant gushing of moans and yelps from the crowds below, as the people reacted to the suggestion. Darumon once again glanced at the people on the streets, realizing that even though it had to be said, to lay down a lesson for Ytani, he didn't actually mean to incite a panic reaction.

"And therefore," he resumes. "My reason for protecting these people. Although it would seem this is also becoming futile by now. Too much has occurred in this time, and I think my time is growing short because of it."

Kaliya held her response as she glanced around the scene. Many of the people down below were huddled in tight groups, some of them clutching their interfaces as they still had their chips enabled and were receiving feedback.

"But, Ytani," Darumon finishes. "If you want to be a god, prove yourself against me first. But not as some flimsy image. This nonsense is not what gods are made of. No one will respect a simple projection. You need to be physical, Ytani, and not as some meager band of minions doing your work. A true leader goes out and makes his own name. And if you're still standing from it, then you can present yourself to my Master and see what he has to say about it. And I will see you in whatever afterlife he arranges for you."

The Marshal now pulls back and brings his focus to create another rift to pass through. The people on the ground all stare as the otherworldly phenomenon envelops his body and carries him away.

Kaliya watches as he makes his exit. She briskly glances at the people below before she redirects herself to her Ytani image, again forming the fiery whirlwind and ascending back up to the sky.

Ayene stepped out of the shadows after recording those final moments and simply shook her head.

"In all the nether-space, if this is what it looks like to see gods facing off, I'm glad one of them was only a projection."

✦✦✦✦✦

"Now wait just a moment!" Kailen shouts. "He REGRETS what he did? Cu'Nar's Pity! Did I hear that right?"

"I was standing right in front of him," Kaliya notes. "And although he was burning up at Ytani, his eyes told me he felt the pain of loss inside there. He also apparently feels his time is coming to a close soon, likely for all our sensations and the people growing wise to it by now. And certainly after this meeting and the things said there."

"My Lord," Ayene adds. "How are we going to respond to this? I mean, we have those prophecies, and they apparently tell us there's an ending coming up, but this could change our approach significantly."

"Yes, it could," he admits. "And it becomes even more puzzling for us as to how this approach will be made. I had a number of ideas circling through my mind before this, but I feel as if many of those just got thrown away. I may have no other choice but to play this mostly by ear to feel my way through it."

"Well," Kaliya resumes. "One thing we got out of it is we're going to have to work Sargeras some other way. I don't think Darumon will help us...at least not directly, or without some special influence. And trying to draw Sargeras out by any other means might actually expose the Prodigy Gift, and well... Whoosh..." she waves her hand figuratively. "There goes Azgarén."

"Yes, this would be a problem."

"And at this time, I have no idea what sort of influence Ytani can invoke, or even you, for that matter, to bring him out. So, if we're speaking of personal knowledge coming at the last moment, I hesitate to ask who to look for."

"Very well, but at least we have a date with Darumon, and this is one objective met. Perhaps my approach can find a clue along the way. Meanwhile, we must prepare ourselves."

"I also made that mention of Ytani making noise as a hint to the people that taking shelter during this time would be a highly recommended thing to do. This will hopefully ensure they actually listen and follow instructions."

"Good, and therefore increasing our chances of them taking their medicine and being protected from that feedback effect. Then our plan must be to bring Miss Ur'paran out to the new conservation site for its grand opening and position her to begin recording our show as it unfolds. This will follow with Marelle making one final incursion, but on this occasion, we will not engage anyone or anything. We will simply have her make a showing. However…"

He pauses to wave a finger as he leans back in his chair to consider his thoughts.

"She should not make a fast approach. We need to delay for time here. So, she will make a casual approach, allowing us time for Commander Geilv to respond at Central Command by sounding a local alarm. This will likely bring Darumon's attention to the fact, and along the way I hope they will sound a global military alert. We will then follow with the public alert, and Miss Ur'paran needs to be active to reinforce the notion on her live broadcast."

"And this invokes our world panic," Kaliya nods, "where they rush for the pills, and then the shelters."

"And hope we do not have any major accidents along the way. Marelle's delay will hopefully allow them time for this, and our play must not take too excessively long before that drug runs out on us."

"Yeah, the OTHER problem…"

✦

Another year was at end, and once again the MC was giving his oratory to the graduating class. On this occasion, Haran had finally completed all his courses and stood proudly among the ranks of students awaiting their completion papers. As the ceremony proceeded, his name was called to the front.

"Mage Elder Haran Carronel…"

He steps forward and approaches the dais, offering the traditional salute and kneeling to receive his oath.

"On this day," the MC declares. "You who have come before us do hereby honor us with your devotion. Now, the time has come for you to choose, with final determination, your course to become a member of our brotherhood, the Order of Tyr, fully and completely, and for the duration of your lifetime. How do you plea?"

He perks up and speaks boldly to the assembly.

"As the first of my generation that once held such high hopes to study these lessons in the old academy of Rolsklinde, and for all those who came before, but never truly achieved their dream, and to the honor of my family who supported me in those early years, and my friends, and my elder sister who so often held my hand when I was feeling low,

I plead yay, that I will carry this to a new generation and inspire them to achieve their highest aspirations, as others have done for me."

The congregation ushers up a sturdy applause, along with whistles and cheers, as the MC smiles brightly and turns to Thaelyn for his opinion.

"Very well stated, Haran, I am sure we are all proud of your achievement."

The MC then closes with his traditional statement.

"Then in the eyes of our gods, rise, Brother of the Order, Haran Carronel."

Haran receives his completion record and returns to his former position until the end of the ceremony, reflecting on his time in the academy and already feeling a little nostalgic that it was over, but now to look ahead to greater prospects. As a Mage Elder, he could hold such positions as to decide policy for the Arcane Sciences, research and invent new concepts in the application of magic, whether for civilian or military use, also to teach younger generations, and even to govern the legal aspects of licensing for their citizens. It was a proud accomplishment, but his first duty was a more serious one, and it would be played out on a battlefield.

◆◆◆

Azina was visiting the Director's office for a social call during her break. Business had been building up in recent times, as Kaliya's Ytani showdown came to a climax.

"Ghantil, did you see that last news report with Ytani and the Marshal?"

"Yes, I did. Wow, that was a contest of words."

"Yeah, and since then we're getting a lot of additional people coming in for the inhibitor drug. All those who were resisting before are getting nervous."

"I just hope we're getting full coverage. I'm dreading to see what happens after this when we start taking tally of all those who refused to cooperate with our medical alerts and warnings."

"We can only do so much, I guess," she shrugs. "We've been giving instructions to our medical clinics to stay open during this final event and maintain a good supply of the drug in case we have any last-minute shoppers. They're also stockpiling a lot of emergency pharmaceuticals and calling in all their staff in case we have any emergencies. That, and all the law enforcement services, and I hear many of the military bases will go active once this is done to offer disaster relief services."

"Disaster relief…but on a planetary scale," he muses. "We've never had anything like that before."

"And I hope we never have it again. But this just brings us back to the beginning for the rest of it, like the Council, or lack thereof, meaning we have no true government in this world. And then we have the mayhem that's likely to occur when the world realizes all these little pieces we've been holding back so far, like the Eracyodines and who it was that actually altered them."

"I think that should have been revealed clearly enough with Latena's last interview. We have her statements about hidden conspiracies and shadow authority bodies, the artificial evolution, and someone interfering with our research. And everything is pointing in his direction as the one behind it. Even the Marshal's own statement, which would essentially confirm it. Although I hear some are still afraid to actually commit to the idea for the obvious implications."

"Yeah, it's scary to think of. He created us, and he's the one who's been managing us during all this time. It's not a nice picture. But it's a part of our history now, like it or not."

✦✦✦✦✦

A few days had passed since Kaliya's last Ytani play. The activity level in Rolsklinde was heavy today, as troops were moving to-and-fro while they assembled for deployment.

Thaelyn and his officers were in a final conference in the WIC building, along with a host of others who held special roles for the coming engagement. They each needed to check in before arranging themselves.

"Commander," he begins. "Do we have your Elder Council ready?"

"Yes, Your Lordship," he responds. "I was briefing them earlier. It goes without saying they are stunned that we are arriving on Azgarén after what seems like only a blink of an eye since our activities here."

"Yes," he smiles. "As might be expected for how you traditionally direct your accomplishments. But just wait until they arrive, and no doubt see what work we made in this time."

"Cu'Nar's pity!" he chuckles. "That'll be the end of them. A world in the midst of a planetary revolution, turned upside-down from all our little games, and this is in addition to already being upside-down due to Darumon and all his efforts. I don't think I want to see their horns after that."

"Or what's left of them," Kaliya smirks.

"This also makes me wonder what the world will look like by the time my second child arrives."

"It should be a most interesting moment, Commander," Thaelyn considers. "Along with the stories your first child will have to offer the next."

Thaelyn now turns to his other visitors who were waiting their turn.

"Your Grace," Sehnisavain asserts. "Our people are ready and will join you at the appointed time. Adept Mynae and her team have trained hard and feel they are sufficiently practiced enough to call forth their little play. She tells me that even though it might seem a small thing, she will be contented with her contribution."

"Good, I am pleased. There are many wounds to heal here, some of which run deeper than others. We each have our own to attend, but most importantly is to remember we are a family together."

"Of course, Your Grace, and a better family I cannot imagine for our people," she submits with a bow before departing.

"Priest Malorn, how do you feel today?"

"Perhaps a bit nervous, but overall, at ease with myself for the small role I might offer. All I require is that quick hello. After all, he surely must wonder whatever became of me," he smiles brightly.

"Most likely, he expects those dwarves are what became of you," he grins.

"Perhaps so, and all the more reason to let him know I'm still so much alive!"

"Powers help us. And Haran, you also have your place. When Kaliya is ready to go out, you must bring up the appropriate conditions to allow for her little performance. This actually serves two functions. It provides her with the conditions to demonstrate her new skills, and it also provides cover for our little surprise."

"Right, my Lord, this shouldn't be too difficult."

"And while this part may not be so difficult, your next one will require you to pay very close attention to detail. When Aelwyn goes out, you are her guardian. No doubt, if he should behave as I suspect he will, Sargeras will be none too pleased at her interference."

"And for this, I need to put forth my finest effort. I've been envisioning this for a while now, and I feel I know exactly how to go about it. I also took an extra glyph from the runemancer to help augment my focus."

"Excellent. Next is Marelle, you also have essentially two roles to play. Your first is to make our showing, and this will invoke a world panic that Ytani is coming…again. And this time to presumably make his noise."

"If only they knew it was US making the noise. If you thought they'd have a panic attack before…" she snickers.

"Yes, and especially with you in the pilot's seat," he grins. "Now, you must remember we need time for the alarms to sound and people to find their places. That medicine is the most important. So, make a relaxed approach."

"Got it, only about half speed at mag-2, which would be for stellar travel, and this time without the cloak, so they can see us coming and know where we're heading."

"Correct. But now, once we are on the ground, I will have you form up across their field, likely in front of that control booth window. Do not make any aggressive moves. Simply make it appear as though you are claiming that space out there as part of a presentation. This is where you will call in and announce yourselves, and then mention a call to be received by your so-called superior."

"Which he'll naturally assume to be Ytani, in this case," she muses. "But, Gods' pity, when Kaliya told me about him on that video…" she sighs and shakes her head. "How do you think he'll react when he realizes it's you instead?"

"I have no idea, Marelle, and this concerns me from multiple directions. I was reviewing the recording I made of our conversation during his pull-out after our battle here. His attitude towards me was very severe, same as for the Estelar. If he still carries any of this, I will need to counter it appropriately. But Adalon's prophecies tell us we will see our conclusion, one way or another."

"Right."

"Speaking of which, your other role is with her, as you will be the one to deliver her into the region. Once your play on the field is complete, you will return home and change to the other ship. We will contact you when we are ready."

"Sounds good. I'll be there."

"Now, Relissa," he continues. "I know you were hoping to carry some small role here, but this engagement leaves us with very few possibilities for a ranger. However, I will ask you for one special favor."

"Aye, sounds fair enough," she nods.

"I need you to mark a rune for me. This one is special. I am going to assume Darumon and Sargeras will take up positions just opposite us on the other side of that river. It makes sense if they want the best view down the middle of our playing field. Therefore, I need you to find a way across there to the lower end of those hills and mark a rune in a discreet location. If nothing else, perhaps you can ask one of the foremen to offer you a ride. Part of our attack must be standing right next to him, as this is where we will make our final move."

"Part of it, ay? And who's playing that part?" she raises her brow.

"Aerlie and I must arrive in that location, as we carry a key component, but I can say no more on this. You must simply trust that I have a plan for it. Keep the rune with you. I will call on you to open it for us when the time is right."

"Aye, sure I will," she agrees sullenly.

"Fear not, Child," he soothes. "Despite what you once thought of me for taking this course, I am not one to charge blindly into combat. And you should know this by now. It simply must be done, and curiously, Adalon foresees it, which causes me to wonder who ultimately arranged it. This cannot be an accident or a coincidence."

"Aye, she's a sly one. Well, you know I'll stand by you till the…um, well, maybe I shouldn't say it that way, but you know me."

He smiles at the young elf's quirky manners before continuing.

"Commander, you will take up a role inside the control room, along with the General. We have several operations that need coordinating from there, not the least of which are the signaling measures I wish to employ to direct the attention of our guests into new segments of activity."

"Right, this is interesting," Kailen reflects. "I'm trying to imagine a row of trumpeters announcing the commencement of our activities on a living game board for the amusement of a Primordial and his servant. This should be fun to watch."

"Not only that," the General adds. "But we also have the loudspeaker system we installed that is connected to our com-link and the relay network back home on Tae'Eladar, as well as here."

"Yeah, and I'm still trying to understand why you commissioned the installation of this network around so many cities, and what relation this has with our battle plans."

"Ah, but Commander," Thaelyn croons. "What is a contest without an audience giving praise…the revelry of shouts and applause, and a proud ovation to honor the triumphant?"

"Uh huh… Somehow, I think you're yanking my tail with that one." They take a moment to share a quick laugh at the thought.

"Kaliya and Ayene, I want you to pass the word along to our friends on the other side. We need Miss Ur'paran in position for her special live presentation. She will be the one to document this as part of your local history, and ours as well, I suppose. We will ask the Director and his attentive young assistant, Miss Nur'ten, to attend and act as spokespeople for the new conservation center, at least in the beginning."

"We have a list of people we want to include in this," Kaliya admits. "Latena has expressed an interest to be present, since this will essentially wrap up her political agenda to present the Stormhooves, as well as to introduce you to the people of Azgarén. We expect this will coincide with those final few details to lay out. Also, she tells us she's been doing a bit of research on Tae'Eladar's system of politics, and while she hasn't told us what she has in mind for Azgarén, as there are still a lot of pieces to set down, ours makes a very good example of a functioning system to work from."

"Ah, how nice," he smiles. "Well, I would certainly find it favorable if she would wish to borrow a few ideas from us."

"We also want to bring in Kita to represent the ACI. We'll be going public after this."

"Of course… And then Ayene, I will have you interact with Commander Geilv and his people to help coordinate the alarm bells, and eventually you will join the rest in the news cluster to offer whatever support is needed, at least until we are ready to come out of hiding with these final details. Some of this is likely to be played out ad hoc, so stay alert. I think I would also like someone to serve as a runner, just in case."

"In projected form?" Ayene wonders. "I could assign Navina for this. She's a recognized face for the ACI in case she needs to go up to the Commander for any reason. Ileani knows her, as well."

"Good, and I think it would be wise if we could have the Commander join the news team, perhaps to use their cameras to help him monitor the game field better. Next would be Petrith. On our launch, we must send our alert signal to the people, this time delivering a real alert, not a practice one, and ensuring they understand this is the time to ingest their medicine."

"I'm all set for that," he assures. "We have two recordings programmed into the network, the practice one and an official message. I just need to remember which buttons I assigned those to," he contemplates teasingly.

Thaelyn glares at him uncertainly, and then glances at the General.

"General, watch him closely."

"Absolutely, my Lord," he grins.

"The only other item I can think of at this time would be Adalon and her role. And though I feel she probably understands her role better than most, as I would expect she has pondered her prophetic sight deeply during this time, I suspect her assignment was given by the Maker. So, whatever SHE has in mind will follow behind Adalon's play."

As Kaliya considers these words, she suddenly pulls out her transcom and calls up a data document she kept in there with some of her notes. The others watch as she begins referencing the file.

"The Forgotten One, whose guile intrigued, so many brought to mind; shall meet his match on field of play, with Silver Wings aligned."

"Are we reviewing her prophecies again?" Thaelyn muses.

"I'm asking myself how it might look in the end. We have that one, followed by this other one: Two lost souls will meet at last, the Master and His Slave; hidden tidings are revealed, where the Forgotten One is knave. And finally: The Hooves of Storm will make their name, where Two become as One; He will fall beneath the wings, what chaos he hath done. This tells me Adalon does something, then we have these two lost souls meeting, and I guess the final play, whatever that is."

"With Silver Wings aligned," Ayene offers. "This surely must reference Adalon being on our side, aligned against him and his side. That Master and Slave business is scary to think of, and it tells me someone new shows up. And the Hooves of Storm making their name," she chuckles. "I think you already made a name a few times, but for what you have in mind out there this time, in all the nether-space, what a name!"

Chapter 13

PRELAUNCH

The sun was just peeking over the horizon on Tae'Eladar, as a pair of silver cat-like eyes watched from the crest of a mountain summit. The range overlooked the city of Bya'an Tamoranth, and the eyes belonged to a mature adult silver dragon. He had been lying there all night in deep contemplation, watching for the sunrise that would signify the start of a new day. But unlike any ordinary day, this one would see his mother go out to battle. This might not normally affect him, if it were not for the significance of this particular occasion.

He slowly pulls himself to his feet and retreats down the embankment into a shallow canyon where the large entrance of his lair was found. He enters inside and winds his way down a curved ramp leading into a series of massive chambers, one of which served as their living space.

"The sssun risesss, Mother. The time has come."

"I know, my ssson," she answers soothingly. "You worry for me…"

"It has been… A long time… Sssince you lassst… Went to battle…"

"My dear Ikurin…" she chuckles. "Thisss does not mean… I have forgotten… How to fight…!"

"No… But you have… Never fought… A battle… Sssuch as thisss…"

"Fear not for me… My ssson…" she asserts confidently. "I once created… The Draconicsss… To bring down… Sssuch as they… Should they ssstep… Out of line. And let usss not forget… I am more… Than the sssum of my partsss…" she laughs.

"Indeed, Mother! But jussst as you might teach me... Do not let thisss... Cloud your judgment..."

"Oh!" she balks satirically. "Are you now... Preaching to me...?"

They both share a laugh together at the humorous retort.

"Thisss moment... Has long been coming," he reflects. "Is thisss truly... The lassst...?"

"I have foressseen it. The othersss... Are dessstroyed... Or entombed. He will not... Be permitted... To perssssevere... In his freedom. He will either... Sssubmit... Or join the ressst..."

"As you sssay, Mother," he offers. "Then be ssstrong... Be ssswift... And be sure..."

"Of thisss... You can be certain..." she affirms confidently as she turns to leave. "He will know... What he has wrought..."

The elder dragon lumbers along the cavern, making her way outside onto the surface of the mountain peak. She climbs to the top and spreads her enormous wings, stretching them wide to limber up, after spending so much time cooped up in her lair. She begins flapping, stirring up gale force winds in the process, and leaps into the air, then flies off in the distance towards the Bahlaie Research base.

From the ground, the sight was a rare privilege to see, as Adalon was very seldom observed outside in the skies. Her sedate lifestyle kept her in her chambers most often. There, she would spend long periods in deep thought and contemplation.

She sailed over the land, looking down at the cities and towns reaching off in all directions. The capital city of Bya'an Tamoranth was one of the most glamorous in the kingdom. And then came the green pastures of the nearby countryside and farming communities, soon followed by forests and more mountains. In the distance was the military research center, including several hangers and industrial plants, and the large open space of the landing strips and launch pads.

She circles around to a clear area, leaving ample room for her to land without blasting away any of the local buildings from her wing bursts. She descends while flapping vigorously to slow her speed and coming to rest with only a soft quaking of the ground. She then strolls gently towards an assembly of workers, where a tall scaffold had been erected.

"Adalon!" shouts one of the ground workers. "So good to see you! How do you feel about taking down a Primordial today?"

"I am ready... Jussst show me the way..."

"Right to that! We'd like to set you up with a little something so we can maintain contact with you as we move forward. We designed a special com-link device for you."

"You would ssset... That odd thing... Upon me?" she laughs. "What sssight is thisss... Sssuch a beasssst as I... With sssuch... Ornamentation. What would the othersss... Think of thisss...?"

"I think they might each want one for themselves, after seeing how good it looks on you!" he chuckles.

She laughs boldly at the notion.

"Flattery... Oh, how I love it! Very well... How does it work...?"

"We strap it around you on one side, make it nice and secure, where one end reaches up near your ear, the other down close to your mouth, but off to the side so it won't get in the way. It's voice-activated, turning on as needed when you speak. And the receiver is active fulltime, so you can listen to what's happening around you."

"Excellent. Thisss will afford... What I have to sssay... To be heard... By all..."

She positions herself conveniently to the scaffold and lowers her head within reach of the workers. They attached the device using straps around her horns and spines on one side of her head, making sure it was all tight. By the time they were finished, she looked like a Draconic DJ ready to give a performance.

"All set," the worker calls up to her. "Now we just wait for the time when they call you."

"Waiting is what... I have done... Too much of. I am anxiousss... To sssee thisss through. And then to ressst. Finally, to ressst..."

She moves off to the side of the base and reclines, watching the activity on the ground as she ponders her moment.

Thaelyn and his officers had relocated themselves to the new control room of their command base on Azgarén. Kailen and the General were taking up their positions by the forward console which overlooked the field outside. Professor Cogswoggle stood ready with the Harvester controls for the shield wall and arcanic flow emitters. Petrith was at a rear console which handled the communications. He had an array of monitors on the wall with local news broadcasts and closed-circuit video feeds, along with com-links for all the important players.

Aerlie and Aelwyn waited inside the room, standing off to the side to keep out of the way for now. Relissa and Haran hovered in another corner waiting for their turn, while Ayene and Navina stood nearby watching the people assemble and preparing for their roles. So far, they were still physical, but they had chairs waiting in another area of the base to perform their projection when the time was right. Lady Sehnisavain and her people, along with Priest Malorn, were also standing by and waiting for their special moment.

Kaliya was briefly inspecting her unit inside the staging area, along with a large number of standard Order troops. Several battalions had been arriving and packing themselves tightly inside the staging area down below. The large chamber deep inside the mountain was going to be crowded, at least until the first group was deployed onto the field during their battle play. Monitors were positioned at several locations in the staging area, as well as the observation deck, to display the activities outside to those in attendance.

The Daanen-Aryku Elder Council was just arriving through the gateway node, led by Tyanna and Túfula. Ankhia and her sister, Sulíma, followed close behind, along with several others, as they all headed up to the observation booth. As they proceeded through the building, Sulíma and Túfula were bringing the Council up to date on a few details.

"Grace of the cu'Nar," Elder Girhani praises. "What is all this? Where are we?"

"Inside a mountain," Túfula responds. "We're in the Bintavyan Valley, just west of Capitol Prime. This places us in near proximity, but just far enough away that we hopefully won't cause any serious trouble with the city itself."

"Not cause trouble with the city? It's my understanding we're here to oversee some sort of battle, right?"

"Yes, but the people are innocent in this case. Just like everything else Darumon touched along the way, they're also victims, and maybe more so because they didn't even know of it until recently. Even now, they still don't know the full truth of it."

"Túfu, forgive me, but when you say they're victims, and when I compare this to all our experiences being chased by their military, losing so many people in so many villainous attacks, it's a little hard to believe these…Suuden-Aryku…can be victims of any kind."

"I know, Elder Girhani, and this is our curse…the curse of ALL our people, as we're also Suuden-Aryku. But we developed so much hatred for THEM that we began calling ourselves by another name just to make us seem like a different race entirely. We are a part of this society, but these people don't even know their own history, to say nothing of what Darumon did to them during this time, as he kept so many secrets that not even his custom-made military knows what they were doing out there."

"How do you mean?"

"The first thing you need to understand is we never had a true military body, one that was designed to aggressively go out and hit things. Therefore, we took offence that they now had one, and we were the ones they were hitting. This now makes us think the entire society was converted to monsters, when all we ever saw was a military whose purpose was to go out and hit things, like any true military should."

"Uh oh. All right, I see your point. We misinterpreted what actually happened here because we never did anything like this before. It's our pacifist attitude killing us again, like what Kaliya once said."

"Yeah, and that is probably our worst problem. We've come too far as a civilization to allow ourselves to become someone's victims. And yet, we never evolved the survival instinct…to fight in order to live."

"Got it."

"Second, we left way too soon to realize what Darumon actually wanted from us, that he was now creating a true military to go out and hit something. Therefore, we took it for granted that WE were the ones they wanted to hit, not whatever it was he originally came here for."

"Oops! Right, I see it. Another dull-horn pacifist assumption. We centered the focus on us, rather than whatever was his original intention."

"As for the rest, these people were also clueless, for all his storytelling. For instance, he sends one group to do 'this'…" she gestures figuratively with a hand, "…but classifies it behind a tight security roadblock. No one knows what they did, and no one is allowed to ask questions around here. Then he sends another group to do 'that'…" she gestures with the other hand, "…and classifies that one also, so no one knows what it is. Therefore, the military was sent to do things, and most of them, including the HC on many occasions, never knew what it was. He blasted entire worlds to oblivion, using excuses and false allegations, and they never knew the underlying truth because they had no idea who was on the other side of it. And all of it on the active mode of those chips inside their heads that turn them into mindless drones, so they couldn't question it even if they wanted to."

"Grace of the cu'Nar..." she shudders. "Is that how it played out for them? So, all those attacks..."

"Their Council declared us traitors to their glorious cause," Sulíma asserts. "They never apparently cared for Master Velen's faction, as it was too strange for them, and our leaving home was simply a convenient excuse to villainize us."

"Oh, well isn't that nice. And the warning from the cu'Nar?"

"They never heard of it, or ignored it completely. The so-called pursuit of all knowledge, as promised in the Charter of Laws, was a lie. It only applies to whatever the Council wanted, or maybe we should say what Darumon wanted, to evolve us along certain lines. And Metaphysics was one thing he apparently didn't care for."

"I see. And so, when we left, it simply opened up a channel for him to hunt us as criminals or something?"

"Yeah. Also, he apparently offered them his own form of secrets of the universe as a form of payment in exchange for their support to HIS cause, which he described as a noble effort to return stolen property. So, they were made to believe they were doing a good deed on his behalf."

"You're kidding me! And how do we fit in if we're called criminals?"

"We were apparently leading all of his opponents in a continual surge of attacks on our home space. Therefore, he had to build up this massive military to protect Azgarén. And naturally, whenever he found us, he had to advertise the miraculous discovery, and yet another attempt to destroy us. But we always seemed to escape from him. Oops!" she shrugs sarcastically.

"Oh, thank you, Suli!" she shouts. "That just made my millennium."

"Elder Girhani, Elder Vankkar, and most of all, Master Velen, it became known to us, after a bit of investigation, that our faction was never desirable because it was too esoteric for their taste. Our world culture was centered around the discovery and evaluation of empirical study, not mysticism. So, with respect to Master Velen here, he just wasn't regarded very highly among their ranks. Therefore, he became expendable."

"I recall this," Velen reflects soberly. "They just barely allowed me a seat on the Council after a hard debate over the reasoning for my studies, and all based on those same principles of the discovery of all knowledge, as it was promised in the Charter. But I also recall how we were never granted official recognition in that same Charter, as all the other factions were permitted. It was mostly a probational admission until we could demonstrate something tangible."

"Right, and we made sure the people out there knew about this in our own propaganda campaign, as most of them apparently had no idea this is how their politics was being managed. Then, Darumon showed up, and this was the end for our faction, and any other form of rationality to think with your own head. He has been found to be running our entire society, in one form or another, and probably throughout our full history, as an authoritarian dictatorship. The Charter of Laws was recently discovered to conceal hidden phrases and clauses to allow someone to dictate to the rest of us whatever they wanted the people to have or not have, and the Council was simply a front to defer attention. This was to make it seem we had this wonderfully beneficent government making us all so happy to be alive, when in fact it was actually a lie from the beginning."

"A lie?" Elder Vankkar wheezes. "But Suli, how is it no one ever discovered this earlier?"

"It mostly comes down to that famous spirit of the words, which was a cover for the truth to worship the Council as a god entity. What they say, we do, and we're not allowed to question it, or else we have someone come around to pound that spirit of the words back into us."

"So this is why we have it," Elder Girhani muses softly.

"Also, this all began in the days of King Saakerav, someone we were made to romanticize that he did such a wonderful thing for us that we wouldn't ever question it. HE is the one who wrote the Charter, and we think he was actually Darumon in disguise."

"And this represents more of his propaganda," Túfula huffs. "And this totally blew my romance for our old history. He has no true heritage, either before or after, so it's a mystery who he REALLY was or where he REALLY came from, except to say Darumon. And also, it's said during his reign, the propaganda going along with him focused on what a great thing he was accomplishing on behalf of the world he was conquering by military force…very expensive military force. And then, he walks away from it and leaves us with a radical new form of government that was technically unknown to the world at that time."

"That would actually sound a bit suspicious, I suppose," Elder Vankkar nods.

"Right," Sulíma affirms. "So, the Charter was written in such a way where if you had your horns turned the right way for it, you could probably see it. But dull-horned us, we were all told to believe in the spirit of the words. It's like taking something on faith."

"Yeah," Túfula smirks ironically. "Us, Father, who were never permitted to hold a formal religion, but told to hold faith in the spirit of the words of a Charter that's presumably here to help us. Effectively, this is saying not to bother reading between the lines, just do as you're told."

"Unbelievable!" Elder Vankkar scorns. "And I recall this mention of the spirit of the words so often repeated in our schools, even after we left."

"This also accounts for how Master Velen's faction never got the formal recognition it should've had within the Charter. We were intended to grow and evolve along certain tech trees to serve Darumon. We might see some collateral effects passed down to us, but ultimately it had to lead him on his grand crusade to fight his old enemies. Then, when the cu'Nar came and carried us away, this basically killed the last hope for the faction to hold any credence. From here, it became a forbidden topic."

"Amazing. And also very disappointing for our society that believed in what the Charter was telling us."

"On the positive side, however, some part of it did actually survive, but in secret. So it's not completely dead," she smiles softly.

"All right, that might suggest a small glimmer of hope."

"Meanwhile, the Prodigy Gift became a hot topic soon after we left, but not for anything Master Velen was claiming. They dubbed it a horrible alien parasite thing trying to steal bodies, so they mandated a corrective medical implant in the full population in order to cover it up. This also took away their emotional capacity, it seems."

"A medical implant," he muses. "Is this that thing you mentioned once in my study? But how do you cover something like this with an implant?"

"It apparently interferes with the initial discovery of the Gift. And those early children who all died, were actually killed...murdered by Darumon, along with countless others at random throughout the population to create a world panic. This caused them to take whatever Darumon and his god-entity Council pushed at them, meaning these chips and the biotech seeds as an emergency escape procedure to evacuate the planet at all costs from this alien thing no one could identify."

"Túfu! How does a society of professional scientists allow themselves to fall into such disarray as this?"

"One, no one could MEASURE the Prodigy Gift. When you come from a society that demands everything be measured in numbers, to suddenly find something that does NOT, even though you are ALSO denied a religion or the belief in anything supernatural, suddenly it makes you behave as children frightened by ghost stories."

"Oh great!" he sighs.

"Two, when you have an alien super mind promising the secrets of the universe, and a dictatorship Council everyone places their faith into as a god entity, that society of scientists, which doesn't otherwise do anything UNLESS that god entity tells them to do it, suddenly becomes puppets for whoever controls the show."

"Wonderful…" he moans.

"And finally, three, where you have random deaths occurring in the streets without rhyme or reason, and you simply don't know who will be next. Plus, you have a state-controlled media feeding you all this sensationalism to spur things along. So, you really don't have a true possibility to think for yourself."

"A state-controlled media?"

"Yeah, part of that spirit of the words. He was controlling what our free and open society was listening to during this time with people inside feeding everyone fabricated news."

"Oh really!" he blasts. "So, even if we did have something important to say, it didn't get out?"

"Not unless it served him in some way. Those early deaths were reported for the sensationalism of the death, but not the people realizing what might be occurring to the children along the way. Even if they did discover something, it was buried."

"I swear to you…" he moans and covers his eyes.

"Túfu," Velen wonders. "You mentioned that underground movement of our faction. Did they discover anything new in this time?"

"Not really," she relents. "By this time, Darumon had his chips in their heads, which effectively turned off the Gift. We found out there was a secret study going on, but with no true results. We figure those chips probably left a lasting effect, even after they were turned off, that prevented our society of empirical-minded scientists from rediscovering anything as esoteric as ghosts," she giggles.

"I see, and such a pity, as by this time they could potentially have solved the mystery."

"Assuming that state-controlled media would actually allow it through," Elder Vankkar issues. "Although, by now, if they should ever take any lessons from Kaliya, they'll have more than they can handle for their data set."

"But now, Túfu," Elder Girhani resumes. "What is this place? Did you people build it?"

"Partially," she accedes. "We recruited the aid of some dwarves for most of the digging, since they're so good at it, but a large part was a combined effort of Thaelyn's scientists and our technicians for the new technology we created together, and much of the work outside was a local Suuden'kai workforce we hired."

"What?" she shrieks. "Are you saying we actually got some of them to work for us, after everything else you just said?"

"Yeah, it would seem that no matter how tightly you try to control a society, there are still a few people out there who just don't want to sit on their tails for it," she grins.

"Really!" she chuckles ironically. "Well, I suppose I can't argue with that. All the better, I suppose. Maybe you can actually use this to your advantage over time."

"Yeah, we found a few who were especially useful. One of them is Ileani Ur'paran, a local news reporter. She's been helping us deliver a few pieces of our own propaganda to overcome Darumon's media machine."

"Oh? And how has that been working for you?"

"Oh, Elder Girhani, we have copies of her NEW sensationalism, and you'd be amazed. Let's just see what it looks like when we sit down. We have a local feed waiting for us up there."

"Uh oh, suddenly I feel my horns tingling."

"Túfu," Elder Vankkar begins. "Just how did His Lordship actually find his way here? Can you tell us now that we're standing here?"

"Well," she responds. "You know how Kali brought everyone across to Ruuki uy'Daan, right? Darumon left behind a little trash in the form of some old mini conveyor units he was using to import all those orcs over to Therinë. One of them also pointed at a world called Morndindor, where he once tried using them as an assault wave, but it didn't work. However, he later took that world and had a mining operation over there by the time we arrived, and we found another Prodigy Child who brought us here."

"Really! Now that's interesting! So, even without a proper space industry, he was hopping over worlds until he finally arrived here.

Opadna, I think we're in trouble here. If these people don't even need star cruisers to travel between worlds, where does that leave us?"

"In their dust," Elder Girhani relents. "Unless we can pick up to meet them somehow."

"And along the way, we found another Prodigy Child? Which means we now have two of them working for us…cu'Nar help us for whatever that means," he chuckles.

Sulíma and Túfula both laughed cheekily at the suggestion, since the Elder Council had not been told of the Stormhooves yet. They led them up to the lounge and found a comfortable place to sit, with a view outside and a video monitor displaying the local news broadcast.

"Well, this is certainly comfortable," Elder Vankkar satirizes of the leisurely surroundings. "Will we have a snack plate and drinks with our entertainment?" he jests.

"Actually," Sulíma mentions. "We do have a refreshment bar back there, so if you're thirsty…"

"I was joking…" he looks around.

"I'm not…" she smirks. "After all, I'm told we have investors who helped finance this place, so we designed it to hold some sort of future potential after we finish the battle to liberate our world. And Thaelyn isn't one to squander his resources."

"Investors…" he shakes his head.

"To liberate OUR world?" Elder Girhani muses curiously.

"Yes, OUR world," Sulíma asserts firmly. "Because it's just as much ours as anyone else who holds their ancestral history here."

"Yes Ma'am… Will you also be bucking for my job when this is over?" she grins.

"Um, I'll think about it," she smiles.

As they sat down and peered out the window, they could see a group of trumpeters and drummers assembling on the ground just outside. They had microphones set up to broadcast their music across the field through a loudspeaker system mounted on some of the spires. Aside from that, the field was empty at this time, with everyone taking up hidden positions inside the mountain facility.

The final few people were arriving through the gateway inside the facility and working their way up to the observation lounge. Among these was Vonafel, carrying her trademark obsession of Adalon's prophecy book in her arms. She glanced around at the strange sights as she meandered her way upstairs to the lounge and found a convenient seat to one side where she could see the action through the window.

"All right, Adalon," she mumbles to herself. "I'm here now, just like you asked. What do you have in mind this time?"

In the control room below, Thaelyn and his senior officers surveyed the field quickly and glanced around the room to make a final check before their launch. He nods to Kailen and the General to check their links.

"Specter Prime," Kailen calls into the com-link. "What is your condition?"

Marelle and her team were loaded and ready in their combat squadron and sitting on the tarmac at the BRC. On the field, she could see Adalon waiting and watching. She responds to the call.

"This is Specter Prime; we are on deck and ready."

"Understood, stand by your position..."

"This is General Gabarleine to our temple authority. Are the people assembled?"

"Yes, General," responds the voice on the com-link. "The congregation is ready outside, and we have confirmation from the other major cities and towns that they are similarly prepared."

"Mister Girhani," Thaelyn directs. "How does our feed from the control booth at Central Command look?"

"We replaced the old spy-cam with a live video feed earlier today," he reports. "And the signal looks good for us so far."

"Excellent. Then Ayene, I believe the time is upon us."

He glances out the window at a news van with Ileani and her people setting up their equipment. The Director and Azina were also present, as was Kita from the ACI, and Latena to offer her role when the time was right. The Director also had a number of medical interns on hand to take care of any emergencies relating to the seeds or anything else that might occur out there.

"You should go project yourselves now," Thaelyn directs at the two women. "Ayene, I will have you go out there and inform them that we are ready, and to begin their interview. Corporal Lar'akan, we will have you act as a messenger in case we need to pass any important instructions along the way. Then, Ayene, once the news crew is working, you should go to Central Command and begin our work there. And perhaps you should stay in the area in case we have any special needs arise that we should accommodate."

"Absolutely!" she salutes and leaves the room.

Navina follows behind Ayene as the two of them retire to a separate room for privacy to project themselves.

◆

The Director and Azina were stationed among the group with the news team. Ileani had organized her crew, which included four cameramen, some inside the vehicle operating remote drones, and others outside with cameras and directional microphones to pick up the sounds at distance. The van had established a communications link to their headquarters in the city, and the people at CPComm were preparing for another special live report to occur soon.

"Ghantil, my nerves are jumping."

"Not just yours, Azina. I think many of us are feeling that right now. Just stay close, we'll see it through together."

"You're not the only one, Azina," Latena offers. "But at least, when this is done, you get to go back to a nice calm medical lab and continue whatever work it is you do over there. As for me," she sighs heavily. "I have a world to lead into a new Era. This is enough to cause my horns to go flying halfway across the continent."

"But do you think you will be doing this all alone? Won't you have some kind of help?"

"Oh, I'll have help, all right. But I've become the lead revolutionary bringing us into this new moment of history. That's a big job, and who am I but a recent university graduate. I'm lucky to have support for this point, and some of it with the lessons I need to get things moving in the right direction. But we're so pressed for time to get something working, and meanwhile the rest of our world is teetering on the brink of collapse."

"I don't envy you, Latena. And we haven't even pulled out the final few bits for the public news sensations. That's coming up just as soon as we get going here."

"Some of it has to follow after the Marshal and Sargeras are down," Kita affirms. "This is where I need to step in to finally announce ourselves."

"Yeah, and hit the people with another bombshell or two."

"Yes, well, these things need to come out to finalize where we stand and why we need to make these movements, like with Latena."

A bird soaring overhead spies the group and descends for a landing.

It circles several times, lining itself up to find a convenient perch, and then settles neatly onto one of Azina's horns.

"Hey!" she protests as she tries to duck away. "What is this now? Ghantil!"

"Hold still, Azina," he ushers. "It looks like you've just become a park statue," he grins.

"Oh, thanks. What is it?"

"It's one of those birds, a hawk as they call it."

"Probably another of Relissa's little friends, no doubt she's playing another joke on me."

The bird perches contentedly on the girl's horn, glancing around at the attention being given to it by the people nearby, including the news team.

"Azina," Ileani states cautiously. "That...thing...looks dangerous. Those claws and that beak..."

"It's alright, Miss Ur'paran," the Director reassures. "These are often used as trained assistants to some of our friends. You shouldn't be afraid of them."

"That's right," the bird squawks. "Unless they start talking, then you should be afraid."

The bird follows with a cackle, while Ileani freezes her reaction, unsure how to respond to the notion.

"Oh, wonderful..." Azina mutters. "Ayene, is that you?"

The hawk bends over to peer into the girl's eyes.

"Oh, hey! I didn't recognize you down there."

"Yeah, sure!" she yips. "Get down here! I swear, Ghantil, having a friend like this..."

"Well, this is surely what makes life interesting," he muses. "And even more so for where our lives are undoubtedly heading."

Ayene folds herself to the ground in front of them and reshapes back to her natural form. Ileani simply shakes her head, along with her camera crew.

"I think you people are having too much fun with this thing," she moans. "All right, so what's the plan? Are we getting ready to go live?"

"Yes, we are," Ayene asserts. "All our pieces are in place, so we just need to begin the show, and then I'll flash over to Central Command and start up the action there. Your cues will be when you start hearing the raid sirens."

"Right, and that's when all sanity goes to the nether-realms. So, let's make sure we all have our scripts. Director, you're playing our spokesperson for the conservatory. Miss Kaetaal, you and Latena will hold back until later. Ayene, will you be in this shot at all?"

"I will be, once the Marshal and Sargeras are outside. They shouldn't have access to a news feed at that point, so they won't be able to listen in on the conversation. The Director will announce the conservatory as a project to bring our world into a new Era of restoration, but I'll need to explain what it is we're actually restoring and why. Then we have our game."

"All right."

Ileani turns to her news team and applies an earpiece to listen in on the newsroom announcements. She then takes up her microphone and calls in.

"CPComm, this is Ileani, do you hear me?"

"Yes, Ileani, we're here and waiting for your signal. What's the situation out there?"

"We're ready to go live just as soon as you open us up for it."

"All right, stand by. We're going to a commercial in a moment, and then we'll bring up our special announcement bulletin."

Ayene moves away into the background, as Ileani and her team wait. She then flashes away from the scene to attend to her next duty.

Latena felt a flurry of butterflies rolling around in her stomach by this time as the anticipation built up. She also moved away from the group for a little privacy and pulled out her trans-com to make a call.

"Hello?" ushers a youthful female voice.

"Auryn, we're getting ready out here. Where are you right now?"

"Latena? Oh! We've been gathering up a lot of people here in the downtown civic center. I've been waiting for your call. What's going on so far?"

"We're getting ready for a news flash of the conservation center, and shortly after that, all the nether-space will bust loose on us as the world comes under attack by Ytani again."

"All right, our people are still assembling. We're waiting for a few more hover coaches to arrive from out-of-town, but the last call was they're not too far away. Meanwhile, we have a vid-com on a wall nearby, so we can watch what's happening from here. Then, once we're assembled, we'll get ready to meet you out there."

"All right, but my suggestion is to wait until the fireworks settle a bit before moving again. We don't want any accidents when the feedback thing hits."

"Got it! And then we'll meet you out there to go public with our new movement."

"This should be fun to watch," she chuckles. "I'm ushering in a new Era with a political revolution, and you're bringing in a religious one. Between the two of us, this world isn't going to be the same."

"I don't think it's supposed to be."

◆◆◆◆◆

Around the world on the global news channel, as well as broadcast alerts on other entertainment channels to redirect the public's attention, the news group at CPComm gears up to make an important announcement.

Inside the observation booth, the Daanen'kai Elders, along with their friends and family, watched the local news channel as it wrapped up an intermission. Then a station announcer comes online with a special notice.

> *"We are interrupting our regular programming to bring you a special live World Event presentation, the grand opening of a monumental new conservation center in the Bintavyan Valley, just outside of Capitol Prime, and hosted by our own Ileani Ur'paran."*

The Daanen'kai Elders all glanced at each other incredulously at the apparent influence Thaelyn and his people must've achieved to invoke such a deep integration as to control the local media streams with such a clearly sensational announcement.

Ileani had set herself up with the cameraman and positioning the base in the background.

"Ileani," the set coordinator affirms over her earpiece. "We're going live in three, two, one..."

> *"This is Ileani Ur'paran for C.P. News. Greetings everyone, and welcome to our special broadcast as we introduce this truly extraordinary moment in our world history. Behind me is the recently completed Lajad-Torak Restoration Conservatory, located here in the Bintavyan Valley just outside the grand city of Capitol Prime.*
>
> *This is a special moment for us here at the Conservatory, as this*

project, which was conceived by a cooperative effort between our top experts and science professionals, and made possible with the support of several prominent financial institutions, and many generous donations given by concerned citizens, has been brought into reality as a symbol of our motivation to make right so many of the wrongs we have seen evidenced in recent history.

Not only do we hope to symbolize the restoration of our natural world for all the harm once caused by the old war protocols imposed by the Council, but we also hope to demonstrate a new way to see ourselves and our responsibility over what we own…"

The broadcast was being delivered to vid-coms in homes and office lunchrooms around the world. It was aired on the large display boards in the commercial districts, and inside shopping malls. Anywhere you might find people, they needed this to be displayed in order to achieve maximum visibility.

Ayene had arrived in Commander Geilv's office for her visit to bring his attention to the day's events.

"Commander, we need your participation out there."

Geilv perked up at the sudden announcement. He had been sitting at his desk trying to focus on his work, but not very effectively, as his nerves were tense in anticipation of her arrival. He jumped out of his chair and the two of them rushed to the control booth.

On their arrival, Captain Ta'yeen lurched around when he saw Ayene hurriedly leading the Commander into the room.

"Sir! Are we expecting something today?"

"Ask her, she's the one with the details."

"All right, um, Lieutenant Ti'van? What do we have today?"

"Well, first, Captain," Ayene smiles. "It's now Captain Ti'van. I finally got that long-awaited promotion."

"Really? Well, congratulations. What was the special occasion for it?"

"My role in capturing that heavy cruiser, among other things."

"Uh huh… So, you take down a cruiser and they promote you."

"Well, there were a bunch of other things included, but that certainly tipped the scales for me."

"All right. Congratulations, anyway…I think. But now what?"

"Now, we prepare for battle. How is that team you were training with those weapons?"

"Still alive, I'm glad to say, but as for skill levels, I'm not sure how to rate them."

"Just so long as it looks good. Tell them to follow our example. Some of our people will offer visual clues and demonstrations you can copy from. We need this to look as clean as we can. Beyond that, Ytani is ready for his final show."

"He is..." he glances warily at Geilv. "And do I dare ask what this show will be like?"

"We're not planning anything hostile this time," Ayene offers. "That last conversation with the Marshal surprised us for what words he shared. We're a little unsure what to expect out of him on this occasion, but we need to push forward anyway. So, our goal is to have Ytani appear in our skies, and this will put our military on alert. First, this base, then global, and this will follow with the public raid sirens. We have Ileani out there making a live broadcast, and this will integrate with our show. Our ships will make a slow approach, comparatively speaking, to give time for the people to take their medicine and run for safety."

"All right, I understand. And that medicine...I suppose this also means us here, right?"

"Everybody who still has the seed."

"Yes..." he sighs as he glances at his body. "I'm not so sure I like the idea, but if this is the only way."

"At least until you can schedule having it removed, but the waiting lists are growing huge by now, I think."

"Wonderful, but that's another thing. Commander, do you have anything to say?"

"My only thoughts are to gather up our people on the ground and prepare them with the troop transports. We're going out to the valley, as I recall, right?"

"Yes Sir," Ayene affirms. "There's a news team out there, and we recommend you join with them and use their monitors to oversee the operations."

"Sounds good... Then let's get going."

Ayene turns to face the small ventilation duct over the door.

"My Lord, we are ready here."

She then turns back to the others in the room, where each of them was now peering up into the small space to see what she was talking to.

"In all the nether-space," the Captain groans. "How did you get that thing inside there?"

"The projection skill isn't limited to size or what small space we can squeeze into."

"I swear..." he shakes his head.

In the control room at the base, Thaelyn and his officers received her message over their video feed and went into action.

"Specter Prime," Kailen announces into the com-link. "You are now clear to launch."

"This is Specter Prime, acknowledged."

Marelle called out to her team, and they began lifting off the field at the BRC. She pulled them into formation, where each flight took up a position surrounding her ship in a triangular pattern, and together they took off into the blue. As they reached their jump point, they made ready for their move.

"Spector Squadron, link up," she issues.

Each of the ships link into her main navigation carrier signal and the computer arranges them into a tightly packed formation. She instructs her computer to select Azgarén as its destination, and the group collectively charges up.

"Here we go people," she utters through the com-link.

She hits the jump actuator and the entire assembly flashes out of sight.

✦✦✦✦✦

Ileani continued her interview on the news program.

"With me today is Director Ghantil Bak'vayn of the Ark'ravan Research Center to give us his explanation of this facility and what we hope to learn from it. Director, first of all, you are better described as a medical professional, rather than a conservationist. What can you tell me of the original concept behind this facility?"

"Miss Ur'paran, I have long believed it should be the duty of every citizen to hold themselves responsible for their actions and what we make of our lives and our homes. I was no less pleased by the old Council mandates for the industry that so flagrantly defied the environmental protection laws, but at the same time, I was also appalled by our people for not reacting to this so much earlier. I watched as our world turned from a lush green living body into what we see today. I don't know what it'll take to set things right

again, but we most certainly need to spend every effort to see it done. And now that the people of this world have had their eyes opened to these facts, I think we need to drive it home that we are as much responsible for this, and so many other errors, that we cannot and should not cast blame solely on someone else."

"That someone else being the Council, perhaps?"

"Most certainly the Council, as they are clearly the ones who established those mandates. But even the Council is composed of citizens who, at one time, were just as permissive of this as any other. I don't think it's fair that they alone should take the blame, as this is the home of ALL our people, not just those in the position of decision-making. Therefore, I must hold every one of us accountable, each for our own small part. It is the only fair thing to do."

In the Saakerav base, a signal comes in on one of the consoles.

"Commander!" calls the tactical officer. "We have a jump signature. Sector Sixteen!"

"All right, people, by the book," he notes. "First, do we have any bodies out there, and what kind."

The officer runs a quick scan to pinpoint the site.

"I'm showing a cluster, but they just barely show up on the screen. They must be very small vessels."

"But you're getting blips, not empty space?"

"Yes Sir! And I'm showing them in motion, coming this way at moderate speed."

"I see. All right, Central tells us we are NOT to engage, as we don't want to lose any more ships. This is apparently the work of the ACI, not any repugnant young man named Ytani. Send word down below to tell them we have inbounds."

"Yes Sir."

Again, Ileani continues her interview with the Director.

"And what do you hope to accomplish with this new center? How

do you think this one facility can undo so much harm when so many others have just barely managed to maintain a status quo?"

"In truth, the world as a whole will require more than just what any one facility can provide. But this one will serve as a symbol for a new beginning, where we finally make the connection of our responsibility of who we are as a society. There are qualities within us that need to be recognized, and our place amongst the grander scheme of things needs to be understood that we are not simply bodies that occupy this space, but custodians who hold a place of importance, with minds, manners, expectations, and desires that must be carefully managed such that we do not make mistakes like these again. We cannot! As we clearly hold a potential unlike any other, and this in itself demands careful scrutiny over how we use it and what repercussions we leave in our wake."

In the observation lounge, Elder Vankkar watched the video stream.

"Cu'Nar's pity, who wrote his lines, because that sounds scripted to me."

"Oh Father," Túfula huffs playfully. "Must you always be so cynical?"

"It's a habit, Túfu. It grows on you after a while when you sit in the chair I occupy."

✦ ✦ ◆ ✦ ✦

Inside Central Command, the Captain was on the line with the space dock. When he finished, he turned to Geilv to report, and tried to make the presentation look official.

"Commander Geilv, Saakerav informs us we have inbounds from Sector Sixteen. They believe it could be more of Ytani's forces, and they are heading this way directly."

"Is that so," he roleplays. "Then Ytani is making good on his promise, is he? The Marshal wanted to be present for this occasion, but we also need to put our people on alert. Sound a general alarm, and then call the Marshal to pass the word."

"Yes Sir!" he replies.

The Captain turns and instructs the officers in the room to sound a base alarm while the comms officer calls in to the Marshal.

✦ ✦ ◆ ✦ ✦

The Director continued his statement on the news camera.

> *"In recent times, especially, we have discovered ourselves to hold a unique capacity to influence our environment and the lives of others in such ways that if we cannot hold the responsibility over our own, we certainly cannot qualify ourselves to hold it over anything else. Therefore, it becomes obvious that we must learn to behave like the sophisticated form of life we have always believed ourselves to be. More than that, it must begin at the most fundamental levels, and hold true throughout all other aspects of our lives and livelihoods, and well before we afflict ourselves upon anything else out there."*

"Grace of the cu'Nar, Santari…" Elder Girhani whispers. "Scripted or not, where did he even get it, because that sounds like they must've had some sort of revelation over here."

As Ileani and her team were conducting their interview, the distant sound of a wailing siren began to echo across the fields. She turned to follow it as it rose up from the southeast of her location.

"CPComm," she begins. "I'm hearing a siren out here somewhere. Are we having another drill in the city today?"

"We don't show anything scheduled for today, Ileani. Where do you hear it coming from?"

"I think…let's see. Wait, I think it's coming from Central Command. Do we know what's going on out there?"

"Give us a moment and we'll see if our local correspondent has anything to say."

⟡

Ayene oversaw the initial stages of the alarms going off in Central Command, and the comms officer had called the Marshal's attention to the inbound ships being tracked by the space dock overhead.

"Commander," she submits. "I need to go into hiding for now. I'll stay close to watch, but as far as anyone here is concerned, I don't exist, got it?"

"Yes, Captain," he nods.

She turns to survey the wall above the forward console and places her focus on a tiny point. She then folds her image out of sight to take up occupation as a nondescript spot on the wall.

Geilv and the Captain both watched her flash into a streak aimed at the wall and disappear. They leaned forward to peer closely at the wall, but the spot was virtually imperceptible as it blended with the native colorations.

"I swear to you, Commander," the Captain states flatly. "If they can hide themselves so perfectly in plain sight, it's scary to think of for any sort of spy activity."

"That's probably the point."

On the streets of the city, people were in motion as they walked along between the offices and shopping venues. On occasion, they would pause in front of the large video display boards in the public plazas and on the sides of the tall commercial towers. Others were watching the news from local cafés and inside shopping malls, and some were taking time during a work shift break in a lounge area to catch up on the news and watch the special program being broadcast on the air. But with the announcement of the alarm at Central Command, some of them began to slow their pace to listen more intently.

"Ileani," states the resident anchor at C.P. News. "We're receiving a report from our correspondent at Central Command that the base has just gone on full alert. Apparently, Saakerav Station has detected inbound objects arriving in our local space. They think it could be Ytani again."

With the announcement of that name, the people on the streets all halted suddenly and now turned their full attention at the monitors and large video displays. Shoppers in the malls had stopped their casual browsing and stepped around to the nearest monitor. Patrons at the cafés were setting down their drinks, and the average person who might be watching the broadcast piped in through their trans-com or data tablet also came to an abrupt standstill. Hushed whispering was beginning to well up among many of them as they continued to listen in.

"Oh no, not him again!" Ileani feigns. "Do they think he's following through on his last message?"

"This is the general belief, Ileani," the station anchor admits. "But they're still analyzing it. This group apparently arrived in the outer band and they're making what seems like a casual approach."

"A casual approach…to Azgarén?"

"Yes, but it could be they're simply looking for more ships to harass."

"And what is Central doing about it?"

"As far as we understand it, Central is concerned over losing any more ships to these people, so they're holding back to observe their actions so far."

"But CPComm," her voice surges, "if they're not moving to intercept, what about us down here?"

* * * * *

"What do we have out there?" the Marshal asks urgently as he arrives in the control booth at Central Command.

"We have inbounds from Sector Sixteen," Geilv reports. "The same arrival zone as Ytani's forces have been using. They're coming this way, although only at a moderate rate of speed, it would seem."

"A slow casual approach, is it? He must feel very confident in himself by now. Are we moving any ships to intercept?"

"At this point, I don't want to lose anything else, and he's certainly demonstrated his capacity to take down everything he's come into contact with."

"Then you intend to let him simply have his way with us this time?"

"I'm going on the impression he is coming to make his presentation with you personally, based on your last exchange. We're able to track him this time, which must mean he is not using his cloaks on this occasion."

"Yes, this would stand out. And therefore, the casual approach that is so visible on our scanners. But we shouldn't be too lax, Commander. He also promised to make noise. Take us to a full global alert. We should bring everyone into action in case we find ourselves defending our space."

"Affirmative," he nods.

Geilv now orders the Captain to issue the directive.

* * * * *

"Ileani," the station anchor submits. "We are now receiving additional calls in here. It would seem Central Command has just issued a global military alert. Every military base planet-wide is going active. Central has confirmed that these invaders do seem to be making their way directly for Azgarén."

On the streets of every city, people were now gathering into groups in front of every available video feed they could find. Shoppers in the malls were clustering around the public monitors. People passing by on the sidewalks were being called inside the local cafés, while others were huddling around those watching their tablet devices. The large plazas and their huge display boards were accumulating masses of pedestrians as the news seemed to be making a sudden turn for the worst.

Marelle and her team continued their approach through Azgarén local space. There were no other ships in range, and nothing showing up on the scanners to interfere with them.

"This is Specter Prime, all clear so far. How does it appear on the ground?"

"Specter Prime," Kailen responds. "So far, the military is on full alert, Darumon is watching your approach on their scanners, and we have an indication that the public is quickly becoming restless."

"Understood…those poor people… Just wait till the next step hits them."

"Speaking of which," Thaelyn ushers. "Mister Girhani, if you please, I believe now would be a good time to issue our public alert."

Petrith nods and calls up his emergency broadcast network tap. He orders a prerecorded official alert message, and then submits the order to the network.

In cities all around the world, the raid sirens suddenly fired up. They shrieked with intermitted wails mixed with vocal instructions in a sturdy male voice.

> *"Attention all citizens! This is an emergency. This is not a drill. Hostile forces are advancing into Azgarén local space. All citizens must seek immediate shelter in their nearest designated safety zones. All vehicles must be grounded and removed from the roadways to allow for emergency traffic only. All citizens in possession of the An'gamu Seed are instructed to ingest their medical rations at this time. If you do not have a medical ration, you must seek out the nearest medical facility and obtain one immediately!"*

In the city plazas, shopping malls, and cafés, where the people had paused to observe the large displays and the urgent reports, now panic ensued as they all began dashing around trying to orient on the nearest shelter. In the office buildings, when the raid sirens sounded, and the blaring announcement echoed through the structures, workers jumped out of their seats, grabbed their personal belongings, and scrambled to find an exit.

People fumbled with pockets and handbags looking for their antidote ration, then yanking it out and frantically fidgeting with the wrapper, eventually to stuff the whole thing in their teeth and tug at the broad flat tablet inside. Many would then grab the nearest bottle of water and slam it to their face, splashing half of it across their cheeks as they gagged on the pill trying to swallow it. They wobbled as they choked on the item, reaching out to steady themselves on walls and furniture, then staggering into the frenetic stream of foot traffic.

"Ileani!" the station anchor urges. "The raid sirens have just gone active. We're receiving reports from all major cities that we are on a planetary emergency alert! The announcement says this is not a drill; it's the real thing this time. We have reports of the public fleeing in all directions and taking shelter."

"All right, CPComm," she responds sternly. "We have instructions to stay online as part of the emergency procedure to direct the people. One moment..."

Ileani diverts to find her handbag, which was sitting on a nearby chair. She grabs it and pulls out a data tablet, then calls up a special document. She starts reading it to the camera.

"This message is part of the Planetary Emergency Broadcast Network to all citizens worldwide, with no exceptions. Azgarén is being invaded by forces presumed to be hostile. All citizens are ordered to seek immediate shelter in your nearest available safety zone. All vehicles must come to a rest on the side of the road to prevent accidents and allow for emergency traffic only. In addition, those who are still in possession of the An'gamu Seed are ordered to ingest your medical supplement at this time. The medical community further advises that if you do not have your supplement, you must seek out your nearest clinic to obtain one immediately as a priority. The supplement is deemed necessary for survival in case of an attack that can affect the Seed and that aura effect it creates."

In the observation lounge at the base, the Daanen'kai Elders watched with bated breath as the scene took on a very serious note of urgency.

"Túfu," Elder Vankkar emits nervously. "What are we looking at here? Why is she talking about emergency this and medical that?"

"It gets complicated, Father, so just hold on to your horns, we're in for a ride."

✦

Inside Central Command, the Marshal was still watching the scanners.

"Only about halfway now," he muses. "Either he's simply toying with us, or he wants to draw it out to satisfy his overinflated ego. He probably thinks we're sweating for all the anticipation."

"I wouldn't know, Marshal," Geilv responds discontentedly. "This sort of mentality is completely irrational."

"Absolutely, Commander, but with a military force like his, we can't take anything for granted."

"Agreed, and therefore his promise of making noise. I wonder what sort of noise he has in mind. I would place our security forces on alert, but I suspect if he can take down our larger ships, the smaller ones would not likely last long."

"Unfortunately, I might have to agree. But I suspect we may have one other issue to contend with, and that being his military even if we are able to remove him. If they have an index to our local space, they might try additional raids against us in retaliation of us dispatching their glorious leader."

"If this is the case, we will need to locate their base, and this might then bring us back to the beginning of either tracking or capturing one of their ships."

"Yes," the Marshal accedes. "And for this, we might need to apply some new technology to give us that additional edge. But let us first see what they look like. This could possibly give us a clue for later."

"Speaking of which," the Captain offers. "According to those reports, I got the impression the ships were able to see them, even though they could not track them on their scanners. So, if we can get a visual on them, this cloaking technology of theirs might be better described as a stealth shield. If this is the case, perhaps an image-recognition circuit could work as a countermeasure."

"Good point, Captain, so we will keep this in mind for later. Perhaps our people could put together something like a drone unit with our beacon pod and a magnetic clamp to attach itself to one of their vessels. This would at least provide us with one option. But at the same time, I am still puzzled by something."

"What is that, Marshal?" Geilv asks.

"These minions of his seem rather obedient to follow his orders. However, this now brings something to mind. Prior to this, they only launched minimal raids on us when they clearly could've done much more. If their purpose is to cause any real trouble for us down here, they could've done so in the beginning. Say, for instance, if they wanted more than simply his female tribute. He seemed to hold the opinion that a god could, and perhaps should, hold the right to demand any form of tribute, and for this point I might also include material wealth."

"Maybe."

"These followers apparently hold the power to bring down our ships, but they didn't come here to ransack any ground targets, not even to take his female tribute by force. Even now, if they actually held any true interest in making noise, I think they would be approaching at full throttle, not this lazy attitude. There is something wrong here. So, I need to ask, is Ytani simply toying with us for his own wants, perhaps for the purpose of making his noise? And what about THEM, do they not have any of their own interests down here?"

"This is a curious proposition," he considers as he glances cautiously at the Captain.

"Keep in mind, Commander, he failed on each occasion to give us a proper delivery site. Even if we say he was keeping his location a secret, he could've used a common waypoint for an exchange of some kind. For this point, I am reminded of Morndindor. We all know where that is, and if he originally met these people there, they should be able to find their way back to it. Why not use this as a delivery point if he doesn't want to give out anything else?"

"So, you're suggesting here he just likes to hear himself talk, I suppose…maybe to make these public displays to boost his own ego?"

"This does seem to fit the pattern more than what I'm looking at here on this scanner. He clearly doesn't hold a clue over what a true god should look like."

In Thaelyn's base, he and his officers studied the monitors with their hidden spy-cam feeds.

"My Lord," the General muses. "He's putting it together."

"Yes, General, we can certainly credit him for his guile. If he could be anyone else, I might find it interesting to sit down for a friendly chat about such matters. Unfortunately, I doubt he would desire this as much."

They continued to watch the conversation in the control booth.

"Marshal," the Captain interjects, hoping to defer the interest. "Didn't we hear once he was only a child when he was assigned to that base?"

"Yes, he was, actually. Do you have a suggestion for this point?"

"Well, his behaviors have demonstrated a level of immaturity. What sort of education did he receive over there, if any, and what sort of values do you think he might have as a result? A mature adult, for example, fully educated and possessing adult-level valuations might realize material wants, but his seem much more physical, as a child who likes playing with toys."

"Yes! Good! You have a very interesting point, Captain. But these minions of his?"

"I suppose that part would be highly subjective as to how they define value to begin with, especially if they come from some other universe where you might have a completely different foundation of the concept."

"Perhaps. You know, you may hold a valid point. Not all species find value in the same material resources."

In Thaelyn's control room, they all nodded.

"That was a clever play," he accedes softly as he glances around the room. "Mister Girhani, do we have an estimate for the public retreat into their shelters?"

"By this time," he responds. "I think most of them are inside, and Ileani has been working with her people to continue directing the emergency alert. The interview is on hold for now."

"Very well..." he nods. "Commander, perhaps you can contact Marelle and pass along some of these words to inform her of our observations."

"Absolutely..." he affirms.

✦

Marelle made a steady line towards Azgarén. The planet was now coming into view outside her window. As they made their approach, she began a preload cycle in her jump drive indexer.

"Base, this is Specter Prime, I'm coming into position for a quick orbital mark. I'll use this for later when we bring in the big ship. Then we'll continue down for our little presentation."

"Acknowledged, Specter Prime."

"I'm also thinking about the dear old Marshal. That poor guy, he doesn't think we know how to make noise. So, what if I just pop in for a few flybys. After all, I don't want us to appear as a bunch of liars."

"Um, Marelle, are you sure about that?"

"Oh, come now. After all, how many times have I had to assault a planet? Besides, I want to make good on all that training I got back home."

"Oh great."

Her squadron continued along uninterrupted, until they arrived in a low orbit position. They slowed to a stop, and she hit her indexer to mark her current location.

In the Saakerav Station, they were watching the small fleet of combat vessels making their pit stop.

"Sir," the tactical officer emits. "They came to a halt out there, and I'm detecting a buildup of Abnormal Energy in one of them."

"Can you tell what it's doing?"

"Sir, I don't even know what that stuff is supposed to do, let alone what it's doing now. But the scans show it just released a wave of it around the lead ship, and now it's settling back again. And Sir, the fleet is in motion again, now going down to the planet."

"Then whatever it was, maybe it was related to a transition of some kind…space travel versus planetary movement."

"No idea, Sir."

On the ground, Ileani was in contact with her station trying to monitor the progress of the inbound fleet.

"Ileani," the station anchor issues over the broadcast. "Central is telling us they are now entering the upper atmosphere. They're apparently right above us somewhere and coming down."

She and her team all look up in the sky trying to spot anything flying around up there.

"I don't see anything big, like cruisers. If they arrived way out in the outer band, they had to be using inversion drives, right? I'm no propulsion engineer, but you need something big for that, if I'm not mistaken."

"That's right, Ileani. Our people here are wondering what sort of ships might be capable of both space travel AND planetary travel if they were using inversion drives out there. But our correspondent at Central says they're making a quick descent right now, which has to mean at least supersonic, and you can't do that unless you have some very special propulsion."

"And for that, you need space to carry it, but I don't see anything yet…um…wait a moment, I think I saw a glint up there."

Ileani and the others in the news crew now try to squint at what appeared to be a small cluster of objects emitting occasional flashes of sunlight off their hulls. The group was still at very high altitude and moving fast.

"Yes, up there, get a camera on it," she directs one of her crew. "It's still very far away, but it looks like it's making a series of turns as it's coming down. They look like they might be coming down over the ocean."

She turns to examine one of her monitors for the camera they were aiming at the inbound squadron. They had the camera on maximum zoom, and the image still appeared as small dots.

"What are those things? Did they launch a squadron of combat fighters at us?"

"Ileani," the anchor informs. "Our correspondent at Central has just confirmed with us that the invasion force is a cluster of combat vessels that seem to cross the line between a heavy fighter and small corvette class category."

"Wait a minute! A heavy fighter with an inversion drive?"

"And apparently jump drives, as these are the same ones that jumped into our local space and took down our ships."

"Excuse me!" she shrieks. "How in all the nether-space does a group of fighters, heavy or otherwise, take down a heavy cruiser and an escort flotilla?"

"We don't know, Ileani, but Central also tells us they were using some sort of cloaking technology to block our targeting scans."

"So, let me see if I have this right. Jump drives, inversion drives, a cloak…and all of this in a heavy fighter frame?"

"That's right."

She urgently returns to studying the sight in the sky as it eventually descends below the ridgeline of the mountain in the foreground. The crew now waits for a new sighting as the ships come back into view.

The Director and Azina were both watching from behind the news team when Marelle's squad finally made its appearance coming over the mountains.

"Look, up there!" Azina shouts and points at the odd craft passing overhead.

Ileani aims the cameraman at the sight. In the sky above was a formation of small ships of an unknown, but otherwise gracefully artistic design. They flew directly overhead in the direction of the city.

"CPComm, do you see that? They're heading for the city!"

Inside the observation lounge, the visitors gazed out the window at the clearly foreign craft zipping across the sky above.

"Túfu," Elder Vankkar taps her shoulder urgently. "Who do those belong to?"

"Us..." she responds casually.

"Huh?" he blasts abruptly. "What do you mean us?"

"Well, maybe I should say, His Lordship."

"That's even worse! His society isn't even space capable. I thought they were only Industrial Age."

"Yeah, that's the really cute part of it...they still are. As for space capable, they weren't...until recently."

"Great cu'Nar above!" he shouts. "And they're already capable of building THOSE?!"

"Túfu," Elder Girhani asserts. "I have to agree with that reporter out there. How do you squeeze an inversion drive, to say nothing of a jump drive, in something that tiny?"

"With magic!" she grins and flutters her fingers.

"Oh please...not more of that."

"And why are they heading for the city?" Elder Vankkar wonders.

"Well," Túfula considers. "I don't know the game plan that well, but with Marelle flying lead, anything is possible," she giggles.

"Uh huh...and who is this Marelle?" he eyes her warily.

Marelle led her group over the valley and across another set of hills. Ahead of them now was the large metropolis of Capitol Prime.

"All right, team, let's break formation and have a little sightseeing tour. Try not to hurt anything, and remember not to feed the local wildlife."

The squadron broke up, and each ship veered off in a different direction.

Inside Central Command, they were getting calls from the local security forces.

"We're picking up those ships flying recklessly in-between the skyscrapers downtown!" the voice shouts. "Some of them are zigzagging between the towers while others are making spirals around them! We've got one flying low to the ground along Central Boulevard weaving between the traffic signs and under bridges! Sir, this is intolerable! They're violating every traffic law we have on record!"

"Are there any other vehicles on the road?" Geilv asks.

"Well, no, the emergency condition brought all the normal traffic to a standstill. But still, it's the principle of the thing!"

"At this moment, I wouldn't recommend you try doing anything about it. Those ships are armed and dangerous."

"Yes Sir…" he pauses briefly. "Oh no… Now one of them is playing with the skywalks!" he screeches.

Marelle was flying a wave over the first of the two skywalks, then diving below the second one and pulling into a loop around it before continuing on.

"Oh, I so wanted to do that in real life!" she croons. "I wonder… Do they have that tunnel?"

"Um, Marelle," Kailen moans on the com-link. "Is that really necessary?"

"Hey, like I said, I need to live up to my training."

"Yes, and I recall your flight instructor…or what's left of him."

"Oh, Commander, he's just fine. He's in need of psychiatric therapy, but he's fine!"

She soon sights the main highway leading in from out of town and descending into an underground tunnel system.

"Ooh! There it is!" she squeals.

She makes a quick run for it and spirals into a plunge through the tunnel opening.

In Central Command, the security officer on the com-link is screaming by now.

"In all the nether-space! That one must be insane! It just dove into the Iv'namak Expressway!"

Marelle was using her strafing pad extensively now, zipping left and right around the underground features of pillars and lane partitions as she navigated her way through the long underground passage.

"Ileani," the station anchor announces. "We're receiving word from C.P. Security of the unknown ships playing some sort of game around the city. The reports tell of circling around the buildings, weaving recklessly through the streets, looping around the twin skywalks, and one of them apparently dove inside the Iv'namak Expressway. We haven't heard anything about it yet, but some of us are wondering what sort of lunatic would try flying a ship of that size, and at the speeds they're travelling, through the underground highway system."

"You must be kidding me!" she shouts. "Inside the tunnel?"

"That must be Marelle," Túfula muses softly as she listens to the report. "Only she would try something like that."

Elder Vankkar glared at his daughter incredulously for the statement.

"Just what is it you brought us here for, a liberation battle or a comedy show?"

Marelle finally spies the exit of the underground highway and surges through the opening in a graceful spiral climb before angling back towards Central Command.

"All right, boys and girls," she issues over her com-link. "If we've had enough, we should make our presentation."

The squadron forms up again and takes off in the direction of Central Command. Each Flight circles around from a different side and orients across the tarmac to hover in a stationary position, forming a broad triangle arrangement. Marelle then swings a loop and slides laterally on her strafing control into view ahead of the group. They now faced the window of the control booth and the people inside.

Both Geilv and the Captain glared at the scene outside as the squadron took up a position to occupy the field. But Marelle's entrance left them with a notable impression.

"Lateral strafing action," the Captain muses privately. "That would certainly make them maneuverable. If those things are capable of moving in any of the three-dimensional axes, and using inversion drives, that would blow our security shuttles right out of the sky."

"It also gives us an idea of what they might call making noise," Geilv admits. "Maybe also their value quotient...exhibitionism."

The Captain turns to the console with the scanners and studies the monitors.

"They definitely have inversion fields around them, but..."

He peers closer at one of the monitors and works a camera control for a better image.

"Commander, is it just my eyes, or is there something else here."

Geilv turns to examine the monitor, followed by the Marshal.

"Look here," the Captain points at the monitor. "It's just barely perceptible on the screen, but I think I see some kind of bubble effect around it. Is that the inversion field, or something else?"

The Marshal studies it carefully and glances out the window for reference.

"I don't think that's the inversion field; not if they're stationary. It would barely show up as a faint distortion ripple in a station-keeping mode. No, that's a shield emitter! Those little mongrels have shields on them!"

"That might explain the last attack," Geilv considers. "If we say the Naal Balai actually landed a few hits close enough to strike them, those shields might have simply absorbed the effect."

"They would have to be very sturdy, Commander, but then, for everything else they have in there...blast! And this might also deter us from applying a beacon pod. I doubt it could even get inside there. It would have to represent a shock barrier, not simply an energy barrier, and this means it might represent a virtual wall."

"A wall," the Captain shakes his head. "If a ship can encapsulate itself in something like that, and be so well protected from anything on the outside, it would be nearly indestructible."

"That would represent some remarkable technology," Geilv ponders quietly.

Marelle waited a few moments as she observed them inside the booth. Once they seemed to return their focus on her fleet outside, she began creeping forward to take a lead interaction role. She engaged her com-link to call in.

"Central Command, are you receiving?"

The Marshal lurched over to the com-station to answer.

"This is Marshal Darumon," he growls. "Who are you, that you would come here and raise so much havoc in our space?"

At this time, Marelle decides to see if she could break up the tension a little with her own form of greeting, at least in part as a result of the previous conversation they had shortly before on Darumon's observations.

"We are here in the service of Ytani the Overbearing," she lauds. "Ytani the Misbehaved, Ytani the Ill-tempered...and general all-around bad guy who doesn't play nice with others."

Darumon drew back incredulously at the ridiculous greeting. He turned to peer through the window at the curiously diminutive pilot inside her ship, and although he couldn't see her features through her helmet visor, the greeting itself seemed like a joke. He turned to Geilv, who could only shake his head and shrug, and the Captain who simply stared blankly out the window. He then returned to the com-station and approached it more cautiously.

"How am I supposed to interpret that statement?" he asks. "Are you actually serious, or simply playing me the fool?"

"Well, if you knew him like I do, I think you would probably have to agree."

"Yes! I most certainly would. And what is your purpose here if you regard him in such terms?"

"Oh, that! Ahem… We have come to make mischief and mayhem, to steal candy from children, and to make funny faces at you through the windows. Tremble in fear before us! Har!"

Darumon simply glared at the com-link, subtly shaking his head. He almost felt a tiny mote of humor welling up inside him, and a few hidden chuckles seemed to emerge, but his overall rage was not as easily abated.

"Cute… And what about Ytani himself? I was expecting to see him out there. Did he have a change of heart perhaps, sending you to torment me rather than to demonstrate his grand nature of godhood personally?"

"Ah yes. First of all, I think his piloting skills are not quite as proficient as the rest of us. He was apparently only a civilian, to my understanding."

"Yes, this much I do recall."

"Other than that, he had a prior engagement a while ago that he just couldn't escape from, and this had the unfortunate effect of, shall we say, scattering his attention such that he may be unable to collect himself in the foreseeable future. However, I do carry a message for you…if you're interested."

"Oh, but of course!" he mocks. "I'm always open for a moment of idle prattle. And what sort of message did you wish to deliver?"

"The message is that you'll be receiving a call…any moment now… from a favorite admirer who wants to say Hi. Where it goes from there, well, I have no idea. After all, I'm just a pilot sent on an errand… nothing personal to you or anyone else here."

"Oh! Nothing personal?" he blasts. "You come in, attack our fleets, and it's nothing personal?"

"Technically yes, Marshal," she asserts firmly. "We used nonlethal methods to disable, not destroy. We don't simply blast things without justifiable reason. Making noise, on the other hand…well, that can be fun if it's in the right context, and doesn't otherwise break anything critical."

"The right context?"

"Yes, Marshal, some of us hold certain standards for the context we apply with our actions. But Ytani, if you are so familiar with him, is another thing. If that kid can't even give you an accurate depiction of where to send his trophies, that's not my fault. And yet, I'm not going to break anything on his behalf, either. Although, I will admit, we did need to demonstrate there is a body out there with some capacity. This much was necessary, especially after what we saw you people do to that one world we passed by."

"I see. Yes, that might stand out."

"And we are fairly sure you are responsible, for all of Ytani's ranting."

"Do you wish to lodge a complaint about it now?"

"I think it should be obvious if you consider the loss of life and the environmental damage. But in the absence of actually witnessing it personally, it becomes problematic, if only to base it on the ravings of some kid with too many hormones. He seems to like to tell outrageous stories."

"Yes, I suppose that might cause some concern for his integrity."

"As for the rest, I will emphasize again, we used nonlethal force, keeping your people alive. Material objects can be replaced. Keep this in mind if you should want to repeat the last action, as we MIGHT be watching for another one."

"I see, and I understand. And I suppose I must also admit I regret that action, for the end result it gave. And would this relate to you simply coming in for those limited engagements, and then departing?"

"It would. We had no further interest in anything down here."

"But what about our heavy cruiser?"

"It has been relocated temporarily for safety reasons. That is a fine piece of hardware, Marshal, well worthy to keep in one piece. But Ytani, well, he is a temperamental fellow, you know. We certainly wouldn't want him getting any funny ideas about it."

"Uh huh..."

"But anyway, now that my work is done, I should be off now. Ta-ta, and have a nice day."

Marelle closes the link and backs away to rejoin her group. The people inside the control booth watch as she takes up her previous slot in the formation.

"Specter Squadron, link up," she issues in her local com-link.

The group now links their flight controls to her lead carrier signal and the formation pulls into a tight configuration.

"What are they doing out there?" the Captain wonders openly.

Marelle powers up their collective jump drives and the body begins to glow.

"Sir," the tactical officer emits. "I'm detecting a large build-up of that Abnormal Energy."

"They're jumping," the Marshal muses softly.

"A group jump maneuver?" the Captain winces. "In all the nether-space, that requires some special control features."

In another moment, the collection of alien combat craft flashes out of sight in a large ball of energy, leaving only a rippling effect of the dimensional space closing in behind them.

"I swear to you," the Captain moans. "If we should ever have the opportunity to study that, it could revolutionize our technology."

"Yes, it could, Captain," the Marshal affirms. "And perhaps, at some moment, you might find that opportunity. But you might need to throw out some of that other technology along the way. Now, I'm wondering about that message. If Ytani didn't feel so bold to actually show up here, is he hoping to torment me from elsewhere or…" he trails off. "No, not him… Someone else is here."

Both Geilv and the Captain gaze at him as his eyes seem to drift off into the distance.

Thaelyn and his officers were clustered around the monitors in their own control room at the base. They studied the spy-cam video of Darumon for his reactions as Marelle made her presentation. But now Thaelyn could feel his time was upon him, and he had to move quickly to contain it.

"He is a clever one," he muses, "and quick to realize his environment. He is beginning to realize it is not Ytani who has arrived, and I suspect he is reaching out at this time to identify me in this place. Mister Girhani, we need to press forward. Call us in."

Petrith reached over to the local com-station to engage the link. He opened a channel as an outside call broadcasting to interact with the receiver at Central Command.

"This is Base Zero to Central Command," he announces into the link. "Are you receiving?"

The Marshal was instantly pulled out of his thoughts at the sound of the incoming message. He rolled his eyes uncertainly at the com-station. Geilv and the Captain also turned to examine the com-station for the strange codenames and professional appeal.

The Marshal stepped in closer, seemingly hesitating to answer the call.

"This is Darumon, who am I speaking with?"

"Stand by…"

Now Thaelyn steps in to make his announcement.

"Ah, my dear Marshal Darumon!" he rejoices. "How pleasant it is to hear your voice again. I trust you have been well during this time?"

The Marshal glared at the com-station for the preposterous introduction. He briefly glanced at the other officers next to him, but neither of them held any better knowing than he did.

"This isn't Ytani, is it," he asks tenuously. "Somehow, I doubt it is, not the way he tends to behave."

"Indeed, it is not. But fear not, Marshal, for he, with all of his alleged godliness, met with an appropriate requiem."

"Oh, he did. But this simply leaves me to wonder who YOU are now, further that you apparently knew him…" he stalls in his statement momentarily, "…and for how long you knew him that you might be the one responsible for his supposed requiem."

"You are indeed an opponent worthy of your guile, Marshal. But in answer to your question, at least in a direct sense, I once came to realize his sins, and was made to pass judgment on him. The rest was a function of my people to carry it out. Outside of that, I am one you once met and took only a parting interest in, believing me not to hold any significant capacity to trouble you as you marched your way across Creation in search of your trinkets. Perhaps this might be enough to spur your recollection?"

The Marshal continued to glare at the com-station as he mulled a variety of possibilities. But as the choices narrowed themselves down, he began to feel a cold shiver rush through him.

"Someone I once met…" he mumbles. "I dare not mention any names, as there are a few I would not wish to meet again. Especially for the terminology you are using."

"Perhaps, and yes, I do recall such words mentioned once. But unfortunately, there are those of us who hold certain responsibilities, and dimensional folds notwithstanding, we will see to them. I am Thaelyn, King of Tae'Eladar. Good greetings to you, Marshal, for I have successfully found my way here to this place you once thought to be well outside my reach."

Now the Marshal loses it. That cold shiver he had before suddenly turned into a flood. He stumbled back a step as a shudder rumbled through him, and he began emitting a series of mournful wails.

Geilv and the Captain found themselves passing their glance between the Marshal and the com-station, unsure which of these was the most striking.

"Him?" Geilv wheezes. "But how did HE get here?"

But before an answer could be given, the Marshal begins doubling over and bellowing at the top of his lungs.

"NO!" he cries morbidly and nervously shakes a finger at the com-station. "Not you! Anything but you!"

He then starts throwing a tantrum on the nearby equipment. He pounds both fists into an adjacent console, forcing the operator to jump out of his chair and back away.

Geilv quickly darts his eyes around the room and starts issuing gestures for everyone to vacate the area. He pushes the Captain towards the door and the collected assembly begins hurriedly evacuating the room. He then takes up shelter around the corner of the door frame as the Marshal continues throwing a fit.

Darumon grabbed one of the forward control panels and rips it out of the console. He then hurls it through the window, followed by a chair. He then turns to another console at the rear of the room and tears it out, tossing it across the room at a side window, but hitting the wall instead. And all the while, still wailing as an animal in extreme pain.

"No…No…No…" he bawls.

He finally collapses to the floor, still pounding his fists as he slowly loses his energy to continue fighting, and where his tantrum descends into sobbing.

Thaelyn and his people gazed uncertainly at the monitors with their spy video. The display was shocking and entirely unexpected.

"Gods above, my Lord," the General whispers. "When Kaliya said we may have broken him once before, could it have run so deep?"

"Perhaps it is the accumulation of so many related events. It would surely bear an overwhelming burden after a while."

"Given everything we've ever experienced out of him," Kailen offers. "I would never have expected this, burden or otherwise."

When Darumon's bawling seemed to settle enough, Thaelyn stepped in to interact again.

"Marshal?" he intones cautiously.

Initially, there was no change in his appearance on the screen. He merely continued to pound a fist softly on the floor and moan to himself.

"Oh, my beloved Master," he blubbers. "I tried so hard, but it was simply not meant to be. They've come for us now. It's over."

"Marshal?" Thaelyn tries again. "Are you able to respond?"

"Yes, Celestial, I am here. Where could I possibly go at this point? There is nowhere else left for us."

"What did we just see occur?"

"What just occurred?" he groans. "He comes halfway across Creation to finish what he started, and he asks me what just occurred."

"My apologies, I realize the question may be rhetorical, but the reaction was unexpected."

"Maybe...maybe not..."

Darumon slowly pulls himself off the floor and grabs a nearby chair. He wheels it around to the com-station and hoists himself into it.

"But all things considered," he continues dolefully. "Maybe it's just as well by now. Maybe it's better to see you than anyone else at this moment."

"I, uh...very well, perhaps..."

"I suspect you can see me at this time, am I right?"

"In fact, I can. I will admit I have a small camera located in a hidden recess which gives me a rather tidy view of the room you are in."

"Of course, you and your spies. I still recall your activities in Rolsklinde. And for this, you need access, and for this you need time, and for this, I suspect you have been here for much longer than that last visit by that insolent young man. And for THAT, you also need to KNOW him, which means you need to know about Morndindor. And then, let me see...this might also bring us back to the weapon I was producing there. Do I dare ask what became of it?"

"You may if you wish. You once stated how this knowledge is only for those of the higher echelons, and for this I would most certainly agree. But I happen to know a few in those positions who confided in me a few secrets. They also assisted in providing a Door to a distant gravastar, located somewhere here in this fold as a disposal technique."

"A gravastar! That would certainly do it, although I would hesitate to see the local space afterwards."

"As would I, but they told me the surrounding space was long in a state of decay, so the collateral damage would be minimal."

"Of course, they would certainly never use something that held any current potential. But then we have the story of how you overcame the most obvious hurdle, or did someone amongst them simply provide you with another Door into our local space?"

"Actually, no," he responds enthusiastically. "The Estelar were largely under instruction to keep at distance during this time, which left me with only my own devices. But as you surely observed of us on Therinë, we were not in possession of that level of prestige to accomplish this much."

"Yes! This much I recall. And as I reflect on that last conversation we shared, you placed some emphasis on your current wherewithal, and also how this would most certainly change over time. However, this is not such a great measure of time for a society to make such advances, unless…" he coughs subtly, "…they had a little help. But this would also defy your normal manners; if I understand your kind correctly."

"It would. Our native society must take the natural path to this achievement, but I had to make a few exceptions to this rule for our military in order to find our goals."

"Only a few?" he chuckles weakly. "Combat craft the size of heavy fighters, but with inversion and jump drives, shields and cloaks…let me see. I know you used portals and invisibility cloaks often during your engagement on Therinë, and this could potentially translate into higher forms. And…oh! That shield of yours. I saw it in play inside the city during that encounter with the tanar'ri. That was a rather clever invention."

"Yes, we are rather proud of that one. It is one of the official creations of our military that occurred during our war with that nation of orcs I suspect you deposited once on our soil."

"Yes, I admit, it was during my early investigations of that world. I saw it was accumulating a variety of mismatched species, so I thought I would throw one more into the mix to see what sort of effect it might have. But it would seem it did not really make that much of a difference overall, and certainly not after you arrived."

"Indeed, we did have a number of issues with them over the course of our history, but in the end, they simply made too much of a nuisance of themselves such that we could no longer tolerate it."

"Then tell me if you will. How does your world appear in the present day? Humor me with a little story, will you? I think we both know where this is taking us. But allow me a moment to enjoy that refreshing Challenge of Creation one last time."

Thaelyn and his officers were all studying the monitor during this time. But with Darumon's odd request, they began exchanging glances in nostalgic amusement.

"Why, of course, Marshal. Perhaps a brief story would pass the time nicely. I arrived roughly three-quarters of a millennium ago at the suggestion of another who thought I might find an interesting challenge to bring the world into better harmony with itself. Naturally, as you can probably expect, one such as I, arriving in a place such as that, would carry a few curious permutations."

"Oh, I'm sure it did!" he chuckles. "A Celestial in a Prime world filled with mortals. Assuming you gave them the proper education on these matters, I might expect them to perceive you as nothing less than a messiah!"

Geilv and the Captain were both peering around the door as Darumon carried on his conversation when they took a moment to glance at each other for their impressions of this suggestion.

"In truth," Thaelyn responds. "Many of them did. But it was not my purpose to bring them into worship over my station. I presented myself as a fellow seeking to teach and bring them into a new Era, not for my benefit, but rather for theirs."

"But excuse me, Celestial; did you not say you were their King now?"

"Yes," he chuckles. "As it turned out, one thing led to another, and I found myself ascending a hierarchy of authority and power in that world. As I travelled across the face of Tae'Eladar, I had to put down many wrongdoings and errant authorities. This naturally brought more people to my side until I simply found myself attaining a position of my own authority. It was a long hard battle, but the people of Tae'Eladar have this curious expression that tends to go around."

"An expression," he leans forward as he develops an interest in the topic. "What is this one now?"

"It goes as…by blood or by deed…meaning to say you might come into power either as a blood relation to a previous ruler, say as a King followed by his son, the Prince, or you might come into it by one or more great deeds, and this would elevate you to a position of such honor that the people will follow your example."

"And by your depiction, it would seem you took the 'by deed' approach."

"It does indeed seem that way. In the end, I brought many nations and other detached societies into a single world body. I taught them how to integrate themselves, each with their special qualities, to create a society that not only finds harmonious coexistence, but that also unites their unique character traits to augment the final result."

"How interesting, but this would be a difficult one to manage, at least in the beginning."

"It was, you can be sure of that. But I learned to be very wise with the management of my resources, and this has brought us forward to the present day. Tae'Eladar is currently in an Early Industrial Age, and I have found, on a few occasions, the keen ingenuity of our people has forced me to artificially regulate them somewhat for their own growth rate, as they tend to be so ambitious," he chuckles.

"Really!" he laughs. "And so, you are able to create such as these combat vessels we saw out here."

"I will admit we had a bit of influence from the Daanen-Aryku for this much. They provided us with some of their space travel technology, and between the two of us, we combined a few elements of this and that to create a rather curious example."

"Curious is certainly a word for it. But now, how did you find your way out here, especially if the Estelar were not involved?"

"For this, we need to reflect back on Therinë a moment. After you left, I found myself occupied with a large rebuilding effort. The city of Rolsklinde was a total loss, but as I believe I mentioned once before, I had my spies up there giving me enough detail that we knew something was liable to happen, so we arranged a citywide evacuation. On Tae'Eladar, our prosperity allowed us to offer a lot of emergency aid, and we used this to carry us until we could reestablish a few local amenities."

"This would have given you an excellent boost to get started."

"Oh, it did. But as I am sure you probably already know, the Naarg uy'Sodrad was a wreck. Their propulsion and navigations systems were a complete loss, so there would not be any possibility to use that."

"Yes, and this is where I expected you to be limited to that world."

"And with good reason, too…except for a small element of luck that happened our way. Among Velen's people was a young lady who exhibited a most curious Gift, one I would not expect to find in a mortal creature, and certainly not one from such a young breed as these Suuden-Aryku are thought to be."

"Uh huh…and I think I can already see where this is going. Are we speaking of his famous Prodigy Gift here?"

"We are, and this particular individual was born on Ruuki uy'Daan, the world that came just before Therinë."

"This is interesting, but then, how did you use it?"

"First, she required some training…"

At this mention, Geilv quickly flashed a stare at the Captain.

"Training?" he whispers. "Are THEY the ones training everyone?"

"If they're some sort of godlike society," the Captain returns softly. "They might certainly qualify."

"Of course," Thaelyn continues, "simply training her for the Prodigy Gift is one thing. But if our goal involved travel to Ruuki uy'Daan, at least as a means to settle our issues with those orcs, she needed a means to bring the rest of us across. For this, she also trained our Arcane Sciences rather extensively."

"Ah…" the Marshal croons. "So, you finally managed to teach them what magic is about. This must've been fun; they tend to be so rigid in their train of thought."

"Yes," he chuckles. "Her initial impression of it was that of a primitive form of mysticism. But we quickly corrected that with a few demonstrations. She actually became quite good at it, after a while. Then she equipped herself with some custom apparatus and marked a portal rune for us on Ruuki uy'Daan."

"Clever. And so now you have access. But so far, this is only Ruuki uy'Daan. It is not here on Azgarén."

"Indeed, but you are probably forgetting those mini conveyors you left behind, one of which led us to Morndindor."

"Oh blast!" he slaps his head. "But of course! And there we have our link. So, you hop from one world to another using your portals, and not until after you arrive here do you bother with anything like spacecraft."

"Incredible!" the Captain croons as he steps back inside the room. "Am I interpreting this correctly that these portals function perhaps like a conveyor?"

"Yes, Captain," the Marshal accedes. "This would be the equivalent if using that Abnormal Energy your people are so fascinated with recently. You don't need to fight over the principles and limitations of physics, as the mind simply interprets how you want to use it, and there you are. And you can accomplish this much earlier in life. If they have this at only their Industrial Age, this can give you an idea of how a society in that environment might evolve, and it does not follow your example."

"I recall those flying animals of theirs," Geilv submits as he joins the conversation. "They were used as mounts of some kind, but our scans showed them using some sort of envelope that allowed them to travel supersonic."

"Supersonic!" the Captain wheezes.

"Indeed," Thaelyn issues through the com-link. "And the principle is a junior version of a spatial inversion drive, so we simply adapted it accordingly."

"Unbelievable! Are you the ones behind so many of our recent news sensations?"

"We are. The ACI is our creation. We arrived here a few years ago, about a year prior to the Marshal's visit to the mining base, which we owned at that time. We had our own crew impersonating the base staff and feeding just enough detail to turn you away from that world, thereby liberating those unfortunate people who now need to struggle in a deteriorating environment, although we are working on correcting that now."

"And now you are here," the Marshal surmises. "That is quite a trek, and with some very difficult obstacles to overcome. Eh, one final piece. From Morndindor to here, did you use the conveyor we had in that base? If you arrived so much earlier, it could not have been through the Ghan'aju, and the conveyor would bring you directly inside here."

"This is true, but we found another Prodigy Child in that base, so we used her much like the first one to give us access."

"Ingenious, I must admit," he tosses his hands up. "To travel across worlds in such a manner is a privilege for some. These people do not yet know what this Gift is, but I suspect they will learn soon enough. And at this time, I suspect, for all that you have apparently done here, you must have realized many side follies along the way. The Eracyodines, for instance…I suspect that one would tend to stand out, if you ever had such opportunity to hear the story."

"Yes, this one stood out rather quickly to us, and when combined with these Gifts, this clearly hinted at an external element getting involved. You once used such a mention with me and mine if I recall."

"Oh, that…yes… Excuse me, but I was under a lot of stress at that moment, and your arrival didn't help matters. That, combined with the sorts of attitudes my kind tends to carry, and well…"

"Very well, Marshal, I will excuse you for this. We are two very different breeds, you and I."

"Indeed! Perhaps now I could grace you with a little story of my own."

"But of course! What do you have to offer?"

"Ours is…was…" he sighs, "an ancient society, Celestial. We are what we might call a precursor society to your Estelar. I'm a younger member amongst my kind, but I recall stories handed down by those who were much older. There was a time when we once presided over the Seas of Creation as its governors. It is said we fought a long hard battle against many competitors to reach our position of authority. And finally, as we ascended into that divine station, we found one final obstacle, our own precursor."

"So, yours is not the first, in this regard."

"It would seem that way. And it also makes me wonder how many more there could have been. We came into power by deposing those who came before us, so this could be a cycle amongst such beings as ourselves. Be aware, Celestial, as you may one day find a younger one coming up from behind you to take your place one day."

"Very well, I will take this under advisement and share these words with others."

"We maintained our station for many long epochs. In those early times, we were fascinated to observe the younger species, those that showed promise, and occasionally culturing them for the experience, even the pleasure, of developing elaborate societies with fascinating qualities. But here we come to our longest standing problem. On one side, we might find some of them simply fail for one reason or another. It could be war; it could be natural causes. Life, as an element, tends to ebb and flow…never-ending. But on the other side, we were very covetous of our station. It meant a great deal to us to hold such a prestigious position of authority. And we certainly would not want any new competitors to come along and steal it away from us."

"I can most certainly understand this. And I am sure yours would not be the only example."

"Indeed. Therefore, even though we might find fascination in this thing we call the Challenge of Creation, to observe and study younger forms of life evolving up that same ladder, we could not allow them to eventually compete with us. We regarded it to be as much a sin to forfeit our position as it might be to simply put them down for the rivalry aspect. One way or another, it would come to this, with the only stipulation being the time for them to develop into a comparable body to challenge our own."

"And here we now have what the Estelar so often objected to, once they did find their way up there. From their perspective, they apparently found you…denying…those younger forms the privilege to evolve. But we must surely take this into context as a society that once held this covetous perspective of a sole occupancy."

"Yes. I once held a conversation with the Commander here on this topic," he glances over his shoulder at the two officers. "And then, after so long a time, our glorious civilization began to decline. Over the course of so many epochs, life became very mundane and tedious for some. Watching one eon after another passing, it leaves you with a diminishing sense of ambition after a while. All those younger species you once found so much interest in no longer held such value…you have seen so many of them by now. And this was further compounded by that rivalry aspect. The continual need to safeguard against it. It was as perpetual as the element of life itself."

"Yes, I believe I can see the direction here. If you are a society that cannot coexist with another at the same level, this might become something of a trap for you, backing you into a corner from which you must fight each and every other example that emerges out there."

"Exactly. And we did. But with so many, it became tedious to the point where the simple fascination of life was lost to us. Our existence became virtually mechanical to cull anything that might offer a threat. And even our attitudes reflected the lack of dignity we once held. Ours was a very aristocratic society, and ruled by a privileged few. But that aristocracy, as you can probably guess, brings its own burdens, as they who hold such a position can become rather, um…pompous."

"It can most certainly follow this way. Oh, I can tell you a few stories about certain rulers we once had on Tae'Eladar."

"I'm sure you can!" he smiles. "By comparison, my kind is a servant body, custom grown to serve our masters. We hold them very high, and we must be very subservient to them. I am not against this, and I do love my master very much. But as I reflect on the stories I once heard from the elder members, I would sometimes try to imagine how it once was for us."

"I think this is quite reasonable. That bit of nostalgia, maybe even some romance. Am I right?"

"Yes, it would seem we all carry a small piece of this," he chuckles softly. "No matter how high you climb, you might still feel for the early days. But eventually, we come back to our decline. And due to this… somewhere, somehow, the first of them came. It was likely outside our supervision, as I am sure there were gaps opening up by this time, but a young society finally succeeded in emerging. I recall reports that would sometimes echo along our pathways of knowledge where someone new had appeared, and this new society was now opposing us for our beliefs and social culture. This is where those of us who remained began to vanish in earnest, as your Estelar were now hunting us."

"I once shared a bit of old history with a few of my contacts to fill in some of these pieces. After we found you on Therinë, and Velen's people told us their story of your arrival here, I needed to understand these old stories more fully. The Estelar generally do not wish to talk about it much by now, as it represents a painful and unpleasant memory."

"Painful? Hmm, maybe. Would this relate to your famous Measure of Balance? All life is regarded as precious. Yes, I suppose I can see it, although it is bittersweet as we were on the wrong side of it."

"It would certainly seem that way. Especially if you consider the games you played in those later moments."

"Yes, and then there was that. But they came much later. As I said, I am a younger member, and during my lifetime, all I saw was the decline of our empire. My Master is also a younger member of that society; once born, I believe, in that fold where your home is found… what it once was before the Rending."

"Indeed!"

"It was a stale fold. Ancient and decaying. A rather depressing place to live, but it was all we had by that time."

"A stale fold?" Geilv wonders as he listens in.

"Yes, Commander," Darumon responds as he glances over his shoulder. "This is to say, a universe that is so old, everything is dying. You might only have the last remaining red dwarf stars still shining by that time, and little else to look at."

"Incredible. That would be a rather dismal place to call home."

"It was the last bastion of our former empire, and we were the last of our kind living there, hoping to escape from these newcomers… Hoping they would simply leave us be in that place."

"But it seems this is not what happened, correct?"

"Indeed, you are right. When the Estelar found us in that place, here is where they found us performing what they would likely describe to be the worst of our offenses. Our boredom, combined with our aristocratic pomposity, and further influenced by this extreme measure of time diminishing our senses and respect for life, rivalry or otherwise, drove those who remained to find any kind of entertainment they could imagine. And in a stale Fold, where there is nothing else of interest to look at, we had to create our own."

"This would surely offer an explanation," Thaelyn accedes.

"This was made worse, as our need to entertain ourselves simply prompted us to create contenders in a game to compete one against another. After all, we regarded them as nothing more than creations, like laboratory specimens, and not deserving of an independent existence. They did not evolve into it. They were a product."

"Yes, I can see this perspective. Some might suggest this would incite a controversy simply for the ethics of creating life and labeling it as something less than that."

"It could, I suppose. Look at the An'gamu Seed as one example. It might not hold an independent form of cognition, but it is also regarded as a simple product of science. But ultimately, once they found us, we knew our time was at an end. Just as we once overthrew those who came before, yours finally did the same to us."

"And this generally brings us to where we stand now?"

"Yes, but with one small exception. Neither I nor my Master was willing to accept this at the time. We didn't want to see the last of us fall, but at the same time, it WAS the last of us. We were a dying breed, and this in itself was already depressing to some. How would you feel if your final days were upon you, and not only for you, but all of your kind the same?"

"I suppose I would not be at all pleased over it. The memories, the nostalgia, the stories told by those who might still recall brighter days…"

"Precisely!" he nods. "And that fold was not a place we wanted to be buried in. It was effort enough for us to breathe renewed life into even a handful of worlds, but it was also a vain effort at reliving some of our past glories. And here is where your beloved Estelar came down on us like a plague for it."

"Indeed, and this is what we refer to as the final Celestial War."

"Yes, although I personally wouldn't call it much of a war. You clearly held the upper hand, from what I recall. But I didn't want to fall victim to that. It was too abrupt an ending to too dreary a life.

And my Master, well, he felt the same, but much like all the others, he was simply offended that someone might finally be coming for us. It represented the closing of another chapter, the end of one generation and the beginning of another, and we didn't want it to be ours."

"I believe I can understand. You desired life, but your life, in this case, was rather limited."

"Yes," he sighs. "Thaelyn, I once promised my Master I would struggle until the end of time, if I had to, so I could bring him back from the edge. I had hoped, maybe…just maybe…I could reverse the process. Maybe this would not be the end of our moment. But it is clear to me now that all I did was to delay the inevitable. The younger ones have won…again."

In the command base, Thaelyn and his officers watched the video feed and listened to the words, and they each felt a certain sense of melancholy for the moment.

"Marshal, by your statements, do I hear the equivalent of a surrender in all this?"

"My kind does not tend to use titles, Thaelyn. I am simply Darumon, a most faithful servant to my beloved Master, Sargeras. As for a surrender, yes," he hangs his head. "I realize now it was a futile effort to bring us back. Even if I were successful in any part of my plans, what would it bring, but more like you to see it finished. The events that occurred near that city…I believe you call it Sigil…it was a clear enough indication that not only do they know we exist, but we are so insignificant in their eyes that they would not even bother coming out here to finish us personally. I recall words spoken…solitary iteration. This is how they feel about us. So, with respect to you, it would seem you are the only one to take up this goal, and that's a little disconcerting for one like me."

"I understand your meaning, but before we go too far with that statement, I should admit to something. Those words you mention were to keep you from trying anything new, which at this point might include another attempt, and also to simply run away to another hiding place. I will admit, there are those who might think you are not worth pursuing, if only to consider it is simply the two of you, and here in this barren fold. But on the other side of it, we were concerned you might try escaping again, which we did not want."

"While that may be true, I don't think there is any place else for us to run. We chose this hole in Creation as an escape where they might not even take notice of us. Even if we were to go elsewhere, we would only find more of you, and even worse, we would stand out that much more prominently. Furthermore, now that they are aware of us, I suspect we have one or more of their apparition pools watching us by now, and they would simply track our movements from here."

"Apparition pools?" the Captain wonders.

"You can associate these with surveillance cameras," Darumon responds. "But on the scale of gods that can peer into any space, in any universe, and follow you wherever you go."

"Oh wow, now there's a concept."

"They do not exist in such a fold as this. They make their homes in what we most often describe as the Fifth Fold, and this is much higher than where we are now, even beyond your nether-space, which is the Fourth Fold to us. So, peering down into a common three-dimensional space like this is as easy as for you to observe a drawing on a sheet of paper."

"And there goes what little sense of security I had remaining," he moans.

"But Darumon," Thaelyn asserts. "I must now ask where we go from here. Because, with respect now to you, if your ambitions are to create such as the Agent of Unmaking and potentially threaten the rest of Creation with it, we certainly cannot have any more of that."

"Oh, indeed," he passes around the room. "I'm sure there are a lot of things you can't, and won't, have any more of where I'm concerned. Just pick any world I visited, and you have part of your answer. Even this one, as your kind would certainly not permit such levels of tampering as what I did here."

"While this may be true, I might offer a subtle mention that they are indeed a rather noteworthy creation, if you do so like to dabble in such things."

"Do you think so?" he perks up. "They do hold a few fascinating qualities," he glances at Geilv and the Captain. "I was never the one to actually create anything myself. It was always they like my Master who chose the pattern for a new species. My method, on this occasion, without the dynamistic flows to assist me, was rather crude. But the result seems to be developing a few features that could carry it into a new station one day."

"The Prodigy Gift, for instance?"

"Yes! As much as it might disturb me that they have it at all, I will also admit, from the perspective of creating something, this is one Gift to be respectful of."

He pauses to look into the eyes of both Geilv and the Captain. The two of them briefly exchanged glances, and then returned to Darumon.

"My children..." he mumbles. "They may not like their Father, but it cannot be denied any longer. And my role in all this was atrocious."

He closes his eyes and hangs his head again.

"Thaelyn," he resumes. "Our time is over. It was over an epoch ago, and I just didn't want to admit to it at the time. But now I must. I feel my time is close at hand, and so is my Master, and you must be the cause of it. How do you plan to reconcile this matter? I am sitting here, and you could've very easily brought me down by now, probably on many occasions, even as far back as Therinë. Why haven't you?"

"We had to follow a careful path to arrive here and to ensure what we found along the way. We also have all these people and the turmoil they had to live under. With or without my ability to deal with you and Sargeras, I must also consider them, and whatever repercussions might fall their way."

"Yes, naturally. They would quickly fall into chaos in my absence, for all I have done here. Speaking of which, what will you do with them after this is done?"

"That largely depends on the choices to be made as they begin to realize their history, their present day, and what sort of future they might have ahead of them. It is difficult to say how this will unfold at this time."

"Yes, perhaps, but if you understand any part of their heritage, and these Gifts they are realizing, and whatever else they might carry, perhaps you could offer some guidance. This is your way, after all, and they will likely need it."

"Indeed, Darumon, as I did on Therinë and Morndindor, and even on Ruuki uy'Daan with what remained of those orcs, if they would accept it from me, I will offer it. As for you and Sargeras, well, we had originally planned a little treat to see if we could entice him outside."

"A treat? How does a Celestial define such a thing as a treat to one like him?"

"In the form of a game, just like the old days. If this is what brought you any form of pleasure, surely, he might find it worthy to come out of hiding for us."

"But a game, like a contest?" he balks. "I would think your kind would find this offensive, to say the least."

"We would, but I am not actually speaking of one involving bloodletting. More like a tournament match."

"Ah! So, you set up two sides for a good show, but not a Deathmatch, as we once did. I see it now. And where would this take place?"

"Are you aware of the Bintavyan Valley just west of your location?"

"So close?" he shouts. "In all Creation, you are indeed brazen!" he laughs boldly. "And yes, I recall some sort of construction project out there recently. Incredible! Did you build an arena of some sort?"

"In a manner of speaking..."

"Yes, of course!" he smiles tenderly. "But here is where we have a problem, Thaelyn. While I may admit we are at the end of our time, I cannot consciously commit any deed that would intentionally bring harm to my beloved Master. My kind is not made that way. Each of us is a custom creation for the sole purpose of serving our individual master, and very subserviently."

"I believe I can understand this part. Therefore, you are prohibited from performing any deed that could invoke harm. And this is not by a simple rule, but rather by your nature, correct?"

"Yes."

"This is a rather curious scenario, to see a custom race created for such a purpose. But then, if we are speaking of a society like what you mentioned, it might actually fall into place better for the stratified nature of it."

"It would. And our loyalty is absolute. Each of us was slightly different in form, but we all shared one common lineage of dedication to our masters. Therefore, if you are hoping I will go in there to bring him out, I cannot do this. All I can do at this point would be...oh..." he reflects thoughtfully. "Perhaps if to give a statement...in theory."

"A statement in theory..." he muses. "This is interesting. How might this statement appear...in theory?"

"In theory, yes... These games were most often arranged between such like my Master...his kind. In the absence of that, his loyal servant might come to him with the proposal, perhaps on behalf of another, and offer this to him as a glorious gift to his most beloved Master, to please him with the entertainment of the spectator sport he so enjoys."

"How does one like this servant approach one such as Sargeras?

I presume you have some manner of protocol you employ for these occasions?"

"Oh yes," he affirms. "As I said, we love our Masters, and we are very servile in their presence. I hold the ability to alter my form, and I generally approach him in a factor that is somewhat diminutive of his own. We speak verbally, just as we are here. This is actually my... um..." he glances uncertainly at the two officers in the room. "This is my native language we are using here. It became a habit after a while for us to use this with our creations to simplify our interactions down to a common standard."

"So, we don't even have our own language?" the Captain winces.

"Captain," Thaelyn interjects. "I would not criticize this as much. A language, by itself, should not be a cause to decry any derogatory statements. I might even suggest just the opposite, for this point, as we have in our possession a tiny piece of a forgotten moment in history. This might be just as much cause to feel ourselves unique."

"All right, I suppose I can accept that. Thank you."

"That was actually a very kind statement," Darumon offers. "I thank you as well. If it means anything, they do have their own written form, but the spoken form is the same."

"A written form. Would this relate to that ancient rift frame we found on Tae'Eladar leading to the Outer Planes?"

"Ah, did you discover a lost artifact?" he chuckles softly. "Yes, I do believe I left a few inscriptions there to help identify the work. That would be an example of our written form."

"How interesting..." Thaelyn muses thoughtfully as he glances around at his officers. "But now, as for this...theory...of yours, allow me to ask you this. Would such a being as Sargeras be able to tell the difference between your natural body and, oh, let us say something along the lines of a metaphysical manifestation, such as what we might see in the Prodigy Gift."

"This is a truly interesting question...in theory. My form is anchored in corporeality, with a sizable portion of ethereal composite, and in some ways similar to your Celestial bodies."

"Indeed, this much I believe I can understand, though if you can also change this form, it must carry a fair amount of configurability."

"It does! But as opposed to his which is entirely ethereal. Although his current manifestation is quasi-material to persist in this domain. But if it appears in the form of his favorite servant, I doubt he would take notice, especially as he would never expect to see such a young species as these with such a Gift as this…they simply aren't made that way, you know."

"This much I can certainly attest to," he chuckles softly.

"Therefore, I feel as though one could possibly go up to him in this form and make this interaction, and he would simply accept it as if it were the original."

"I see…"

In the command base, Kaliya and Kailen glared at each other, along with Navina, Aerlie and Aelwyn.

"Cu'Nar's pity," Kaliya whispers. "And here we have our personal knowledge."

"And from the LAST place I would expect it to come from," Kailen mutters softly.

"I would go even farther. This is beyond the last place, if such a thing can exist."

"Darumon," Thaelyn resumes. "Given this, I feel I should ask one final question. What might be your next course of action once we are finished here?"

"I suppose my next action will be to attend to my Master's needs… whatever those needs might be, until I can no longer give my service to him. If, for instance, he should take an interest in a new game for some odd reason, my next duty would be to see about our contestants, perhaps to arrange them in this lovely new arena we recently built for the occasion."

"Yes, perhaps so. Darumon, this conversation was a truly fascinating one, and not only for the storytelling and the knowledge we shared. I must say it has opened my eyes to a precious bit of old history, some new perspectives on old interpretations, and a meeting of minds that come from very different generations. But as I must now focus on my duties, I feel I should be on my way. Perhaps we might find an occasion to see each other again for some light entertainment."

"Indeed, Thaelyn, and I thank you for the polite banter. I would find it most curious to see what sort of show you might have to put on, if it should interest you to do so."

He ends the link.

Darumon sat there at the com-station for several moments in deep contemplation. Geilv and the Captain moved back a step to give him room, should he desire to get up and leave, but all he did was stare out the window. Then, gradually he began to rise up and leaned on the console a moment longer as he tried to pull together the last of his resolve. He gazed at the com-station in front of him, then at the adjacent consoles around him, slowly panning his gaze at the rest of the control booth and the destruction he had wrought. He sighed sullenly before turning to face the two men in the room.

Geilv waited for his reaction after the lengthy conversation he shared on the com-link. But when Darumon did not respond immediately, he felt he should attempt to initiate an exchange of some kind.

"Marshal?" he asks calmly. "Do you have any instructions?"

"Marshal…" he reflects solemnly. "Let us do away with the false imagery. I am no marshal, Commander."

"Should I simply address you as Darumon, then?"

"It is my name…why not?" he shrugs. "Commander, you heard it as much as I did. It would appear as though we may receive a challenge to a game. The question is how well you will play, maybe also if you will play at all. But this would be the answer to your people's miseries, to finally be rid of us."

"Darumon, I am uncertain how to respond to that under these conditions."

"Oh? Let us do away with your false imagery, as well. I suspect you know full well who they are, and were conspiring with them during this time. But oh, do not mind me. You have grown up now. Surely, you can make a few of your own decisions."

"In truth, I was not expecting to see him again. I only knew of an agency calling itself Azgarén Central Intelligence that came into service recently, claiming it held relations with some outside body. This is that planetary security agency you may have heard of in a few recent news broadcasts."

"Is it now! How very clever of them…and very efficient too. This now causes me to reflect on this long series of news sensations…" he chuckles ironically as he scans the room again. "So many, so sudden, as if someone came along and pried your eyes open to see what the world has become after all these fabrications kept you so…um…" he trails off as he considers the word he might use here.

"Domesticated?" Geilv offers.

Darumon jerked up to meet his eyes again, frowning as if that word might seem offensive by now. He briskly glances around the room again before continuing.

"Commander, I would wish to share a few of my personal thoughts, if I may."

Geilv studied him, but Darumon did not appear his usual self by now.

"What thoughts are those?"

In the control room of Thaelyn's command base, the group continued to watch the video as this new sequence took place.

"I was never made to be a father," Darumon admits. "My kind is not intended for that purpose. Recall what I said before. Each of us is a custom creation for our individual masters. We are not an evolved species with a life of our own. Further is that we are linked to them. Their existence becomes our existence. We might hold many roles, but in the late stage of our empire, and within my lifetime, I served just one primary purpose, to train our creations for a form of entertainment sport. He and his kind would create a species, perhaps like yours, but in this case better designed for physical combat, and mine would train and condition them for battle. To take a personal interest in them was generally forbidden, and they would not likely survive that long anyway."

"Would this reflect on that one statement you made about being conditioned not to hold feelings of any kind?"

"It would," he nods.

He glances around the wrecked control booth again before continuing.

"Except for all of this, I suppose. I do seem to have a temper."

"So I've noticed," he chuckles gently. "And so have most of our ground crew outside your office window."

"Yes, and you should see the inside by now. Anyway, as I said there," he directs to the com-station again. "I once promised my Master that I would struggle until the end of time to bring him back. I must be entirely subservient to him. This is my sole reason to exist. And at this moment, it is really the only thing left for us…simple survival. But survival in an environment where everything is trying to destroy you is not a friendly place to be. Especially if they are so determined to see it through to a complete and final end."

"And here is where you spoke of hoping to rejuvenate your society. That long eternity of time tearing you down from your former prestige, none of which you ever personally experienced."

"Yes, Commander. It was a vain hope, but it was all I had. Even if I were successful in finding freedom for our people… Even if I were successful in liberating our remainder population... Even if I could...somehow...share my discoveries, my perspectives, the hindsight interpretations of our failures...would any of them listen? Or were they too far depraved for it by now."

"But even so, I think you would again have that trap you spoke of."

"Yes. The eternity of time tearing us down again. Ours was a society that could not tolerate competition. We did not wish to share our position with anyone else. So, even if I could bring us back somehow, no doubt it would simply fall back into ruin, as it did before. Someone else would rise up, and here we go again. But in this case, as we are no longer such a widespread society, and therefore to govern so much of Creation out there, that new rival would likely come into it much sooner."

He pauses to glance outside the window.

"Commander," he continues. "You must understand this. When I first came here and found your early ancestors, those Eracyodines, I saw nothing more than raw materials. I had a plan, within reason, but I needed a species to assist me. Therefore, I used yours, elevating them to a level of sentience that I could shape to serve my needs."

"How did you actually do this?" the Captain wonders.

"Without the dynamistic flows to aid me, I was left with nothing more than my own body. As unpleasant as it might sound, I had to mate with them."

"To mate with them..." he winces. "You can do this with an entirely different species?"

"I can, although it is also forbidden. My body carries a rather unique ability to serve as a universal platform to interact with many other forms of organic life...animal grade, you know...so long as they hold a minimum station of evolutionary achievement. But to hybridize myself with anything else is severely repulsive to our kind, especially our masters. They would take great offence to it. Nevertheless, it is all I had. I knew this would cause a few complications, and it would seem those are coming forward now. And yet, while on one side I was unsettled by this, as my Master would never permit such a thing, a small part of me was also fascinated by it, maybe even a little bit...fulfilled."

"Fulfilled... Interesting. Is this to say we actually please you, as a creation?"

"A creation..." he ponders briefly. "My kind is not intended to create something. This is not part of our role to play. But unlike all the others, where my Master and his kind were the ones doing the work, this one was mine. It became personal. I did this, and it carried a different feel for me. I had become a father, in a literal sense of the word. But again, this is not a role for us to play. We are not conditioned for it. Just the opposite…when you consider everything else. We are not permitted to feel for our creations, and we are not permitted to become attached to them. But in the absence of my Master governing the occasion, I allowed myself to finally feel that which we were denied all this time. I became personally attached. I experienced that ancient romance of our kind, the Challenge of Creation. To observe that young race struggling to rise up. It was my dream come true."

The Commander and Captain Ta'yeen both watched Darumon's face pucker softly.

"Captain," he continues. "I was never a father before this, but here I am. And you, Commander, demonstrated your strength to me that day you finally stood up to challenge me. You…your people…" he sighs. "Even if you did have outside help to open your eyes, and I suppose at this time it might be necessary, but once you began moving in that direction, you showed your truer value as a warrior race, whether you might realize it or not."

"A warrior race," Geilv wonders. "But we're not really a militaristic society."

"Not all wars are fought on a battlefield, Commander. There are many other challenges out there, and to fight them is to grow in strength, whether it be physical or intellectual. Clearly, your society is not engineered the same as ours. Yours is better to take a polite, maybe a more cooperative approach. Although, I would still caution you, warrior or not, you do need to ensure your position above any who would try tearing you down."

"Of course."

Ayene was still portraying a spot on the wall to oversee the interactions in the room, but when Darumon began his dialog, she listened closely, and now felt a need to show herself. She folded her image from the wall to the floor and returned to her natural form.

As she came into view, both the Commander and the Captain jerked at the sudden arrival. Darumon didn't feel it, neither did he see it, as he was turned away from it, but as he studied their reactions, he turned around to find her. He squinted at her image projection and raised a hand to it as if trying to examine its integrity.

"So, a few of you have actually begun to train it, have you?" he smiles gently.

"Yes, Darumon," she replies. "I'm the one he found on Morndindor. I'm working for His Lordship these days, part of that ACI body, so he's already helping us learn. But I can't believe what I'm hearing now!"

"Perhaps not, and maybe I'm the last person you would want to hear it from. But you are my children, like it or not, and you have turned out to be a fine creation."

"But excuse me, how do you define your actions where the Tav'ageen Anomaly is concerned?"

"Yes, that..." he turns away and shakes his head. "I knew there would be complications, but that one... By the love of the Master, that was unexpected!" he chuckles. "I was fascinated that such a thing would even be possible in such a young species as yours. But here we have a serious concern, and it relates to my Master again."

"That vulgarity of the hybridization?" Ayene muses.

"Yes, very good," he nods. "My sole reason to exist must be to serve him. It was necessary, and ultimately inevitable for me to rescue him from his hibernation. I worked long and hard to develop your society to aid me, and this held value, at least where my work was concerned. But you were also my children. And by this time, I had become lost in that devotion. But my duty to my Master had to come first, and I knew he would never permit such a thing as this to continue. I had to bring him out, but I could not allow him to see this. Therefore, I had to hide it, and further to turn you away from it, to discourage you from any further study. He could not see THAT, either. It would mean the end of you as a species."

"I see. And this is what some of us were speculating on recently."

"A few had to be sacrificed to preserve the many. But I will have you know," he waves a finger. "I did not take pleasure in it. And yet, my duty to my Master was still paramount to me. He was ill from so long a time in hibernation. And in this fold, he could not survive for long without something to sustain him. And I dared not travel far outside and risk myself along the way."

"You said your existence is based on his?"

"Yes, and if his fails, mine also fails."

"Oops! So, we have that survival issue again."

"And then we have Elder Nazég. He was right to study this in his faction, although in this fold, he would find himself handicapped for the lack of the flows. Still, for as much as I needed to hide these Gifts of yours from my Master, I needed HIM to stop revealing them."

"And um, what about that long pursuit?"

"And then we had that, and I must once again defer to my Master. I needed an excuse to pursue my goals, and those goals had to bring you to that place where I could take my own action. That vain hope of restoring our former society…if such a thing could even be possible by now. You did not know where to travel, and neither did you hold the practice along the way. And I could not…directly…inform you."

"Would this also relate to your reference once that we are already a very mature society, maybe borderline to Sargeras's tolerance level, and you hesitated in teaching us anything new?"

"It would! But it would seem moot by now."

He again pauses to glance back outside at the field.

"We built a world out there. We raised it up from the dust and created a marvelous civilization together. At this moment, your reach spans this galaxy and even more. But this is only the beginning for you. You can do much more than that. That other universe can teach you things you will not find here. And that…Abnormal Space…nether-space, the Fourth Fold, call it what you will, now that you know of it, you might find yourself spending a lot of time out there," he smiles compassionately. "And the Gifts you are discovering will carry you even farther. But they are potent, so be careful with them."

"Oh, absolutely! You can be sure of that!"

"As for the maturity, for all of your achievements in science and technology, you are still lacking one important piece, and this relates to the dynamistic flows. Learn that, and you will be complete as a species to rival the best. From there, I cannot be sure where you will travel, but this one universe is only the beginning for you."

"And you?"

"I feel my own end coming…very soon now. Something big, something ancient…and also, very curiously, something familiar, but I can't be sure what it is. It's hiding itself from me."

Ayene gazes at him inquisitively, and quickly flashes at Geilv.

Darumon sighs again and looks Geilv in the eyes.

"I know my crimes, Commander. I freely admit to them, and I do regret so many of them now. It would seem our time is truly at an end. There is nowhere else to run, and they have finally come for us. But while I may admit to this, my Master is another thing. He is not privy to these affairs, and I suspect, much like all the rest, he is too deeply mired in our old traditions. He was born into it, after all. It is all he ever knew. Be aware of him, Commander. His focus may be drawn to the game, but do not make yourself a direct target in his eyes."

"I will take your words under advisement," he nods. "But what about this game. How does it work?"

"I suspect he is offering us a last gasp before oblivion finally takes us. In the old days, it was a gladiatorial match. Whole armies would face each other on a battlefield, often custom made to offer strategic challenges and chokepoints. The victor would earn the praise of his peers for all our work. The loser...well, let us not speak of that here. If you want to learn more about it, maybe you can ask that Celestial."

"And we're expected to do this now?" the Captain emits.

"My interpretation is he wants my Master exposed and probably away from the city to prevent any collateral damage. I doubt my Master would allow himself to go down so easily...or cleanly. But he will expect you to perform admirably, so make a good show of it. At least give him this much...if this is to be the last time for us."

"I suppose, although I'm a little concerned about the whole idea, especially if this other person is the one setting it up. This leaves us with something of a disadvantage in knowing how these things are played."

Darumon ponders the situation briefly, and turns to Ayene again.

"It's alright," she offers. "We'll help them through as best we can. Our team has a few ideas they're toying with, but ultimately, we have to win the fight."

"Naturally. The only thing after that is the future of your race. They might wish to claim you for themselves, or perhaps attempt to recondition you for another purpose. I find it unlikely they would simply walk away after all this. You are too fine a prize to ignore."

"You make us seem almost like a trophy."

"I do not wish to demean you, but in some ways, maybe you are. Simply look at yourself in a mirror, and you will understand my meaning. A species like yours would not exist for half an epoch at best, and yet here you are...very young, but with qualities that could easily place you on a much higher pedestal. Dare I say it, but you could perhaps compete with the Celestials themselves, if not for your youth and inexperience."

"What do you know about them," the Captain asks, "and these Estelar, for that matter?"

"In my time trying to study them, I have learned they tend to nurture younger species. Their stand on these matters is very different from ours. They hold a belief that young species like yours will one day grow and mature into higher forms. This concept is offensive to our kind, as we held a much more solitary decree of authority, but that is another matter. You should ignore this coming from me, as this is also moot now. Instead, if you should hold the power to survive beyond this… and if you have any such interest within you…" he gazes longingly into their eyes, "…make your Father proud."

His face now puckers more determinedly as he turns and shuffles out of the room, but then abruptly halts partway through the hall and turns back again.

"Commander, I must attend to my Master now, just in case he hears any mention of a game out there. And from this moment, at least within his eyes, I must become indifferent to you again."

"I understand."

He turns around again and departs from the building.

Ayene peered around the door at him as he left. Once he was out of sight, she rolled back around the wall and glared at the two men.

"I swear to you," she urges nervously. "I sincerely swear… I would NEVER, in my LIFE, have expected to hear THAT come out."

"You're not the only one," Geilv relents. "And I have at least as much a reason not to want to hear it, and yet, now I feel lost in my personal thoughts for it. But now, what are we to do next?"

"I don't know…"

She steps out into the room and stares up at the ventilation duct.

"My Lord, I need advice over here. Maybe you could send Navina with a message."

Both Geilv and the Captain stepped further inside to again glance up at the duct.

"Just out of curiosity," the Captain muses cautiously. "How long has that been in there?"

"Years, Captain, ever since Morndindor."

"That's a bad sign for our side that we didn't take notice in this time."

"Why would you even expect such a thing?" she shrugs.

In the control room at the base, Thaelyn and his people were similarly in awe at the speech just presented by Darumon.

"Yes, Ayene," Thaelyn muses quietly. "I must agree with you. That was unexpected."

He turns to the other members in the room to gauge their expressions.

"I will not enjoy this moment," he submits openly. "This provides us with that final piece of the puzzle for his recent manners. He is remorseful over his deeds and feels empathy for what he created. Although, he is also torn between that and his responsibility to Sargeras."

"Responsibility," Kaliya muses. "And that old conditioning, which is probably causing conflicts with his other feelings."

"His conditioning... His hindsight of their decline, with their manners and attitudes along the way, and what it did to them... That trap, as he calls it, and his vain hope to bring back those better days. Powers behold, that is a heavy burden to carry."

Thaelyn pauses in contemplation of the sequence just played out. He then glanced around at the company of people in the room with him.

"Mister Girhani, I hope we have a recording of that dialog."

"Absolutely," he responds confidently. "Everything here is being recorded."

"Good. I currently have several thoughts on my mind. Our conversation should be shared with others, and in particular I would wish to submit this to Torm and the other Estelar. A piece of old history to fill their libraries on how it all began, and further as a warning for that trap. If it happened to the Primordials, it could possibly happen to others."

"I agree," Aerlie nods. "This must surely be passed around so they might know of it. If the eternity of time can do this to one, it can do this to others. Although, granted, the Estelar do not carry this same rivalrous attitude, but still..."

"Indeed. And then we have this other part. That missive is simply too valuable to hold back, and I feel it should be shared with the masses. These are the parting words of a Father to his Children, and I would be remiss in any role I might play for my own if I did not allow them to see this. They must see this, as they must know his inner thoughts, even if he could not express them openly."

"So," Petrith considers. "You want to publish this, maybe with Ileani out there?"

"Yes, but not yet. We still have our more immediate demands. Instead, save a copy of it on a chip and keep it ready. When we are finished here, we will give a special review."

He next turns to find Navina.

"Corporal Lar'akan," he begins again. "I need you to go over there and pass a message for me. If we can use a projection as our agent to interact with Sargeras, I will have Ayene do it. Her presence in that room would likely give us the best result for imitating his image. She will need to portray the humble servant offering a fine piece of tribute to her most beloved Master in the form of a game, and ask him to find his own way out, thereby to meet the real Darumon along the way."

"Yeah, good luck with that," Navina winces.

"And when you are finished, go out there to our friends and give a private briefing to let them know what just happened. If we are to give our presentation, we should do so appropriately."

"Got it. All right, give me a moment."

She salutes and quickly flashes out of sight.

Thaelyn now turns to Kaliya, and saw her eyes were becoming moist, if only a little bit. He lays a hand on her arm, and the other one on Kailen's.

"Strength, my friends, Fate must play its role. I think it is out of our hands now. He knows what is coming for him. He can sense it, so it must be true. Commander, check on Marelle for us to ensure she is ready. Kaliya, I will have you check on your troops, and also pass this message along to them. I want them to know about this. Relissa, perhaps you could be of use in sharing it with Lady Sehnisavain out there, and our other participants. Let us go lightly on him if we can. There is no sense in adding insult to injury here."

"Aye, will do," she nods eagerly.

"We will commence our formal activities once Ayene is finished and joins the news team out there."

Chapter 14

STRATAGEM

In the various shelters where the people were hiding from the raid sirens, many of them were watching the local vid-coms that were installed to assist in monitoring the events outside. The crowds huddled together, and quiet murmuring resonated amongst them as they tried to comfort each other in the face of the crisis occurring around them. Many were frightened and experiencing feedback from their chips, as they listened intently to the continuation of the news report.

"Ileani," the station anchor announces on the video feed. "Our correspondent at Central Command has informed us that the alien vessels have departed the area, and the Marshal apparently shared a lengthy conversation with someone on the com-link. However, the military is still encouraging all our citizens to remain in the shelters until a full dismissal of the alert condition is given, especially in Capitol Prime. Apparently, we're not done yet."

"CPComm, do we know what is occurring out there right now?"

"Our last word is we are expecting an engagement of some sort, and this will involve our military making a maneuver in the defense of our world and our people. Therefore, it is imperative for our people to follow their safety regulations, and once again to ensure they ingested their medical rations."

"Right, and if they didn't have one prior to this, I would strongly recommend they make an effort to acquire one immediately, as this is regarded as a priority procedure."

In Central Command, Ayene, Commander Geilv, and Captain Ta'yeen waited patiently in the control booth for word to be delivered for their next instructions. As they browsed the wrecked control stations, a small bird flew into view and landed on the sill of the broken window in the front of the room. This drew the attention of everyone present.

The Captain halted as he saw the otherworldly creature, and more so that it seemed to have a utility belt wrapped around it with a trans-com arranged as a backpack feature. He leaned in to examine it more closely.

"Am I seeing that correctly? Is that…thing…carrying a trans-com on its back?"

The bird turned to look at him and cocked its head inquisitively.

"Hey!" it squawks. "We're a very progressive species. We need to stay connected; you know?"

"Uh huh…that's what I thought. This is going to cause my horns to lose their curl after a while. So, who are you?"

The bird folded itself to the floor and reshaped itself to a young female officer wearing a foreign military uniform.

"I'm Corporal Navina Lar'akan of the Order of Tyr, in the service of Thaelyn, Lord and King of Tae'Eladar," she finishes with a polite bow.

"Not a bad presentation, Corporal," Geilv offers with a gentle nod. "So, how do you represent the ACI if you're actually with his military?"

"At present, it's sort of a joint operation, and some of us are serving double-duty, largely due to the Prodigy Gift, which offers us a wide variety of possibilities for how we can apply our service."

"Yes, so it would seem. You can apparently appear and disappear anywhere you set your sights on."

"The potential is extreme, but so are the responsibilities. Studying and serving within his military Order offers some very fine examples of training and discipline, as well as moral structuring and respect for our roles."

"That sounds like a fine service for someone with such a Gift as this. And based on what the Marshal just said about them, and us as well, I can only imagine the standards you have to live by working for a Celestial."

"Indeed, and his are rather well refined. Many of us started out very angry, injured, and severely distressed over our experiences with you and your military hunting us, and killing so many of our family members. We wanted to see you all burn for it. But when he called us into action, and began to teach us his values, it turned things around for us. Suddenly, we realized our miseries were not the only miseries we had to contend with. We did not know of these seeds of yours, or these chips, or anything else he apparently did to you after we left home. All we ever saw was the end result of whatever it was he had in mind to do out there. We became his punching bag, for whatever reason."

"Miss Lar'akan, I don't know if you would accept this from me, but I feel just as bad, maybe worse for my part, and that I allowed it to carry so far without trying to investigate sooner. I did take notice of occasional discrepancies, but…"

"He simply put you on active to keep you under his thumb," she finishes. "We cannot blame you, Commander. Not now. Not after all we have learned since then. Him, yes. Your Council, possibly. But it would seem this story became ever more complex than when it first started out. Now, we find ourselves with a legacy like no other, and a duty to uphold, unlike any I can imagine for any normal society."

"Is this part of the teachings that Celestial gives out?" the Captain asks.

"Part of it, yes, and he carries them down from the Estelar themselves. He serves as a role model for all of us, his entire society, as it turns out. Every member of his military Order needs to pass a certain degree of refinement for their spiritual purity before they can apply for service. This, in itself, virtually guarantees a level of perfection for our membership and our service potential. From there, we must serve as role models for everyone else. As such, his world has become a utopian paradise. No war, no crime, nothing bad to spoil people's lives."

"Amazing, but does this also involve assaulting heavy cruisers?" he muses wittily.

"Warfare can never be completely ruled out, as we must still preserve lives and promote our philosophies whenever we can. Life is precious, and surely worth fighting for. But a decision might need to be made for which is of greater importance…the few, or the many. And we are fighting for an entire world here."

"Yes, you are."

"Admittedly, assaulting star cruisers is not a common component of our rulebook," she smiles. "But that one example was actually a landmark occasion for us. It was in part a test of our skills, our teamwork, the combination of using physical and projected members for different roles, and also to uphold our respect for life by using nonlethal methods over harmful ones. We are an Order of Knighthood within Thaelyn's service, and that carries its own demands for our level of prestige and the results we bring, as well as who and what we must represent along the way, to demonstrate our respect for him, as well as to earn his respect for us."

"Earning respect in both directions?"

"We call it the Sacred Trust, to honor and be honored, each for our contributions to and from the whole."

"You even talk different from the rest of us," he smiles gently.

"His culture grows on you," she grins.

"I always had a soft spot for our ancient military lore," Geilv admits. "This would make a fascinating, if also a nostalgic study from the historical perspective to compare with our own."

"Then you will most surely want to participate and watch closely as we play our game out there. And speaking of which, Captain Ti'van, His Lordship has instructions for you."

"That's what I was afraid of," Ayene chuckles.

"He says that since you were present here, you would hold the best first-person knowledge at this time to imitate Darumon's image. Therefore, he is asking you to go to Sargeras and represent Darumon offering this most gracious gift of a game. But he'll need to make his own way out, and to find the real Darumon along the way. You'll probably need to offer an excuse of some kind, maybe to arrange your so-called contestants."

"All right, sounds simple enough. Go up to the one creature in all Creation I would rather not meet in person, and offer him a gift in the guise of the one OTHER creature in all Creation I would rather not meet in person."

They all share a round of laughter as Ayene tries to envision the scenario.

"Meanwhile," Navina continues. "He's passing the word around of what Darumon said. He feels his statement needs to be shared with the world, but only after all else is said and done. This becomes an integral part of our heritage, and we cannot allow ourselves to forget it."

"I agree, although this is a hard one to live with."

"Now, I need to go out and meet with that news team and share this with them so we can adjust our approach. He wants to modify his posture where Darumon is concerned. We'll wait for you to arrive before we proceed."

She offers a quick salute and flashes out of sight, leaving Ayene to consider her latest mission.

Geilv studied the interaction, as it represented a unique opportunity to witness a foreign military organization and how they behaved, which was noticeably different from theirs.

"I find myself curious over how you people train in your service."

"It's a lot different from what we have here," Ayene admits. "Their culture is a lot different too. If you thought I twisted your horns on a lot of occasions, this is a way of life for them. They're like a family, a brotherhood, or a fellowship of people serving a common cause, but more intimate than our example. It's what gives them their special character. And trust me, it's a bold one!" she chuckles. "Now, Commander, perhaps I can ask for a small favor on your part."

"What's that?"

"You know him best, so let's put together an image to be sure I get it right. This is a critical step, and I don't think I want to take any chances."

Ileani was attempting to fill in the time with a side interview, using the Director and his experiences at the ARC. They were currently discussing the strange genetic coding found inside the An'gamu Seed design.

"...And this led us to believe that if a certain impulse effect was delivered back across this organic network, it could represent a type of feedback that could hit each and every person still in possession of the Seed."

"And for reference, Director, what sort of effect do you think this might have on a person?"

"Granted, there is no way of knowing without actually seeing it, but our best guess might resemble what happens during the procedure we recently developed to remove it. This drug we are releasing is the same one we use during the removal procedure, and this essentially dampens the feedback signal the Seed gives off as it dies. It resembles a strong bioelectric shock reaction, and when it hits most of the organs, it can cause a variety of fluctuations, but those organs can usually recover without too much trauma. However, with the brain, it can lead to a person entering a mild to medium coma. And as we all know, if

this is not treated immediately, the victim could suffer even worse symptoms, including respiratory failure and other life-threatening conditions. But if to use the drug as an inhibiting agent, the symptoms are lessened. They may not be alleviated completely, but the effect is survivable without any critical medical attention. Therefore, our advisory for everyone to use it during this time."

Navina was just arriving in her bird form and landed on the news van to oversee the activity before entering into it. Azina took notice of the bird's arrival, as it flew in from above and settled into place, so she diverted from the interview to stroll over to it.

"Ayene? Is that you again…with your cute little backpack?" she grins.

"Actually no, not this time," Navina responds in her birdlike voice.

She folds to the ground and reshapes to her natural image.

"I'm Navina Lar'akan. I have some information I need to share with everyone here, but so far off-camera and private."

"Uh oh, what happened? When you start passing things around in secret, I can feel my horns tingling."

"Right, well, hold on and listen to this. This is from Central Command in their control booth when Thaelyn was speaking to Darumon…"

✦

"All right, I suppose this is as good as it gets," Ayene emits in a simulated gravelly voice as her new Darumon image. "Wish me luck, Commander, we need this to work."

She now flashes out of the room.

Ayene had never actually been inside the tall black monolithic structure that was Sargeras's sanctuary in the middle of town. She folded herself in front of it and searched for a convenient entrance. She found a door leading in on one side, but it was locked. There were no windows to peek in, so the only alternative was to reshape herself as something small to slide under the door.

She takes up a temporary new shape as a sliver of paper, and then wriggles her way through the crack under the door, coming up the other side. She was now in a hallway, which looked like it might be used for maintenance. She resumes her Darumon image and proceeds down the hall until she comes to a large double door that looked important, but again it was locked.

"I swear, who would ever try to break into a place like this for any reason? Other than me, that is," she giggles.

She again chooses to slide under it as a sliver of paper and comes up in a huge auditorium. She immediately resumes her Darumon image as she surveys the room.

The chamber was enormous, accounting for the greater interior volume of the building. It was broad and tall, and represented the main audience hall where Sargeras sat. In the center was a massive throne-like chair with an equally massive body sitting in it, seemingly at rest.

Ayene gazed at it uncertainly, as this would represent the first time she, or anyone, would've seen Sargeras, or any Primordial for that matter, this close. His form was intimidating, to say the least, but she knew she had a duty to perform, and in her new Darumon shape, she had to get it right. So, she made a cautious approach, trying to recall Darumon's words along the way. Among these was the size factor to meet Sargeras more or less eye to eye. She made her way to a clear area, and then tried reimagining her shape with a magnified scale.

Now she represented a giant-sized Darumon, but not as big as Sargeras himself. Her next objective was to draw his attention in order to make her offer. She approached him reverently.

"Master?" she announces gently. "I hope I'm not disturbing you too much, you seem so peaceful sitting there."

Sargeras slowly came to life as he lazily opened his eyes to look around, there to see his faithful servant hunched over penitently and waiting for him.

"Ah, my dearest servant," he croons in a bold reverberating voice. "Have you come to offer your kind words to me once more?"

"Oh, but of course, my beloved Master, you know this is what I live for. And even more, as this time I have something special for you. But it may require you to come outside for a leisurely walk," Ayene grins expectantly.

"Something special outside? And what might my mischievous little servant have planned for his weary Master?"

"Oh, my Master!" Ayene chuckles cutely. "You spend so much time here, and this place is so lonely, and I so often wished to please you with something special. So, I worked very hard to think of a solution, and do you know what I created? Oh, I think you will never guess."

"Really! Is my dear little servant taunting me now?" he muses jovially. "Then tell me, Darumon, what is this grand thing you have in the wait."

"Yes! And a grand one it is, or at least for what I was able to bring together in this barren place. I have arranged a game, Master! A little entertainment for my dearest Master, to help remind him of our better times…you do recall those moments, right Master?"

"Indeed, and I often find myself drifting off to those moments. We had such fine creations in our day, especially those last ones. Oh, Darumon, do you recall them? They were a truly masterful creation, and so successful in the games. How many times did we see them take their victories?"

Ayene was suddenly becoming curious as to the subject matter here, but she couldn't allow herself to drift too far off the mark, or else it might show a failure on her part for her acting role.

"Oh, but yes, my Master," she feigns. "They were perhaps the best of the best. And I worked so very hard to train them…"

Ayene pauses in her statement, wondering silently if she could prod for a little more detail, but it had to be a gentle prod. She reflected on Darumon's statements earlier with Thaelyn about evolving younger societies.

"But you know," she continues delicately. "I think perhaps they also carried a little of their own innovation. This surely offered a small amount of its own contribution."

"Yes, I believe you are right," Sargeras affirms. "Especially that matriarch of theirs. She was a masterful tactician. I think it was a good choice for us to preserve her for our future exploits," he chuckles softly. "She most certainly earned enough of them for us."

Ayene was now very curious as to this reference, but at this point, she felt as though she didn't dare press any harder. She couldn't let on that she had no idea what they were talking about, and she also had a job to do, and this had to come first. But before she could reply, Sargeras continued his own reminiscing.

"Do you remember, Darumon?" he asks distantly. "Those gifts we gave to her as part of our little…secret," he grins mischievously. "But like everything else, she too is lost to us."

This statement truly intrigued Ayene for the meaning, but again, she dared not make any outward signs of unknowing, or else it might spoil her image. But for this one individual to hold such a lasting impression, she must've represented something more than a simple minion character.

"Yes, she was special, to be sure," she reflects sympathetically. "And more so that she might still hold your attention. I can see it in your eyes, my dearest Master. But the misery of this long passing has worn on you. I think you reminisce too much on what was lost. I know it hurts, but let us try redirecting ourselves to a little recreation to lift our spirits. We are here in this place, and although I realize it is nothing as compared to what we once had; still, we are together, and I made this special treat for you."

"Is it true, Darumon? You would go to such efforts for me?" he smiles warmly.

"Oh, my Master, I think you jest now," she grins joyfully. "Come! I have still to arrange some of our contestants, but the game awaits an audience!"

"Well then," he pulls himself forward. "Where is this game you devised for us, and who is playing?"

"We have two teams, one is assembled from the local society, and the other is a visiting body. I searched long to find someone I felt might offer a little intrigue, you know, to make things more interesting. I do not know what challenges he might offer, but he represented someone who might hold a bit of surprise for us. We built a small arena just around this line of hills to our west, in a valley beyond. We have lots of open space out there, so there is plenty of room for future expansion."

"Future expansion?" he wonders. "Do we have in mind something for later, perhaps?"

"Well, I realize this little thing is nothing as compared to what we once had, but then I must remind myself that all things tend to start out small, and then build as we progress along."

"Ah!" he sings. "I understand. The Challenge of Creation... Oh, this does bring back a few good memories. Very well, my faithful servant, did you say you still needed to attend to a few matters?"

"Yes, I need to be sure the final pieces are in place, so if I could simply ask you to find your way out of the city here, and to the south. You will see a large military base out there. This is where you will most likely find me attending to these last few pieces before we can be on with our newest attraction."

"This is fair enough. Then you should be on your way, and I will meet you there shortly."

"Excellent, my Master! Oh, I can hardly wait to see what we have in store."

Ayene felt a subtle sense of relief that this part was over, but now she needed to make her exit, and not knowing how Darumon might otherwise do this, her only option was back the way she came. So, she returned to the door and shrank her image to fit, then hoped the inside had the lock she could turn to open it properly. She found the lever, and then a small button to unlock it, so she quickly opened the door and passed through out of sight. Once she was safely inside the corridor again, she folded her way out of the building. She made a quick diversion to the base control room where she would find Thaelyn to report in.

"My Lord, I just finished with Sargeras. In all the nether-space, if I were physical, I'd be sweating by now."

"How did it go for you in there?" he asks. "Did you experience any trouble?"

"No trouble, just a curious bit of dialog, where he seems to spend a lot of his time recalling old memories, and apparently in deep depression."

"I suppose this is to be expected by now, given our discussion with Darumon a short while ago."

"Yes, but I also got a few curious pieces of something out of him, if only in passing. He seemed focused on whatever was his last minion species for his games. They were apparently a superior creation, winning lots of games, and their leader, whom he described as their matriarch, was a truly masterful tactician. He really seemed to like her."

"Indeed! So, they tend to play favorites on occasion?"

"Yeah, so much so, that he and Darumon apparently had a private little secret where they granted some kind of special gift to…preserve her…for what I'm guessing to be extended service to win additional victories."

Thaelyn glared at her for the curious statement. But the moment was quickly jolted by the sudden eruption of laughter out of Kailen, whose bold outburst drew the attention of the room.

"Incredible!" he chortles. "Is this to say he was using her to CHEAT in his games?"

"Buggers!" Relissa shakes her head. "That ties it for sure."

"This would be a most interesting story to pursue," Thaelyn muses. "But I doubt we might have the opportunity. Not with where we stand or where we are going. Still, it does afford us another small glimpse into the lives of those beings from so long ago."

"Yes, it does," Ayene nods thoughtfully. "Anyway, I need to get back to work."

"Very good, as you were."

She flashes out of the room and arrives back at the news van just as Ileani was wrapping up her interview with the Director relating to the seeds.

> *"But Director, do we know anything more about how it works? I recall Miss Ta'yeen and her theories about this life support function, and this would simply force us to point a finger at the Marshal again, like for so many other things at this point. But was it really necessary to force this on each and every one of us, which now seems to be placing us into this vulnerable condition? Couldn't there be another solution?"*

As Ayene oriented herself after arriving, she listened in to the conversation. This would normally account for part of her news release, so she stepped forward to interact.

The Director and Azina both took notice of her arrival, as she came in behind the cameras. Ileani then followed their gaze when they both seemed suddenly distracted by something. And as she turned around to see Ayene arriving, she realized the show was about to begin.

"Perhaps I could take this one," Ayene offers.

"Of course," Ileani nods.

They rearrange themselves with Ayene now in the scene, and the conservation center still in the background. Ileani gave a new introduction to begin this sequence.

"With me now is Captain Ayene Ti'van. Captain, we were just going over the An'gamu Seed and that strange alien coding that was discovered inside, and also locked behind that military grade security code. And since you only just now arrived, let me recap that I was speaking with the Director here about the need to use this, for whatever reason, like if we consider Miss Ta'yeen's theory of a life support engine for Sargeras, and if this was so necessary, thereby placing our world population in the current condition of this threat potential, or could there have been a better solution. Can you give us your opinion about this?"

"Ileani, yes, at this moment in time, I can give you answers to several things, and on multiple levels. We are at a threshold moment in our history here, and it is time for the people of our world to realize a few details that have been hidden from them until now."

"Oh dear...here we go."

"You are one of the people working for us alongside that planetary security agency we established a while back to investigate so many of the wrongdoings in our world. We have been releasing our sensations through you as a way to slowly bring our people up to a full understanding of those bits of knowledge that were being kept away from us due to that famous hidden shadow authority Miss Ta'yeen over here was speaking of in her conspiracy theories. Although, even without her, we would still have informed the people of this. But her discovery, which was really by accident, but so convenient, simply allowed us to employ one more agent to our greater needs to unravel our society from that shadow authority's grip."

"So, her discovery was by accident?"

"Yes. Apparently, she just finished her studies at the U over here and was going in for her preparatory for the seed. But when she discovered it was cancelled, well, one thing led to another, and she, like a young girl might, had the horns, and enough swing in her tail, to actually ask questions and pursue it to a final conclusion. Unlike a lot of people around here, it seems."

"Ouch, but I suppose I might need to agree. I've heard it said once or twice our world population tends to behave as herd animals following a leader off a cliff, if told to do so."

"Yes, especially if you consider how they tend to worship the Council like a god entity that can do no wrong. This is why we are standing out here now, and hopefully, with all or most of our world population huddling in shelters waiting for the END of that world. There is a reason for it, and it reflects right back to that world population not doing as it is told unless, like Latena once said, you put a gun to their head. The Tav'ageen Scare did this once, and we need to do it again just to be sure we have their attention. This is no joke, and it WILL affect everyone in our world."

Throughout the world, in each of the shelters, people started whispering and glancing around at each other's opinions of this curious suggestion. After all had been said from all the previous sensations, many of them were becoming curious as to the reason for using such drastic measures just to draw their attention to something advertised as a simple conservation effort.

"But Captain, I'm sure many people will ask what relation this has to anything, as it was largely caused by that young man Ytani and his threats, and those friends of his, whoever they might be, who launched a series of raids in our local space. Can you explain this to us?"

"The relation circles around the people taking their god entity Council and its mandates over any rational thought. Instead of demanding conventional technologies to evacuate the planet, they allowed themselves to be infested by the seeds, with their secret hidden code. This is one thing. Next is to take an alien creature simply on his word that he has anything at all to offer, and again, following this on faith, much like bowing down and worshiping a god entity, and further, waiting an eternity for it, while our world is polluted to all the nether-realms, and this again forcing us to continue the seeds. Third is to say we, as a society who should be permitting ALL forms of knowledge as our domain, discredited one such candidate and chased him away, again based on that alien creature who made his claims without sufficient evidence to prove it. And finally, like the pacifist society we are, we simply didn't know what questions to ask in order to realize why it's taking that eternity to find our answers."

"Ouch, but I have to agree. We did it to ourselves."

"Now, as for Ytani. He WAS an agent working for the Marshal, or perhaps I should simply call him Darumon, as he is no marshal of any kind. His kind doesn't apparently use titles, as he is simply part of a servant race to such beings like Sargeras, each one a custom creation for their specific master."

"Interesting."

"Anyway, Ytani once worked for Darumon at a top-secret mining base until one day that mining base was discovered by our people and shut down. Ytani was found guilty on multiple counts of abuse, and even murder, where he was using the base staff as his personal pleasure victims. He developed a kind of mania along the way and started abusing the female staff members, and even killed a few, but none of us, or even Central Command knew about it."

"That sounds bad."

"When we found it, we dealt justice on behalf of his victims, but we had to do so quietly, because we were also hiding from Darumon at that time. HE is our enemy here, not any insurgents. And so, here we go with the story..."

Ayene allows a pause in her statement before proceeding to this next stage.

"We need to establish for ourselves a few terms and definitions as we go along. Sargeras is part of a now-dead society of beings of such extreme evolutionary advance, many lesser beings, maybe along our scale of development, might call them gods, if only for how far they've travelled in this time. So, religion or no religion, gods DO exist. But they are not the first, and neither the only example out there. And this particular society has a rival."

"Would this count perhaps as that insurgent body Darumon spoke of once?"

"It would, and his anguish with them is based on HIS society being dead now. This is revenge we speak of, not justice."

"Um, all right, but to be described as dead…I would think there might be a reason for this, right?"

"There is, and THAT was justice."

"Yeah… Although you once told me this in private as part of my role, now we need to bring it to the people. All right, go ahead."

"First, beings of this level of development do not normally make their homes in common three-dimensional space. We tend to toy with the term nether-space as a fantasy domain you simply don't want to find yourself getting lost in. But unfortunately, this is apparently one of those sciences the Council, likely under the influence of that shadow authority, explicitly denied us to question or study. It's real. Four-dimensional, and even five-dimensional space are both endpoint destinations where, if you have the proper knowledge and capacity, you can travel there."

Inside many of the shelters around the world, a series of urgent moans and hushed mumbling erupted as they considered this clearly sensational statement.

"Several decades ago," Ayene continues. "Darumon led our military into that space we might otherwise call nether-space, although he did not give us a proper definition for it. Simply to say, 'We need to go here because I said so, to find something I need.' And that was all. So, for all his promises of great wisdom, he didn't even define what we were doing for him."

"Well, that was certainly considerate of him," Ileani huffs.

"Let's keep this thought in mind a moment, as I have something else to say on it later."

"All right."

"Anyway, it actually required a few of our people, with more assertive aspirations, and horns that were not so tightly wound up due to all his rhetoric, to look out a window and ask what they see, then to apply a little speculation to the idea. But even that might not be enough, as our society, so strictly conditioned to worship our god entity Council, might not even consider the idea, especially if THEY say it isn't so. Therefore, it finally required an outside influence to teach us what we were missing."

"An outside influence?"

"Yes, people with the knowledge to actually define such things, and who are a bit more generous to give it out."

"Uh oh…"

"Therefore, the beginnings of what would ultimately become our planetary security agency…a counterforce to Darumon and his efforts. We learned who these people really are."

"Wow. And when did all this actually occur?"

"We can say there was an official and an unofficial beginning, so allow me to continue. First, who are Sargeras and Darumon in reality. There is a history here, which dates back so long ago, our entire world probably didn't even exist, to say nothing of our species. For this, you need to go back in time a very long distance, and not easily measurable on our terms. We might think we are so wise in the ways of science, but in reality, we are like children, just barely learning to crawl in a much larger environment than we ever thought possible."

"This would certainly unravel a few horns."

"Yes. If you thought that…accidental…leak of the new universe was sensational, this is smalltime news as compared to what's really out there. The Seas of Creation, as beings of this sort would describe them, is a vast multidimensional environment of MANY universes and other pockets of space. Ours is just one of those. But beings like these tend to make their homes across all of that, and the terminology they use is therefore adjusted to compensate for a new standard of perception, one that might raise the foundation we would otherwise use here, where simple terms we apply for basic items are redefined to a new level of interpretation, and the fancier terms we might use for our more elaborate inventions simply fall into the background."

"Can you give us an example?"

"One example we found in use amongst such beings is where a dimensional rift, like what we might create in a jump event, or in the operation of a conveyor, is simply a Door to them, they use them so commonly. Another might be to describe a dimensional layer of space, such as a universe like ours, as a Fold of that space, one among many."

"Wow, all right, I think I'm getting the picture here. And you know, in a way, this makes me recall the Marshal's…or maybe I should say, Darumon's famous statement of 'things out there' that we might not be ready for."

"In a very real sense of the word, you are right. And our people would be very wise to listen to that one document more than anything else he gave us, because on this one occasion, he was trying to teach us something. But he also had his own issues with teaching, and this reflects on his master and how HE might feel about it."

"Oops. As if to say, Sargeras doesn't like teaching things?"

"Something like that. And so, we continue. Inside Central Command, when those alien vessels came soaring overhead, we had a little confrontation where we had, shall we say, a meeting of minds between Darumon and these people who arrived recently. But when I say, arrived recently, I'm not talking about Ytani here. He's dead now. I'm speaking about the real people our agency is working with to save our world, and when THEY arrived…at least unofficially. And this occasion today wasn't it. They've been here a while already. All those sensations we had you broadcast in the news, starting with those protests on that dirty industry, and even a few things before that, is their work, funneled through those of us actually operating in this world to correct for Darumon's games on our people."

In the many shelters, people once again rose up with murmurs and rumblings relating to the many sensations and their implications, but now mixed with this new realization of where it was all likely coming from. And it didn't sound local.

Ayene continued for the camera.

"The story we have here is complex, with many elements involved. But during that meeting, and the resulting conversation, we found ourselves with some very interesting new details, and I would even say very privileged details, as it now relates to a society that is long dead and buried. But here we are with this remarkable opportunity to learn something about who they once were. I doubt anyone else, except possibly for that rival society out there, would be privileged to know this by now."

"Really! This could be interesting."

"We don't know their name as a society. This rival society, who calls itself the Estelar, only refers to them as the Primordials, which is a term we interpret to be derived out of that rivalry, and not a polite one."

"Oops, that doesn't sound good."

"No, they're hardcore enemies to each other. But here we have

Darumon, who was in conversation with the leader of this group who arrived in our world. And according to the stories being told, his... which is really to say Sargeras's society... After all, recall that Darumon is only a servant being, and apparently a custom-made one for Sargeras, but this ancient society of godlike beings once ruled all the Seas of Creation as an overseer body. But by the sound of it, we might think them to be very supremacist and authoritarian."

"I see."

"At least as it is told by the perspective of the Estelar, who likely only knew them in their later moments."

"Oh? Would there be another perspective?"

"There would, and here is where we might describe ourselves as privileged to know of it."

Ayene glances around the scene as she prepares to summarize this part.

"In the beginning, they were apparently a society much like many others. They had laws. They had policies. They were also governed by a form of aristocracy, rather than a democratic form of authority."

"Really! So, a society on that level can still be ruled by an aristocratic body?"

"I suppose so. But they were also a very independent body, constantly in competition with anything and everything else out there. The fight to the top was exactly that...a fight, where only one could win."

"Uh oh."

"This resulted, eventually, with them winning the prize. But only after meeting one final challenge, another precursor race that was itself in a state of decline."

"Another precursor. This suggests a type of cycling effect, one to another."

"It does. After that, they tried to hold a role to oversee the rest, watching, maybe even to guide younger races to some degree. They found it entertaining, perhaps fascinating to watch, as it might reflect a little on their own history. Much like a romance, if you will. But here we have a problem. Rivalry again."

"Rivalry...from those younger races?"

"Yes, as they would eventually rise up and try to take over. And the prize, if we can call it that, of holding that top position was simply too good. It was worth killing for. To do otherwise was the same as committing suicide of your own, as you are going down at the same time they are coming up."

"Oh no."

"So, one way or another, you need to preserve your position of authority, or else lose it. And for them, this meant hitting them sooner, rather than later. Here is where the Estelar took offence, as they perceived this as denying the younger races the pleasure to evolve, when in fact it was more about survival, trying to cull their future rivals before they could effectively rival them."

"I see," Ileani muses. "From this perspective, I suppose I can understand the principle, as unpleasant as it may be."

"However, as their civilization grew older, the tedium of managing those potential rivals, constantly watching for every other form of life out there among all those universes, wore on them. Darumon once described it as a kind of trap, with changes of attitudes along the way, where life, as an element, loses its luster…there's simply so much of it out there, and every example a potential rival, that you become numb to it after a while."

"That would carry it to the extremes, I think."

"It would. At the same time, many of them simply grew tired of their perpetual existence, as these beings are truly immortal by now. As such, they sought their rest, and this began the decline of their civilization. And THIS gave way to open up space for some of those younger societies to finally reach the top, NOW to rival them on their level. It was the beginning of the end for them."

"Oops."

"We need to think in terms of eons here, Ileani. These are ancient societies we speak of."

"It would appear that way!"

"Unfortunately, that trap is a cruel one. At least for this one society of aristocrats, whose attitudes changed so much, and for the glamour of holding such a prestigious station as godhood, that it went to their head after a while. Here is where that rivalry turned to supremacy, as nothing else out there was worthy enough to hold ANY station."

"Any?" she winces.

"This might then answer the one about Sargeras teaching anything. We're already too high on the ladder. He wouldn't want to see us go any higher."

"Uh oh. And how would this relate to receiving those promises of great wisdom?"

"It negates the whole idea. But ultimately, this is what leads us to the first members of the Estelar."

"Right. So, here we go again with another rivalry. But this time, a real one."

"Yes. Likely, they are not the only ones by this time. But unlike the others, this one chose not to rival its own competitors. They group up as a peer body."

"Ah! Now THAT is interesting. This would break that original stereotype mold, wouldn't it?"

"It would! As now you have a conglomerate body developing a fascinating new philosophical belief system, which they call the Measure of Balance."

In the downtown section of the city, Sargeras rose from his chair and lumbered forward to the front of the chamber, where he waved a hand across the massive door. It began to slide open as a series of large slabs parting ways from top to bottom along heavy tracks. He peered outside at the city, and then stepped forward, for the first time since his arrival, into the outdoor environment. He paused to examine the local surroundings as well as the climate itself.

"This species is not very adept at maintaining their home," he muses to himself. "Perhaps I should speak to Darumon about this. If they are to represent themselves as proper contestants, they should at least remain healthy."

He now turned and followed the streets to the south and out of the city.

In the command base, Petrith watched the monitors.

"My Lord, he's coming."

Thaelyn and the others take a moment to redirect themselves to the closed-circuit video feeds of their surveillance cameras watching Sargeras making his way outside.

"Good, and so it begins," he nods.

Ayene continued her interview for Ileani.

"We might say this belief system became something like a rule of law for them. It is by mutual agreement amongst all of them that this is how things should be, in order to maintain cohesion and harmony amongst all things within the Seas of Creation. And they would then teach this to younger societies, at least those who might be high enough to qualify for it, as well as to enforce it on anything else out there high enough to influence anything. This would then reflect on those Primordials."

"And naturally," Ileani concedes. "This is where that rivalry would come in, as I doubt a body of supremacist aristocrats would care for someone else telling them what to do."

"Exactly."

"But a rule of laws on the scale of a god society? Ooh! That sounds exciting just by itself. How does it look, do we know?"

"We do!" Ayene smiles warmly. "Some of us, who are involved in this, have also taken up our own form of worship as their new students."

"Worship? Like an actual religion?"

"Yeah, it's funny. You rise up out of a primitive society, thinking you need to throw away your old religions, as your science denies the existence of a god image, only to rise up so high, you meet the actual gods themselves," she chuckles ironically. "These Estelar sometimes take in one or another of the Child societies as students. Much like we have our schools, they might have different levels of graduate studies for older or younger societies. Best of all, once you graduate up to something very near to their own level of evolutionary advancement, you may actually join with them as part of that peer society. This way, they get fresh members, even if the older ones drop out."

"Oh! Yes! And that would surely solve the problem of that cycling effect, I think."

"Yes, it would," she nods. "But this rule of law is interesting. The Measure of Balance… They divide the principles into polarities. Positive and negative. These two forces must stay within reasonable balance in order to keep the nature of all existence harmonious, whether relating to matter and energy, or even life and death. Nudge it too far to one side, and you might experience discord, and maybe a collapse of some kind. But most of all is with life itself. To them, life is regarded as a precious element, that should be allowed to grow and evolve, based on the influences of these two sides to ensure it has a fair fighting chance. But NOT with such limits and punishments as Sargeras and his kind placed on things. Now, Ileani, can you begin to see why someone would take exception to them in that top seat? Rivalry is not the issue here."

Ileani gaped at Ayene, and she was speechless for a long moment.

"Taking exception…" she mutters. "To the point of wiping them out? And based on these laws…"

Her face grew pale for the implications, as she reflected on the earlier statements of these Primordials now being a dead society, with this being the reason, and she simply stared ahead blankly. Furthermore, the sensation was rushing through each of the shelters, cascading amongst all the people watching the broadcast.

Ileani had to force herself back into conversation.

"Um, yeah…" she wheezes. "So, this is where it came from, and where it went afterwards, until finally it chased Sargeras and Darumon to our front door?"

"Essentially yes. As a god society that holds such power over life and death that you can very literally wave a hand and it goes poof, you can't allow room to negotiate. It's all or nothing at that point."

"Yeah, I suppose it goes with the territory."

"Therefore, there were never any insurgents. Darumon wanted revenge, in honor of his master and all the others of his former, and to him, glorious society of overseers, that fell into such horrid, and again to him, ruin, that he had nothing else to live for. He was hoping to return them back to it. Simple survival, that's all."

"All right, wait." she muses overtly. "To him…survival… I'm getting the impression here that we need to see it from the other side for a moment. First, I recall you once said he is essentially in exile. And clearly, he and his kind are being hunted to extinction. So, if we look at it from his perspective, HE saw it as a horrible loss, something he held a lot of pride in, but taken away by people with a very different opinion of things that his didn't agree with. This was further complicated by that trap, as you call it, and the decline they suffered."

"Yes. It's hard for us to see it this way, as we might not hold the same values, but as he said, he was a younger member of that society that never had the opportunity to really enjoy that level of prestige the older ones recalled from their better days. Therefore, his misery of being born into a dying society. And being ones who chose to rival everything, rather than to coexist with them, this would naturally lead to a lot of other things, not the least of which is someone taking exception to their manners."

"Wow. Yes, that does put things into perspective. And I might further suggest it makes a good lesson. Be nice to your neighbors…or else!" she chuckles ironically. "All right, I can't criticize him for simply wanting to survive and return back to his better days. But at the same time, what he did here wasn't much better."

"This leaves us with what is likely a long campaign by the Estelar to enforce their values on these Primordials, and probably meeting similar results all along the way, as one pocket after another falls, until we come to what might be the last of their kind, in the last bastion of their former imperial holdings. And by the sound of it, not a nice example of one."

"How do you mean?"

"He used some terms here which will need definition. A stale fold, meaning a universe that is so old, it's basically dead by now. Imagine a universe that might be hundreds of billions of years old or more, with only a few remaining red dwarfs by now."

"Ouch! Yes, I know the theories. The astrophysics faction wrote a few papers on that once. And this is where they were holding up?"

"Apparently so. Unfortunately, here is where their supremacist behaviors and monotonous tedium gets worse with the younger societies."

"Worse!" she shouts. "How can it get worse if you're not allowed to grow up past a certain point?"

"In a dead universe, you don't have anything to play with. So you make your own."

"Oh dear."

"But in this case, with such an attitude that it's now a simple product of invention, not a true lifeform to carry a life of its own."

"Oh DEAR!"

"And here is where you use it for a game of gladiatorial sport, matching whole armies simply to watch them tear each other apart."

Ileani glares at Ayene and stumbles back a step. She then grabs her horns and screams. The sentiment was echoed in many of the shelters, as the people felt a similar sense of revulsion and outrage. Of course, for many, it was quickly muted when their chips hit them with the feedback shock.

In the observation lounge, the visitors simply shook their heads.

"That doesn't get any better," Sulíma moans. "No matter how many times I hear it."

"Is it supposed to?" Túfula offers.

Outside, Ayene tries to pull Ileani back into focus to continue the interview.

"We can't be sure how long this went on," Ayene reflects. "But what we understand of this story, based on information given to us from the other side, is they first tried to confront these last few Primordials to make them stop, but it ultimately descended into one final battle to finish them."

"Not that I think I really want to hear it," Ileani shudders. "But what did those people actually do?"

"Each of these Primordials had a pet world, likely collected together manually out of the leftovers of that universe. On these worlds, they created life...full environments I would imagine, including some form of sentient species as a pet society. But they weren't trying to evolve them. Instead, they were using them as a type of warrior caste to compete on a custom battlefield with a fellow Primordial and his creation, and simply for the entertainment value."

"That would certainly seem nasty."

"But it actually gets worse, as the loser between the two sides would see the remainder of their species wiped from existence to be replaced with a new random creation for the next game."

Ileani gawked at Ayene for the suggestion.

"I can't believe what I'm hearing! To think a god entity of any kind would do something like this! That's not even fair! And I'm not simply saying it for the atrocity of the thing, but they don't even get another chance at it? Just simple...probably simple creatures, not even as high as we are, right? Probably much less if they're only used as, uh... What word to use here. Battle, um... Thralls?"

"It'll do, Ileani. And as our people would describe, you need to consider the numbers here. If your goal is to preserve life, which is to say innocent life, those examples that may hold promise of any kind... Natural disasters and such notwithstanding, as bad things can happen to all of us. But if it is within your power to do anything at all...that which is offending it must be destroyed. And on the scale of a god, whole universes are now measured in that number, Ileani. Not simply one lonely little world like ours."

"In all the nether-space, Ayene, that's a big statement. I can't argue with you, but it's so...BIG."

"This brings us to where we are now. Our society holds a responsibility, pacifist or otherwise, as we DO hold the power to affect the lives of other worlds. Just look at what Darumon did out there with all his so-called insurgents. Ours is a society that should hold higher morals, and an affirmative direction to promote those values. We can travel across the galaxy and back again, and what do we do with it? Anything? Some might say it's not our business to interfere with the affairs of another society, and maybe they're right. But justice is still justice. And if we can reach out and offer our aid, we must do exactly this. And here we come to the REAL reason we are assembled out here today, with this fabulous conservation center..."

Ayene smiled pleasantly as she glanced over her shoulder at the structure behind her. But even though the reasons were known to Ileani, she still needed to clarify the statement for the camera. And she was getting a little nervous by now.

"Ayene, you're not going to drop another bombshell on me, are you?"

"No, Ileani, not this time. You already know the answer. It's all those people who are supposed to be huddling in the shelters out there who will get the bombshell this time. After all, how else do you get a full planetary society of noncompliant dull-horns to do anything unless you point a gun at their heads. Especially if none of them believe in a religion, gods, mysticism, supernatural this or that, and such absolute complete nonsense as metaphysics. I mean, after all, we threw away the one guy who could actually explain who and what Sargeras and Darumon really are as extradimensional beings," she shrugs nonchalantly.

"Thank you, Ayene. Such a nice little rub."

Ayene now turns in the general direction of Central Command in the distance as she prepares her next statement. She could just make out a couple of towering figures moving around out there.

"Right now, Sargeras and Darumon are both coming this way to participate in this event we have arranged out here."

"Whoa!" Ileani shrieks. "Sargeras is outside?!"

"Yes, called to the attention of what we have behind us."

"In all the nether-space!"

Ileani now followed Ayene's gaze, searching across the fields and into the distance, and she could also just make out the exceptionally tall figures.

"CPComm! I see them, way off in the distance, over by Central Command. In all the nether-space! They're huge!"

In the many shelters around the world, a collective series of gasps and anxious cries erupted out of the masses of people, as the camera turned around and zoomed on the scene in the distance. This was followed by hushed whispers and nervous rants at what might be about to happen next.

Sargeras was just arriving outside the military base, where he happened to take notice of Darumon directing the loading procedure of the troops into their transports.

"Ah, there you are," he calls. "Are we nearly ready, my faithful servant?"

Darumon turned to quickly glance over his shoulder as Sargeras made his appearance.

"Ah, Master! I am so pleased to see you taking a much-needed stroll. Yes, we are nearly ready. I am just seeing to the last of them. Once this group is loaded, I believe we can move ahead. It is not that far, just around those hills. I think the walk will be good for you. You spend too much time in there. You need to move around now and then."

"Perhaps you are right, and it does feel good. But Darumon, this environment seems a bit…sullied. You should probably see to it soon. I can hardly imagine this species can tolerate such levels of toxins as these."

"Ah, but of course, and as a matter of fact, efforts are already underway. I must admit, when we first arrived, they were so overjoyed to assist us that they became a little, eh… Ambitious! With their industry. But this should not concern you, as they are a hardy group. Still, I am aware they are working to replace that old industry to correct for this unfortunate condition."

"Good, then where is this arena you mentioned that will host this game of yours?"

"Yes! If you would just follow me, I will show you!"

Darumon now begins leading Sargeras across the fields towards the southern end of the hills separating them from the neighboring valley.

Ileani stared at the scene, which from her perspective was barely on the horizon from their location. She turns again to Ayene.

"Ayene, how did you get him to actually come outside? I mean, he's never done that before, not in the full length of time he's been here!"

"First, it's necessary for him to be outside, so we can target him without a lot of collateral damage. This is one reason the people, especially those in C.P., are hiding in shelters. To get them out of the way. Someone like him, if he should realize what's happening, probably won't go down cleanly."

"Uh oh..."

"Next, it's necessary for ALL the people to be in shelters, if only to clump them together for mutual support. We believe those seeds carry a nasty trick in them. Whether this is by design, or simply incidental, we don't know, but we think taking him down could result in a feedback effect through that energy aura we've been trying to advertise by way of your news reports. And by the way, we need to apply another definition here, while we're on the topic. Everybody..." she turns to the camera. "Pay close attention to this. Sargeras, and indeed, I suppose, any form of life that evolves up to that point, including such examples as the Estelar, require a special support environment to survive. And this isn't found in a typical three-dimensional universe like ours. You've been hearing the words Abnormal Energy on several occasions, right?"

"Yes Ma'am," Ileani affirms.

"The real name for these energies is Dynamistic Flows. In that extradimensional space, this is a common feature, as this is where it originates. In a three-dimensional universe, say like ours, if we are within the reach of this source, we might also feel it, as it can descend down to our level, and beings like us might also find a way to use it, if only slightly...by comparison."

"By comparison?"

"We are simple creatures, by comparison to them, so our ability to use it would also be simpler. But THIS universe doesn't have them. It's what they call 'barren', meaning devoid of those flows, and this is actually NOT a common thing, as most places DO have them."

"So, it sounds like we are missing something a lot of other people might have available to them."

"Yes, and this actually handicaps us for our scientific and technological development. We are limited to ONLY the classic laws of physics, but this is only one side of the coin. The OTHER side is where the good stuff is, unfortunately for us."

"Just for reference, why would you say unfortunately? I thought we were doing very well for ourselves."

"Well, yes, you're right, but it was a long hard road, and with a lot of bumps in the way. But if to use this other stuff, you could bypass a lot of that, because a society who is skilled in these energies, which some call arcanic energies, can do actual real magic…the sort of thing our science would otherwise deny exists. They could solve many of the same problems…very differently than with our methods…and achieve certain developments and inventions much earlier in life. And the laws of physics no longer apply, at least not completely."

"Oh dear…and therefore the handicap. They could probably excel beyond us in a fraction of the time we were riding that long hard, and bumpy road."

"Right, and this is also what might power the capabilities of a god society. Because they evolve into this as a primary home space. And now, this brings us to where we are here in this world. Sargeras needs this as his life support. Therefore, the seeds. I would imagine, once upon a time, some tail-crazy geneticist got the idea to invent those early generation seeds, maybe just to see if he could do it. I would further suggest Darumon might have been an influence to make it so, as a prelude to modern times. Why else would we need something no one ever wanted, to colonize something we were never allowed to colonize?"

Inside the observation lounge, the Daanen'kai Council members all glanced at each other for the strange reference.

"Never allowed to colonize?" Elder Vankkar wonders.

"We were never allowed to leave home, Father," Túfula responds. "We never actually colonized anything, so how is anyone to know IF we have the tech for it, let alone how advanced it might actually be. This is one argument that may have driven these loose-horned people to take those seeds, rather than normal colonization tech. They probably had no real idea we even had any, as we never used it."

"Delightful… But why would this be an issue to begin with?"

"A big world panic scare. Remember I told you about this before? Those medical implants, and the seeds. They had this horrific world panic, and instructions from Big Daddy Darumon and his superior alien wisdom to simply run away screaming…and oh, here, take this seed with you for survival in all those horribly alien environments out there."

"Oh, how nice of him!"

"Well," Elder Girhani muses. "That's one way to encourage people to take something they wouldn't otherwise touch."

"And also the reason for that statement," Sulíma adds. "To put a gun to their head."

Ayene continued her interview.

"But Darumon needed a lot of coverage to make this work. I would imagine, if you look at it in hindsight, these things, individually, might not create a lot. So he needed quantity to create this aura effect for Sargeras to tap into. It likely creates an artificial layer of these same dynamistic flows, or something similar, for him to restore himself with. Then we have these stories. First, we have the Tav'ageen Anomaly, which is a central focusing point for a lot of this. I'm going to say this was coincidental, and while it might have made a convenient excuse, it was also an unfortunate one for the results we saw."

"You mean the Scare, and those death syndromes," Ileani reflects.

"At the very least. He comes along, tells us his stories, frightens us with the Scare, we all take those seeds, thinking we need this emergency evacuation of the planet from this alien parasite thing he claimed was out there, but oh no, here come his famous insurgents. Now we're stuck here...as if he ever REALLY intended us to leave home in the first place. After all, we're being used as life support for his master, and he's HERE, not on some myriad of other worlds."

"Of course..."

"But we still need an excuse to keep the seeds, even IF our people did finally realize all the other techs we had available. So, along with those really nasty insurgents, we need OUR really big military, and for that...?"

"Naturally...that dirty industry, with the excuse that we're leaving home anyway, so don't worry about the pollution."

"Good. And the perpetual storytelling that...any day now...things will continue forward...just keep tucking your tails and wait for it."

Inside the observation area, Elder Girhani shakes her head at the scenario.

"I swear, and I thought we had it bad. This is simply awful, especially as I look up into that sky."

"Túfu," Elder Vankkar wonders. "What kind of story did he give relating to those insurgents that caused so much hysteria?"

"According to Darumon," she notes. "He and Sargeras were hiding from insurgents that threw them out of power in some fantasy world they used to own. We were supposed to help reclaim it. Unfortunately, Master Velen and his faction apparently took to the other side, rather than this most generous benefactor and his wonderful promises."

"Oh, well I'm so sorry to hear that," he huffs.

"And here we have that traitor statement," Elder Girhani moans.

Ayene continues on the video feed.

"This leads us to those chips as his secondary answer to the Tav'ageen bit. But does he ever tell us what this alien parasite thing really is? No. And does he allow our science factions to continue studying it? No. He was hiding from us during this entire time, with his shadow authority government, and managing our society along certain specific lines. But when THAT came out, and only after a few episodes, where he began to worry if we might finally learn something about it, here he comes, along with his poor, and at this moment in time, suffering master, to ask for help, and more importantly, to distract us from our research. He needed to take control of it...his way."

Again, in the observation booth, Elder Vankkar started getting shivers running along his spine at the implications being developed here.

"Um, Túfu," he hesitates. "This thing she's calling the Tav'ageen..."

"Yes, Father, it's the Prodigy Gift, their name for it, which is more a medical term at this point, because they initially thought it was a disease or something."

"Oh wonderful. But all right, I suppose, without him explaining it..." he thumbs at Velen, "...I guess anything is possible."

"Ayene," Ileani asks. "I feel a need to ask about this statement... to take control his way. We have the chips, but we also have that last meeting with Ytani, and this seems to have raised a few new issues I would like to clear up, if I can."

"Yes, we do need to clear this up. Sargeras and his supremacist attitude, and us with a really, REALLY godlike Gift he shouldn't become aware of...not even accidentally, like if he should hear people speaking of it on the street."

Ileani's eyes bulged as she glared at Ayene.

"Would this relate in any way to that statement he made of wiping whole civilizations away?"

"It would, and we are already a very mature one for everything else we have. And this is without the application of those dynamistic flows and whatever THAT might do to the equation."

"Oh wow, that spells it out a little, especially with what you said earlier about their tolerance levels."

"Yes indeed. This is now where we bring out that old seed research, giving it a new life, especially with this custom programming hidden behind that security lock, which he did NOT want us to learn about, as it contains exactly that code to generate this aura effect. And surely, not only would this be VERY proprietary, but it would also hint at something entirely unrelated to living on inhospitable worlds. It might also clue us in on something else he was hiding, in this case relating to this Abnormal Energy we would not otherwise know anything about."

"Do you think we could actually learn something, even if we did know what it was?"

"I don't know if I could answer that for this example, or how it relates to the natural stuff. I would think it might be very problematic to synthesize something that otherwise has a naturally occurring extradimensional origin."

"Ugh…yes, all right."

"So, it might be more of a hack in this environment. Just enough to do the job. And then, everything that came after was largely a maintenance effort to keep it that way, until one day he might feel we were ready to take his fight home."

"And how do you think WE, of all people, could do that? Do we actually hold such potential to fight gods now?" she chuckles mildly.

"I would hardly think that. But this is where that mining venture would come in that Ytani spoke of. He was an image we created using this same Gift to portray that figure on the streets. The reason was first, to reveal a few additional clues to Darumon's antics out there, using a scapegoat image to redirect HIS attention, as this would be delicate, and we didn't want him targeting anything he could set his sights on locally."

"Got it."

"Next might be to open up a few of his secrets, like where he was taking us on his grand crusade, such as other universes and nether-space, to break some of those science roadblocks on the issue."

"And got that one."

"And further, to give him a real threat potential to worry about, while we sneak in behind him and Sargeras, as HE was trying to do to the Estelar."

"Ooh, nasty."

"Therefore, once we hit a threshold, and had all the pieces in place, we launched today's event. And after we got what we wanted with our result over in CC, I impersonated HIS image inside Sargeras's sanctuary building to lure him out, as Darumon himself couldn't do it."

"Hold on a second…couldn't do it? As if to say, you gave him an ultimatum or something, and either he refused or simply could not?"

"Ileani, here is where I need to reveal a few tender items, and these came up during that same conversation a moment ago over in Central Command with those people. We have a video taken of a conversation that took place shortly after they left, and we would like to play this for our audience a bit later, and I strongly encourage the people to stick around and watch it, as this is important. Darumon could not perform this deed because, as a loyal servant who is custom-made to SERVE his master, not bring harm to him, he could not consciously go in there with a message that would ultimately lead to his demise. It's that simple."

Ileani reeled back in shock as she pondered this suggestion. She found it hard to respond, as the concept itself carried a hidden allusion.

"Couldn't do it...to intentionally bring harm... Ayene, how am I supposed to interpret this. It almost sounds as if he expects this outcome by now, and he is essentially...um..." she hesitates.

"Surrendering."

"Surrendering!" she shouts. "HIM? Surrender? In all the nether-space, after everything else you just said? I... I... For the love of... I swear! I think I might be ready to get down and pray to one of those gods of yours now!"

"I can give you a name, if you would like to call it out in praise," she smirks.

Ileani glares at her sternly, then turns to the camera and raises her brow intriguingly. Ayene continues.

"He essentially surrendered some time ago. Do you recall Latena's second major interview? This is the follow-up after that first Ytani incident up in that tower observation deck."

"Yes, she came in with her ideas of what he was doing with that strange shape-changing thing, and whatever."

"Good. Our purpose here has always been to reveal one after another of Darumon's secret dealings. We couldn't just come out on his regulator-controlled media stream, as he wouldn't expect, or desire REAL news to be broadcast. So we had to simulate news he would expect his people to allow, as part of our own movements, at least within reason. And only on your LIVE broadcasts, which couldn't be censored or altered by his people, would we bring the really big sensations."

"Right, and wow, Ayene, did you hit us with a few of those. I think, between the election fraud and the Council Grand Hall roof collapsing, most of us needed therapy," she chuckles. "And then to see HIM..."

"Well, Latena's interviews were part of our plan to leak certain details. And in this case, with her being a conspiracy theorist, which was a sweet thing to discover, and since we had already dismantled so many of his machinations, the details we had to nail home were to tie up a few loose ends, at least some of which were for the HC, who was basically under his own management by Darumon, where he could finally make a stand and deal with it."

"Um, wait, I think we need to touch on this, for our viewing audience. Commander Geilv, the HC of our world military body… under management?"

"Yes, you're right. One of the mandates the Council passed was a top-secret military neural implant chip. Our people were never allowed to know about this. It was initially advertised as a training aid for our young military of dull-horns who don't know how to fight. After all, our otherwise highly refined society of intellectuals hasn't seen warfare in our world for a thousand millennia. What do we know about it after so long a time of peace? And with so many of us being pacifists anyway, since it is much more to our nature. Our ancestors were herbivorous prey animals, not predators, and we are STILL prey animals, as none of us truly has the predator instinct."

"All right."

"So here we have the justification, and then passed, as most things are, by the Council, and the rest of us following along as a herd driven off a cliff by it."

"Oh great…"

"In reality, it was a mind control device. Push a button, point a finger, say 'kill', and the person goes off without care or concern, and especially without the ability to question or analyze anything, and performs exactly that."

"I swear, Ayene…that monster, and what he did to our people. I don't care if he had this great cause to serve his master in the honor of his people and his desire to return them back again, this takes it too far!"

"I might have to agree. But Ileani, I must also say WE, as a society that did NOT have mind control chips in our brains, but still allowed ourselves to be mind-controlled by everything else he did, need to realize our own responsibility for allowing this to actually go that far without pushing for a few answers. All that tail-tucking we were told to do, and we did it. If we are to describe ourselves as such refined intellectuals, we need to behave that way, and NOT simply take someone at their word, OR to listen to a god entity Council, thinking they can do no wrong.

We blindly ignored the fact that they were in those same offices for so long, they should've died of old age sitting on those seats."

"Yes, Ayene, I agree, this was a shameful act of ignorance on our part, at the very least."

"And even the HC had one, and often in active mode to keep him under control, as he apparently did try to ask these questions, and this was his reward. Do as I say, or else, bam, active mode of the chip to keep you quiet."

"Oh dear, that poor man. And for how long?"

"Most of his career in that office."

Ileani closes her eyes and turns away as she mourns the situation.

"And so, Darumon, and our military...what were they doing under the claim of fighting insurgents?"

"Cleaning house...all across our galaxy, simply for target practice for our young military who doesn't know how to fight. At least until we were tough enough to go after gods. But this again reflects on that mining base and his super weapon to fight them with. So, Ileani, and to all our people out there, our society, mind control or otherwise, is responsible for mass murder on a galactic scale. I'm not sure if there's a law big enough to cover something like that. So we will now need to spend the rest of our existence, as a species, working to pay it back somehow. This becomes our legacy."

In the raid shelters, the people were now moaning over the horrific tragedy and the heinous criminal motives that might perpetrate this act. But not only that, as these statements didn't limit it to only the military. Each person had to take some part of the blame for allowing it to go so far in the first place. And while Ileani also knew this, she still felt moved by it. She allowed herself an opportunity to reflect, as she lowered her head in consideration of these words before continuing.

"I don't want to be a part of a society that is responsible for something like that. But I guess we have no choice...here we are. Captain, is there any sensible reason why he would do this, or is it simply more of what got him and Sargeras in trouble with these others? You mentioned something about surrendering. What was that about? How did it happen?"

"Our work to disable Darumon's military control started sometime before we came to you. We needed this under OUR control, so we wouldn't see it used on our world population for all our other efforts. This eventually resulted in Geilv finally realizing Darumon's abuse of those chips, and what he was apparently using our military for, so he ordered them all turned off."

"Good!"

"But he still needed to play the game like business as usual, to keep Darumon in line. Then, after Latena's second interview, where we released a select few statements, Geilv was able to apply these, since so much was out in the open by now, that he could justify his realization, and turn his guns on Sargeras's head. This caused Darumon to completely buckle. The loyal servant who cannot do anything to threaten his master. If only we knew this way back in the beginning."

"Wow! Yes! That might have saved some trouble."

"But Ileani, I need to temper this statement with a few additional words. Darumon, by this time, was going haywire for all our sensations, our news leaks, Latena and her statements, and everything else. He was at the end of his wits by this time. Recall those words of hoping to bring his master back, in many ways from the dead, along with anything else he could muster, for the glory of his old lifestyle."

"All right, that alternate perspective again."

"He was a broken man by this time. His dreams shattered. His rage, perhaps as part of that old attitude his kind was once born with, wanted to see Latena made to disappear. But this was at least as much for her rabble-rousing over this newest conspiracy theory relating to the Tav'ageen Anomaly and Ytani."

"Yes, I think I can understand this part. We would be speaking of Sargeras again and his opinion, right?"

"Yes, those chips are there for a reason, a cover-up, like Latena said. But not for us... Well, not entirely. But in front of HIM. He did it at least as much to protect US from his master, as well as himself for what he did to create us."

Inside the observation booth, Sulíma and Túfula were leaning forward to listen in to the broadcast. But when this statement came out, they both jerked back and drew in sharp gasps.

"What?!" they yelp in unison. "Our protection?!"

They glared at each other, and then at the monitor again.

"Kali said something about that last Ytani impersonation she made," Túfula recalls. "And also some of those conversations with their HC, but this..."

"Unbelievable!" Sulíma blasts. "I wouldn't expect this, Túfu. Not after so many other things."

Ayene continues on the news feed.

"But this isn't all of it, Ileani. A few other things came out during this conversation we had over there. If you think this much is surprising, hear the rest of it. He held feelings for us as his creation, something he was never allowed to have for anything else. And in fact, his kind, for those games they once played, are specifically conditioned NOT to hold feelings for anything. It's simply not allowed."

"I see," Ileani accedes. "But what sort of feelings, in our case?"

"This is apparently a very private secret he held. According to him, during those old days, with those Primordials creating life for this game, and probably the only thing he experienced in his lifetime, his kind was used to train them, maybe a bit like circus animals. It was a job for the pleasure of their masters, and these creations would probably not last long enough to develop feelings for anyway. So, don't bother. But when he came here and made us, this was HIS work effort, not his master's. And in the absence of his master watching over him, he allowed himself to indulge in that which he was denied before. And along the way, he became fascinated with what he called the ancient pleasure of watching a young species grow up, which to him would be a fable from a bygone era."

"That's interesting…I suppose. So he was granted a kind of luxury he never had before. Does this mean he held some kind of parental instinct? If so, he was extremely poor at expressing it."

"Yes, this much I can agree with, as his kind was never made to be a parent of any kind. But he was heard to complement us once in a conversation with Geilv, and during this conversation, he offered a few words for his private feelings, realizing by this time, now that his longtime rivals have finally arrived, and his time was at an end, that he wanted to reveal what he couldn't reveal before. This is that video we'll play for our people later on. We want them to hear it."

"All right then, we'll review what he has to say and consider his words. Although, I personally can't guarantee my reaction to it."

Ayene pauses to glance in the direction of Central Command again. By this time, a fleet of troop transports had lifted off and were making their way across, with Darumon and Sargeras leisurely strolling along. Ileani follows her gaze.

"They're coming now."

"Yeah," Ayene states. "We need to finish this up before they arrive. So, listen carefully. Once again, this is for all our people out there. This facility behind us is not simply a conservation center to preserve some odd little animal species. We have tons of those already. In fact, by this time, I doubt there's any natural wildlife still out there that hasn't already been moved to a facility somewhere. No, this one is for US… our people…our world…our right to exist as a species, and the reason behind this is due to our Creator, if you reflect on that old religion, along with his master, still living here and posing a threat to our continued existence. We, as a race, must now evolve, and as it turns out, give our dear Creator the old hoof in the tail."

"Oops!"

"But doing so will not be easy. Darumon has already admitted defeat, but Sargeras is oblivious to what waits for him out here. HE now becomes our problem. I doubt he is aware of what Darumon did to create us. He probably thinks we're a natural species that just happened to open the door for him."

"Why do you say this?"

"This reflects on another statement Darumon made in there during this conversation. For him to hybridize himself with anything else is considered offensive and even vulgar to his kind, and such like Sargeras, I suppose. They don't apparently like the idea of mixing their blood with anything else. The result is then regarded as an abomination that needs to be purged immediately."

"Yikes!" Ileani retracts sharply. "That could be a problem!"

"Therefore, Darumon had to hide this fact, for his own safety, in case he should be punished for it, and ours as well. But he knew his methods, which in this barren fold universe had to involve his own body, might cause a few complications, as the hybridization aspect would create a few side effects, like our ridiculously long lifespans, and more recently, the Tav'ageen Anomaly."

"Oh dear…"

"Cu'Nar help us!" Elder Vankkar wheezes. "Is she saying it's in all of us?"

"Yes, Father," Túfula admits. "Those early examples are simply forerunners who found it first."

"But Túfu," Master Velen emits tenuously. "What does this say about us as a species? I was originally under the impression it could be an indication of a form of transition, but this…"

"Master Velen, you're only half right. I'm sure you couldn't possibly know about the hybridization aspect, but we're not simply beginning a kind of transition, we're already half-god, possibly in a similar state to the Celestials by now. But we are a species that is still very young and not even ready for it. I suppose, if you had the chance to study it further, you would've figured it out…within reason, as you might still need a Celestial to compare with. But Darumon, and likely through his puppet Council, were trying to hide it."

Ayene continues the interview.

"So, he comes here, interbreeds with those Eracyodines, and creates us. He then raises us up, while we are essentially inbreeding ourselves, half-brother and half-sister, which no doubt refines this quality of his side of the family, to create these curious complications we have no idea how to identify…not unless you involve someone like Elder Nazég and metaphysics, as this now becomes the science you need to interpret it. We are capable of using telepathy, clairvoyance, precognition, probably ESP, and who knows what else beyond this one projection skill."

"In all the nether-space!" Elder Girhani screeches. "All of that? Master Velen, were you aware of these other qualities?"

"They were suggested as part of our theories," he reflects. "But we did not have the time or opportunity to explore them. And then those two arrived, and we departed. Since that time, we simply did not have as much opportunity to do the study I had hoped for."

"Well, someone did!"

"Kali and her people…" Sulíma offers. "They probably uncovered more of this in the last few years than Master Velen did in his entire lifetime."

"Oh dear cu'Nar! Santari, if you were ever afraid of these things, I think you just found a new volley of them."

"Yes," Elder Vankkar nods. "And I think I want to find a new world to hide on."

Again, Ayene continues her lecture for the camera.

"When Darumon published that paper of his famous 'things out there' message, our people should probably pay close attention to it, as this is one occasion when I think he was hoping to teach us something, at least inasmuch as he could without getting anyone in trouble with his master and his tolerance levels."

"Meaning to say," Ileani speculates. "All those things he apparently did NOT allow us to know beforehand, like those sciences his pet Council was hiding from us?"

"At the very least. Our efforts to thwart him and his attempts to control things, instead forced him to reconsider some of his inhibitions, if only to create excuses for why the Council seems to be missing, and what they're doing out there. He was trying to resolve all those protests and the people coming to these new realizations he worked so hard to hide. He was losing control, and he wanted to gain it back again, but we weren't going to allow this."

"Yeah, you can be sure of that much. We're in the middle of a world rebellion," she chuckles.

In the many shelters around the world, the people were fixated on the monitors. Many subtle conversations were erupting among them relating the earlier news sensations to these statements here, and the potential implications that could result from it.

Ayene offers her rebuttal for the camera.

"But Ileani, our people need to understand something when I say we need to evolve. I'm not simply speaking of learning our lessons to ask those questions we need to ask, and NOT tuck our tails on command. We are in possession of qualities we should not be in possession of, if only for this hybridization aspect. This alone raises us, as a species, to something we are not ready to achieve. These Gifts, collectively, should not be a factor in us at this moment in our evolution. A species can evolve them, but ours came much too soon, and most of them are fantasies for us, not something we can cope with in reality."

"That sounds bad for us as a race at this point in time."

"It is. Except for our immature knowledge base, we could actually qualify for an early generation Celestial race, which is a race that is partway to godhood, and likely already living in that extradimensional space."

"Seriously?!" she frowns.

"Yes, all these Gifts I spoke of are Celestial grade gifts. Common mortal people would not likely have them. Certainly not to the extremes we are discovering here. Those of us who are learning them, are learning FROM Celestials. They are our teachers."

"Oh dear...I'm feeling a little faint now."

"Furthermore, when you were asking, almost joking about some of us taking up worship for these Estelar, THEY are the teachers of the Celestials."

"And now I'm feeling a little MORE faint. Does this mean WE need to take up study with them now?"

"Probably so, as we certainly qualify for it by now. Therefore, we must evolve to meet this demand, and it IS a demand by now. This includes not only the knowledge base, but the maturity levels and responsibility, the respect, and the morality that goes along with it. Once the medical community turns off those chips, boom, a full society of people like Ytani. His portrayal would be an example of what NOT to do with it."

"This much I would certainly agree with."

"But until we can attend to this, we must first graduate to that point. This is our maturing period. This is where we come full circle from the beginning, and why our people should be neatly tucked away inside shelters. We're finishing what was started an epoch ago."

Ayene glances across the field to see Darumon and Sargeras coming around the corner of the hills into the valley. Ileani follows her stare and directs her camera to the sight.

"CPComm, they're almost here. They're just coming into the valley and moving north along the river on the opposite side."

"Ileani," the station anchor responds. "We're a little concerned over the reasoning here. Can you get us an explanation of why they're assembling out there and what is actually about to happen? Because I still recall that statement telling us the conservation center is about preserving us as a species."

"Right, um, Captain, can you help us understand this quickly?"

"Ileani," Ayene asserts. "This facility is a battleground arena. The field out here is a type of game board where two armies will meet and do battle for the survival of our world. This is what got those last few Primordials into trouble in the old days, a game where two sides fought to the death for entertainment. But in our case, we're not going as far as that. We do need to put on a good show to demonstrate ourselves, but this is much more like a stage play until we can drop our little surprise on him. He just isn't allowed to know this yet, or else he might try running again. However, we DO need him outside for it, otherwise he might take the city down with him. Therefore, the game, as a lure to call him out."

"Oh wow! Now there's an explanation. And the people who might live in that city...?"

"...Would probably go down with the city itself. It's unlikely he would care, so long as it serves him somehow. This is also where the seeds and the medical supplement come in. Like I said, if we take him down, it might cause a reflex in that organic network aura effect, and zap, there goes our population. So, last warning... If anyone hasn't taken their medicine, they're likely to be in trouble soon. My best advice, if you missed it before, is to get to a medical center now for a dosage, or maybe just sit there and wait for the big hit, so the med-techs can take care of you as soon as you hit the floor."

"That's very good advice. And I'm aware the medical centers are all being held open for any emergencies during this time."

"And once again, this is why our people should be huddled together, for the mutual support in case anyone does go down and needs more serious medical aid, and with others nearby to offer assistance. And THIS is why we have the raid sirens, to make it happen. Most people don't pay attention to the more important details unless you have an apocalypse coming."

"Thank you, Captain, for the note of encouragement," Ileani chuckles ironically.

"I know. I was probably one of those at one time. But this is serious. Unless you have sirens going off in your ears, your data-pad is probably the most important thing in your life. Therefore, Ytani the Great…" she waves her hands theatrically, "…had to make noise in our streets to draw the people's attention. The image was at least as much a lure to distract the Marshal, as it was to draw OUR attention to something big happening. And it had to be noticeable enough, as well as obnoxious enough, to make them pull their noses OUT OF their data-pads to pay attention to it. If we were made so often to jump off a cliff on someone's orders, we had to create a situation to turn that around, but also on the same scale."

"Got it."

"BUT…Ileani. Here is a clincher for you. We had to do this, not the Estelar themselves. Having someone like a member of the Estelar showing up would probably stand out in the eyes of a being of similar proportions, and we hold the opinion Sargeras wouldn't stick around long enough if that should happen. So, we needed to turn their attention elsewhere. For this, we needed a distraction, and therefore, the game," she turns and waves a hand at the field behind them.

"I see. That's a rather elaborate distraction. An expensive one, too. And all this just to distract someone. Wow. So, what is it we're looking at now?"

As Ileani spoke, a series of large troop transports began setting down nearby and unloading wave after wave of soldiers. The interview became suddenly distracted as Ileani gawked at the arrangement of people wearing what was clearly medieval style armor and carrying swords and shields.

"In all the nether-space!" she shrieks. "You've got to be kidding me! Ayene! What is that over there?"

"Your side of the game board," she grins.

"Our side?!" she screeches. "But…but… In all the nether-space! What are they wearing?"

"Game gear, for lack of a better word," she chuckles. "It makes for such a pleasant little entertainment scenario. We think Sargeras will enjoy it."

In the observation booth, Elder Vankkar gaped at the monitor, and alternated with his view out the window.

"Are you people actually serious?" he balks.

In each of the raid shelters, the people marveled as well as puzzled over the ridiculous arrangement of attire. For most, it didn't look like it could be real, and for some it almost seemed comical.

Ileani felt weak and stumbled back a step. She moaned faintly and slapped a hand against her brow as she gaped at the scene in front of her.

"Ayene, please, for the love of what's left of my horns… Why are they wearing that archaic equipment?"

"We're not the only ones with a romance, Ileani, and the Primordials enjoyed their games as physical hand-to-hand combat."

Commander Geilv and Captain Ta'yeen unloaded from their transports and made a direct line to the news van while still giving orders for their troops to take up their positions.

"What are those spires supposed to be for?" the Captain wonders.

"I don't know," Geilv muses. "But I'll bet it's some kind of containment feature."

He turned to observe the large mass of soldiers marching across the field.

"Listen up, people," he issues on the com-link. "We seem to have a channel running through the field between those two rows of spires. Advance from the river and take a formation in a defensive line."

Thaelyn and his officers watched as the Suuden-Aryku troops were being deployed onto the field. He then turned to the gnomish Professor standing at the control panel.

"Professor," he asks. "How is our charge?"

"We are at full power in the capacitors, with a fair amount of overflow right now. My last readings actually looked very promising.

It seems those little arcanids are making themselves nice and comfy in there. The gathering probes are pulling out more than previously calculated, probably due to all these people standing around that are offering additional incentive to generate a greater surplus."

"Excellent, then I will ask you to bring up our walls, if you please."

"Right-a-diddly-do, my Lord!" he chirps.

He hits a few buttons and pulls a lever to energize the shield walls. As before, during the testing phase, the spires began to form a cloudy haze of energy wrapping around them.

Azina was watching and waiting for this. When she took notice of the swirling haze, she pointed assertively.

"There go the walls!" she shouts.

As Ileani turned the cameras around, the spires were crackling with static energy, which quickly erupted as bolts shooting between the spires and expanding into a continuous wall-like projection. She flinched at the sudden eruption of energy, letting out a yelp as she ducked away.

"What was that?" she emits breathlessly.

"That's a shield wall," the Director offers, "to close off their flanks. This forces the game into a predetermined channel."

Geilv gazed at the battlefield, and the curious arrangement of the walls.

"That resembles that thing they had around their outpost on Therinë."

"Commander," the Captain mutters. "Didn't I hear it said these people were supposed to be only Industrial Age?"

"Yes," he nods. "But we also have that Abnormal Energy thrown into the mix, and that stuff must be capable of working miracles. Their evolution might take a very different path than ours. We shouldn't take anything for granted here, regardless of their technological Age, as it wouldn't resemble ours."

"Yeah, but that's a little scary for what I'm seeing. If they're engaging us with medieval weapons, but using shield emitters that might even excel beyond us. And then to include those ships of theirs..."

"I know, so let's just play it as best we can. Once it's over, maybe we can sit down for a nice long talk. I think we might need this regardless of anything else, for the condition of our world, which seems to be their work."

Ileani and her team watched as the two officers arrived in their group. Latena had been hanging in the background until now, but as the Captain arrived, she rushed forward for a quick embrace. Ileani smiled in amusement as she made a tender approach.

"High Commander Geilv, and um…" she raises her brow.

"This is my uncle," Latena smiles. "Captain Tunil Ta'yeen."

"Ah, thank you."

"Latena," the Captain eyes her suspiciously. "What are you doing out here?"

"Uncle, I'm here to be a part of THE most important day in our history. This is the day we find our freedom, and I'm already planning on calling it the day of the Azgarén Emancipation, which we'll make a national holiday."

"Aren't you moving just a little ahead of yourself?"

"Well, maybe a little, but I know a few things, so it's just a matter of waiting for it."

"And what about your parents in all this?" he asks. "I don't want to hear your mother screaming at me again for all your wild antics."

"I know, but if they're doing as they're supposed to be doing, and in the shelters watching the news feed, like all the others, all I can say is…" she turns to the camera and waves flirtatiously. "Hi Mom, hi Dad! By the way, I'm starting a planetary revolution with the help of these people behind us here. Nothing personal, it just needs to be done," she smiles innocently and shrugs.

In the observation booth, Elder Vankkar felt his jaw drop at the overt play.

"Cu'Nar help us all. And I thought Kaliya was bad. She looks to be about the same age or so."

"I know her," Túfula grins. "We met at the academy when she was taking language classes. She's ambitious, and probably worse than Kali ever was. She's barely out of her university studies and already turning the place inside-out. She's a politics student, so you would probably get along great in a debate forum."

Darumon and Sargeras had arrived at a convenient location across the river from the arena, with a perfect centerline view down the middle.

"This looks like a good location," Darumon considers. "What do you think, Master?"

"Such a quaint arrangement, and so tidy!" he gloats. "Indeed, this is a fine bit of work. Just like old times."

Thaelyn and Aerlie both stared out the window at the two colossal figures. For all the stories of the Primordials, this would represent the first time anyone had seen one since the Celestial War.

"So curious, Thaelyn," Aerlie muses. "Are you paying attention to their interaction?"

"I can hear them through your ears. This is a rather interesting moment, to actually pay witness to one such as these."

"It is, and I am noticing how Sargeras behaves a bit like a portentous luminary."

"We already know from our discussion with Darumon that his kind did most of the leg work, so it might follow that the masters, in this case, may behave more like pompous lords at a pit fight."

"Yes, and this would represent the first time anyone has seen them since the old Celestial War...a little more of that lost history now coming into play."

"Indeed, and perhaps we are blessed with this opportunity. One generation beholding another, but in this case, with the chance to study, rather than simply encountering them before overtaking them."

Darumon looked down at the troops on his side as they formed a defensive line. From here, he could clearly see how they were outfitted. He squinted as he leaned in for a better look, trying to understand if he actually saw what he thought he saw.

"How interesting," he muses quietly. "I wonder where they found those old relics. Then again, I wonder if I should even bother to ask," he glares at the control booth where he could see several people gazing out onto the field. "But now, do they know how to use them."

Sargeras had been overseeing the gathering as they marched in from the outer field. He similarly noticed the curious accouterments, which seemed out-of-place, but also very nostalgic for the occasion.

"Ah, Darumon," he welcomes pleasantly. "Look at what you brought to me, how charming of you to remember."

"This?" he blurts unexpectedly. "Oh, but of course! After all, what is a game without the classic appeal of dueling! The clash of metal on metal, the vigor of the sport... Oh Master, did you think I would forget?" he grins courteously.

Darumon offers up a carefully disguised chuckle as he tries to imagine the scenario that might be ready to play out in front of him. He then turned to glance at Geilv and the others in the news van.

"And no doubt we have another live news sensation in the making," he whispers to himself. "Very well, at least we will not go down in obscurity. Perhaps I will take this with a mote of gratitude that we will not be forgotten...not completely."

Aerlie could see his lips moving with her extra-sharp Avariel eyes, and she was attempting to project her clairvoyant perception to listen in on his quiet mumbling. And for a moment, she felt a note of sympathy. She drew back and sighed sullenly.

"You are right, Thaelyn, this will not go pleasantly."

"But it must go, nonetheless. Are you able to perceive anything?"

"Yes, if only to use a few of my Celestial skills along the way. He is preparing himself for his final moments out there, while Sargeras still appears oblivious to the plan."

"I see. This is good, at least for our purposes where Sargeras is concerned. I simply hope we can maintain it this way."

Geilv studied his people as they assembled on the field. Their appearance seemed a little ragtag, so he decided to spice things up with a bit of theatrical appeal.

"I need you people to show yourselves up a bit," he calls into his com-link. "We're here to fight a battle to impress our Creator. Let's hear your battle cries! And wave your weapons in the air as if you're anxious for a fight!"

Ayene glared at him, along with the Director, Azina, Ileani, and the rest. He looked back at them and shrugged.

"Well, we need to make a good show. These are our instructions. So, as the field commander, I need to apply a little motivation."

"Yes Sir!" Ayene smiles eagerly.

The Suuden-Aryku soldiers on the field started waving their swords in the air and banging them against their shields, while letting out a series of howls and war cries.

Sargeras peered down at them and beamed in anticipation of the fight. Darumon studied them carefully, and cautiously glanced at the Commander in the news group. He then offered a subtle smile and nodded.

"Yes," he admits. "I think we might have ourselves a curious little show. But oh, Master, I suspect we might also have one or more hidden surprises. Our opponent is a clever one. Surely, he would not come all this way for some boorish little display."

"Do you know of him, Darumon?"

"We met once upon a time as I was conducting a bit of travelling. He spun a clever ruse or two, and I took notice of this. One does not see such very often, you know."

"Indeed, and this brings me back once again to that one we had in our service. Oh, she was a fine example of this."

"Her again? Yes, I recall that one clearly. She most certainly did stand out. This is a rare breed we speak of here. So, I must ask myself, what does this little one have to offer?"

Thaelyn and his officers waited for the Suuden-Aryku to fully assemble on the field. When the time seemed right, he turned to find Navina in the room after she returned earlier from her errands.

"Corporal, go out there and inform Ayene the game is about to commence."

"Yes, my Lord," she salutes and folds away again.

She arrived in view of the news team as they were overseeing the field and the Suuden-Aryku contestants. Ileani and Ayene were in the camera when Navina popped into view. This naturally caused Ileani to jump at the sudden arrival, but she was getting used to it by now.

In the observation booth, as well as in the shelters, the people took immediate notice of Navina's arrival in front of the camera.

"Who is that?" Elder Vankkar asks.

"That's Tana's mother," Sulíma responds. "Navina Lar'akan."

"Navina Lar'akan…one of ours?"

"Yes, but now working for Thaelyn."

"And she's projected?" Elder Girhani wonders.

"Yeah, a lot of our people who are working for him are doing that lately."

"Incredible. And none of them were originally Prodigy Children?"

"No, but they did have to go through some special training to discover and use it. They have classes at his academy now."

"You're kidding me!" she shouts. "Actual classes?"

"And the curriculum is growing."

Navina approached Ayene to pass her message.

"Captain, His Lordship says we are ready to begin."

"Excellent, then without further ado, let's be on with our announcements."

She calls Ileani to begin the next segment, and they arrange the cameras again. On video monitors around the world, this new sequence was taking place.

"Captain Ti'van, can you explain to our viewing audience at this time what we are looking at?"

"Absolutely!" she emits enthusiastically. "As we said before, this is a battlefield arena, and so far, the High Commander and his people are arranging their contestants. As you can see, they are outfitted in a classic array of chain and plate mail armor, and wielding a sword and shield, just like in the good old days of a royal tournament."

"But we don't have any royalty in our world anymore."

"Minor detail," she shrugs. "It's the thought that counts. And I believe I overheard a moment ago Sargeras praising the arrangement. So, if it pleases him, that's all that matters. And he is part of an old aristocratic society, you know."

"Yes, I suppose so."

"As for our opponents, visiting us today is His Royal Majesty, Thaelyn, King of Tae'Eladar, along with his entourage of contestants to challenge our illustrious military in a battle to make history."

"Um, Ayene, you sound excited for the occasion."

"Well, we need to throw in a little theatrical showmanship."

"Yes! I recall a little of your theatrics from all those previous sensations we aired. And I lost my horns on each occasion!" she chuckles.

"But hey, this is a momentous occasion in our world history. How many times do you think we get to fight for the survival of our species?"

"Uh huh... And where is this place called Tae'Eladar, and do they also use this form of equipment?"

"They do, as it turns out, at least partially. Tae'Eladar is a world located in yet another universe out there aside from the one the Marshal discovered once with his mining exploits. He sort of made an accidental discovery along the way and found a most curious opponent in His Lordship. Now, as you can see, we have arranged this extraordinary event that could very well change the world as we know it."

"Wow, Ayene, you like to talk big. You and your, well, she was also a Captain, right?"

"Yes, but she also got a recent promotion, so she's a Colonel now."

"Really! Wow, you people move fast. What was the reason for her promotion? How many times she could send my horns flying?"

"While I'm sure that contributed, the tipping point for her was that same heavy cruiser we took over."

"The cruiser," she muses. "Um, just for the sake of discussion, how many people did she lead onboard a warship in full battle-ready condition and expecting trouble?"

"A single company, which counts at roughly two hundred soldiers."

"And the crew complement of that ship?"

"I'm told it was around fourteen hundred, many of whom were likely armed and expecting that trouble, once they sounded the alarm for the hostile intrusion."

"And the losses along the way?" she raises her brow.

"None. We took the full complement prisoner before they even knew what hit them."

Once again, in the observation booth, Elder Vankkar reacted to the statements.

"And they're only Industrial Age!" he moans softly. "But able to take down a seven-to-one ratio opponent on full alert."

"Don't ever underestimate them, Father," Túfula grins. "But this one was special. It's a special unit recently developed for the occasion."

Ileani continued her interview for the camera.

"In all the nether-space, Ayene. You people are dangerous. And you're out here challenging our people to a contest of some sort?"

"Yes, but this one is just for show. We're hoping to demonstrate some part of our technique."

"Technique. Right. So, we have this world-shattering event out here in the form of a contest between two warring sides doing battle on behalf of our world population. And if I'm interpreting it correctly, this is to win our freedom? All right, so how do we get started?"

*"We shall begin with the official announcement of our visiting troops!
May I present to you, the Most Noble Order of Tyr, in the service of
the royal throne of Tae'Eladar."*

"And here we go," Thaelyn observes. "General, we seem to have a
line of opposition forming up on our outer frontier. Ready the troops!"

"Yes, my Lord!"

The General signals the troops who were hidden away inside their
staging area. He makes a brief announcement over the intercom to
prepare the first line.

In the news van, Ileani and her team were refocusing their cameras
on the battlefield and launching a series of drones for better angles on
the field, as well as a few to observe Darumon and Sargeras for their
reactions.

"This is Commander Geilv," he calls to the soldiers over the com-
link. "We need to form up a solid front line. Take up your positions
just like you did during your practice. Remember to hold your shields
up and ready your weapons."

"Acknowledged, Commander," returns one of the field officers.
"Listen up, people. We'll form up our positions in rows. If anyone is
sent down, the rearward rows pull them aside, and then fill in their
place. We're taking a wall formation."

The Suuden-Aryku soldiers attempt to form up a solid line,
representing a wall using their shields. They were mostly drawing
from the impromptu practice they had during this time, which involved
a number of lessons from historians who studied the ancient forms of
warfare. But their arrangement was still a bit sloppy and amateurish.

"General," Thaelyn asserts as he points to the line-up on the field.
"When we send our people out, see if you can get a few to give some
visual instruction to improve their form out there, will you?"

"Of course, my Lord..."

"And now, let us begin," he declares. "Mister Girhani, call out the
March of the Order."

Petrith issues the instruction through his intercom to the trumpeters
on the field, which were situated just in front of the control room, and
offside from the ramp leading out of the staging area. They began by
sounding off a sequence of long horn blows as the attention-getter,
followed by playing the familiar marching hymn of the Order.

The sounds caught the attention of the Suuden-Aryku troops on the field, as well as the Commander and the others in the news group. It also brings the attention of Darumon and Sargeras.

"Ah, how pleasant," Sargeras relates warmly. "They even brought a serenade for the opening engagement. I have not seen such as this in a long while."

Darumon turned to look up into his Master's eyes and smiled apprehensively.

A parade of troops marched out from the ramp under the control room and onto the field. The front row carried a set of banners, which they placed into mounting posts on the sides. The banners held the traditional heraldry of the Order; that of the dragon shield, the hammer and balance, and the vines grappled in the talons below. The scene was being observed by a remote drone hovering over the field and zeroing in on the arrival of the foreign soldiers.

"They seem somewhat diminutive, Darumon," Sargeras observes, "even by comparison to our own."

"Yes, Master, but I suspect their skill may offer an interesting bit of sport for our side."

Commander Geilv watched the arrival of Thaelyn's troops and studied the monitors for their positioning. The Suuden-Aryku had aligned themselves across the field, waiting uncertainly to see how their opposition would form up.

Thaelyn studied the procession of his troops as it marched forward onto the field in tune to the music, reaching partway, and then halting in a formal presentation as the music ended. Then a field officer started calling out orders to the assembly.

"Order, forward!" he shouts. "Take up your lines and form a staggered wall."

The Order troops strode up, forming another line just inside the forward edge of the game field, as marked by the walls. They took up a staggered row, some kneeling while others remained standing, erecting their shields as professional soldiers accustomed to using such gear, and forming a long defensive wall.

"Commander," Ayene whispers in his ear. "You might want to pass the word to your people to take a few lessons from our side on how to do this. I know you have no idea how to fight with swords, but at least try to make it look like you do."

He nods and passes the word through the com-link, instructing the Suuden-Aryku forces to tidy up their appearance according to the example of the Order troops. The game was beginning.

Thaelyn observed from his window as the two lines took up their positions, and then nodded to Petrith.

"Begin Round One."

Petrith issues a signal to the trumpeters to blow one loud horn as the announcement to begin the first stage.

The Order troops jumped to their feet and rushed forward to meet the Suuden-Aryku. The Suuden-Aryku also leapt forward to engage, but with somewhat less enthusiasm due to their inexperience in this combat style. The two sides clashed in the middle with the front lines pressing against each other.

The Order was playing gentle, swinging their swords to aim carefully at the Suuden-Aryku shields, landing solid blows, and then turning their shields up for the Suuden-Aryku to strike back. The Suuden-Aryku were only just barely experienced in this manner of combat from the brief training period they received. It quickly became apparent that the Order troops might need to give a bit of occasional coaching.

"Hold your shield more to the front," the warriors whispered to their adversaries. "Watch your feet, left one forward, right to the rear. Shift your weight. Use your shoulder when you swing. Twist at the midsection. That's more like it!"

The clashing of metal continued along the full line of combatants, while Commander Geilv watched, alarmed for the vigor of the ordeal, and concerned for any injuries that might occur amongst his soldiers. Even though it was intended as a show, and using blunt weapons, when considering the seed entity and how it behaves, even a small cut could be dangerous. Fortunately, the Suuden-Aryku armor was carefully designed to offer generous protection.

The Order field officer, a Colonel in this case, also paid close attention to the action, and slowly starts calling out a series of coded instructions. The Order troops were lined up in an alternating pattern where each was assigned a special code to be called out at certain intervals, and each was equipped with headphones to listen in to the Colonel's orders.

"Blue, go to Ram," he issues into his shard-com headset.

As their codename was called, they altered their tactic by feigning a conspicuous death scene and falling to the ground, where the next in line would pull them away and take their place.

The Suuden-Aryku soldiers gazed at the fallen victims, glancing quickly at their swords, and wondering if they actually killed them, or if it was only part of the game.

"Commander," calls a field lieutenant. "My opponent just fell down, he looks dead."

"Keep your mind on the next one. It's far more likely he's faking it, but you can't let your guard down."

"Affirmative!"

The soldier then turned to the new warrior now facing them down.

Additional Order troops continued to pull the fallen out of the way, clearing the field of the stricken bodies, and bringing them back inside.

"Yes, their skill is impressive," Sargeras ponders of the slain contestants. "But clearly size is against them."

Darumon wasn't so sure. He took notice of the type of armor Thaelyn's people were using. It wasn't the adamantium he saw that first day on Therinë. This appeared to be a more traditional material, like steel and leather. Even the weapons appeared normal.

"Hmm, yes," he conjectures. "Size is one thing, but the equipment they're using is another."

"Oh, do you think there is a deficiency here? As for me, it seems quite ordinary, and with a pleasantly nostalgic allure."

"Yes, most assuredly... As I study it carefully, I can see it is quite adequate. But like I said, he is a sly one," he chuckles roguishly. "I think he is holding something back."

"Ah, my most faithful servant, are you hinting at some clever surprise in the wait?"

"Yes, a surprise, no doubt. But what is it he's holding back?"

The Colonel calls out another one.

"Green, go to Ram."

Another selection of troops feigns a mortal wound and falls to the ground, only to be pulled away and replaced by more waiting behind. The action continues this way with more code words called out and more Order troops falling to the side. The Order side seemed to be thinning.

In the news group, the Commander continues to watch, alternating between the scene on the field and that on the monitors which gave him a bird's eye view. The Director and Azina also studied the action.

"Ayene," Azina notes. "Not to be criticizing or anything, but your side looks like its losing."

"Yeah, so far it looks like we've had a full cycling of the line with fresh troops. That's not a good sign. I guess the Commander's team is doing quite well for itself out there," she grins mockingly.

"Captain," he mutters softly. "You know darn well we have no idea how to fight like this, and I still recall Therinë."

"I wasn't there, personally, but I think I know your meaning. All I can say is we need to apply some theatrics. After all, we have to impress our Creator. And besides, Azgarén is a far cry from Therinë. We don't have the flows here…yet."

"Yet?"

"Yet…" she smirks.

Thaelyn was monitoring the action closely. The line was growing thin by now, with only one row on the front and a small number of replacements. He waits for one more Ram procedure to feint the next group, and then gives his order.

"Petrith, sound the End of Round."

Petrith sends a signal to the group of trumpeters to blow three short horn bursts. The Order troops retract their swords and hold their shields in a full blocking position, and then back away. They then retreated back inside the structure, leaving the Suuden-Aryku wondering what was coming next. Many of them were glad for the break in the vigorous activity.

"Commander," calls the field lieutenant again. "Any ideas what we're supposed to do now?"

"Negative. So, take a moment to catch your breath and reestablish your line."

The Suuden-Aryku paused to regain their composure, while repositioning themselves back to a wall formation to get ready for whatever was coming out next.

As the last of the Order troops disappeared inside the structure, Sargeras and Darumon waited in anticipation for the next move.

"I wonder how long these lazy oafs down there can hold up," Darumon considers silently as he examines the Suuden-Aryku's beleaguered postures. "This is more work than they've likely seen in half their lifetimes."

Thaelyn and Aerlie both looked up at the two spectators, trying to gauge their readiness for the next act.

"We seem to have their attention," he suggests. "But now, let us see if we can glue it firmly in place."

He turns to the Professor, who was standing patiently at his side by the control panel.

"Professor, it is time. Open up the emitters. General, send word to Lady Sehnisavain and her group. Their moment is next."

The Professor engages a control on the panel and the meters begin to rise as the flow of arcanic energy is released onto the field.

Ileani turned to Ayene for another brief narrative.

"Ayene, can you tell us what is coming next?"

"Now we have a brief intermission with a little halftime entertainment for our audience," she thumbs at Darumon and Sargeras. "This also gives the two sides a moment of rest before the next stage."

"Halftime entertainment… I'm almost afraid of what that means."

"Yeah, hold that thought, Ileani, because Round Two is where things get serious. Commander, I'll give you fair warning, your people are going to receive some rough handling soon."

"Anything to cause injury?" he wonders. "Remember those seeds, Captain."

"Yes Sir, we are well aware of those. But here is where we need to turn things around, and it has to look real."

"Right."

Thaelyn and the others waited as the magical energies flooded the field, watching the gauges on the panel and the barely perceptible flows coming out of the emitters. Then he turned to Petrith for the next phase.

"Mister Girhani, sound the Jubilant Auspice. And Haran, make ready for your first act to follow the elves."

"Yes, my Lord," he responds as he examines his new mage staff.

Haran's staff was another specialty creation. It was somewhat taller than him, and ornamented with twisted shafts of teak and rosewood, accented with gold trim, and crowned with a headpiece set with glowing gems which emitted a soft blue-white aura. This was the staff of a battle mage, not some common item used simply for walking.

The trumpets outside began a mockingly proud melody, prompting Lady Sehnisavain and her group to come out into the open. Among the members were Adept Mynae and her team who moved alongside her. Priest Malorn also strode along with the group, dressed in his finest priestly robe, which was a pale gray with blue lining on the collar and cuffs.

"Who are those people?" Ileani asks.

"Here we have an assembly of representatives," Ayene asserts. "That one man out there is a priest and a former resident of Therinë where Darumon was once impersonating a local governor to deceive them in many ways similar to what he did here with us. He's a survivor of a calamity, and just wants to say Hi, as far as I know."

"Oh, is that all, to say Hi?"

"Yes. He misses his dear old Governor, and wanted Darumon to know he's still alive…when he shouldn't be."

"Wow, nice people we have out here. And those others?"

"Former slaves, also from Therinë, that Darumon took once and used to devastate the rest of them."

"Um, and why are they all here now?"

"Because Therinë is now part of Thaelyn's kingdom, along with all of its residents, and Darumon left a lot of bad feelings along the way."

"Wait, this Thaelyn took an entire planet as part of his kingdom?"

"What was left of it… Another example like all the rest, blasted nearly to nether-space."

"Wonderful. Is there any world out there that wasn't blasted to nether-space?"

Lady Sehnisavain and Priest Malorn both approached into view, as Mynae and her team lined up along the water grate running across the field.

"Priest Malorn," she offers. "Perhaps you would like to go first?"

"Oh, dear Lady Sehnisavain, you are most gracious to ask."

"Yes, well, our performance will take a bit longer, and yours is rather simple. It just seems natural this way."

"Yes, I suppose you hold a good point there. Very well then, wish me luck that I do not return charred beyond recognition," he grins brightly.

He proceeds to step forward into view and takes up a prominent position.

"Ah, hello there!" he shouts boldly. "Is that you, dear Governor? My goodness, you look rather well, despite all that has occurred."

Darumon peered closely at the little man on the field. At first, he didn't recognize him for the strange attire, to say nothing of expecting what was clearly a human speaking the native tongue.

"Who is that down there?"

"Ah, but of course, perhaps you might not recall so precisely. I had a slight change of profession, you see. But surely, if you look closely enough, you will recall all the wonderful times we shared together… back in the fine and lovely city of Rolsklinde!"

Darumon continued squinting at the little figure, but at the mention of the city, the realization dawned on him sharply. He retracted suddenly and gasped.

"Dean! In all Creation, is that you? You're still alive?"

"Oh, indeed, and it is such a joy to hear you recall my name. Yes! I just barely managed to escape from there...one way or another. Feet first, as I recall. But with a little help, I managed to make a full recovery and now...ooh! Just look at me! I'm a priest now!" he jumps buoyantly.

"A priest! You? That would not be my expectation. You were the least likely to turn to a religion."

"Yes, well, you might say I had this life-altering event. Call it... oh...death. But then this funny thing occurred. Well, I suppose you wouldn't be as interested in such a thing as a resurrection, but it truly changed my perspectives on a few things."

"A...resurrection..." he gasps and pulled back as he felt a brief moment of fainting welling up.

"Anyway, since we had this moment, I just had to come out here and show you my new gown. Isn't it grand?" he flashes at his formal attire.

"Uh huh...grand..." he nods uncertainly.

Ileani watched and listened to the dialog through her monitors. She turned to Ayene grimacing at the brief interlude.

"Ayene," she murmurs. "Death? Resurrection? What does he mean?"

"He was a victim of an attack on his home city. He died. But Thaelyn had previously granted him a special consideration for his service to help others, and his priests made a deal with one of the Estelar to bring him back."

"They can do that?" she wheezes as her eyes bulge.

"Yes, but usually only on special occasions. The terms of life and death must follow the same natural balance as all other things in Creation, so this is much more like an exception to the rule."

"Unbelievable. And now he's a priest?"

"Yes, as thanks for his gift of renewed life. Now he serves to help others."

"These people must hold a very deep sense of duty," Geilv suggests.

"Everyone in Thaelyn's service is like that."

Priest Malorn now retreats back several steps while Sehnisavain steps forward.

"Do you know what you're going to say, Lady Sehnisavain?" he asks.

"I did once, but when Relissa came outside with that new message,

I think I might need to make a few changes. Still, a lot of people died needlessly, and this brings its own pain."

"Naturally, and these feelings run deep, to be sure. Just know that Ilmater weeps for you, as much as you might weep for others."

"Thank you."

She steps forward into view and glances at Mynae and her team who stood ready at the water channel.

"There was a time when my people lived a full life in a world at peace," she calls out sternly. "Free from the scourge of war and devastation. We knew not such history as what you might represent, as it came far too long ago for our kind to learn of it. And yet, a fragment of this history crept down upon us and laid waste to that which was not a part of it. Now, what remains of our people must struggle to restore our vitality. Thankfully, we found again what was lost, and returned ourselves back to our ancestral ways. But the pain of our experience will haunt us for as long as it continues to stain our soil. And for this, we present ourselves here, to demonstrate to you our fidelity to our native heritage."

Thaelyn and the others listened to the announcement and nodded.

"Very cleverly stated," he affirms. "And largely in a third person context so as not to point any direct fingers."

"And also," Aerlie adds. "With a subtle positive spirit of survival."

Darumon glared at the little creature cursing at him. On the one hand, he felt a silent ire as he began to realize who it was screeching at him. But on the other hand, he knew this was one of his crimes he had only recently begun to feel so remorseful over. He closed his eyes and discreetly nodded.

Sargeras studied the elder High Elf as she shouted out her agony.

"I recall that one," he mutters. "Her echoes faded, became lost, and finally died. But she still lives? What force took her away from us, Darumon?"

"Faded and died? How curious..." he feigns. "But, oh, this was stretching across a boundary of folds. I recall how you were just barely able to maintain it in this harsh place. I hope I did not stress you too much, my dearest Master."

"Well, the boundary was difficult, yes. But they... Actually, maybe I should admit, for the quantity..."

"Yes! And there were a good many of them I asked you to watch for me. But in actuality, once I had finished with them, it was no longer necessary to keep them in that particular service. They were dismissed to another location, which probably carried them outside your convenient reach. Surely, that must be the cause."

"Ah, perhaps. That might explain it."

Inside the control room, Aerlie let out a mischievous chuckle, which caught the quick attention of the other officers.

"Oh, Darumon," she mumbles. "That was good."

"My dear?" Thaelyn turns to check on her. "Do we have something of curious import?"

"Him, up there," she points at the two giants. "Sargeras recalled Sehnisavain during her outburst, and was asking how she became lost in his mind control effort. He thought she should be dead, due to his sensation, but here she is."

"I see. This is actually very interesting, to hear of it from the other side."

"Right, and then we have Darumon. He was attempting to downplay it, first to cross a dimensional bound, thereby making it hard on his poor weak master in this barren fold. Sargeras almost argued the point, until he reconsidered that it was indeed hard, but also for the quantity he had to spread across. So, Darumon quickly catches this and says he simply dismissed them to another service elsewhere outside his convenient reach."

"Oh my goodness!" Thaelyn chuckles.

"Cu'Nar's eyes," Kailen shakes his head. "All right, he must've received a private lesson from someone we know. Has either Kaliya or Ayene been moonlighting somewhere?"

They all let out a quick laugh as they continued to watch the field.

Sargeras continued to survey the scene with the elves, until another thought came to him.

"But Darumon, how is it possible they could find their way here?"

"Here?" he gushes. "Hmm, yes, I suppose I must admit. But this is likely due to being dismissed from my service once. They simply found a new service elsewhere. You know, Master, some of them do that."

"Ah! Yes, you are surely right. These smaller ones do tend to seek gainful employment on occasion."

Aerlie shakes her head as she continues to listen through her projected thoughts.

"Oh yes, gainful employment... As if YOU would never think of such a responsible thing."

By this time, Sehnisavain had moved closer to Mynae's team, ready to give her direction.

Ileani again watched and listened, and again turned to Ayene for an impression.

"She doesn't sound at all happy."

"No, but if your full society was devastated, would you be happy for it?"

"No, I wouldn't. And here I thought we had it bad."

Geilv was struggling to interpret the situation, as the voice vaguely stood out to him.

"Captain, who is that out there," he asks.

"She's Lady Sehnisavain of the High Elves of the city of Kynesoth."

"What?" he gasps. "But how? Last I heard; that city was found empty. It was supposed to be evacuated. The Marshal wanted to keep them as his pets. But before we could evacuate them, they all vanished. I recall speaking to someone who sounded like they were delusional, and then ran off. Then, when our people arrived, the city was found empty with the gates locked on the inside. How?"

"Thaelyn essentially captured that city using a few clever tricks to convince them they were following the wrong god. He then persuaded them to follow him into a form of redemption using their original religion, part of which revolves around a racial pantheon of these Estelar, and part of which involved a being called a dryad to cleanse the dominating influence Darumon and Sargeras placed on them. After that, it was a play on the com-links to make you think their gods came and took them away in order to send Darumon running the other direction."

"Interesting. Another play on the com-links. So, he was using our technology against us, and on multiple occasions. I need to watch him for that," he chuckles. "But it certainly seemed to work. It looks like he's been working hard to undo everything the Marshal ever did, including here."

"Yeah, Darumon used every nasty trick he could play on those people. He broke their religion, removed their holy symbols, and drove them mad with his telepathic mind control. Elven society holds a very close bond with nature and other natural entities. To disturb this is to harm their spiritual bonds with all other forms of life."

"That sounds despicable!" Azina grimaces. "I can only understand part of what you're saying, and already I want to pull my horns out for it. He treated them like dirt, and he wanted to keep them around for more?"

"They understood how to use this Abnormal Energy," Geilv admits. "They call it magic in their language, so they held value for this point."

"Uh huh…" Ileani muses as she studies the monitors. "So, what is it they're doing out there, because it seems a little strange."

Ayene examined the monitors as the line of elves along the water channel began weaving their hands in odd circles.

"That's what we might also call magic, Ileani," Ayene grins sheepishly. "This is where that Abnormal Energy comes in. Or rather the dynamistic flows, or arcanic energy, depending on who you talk to."

"Uh, but wait, didn't you once say we don't have that here in our universe?"

"Yeah. We're using some very special technology, which is generally on loan to us for this engagement, and it can supply an area effect with a temporary charge."

"Oh wow, and what sort of, um, magic, are they, um, calling up?"

Ayene simply smiled and returned to the monitor.

"Commander," ushers the field lieutenant on the com-link. "Can you explain what we're looking at? We can hear something like chanting."

Darumon gawked at the obvious display. Although he recognized it, he couldn't allow himself to believe in it.

"What in all Creation are they doing down there! That's not supposed to be possible on this world."

Mynae and her team coordinated their efforts, speaking out the incantation over the water until a bulge began to rise up out of the grating.

"Commander!" the lieutenant returns more urgently. "There's something coming up out of the ground over there!"

Mynae's team was bringing up a significant wave suspended above the grating. It was as tall as a man and represented a healthy amount of water to knock a person off their feet, and then some. Darumon watched, shaking his head at the implausibility of the act.

When the spellcasting was finished, Mynae's group sent it away. It went splashing along as a mini tidal wave flowing across the soil. The Suuden-Aryku gaped at it, with several of them looking around for someplace to take cover, but the area was entirely open space.

Ileani and the others in the news group watched on their monitors as the wave moved swiftly, and seemingly intentionally at the line of soldiers, and not diminishing in any way for the duration of the travel, as normal water would, until finally it made contact, splashing heavily against them. The rush of water swept them off their feet and carried them away, in many cases knocking their weapons out of their hands and drenching each of them thoroughly.

Sargeras looked down at the strange anomaly, where he witnessed the Suuden-Aryku scattered across the field from the edge of the line almost to the river, as the wave struck, and then drained off. The disarray of his wet game pieces being knocked around so absurdly by such an inane maneuver struck a note he had not felt for a long time. He began at first to smile, and then started to laugh.

Darumon was dumbfounded by the demonstration of a force that should not exist in this world. But the merriment now gushing up from his Master could not go unnoticed. It was obvious that Sargeras found this very amusing, and so Darumon felt compelled to join in and mimic the moment of indulgence.

He offered up a cautious laugh to appease his Master, but after a few rounds, he modestly covered his face and turned away in despair, trying to conceal his expression from Sargeras's view. Sehnisavain and her team, along with Thaelyn and his officers, all studied him, and understood he did not share his Master's sentiment on this occasion.

The Suuden'kai soldiers picked themselves up and tried shaking out the water that was now squishing inside their armored suits, then went in search of their lost weapons to reequip themselves. When Sargeras's laughter started echoing out, they all turned and looked up at him in disgust for taking such pleasure at their misfortune.

They then turned to see Darumon. The field lieutenant was discreetly looking over her shoulder at him, hoping not to stand out for a direct gaze. She tried catching his glance, and then offered a subtle nod to acknowledge his misery. He took notice of her kind gesture, and returned a similarly gentle nod back. And while he could not make the display very apparent, deep down, it helped to soothe his feelings.

Meanwhile, Geilv passed his glance between his people and Sargeras, feeling a similar sense of revulsion for the Primordial's reaction.

"I need a report!" he urges into his com-link. "Can anyone respond?"

"Yes Sir, we're here," replies a voice through a series of coughs. "We're alright. Soaked from horn to hoof, but otherwise unharmed. What was that thing! It looked like it came at us with an intelligent sense of purpose."

"It did," Ayene suggests. "That was a line of water elementals, a conjuration to bring forth a type of living essence into an elemental form, in this case water."

"Elementals!" Geilv asserts. "I know that word. The Marshal once tried explaining it to me. Thaelyn's people were using them on the battlefield against our troops. They were dangerous, too."

"Generally speaking, they can serve many purposes, not all of them military. Like with all things, whether with magic or any other form of knowledge or technology, there are many forms of practical application, some of it military, but much of it civilian. As for being dangerous, this depends largely on the instructions you give them."

"So, you can order them to perform tasks for you?"

"They're essentially intelligent, or maybe semi-intelligent living entities, albeit often temporary to exist in our native environment, and controlled by the mages who conjure them."

"I swear, I'm going to need to visit one of his academy classes before this is done, simply to understand some of these terms. All right, so we're using magic now. This doesn't sound good. We had a hard time of it on Therinë, from what I recall, and we were fighting for real on that occasion."

"How did it go for you?" Ileani wonders.

"Once his people showed up, we suffered consistent losses, and I don't think any of his people took any real damage."

"But wait, what kinds of weapons were you using on that occasion? Not swords, I would think."

"No, our usual plasma rifles, but it didn't change anything. That shield you see up there comes in a portable version, and it's impenetrable."

"Impenetrable!" she shouts. "And did I hear you say they were only Industrial Age?"

"That's right. Now go figure the rest. If a society of ONLY that level of recognizable technology can create these things using this magical technology of theirs, we're in a bad situation with ONLY our own science and all the things we worked so hard for."

"In all the nether-space, suddenly I don't like living on Azgarén!"

In the observation booth, the Daanen-Aryku Elders shook their heads in disbelief at the sights outside and the statements coming through the news feed. This was further reflected in the general public still hiding in their shelters around the world.

Sehnisavain and her group watched the Suuden-Aryku stagger to their feet again. She felt their pain, but also realized her work was done. Sargeras was very involved by this time. She called for Mynae and her team.

"And so we have it," Mynae considers. "He may be laughing at it, but it serves a larger purpose. And it delivers a word for us that we do not so easily back down."

"Very good, Mynae," Sehnisavain smiles. "We should move away now."

Thaelyn now prepared for his next sequence. He turned to observe Haran, Relissa, and Aelwyn who were standing nearby waiting for their turn.

"Aelwyn, how do you feel about your part? It is coming soon."

"Yes," she responds calmly. "I am standing here immersing myself in a minor sensation of meditative reflection, trying to build my strength."

"Good, and Relissa?"

"Aye," she nods anxiously. "I'm still here...so far. But I think my shadow went skittering off a while back."

"So long as the greater part of you holds your ground, I think we are in a fair condition," he smirks. "But now, Haran, it is time to move forward while Sargeras is so deeply immersed. Give us a little... atmosphere...will you?" he grins.

"Absolutely, my Lord!" he smiles confidently.

He leaves the room and exits outside, marching out onto the field just beyond the water channel for better positioning.

Ileani and her news team observed the lone young man taking up his position, with his ornate mage's robe and long decorative staff in hand.

"Ayene," she wonders. "Who, or what, is that?"

"Which do you prefer, the who or the what?" she grins.

Ileani glares at Ayene and waits for an answer.

"Oh, all right," Ayene relents. "I can see you still need practice with the humor."

"For everything you're throwing at me today, I might demand another sweet treat as payment."

"Certainly. He's a mage, like those others who came before. This is a type of profession for someone who studies the art of magic, or Arcane Science as they call it. In this case, he's top of the line, a Mage Elder."

"That sounds scary for the demonstration we had just a moment ago. And what role does he play?"

"He actually has a couple of roles during this game, but for now, he is going to set us up for Act Two, the final play out here. Just watch."

"I'm not so sure I want to," she emits tenderly.

Haran sets himself into position in the upper center of the field.

He gazes calmly at the Suuden-Aryku, and then turns his eyes up to meet with Darumon.

"Greetings, Darumon," he shouts. "Or maybe I should say Governor Dramon. You might not know me, and for that I am sorry. But perhaps we could make a small introduction."

"Indeed, little one!" he taunts pretentiously as he glances sideways at Sargeras. "And just who are you supposed to be, all dressed up so fancy."

Sargeras turned to observe his servant with his abnormal interactions.

"Darumon? This seems a bit unusual for your behavior."

"Oh, my Master, it is all in the joy of the moment. A little provocative interplay, you know."

"A little…" he ponders briefly. "Ah, yes, I think I see it now. Such a curious invention, I do not recall this before."

Darumon turns back to Haran on the field in anticipation of his response.

"The name is Haran Carronel," he resumes. "I used to be a student at the old academy in Rolsklinde."

"Oh, were you now. But as I recall, those students didn't often rise up to a very high position of scholarly esteem."

"Maybe not, but then their study materials weren't quite up to par, either. But I found some supplemental study elsewhere, and this allowed me to achieve a bit more for myself."

"Really! And would you care to show us a little of this advanced study of yours?"

"Oh, absolutely! Just give me a moment to call out my chants."

"This should be fun to watch," he chuckles mockingly.

Sargeras found himself drawn to this new interaction as a form of playful encouragement.

Haran began twirling his staff, first using both hands to make several spins in front, then around his body, and finally over his head as he started chanting. He traded it into his right hand where he aligned and brought it down firmly to stamp hard on the ground. Sparks shot out in all directions, and a roll of thunder echoed through the soil.

"What…" Ileani murmurs nervously. "Is that thing powered somehow?"

"Maybe so…" Ayene grins.

"Ayene! I'm actually becoming fearful of this thing you call magic."

"Ileani, I've already been there and lost several sets of horns along the way. All I can say is, until you've seen these people in action, you had better grab what's left of yours and hold on tight. A Mage Elder doesn't play with small-time fireworks."

Darumon eyed Haran warily, recognizing the prominent display of magic.

"Such a fascinating display, don't you think, Master? I mean; if you consider where we are right now."

"Indeed, Darumon," Sargeras admits. "Where did you find these people? Surely, they could not be found locally."

"Well, as I said, I did a bit of travelling during this time, and as I put together a few ideas here and there, I realized, what sort of proper entertainment can one find in such a place as this?"

"This is very true, but then, how would these down here stand up to it if they are in fact of local origin?"

"This is a curious question to ask, but so far we haven't actually seen the next wave come out yet."

"Ah, and therefore that hint of a little surprise, perhaps?"

Haran made a cursory glance over the scene, and then went into his act. He begins a vivid waving of his staff, accompanied by a vigorous chant, followed by more twirling over his head. He spins on his heel, then realigns, orients it in front and tamps once again center forward, sending a shockwave through the ground. A wind begins to blow, seemingly drawn inward from around the valley towards the arena.

The effect is immediately noticed by those on the field, including Ileani. She instinctively turns into the breeze as if to find its source, but there is nothing apparent. She then turns to glare at Ayene, who simply shrugs.

"Like I said. So, don't look at me, I'm just a projection. I don't actually feel it."

"Lucky you…" she groans.

Haran continued his dance, repeating several of the steps, making multiple spins, swinging his staff, and tamping again. The chanting built up the energy around him and within the staff, and his vocalizations were reverberating. Each time he pounded the staff into the ground, more sparks and thunder spread into the earth. The winds grew, and a distinct chill entered the air.

"Ileani," announces one of her cameramen. "I'm having difficulty keeping the drones stable in this wind. It's picking up too much."

"Try positioning them under the shelter of those walls. That might shield it."

By this time, a rumbling sound echoed at Haran's feet and waves of static energy were rippling around him in a wide circle, with small wispy tendrils branching up and weaving as if blown by a delicate breeze. As he finished one final sequence, he grabbed the staff at a point approximating its lower one-third mark and spun a determined circle, sweeping it low to the ground to collect the energy into a stream. And as he came forward again, he jabbed the staff sharply skyward, drawing the collected energy around him into a tight funnel that reminisced of lightning, but not a simple bolt. Rather an inverted vortex reaching into the sky above.

Ileani, Azina, and the others in their group jumped at the sudden flash, letting out yelps and cringing away from it.

"In all the nether-space!" Azina shrieks. "What is he doing? He should be dead after that! That's enough to fry a person!"

Ileani's eyes were fixed on the sky overhead, which quickly took on a spiraling pattern to match the intensely swirling winds. Clouds were forming…thick dark clouds.

"That shouldn't be possible," she mutters timidly.

"That's really a matter of opinion," Ayene corrects. "And this is what we call magic."

"So, it is real after all."

"In certain places, yes…"

Haran went into a new routine to exaggerate the effect, making a single rotation in a crouch, then jutting upright and lifting his hands high. A faint column of wispy energy could still be seen around him as he delivered more into the atmospheric disturbance above.

Ileani studied her monitors closely.

"Do I see something in there?" she points at the video.

Ayene peers in closely.

"Yeah, that would be the energy again…or still. We're flooding the field out there from a device we have inside, and he's calling it into his service."

"But how?"

"It follows the will of the mind."

"Something like thought-controlled?"

"In a manner of speaking, but we don't really use that term here. In the natural element, the mind holds the power to influence its surroundings using this as a resource to apply our perceptions onto the fabric of Reality around us."

"But Ayene, that doesn't even sound real to me."

"I'm not surprised. And this is what the Council rejected so often. According to our empirical sciences, this shouldn't exist. You can't measure it with numbers. This is a different study altogether, and it would appear very alien to us. It's mental, conceptual, the power of thoughts. And once you understand it, many things become possible that might not be otherwise. You can shortcut, and even bypass, the traditional laws of physics with this stuff."

As Haran continued his exercise, the cloud formation spread out in all directions, covering the entire valley. The sky turned dusky gray as the clouds blotted out the sun, and the winds swept around the arena and angled upward into the central vortex.

"Well now," Darumon reflects intriguingly. "Isn't that interesting? He created a storm. I wonder what he has in mind. Perhaps he hopes to assault us with rain."

Sargeras erupts with a brief laugh at the notion.

"Oh, Darumon, that would be a curious twist. But what I wonder is what else is waiting for us, as I suspect this might reflect on some new sequence we are about to witness."

Haran moved off to the side as the storm continued to perpetuate. The air grew cold as the winds picked up the ambient moisture. No part of the sky was visible now, only the heavy cloud cover swirling overhead, which reached across each of the surrounding mountain ranges, past the city on one side and towards the shoreline on the other.

"Kaliya," Thaelyn asserts. "Your move..."

"The Hooves of Storm will make their name..." she recites. "And in a very literal sense of the word."

"Indeed!"

She calls on her people, who were arranged in the underground staging area and ready for their debut presentation. Now was the time to assemble. She turned to leave the room and make her own presentation first.

Darumon and Sargeras both gazed upwards, observing the cloud formation, when Kaliya emerged onto the field, strutting forward to roughly the same location as where Haran stood during his demonstration. Here, she would begin her first act.

"Greetings, Darumon," she ushers boldly. "And you as well, Sargeras. We are so glad you could join with us this day."

"Are you now," Darumon taunts assertively. "And just look at you, in that flashy bit of armor. Do we have a name to go along with it?"

"But of course! I go by the rather prestigious name of Kaliya Nazég!"

Darumon's voice caught in his throat at the mention of that name. He briskly flashed at the Daanen'kai Elders visible through the window before returning to her.

Inside the observation booth, each of the Daanen'kai visitors leaned forward in a moment of anxiety and anticipation of her appearance outside.

"Kaliya!" Elder Vankkar mumbles. "What is she up to this time!"

Geilv examined the figure on the monitor and reflected on the name. "Nazég?" he whispers. "Captain Ti'van, is she…?"

"Related? Yes, she's his daughter."

"They're coming home again? But how did they get here?"

"Portals, Commander. And they're bringing back the knowledge they were called out to discover."

Inside the shelters, the people gazed at the scene and began murmuring again, this time over the name and the clear implications of all the news sensations relating to the former Elder.

Ileani, Azina, and the rest, all turned their attention to the lone female out on the field, each of them quietly reflecting on their past experiences and interactions with her.

"Bringing back knowledge?" Ileani wonders tenderly.

"Yes, in a manner of speaking. Although they probably didn't know this at the time; because the owners of that ship didn't explain it to them fully when they first arrived, but one could say they were called out on a kind of pilgrimage to seek aid and discover knowledge. Now they're coming home with it."

"Uh huh… And you said she's a Colonel now?"

"Yes, she is," Ayene affirms.

In the booth, Elder Vankkar reacted to this statement on the monitor.

"A what?!" he shouts. "How in all the nether-space did she make Colonel? That's, um… That's…" he attempts to count on his fingers. "Well, that's a lot higher than a Lieutenant!"

Darumon forced himself back into focus to continue his banter.

"Is that so? But now tell me, what can this little one in her fancy armor do for us? Does she hope to make a little dance and blind us with her shiny apparel?"

"A dance?" Kaliya muses intrepidly. "Oh, certainly! But I hope to blind you with more than my simple apparel. Maybe if I also mention we took up a religion out there, can you believe it?"

"A what?" he balks. "You? A religion? Incredible!"

"And now I'm a Paladin of Oghma!" she shouts.

Kaliya now draws out her sword-staff and twirls it in one hand, then pulls herself to attention while she raises her other hand to call on a divine protection chant. A tall pillar of light erupts around her and envelops her body in a brilliant holy aura. The obvious display, and the mention of the name, caused Darumon to yelp and fall back a step.

"Darumon," Sargeras whispers. "What am I observing down there?"

Darumon was speechless as he gazed at Kaliya's divine armor pulsing around her body.

In the news van, Ileani and the others watched the scene.

"Ayene," the Director mentions. "Is this what you were speaking of as you visited my office that day?"

"It is," she nods. "This is what it looks like from the other side."

"Is that more of this magic of theirs?" Ileani wonders.

"This isn't the same as arcane magic. This is divine magic, and powered by a true deity."

Ileani felt shudders running through her as she turned to gape at Ayene.

"A d-d-deity?"

"The result of worshiping them, at least in her case. To be a paladin of a god is to serve that god and all he represents, and to borrow from him his strength and his spiritual energies, which empower you with certain supernatural abilities. Paladins are regarded as the highest form of noble knight, a type of holy warrior that is part priest, and highly revered by the people as those who demonstrate a level of virtue and honor that is often unparalleled within any military unit. And she trained a full army of them for the occasion."

"Grace of the cu'Nar!" Elder Girhani gasps. "Is THAT what they were doing out there?"

"A paladin? Her?" Elder Vankkar adds.

"An army…of supernatural…holy warriors…" Ileani wheezes. "And worshipping who…or what?"

"Lord Oghma," Ayene states confidently. "Sage of Wisdom, Adherent of Inspiration, and a member of the Estelar. And she's bringing this knowledge back home for the rest of us to realize."

They turned again to Kaliya on the field, where Darumon was still recovering from his shock.

"Eh, yes...most interesting..." he admits. "But a bit of flash is hardly the sort of dance I would expect to see make any real challenge here. Do you have anything else to offer?"

"Indeed, I do!" Kaliya decrees heartily. "Allow me to call out a few of my dance partners to join me. And along the way, we hope to inspire a little nostalgia. I think you might like that, a fond memory reborn to a modern Era as a way to show how happy we are to be home again!"

Kaliya turns to her helmet shard-com.

"This is Colonel Nazég. The stage is set, my Lord. On your word..."

"The word is given," Thaelyn asserts with one more cursory glance around the room. "Mister Girhani, sound the Triumphant Return."

Petrith puts another sound bite on the speakers, this time an uplifting musical portrayal of pride and chivalrous honor.

Kaliya gives another announcement into her com-link.

"Homeward bound troops," she shouts. "Present forward!"

The Stormhooves began a marching procession from the bunkers onto the field. As with the first lineup, the front row carried banners on both sides, and as they emerged into view, the flag-bearers placed their banners into the mounts next to the original Order banners left behind from earlier in the campaign.

Darumon gawked at the proud display marching into view, and all of it adorned in a similar array of shining armor.

"That must've cost a bit," he muses silently. "But if he's willing to go this far...and they're not even his own people...or are they by now?"

Elder Vankkar also stared at the procession outside the window.

"Cu'Nar's grace! Look at all of them. That must represent half our population out there. No wonder we seem so shorthanded lately. They all signed up on his side," he chuckles.

"Well, Elder Vankkar," Sulíma retorts playfully. "If we could get the other half to sign up, we should be good to go again."

"Yes, but excuse me, little lady, that might put someone like me out of work."

"Oh, come on, I'm sure you can find something else to do with yourself. Maybe you could finally get around to chasing Elder Girhani's tail a little."

Elder Vankkar glared in astonishment at the youthful lady, while Elder Girhani began giggling impulsively.

Outside by the news van, Geilv watched the parade of new contestants coming out. He was now becoming worried over the grade of equipment they were carrying.

"Um, Captain Ti'van, how does that armor compare to our own?"

"You mean the native stuff, or this steel plate we're using today?"

"Well, either, I suppose, but mostly what's in use out there right now."

"Yeah, either way, it's probably the same. This is adamantium, that stuff the Marshal was mining on Morndindor. If used properly, like for industrial applications, it's far superior to steel in many ways, and it also carries an arcanic charge that allows you to enchant it with additional properties. Steel would just break against it."

"Uh huh…that's what I was afraid of. And how should I interpret this for our game play out there?"

"Well, you recall my mention of rough handling."

"Yes, and you recall my mention of seeds."

"That I do, but we still have a show to put on. This is as much to present an image for a new military unit as it is simply to bring out the next team. Besides, it's not the armor you should worry about, it's the weapons. They're made of a similar material called mithril, and also enchanted, but I'm aware the bladed ones carry a special sheath to blunt the edges."

"Good. But next is this. As I look out there, the general frame of those people looks like they could be our own. Are these Elder Nazég's people now?"

"Yes, they are. They represent an elite Special Forces unit with some remarkably unique training as compared to your average military. These are the ones that took down that heavy cruiser with only a single company."

"In all the nether-space," he gasps. "And you expect our people to hold any chance against them out here?"

"Um, technically speaking, do you actually want an answer to that?" she smiles timidly.

"No, thank you. But are we speaking of Elder Nazég's work to create this, or this King of yours? Because if it involves this magic…"

"Right. As I understand it, Elder Nazég is quite a dedicated pacifist. So, any mention by Darumon claiming he was part of something militant couldn't be farther from the truth. This here is part of Lord Thaelyn's military, a new branch recently created just for us."

"A new branch? Why would he do this?"

"There are a couple of reasons here, Commander," Ayene affirms. "First is to honor a piece of our history, and to inspire future generations of our people. We were made to romanticize certain aspects of our history, maybe as part of Darumon's propaganda campaign to control us. So, we're going to play on that and give new life to it, this time with a proper meaning, one that you CAN romanticize over with justifiable cause."

"All right, this sounds very altruistic of him."

"Next is to serve as a guiding light to lead our people for our newfound legacy and all our near-godlike gifts. It's no accident for us to choose this. They will set the examples, and the rest will follow. They will teach, and the rest will learn. And they will help our people create a new society with new values and new standards of excellence. And Commander, regardless of whatever you, I, or anyone else listening to this may think; like it or not, we MUST pay attention. We're not just simple people who can take it or leave it when you consider the Prodigy Gift. It's in every one of us. Therefore, it becomes a dire responsibility for us to pay attention to this day and the lessons we will learn here. As I was saying to Ileani here a moment ago, we are in possession of something we're not ready for. We're too young as a species, and too backwards in our beliefs. So, the time has come to grow up, because if it takes a Celestial to teach you what this is, then you need to start behaving as one in order to use it."

"You know, Ayene," Ileani mutters. "Despite what you said to me before, I still say you like to talk big!"

"Yes, but Ileani, this actually is big. Do you at least understand the implications here? We stand on the edge of godhood. Do you know what it takes to hold that position by natural means? Hundreds of millions of years of evolution, and what do we have so far? AND, we have ridiculously long lifespans, which exaggerate the numbers even more for how long we need to wait for that same evolution, due to our long reproductive cycles as compared to anything normal. And by normal, I mean with lifespans measured in decades, maybe centuries at most, but not tens of millennia."

"Ouch!"

"In order to qualify for this Gift, our species would have to be many orders of magnitude more advanced to receive it naturally. But look at us. We lose our horns if someone simply comes along and flashes a little bit of magic at us, or anything else that doesn't fit our limited perspective of what we think to be wisdom. Gods wouldn't do that.

Celestials, who are half-god by themselves, also wouldn't do this. And yet, here we are, nearly on that same level and with no idea what it means to hold it. A Celestial society would normally LIVE in that fourth-dimensional space, and founded on such like metaphysics as a standard principle. And we simply make fun of it in our language."

"Oh dear, I feel a tail spanking coming on now."

"You're not the only one, I'm sure. Therefore…" she waves her hand at Kaliya's army. "Here you have it…our saviors, trained by a Celestial and following the wisdom of a true god. Do you see that banner over there? Do you know what it symbolizes? Take a closer look."

Geilv turns to find the banner the troops set down on their way out, but from his vantage, he couldn't make it out clearly enough.

"Miss Ur'paran," he submits. "Can you bring one of your cameras to zoom on that flag out there?"

"Sure…"

She directs one of her cameramen to reposition a drone for a better angle.

Elder Vankkar listened to the news feed and found himself reflecting on Ayene's words. He also wondered about the banner, so he turned to look out the window at the two banners installed just outside. Among them, he took notice of Thaelyn's military heraldry, which he recognized from his studies in the library at Bya'an Tamoranth. But as he focused on the newer one, he couldn't be sure if his eyes were seeing it correctly.

He let out a yelp and jumped out of his chair, then crawled along the floor to the window. He stared outside at the banner waving gently in the winds and let out several quick wails as he turned to the other members pointing anxiously at the imagery.

"Santari," Elder Girhani emits urgently. "What is it?"

"Do you see it? Out there! Do you?"

Elder Girhani hurries out of her seat to the window to join him. She peers outside at the banner.

"Yeah, what about it?"

"Oh dammit, didn't you pay ANY attention in history class?"

"Sorry, but history really wasn't much of my specialty."

"Velen, surely you must recognize it."

Velen leaned over to peer out the window. Tyanna also lifted forward to peek at it, and while she understood, as she was part of Thaelyn's special circle, the rest were ignorant so far, due to the threat of Darumon's security risk.

"Fascinating," Velen muses softly. "But why that? That was in a completely different Age."

Elder Vankkar glances up to his daughter, who joined by his side at this time with a bright grin.

"Túfu! You little rascal, you know something, don't you!"

"Maybe…" she replies innocently.

"Don't give me that 'maybe' business, I know you too well. What do you know about this?"

"This runs a little deep, actually."

Back outside in the news van, Ileani had a camera drone aiming right at the banners. As with Elder Vankkar, the first one was clearly a foreign symbol, but the second one sent shivers through Commander Geilv.

"But that…is not…possible," he wheezes. "You say he chose this to honor US? But why this?"

"Actually," Ayene offers. "It was Kaliya who chose this, but it was based on the recommendation of a certain individual with prophetic vision, who used a metaphor to symbolize it. She called it the Hooves of Storm. And since our people have been made to romanticize this so often, I guess it makes sense to bring this into reality again. Therefore, she reinvented it."

"Hooves of Storm?" Azina winces.

Kaliya's troupe had now fully assembled out on the field, and she was ready to make her proclamation to the world. She set herself up in front and stood tall and proud. Her com-link was again interfaced with the loudspeaker system to broadcast her words openly, causing her voice to echo across the field.

"We are the Mind of the Enlightened. We are the Thunder of the Stampede. The Arm of Justice, the Voice of Virtue, the Wardens of the Righteous, and the Stewards of the Undaunted. We are the Stormhooves…reborn!"

Elder Vankkar slowly collapsed to the floor and covered his mouth at the presentation given so proudly. His emotions were welling up inside from his romance to a bygone era thought never to be seen again.

In the shelters around the world, an uprising of conversation began to echo among the crowds as they tried to recall the era so often represented with high prestige and glorious achievements. It was the beginning of their current Enlightened Era, if not for the recent news sensations that so heavily tarnished it. But then, some of them began to apply Ayene's statements just preceding this, and it seemed to give a new direction to it. And yet, so far at least, these were just words. The application was yet to be seen.

"Stormhooves!" Azina shrieks. "But doesn't this date back to King Saakerav again? And didn't we already conclude he was Darumon in disguise?"

"Yes, and we did," Ayene states. "But aside from the fact of who King Saakerav was and who might have been impersonating him, he did give us something of benefit, and that was to bring us together into a new Era...of some kind. Thaelyn's world was also broken into many nations at one time, and HE brought them together with HIS authority. But rather than walk away from it, he stayed on, and he taught them new wisdom, new values, new ways to live and work together as if they were a family, and these represent many different races. He also taught them how to interact with their gods on a much more personal level than you'll find for most other societies who might have any contact with the Estelar. So, the concept of them learning the secrets of the universe now comes into practical play, just not all at once. They have to grow into it, piece by piece. And he's also annexed three additional worlds on his way here, all victims of Darumon, and now he's rebuilding them. This is who and what a Celestial is; in case you need it spelled out for you."

"Three new worlds...in how much time?"

"A mere handful of years. Barely a flicker for how long it takes us even to unravel our horns."

"Oops..."

"Of course, this was due to the campaign he was on to arrive here. This might not necessarily be the case in normal practice."

"Yes, I suppose."

"And you already saw what they accomplished as the result. Now reflect on us a moment...who we are, where we came from, and how long it took."

"And another Oops..."

The whispers and murmuring in the shelters suddenly got a bit louder as these implications began to settle. This represented a level of progress that was completely contrary to their old Council, Darumon's promises, or anything else their native science factions might otherwise be able to provide. It also represented the promise of new forms of knowledge they might never have known about before, namely the magical studies. This also led some to ask if they might even be able to keep up with it for the speed and rapidity these others were taking to see their advance well before their technological Age would otherwise allow for it. And all this was nearly within reach, if only to make this first hurdle and see where it might lead them.

"Ayene," the Director begins. "Not that I wish to argue, but we're speaking of an entire world here. Do you think she can actually lead all of them with these new principles of hers?"

"She, like the rest of us, doesn't really have a choice, and I believe you already know this, Director. We are already creating a series of new standards and protocols that need to be established worldwide for all our citizens. The Prodigy Gift demands this, not any one of us. It is not simply for our own protection, it is for our people to realize we have a level of responsibility we must live up to, and we are speaking on the scale of gods, not mortal people."

"But we're not actual gods, are we? I mean, I wouldn't dare describe us as such."

"No, but we're not mortal people either. Not in the traditional sense. This is why we are forced to realize who we are, where we come from, and what it means for us as a species. We could say, due to Darumon's practices at hiding so much, we lived a very sheltered life, unknowing of our true nature or where we should be right now, if given a normal evolutionary climb. Therefore, the Stormhooves will carry us forward, leading us by example, and people like Latena over here will shape our new world to give us the rules we need to live by."

He glances at the young girl who was standing nearby with a proud smile.

"But isn't she also working for you?"

"We can say she's sponsored and supported by us to give her the resources to conduct her campaigns. I understand she's also borrowing a few ideas here and there from a political system that actually works. But this is not to say, from one political body to another, we're trying to take over, like with a hostile coup. Normally, a species like ours, at this stage of our development, and not counting our immaturity to actually understand who we are, might already be recruited by the Estelar as an apprentice society. We could say this is a mandatory conscription, if only because the Measure of Balance is paramount, and any society high enough to affect things on that level will be expected to participate. I dread to think of any who might otherwise refuse, as this might now reflect back on those Primordials. The Estelar are the governing authority, and I seriously doubt they're ready to allow anyone to come in and give THEM the hoof in the tail treatment."

"Oops!"

"Ghantil!" Azina blasts. "That's supposed to be my line!"

"Sorry, Azina, but I guess it was my turn this time," he smiles.

"Therefore," Ayene continues. "Like it or not, we DO qualify, and I think it is fairly safe to say, we WILL be required to evolve to that level, filling in those missing pieces so we don't kill ourselves with these Gifts we weren't ready for. You'll see in a moment what I mean once those people out there go to action. This is what you get when you complete the picture with those teachings Darumon didn't give us."

"Um, right... Well, I will admit, I am a bit curious to see what they have to offer that is so special it can take down a heavy cruiser with so few people."

"Good! And this is where we are now. The Stormhooves are here literally to make their name in this battle. But unlike the originals, this time they're equipped to fight gods, not mortal men. So, if the original Stormhooves were legendary, this one will be mythical. And that is no understatement, Director. They will travel places and do things only a Celestial body would achieve."

"Ayene," Ileani interjects. "I'm only catching on to part of this. You people called me in to this little game of yours, and like so many others in our world, you twisted my horns up tight. But can you tell me, how does an army of any kind fight a god...assuming I could understand what a god is supposed to be, as I'm not religious. And how does this relate to the show we're putting on?"

"First," she replies calmly. "You need to remember, this particular game is being played by proxy, which is already an issue to keep our guests entertained. As for fighting a god, these people aren't your average army. Religious or not, gods are indeed powerful creatures, but then so are these," she thumbs at the army on the field. "We're not normally a militaristic society, so our perceptions of one might be a bit underpowered. But Thaelyn is a soldier in the proper sense of the word, and he knows how to teach people to find their best advantage. This is one of his gifts. These people are trained in advanced forms of combat, which includes a variety of weapons, as well as a form of martial arts combat. I doubt anyone in this world even knows what that is, so we're about to get a crash course on it soon...some more so than others," she giggles cautiously.

Geilv glared at her for the implications.

Ayene continues, "They're also trained in advanced forms of magic, like those mages we saw out here earlier, and as paladins, they also possess a number of divine skills. Combine all of that, along with a few trade secrets his military provides their people, and you have a very fine example of a super soldier."

"A super soldier? As if to say, like um…"

"Augmented."

"Uh oh…" she mutters timidly. "Are we speaking of something like cybernetics or something?"

"No, and I think they might actually hold objections to artificial devices anyway. These are both arcanic and divine enchantments, some of them permanent, and others temporary for the need. Do you see her out there with that glow? That's an enchantment, in this case temporary for the occasion. But there are others applied to the body to permanently enhance her in a variety of ways. As such, you can't kill her by traditional means."

"Yikes! Yeah, maybe that does hold some potential. But is it enough to take on a god?"

"Granted, this is their debut occasion, but for all they train as a body, I would likely say, they could cause a lot of damage, at least as a group. I've heard stories of Thaelyn's people taking on creatures from the nether-realms, and although they were tossed around like rag dolls, they simply stood up again and charged back into it until their target was down. THAT is dedication, as well as durability. And her people are no different, perhaps even better for the added conditioning. I might also say, even though we're not normally militaristic, we can be trained for it, and they worked hard for all this."

"Wow, and trained by a Celestial which, as you say, is also half god. Well, I think that should make life a little more interesting around here."

Elder Vankkar was sitting on the floor near the window as he continued to listen to the news exchange on the monitor and staring at Túfula, who was kneeling beside him.

"And all this by that little tender-hoof," he points out the window, "who couldn't even run a simple patrol without stumbling on something. No offence, Velen…"

"It's alright, Santari," he smiles. "She just needed to find the right moment. And it would seem we had someone watching over us along the way."

"Not simply that," Túfula adds. "But she's grown many times over and won several special honors for her work so far. She's creating a new military, complete with its own special merit awards. Thaelyn once said this will require its own special training and study courses just to fill the hoof-prints she leaves behind."

"You're kidding me!" Elder Vankkar gasps.

"She's been declared a hero, a legend in her own time, and an inspirational leader. Many of our people are now following suit, including Petrith. Suli and I are taking civilian courses, and yet, even we are fascinated by it. So, all I can say about her being a tender-hoof is she was working the wrong service. She's an offensive trooper, and the Sentinels are better described as defensive. They're no good for any kind of real warfare. It's no wonder you people were trapped inside that wreck of a ship."

"Thank you, Túfu, but I suppose you have a point. And she did want to take the fight to them. We just didn't follow."

As Elder Vankkar surveyed the field outside, he reflected on the old memories of the stories he used to tell at his daughter's bedside. He wrapped an arm around her and pulled her in for a gentle hug before returning to his seat.

✦✦✦✦

Darumon glared at the audacious display below, first to study their presentation and military prose, then to reflect on the name they were using.

"Stormhooves, is it?" he mutters privately. "A bit of nostalgia, yes. And it certainly did carry us long enough. But for her to reinvent it... Yes, I think I can see it now. This could serve them well, especially if he's the one behind this reinvention. Very well, I can accept this. But just what are they capable of? We do still have a few standards to set, even for a reinvention."

As their local conversation came to a close, Commander Geilv spent a moment to study this new lineup. These were clearly different from what was used before. Their armor shimmered with a surreal glow. The males looked like they were outfitted for an apocalypse, and the females gave the appearance of being ready to tear their opponents apart with their bare hands, to say nothing of whatever it was strapped to their backs.

829

"This is Commander Geilv to all forces," he announces soberly into his com-link. "This looks serious."

"Oh really, Commander?!" yelps the field lieutenant. "What was your first clue? With respect, that is."

"I understand, but we still need to make this look as good as we can. These are described as an elite Special Forces unit, the same ones who captured the Naal Balai with only a single company."

"A single company versus a heavy cruiser on battle alert? Sir, we have an army of them out here. My horns just ran off back to base, and the rest of me is ready to follow."

"Granted, but put on your war face again, and let's hear your battle cries. Sargeras is watching, and we need him to keep his eyes on the field."

"Yes Sir! All right you people, let's show these fancy-tails who the home team is!"

The Suuden-Aryku troops gathered themselves up again and started letting out their whoops and shouts, although at this moment their hearts really weren't into it.

As Kaliya waited for her troops to form up, she observed Sargeras and Darumon on the far side of the river for their reactions. Sargeras appeared glued to the scene, carefully examining the new lineup on the field as if trying to judge their worthiness in comparison to his side.

"Darumon," he mentions privately to his servant. "These are much different from the previous contestants. Could this be one of those little surprises you were expecting?"

"Yes, this might certainly qualify. It would seem he acquired a few of our own examples for a bit of cross-training. But now this makes me wonder what sort of training he actually did provide, or is it limited simply to this flashy armor."

"I would suspect if he went to this level of exercise to equip them, he might have also provided something else into the mix."

"Perhaps, so I am curious to see what it is now."

✦✦✦✦✦

Inside the control room, Thaelyn begins his next set of orders.

"Commander, it is time to send word to Marelle. Have her make our package ready and begin on her way."

"Yes, Your Lordship," Kailen replies as he calls up Marelle on their shard-com link. "This is Base Zero to Mouse-catcher. Are you receiving?"

"This is Mouse-catcher, standing by," she responds from the bridge of her new command.

Marelle had long since returned to Tae'Eladar after her run on Azgarén. Her team had now reorganized themselves, and her ship's crew was assembled on the large transport vessel. They were now on standby waiting for their cue.

"Mouse-catcher, you are ordered to retrieve your package and make it ready for delivery."

"Understood, we will begin immediately."

Marelle closed her link and began issuing orders to her crew.

"Helm, power us up. Bubble control, make ready for acquisition. Comms, hook me up to Adalon."

"Yes, Captain, the link is open."

"Adalon, the time is now. Are you ready out there?"

"I am ready..." the large dragon resounds keenly.

Adalon was still lying on the field outside the Bahlaie research base as Marelle brought her ship up to full power and began lifting off. The great beast eyed the ominous craft warily as it took to the air.

"By the Powersss above... Whoever designed that thing..." she chuckles tenuously. "Sssuch ingenuity... And by sssuch a young sssociety... And under sssuch impromptu conditionsss. If I were not aware... Of the geniusss behind it... I might be... A little dissstressed..."

"No doubt, if I were in your place, I might feel the same. Have you ever seen a society with a vessel like this one before?"

"Of thisss particular design... No. Thisss one would certainly... Draw it'sss own attention... For it'sss uniquenessss of form. Not to mention... For who built it and why. Neverthelessss... If I did not know... Of it'sss purossse... And it came for me... I am uncertain... Of what my ressssponse... Would be..." she laughs boldly.

"Well, try to hold on to your reflex reactions for a bit longer. Pull your wings in close and coil up your tail."

The odd vessel had lifted into the air and was now gliding across the ground towards the large creature. Adalon retracted her wings and pulled her tail around close to her body. Marelle instructed her crew to carefully position themselves above the beast as the suspension sphere control station aligned its targeting reticle, coordinating with the helm for a perfect alignment.

"Ready here, Captain," the officer advises.

"Good, let's make this one count. Acquire the target and pull it in gently."

The bubble projection emitters cast out their net to envelop the waiting prey. Adalon felt herself being wrapped up as if in a confined cage.

"Adalon," Marelle asks. "How are you doing down there?"

"It feelsss... Very tightly confined... Not at all comfortable... But sssecure. I have not felt... As cramped as thisss... Sssince I was lassst... In my shell! I never thought... As if I might sssuffer... From claussstrophobia... But thisss would certainly... Offer good cause..."

"All right, try to hold on. We'll get you delivered as quickly as we can."

"Indeed. Hurry up... And bring me there... Ssso I can ssspread... My wingsss again. I am anxiousss... To sssee thisss through..."

"Good. Helm, take us up to our jump point."

Kaliya waited on the field for Thaelyn's final word. She heard on the com-link that Marelle was on the way, and she knew timing was important here. Finally, a new message came across.

"Colonel Nazég," Thaelyn issues. "Begin Round Two."

"Acknowledged," she responds as another horn bellows out from the herald trumpets behind her. "Stormhooves, this is our moment. Charge up!"

The full array of soldiers now lifted their hands to call on the same divine chant as Kaliya was wearing. Row after row of glowing pillars erupted to envelop the troops with holy auras, setting the field ablaze with their divine illumination.

Darumon gazed at the display on the field.

"All of them?" he mumbles quietly. "Such a curious sight, and clearly an indication they are well cared for."

The Suuden-Aryku had returned to their wall formation, although very uncertainly for the appearance of their new opponents. They expected they would not last long if that horde should ever charge forward.

Kaliya examined their defensive wall, which this time appeared a little more professional due to their previous experience with the first set. She takes up her first tactic.

"Thunderhooves, let's take down that wall. Present forward and show them what we do to objects in our path."

The troops arranged themselves with a row of males forming up a solid line. They pulled out their hefty weapons and held them aggressively in their hands, then let out a roar as they charged forward.

"Commander!" the voice shouts on the com-link. "In all the nether-space, what are those things they're carrying?! If we get hit by even one of those…"

"You will hold your ground," he responds sternly. "Just remember your briefing earlier. And pray…" he finishes looking tentatively at Ayene.

"Ayene," Azina mutters. "What are those things? They look like giant hammers or something."

"Those are called dire maces," she informs. "And yes, they're heavy, they hit hard, and in the hands of a strong warrior, can do a lot of damage."

"And what does this mean for our people?" Ileani wonders.

"Just remember, we're not here to hurt anyone, but we do need to make a show."

"A show?!" she shrieks. "Using that? What kind of show are you hoping to make, how to sink foundation supports without the need for a pile-driver?"

The forward line closed in, now twirling their weapons in circles over their heads. The nervous Suuden-Aryku cringed at the idea of where those things might make their landing. But before the front line made contact with the Suuden-Aryku's defensive wall, they halted suddenly, bringing their maces down in a powerful overhead slam to the ground.

A massive eruption of thunder echoed through the earth, and the ground buckled under the fierce blow. A rippling wave surged through the layers of soil as an intense shock quaked the land. The tidal forces struck the line of Suuden-Aryku harshly, knocking them fully off their hooves and flinging them through the air, and further to propel them as the wave continued rolling towards the river.

As the earthquake hit the shoreline of the river, it sent a swell splashing across to the opposite side, eventually to impact near the feet of Darumon and Sargeras.

"Most interesting," Sargeras notes to himself. "Were you aware of this capability in these people, Darumon?"

At first, Darumon was speechless, but he quickly realized he had to pull himself together to respond to his master.

"Fascinating," he croons. "And truly a vivid demonstration. Clearly, they are using enchanted weapons. Potent ones, I might add. And no, this is a new one. What else do they have? That was only the males."

"I need a report!" Geilv shouts into his com-link. "Someone give me a report!"

"Commander," responds the weary voice of the field lieutenant. "I think we're alright, no injuries, maybe a few bruises, but nothing serious. What in all the nether-space did they hit us with? How do we defend against earthquakes?"

"I think that was just a wake-up call, but be on your guard. There's another line coming at you."

"I don't think I want to see what they have in store, thank you very much."

Kaliya issued her next order. This would be her special revue.

"Stormmaidens, forward! Let's light up the sky!"

The Suuden-Aryku slowly gathered themselves off the ground, but before they had a chance to reestablish the wall, Kaliya was taking up a position in front of the female line, much like the Grand Marshal of a parade while the rest moved into play. The males, in the meantime, halted their advance, much to the curious surprise of the Suuden-Aryku.

"Commander," the lieutenant reports again. "This front line must be waiting for something. They're kneeling down and holding their position."

"That just means they're waiting for the rest to catch up. Hold yourselves firm, people, this looks like it's going to get rough."

"Right now, I wish I had a religion, because I think I would be praying to something."

"You should hear it from where I'm standing. These people already have one."

"Great! Maybe they could give me a few lessons…if I survive that long."

The female line advanced partway along the field, but halted behind the males. They pulled out their sword-staffs, twirling them around in front, as Kaliya went into her dance.

She began twirling her sword-staff in circles, first in front, and then behind, over her head and off to each side, pirouetting as she swung it widely in one hand and trading off to the other one. The rest of her team mirrored her movements.

"Oh, come now!" Azina barks. "I'll bet she's just showing off, right Ayene?"

"As I understand it, she used to do gymnastics as a girl, even to win a few awards, so maybe just a little," she grins.

"Uh huh…and now she uses it on a battlefield. That must've been some childhood she had to go through. And should I ask what she's twirling around?"

"Only if you want to know it's called a sword-staff and has a razor-sharp edge to it, plus it's enchanted with ice and lightning effects."

"Right, and thank you, but it was actually a rhetorical question."

"Naturally," she smiles.

"Enchanted with ice and lightning?" Ileani wonders. "How do we describe this in terms those of us who still have our horns attached could understand?"

"There are different schools of magical study, and this falls under what we call elemental magic. There are four primal elements in nature…earth, water, air, and fire. Each of these carries its own qualities and effects. Those dire maces have earth and fire, meaning they can invoke these types of effects, like an earthquake or a firestorm. Water and air, like what's used on the sword-staffs, can invoke a freezing or electrocution effect."

"That sounds exceedingly dangerous, and not only for that razor-sharp edge. So, even if it doesn't slice you in half, you could take other forms of damage from it, right? Is it actually necessary to include these?"

"Not everything out there is as fragile as our form of life. Some forms have very strong resistances to certain types of damage. So, the additional effects can hit them one way where another doesn't even get through."

"Well, not having ever met something like that…" she shakes her head. "And I hope I never do."

As Kaliya wrapped up, she and the others took their weapons in both hands, leveling them out and lifting them up ritualistically as they began a chant.

The Suuden-Aryku were bedazzled by the display, and unsure if they should even bother taking up a formation again. The scene was in full view of multiple camera drones playing across the monitors for the news team. Azina and Ileani both stared in anticipation of what these women had in mind, especially after the display the males put on just a moment before. Commander Geilv and Captain Ta'yeen, along with the Director and the others in the group all waited, then soon to feel chills dashing through them as they saw it.

The line of female warriors began to glow with a clear electrical build-up, sending out static bolts in a wild spray along their bodies. They held their weapons over their heads and began to levitate off the ground, with the surging electrical fields increasing in intensity as they lifted higher.

Azina shook her head incredulously.

"I don't think I'm going to like this," she whispers.

The Daanen'kai Elders inside the building shared the sentiment. None of them could have anticipated how proficient the troopers had become using magic, and especially in this short period of time.

The line continued to rise, and their bodies glowed brightly, then suddenly flashed into potent electrical bolts rocketing upward into the cloud cover above. The crashing of thunder accompanied their movement, and the line divided into two parts, spreading in opposite directions across the swirling clouds, then to circle back along the field.

Darumon gazed at the spectacle in awe.

"Well now, that was unexpected."

"Indeed, Darumon," Sargeras accedes. "And if they are so proficient, this does not bode well for our side."

"Hmm, maybe. But to do this up there for a bit of a light show, this isn't quite the same as on the ground, now is it?"

"Do you think they have something else in mind?"

"Perhaps. You did mention a word about these clouds for something, right? So, call it a curious fascination of their showmanship."

Sargeras nods as they continued to watch.

The Suuden-Aryku shuddered at the sight, staring up at the extraordinary display in the turbulent clouds. Echoes of rolling thunder continued to resound throughout the valley as the glowing orbs seemed to make a circular pathway towards the rear of the battlefield.

"Yeah," Azina considers. "This definitely gives the name Stormhooves a whole new meaning."

"Commander," the field lieutenant mumbles on the com-link. "Um, a question, if I may... How, in all the nether-space, are we supposed to fight that!" she screeches.

"I honestly don't know, Lieutenant," he responds hesitantly. "I can't think of anything that could oppose a power of this sort, not in our world or any other. These people were just now described to me as capable of fighting gods. Now I think I understand why. They're here to set a new standard for us, all of us it would seem. So, just hold your line, as best you can, and if you go down, stay there. That's an order!"

"Is that before or after they come back down, because I'm almost ready to faint."

Kaliya's female detachment was rounding the rear of the battlefield, and now aligning for a return forward in a line down the middle.

"Here they come!" the Lieutenant shrieks.

In orbit above the planet, the Saakerav station was monitoring the news broadcast the same as those on the ground. The base commander, along with his crew, watched in awe of the fascinating show being presented below, when an alert signal comes in on the scanner array.

"Commander, we have a distortion wave. I'm showing a jump signature. It's close by, low orbit, just down-spin of us."

"A jump signature? What kind? Are we expecting anyone?"

"Not that I'm aware of, and this is an odd location for an entry point."

"What size?"

"Midrange cruiser... I'm getting a ship on screen. What the... Commander, it's that odd transport vessel again."

"You mean the one that arrived once before with the cargo for Central?"

"Affirmative, along with what appears to be a fighter escort."

"An escort! What in all the... Get me Commander Geilv."

Marelle directed the vessel as it made its entrance into Azgarén space, directly over the planet at the location of her most recent index site, which she made during her previous visit with her invasion force.

"This is Mouse-catcher to Specter Squadron," she orders. "All ships, take up a shield formation."

The fighter escort arranged themselves as a hemispheric shield circling around the front of the vessel, and together they moved downward from their low-orbital arrival point into the upper atmosphere.

"Steady..." Marelle urges the helmsman. "Ease us through."

The Suuden-Aryku on the ground watched the skies, trying to follow the movement of the lightning bolts, not sure what to expect out of it, but strongly worried over being struck by one, which could be deadly.

A call comes in on the com-link.

"This is Commander Geilv."

"Commander, this is Saakerav base. We just picked up a blip appearing in low orbit and now heading down toward the planet surface. It's that transport ship again, along with a fighter escort."

"Did they make contact?"

"Negative, Sir… They appeared and immediately began moving downward. We tried scanning them, but our scans are coming up with anomalous readings."

"What sort of readings?"

"Sir, I'm not sure how to interpret this. The scans can't seem to accurately penetrate that cargo suspension field of theirs, but it looked almost as if they're transporting something biological. And it's huge!"

"How huge are we speaking of, Saakerav?"

"Our analysis suggests close to eight hundred tons. What sort of biologic could measure that large?"

"Incredible! And this ship was carrying it as cargo?"

"Yes Sir! What should we do about it?"

The Commander pauses to look up at the sky again, but the cloud cover conveniently obscured any possibility to see an inbound ship, or anything else approaching from above. He turns to Ayene for an answer.

"Captain Ti'van, Saakerav Station is reporting an inbound ship carrying something they think is a biologic. What do you know of this?"

"It's a special package to help us finish this game," she glances at Sargeras and Darumon for emphasis.

"But they said it has something measuring eight hundred tons!"

"Wow, that's a big package. Adalon would be proud."

Azina jerked around at the mention of the name.

"Adalon? That's the name of that prophetess, I think, right?"

"Yes, it is."

"But…wait a minute…are you actually saying SHE is coming here?"

"In the flesh…"

"And she weighs eight hundred tons?!" she grimaces.

"I never met her in her natural form, but I did meet her once in an avatar form. I've heard some people say she's roughly the size of a five-story office building. So yeah, she's a very well-built example of her kind."

"Well-built?!" she shrieks and grabs her horns.

Kaliya's cloud-borne electrical dance was beginning to align itself over the heads of the Suuden-Aryku troops. The polarization and growing intensity of the surges above did not go unnoticed by the people on the ground. Flashes formed and glowing nodes erupted in a random scatter near the end of the battlefield, sending streaks of lightning to the ground, impacting on the surface, and rematerializing into the female troops.

The field lieutenant let out a shriek, as did many others, at the near proximity of the fearsome strikes and the sudden appearance of their opponents out of the plasmatic haze. The lineup of males then lifted up and made a new charge while the females were intermingled amongst the Suuden'kai soldiers, already in striking distance and combat ready.

Kaliya and her team began with their martial arts attack sequence, twisting and jabbing with fists and elbows into flanks, knees to the lower abdomen, and foot sweeps to knock them down. The maneuvers were not as violent as to cause actual injury, but rather to invoke reactionary impulses within their opponents.

The Suuden-Aryku found themselves in a new struggle. Their shields were useless for defense, as Kaliya's team used unfamiliar combat techniques, including spinning, kicking, and sequential movements of hands and arms to disarm their equipment, leaving them exposed for another maneuver to simulate a finishing strike. Ileani and her news team watched in horror the expertly coordinated attacks, as Kaliya's troops tore through the Suuden-Aryku lines, leaving the soldiers dropping like flies.

Darumon also studied the scene as he tried to follow the unusual combat art.

"This is a new one," he muses. "Their method is entirely different from anything I would expect out of them."

"Yes," Sargeras agrees. "They seem to have received some very advanced training, and they do not appear to be using the flows to augment themselves in this case. You may have been right, Darumon, that earlier display was simply for the glamor. They do not seem to require it on the field."

"And this would make them rather dangerous, with or without the flows. And I think if to involve that other aspect would simply exaggerate the effect. I must admit, it makes for an impressive display."

"Impressive, yes, but unfortunately, our side is losing rather rapidly. I wonder; have you ever considered teaching our side to use the flows?"

"As a matter of fact, the thought did cross my mind a few times. But of course, to do this would first require bringing them to a location where they could train, and also to condition them to understand the nature of it. Living in this fold, as I'm sure you can understand, they would require some special handling simply to interpret this aspect."

"Of course. But if these others were able to do this, it certainly seems feasible."

"Indeed, it does. Perhaps we can consider this for later. I suspect this fellow out here is simply demonstrating what can be made if they were to apply themselves."

"Do you think so? Is he some manner of trainer, perhaps?"

"I suspect he is, to some degree, and with a most curious approach to it."

As the Suuden-Aryku troops were laid out on the field, Azina pulled herself away just long enough to frown at Ayene before turning back to the monitor.

"And to think," she mumbles. "I once wanted to know the secrets of the universe. Now, I think I just want to go back to the way it all was."

"It'll be fine, Azina," Ayene responds softly. "Just hold on long enough to see it through."

"I really hope you're right. This looks a lot worse than what Darumon did to us."

"Not necessarily. A lot of innocent people died because of him."

"And this? How do you describe this?"

"First, they're not dead, just ask the Commander over here. He's still talking to them. Second, it's to hold Sargeras's attention until our final pieces are in place. This is our greater goal here."

"Our greater goal..." she wonders hesitantly.

"Azina, I'm sorry if this offends you, and you're probably not the only one. But our life in this world has been exceedingly monotonous as a society that knows virtually nothing about anything outside our own. Life just isn't that simple. We really are a domesticated breed. But today, we will learn how to live for ourselves, and this also means to learn how to fight for it."

Azina glares at Ayene for the statement, but then relaxes. Ileani also listened and reflected on her role during this time.

"She's right," she considers. "As one of those who kept reporting on all that monotony, I can attest to how boring it got. He had us right where he wanted us, and for better or for worse, we really were under a tight control effect. We never interacted with anything outside our world, never even knew of most of it, and never had to fight for our own survival, as it was generally hand-fed to us to keep us docile."

"Especially if you consider Saakerav," Latena adds. "That was the day we truly became domesticated, as we lost our will to fight at all. He may have given us our unity and led us into a new Era, but it was an Era with an ulterior motive, and not our own. Now we must realize we can be a liberated society, but this also carries certain responsibilities as well as obligations, and not all of them peaceful. We may now have that chance to investigate other worlds, and even other galaxies, but don't you believe for one moment it's all rainbows and ribbons out there. If we want to learn the secrets of the universe, we'll have to struggle for each and every step to earn our right to it. Gods don't simply hand out this information on a platter. They're not supposed to, and they're not going to. We have to prove ourselves worthy of it, and it all comes down to proving ourselves strong enough to earn it."

"But Latena," Azina winces. "Do you mean through combat?"

"Azina, when I was on Tae'Eladar taking my lessons in their language, I also learned a few things from some people I met over there. These gods of theirs teach that philosophy Ayene spoke of: The Measure of Balance. Generally speaking, it says life is not a free ride. The positive side encourages growth, but the negative side throws hardship and challenge at you. This is to test your resolve to actually grow. As for us, a free ride is all we've ever had here. When we speak of what we might call Survival of the Fittest, it's a rule that goes all the way to the top, with no exceptions. You're a pacifist, and while there's nothing wrong with that, even you need to fight for something on occasion. When was the last time you were in your research lab trying to learn something. Did you simply ask your research computer…what is the answer to 'this'…and it popped out a miraculous result? You have to fight, in your own way, to get what you want. It's all part of that same growth experience, a struggle to achieve something. In fact, we all made a big mistake taking Darumon's promises of free wisdom. It doesn't work that way."

"Well, all right, I suppose…if you put it THAT way."

"Our ancestors were not a predator species. We still aren't. But here we are, a sentient lifeform, struggling to survive, and we WILL survive, but it won't be easy, and it certainly won't come cheap. I wouldn't suggest combat to be our first choice, but we do need to fight to achieve our results, whether on a battlefield, in a classroom, in a laboratory, or even in a political forum. Whoever we are, whatever the reason, if it comes down to it, we may have to fight, if only to keep ourselves from being pushed around by someone bigger."

She pauses as they again glance out on the field at the carnage. The Suuden-Aryku troops were mostly on the ground by now.

"Fortunately, today," she continues. "The bigger ones are our own people and here to teach us these lessons. But we had it very easy in this world, largely because we had Darumon protecting us as his investment for his own purposes. So, if we are to claim our new liberty, we're also saying we don't need him, or anyone else to watch our tails. But at the same time, since we have this opportunity, I think we should make friends wherever we can find them, and do so with all due diligence, as there is a clear advantage to this. Thaelyn and his people are unique in many ways, and they can teach us our own value as a species."

"All right," Azina asserts. "I think I can see the value of this, especially for all he's done for us during this time. Most of these news sensations Ileani put on were his work behind the scenes giving us the answers Darumon was otherwise hiding from us."

"Right. And I would also suggest associating ourselves with these gods of theirs. Velen's people have apparently already done so, and this gives them power, as well as confidence. Just look at them out there," she points at the field. "These Estelar are a nurturing society of parental figures. To associate with them would help us as a society that is unfortunately blessed, or cursed, depending on how you look at it, as being half-god in our own way, and yet we're simply too young to know what to do with it. We NEED them!"

Azina withdrew from the firm declaration as she tried to visualize the Prodigy Gift and all she and the Director had learned of it so far.

"And finally," Latena concludes. "As Ayene said earlier, if we can qualify ourselves to be on that same level as a Celestial society, maybe a young Celestial society, we need to understand the responsibilities to hold that station. And simply sitting on your tail is not the responsibility we're speaking of here. WE become the parental body to teach others. And this might also include using assertive measures to defeat the villainous and protect the innocent."

In the shelters, the people listened to Latena's statements, and although the newness of the situation had not fully settled into their minds for the magnitude of the Prodigy Gift and its implications, the testimonies being expressed during this time were starting to build a picture of something they clearly were not ready for in their lives.

Elder Vankkar was watching the monitor, as the camera crew was filming everything being said, and alternating between this and the scene outside. He listened to Latena's argument and felt a moment of his own sentiment.

"That girl knows how to debate."

"She's a graduate from the local university," Sulíma offers. "A political science and history major, and also a conspiracy theorist and political activist."

"An activist? So, that statement she made a little while ago about starting a revolution…"

"Yeah," she affirms eagerly. "She's got the whole world in a complete state of turmoil right now. The old Council has been tossed out, the Charter of Laws has been torn down, and she's apparently working with an army of legal specialists to write a new one, as well as trying to decide on a new form of world government."

"Just what have you people been doing over here in this time?" he retorts in amazement.

"Some might say payback for tossing Master Velen out," she smiles. "And in the process, remaking history to correct for the reasons behind it."

Thaelyn and his officers also listened to one of their monitors.

"That young lady continues to impress me," he nods. "If we are not careful, she might find herself in the position of authority around here."

"She's a little young for that," Kailen muses. "But I suppose these things can happen. And you might find a strong ally if she holds up to that promise of making friends."

"Yours would be a most intriguing ally indeed, Commander. And she does make a solid point where the Prodigy Gift is concerned. As a society that is still quite young, you could do with a little support from those in the know."

They turned to look out the window again to see the battle was coming to its final moments.

"We should check on Marelle again," Thaelyn submits. "She should be just about ready. Then we must make our final move."

"Absolutely, Your Lordship."

Kailen calls up the ship on his local link.

"Mouse-catcher, this is Base Zero. What is your current condition?"

Marelle turned her attention to the com-station which opened the link for a general response.

"This is Mouse-catcher making our descent over the western ocean. We are nearly at our release point. How is it going down there?"

"The final dance is wrapping up. We're ready to move forward."

"Understood. I believe we are arriving at our drop site. Helm, decrease velocity; bring us down to our release threshold."

The immense vessel had plunged lazily through the layers of the Azgarén atmosphere, along with its escort, turning a slow spiral and descending into the denser layers until it reached a safe altitude for Adalon to carry on independently. It leveled out and aligned itself towards the battlefield on the distant horizon, then slowed its forward momentum to a relative crawl. The spatial inversion field was at minimal power for the release of its cargo.

"Fighter escort, disperse. Bubble control, drop it down."

The suspension bubble was lowered through the distortion field into real space under the vessel, allowing it to anchor to the native environment. When it had reached its full exposure, Marelle gave the final order.

"Make ready... And now, release!"

The control operator deactivated the field and Adalon was away. She dropped freely from the vessel, spreading her wings to catch the breezes and began gliding towards the battlefield.

"Base, the package is delivered," Marelle announces on the com-link.

"Acknowledged, Mouse-catcher... Now make for your landing site."

Adalon felt the freedom of flight again, stretching her wings fully and focusing her sights intently on the objects now coming into view ahead of her. She quickly spotted the enormous storm clouds over the battlefield and set herself to make a low and stealthy approach.

"Finally... After ssso long..." she reminisces. "Sssargerasss... I come for you. The circle closesss at lassst..."

With this statement, Adalon angled herself into a dive to pick up speed.

✦ ✦ ✦ ✦ ✦

"Darumon," Sargeras mutters privately. "This is clearly not going well for our side. And I am still concerned over these unusual auras I am seeing down there. This is not a typical application of the flows. There is another form of energy involved, and it is beginning to disturb me."

"Oh?" he feigns. "But Master, these little ones are not well known for observing anything outside what might be found within this fold. What could it be that this scene, for all its curious surprises, might appear so disturbing?"

"I am uncertain, especially as you put it that within this fold there could not otherwise be anything of particular concern. But those energies…how they reflect upon this space… They seem to resonate something…unsavory."

"Hmm, well, I suspect this battle is due to close soon. I have my doubts there will be much more to see down there once the current contest is over."

"Perhaps, but I would like to know where these people came from, and who trained them. These techniques are certainly very effective, but this aura…hmm…"

Darumon glanced discreetly at his Master, trying not to make direct eye contact. He knew the answer to this quandary, but he dared not invoke any further speculation. To do so might not only bring repercussions for who he supposedly invited into this game, as Sargeras was still under the impression this was Darumon's work. But also, he did not wish to fight it any longer, as the outcome was sealed. It was just a matter of waiting for the final moment to arrive, and he sensed it was coming even now.

Aerlie was studying them for their reactions.

"Thaelyn, I think we are running very close now," she remarks tensely. "He is becoming distressed."

"Sargeras?"

"Yes. I can only barely distinguish their murmurings over the other noises out there, and I'm trying to project my thoughts into the vicinity to see if I can pick up their musings. Darumon is attempting to conceal his knowing, but I doubt it'll last long. From the way their lips are moving, I'm interpreting Sargeras is disconcerted over the holy auras Kaliya's people are emitting."

"Yes, this might stand out. Then we should move quickly to contain it. Adalon is on her way, so we should be ready on our side."

He turns to the others in the room to begin the closing sequence.

"Aelwyn, gather yourself and Haran, and make yourselves ready. Go outside and wait for your moment. Timing will be critical here."

Aelwyn was standing next to him watching the scene through the window. She turns and nods.

"My dearest Spirit-brother, I wish you to take great care in your own actions. You may have the most difficult role of any of us in this game."

She lays a hand on his temple and passes her glance to Aerlie, laying the other hand on her shoulder, before turning to stroll out the door, drawing Haran with her as she moves outside.

"Relissa," Thaelyn continues. "Do you have your rune?"

"Aye, but jiggers, I'm worried about this now."

She pulls out a portal rune from her pocket, holding it firmly in her grip, though she could feel her hands sweating by now. Thaelyn could easily see the girl's distress, so he now lays a hand on her shoulder to calm her.

"Do you recall what I once said about placing your faith in me?"

"Aye, and do you remember what I said after that?" she attempts one of her quirky grins.

"Indeed!" he chuckles fondly. "But now is the time to see this through. Open the portal for us, please."

Her butterflies were spinning somersaults in her stomach by this time, but it was something that had to be done, and she was the one to do it. She looked at the rune in her hand and began stretching it out, making it ready to cast her enchantment on it. But before she committed to the deed, she reached forward and wrapped an arm around Thaelyn to offer a generous hug and a peck on the cheek, then followed with Aerlie before returning to her casting posture. She took a deep breath to collect herself and started the spell weave. The energies circled around the stone, soon to erupt into a spiraling column and then to settle back into a swirling ring.

"Here you go," she relents. "Try not to trip on any oversized feet."

Thaelyn gazes one last time at Kailen and the General, both of whom were waiting with dire anticipation.

"General, check with our people back home. I will flash you when we are in position. At that time, we will begin our observance."

"Yes, my Lord, and do take care out there."

Thaelyn reached out and brought his hand down on the rune stone, flashing out of view. Aerlie followed close behind, and then Relissa dismissed the enchantment and turned to stare out the window again. The General called up a link on his shard-com.

"This is General Gabarleine to our temple authority. We are nearly ready here. I will send word in a moment to begin."

"Yes, General," the priestly voice responds. "We are ready and waiting on this side."

"Colonel Nazég, are you aware of our status here? His Lordship is taking his position."

"Acknowledged, General," Kaliya emits. "I've moved away from the conflict so I can oversee our operations better out here."

"Good, stand by."

Relissa shook her head at the audacity of the scene outside as she leaned on the console.

"If someone were to tell me a few years back that I'd be standing here watching a tournament against peeps like these to entertain a god that shouldn't even be alive, I would've smacked them a good hard one where it hurts."

"Indeed, Relissa," the General admits. "I think I would feel the same, if this were to come forward in those early years on Tae'Eladar."

"Aye! That's a good one. But buggers deluxe if I know anything about how this is going to turn out."

<hr>

Commander Geilv and the others in the news group watched as their line of soldiers thinned out rapidly. He made another call on his com-link to his field lieutenant.

"This is Commander Geilv. Lieutenant, do you have a report out there? What is your condition?"

"I'm down, Sir," she replies with a sigh. "That didn't take long."

"Are you injured?"

"Only my pride… I always thought myself to be a good soldier. But these people move so fast, I can't keep up with them. One moment, I'm standing there, and everything around me is a blur, then the next thing I know, the world is spinning in a bigger blur, and I was flat on my back. I felt like a rag doll."

"At ease, Lieutenant, we're not actually supposed to win this one."

"Understood, but it would've been nice if I could've landed at least one hit on somebody."

"Don't worry about it. Maybe we can learn a few new tricks out of this. Until then, keep on standby."

"Affirmative, Sir."

He glanced at Ayene for her reaction, hoping she would have something to offer, but she could only shrug consolingly.

"We should be close to the end by now," she considers. "I can't imagine they would be too much longer, especially with that transport on its way."

At the far end of the row of hills, south of the battlefield and well out of noticeable view of anyone important, a flash delivered two alien figures to the local terrain.

Thaelyn and Aerlie arrived at the predetermined site where they would take on their unspecified role to bring out the final scene of this outrageous act. They were standing well behind Sargeras further along the base of the hillside, far enough away that he would not likely take notice of them, assuming he was paying any attention to begin with. But his mind was clearly directed at the carnage below.

"Thaelyn," Aerlie whispers gently. "We've never done anything like this before."

"No, but as with all things, there must be that first time. I still find it amusing that this fell into place so conveniently."

"The Maker, it must be. She must've seen it coming and took advantage of it."

"But this still does not answer the line in the prophecy about the Master and the Slave. I am expecting someone else to arrive still."

"Probably only after we act as our own distraction."

"Very well, my dear, then let us be on with it. I sense Adalon is very near by now," he glances in the direction of the western line of mountains.

"Yes, I know. All right, I am ready, my love."

Thaelyn peers over his shoulder at the conservation facility and telepathically flashes an image at the General inside the control booth. The General perks up and turns to the approximate direction of the rune portal exit point, and nods conspicuously.

Kailen observed the General's unexpected reaction and shook his head.

"Telepathy," he muses softly. "And to think, here in the hands of a society that is not even as advanced as ours, and yet so much more accustomed at using it."

The General simply smiled as he engaged the com-link again.

"Temple authority, the time is now. Bring our people into service."

"Right away, General," she shouts enthusiastically. "Let the bells ring out!"

Petrith now reconfigures the loudspeaker system to broadcast the signals coming from Tae'Eladar. A new melody began to ring out of the speaker system. The sounds were those of steeple bells chiming in a rhythmic tune. The uncharacteristically uplifting song defied the general scene and harsh nature of the action on the field. When the music began flowing outwards, Thaelyn and Aerlie moved in for an intimate embrace, clasping their hands firmly and pressing their lips together. And as they leaned into one another, a hallowed glow enveloped them.

The new music sounding out caused Darumon to redirect his attention towards the control booth, trying to interpret the reason for this outlandish new presentation. Sargeras was similarly bemused by the abnormal nature of the overture. He turned to Darumon for his impression, but his loyal servant was clearly perplexed.

"Master," Darumon begins tenuously. "I can feel your questions already, but I cannot say what this is now. It certainly does not follow with what we are seeing down there."

"More surprises, perhaps? I am becoming very curious of our competitor."

"Curious…yes…but this…"

He begins nervously scanning the skies, but the cloud cover was clearly concealing anything from the view above.

"So convenient," he mumbles to himself. "And so intentional, I suspect."

He made another glance around the field below, trying to judge if anything had changed. All seemed the same as it was a moment ago, if only for an obvious rise in confusion on the part of the players on the field over the strange music.

"They don't seem to be expecting this part."

Sargeras glanced at his servant and followed his gaze. He could see the action slowing, not that there was much left to do down there, and several people were glancing around in clear bewilderment.

"It would seem he is bringing up a surprise even they were not anticipating. How interesting. I wonder what it is."

Aelwyn and Haran had arrived at the upper end of the field. Much like Aerlie, Aelwyn was trying to project her Celestial senses to interpret Darumon's and Sargeras's musings.

"How interesting," she notes. "General," she calls into her headset. "This is a clever turn of sequencing."

"How do you figure?" the voice returns.

"I am sensing their confusion over the similar confusion of our people on the field, as if to say, no one knows what is happening," she giggles.

"That doesn't surprise me, as I'm sure they don't!"

"Yes, but my meaning here is this will make our people blameless for any premeditation of this sequence."

"Ah! Yes! This should throw a curious twist into it."

Relissa and Kailen stared out the window, along with the General. Relissa's training in surveillance allowed her to see it first, as she was also expecting it to arrive at the foot of the range where her portal came out.

"Jiggers," she croons. "What's that business over there?"

Kailen followed her mention.

"Cu'Nar's eyes..." he moans.

The General went silent and was modestly gaping as he studied it. He instinctively knew what it represented, but it was much too large to be anything predictable.

Commander Geilv and the Captain were also stunned by the strange new music. Azina, the Director, and Ileani with her news team, each were incapable of reconciling the nature of the tune. Even Ayene was puzzled by the abnormal presentation. She cocked her head and slouched her shoulders as she gawked at the field and the spires that were emitting the strange sounds.

"Huh?" she wheezes. "What in all the nether-space is THAT supposed to be for?"

"Ayene?" Azina mumbles. "What kind of music is that?"

"Those are steeple bells from their temples. But they only chime that stuff when they're doing their, um...uh oh..."

She quickly perked up and began urgently scanning the area for anything out of place, until she found the lower end of the hillside.

"Look there!" she points emphatically at the sight.

Her direction brought the attention of the full group along with her. Ileani turned one of her cameras around to see a tall pillar of divine light erupting out of the ground.

"And what is that now?" she asks timidly.

"Something's coming!"

The Daanen-Aryku members in the observation booth had no idea what the music was about, but it soon became apparent, as they had the best seats in the house to see what was happening out there. They all turned to study the anomaly. Kaliya also turned to it, as she waited expectantly for the final play.

Darumon was still gazing at the display on the field as he puzzled the notion.

"Master, at this moment, I feel, um…"

As he nervously tried to formulate his thoughts, he began to sense something strange occurring nearby. He turned to examine his Master, but as he redirected his gaze, his attention was drawn to a sight appearing further along. He didn't need long to identify it, but as the realization set in, he felt his spirit sinking.

"Oh…dear…" he moans softly.

Sargeras could sense something was wrong in Darumon's sudden change of demeanor. He quickly spun around to follow his direction, there to observe the pillar of spectral energies reaching up to the clouds. The column expanded outwards, growing in diameter and intensity, and it further seemed as if it emitted its own choral hymn, which grew in its tonal force along with its girth and the brilliance of the light.

"Ayene," Azina whines. "I'm with Ileani. What IS that thing?"

"I can only guess at this moment, based on some of my past experiences. I saw something like this before, if only on a smaller scale. That's a divine pillar. Something is coming, and by the size of it, it has to be big!"

The battle scene on the ground slowed as the contestants took notice of the abnormal glow permeating the region. The Stormhooves broke off their attack and withdrew. The few remaining Suuden-Aryku who were still standing collected themselves, only to halt as they turned to see the divine pillar, which had grown substantially by now.

"Does anyone know what that is?" the field lieutenant asks cautiously as she props herself up from her stricken position on the ground.

"I can only give a hint," responds one of the troopers. "And it's not of this world."

"Yes, well, you're not of this world, either."

"Um, technically we are, just not recently."

"All right, fine, but apparently you didn't come back alone."

"Would you have preferred we stayed away so you and your corrupt Council could continue to describe us as traitors?"

"Um, actually, all right, forget I said anything. Maybe I'm just upset for the beating I took."

"Fair enough… What if we treat you to a drink or something to smooth things over?"

"A drink?" she muses. "Well…um…" she mulls indecisively as she studies him. "Maybe…but only if you show me how you do some of these tricks of yours."

"I suppose I can do that."

By now, the column had peaked, and the glare obscured what might be inside. But as it began to fade, the outline of a body appeared. It was kneeling at rest, but soon rose to a standing position, taking up the shape of a being of immense proportions, easily matching that of Sargeras himself.

The column faded from sight, but the body still emanated a residual glow. It bore the appearance of a male of very pale features, silvery-white hair reaching below the shoulders, a medium-length beard, and aged contours. His eyes were closed, as if blind, and he was missing his right hand. And he was dressed in a long flowing magistrate's toga of pure white.

No one on the field was able to speak. The people inside the building were stunned, as were the news crew and their guests. Ayene felt compelled to move away from the group to give her space, while Azina, Ileani, and the others were frozen in place.

Darumon was struck with fear in the shadow of this new participant, but feeling a subtle sense of closure fast approaching. Sargeras, on the other hand, turned to face it with a rising sense of muted antipathy.

The being stood there, motionless, absorbing the ambient energies from the voices playing over the loudspeaker. His body shimmered with waves of praise and jubilation asserted by the worship being directed at him from the songs sung in his honor.

"He's one of them," Ayene mutters.

Ileani turned abruptly to the young officer.

"One of who, or what?" she asks curtly.

"I've never actually seen one, only icons in their temples. I've heard they normally hold very alien forms in their natural element, but will sometimes take up shapes in something familiar when presenting themselves to people like us. But he must be one of the Estelar."

"You mean one of those other godlike beings?" she responds nervously.

"But Ayene," Azina interjects mutedly. "I thought you said they didn't dare try their own approach for fear he might run."

"The general idea was to distract Sargeras for a hidden advance. Well, I think we succeeded."

"Yeah, but now what," Ileani wonders.

Sargeras waited for some reaction, but his patience was wearing thin. It was already frayed by the absurdity of the contest they were watching below, so he decided to take the first word.

"And what is this we have here?" he exclaims harshly. "Does it have a name?"

The glowing form of the divine being straightened up proudly, drew in a deep breath, and announced himself with a voice that boomed like the detonation of a massive bomb.

"I AM TYR, LORD OF JUSTICE!!"

Azina felt the pressure wave of the shockingly loud voice. It startled her, causing her to let out a wail and topple over backwards. The Director jumped and shuddered while Ileani, Latena, and Kita cringed and yelped in fright. The military officers at the post flinched and ducked, but managed to hold their stance a little more stoically than the rest.

The players on the field shrank at the shocking explosion of Tyr's voice. Kaliya's people reflexively moved away from their quarry and lowered their weapons, then fell to their knees. Lady Sehnisavain and her elven crew also bowed down in reverence. The Order soldiers who were still inside the underground bunker all rushed out and kneeled on the upper field. And the officers inside the building also lowered themselves in a moment of silent prayer.

"Ghantil," Azina whimpers idiotically as the man tries to help her up. "Do you think everyone heard that?"

"Yeah, I think the whole continent heard it."

Ayene was nearly trembling, even in her projected form.

"But he...but that...him..." she stutters, and then falls to her knees.

Latena and Kita both observed Ayene and nervously glanced at each other. They quickly rushed up and joined by her side on the ground, along with Navina.

Azina, the Director, and Ileani glared at the group, and felt a similar compulsion to kneel down, and this was followed by the Commander and his Captain.

"Captain Ti'van," Geilv ushers tenuously. "Would this have anything to do with that ship coming down?"

"No Sir, that's supposed to be Adalon. She's a Draconic."

"I don't know what that is, or this either, for that matter. But does this at least mean the fight is over for our people out there?"

"Yeah, I think so."

Inside the control room, the officers gazed out the window.

"Buggers," Relissa gasps softly. "That's all I can say. Just buggers."

"How is this possible?" Kailen mutters. "General, do you know anything about this?"

"All I can say is…Great Gods, in a literal sense of it. There is a history little-told back home that when Tyr died, Torm came to us and told the Lord and Lady they were to receive something he bequeathed unto them. But dear gods above, was it his holy essence?"

"What does that mean?"

"It means the remains of Tyr, as a divine being, was transferred into the two of them. They became his vessels, and each carries a part of his spirit now. And my guess is, if brought together, they can remake him, if only for a time."

"That's just plain weird, from my perspective, and astonishing from what I'm seeing out there."

Some distance to the west of the game field, behind the mountains that housed the conservation center, and away past the coastline that lay further beyond, an enormous creature flew low to the waterline. For its great bulk, it seemed to soar along gracefully, but its wake left a large surge in the sea behind it.

Adalon was nearing the shore where she could see the row of mountains in the distance beneath the crown of dark clouds. She was only just entering the edge of that cover, closing in on the beaches.

In a small community along the beach, the local residents were mostly huddled in their homes. Others had been visiting the beach earlier in the day with their families for a refreshing break and a little sport. But when the alarms came in, most of those had retreated to the spas and beachside cafés for safety, there to watch the series of events unfold on the vid-com news broadcast.

One such group of adults was sitting around a refreshment bar in an open-air café, packed tightly and glued to the local news channel. Like with so many other members of the population, they were in fear and awe of the developing events, and now they were witnessing the standoff between the two godlike giants.

Their children, however, had become restless after a while, and decided to sneak off to a game court located down on the beach. They took along a ball and hoped to spend some time kicking it around in a vigorous game similar to soccer. They were deeply immersed in their sport, enjoying a good time passing the ball along the ground, each team trying to score a goal on the other side.

"Over here!" calls one child. "I'm open, pass it here!"

The ball is exchanged between the two and they maneuver it down the game field, dodging the others and passing it between teammates. The last one finds himself cornered by members of the opposing team and looks for an opening to send it along.

Another boy runs around behind the group into a clear path and waves.

"Here!" he shouts.

The first boy dodges to the side and makes a quick pass through the opening.

"Garid, over this way," shouts another teammate.

He looks off to the side to find a young girl waiting near the goal post. If he could pass it off to her, they might score a point. He carries the ball around an incoming blocker, turns and makes ready for a pass, but stalls when something catches his eye.

The spectacle was unusual, as they don't normally see aircraft flying so low just offshore. He is distracted by the object, and it causes him to halt his motion unexpectedly. He stares at it, but his sudden change of behavior results in a collision with another boy who was moving in to steal the ball. They knock each other down.

"Toba!" shouts the girl. "That wasn't nice."

"I'm sorry, he stopped right in front of me," the other boy remarks.

She rushes over and bends down to check on the fallen player.

"Garid, are you alright? Garid?"

The boy was awestruck by what he saw coming in from offshore. His eyes grew wide, and his voice sputtered.

The game was at a standstill as everyone watched Garid's expression change from shock to horror. The girl turned to find what he was looking at, bringing her eyes around to the gigantic silver monster gliding just above the surface of the water. Her first response was a strained gasp, and then she let out a boisterous scream. She scrambled to her feet and dashed off to the snack bar to find her parents.

The startling outburst invoked the rest of them to lurch around and see the otherworldly creature, and soon the full assembly was shrieking and running up to the buildings.

Inside the café, the adult members were keenly centered on the vid-com and the dire events taking place only a modest distance away across the coastal plain and the mountains bordering them and the valley. When the screams and shouts came rushing in, many of the adults tried to shush the children so they could continue watching the broadcast...at least until a massive shadow came over the region, followed by a blast of gale force wind.

Tyr and Sargeras were staring down at each other on the opposite side of the river. Darumon stood behind his master, vainly hoping to delay the inevitable for a few moments longer. Sargeras studied Tyr's form, taking note of the unusual attributes.

"Now I understand those auras," he spurns. "A clever ruse, perhaps? A hidden movement to follow us here? But what manner of ludicrousness is this? Is this all they can send, one lame contestant? Am I not worth more, or have they fallen so lax that they now only lay on their overstuffed gullets? Is it not enough that you ruined our game once? Nor that you pursued us across the Seas of Creation for your sport? Must you persist in despoiling the pleasure we take from these small creatures?"

Darumon glared at his Master from behind Sargeras's back, and then glanced sideways at the Suuden-Aryku on the field and the news team across the way. He did not share this sentiment, not at this moment, but he could not overtly display anything else, not while his Master might see it. He took notice of some of the Suuden'kai troops on the ground sitting up by now and knew it was all just a play. So, he singled out Kaliya in the mass on the field and discreetly waved a hand to draw her attention.

Kaliya had her eyes on Tyr and Sargeras, but when she took notice of Darumon waving at her, she quickly turned her attention to him.

He signaled with a finger pointing at the people on the field, then darted his eyes around, as if looking for a convenient exit, and aimed at the north shield wall.

Kaliya quickly picked up on the meaning and nodded. She then called into her shard-com to give her orders.

"Stormhooves, we need to clear the field. Get these people up and move them around the north wall. Use it like a shield and pray nothing big comes your way."

The troops immediately sprang to action, sheathing their weapons and helping the Suuden'kai soldiers up, then ushering them hurriedly around the wall.

Kaliya supervised the action, then glanced around the field taking notice of the original Order troops on the upper end, along with the trumpeters and a few others who came outside.

"I need all remaining assets to take shelter back inside. I want all nonessential persons off the field immediately."

Tyr stepped forward to bring himself into a better position around the hillside as he prepared to make his presentation.

"Long ago it was," he begins with his voice still echoing, though not as severely now. "We did travel the Face of Creation to find thee and thine in that darkened place, where thou didst commit thy sacrilege upon the Children of thine own hand. We did then place upon thee our canons to reform thy ways, and thou didst reject us bitterly. We, who once arose in the far mists of Creation, who made ourselves aware of the Wisdom of the Ages, will not stand idly by as thou dost once again return to this blasphemy of thy former comportment, as neither we shall permit this of any other. So it will be, by the commandment of they who do now preside over the Face of Creation."

"Preside over it?" Sargeras shouts. "Stolen is a better term, taken out from under those who did not desire you in the first place. We did not ask to be subjected to your rules. By what right do you have to intrude upon our space?"

"Thy space?" he balks. "There is a lost notion amongst the Seas of Creation that thou didst once take this from another. Nevertheless, this notion is no more, and now it is ours. It does not demand any right, but a simple principle of merit, and adherence to the virtues of dynamism. If thee and thine wouldst practice this in any form, thou must also uphold the responsibility for such. But thy society did not, instead to bring suffering and torment. Thou wouldst create thy servants purely for thine own amusement, and when this came to pass, they would be dismissed with no more concern than the performance they gave. This is unbefitting of any being who would dare claim to hold such prestige as thine own."

"Oh, is it now!" he snaps. "And who are you to make this claim? Our kind once held mastery over the Seas of Creation. We were the ones to determine IF and WHEN any species might be worthy of concern. And only in those cases where they might show enough promise would we permit them the luxury of demonstrating it. This is the only way it should be! And you should hold no authority over us to dictate otherwise."

"Incorrect, Primordial!" he thunders. "Thou wouldst place so much authority in thine own hand to determine the worth of others, but thou dost not include thine own in this equation? This is precisely the reason for the punishment we did once bring down upon thee. The Measure of Balance does not permit the temptations of the individual or the group, despite what factional belonging they may claim for themselves. It must encompass all things, even thine own, whether thou dost desire it or not, and whether thou may come under our authority or not. Thou shouldst hold no more privilege to determine the worth of others as thou wouldst claim of ours against thee. The statement is self-defeating, and rife with arrogance. And now that thou dost find thine own determination of worth brought into question, thou wouldst dare speak of thyself so righteously? Thou didst not bequeath this unto others; therefore, thou dost not deserve it for thyself!"

Sargeras screamed in outrage at the derisive contention.

In the news group, Ileani and the others cowered behind their instruments.

"In all the nether-space," she shudders. "Is this how gods do politics and law?"

"Well," Ayene mumbles. "It certainly does bring home why they're called gods."

In the many raid shelters, the people were similarly quivering at the surge of emotions being played out by the two god entities. But at the same time, many were also taking note of the statements being made and their implied meaning. And clearly, Sargeras was showing his true colors. This naturally followed with arguments over the long-term assertion of him being a benefactor of any kind.

"Therefore, Primordial," Tyr concludes. "Thy demeanor of opposition to any rule notwithstanding, thou cannot expect to hold such authority to determine the worth of another without once expecting the same of thine own. And when it did finally come forward, thy breed did reject this notion, and for that same arrogance that thou dost think thyself to hold absolute authority over all other things. Life is precious, whether thine own or that of another. And when thou dost disrespect that life, thine own may become forfeit. Such is the Measure of Balance, and unlike thee, we do place this even above our own, as we are no less for it."

"I will not be told what to do!" he rages. "Not by you, nor any other. We should've been paying closer attention. This is our only failure, to prevent YOU from coming up. But I will not fall like the others did. They let themselves be drawn into that fight, the fools, when we should've receded so we could plan your proper removal."

"Primordial, this argument is futile!" he scorns. "Thy breed was in demise even before we found it. And our memory of thine actions, even from those early moments after we did find thee and thine, only necessitated our own. Irrespective of this, it was highly unlikely thy breed could make a proper return when we did already hold authority over the greater portion of Creation. Any further attempt at this blasphemy would have only quickened thy demise. It was a matter of Fate that brought us forward, and thine own breed down. And thine arrogance was made further apparent with the delivery of the Agent of Unmaking upon the realm, thus laying catastrophic demise to all that remained after thy craven retreat. We, the Societies of the Estelar shall not tolerate this level of desecration, despite any claim of authority thou might place over anything!"

"Craven?!" he shrieks.

Sargeras was infuriated by this time. He lunged at Tyr, hoping to grapple him and rend him apart physically. Tyr simply ducked to one side and spun around to deliver an elbow jab into Sargeras's flank, knocking him to the ground.

Sargeras pulled himself to his feet again and tried another approach. He retracted his arm as he summoned up his strength, and then launched a powerful spray of plasma flame at Tyr.

Tyr could see something was coming, so he quickly called up a shield to deflect it away from his body. This diverted the spray as a shower into the southern shield wall along the arena, scorching the ground, but simply bouncing off the shield itself.

Kaliya, Aelwyn, and Haran were all standing on the field when the bolt impacted in front of them. They cringed reflexively, but relaxed as they saw the wall absorbing it.

"Thank goodness for that!" Haran chuckles weakly.

In the news team, Ileani and the others were feeling very exposed.

"Commander," the Captain states anxiously. "Suddenly, I don't think this is a safe place to stand around."

"Yeah… Captain Ti'van, do you have any suggestions?"

"Um," Ayene ponders quickly. "Wait…Navina!"

Navina had moved into the background near the news van. When she heard her name called, she rushed forward.

"Yes, Captain!"

"We need protection out here. How well can you form up a wall, like the shield wall over there?"

"Me? Against that?" she points nervously at Sargeras.

"Well, you're not physical, but you CAN create a barrier."

"Oh great, now here's a good test. All right, I'll give it a go."

She moves forward and struggles to imagine a suitable image. She then reimagines her shape as a broad glass wall circling in front of the group and arcing over their heads to offer protection from anything raining down from above.

"Incredible!" the Captain wheezes. "And so impromptu…"

The Daanen-Aryku in the observation booth, as well as the people in the shelters, all reacted in awe of the improvised creation formulated to serve the need.

Elder Vankkar shakes his head at the sight on the monitor.

"And she says we're only HALF god?"

Darumon held back, mostly because he didn't want to tangle with an Estelar directly, as the imbalance was clearly against him. But in so doing, he also felt a nagging sense of failure at assisting his Master in a time of need. And yet, this wasn't his place, as he felt something else coming for him instead. He turned to survey the area of the western mountains. There was nothing to see at this time, but he could feel something just on the other side.

✦✦◆✦✦

Adalon was sailing over the coastal plain, advancing quickly on the mountain range that divided her from the battlefield. Her passage did not go unnoticed by the people on the ground, as her presence was felt by the gushing of air left in her wake. She flapped her wings vigorously to rise over the slope, and then slowed to settle on the leeward side of the summit, just below the ridge to conceal her from view. She grappled with the rocky outcroppings as her great bulk thudded against the peak, sending shockwaves into the mountainside.

In the observation lounge, the Daanen'kai Elders could hear the dull crash and felt the shifting of rock.

"What was that!" Elder Girhani yips as she looks around the room. "Did we just have an earthquake?"

Adalon clawed her way up to peek over the top. She could see Darumon, who was still opposite the arena on the far side of the river. But Tyr and Sargeras had traded places as they scuffled. She then pulled herself onto the ridgetop and stood upright, proudly overlooking the field below.

Sargeras tried again to rush Tyr, aiming low to avoid a deflection this time. Tyr crouched down as his opponent plowed into his midsection, then slammed a knee into Sargeras's face. He lifted Sargeras up and swung a lightning-charged two-fisted strike into his jaw, sending him tumbling back toward the hillside.

Azina watched and shook her head.

"Is this how gods fight? It doesn't seem that much different from the rest of us…except for the flames and lightning, and stuff."

"You're asking the wrong person, Azina," Ayene relents. "I wouldn't know, personally. But I guess it all comes down to whatever is natural."

Adalon peered down into the valley at the two brawling godlike beings. They had traded places again, with Sargeras back where he started.

"Darumon, come to my side!" he asserts. "Together, we can take this one down, and then depart from this place. We will plan our comeuppance for another day."

"Comeuppance…yes…" he hesitates. "Um, Master, I would not fare well against one of those."

"Nonsense, Darumon. Remember, we are in this barren fold. He would not pose a sufficient match for the two of us."

"Right…you are most certainly right…" he pants nervously. "But I feel there is…"

Adalon now takes this opportunity to announce herself. She draws in a deep breath and bellows out a tumultuous roar. The air shook violently, and the land trembled under her powerful blast.

Darumon instantly jerked around to find the statuesque creature perched on top of the mountain, a living monument of glimmering silver scales.

"...Something else..." he trails off. "Oh no. One of them..." he whispers. "But of course, it has to be. They're the enforcers, after all."

Ileani, Azina, and the rest of the crew also spun around at the shocking outpour. They struggled to focus their eyes on the unrealistically gigantic figure that seemed nearly as big as the mountain itself.

Ayene gazed at the ominous sight in amazement.

"Wow," she gasps. "Five-story office building was right."

Azina felt a moment of terror. Her body froze, her voice caught in her throat, her eyes bulged, and her hands trembled as she lifted them to her face. Then she screamed fiercely.

Ileani was no better, but an adrenaline rush and her duty as a reporter was the only thing driving her now.

"Cameras!" she shouts. "Get them up there! Follow it! CPComm, are you getting this?"

Commander Geilv gaped at the sight of the huge creature. The Captain was standing next to him and nearly speechless.

"Commander," he mumbles uncertainly. "Would that account for an eight-hundred-ton biologic?"

"Uh huh... That'd be a good place to start. And worse, if these are the sorts of real opponents to Darumon and Sargeras, we wouldn't stand a chance against them."

Adalon leapt off the ridgetop and soared down towards her first target.

Velen and the Elder Council barely had time to interpret the thunderous upsurge that shook the building before a gigantic shadow passed over their heads. Through the observation booth window, they could see the impossibly wide underbelly of the winged creature descending from above.

"Great cu'Nar!" Elder Girhani yelps. "What in all the nether-space is that?!"

"Not the cu'Nar," Sulíma yips. "That's for sure!"

Velen gazed at it with a sense of paralyzing fear, but this was soon replaced by the sudden realization of its identity. He just barely recognized it from a vision he once had.

"Silver wings..." he mumbles.

Sargeras reeled back at the impossible sight.

"What manner of beast is that?!" he roars.

He promptly judged its direction, darting his eyes at Darumon and back again.

"Darumon, beware! It comes for you!"

Darumon was paralyzed with fear and resignation, as he realized in this final brief moment, this is what he saw coming in his visions. But before he could find anywhere to duck out of the way, Adalon swooped up and slammed into him.

The momentum of her body hammered him, and echoed shockwaves through the air. She gripped him in her claws, lifting him briefly, and then crashing down on top of him with a staggering thud.

Kaliya followed the precision strike as she began to recall the prophecy. She was watching it play out right in front of her, and her curiosity begged her to interpret the lines.

"He will fall beneath the wings," she ponders. "I wonder if she meant Darumon. What chaos he hath done…meaning all of his ill deeds."

Azina and the Director, along with the rest of their group, all felt shudders ripple through them as they listened to the impact. They watched Adalon as she stood on top of Darumon glaring down into his eyes.

Darumon was stunned from the blow and coughing up blood. He gazed at the enormous beast through his blurred vision, and for the first time in his life, outside of the imposing form of his Master, he felt small.

"Greetings, Draconic," he sputters. "I saw you coming."

"Indeed, Darumon… I know thisss. But at the sssame time… You know of thisss form…?"

"I did some study once…very discreetly, you know. It's a fascinating place out there, but a bit dangerous for one such as I."

"Yesss… It is at that."

"In all the nether-space," Azina murmurs. "It talks?"

"That's Adalon, Azina," Ayene notes. "She's a Draconic. They're a sentient race, and supposedly very old."

"It has been… A long time…" Adalon continues. "Do you remember me…?"

"I do feel something familiar," Darumon relates. "But I can't be sure what it is. And I feel you know this, and are hiding it from me intentionally."

"Of courssse…" she muses. "I did not wish… To reveal mysssself… Prematurely. You would not recognize me… As I am now. But perhapsss… If I offer… A sssmall reminder…"

"That would be nice."

"The lassst time we met… You asssked me… Why I had… My

people... Digging holesss in the ground. I anssswered... It was a sssurprise. Well, Darumon... Are you sssurprised...?"

Darumon was uncertain as to the association, as he couldn't immediately recall interacting with anything and asking about holes in the ground.

"I'm still not sure if I can place it."

"Granted. As it surely was... A long time ago. I am one... You once knew. The leader of my people. But perhapsss... The reference may be lossst... Unlessss we alssso asssk... How many... Immortal creaturesss... You have ever known... In your lifetime. Whether by natural... Or even unnatural... Assssertion..."

She let that sink in a moment to see if it stirred any old memories. Darumon studied her. It was true he didn't personally know hardly any immortal creatures, outside himself, Sargeras, and any members of the Estelar he ever researched. But as he gazed into her cat-like eyes, something began to spark.

"Unnatural assertion?" he whispers. "Digging holes! Wait a moment! You? But that can't be... How can you be here now?"

"I sssurvived... Because of my giftsss. Did you think... I would let... My kind fall... Ssso easily... To your gamesss...? I used thisss... To keep them alive... And I used it... To preserve them. And now... Here I am. I have watched you... For a very long time. You were never lossst to me. I observed... And recorded... Everything you did... In thisss world... And elsssewhere. And now... I am the law... To bring judgment... For all the sssacrilege... You have brought... To ssso many othersss..."

"Of course. And so it is. This becomes my Fate."

"Do you have... Any wordsss... For yoursssself...?"

"Does your Sight reveal any of the recent history of our interactions here?"

"It does. Like your commentsss... Within Central Command... As well as... Many of your private musingsss..."

"Good. At least you have that much. Then I will admit, I regret so many of my actions. So much loss and so much waste. I have come to understand a tiny piece of something I once only dreamed of, and it revealed to me a greater meaning. But my habits, combined with the lifestyle of our kind...the attitudes, the conditioning...it simply drove me into familiar practice, dispassionately and irresponsibly for the obvious outcome. It would be impossible, at this time, to replace any part of it. Therefore, all I can do is submit myself to your judgment... final and forever."

Kaliya could hear the exchange through Adalon's headset, along with the General and others inside the control booth and elsewhere. She decides to step forward to offer her thoughts.

"Adalon, is this actually necessary, if he feels so bad about things?"

"It mussst be, Kaliya..." she turns to look back along the field. "And for multiple reasonsss. He will find... No ssssolace... Among they... Who now own... The ssSeas of Creation. And the Measure of Balance... Mussst find itsss recompenssse... For the desssstruction he wrought. But for his confesssssion... I will offer mercy... And deal a ssswift blow..."

"As you say. But I think a moment of requiem might be in order on behalf of his realization."

"If you wish it... I will not argue. He is... After all... Your father..."

Adalon now returns to gaze back down at Darumon.

"The Measure of Balance... Is intended to protect... All that we can reach... And to hold resssponsible... All they who can reach it... Sssuch that... The element of life... Among other thingsss... Is not disssturbed... Beyond a natural tolerance. Life may ebb and flow... And perhapsss... Sssome may feel themsssselves... Grow numb to it. But this is... Inconsssequential... To the greater principle... That it is what it is... And should alwaysss be. It is not... For any of usss... To judge differently..."

"Naturally," Darumon concedes softly.

Azina and the others in the news group watched and listened, as the voices echoed across the field, and were also picked up on their drone microphones.

"I swear, Ayene," she shakes her head. "Regardless of the tail-spanking you gave earlier, listening to her speak of a rule that seems to go way over the rest of us, really says something."

"It does," Ayene nods solemnly.

From inside the control room, Relissa and the others gazed at the scene.

"All right then," she mutters. "So, I guess they knew each other from somewhere."

"Yes," the General wonders. "But where and when did they ever meet?"

Adalon places a claw to brace herself against his shoulder. She then plunges her maw down onto his neck, gripping it firmly and yanking sharply, thereby neatly snapping it. She could feel his lifeforce quickly seeping away. She then pulled back to examine him as he released his final breath.

Sargeras watched, but he felt helpless to assist his longtime servant. The size, apparent strength, and clear ferocity of this creature was enough to keep him away from it, even though he wanted to act. The armor plating of the scales also denied an easy solution to throw something at it, like more fire. But the dialog intrigued him. It hinted at something he clearly was unaware of during his long sleep. But the references as to the relationship were a mystery to him.

The people in the shelters watched and listened. Much like with Azina, they felt the majesty of the words, but in their culture, and for so many of them who were not travelling in those same circles as the most immediate players, it felt almost alien.

Kaliya gazed at the scene as Adalon retracted from her prey, moving back several steps, and leaving the body to rest. She hung her head briefly in thought, and then got on her shard-com to give new orders.

"Stormhooves, get out here! And see if you can bring a few of those others with you. Kailen, will you join me for a moment? I want to give a final salute to our father. That is, that one over there, a moment of silence in his memory. Can we?"

"Kaliya," Kailen replies on the com-link. "You are turning into more of a savior symbol than Thaelyn likely was to his people once," he chuckles softly. "Give me a moment, I'm on my way."

Kaliya waits as her troops reassemble back on the field, much to the curiosity of the news team and its viewers since they couldn't hear the conversation she just made. Ayene watched the action, along with Azina and Ileani. Sargeras also took notice of the activity, along with Tyr, and even the people inside the observation booth studied it.

"What is she doing this time?" Elder Vankkar wonders privately.

Kailen called up Petrith, and together they rushed outside to join as the assembly formed up, along with a mass of the Suuden'kai team. They all turned and began to kneel in silent salute.

Ayene gazed at the scene and quickly realized what the girl was doing.

"In all the nether-space!" she gushes. "Navina, get down here!"

Navina's wall image quickly returned to normal, and the two of them moved into the open and kneeled to join the ritual. Azina gawked at the gesture, along with Ileani.

"Um," the reporter hesitates. "What are you doing?"

"It's a silent salute to the fallen," Ayene responds. "I would recommend anyone who holds any decency to join in."

"Join in? A silent salute…but to HIM?"

"Ileani!" Ayene glances back at the woman. "Were you listening to what Adalon said a moment ago? Life is a precious thing, and it doesn't technically matter who it belongs to. Therefore, this is what you do to honor a fallen soul who realized his own errors in life and essentially asked for forgiveness. Adalon gave a merciful execution, meaning she understood. And since he WAS our father, in a sense of it, we must now honor what he gave us, which is life, and a number of extraordinary Gifts, to which we must now uphold our responsibility, and our heritage to what he made of us, for better or for worse, that this now becomes our legacy. Therefore, we will offer a moment of salute to our Creator."

"I swear! You people!"

Now she rushes over, followed by Latena, Azina and the Director, and the rest, to join in the service.

Inside the observation booth, Sulíma and Túfula both gazed at the monitor, and then at each other.

"Suli?" Túfula emits tenuously.

"Túfu?" she replies back cautiously.

"Yeah! Suli!"

"But… Túfu?"

"Suli! We have to."

Now the two girls jump forward to the window and kneel, much to the surprise of the rest. Elder Vankkar gapes at the duo in amazement.

"I'm actually with that reporter out there," he balks. "Seriously?"

"Yes, Father," Túfula admits. "We must. She's right, this becomes our legacy, for better or for worse, and like it or not. We wouldn't exist otherwise, at least not as we are. Dinner for something, two million years ago, maybe. But not who we are today. And if we are a young Celestial society who must learn our role in that Measure of Balance Adalon spoke of, this is where we begin our lessons."

"In all the nether-space, what has happened to the world around us?"

Now the rest of them rise from their seats to kneel. Velen also joined, although his actions, for his great age, were much more difficult, leaving the two Elders to assist.

The scene now playing on the monitors invoked a new sensation amongst the populace in their shelters. Many of them could only gaze in awe at the apparent sense of duty, although it was also an unknown, and in this case, an unexpected form of behavior to give this sort of funerary service, especially for someone otherwise described as the enemy. Nevertheless, as the message began to sink in, several of them stepped forward to join the ritual. This was followed by a compulsive drive to bring even more to take up the ranks.

Sargeras stared blankly at the scene, as the meaning was essentially lost on him, not knowing the history of these people. He then turned to glare at Tyr for his reaction, but Tyr, who was similarly amazed, and even impressed, simply looked back and shrugged.

Adalon had moved away from her prey by this time. She watched Sargeras carefully for his reactions, as well as Kaliya and her service on the field.

"You have learned your lessssons well… Tall One…" she mutters softly.

She stepped over to the river where she dunked her claws in the water to rinse off, then wiped her face and dunked her snout to finish up.

The news team watched as she tidied herself up.

"Well," Azina muses. "At least she's hygienic."

"I guess she takes a lot of pride in that shine," Ayene smirks tenderly.

The scene went unnervingly quiet as Adalon took up a position on her side of Sargeras, while Tyr stayed on the other side. She was careful to move slowly, and not make any outward signs of aggression. She finally sat down with her gaze firmly set into his eyes.

Kaliya finished her salute, as she also watched Adalon taking up her position. Now she felt as if she should return the troops back into their shelter. She sent them back around the north shield wall, while Kailen and Petrith returned inside. The rest of the people also went back to their original positions.

Sargeras found himself trapped between these two bodies, and time seemed to stand still for a moment. He stepped further away from Tyr, while keeping a close eye on the large silvery beast, unsure which of them would advance first.

His confidence at fighting Tyr in this barren fold faded. The absence of the dynamistic flows, which might otherwise cripple Sargeras, would do the same for Tyr. But Sargeras felt his oats during this time, if only for the seeds feeding him. Now, he had both of these opponents to himself, flows or no flows. And the silvery creature was not as likely as dependent on them.

"Sssargerasss…" Adalon announces. "We meet again…"

Relissa watched from the window in the control room.

"What?" she blurts spontaneously. "Jiggers! What is this 'again' bit now?"

"I have a feeling we are about to receive an education," Haran admits through his headset.

The Daanen'kai Elders exchanged brief glances before returning to the scene.

Sargeras gazes at the creature vacantly.

"Again? I do not recognize you. Nor do I know this form directly. In fact, I have not involved myself with anything for nearly an epoch."

"Perhapsss…" Adalon admits. "But you should know… What we once were… An epoch ago…"

"Holy buggers!" Relissa moans. "That predates a few things."

"Once?" Sargeras muses perplexedly. "I should not think anything from that period would even exist in the modern moment."

"Mossst of it… Does not by now," Adalon affirms. "Not after your kind… Unleashed… The Agent of Unmaking… Into that fold…"

"And therefore, I cannot see how you can regard this as any form of reunion. You do not even appear as one of THEM," he directs over his shoulder at Tyr.

"Indeed… Perhapsss thisss is true. And yet… Though I am… A younger member… I am very well… Ressspected… For my age…"

"A member?" Relissa whimpers. "She's a member…of them?" she glances at Tyr.

"I'm developing a rather suspicious opinion here," the General considers.

"Aye!"

Tyr began peering around Sargeras to glare at Adalon. Ayene watched and took notice of his apparent surprise.

"Well now…" she wonders. "Isn't that something! That old lizard… as Aerlie likes to call her."

"What do you mean?" Ileani asks.

"I think she's hiding something from us…from everyone. And now, here she is."

Sargeras frowns at Adalon for her suggestion.

"But what association does this have to anything I might be familiar with? Everything in our former fold was destroyed, and you were not present at that time."

"...In thisss form," Adalon corrects. "Thisss is a new creation... Sssince that time... And carefully guarded... Made for a purpossse... One that carriesss meaning... Which directly relatesss... To you and your kind... My former Massster!" she hisses.

Sargeras straightens up and staggers back a step.

"Allow me... To introduce myssself," she continues. "I was once... Your Chosen One... Created by your hand. The one who brought you... Ssso many accoladesss... Amongssst your peersss. The one you took favor on... And bessstowed upon me... Your ssspecial giftsss. Sssecrets you withheld... From the othersss... Ssso you could cheat in your gamesss. I am Kuroku... Of the Ikoko clan... Of the ssSarrukh!"

Relissa felt faint at this time. She sat in a nearby chair and leaned her elbows on the console, then laid her head in her hands.

Ayene gaped at the mention, and even though she was a projection, she could feel herself turning pale.

Kaliya shook her head in disbelief, and Kailen gazed blankly at the scene.

"Dear cu'Nar, help us all," he moans timidly.

"Kailen," Kaliya responds on her com-link. "They already tried once. And SHE is the one behind it. But if she's originally Sarrukhan, this must date back a very, VERY long time ago."

"Aye," Relissa adds. "The Maker... There she is...your secret entrant, the Master and his Slave."

"Unbelievable!" Kailen notes. "And this also gives us a link to those Sarrukh. They're her original people."

"And his last creation..." Kaliya recalls. "Like Ayene was saying earlier about Sargeras in his sanctuary, still thinking about them. Well, Thaelyn's going to get his wish, I think. That story of the back history."

Vonafel had been sitting pensively in the lounge area behind the others when the name was mentioned. She instantly had a flashback from her studies.

"Kuroku..." she whispers silently. "Her? And she's originally a Sarrukh? Oh, dear gods. And then we have Tae'Eladar and all of us."

Sargeras lurches into a defensive posture at the mention.

"Impossible!" he shouts. "That was an epoch ago. You should no longer exist. Your world should no longer exist, the same as all the others!"

"Oh, but of courssse," Adalon scorns. "And thank you for your concern. You were ssso quick... To essscape... That you forgot... To carry usss with you. We who were heralded... As your finessst championsss. You ssspeak of holding... Authority... Over life and death... That which is worthy or not. But you do not even care... To think of that... Which ssserved you ssso well. Sssuch hypocrisssy!"

"We didn't have the time or opportunity to bring you along. We barely got out of there ourselves."

"Ssso be it. But you should have ssstayed. It would have sssaved me... Thisss epoch... To pursssue you... Acrossss Creation... For all your crimesss. The othersss found their Fate... As it was befitting them. But you had to run... Like a coward... And into thisss place... Above all othersss. The Powersss... Dessscribe thisss fold... As a sssanctuary. A protected ssspace... That even THEY mussst ssstay out of. You defile it... Sssimply by ressssting here."

"As if that matters to me," he snaps. "It was the only place we had to hide from them."

"Perhapsss thisss is ssso... And perhapsss they would not... Concern themssselves... With you in thisss place. But here we are... And you are no more welcome... In thisss fold... Than any other..."

"And are you now here to correct this? Is all this part of a game YOU created?"

"It is..." she affirms. "I am... The driving force... Behind all thisss... Around usss... That made itsss way... Into thisss place... To draw you... And your ssservant... Out of hiding. Jussst as he... Built thisss world... I built my own. Jussst as he... Raised his armiesss... I raised my own. And jussst as he... Once hoped... To take revenge... On the Essstelar... I made my plansss... To finish... What was once ssstarted... An epoch ago. You may have hidden... Yoursssselves... Away from them... But you could not hide... From me..."

"And just how is it you knew about us, and they did not?"

"You sssucceeded... In essscaping... Sssight-unssseen from them. But I used my giftsss... Oh former Massster. Those you once... Gave to me... To ssserve you in your gamesss. But I learned waysss... To use them... Outsssside of that..."

"Really!" he huffs. "So, I'm not the only one cheating here, it would seem."

"I sssuppose… The term is sssubjective. You used it… To improve your ssstation… Amongssst your peersss. A sssimple product… Of your vanity. I used it… To preserve my people… Even through… Your Agent of Unmaking. I was trying… To sssave… That which I held value in…"

"Then let's talk about that a moment. How is it you could survive that occasion? How is it even possible you could still be alive after all this time? Your kind is not immortal. And what is this form you take? How did you accomplish this…or did THEY do it?" he glares briskly at Tyr.

"Good…! Let usss share… A little ssstory-telling… To explain… Sssome old hissstory…"

"Oh buggers!" Relissa whines. "Kaliya, I'm going to get you for this! And I thought all my schooling was done by now."

The General reaches over and pats her on the shoulder as they continue to listen.

Adalon pauses to glance around the field at the others. She spies Kaliya, Aelwyn, and Haran outside, the officers in the control room, those in the observation booth, and finally the news team.

"I once made a promissse…" she reflects. "And now… The time has come… To uphold it. Firssst… Although my people… Are not immortal…" she pauses to consider the statement. "Were not… And largely… Ssstill are not… But their time approachesss… You… My former Massster… Once gave thisss to me… As one of your sssecrets… Along with the Gift… Of Long Prophecy. Do you recall thisss…?"

"Yes, I recall this now. And I am beginning to believe it was a mistake to do so."

"Oh no…!" she rebuts sharply. "It was no missstake. How could it be… A missstake… When it ssserved you ssso well… In the gamesss. You enjoyed it… Far too much… To proclaim it… A sssimple error in judgment. At no time… During our victoriesss… Did you ever reproach… Your decision…"

Sargeras sighed, and his posture slumped, as he realized this was far closer to the truth than he might wish it to be.

Adalon continues, "As for how… We sssurvived… That insssane deployment… Launched by the othersss… We had help… And that help came from… An unlikely sssource… And due to… An unexpected encounter…"

She pauses to glance around the field, where she can see she had the full attention of everyone involved.

"You gave me inssstruction... To use my giftsss... To foresssee... The future encountersss... Of our gamesss... Ssso I could plan our attacksss... And achieve our victoriesss... On your behalf. But in ssso doing... I found it necessssary... To peer into... The private livesss... Of our future opponentsss... To sssee how they live... And to undersssstand their mannersss. In doing thisss... I became familiar with them... Even curiousss... To sssee how they recover... From their failuresss. But do you know... What I found... As I peered... Back into those worldsss... After the game was complete? I sssaw their own Masssters... Wave a hand... And extinguish... Their entire ssspecies... Sssimply to create... A new one... In their place... For the next game..."

In the news group, Azina and Ileani both grimaced at the notion. They glanced at the rest of the people clustered around the van and saw similar expressions of revulsion.

"So much for him being a benefactor of any kind," Azina sighs.

In the shelters, the people also recoiled from the statement, and many were whispering to each other about the implications of any godlike being who would behave in such a way for any reason.

"Thisss was our worth..." Adalon continues. "To our mosssst beloved Masssters. We are permitted... To exissst... ONLY if... We perform well... For your pleasuresss. My love for you... Turned very quickly that day. It sssoon became... A matter of sssurviving... For the sssimple assspect... Of exisssting..."

"And of course," Sargeras retorts. "I suppose this offends you, especially after all else has been said so far."

"Would it not... Offend you... If you were in... Thisss sssame position... Oh former Masssster? But wait... I think it does... Because NOW you are here. How ironic thisss is. And then came that moment... Where I had... A little accident..." she snickers.

"An accident?"

"For lack of a better word..." she accedes. "I foresssaw the coming... Of the Essstelar. Although... In the beginning... It was indisssstinct. I foresssaw their arrival... I foresssaw the encounter... And I foresssaw the battle... Including your releassse... Of the Agent. But as I pondered... These incredible visionsss... My mind wandered... Until it sssstrayed upon… One of them. His name was Helm… The Guardian… The Watcher… And he became my contact…"

"Jiggers!" Relissa yips. "She had something special with him?"

"I shared my thoughtsss with him. I did not want… My home… And my people… To be torn asssunder… As all the ressst… After you let looossse… That weapon. I warned him… And told him… To share thisss… With the othersss… To ensure they found victory… Over yoursss. But I alssso asssked… That he reward my home… With sssalvation… To protect usss from oblivion. As sssuch… He erected a shell… Made of Imberium… Around our home… And thisss provided usss… With our sssanctuary…"

"An Imberium shell…yes," Sargeras muses deeply. "It would need to be maintained during the initial blast effect, but this would certainly explain the survival of your world against the Agent. And then your species perpetuated, perhaps evolved in some way?"

"We did… Although thisss form… Is not a part of that. The Essstelar… Are far more permisssssive… Of natural growth… And encouragement… To overcome our challengesss… Than your kind… Might ever care for. They alssso grant… At leassst on occasion… For one to excel… Beyond their limitsss… To achieve greatnessss. For thisss… I asssscended… To join with them…"

"In all the nether-space," Ayene wheezes. "So, she started out a normal person, even with all those gifts, but then ascended to godhood?"

"And then… I created these…" she raises a foreleg and extends a wing to examine herself. "Thisss is my work… To create my own… Masssterpiece…"

✦ ✦ ✦ ✦ ✦

Marelle had guided her ship in a wide arc for a landing in the southern field below the conservation center. The large open space allowed for ample room to set the huge transport vessel down, along with its fighter escort.

The grappling claw splayed out and lifted upward, preparing to serve its secondary role as a set of makeshift landing gear, affording the body to lower itself to the ground, like a giant six-legged insect coming to rest. The smaller ships set down gently around it.

Marelle and her crew then proceeded to debark, while the combat pilots each exited from their vessels, and the group made haste up to the shield wall and through a small side entrance in the mountainside leading into the base.

The sudden commotion drew the attention of Adalon, then Sargeras and Tyr, although it was a minor diversion for them. But for those in the news group, it turned a few heads.

Commander Geilv and Captain Ta'yeen, along with the others, quickly took notice of a large body of people moving along from behind them.

"Who are these people!" Geilv wonders. "And where did they come from?"

He and the Captain both turned to find the fleet of odd ships, which apparently came down largely undetected, for all the other commotion going on in front of them. They studied the configuration of the transport ship, and how it appeared as it sat on the ground.

"Fascinating," he notes to himself. "That claw doubles as landing gear."

"That must be an interesting experience to pilot," the Captain muses. "I wonder if they would permit us a close inspection of their ships. I would sure like to know how they managed to squeeze a spatial inverter and jump drive into a pocket-sized combat craft."

Ileani directed one of her cameras to examine the new arrivals. In addition to the ships, she saw a lone well-dressed officer heading their way. She had never before seen such an example as this, with pale pinkish-tan skin, auburn hair, but no horns or tail; clearly an alien lifeform…at least to her eyes.

Marelle diverted briefly to check in with Ayene at the news van. As she arrived, she noticed there were many eyes on her, as well as cameras. She waves for Ayene to come over.

"Ayene," she whispers. "What's the story out here? We've been listening on the com-link, and so far, it's blowing our minds."

"I don't really have anything else except I suspect these new parts are unknown even to Tyr up there, the way he's reacting."

"You're kidding me! You'd think, at the very least, he would know what this is about. How are things on the ground with you and the others?"

"Stable. A lot of emotions, but otherwise under control."

"Excellent. I don't want to distract things, so I'm heading inside."

She turns and makes a casual sprint towards the door.

✦✦✦✦✦

Vonafel found herself leaning forward in her chair with increasing enthusiasm as she listened attentively to the news feed being broadcast from the drones and other cameras outside.

Sargeras was examining Adalon carefully as he tried to interpret the meaning of her unusual form.

"You said this was some manner of response due to us, I believe. What purpose does it serve?"

"Thisss race is called... Draconic... And they are... A Guardian Race... Designed to protect othersss... From those like you... And even them..." she directs at Tyr. "Should they ever... Ssstep out of line... And behave with sssuch mannersss... Where they try to take... The authority... Of life and death... Into their handsss... Without sssolid principle..."

"Wow..." Azina mutters. "So, she's the answer to people like him."

"Law enforcement amongst gods?" Ileani muses.

"Well," Ayene relents. "I suppose you still need it, no matter where you stand."

Vonafel felt a shock hit her. She jerks around to her stack of books, which she had lying next to her chair. She grabbed Adalon's prophecy book and flipped to the final page.

"A Guardian Race?" she whispers anxiously. "Is that what they're for? Law enforcement, protectors..."

"The Essstelar have learned... To ressspect me..." Adalon resumes. "They honor me... As I follow... Precisssely... In Helm'sss path... As he was... A well-honored member. But now... We should return... To you and your ssservant... And your hidden retreat..."

"Yes, this should be interesting," Sargeras wonders. "If you were not a Power at that moment, and they did not know of us, how did you find us?"

"It is actually quite sssimple. I had help... From a race... Of Positive Primesss..."

"And there we have the cu'Nar," Kaliya throws her hands up. "Folks, it's all coming together now..."

"Um, Ayene," Ileani hesitates. "Positive Primes?"

"They're beings of an elemental nature," she responds. "Like those we saw earlier, but in this case made of positive energy. This is the race that delivered Velen's ship, and probably on her behalf to help him escape. Velen's people call them the cu'Nar. And we have speculated that ship might have been built by these Sarrukh, so I think this is very likely by now."

"I recall that name…cu'Nar. Kaliya's eyes glowed as the result of them apparently sharing some of this energy with her people."

"Right, supposedly as a means of cleansing them from something, and probably relating to our origins from Darumon."

"How would Positive Primes aid you in this case?" Sargeras asks.

"I foresssaw your departure…" Adalon recalls, "In the child moon… That once circled our home. Helm acquainted me… With these beingsss… Ssso I could learn… To interact with them. From there… I had them follow you… Through the rift… Your ssservant opened… To carry you away. They began to ssserve me… As messsssengers… And sssspies… From that moment… And until the current day…"

Elder Vankkar sighed and glanced around the other Daanen'kai members in the observation booth.

"We were just more pieces of the puzzle, I guess."

"But important pieces, Father," Túfula explains. "We brought word to Thaelyn because she was in hiding at that time. Also, she probably needed us for our Prodigy Gift."

"But what does this mean in the longer term for us?"

"I don't know. But being part of Thaelyn's kingdom is certainly a nice place to live."

"And so, these…spies…of yours," Sargeras muses. "They informed you of where we went. But why did you not apparently share this with them?" he again glances at Tyr. "You could not have been capable of anything on your own, not at that moment."

"I was not…" Adalon admits. "But I was alssso… Very patient… And did not expect… You or your ssservant… To make any movementsss… Until the memoriesss… Were lossst in your opponentsss. Thisss required time… And I had plenty of it. Therefore… As you ssslept… Ssso I waited… Until othersss grew… To take by my ssside. I assscended to join… The Essstelar… And I created… The Draconicsss… As my firssst achievement. I became known… As the Maker… Of Guardian Racesss…"

Vonafel felt another shock rush through her as she followed the dialog and referenced her book. She let out a brief wail.

"First?!" she yelps.

Ankhia glanced over to see the elder elf in a nervous fret.

"Vonafel? What's wrong over there?"

"A Guardian Race!" she screeches, as she points vigorously at the book. "That's what she's doing here."

"All right," Haran muses into his com-link. "So, she was once a Sarrukh, then ascended as a goddess, took the name Maker Kuroku, created the Draconics, but then how did she find her way back down here as one of them?"

"Wait," Kaliya interjects. "Adalon was born about the same time as Thaelyn. So, this is the Maker going into hiding and taking on a new form, and everything she did after was to engineer this situation we're in now."

"I would imagine she might need a little help for that."

"That seraph of hers, I'll bet! And I'll bet she has an army of them back home to help even further."

"A maker of guardian races," Sargeras grumbles. "And then what? You became so proud of your achievement that you took up as one of them?"

"Gently now…" Adalon cautions. "Let usss not… Cassst inssssults… Where they are not… Warranted. For me… Thisss form… Ssserves a purpossse. For one… It ssserves as my example… In your eyesss. I wanted you to sssee… How your former ssslave… Has evolved… And what she has created… In thisss time. If you were… A proper Creator… You might be proud… Of your creation. But knowing you… Thisss is more likely… To bring revulsion inssstead…"

"Now there's a rub in the face," Ayene winces.

"I'm not so sure I want to be standing here right now," Ileani mumbles.

"Yeah, um, Navina? Maybe we should put that wall back up."

"Uh huh…" she relents. "Do you think it would actually help, under these circumstances?"

"It can't hurt."

Navina nods as she takes up her wall simulation again.

"For another…" Adalon continues. "I once promisssed… My people… I would ssseek vengeance upon you… For your lack of devotion to usss…"

"There's that mention of vengeance," Kailen notes. "She's the one calling for it, at least as much on her behalf as probably everyone else's."

"Thisss is as much… My fight… As it is any other. I held thisss back… From the Essstelar… Ssso I could make… My own arrival here… To finish what began… Ssso long ago. Thisss circle will now close... My former Massster. Your kind... With your irreverence for life... Will no longer be tolerated. My purpossse... Is to build... Guardian Racesss... One after another... To prevent thisss unfortunate cycling... Of Masssters like you. The Measure of Balance... Is a fine example... Of fairnessss to all thingsss... And I for one... Intend to ensure... It ssstays that way..."

"She sounds more dedicated than all the rest combined!" Kaliya muses.

"She's got enough cause for it," Kailen accedes.

"Ah, I see it now," Sargeras affirms. "You bring all this into play just to lure me out of hiding, so that you can test yourself against me. The Master against his slave, is that how you want it, Kuroku? Do you think yourself grown up enough to challenge me?"

"The better quessstion is... Do you think... You can challenge me. The Draconicsss... Were made for thisss. I would advise you... Not to underessstimate them..."

Adalon now stands up and takes an aggressive stance, but holds her position waiting for Sargeras to make the first move.

"General," Relissa whimpers. "Did I say buggers a little while ago?"

"Yes, you did, Relissa. And I recall it was the only word you could conjure forth."

"Aye. Then let me say it again. Buggers!"

"I think I would have to agree with you on this one."

"Ayene," Azina whines. "I think I'm sorry I met you. If I could've known what was waiting for me back then..."

"It wouldn't have made any difference, Azina. We'd still be here."

"Well, um, I guess you have a point."

"Azina, it's not about you, it's not about me, and it's not about any other person on this planet. This obviously goes well beyond any of us. Unfortunately, we got stuck with something that shouldn't have existed in the first place. So, the only thing I can say is what's been said before. You need to turn your horns around, stand tall, straighten your tail, and realize we are at a crossroads here. Our very existence is due to creatures that should've died out a billion years ago."

Azina sighs as she glances at the body of Darumon, and then Sargeras lining up with Adalon.

"Right, and I suppose, if it were not for that, the Eracyodines probably would've been eaten by something bigger. They weren't made to take control by natural means."

"Yeah, probably… But now we have a chance to find out what we're truly made of. And at the moment, it seems half of it carries godlike qualities, which changes a lot of things for us. The REAL trouble is we weren't ready for it, and for that matter, we don't even seem to know how to hold up to the responsibilities of the things we do have."

"Is that before or after having a dictatorship keeping us tied up like animals."

"Yes, there's that too. Our pacifist nature, the lack of imagination, and our blind determination to follow such narrow perspectives, and then our tendency to follow the herd without asking where we're going. This, compounded by our ridiculous longevity and our sluggish habits, caused us to simply ignore the important details when it was necessary to ask about them. And to make matters worse, we didn't even bother asking about them even after ten millennia of suffering with the results, only to find we had jumped off a cliff and were now laying broken on the rocks below."

"Right, I get it. So, in other words, I should've been more like Latena over here. Either that, or I should simply keep my mouth shut, because otherwise I might find my hoof jammed halfway down my throat."

"Exactly…" she nods and pats the girl on the shoulder.

Azina gazed at her friend and sighed deeply. She knew Ayene was right, as she was asking these same questions once upon a time, although she didn't have the means to act on them.

Ileani and the others watched and listened in. Commander Geilv felt the worst for it, and all the things he had experienced and been made to do during his career. Ileani also felt a pang of guilt for her part as a journalist hoping to report on newsworthy topics, but only to be stifled by the regulators.

In the shelters around the world, the people reflected on these same words being broadcast over the network. Murmurs and whispers arose from the audiences as they each reflected on their roles, however great or small that they held some part in allowing this to go so long.

As Azina considered the statement, she could only shrug and redirect her attention to the scene ahead of them.

Sargeras glared at Adalon and quietly questioned the merit of holding this particular fight. On one side, he had Tyr, and on the other was Adalon, and this clearly wasn't a good place to be in. He glanced at both of them, wondering which would move first.

Aelwyn was suspecting by the look in his eyes that he might not hold the will to carry this challenge. She quickly turned to Haran to draw his attention.

"Haran, come quickly. We should move into position. I need to prepare, and you need to hold him back."

"Right," he asserts.

They rushed forward from the rearward portion of the field to find a better vantage with a clear view of Sargeras around the walls.

"If there is one thing I ever learned from you, Kuroku," Sargeras muses uncertainly. "It is never to find myself in one of your traps. I took special delight in watching you play this on so many others, but to be the victim of one is not my choice. If you want a piece of me, you will have to hunt for it. Tell your spies, now that I know of them, that they should be extra careful to come too close, or I'll simply wipe THEM from existence."

He briefly glanced at Tyr, who simply folded his arms and did not seem to be making any special movements. Sargeras then began to delve into his inner mental focus.

At first, it seemed as though he was simply drawing strength, and indeed the ambient energies from the seeds seemed to be coalescing around him. A visible aura began to develop, and he soon turned to channeling it.

"Um, Ayene, what's he doing?" Azina asks tentatively.

"He's trying to escape from us! Dammit, we expected this of him. Now it's Aelwyn's turn."

"Aelwyn?"

"Over there in that fancy robe," she points. "She's already moving into position."

The group directs their attention to a man and a woman moving quickly to the middle of the field, where Aelwyn takes up a convenient line-of-sight with Sargeras, and Haran moves in front of her, already beginning a modest preparatory chant.

Sargeras could be seen beginning to form a ripple in the spatial continuum around him. They all watched as he was clearly attempting to evade from the scene. Then Aelwyn engaged her role. Her eyes glowed, her voice seemed to resonate, and she developed a subtle aura around her body as she began her chant.

"Space will become rigid, inflexible, crystalline, locked and unalterable by hand or mind, and he who would pierce it shall feel the needling thorns of Reality played back at him!"

As she finished up, the rippling waves forming around Sargeras altered dramatically, at first crackling, and then welding back together into new patterns. The effect spread outwards as a wave where space itself seemed to freeze over in strange, inexplicable designs, surrounding Sargeras in a large spherical cage that resembled a spectral form of crystal, and riddled with spikes penetrating inside.

"Aargh!" he screams with loathing.

Azina and the people in the news group ogled the stunning display of mental prowess invoked on the field in front of them, and were just barely able to perceive what happened.

"What did she just do?" Ileani wonders.

"Blocked him…" Ayene responds.

"But how can someone hold that much power in such a little body?"

"I can't be sure if size actually matters, but she's a Celestial. The corporeal portion we see out there is only part of her whole essence, some of which is extradimensional."

The Commander briefly glanced at the Captain at the mentioning of the word, and further wincing at the exotic definition.

"Extradimensional?" he whispers. "Just what sort of society do they have over there? And what exactly is a Celestial?"

"As for the society," Ayene asserts. "It's a varied one. You can be sure of that much. And strangely, they live and work in perfect harmony, despite the many differences they share, even if you consider Kaliya and her people. They are very xenophilic, and closely bonded. Compare that with us who have virtually no experience living and working with anything outside our own. Then, a Celestial is best described as an intermediate form between us and them," she points at Tyr. "Part corporeal, as they still hold a vestigial component, and the rest of it the early part of a divine ascension. They would be a working example of metaphysics in action."

Sargeras staggered a moment after his hit, and hastily turned to investigate his two opponents.

"Who did that!" he demands.

He first checks Tyr, but the proud being simply shrugged, and did not show any signs of tampering. He then looked at Adalon, but she only crouched on her haunches, laughing subtly.

"Lose sssomething…?" she chides gently. "And even if not… Do you think… I would ssso easily… Allow you… To ssslip away? You ssspeak of trapsss. You ssspeak of ssspies. But you may alssso… Want to include… My ssseraphim ssservants… Who are watching… Your every move… With their apparition poolsss. They can follow you… Even through your rift. Try to essscape from me… If you dare… But I will not wait… Another epoch… To follow you. I can fold ssspace myssself…"

Sargeras was trying to ignore Adalon's taunts as he continued to search the grounds for the source of his obstruction.

"What insolent speck is responsible for that?" he rages. "I sense you!"

He turns to the field, following his senses until he homes in on Aelwyn.

"Here I am, you Ancient Terror!" her voice booms. "Look here at the Children of the Powers. My Father blessed upon me authority over the fabric of Reality, and I will use it this day to keep you in your place! You will take your punishment and be done with it, Coward! You have been running for far too long. On this day, you are found, and on this day, you will meet your judgment!"

"Impudent bug!" he bellows. "You would dare speak to me in such form?"

"I will speak to you in whatever form is appropriate, especially for one who would never permit another to reach such prestige as to threaten your own."

"Yes, to threaten! This is the cause of it. We would never allow such as you to rise up and take our place. But it would seem someone fell lax."

"Fell lax? Like those precursors you so promptly displaced? It was simply a matter of time. You cannot hold it back forever, especially if you fell into such habits as these games of yours. Fell lax? I think the greater portion of your society fell lax. And they, who fell so far as to lose all interest, fell into oblivion shortly thereafter."

"Are you now to insult our entire race? We once held dominion over the Seas of Creation. It was OURS to do with as we pleased!"

"Yes, WAS is the word for it, and now look at you. What is left of this great empire, but one lonely member who cannot even find safe haven for himself without some ancient grudge following close behind," she points at Adalon. "I would imagine you made a great many enemies along the way, because you show no respect for any other. If you were now to recognize your own Fate, you would follow those who went before you. But instead, you resist, hoping to perpetuate the suffering your kind so often brought. And here is where you will feel your own pain."

"Unbelievable! You are an abomination! To think that any of the higher echelons would spend their toils on one such as you is unbearable! And worse is to think you hold such powers as these. This is not for the likes of such insignificant playthings. Be away with you, pest! Go back to your wretched Father!"

Sargeras swings an arm around at her, retracting it as he made ready for an attack.

Haran was standing with his shield spell ready to engage. When he saw Sargeras launching his attack, he popped in front of Aelwyn, braced his footing, and cast the final chant. He positioned his hands to project a large barrier, and the energies sparked and coalesced into a chute-like structure.

Sargeras's hand charged with a fiery inferno. He jabbed it at Aelwyn, sending an intense jet of flame rocketing forward. But rather than hit Aelwyn, it struck Haran's shield, which deflected it harmlessly into the air above.

Haran leans into his conjuration, placing all his strength into his concentration, carefully and precisely calling out his maintenance chant to keep it up. Aelwyn ducked down behind him, and as she observed his success, she took a small sigh of relief. She looked around at the others in view, and saw they were all staring in shock and awe.

Azina covered her eyes, only barely peeking through between her fingers. She briefly considered running for cover behind the news van, but considered it probably wouldn't be enough.

"What is he doing?" Ileani wheezes. "Is he insane?"

"Ileani," Ayene emits. "He's as much a soldier as the others. He's doing what he must, and that is to protect her with his magic. These people do not back down, not EVEN in the face of gods."

Geilv winces at the display, and glances at Ayene for her statement.

"That's a level of dedication I think rises above anything we ever experienced."

"And probably the reason the Marshal stuck chips in our brains. We don't know how to follow this level of dedication. We tend to lose our horns with something as simple as a little news sensation."

"Yeah, and thanks for reminding me of that," he retorts. "But you also said she's a Celestial?"

"Yes, although in her case not as highly practiced in this level of magic. Her specialty runs along metaphysical, parapsychological, and empathic studies. She's the one who's been training us in the Prodigy Gift."

"Fascinating. And this seems to follow nicely in Elder Nazég's path."

The group watched breathlessly as the condensed stream of fire stretched out from Sargeras's hand straight across the field and slamming into Haran's shield. Azina unconsciously shook her head at the portrayal of strength being demonstrated on the field today.

"If I should be lucky enough to have children," she muses. "This would be the story of a lifetime for them."

"And considering how long we live," Ayene smirks. "That's saying something."

Sargeras was infuriated, not only by the insolence of that first small creature, but now the other one currently defying his wrath. He continued bearing down on Haran's shield, believing it could not possibly hold up forever.

Aelwyn knew she had to do something, or else Haran might run out of strength. She stood up behind him in the shelter of his shield and began again.

"Very good, Ancient One, spill your wrath upon this small Child who so boldly defies you. Show me your deepest ire, I demand it! Teach me how you would treat those who show you such irreverence...you who bears no virtues unto yourself. Who is the impudent one? Is it I, who stands here in my place confident in my authority, or he who gloats over his pride, but then runs from his own condemnation?"

"You will know your place, little one!" Sargeras roars. "We were once THE authority on life."

"My place is exactly where it is. Do you not listen to your own words? ONCE the authority. But that authority has expired! And clearly, it was unwelcome to begin with. Cast not your blasphemy at me, Ancient One, as we are born for a purpose, to bond life together. When did you ever earn such a privilege as this? To be a Power is to hold responsibility for what you have earned, but your kind never found value in this. Your own history is one to condemn any that might rival you, even though they ought to hold just as much privilege for their own as what you once claimed for yours."

"Privilege! Ours is a station only for those who are worthy!"

"Yes! Worthy, by removing they who were not. And further preventing they who might also aspire to it, but are denied. Who is to say what is worthy? You? Your standards are not the only example!

Look at you, spending your ire for your lost pleasures on this little one. A form of life so privileged that it offends your senses, such that you would spend the last of your strength to banish it. Well, if this is how you choose it, then you should see what else exists in the great Seas of Creation to offend you. Colonel Nazég, why not give him a little demonstration of your own?"

"Absolutely!" Kaliya shouts. "Stormhooves, First and Second Platoons, front and center! Take a sequential formation."

A large group of her troops now breaks away from the cluster guarding the Suuden'kai soldiers on the sheltered side of the north wall. They rushed around onto the field and took up positions as two successive rows of offensive lines.

Velen and the Daanen'kai Elders all leaned forward when Kaliya gave the command to bring her people back out. Tyanna frowned deeply to see her one and only daughter taking a stand against that behemoth.

Sargeras eased up on his attack directed at Haran and Aelwyn as he saw the Stormhooves moving into view. He suddenly became curious, recalling their display of magic earlier during the play. He relaxed himself from his previous target to examine this new group. But his disdain for the lesser species, which was further compounded by his lifelong experience that none of them were ever allowed to develop so highly, caused him to cast doubt that any such as these could actually bring harm to one such as him.

"And what do these little ones think they can do?" he scorns. "Does this pittance actually feel itself so mighty that it can offend one of my magnificence?" he chortles abrasively.

"You might want to reconsider your words, Sargeras," Kaliya hollers. "There may have been a time when you never allowed any like us to threaten you, but these are not those same times. First Platoon; hit him hard and heavy! Second Platoon, stand by."

Ileani and her news team followed the new activity, also curious as to what they had in mind by coming back into view. They continued to film the affair, and the populace who were watching on their vid-coms had almost forgotten this was a real-life battle for the fate of their world. Of those who were hiding in the shelters, a few were even taking bets on who would go down first.

The females begin by conjuring a potent spell. Their motion swept in rhythmic arcs and circles, twirling their hands in spirals from the ground upwards, while their bodies built up a powerful electrical charge.

The males, on the other hand, took out their large dire maces and stepped back to afford themselves some room. From there, they began spinning their weapons over their heads and around in circles, to build up momentum for a heavy toss.

Ileani and her news team, along with Azina and the others in the group, all studied the motions. It seemed like so much fantasy to actually watch this unfold, but that fantasy was about to meet with reality.

The female line had built up a powerful charge within their bodies. They took aim with both hands outstretched, letting loose an array of fierce lightning bolts. At the same time, the males let go of their maces, causing them to soar through the air as flaming guided missiles, impacting against his body with fiery explosions.

Sargeras screeched and stumbled backwards against the hillside, then falling onto his rear quarters as he attempted to catch himself with a hand. He was at least as surprised at the ferocity of the attack as the effectiveness of the result, and it left him briefly stunned.

Commander Geilv stared at the display, for the first time truly seeing a proper form of magical attack in action.

"In all the nether-space," he mutters silently. "No wonder we didn't stand a chance against them on Therinë."

Ileani and her news team zoomed in on the action, with cameras on both Sargeras and Kaliya's team, until she took notice of something unexpected. The male members raised their hands, and their mace weapons reappeared out of seemingly nowhere right back into their grip.

"But that has to be impossible!" she wheezes as she points at the monitor.

"Those weapons are enchanted," Ayene mentions soberly. "So, it IS possible, in this case. They're keyed to their owners, so they can be recalled simply by thinking about it. Magic can do some fascinating things."

Sargeras growled intensely as he dragged himself back to his feet and scowled at the little things below him.

"It would indeed seem you have learned a few tricks, but can you fend off against this?"

He swings his arm back around at the group. Kaliya instantly knew what to expect out of him.

"Front row, shields!" she shouts.

The front row of troopers takes a quick defensive stand, holding up their shield arms and engaging their projectors. A wall of tower shields, using the same technology as the rest, instantly pops into view, serving as a barrier to guard their forces.

Sargeras directs his hand at the body of soldiers, and a spray of fire leaps out from it, sending off a storm of projectiles and flame at the mass below. Azina and the others grimace at the display, but the assault simply deflects off the wall formation, leaving the soldiers underneath completely unaffected.

"Second Platoon…" Kaliya orders. "Let's see some fists, two above, two in front, and follow with ice cones and smites."

The second lineup now goes active, with each of them conjuring up something from behind the shelter of the defensive wall. The first of these to let go was a group of troopers conjuring ethereal fists.

Ileani and the others in the news van watched as a new wave of strikes launched out. The first of these was a set of giant fist-like apparitions appearing and coming down from above. They struck Sargeras with such force that it seemed to ripple through his body, forcing him to his hands and knees. His fiery attack was interrupted as he went down, and he was soon hit by a second volley striking his face and chest, knocking him backward and laying him out on the hillside.

"Ouch!" Azina wheezes sympathetically.

This attack was quickly followed by several cones of icy projectiles spraying out, striking him with their thorny spikes and covering him and part of the hillside with a layer of frost. He was next hit by several divine smites of energy raining down on him, each of which inflicting a moment of crippling pain.

Sargeras twitched and yowled in agony at this latest assault, and the people in the news van cringed at the magnitude of the display. But Commander Geilv and Captain Ta'yeen both reacted as a subtle twang seemed to zap through their bodies. They buckled and clutched the rear of their heads.

Latena was standing behind the others as they observed the fight, when out of the corner of her eye, she could see the two men taking what appeared to be a feedback hit. She jerked around to study them as they tried to stabilize themselves.

"Azina! Director!" she shouts.

The two medical professionals pulled their gaze around to catch the Commander and his officer just starting to pull their posture upright again.

"We need med-techs over here," the Director shouts.

The medical team that had been standing near the van rushed into position to help the two military men as the others felt generally helpless to do anything. Ileani observed the scene as a cold shiver ran through her.

"The feedback?" she gasps.

"This might constitute our evidence," the Director asserts. "I would imagine everyone with the Seed just got one."

"Oh wonderful…"

On the field, the Suuden-Aryku troops also felt a shock rumbling through their bodies and terminating at the base of their skulls. The people in the shelters also felt it, and many were starting to panic for the implied meaning.

"Colonel," ushers a voice on Kaliya's com-link. "The Suuden'kai troops look like they took a hit from that last one."

"Acknowledged," she offers. "But unfortunately, we're not done yet."

Sargeras slowly pulled himself back to his senses and he attempted to prop himself up. He first glared at both Tyr and Adalon to check their movements, but the two of them were holding their ground. He then peered down at the field again to see the troopers relaxing in a defensive stance. He suddenly felt uncertain at challenging them again.

"Such potent little ones…" he mumbles. "Surprisingly potent… And they actually allow this?" he glances at Tyr again.

"They not only allow it," Kaliya affirms. "They encourage it. Ours is a very different relationship than anything you might have ever permitted. They encourage the younger races to grow, one day perhaps even to join with them on their level. But unlike you and yours, we don't play this game of pushing out the older ones. We form up as a peer society."

"Intolerable!" he grunts as he comes to his feet again. "To pollute the higher echelons with such juvenile refuse…"

"Thou wouldst be wise to mind thy words, Primordial," Tyr asserts. "That juvenile refuse did once remove thine own glorious empire of grand perfection. Be that thine example of what potency life doth carry unto itself. It was by thine own words that thou wouldst never permit this, and therefore thou must know of its potential. But by thine own declaration of perfection, thou dost once again proclaim thy tendencies of prejudice."

"Prejudice…" he grumbles. "We once decided who was worthy or not, but none could ever be so worthy of what we achieved. Even those forebearers we deposed once were unworthy of their title, as they fell into such crippling decay that they could not even maintain themselves."

"And thine own did not the same?"

"As I said, someone fell lax. It wasn't my fault you were permitted to rise up."

"Primordial, dost thou not even listen to thine own proclamations? Someone fell lax. This is to say thy kingdom fell into ruin no different from thy forebearers. It is also to say thy people fell into similar despair and destitution, that thou could no longer uphold thine own prestige or domination of Creation. Therefore, as it was said, it was simply a matter of time for our own to come forward and replace thee."

"So it would seem, and then you raise all your pets to join you. Such a fanciful existence you are creating here."

"Better that they join us rather than replace us. Those higher echelons can be enjoyed by more than our own."

Sargeras again glares at the Stormhooves on the ground, trying to judge their worthiness as a species. He singles out Kaliya on the field, as she was clearly the one leading this military body.

"And then we have you, little one. You seem quite confident in yourself. Are you the leader of this band out here?"

"I am she who created the Stormhooves in their modern incarnation," Kaliya declares. "And we carry a number of qualities that do make us rather proud. Do you wish to argue this?"

"Oh, and I see you must be as brazen as this other one," he directs at Aelwyn.

"We tend to carry this quality as we are backed by some very powerful allies. They teach, and we listen. We are their Children as much as we are their students."

Sargeras pauses a moment to glance at Tyr, realizing his kind were those allies. But at this moment, it was quickly becoming clear he was not only surrounded, as well as overpowered, his final moments were closing in on him.

He glared at Kaliya, mulling her words, and fuming at the implications that he could be beaten by a mere mortal creature. It might be one thing to have another Power overcome him, but this was simply humiliating.

"Little one, I may not last beyond this day, but if there is one thing I will not tolerate, it is such an insignificant bug like you to best me."

"Oh? This should be fun," she retorts brashly. "Do you want to test me one-on-one, Sargeras? Go ahead!" she shouts. "Give me your finest and let's see who wins! If I need to demonstrate our power to exist over yours, then try to erase me from existence. Let's see whose mind is the more determined!"

"You would actually challenge me to a test of my authority over Reality?"

"If you dare," Kaliya scorns. "You obsolete BEAST!"

Sargeras screeched in outrage. His bellowing echoed around the valley.

Ayene gaped at the monitor as she watched in horror this unwieldy turn of events.

"Kaliya!" she shrieks at the video. "That's exactly what he said NOT to do!"

The Director, Azina, Ileani, and the others all briskly gazed at her for the statement before returning to the monitor.

"And this time," the Director adds. "She definitely IS crazy."

The Daanen-Aryku inside the observation booth all cringed and recoiled at the display.

"Kali!" Sulíma shouts. "What are you doing out there?!"

Sargeras stretches out his hand and takes aim directly at Kaliya, this time focusing his mind on her physical manifestation.

Kaliya immediately reacted, and she drew in her concentration to counter him. This would become a contest of the mind alone, and the prize was the determination to exist.

"You will NOT force me out of this place," she roars. "For I have learned the nature of existence and how to manipulate it to my own design. In this space I have WILL! And my will CAN alter this space!"

Tyanna gazed tensely at the video monitor as she watched her daughter exhibiting a power not previously known to them. The imagery showed Sargeras attempting to will her out of existence, as so many other Primordials have done to their creations in the past. But even though the image seemed to be wavering slightly, Kaliya was forcing it back into Reality. Even more than this, Kaliya raised her own hand and fought back, and now they could see faint rippling effects waving between them.

Ileani, Azina, and Commander Geilv, among others, all studied the scene with anxiety and apprehension. Ayene worriedly glued her eyes to the monitors to observe what was becoming clear as the fabric of Reality now twisting in a line between the two opponents.

Sargeras continued pressing his attack, but Kaliya's struggle was forcing his will away from her. The rippling effect was driven off her image and into the space between them. A darkened void was developing in the air, with occasional minor streaks of charged energy flashing out of it.

"If either of them loses control of that…" the Director mumbles.

"At this moment, Director," Ayene replies anxiously. "I might actually have to agree with you."

Sargeras found his struggle to be weakening, in part due to his diminishing strength after all his other efforts, and in part for a developing sense of doubt in this contest. This opponent was exhibiting a strength no other in his experience has ever demonstrated before, and this hinted at whether this contest could actually turn against him. He was now fighting to preserve himself as much as he was fighting to erase her.

Kaliya could sense she was overpowering him, and she found new strength in this. Her confidence grew, and she centered her mind on a new focal point. She brought her other hand up and directed herself at her selected target. She called in the remaining ambient arcanic energies still on the field to further bolster her strength and pushed even harder, anchoring her advance on the trueness of her own existence driving his back. This pushed the void bubble in his direction, and the lightning surges increased.

"What is she doing out there?" Tyanna whispers. "Where is she going with that?"

Velen gazed silently at the scene. His body was unconsciously tensing up in a sympathetic struggle to support his daughter.

Tyr and Adalon both studied the scene in awe and hesitation at Kaliya's surge of power, until finally the struggle broke from Sargeras's grip. The bubble collapsed into a potent bolt of energy shooting back at Sargeras and striking firmly against his left hand, which he was using to exert his own attack. He screamed in agony and stumbled back again, collapsing once more onto the hillside.

Within the group at the news van, Geilv and the Captain both yelped and doubled over, once again slapping their hands around the back of their heads. The Suuden'kai soldiers on the field each experienced the same reaction, many of them stumbling to maintain their balance. This was further reflected among the general public hiding in the shelters.

Azina took immediate notice of the two officers nearby.

"Again!" she yips. "Set those two on the ground!" she orders. "Ileani, we need to inform our people to sit down at the very least, before they fall down and hurt themselves."

Inside the control room, Petrith listened to the news report.

"General, she has a point. Those soldiers out there should be set on the ground."

"Good, make it so," he nods. "Send word to our people to assist. Relissa, perhaps you could go out and call the Priestess and her people to offer some comforting aid."

"Aye!" she responds and dashes out of the room.

Ayene gazed at the scene between Kaliya and Sargeras, trying to judge what just happened. Kaliya still appeared to be standing, but as Ayene turned to look at Sargeras, he was clutching at his arm. As her eyes focused on him, she wheezed, and her jaw dropped.

"In all the nether-space!" she shouts. "Look at him!"

Ileani, Azina, and the others quickly turned around to examine Sargeras as he tried to upright himself on the hillside. His left hand was gone, reduced to a simple stump at the wrist.

"What happened to him?" Azina yelps.

"She turned it around on him! He was trying to force her out of existence, but she turned it back and hit him in the hand."

"Wait! Ayene, are you trying to say she caused his hand to vanish simply by thinking about it?"

"Yes, Azina, exactly! This is what she was talking about once in your office. The riddle of metaphysics, the mind altering the state of Reality. And I know she can do this because I've seen her create stuff out of thin air before."

"In all the nether-space, Ayene, what does that say about her?"

"It says she is the Prodigy symbol for the rest of us. She just demonstrated Elder Nazég's principles for us! Eat that, Council!" she laughs boisterously.

Velen, Tyanna, and the other Daanen-Aryku in the observation booth gazed at the monitor in astonishment.

"Grace of the cu'Nar, Velen," Elder Girhani muses softly. "What has she become?"

Velen turns to his wife hoping to find the answer, but all she could do is return an astonished stare.

Adalon peered around Sargeras's form in amazement.

"Inpressssive...!" she extols. "And here... They make their name..."

Kaliya retracted from her assault. Deep down, she felt an elated sense of accomplishment, though she also felt worn by it.

"That was for you, Darumon," she whispers. "You may not like how it was applied, but still, I hope it makes you proud of your creation. We are more than even you might have predicted. We'll see it put to good use, if it should ever come out again."

She eyed Sargeras carefully for his next move, but she suspected he wouldn't want to try anything else. Not in her direction. He was clearly even more worn for the effort, as well as the defeat. He surveyed the scene unpretentiously, until he landed his gaze on his small opponent again.

"Such a thing as you cannot…should not exist!" he states feebly. "Just what manner of creation are you? How can one of such puny design hold such potent authority over the threads of Reality?"

"I'm sure there was a time when your kind once held such a station before you ascended further to take your role over your predecessors. We are simply the next generation on our way up. Evolution can do that, you know."

"Yes, it can. But yours does not represent one of such station to hold this level of power as yet."

"I suppose we must admit to this, to some degree or another. But I'm sure we're not your average creation, either. And further, we should probably include that ours is not solely an evolutionary trait. My skills must take into account more than just one feature. We have our innate qualities, plus some very encouraging forms of training and conditioning, and also a few augmentations. You won't find this just anywhere."

"Then, this is to say, they do not simply create tiny things that fumble around in their native soil?"

"Technically speaking, the Estelar don't actually tend to create anything. They let nature take its course, and then choose one or another to assist with a bit of nurturing. I believe I once heard a term your kind might use, the Challenge of Creation."

"Yes! But this was in our earliest moments. Even at that, we would not permit such to travel as far as this."

"I understand yours was a very proud society…proud of your achievement, proud of your station. But nothing lasts forever. Not for your predecessors, who probably held similar pride at one time, and not for you, it would seem."

"So it would seem."

"As for us, well, we hold a few qualities that you might not find in your common source material. This likely gave us a jump start, and we simply took it from there, once we realized what we had and how we should apply ourselves."

"Such a curious example. Very well, I find myself no longer able to argue the point," he turns and wearily glances at Tyr again. "I must retract my earlier statement. It would seem you have indeed been busy during this time."

"At last," Tyr responds softly. "Thou dost finally see the course of our proceedings."

Sargeras sluggishly pulls himself to his feet again. He watches Tyr, and then turns to observe Adalon, who was still standing ready for her moment.

"Which of you wants me? Kuroku, I suppose, as you have the longest grudge to hold. You came all this way to see me finished. Be that as it may, but do not expect me to simply stand here for it. If I am to uphold the prestige of my kind, you must take from me what we once took from our forebearers. We held our position of authority with pride. If you should do the same, you must demonstrate your worthiness."

"I underssstand, Sssargerasss..." she asserts. "By all meansss... And ssso much the better. You will fall... As a warrior. The lassst of your kind... To conclude... An ancient moment... With final determination..."

Adalon prepares herself as Sargeras finds his feet again. Tyr moves to one side to give them space. Sargeras takes a moment to collect what strength he has left, and then launches a new attack. He uses his right hand now to charge up another fiery barrage, this time of molten shards, hoping to chip away at her scaly armor.

Adalon turns to allow the broadside of her flank to take the hit and raises a wing to shield her face. She then draws in a deep breath in preparation for her counterstrike. She redirects her gaze at him as she lets loose a powerful blast of icy breath, encasing him partway within a thick frozen block. This once again interrupted his attack and immobilized him briefly.

"Even ethereal bodiesss... Have a freezing point..." she muses. "If only to reduce it... To Absssolute Zero..."

Wispy vapors drifted away from Sargeras's body as the condensation of the local air wafted downward and away from his feet. Ileani and her group all gazed at the enormous shape that seemed encased in a block of solidified gasses, which were just starting to sublimate away.

Adalon now lunges at him, extending the claws on her forelegs and slashing at him. She took several swipes to cut through her own block of ice until she hit his body. And as she cut into him, the Suuden-Aryku took another minor hit for the damage effects feeding back through their seeds.

Azina glanced at Geilv and the Captain, who were now toppling over on the ground.

"This isn't going to be pretty!" she yips.

"I'm calling an alert," the Director announces.

He made a call to the ARC, placing the staff on special alert. This was then issued as a global emergency to all the clinics and labs around the world. Medical technicians and interns were now equipping themselves with emergency supplies and heading out to every raid shelter on file to begin offering support.

Adalon rears up on her hind legs, using her tail as a tripod to stabilize herself. She began conjuring up a spell, then throwing it down at Sargeras's feet. It erupted in a whirlwind pillar of fire to burn away the remainder of the ice. But before Sargeras could recover his senses, she lunged at him again, this time grabbing his arms in her claws and flapping her wings vigorously to take off. The gale force winds generated by her wing bursts kicked up clouds of dust and debris from the ground.

"Watch that stuff!" Ileani cautions to her cameramen.

Sargeras tries faintly to struggle against her as Adalon uses her added lifting force to drag him along with her. She continues flapping, now increasing her vigor to gain lift, and as she leaves the ground, she curls forward to grab his lower body with her rear claws.

"That's some serious lifting power," Azina muses.

Ileani and her news team found themselves trying to dodge the winds with their drones and protecting the other cameras from the flying debris. Azina, the Director, and the others by the news van took shelter under Navina's glass barrier shape, as it was the only thing protecting them by now.

Adalon managed to lift Sargeras well away from the ground by this time, even though he was still struggling to escape from her. He cursed her through the flapping of her wings, although the sounds were muffled under the strain of his capture. She circled around over the hills, across the river, then looping back, and then stalled, letting her wings go slack and dropping out of the air. They impacted into the hillside with a thundering crunch.

All the observers flinched intensely as the booming thud sent dirt and rocks scattering across the ground and emitting a quake they could feel even at a distance. And with this horrific crash came another feedback hit, an even bigger one this time.

The Commander and the Captain again clutched their heads. The medical team tried to assist, but they felt helpless overall as the fight was still ongoing. The same scene was occurring in the shelters in cities around the world, as the people also felt the hit. There were shrieks and moans as people began to collapse into heaps. Some were able to stabilize themselves on the floors while others simply toppled over.

Adalon recoiled quickly from the collision, while the giant underneath her was severely dazed from the heavy body slam.

She now goes into her frenzy, snatching his arms in her jaw and gnashing at them, tearing into them, and ripping the fleshy material away. Even though he was technically an ethereal creature, his manifestation simulated the qualities of a corporeal body, and this reflected on his underlying nature. She continued to dig into him with her claws, tearing away at him as she unleashed nearly an eternity of rage for all he and Darumon had done to her kind in past ages.

Tyr had backed away even further by this time, granting her plenty of room for her maneuvers. He scanned the scene below him with the Suuden-Aryku and their attendants. The bodies were laid out across the ground by now, writhing from the feedback hits. He could see priests moving in to give aid to the soldiers, and the Commander and the Captain on the ground with the news personnel. He could only imagine the scene in the raid shelters, but that would have to wait, as it was currently outside his capacity to contend with at this time.

Azina was divided between the monitors and the actual scene across the river, even though the action was exceedingly brutal and unpleasant to her senses. She wondered how long this would continue.

Adalon ripped away at her prey. She reeled up and bellowed a howling roar, letting out her anguish over the long memories of her people's suffering, and all those who came before and since.

"Thisss is for you... And all the othersss...!" she blasts fiercely before diving back down with renewed vigor, biting and clawing with primal fury.

The moaning of Sargeras's cries subsided as he descended into traumatic shock. So too did the general effect of the feedback reverberating through the Suuden-Aryku. Adalon continued her seemingly irrepressible assault, laying into him for many moments longer, and leaving a spray of gore across the hillside as the lone Primordial took a ghastly amount of damage, until finally her energy ran out.

She slowed down, panting and exhausted, and glaring at his remains. She studied him for a moment, as if trying to judge his condition by this time. He was motionless and silent. She glanced around the area at what she had done, and as the realization settled for the untamed level of carnage she had wrought, she closed her eyes and whined riotously.

She hastily retreated from his body and moved away on the hillside. She examined herself. Her claws were filthy, and her mouth tasted foul. She soon realized she had lost control of herself, and she abruptly turned away and hid her face under a wing. There, she began to weep.

Kaliya and the others on the field gazed in wonder at the sight, not only of the amount of destruction Adalon left behind her, but now of her reaction. They all felt compassion for her, as they also began to realize she got carried away with her rage.

Tyr moved in closer, carefully circling around the mess so he could approach alongside her. Azina watched, along with Ileani and her cameras. Like all the rest, she took careful notice of Adalon's change of demeanor. But she also had a sudden curious thought come to mind as she observed Tyr seemingly navigating so expertly around the scene as if he could see, even with his eyes closed.

"Ayene," the young intern begins. "Is he actually blind? His eyes are closed, and that usually means blindness."

"I don't know the history behind it," she admits. "But as a god, he would have more than just your average physical senses. The Celestials have a form of Sight that extends beyond just vision. I would imagine he's using something like that by now."

"So, eyes or no eyes, he can still see somehow. I wonder, do you think he would let me come close enough for an examination?"

"Does it include dissection?" Ayene smirks.

"Um…" she hesitates pertly and rolls her eyes.

Tyr arrived by Adalon's side and knelt down next to her.

"Sister Adalon," he offers privately. "I have never seen thee in this state before."

"I am sssorry… That ssso many… Had to sssee thisss…" she emits breathlessly through her sobbing. "It is ssso very… Unbecoming of me.

He warned me… Ssso many timesss. I thought… I could contain it… But in the end… It came down… To ssso many memoriesss… And to witnessss… Ssso much sssuffering… Of ssso many people… On ssso many worldsss. I felt their pain… As I reflected on my own…"

"He being…Helm, perhaps? Yes, I believe I understand."

"Adalon," Kaliya emits into her com-link. "Can you hear me up there? Is that thing still working, after all that?" she chuckles.

"Yesss… Tall One. And even without… Thisss communicator…"

"Right, well, listen. I don't think there is any one of us here who would blame you for what just happened. We each felt a piece of it just from the way he spoke to us. Now, I realize, this might not be a very becoming scene to put on, and I'm sure you have a long history of one kind or another; therefore, you have a lot of pride in yourself, respect amongst the others, and an image to uphold. But cu'Nar's Grace, Adalon, if you're dating back all the way beyond the Celestial War, you can't just expect yourself to hold that much in when it finally comes time to do the deed. You probably have every right to it, especially as you say you and your people had to fight simply for the right to exist at all. What can anyone expect after that?"

"I thank you… For your wordsss… Kaliya. Perhapsss… You are right… But it ssstings… Nonethelessss…"

"All right, so it stings. But I bet it won't sting nearly as much as the rest of us putting a wax and shine back on those scales of yours after the flame job you took," she chuckles gently.

Adalon perked up to look over her shoulder at the lonely figure on the field. If a dragon could smile, she was beaming at the generous offer of levity just made.

"Sssuch an adorable Child," she mumbles. "Indeed… You do ssset the example…"

She now glances at the mutilated body of Sargeras again.

"We mussst clean up now…"

She rises to her feet and strolls down to the river again to rinse off. Once she felt better for her appearance, she raised her head to the sky, peering at the swirling storm overhead. She then turns to Tyr.

"Perhapsss you can asssssist… With these cloudsss. We have no further need… For thisss…"

Tyr rises to his feet and glances upwards. He waves a hand in a wide arc, and the clouds are blasted away with a thunderous boom in a rapidly expanding circle around the area.

"Wow," Azina croons. "Now that's a godlike power."

"That one is impressive," Ayene nods.

Adalon turns her attention skyward again, this time in a moment of contemplative summoning.

"Um, now what is she doing?" Ileani wonders.

Before Ayene could answer, a brilliant divine pillar descends out of a planar rift in the sky above and reaches down to the ground near Adalon. The beam seemed to sparkle, as a glowing orb travels along its length.

"I think I know what that is," Ayene muses. "That's got to be her servant again. I met her once before; I think the name was Thaliel."

The orb settles on the ground and reshapes itself into an exceedingly tall female figure of pale features, and with large white wings on her back.

"Maker," Thaliel begins. "We are ready if thou dost require it."

"Yesss, Thaliel... Bring them down... And carry thisss away from here. Let no part of it... Taint thisss land..."

Thaliel bows and calls on additional seraphim to assist. A pair of large planar rifts opens over the bodies of Darumon and Sargeras, and a small army of other seraphim descend around the slain opponents. They wrap the bodies in glowing envelopes of energy and begin lifting them back up to the rifts to carry them away from the scene.

Latena and the others in the news group watched in awe at the otherworldly creatures performing their duty. She steps forward to the monitors to study the imagery before looking up at Adalon and Tyr as they both sat down for a rest.

"And here we have the day of our liberation," she muses wearily. "We are free."

Chapter 15

THE FINAL PROPHECY

The scene outside was coming back under control by now. Lady Sehnisavain and her people were attending the fallen Suuden-Aryku, who were just now beginning to regain their senses. Azina and her team continued to give aid to the Commander and the Captain near the news van, while the Director coordinated with his people from the ARC and other medical labs.

Around the world, the people in their raid shelters were slowly returning back to life. With the fall of Sargeras, they all took a stunning blow from the feedback effect. They were piled into heaps on the floors, some had briefly blacked-out, and many were dazed, but now they were showing signs of movement again.

Navina restored her image from her wall simulation, and both she and Ayene returned inside the control room to check in. Kaliya surveyed the field, sending Aelwyn and Haran back indoors, and calling the rest of the troops back outside to give them an opportunity for fresh air and room to stretch, rather than being cramped inside the small underground staging area.

"General," she ushers on her com-link. "We should be able to bring down the wall by now, what do you think?"

"Absolutely, Colonel," he affirms. "Professor, if you please."

The gnomish Professor nods and begins working the controls to deactivate the shield walls and power down the arcanic emitters on the field. The shield retracted with a loud crackling as the wall separated into bolts of energy receding back into the spires. The sudden ruckus startled the people on the ground as they all turned abruptly to see the wall coming down.

"Well," Latena muses. "I guess they're open for business."

She pulls out her trans-com and makes a quick call.

"Hello?" ushers a gentle female voice.

"Auryn, this is Latena. Where are you right now?"

"Oh, Latena! Yes, we're still at the civic center. Some of our people took a hit from the feedback, and they're just getting back up again, then we'll be on our way. What's happening out there?"

"We're basically recovering from all this excitement, but I'm going to get on my soapbox again in a moment with my final political speech. I need you out here at that time to support me."

"All right, we'll be on our way shortly."

They end the link and Latena turns to Ileani next.

"Ileani," she whispers. "I have a speech to make, once the people are able to listen to it again."

"All right," she nods. "What sort of sensations are you hoping to make this time?" she smiles timidly.

"This is where we must find our new direction as a world society. We need to know what to do with ourselves now that we're free, but with Gifts we shouldn't otherwise have, and who to talk to about it. I don't think we can do this alone. If you think Ytani was bad as an individual, now think of an entire world like this."

"Yeah, and it's not a pretty thought. So, in other words, I'm going to lose my horns one last time."

"You should probably just get used to picking them up off the ground from this moment. This is the first day of an entirely new future for us."

Marelle and Relissa were coming outside to check on things with the news van. As they strolled over, the Director, Azina, Kita and Latena all took notice of them, recognizing them from their earlier encounters. But Ileani became very curious over this odd couple and hoping this time to share at least a few words.

"Director?" Marelle begins. "What's the situation from the medical side?"

"Problematic," he sighs. "I have our people on emergency alert, and visiting as many of the shelters as they can, but the numbers are a problem for us. All we can do is hope everyone got their medical rations, and those who didn't will be brought to a clinic for treatment."

"All right..." she glances around the group. "Four billion people... that's a lot to ask for."

Commander Geilv and Captain Ta'yeen were sitting on the ground, still trying to shake off the last of the stunning reflex hits. Marelle kneeled down by them to check on their condition.

"Commander, how do you feel?" she asks softly.

His eyes were still droopy, but he was able to respond by slowly rolling them around to look at her.

"I think...I know you..." he puffs. "Your voice..."

"I'm Captain Marelle Carronel. I'm the one from that transport, and also the combat ship outside your window at Central Command."

The Captain turned to the sound of her voice and tried entering the conversation.

"Were you the one...flying those...wild...antics...in the city?"

"Um...yes?" she grins gently.

"In all the nether-space...you must be crazy..."

"Yes, well, some of the pilots I helped train thought I was a bit excessive, and you probably wouldn't want to speak to my flight instructor. But this is just how we work back home. We're not as sedate as you people."

"Sedate? Is this how you see us?"

"That is, other than Kaliya out there," she directs back towards the field. "She and her people had to learn to put their tails in overdrive just to keep up with us. In comparison to that, the rest of you move rather slowly."

"Uh huh... Well, I suppose...if you can go from...um...Industrial Age to space flight...so quickly...we're in a lot of trouble."

Ileani came around with one of her cameramen to see if she could participate.

"Um, Captain," she utters cautiously. "Are you able to give us a few words?"

Marelle turns to the reporter as Ileani tries to compare her and Relissa.

"You two don't look like the same race."

"We're not," Marelle smiles as she stands up again. "I'm what we call human. This here is a friend of mine, Relissa Moonshimmer, and she's a Night Elf."

"A Night Elf..." Geilv mutters. "I know that name. Are you from Therinë?"

"Yes Sir, both of us. Therinë is now part of Thaelyn's kingdom, as is Ruuki uy'Daan and Morndindor."

"All of them? What did he do, annex them as he pushed along?"

"Essentially yes… The people of Solinaia, her home city, joined the kingdom shortly after he reunited them with their old religion and the people of Tae'Eladar. Rolsklinde, my home city, joined up, along with the High Elves of Kynesoth, just after you left, as he was collecting all the people into one society again."

"One society?" Ileani muses. "So, all that talk we had earlier of his society holding different people, including some of our own… Does he do this often, that is to say going out, finding new people, and bringing them together into one body?"

"This would constitute as our first time off-planet. But I suppose the answer would be yes, if he found someone who might fit well into the picture. You need to be capable of supporting his philosophies in order to find a place within such a society. But he works it so that everyone supports each other for their special abilities and talents."

"But if this is your first time away from home, where did all these different people originally come from?"

"Tae'Eladar became something of a collection point where multiple races migrated and formed a type of community together. Thaelyn arrived later to cement things together even more. We have elves that came from one world, dwarves from another, and also halflings and gnomes coming along for the ride. We humans once thought we were native, but more recently, which is to say a few centuries ago, we found out we were seeded on Tae'Eladar by the Sarrukh," she pauses to glance at Adalon. "Her work, it would seem, in preparation for this here."

"Do we know where you originally came from?"

"We do, as they left behind some technology and documentation of what they did. But the last time anyone checked on it, that world was a few steps behind us, so we're leaving them alone for now."

"And how many worlds does he have by now?"

"It's all largely due to this war. It began with Tae'Eladar, then Therinë as his home was invaded by Darumon using a race we call orcs. They came from a world called Ruuki uy'Daan, previously the home of Velen's people before Darumon pushed them to Therinë."

"And just for reference, where are these worlds? Are they here in our home galaxy, or that other universe we heard about recently."

"The other universe…and Tae'Eladar is in another one after that.

Then, once we found a way to Ruuki uy'Daan, using Kaliya and her Prodigy Gift to lead us, we had to deal with the remainder of those orcs."

"I'm a little concerned if I should ask this or not, but how did you… deal…with them?"

"Compassionately…" she affirms. "Once we arrived and convinced what was left of their race by then to stop worshiping Sargeras…or Darumon…whichever it was, as their god, we had to make a choice on what to do with them. Their society was running very thin by that time, and their culture was polluted by Darumon's influence and your technology changing several aspects of life for them. Therefore, Thaelyn decided the only way to set things right was to relocate them to another world to start over."

"Relocate? Why?"

"The Estelar have a very strict philosophy called the Measure of Balance, which basically says everything needs to balance in harmony with itself, and all things come at their own time. These orcs were a primitive tribal society, essentially Stone Age, and yet Darumon taught them how to use advanced magic to open portals, and how to use your conveyor technology, among other things, which he left on their world. This violated that policy and corrupted their society. Now, if left to their own devices, and being generally warlike, they could use this to invade anything they could lay their sights on and make trouble without end. The only way to fix this was to remove the magic from the equation, as well as the technology. So, Thaelyn moved them to a world outside the flows that power the magic and away from the other polluting influences. This allows them to go back to their original ways, but this time using more traditional methods and no shortcuts."

"A bit like resetting the clock to a moment before the corruption occurred."

"Right, and with nothing else happening on that world, we simply claimed it as the spoils of victory."

"Why is it called Ruuki uy'Daan…Land of Exile?"

"This was the name used by Velen's people, as they regarded themselves to be in a form of self-imposed exile away from home. They also began calling themselves Daanen-Aryku, at least in part for this reason as, um…well, their unfortunate experiences with you people."

"Us? Does this relate to Darumon's pursuit and constantly describing them as traitors? My apologies for bringing this up, but I feel I need to clarify."

"Yes, of course. They had no idea about your Council's opinions on this side. All they ever saw was your military appearing out of nowhere and assaulting them for no apparent reason, and ruthlessly killing so many innocent people who did absolutely nothing to you. But worse were these seeds and the effects of all those chips. In their eyes, you were grotesque monsters behaving as cold-blooded killing machines. That's all you were, and all thanks to siding with Sargeras. They didn't even have Darumon's name attached to it at the time."

"Wow…that's simply…" she closes her eyes and looks away. "When I consider so many other things we brought out during this time, I'm not even sure what to say about it."

"A lot of people got hurt on all sides here. I would imagine some part of it can begin to heal by now, but it won't be fast, neither will it be easy, especially for those of us with the ridiculously long lifespans," she smirks.

"Yeah, and thanks for the gentle rub. How long is yours, by comparison?"

"My people measure ours in decades, maybe the better part of a century. The elves might run for several centuries."

"Interesting, and this seems like it might better fit with some of the animal species we have here. Ours is uniquely different, and no doubt due to our unusual, um…heritage. So, your people on this first world joined his kingdom, and you claimed the next one because, I suppose, it was empty by now, right?"

"Right. Then we have Morndindor. One of those custom conveyors pointed to that world where we found the original home of the dwarves. This was also Darumon's mining operation. That world was devastated by bombardment down to one surviving city. So, in thanks for us saving so much of whatever remained over there, they also joined up."

"It would seem like these worlds came into your possession at least as much out of thanks than anything else."

"Yes, this is generally how it worked. Thaelyn leads by example, and the people simply come to him. I think the only example of him using military force would be on Tae'Eladar itself, where he basically had a divine mandate to take control, and this didn't leave any room for exceptions. The Maker had plans for that world, and it had to be united to see it through. He used political methods whenever possible, but there were those few here and there that didn't want to cooperate. You know, corrupt leaders and criminal elements."

"Of course, but now, as for us here…" she glances around the field. "You people played this elaborate game to liberate us and to bring down the Marshal and Sargeras, but what does this mean for our people and our world? Where do we go from here?"

"When Thaelyn first arrived on Therinë," Relissa begins. "We all thought he was wacky for taking on someone like Sargeras. Kaliya and her people told us the story that sent them running off, and it put a literal fear of god in us. But he was all the way over here. Still, your military was making a lot of trouble for us, them on one side, the orcs on another, and Darumon apparently corrupted the High Elves on a third side."

"That sounds like a very bad place to be in."

"Aye! But when Thaelyn came along, we didn't quite know what to think of him. We'd never heard of such a thing as a Celestial before. Then, he started fighting our war for us. It became his war, at least as much for what those orcs were doing, but the others came soon after. He sent spies to learn what happened to the High Elves and pulled them back to our side. He also sent spies into Rolsklinde to learn why their Governor wouldn't fight all the bad things out there, and learned he was actually in cahoots with your Suuden'kai military. This made him an enemy who was lying and feeding the rest of us a load of rubbish for what happened to our world."

"A little like Darumon did here, I guess."

"Aye, he was impersonating the bugger. But once we got rid of all that, our people came together to follow him, and we began to rebuild our homes and cities. But Thaelyn…" she whistles. "When he started putting together who Sargeras was, he just couldn't let it slide by. He had to take this all the way. It was offensive to see a Primordial still out there, especially after all the trouble Darumon made back home. Now, we know he made a lot of trouble here too, and Thaelyn doesn't leave people hanging. He sent his people here to help you understand all your own mistakes and learn what Darumon did to you. But now that we're here, the rest is generally up to you. If you want more, you can ask real nice, and I'm sure he'll do what he can for it. But like Ayene said here earlier, there are a few things you just need to come to terms with, like it or not."

"And this would reflect on the Prodigy Gift again, I suppose."

"Aye, that's a good one, to be sure."

In the downtown section of the city, a caravan of hover coaches was preparing to leave the local civic center. A large number of people were loading up, each of them dressed in a very peculiar style for the local fashion. They were all wearing priestly robes of a unique design for the Suuden-Aryku. The robes resembled three-quarter length coats, very clean and professional, in parchment white over deep blue shirts and pants. They had tall collars, parted in three sections, and the edges curled over like a partially unfurled scroll.

"All right," Auryn announces. "Let's check ourselves one more time. Do we have everyone? Good! And do we have our new scriptures? What about the candles? Remember, we want to make a good impression for these people."

"Auryn," her mother intones wittily. "Don't you think you're getting a little overanxious here?"

"This is really important for us, Mom. Latena is counting on me…all of us, really…to make a good show for it. This is where we make our own statement. It's something our world hasn't seen for a thousand millennia."

"Well, I suppose that does make it rather important, as we are bringing something back after such a long time that no one would even remember it."

"And not only that, but it's a new religion with a new god, and I'm sure he'll be watching."

"But Auryn, I think he will not be paying quite as close attention to our dress code or our supply stocks. I think he will admire us even if we don't appear absolutely perfect. After all, these beings are as much teachers as we are their students."

"Yes Mom, but I'm hoping to make a good grade for our class presentation," she grins.

"Oh! In all the nether-space, all right, let's get going."

The last of them load up inside their vehicles and begin on their way out of town.

◆◆◆◆◆

Kita had been studying her data tablet while Ileani finished up with Marelle and Relissa. Now she felt the time was approaching to come forward to speak.

"Ileani, I need to make my own announcement here, before we

get involved with anything else, like Latena and her speech. I have instructions that the ACI is going public now."

"Oh, all right... Do you want to do this here?"

"Yes. And Relissa, Navina said something earlier about a chip with a video you wanted to present online."

"Aye, I'll go fetch that for you."

Relissa takes off in a dash back to the control room while Kita moves forward for her official presentation. Ileani positions herself and her cameras to begin the next segment of the broadcast.

"CPComm, what's the situation over there?"

"We're slowly pulling our horns back around, Ileani," the station anchor admits. "Some of our team was sent to the floor during that feedback hit, but we're still here."

"Good, let's tidy up and get moving again."

"We're ready here. Go, Ileani."

Once again, on the video monitors around the world, the official news began to pick up again as the people returned their focus to the broadcast.

"This is Ileani Ur'paran, still live at the Lajad-Torak Restoration Conservatory, here in the Bintavyan Valley just west of Capitol Prime.

This day is turning out to be a crazy one for us out here, as I'm sure it is for many others. Both Marshal Darumon and Sargeras have been destroyed by members of the opposing faction they were hiding from during this time, meaning to say a rival godlike society called the Estelar. We just witnessed a rather extraordinary display of skills and other talents, many of which don't have an easy definition for us in our world, but I think it goes without saying, if anyone wanted something new to study, here it is.

We have yet to make an official meeting with the leaders behind this military body that somehow infiltrated our world sight-unseen by us, and more importantly, by either the Marshal or Sargeras, as they intended to make a silent approach to prevent them from escaping to places unknown. During this time, I should also admit that we at CPComm were under instruction to cooperate with these efforts, and I, for one, was employed on multiple occasions to assist in releasing some of these critical details to the public, but to do so in such a manner as not to draw any direct attention by the Marshal. The reason being he was considered a risk factor if he should wish to take some form of counteraction. And considering what occurred during the Tav'ageen Scare, this could be dangerous.

With me now is an agent for that planetary security agency we mentioned once or twice during this time. They too had to remain very secretive, and largely for this same reasoning. But now that we're here, I'm told they have an announcement to make."

Ileani now passes off to Kita as she pulls up her tablet to make her speech.

"My name is Special Agent Kita Kaetaal of Azgarén Central Intelligence. We describe ourselves as a planetary security agency designed to serve as a counterintelligence service, along with antiterrorism and anticorruption at all levels. Our authority generally supersedes the traditional law enforcement and civilian security agencies, as we must oversee security on a scale that can threaten government and military activities, national security, global citizen security violations, and threats both foreign and domestic by bodies that cannot be so easily traced using common investigative methods.

Among other things, we may employ what we shall heretofore describe as our Prodigy Gifts, in plural, which not only includes the projection skill, but also telepathy, as well as any and all other Gifts we may be privileged to possess as part of our unique heritage in order to see to our goals. As a society that is clearly in possession of these skills, our laws must now extend to cover their application, whether the inappropriate use by felonious agents, or the legitimate use by law enforcement bodies. Our activities will coordinate with other law enforcement agencies, as necessary, plus legal and political entities to establish new laws and procedures for when, where, how, and why to use any or all of these Gifts. We will also assist in the development of new technologies to investigate improved services, devices, and security procedures, to prevent the illegal and immoral application of these Gifts that could represent a security risk to our world population."

In the observation booth, Elder Vankkar winced at the presentation. "Well, they're bringing telepathy out of the closet. I'm not so sure how I feel about that, but if they're already planning a top-level security agency to oversee how it's used, I guess it can't be too bad. But now I worry if this could be the beginning of a new kind of repression."

"Oh Father!" Túfula slaps him teasingly on the arm. "Must you always be so negative?"

"I'm sorry, Túfu, but it's my job, and it tends to grow on you after a while."

"Personally, I don't think we have to worry about this. Not if it's coming from Thaelyn and his teachings. Clearly, if everyone can use it, it goes without saying they'll have to learn how to use it right. It works both ways, you know, and this is the law enforcement agency to govern it."

"All right, Túfu," he accedes. "I suppose if it's in us, we have to accept it, like it or not. But like they said earlier, we're not mature enough to know how to use it right. So, how do we correct this?"

"We need to grow up…and fast," she giggles.

Kita continued on the video feed.

"We were not established by the Council, or any other existing official government agency, but instead we are effectively, as ironic as it might sound, an insurgency force taking control of our world away from that which took it away from us. We are led in part by Colonel Kaliya Nazég and the Stormhooves as a liberation force. The Stormhooves is an Order of Knighthood and an elite Special Forces military unit dedicated to a member of the Estelar named Lord Oghma. They are trained on Tae'Eladar under the supervision of the Order of Tyr, which is the native military body serving His Majesty, King Thaelyn.

Although they are technically a part of his military body, they are offering themselves to the service of the people of Azgarén to represent a standard of excellence that others may follow their lead into a new Age for our people. To this end, they desire to position themselves as a government-level authority figure to teach and to regulate the methods and manners of how the Prodigy Gifts may be used. Their teachings are handed down by the Estelar and the Celestial Races, both of whom are of such advanced levels of sophistication that these skills may come naturally for them over time, whereas ours did not. It is their firm belief that not only can they provide a valuable service to our people, but also a necessary one. This is to ensure the proper delivery of discipline and culturing, where we will learn to understand the responsibility and respect for our fellow citizens, and any other forms of life we may ever encounter."

In the shelters around the world, the people were once again listening to the news broadcast, and many of them began whispering about the implications of the Stormhooves taking up a position of government authority. This naturally followed with more discussion relating to the statements of the Prodigy Gifts and the dire need to evolve their society to meet the apparent demands. Overall, it didn't sound like they would have much choice. Their heritage was forcing the situation.

"We are also led by a former member of our own military, who gave himself fully into this service, and supports these same statements. He was a former Fleet Commander in the Azgarén Space Navy, now turned Director of the ACI, and also working alongside Thaelyn of Tae'Eladar. His name is Lajivi Kriv'tik."

On the mention of the name, Commander Geilv instantly perked up.

"Lajivi?!" he blasts. "Is THAT what he's been doing out there? In all the nether-space, I should've guessed! Where is he right now?"

Kita is interrupted by the outburst as she turned to face the Commander. She smiles tenderly as Ileani turns one of her cameras at Geilv to include him in the picture.

"He's right behind you, Commander. Or perhaps you didn't take notice of it during this time."

Geilv felt a sudden cold spike as his anticipation at seeing his old friend hit home. He delicately turned to look over his shoulder, but he didn't actually see anyone standing there. Then he took notice of a bird sitting on the roof of the news van. It seemed a little out of place.

Ileani followed his gaze until she also noticed the bird, and reflected on Ayene's earlier antic with Azina.

"Oh no," she moans. "Not another one."

The bird leapt off the vehicle and gently glided to the ground. The cameras watched as it seemed to blur momentarily and change shape, growing rapidly to a man-sized form in a neatly attired suit.

Kriv'tik stepped out of his projected bird form as he altered his image back to his normal shape. Geilv stumbled back a step and clutched at his chest as his breath caught in his throat.

"Lajivi?" he wheezes.

"Easy does it, my old friend. You're not as young as you used to be. But then again, neither am I," he chuckles.

"But are you another projection?"

"Yes, strangely, it seems you CAN teach an old bull a new trick on occasion. It took a few tries, but most of our membership is doing it these days and signing up for new service. We're entering a new Era, Teranu. The old ways will need a serious revision."

Geilv smiled sentimentally and reached out a hand. Kriv'tik extended his, and they exchanged a firm handshake and a pat on each other's shoulders. Ileani felt a moment of thoughtful reprieve before returning to Kita. The young agent continued her report.

> *"Now, we realize, some of these statements might suggest an image of a new form of take-over. However, in the absence of a proper government to object to it, and with the people in such need for efficient guidance by authorities who are knowledgeable and assertive to support our modern demands, we find ourselves in a position where we must adopt something entirely new. This is where Miss Latena Ta'yeen comes in. We have been supporting her during this time to bring the people into alignment to realize this need, at least as much for those details we could publicly declare while in the presence of Darumon who was still watching over us. But now, with him out of the picture, we can come out with one final detail not previously mentioned."*

"Here we go..." Azina moans in the background. "Everyone, hold on to your horns."

> *"The Council has long been described to be in this deep deliberation. The truth, however, is not as polite. According to military as well as public records, the last time any Council member was seen publicly occurred during the press release of the Tav'ageen Suppressor chip, back in 9765.31 CTD. Presumably, according to the information given to our people by press agents and others, sometime after this, they went into this deliberation. But as the recent news sensations revealed, that deliberation was NOT inside the Grand Hall building as everyone thought. Then we have what some call this ridiculous excuse by the Marshal that they were in some lonely research lab*

conducting this all-important work in secret, and using a miracle longevity drug to keep them alive during this full period.

In actuality, during the Tav'ageen Scare, the Council was sequestered away as part of a secret quarantine procedure to protect our government body. Even High Commander Geilv believed this was so. But apparently, the Marshal was keeping secrets even from him. The research base was an old Sentinels' lab located on a barren moon in a distant star system. It was out of service until this time when it was repurposed for the occasion. But sometime after that final public appearance, when we all thought they were conducting this deliberation, that base, codenamed Site One-Alpha, was supposedly destroyed by the Marshal's insurgents."

In the raid shelters, the people were suddenly rising up with moans and shouts over the obvious implications, while others tried to hush the outpour to listen to the rest of the report.

"We are aware that Central Command recently sent a scout vessel to the location to investigate. But this was only after the incident at the Grand Hall. What they found was a destroyed research base, and a lunar surface littered with debris, as well as bodies. A careful examination was carried out and discovered not only was the full Council membership included, but also their immediate family members, meaning those who might be first to take notice of their loved ones gone missing from home. The barren environment allowed the investigation to conduct forensic tests to determine the nature of the attack, and the results resembled weapons' fire consistent with our own period designs. This suggests it was our own military that destroyed our Council, and likely while under the effects of that military control chip in active mode, so no one could question it."

The outpouring in the shelters grew in intensity as the people began grumbling over the obvious criminal actions and loss of life, on top of all the lies, deception, and excuses.

"Therefore," Kita continues. "We are literally without a government of any kind. As such, the ACI will offer itself to serve as a crutch, along with the Stormhooves, and the efforts currently underway by Latena Ta'yeen and her people, until a decision can be made for a

replacement. But regardless of what form of government we create together, there are those of us who believe we will need to associate ourselves with these other societies to afford us the guidance we need as a young race that, technically, should not even exist as we are. Otherwise, we would be holding a position right alongside them, had our history followed a natural course. We are a race of half-gods, some have said to be on par with the Celestial societies, if only a younger variety. And as such, we need others of our own kind to show us how this is done. Unfortunately, our limited perspectives that so often prefer to deny those aspects of what a Celestial actually is, will need to be modified. If the people, and the Council, once denied acceptance of such a concept as Metaphysics, this must now become our new living standard."

Kita turns to find Relissa in the news group. The young dark elf had returned from her errand with a holo-chip in her hand. Kita reaches out to take it. She holds it up to the camera.

"Here in my hand is a holo-chip taken from our recordings inside the facility behind us. It is from a spy camera we have positioned inside Central Command in their control booth at the time the Marshal carried a conversation with our people who were impersonating Ytani's forces. Just after that, as I understand it, the Marshal shared a private word with the HC. This represents that conversation, which all of us, including the Stormhooves and His Majesty, agree should be shared with the people. At this time, the people may not hold much sympathy for the Marshal after all he has done. But if you take a moment to reflect on these words, regardless of anything else, you might begin to see it from his perspective."

She hands the chip to Ileani, who then passes it along to her technician at the camera broadcast controls. He plugs it in and makes a brief review to find the beginning of the recording, then broadcasts it on the air.

The image was clearly from a hidden perspective looking down into the room. It portrayed Darumon facing the general direction of the camera, with Geilv and the Captain in the near foreground.

Kita and Latena, along with the others in the news van, all watched the monitor to see what it had to say, as this was their first time witnessing it. In the observation booth, the Daanen'kai Elders also leaned in to listen closely, as did the people in the shelters, many of whom were still grumbling over the Marshal's previous misdeeds.

> *"Commander, I would wish to share a few of my personal thoughts, if I may."*
>
> *"What thoughts are those?"*
>
> *"I was never made to be a father. My kind is not intended for that purpose. Recall what I said before. Each of us is a custom creation for our individual masters. We are not an evolved species with a life of our own. Further is that we are linked to them. Their existence becomes our existence…"*

The people watched as the video played out. At first, there was antipathy at simply seeing Darumon's face by this time, but as the video continued, the audience went cautiously silent.

As Latena watched, she couldn't help but to reflect on that statement. "His existence is based on Sargeras's existence?" she murmurs.

The dialog in the scene progressed.

> *"…I once promised my Master that I would struggle until the end of time to bring him back. I must be entirely subservient to him. This is my sole reason to exist. And at this moment, it is really the only thing left for us…simple survival. But survival in an environment where everything is trying to destroy you is not a friendly place to be. Especially if they are so determined to see it through to a complete and final end."*
>
> *"And here is where you spoke of hoping to rejuvenate your society. That long eternity of time tearing you down from your former prestige, none of which you ever personally experienced."*
>
> *"Yes, Commander. It was a vain hope, but it was all I had…"*

Soft murmuring could be heard echoing through the shelters as they continued to listen.

> *"…Ours was a society that could not tolerate competition. We did not wish to share our position with anyone else. So, even if I could bring us back somehow, no doubt it would simply fall back into ruin, as it did before. Someone else would rise up, and here we go again…"*

The news team glanced at each other as they continued to watch the replay.

> *"Commander, you must understand this. When I first came here and found your early ancestors, those Eracyodines, I saw nothing more than raw materials. I had a plan, within reason, but I needed a species to assist me. Therefore, I used yours, elevating them to a level of sentience that I could shape to serve my needs…"*

Many of the people found themselves wincing at the depiction of Darumon's hybridization of their species. Even though it had been said before, to hear him admitting to it was another thing.

> *"…My body carries a rather unique ability to serve as a universal platform to interact with many other forms of organic life…animal grade, you know…so long as they hold a minimum station of evolutionary achievement. But to hybridize myself with anything else is severely repulsive to our kind, especially our masters. They would take great offence to it. Nevertheless, it is all I had. I knew this would cause a few complications, and it would seem those are coming forward now. And yet, while on one side I was unsettled by this, as my Master would never permit such a thing, a small part of me was also fascinated by it, maybe even a little bit…fulfilled."*

In the observation booth, a sudden twist of emotion began to enter their thoughts.

"He was actually fulfilled?" Ankhia mutters. "Him? For all the things he did?"

> *"…My kind is not intended to create something. This is not part of our role to play. But unlike all the others, where my Master and his kind were the ones doing the work, this one was mine. It became personal. I did this, and it carried a different feel for me. I had become a father, in a literal sense of the word…"*

"So he did hold a parental instinct," she whispers softly. "If just barely."

"But he wasn't very good at showing it," Elder Girhani emits.

"He was denied feelings of any kind," Tyanna considers.

"…I experienced that ancient romance of our kind, the Challenge of Creation. To observe that young race struggling to rise up. It was my dream come true."

"Cu'Nar's pity," Túfula moans. "He was fascinated by watching us."

"…I was never a father before this, but here I am. And you, Commander, demonstrated your strength to me that day you finally stood up to challenge me. You…your people… Even if you did have outside help to open your eyes, and I suppose at this time it might be necessary, but once you began moving in that direction, you showed your truer value as a warrior race, whether you might realize it or not."

As the video progresses, it comes to the moment where Ayene makes her appearance in the room.

"So, a few of you have actually begun to train it, have you?"

"Yes, Darumon. I'm the one he found on Morndindor. I'm working for His Lordship these days, part of that ACI body, so he's already helping us learn. But I can't believe what I'm hearing now!"

"Perhaps not, and maybe I'm the last person you would want to hear it from. But you are my children, like it or not, and you have turned out to be a fine creation."

The video continued with Ayene's questions relating to the Tav'ageen Anomaly.

"…My sole reason to exist must be to serve him. It was necessary, and ultimately inevitable for me to rescue him from his hibernation. I worked long and hard to develop your society to aid me, and this held value, at least where my work was concerned. But you were also my children. And by this time, I had become lost in that devotion. But my duty to my Master had to come first, and I knew he would never permit such a thing as this to continue. I had to bring him out, but I could not allow him to see this…"

Inside the observation booth, they all reeled back.

"And there you have him hiding it," Sulíma accedes. "Protecting us from HIM."

"…A few had to be sacrificed to preserve the many. But I will have you know, I did not take pleasure in it. And yet, my duty to my Master was still paramount to me. He was ill from so long a time in hibernation. And in this fold, he could not survive for long without something to sustain him. And I dared not travel far outside and risk myself along the way."

"You said your existence is based on his?"

"Yes, and if his fails, mine also fails."

Out by the news van, Latena studied the clip.

"In all the nether-space!" she gasps. "He's as much a slave as anything else out there. If he does NOT serve his master, he dies because of it!"

"Now that's motivation for you," Azina murmurs.

The video progressed to Ayene asking about the pursuit of Velen and his people, along with his concern of their race already being so mature, and the worry over teaching more.

"We built a world out there. We raised it up from the dust and created a marvelous civilization together. At this moment, your reach spans this galaxy and even more. But this is only the beginning for you. You can do much more than that. That other universe can teach you things you will not find here. And that…Abnormal Space… nether-space, the Fourth Fold, call it what you will, now that you know of it, you might find yourself spending a lot of time out there. And the Gifts you are discovering will carry you even farther. But they are potent, so be careful with them."

"Oh, absolutely! You can be sure of that!"

"As for the maturity, for all of your achievements in science and technology, you are still lacking one important piece, and this relates to the dynamistic flows. Learn that, and you will be complete as a species to rival the best. From there, I cannot be sure where you will travel, but this one universe is only the beginning for you."

As the Daanen-Aryku continued to watch, Sulíma felt a need to cover her mouth from a strange upwelling of emotion. Túfula was not far behind, and even the Elders felt a sensation rising.

"In all the nether-space," Elder Girhani mumbles as she glances at the others. "That turns things around a bit. He admired our progress, and desired more, if only for his master getting in the way."

The recording continued as Darumon reflected on the game to be played outside, and the final destiny of the Suuden-Aryku as a race.

"...A species like yours would not exist for half an epoch at best, and yet here you are...very young, but with qualities that could easily place you on a much higher pedestal. Dare I say it, but you could perhaps compete with the Celestials themselves, if not for your youth and inexperience."

Now Sulíma felt tears coming to her eyes. This represented an actual compliment. Ankhia wrapped an arm around her younger sister, as much to comfort her as it was to gain comfort from her.

In the shelters, many of the people were reacting similarly. The message was becoming clear, despite everything else he represented.

The scene continues with Captain Ta'yeen speaking.

"What do you know about them, and these Estelar, for that matter?"

"In my time trying to study them, I have learned they tend to nurture younger species. Their stand on these matters is very different from ours. They hold a belief that young species like yours will one day grow and mature into higher forms. This concept is offensive to our kind, as we held a much more solitary decree of authority, but that is another matter. You should ignore this coming from me, as this is also moot now. Instead, if you should hold the power to survive beyond this...and if you have any such interest within you...make your Father proud."

Sulíma and Túfula both felt their emotions taking over. Sulíma slid her hands over her face and whined softly as she hunched over, while Túfula covered her eyes and leaned to the side with her lips trembling. Ankhia was speechless and gaping at the monitor. The two Elders gazed at each other, and then the rest.

"How am I supposed to interpret that?" Elder Vankkar whispers somberly.

Velen could only gaze at the monitor blankly and shake his head.

The audiences in the shelters were stunned at what were clearly a father's last words to his children. It wasn't the sort of father most of them wanted, but the words surely carried a hidden feeling of affection from a being not otherwise allowed to express it. They held their focus on the monitors, silently contemplating the meaning of his message.

Kita, Azina, Ileani, and the rest were also shocked, even though they had been forewarned by Ayene and Navina at the beginning of the show. As for Latena, this simply solidified her position. She knew what she had to do.

"I need my podium," she asserts. "I need to make my new political speech. Relissa, can you help with that?"

"Aye!" she responds and goes rushing off again.

"Ileani, get those cameras turned around."

Ileani found herself being yanked back into reality as Latena exhibited a surge of new energy. She redirected one of her cameras at the young girl.

"We need people out here," Latena asserts into the news feed. "We need our citizens to get off their tails and into whatever vehicle they can find, and come out here to represent our public. If you live in C.P., or maybe over here on the coast, get moving. We need to show our appreciation for what these people behind us have done for our world. Not only do we owe them our freedom, we can probably also say we owe them our lives, our very existence."

"Um, Latena," Ileani interjects. "Can you possibly clarify your meaning here? To owe our existence?"

"The alternative is to be owned by Darumon, Father figure or otherwise, to be used for whatever his servitude to Sargeras demanded. And by this, think of the word slaves, if your horns can hold up to it. Our idea of a free and open society was largely an illusion. While Darumon might have desired us to go higher, his servitude to Sargeras limited his options. And it's clear to me that HE was as much a slave as any other, especially if his very existence depended on it. And with no other choice but to survive against impossible odds, this can explain a lot of things. Although I wonder if any of us pacifists can even begin to interpret what that means if none of us ever held our tails straight enough to do the same."

"Ouch, Latena, but I suppose, after everything else that's been said..."

She pauses to glance over her shoulder at the field behind her.

"We have a legacy unlike any other," she returns to the camera. "Just look at Kaliya out there and her funeral service. That was a demonstration of a principle, one that our society has very likely lost due to King Saakerav and his policies to drag us into his Enlightened Era which spoiled so many old beliefs and traditions. A Celestial race is a highly refined, and often revered society of beings. If this is our direction, we need to return to those old beliefs and reacquaint ourselves with their values. And to all the nether-realms with that technocratic society that refuses to believe in anything that isn't otherwise measured in numbers. This means, we have not one, but multiple obligations to uphold, and not just for our own. These aren't optional, people. This is simply who we are, and it'll require a full refit of our social values to realize what to do with it."

She abruptly breaks off and begins marching up to the shield wall spires to assist in setting up the podium pieces, which Relissa and a few others were now hauling out from a storage area inside the building.

Ileani glared at the girl for her sudden enthusiasm, and then glanced at Azina and the Director. She next turned to the Commander and the Captain.

"She's your niece, right?"

"Yeah," the Captain relents. "And I can already hear her mother ranting."

Inside the observation booth, Vonafel had moved closer to the Daanen-Aryku members to watch the video and gain a better understanding of these new players.

"Who is she?"

"That's Latena Ta'yeen," Sulíma informs.

"She seems full of energy. What is she doing?"

"She's a political activist who's been campaigning for a new world government to replace the old one. According to everything that's been said so far, we need to carry ourselves into a new Age of some sort due to our Prodigy Gifts and everything else we have piled on top of our horns."

"Campaigning? A new Age..."

Vonafel glances down at her book and opens it again to the final page. She studies the one remaining quatrain.

"Does the word 'Era' hold any meaning to you?"

"Well, yeah, I suppose it does," Sulíma offers. "If we put it into this context, our people have long held the belief we were in an Enlightened Era due to our transition from many nations into one big world society turned to science. But here is where we have our troubles with our old government that was actually a dictatorship, and all because of Darumon."

"And that's gone now…" she trails off. "But there should be more than one. It's in plural here."

"What's in plural?"

"People…crusaders of some sort."

✦ ✦ ✦ ◆ ✦ ✦ ✦

In many of the local raid shelters, those in the city and the nearby communities, the people all glanced around at each other after Latena's proclamation. They realized she was right, and many of them felt the same need to offer their thanks. Some also hoped to meet their saviors personally, at least in part to make their personal offers as it was to finally learn something new about the universe around them. And this example certainly did offer some fascinating new tidbits.

"We need to get out there!" shouts a man. "Let's all get to our shuttles and make our way to the valley. Call your friends, your family, anyone you know who lives nearby. We need to show ourselves!"

"With so many of us travelling," replies a woman. "It will be madness for all the traffic."

"We should find someone with hover coaches," calls yet another. "Are any of the public transit lines working?"

"If not," yells another male. "We should call them and get a few of THEIR tails moving! Come on!"

Soon, a flood of people began pouring out of the shelters and onto the streets. They each sought out their individual hover shuttles and offered others to join in as they carpooled away from the area. Calls went out to spread the word, and life quickly turned chaotic for travelers trying to exit the city.

"I have a brother in C.P. Security," shouts someone. "We are going to need some assistance out there to control the traffic."

The city rapidly came back to life as the streets filled up with a mass migration leading out of town. Volumes of elevated traffic lifted up and shot through the air as a cloud of hover shuttles spread out, generally ignoring the marked traffic guides, and seeking whatever was the most convenient passage through the area.

✦ ✦ ✦ ◆ ✦ ✦ ✦

Adalon and Tyr were still resting on the hillside, even though they knew they needed to join the others and offer some form of greeting, at the very least. They watched the news people conduct their work, realizing they were processing a series of objectives with Marelle, Relissa, Kita, and the holo-chip. These were necessary steps to bring a few pieces into play before anything else could take place. But as Latena started rushing away towards the wall, and when Relissa came out with help to assemble the podium, they knew it was time to become active again.

"They are becoming… Anxiousss…" Adalon emits as she watches the scene. "We need to give… Our ssstatements…"

"I know, Sister Adalon," he replies. "But now I ask of myself what we will say."

"The wordsss… Will fall into place… As they mussst…"

"Yes, and when thou dost begin speaking in such terms as these, this is where I begin to worry," he smiles.

The two of them rise up, with Adalon slowly lumbering her way towards the river. Tyr holds back as he watches her, and again gazing at the scene below, with Latena vigorously directing the assembly of the podium.

"What hath that young lady in mind this time," he wonders silently.

Ileani called some of her cameramen to move closer to the action as the podium was set up. She began issuing directions to arrange a press conference in front of it.

Kita, Azina, and the Director followed along, as did the military officers, bringing the major portion of their group from the news van into proximity as the activity levels clearly showed a change of direction for this presentation.

Ayene and Navina both returned outside, this time in their physical forms, as they had no more need of their projections. Navina was dressed in her Order military uniform while Ayene was in a cadet uniform, as she was still a student at the academy. The two of them joined with Kaliya as they made their way to meet with Ileani.

Inside the control room, the General and Kailen also made themselves ready to join the meeting.

"Commander," the General begins. "You should call on your Elders upstairs. This is the moment of your homecoming," he smiles.

"Simply to hear those words seems so strange, even alien to me," he relents. "But here we are."

He turns to leave the room as the General and Petrith move to join the rest outside.

Azina, Ileani, and several others also took notice of Adalon and Tyr rising up and preparing for something. They watched as Adalon made her way to the water's edge and began glancing around, as if she had intentions to cross the river. But this river was much too wide to simply step over, even with her great size.

"Can she swim?" Azina wonders.

"As big as she is," Ileani considers. "She could probably walk across the bottom of it."

"Nah," Relissa smirks. "That's too boring."

"Oh, boring, is it?" Azina retorts playfully. "Then what do you suggest? Maybe she flies across?"

"If she does," Ileani winces. "It'll generate so much wind, it could blast apart everything we have over here."

As they continued to watch, their cute remarks turned to shock and awe when Adalon began stepping out onto the watery surface. And when her foot met with the water, the surface froze over instantly into a solid form to support her weight. She then followed with the next foot to continue the crossing, creating what appeared to be a frozen bridge that allowed her to simply walk across the river.

"What is she doing?!" Azina shouts. "And how does she do that?"

"Aye," Relissa quips. "That's a fun bit we learn back in Mage School. You might not believe it, but they teach us how to literally walk on water over there."

"I'm getting a headache from all this," Ileani moans.

Adalon continues stepping slowly across the river, with each foot creating its own ice patch underneath it, which vanished as she lifted up and moved to the next spot, until finally she had arrived on the near side and searched for a comfortable position between the two rows of shield wall pylons.

Kaliya saw that she wanted to find a place to set herself down, but the field had those bulwarks in the way. She lurched forward and started shouting orders to the troops standing around the field.

"Everyone, let's pull up these barriers and move them aside. Stack them up over there in the far corner," she points at a location to the side of the control booth. "Quickly now..."

The field became a flurry of activity as the troops began lifting up the barricades out of their mounting slots and carting them away, leaving the space clear for the large beast to lay down.

"You couldn't pay me enough to run around under the feet of that thing," Azina murmurs.

"Do they actually get paid for something like this?" Ileani winces.

She and the others in the news group backed away instinctively as the behemoth creature loomed directly over them, moving into position, and plopping down with a thud that reverberated through the soil. She appeared even larger from this perspective than before, and it was startlingly intimidating.

Kaliya circled around in front of Adalon and held up a hand to her. Adalon lowered her massive head within reach for Kaliya to lay her hand against the creature's immense muzzle.

"That doesn't even look safe," Azina grimaces. "What if she gets hungry?"

"She doesn't eat people, Azina," Relissa admits. "They have their own society and their own types of food. Some of it actually sounds a mite tasty, if not for the fact that one piece might be a month's supply for peeps like us," she chuckles.

Tyr was just about ready to relax from his manifestation. He pulled away from the hillside and prepared to depart, indulging himself in one last thoughtful recollection before vanishing from existence again. He then descended into deep contemplation, clasping his hands together, or at least as best he could with one hand and a stump, and bowing his head. His body began to glow, enveloping itself with another divine column of brilliant light, and once again obscuring his form in the intense glare.

Relissa perked up as she studied the spectacle, tapping her hand against Marelle's arm to draw her attention and pointing across the river. The rest of the group soon followed as they watched the column shrink, and then finally appeared to divide in half.

Kaliya studied the phenomenon in amazement.

"The Divine Justice, one divided by two. That's not something you see every day, not even on Tae'Eladar."

Relissa could now see two figures emerging from the fading pillars of light. They appeared to be dropping to the ground, as if exhausted.

"General!" she shouts. "We need a guard contingent out here!"

She grabs Marelle's arm and together they start rushing towards the river. Along the way, Relissa calls to her pet wolf, which was hiding just inside the ramp leading down to the staging area. She blows a sequence of ascending musical whistles, and he came dashing out, much to the surprise of Ileani and the others who were not accustomed to seeing such an animal.

A large group of Order troops assembled and began rushing along to follow Relissa and Marelle. Ileani grabbed one of her cameramen and took off to follow them, keeping at a comfortable distance so as not to interfere with their operation. Latena, Azina, and the Director pursued further behind.

Relissa and Marelle were first to arrive at the water's edge on their side of the river. They peered across at the two beleaguered nobles. The rest of the troops began clustering together just behind them, along with Ileani and her cameraman, then Latena, Azina, and the Director.

"We need to get across here," Relissa emits urgently. "Let's form up a bridge. Line up, people, let's go!"

"Do we still have enough of the flows out here?" Marelle wonders. "I think they turned it off a while ago."

"Just barely, I think. But I also feel those seed energies a wee bit. Maybe it'll do as a substitute."

"If you say so…"

The troops began stepping out sequentially onto the water, forming up two lines just opposite each other and barely a pace apart. They used the same trick as Adalon to create a solid surface under their feet, forming a bridge-like path reaching well away from the shoreline. More troops arrived and made their way out to extend it further.

"I swear," Azina yips. "Nothing stops you, does it!"

"Not in this lifetime," Relissa chirps.

"Relissa," Marelle urges. "Let's shoot across there and help them."

"Aye! Excuse us, peeps."

She and Marelle each raised a hand to form a circle with their fingers, targeting a bullseye on the other side of the river while the troops were still arranging themselves. They then made a forward sweeping motion with their other hand, and their bodies flashed into glowing wisps, shooting out from their position and across the river.

Azina yelps at the sudden transformation, then struggles desperately to follow the rapidly moving dots of energy until they made impact on the other side, reconstituting back into their original bodies.

"In all the nether-space," she shrieks. "Doesn't anyone walk on that world of theirs?!"

Relissa and Marelle dashed over to assist Thaelyn and Aerlie on the ground as they waited for the bridge to complete.

Relissa's pet wolf was the first to arrive, following along as the bridge reached across the river. She gave it a brisk command to go on local patrol, not that there was anything to guard against, but as a standard procedure to support a fallen man.

Commander Geilv and his Captain remained behind, studying the precision, dedication, and efficiency of the Order troops, and reflecting on his own people for comparison.

"This magic of theirs must be extremely versatile," he considers. "It seems these people don't have any special need for anything it can't otherwise provide for them."

"Yes, Commander," the Captain concedes, "which leaves us at a clear disadvantage for almost everything. It's no wonder they're ONLY Industrial Age. My guess is they don't even need that much."

Lady Sehnisavain sent a group of her younger clerics to lend assistance, as they had far more energy than she did for the hasty jaunt. They crossed over and began examining the two nobles, offering revitalizing chants to bring their energy levels back up.

Ileani angled her cameraman at the scene while she tried giving an overview of what she was observing.

"CPComm, this is amazing what I'm looking at out here. I don't actually know who these two people are, but the amount of attention they're getting suggests they must be very important. I see what appears to be a male, and he looks somewhat similar to these others that call themselves human. But the other one appears female, and I actually have no idea who or what she is. Do you see it? She has wings on her!"

"Ileani," Latena steps in. "Maybe I can help."

"Yes, please, Latena. Can you tell us who these two people are?"

"The male is Thaelyn, and the other one is Lady Aerlie, his Queen. And yes, I happen to know they are different races, and this does sometimes occur on their world, so it seems. I guess love really is blind to such things as what race you belong to."

"Really! Do they have any children that you know of?"

"I'm not aware of any at this time, but they're both Celestials, so I guess time is truly on their side."

"Amazing, but now for the big one… Where did they just come from, and where did that other one disappear to?"

"That one I cannot answer, so I can only hope someone will come along with it in a few moments."

The Order troops rushed across the newly completed bridge while those standing along the sides held their position to keep the icy lane open. The bridge did not resemble your classic form of ice, rather an odd crystalline structure with a heavily textured surface that apparently held itself rigid without the typical slippery nature ice is so well-known for, allowing the people to make a hurried step across without skidding.

Once on the other side, the troops took up a broad circular formation around the two nobles, turning outwards and presenting their swords against their shoulders in an official guard stance held at attention, which again was standard procedure for protecting their royal sovereigns in unfamiliar lands. The regal pomp and circumstance of their performance was not lost on the Commander, or any others who might recognize this manner of presentation from their ancient history.

Ileani found her view obscured as the troops formed up. All she could do now was to wait until they were back on their feet and moving across the river.

The elven clerics assisted in helping Thaelyn and Aerlie find their strength again, although it was clear the two of them would likely sleep for a week before they were fully recovered. Several long moments passed, and they finally stood up, assisted by some of the guards, and with a couple of clerics helping Aerlie with her wings, as she was still too weak even to hold those up. The circle opened up and a procession slowly marched out from within, with Thaelyn and a guard helping him, then Aerlie and another guard assisting her.

They filed through the troops supporting the ice bridge, gradually making their way across, with the remainder of the guards following behind. The contingent reeled itself in as they progressed across, with the outer bridge support retreating behind the rest, until the full troupe had completely retracted itself to the near side again.

Relissa and Marelle followed behind Thaelyn and Aerlie amongst the cluster of guards. The group made its way directly towards the conservation center building, where they hoped to assemble for their official presentation.

Ileani followed at a distance, still trying to keep out of their way, as it did not appear either of them were in the right condition for any sort of interview yet. Azina and the Director continued at her side, keeping behind the camera and observing the scene.

Commander Geilv and the Captain were watching the procession across the field as the guards made their way back. Geilv knew the time was soon approaching when he might finally have an opportunity to meet with Thaelyn, after all he had heard of him. At the same time, the General and the others from inside the building were emerging to join the activities. So far, they were holding back and huddling in a group near the door. Then, as Velen and the Daanen'kai Elders appeared, the Captain took notice and tapped the elder officer on the arm to draw his attention. But when Geilv turned to see Velen, his heart sank. He knew who it must be by his manner of dress, even if his face seemed unfamiliar due to the long absence and the stress marks.

"Is that him, do you think?" the Captain whispers.

"I think so. I can just barely recognize him anymore, for the length of time passing. He looks worse than I feel at the moment."

Latena followed alongside the guards trying to spy Thaelyn within the mass. Once she had a moment to peek at him, she decided to rush forward to meet Kaliya, who was still standing near Adalon.

"Kaliya," she emits softly. "Thaelyn doesn't look well. Do you think he'll be able to speak to the people? I hope to have a bunch arriving here soon, if those slack-tails know what's good for them."

"I'm sure he'll be alright," she muses. "He's tough. Just give him a few moments to recover. I would imagine that experience probably takes a lot out of you."

"Just what did he do out there?"

"One of the cu'Nar's messages to my father told us of someone representing the Divine Justice who would come save us. But the statement also said he was one divided by two, whatever that meant. Then, Adalon gave us a prophecy telling of two becoming one during this fight. Well, I think that gives us our answer. Tyr died a few centuries ago, but gods aren't corporeal beings like we are, and their spiritual essence can be absorbed by other creatures, like other gods or even beings like us. We think the two of them became his vessels."

"Wow, I'm only barely able to pick up your meaning, and it already sounds fantastic. Does this make them gods now?"

"If my understanding is correct, it could, if they chose that course. But they don't seem to be doing that, instead keeping as they are. Nevertheless, I'm sure they hold a lot more under the hood than you might imagine, even for Celestials."

Ileani returned to the podium and repositioned her cameras. She glanced at Kaliya and Latena as they shared their private words. And then, when Thaelyn and Aerlie arrive in the area, Kaliya stepped over to meet them.

"My Lord, how do you feel?"

"Other than ready to place you down for a substantial mark on my list...?" he murmurs faintly.

"Um, oh dear...what did I do this time?"

"My dear ambitious young velvet-horn, you were brazen enough to actually challenge a god directly. And worse..." he raises a finger, "...based on manipulating the fabric of Reality. Even if he was in a weakened condition, this is worthy of its own chapter."

"This reminds me of a young girl I once knew," Aerlie adds. "Where is she now, I wonder, who was once so afraid of jumping on the backs of dragons?" she smiles.

Kaliya gazes at Aerlie for a moment as she tries to muddle the meaning, until suddenly a memory flashes back of an old conversation she once had during an anatomical exam she underwent back in the academy.

"Oh, dear cu'Nar, you're right! Well, those days are long behind us now, I guess," she chuckles faintly. "But now, how do we mark it for my victory?" she grins timidly.

"Oh..." Thaelyn moans. "Powers help us for that component alone. You have managed to exceed even your father's predictions."

"Right. Well, anyway, later for that. What about you personally, both of you?"

"Very weary, but then I suppose this much is obvious by now."

"Yes, it is, and I would recommend you take a few moments of rest before exerting yourself again. Maybe the two of you could sit down in the lounge and enjoy the show. We're still waiting for an audience, it would seem, so let's take advantage of the lull."

"An audience?"

"Yeah, Latena apparently made a statement to call some people out here for another of her speeches."

"Indeed! I wonder what she has in mind this time."

"I don't know, but I'm going out with my own little story to bring things current. So, why don't the two of you go upstairs and have a drink while we set things up."

"Are you now giving orders to me, young lady?" he smiles feebly.

"Yes!" she smirks. "And you can put me down for yet ANOTHER mark if you like. But if to use Relissa's words," she briskly glares at the girl standing nearby. "You're not in the right sorts to be jumping around."

"'Ere now!" she yips. "You need to put a little more twinkle in your eye for it."

Thaelyn grinned and silently laughed at them. He then glanced at Aerlie, who also appeared very amused.

"We are so very blessed," she smiles. "Perhaps we could take a moment, Thaelyn. We've certainly earned it by now."

"Very well," he concedes.

"While you ressst..." Adalon offers. "I can give my ssstory... As well. It will occupy our time... For a moment..."

"Excellent, Adalon," Thaelyn affirms. "And I would be very interested in hearing it. I would imagine you have a lot of history behind you."

Thaelyn and Aerlie give their instructions to take them inside where they can find some relaxation. The elven clerics followed along to continue their therapy.

Ileani and her news team followed them with their eyes, realizing they needed rest, but now asking themselves what comes next.

Latena also watched and listened. She had to agree with the decision, but as she saw them passing through the door, she instantly took notice of Velen and the others standing there. Suddenly, she felt very humble. She stepped over to Ileani and tapped her on the shoulder.

"Look there," she points discreetly.

"Yes, I see him. In all the nether-space, is that him, after all this time?"

"What's left of him, by the looks of it."

Latena felt herself being drawn forward. She clasped her hands and lowered her head as she approached reverently. Ileani turned her cameras on the scene as the young girl made a timid approach to the elderly official.

"Would you be Velen Nazég?" Latena asks.

Velen gazed down at the young lady and smiled gently.

"That I am," he responds in his typical frail voice. "I am rather impressed by what I have seen in the news broadcast thus far. But at the same time, I wonder where it will ultimately lead, if this world has no government to carry it, and so many obstacles to overcome."

"Oh, don't you worry about that, Elder Nazég. We have a lot of people currently working on our answers, and I have a few good ideas circling around my horns to throw into it," she smiles.

"Miss, um, Ta'yeen, is it? You seem quite full of energy. If you don't mind my asking, how old are you?"

"I'm just two, but don't let that fool you. I graduated with top honors at the university here in C.P. with a dual major in political science and political history, plus a minor in social history."

"That's quite an achievement," Elder Vankkar notes. "But did we also hear that you're some sort of an activist?" he grins.

"Yes, and for good reason. The Charter was corrupt, but it wasn't until I, um, sort of accidently bumped into these people when anyone would actually listen to me."

"And according to my daughter here," he glances at Túfula standing next to him. "You have this world turned on its horns by now."

"Yes, but now it's time to put things back into some sort of working order. Now that Darumon and Sargeras are out of the mix, we need to find our new direction. But Elder Nazég, I wanted to offer a few words to you, personally," she pauses for a deep breath to collect her strength. "I don't know if I could ever express, at least not sufficiently enough, how the people of our world might feel at this time, or SHOULD feel, if they know what's good for them. And I'm only aware of a small part of what must've happened to you out there, from what Kaliya told me. But I think the people of the world owe you a huge apology, if it could ever hold enough meaning to cover for any part of your suffering."

"I thank you very much, Miss Ta'yeen," Velen nods. "There may never be enough to repay for all the lives lost…so many. But from what we've been listening to inside here, it would seem you had a considerable amount of your own woes to deal with. This will remain with us for a very long time."

"And we can never allow ourselves to forget it. We will see that it receives an appropriate memorial, and this memorial needs to represent many things for our people. The way I see it, we could possibly say you were called away on a type of pilgrimage for us, even if no one truly knew about it at the time. There may have been lives lost along the way, but they cannot be said to be lost in vain, as what you brought back to us is worth more than the sum of its parts. We have learned who we really are. We learned where we came from and why. We learned there is a hidden quality to us that needed to be exposed, and then understood, but only with the wisdom to know what it means for us as a species and a society of individuals who were not ready for it. And we now know that we have a future, where not only must we hold responsibility for what we are, but also what we might do with ourselves, and it cannot be limited to just our own interests. If we can declare ourselves to be so high that we may compare with Celestials, we must then understand THEIR role, and follow in the same hoof steps. It's not just about us now."

"You know," Elder Vankkar muses. "You could put someone like me out of business with a speech like that."

"Yes," Velen chuckles. "You are a very passionate young lady, Miss Ta'yeen. I think you will go far in whatever professional career you may choose for yourself."

She smiles sweetly as she bows her head and withdraws.

A number of large hover coaches had been arriving on the outer portion of the field in a large parking lot that had been established for the conservation center. From these were unloading a few hundred people in their priestly robes, and so far, simply collecting themselves in a group.

Auryn's gathering was assembling itself at the edge of the field facing the conservatory. She pulls out her trans-com to make another call.

A subtle ringing issued out of Latena's unit as she was returning to the news group. She ducked behind the cameras to answer the call.

"Yes?"

"Latena, this is Auryn, we're here. Can you see us?"

Latena turned to survey the area. She could see the mass of people in the distance, with one of them waving vigorously at her.

"Yes, I see you. All right, listen, I hope to see a lot of people showing up soon. Did you happen to notice any traffic heading this way?"

"We were well ahead of anything else, but several of us got calls from friends in the area. Apparently, that message you made is getting passed all over the place. From what we hear, there are a huge number of people moving around right now. I would imagine we'll see them arriving soon, but it's going to get crazy out here for all the traffic."

"All right, um…" she pauses to think. "Wait, maybe if I ask Kaliya or Ayene for some help. They can send a few people out there to direct the flow."

"Great! Meanwhile, where do you want us?"

"Let's keep you in the background until the place fills up. If you're going to make your showing, you need to do it in full view of everybody. This is the day we ALL meet our new gods."

"Got it, just give the word when you're ready."

They end the link and Latena goes in search of help. She sees Kaliya entering into discussion with Ileani and preparing to give her story, so she turns instead to find Ayene standing off to the side enjoying the sights.

"Ayene!" she whispers urgently. "I need some help from you."

"What is it?"

"Auryn is out there with her group. We're getting ready for a special presentation once we get an audience out here. But she tells me she's hearing word of a LOT of vehicles coming this way, and we're going to need some sort of traffic control. Can your people offer anything?"

"Absolutely!"

She turns and starts calling up several platoon leaders to give them their orders.

Meanwhile, Ileani begins her latest interview, this time with Kaliya.

"A Colonel now, is it?" she smirks.

"Yeah, these things happen," Kaliya shrugs.

Commander Geilv stepped forward to join the session briefly. He studied Kaliya, who by this time had removed her helmet to interact with everyone, and for the first time he saw the face of a member of Velen's people, glowing eyes and all. He gazed at her curiously, and also taking notice of her youthful features.

"A Colonel," he muses. "That's a different line of service from what we tend to use."

"Thaelyn's service tends to be more ground based, an army as opposed to yours which is more of a navy. Although, we were speaking recently where the Stormhooves will probably end up as a hybrid of some sort, and this may require revising our ranking system."

"This sounds reasonable, especially when you consider the Naal Balai. You apparently did a very efficient job on that one. But still, as a Colonel, you look entirely too young for it. How did you manage that?"

"First, their service tends to move a bit faster than ours. In fact, many things move faster for them than anything we have here. Also, well, after all the attacks, there's not much left of us."

"Yes..." he closes his eyes and hangs his head. "I've asked myself about this a few times, but the answer was never very pleasant."

"Um, Colonel," Ileani begins. "Or can I just call you Kaliya, since we have something of a past together?"

"Sure, Ileani…" she smiles.

"Just for the record, even though I know who you are from our past interactions at CPComm and other places, can you give us your full name for our viewing public?"

"Of course, I'm Kaliya Nazég."

"And I see over there we have what can only be described by now as a living legend, in one form or another, Former Elder Velen Nazég. Can I therefore assume you and he are related?"

"Yes, he's my father."

"Wow, your father. By this time, I would've expected something at least a few generations away. No offence, but simply for the time offset."

"Yes, this might be true, but we had a lot of problems along the way."

"And would this represent a return home for your people?"

"Yes, a return," she sighs. "But not a pleasant one for the journey we had to suffer."

"All right, then let's touch on this. Can you explain to us from your side what you experienced?"

"As the Commander here already noted, I'm rather young at just barely four. I was born on Ruuki uy'Daan, and at just half a century, I watched as we took Darumon's final assault on us, using his orcish minions who were native to that world. They hit us by surprise and devastated our population. I spent the remainder of my life growing up on Therinë, in what was essentially a warzone, as he and your military laid siege on that world, and devastating yet another population."

The Commander turned and grimaced as he tried to envision the scene. Kaliya reached out to lay a hand on his arm to comfort him.

"Yet another…" Ileani muses. "Out of how many worlds, I wonder."

"I'm actually afraid to ask that question," Kaliya asserts, "after listening to Commander Kriv'tik and his stories. But if we go back to the beginning, my father received a warning from a race we began to describe as the cu'Nar."

"Why that name? Is this their actual name, so coincidentally to sound like the words 'they who follow' in our language?"

"No, this is our name for them, as they were apparently following Sargeras. They don't speak a language we can easily interpret. And so, with nothing else, we dubbed them cu'Nar. Adalon here," she glances over her shoulder, "or maybe I should call her Maker Kuroku, since that seems to be her original name, described them as Positive Primes, and they apparently serve her as spies and messengers who were watching Darumon and Sargeras during this time."

"This is what she was revealing to us during her interaction with Sargeras."

"Right. They delivered that ship to us and told us to leave. My Father tried to pass this to the rest of the Council, but apparently, they didn't listen."

"And then we have this history," Ileani submits. "Where, on our side, they and the Marshal described you as traitors, but instead you were told to run away by someone who apparently knew who these two were in reality."

"The story is as unfortunate as it is impossible for us to have realized what it was at that time due to the origin being so old and so far-removed. Along the way, as you and I have spoken about before, the cu'Nar shared some of their positive energy with our people to purify us from what we believe to be an aftereffect of being born by Darumon and whatever essence his kind shares. We suspect between them and the Estelar, there may be some form of incompatibility, and the Maker wanted it purged."

Kaliya glances up at Adalon for her opinion.

"Indeed..." she affirms. "But it runsss... Even deeper. During their rule... They caused... Ssso many othersss... To sssimply vanish... From exissstence. Now their time has passssed... And I want to sssee them... Take the sssame for it..."

"You must really hate them," Ileani mentions.

"I do... And for good reason... One you should undersssstand by now... If you were lissstening... To Sssargerasss..."

"Yes, I was paying attention to him, as I think we all were. He never came out to speak at any moment, so this would represent the first time. And it was enough," she chuckles sardonically.

"As for Darumon... While I disssliked him... No lessss... I alssso feel... His wordsss... As a father... To his children. But thisss is a new Age... And the Essstelar now rule... The sssSeas of Creation. If you are to blend... With thisss body... You mussst undersssstand... How it worksss. They are carefully aligned... Along polaritiesss... Of Positivity... And Negativity. Each of these... Consssstitutes... The equation within... The Measure of Balance... And we need both... To maintain the harmony... Of all thingsss..."

"I believe I recall this Measure of Balance stated during your encounter. And although we already had Ayene speaking of it, may I ask how you would describe this?"

"All thingsss within exissstence... Mussst balance. Thisss includesss sssuch... As matter and energy... To maintain the equilibrium... Of the forcesss... That bind Creation together. The processs of Nature... May sssee to thisss... Even without our help. But another element... That mussst be included... Is that of life and death. These forcesss... May find their way... Out of balance... If they are not challenged... To ensure their integrity. The ssside of Positivity... Is to nurture... And sssupport... To offer charity... And compassion... And to encourage... The weak... To overcome their limitationsss. The ssside of Negativity... Is to tessst... And interrogate... The resultsss... To challenge them... That they will demonssstrate... Themssselves... To be sssturdy enough... To sssurvive... In the face of adversssity. Persssseverance... Is not for the weak... Who cannot grow ssstronger... As life... Holdsss no favoritism..."

"Wow...that goes a little beyond any of the beliefs or philosophies we have here. I'm not even sure if Elder Nazég's faction went that far."

"But here we have... A mossst curiousss... Permutation. Yoursss is unique... Amongssst the Child Racesss... As you have originsss... That contain... Thisss ancient esssscence... From a bygone Era. As a compromise sssolution... To thisss impurity... We will add the esssscence... Of the Elemental Primesss... To align you... More appropriately... In accordance... To our interpretation... Of the Measure of Balance. In thisss case... We will choose... The Positive ssside... Which I perssssonally prefer..."

"Just for the sake of argument, why would you choose this in our case, preference or otherwise?"

"Sssuch an interesssting quessstion. If to exclude my preference... You are not... An aggresssssive sssspecies... Therefore the assspect... Of using you... To challenge othersss... May not sssseem appropriate. You are intellectualsss... And therefore your aim... Is much more consssstructive. Then we mussst consssider... These Giftsss... Which hold conssssiderable potential. And I think... A more consssstructive purpossse... Would be far more... Appealing... Essspecially when you consssider... Where they came from. Their kind did... Enough desssstruction... Already. Let usss turn thisss around... And find a better use for it..."

"All right, fair enough..."

The conversation returns to Kaliya as she continues her story.

"The cu'Nar came to my father and told him Sargeras was bad. But the cu'Nar do not speak in any form we can easily relate to. They're telepathic, and their language is what we call conceptual, meaning in the form of images and thoughts, which requires a considerable amount of interpretation to understand. They also used a peculiar term, which we interpreted as the word Titan, to describe Sargeras. But this word, to us, holds very little meaning, other than to say it's something big and powerful. Regardless of this, and without the support of the rest of the Council, my father had to call as many of his faction members as we could carry and leave."

"How many was that?" Ileani wonders. "I think our history tells us you carried off a large number of faction members, but I'm not sure if anyone remembers the count."

"According to our own history, it numbered around three hundred thousand."

"Three hundred thousand?!" she shouts. "How could you possibly pack that many people into a single ship?"

"It was a huge ship designed to carry large numbers of people," she shrugs. "It was basically a mini city, a fully self-contained colony vessel, complete with internal food production, several research centers, industrial workshops to produce tools and equipment, a full-featured medical ward, compact living quarters, community and recreation areas... It wasn't luxury living, but it certainly offered everything you need to bring a large volume of colonists to a new world and sustain them until they could establish themselves with the native resources."

"That's incredible! Something like that would be a fabulous design concept for us to use later if we should ever want to colonize anything."

"But the curious thing about it was everything was engineered on a tech level we could associate with, and also coded in our native language."

"Excuse me? And this was delivered to you by what was essentially an alien race, and one that doesn't even speak as we do?"

"Yeah, and one that doesn't technically seem to need spaceships to move around. They just came and went as they pleased by some other means we didn't understand. This left us to wonder who built it, and why they simply donated it to our cause. Whoever it was," she glances up at Adalon again, "must have some fantastic resources behind them, and further, I suspect they speak the same language as we do."

Ileani followed Kaliya's direction and gazed at the huge dragon in the background.

"Speaks the same language…" she hesitates. "Speaks the same… as WE do?" she winces.

"Yes, during Darumon's conversation with Thaelyn, over in Central Command, he admitted that this is HIS language, not ours. His kind used their native form to teach their creations a consistent interface, rather than inventing something new each time."

Ileani covered her eyes and shuddered.

Latena glared at Kaliya for the assertion.

"Wow, that hits a little hard," she admits. "It really nails home the idea of being someone's pets."

"Yes," Kaliya nods. "But Thaelyn would tell you how language is not something to find offensive or defamatory. Instead, maybe we should find a certain level of pride in carrying a little piece of an ancient and otherwise forgotten history in us. Besides, our written form does seem to be our own."

"So," Ileani resumes. "This, in addition to that message Darumon left for us as his children, I suppose, should inspire us rather than insult us."

"Yes, this is how we might wish to see it, as one more aspect of our uniqueness."

"Would this perspective also relate to that funeral service you gave so suddenly out there?"

"It would. Naturally, we knew of that message when it came out, as we were watching that spy-cam feed up here in this control booth. We then shared this with our people out here, as many as we could, and this also influenced our actions during this event, including that final moment. But it also runs into another perspective, a philosophical one, and this relates to our lessons on the Measure of Balance."

"How so? He was basically our enemy during all this time. And even though Ayene over here slapped my tail when I tried arguing the point…" she grins.

"Oh, she did?" Kaliya smiles. "Yes. I got mine slapped once, and for very similar reasons. The Measure of Balance teaches us that life is precious, and it doesn't really depend on who it belongs to. Evil may be our enemy, and the errant deeds of they who perpetrate that evil. But life, as a simple essence, in and of itself, is not a thing to be judged as right or wrong. It could follow a path along the road of Fate, leaning to one side or the other, just as easily as it could sidetrack off of it entirely. We had those orcs once, who virtually destroyed our homes on Ruuki uy'Daan, and further contributing to the mess on Therinë. I grew up with such dispassion against them, I wanted every last one of them to burn as much as they had burned everything else, and irrespective of their personal guilt for actually burning it. Then, I found myself being corrected that they were clearly corrupted by another influence, and this even went so far as to override their own cultural values to know better."

"Wow. That would be a hard yank of the tail."

"It was. This is where I found myself thrown into these new lessons, as well as a considerable amount of therapy for my own issues, and I learned about this philosophy that tends to rise above any of us here. All of Thaelyn's people follow this rule. They will fight hard against any injustice, but not simply to destroy whatever is causing it. They would prefer to reform, if possible, rather than destroy. Therefore, those orcs, what remained of them, on Ruuki uy'Daan, had to be made aware of their errors and returned to something more appropriate."

"And this would reflect on that philosophy to preserve and nurture life, maybe with the result of that adversity which brought them through this in the first place, now opening up the realization."

"Exactly."

"You carry a very interesting perspective, Kaliya. All right, I'll think about this. But returning back to your strange, and so conveniently configured ship, and you think SHE did it?" she points at Adalon.

Kaliya lets out a compulsive giggle as she responds.

"Based on what we got out of today's activities, I'm getting a few ideas, and it might begin with the Sarrukh. Around thirty-five millennia ago, about the same time as Latena's mention of Darumon hindering your expeditions to our neighboring galaxy, someone came out of absolute nowhere into Tae'Eladaran space, which itself would be a preposterous notion, and restored an otherwise dead world back to life."

"Um, wait, can you clarify one or more of those statements for me? Why would this be a preposterous notion?"

"Yeah, I figured you might ask this one," she smiles. "Tae'Eladar is in a universe by itself…well, almost by itself, as we believe the Estelar are trying to reclaim some portions of it. The rest of it is the result of the old Celestial War between the Estelar and the Primordials, the last battle where the Primordials set loose a doomsday weapon that destroyed everything else. It was the same kind of weapon he was producing at Morndindor. But Tae'Eladar was saved by enclosing it inside a special shell. As such, there's no physical way in or out, so you need a jump drive to go anywhere. But here is where we have our preposterous side, because you need to know of it to find it."

"Ah, a jump index, right?"

"Right. But in an independent universe, and with no other way of arriving there, this is impossible...unless you knew of it beforehand, maybe because you originally came from there."

"All right, help me with this part now."

"According to Adalon's statements, this must've been her original home, therefore the original home of the Sarrukh. This gives us part of our answer, as they might remember it. Now we have this incident from thirty-five millennia ago, which we associate with Maker Kuroku. We know she refurbished that world from the native history. We also know she called in...someone...with the name Sarrukh. We have some left-over evidence that gives us this story. What we did NOT know at that time was the relationship. But the timing is important here. The Maker was clearly watching Darumon, ever since the time of the war, and saw he was starting to restrict our people. Therefore, he probably had in mind to reel us in for his master plan. This might have served as a trigger for her to call in the Sarrukh, who in the modern day would be..." she whistles and rolls her eyes.

"I think I catch your meaning," she smiles. "How long ago was this war?"

"The Estelar describe it with the word Epoch, and the scholars on Tae'Eladar, who sometimes take their lessons from certain Celestial teachings, typically associate this as roughly a billion years."

"Wow! So, a society as old as that..."

"...Would probably be godlike in their own way, or very close to it by now. And certainly, high enough to take a world in a deep ice age and restore it to full life, seeding it from another source to give it a jump start, and poof, instant world to play with."

Ileani went silent as she tried to envision the scenario. She simply closed her eyes and shook her head.

"And this is where we might be if we had the normal evolution to go along with all our special attributes."

"Probably so," Kaliya nods. "But if you have something like this, building a ship like the Naarg uy'Sodrad might not be so difficult. Then we left home, and without any prospect of returning at all. We actually regarded ourselves to be in a form of self-imposed exile and started calling ourselves Daanen-Aryku."

"Yes, we had a couple others out here a short while ago speaking of this. And here is where the Marshal probably starts giving chase, calling you traitors and starting all sorts of trouble out there with his so-called insurgents."

"We never knew the part about these insurgents. All we knew from our side was we would settle on a world for a few or several centuries at a time, build a city, try to make new homes for ourselves, and then boom, here comes your military out of nowhere and blasts us to nether-space. We lose some portion of our population, the survivors make a mad dash to the ship, which strangely never came under attack, and we leave to find a new world. Then the process repeats, and it continued this way for something like eight millennia."

"Strangely never came under attack," Ileani muses. "Something the size of a small city, capable of holding three hundred thousand people, plus full facilities to survive almost anywhere you go, and it never came under attack. Wow, our military must be terrible shots for all our wonderful technology," she chuckles sarcastically.

"It was probably those military chips. We heard they were originally described as training aids, but I guess they didn't work," she shrugs innocently.

"Uh huh… But this is only eight out of the nearly ten millennia since that time. What about the rest?"

"Whenever we might see your military, like in the case of a ground assault, they appeared and behaved as monsters to us due to these seeds and those chips, neither of which we knew about or understood. Then, on one of these occasions, we were so desperate to escape from you, we decided to make a wild jump."

"A wild jump!" she gasps. "If I'm not mistaken, that's an extremely risky maneuver!"

"Yes, it is. But now, try this one on your horns. Whoever it was that programmed our jump drive brought us not only to a valid destination within a viable universe, but also within easy proximity of a star system with a habitable planet inside. Now, what do you think of that for an impossible deed?"

Ileani gaped at the suggestion, as not only was it simply impossible, but it was literally astronomical, and then some.

"How…" she wheezes.

"We had a spy onboard doing the work. We believe this same spy was also the reason your military…miraculously…found us each time we jumped to a new unknown world. And that spy had to be Darumon, as we later came to learn he can alter his form to impersonate other people, as well as fold space to provide for his own transportation."

"Oh, well isn't THAT convenient!" she snaps. "And he told US he was chasing you halfway across the galaxy trying to find you, but YOU were constantly evading us."

"Yes, well… This new world was in that other universe you've been hearing about recently, and we called it Ruuki uy'Daan as we felt this might be our final home, but one of exile. And we had fourteen centuries on that one before he grew tired of us again."

"What was so special about this world that he brought you there? You said something about those orcs, but is there another reason, or is that it."

"The orcs, yes, and he apparently owned them for a very long time, once using them as an early invasion of Tae'Eladar to see if it could start any trouble. This came about roughly ten millennia ago, when he became active on these other fronts, including here."

"How nice."

"We also learned he…stole…some of the local population from there to deliver into Therinë, luring them away with the promise of greener pastures. This was apparently to prime that world for later."

"And that sounds even nicer. Then he returned and apparently devastated that world to bring things under control."

"Right. And here is where he eventually dropped us for safekeeping while he went looking for his minerals to harvest."

"Great. But sending those orcs to Tae'Eladar. Is this to say he had some future plans for it?"

"Who knows at this point. Maybe he was hoping they could soften things up for him if he should ever return later. He was apparently travelling and conducting research on his old enemies at the time, and he used Therinë as a staging post for his forward operations. But this was clearly spoiled once Thaelyn came along."

"I see."

"Then, I was born, and at half a century started showing my Prodigy

Gift, which he apparently didn't want to see. So, he decided to finish with us by having his orcs attack us blindsided, pushing us off, and this time sabotaging our ship to crash on Therinë. We were there for three and a half centuries until Thaelyn came along."

"How horrible, and I'm very sorry for all this. How many are there of you these days?"

"The only survivors of the original expedition are my mother and father. The rest of us are at least several generations removed after so many repeated hits, killing so many people, and then an urgent repopulation effort on the next world to compensate, then to see a repeat of the loss and repopulation. What remains now are mostly a younger generation, and only numbering around ten thousand."

Commander Geilv grimaced morbidly at the figure. He covered his face and turned away whimpering as he stumbled back a few small steps and doubled over.

Kaliya watched and sighed, as she could sympathize with him. She stepped over and wrapped an arm around him, followed by Captain Ta'yeen. They tried to comfort him as he essentially collapsed to the ground.

Ileani and the others who had gathered in the group by this time also felt sympathy for the elder officer.

"There is great pain here..." Adalon begins. "Thisss much is certain. And it does not end with yoursss... As there are many othersss... Out there..." she glances upward. "Whole worldsss ruined... Whole sssocieties lossst... And I have ssseen... Ssso many of them..."

Ileani turns to Adalon now, hoping to distract some of the agony on the ground by inquiring about her story.

"How do you prefer we address you," she wonders. "As Adalon, or as Maker Kuroku?"

"Either will do," she accedes. "I am not... Essspecially particular. My native name... Is Kuroku... Of the Ikoko tribal clan... Of the ssSarrukh... From the old daysss... Of our early hissstory..."

"I'm almost afraid to ask how long ago that was, especially considering if you date back before that war Kaliya spoke of. Can you tell us something about your people?"

"Ours was the lassst... And perhapsss the bessst... Creation... Of Sssargerasss... Although I sssay that... Not knowing... Of the othersss. But consssidering... Our sssuccesses... In his gamesss... I think it is fair..."

"Were you a technological society, like ours?"

"No. Our Masssters... Did not generally... Permit sssuch advancement. We were intended... For the gamesss... Not to evolve... Into higher formsss. Therefore... It was not worthy... Of their time... To invessst... In sssuch teachingsss. Ours began sssimple... As ssso many did. But our victoriesss... Granted us... Certain boonsss... To learn new ssskills. In time, we grew... Into an Age... To work iron... Whereas othersss... May only know... Copper or bronze. But unlike your ssspecies... Ours was built... For warfare... With toughened hidesss... And sharp teeth and clawsss. Everything elssse... Was sssimply to add... On top of that... For the benefit... Of improving oursssselves... For the next game..."

"It sounds like your only purpose was to fight. But then, if I understand correctly, you were given some gifts of your own?"

"I was born... To a tribal matriarch. I would be her heir... When her time had passssed. I was quick to learn... And very sssavvy... And I developed... Many interesssting tacticsss... To play on the field of battle..."

"What kind of battlefield was it?" Captain Ta'yeen asks.

"The battlefield was... A wildernesss range... Cussstom made... And often ssset... With landssscape featuresss... To offer ssstrategic bonussses. To they who were... Clever enough... At using thisss... To their advantage... They could take the lead... And win the battle. I learned thisss quickly... And led my people... Into many sssuch victoriesss..."

"It sounds like you were a very talented individual," Ileani muses.

"In a very literal sssense... It was truly... Live or die out there. I sssuppose... I got lucky... In the beginning... And I learned from it. And then... I took notice... Of the tacticsss... Played by our opponentsss... As we ssspied on them... To dissscover their sssecrets..."

"'Ere now," Relissa teases. "Are you saying you cheated just a wee bit?"

Adalon let out a hearty laugh.

"And thisss... Coming from a ssscout...! But as you know... Information is vital... To win any contessst..."

"Aye it is!"

"In time... I grew older... And gained more influence... Among my people... To lead larger armiesss... With more complex ssstrategies. Here is where I gained... The attention... Of my Masssster..."

Adalon holds a moment in contemplation. She closes her eyes as she reflects on the occasion.

"I thought it was sssuch… A grand gift… From my god…" she mulls wistfully. "It lifted me… Above all othersss. It made me… A god-queen… Amongssst my people. Highly exalted… That I could lead… Our entire world population. They all united… Under my rule… And our victoriesss… Became legendary…"

She opens her eyes again and returns to the reporter.

"But it was all a lie. The Giftsss were real… But their purpossse… Was a cheat. And my Massster… Was taking glory… For his creation… When he did not even play… By the rulesss of his peersss…"

"Wow!" Ileani winces. "That sounds bad, especially on the scale of a god."

"At firssst… I did not know thisss. But as I learned… New waysss… To use my Giftsss… I sssaw what became… Of those who lossst… And through thisss… I learned who we were… In the eyesss of our godsss. From that moment… The gamesss… Were not about pleasing… Our Creatorsss… But sssimply to sssurvive… Using any meansss necesssssary…"

"And here is where so much of your anger seems to come in, not that I would ever blame you."

"Indeed… And I watched… Ssso many othersss… Wiped from exisssstence. It frightened me… And outraged me. I was a warrior… In the truessst sssense… And honor is my creed. I would choose… To earn my place… Through fair and laudable deedsss. Not by falsssehood… And disssreputable meansss. But when faced with the choice… Of the extinction… Of my own people… I was forced to do… As he desired… And sssend… Ssso many othersss… To their doom insssstead…"

Inside the observation booth, Thaelyn and Aerlie both watched and listened to the exchange outside. They gazed at each other mournfully.

"Such an existence, Thaelyn," Aerlie whispers. "It makes you wonder about all the bygone Eras that came before, and how many others may have suffered because of those Primordials."

"Yes," he nods. "And this again causes me to ask about the Estelar. When, where, and how did they originally come to exist, if they were once under this same oppression. And could their philosophy of the Measure of Balance also be due to some aspect of it. We know now they did carry a memory of them. And so, perhaps this is their way to correct the situation."

"Therefore, the peer association we see today. They maintain a system of checks and balances, and careful culturing of the younger races to condition them properly, that they will follow in kind when their time approaches. But I think Sargeras was also correct when he said someone must have become very lax. Their society may have begun to fail, much like their forebearers, but their pride overrode their better judgment to ensure themselves by leaving behind something akin to an heir to follow them."

"Indeed, you are correct. This also causes me to recall Darumon and his story. That trap, as he called it. But the Estelar, with their method, WILL leave heirs behind, even if those original few should one day follow that course. The Celestial races, for instance, will take their place one day, and carry this to another generation. We simply need to ensure we do not become numb to the eternity, as they once did."

Mynae was just returning through the gateway in the lower portion of the facility after a quick trip back home to Tae'Eladar. She was carrying a tightly wrapped bag. She rushed up the stairs to the observation booth where the others were still sitting and enjoying the sights outside.

"My Lord, here we are…"

She sets the bag down and pulls out two bottles with a purplish liquid inside. She hands one to each of the nobles.

"And what manner of concoction do we have here?" Thaelyn muses jovially as he examines the item.

"Well, surely you recall that I work in an alchemy shop, right?" she smiles gently.

"Indeed, I do, and you seem quite content there. Is this one of your products?"

"It is. It's a revitalization potion, and quite popular with certain industries, especially heavy industry, like mining and construction work. We have a brisk business in those areas to keep the workers on their feet during their long work shifts. Anyway, this should give you a little fix so you can go out there and finish what you started."

"What do you think, Aerlie?" he glances at her warily. "Do we dare indulge ourselves in the unknown?"

Aerlie studies the odd bottle and turns to Vonafel, who was sitting nearby and simply relaxing after the main event.

"Vonafel, what do you think?"

"Coming out of this winyamo?" she casts playfully. "If she would send water elementals after those people out there, just to play into the good spirits of a Primordial, I hesitate to see what else she has in mind."

"Oh, you!" Mynae sneers mockingly. "Ianter!"

They share a quick laugh together as Aerlie considers the strange brew.

"Well, Thaelyn," she smiles. "I suppose it can't be any worse than the rest. After all, what we just did outside was also a first, and it was in public!"

"Dear Powers help us…" he chuckles. "Are we becoming exhibitionist?"

They each pop open the bottles and begin drinking down the contents, then handing the empty glassware back to Mynae.

"Good," she asserts. "Now, give yourselves a few moments for it to hit bottom," she grins.

Back outside, Adalon was still reflecting on her experiences.

"After the fall… Of our old Masssters… We gave oursssselves… To offer thanksss… To the Essstelar… As our new godsss. But our relationship… Was not your ordinary worship… Of deitiesss. We learned from them… And shared many lessssons. My contact… Was one we called Helm. We gave much of our ssservice… To his honor… For protecting usss… During the cataclysm… Of the weapon. I continued to lead… Our people… From one Age… To another… Until one day… I foresssaw the coming… Of the Great Age of Ice… That would sssmother our world…"

"That sounds bad," Ileani offers. "What did you do about it?"

"The only thing we could do… Was prepare to leave home. We were old enough. We had a proficient… Ssspace indussstry… Albeit limited… To our home inssside the Shell. But we needed an essscape. We had two choicesss. I could call on Helm… To offer an exit… Or I could use my asssociation… With the Positive Primesss… To give usss… Our firssst dissscovery. And ssso, I chose them… Which allowed usss… To find our way… Without the ssspecial asssssistance… Of the Essstelar. It ssseemed more appropriate… As we were plying… Our own ssstrength… To find a sssolution…"

"Still a little of that old warrior attitude, perhaps?" she grins tenderly.

"Indeed!" she chuckles. "I was an old-timer… Among my people. I governed them away… From our earlier… Warrior classss… As I wanted them to excel… At higher goalsss. But as for me… I ssstill lived… Too much in my own passst. When the time came… For them to leave... I could not join them. I felt my time... With my people... Mussst come to a close. My children had grown up... And it was time for them... To leave home. And I... As their Mother... Had to find my own direction..."

"Oh dear..."

"It was a sssad day for usss... But I encouraged my children... To venture forth... As a new sssociety... Now borne... To the ssSeas of Creation. There would be no more... Limitsss... To their power... And they would grow... And evolve... Into new formsss... Perhapsss one day... To join with the godsss themssselves..."

"Jiggers, Adalon," Relissa winces. "And where are they now?"

"Out there..." she gazes skyward. "They have ssspread... Far acrossss... The ssSeas of Creation... And I am ssso... Very proud of them. But as I assscended... I brought with me... A group... Of volunteersss... Who chose to ssseparate... From the ressst. And together... We created... The Draconicsss. Thisss would be... My ssssecond brood of children... And my firssst... Contribution... To the ssSeas of Creation... And the Measure of Balance... That we will not ssssee... Sssuch like the Primordialsss again..."

As Adalon wrapped up, Ileani felt an urge to give her applause. She was quickly joined by the rest as they all offered their comforting support.

"You know," she admits. "I would imagine, for all the time you spent out there, you must have some fascinating stories to tell."

"Oh... But I do..." she asserts energetically. "I kept... A careful collection... Of memoirsss... Filled with my hissstory... And my teachingsss... And ssso many experiencesss... I shared along the way. It is in... A private library... Back home... Where I live... In the Outer Planesss. I had long hoped... That one day... I could share thisss with othersss. But my commitment... My promissse... My obsssession... To pursssue my old Massster... Kept me very... Isssolated... And reserved. I think perhapsss... It is finally time... To find my peace... And redirect myssself... To the future..."

Thaelyn and Aerlie were finally feeling themselves ready to join in again. They made their way outside to participate in the show.

"Adalon," he calls enthusiastically. "That was a truly extraordinary story, and I would most certainly wish to see some of those volumes of yours. But do they come in sizes one of us could actually carry?" he chuckles.

"Ah…" she croons. "Does he return to usss…?"

Kaliya stepped forward to meet the two nobles as they emerged outside. She studied them carefully, as they seemed to have an unusual bounce in their step when compared to earlier.

"Um, my Lord, are you feeling alright?"

"Indeed, I am actually feeling quite invigorated. Young Mynae in there passed us one of her special alchemical formulas, and it seems to have made its mark. I feel as if I could take on another war, if only one would come my way."

"Oh, cu'Nar help us!" she blurts nervously. "No, not today… Let's give everyone else a rest first," she chuckles.

Ileani perked up instantly as she saw the two people coming into view. She stepped forward hoping for a quick introduction.

"I, uh…" she flusters with a quick bow. "Well, um, first, I hope you're feeling much better after the way you appeared a short while ago. And I hope maybe you can give us a few words now?"

"Of course," he affirms. "And I am sure we have a considerable amount of work ahead of us to bring your world back into some semblance of harmony with itself. Especially after so many of our news sensations, to which you were so graciously instrumental, and also young Miss Ta'yeen's efforts at essentially disrupting all your political affairs."

"Yes, and apparently so much of this with your secretive background work. You know, Your Majesty, one might actually think YOU were trying to take over our world," she grins cautiously.

"Although I will admit, some have suggested these words, in one form or another, but I would not pretend to make such efforts consciously. This is your world and your people. If you were to choose this unto yourselves, I would be most honored for it. But this is another discussion entirely, I should think."

"All right, but now, I'm sure many people would like to know what happens next. The Marshal and Sargeras are both gone, but our world is a wreck. The Council is apparently dead on some lonely moon no one knows about. The primary document we once used as our Charter of Laws has been thrown in the refuse bin. And our people have been forced to realize our entire history was likely engineered, at least in part to hide our real history that we were artificially evolved and are very literally half god, which is both amazing and frightening at the same time. Ayene and this Special Agent over here," she glances at Kita, "both say we need to grow up with the help of others who are already there, but Your Majesty, how does someone actually do this?"

"Indeed, I understand your concern, as well as your fret," he sighs and nods. "Let us begin with this. First of all, with respect to you and yours, you are not only a young society, but also a very inexperienced one, even for your years and apparent expertise in space travel. You have lived a very sheltered life, probably due to Darumon keeping you so close to home, that you have little or no true experience of working with others outside your own. Velen's people may have encountered a few here and there, but they were also very isolationist, and found it difficult to associate with anything, perhaps in part due to the circumstance of being hunted by your military. Therefore, if you are to live and work with anything at all, you must first come out of your collective shells and realize there are indeed other forms of life out there and some of them quite different from your own."

"All right, this is reasonable."

"Now, there are societies out there we generally refer to as the Celestial Races. These are societies that are most often many orders of magnitude more mature than your own. But I should also stipulate this with a small mention. We may be speaking of two flavors here, which we refer to as the natural as opposed to the hybridized forms. The hybridized form would actually fall more in line with your own, being half something from a much higher echelon. Aerlie and I are also hybrids, as we are mixed between the Estelar and one or another of the mortal races. Mine is called Aasimar, and I would be half human. Aerlie is Eladrin and in her case half elven. There are others out there, made by one or another of the Powers from some Child Race they might hold special interest in, and we largely serve as interfaces between the two."

"Wow, that's interesting. And the natural ones, would they be more like a full civilization that just happened to evolve that far on their own?"

"This is correct, very good. But to arrive there often takes at least tens, and sometimes hundreds of millions of years for most societies. Yours, at a mere two million, is still regarded as very young, even though you clearly hold features of a much older one. If we put aside your Prodigy Gifts, your simple longevity alone would come into play as one feature I would not expect in…well, in any normal society at only two million years advancement."

"You say any normal society. Could there be another kind?"

"I might suggest that if a society spent an inordinate amount of its efforts artificially engineering itself, where it might develop some curious qualities as the result, this is one possibility. But this would no longer represent a natural form of evolution, and I do believe in taking this course."

"All right, but if these other societies are so much older than we are, how would we ever possibly fit in with that? Even if we are half-god, being so young, we might actually seem more like children by compare, right?"

"In many ways, you would. By that time, those societies have travelled much farther and experienced much more of the Seas of Creation than where you stand presently. Perhaps I should also mention, some of those societies can become rather pompous after a while," he chuckles. "But as a fair compromise, having close relations with our own would certainly offer some fine examples to work with, and it would provide you with the teachings you need to go even further. Our society, much like what Adalon described of her people, holds a very close association with our local body of Estelar, unlike most others who tend to interact in a more indirect manner."

"How does this indirect manner tend to appear?"

"More like your traditional religions where they are generally regarded as a form of mysticism. You might have priests of some sort worshiping something they believe to be a god figure, but without any definitive proof of what that god figure truly is. It could be nothing more than an idol, a depiction of imagery, or words written on a page of scripture. In this way, if the Estelar should wish to guide you on a certain path, they may not necessarily reveal themselves directly to your eyes, instead only to interact with selected individuals, rather than a greater body. This interaction might be in the form of visions, whispers, dreams, or some such, which would then be shared with the masses as a type of gospel the people take on faith. However, for some societies, this can also raise questions over the validity of those individuals and their statements."

"Ah, I think I see it now. And this might also follow with our society that once turned away from it, with or without Darumon's influence as King Saakerav, as we didn't have anything solid to define it by."

"Indeed. But as one who is a hybridized form of Celestial, I not only interact with them as part of my personal family, but I also share this with our people to teach them the higher virtues we receive as part of our own teachings, and I guide them on their paths as we move forward together. And if we should ever be so fortunate as to meet others along the way, such as your people, we would wish to share some part of this with them as our role within the Measure of Balance. Kaliya and her people, many of them, have already joined with our society as full citizens by now. This is a clear suggestion that you and yours could do the same if you were to find a similar interest in this. But I think I should also caution that our society is not quite as highly advanced as yours in the present day. Therefore, we would need to proceed cautiously together until we can find our internal equilibrium of cultures."

"I believe I understand. I recall it said you were only in your Industrial Age over there, although with some fascinating permutations due to your magical technologies. How long do you think it might take for them to reach something approximating our level?"

"Here we have a conundrum that often twists your people's horns around, if to use one of your curious little phrases," he grins.

"Uh huh… Kaliya and Ayene have done this so many times, I don't think I could ever untwist them by now."

"Yes, well, the people of Tae'Eladar tend to move much more rapidly, at least in part due to their shorter life cycles demanding faster returns. If we consider, outside of this war effort, and also outside of discovering Velen's people, or yours for that matter, we might say our rate of development, which I have been trying to carefully regulate so we do not overextend our cultural advance, might carry us an anticipated two, maybe three centuries at most, before we find proper space travel, such as for interplanetary, or even interstellar excursions. Not simply to reach space, as if to use such as rockets into low orbit, but a more determined form of it."

"All right, got it. But you're right, this is enough to twist up a person's horns really tight. That's barely a flicker of time for us."

"Indeed, and now made worse with all we had to go through to arrive here. Velen's people are already influencing ours for their higher esteem. As we drew more of his workforce away to join our military effort, we donated some of our own to supplement his native occupational demands for such as industry and manufacturing. This has already elevated our people's understanding with their level of technological appeal, and naturally this increased wherewithal will surely filter back to the rest. Therefore, all I can say is our ultimate climb is significantly reduced. In fact, as I reflect on our own High Commander over here," he directs at Kailen. "He just recently had a new son, but I suspect before that boy is even halfway through his education, we will be entering that next stage of our development."

"In all the nether-space, please don't tell me that!" she chuckles.

"Now, my people fully understand the need to measure themselves for any new growth. This is a lesson I was careful to teach them over the course of my tenure. Therefore, even with your influence, I think we might be able to govern it, within reason. And fortunately, we are already high enough that the jump ahead may not be as great. Still, it will be a jump."

"Yeah, for yours and ours both, I think. We might have our sciences, but you also have this magic of yours, and if we can get our hands on any part of that, like what you apparently taught Kaliya and her people, this will also be a jump for us…and more reason for our horns to drop off," she smiles.

"This is true, and at the same time, it offers each of us a curious sense of camaraderie, as we must now grow into each other. If we were to form any kind of bond, we could make small steps along the way until we find our balance, and then carry forward from there in a more conventional manner."

"Now that's an interesting proposition," she nods.

Latena was getting another call on her trans-com by this time. She receded away from the bustle of the interview to take the call.

"Yes?"

"Latena, this is Auryn again. I'm watching you over there on my tablet. I have a news feed playing here. It's absolutely fascinating so far, but I think you might want to get up on your platform soon. I'm looking back towards the city, and I see a lot of vehicles coming this way."

"Ah! Good! Then let me get to that now. I need to prepare my new statement."

"All right, and you'll let us know when it's time."

"Yes, I'll try to work in something to signal you. That's when you make your move."

"Got it."

She rushes back over to Ileani to whisper in her ear.

"It's time. I need to go on the air."

Ileani turns to the young girl and nods.

"CPComm," she announces. "We have our next segment coming on now. Miss Latena Ta'yeen would like to take this moment to offer our people her latest statements relating to where we are now, and her propositions for our people in relation to all we have seen and heard during this time."

Latena climbs up on the elevated platform while Ileani repositions her cameramen for a better angle. Thaelyn and Aerlie glance curiously at the young political hopeful as she positions herself, and they move back to allow her some space. They join with Kaliya, Ayene, Relissa, and Marelle, among others on their side, while the Daanen-Aryku Elders and Thaelyn's officers lined up on the other side.

Latena takes out her data tablet and pulls up a document she had been working on recently to use as her reference. She felt a little nervous about making this presentation, and she would need to improvise a bit, due to the recent events and what influence they would generate. But she felt in her heart this was the best, and perhaps the most reasonable course of action she could ever hope to offer to the people.

"Citizens of the world," she begins. "We find ourselves today at a turning point in our history, one unlike any other we can truly describe by rational means. Many independent elements brought us to this moment. If we reflect on all we have learned on this day, and all those moments during these past few years that ultimately defined the events of this day, we find ourselves with a decision that is not only imperative to make, but it cannot be avoided now. We need to set our future direction as a race."

In the distance, at the far end of the field where the local highway passed along from the city towards the coastline, a large mass of hover shuttles, coaches, family vans, and other vehicles, began to emerge into view from both the city as well as the coastal town on the other side. Several platoons of troops stood ready to direct the flow into a makeshift parking area, although the space would likely fill up quickly.

As the swarm of public citizens made their appearance, Thaelyn took notice of the sight just coming into view. He turned to gaze at it uncertainly. The flow was clearly an intentional delivery of people into attendance, and all too conveniently for the service Latena was so anxiously putting on display by now. He then turned to gape at the young political activist, discreetly pointing a finger between her and the arriving mass, and finally to glare at Aerlie, who could only shrug as she seemed rather amused at the sight.

"Throughout our history," Latena continues. "All we ever believed about ourselves was that we were a simple society of people, living our normal lives as best we could. Perhaps, in many ways, we still are. But to call us simple no longer applies, not when you consider the Prodigy Gift…or Gifts, as Agent Kaetaal calls them. This alone elevates us to a level where we have no other choice but to admit we hold capacities that need to be understood, as well as contained within certain parameters, not only for the legal implications, but also as a society that is no longer simple in any way. To have a government agency assisting with this is certainly a very reasonable objective. A form of law enforcement, a form of political regulation, these become obvious to us as a society that understands the need for law and government. But do we understand how to create this for ourselves? At this moment in time, I think for all that has been said, we do not. Therefore, help would certainly be a welcome offer. And that help must come from those people who are already there and have the experience to demonstrate these methods."

Many of the vehicles were landing by now, and people were beginning to flock into the area, taking up space behind Ileani and her cameras as a spectator audience. Thaelyn began to feel a subtle sense of foreboding as the masses accumulated. He could feel a certain alteration in the energy levels developing around him.

Latena carries forward with her lecture.

"It makes perfect sense that we should bring ourselves into a form of bonding with those who are so much like our own, even if we are considered young. Youth will mature in time, and this should not hold us back. It also makes sense what was said that we hold so little experience with anything outside our world, and this must also change. The display we saw on the field out here today is clear evidence that there are factors in existence we know nothing about, but that a society like ours SHOULD know about them, and therefore we must learn. But do we go this alone, or do we go hand-in-hand with those who not only know how to teach us, but can also serve as role models. Such as the Stormhooves would be an excellent example to lead us by demonstrating how to behave in those ways more becoming of our fuller nature. But again, we are not simple people who should limit ourselves to our favorite romance of watching a few programs on the vid-com, then to say this is all that we need. We need to LIVE this life, to be a PART of these people, to place ourselves not only on their level, as it might be becoming of us, but to join with them, as we do not seem to belong to anything else. Our heritage denies us that luxury. We are not as other Child Races ought to be. We carry something that is not found elsewhere."

As Thaelyn listened, he reached out urgently to tap on Aerlie's arm.

"Aerlie," he whispers. "Where is she going with this? All I said before was that we would do well to make an association, but…"

"I don't know, Thaelyn, but she seems to have a direction in mind."

"But Aerlie…" he frowns as he trails off.

"I must reflect a moment on Darumon's final message to us," Latena resumes. "We might not want to think of ourselves as the children of that particular individual, but here we are. And regardless of whatever else he did to us; he apparently did hold a hidden sense of accomplishment as he watched us growing up. He was limited in his display while under the eyes of his own Master, but those final words of his spoke to me, as I hope they did to others. We do not belong on our own. We belong to those we more accurately represent, and as a young society still in need of growing up, we must take to a new father to guide us."

Thaelyn now felt a sudden spike rush through him at the assertion. His mouth fell open even more at the implications of where she was going with it.

"If we can compare, as Darumon said, to such as the Celestials, then it is the Celestials we must immerse ourselves amongst in order to learn from them. The Gifts we hold demand nothing less…especially after that little demonstration Kaliya made earlier. In all the nether-space, if we can do THAT much," she shakes her head. "Therefore, we ARE on that higher pedestal, and living out here in the middle of nowhere is nowhere for such people like us to live. This may be our home, but our family is in a different neighborhood."

Thaelyn felt an urge to step forward and interrupt her, but his feet seemed stuck to the ground. Aerlie leaned over and took his arm to steady him, as she sensed his discomfort.

"We have before us several demands we must acknowledge. One of these is from Maker Kuroku behind me and this issue of these cu'Nar and their so-called blessing to purify us from this ancient essence. If something like this makes us more compatible with others like ourselves, this is a family I think I would want to be a part of. Furthermore, we may not have much of a choice if a goddess is telling us we need it. Because personally, I'm not one to argue with something the size of an office building," she chuckles.

Adalon lets out a bold laugh at the jovial comment. Latena glances up at her and smiles.

"Besides, I think it might be nice to have glowing eyes. It offers a cute little sparkle, and maybe it would inspire us to regard ourselves with higher esteem and higher obligations to see this reminder every time we look at ourselves in the mirror."

The people assembling in the audience all listened and let out a cheer for the suggestion.

Thaelyn cocked his head and the curious level of support Latena was generating out on the field as more people joined up.

"Powers help us…" he mumbles. "If she is doing what I think she is doing…"

"We are a world in great need of many things," Latena continues. "We still need to clean up our environment. We still need to remove the remainder of the seeds, and I would further suggest these horrid little cranial gadgets," she taps the unit on the side of her head. "Neither of which serves any valuable purpose. But more importantly, we need to reorganize ourselves as a society, with a new government and new laws. We need a new social order, a new culture, new philosophies, and new symbols of status to direct our motivations. But where do we find this, except once again from those who know, that family which already lives according to these principles, a Celestial family, and they who already follow them."

"Uh oh…" Thaelyn moans privately as he watches her and rolls his eyes to the crowds who were listening.

"Here we find ourselves with the greatest challenge, and yet this is also our greatest opportunity. If we are to say we need to join with a higher body, this is also to say we should not remain an independent one. We are children, but not ordinary children. We are half-gods, but not ordinary half-gods. We are the creation of something that should never have existed in our modern day, but in our modern day we cannot avoid realizing our heritage as that which belongs to a similar nature. But as children, we cannot simply go out there and join with those who are so obviously that much more mature. Instead, we must join with those other children who are still growing up. We must learn from them, go to their schools, live by their principles, honor their traditions, and as our time approaches, we may one day find ourselves ready for our destiny, not only as our maturity comes around, but also for the new culturing we receive along the way."

Again, the people rise up in cheers and applause at her encouraging statements.

Inside the observation booth, Vonafel was still watching the scene outside. She studied Latena carefully during her presentation.

"That's clearly one of them," she mutters privately. "It has to be, and if I'm interpreting her correctly, she's calling for the end of this older Era. But it said Crusaders…in plural. Who is the other one?"

Thaelyn was getting worried by now. This scene was suddenly turning out as if he might inherit yet another world, and this one was a rather exceptional example for the people and their capacity. He wanted to draw her attention, but she simply continued her speech.

"But to learn from them is not enough, as we must also learn from those who teach the rest…the Estelar. These are the Fathers above all other Fathers. Even the Celestial Races follow their wisdom and guidance. If this is their place, it must also be our place, and for this, we must learn to understand and follow their teachings, no different from any other. But ever since the days of King Saakerav, we were discouraged to follow any form of religion. We believe there was a reason for this, and that reason may again be Darumon, as HE was our Creator god. But he probably didn't want us worshipping him in the sight of his own Master. So instead, we were turned towards science and empirical study to redirect our people away from any sort of religion. But the Estelar are real, not fictitious idols. And they teach many others, so why not us. And apparently, Kaliya and her people have already become their students, so why not include us as well!" she shouts.

Latena now angles her view off to the side where she could just make out her friend in the distance. She raised her hand as her signal, and Auryn waved back.

"All right everyone," Auryn asserts anxiously. "This is it, let's go!"

She arranges her people in a column, some of whom were carrying candles set within hurricane glass holders, and others were holding up their new scriptures. They began a procession marching forward reverently and raising their voices in jubilant song.

The masses of visitors all turned at the astonishing sight of people in strange robes moving along in such an archaic manner. It was like watching an old historical program on their home vid-coms, but here played out in reality, and apparently for a real purpose.

Thaelyn followed Latena's curious gesture until he found Auryn's group on the field. He glared at it, dumbfounded by what he thought he saw. He stumbled forward for a better view until Aerlie came alongside him.

"Ah look, Thaelyn!" she croons. "And she brought some of her friends with her!"

Thaelyn frowned at the unexpected statement. He turned stiffly to see his wife's face with a bright grin stretched across it.

"Huh?" he blurts breathlessly.

Aerlie continued to smile innocently as she began moving forward to greet the new arrivals.

"Wait! Aerlie! Who are these people?"

"Why, they appear to be pilgrims."

Thaelyn's eyes bulge and he slumps forward as he tries to fathom this impossible suggestion.

"Pilgrims?" he whispers hesitantly. "Pilgrims? P-pilgrims…here, pilgrims? Out of these people…PILGRIMS?!" he screeches.

Aerlie again turned with an innocuous smile before receiving the first of them into a combined service.

"Pilgrims!" he shouts. "And you KNEW about it!" he points assertively.

"Well, look at that," Ileani muses jovially. "So, I'm not the only one who gets their tail yanked."

"Oh, indeed, young lady! I am surrounded by it! You should see some of the unmentionable antics they play back home."

He turns desperately to find someone else. He glances over his shoulder to see Kaliya silently giggling.

"You!" he points and shrieks. "You had some part of this, it must be!"

"All I did was to mention a name," she shrugs. "She followed along behind Latena as they, um, stumbled into the ACI's basement and bumped into that rune stone."

"Oh, truly?!" he groans emphatically. "How unfortunate! And so innocent… General!" he waves his hand. "We seem to have a problem over here."

"Oh indeed, my Lord!" he returns wittily. "It would certainly seem we are chest-deep in our usual mires. Do we have a need for a list, perhaps?"

"Oh, this goes well beyond that," he waves a finger. "First, I think I am going to order a full volume to be assigned to this one," he points to Kaliya.

"Um…" Ayene raises a hand. "What about me?" she smiles gently.

"Oh, but of course!" he throws up his hands. "No doubt, you held more than a few roles. And Powers help us, for the length of your lifetimes, I can surely expect a great many more. And General, I have a special one for her," he points at Aerlie. "It dates all the way back to that day she brought in that bottle of blue. Do you recall that one?"

"Oh, my goodness!" he lauds vigorously. "But of course, and what a day THAT one was!"

"And now HER," he points at Latena. "I cannot even be sure how to classify this one. Barely out of school and already inciting a world rebellion...successfully!" he darts his finger upward. "And now this..." he redirects at the congregation.

Thaelyn slumps and lays a hand on his forehead as he tries to catch his breath.

"Miss Ta'yeen, what are we looking at out here?" he thumbs to the side.

"This is a friend of mine from the university," she responds. "Her name is Auryn Táwgari, and she majored mostly in cultural studies. But she and her family also belong to a hidden sect that has tried to hold on to our ancient religion, in this case honoring the Creator, but not very successfully, and neither was it very fulfilling, as they always longed for something a little more, um...tangible. She told me they have these sects in most of the major cities around the world, and when I learned of your people, I called her in to make a study of your religion...with Kaliya's recommendation of the one you call Lord Oghma. She visited Tae'Eladar and met with the Lady, and has been in private study ever since, along with her family and many of their cultists along the way."

"Met with...her?" he wags a finger nervously at Aerlie. "Yes! And how interesting she did not inform me of this. Um, my Dear..." he turns to his wife in an attempt to restrain his passion. "We may need to have a little chat."

Aerlie simply turns and smiles sweetly at him.

Thaelyn turns back to Latena as she continues.

"Now we have a new movement occurring here. If we're going to become what our Fate tells us we must become, we need to go all the way with it."

"Fate?" he gushes. "Oh no. But...but...um..."

"Your Majesty, we already need a new government in our world, but more than that, we need proper direction and guidance, and by that which can teach us who we are as a race that doesn't have a proper background to it. This means we shouldn't be limiting ourselves to a simple little political treaty with you. We need to become YOUR children now. You already have Kaliya and her people, and I believe the rest of us should give ourselves to the same family unit you have created on Tae'Eladar. And if I understand this gift of the cu'Nar correctly, we'll certainly qualify by that time."

"But...but...but...but..."

"Furthermore," she asserts. "If we become citizens of your society, we'll simply take your form of government and make it our own. We need to teach our people a new system regardless, but yours is already a functioning body, and it can get us back on our hooves that much quicker. You have resources, you have backing, and you inspire people to get up and move their tails in ways we never thought possible here."

"Well, yes, but wait. What about that issue of the difference in culture we spoke of a moment ago?"

"You already said it. We're all in this together, so we'll find our way out of it together. How long do you think your people will take to grow into whatever cultural influence we might kick into the equation? Decades? Centuries? That's child's play for us. And with that nether-wild school system you have over there, you'll kick the rest of us in the tail so hard, we won't know how to manage all the new studies you'll be throwing at us. If our science factions were crying over not enough work to do, they'll need to hire armies of new researchers just to keep up with your people."

"I, um...well, I uh..."

"And THIS is what I believe our people need," she returns to Ileani and her cameras. "We have every reason to want this, and I can see no reason to refute it. We are not normal people living normal lives. Therefore, we need to bring ourselves to join with those who are more our brothers and sisters than any other species might be out there. Tae'Eladar is a gathering place of many different people of different backgrounds. We would fit in wonderfully in all that. Just look at Elder Nazég's people. The people of Tae'Eladar barely knew them for only a handful of years and already treat them as welcome members of their society. They do not segregate us due to our unusual appearance or our strange Gifts. They are far more adaptable than we ever could be, and this creates the absolute finest setting in which to teach us how to overcome our limitations as this young species with Gifts we shouldn't otherwise have. And we would become part of a larger family to which we might normally belong, and SHOULD belong, to set the standards we need to live by."

Auryn and her group had lined up in front of the audience, with many of them trying to entice some of the listeners to hear their special message. Auryn decided to break away and join Latena for the interview. As she comes around, she turns to the cameras.

"We have given ourselves to the one we call Lord Oghma," she states affirmatively. "Sage of Wisdom, Adherent of Inspiration, he is a member of the Estelar that actually holds a very solid portfolio of teachings for people like us who dedicate themselves to the sciences and intellectual studies. There is nothing wrong in offering yourself to a god, for as long as it brings you peace of mind and direction of purpose. For some, it offers a form of spiritual comfort, and we do have spirits that need comfort on occasion. For too long, we have been restricted from any kind of religious worship. If this was the work of Darumon as part of his concern to keep himself out of the picture while he was in the service of a higher being, then so be it. But now that we are released from his care, we should bring ourselves to understand who can take over our nurturing, as we are indeed still too young, and now with this newfound knowledge of things we were not ready to know about."

Vonafel leaned forward in her seat, as she was still up in the observation booth, and studied this new face. She could feel a subtle sense of recognition as she listened to Auryn's words.

"Boom," she mumbles. "And here we have Number Two. The end of one Era, and now these two are leading them into a new one. But Protector help us if Adalon is doing what I think she's doing," she glances at her book again.

She gets up from her chair and begins making her way downstairs.

"I hope to go into full study soon on Tae'Eladar," Auryn continues. "They give classes over there, and I hope to be the first of our people to restore a full and proper religion to our world. We do not all need to become priests, but at least to recognize their existence and what they have to offer, to bring our thoughts, if only on occasion, to their teachings, it will give us that final layer of fulfillment and direction, if we are ever to mature into one of them one day," she turns to Thaelyn.

Kailen was standing behind the rest in the Daanen'kai group. He wearily rubs his brow as he slowly shakes his head. He then turns to Velen and the two Elders.

"Uh, Father, I hope you don't mind, but I think we're moving in a direction that's going to carry its own momentum soon."

"And what direction is that, Kailen?" he smiles gently.

He steps forward alongside the platform to present himself. He clears his throat as he tries to formulate his words.

"Um, I guess this is where I start calling you 'my Lord', because I think I'm going to be working for you full time soon."

Velen grinned and chuckled at the suggestion. The two elders glared at each other briefly, until Elder Vankkar finally sighed and shrugged.

"I think we're out of a job, Opadna. I doubt we'll have anything left to govern by the time this is done."

"Barely even now," she winces. "By the appearance of things out here on the field, I'm asking myself who's actually running all that industry back home," she chuckles.

Elder Vankkar then steps forward next to Kailen.

"I, uh…don't know how you might want to represent our people within your government, but I would like to point out my long history within our Council. And since it would seem I'm going to be out of a job soon, I think it's time I apply myself to find a new one."

Thaelyn glared at the group on the other side of the podium, then again at Aerlie who simply smiled and shrugged. He then laid a hand over his eyes.

"I am going to need my medicine again," he moans. "And such a pity, as I was feeling so perky when I first came outside."

As he removes his hand to offer a response, he takes notice of Vonafel coming outside to join the delegation.

"Oh no, not you again…"

"Yeah, me again," she smiles sheepishly. "I think we have our final quatrain. But like with him," she points at Elder Vankkar. "I worry if I'll have any kind of job after this, I put so much time into these books."

"Indeed, but I think after all is said and done, we will have a vivid new history to record. What do we have this time?"

"Um, excuse me," Ileani interjects. "Who do we have here, quickly?"

Vonafel turns to Ileani to respond.

"My name is Vonafel Windsong, and I'm the Senior Archivist at the Royal Historical Archives in the city of Bya'an Tamoranth on Tae'Eladar. My main specialty is the study of ancient historical documents, scrolls, and other writings, but most importantly, I spent the greater part of my life studying the prophecies of Adalon the Silver," she glances over her shoulder at the large dragon. "They represent a very mysterious compilation of musings which seemed to tell a story of a sort, relating to our world and certain specific people in it, namely the Lord and Lady. It was as if someone was writing the life history of who they were, where they came from, and why they are here, but before any of it ever actually occurred."

"Fascinating."

"But more recently, we have this book I'm holding here," she raises it for reference. "This is Book Two of her prophecies. In this book, we have generally more of the same, except when it arrived at the final chapter, where it takes a most curious turn, because now it speaks of entirely new people, places, and events we would know nothing about on Tae'Eladar."

"Interesting, but is this to say you eventually learned something from it?"

"Oh yes, because it turned out to serve as a guideline for how we were supposed to find our way here this day. The people were Kaliya and her Daanen-Aryku friends, and you here on this world. It spoke of Darumon and Sargeras, how they first arrived here and what they did, and it teaches us of the Stormhooves and what they will do, ultimately to finish with this battle we saw out here."

"In all the nether-space, you're right. But that sounds like more than any simple prophecy. It sounds more like a prepared list of objectives."

"Yes, and written by her," she thumbs at Adalon. "She is famous for her cryptic writings and obscure wording. And then we have what she said out there on the field, and what I'm looking at right now," she points at Latena and Auryn. "We have one final quatrain in the book before it ends, and I have long wondered what it means, because it seems disjointed and left hanging. It suggests the end of one thing and the beginning of another, but with no clear finality to it."

"Uh oh…what does it say?"

"I'm afraid to tell," she whimpers. "Because first, it would suggest we are ALL more than what we thought we were. And second, well, I don't know what to do with myself after this."

Aerlie strolls over and wraps her arms around her longtime friend to comfort her.

"Vonafel?" Thaelyn steps over to lay a hand on her shoulder. "What is it? Is it good or bad?"

"My Lord, listen to this and you tell me. But I think our people have a bigger history ahead of us than what we had leading up to it."

She fumbles with the oversized book, and then opens it up to the final page, which lists the final quatrain.

"I'm looking at these two young ladies here, all right?" she directs at Latena and Auryn. "This must be the missing element," she clears her throat and prepares to read. "Young Crusaders bring to bear, an Era in demise; another Guardian Breed is made, when mysterious Gifts arise."

"Cu'Nar's Pity!" Kaliya shouts. "A what?! A guardian breed? Us?" she shrieks.

Ayene steps closer to examine the book, along with Relissa and Marelle.

"Jiggers, girl!" Relissa moans. "You just got your full life of work cut out for you."

"But Relissa, it's not just them!" Vonafel urges. "It says ANOTHER one, but Adalon said out there she's making it her purpose to create one after another of these, with the Draconics only being her first. Well, excuse me!" she screeches. "Would Tae'Eladar be Number Two in that lineup? Look at where we've been, where we are now, and apparently, where we're going with it!"

Thaelyn suddenly went silent at the insinuation. He glared at the book, recalling all his old memories of the past quatrains which generally directed his life, that of Aerlie, their entire world, and the Order of Tyr. He slowly turned to look up at Adalon.

Adalon gazed down at the group of quizzical expressions. She then slowly panned her view around the assembly.

"I am not called... The Maker... For no reason. I know the value... Of my resssources. And I know how... To play thisss game... Sssuch that we... Will maintain... The Measure of Balance... Assssertively... To ensure... We do not fall ssslack... As ssso many othersss... Once did. I will leave... A legacy... Even if I do not... Persssonally... Carry that far. And that legacy... Will uphold our pressstige... And our beliefsss... To carry forward... Beyond any other. You... Who hold sssuch qualitiesss... By joining with our people... Will grow and learn... And augment our own... To provide even more. But before you can fully... Engage in thisss... You will firssst require... An education... And conditioning... To demonssstrate your authority... Over these Giftsss. And for thisss... We musssst begin... With the Positive Primesss..."

Adalon turns away and closes her eyes in a moment of concentration. Very soon after, another divine pillar erupts and reaches down from above. Within its glow, a ball of light settles to the ground, just as it did before, and takes shape. Kaliya and the others watched as another presence began to manifest itself in their local space.

"What do you think," Ayene whispers. "Her again?"

"Probably," Kaliya nods. "She must be the main attendant, so I would imagine Adalon keeps her very busy."

"Yeah, and here comes that idea of being conscripted. Oh well, I'm game for it, if no one else is."

The image took shape as Adalon's primary seraph arrived. Kaliya and Ayene glanced at each other as they both recognized her from before.

"Yes Maker…" Thaliel announces.

Ileani and the other observers gazed at the tall figure in wonder. It was the same one Adalon called into service a short while ago on the other side of the river to remove the bodies.

"What… Who…?" the flustered reporter stutters.

"Thaliel…" Adalon inquires. "Are we assssembled…?"

"They are ready and waiting for thine instruction," she responds confidently.

Again, Adalon angles her head away from the crowd and upward above her. She closes her eyes and seems to enter a light trance.

Kaliya and the others studied her actions. It was clear that she was attempting to summon something telepathically. At first, the scene didn't show any immediate alteration. But then it seemed as if the ambient light began to flicker unnaturally, as if something was gathering it up into bunches, like a farmer wrapping bundles of wheat.

Kaliya panned her gaze around the area. The sight was startling, as she could see a large number of them showing up all around the valley. She turned to one that was making its appearance just above them adjacent to the conservation center. It hovered in the air over their heads. The image began to manifest itself as a glowing shape, with an almost crystalline geometry, but immaterial, as it was clearly made of elemental energy.

"Wow, so that's what they look like."

She briskly glanced at Velen, but he didn't seem able to speak. He stepped forward in awe and slowly began to lower himself to a kneeling position. He was quickly followed by the rest of the Elder Council, and then the other Daanen-Aryku. Kaliya and Ayene also dropped to a kneeling position, as did Latena and Auryn, and her pilgrim attendance.

Relissa and the others all watched the entities in amazement.

"Jiggers, what a day," she shakes her head.

She and Marelle join the others on the ground, along with Thaelyn, Aerlie, and their officers.

Ileani was feeling very nervous at this point.

"Are we doing this again?" she flusters. "Um, can anyone tell me what I'm supposed to do right now?"

"Ileani," Ayene mutters. "Our people don't really know how to behave in front of beings like these, but they are regarded as very old and wizened, and you generally offer your respect by kneeling."

"Uh huh... Well, I don't want to offend anyone...or thing, so..."

Now she goes down, and gestures for her cameramen to do the same.

As more of the congregation knelt down, the visiting Suuden-Aryku also felt a compulsion to do the same. Soon, they were all kneeling, even though for many, it was a strange sensation to kneel to something.

The otherworldly beings floated silently above the land, and the Suuden-Aryku were largely speechless and uncertain how to react. Ileani decides she needed to speak up and gain some level of understanding of what her people were expected to do here.

"Um, I...uh, I'm feeling a little unsure about all this suddenly. I understand your meaning for this delivery, but I just barely managed to wrap my horns around being free from Darumon, and now here we are about to sign up for something I don't think any of us was prepared for."

"I underssstand..." Adalon explains. "But to sssign up... Or not... You ssstill carry... The Prodigy Giftsss... And due to thisss... You need guidance... From those who can teach you. These are not sssuch... That you can sssimply turn... On or off. The potential they carry... Is extreme. And for thisss you will need... An extreme form... Of regulation. The Positive Primesss can begin you... On thisss journey. By taking thisss offering... They will not only cleanse you... Of the incompatible essssence... They will alsssso... Purify you... And align you... To the Positive ssside. Thisss bringsss with it... Collateral benefitsss... Not the leassst of which... Is an inherent adjusssstment... Of mannersss... And perssspectives... That will naturally exclude... Many wrongdoingsss... And harmful behaviorsss..."

"Wait a moment. Are you saying that by taking this, we might actually see a complete cessation of any form of crime?"

"Even the Essstelar... May occasionally make... A missstake... Here and there. But violent actsss... And harmful missschief... Againssst like bodiesss... Will generally ceassse. You will more closssely resemble... The Celessstial Racesss... Where your only true opponentsss... Would be those... Of the Negative ssside... Should you ever encounter any..."

"I think I understand, but um..." she glances tentatively at the nearest cu'Nar entity. "Well, this is for everyone, right?"

"We musssst include... All of you... But only after... You have removed... The ssseed lifeformsss... From your bodiesss..."

Ileani reflexively glances at herself, knowing she had already removed hers some time ago. She then panned around the still-growing audience, many of whom still had theirs attached. She winced at the thought of how this would appear.

Latena could see her worry developing, so she stepped forward again.

"This is our direction in life," she asserts. "This is where our society must travel. We need to evolve. We have a duty to uphold. Maybe part of it relates to Darumon as our father who gave us a parting farewell, and we owe it to him that he made us, but in so doing, he created something even he wasn't expecting. But we also hold this little piece of a forgotten history, perhaps the last of its kind..."

She pauses as she glances around, catching Velen's eyes and quickly recalling his story, and then turning to settle on Geilv.

"And then we have another duty," she continues thoughtfully. "One to which we must ALL atone for. Our sins as a society that allowed ourselves to become responsible for so much death and destruction... whole worlds, whole societies, and all for the promise of something we were never supposed to receive, not in the form it was promised. It may be impossible to actually repair this damage, and we may need to dedicate the remainder of our lives to repent for these sins. But if to join a body with a direction to guard and protect, rather than destroy, maybe...just maybe...we might one day do enough good that we can reclaim our honor as our own form of warriors, just like Darumon said. But our entire society needs to unite behind these virtues. We cannot permit ourselves any longer to follow someone's spirit of the words or the romance of a bygone era. Beings like us, who carry so much potential, MUST represent themselves higher than that."

She now takes a moment to examine the large gathering forming up in the field.

"We are already partway there. We need a new government; we need new culturing and conditioning… Basically, we need to start over as a society that finally realizes who we are and what direction we must take for our evolution. So, we may as well jump in with both hooves and make a good splash at it. If she says we could be the next Guardian Race, I don't know where that'll take us, but we certainly do need help to figure out how to use these Gifts the right way. And to join with others who are already there as Guardians, we would become as a family together, whatever role we eventually take."

Ayene stared up at the alluring image of the nearby cu'Nar entity overhead. She reflected on her academy training, which she had been attending part-time in between her other duties on Azgarén. But now that these were essentially at an end, she would need to delve even deeper to finish her courses and one day graduate. And she wanted to blend in fully with the others.

"Well," she sighs. "I think I know what I want. Adalon, someone needs to go first, I suppose. It may as well be me so I can get on with the rest of my studies. I'm already a part of the Stormhooves, although not a full member, but in training. So, I need to take that next step."

"Indeed…" she accedes. "Then come forward… And present yoursssself… To thisss one here…"

Ayene takes a cautious step towards the entity. Latena and Auryn, Azina and the Director, Ileani and the rest, all followed her with their eyes, many of them watching closely to see what happens.

The cu'Nar entity appeared to bud off a smaller unit which swung around at the young officer. She watched it warily as it made a determined approach at her forehead. She almost desired to reconsider her choice as it made contact and merged inside.

Initially, she felt a mote of warmth spreading within her cranium, but it quickly grew in intensity as an electrical buzz shot through her full body. Her eyes went crossed and slowly closed, and she emitted a low whine. Her muscles froze and she felt numb. Her body began to glow softly as a rippling effect ran the full length of her form, and the numbness was replaced with a vigorous tingling.

Kaliya and the others stared at her as she was held rigidly in place until the glow subsided. When she found herself regaining motor control over her mouth, she attempted to speak, but it was slow and restricted.

"I probably…should have…sat down…for that."

She began to stiffly topple over backwards.

Kaliya was expecting something like this after watching the reaction. She jumped up and grabbed the girl as she came down, then gently settled her on the ground.

"You're a daring one, Ayene," she muses. "First for the seed removal, and now this. Are you alright?"

"Now I know...what the coil...of a static generator...feels like."

"Well, at least you didn't come out cooked."

Ayene smiled gently at the notion, and then slowly opened her eyes.

Latena, Relissa, and the others circled around, while Ileani moved into position to observe the girl's condition. As she opened her eyes, they could see a soft blue-white glow building up.

Thaelyn moved in for a closer look.

"I think at this moment," he considers. "I may wish to make a small exception to our usual procedures for the Spirit test back home. I would like to recheck your grade."

"Aye," Relissa agrees. "I'll bet she gets something better than blue this time."

Latena kneeled down closer and took Ayene's hand.

"Ayene, can you tell me if you feel any different?"

Ayene rolled her eyes at the young girl as she tried to assess her new condition.

"I'm not sure how I would describe it," she emits faintly. "I don't feel any big differences...I don't think. But then I guess I already had enough time among them to convert a few perspectives and attitudes. But things do seem a little, um...sharper in clarity, more determined."

Latena patted her arm and smiled. She stood up and looked at Auryn.

"You know what we need to do," she mutters. "We need to set the example for all the rest. The people need to see it."

"Yeah," Auryn winces. "But can we at least sit down for it?"

"Well, all right, if you don't want to land on your tail afterwards."

Kaliya studies the two girls as they try to build up their courage.

"Adalon, is there some sort of process we need to take here, like a timing sequence?"

"It would be... Advisable... To cycle through them... At only a few... For each entity... To allow them time... To regenerate. I will sssee about... Calling more... To accommodate... The population numbersss..."

"This could take a while."

Kita decided she also needed to take the plunge, so she cautiously strolled up.

"I suppose as a member of the ACI, it falls to me to make my own statement for our planetary future."

"Great, join the team. But what do you think your boyfriend will say to this?"

"He's still recovering after that little demonstration I put on back home in this cute little lace thong I dressed up in once. So I'll need to think of something new this time," she smirks.

"I swear..." she shakes her head. "You must've taken lessons from Suli over here."

Kaliya surveys the area and selects a group of entities on the opposite side of the gathering. She leads the trio of girls forward and sits them down, then waves at the cu'Nar entities to come over. As the entities moved into position, Auryn's parents circled around to watch. Captain Ta'yeen also joins at their side to observe Latena.

"I'm dreading the next call from your mother, Latena. She'll be screaming her horns off before this day is out."

"Yes, well," she concedes. "I just hope she realizes we're entering a new Era and I'm very privileged to be the one doing some of the work."

"Captain," Thaelyn calls. "If it makes matters any easier for you...or her, perhaps...I think I should mention something we were discussing at one time back home amongst our officers. Young Latena here has certainly demonstrated herself as a fine example of a future politician. Regardless of her mischievous nature as a young lady who, apparently, like so many other examples around us," he glances at Kaliya, "that tend to indulge in a bit of random misbehavior, her talents cannot go unnoticed. She has been very instrumental in her role in bringing about this transition in your world. So much, in fact, that we would be remiss in taking advantage of these talents for the future potential of your people, whether in your own form of government or mine, if these out here do indeed follow this course. Therefore, if the people of Azgarén were to choose this course, I would have her take a position to represent them on my High Council."

Latena was peering over her shoulder as she listened, and as Thaelyn finished his statement, her heart leapt nearly out of her chest. But as she turned back around, she saw the cu'Nar entities launching their buds at the group. She barely had time to catch her breath before one of them merged with her body.

Like with Ayene, they each felt the subtle delay before the sharp tingling and shooting electrical surges rumbled through their bodies. But in their case, being in a seated position, when the sensation ended, they simply toppled over onto their sides.

Kaliya glared at the unfortunate bodies still twitching on the ground at her feet. She set her hands on her hips and huffed.

"Is this how it's going to go for everyone? Oh well, who is next?"

"As we proceed on thisss..." Adalon submits. "We mussst alssso attend... To the ressstoration... Of thisss world. We will sssee... The ssseed removal processss... Accelerate... From thisss moment... As we focusss oursssselves... On arranging the resssources. But we mussst alssso clean... The environment... Ssso that they... Who are without... Do not sssuffer... Any ill effectsss..."

"We already have the production of the filter masks," the Director mentions. "But yes, this is merely a temporary solution. We'll need to employ a lot of manpower and technology to clean things up."

"And for thisss... Perhapsss I can offer... Sssome extra sssupport..."

Adalon again turns to glance down at her servant. Thaliel nods affirmatively. She once again closes her eyes and angles her head away, this time straight up into the sky, and she holds it there for an extended moment.

In the Saakerav base, in orbit over the planet, the base Commander and his crew were still watching the events unfold on the news broadcast being piped in from the surface. Then, an alert suddenly rings out on the scanners, and a crewman turns to examine the new readings.

"Sir, we have a blip forming..." he studies the readings a moment. "What in all the... Sir!" he shouts. "I have what looks like a jump signature, but..."

"What is it," the senior officer asks urgently. "What do you see out there?"

"In all the nether-space!" he screeches. "What is that thing! Sir, it's still growing!"

"What are you talking about, soldier?"

The station commander rushes over to the console to look at the scope.

"That's impossible! How big is that thing?"

"It's off the scale, Sir!"

"Where is it?"

"First ring lunar orbit."

"First ring…" he gasps. "And it's reading that big?" he yelps. "Get me Commander Geilv, NOW!"

An urgent ring sounds off in Commander Geilv's pocket and he pulls out his trans-com.

"This is Commander Geilv."

"Commander!" the voice shrieks. "There's something arriving in a first ring lunar orbit! The energy readings are through the roof!"

"What is it, a ship?"

"Sir, I have no idea! It's entirely irrational that anything could generate readings like these. The power flow is immense! You should be able to see it from your location. It's that big!"

The Commander looks up into the sky, along with Thaelyn and Aerlie, and the other nearby members who overheard the exchange. They were followed by Ileani and her news team, then everyone else in the area.

In the sky directly overhead, they observed a brilliant flash of massive proportions. It burst onto the scene like a titanic explosion, radiating outward and filling half the sky. The shockwave from the arrival was enough to send ionizing ripples through the upper atmosphere. When the glare from the dimensional aperture faded, it revealed an immense body looming overhead.

"Commander," Thaelyn utters briskly. "Where did he say that object was located?"

"Saakerav Station said a first ring lunar orbit."

"First ring lunar!" he howls. "Dear Powers, man… Are we speaking of something that is actually the size of a moon?!"

The assembly continued to stare at it. It appeared round, and there was a strong glow on the forward side of it, as if a sea of lights were shining out from the surface.

"Adalon," Thaelyn shouts. "Would you kindly allow us to know what that is?"

"They are my children… The ssSarrukh!"

"Mother of all buggers!" Relissa whimpers.

Well above the planet surface, overlooking the hapless world, was an object rarely seen by mortal men. It was round with a shallow bowl-like depression on one side. The full body stretched as wide as a large continent, thousands of miles across. The rear portion displayed a series of large concentric rings of pulsing energy housed within enormous crevices. The outer perimeter was a rhythmically vibrating ridge of light.

And inside the bowl, looking down on the world below, were structures rising up like pillars of diamond, a gigantic geode-like arrangement on a scale unimaginable to the senses.

Circling within the depression were dozens of major city centers and other structures lining the basin and sides, all aglow, and interconnected with an illuminated web of transport chutes. And at the center was an array of exceptionally tall spires jutting out as colossal sky-rises, towering over the rest as a magnificent capital district.

The people on the ground gazed at it in awe and wonder. The level of technology necessary to build such a thing must be fantastically high. It could potentially house a population measuring in the billions, no longer bound to a home world as they simply bring it along with them, travelling across Creation as they please.

Captain Ta'yeen was nearly breathless at the sight. He moved in close to Geilv for a private word.

"If the Marshal ever said anything about insurgents, this is probably more like what we should expect to see."

"Yeah, and certainly NOT anything we could counter."

On the ground, not far from the podium, appeared a series of three planar rifts. The concentric rippling effects resembled the same as what Aelwyn was using as she returned from her studies, or what Darumon was once observed creating as he made his inspection of the Morndindor base. From within these rifts emerged three distinctly foreign bodies.

They stood nearly as tall as the male Suuden-Aryku and were dressed in a smooth three-quarter length coat and pants, appearing neat and professional. Their four-digit appendages hinted at an ancestry of claws that mostly evolved away into something better suited for more civil applications. Their heads were of average proportion in relation to the body, but with an extended cranium enhancing their features. They had narrow boney ridges cresting over the temples, presumably the evolution of what were once horns into something less prominent. The face had only a slight protrusion for the nose and mouth, and cat-like eyes. The skin seemed dense, but not scaly, and colored a slight bronze hue.

The three visitors each surveyed the ogling masses, and then turned to each other, continuing further to meet with Adalon.

"Matron Kuroku," the first member announces in a somewhat raspy voice. "Our exalted Mother..."

"My children..." she responds delicately.

The three Sarrukh reverently raised their hands to touch the large creature in a moment of silent praise.

"Haran," Relissa mutters. "Will you look at that?"

"She clearly resembles something like a deity to them," he considers. "A holy mother figure. I can barely even imagine their history together, after so long a time."

"And they arrived here using planar rifts," Kaliya notes, "which means they must be extremely evolved by now. Didn't she say something about them being close to a transition?"

"I believe so," Thaelyn muses thoughtfully. "It is a rare occasion to see such a thing as a race at the cusp of their ascendance from a Celestial station. They may be only a few steps away from the Estelar by now."

"I'm trying to imagine the places they've been and the things they've seen," Marelle adds, "if that up there is their new home."

"Perhaps only one of many," Aerlie suggests. "She said they travel all across the Seas of Creation, so they may cover a huge expanse, with many of those vessels carrying them."

"Unbelievable!" Ayene wheezes. "Simply to imagine the power necessary to punch a hole in space big enough to swallow a moon."

"Ghantil," Azina mumbles distantly. "If I should ever ask about learning the secrets of the universe again, I want you to find something large and heavy and hit me with it."

"Azina," he consoles with a pat on her shoulder. "It'll be alright. But clearly, we were talking to the wrong people before this."

The three Sarrukh pulled back from Adalon after their quiet moment together.

"You kept your promise, Great Mother."

"Was there ever any doubt...?"

"Never, Great Mother! Your legacy amongst our people carries its own strength. You inspire others, and your dedication to those who once preserved our race has never faded. We still remember, and we will be sure to carry this for as long as we exist."

The three Sarrukh returned to the attention of the crowd and stepped forward. They circled around the podium towards Thaelyn. The rest of the officers, and the Daanen'kai Elders all came out to join the group as Thaelyn straightened himself for an introduction.

"I am Administrator Amakukituko of the Amaku-Shakona-Nakina Expedition," the lead member announces as he glances at his colleagues.

"I am most humbled to make this acquaintance," Thaelyn offers with a bow. "I am Lord Thaelyn, and this," he gestures to the others, "is my wife, the Lady Aerlie, and then we have High Commander Geilv of the Suuden-Aryku."

"Of course, and we know many of your names already, as our Revered Mother has told us of you."

"Your names carry a hint of your ancient origin, and this origin seems to reflect itself in the Draconics as well."

"They do, as they were once our own people. We kept as many of our ancient traditions as we could, although we will admit that time does take its toll to change a society as it progresses forward."

"And I would therefore imagine you have many stories to tell, perhaps much like her."

"Indeed! We have a rich history, and tales of many travels. We might be willing to share some of these if you are so interested. Consider it the passing of a legacy from one generation to another."

"That would be a most enjoyable moment," he grins.

"But as for this occasion, long have we waited since the time of our liberation to see that creature destroyed. We cannot know how many have suffered because of him or the others, but this was not a duty for our kind. We abandoned war and conflict long ago. Therefore, it was left to our Revered Mother to challenge him with her own creation. And we are content that she chose well. Yours, and theirs, are fine choices to serve a higher purpose. The Seas of Creation are vast, Thaelyn. The society you govern on Tae'Eladar is still in its infancy, but I suspect it will not be long before they are rescuing new worlds from other perils. Be prudent in your rule and the direction you give them. Perhaps, one day, you might find yourself leading them behind us, and then we can be as one again."

"These are fine words, and I do hope we can impress ourselves on those same Seas of Creation as others have done before us."

"And here we come to the reason for our visit. As a service to these people, we would wish to offer our facilities and our resources to restore what was once damaged. Our technology can reclaim entire worlds. Therefore, we feel it should not be as difficult to clean this one."

"This is indeed a fine offer, and I think it goes without saying, the people of this world would welcome it."

He turns to find Latena, who had finally managed to stand up again, along with Auryn. The two of them staggered over to join the group and participate in the conversation.

"I hope you'll excuse me," she emits lightheadedly. "That cu'Nar thing is still buzzing in my ear. But yes, on behalf of our people, we would most certainly welcome your help. We've already shut down most of the original industry that caused it, and retooled some of it for other purposes. But I worry about the damage to our ecosystem. We have a lot of conservation centers struggling to keep what's left of our wildlife, but it would do much better if we could somehow restore that as well."

"We will work with you as best we can," the Sarrukh dignitary offers. "We will examine these specimens and see about replicating them using our own methods for restoring life to a dead, or in your case, a heavily damaged world. But first, let us begin with the initial processing."

He turns to his two associates as they orient their stares upwards at their vessel, but only briefly before returning.

From high above, a swarm of small drone ships begins streaming out of the mother ark. They slithered their way towards the planet in long rivers, spiraling down and spreading out in all directions.

From the ground, Thaelyn and the others, including the Suuden-Aryku, watched as wave after wave of ships soared overhead. The drones began releasing cleansing agents into the upper atmosphere to initiate the detoxification of the pollution layer.

Thaelyn and the others exchanged glances, as they circled around their group for a full impression of the remarkable turn of events. Next, they turned to look at the large assembly of people filling up virtually the entire field behind them. Their work was only just beginning.

Chapter 16

RENAISSANCE

It's a regular day for Ileani in the newsroom as she prepares for her daily report. Life had settled during this past century since the events in the valley, at least within reason. During this time, her news broadcast had changed hands and was no longer called C.P. News. Now she worked for the Imperial News Network, part of a new empire-wide broadcast chain that reported continual slurries of sensations involving social events, political debates, new discoveries, and scientific breakthroughs. If she ever wanted real work to perform, now she was up to her horns in it. She was just getting ready for her latest report as she sat in her anchor chair while the set coordinator gave his signal.

"This is Ileani Ur'paran for INN. In today's news, we have word from the Azgarén Naval Expeditionary Service regarding several potential new discoveries of habitable worlds found in the Katharian Galaxy. Although no advanced forms of life have yet been discovered, hopes are high, as new worlds are explored.

As you may recall from our earlier reports, the Katharian Galaxy is the designation for the local galaxy in that universe where Former Elder Nazég and his people fled as they were being pursued by Darumon during his ill-fated campaign to restore his people's former prestige. The name was given in honor of the Commander of their ship, Sanri Kathar, at the time they made the discovery. Of course, technically,

980

we realize it was Darumon who must've made a covert operation at one time to find his original index to that galaxy, and then to use this in the guise of the navigation officer of Elder Nazég's ship. But according to military records, the data must've been so carefully covered up that it may be impossible to know who was piloting the original expedition.

Meanwhile, on Tae'Eladar, they're getting ready for the launch of their first official entry into space exploration. This new starship, described as a Gryphon Class survey vessel, will mark their first entry into a new technological era…"

⸙

Capitol Prime has flourished since the liberation, as has all of Azgarén. With the aid of the Sarrukh, the pollution was cleaned up and much of the native flora and fauna was restored, mostly from the specimens being kept within the many nature preserves and conservatoriums. The city has been largely redesigned, providing ample green space by lining the sidewalks with trees and planters. Courtyards and parks were replanted, and many of the sterile skyscrapers were brought down and replaced with newer designs that incorporated terraces and galleries, where the sweet smells of flowers and herbal shrubs now permeated the streets and walkways.

In the center of town, where once there stood a stark and foreboding monolithic tower, the sanctuary building once used as the home of Sargeras during his occupation, now the entire area was a large plaza and memorial park. It included a selection of novelty shops and small marketplaces, a druidic temple, and a gateway hub terminal.

However, the most important feature in this plaza was at the center. It was a shrine with a rather peculiar-looking arrangement of trees, non-native to the local environment, but seeming to have settled down nicely in their new home. The largest one, in the middle, was a mature mother tree with a broad umbrella canopy sheltering a host of six daughter trees in a circle. The grove was the focus of attention on a daily basis, as visitors would come and pay their respects to the dryads who lived within their Trees of Life.

Tana Lar'akan was now a fully sanctioned druid, after completing her studies on Tae'Eladar. She now served in the local temple as the high priestess, giving lectures as well as offering blessings and holding special services under the tree. Citizens would stop and visit, sit in or around the circle to chat, and enjoy the refreshing breezes and fragrant scents, while they listened to the druidic chants and basked in the nurturing glow of the dryad auras.

In another part of town was another temple, a larger one, where citizens would go to find spiritual support and healing. Auryn served here as another ranking priestess, the first of her kind in this world. She led some of the local class studies, as well as organized the choir and religious services for their patrons. In another part of the complex was a new Healer's Ward. These facilities were designed to replace the older medical clinics, since their medical profession was undergoing a partial conversion to use the healing gifts granted by Oghma to the priests, rather than the strictly scientific approach of the original med-techs. Here, Azina was offering a mentorship as a full medical technician to a new generation of interns.

"Med-tech Nur'ten," calls an announcement on her vid-com. "We have a minor emergency in Examination Room Three."

"I'm on my way."

Azina hurries down the hall to the examination room, where she can hear the cries of a young boy.

"What do we have?" she asks as she enters the room and steps up to the bed.

"A fracture on his left fibula…"

"Oh? What happened?"

The mother had taken a seat just opposite the bed. She speaks up to answer the question.

"He was apparently trying to climb a tree, Med-tech."

"Climbing a tree?" she smiles curiously. "Now just a moment, we're not really designed for that sort of thing."

"Yes, well, I guess he thought otherwise."

"Well, let's just see about that."

Azina studies the boy's leg. She peers down at it and draws in her concentration, allowing her eyes to radiate with a soft divine light… that is, above and beyond her usual blue-white glow. Her Healer's Sight allowed her to see inside the body and examine the bone directly.

"This doesn't look too serious. You got off lucky this time. Let me give you just a little pinch to ease the pain and I'll fix this right up."

She reaches around behind the boy and presses her fingers against the nape of his neck, sending a subtle impulse into the nerves to disable his sensations from the rest of the body. The boy felt a wave of numbness come over him and he relaxed into the bed. She then instructed the intern to assist in aligning the bone while she folded her hands together and charged up with a divine chant. Her hands began to glow, and she laid them across the boy's leg on either side of the fracture. The glow transferred into the leg, causing the bone to fuse back together neatly. She then returned to the neck and offered a little massage to revitalize the nerves, restoring the full function of his body.

"There you go," she announces soothingly. "And let's try to remember we're not made for climbing trees."

"Yes, Med-tech," the boy responds politely.

"Excellent. Madam, we're all done here."

Azina records the visit on a nearby terminal.

"Here we are. Go back out and speak to the receptionist. She'll take care of you and finish this up, and have a wonderful day."

The boy gently hops down from the bed, carefully testing his newly healed leg before feeling confident enough to walk out of the room.

Azina watches the couple leave and reflects modestly on the old days.

"I wonder, if we should ever encounter another society out there; how do we explain ourselves?"

"What do you mean?" the intern wonders. "Kids who like to climb trees with hooved feet, or maybe our medical services to fix the broken legs that come afterwards?" he chuckles.

"Well, certainly that much!" she smiles. "But the many other traits we possess now. Healing with a simple touch. A form of religion that encourages scientific growth…which might otherwise deny the religion, but not in our case, as we simply move closer to our god. And living as a society of saviors who follow a philosophy of protecting just about everything we may ever encounter out there."

"It's a lot to think of."

"And all of it in barely a century since that moment. It seems like only yesterday."

"Our classic attitude of time perception…"

"No longer!" she retorts. "The people of Tae'Eladar are climbing on our tails now. This is where we have to learn to pick up and run. Our children are going to be in serious competition from here on. By the time they finish one school, they'll have to start over with another one. Maybe learning to climb trees with hooved feet is only the beginning."

In another part of town, in a local junior school, the upper classmen were attending their studies. The instructor steps away from his desk to give a brief lecture at the start of class.

"I'd like everyone's attention, please. Thank you. Today we begin our course in Arcane Science. The studies that'll be presented must be adhered to very closely and with great care to ensure our policy of safety and respect for the Art. Since those first days when we joined the Empire, our people have been taking up the studies of the Arcane and incorporating these practices into virtually every aspect of life here in our world. As we enter the First Circle of study, you will learn how the dynamistic flows are formed, how they can be harnessed, and then channeled. We'll learn the early principles of their conduct and influence on our environment, and also the potential harmful effects if misused. First, who among you can tell me where these flows are originally derived?"

At this moment, the full assembly of students raises their hands. The instructor selects one young boy, and he stands up to give his answer.

"The flows we might see here are created by the arcanids that live in a separate dimensional layer just above our own."

"Very good. Since our admission into the Empire, our leading science divisions have conducted a wide variety of studies on these flows as they are found in other locations, such as the Katharian Galaxy and local Tae'Eladaran space. Then, with the official development of the dynamistic harvester technology by Senior Meta-Tech Sulíma Tad'vaal, we were able to bring samples back home with us. However, it wasn't until later, when she began experimenting by releasing colonies of arcanids locally to see if she could seed our native environment with its own supply, that we truly saw the advancement of our capacity to provide this to our people here on Azgarén."

Another hand goes up among the students.

"Yes, Tanila?" the instructor directs. "Do you have a question?"

A girl stands up to present herself.

"Didn't I hear once how this was a very controversial decision to make?"

"It was! There were some who suggested that by introducing arcanids into our local environment, which did not have any naturally occurring, it could alter the balance of elemental forces. But these were resolved by suggesting the arcanids would ultimately find their own way in one day, and we might not truly know how this would occur under any ordinary circumstances. There was even one argument that said if a society could somehow find its way outside their native universe into another with the flows in it, they would likely try to bring this back regardless, and we are simply following a process much like evolution. Maybe this is how it happened elsewhere, and we are not the first. We don't know, but either way, our world is a very small place in this universe, and we don't plan on spreading this around much outside our own space."

"And so, we maintain the Measure of Balance for what we do to the place."

"That's right, as best we can."

In another classroom, they were preparing for a history lesson. The teacher began her discourse to the students after settling them into their seats.

"Welcome everyone to Azgarén Social History," she announces. "This course will cover the progression of our history as we passed through the so-called Enlightened Era, as first established by King Saakerav and maintained by the Council of Elders, up until the time of the Azgarén Emancipation and the arrival of the Stormhooves. It further covers the delicate legacy of our people and the great responsibility we must uphold, not by choice, but as a birthright we cannot avoid, and this is our relation to Darumon, and the ancient society known only as the Primordials."

The room goes silent with only a murmuring of voices and soft moans. The teacher surveys the classroom and subtly nods her head.

"Yes, I know the feeling," she admits somberly. "I still recall the day it happened. It doesn't seem that long ago, and I suppose it will feel that way for many of us for a long time yet to come," she pauses to glance briefly at her body as she recalls the seed entity she once had. "I was there, one of those hiding in the shelters at the time they came to our world. It was that same day we thought we were coming under attack by some errant young man and this strange ability of his that no one understood. But as we know now, this was simply a wake-up call for the rest of us that everything we were made to believe prior to this was a lie."

A hand goes up to draw attention. The teacher directs a young boy to stand up.

"This is where we were also having a lot of trouble with a kind of revolt, right? The people were trying to throw out that old Council along the way."

"Yes, they were, although unknown to any of us at the time, the Council was already gone, as part of a hidden cover-up by Darumon to take control of our world and our people. But here we come to one of the strangest twists of all, and it was decided by our leaders that this represents a necessary part of our history, never to be forgotten and never to be disparaged. We may each hold our independent feelings on the matter, but it is a part of us, and we must therefore offer our respect to its inherent value."

She holds her statement as she studies their faces briefly before continuing.

"Darumon created us to serve his desires to restore his master's former society, which to him was as much a romance as it was a way of life. It could easily be described as simply trying to survive against all odds, and those odds were dire. But while we might not hold the same feelings for this much, one thing we must admit to is this. Darumon was the father of our race, and for better or for worse of how he behaved in front of us, he held hidden feelings he was never permitted to display openly, largely due to Sargeras, who would object to him holding anything personal over a lesser species."

She pauses to examine the class assembly.

"Sargeras, much like all the Primordials, didn't really care for anything outside their own. They were much too competitive and rivalrous. Also, over the course of time, they had grown especially aristocratic and pompous. And worse, if Sargeras were to learn where we actually came from, he would regard us as an intolerable abomination, being a hybridized form of life as we are. Therefore, Darumon had to take some extreme measures to conceal our origins from his master."

A hand goes up from a young girl before she stands up to speak.

"And this is when he used those chips and things to hide the old Tav'ageen Anomaly."

"Yes, as well as a lot of tricks to hide our evolution. But despite all this, Darumon apparently developed a personal sense of pride in us as his children. Therefore, if we are to claim our prestige as a young Celestial race, it falls to us to make him proud, that we shall go forward and demonstrate ourselves as a species that can do so much more than anything he ever worked with before.”

The room now ushers up a series of oohs and ahs, along with some cheering and applause as their moods were clearly lifted by this encouraging statement.

On Tae'Eladar, the city of Bya'an Tamoranth had grown into a bustling metropolis. People buzzed along the roadways on hover-scooters and monocycles. The city had risen up with towers that included elevated parks and verandas, and the people could often be seen walking by wearing professional business suits and carrying tablet devices with the daily news reports.

On the hill overlooking the city, stood the proud guildhall of the Order, largely as it had always been, with the exception of a few renovations over time to accommodate new architectural standards and amenities. Down the road was the parliament center, a sprawling complex involving multiple buildings and offices for the various political leaders and departments of the local planetary government. There were also chambers for the broader Imperial Parliament, the Board of the High Council, and other divisions to oversee the many races with their mixed cultures and social needs, regardless of what world they lived on.

It was midafternoon and a session was underway in the High Council's inner chamber. A new face had arrived on Tae'Eladar during this time, and he quickly applied himself to his most prolific professional aptitude. He had been appointed with the title of the Council Speaker, which represented the central coordinator over their deliberations.

“Lord Aristan,” ushers an enthusiastic young female member. “I think it becomes very apparent that if we are to participate in that galactic environment, we must associate ourselves with that governing body we found recently.”

“Councilmember Ta'yeen,” he responds assuredly. “But of course, I would wholeheartedly agree. That encounter we had last month with the Azgarén naval expedition was rather unexpected, as I had never actually heard of a governing council body presiding over an entire galaxy. But it is quickly becoming clear, especially if you factor in the human home world also found in that galactic plane, that if we should wish any form of interaction with their world on behalf of our people here, perhaps also to explore and one day find a few colony sites for ourselves over there, we must follow through this political process."

A new hand quickly goes up in the crowd. Aristan redirects to the next member.

"The Floor recognizes Councilman Hardin Bansett."

The man stands up to make his statement.

"Your Lordship, and in accordance with Latena over here, as she is certainly right on the mark for this point, if our people should hold any interest at all in interacting with our lost brothers and sisters on that world…I cannot even be sure what name to give to it at this time, since we're still in the process of reacquainting ourselves with the happenings over there, after our centuries-long absence. I mean, we only recently got permission to re-open the Sarrukhan Gate and use it to establish a new index to travel there. But anyway, as we see those people are substantially behind us in their technological wherewithal, and it doesn't look like it's going to improve anytime soon, especially with the way we keep advancing by so many leaps and bounds…" he chuckles.

The rest of the room joins in with a round of laughter.

"Anyway," he continues. "As I recall from the history of our last visitation, which was several centuries ago, they were apparently in a late Copper to early Bronze Age period, whereas we were, well, quite more than that, and especially in certain areas of study. Now, here we are, entering what some would describe as an advanced Space Age, and they are STILL Bronze Age over there. Your Lordship, this is a critical situation for us in the human community. That world may belong to them, but we still declare a kind of birthright to call it home, at least insofar as it is the home of our form of life, and this statement carries meaning to us here."

"I am sure it does, Hardin, and it also carries a subtle meaning even to me. Although I may be Aasimar, just as Thaelyn and my beloved wife Aelwyn, our origins also involve this to some degree."

"Agreed! But if we should ever wish to interact with them…well, aside from the demands we have over us where the Measure of Balance is concerned, if for instance we could offer some small amount of exchange, and dare I say it, but maybe also consider a bit of…ehm…assistance?" he grins bashfully. "That is, to inspire them to move a little faster on their side. Otherwise, we may as well forget them altogether. By the time they achieve anything to meet us among the stars, we'll already be halfway to godhood!"

The room lifts up with another round of jovial laughter, and Aristan smiles brightly at the notion.

"Well, I cannot be quite as certain as that, but I do see your point, and it is a frustrating one."

"Aye! Our expeditions over there to discover their activities seem to suggest they are more interested in starting wars than to progress their society. This reminds me a bit of our world before Thaelyn arrived. And this also brings me back to my original point. We had this remarkable period of growth because of him, and I might say ONLY due to him… well, and also Adalon, naturally. If it were not for that, we might also be stuck in a darker Age. Therefore, as a representative of the human community, and I think I would not be alone in this, here is a proposal I would wish to make. We most certainly need to become friendly to that new authority…what did they call themselves again?"

"I believe our encounter had them identify themselves as…" he coughs subtly, "…The Coalition of Advanced Galactic Societies. But apparently the representative we met was kind enough to simply allow the more familiar name of Galactic Council. And such a curious one this is. A representative council of so many advanced civilizations all joined together to make fair and equal use of their resources. This is encouraging, but it also represents a lot of competition for us in that area."

"I think, considering we have two other galaxies to play with, I won't cry over it by much if we should be outbid on anything over there. But one or two colony worlds might be nice, if we can muster it, to give us a local base close to our kin. Then, I would wish to propose one or more programs to be considered where we could send, shall we say, advisors. Nothing too grand, mind you; simply a few words in the right ears to…inspire…them to make a bit of progress now and then. And by the way, this would also fit nicely up your alley, Your Lordship! Maybe you could see about directing some of it," he grins mischievously.

Aristan glares at him and raises his brow impishly.

"Is that a curious reference to my Father, perchance?"

"Well, Oghma is the one known as the Adherent of Inspiration, and you certainly do as much for the rest of us around here."

"Indeed, and I feel this now returning back to me. Very well, we can discuss this as time goes by. But we must be sure we understand how we would go about it and what limitations must be placed on us along the way. They are still an independent society and must follow a reasonably natural path. Meanwhile, as for this Galactic Council, since they tend to scrutinize membership based on residency within that galactic domain, this becomes a little problematic, as we are not proper residents."

"Um, what about this…" Latena pops up briskly with a cute smirk on her face.

"Oh no, not you again…" Aristan sighs. "Miss Ta'yeen, I have heard stories about your exploits. What do you have on your mind this time, young lady?"

"Simple. Ancestral heritage… That world is the home of humans as a species. We have humans here that originally came from there, due to the Sarrukh. It's their home, their legacy, and as you said, their birthright, so THEY are going to make a claim of ancestral heritage for ownership, even though they don't live there currently."

"And how do we factor in the aspect that they live on a completely different world AND in a completely different universe?"

"Well, I don't recall anyone mentioning how those early humans ever gave permission to the Sarrukh to abduct them away from home," she smiles sheepishly.

Hardin glances at the youthful girl for her curious statement and couldn't help but to break out in a hearty chuckle, followed by several others. Aristan, on the other hand, gazes stone-faced at her and raises his brow in his personal form of stylized dry parody. He then rolls his unblinking eyes downward, pulls up his tablet, and begins writing something down. Latena could feel her face starting to blush.

"Um, what are you doing?" she asks timidly.

"I am taking down a brief note for Thaelyn. I believe it may be time for him to bring out that famous list of his again."

"Oh no!" she moans and hides her face.

Hardin steps over to pat the girl on the shoulder before speaking out.

"Your Lordship," he announces boldly. "As for her proposal, I will second that motion."

"You must be joking!" Aristan rebukes.

"Not at all! It makes perfect sense to me. With respect to the Sarrukh, our ancestors were stolen away, and it's time to return home. If I understand that First Contact meeting correctly, becoming part of that Council is reserved for those who can claim an indigenous birthplace within a local star system. So be it, we qualify! Give us a chair and a chance for a local colony world to further establish ourselves.

Then, we'll carry out some discreet relations with our brothers and sisters on that world to slowly build them up until they're ready to join us amongst the stars."

"Powers help us all."

✦

Vonafel continued to work in the Royal Historical Archives during this time. Although lately, she was reducing her schedule to only part-time as she was approaching her retirement years. She mostly oversaw the training of younger conservation experts as they continued to restore and study the ancient texts within their halls. But while she spent her time with her assistants, her granddaughter was busy in another section of the building.

The museum had undergone a renovation since the days of the war, and a new memorial had been arranged inside the main hall. As visitors would enter the primary museum exhibit room, they were greeted by a large monument boasting a series of golden plaques circling around a curved backdrop surrounding a special hermetically sealed display box with Adalon's original books inside.

The plaques listed all of her prophecies in sequence, first from Book One, then Book Two. There were several video terminals displaying recitals and video logs with reenactments of the associated historical events, as well as replays of actual news releases from the campaign on Azgarén.

Vonafel's granddaughter was currently giving a lecture to a visiting group of tourists.

"One could easily say our history is a most extraordinary example of engineering," she announces. "Tae'Eladar, as we know it today, would not exist, if it were not for the work of Maker Kuroku. It was locked in a deep ice age, and likely would've remained there indefinitely. Had it not been for the existence of that lone Primordial, Sargeras, and his servant, Darumon, who successfully evaded their Fate at the hands of the Estelar back in the days of the old Celestial War, we would not exist in this world."

She pauses to examine the memorial and the arrays of plaques on the curved wall.

"She waited and watched, and only when she felt the time was upon her, did she go into action, calling upon the Sarrukh, who were as much her original people as they might be her philosophical Children, to return to what was once THEIR home, to restore and then donate it to an entirely new form of life...us. But those early seeds were only the human population. We elves came later, along with others. When we arrived, we found a brood of dragons holding ground here, and thought them to be invaders, so we fought back. But unknown to us, it was WE who were treading on sacred ground, which was protected by the Draconics to guard the Maker's work. This became known as the Age of Dragons in our old history. It would not be until much later, after the arrival of our Lord Thaelyn, when we would learn the truth. But more than that, would be the discovery of these quatrains you see up here," she points at the wall, "representing the Maker's story of our world, and how it was intended to be."

She now directs her audience to the many video terminals.

"Within these archives are the various individual tales of our most noteworthy moments, brought about at least in part due to the prophecies of the one we would come to know of as Adalon the Silver, who in reality was the Maker herself, taking up a hidden alias as she quietly played her own role to pursue that Primordial all the way to his final end. But even though we followed this story through our history, we could not have known the final chapter until we met with our most endeared friends and compatriots, the Suuden-Aryku. Their story brings the final culmination of our purpose in life, as a new example of the Maker's work...a guardian society who would spend every effort to uphold the grand Measure of Balance, to protect and to nurture, and to promote the growth of any deserving society we should have the privilege to encounter."

✦ ✦ ◆ ✦ ✦

It was midafternoon, and a daughter was meeting with her father for a pleasant little reunion at a local café.

"Father!" she jumps up to give him a hug. "How are things in the Council lately?"

"Well, Túfu, they certainly keep us busy. I hear we found a couple potential sites for colonization within the Katharian Galaxy, but I would strongly recommend some biological studies be made to ensure we don't walk into a potential health hazard with alien microbes."

"Yeah, that wouldn't be too nice to have."

"Other than that, dear young Latena is rallying the human faction to justify their claim to their ancient home in that new galaxy we're exploring."

"Do we have a name for it yet?"

"There's still some debate on what to call it, so they're going to organize a few surveys and some careful social interaction at ground level. Maybe we can borrow a name from one of the native languages once we learn something. We'll need to send a few agents down there to make some very discreet contact with the locals, but they're way behind us on technology."

"The way we keep moving forward, I can understand that easily enough."

"One of our first objectives is to study their language and cultural manners. Later, we might see about carefully influencing a few of their people to encourage some positive growth. Otherwise, as Councilman Bansett said, it may be pointless to try anything in the foreseeable future as we'll be so far ahead of them, there won't be any possibility for anything."

"That sounds tricky. And didn't you say once they were broken up into a lot of little nations down there? It sounds like Azgarén or Tae'Eladar in the early days."

"It does, and it may stay that way, unless one day they have someone as powerful and influential as His Lordship come along and change it."

"Not simply as powerful, but also as indomitable. Look at Tae'Eladar in those early days and how many opposed him. I would imagine the same was true back home with King Saakerav. But in that case, Darumon wouldn't be someone you could oppose anyway."

"True, but this world is in a barren fold, same as Azgarén. In fact, our recent calculations tell us it could be a galaxy around two hundred twenty million lightyears distant from our own."

"Really!"

"So, it's unlikely you'll find a Celestial making any visits. We may have to take this the slow and hard way."

"Slow and hard…a far cry from the path we took! Just look at all this, Father," Túfula gazes out at the city and the people passing by on the roads. "It's amazing. They went from something approximating a medieval condition to this in only four or five centuries. I'm barely halfway to my first millennium, and here we are going into a space age together."

"Yeah, but if you ask me, this past century, for all of us, and especially them, was a bit of a rush job. That heavy influence our people made really stirred things up for them."

"I'm sure it was simply a reflex reaction. Fortunately, that elixir of theirs made things go a lot easier. They were already so very progressive even before this, and according to Suli, the transition from gryphons to starships was barely more than applying that transport sphere of theirs from an animal to a constructed vessel."

"And I hear right now, that constructed vessel is getting ready for its maiden flight."

"Yes, and Kali was given the special privilege to take it out for a test run…she and Ayene to represent the closing of a circle, as Adalon might say. Our two societies that were so different, now officially joining together for a combined future."

"Túfu, I must admit I'm a little envious of your generation. You'll go places and see things that the rest of us could only dream of in our youth."

"There's nothing stopping you even now. And also remember, I spend most of my time in the Royal Historical Society, so I don't get out as much."

"Still, you can break away once in a while."

"If I do, I'll also need to coordinate with Suli, or else I'll never hear the end of her rants about spinning my tail without her," she giggles.

"That girl!" he chuckles. "By the way, how is Petrith these days?"

"He's been busy managing his data security agency. The ACI has been developing a number of new security protocols as we see more people taking up studies for their Prodigy Gifts, at least for the telepathy study. The others are still mostly reserved for military use, or carefully regulated for further study, at least until we can close a few more loopholes with the technology to monitor things on the civilian level."

"I still say it's a risky proposition, but at this point, there's nothing we can do except try to stay one step ahead of it."

"Yeah. And continue working to improve the culture of the people. But with life spans like ours, this will take a while."

"Of course," he relents. "I guess I still have a few of my old Elder Council habits. The Voice of Contention, it was always my job to argue these things."

"Yeah, but now you're on the Imperial High Council, along with Opadna. By the way, are you two ever going to have a child together?

It's been almost a century since you got married. I'm waiting for a little brother or sister out of you."

"Túfu, we've talked about it, but it still feels a little awkward when you consider you and Petrith. Even though she's not your biological mother and he's not my biological son, coming together like this..."

"Father, how many times have we had this discussion? We each lost something special in the attack on Ruuki uy'Daan. We may never get over that, but I think it was very appropriate that you two decided to join together. Petrith and I don't mind, and Suli and Kali don't see anything wrong with it, either. You just need to drag her into the temple, get a hot steamy blessing by Lathander, and then go to it," she giggles.

"Now just a moment, I don't think I want anything quite as hot and steamy as that. The younger crowd might go that far, but at my years, I should take things a little slower."

◆◆◆◆◆

Kaliya was in her officer's cabin taking a brief respite from her inspection tour of the star cruiser being constructed at the new Carronel Space Administration on Therinë. She had settled down at her desk and turned on the vid-com to call up her parents, both of whom were partially retired while occasionally giving lectures at cultural conventions.

"Well, this is it," she declares excitedly. "We're finishing up the final inspections and ready to take her out."

"We're both very proud of you, Kali," Tyanna remarks on the com-link. "This is a special moment for many of us."

"Yeah, it essentially levels the field for a lot of people. From here, we can start moving forward as a whole, rather than playing this little game of working the younger society up to meet us."

"And to think of all the places out there you might explore. It just seems so incredible."

"The most daunting aspect of it is we have two separate universes to work with, the one with Azgarén, and then ours here around Therinë. There's not much you can do with Tae'Eladar, since it's inside that Shell, but the rest gives us more than enough to play with for a very long time."

"I would probably advise you go slowly," Velen considers. "Especially in the local galaxy around Azgarén. We cannot know who might have survived from Darumon's heinous affairs, or if they would even remember us after this time, but we certainly wouldn't want to make any trouble."

"Right, I've been thinking about that, assuming they even knew who it was that attacked them. More than likely, they won't trust much of anything coming down from the sky, but we'll keep a close watch for it. I would probably choose some careful surveillance using spooks to simulate the locals, at least until we can gain some perspective on things. But I'm not going that far out on this occasion. This is just a shakedown, and for now only in the local space."

"Very good, then… Well, we shouldn't keep you, and I'm sure you have your work cut out for you."

"Yeah, and we also have a couple of special guests who will be joining us on this occasion."

"Oh, who is that?"

"Aileen and Brianne, they'll be giving a commemorative send-off in their mother's honor, since this is the first official Tae'Eladaran imperial starship."

"That sounds very nice, and also very appropriate. She was truly a unique woman in her day."

"Yes, she was," Kaliya reminisces deeply. "Well, I should be going. I'll talk to you again soon."

They end the link and Kaliya rises from her desk. She walks out the door of her cabin and along the corridor to the magneto-lift, entering inside and selecting the bridge as her destination. The lift hums smoothly as it delivers her on her way. In barely a moment, she arrives on the bridge, which was neatly arranged and fully staffed. She steps out and around to her Captain's chair.

Waiting for her was Ayene, who was serving as the First Officer for this flight. She was standing near one of the consoles to oversee the operations when Kaliya appeared on the bridge.

"Commander on the bridge!" she announces.

The full bridge staff jumps to attention to offer their salutes.

"As you were," Kaliya decrees.

As she approaches her chair, she is met with a set of twin sisters. The two women appeared identical to each other, with placid youthful features, light copper hair well below the shoulders, and strangely colored golden eyes.

"Aileen, Brianne," Kaliya addresses. "This one is in honor of your mother."

"If the spirit of our mother could be watching over us," they announce synchronously. "We are sure she would be very pleased for this occasion."

"Marelle was a good friend for many of us. She showed us the way and pioneered many of the technologies we're using right now."

"And now, in her honor, we carry what she began into a new era for our people."

The twins were a mirror image of each other, not only in appearance, but also their interactions. Although they could respond independently, they often chose to synchronize themselves as they were telepathically linked virtually all the time, seldom taking their privacy from each other for any reason. They were the Celestial children blessed upon Marelle and Roderick after their rather boisterous occasion of conception once upon a time during a curious moment of Tae'Eladar's history.

Kaliya sat down in her chair while the twins took up a position just behind her.

"Ayene, what's our situation up here?"

"All systems appear operational within program specs. We are ready for your orders, Commander."

"Ayene, how many times," Kaliya sighs. "We're friends, so you don't always need to be so formal with me."

"I know, Kaliya," she smiles. "But this one's important!"

"Cu'Nar give me strength. All right, all stations, make ready."

The bridge crew runs another check on their respective stations while Kaliya makes herself comfortable in her seat. She scans the bridge operations, and privately considers indulging herself in a quick cup of tea. She holds out her open palm and sets her focus into the space just above, directing her mind to perform a new trick she perfected over the years.

Within her hand, a saucer forms out of nothingness, followed by a small cup and finally a blend of hot herbal tea filling it. She had developed this talent as a continuation of her experience on the game field, perfecting it over time to apply a finer detail.

Ayene watched and smiled.

"My cups still come out a little fragile."

"You need to apply more substance, maybe a different material. And remember, you sip it delicately, not guzzle it like a common factory worker!" she smirks.

"Uh huh... Miss Manners speaking here," she giggles.

"I will admit one thing, though. This skill could break a society's economy when you no longer have to pay for something."

"Not simply that, but whatever you might call wealth. Just think it into existence."

Kaliya picks up her cup and takes a few sips, and when she was finished, she caused it to vanish by canceling the manifestation of the cup and saucer.

"All right helm, power us up."

The ship comes to life on the large tarmac outside the spaceport.

From a window inside the building, looking out at the sleek vessel, an assembly of observers gazed in amazement, including a mature dark elf and her two daughters, one of whom was nearly an adult, and the other was a young adolescent.

"Mum! Look!" shouts the girl. "They're getting ready."

"Aye," Relissa responds soothingly. "It's a grand one, that. And I'm real proud to see this day. Who would've thought...we came so far in this time."

"I barely even had time to grow up," the elder girl admits. "The schools were changing their books almost before I could finish reading them," she giggles.

"You're right, we were rushing things so quick."

"Barely a century, to be sure," submits one of the other women. "And made more of a spectacle as this Child society seems to have skipped a few steps."

"Aye, Nemelle, so they did. But then, as I hear it, some parts were simply waiting on the side for their right moment."

"Mum," the young girl submits. "Can you tell us the story again? It's so dreamy! The places you went, the things you did..."

"'Ere now, how many times do you need to hear that bleedin' story?"

The young girl giggles while Nemelle simply smiles and shakes her head.

"I think she may never have enough of that one," she offers. "I will admit, even for as many times as I have studied the sensory stones up in Sigil, this one would bring me back on many occasions."

"Maybe so," Relissa admits. "I don't think any of us will ever get over it. But it was enough just to live through it the first time!"

"And yet, we still have one final chapter pending. Our continuation of this world and that last society that has yet to join us on this extraordinary voyage."

"Aye, and then there's that. Have we heard anything new from our spies down there lately?"

"We have managed to map the Underdark substantially by now, mostly by using the Stormhooves in their projected forms, as it is much safer that way. We have identified several large cities down there... nothing like ours on the surface, but for the confined spaces, they are impressive. But it would seem they have mostly kept to their ancestral ways, unlike those of us up here who have evolved substantially in this time. If they ever thought themselves capable of assaulting us with their backwards-thinking armies, they will be severely outmatched by now."

"That's Drow for you, I guess. They never made any effort to come up just to ask questions or take a quick peek at things. Our history is more like them sending their warriors simply to make trouble, never to make peace."

"Indeed, but this must now change. Our world must unite fully. We can no longer tolerate them in this condition."

"Aye, but what about that goddess of theirs? We'll need to give her the walking papers before this is over."

"She should know this well enough already. This world is not hers to play with. This world belongs to the Maker, and it was intended from the beginning to be aligned with the positive side. Besides, she does not hold a great amount of favor with the rest for her practices."

"This doesn't sound like it'll be pretty in the end, but it needs to be done."

Inside the starship, Kaliya examines the activity around the bridge. All seemed operational and waiting for her next command.

"Take us up, slow and steady."

The helm responds by lifting off the pad. A subtle rippling effect seems to slide past as the spatial inversion field carries them away, arcing around in a gentle turn and angling up. It thrusts forward and moves ahead, picking up speed as it makes its way through the atmosphere.

"We're coming into low orbit," the helmsman notes.

"I've got a signal coming in from the new starbase," the comms officer declares.

"On screen," Kaliya issues.

The officer brings up an image on the main screen. Kailen was checking in as the ship was leaving the planetary surface.

"Well, that looks like a fine piece of work," he states merrily. "It's good to see we're finally getting our hooves wet around here."

"Yes, and in time, who knows where this'll lead us. But so far, we just have a few simple runs to make. How are things on the new station?"

"We've been working on several of the lower decks recently, adding new facilities. The project is moving along, and we're expecting a new shipment of parts from the processor further downspin, but it seems they can't keep enough supply on hand for all the construction going on right now."

"Well then, you probably need to get on their tails harder," she chuckles. "How's little Sani in his new school?"

"Kaliya, that poor kid will never catch up if things keep going like this. As soon as he finishes one class, they change the lessons, and then he needs to take an update course."

"Well," she chuckles. "I think it'll stabilize a little from here. It was hard this past century when Tae'Eladar and the other worlds were playing catch-up with us. Now that we're here, it might go along a little smoother."

"You think?" he winces. "All right, I'll pass the word to Ankhia so she can reattach her horns…again."

"Good. And I'll let you know how this run goes once we get back."

"I'll be looking forward to it."

The com-link closes, and the main viewer returns to the forward scene.

"Nav, let's set our first jump point for Azgarén local space."

"Yes Ma'am. Now charging the arcanic capacitors… Ten percent… Twenty… Thirty…"

Kaliya glanced again at the twin sisters as they stood behind her chair and watched expectantly while the count continued.

"Fifty percent… Sixty…"

The bridge operations seemed well-rehearsed, and all systems looked good on this first outing.

"Eighty… Approaching critical dump… Ninety… Arcanic dump… now! We have our rift; the envelope is folding."

From outside, the proud new ship is shrouded in a brilliant glow, and then flashes out of sight, on its way to new adventures for a burgeoning society on the verge of a new Era.

THE END